THE SOUL DRINKER

THE SOUL DRINKER

Drinker of Souls

Blue Magic

A Gathering of Stones

Jo Clayton

Published by arrangement with
DAW Books
1633 Broadway
New York, New York 10019

Printed in the United States of America

CONTENTS

Drinker of Souls

1.

A Thief and His Sister

Aituatea shifted the bend in his legs to ease his aching hip, careful as he moved to keep the bales piled under him from squeaking, the bales of raw unwashed fleeces that were a stench in his nostrils but sheltered him from noses and teeth of the patrollers' rathounds. He raised his head a little and stared at the curls of mist drifting across the calm black water of the bay. A wandering breeze licked at his face, tugged at his slicked-back hair, carried past his ears just enough sound to underline the silence and peace of the night. "This is a bust," he whispered to the one who stood at his shoulder. "She won't come."

"The man on the mountain said . . ." His sister's voice was the crackling of ice crystals shattering. "Look there." She pointed past the huddling godons beyond the wharves, their rambling forms lit from behind by torches burning before the all-night winestalls, the joyhouses, the cookshops of the water quarter. The Wounded Moon was rising at last, a broken round of curdled milk behind the spiky roof of the Temple. She swung round an arm colorless and transparent as glass, outlined with shimmers like crystal against black velvet and pointed across the harbor. "And there," she said. She was all over crystal, even the rags she wore. "Out beyond the Woda-an. A blind ship from Phras, dropping anchor."

He looked instead at the Woda livingboats shrouded in the thickening mist, their humped roofs like beetle shells catching bits of moonlight. A blind ship. The Woda-an hated them, those blind ships. There were torches flaring up here and there among the boats as the Woda-an grew aware of the visitor, clanking rattles starting up, growing louder, fading, sounding and fading in another place and another as they invoked the protection of the Godalau and her companion gods against the evil breathed out by the black ship that had no eyes to let her see her way across the seas. He sneered at them with Hina scorn for the superstitions of other races. *They'll be thick as fishlice at the Temple tomorrow. Where's that curst patrol? I want to get out of this. She won't*

come, not this late. He propped his chin on his fists and watched the
ship. He drowsed, the Wounded Moon creeping higher and higher
behind him. The guard patrol was late. Hanging round the winestalls.
Let them stay there. "Let's get out of this," he whispered. "That ship's
settled for the night. Won't no one be coming ashore." He twisted his
head around so he could see his sister. She took her stubbornness into
the water with her, he thought. She stood at his left shoulder as she'd
stood since the night she came swimming through water and air and
terror to find him while her body rocked at the bottom of the bay. The
black glitters that were her eyes stayed fixed on the Phras ship as if she
hadn't heard him. "The man on the mountain said she'd come," she
said.

"Doubletongue old fox."

She turned on him, stamping her crystal foot down beside his shoulder, her crystal hair flying out from her head. "Be quiet, fool. He could
curse you out of your body and where'd I be then?"

Aituatea rubbed oily fleeces between his palms, shivered at the memories her words invoked. Old man kneeling in his garden on the mountain, digging in the dirt. Clean old man with a skimpy white beard and
wisps of white hair over his ears, tending rows of beans and cabbages.
Old man in a sacking robe and no shoes, not even straw sandals, and
eyes that saw into the soul. Aituatea jerked his shoulders, trying to
shake off a growing fear, went quiet as he heard the faint grate of bale
shifting against bale. He stared unhappily at the blind ship, whispering
to himself, "It'll be over soon, has to be over soon." Trying to convince
himself that was true, that he'd be through dealing with things that
horrified him. The Kadda witch dead and Hotea at rest, which she
would be now but for that bloodsucker, and me rid of her scolding and
complaining and always being there, no way to get free of those curst
eyes. He wanted to climb down from the bales and get off Selt for the
next dozen years but he couldn't do that. If he did that, he'd *never* get
rid of Hotea, she'd be with him the rest of his life and after. He suppressed a groan.

Out on the water the torches scattered about the Woda-an watercity
were burning low and the rattles had gone quiet. Behind him on Selt
Island's single mountain where the Temple was, rocket after rocket
arced into the darkness, hissing and spitting and exploding to drive off
the enemies of the Godalau and her companion gods.

Part of a counting rhyme for a fete's fireworks:

Blue glow for the Godalau
Sea's Lady, sky's Queen
Red shine for the Gadajine
Storm dragons spitting fire
Yellow flash for Jah'takash
Lady ladling out surprise
Green sheen for Isayana
Birthing mistress, seed and child
Purple spray for Geidranay
Gentle giant grooming stone
Moonwhite light for Tungjii-Luck
Male and female in one form . . .

Luck, he thought. My luck's gone sour these past six months. Aituatea repeated to himself (with some pleasure) *fool, fool, fool woman. She never thinks before she does something. Going to the Temple the day after year-turn when she knew Temueng pressgangs would be swarming over the place, sucking up Hina girls for the new year's bondmaids. She should've thought first, she should've thought. . . .*

What happened, he said, where you been all this time?

Thanks a bunch for worrying about me, she said. He heard her as a cricket chirp in his head, an itch behind his ears. I was working the Temple court, she said, reproach in her glittering glass eyes. You were off somewhere, brother, Joyhouse or gambling with those worthless hangabouts you call your friends, and the money was gone when I looked in the housepot and there wasn't a smell of food or tea in the place. What'd you want me to do, starve? It being the day after year-turn, I knew every Hina with spare coin and unwed daughters would be burning incense by the fistfuls. I spotted a wool merchant with a fat purse dangling from his belt and started edging up to him. I get so busy checking out running room and easing through his herd of daughters, I forget to look out for pressgangs. Hadn't been for those giggling geese I might've heard them and took off. I don't hear them and they get us all.

They take us, me and the wool merchant's daughters, across the causeway, me hoping to be put in some little havalar's House where I can get away easy and take a thing or two with me for my trouble, but I see we are heading all the way up the high hill to the Tekora's Palace.

I am cursing you, brother, and thinking when I get home, I am going to peel your skin off a strip at a time.

She was much calmer at this point in the story, drifting about the room, touching familiar things with urgent strokes of her immaterial fingers as if she sought reassurance from them. She hovered a moment over the teapot, smiling as she absorbed its fragrance.

I know I can get loose again easy enough, but the Tekora's a mean bastard with girls that run away. You wouldn't know that, would you, brother? Only women you bother about are those no-good whores in the joyhouses.

Aituatea scowled; dying hadn't changed his sister's habits in the least as far as he could see. Shut up about that, he said. Get on with what happened.

Branded on the face, brother, branded runaway and thief, who'd let me get close enough to lift a thing? So when the Temueng Housemaster puts me to work in the Tekora's nursery, I am ready to act humble before those Temueng bitches when I'd rather slit their skinny throats! She grimaced in disgust. You know what they do to me? Hauling slops, picking up after those Temueng nits, not lifting a finger to help themselves, running my feet to the bone fetching things they could just as easily get for themselves.

Her chirp sounded bitter and full of rage; she was madder than he'd ever seen her, even when he turned fourteen and ran off with the housemoney to buy time with a joygirl, what was her name? He shook his head, couldn't remember her name or what she looked like.

After a month of that, Hotea said, I am about ready to skip out even if it means I have to get off Utar-Selt, live low the rest of the year. You could take care of yourself, brother dear, though I did mean to warn you they might connect you with me if your luck went sour as mine. The nursery garden has a high wall, but there are plenty of trees backed up against that wall. On its other side is the guard walkway and a pretty steep cliff, but I am not fussing about that, I can climb as good as you, brother, and swim better, and the causeway's near. I am thinking about going over the wall that night, or the one after, depending, when fat old Tungjii, heesh jabs me in the ass again. The Tekora's youngest daughter disappears.

Hotea beat her fist several times on Aituatea's shoulder, making him wince at the stinging touches. He jerked away, then clutched at his head as the sudden movement woke his hangover and started the demon in his skull pounding a maul against his temples.

Hotea laughed, the scorn in the soundless whisper raising the hairs along his spine. Fool, she said, you'll kill yourself, you go on like this. You need a wife, that's what, a good woman who'll keep you in order better than I could, give you sons. You don't want our line to die with you, do you, brother?

She shook herself, her form shivering into fragments and coming together again.

Listen, she said, you got to do something about that witch, as long as she lives I won't rest.

She wrung her hands together, darted in agitation about the room, gradually grew calmer as the grandmother ghost patted her arm, ragged lips moving in words that were only bursts of unintelligible noise. She drifted back to hover in front of Aituatea.

The Tekora's youngest daughter, she said, three years old and just walking, a noxious little nit who should've been drowned at birth. On the eve of the new moon they turn the place upside down, double the work on us. I don't think much about it except that I'd strangle her myself if I come across her, she is wrecking my plans because she took off. Three days later they find her face-down in the nursery fountain, shriveled and bloodless like a bug sucked dry. Not drowned but dead for sure. 'F I was scared of leaving before, well! Tekora would tear Silili brick from plank looking for me, or that's what I'm thinking then. The other maids are as jittery as me. We are Hina in the house of the Temueng, that makes us guilty even if we do nothing, and the other bondmaids are too stupid and cowed to say boo to a butterfly. Housemaster beats us, but his heart isn't much in it. And things go on much the same as before. On the eve of the next new moon another daughter goes and I am there to see it.

They order us bondmaids to sleep in the nursery to make sure the daughters don't just wander off. This night is my turn. A bondmaid brings me a cup of tea. I sniff at it when she goes out. Herb tea. Anise and something else, can't quite place it. I take the cup to the garden door and look at it but can't see anything wrong. I sniff at it again and I start getting a touch dizzy. I throw the tea out the door and carry the cup back and put it by my pallet so it looks like I drank it. I stretch out. I'm scared to sleep but I do, up before dawn running like a slave for those bitches, I'm tired to the bone. Something wakes me. I don't move but open my eyes a slit and keep breathing steady. A minute after that I see the Tekamin standing in the doorway, the Tekora's new wife she is, he set her over the others and they are mad as fire about it, but what can they do? Hei-ya brother, I have to listen to a lot of bitching when I am fetching for the other wives, they don't get a sniff of him after he brings that woman back with him from Andurya Durat. No one knows where she comes from, who her family is or her clan, even the wives are scared to ask. And there she is in that doorway, slim and dark and lovely and scaring the stiffening out of me.

She comes gliding in, touches the second youngest daughter on her face and the daughter climbs out of the bed and follows her and I know what she is then, she's a Kadda witch, a bloodsucker.

I lay shivering on my pallet wishing I'd drunk the drugged tea, my head going round and round as I try to figure out what to do. I think of skipping out before morning and trusting I can keep hid. But I think too of the Kadda wife. I don't want her sniffing after me; I have a feeling she can smell me out no matter where I hide. Well, brother, I raise a fuss in the morning, what else can I do? And you better believe I don't say one thing about the Tekamin. The other daughters howl and scream and stamp their skinny feet and the old wives they go round pulling bondmaids' hair and throwing fits. When the Housemaster beats me again, it is just for the look of the thing, and for himself, I suppose. He is scared himself and happy to have my back to take it out on.

I keep my head down the next month, you can believe that. I try a couple times to sneak out of the bondmaids' dorm, but the damn girls aren't sleeping sound enough and keep waking up when I move. Anyway I'm not trying too hard, not yet. The Kadda wife isn't bothering me—except sometimes she looks at me like she is wondering if I was really asleep that other time. I'm thinking maybe I can last out the year and get away clean and all the fetching and carrying and cleaning up don't bother me near so much. Then the Wounded Moon starts dribbling away faster and faster till it is the eve of the new moon again and curiosity is eating at me till I can't stand it. You told me more than once, brother, my nose would be the death of me.

Hotea giggled and the other ghosts laughed with her, a silent cacophony of titters, giggles and guffaws. Aituatea sat slumped in his chair, waiting morosely for them to stop. He wasn't amused by a situation that meant either he had to go after a bloodsucking witch or face having an overbearing older sister at his elbow for the rest of his life.

Another girl is sleeping in the nursery this night, the Godalau be praised for that, but I decide to sneak in there and watch what happens. I tell myself the more I know, the easier I can get away without the witch catching me. Well, it's an argument.

Like it happens sometimes when old Tungjii gets together with Jah'takash and they wait for you to put your foot in soft shit up to your ears, everything is easy for me that night. The other bondmaids go to sleep early. Snoring. I've half a mind to join them, but I don't. I make myself get out of bed. Moving about helps some, clears the fog out of my head. I sneak down to the nursery, jumping at every shadow and there are lots of those, the wind has got in the halls and is bumping the lamps about, but that is just the sort of thing you expect in big houses at night, so instead of scaring me more, it almost makes me feel like I'm at home, prowling a house with Eldest Uncle.

In the nursery the nits are sleeping heavy. The bondmaid is stretched on a pallet, snoring. She doesn't so much as twitch when I step over her and duck under the bed of one of the dead daughters. It is close to the door into the garden and I figure if anything goes wrong I can get out that way. The door is open a crack, wedged, to let the air in and clear out the strong smell of anise. I lie there chewing my lip, thinking things will happen soon.

Sounds of wind and fountain whoop through the room; I almost can't hear the bondmaid snoring. There is a lot of dust under the bed; no one checks there and we don't do more than we have to, but I am sorry about that now because some of that dust gets into my nose, makes it itch like I don't know. After a while I start getting pains jumping from my neck to between my shoulders. I stand it some minutes more, then I have to stretch and wiggle if I want to be able to walk without falling on my face. I am just about ready to crawl back to my bed, muttering curses on Tungjii and Jah'takash, when I hear a kind of humming. I stop moving, hoping the wind noise had covered the sounds I was making. I can't tell you what the humming was like, I've never heard anything like it. My eyelids keep flopping down; I am fighting suddenly to keep awake; then more dust gets in my nose; I almost sneeze, but don't. One good thing, the itch releases me from the witch's spell. I ease myself toward the end of the bed and crick my neck around so I can see the door. I am hidden by the knotted fringe on the edge of the coverlet and feel pretty safe. The Kadda wife is standing in the door.

The humming stops.

The Tekora moves out of the shadows to stand beside his wife. I stop breathing. He looks hungry. I feel like throwing up.

The Kadda wife looks around the room. I get the feeling she can see me. I close my eyes and pretend I'm a frog hopped in from the garden. Even with my eyes closed I can feel her looking at me; I'm sure she's going to call me out from under the bed; I'm thinking it's time to scoot out the door and over the wall. But nothing happens and I can't resist sneaking another look.

The Kadda wife smiles up at the Tekora and takes her hand off his arm. It's like she's taken the bridle off him. He walks to his daughter's bed. He looks down at the little girl, then over his shoulder at the witch. She nods. He bends over and whispers something I couldn't make out that hurts my ears anyway. The girl gets up, follows him out of the room. His own daughter!

Hotea's voice failed as indignation shook her. Her form wavered and threatened to tatter, but she steadied herself, closed her hand tight about her brother's arm. He winced but didn't pull away this time.

The witch looks around the room one more time then leaves too. I stay where I am, flat out under the bed. I am thinking hard, you better believe. No wonder the Tekora is neglecting his other wives. I see he is looking younger. His skin is softer and moister, he is plumper, moving more like a young man. I see that's how she is buying him, then I think, he's running out of daughters, he's going to start on the bond-maids too soon for me. And I think, what odds the Kadda wife doesn't make me the first one to go? None of us Hinas are going to finish out this bond year. I wait under the bed for a long time, afraid she's going to come back and sniff me out, but nothing happens. I creep out from under the bed when I hear the first sleepy twitters of the warblers in the willows outside the door, a warning that dawn is close. If I have to spend the rest of my life exiled, I am going down that cliff. Now. No more this and that and the other. Out. Away. Far away as I can get, fast as I can get there. The last daughter is still sleeping, so is the bondmaid, but she is going to wake soon and start screeching the minute she sees the third daughter is gone. I kick the wedge away and whip out the door into the garden.

The Kadda wife is waiting in the garden for me. I get maybe two steps before she grabs me. I try to jerk loose, but her cold hands are hard and strong as iron chains, and they drain my strength away some-how. It is as if she sucks it out of me. I am scared witless. I think she is going to drink me dry right there. She doesn't, she pushes me back into the nursery and across it into the hallway. I go without making a sound, I can't make a sound though I try screaming; something is pulling strings on my legs as if I were a puppet in a holy play. No, an unholy play.

She takes me high up in the palace to a small room under the roof, shoves me inside and a minute later there is this pain in the back of my head.

When I wake, it's dark again—or still dark, I don't know which. I am hanging on an iron frame like a bed stripped and set on end, my wrists and ankles are tied to the corner with ropes. There is a gag in my mouth, probably because of the open window high in the wall on my right, and a strong smell of anise, I am getting very tired of anise. The mix smells stale, as if it had been floating round the room a long time and that scares me all over again, more than if it'd been fresh. They hadn't eaten the daughter yet; looks like I'm going to take her place this month. My wrists and ankles are burning, my mouth is like leather, my head feels like someone kicked it.

After a short panic, I start fiddling with the ropes and go a little crazy with relief when I find I know more about knots than whoever tied me. I get myself loose and start looking for some way out.

There is no latch on the inside of the door, just a hole for a latch-string or maybe a pin key. Nothing in the room I can use on it. I push the frame over to the window and climb up to look out, I climb care-fully, the frame creaking as if it will collapse if I breathe too hard. I get halfway out the window and look down. There is nothing much be-tween me and the water except a lot of straight up-and-down cliff and the surf is white wrinkles about black rocks. Way way down. The wind is blowing against my face, cold and damp, but it feels good.

Fingers touch my ankle. I know it's her. I kick free before she can drain away my strength again. Somehow I keep myself from falling as I wiggle out the window, so scared all I know is that I have to get away fast. I hear cursing behind me and the squeal of metal as the frame collapses under her. I stand in the window and look down at the waves crashing against the rocks. No joy there. I look up. The endhorns of the eaves are close, but not close enough so I can reach them. Behind me I hear curses and other noises as she drags something to the win-dow. She's coming for me. I take a chance and jump. My hands slap around a horn and I am hanging free. I start pulling myself up. Fingers close about my ankles. I kick hard, harder, but can't get loose. My hands slip.

So here I am. And here I stay till the Kadda witch is dead, down in the water with me, dead, you hear me, brother, you hear?

Aituatea winced as he felt a nip in his left shoulder.

"Look." Her crystal arm sketched in touches of moonlight, Hotea jabbed her finger at the Phras ship.

The ship's dark bulk was suddenly alive with lanthorns shining red and gold behind horn sides, dozens of them lighting up the deck and the swirl of dark forms moving over it. He could hear snatches of speech too broken for understanding, the blast of a horn as one of the figures leaned over the rail to call a water taxi from the Woda-an. The hornblower had to repeat the signal several times before the slide of a red lanthorn marked the passage of a taxi from the watercity to the blind ship.

A slim, energetic figure swung over the rail and went down the netting with skill and grace. Aituatea swallowed the sourness in his throat. A woman. By outline alone, even at this distance, a woman. The Drinker of Souls. He cursed under his breath. The weight of centuries of custom, of his sister's shame and fury, of his own battered self-respect, all this pressed down on him, shoving him toward the thing that twisted his gut. He pressed his hand over his mouth, stifling an exclamation as two more forms balanced a moment on the rail then followed the woman down, small forms, children or dwarves or something. The old man on the mountain hadn't said anything about companions. He glanced up at Hotea. She was staring hungrily at the woman, bent forward a little, her hands closed into fists, her form shivering with a terrible urgency. The strength of that need he hadn't understood before, despite all those scolds, all those bitter accusations of cowardice and shame repeated so often he ceased to listen; he squirmed uncomfortably on the fleece.

The taxi came swiftly toward the wharf, the stern sweep worked by a young Woda girl, the lanthorn on the bow waking coppery highlights on sweaty skin the color of burnt honey. Her short black hair held off her face by a strip of red cloth knotted about her temples, she swayed back and forth in a kind of dance with the massive oar, her muscles flowing smoothly, her face blank and blandly animal, as if she lived for that moment wholly in the body. Aituatea stared at her, his tongue moving along dry lips, a tension in his groin reminding him how long it'd been since he'd had a woman. A stinking Woda bitch. He ground his teeth together and went on watching her. Frog ugly. In his Hina eyes she was a dirty beast, beastly with her strong coarse features, her broad shoulders, her short crooked legs—but she roused him until he was close to groaning. Six months since he'd been to a joyhouse, he'd tried it once after his sister fell in the bay but he couldn't do anything there. Hotea's ghost followed him everywhere as if a string tied her to his left shoulder; he tried to drive her off for a little bit, but she wouldn't go; he thought maybe he could ignore her long enough to get his relief, but when he was with the girl he could feel Hotea's eyes on him, those damn judging angry eyes, and he shriveled to nothing and had to pay the woman double so she wouldn't spread talk about him.

The taxi bumped against the wharf. The strange woman laughed at something one of the children said, a rippling happy sound that jarred against his expectations. Drinker of Souls conjured dour and deflating images. The children's giggles echoed hers, then she was up the ladder and swinging onto the wharf. The children followed. In the moonlight they looked like twins, pale little creatures dancing about the woman, flinging rapid bursts of their liquid speech at her, receiving her terse replies with more laughter. After a last exchange that left the woman grinning, the twins capered away, disappearing into the maze of boxes and bales piled temporarily on the wharf, waiting for the Godalau fete to pass before they were tucked away into the godons. Aituatea heard the children chattering together, then the high rapid voices faded off down a grimy alley. The woman turned to look across the water at the Phras ship where the lanthorns were going out as it settled back to sleep, then she gazed along the curve of Selt toward the many-terraced mountain of Utar. He saw her follow the line of torches burning along the causeway, the lampions that marked the course of the looping roadway, her head tilting slowly until she went quiet, stood with a finger stroking slowly and repeated alongside her mouth, contemplating the topmost torches, those that burned on the gate towers of the Tekora's Palace.

She had long straight hair that gleamed in the strengthening moonlight like brushed pewter, the front parts trimmed to a point, the back clasped loosely at the nape of her neck. She was taller than most Hina, wider in the shoulders and hips though otherwise slim and supple. Her skin was very pale; in the moonlight it looked like porcelain. She wore loose trousers of some dark color stuffed into short black boots, a white, full-sleeved shirt with a wide collar that lay open about her neck. Over this was a sleeveless leather coat; when a gust of wind flipped it back for a moment, he raised his brows, seeing two throwing knives sheathed inside. She wasn't Phras or any of the many other sorts of foreigners that passed through the port of Silili, but he wasn't too surprised at that, seeing what she was.

Behind him he heard the stomp and clatter of the godon guards and the whining of their rathounds. He took a chance and watched the woman to see what she would do.

Poking long spears into crevices to drive out drunks or sleepers, sounding their clappers to scare away ghosts and demons, whooping to keep up their courage, the godon guards came winding along the wharves.

The woman stirred slightly. Touch-me-not spun out from her like strands of mist, real mist spun up out of the water until she was a vertical dimness in a cocoon of white. Aituatea watched, uneasily fascinated, until the guards got close, then dropped his face into the fleece and waited.

As soon as the patrol had clattered past, he looked up again.

The cocoon out by the water unraveled with a speed that startled Aituatea, then his stomach was knotting on itself as she came sauntering toward him, as unstoppable and self-contained as the wind. What's she doing here? Why'd she come to Silili? He hadn't thought about it before, but now he saw her. . . . What's waiting for her here? Old man, you didn't tell us nothing except she was the one who could face the witch. What else didn't you tell us? What else do you know? Crazy old fox, said nothing worth salt.

The old man settled onto his haunches, his dirt-crusted hands dropping onto his thighs. Eyes the color of rotted leaves touched on Aituatea, shifted to Hotea and ended looking past them both at the woolly clouds sliding across the early morning sky.

Hotea drove her elbow into Aituatea's ribs. He lurched forward a step, bowed and held out the lacquer box filled with the rarest tea he could steal.

Ah, the old man said; he got stiffly to his feet, took the box from Aituatea. Come, he said. He led them into the single room of his small dwelling. It was painfully clean and quite bare except for a roll of rough bedding in one corner and a crude table with a chair facing the door and a bench cobbled from pine limbs opposite. He went to some shelves, mere boards resting on wooden pegs driven into the wall, set the box beside a jumble of scrolls and a brush pot, shuffled back to the chair. Sit, he said.

Aituatea glanced over his shoulder. Morning light cool as water, filled with dancing motes, poured through the door and flooded across the table, picking up every wrinkle, wart, and hair on the old man's still face. Though he was uneasy with emptiness at his back, Aituatea slid onto the bench and sat plucking nervously at the cloth folds over the knee of his short leg. He wanted to shut the door but he was afraid to touch anything in the hut and afraid too of shutting himself in with the old man. He twitched but didn't look around when he felt the cold bite of Hotea's hand on his shoulder. His eyes flicked to the serene face across from him, flicked away, came slowly back. The old man looked harmless and not too bright but there were many stories about him and brash youths who thought they could force his secrets from him. Some said it was always the same old man, Temueng to the Temuengs and Hina to the Hinas, or whatever he chose to be.

The hut was filled with a faded tang of cedar and herbs; the breeze wandering in from outside brought with it the sharp aromas of pine and mountain oak, the dark damp smells of the earth, the lighter brighter scents of stone dust and wild orchids. It was warm and peaceful there, the tranquility underlined by the whisper of the breeze, the intermittent humming of unseen insects. In spite of himself, Aituatea began to relax. Hotea pinched him. Stubbornly he said nothing. This visit was her idea, something she came up with when she couldn't drive him into action with bitter words or shame. If she wanted help from the old man, let her do the talking.

The sunlight sparked off her outflung arm. I'm drowned by a Kadda witch, she burst out. Her voice made no impression on the drowsing sounds of the small room, but the old man looked at her, hearing her. I want her dead, she cried, in the water with me. Dead.

The old man blinked, pale brown eyes opening and closing with slow deliberation. With his shaggy brown robe, the tufts of white hair over his ears, his round face and slow-blinking eyes, he looked to Aituatea rather like a large horned owl. The tip of a pale pinkish-brown tongue brushed across his colorless lips. All things die in their time, he said.

Hotea made a small spitting sound. Aituatea looked at his hands, feeling a mean satisfaction. This wasn't what she'd come to hear, platitudes she could read in any book of aphorisms. Not that woman, she said, her voice crackling with impatience. Not while there's young blood to feed her.

Even her, he said.

I want her dead, old man, she said. I want to see her dead. Hotea's hands fluttered with small, quickly aborted movements as if she sought to uncover with them some argument to persuade him to interfere against his inclination. Look, she said, Temueng children have died. Do you think Hina won't pay for those deaths? Ten for one they will. We're guilty, old man, whether we do anything or not. They can do no wrong, they're the conquerors, aren't they? Besides, leave the witch alone, how long before she eats everyone on Utar-Selt? Hotea went still a moment, then her voice was a thread of no-sound softer than usual in Aituatea's head. Teach us, old man, she said, teach us how we can front and kill a Kadda witch.

The old man stared at her a dozen heartbeats, then turned those pitiless eyes on Aituatea. They swelled larger and larger until they were all he could see. He began to feel like weeping softly and sadly as they searched his soul, as they spaded up fear and waste and the little niggling meannesses he'd done to his friends and to his sister, and all the ugly things he'd buried deep and refused to remember. As he stared into the old man's eyes, he was finally forced to see that he would never do anything about the Kadda witch without someone to take the brunt of the witch's attack, that he would keep putting it off and putting it off, growing more wretched as the years passed, as Hotea grew more caustic.

The old man leaned back, his worn face filled with pain as if he had absorbed from Aituatea all that self-disgust and fear. He slumped, his body shrinking in on itself, his eyes glazing over. Kadda witch, he murmured, blood drinker, knows no will but her own, evil, recognizing no right beyond her own needs. I see . . . there's a counter . . . I see . . . He flinched, drew further into himself. Powerful, he said, another power comes . . . an ancient enemy. . . . His eyes moved in a slow sweeping arc, but he was seeing nothing in the hut. Aituatea felt his stomach knot.

One comes, the old man said, husky voice reduced to a whisper. A woman . . . something between her and the witch . . . like the witch . . . no, not the same . . . drinker of life, not blood . . . not evil, not good. . . . Drinker of Souls, she comes the eve of the Godalau fete. Set her on the track, let her sniff out the witch, buy her with Das'n vuor, and point her at the witch. She comes with the rising of the Wounded Moon, will leave before the rising of the sun. The Drinker of Souls, come back to Silili after years and years . . . a hundred years . . . ah! her purposes mesh with yours, angry ghost. He muttered some more, but the words were unintelligible, intermixed with sudden chuckles. It was as if he had to wind back down into his customary taciturnity and something amusing he saw was retarding this return.

Aituatea sat frozen, sick. Three months' respite, then he had to face the witch or face himself. He glared at the old man, silently cursing him for setting the limit so close.

The old man lifted his head, looked irritably at him. That's it, he seemed to say, you got what you came for, now get out of here!

Shadow spread out from him, dark and terrible, killing the light, the warmth. Aituatea scrambled back, knocking over the bench; the smell of cedar choking him, he ran from the hut.

Another nip in his shoulder. Hotea getting impatient. "Go after her. Stop her," she shrilled. "Don't lose her, fool. You won't find her again, you know it. And we've only got till sunup."

Muttering under his breath Aituatea swung down from the bales and limped after the woman. His hip hurt but he was used to that and almost forgot the pain as he hurried past the godons and stepped into the Street of the Watermen. She was making no effort to hurry—it was almost as if she wanted to be followed, had set herself out as bait, trolling for anything stupid or hungry enough to bite. He kept back as far as he could without losing sight of her. The peculiar lurch of his walk was too eye-catching, even in the leaping uncertain light from the torches burning in front of businesses still open, casting shadows that lurched and twisted as awkwardly as he did. She circled without fuss about the knots of gambling watermen and porters crouched over piles of bronzes and coppers, tossing the bones into lines chalked on the flagging. She slowed now and then, head cocked to listen to flute and cittern music coming in melancholy brightness from the joyhouses, ignored insults flung down at her from idling women hanging out second-story windows, walked more briskly past shops shuttered for the night—a herbalist, a shaman's den, a fishmonger, a greengrocer, a diviner, and others much like these. Some cookshops were closed for the night, others were still open with men standing about dipping noodles and pickled beans and pickled cabbage from clay bowls or crunching down fried pilchards. He watched her careless stroll and felt confirmed in his idea she was bait in her own trap. Maybe she's hungry, he told himself and shivered at the thought. He dropped back farther, his feet dragging. For no reason he wondered suddenly where the children were. Now and then it seemed to him he heard them calling to each other or to the woman, but he was never sure and she never responded to the calls.

"Where's she going?" he muttered and got Hotea's elbow in his ribs for an answer. That she was heading the way he wanted her to go, uphill and vaguely north, made him nervous; it was just too convenient; as Hotea said, it happens sometimes that everything goes easy for a while but old Tungjii's getting together with Jah'takash and they're waiting for you to put your foot in it. But he kept limping after her, eaten by curiosity and buoyed up by nervous excitement.

She sauntered past a lighted cookshop. The owner-cook was leaning on the counter, pots steaming behind him, tossing the bones with a single customer. The two men stopped what they were doing to stare after her, then went back to their game, talking in low tones, discussing the woman probably. A shadow drifted from behind the cookshop a moment later. A clumsy shift and Aituatea saw a part of the shadow's face, the hulk of his body, then the follower was in the dark again. Djarko. He snorted with disgust. Took the bait like a baby. He limped after them, careful not to be seen. Djarko's equally cretinous cousin Djamboa had to be somewhere about, they hunted as a team. He spotted the second shadow and smiled grimly. Better them than me. The Godalau grant they satisfy her so she'll be ready to listen before she jumps me.

The woman turned into one of the small side lanes that wound through close-packed tenements of the poorer players, artisans and laborers. Djarko and Djamboa turned after her, almost running in their eagerness. Aituatea followed more warily, trying to ignore the nips in his shoulder as Hotea urged him to catch up and defend the woman from those louts. Defend her? Godalau defend me. He slowed his uneven gait until he was slipping through shadow near as much a ghost as his sister was, avoiding the refuse piles and their uncertain footing, gliding over sleepers huddling against walls for the meager shelter they offered from the creeping fog. He edged up to blind turns, listening for several heartbeats before he moved around them. Apart from the sodden sleepers the lane stayed empty and quiet. Inside those tall narrow houses leaning against each other so they wouldn't fall down, Hina had been asleep for hours. Most of those living here would have to rise with the sun to get in half a day's work before they left for the feteday, the players and nightpeople were gone for now, though they'd be coming home at dawn to catch a few hours' sleep before working the streets to ease coppers from the purses of the swarming revelers.

Hotea pinched his shoulder. "Look," she said. "There."

"Huh?"

"On the ground there." Hotea pointed at a filthy alley between two of the tenements. Aituatea squinted but saw nothing; choking over the lump rising in his throat, he crept into the alley.

He kicked against something. A body. He dropped to one knee and twisted the head around so he could see the face. Djarko. He pressed his fingers against the meaty neck under the angle of the jaw. Very dead. A little farther up the alley he could see another long lump of refuse. He didn't bother checking, only one thing it could be. Both dead. So fast. Not a squeak out of them. Big men. Stupid but strong. Dangerous. Not even a groan. He got creakily to his feet and shuffled back from the body, step by step, lurch and swing, soles grating against the hard-packed dirt. Hotea touched his arm. He exploded out a curse, swung round and would have fled but for the dark figure standing in his way.

"Why follow me?" She had a deep voice for a woman, danger in it he could hear as surely as he heard the pounding of his heart.

He swallowed. His mouth was too dry for speech. Hotea jigged at his shoulder, almost breaking up in her impatience. She dug her fingers into him, spat a gust of words at him so fast it hurt his head. He jerked away from her and flattened himself on the rutted dirt in front of the woman's boots.

She made a soft irritated sound. "Stand up, Hina, I won't talk to the back of your head." The sharpness in her voice warned him her patience had narrow limits.

He scrambled to his feet. "Drinker of Souls," he said. "Will you listen to me?"

She shook her hair out of her face, that silver-gray hair that caught the moonlight in slanting shimmers as she moved her head. "Brann," she said. "Not that other. I don't like it. It isn't true anyway."

Aituatea glanced over his shoulder at the blob of dead flesh, turned back to the woman, saying nothing, letting the act speak for him.

She shrugged. "I didn't tell them to come after me."

"Fish to bait," he said and was surprised at his daring.

"I'm not responsible for all the stupidity in the world." She rubbed a finger past the corner of her mouth, frowning a little as she looked from him to Hotea standing a step behind him. "You were on the wharf watching me."

"You saw me?"

"Not me." She snapped her fingers.

A soft whirr overhead, then two large horned owls swooped past him, low enough he could smell the fog-dampness on their feathers. They beat up again to perch on the eaves of a house across the street, blinking yellow eyes fixed on him. He knew, then, what had happened to the children. He straightened out of his defensive crouch, keeping his eyes on the woman's face so he wouldn't have to look at the owls. "The man on the mountain said you would come ashore tonight."

"Ah. Then he's still there?"

"Someone is."

"You want something."

"Yes. I want you to do something for Hotea and me. I've got something the old man says you want; I'll give it to you if you'll do a thing for us."

"What thing?"

Aituatea fidgeted, slanting a quick glance at the owls. One of them hooted softly at him. "Not here. Not safe." He dropped onto a knee, bowed his head. "Honor my home, saöri Brann. There will be tea once the water boils."

"Tea?" A raised brow, a warm chuckle. "Well, if there's tea. I've an hour or so to kill." She smoothed her hand over her hair. "And who's waiting for me in your home?"

"A few ghosts, that's all. Do you mind?"

"Ghosts I don't mind."

He nodded and started back down the lane, walking slowly and trying to minimize his lurch, the woman walking easily beside him. "They're family in a way," he said. She made him nervous and he spoke to fill the silence. The owls whirred past, gliding low then circling up until they were lost in the fog.

"Family?"

"All my blood kin except Hotea died in the plague. Ten years ago." He turned into a side street heading more directly north. "They're company, those ghosts, though they're not actual kin. They go when their time's up, but there are always more drowned and killed and suicided to take their places."

"They won't like me." A corner of her mouth twisted up. "The dead never do."

"They're ready for you. I told them I was going to bring you if I could."

"Old man been busy about my business?"

"Hotea and me, we went to see him about our problem."

"This mysterious problem. Mmmh, I thought no one would be left to remember me."

"We asked him for help."

"And I'm it?"

"That's what he said."

They walked in silence past the crumbling houses, Hotea drifting beside him. The tenements degenerated into crowded hovels built of whatever debris their dwellers could find or steal. In the distance a baby wailed, two men were shouting, their words hushed and unintelligible, a woman shrieked once and no more, but the street they were on was sodden with silence. "There's a story about where we're going," Aituatea said. "A score of years ago there was this silk merchant. Djallasoa. He built himself a godon up ahead not far from the Woda-an Well. He sold Eternity Robes. Know what those are? No? Well, you find yourself some young girls without a blemish on their bodies to weave the silk, then get enough strong and healthy pregnant women to embroider the robes so the force of the new life will be transferred to them. A thousand gold pieces is cheap for the simplest. Hundred-year robes, that's what old Djasoa's robes were called. Even the Temueng Emperor bought from him. Talk was you never even caught a cold wearing one of his robes." The fog wrapped the three of them in a dreamlike world where the ragged huts on either side of the lane faded in and out with the shifting of the mist. "Djallasoa's eldest son was a bit of a fool, so the story goes, kicked a Woda Shaman or something like that. Old Dja tried to smooth things over. Didn't work. The Woda Shaman came ashore, built a fire in front of the godon and slit the throats of Dja's wife and seven children, then his own. After that there were nine angry ghosts infesting the place. No Hina priest of any sort could drive them off, not even those belonging to the Judges of the dead. The gods refused to get involved. . . ." The lane ended. He circled a thornbush and began picking his way through the scrub along an unmarked path so familiar he paid little attention to where he was putting his feet. "And the other Woda Shamans sat out there on the water enjoying the fuss and refusing to interfere. All the Eternity Robes Djallasoa had stowed in that godon, no one would chance buying them, not with a Woda curse on them."

The wasteland they were passing through was a mixture of thornbush, bamboo, scattered willow thickets and a few stunted oaks. With the fog obscuring detail an arm's length away, the silence broken only by the drip of condensation from limbs and leaves, the crackling of dead branches and weeds underfoot, it was like walking through one of the Elder Laksodea's spiky ink paintings come alive in a dream. Aituatea had a fondness for Laksodea and had several of his paintings, souvenirs of successful nights.

"Why are you telling me all this?"

He turned to stare at her, startled by the acerbity of her words.

"Have we much farther to go? I have better things to do with this night than spend it wandering through drip and scrub."

He pointed at the thinning growth ahead. "To where this stops, then a bit farther." He rubbed at the side of his neck. "Your pardon, säor, and your patience, if you will, but no one knows where Hotea and I live. It's safer that way. And I merely thought to help pass the time with the story. If you don't want to hear more. . . ."

"Oh, finish it and let's get on."

He bowed, started walking again. "Guards wouldn't stay around the godon at night. The silks inside were safe enough, not even Eldest Uncle wanted to face those ghosts and he was the wildest thief in Silili. Finally old Djasoa and the rest of the clan fetched a gaggle of exorcists and deader priests waving incense sticks, hammering gongs, popping crackers, making so much noise and stink they drowned out the ghosts for long enough to haul out the silk. The Eternity Robes they burned in a great fire by the Woda Well, the rest they took away to sell to foreigners who'd haul them out of Tigarezun, the farther the better. And the godon was left to rot. Old Djasoa wanted to burn it, but the other merchants raised a howl, it was an extra dry summer and they were afraid the fire'd get away from him, so he didn't burn it. So there it sat empty till the plague. You know about the plague?"

"You said ten years ago?" She shook her head, pushed aside a branch about to slap her in the face. "I was half a world away."

He stepped onto the crescent of land picked clean of vegetation. "We turn east here. It was bad. The plague, I mean. The Temuengs ran like rats, but they made sure no Hina got off Utar-Selt. Ships out in the bay rammed anyone who tried to leave and they put up barricades on the causeway." He pointed out a low broad mass, its details lost in the darkness and the fog. "The Woda Well. This is Woda land. No one else comes here now. When there was sickness in a house, the authorities burned it. Temuengs sent orders in and Hina ass-lickers did the work. So when our family started getting sick and oldest grandmother died and Hotea knew it wouldn't be long before someone came with fire, she sneaked me out and brought me to that old godon, figuring the ghosts wouldn't get sick, being already dead, and would keep snoops away. They were getting ragged, those Woda ghosts, already been around longer than most earth souls, it'd been what? ten years, more, but they made life hard for a few nights. We couldn't sleep for the howling, the blasts of fear, the cold winds that blew out of nowhere, the stinks, the pinches and tickles, but nothing they could do was worse than what was happening outside. We're almost there, you can just about see the godon now. Hotea had to go out and leave me alone a lot so she could scare up food and clothes for us. With nothing to do, shut up in that place, I started playing with the child ghosts even if they were Woda-an and after a while we made our peace with the adults, and by the time the Woda-an ghosts wore out, others moved in with us. No one likes ghosts hanging around, it's a scandal and a disgrace. If they can afford it, they have the exorcists in to chase the ghost away, a loose ghost about the house makes gossip like you wouldn't believe. So there are usually a lot of homeless ghosts drifting about. They hear about us and come to live in the godon." He heard a scrabbling behind him, swung around. Two mastiffs came trotting from the fog and stopped in front of him, mouths open in twin fierce grins, eerie crystal eyes laughing at him. With a shudder he couldn't quite suppress, he forced himself to turn his back on them and start walking toward the small door in the back wall, but he couldn't forget they were there; he could hear the pad-scrape of their paws, imagined a rhythmic panting, convinced himself he could feel the heat of their breath on the backs of his legs.

He shoved the door open and went inside. There was a narrow space between the guardwall and the godon itself, space filled with clutter slowly rotting back into the earth, bits of bone, boxes, rope, paper, silk scraps, fish bones, scraps of canvas, old leaves. The godon itself was a hollow square with red brick walls and a roof of glazed black tiles shiny with wet. Drops of condensation dripped from fungus-blackened endhorns, plopped desultorily into the decay below. Aituatea dealt with the puzzle lock on a small side door, held it open for Brann and the mastiffs, followed them inside.

At the end of a cold musty passage, moonlight was a pearly flood lighting the open court beyond, playing on mist that had crept inside or been sucked in by the breathing of the old godon. Brann stood silhouetted against it a moment as Aituatea pulled the door shut and barred it, but was gone by the time he turned around. When he reached the end of the passage, he saw her standing in the center of the court looking up, the moonlight dropping like watered milk on her pale porcelain face. The ghosts were diving down at her, bits and fragments of mist themselves, flicking through her and dashing away. She stood quite still, letting this happen as if it were a ritual that bored her but one she was willing to endure for the calm she expected afterward. The mastiffs were chasing each other and any rats they could scare up in and out of the swirls of fog, in and out of the dank caverns of the ground floor bins. They came and sniffed at his knees, then flipped around and went to circle Brann.

"Second floor to your left," Aituatea said and started for the stairs. The mastiffs trotted past him and went thumping up the stairs, dog mastiff, bitch mastiff, paw matching paw on the soggy slippery wood.

Aituatea went a short way along the second floor gallery, unbarred a door and swung it open. The room inside was dark, warm, odorous—cedar and sandalwood, lacquer and spices, smoldering peat and hot metal from the covered brazier. He bowed, spread his arms. "Enter my miserable rooms, säori Brann." He swung around and went into the dark, turning back the shutters on the window opening on the court, lighting the lamps scattered about on wall and table. He dipped water from the covered crock, set the kettle on the coals, blew them alive, came back to his guest.

Brann was settled in a low armchair, one leg tucked up under her, the other stretched out before her, her hands resting on her thighs. Her hair was darker in the rosy lamplight, more gray than silver, her eyes were a clear light green like willow leaves in early spring. The mastiffs were children again, sitting crosslegged at her feet, staring with the owl-eyed directness of real children. They had ash-blond hair, one a shade darker than the other, bowl-bobbed, fine, very straight. As he'd thought before, they looked like twins, so asexual in these forms that it disturbed him to remember one of the mastiffs had definitely been a bitch.

"My companions," she said. "Jaril." She leaned forward and touched the head on her right. "Yaril." She stroked her hand lightly over the paler head on her left. "This is a nice little nest. T'kk, friend Hina, it's more than enough to hang you." Her eyes moved over the scrolls on the walls, the jewel rugs on the floor, the other fine things visible in the lampglow.

"I'll be dead anyway if the Temuengs get this far."

She tapped fingers on her thigh. "It's rather crowded in here." He dropped into the chair by the brazier and sat watching her. She saw them all, that was obvious. Moonfisher drifting in rags near the ceiling, used to be a powerful fishcaller, brought in heavy boatloads until a storm caught him and drowned him in sight of land. Eldest Grandmother crouching by the door, a tattered patchy ghost, she'd fade out soon, poisoned by a daughter-in-law who was tired of being run off her feet. Elder brother sitting in front of the window, strangled by a Sister of the Cord when he blundered into a forbidden ritual. Little brother, drowned, hovering behind the chair, peeking out at the shape-changers. The headless woman no one knew about, the gambler, the dancers, the several whores, the little sister, even the crabby old Temueng who sat in gloomy silence in the corner. Though Eldest Grandmother started muttering angrily beside the door, glaring at Brann, who ignored her after a flicker of a smile in her direction, the others came drifting around her, circling gradually nearer. One by one they darted to her, stroked her, tasting her through their fingers. As if the taste pleased them, they quieted, grew content, the frazzled edges smoothed away.

Aituatea checked the pot but the water wasn't close to boiling, then he sat staring down at his hands, reluctant, now the time was on him, to speak the words that would commit him to the attack on the Kadda witch. The ghosts gathered around him, his family, patting him, murmuring to him, giving what strength and support they could. Why not get it over with. "I don't know why you came to Silili."

"No." She smiled, drew her thumb along her lower lip. "You don't."

"Well, it doesn't matter. There's a Kadda witch in the Tekora's Palace. His wife."

"Then the man's a fool."

"I won't argue with that. Anyway, she's the one responsible for Hotea's drowning. We want you to help us get rid of her."

"The Tekora's Palace." She laughed, a warm savoring sound. And he remembered the way she looked at the gate torches. He got to his feet and crossed to the back of the long room, going behind the screen that shut off the corner where his bed was. The dark red lacquer box sat where he'd left it among the hills and hollows of the crumpled quilts. He looked at the unmade bed and wondered if he'd ever get back, bit his lip, lifted the box and carried it to Brann. He set it on the low table by the arm of her chair, then backed away. He glanced at the brazier but saw no steam and resettled himself in his chair. "The old man said that would buy you."

She lifted the box, set it on her legs. After eyeing it warily a moment, she lifted the lid. Her indrawn breath was a small whispery sound. "Das'n vuor." She lifted the black pot from its nest of fine white silk and ran her fingers over it. A strange tense look on her face, she turned it over and passed her fingers across the bottom. "His mark," she whispered. "The last firing." She set the pot back and lifted one of the cups, sat cradling it in both hands. "That you found this one . . . *this* one! I remember . . . Slya bless, oh I remember. . . . I held this cup in my hand after my father took it from the kiln. I went up Tincreal with my father, we carried the last cups to their firing; we stayed there all day and all night and the next day till just after noonsong. The first three he took from the kiln he broke, they weren't good enough, this was the fourth, he set it in my hand and I knew what perfection was, for the first time I knew what perfection was. . . ." She shook her head as if to clear away fumes of memory.

"Old man said it would buy you." He repeated those words, knowing he was being crude, perhaps angering her, but he was shocked at seeing her unravel. He wanted her to be powerful, unshaken by anything, as she was when he first saw her. Otherwise how could she stand against the witch?

"Old man, he's right, damn his twisty soul." She eased the cup into its nest and folded the lid shut. "You've bought me, Hina. I'll fight the witch for the pot and for more reasons than you'll ever know. Mmm, tell you one thing. Would have done it without the pot." She grinned at him, her hand protectively on the lid. "Don't try to take it back, I'll bite. Seriously, I'm a sentimental bitch when I let myself be, Hina, and I've been watching you and your sister. You could have worked yourself free of her easily enough, a little thought and gathering the coin for an exorcism, who would ever know? My companions tell me you didn't even think of exorcism. I like that. Well, that's enough, what are you planning?"

"Can you climb?" Hotea pinched him. "So we hear from you again," he grumbled. With a spitting crackle of indignation she pointed at the steam shooting from under the kettle's lid.

"I was born on the side of a mountain that makes the hills round here look like gnat bites," Brann said and laughed.

"Good." He chose a teapot he thought of as his garden pot, the one with bamboo and orchids delicately painted round the five flat sides. As he rinsed the pot, he glanced at her. Her head was against the back of the chair, her eyes half closed, her hands relaxed on the chair arms. He measured out two scoops of black tea, added hot water, took the pot to the narrow table by the screen, set out the shallow dishes for the ghosts.

"Why are you doing that?" Her voice came to him, lazy, relaxed. When he looked at her, she seemed half asleep.

"For the family," he said. A wave of his hand took in the hovering ghosts clustering over the bowls lapping up the fragrance. He came back to the table, filled two cups, frowned at the children. "Do they want tea?"

She shook her head. "No." She took the cup he handed her, sniffed at the coiling steam. "Mmmm." Green eyes laughing at him, she said, "Steal only the best."

"Right." He dropped into his chair, gulped a mouthful of the tea. "Old man said you and the witch are ancient enemies."

"Oh?" Her eyes narrowed. "Do you know her name?"

"No."

"Yes." Hotea darted forward. "Yes. The other wives, they cursed her by name and worse. It's an odd name, can't tell clan or family from it. Ludila Dondi."

"Ah. The Dondi."

"You do know her."

"We met. Briefly. A long time ago. Not love at first sight." She rolled the five-sided cup between her palms. "She was just a fingerling then, but nasty." She emptied the cup, set it carefully on the table. "Talk, young Hina. I'm due back on the ship by dawn and I've other games to play." She set the box on the table, leaned forward, her eyes bright with curiosity and anticipation. "I'm listening."

The willows tilted out over the water, their withes dissolving into mist. The boat was a miniature of the flat-bottomed water taxis with barely room for two and a ghost but the children had shifted form again and gone whiffling away as owls. Brann seated herself in the bow, settled the box at her feet on dry floorboards. Aituatea fumbled at the sodden rope, finally working the knot loose; his hands were shaking, but excitement outweighed his fear. With Hotea floating at his side, he shoved the boat into deeper water and swung in. A few minutes later he was propelling them through mist with nothing visible around them but the grayed-down wavelets of dark water kissing the boat's sides.

After half an hour's hard rowing, he'd rounded Utar's snout and was struggling south along the cliffs, the rougher chop on the weather side of the small island making the going hard. The fog was patchy, shredding in the night wind. Finally, Hotea pinched his arm and pointed. "There," she said. "The nursery garden is up there."

" 'Bout time." With Brann fending the bow off the rocks, he eased the boat through the tumbled black boulders to the beach.

While Brann held the boat, he tied the painter to a knob on one of the larger rocks, then pulled a heavy cover over it, canvas painted with rough splotches of gray and black that would mask the boat shape from anyone chancing to look down. As he waded beside Brann to the tiny beach, the owls swooped down, hooted, a note of urgency in their cries, and swept up again. A moment later, voices, the stomp of feet, the sounds of a body of armed men moving came dropping down the cliff. Brann dodged into a hollow that hid her from above. Aituatea joined her there, all too aware of the heat of her body through the thin silk of her shirt, the strong life in her more frightening than arousing.

"How long before they come round again?" she whispered.

"When Hotea was in the Palace, the round took about an hour, no reason to change that. Plenty of time to get up the cliff."

The cliff was deeply weathered, but most of the hand and footholds were treacherous, the stone apt to crumble. In spite of that, Aituatea went up with reckless speed, showing off his skill. He wasn't a cripple on a cliff. He reached the top ahead of Brann, stood wiping the muck off his hands and examining the garden wall as she pulled herself onto the guard track.

The wall was twice his height, the stones polished and set in what had once been a seamless whole, but a century of salt wind and salt damp had eaten away at the cracks, opening small crevices for the fingers and toes of a clever climber. He kicked off his sandals, shoved them in a pocket of his jacket, looked at Brann, then started up. As soon as he reached the broad top, he crawled along it until he was masked from the nursery door and windows by the bushy foliage.

Brann came up with more difficulty, needing a hand to help her over; again he felt the burning as his hand closed about hers. She smiled at his uneasiness, then sat on the wall and pulled on her boots.

The owls circled overhead, dipped into the garden, flowing into mastiff form as they touched ground. The dogs trotted briskly about nosing into shadow until they were satisfied the garden was empty, then they came silently back and waited for Brann to come down, which she did, slithering down the foliage with ease and grace. Aituatea climbed down as well, dropped the last bit to land harder than he'd expected, limped toward the doors, Hotea a wisp fluttering beside him. Though she was silent now, he could feel her agitation. This was where the witch had caught her. "Sister," he whispered, "scout for us."

Hotea slipped through the wall, emerged a few minutes later. "Empty," she cried. "No children, no wives, no bondmaids. All gone. Not one left." Her crystal form trembled. "The bottom of the bay must be solid with bones."

"Just as well." He took a long slim knife from a sheath inside his jacket, slid it through the space between the doors, wiggled it until he felt it slip the latch loose and the door swing inward. Brann touched his arm, a jolt like a shock-eel. Swallowing a yelp, he looked around.

"Let Yaril and Jaril run ahead."

He nodded. The mastiffs brushed past him and trotted inside, their nails making busy clicks on the polished wood floor. Brann glanced about the garden, moved inside, silent as the ghost she followed. Aituatea pulled the door shut behind him and limped after them.

The air in the maze of corridors was stale and stinking, a soup of rottenness, thick with the anise Hotea had learned to hate mingled with other spices. Those corridors crawled with shadow and dust rolls that tumbled along the grass mats, driven by vagrant drafts that were the only things wandering the palace. Most of the rooms were empty; there were a few sleepers, some court parasites, men and women drugged by ambition and stronger opiates, refusing to know what was happening about them. Aituatea moved through this death-in-life, his fear and reluctance banished by the demands of the moment; there was no turning back and a kind of peace in that.

Up one flight of stairs to the public rooms. The eerie emptiness was the same, the same death smell, the same staleness in air that was paradoxically never still. They went swiftly through this silence to the stairs leading up to the rooms the Tekora kept for himself.

The mastiffs sat on their haunches beside Brann, stubby tails thumping against the mat. Hotea flitted back to them. "Guards," she said. "Standing on either side of the Tekora's sleeproom door."

Brann touched the corner of her mouth. "They alert?"

"Not very," Hotea said, "but awake."

"Mm. Means he's inside. But is the witch with him?"

"I'll see." Before Brann or Aituatea could stop her, Hotea flitted back up the stairs.

"T'kk, young Hina. Pray the Dondi is sleeping or not there, otherwise your sister could bring the roof down on us."

"She won't think before she does."

"And you think too much, eh?"

Aituatea ignored that as he gazed up the stairs, anxious about Hotea.

Seconds later she was back, a streak of subdued light plunging down the slant, a waterfall of woman ghost, halting before them in a swirl of crystal fragments that rapidly reassembled themselves into Hotea-shape. "They're in bed, both of them. Asleep, I think, I only poked my head in for a second. They ate someone tonight, the smell of it is sickening thick in there."

"Asleep. Good. Let them stay that way." She led them around beneath the stairs so the sound of their whispers would not carry to the guards. She settled herself with her back to the wall, waited until Aituatea was down beside her, squatting, fingers rubbing at his sore hip, preferring the pain to the thoughts in his head; it was almost a sufficient distraction. "Bit of luck," Brann murmured, "finding them asleep and sated." A quick wry smile. "Not so good for whoever they ate, but we can't change that. I am very glad indeed that the Dondi's asleep. Even so, be warned, she limits me. I don't want to stir up resonances that would wake her too soon." When Aituatea indicated he didn't understand, she sighed but didn't try to explain. "First thing is taking out the guards." She flipped back the edge of her leather vest, showed him the twin blades sheathed inside. "I can pick them off, but I can't be sure of silencing them, takes time to bleed to death. Any ideas?"

Aituatea nodded, reached inside his jacket, felt a moment among the pockets sewn into the lining, took out a section of nested bamboo tubes. "Carry this for tight holes. Haven't had to use the darts yet, but I can hit a hand at twenty paces. Sister, where are they? what armor?"

Hotea knelt beside him. "About a dozen paces from the landing, my paces, not yours." She held out her arms, wrists pressed together, hands spread at an angle. "That's the shooting angle you'll have from the nearest shelter. They're not looking toward the stairway, didn't the whole time I was watching them, though that wasn't very long." She shifted restlessly. "It's a tight shot, brother, even you'll have trouble. They're trussed in studded leather and iron straps and wearing helmets." She framed her face with her hands, her brow and chin covered. "That's all you got."

"Hands?"

"I forgot. Gloves."

"Tungjii's tits, they don't make it easy." He pulled the tubes out until he had a pipe about a foot long. He looked over his shoulder at the dogs; they were on their feet, crystal eyes bright and interested, tongues lolling. He breathed a curse, brought out a small lacquer box, held it in the hand that held the pipe. "Them. If I miss, can they take out the guards?"

Without answering, Brann pushed onto her feet and went around to the foot of the stairs. The mastiffs sniffed at Aituatea's legs as he stood beside her, then went padding up the stairs as quiet as cats slow and flowing so their nails wouldn't click on the wood. Near the bend in the flight they misted out of shape and reformed into long brindle snakes that flowed silent and nearly invisible up to the landing.

Aituatea followed them up the steps, narrowing himself to the need of the moment. On the top step he knelt and eased around the corner, concealed in the shadow not lit by the lamp suspended above the sun-door, picking out gleams in the many layered black lacquer and the gilt sun-shape inlaid in both halves of the double door. He popped one of his poison thorns in the pipe, careful not to touch the gummy tip, got a second dart from the box and set it on the floor by his knee. Ache in his hip forgotten, chill in his belly forgotten, he focused on the expanse of cheek and sent the dart winging with a hard puff. As soon as it was on its way, he reloaded the pipe and sent the second at the other guard.

One then the other slapped at his face, eyes popping, gave a small strangled gasp and started to crumple. Aituatea was on his feet and running as soon as he saw the first man waver, knowing he wouldn't get there in time to catch both.

The shape changers flowed up from the floor by the guards' feet, children again, caught the collapsing men and eased them down quietly. Aituatea touched his brow and lips in a gesture of congratulation. They grinned and bobbed their pale shining heads.

He stepped over a recumbent guard and eyed the double door, brushed his hand along the center line, felt the door yield a little to the pressure. "Sister," he breathed, "what sort of latch?"

Hotea oozed partway through the door, then pulled back out. "Turnbolt. You'll have to cut the tongue."

He scowled at the gilt sun. "And hope the noise doesn't wake them. Some hope."

Brann touched his shoulder. He jumped. "I wish you wouldn't do that."

She ignored that as foolishness. "Be ready," she whispered. "Yaril will throw the bolt for us, but her presence in the room will wake the witch."

The fairer child changed into mist and flowed under the door. A second later he heard a muted *tunk* as the bolt tongue withdrew, then a wild, piercing yell.

Brann leaped at the door, hit the crack with the heel of one hand, slamming the doors open. She charged in to stand in front of Yaril who crouched on the rug, eyes steady on the witch.

Ludila Dondi arose from the bed, her face ugly with rage, her naked body yellowed ivory in the dim light, like a tiger in her ferocity and the vigorous agility of her leap. When she saw Brann, she checked her lunge along the bed, so suddenly she was thrown off balance. "You." She slid off the bed and came toward Brann, feral yellow eyes fixed on her, ignoring the others.

Jaril took Yaril's hands. After a brief, silent consultation they rose as spheres of amber fire, lighting the room with a fierce gold glow.

The Tekora kicked loose from the quilts and rolled off the bed, standing naked as the witch but not so readily awake and alert. Aituatea watched him with a burning in his belly. No old man any longer, the Temueng was firm, fit, supple, a man in his prime, a vigor bought with the blood of his own children, a hideous vigor that had cost Hotea her life.

The Tekora eyed the two women, reached up and with a soft metallic sibilation drew from its sheath the long sword hanging above the head of the bed. He swung it twice about his head, limbering his arm. A glance at Aituatea, a head shake dismissing the Hina as negligible. He started for the woman.

The Dondi and Brann were moving in an irregular double spiral, gradually working closer to each other, each focused so intently on the other no one else existed for them.

Hotea fluttered about them, turning in wider loops, silent but radiating fury.

The firespheres vibrated more rapidly, then one of them darted straight at the Tekora's face. He lifted his free hand to brush it aside, yelled as his flesh began to blister, swung round and swiped at the sphere with the sword, slicing through it but doing no damage. It settled to the floor in front of him, a mastiff as soon as it touched down. The dog came at the man, growling deep in her throat. Bitch mastiff. Yaril. Aituatea snapped the knife from the sheath up his sleeve, sent it wheeling at the Tekora.

It sliced into the large artery in his neck. There should have been an explosion of blood and a dead man falling.

Should have been. The Tekora plucked the knife out easily and flung it away. The wound in his neck closed over. He lifted the sword and started for Aituatea.

Aituatea looked rapidly around, caught up a small stool and hurled it at the Temueng, it caught his elbow, his fingers opened involuntarily and the sword went flying to land in the tumbled covers on the bed. The Yaril mastiff went for his throat but he got his arm up in time and the curving yellow teeth closed on that instead of his neck; Yaril began gnawing at the arm, kicking at his gut with her powerful hind legs.

Aituatea backed off. Ludila Dondi was chanting as she circled, a drone of ancient words with a compelling complex rhythm. When the doors flew open and he saw her coming up out of the bed, he thought she was completely naked, but now he saw the mirrors on the silver chain about her neck, the tinier mirrors dangling from her earlobes, others set in wristlets on each arm. She moved her body, her arms, her head in counterpoint to the rhythm of the words, dancing the glitters in a web about herself, trying to weave a web about Brann.

Brann stalked her, avoiding the wild yellow eyes, avoiding the mirror lights, gradually tightening the spiral.

Firesphere Jaril darted at the Dondi, shattering the rhythm of her lights and each time he dived, Brann got a little closer.

The Tekora flung off the mastiff, his torn flesh closing. He threw himself at the bed, came curling up with the sword, rolled onto his feet again. With a grunting roar he charged at Brann.

The mastiff Yaril was suddenly a long snake that whipped itself up and around the Tekora's legs, wrenching him off his feet, dissolving before he could cut at it with the sword he still held.

Firesphere Jaril came an instant too close to the witch, touching one of the mirrors; the sphere tumbled through the air, melting through a dozen shapes before it was a boy curled in fetal position on the rug. His fall distracted the Dondi for a second only, but it was enough. Brann's hands slapped about the Dondi's ribs; she hugged the smaller woman tight against her, caught her mouth, held her mouth to mouth, muffling the witch's shriek of rage and despair.

As Yaril melted, Aituatea was on the Tekora, the foot of his good leg jammed between arm and shoulder, hands in a nerve hold on the Temueng's wrist. The Tekora writhed and struggled but couldn't break the hold. Aituatea dug his knuckles in. The Tekora's fingers opened. Aituatea caught the sword as it fell, leaped back, took the Temueng's head off as he surged up, the sword answering his will like an extension of his arm. He swung it up, whirled it about, grinning, suppressing an urge to whoop; but all too fast his elation chilled. The Tekora's headless body stirred, hands groping as it got clumsily to its knees. Something bumped against his foot. The Tekora's head, mouth working, teeth gnashing as it tried to sink them in his flesh. He kicked the head away, wanting to vomit. A hand brushed against him, tried to grab hold of him. He sliced through the body's knees, kicked the severed legs in separate directions. The body fell, lay still a moment, then the stumps began moving. They found no purchase on the silken rug until the torso raised itself onto its elbows and pulled itself toward him. He cut off the arms at the elbow, groaned as the hands started creeping toward him. He kicked them away but they started crawling for him again.

The kiss went on and on, the witch withering in Brann's arms—but withering slowly, too slowly, there was too much life in her. Yaril landed beside Jaril, changed. She reached toward the boy, fire snapped between them, then Jaril was up looking around. A look, a nod, then they joined hands and two firespheres darted into the air. They threw themselves at the Soul-Drinker, merged with her until her flesh shimmered with golden fire and the three of them finished drawing the life out of the Dondi.

Brann dropped the woman's husk, the fire flowed out of her and divided into two children, sated and a bit sleepy. She stared down at the thing crumpled at her feet and shuddered.

Aituatea kicked away a creeping hand, walked over and stared down at what was left of the Kadda witch. An ancient mummy, leathery skin tight over dry bones. "Never seen anyone deader."

Hotea came from the shadows. "Put her in the water; she has to go in the water." She rushed to the nearest window and tried to pull the drapes aside, but her hands passed through the soft dark velvet. She shrieked with frustration and darted back at them. "In the water," she cried, enraged.

Brann nodded. "This one's too strong to be careless of, let the water rot her and the tides carry her bones away. Open the window for me, or would you rather carry that?" She waved a hand at the husk.

"Gahh, no." He stepped over a wriggling leg, a crawling hand, circled the silently mouthing head, pulled the drapes aside and opened the shutters.

Wind boomed into the room, cold and full of sea-tang, blowing out the lamp, stirring the silken quilts, almost snatching the shutters from him. It caught at the shorter hair by Brann's ears, teased it out from

her face, bits of blue-white fire crackling off the ends. She wrinkled her
nose, brushed impatiently at her hair, her hand lost among the snapping lights. "Hold your head on," she muttered at Hotea who was
chattering again and jigging about her. She lifted the husk, grunting
with the effort, carried it to the window and eased it through. Hotea at
his shoulder, Aituatea stood beside her and watched the husk plum-
meting toward wind-whipped water as Hotea had half a year ago,
watched it sink.

Hotea gave a little sigh of satisfaction, tapped her brother on the
cheek. "A wife," she said. "Mind me now, get you a wife, brother."
Another sigh and she was gone.

Aituatea rubbed at his shoulder. Rid of her. He stared out the window seeing nothing. He'd cursed her silently and aloud since she'd
come back dead. And he'd cursed her alive and resented her. She'd
taught him most of what he knew, stung him into forgetting his short
leg, scolded him, comforted him, kept him going when times were bad.
Always there. And now he was rid of her. Alone.

"Hina." He heard the word but it didn't seem important. "Hina!"
Sharper voice, a demand for his attention.

"What?" He turned his head, searching vaguely for the speaker.

"That sword. The one you've got the death grip on. May I see it?"

He looked down. He was leaning on the long sword, the point sunk
into the rug, into the floor beneath. He had to tug it free before he
could lift it. He gazed at it, remembering the aliveness of it in his
hands, shook his head, not understanding much of anything at that
moment, and offered it to her.

She looked down at her hands. They glowed softly in the room's
shadowy twilight. "No. Better not. Lay it on the bed for me." She
hesitated a moment. "Hina, let me touch you."

"Why?" Apprehensive, still holding the sword, he backed away from
her.

"Slya's breath, man, you think I want more of this in me? Got too
much now. Listen, you're tired, sore, we've still got to get out of this
and down the cliff. I can give as well as take. You'll feel like you've
been chewing awsengatsa weed for a few hours, that's all. All you have
to do is take my hand." She held out a hand, palm up, waited.

He looked at her; she seemed impatient. His hip was a gnawing pain,
he'd used himself hard this night, his shoulders and arms ached, he had
toothmarks on one foot and cold knots in his stomach. "The weed,
huh?"

"With no hangover."

"I could use a look at Jah'takash's better side." He tossed the sword on the bed, closed his hand about hers.

A feeling like warm water flowing into his body, gentle, soothing, heating away his aches and pains, washing away his weariness. Only a breath or two, then she was pulling free. He didn't want to let go, but was afraid to cling to her. He opened his eyes. "I owe the Lady of Surprises a fistful of incense." He looked from the sword—a long glimmer on the silk of the quilt—to the sheath on the wall above the bed. "That's what you came to Silili for, isn't it." He climbed on the bed, pulled the sheath down and slid the sword into it, jumped back onto the floor.

"Right. The Serpent's Tooth, Sulinjoa's last sword, the one he forged for what's-his-name, your last Hina king. It always cuts the hand that owns it, so the story goes. His wife, she was supposed to be a demon of some sort, she cursed the sword when he quenched it the last time in the blood of their youngest son." She took the sword from him, no hesitation now, pulled it from the sheath, clucked at the bloodstains along the blade, used the edge of the drape to wipe it clean, moving the velvet cloth gently over it, then held the blade up to the moonlight, clucked again at the marks the blood had left. "Have to work on this once I'm back on the ship." She slid the blade with slow care into the sheath. "Your king took off Sulinjoa's head with it so he'd never make a finer sword for someone else. The Temueng who made himself Emperor, he used it on the king and gave it away to a supporter he didn't much like." She chuckled. "That one didn't last long either."

"Who'd want it with that history?" Aituatea eyed the sword with revulsion, then remembered how it'd felt in his hand. He shook his head.

"The man who's going to pay me five thousand gold for it." She looked down, grimaced and kicked away the hand that had brushed against her foot. "No friend of mine which is just as well, looks like the curse is still going strong."

Aituatea grunted and went hunting for his knife, unwilling to leave any piece of himself in this place. When bright light suddenly bloomed about him, he glanced up. A firesphere floated above him. "Thanks," he muttered. He found the knife leaning against the side of a cabinet, wiped it on the rug and tucked it away. The light vanished.

Brann was leaning out the window when he straightened. She drew back inside. "Dawn's close. We better get out of here."

Giggles flitted by Aituatea. From a shimmering point above the bed, finger-long gold bars, silver bars, rings and bracelets cascaded in a heap on the silk.

"Yours," Brann said. "Courtesy of Yaril and Jaril. They thought you ought to have some compensation for your latest loss."

An owl was suddenly in the room, hovering over the bed, a plump leather sack clutched in its talons. Its hoots like eldrich laughter, it sailed through the window and disappeared into the night. A second owl with a second pouch appeared, flew after the first.

Aituatea passed a hand across his face, disconcerted. In the events of the past moments, he'd forgotten the sense of dislocation that had chilled him when Hotea vanished. Now he resented both things, being reminded of that loss and having his feelings read so easily. But this was no time for indulging in resentments or grief. He shucked a case off one of the pillows, raked the gold and gems into it, tied the ends in a loop he could thrust his arm through, leaving both hands free. "Back the way we came?"

"Unless you know how to get past the causeway guards." She tucked the sword under her arm and started for the door. "You can take me out to the ship if you will. She's due to lift anchor with the dawn."

The fog was blowing out to sea, the wind changing from salt to green, the smell of day and land and coming storm on it. As Aituatea worked the boat toward the willow grove, he saw the sky flush faintly red behind the Temple roof. More than one kind of storm coming, he thought. When someone steels himself to look into that room and finds the Tekora in still wiggling pieces. Hei-yo, Godalau grant they blame the Kadda wife for it since she won't be around. No way to tie me to it, not now, not with Hotea all the way gone. He tied the boat up, splashed through the shallow water to the shore. In the distance he could hear drums and rattles, the Woda-an celebrating the departure of the blind ship. Drinker of Souls, you're not a bad sort, but I hope I never see you again. Tungjii bless you, though. Never thought I'd miss Hotea like this. Aching with loneliness, he pushed through the dangling withes and trudged up the slope toward the abandoned godon.

In the warm and scented room, he sat with the brazier providing the only light, a bowl of wine in one hand, a stone jar of wine on the table beside his feet. He'd put his dirty bare feet on the table deliberately, meaning to provoke Eldest Grandmother into scolding him. The sounds she made in his head were no longer words but they were comfortably familiar. He sipped at the wine, thinking about Brann, wondering who the fool was who sent her after that cursed sword. He thought about Hotea. She's right, I should find me a wife. Someone who could stand to live here, definitely someone who knows how to keep her mouth shut. He stretched out in the chair until he was almost lying flat, crossed his ankles and balanced the wine bowl on his stomach. Not till the storm's blown out. Both storms. He took a mouthful of wine, let it trickle its warmth down his throat, smiled sleepily at the ghosts that were gathering about him. He thought he could see some new faces among them but was too lazy to ask. It's over, he thought. Really over. Me. Aituatea. I killed the Temueng Tekora. Sort of killed him. He grinned.

"Let me go off a little while and look what happens. Drunk. Disgustingly drunk."

He jerked up, spilling the wine, looked wildly about. "Hotea?"

Her crystal form was hovering over the brazier, picking up red light from the coals. "You got another sister I don't know about?"

"I thought you were gone to rest."

"Not a chance, brother, not till I get you safely wed to the right woman." She gathered in several female ghosts and led them to surround him. "Listen, Kellavoe's youngest. Word is her hands are almost as good as mine, can strip the eyelashes off a dozing dragon. Living with her uncle these days since the Temuengs hanged her father and you know old Kezolavoe, meaner than a boar in rut, but she doesn't complain. Good girl. Loyal to her kin. Be doing the child a favor, getting her away from him. . . ."

"Ohh-eh, slow down, I'll take a look at the girl, but after the storm, if you don't mind, sister." He got to his feet, went to set out the dishes for the ghosts. "Why don't we all celebrate? Sniff some wine and help me tell the tale of the raid on the Tekora's palace." He began filling the dishes with wine, feeling his body and spirit relax into a familiar irritated contentment. Plenty of time, good friends and a growing family. He looked about, counted shapes and set out another of the shallow bowls. Definitely new faces in the mix, some Hina, some Temueng and a Woda-an. He stepped back, lifted his bowl. "To family ties," he said. "Old and new."

The ghosts sighed, bathed in the wine's fragrance and exuded a contentment to match his own.

2.

Brann's Quest—
The Flight from Arth Slya

Brann sits awake. Bleeding into memory, all the sounds about her, water sounds, muted shouts from deck and masts, ship sounds, board and rope talking to the dawn, wind sounds, *sighs* and long wails. She sits at a small table, dawn's light creeping in, painting images across her body. The mix of sound and smell reinforces the quiet melancholy that awakened her and drew her out of bed and to the chair, her hair falling about her face, the das'n vuor pot held between her hands. Black deeps on a base as thin and singing as fine porcelain, the true das'n vuor from the fireheart of Tincreal.

She breathed on the pot, rubbed at the surface with a soft rag. Whoever had you took good care of you. Well why not? You're a treasure, my pot, ancient though you are. Almost as old as me. A hundred years, more. Doesn't feel like it's been that long. The years have flown, oh how they've disappeared. She put the rag down and held the pot tilted so she could look down into the black of it, seeing images, the faces of father, brothers, sisters, cousins, uncles, aunts, of her mother suckling long dead Ruan; saw herself, a thin energetic girl with mouse-colored braids leaking wisps of fine hair. A long time ago. So long she had trouble remembering that Brann. She drew a finger across the black mirror, leaving a faint film of oil behind. Is the road to Arth Slya open again? Are the Croaldhine holding the tri-year fair in Grannsha? I'd like to see it again. Jupelang—I think he's the one—said you can't step in the same river twice. Even so, I'd like to see the valley again no matter the changes or the hurt. No place for me there, but I'd like to walk the slopes of Tincreal again and remember that young Brann.

She smiled with quiet pleasure at Chandro shipmaster when he rolled over half-awake. More memory. Sammang, my old friend, you gave me a weakness for sailing men I've never regretted. Blinking, Chandro laced his fingers behind his head and grinned at her, his teeth gleaming through a tangle of black, the elaborate corkscrews he twisted into his beard at every portcall raveled into a wild bramble bush. He yawned, savoring these last few minutes in the warm sheets smelling of both of them, a musky heated odor that mixed with memory to make a powerful aphrodisiac. She started to put the pot down and go to him, but the mate chose that moment to thump on the door.

Chuckling, Chandro rolled out of bed, stood stretching and groaning with pleasure as he worked sleep out of his big supple body. He patted at his beard, looked at her with sly amusement. "Save it for later, Bramble love, won't hurt for keeping."

She snorted, picked up the rag to clean her fingerprints off the pot.

When he was dressed, his beard combed, he came over to her and looked down at the gathered blackness in her hands. "Das'n vuor. I could get you a thousand gold for that." She snorted again and he laughed. "I know, you wouldn't part with it for ten thousand." He brushed her hair aside, kissed the nape of her neck and went out, whistling a saucy tune that brought a reluctant fond grin to her lips.

Quietly content, she burnished the pot.

In the black mirror her woman's face framed in white silk hair blurs, elongates into a skinny coltish girl with untidy mouse-colored braids and grubby hands that look too big for her arms. She sits in a grassy glade among tall cedars, a sketch pad on her knee, jotting down impressions of a herd of small furry coynos playing in the grass. . . .

On the day of Arth Slya's destruction, Tincreal burped.

Brann leaned over and flattened both hands on the grass beside her, feeling the rhythmic jolts of the hard red dirt, relishing the wildness of the Mountain. She tossed her drawing pad aside, grabbed for a low-hanging limbtip and pulled herself to her feet, her eyes opening wide as she felt the uneasy trembling of the tree. Around her the cedars were groaning and shuddering as the earth continued to shift beneath them, and birds spiraling into air stiller for once than the earth, a mounting, thickening cloud, red, black, blue, mottled browns, flashes of white, chevinks and dippers, moonfishers, redbirds and mojays, corvins, tarhees, streaks and sparrins, spiraling up and up, filling the air with their fear. She gripped the cedar twigs and needles, starting to be afraid herself as the groaning shift of the earth went on and on, shivering. After an eternity it seemed, the mountain grew quiet again, the rockfalls stopped, the shudderings calmed, and Slya went back to her restless sleep.

She opened her hand, looked at the sharp-smelling sticky resin smeared across her palm and fingers, grimaced, ran across the grass to the creekbank and her sunning rock, a flat boulder jutting into the water. She stood in the middle of it watching the otters peel out of their shaking pile and begin grooming their ruffled fur, watching the birds settle back into the treetops leaving the sky empty except for a few fleecy clouds about the broad snow-covered peak of Tincreal. This was the first time she'd been alone on the Mountain during one of the quakes that were coming with increasing frequency these warm spring days. A warning of bother to come, the Yongala said, pack what you'll need if we have to run from her wrath; and Eldest Uncle Eornis told stories of his great-grandfather's time when Slya woke before. With an uneasy giggle, she clapped her hands, began the Yongala's dance on the rock, singing the sleep song to the Mountain and the Mountain's heart, Arth Slya, Slya's Ground, to Slya who protected, who warmed the springs and kept the Valley comfortable in winter, to Slya who made fire for her father's kilns, to Slya the Sleeping Lady, powerful protector and dangerous companion. "Slya wakes," she sang. . . .

> Slya wakes
> Mountain quakes
> Air thickens
> Stone quickens
> Ash breath
> Bringing death
> Slya, sleep   sleep, Slya
> Yongala dances dreams for you
> Slya turns
> Stone burns
> Red rivers riot around us
> Day drops dark around us
> Beasts fly
> Men fear
> Forests fry
> Sleep, Slya   Slya, sleep
> Yongala dances dreams for you

At once exhilarated and afraid, singing to celebrate and to propitiate, Brann danced her own fears away, then went hunting soapweed to wash the blackened cedar resin off her hands.

Go back, start again at the day's beginning, the last morning Arth Slya was whole.

On that last morning that seemed much like any other morning, Brann came into the kitchen after breakfast and her morning chores were done. Gingy-next-to-baby stood on a stool by the washtub, soapweed lather bubbling up around his arms, scrubbing at pots and plates. He looked round, snapped a glob of lather at her. "You," he said. "Hunh."

"It's your turn, mouse, I did 'em yestereve." She wiped the lather off her arm, went over to ruffle his short brown curls, giggled as he shuddered all over and whinnied like a little pony, then went to the food locker. "Shara."

"Mmm?" Her younger sister sat at the breakfast table tending a smallish plant, nipping off bits of it, stirring the dirt about its roots. She was only nine but her Choice was clear to her and everyone else; she was already, though unofficially, apprenticed to Uncle Sahah the farmer and spent most of her days with him now, working in the fields, silent, sunburned and utterly content. She set the pot down, looked around, her green eyes half hidden by heavy lids that made her look sleepy when she was most alert. "What?"

"Did Mama order more bread from Uncle Djimis? No?" She held up the hard end of an old loaf. "Well, this is all we got left. And I'm taking it." She put the bread in her satchel; it was stale but Uncle Djimis's bread had a goodness that stayed with it to the last crumb. She added a chunk of cheese and two apples, slipped the satchel's straps over her shoulder and danced out, her long braids bouncing on her shoulders. "Be good, younguns," she warbled and kicked the door shut on their indignant replies, went running through the quiet house to the back porch where her mother sat in her webbing hammock swinging gently back and forth as she nursed baby Ruan, humming a tuneless, wordless song.

"I'm off," Brann told her mother. "Anything special you want?"

Accyra reached out and closed a hand about Brann's fingers, squeezed them gently. "Take care, Bramble-all-thorns, the Mountain's uncertain these days." She closed her eyes, keeping hold of Brann's hand, hummed some more, smiled and looked up. "Coynos, as many different views as you have time for, some of your other four-foots, I'm thinking of a tapestry celebrating the Mountain." She lifted a brow. "And be back to help with supper."

Brann nodded, then clicked her tongue. "I forgot. I was going to tell

Shara to order some more bread, I've got the last in here." She patted the satchel. "Shall I stop in at Uncle Djimis's on my way out?"

Her mother lifted heavy eyelids and sighed. "I'll never remember it without Callim here to remind me. What do we need?"

"Well, a couple loaves of regular bread. And some honey-nut rolls for breakfast tomorrow? Hmmmm? Please?"

Her mother chuckled. "All right, a dozen honey-nut rolls; tell Shara to fetch them before you leave."

"Thanks, Mum." She started toward the door.

"Be just a little careful, whirlwind, don't let the Mountain fall on you."

"Won't." She dashed back through the house, stuck her head into the kitchen, "Shara, Mama says you should fetch the bread and stuff," went charging on through the house singing, "Won't, won't, won't let the Mountain fall on me, won't won't won't," but went more sedately down the white sand road, waving to uncles and aunts and cousins by courtesy and blood who passed her walking along to the workshops that lined the river.

Uncle Migel was at his forge, a pile of work already finished; it was his day to turn out all the finicky little bits the Valley needed: nails and rivets, arrow points, fishhooks, scissor blades, screws and bolts and suchlike. His apprentices were scurrying about like ants out of a spilled nest, the two elder journeymen wreathed in clouds of steam. "Eh-Bramble," he boomed, "bring your old uncle a drink."

She tossed her braids impatiently at the delay, but Valley rules definitely dictated courtesy to adults. She lifted the lid off the coolcrock her father's apprentice Immer had made and brought Migel a dripping dipperful.

He gulped down most of it and emptied the rest over his thinning black hair. "Made your Choice, yet, Bram? Time's getting short."

She nodded.

He pulled a braid, grinned at her. "Not talking, eh?" He laughed when she looked stubborn, his breathy all-over laughter, then sobered. "On the Mountain, are you? Good. Venstrey there—" he jerked his head at one of the journeymen—"he wants a sleeping otter for the hilt of a knife he's working on, stretched out straight, mind you, one curled up nose to tail would make an odd sort of hilt."

She nodded, hung the dipper he gave her by the thong in its tail and went on down the road.

As she came ka-lumping down Uncle Djimis's steps, her mother's apprentice Marran rounded a corner of the house with a pair of hot sweet rolls. "Eh-Bram, catch." He looped one of them at her.

She stretched up to catch the roll—and nearly fell off the bottom step, keeping her face out of the dust with a flurry of arms and legs, a clownjig that didn't improve her temper. "Marran, you idiot, you make me break my neck and I'll haunt you the rest of your days."

He gave her his slow, sweet smile, but said nothing. He seldom had much to say, but few Valley folk, male or female, young or old, could resist that smile. This was his third year in Arth Slya and he was settling in nicely; her mother said he was going to be the best weaver and tapestry maker Arth Slya had seen in an age of ages. If her mother did decide to make a Mountain tapestry using Brann's sketches, it'd be Marran who drew the cartoon and did much of the work. He'd turned fifteen only a month ago and was young for it, but her mother was planning to make him journeyman on the Centenary Celebration for Eldest Uncle Eornis. Brann's Choice Day. Her eleventh birthday. Going to be a busy day.

She kicked some sand, sneaked a glance at Marran, who grinned when he caught her at it, then went stalking away down the road, stuffing the roll into her satchel, hmphing and grumping, half-annoyed and half-delighted at the attentions he kept pushing on her. Her mother and some of the aunts were beginning to plan things, she caught them time after time looking at her and Marran with heavy significance that made her want to bite.

She climbed to her father's workshop and looked inside. Cousin Immer was in one of the rooms fussing over designs for a set of plates one of the uncles wanted for his daughter's marriage chest. Problem was the uncle and the daughter had very different notions of what each wanted and Immer, who was inherently kind, was struggling to design something both would agree on. He was a fusser and sometimes snappish but Brann was very fond of him; even when he was impossibly busy he always found time and patience for a pesty little girl. She went to stand at his elbow, watching him patiently flowing color into outlines. He was putting the same design through various color combinations to show the embattled pair. She patted his arm. "Slya bless, maybe this will work."

He sighed. "If it doesn't, I surrender, Bramble. The Yongala can arbitrate for I don't think either will settle for less."

She patted his arm again and went to putter about the workshop, cleaning tools, straightening the storage niches, sweeping up the small accumulation of dust and the large accumulation of cobwebs, enjoying herself, no one to fuss at her for getting in the way, no impatient older brother chasing her out. As she maneuvered the pile of debris toward the door, the floor trembled and sent dust jigging—only a tiny twitch of the Mountain, soon over. "Sleep, Slya, Slya sleep," she sang as she pushed the pile of dust and scraps together again, swept it out the door.

Enjoying the bright crisp morning she stood in the doorway, looking up through the green lace of birch leaves to a sky clear as the water in the creek singing past the workshop. She breathed the cool air, shook the broom and leaned it against the wall, fetched her satchel and went climbing up the creek, hopping from rock to rock, heading for her favorite sunning place where the boulder pushed the creek aside. She could lie there, her head hanging over the edge, and watch the bright fish dart about. Or sit watching her four-foots coming down to drink. When she was sitting still as the stone beneath her even the fawns came down with their mothers and played on the grassy banks.

On the morning of Arth Slya's destruction, she sat on the stone and watched bright blue moonfishers darting about in a screaming fight, two after the flapping fish in the talons of a third. It seemed to Brann they always found more delight in stealing from each other than in catching fish for themselves, though to have those thieving fights, some moonfisher had to abandon principle and snag his own fish.

When the fight was over and the triumphant moonfisher flew off with his prize, she dipped up water and splashed it over her face; the sun was starting to get a bit too hot. She moved into the glade where the shadows were cool and the air tangy with cedar, took out her sketchbook and waited for the family of coynos that usually showed up about this time.

On Arth Slya's last day, the Mountain twitched and growled and sent rocks sliding and Brann grew afraid, calming her fear with the ritual dance, the sleep song, then went to wash the blackened cedar resin off her hands.

Once her hands were clean, she wandered about the slopes of Tincreal, too restless to sketch. She missed her father. She loved her mother and knew she was loved in return, but her mother wasn't company in the same way, she was mostly absorbed by her work and the new baby, Ruan firehair who slept in a basket beside the loom, listening to the hiss and thump as Brann had listened when she was a baskling, breathing in time to the sounds of the weaving, lulled to sleep by this constant comforting song. Brann was jealous of Ruan and hated the feeling, knew fairly well what the rest of her life was going to be and rebelled against accepting that, needed time for herself, knew the folk were letting her have it and was furious at their complacent understanding. In the Valley everyone knew everyone else's business, knew what each would do in just about every circumstance before even he or she knew. Her eleventh birthday was a month and a half away, the Time of Choosing. It fell on the same day as Eldest Uncle's, his hundredth, and there was going to be a grand celebration and she would share it and at the end of it she would announce her choice for her lifework. And just about nobody would be surprised.

Life in Arth Slya was pleasant, even joyful when you felt like fitting in, but when you didn't, it was like a pair of new boots, blistering you as it forced you into shape. Her father and her two older brothers had left with the packtrain going to Grannsha for the tri-year Fair. She'd wanted to go with them, but her mother was stuck here with a baby too young to travel and Brann couldn't go if her mother didn't. She thought it was stupid that she couldn't go, but no one else saw things her way. Not that she made a great fuss about it, for this was the last summer she could spend free, the last summer before she was officially apprenticed with all the work that meant, the last summer she could ramble about the Mountain, watching animals and all the other life there, sketching in the book Uncle Gemar the papermaker had sewn together for her, with the ink and the brush Aunt Seansi, Arth Slya's poet and journal keeper, had taught her how to use and make.

From her sketches her mother had woven for her a knee-length tunic with frogs and dragonflies in a lively frieze about the hem, dark greens, browns and reds on a pale gray-green ground. As time passed others found worth in her drawings. Sjiall the painter and screenmaker saw her plant and insect studies and went into the mountains himself searching for more such. Her father and Immer let her design some of their embellished ware. Uncle Migel seized on several drawings of otters and wolves and graved them into his swords and knives and sent her back to the slopes with specific commissions. Uncle Inar the glassmaker and Idadro the etcher and inlayer added her notes to their traditional forms. She could choose for any of them; they told her so. Thinking about their praise made her flutter with pleasure.

Though she was irritated and sometimes unhappy about the life laid out for her in the Valley, she found the outside world frightening. What little she knew about it, from candidates who made their way to the Valley, repelled her. Very few girls came, and those that did had stories to put a shudder in back and belly. She watched the boys shivering at a scold, or turning sullen with shaking but suppressed violence, watched the way they guarded their possessions and thoughts, their despair if they weren't taken as apprentices. Even those candidates accepted took several years to open out and be more or less like everyone else. Another thing—since the last Fair the trickle of younglings into the mountains had dried up entirely. The Valley folk came back from that Fair with rumors of trouble and reports of a general uneasiness on the Plains. Legates from the mainland were in Grannsha making demands the Kumaliyn could not possibly satisfy, so the stories went. Still, no one expected trouble to come to Arth Slya, they were too isolated and hard to get to; there was no road most of the way, only a rugged winding track that no one in his right mind would try to march an army along.

She wandered back to her boulder, sat eating one of her apples and watching the antics of otters who'd made a mudslide for themselves and were racing about, sliding, splashing, uttering the stuttering barks of their secret laughter. Her hand dropped in her lap as the otters abruptly broke off their play and darted into the trees.

Two shines like smears of gold painted on the air flickered about the treetops, then came jagging down the stream, switching places over and over, dropping close to the water, darting up again. She stared at them, fascinated by their flitter and their glitter and their eerie song, a high swooping sound alternately fast and slow, sometimes unbearably sweet. She sat on her heels, smiling at them, bits of sun come to earth.

They jerked to a halt as if they'd somehow seen her, swooped at her, swinging closer and closer in tightening circles, then darted at her, plunged through her again and again. She gave a tiny startled cry, collapsed on the warm stone.

She woke as suddenly as she went down, a few heartbeats later.

Two children sat on the creekbank watching her from shimmering crystal eyes, pale little creatures with ash-blond hair, bowl-bobbed, silky, very straight, one head a shade darker than the other. They were so alike she didn't know how she knew the darker one was a boy and the other a girl. They wore shirts and pants like hers and apart from those eerie inhuman eyes were much like any of the children running about the Valley below. The girl smiled gravely at her. "I'm Yaril. That's Jaril. You're Brann."

Brann pushed up until she was sitting on her heels again. "I didn't tell you my name."

Yaril nodded, but didn't answer the implied question. Jaril wasn't listening. He was looking at everything with an intensity that made Brann think he'd never seen anything like blue sky and wind blowing cedars about and butterflies flitting over the stream and dragonflies zipping back and forth, otters crouching across the creek, black eyes bright and curious, fish coming up to feed, breaking the water in small plopping circles.

"Where'd you come from? Who're your folks?"

Yaril glanced at Jaril, rubbed at her small straight nose. "We are the Mountain's children."

"Huh?"

"Born of fire and stone," Yaril said, sounding awed, portentous.

Brann eyed her skeptically. "Don't be silly."

"It's true. Sort of." Yaril stared intently at Brann.

Little fingers began tickling the inside of Brann's head; she scowled, brushed at her face. "Don't DO that." She pushed onto her feet, jumped onto the grass and began circling around them.

"Don't be afraid, Brann." Yaril got hastily to her feet, held out her small hands. "Please don't be afraid. We won't hurt you. Jaril, tell her."

Brann kept backing away until she reached the trees, then she wheeled and fled into shadow. Behind her she heard the high sweet singing of the sunglows, a moment later bits of yellow light were dancing through the trees ahead of her. The patches of light touched down to the red soil, changed, and Yaril stood with Jaril waiting for her. She turned aside and ran on, blind with terror. The shivering song came after her, the shimmers swept through her, caressing her, stroking her inside and out, gentling her, trying to drive the fright from her. She collapsed in the dirt, dirt in her mouth and nose and eyes, the last thing she remembered, the taste of the mountain in her mouth.

She woke with her head in Jaril's lap, Yaril kneeling beside her, stroking her forehead. She tried to jerk away, but the boy's arms were too strong even if she couldn't quite believe in the reality of those arms. She lay stiff as a board waiting for them to do with her whatever they'd planned.

"Hush," Yaril said. "Hush, Bramble-all-thorns, don't be afraid of us. We need you, but we can't help that. We won't hurt you. Please believe me."

Jaril patted her shoulder. "We need you, we won't hurt you," he said, his voice a twin of his sister's, a shade deeper than hers as his hair was a shade darker. He grunted as the Mountain rumbled and shifted beneath them, the third quake that day. "You ought to warn your folk, Bramble-all-thorns; this hill's getting ready to blow. . . . Mmmmh, in your terms, Slya's going to wake soon with a bellyache and spew her breakfast over everything around."

Brann wiggled loose, got shakily to her feet. She looked for the sun, but it was too low in the west to show over the trees. "Sheee, it's late. Mama will snatch me bald." She started downhill. Over her shoulder, Valley courtesy demanding it, she said, "Come on. It's almost supper. You can eat with us. Mama won't mind."

The children caught up with her as she reached the stream and started down along it. "About that supper," Yaril said. "We don't eat your kind of food. Maybe I should explain. . . ." She broke off and looked at her brother. "Not time yet? I don't agree. You know why. Oh all right, I suppose it is a big gulp to swallow all at once." Yaril blinked as she met Brann's eyes and realized she was listening with considerable interest. "Pardon us," she said, "we forget our manners. We'll join you gladly, if not for supper. And warn your people about the Mountain."

"You keep fussing about that. Slya's waked other times, we know her moods, we've lived with her a thousand years and more." She began hurrying through the lengthening shadows, taking care where she put her feet, jumping from rock to rock, flitting across grassy flats, sliding on slippery brown needles, keeping her balance by clutching at trees she scooted past, landing with running steps on the path that led from the high kilns down to the workshop.

When she reached the workshop, she ran up the steps, pushed the door open. "Immer, suppertime."

No answer. Puzzled, she went inside, ran through the rooms. No one there. That was funny. She clattered down to the children, beginning to worry. Immer always worked until the light quit. Always.

The way to the Valley was broad and beaten down from here on, passing out of the trees at Lookwide Point then through a double switchback to end at the landing on the River. A cold knot in her stomach, Brann hurried along the road, but slowed as she came out of the trees, walked to the edge and looked down into the Valley. She could see most of it spread out before her, the River running down the middle, the scattered houses and workshops, the fields with crops, cows, sheep or horses in them, even the broad patch of bluish stone that was the Dance Ground with the Galarad Oak growing on the western side, the one Brann thought must be the biggest and oldest tree in all the world. There should have been children playing on the white sand road and in between the houses. There should have been workers coming in from the fields, others standing by the workshops. There should have been old folk sitting on benches by the River to catch the last of the day's heat, the first of the evening's cool, chatting and telling stories, hands busy at small tasks. But there was none of that.

Soldiers were herding her folk onto the Dance Ground, where the Valley daughters were due to meet with the Yongala to dance the Mountain back to sleep. Brann ground her teeth together to stop her jaw from trembling, but the shake had gone deep into the bone. She closed her eyes. She couldn't bear to see more. That's why Slya's restless, there's no one to dance her pains away, she thought and felt a kind of relief. Easier to think of Slya than. . . . Dance her pains away and ease her back to sleep. Yes, yes. That's it. Slya dreamed this and sent her children. She turned her head, opening her eyes when she was looking away from the Valley, gazed at Yaril and Jaril. They *are* the Mountain's children. Slya sent them. She clenched her hands into fists, the shaking wouldn't stop, jerked her head around to look into the Valley again. Can't see . . . got to get closer. Away from the road. Harrag's Leap. Yes. That's it. Where the mountains squeezed the Valley wasp-waisted, not far from the Dance Ground, was a vertical wall of granite Arth Slya folk called Harrag's Leap after the smith who went crazy one day a few hundred years ago, swore he could fly and jumped off the cliff to prove it. Brann plunged back into the trees, running as fast as she could without falling. It wouldn't be so good to break a leg up here; who'd ever come looking for her? Finally, breathing in great sucking gasps, she flung herself down on the flat top of the cliff and looked over the rim.

She was close enough to make out the faces of those crowding onto the Dance Ground, close enough to hear what was being said, but outside of a few orders from the soldiers, no one was saying much. They looked as bewildered as she felt. Why was this happening? Who would gain anything from bothering Arth Slya? Her mother was there, holding Ruan, looking angry and afraid. "Mama," Brann breathed.

Suddenly she wanted to be with her mother, she couldn't bear being up here watching, she wanted to be down there with her uncles and cousins and aunts, kin by kind if not blood. Sobbing, she started to get up, but two pairs of hands held her where she was.

"You can't do her any good if you get caught." One of the children was speaking, she couldn't tell which. "Think, Bramble, your mother's probably rejoicing because you're out here on the Mountain, at least she knows you're safe. Look, Bramlet, look close. Where are the children? Do you see Gingy or Shara? Do you see anyone your age or younger except for little Ruan in your mother's arms?"

She shuddered, went limp. They let her go and she scanned the crowd below. Gunna, Barr, Amyra, Caith, a dozen other younglings, but they were all fifteen or more, past their Choice. Nobody younger. Except Ruan. And even as she watched, one of the tall black-haired invaders shoved his way to her mother, took Ruan from her, kicked her feet from under her when she fought to get her baby back, elbowed and slammed his way out of the crowd, drawing blood with the clawed back of his gauntlet.

And as she watched, Yaril and Jaril crowding close to her, holding her, the soldier carried Ruan to the Galarad Oak and he took her by the heels, and dashed her against the broad trunk, held her up, shook her, slammed her once again against the tree, harder, then tossed her on a heap of something Brann had missed before, the bodies of the Valley's children.

She trembled. She couldn't make a sound, she couldn't cry, couldn't anything, couldn't even feel anger. She was numb. She kept looking for faces she knew. The old were gone like the children. The young and strong, they were all there, some with bandages on arms and legs, men and women alike, one or two sitting, heads on knees. None of the old ones. Yongala Cerdan wasn't there. Ancient Uncle Gemar who made her sketchbooks wasn't there. Eornis who shared her birthday, he wasn't going to see his hundred after all. Lathan, Sindary, Fearlian, Frin, Tislish, Millo and on and on, a long litany of grief, a naming of the dead. She didn't understand. Why? What could they gain? Why? She watched soldiers going in and out of the houses, driving out anyone trying to hide, plundering the houses and workshops, destroying far more than they carried away. Why? What kind of men were these who could do such things? She watched a knot of them kicking and beating Uncle Cynoc who was Speaker this year, yelling to him about gold, where was Arth Slya's gold. He tried to tell them they had it all, the bits Inar and Idadro and Migel had for inlaywork and decoration. They didn't listen. When they got tired of beating him, one of the soldiers stuck a sword in him and left him bleeding, dying. She watched another knot of soldiers pulling some of the women, her mother among them, from the Dance Ground. The children tried to get her away, but she clutched at the rock and wouldn't move, watched the things the invaders were doing to her mother and the others. She whimpered but wouldn't look away from the devastation below, watched the deaths and worse, some of the acts so arbitrary and meaningless that they seemed unreal, so unreal she almost expected the bodies to stir and walk away when the play was over as they did in the magic battles at the equinoxes, battles that ended with all-night dances and cauldrons of mulled cider and a feast the next day. But these dead stayed dead, bloody dolls with all the life pressed out of them.

Night settled over the Valley, obscuring much of what was still happening down there, doing nothing to block the sounds that came up the cliff to Brann. She listened, shuddering, as she'd watched, shuddering. Again the children tried to get her away from the cliff edge, but she wouldn't move, and they couldn't move her. All night she lay there listening even when there was no more to listen to, only a heavy silence.

Under her numbness resolve grew in her. There had to be a reason for what was happening. In her memory, a gilded, winged helmet, a blood-red cloak, a glittering figure moving through the drabber browns and blacks of the rest. He it was who by a nod had given consent to the use of her mother and the other women, who had supervised the looting of the houses and shops, who had stood by while her folk were roped together in groups of eight, then herded into the meeting hall to spend the night how they could. He knows, she thought, I have to make him tell me, somehow I have to make him tell me.

As the night dragged on Yaril then Jaril went somewhere, came back after a short stretch of time. Brann was dully aware of those departures, but had no energy even to wonder where they went. She huddled where she was and waited—for what, she had no idea, she wasn't thinking or feeling, just existing as a stone exists. She got very cold when the dew came down, but even that couldn't penetrate the numbness that held her where she was.

The night grayed, reddened. Some of the soldiers went into the meeting hall, brought out two ropes of women, her mother among them. Brann strained to see through the dawn haze. Her mother's shirt and trousers were torn, tied about her anyhow. She moved stiffly, there were bruises on her face and arms, her face was frozen, but Brann could see the rage in her. She'd only seen her mother angry once, when a new apprentice who hadn't learned Valley ways yet jumped Brann's oldest brother Cathor over some silly thing, but that was nothing to the fury in her now. Once they were cut loose the women were put to fixing food for the soldiers and later for the captives.

The morning brightened slowly. The smells of the food reached Brann and her stomach cramped. Yaril went off a few breaths and came back with food they'd stolen for her. For some minutes she stared at the bread and cheese, the jug of buttermilk. Hungry as she was, it felt horrible to be eating with the things that kept replaying in her head, things she knew she'd never forget no matter how long she lived.

Yaril patted her shoulder. "Eat," she said. "You need your strength, little Bramlet. Wouldn't you like to get your mother and the others free of those murderers? How can you do that if you're fainting on your feet? You're a practical person, Bramble-all-thorns. There's nothing wrong with eating to keep up your strength."

Brann looked from one pale pointed face to the other. "You think I really could get them loose?"

Yaril nodded. She fidgeted a moment, seemed to blur around the edges, but her nod was brisk and positive. "With our help. We'll show you how."

Brann took a deep breath and picked up the jug. At first it was hard to swallow and her stomach threatened more than once to rebel, but the more she got down, the better she felt.

As she finished the hasty meal the movements below began to acquire shape and order, the soldiers lining up the roped-together villagers, getting pack mules and ponies loaded and roped together. Yaril whispered to Brann, "You want to make them pay. You can. Let them go ahead. It's five days out of the mountains. We'll help you get ready. Let them go thinking they won. Listen to us, we'll tell you how you can make them pay for what they've done." Soft nuzzling whispers as Brann watched the soldiers take brands from the fires and toss them into the houses along the white sand road, as she watched them march away, the roped slaves forced to march with them, the laden packers ambling along behind.

Brann huddled where she was, breathing hard, almost hyperventilating, while the leader mounted his horse and started off at an easy walk, and the soldier-pacemaker's voice boomed through the crisp morning, all sounds magnified, the flames crackling, the scuffing thud of marching feet, the jangle clink of the soldiers' gear, the rattle of the small cadence drum that took over for the pacemaker's voice. She wrapped her arms about her legs and sat listening until the sounds muted and were finally lost in the noises of river and wind. Then she lifted her head. "How?"

Yaril and Jaril gazed at each other for a long breath. Finally Yaril nodded and turned to Brann. "There's a lot for you to forgive. We said we wouldn't hurt you, Bramble, but . . . well, you'll have to decide how much harm we did out of ignorance and need." She coughed and her edges shimmered as they had before. Brann clenched her hands until her ragged nails bit into her palms, bit her lip to keep from crying out at this dallying, in no mood to sympathize with Yaril's embarrassment. "We changed you," Yaril went on, keeping to her deliberate pace though she had to see Brann's impatience. "We had to, we don't say it was right or a good thing to do, but we thought it was the only thing to do. You were the first thinking being we saw in this reality. We didn't mean to come here. We were borne into your reality—your world—by accident through fire. I know, I'm not making sense, just listen, there's no hurry, we'll catch up with them easily enough. Listen, Brann, you have to understand or you can't . . . you can't deal with what we made you. And we can't change that now. We're melded, Brann, a whole now, three making one. We came through the heart of fire changed, Brann. Among our own kind we're children too, unfinished, malleable. Think how you'd feel, Brann, if you woke one morning without a mouth and could only suck up food and water through your nose, and your hands were gone. How would you feel with hunger cramping your stomach and food all around you that you couldn't touch? How would you feel knowing you would fade and die because you couldn't eat? And then if something inside you, something you knew to trust, said, 'that person will feed you, but only if you change her in such and such a way,' what would you do?" Yaril shimmered again, her crystal eyes glowing in the morning light, pleading for understanding.

Brann moved her lips. No sound came at first, finally she said, "You're demons?"

"No. No. Just another kind of people. Think of us as what we said, the Mountain's children. Truly we were born through her. Where we . . . oh, call it began, where we began we ate things like sunlight, umm, and the fires at the heart of things. We can't do that anymore."

Brann pressed her hand against her stomach, licked her lips, swallowed. "You . . . you're going to eat me?"

"No, no! You didn't listen. You have to know this. Maybe it'd be better to show you." Once again she exchanged a long glance with her brother, once again she nodded, turned to Brann. "Wait here, Bramble. When we drive a beast from the trees, take it between your hands and drink."

Brann shuddered. "Its blood?"

"No. Its life. Just will to take." Yaril got to her feet. "You'll know what I mean when you touch the beast, it's coded into you now." She flowed into the form of a large boarhound and trotted into the trees, Jaril shifting also and trotting after her.

Brann sat, feeling cold and horrified at the thought of what she was going to have to do. She heard the hounds baying somewhere in the distance, then coming closer and closer, then they were on the stone driving a large young coyno toward her. In a blind panic it ran at her and if she hadn't caught it, would have run off the lip of the cliff. Without thinking, acting from new instinct, she moved faster than she thought she could, trapped the lean vigorous body between her hands and did what Yaril told her, *willed to take.*

A wire of warmth slid into her, heating her middle in a way she found deeply disturbing though she couldn't have put into words why it was so. In seconds the coyno drooped empty between her hands. She looked at it, wanted to be sick, sent it wheeling over the edge of the cliff. Then she remembered the soldier tossing Ruan on the hill of dead children and was sorry. She put her hands over her face, but found no tears. The male boarhound picked his way over the rough stone and pushed his cold nose against her arm. By habit she stroked her hand along the brindle silk of his back, scratched absently behind his soft floppy ears. "That's the way it's going to be?" The hound whined. Brann scrubbed her fist across her eyes. "I'm all right, don't worry. Worry? I s'pose you do or you wouldn't explain, you'd just make me do things. What now? Was that enough or will you need more? Go ahead. I'm going to think about it like cleaning chickens for supper. Go chase some more beasts here, I'll sing the Blessing while you're gone." She looked over her shoulder at the cliff edge and swallowed, tightened her hand into a fist again. "Slya says all life is sacred, all death must be celebrated and mourned." She spoke gravely, feeling the weight of custom falling on her thin shoulders. Jaril rubbed his head against her arm and trotted off after his sister.

A day and a night and a day passed, Brann and the children learning the rules of their new unity. A day, a night and a day, gathering the lives of small beasts and large, joining hands to share that feeding. Brann shunting aside grief, rage, impatience, fear—except in dreamtime when memory turned to nightmare. The children scavenging for gear and food, tending the stock when Brann remembered the need. "The cows will dry up," she said. "Can't you do something?" "Bramlet," they said, "we're only two. At least the beasts will be alive." A day and a night and a day drifted past, and then another night. When the sun rose clear of the horizon, she started after her folk.

Brann rode a wild black werehorse down the mountain, black mane stinging her face, brother and sister melded into one, carrying her and the gear they'd salvaged from the gutted houses. Down the mountainside, going like the wind, Brann as wild and exhilarated as the great beast under her. Down the mountainside through the bright cool morning, lovely lustrous morning though Arth Slya was dead and lost. Day ought to weep, sun ought to lurk behind a thick weight of cloud, trees ought to droop and sigh, river to gloom and gray, but it was not so. And no more than day and mountain and sky could she mourn. She thrilled at the driving power of the great muscles between her legs, muscles fed as she was with the lives of wolves and coynos. She laughed aloud and laughed again when the werehorse bugled its delight.

Late that afternoon they came to the first of many cataracts. The werehorse stopped beside a storm-felled ash slowly rotting back into the earth, collapsed into brindle boarhounds after Brann swung groaning down, sore muscles protesting, chafed thighs burning. The hounds walked out of saddle and gear and trotted away. Brann stretched and groaned some more, then went through the gear, found the hatchet and went about collecting downwood for a fire, wobbling on legs that felt like wet noodles, splaying her knees to keep her thighs apart. When she had the fire going and the kettle dangling from an improvised tripod, she stripped off her clothing and found an eddy by the ash tree's roots where she wouldn't be swept away. She sat on a water-polished root, dabbling her feet in the river, watching the roughened redness inside her thighs fade to pink, the pink to the matte white of healthy skin. She'd burned her finger getting the kettle to hang properly from the tripod. The burn blister had dried and, as she watched, the dry skin cracked and peeled away leaving no sign at all of the burn. Some change, she thought. She slipped off the root, dunked herself all the way under, crawled out of the water, stretched her dripping body along the hard white wood of the ash tree's trunk, the sun warm and welcome on her back and legs, dozing there until a hiss from the fire told her the tea water was boiling. She pulled her clothes back on, feeling a mild curiosity about when the children would return, a curiosity that faded as she made the tea.

She sat with the hot drinking bowl hugged between her hands, her face bent to the fragrant steam rising from the tea. Her father's work, that bowl, with the goodness her father put in everything he made. She sipped at the tea, listening to the cries of the hunting hounds, wishing her father were there sitting beside her on the ash trunk. Sipped again, trying to wash away the lump in her throat, dismissing the horrors, thinking instead of the good times. When her father took his impling to his workshop with its smells of dry clay and wet clay, of powders and glaze mixes, cedar cabinets and oak tables, the whirring of wheels, thuds of the kicks that kept the wheels going, Immer's humming, another apprentice's sweet whistling, jokes tossed about, laughter, shouts —sounds and smells set as deeply into her as the thumps and clacking of her mother's loom, her mother's tuneless burring songs. Good times. When she shared her birthdays with ancient Uncle Eornis and he fed her cake and cider and told her the exciting scary stories she loved. Tough old man, should have lasted a dozen more years. Everyone in the Valley was making something special for him, she'd done an ink drawing of moonfishers in a scream fight. Her father spent two years on his gift. A das'n vuor pot and a hundred das'n vuor drinking bowls, one for each year of the old man's life. He broke pot after pot until he was satisfied, broke bowl after bowl. Most of them looked fine to Brann, but he pointed out their imperfections, made her see them as he did, feel them, patient with her until she finally understood what he was talking about. And when he took the last bowls from the firing, he broke three, but wiped the fourth carefully and set it in her hands. She looked deep and deep into the black luster that seemed to drink the light, rejoicing in the shape that had the rightness of the Galarad Oak, or the Yongala dancing when Slya filled her, a rightness that whispered deep within. As if a light was kindled inside her, she knew why her father could judge so quickly and surely the worth of his work. Shine and whisper filling her, she felt as if she should hook her toes under something or she might just float away. Her Choice was made. More than anything in all the world, she wanted one day to make a thing as right as the bowl cradled in her hands. She gave it back to her father and sighed. He put it carefully into its nest of silk, then caught her up, lifted her high, swung round and round and round with her, laughing and proud, his spirits suddenly released as his labor was finished at last, astonished and enraptured by what his hands had made, rejoicing at her Choice. He might never do anything quite as splendid again and it was somehow fitting that his daughter marked it with the gift of her life, yet more fitting that his greatest work was born of love and cele-bration and not done for gold.

She refilled the bowl and gulped at the tea, burning her tongue with it, squeezing her eyes shut to hold back tears, "He can't have it, I won't let him, can't have them," remembering with helpless fury soldiers carrying things from her home, the chest with the das'n vuor pot, the chest with the hundred bowls, the Temueng pimush in the gilded hel-met hovering over them with a hungry look, putting his hands on them, claiming them. "No!"

The hounds' bellowing grew louder, closer. Brann put the bowl down, stood crouched, waiting.

A yowling, spitting black beast ran from the trees, swerved when he saw her, a malouch with claws that could strip the flesh from a tough old boar. He yowled again and switched ends, but the hound bitch was too fast for him, dodging the claw strike with a speed that blurred her shape into a brindle streak. She tore at his hind leg, sprang away again. As soon as Yaril distracted him, Brann leaped, slapped a hand against the side of his head. The malouch writhed around, his claws raking her arm, then he froze as she started the pull, a black statue of hate unable to move, unable to make a sound. Ignoring the blood and pain from her torn arm, Brann set her other hand on him. His life flooded into her, hot and raw, terrible and terrifying, waking in her that queasy pleasure that she hated but was starting to need. At last the malouch was a scrap of fur and flesh melting from between her hands.

Children again, Jaril and Yaril took Brann's hands and the fire passed from her. She began to feel clean again though some of it re-mained with her; the malouch had clung to life with a fury that sad-dened and sickened her and she wanted to rid herself of everything she'd taken from him; she tried to hold onto the children, tried to force all of that stolen life out of her, but they melted and flowed through her fingers and flitted away to shimmer over the scatter of gear, then they merged and the werehorse was snorting and stamping impatiently, the children eager to be on their way.

She drew her fingers down the torn arm. The wounds were already closed, ragged pink furrows visible through the rents in her sleeve. With the knife from her belt sheath she cut away the bloody rags. She tossed the sleeve into the fire, thought a minute, cut the other sleeve to match. She knelt beside the river and washed away the dried blood. By the time she was finished the furrows had filled in, even the pink flush was gone. She looked at the arm a moment, then bent again, scooped up water, splashed it over her face, drank a little. The children melted apart and moved beside her, throwing questions, demands, pleas at her, as she walked about the glade, kicking leaves over the body of the malouch, smoothing out the rips in the sod he made with his claws, repacking the saddlebags with slow meticulous care, dismantling the tripod, dousing the fire, burying the blackened bits of wood. She said nothing to them, refused stubbornly to acknowledge their presence, walked heavily to the riverbank and sang the mourning song for the malouch and for the wood she burned, sang the praises of the living river, the living forest. A week ago she would have done all this— restored the land, sung the praises—because she'd done similar things a hundred times before, because she rested comfortably in the support of ancient custom. This time it was a way to shout at the murdering invaders that nothing was changed, that Arth Slya still lived as long as one of Slya's children lived and followed Slya's way.

When she turned away from the river, the werehorse was waiting beside the fallen ashtree. She saddled him, tossed the bulging bags in place, tied on the spade and hatchet, then stepped onto the ash and pulled herself onto his back. He trotted to the track, did a few caracoles to loosen up, then started racing down the mountain once again, crystal eyes having no trouble with the thickening shadow. Down and down. . . .

Until she saw a body flung beside the track, a boy huddled round a gaping wound in his chest. She screamed the horse to a halt, flung herself down and ran back. Kneeling beside the boy, she pressed him over. "Marran," she whispered. She brushed dirt and leaves from his face. His eyes were open, dull, shrunken. She tried to shut them, but her hands fumbled uselessly. Behind her the horse stomped impatiently, then whickered and nudged her with his nose. "Stop it," she said. "Don't bother me."

She gave up trying to straighten Marran, sat on her heels and looked about, her tongue caught between her teeth.

Yaril came round her, squatted beside Marran's body. He put his hand on the boy's face, drew it back. "Dead over a day, Brann. Nothing you can do."

Brann blinked slowly, brushed a hand across her face. "It's Marran," she said. She got to her feet. "Help me fetch wood." With clumsy hands she untied the hatchet from the fallen saddle and started away. "We've got to burn him free." She cast about for dry downwood. Yaril and Jaril ran beside her, trying to talk to her. "We're getting close to the Temuengs; it's dark, they'll see any fire big enough to burn a body; he's dead, how much can it matter when you put him on a pyre? Free your people and let them take care of him, Brann, Bramlet, Bramble-all-thorns, it won't take that long, if we go on now, you can have them free by dawn, back here before dusk, come on, Brann. . . ."

Brann shook her head, her mouth set in a stubborn line. She wasn't going to be stymied from doing what she clung to as right; if she let one thing go, the rest might slip away from her little by little. Bewildered and uncertain, alone with nothing but memory to guide her, all she could do was hold by what she did know. That this was Marran. That she owed him his fire. She trembled, her knees threatening to give way, caught hold of the branch waving in her face. Wood. Yes. She pulled the limb taut and lifted the hatchet.

One of the children made an irritated humming sound, then they were both in front of her, holding her by the arms, taking the hatchet from her. She tried to pull away but their hands were locked to her as if their flesh was melded to hers. Their fire came into her; it pinned her in place as if her feet had grown roots. She cried out, tried again to wrench free; they held her; the fire held her. Frightened and frantic, she writhed against that double grip until Yaril's words finally seeped through her panic.

"Wait, wait, listen to us, Bramlet, listen, we can help you, listen, we'll help, we understand, listen. . . ."

She grew quiet, breathing heavily. The grip on her arms relaxed; movement restored to her, she licked dry lips. "Listen?"

"Let us make fire for you."

"Wha . . ."

"Go back, sit by the boy and wait. We'll make a hotter, cleaner fire for your friend, Bramble, he'll burn in mountain heart. Wouldn't you rather that, than green and smoky wood?"

She looked from one small pale face to the other; the drive went out of her, she turned and fumbled her way back to Marran's body, stood looking down at him a moment. "Mama. . . ." She backed away to give the fire room and sat in the middle of the tampled track, her arms crossed tight across her narrow chest.

Yaril and Jaril came from the shadows and took up places facing each other across the body, with formal movements like the paces of a dance, dissolved into light shimmers that bobbed up and down like bubbles on a string. Brann heard the swooping sweet song again, Jaril's deeper notes dominating, looked at Marran half in shadow, half in moonlight, looked away pushing her grief back, shutting it away inside her as she'd done with the rest of her anger and pain, not noticing how frequently she was doing this or realizing how much trouble she was piling up for herself when the rush of events was over and there was nothing more to distract her from all that she had lost or from the cold shock of what her future held for her. The shimmers vibrated faster and faster, waves of color—blue and green and crimson—passing across them top to bottom, faster faster faster, the song rising to a high piercing scream. They darted away from each other, whipped around and came rushing back, slamming together into a blinding explosion. Blue fire roared up in a gather of crackling tongues. Hanging first in midair, the fire lowered until it touched, then ate down into Marran, racing up and down his contorted body, consuming flesh and bone until there was only ash.

The blue flame paled, broke in half, the halves tumbled apart, and the children lay on the leaves, pale and weary.

Yaril sat up. "We have to hunt before we can go on." Jaril rolled up, nodded, flowed immediately into the hound form and trotted away, Yaril following after, most of the spring gone out of her legs. The burning had cost them.

Brann watched them go, sat where she was for a few breaths longer, then she got to her feet, stretched and began to sing the mourning song for Marran.

About an hour before dawn, the werehorse slowed to a walk, hooves flowing into clawed pads as each one left the ground. It ghosted on, step by slow step, through the starlit quiet until the sound of a man's voice raised in idle complaint came drifting up the track. Brann swung down, pulled the saddlebags off and carried them to a tangleroot, stowed them in the trunk hollow, struggling to make no sounds. She came back, eased the buckles loose and slid the saddle off, teeth tight together, moving as smoothly as she could so nothing would rattle or clink. By the time she reached the huge tree, Jaril was there to help her lower the saddle.

They crept around the perimeter of the camp clearing until they found a pepperbush growing crookedly out from the roots of a sweet-sap where a thin screen of toothy leaves let them see without being seen.

The captives slept in the center of the cleared ground, the ropes knotted about their necks tied to stakes pounded into the hard soil. Perhaps on the first two nights some had lain awake, too stunned by grief and fear to sleep, but this night they all slept, heavily, noisily, with groans and farts and snores and sobs and the shapeless mutters that sleepers make when they're speaking into dream.

Two men slouched heavily about the edge of the camp clearing, passing each other at roughly fifteen-minute intervals, occasionally moving among the ropes of captives, prodding those who groaned and snored too loudly. The rest of the soldiers were rolled in their blankets in two rows on the river side, the pimush slightly apart from his men.

Yaril eeled up to Brann's shoulder, breathed, "Jaril's started for the far side. I'll tell you when he's ready. All you have to do is get close to that sentry, touch him before he can yell. Then we can take the rest."

Brann started sweating. Abruptly deserted by rage and grief, no longer comfortably numb, she had to face the reality of those men whose life forces she was going to suck away. For all her eleven years her parents had taught her reverence for life. Slya's strictures demanded awareness of responsibility for all life stopped; she remembered how desperately the malouch had clung to life and how easily she'd stripped that life away and how nauseated she felt about it later. But there was no going back.

Yaril wriggled close, warm and alive in her eerie way. "Look at his face, that sentry coming toward you," she breathed.

When the guard came out of shadow, she saw the face of the man who'd taken Ruan by her heels and swung her twice against the Oak, thrown her away like a weed onto a compost heap.

"Be ready," Yaril said, her words a thread of sound by Brann's ear. "When this one has his back turned Jaril will bite the other."

The sentry walked past her. "Go." Urged on by the whispered word, Brann raced after the sentry, slapped her hand against the bare flesh of his arm before he had a chance to cry out, landed her other hand, began drawing the life from him, the fire hammering into her differing in quality and force from that she'd taken from the smaller, less deadly beasts. This was a predator among predators, a killer born as much as bred, only slightly tamed by the discipline of the Temueng army. She read that in the flash as his life-force roared into her. A second later he fell dead. Breathing hard, struggling to quell her nausea, Brann looked for the other sentry. He was down also, silently dead. In their serpent forms the children distilled from their substance a venom that killed between one breath and the next, a minuscule drop in poison sacs yet enough for the death of a dozen men.

"It's time," Yaril whispered. "Don't think, Bramlet, just do. It's the only way to keep your people safe. These murderers have earned death, more than you know." She touched Brann's arm, then ran ahead of her to the lines of sleeping soldiers. A shimmer of pale light and she was a serpent crawling in the dust, in the dim starlight, dust-colored and nearly invisible except when her viper's head rose above a sleeping man and darted down.

Brann nerved herself and followed. Man to man she went, setting her hands on those the children had not touched, taking their life into her, a burning unending river flooding her. She drank and drank until there were no more lives to take, trying as she stooped and touched to ignore the pleasure currents curling turgidly through her. It didn't seem right. Her vengeance should be pure, untainted by anything but righteous wrath.

The children rose from serpent form and came to her, their hands melting into hers as they took and took from her until she could think coherently again and move without feeling bloated and unwieldy. She turned to look at the dead. Two rows of them, fifty men falling to snake and whatever it was she was now, with hardly a sound and no struggle at all, they might have been sleeping still. Silent herself she went to stand beside the Temueng pimush, the leader of these invaders, the one who'd given the orders for all they'd done—calmly asleep, untroubled by dreams or remorse. You know why, she thought, but how do I ask you, what do I ask you? He made a small spluttering sound, moved his hands. She jumped back into shadow, but he didn't wake. Jaril tugged at her arm. She leaned down. "What?" she whispered.

"Take from him but not all, enough only to sap his will so we can move him away from them." He nodded at the sleeping captives.

Brann looked down and was surprised to see her hands glowing in the hushed darkness before the dawn, rather like the round porcelain lamps her father made for nightlights. She knelt beside the pimush and took his head between her hands. He started to wake but faded into a daze as she pressed the slow drain. "Enough," Jaril said, touched her hand. She sighed and sat back on her heels. "What now?"

"Into the trees. He'll walk if we prod him."

With the children's help she led the pimush a short distance from the camp clearing and propped him against the high roots of an old oak. "That's done. Where from here?"

"Give him back."

"Huh?"

"You want him able to talk, don't you? Reverse the flow. All you have to do is touch and will, Bramble, it's as easy as breathing."

"Which I think you don't do."

Jaril grinned at her. "Not like you, anyway."

She rubbed a grubby forefinger by the corner of her mouth. The Temueng was tall, head and shoulders higher than most Arth Slya men, the flesh hard and tight on his bones. She shivered. "He looks like he could snap me in two without half trying. Shouldn't we tie him or something?"

"No." Jaril changed, flowed upon the Temueng's chest, coil by coil, his broad triangular viper's head raised and swaying, poison fangs displayed and ready. Yaril moved around until she was kneeling by the Temueng's right arm, drawing over her the feral look of a hungry weasel. It sat comfortably on her delicate child's face, made her more terrifying than a raging male three times her size. Brann looked from child to serpent, wiped her hand across her face, scraping away a new film of sweat. "Why don't I feel safer?" she whispered, then giggled nervously.

The dawn breeze was beginning to stir, rustling among the leaves, here and there a bird's sleepy twitter broke the hush. Yaril clicked her teeth. "Brann, you waiting for it to rain or something?"

Kneeling beside the Temueng, Brann put her hand on his brow and found that Jaril was right, it was easy; the fire crackling under her skin went out through her fingertips into him. His pale face darkened, flushing with renewed vigor. She jumped hastily to her feet and moved back a few paces.

He opened his eyes. The flush receded leaving him pale as he saw the serpent head rising over his; he stiffened and stopped breathing.

"Man," Yaril said.

"What?" His narrow dark eyes flicked about, going to the viper swaying gently but without that extra tension that meant readiness to strike, to the feral child showing her pointed teeth, to Brann filled with moonfire. He didn't move; he was afraid, but mastering his fear, calculating, seeking a way to slide out of this peril.

"We are Drinker of Souls and the Mountain's Children," Yaril cooed at him. She caught hold of his hand, the strength in her dainty fingers as frightening as the rest of her. She folded the hand into a fist and wrapped her hands about it, gazing at him with an impersonal hungry interest. "You killed our mortal cousins and took others away. You bloodied and befouled our mother. Why?" Her high light voice was calm, conversational. "Answer me, man." She tightened her hands about his fist, watched him struggle to keep still, sweat popping thick on his long narrow face. "Why?" She eased her grip. "Why?"

"It was something to do," he said when he could speak again. "To pass the time."

Yaril gestured at the viper and it changed to a giant worm with daintily feathered wings little larger than a man's hand flirting on either side of an angular dragon's head. Forked tongue flicking, a whiffing and fluttering of the opalescent feathers, the great worm grew heavier and heavier on the Temueng's chest, the coils spilling off him onto the roots of the oak. As the pimush stared, mouth clamped shut but eyes wide with the fear he couldn't deny, smoking oily liquid ran down one of the dragon's dagger fangs, gathered at the tip, then dripped off onto his chest. The venom burned through his shirt and into his flesh. His body jerked and spasmed as much as it could, one hand held prisoned by Yaril in a grip he had no chance of breaking, legs and lower body pinned by the punishing weight of the worm.

Yaril passed her hand across the bubbling liquid, drew it into herself. The pain subsided, the man lay still again. "Why?" she said. "We sent the tribute to Grannsha every year without fail, the compact between Arth Slya and the Kumaliyn has never been broken though a thousand years have passed since it was made. Why did you come to Arth Slya?"

He licked his lips, gave a sudden wild shout.

"Your men are dead." Yaril patted his hand. "Only their ghosts to answer you. Call again if you want. Call all you want. Only the captives can hear you and they're staked to the ground. Why have you destroyed Arth Slya?" She tightened her grip on his fist again, watched him struggling to hold back groans and fight off the feeling of helplessness the worm's weight and her unlikely strength were waking in him. She eased the pressure a little. "Speak true and you will die quickly and easily. Lie or refuse to speak, then my brother's venom will consume you bit by bit and the Soul Drinker will see you stay awake for all of it."

His dark eyes darted about, he was fighting a last battle with himself, desiring defiance but too intelligent to waste his strength hiding things that had to be common knowledge in the villages below. With a visible effort he relaxed. "All dead?"

"All. Slya watches over her children."

"Easy they said. Round up the young and strong, no kids or dodderers. . . ." The breath hissed through his stiff lips. "Nothing about no arsehole god getting her eggs in a twist. Your Kumaliyn's skipped. Abanaskranjinga Emperor of the Temuengs rules here now."

"So. Why come like wolves? There were no soldiers in Arth Slya."

"Why ask me? I do what I'm ordered. Good boy, pat 'im on his fuckin head."

"Why come like wolves?"

He sneered. "Old Krajink's not about to let a little bunch of mud dawbers nest free, thinkin they can make it without him. Maybe other folk they get the idea they got rights. Mudfeet, mudheads stompin up trouble, just get chopped, but Krajink he's got to pay us to do the choppin and he parts with silver bits like grasslion from his meat. Cheaper to stomp first. Don't mess up trade or plantin and harvestin. Cheap way to get valuable slaves. Trust ol Krajink to see that. He figures your Arth Slya artisans might as well be making their junk for him where he can keep an eye on them. Figures maybe he can make Durat a rep as big as your dawbers got."

Brann took a step toward him. "Slaves," she spat. "Half my folk dead so that . . . that . . . he can prance around claiming their work!"

He raised his thin arched brows, the sound of his voice insensibly seducing him into speaking further, turning this interrogation into something like a conversation. "So what's new about that, bint? In old lardarse's head we're all his slaves. We hop when he pulls our strings. Don't hop, get the chop. Why not? Do the same, us, to folk beneath us."

Brann stared at him, not comprehending much of what he was saying. It was a world totally other than the one she'd grown up in. All she got from the speech was the ultimate responsibility of the Temueng Emperor for the destruction of Arth Slya. "The Fair," she said. "What happened to the Arth Slya folk at the Fair?"

"On their way, bint. On ship to Andurya Durat."

Brann put her hands behind her back, clenched them into her fists, struggled to keep her voice steady. "Were any of them killed?"

"And get chopped for wasting prime meat? Uh-uh."

Brann closed her eyes. Her father and her brothers were alive. Captives, but alive.

"Bramble!" Yaril's voice.

Jolted out of her daze, Brann came round the Temueng's feet and stopped beside her. "What?"

"That all you wanted to know?"

"Yes . . . um . . . yes."

"Well?" Yaril gestured impatiently.

Brann rubbed her hands down the sides of her bloodied shirt, blood from her wounded arm, long dried. It was different somehow, looking into his eyes, listening to him talk, seeing his fear, seeing him as a person, *knowing* him. With all the harm he'd done her, she shrank from taking him; the revulsion she felt was almost more than she could overcome. She reached heavily toward him, saw the leap of fear in his eyes, saw it dulling to resignation. Her hand fell. "I can't," she wailed. "I. . . ." An immense hot fury took hold of her, drowned her will, worked her arms, set her hands on his brow and mouth and drew his life in a rushing roar out of him.

Then he was dead and that *thing* went wheeling away. It wasn't the children; as wobbly as her thinking was, she was able to understand that. Cautiously Yaril came closer, reached out. A spark snapped between them, then the strong small hands were closed on her arm, and Yaril was pressing against her, warm and alive, murmuring comfort to her. Another spark snapping, and Jaril was smoothing his hands along her shoulders, gently massaging her neck and shoulder muscles. They worked the shock out of her, gave her the support she needed until she was able to stand.

Yaril stood beside her, holding her hand. "What was THAT?"

Brann moved her shoulders, flexed her fingers, the children's hands comfortably human around them, even a little sweaty. "Don't know. I think . . . I *think* it was Slya filling me."

"Oh." There was complete silence from both children for a few breaths, then calm and deliberately prosaic words from Yaril. "We better go turn your folks loose."

As they walked through the trees, Jaril looked up at her. "What do we do after this, Bramble? Go back to the Valley with your folk?"

Brann stopped. "I thought . . . before I knew about Da . . . do you think we could get him loose too?"

Jaril grinned. "Why not."

Brann stopped in the shadows of some stunted alder bushes, an unseen hand restraining her, a wall of air keeping her back from her mother and the rest of Slya's folk out in the clearing. No words, no warning, nothing tangible, but she was being told Arth Slya was no longer for her. She dropped to her knees, then swung her legs around so she was sitting with her hands clasped in her lap, looking into the camp clearing through a thin fan of finger-sized shoots and a lacy scatter of leaves. The children exchanged puzzled glances, squatted beside her without speaking.

Uncle Migel was on his knees beside a stake, looking about. He scrubbed his hand across his mouth, fumbled on the ground by his knees, came up with a dirt clod, snapped it at a soldier lying rolled in his blanket. He grunted as the clod hit, splattering over the man and the ground around him. "Not sleeping," he said. He put two fingers in his mouth, produced an ear-piercing whistle, waited. "Unh, looks to me like they're all dead."

"How?" Her mother's voice.

"All?" Aunt Seansi kneeling beside her mother. "I'd say so, Mig, that whistle of yours is most likely waking folks in Grannsha."

Wrapping thick-fingered hands about the stake, Migel rocked it back and forth, and with an exploding grunt, pulled it from the ground. He got to his feet, his ropemates coming up eagerly with him, all eight of them moving out and around the stakes to the line of bodies. Migel kicked a soldier out of his blanket, got his belt knife and cut himself loose. He sliced the loop of rope from his neck, then tossed the knife with casual skill so it stuck in the ground in front of Brann's mother, who grabbed it with a heartfelt "Slya!" and began slicing her rope loose from the stake. When she was free, she passed the knife to Seansi and marched over to the pile of wood the soldiers had cut the night before, hauled sticks from it to an open space where she used the sparker she found on a soldier to get a fire started.

Brann watched the swirl of activity and noise in the clearing, warm with pride in the resilience of her people. Harrowed by the shock and violence of the invasion, bereft of hope, marched off to a fate not one of them could imagine, waking to find silent death come among them with no idea of how or when it struck, whether it would come on them later, not a one of them sat about glooming or complaining but each as soon as he or she was freed from the rope saw something to be done and did it. Time for fear and mourning later. Now was time for food in the belly and scalding hot tea to get the blood moving. Now was the time to get the mules and ponies out of their rope corral, now was the time for caching the loot from the Valley where they could find it later. In a hectic half hour the camp clearing was picked clean except for the bodies of the soldiers (the body of the pimush was added to the pile when they found it; they passed close by Brann and the children, but whatever kept her from entering the clearing kept them from seeing her). Then they were mounting the mules and ponies and riding away, those that had no mounts trotting beside the others. After a short but heated argument, they left the pimush's horse and gear behind. Her mother wouldn't have the beast along, Uncle Migel wanted to take it. Inar and Seansi and a dozen others talked him out of that, the beast was a high-bred racer too obviously not Valley-bred. Migel kept sputtering that anyone getting close enough to the Valley to spot the horse would be too damn close anyway. But the others countered that it only took one snooping outsider to get an eyeful of racer and report his presence to the Temuengs. If he wanted such a beast, then he should buy one the next Fair on. As they left the clearing, the Mountain chose to rumble a few breaths and go quiet, almost as if Slya were laughing— the soldiers dead, the people returning to rebuild their homes, and Brann aimed like an arrow at the Temueng Emperor.

As the morning brightened and grew warmer with the rising of the sun, Brann sat staring at the empty clearing, not seeing it. She wasn't tired, wasn't sleepy, only empty.

"Bramble." Yaril's voice demanded her attention. She looked around, eyes unfocused. "Here." Yaril put a hot mug in her hand. "Drink this." When Brann sat without moving, staring at the mug, the changechild made a small spitting sound like an angry cat, wrapped her hands round Brann's and lifted the cup to Brann's lips.

The scalding liquid burned her mouth but Brann kept drinking. When the mug was empty, Yaril took it away and came back with more tea and a sandwich of stale bread and thick chunks of cheese, scolded her into eating them. Food in the belly woke her will, gave her the energy she'd not had; the emptiness she'd been suffering was of the body as well as of the spirit; she realized that when Jaril brought the pimush's horse to her, the beast wearing her saddle and the pimush's bridle, the rest of her gear in place with some additions. He was a fine lovely beast—no wonder Uncle Migel had coveted him—prancing, nostrils flaring but tamed by the touch of Jaril's hand when Brann was ready to mount.

"Up you go," Jaril said. He caught her about the legs and tossed her onto the snorting beast, his strength once again surprising her; having seen him as a frail child or an insubstantial shimmering hanging in midair, she could not help letting her eyes fool her into underestimating him. She settled into the saddle, began settling the horse, stroking him, comforting him, teaching him that she wasn't about to allow any nonsense from him.

Then she was riding away down the mountain, holding the horse to a steady canter when he wanted to run. Brindle boarhounds trotted beside her, or disappeared into the trees on scouting runs. The track continued to follow the river, clinging to the sides of ravines where she drowned in the boom of cataracts, departing grudgingly from the cliffs where the river fell in rainbowed mists. Down and down without stopping, eating in the saddle, drinking from the pimush's waterskin, ignoring the continued chafing of her thighs, the cramps in fingers, arms, legs, down and down until the pimush's horse was leaden with fatigue, until they were out of the mountains and in gently rolling foothills.

When the Wounded Moon was an hour off the horizon, she curled up in a hollow padded with grass and went to sleep, leaving the horse and her safety to the children. She slept heavily and if she dreamed, she remembered nothing of it later.

She woke with the sun beating into her eyes, sweat greasing a body drastically changed, woke to the pinching irritation of clothing that was much too small for her.

She sat up, groaned. Hastily she ripped off what was left of her trousers, most of the seams having given way as she slept, breathed a sigh of relief, tore off the remains of her shirt, bundled the rags and wiped at sweat that was viscous and high-smelling. Her hair was stiff with dirt and dried sweat. When she tried combing her fingers through it, it came out in handfuls. She rubbed at her head with the wadded-up shirt; all the hair came out, mouse-brown tresses dead and dark, falling to the grass around her. She kept scrubbing until her head was bare, polished bare. Throwing the shirt aside, she ran her hands over the body the night had given her, the full soft breasts, the narrow waist, the broader hips, the pubic hair glinting like coiled silver wire in the sunlight. She wanted to cry, to howl, lost and confused.

A hand on her shoulder. She jerked convulsively, cried out in a voice she didn't recognize, flung herself away—then saw it was Yaril. Yaril holding neatly folded clothing. "Jaril's fixing breakfast next hollow over. You better get dressed. Here."

Brann shook out the shirt, looked from it to Yaril. "Where . . ."

"Brought it with us. Just in case."

Brann looked at the shirt she still held out and snorted. "Just in case I grew a couple feet taller and a dozen years older?" She bit on her lip, uncomfortable with the deeper richer voice that came out of her, a woman's voice—not the one she knew as hers.

"Just in case you couldn't go back to Arth Slya. Just in case you needed to free your father and the others as well as the ones the soldiers had taken. Seemed obvious to Jaril and me that the Temuengs would round up the Fair people before coming after the villagers."

"You didn't say anything about that."

"You had enough on your mind."

"You did this to me. Why?"

"A child of eleven. A girl child," Yaril said. "Think, Brann. Don't just stand there glupping like a fish. Put that shirt on. Who'd let such a child travel unmolested? Chances are the first man or woman who needed a laborer would grab you and put you to work for your keep. Who'd bother listening to a child? And that's far from the worst that could happen. So we used all that life you drank and grew you older. You haven't lost anything, Bramble-all-thorns, we've stabilized you at this age. You won't change again unless you wish it."

Her head feeling as hard as seasoned oak, Brann stared at her. "What . . ." She pulled the shirt on, began buttoning it, having to pull it tight across her newly acquired breasts. "Stabilized?"

"You know what the word means. Put these on, they belonged to Mareddi who's about your size so they should fit."

Brann stepped into the trousers, drew them up, began pulling the laces tight. "But I don't know what it means when you use it about me."

"Means you'll stay the age you are until you want to change it."

"You can do that?"

"Well, we have, haven't we? Like we told you before, Bramble, we're a meld, the three of us. You're stuck with more limits than we have, but we can shift your shape about some. Not a lot and it takes a lot of energy, but, well, you see. Here. Boots. Mareddi's too. Might be a touch roomy."

"Weird." She ran her hand over her head. "Am I going to stay egg-bald? I'd rather not." She pulled on the boots, stomped her feet down in them.

Yaril giggled. "I could say wait and see. Well, no, Bramble. New hair's already starting to come in."

"I'm hungry." She looked at the blanket she'd slept in, nudged it with her toe. "What a stink, I need a bath." Shrugging, she started toward the smell of roasting coyno.

On her second day out of the mountains she came to a small village where Jaril bought her a long scarf to cover the stubble on her head, also more bread and cheese, some bacon and the handful of tea the woman could spare. Brann hadn't thought about the need for money before and was startled when he came up with a handful of coppers and bronze bits, though she had wit enough to keep her mouth shut while there were strangers about to hear her. Later, when she was riding down a rutted road between two badly tended boundary hedges, she called the hound back and pulled Jaril up before her. "Where'd you get the coin?" She smiled ruefully, shook her head. "I forgot we couldn't travel down here without it."

"Soldiers' purses, pimush's gear. They won't be needing it anymore, and we will." He leaned back against her, awakening a strong maternal urge in her, something that surprised her because she'd never before felt anything of the sort.

"Another thing you didn't bother telling me about."

"You were too busy glooming to listen."

"Hunh."

He tilted his head back, looked up at her with a smile too much like Marran's for her comfort, then he slid away from her, hitting the ground on four hound's feet, trotting ahead to rejoin Yaril.

As the days passed, she rode through village after village clustered about manorhouses with their keeps tenanted by Temueng soldiers. The fear and anger was thick as the dust cast up by plows and plodding oxen, the villages quiet and hushed, the children invisible except for the ones working with their parents in the fields—a kind of desolation without destruction that reawakened anger in her, a fury against the Temuengs whose touch seemed as deadly as the change-serpents' poison. She even found herself blaming the lack of rain on them, though the dry days and nights let her sleep outside, which was necessary because of the presence of the Temuengs in the villages and the sullen, mistrustful Plainfolk.

Toward evening on the seventh day after she left the mountains, she reached the wide highroad from Grannsha to Tavisteen and turned south along it, dismounted and walked beside a horse stumbling with weariness, the hounds trotting in wide arcs before her, noses and ears searching for danger. Now and then one of them would run back to her and pace alongside her for a while, looking repeatedly up at her, remnants of the day's light glinting in the crystal of their strange eyes. The sky was heavily overcast, thick boiling gray clouds threatening rain with every breath. The river swept away from the road and back in broad tranquil meanders, the color sucked from the water by the lowering skies, the sound muted by the ponderous force and depth of the flow.

She was about to resign herself to a wet cold night when she came on a large rambling structure built between the highroad and a returning sweep of the river, an Inn with a pair of torches out front, torches that had burnt low because it was long after sundown. The hounds came back, altering into Yaril and Jaril by the time they reached her. "What do you think?" she said. "Should we stop there?" She drew the flat of her hand down her front, sighed. "I'd really like a hot bath."

Yaril scratched at her nose, considered the Inn. "Why not, Bramble. It looks like it gets a lot of traffic. The folk there won't be surprised by strangers."

"You're the moneykeeper, J'ri, can we afford their prices?"

He looked thoughtful, then mischievous. "Why not. 'S not our coin, we can always steal more." He dug into the saddlebags, handed the purse to Yaril and took the reins from Brann. "You two go on inside, let Yaril do the talking and you stand about looking portentous, Bramble." He giggled and dodged away from the sweep of her hand. "I'll get Coier bedded down, he won't mind a dry stall and some corn for dinner, oh no he won't."

The door opened at Brann's touch and she went in, looking about as impassively as she could. Beside her, Yaril was gawking at the place with far less restraint, her child's form licensing freer expression of her interest. A long narrow entranceway with open arches on each side led to a broad stairway at the far end, a horseshoe-shaped counter by the foot of the stairs. Yaril ran ahead of Brann to the counter, beat a few times on the small gong set by the wall, then engaged in an energetic sotto-voce debate with the sleepy but professionally genial man who emerged from the door behind the counter. Brann watched from the corner of her eye, trying to show she knew what she was about, ignoring the men who came to the arch-door of the taproom and stared at her with predatory speculation. She grew increasingly nervous as Yaril prolonged that debate. If she'd been here with her mother and father, as she could've been, she'd have been excited and absorbed by the newness of it all, protected by the arms of custom and love; now she was merely frightened, asea in a place whose rules of conduct she didn't know. She reached up, touched the scarf still wound about her head. Already she had about an inch of new hair, silvery white and softly curling like downfeathers on a duck. It itched, needed washing as much as the rest of her. Seemed weeks since she'd had a bath. She gazed down at thin wrists that looked as if a breath would snap them, at long strong hands tanned dark that were dark also with the grime water alone wouldn't get off. Soap and a hot bath. She sighed with anticipated pleasure.

Yaril came trotting back. "I thought you'd like to eat first while he's getting the water heated for your bath." She led Brann into the taproom and settled her at a table in the far corner. Jaril came in, looked through the arch, began helping Yaril fetch food and eating things, acting as beginning apprentices were expected to act, serving their masters' wants and needs. The clink of the coin the children had taken from the soldiers had bought her a measure of welcome, the children's act brought her a grudging respect as one who might have a dangerous amount of power however odd she looked. Even that oddness had its good points, setting her apart from the general run of women on their own.

As soon as she was settled behind the table with the wall at her back, she felt better, as if she'd acquired a space all her own. And when the children brought cold roast chicken, heated rolls with cheese melted into them and a pitcher of hot spiced wine, she began to eat with the appetite engendered by her long ride. The children knelt beside her, hidden from the rest of the room. When most of the wine was a warm mass in her stomach and the first edge of her hunger had been blunted, she looked down at Jaril. "Coier all right?"

He nodded. "Good stable. Clean, fresh straw in the stalls, no mold on the oats."

"Good." She put down the wine bowl. "What about you two, do you need to eat?"

He shook his head, the fine hair flying into a halo about his pointed face. "After that last meal? No. We shouldn't need more until the Wounded Moon is full again."

"Oh."

She finished the rest of the food and sat holding the drinking bowl cradled in her hands. Her body ached. She still wasn't quite used to the altered distribution of meat on her bones, though as time wore on new habits were beginning to form. That was a help, but she was more and more worried about her ability to make her way in this other world; she was woefully, dangerously ignorant about things these people didn't waste two thoughts on. The money Jaril carried, for example. The only coin she'd ever held was the bronze bit Marran called his luck piece. The children seemed to know what they were doing, their experience at traveling seemed to be much greater than hers, but she felt uneasy about leaving everything to them. Arth Slya encouraged its young ones to develop self-reliance within the community. They had to know their capacities, their desires and gifts, in order to make a proper Choice, whether that choice be centered in the Valley or elsewhere; that knowledge and contentment therein was even more important to the well-being of the Valley than the proper choice of a lifemate. Even after Choice, if the passage of time found the young man or woman restless and unsatisfied, they were encouraged to seek what they needed elsewhere; apprenticeships were arranged in Grannsha, usually at Fairtime, in Tavisteen, or somewhere on the Plains, the young folk leaving to be dancers, players of all sorts, merchants, soldiers, sailors. She had cousins all over Croaldhu, probably scattered about the whole world, but they all had help getting to know how to act, they had people around them to encourage and support them. Such practices had kept Arth Slya thriving for more than a thousand years. A thousand years. Impossible that in so short a time as a day such a way of life had almost ceased to exist.

She sipped at lukewarm wine and noticed for the first time the singular hush in the taproom. At first she thought she'd caused it, then she saw the three men at the bar, their backs against the slab, tankards still full in their hands. They were Temuengs with pale northern skins the color of rich cream, straight black hair pulled back and tied at the napes of their necks, high prominent cheekbones, long narrow eyes as black as the shirts and trousers they wore. They had a hard, brushed neatness, no dust on them, no sweat, not a hair out of place, faces cleanshaven, nails burnished on hands that looked as if they'd never done anything Brann could think of as work, a disturbing neatness that

Drinker of Souls

spoke of coldness and control, that frightened her as it was meant to do. Yaril sensed her unease, dissolved into the light shimmer, crept around the edges of the room, then darted through the men and away before they could do more than blink, flicked back along the wall and solidified into Yaril standing at her shoulder. "Watch out for them," the girl whispered. "They have leave to do anything they want to anyone, they're the enforcers of an Imperial Censor." Yaril patted her arm. "But you just remember who you are now, Drinker of Souls."

Brann shivered. "I don't like . . ." she started in a fierce whisper. A pressure on her arm stopped her. She looked up. A fourth man had come from somewhere and was standing across the table from her. He pulled out a chair and sat down.

"I don't recall requesting company," she said. Jaril was on his feet now, standing at her other shoulder; she lost much of her fear; with the children backing her, this Temueng was nothing. She leaned back in her chair and examined him with hatred and contempt.

He ran his eyes over her. "What are you supposed to be?"

"Drinker of Souls." The phrase Yaril had used came out easily enough. She looked at his frozen face and laughed.

"Who are you?" He spoke with a deadly patience.

She giggled nervously, though he and his armsmen were not very funny. She giggled again and the Temueng grabbed her arm, his fingers digging into her flesh. He tried to twist the arm, to retaliate for her laughter—somewhat to her own surprise—she resisted him with ease and sat smiling at him as he strained for breath, getting red in the face, his menacing calm shattered. But he wasn't stupid and knew the rules of intimidation well enough. If a tactic fails, you quit it before that failure can make you ridiculous, and slide into something more effective. He'd made a mistake, challenging her with unfriendly witnesses present. He loosed her arm, sat back, turned his head partway around but didn't bother looking at the men he spoke to. "Clear them out," he said.

She watched the enforcers clear the room and follow the Plainsfolk out, stationing themselves in the broad archway, their backs to the taproom. She frowned at the Temueng, knowing she would kill him if she had to. Her gentle rearing and Slya's strictures of respect seemed a handicap down here, but she wouldn't abandon either unless she was forced to. She had horror enough for nightmares the rest of her life.

He jabbed a forefinger at the children. "You two," he said. "Out."

"No," Brann said.

Yaril's nostrils flared. "Huh," she said.

"Yours are they, ketcha?"

"We are the Mountain's children," Yaril said, "born of fire and stone."

He looked from one to the other, turned his head again. "Temudung, come here."

One of the three standing in the doorway swung round and came across to the Censor. "Saöm?"

He pointed at Yaril. "The girl. Stretch her out on the bar. Then we'll see if the mountain has answers."

"Censor," Brann said softly, though with anger. "Take my warning. Don't touch the children. They aren't what they seem."

Yaril snorted. "Let the fool find out the hard way, mistress."

The enforcer ignored that exchange and came round the table, hand ready to close on Yaril's arm and snatch her away from Brann's side.

Then it wasn't a delicate small girl the Temueng was reaching for, but a weasel-like beast the size of a large dog that was leaping for his throat, tearing it and leaping away, powerful hind legs driving into his chest, missing much of the geyser of blood hissing out of him. Brann grimaced with distaste and dabbed at the bloodspots on her face and shirt with the napkin the host had provided with her meal.

By the time the Temueng slumped to the floor, the weasel had shrunk smaller, a darkly compact threat crouched on the table in front of Brann, long red tongue licking at the bloodspots on its fur.

"I think you'd better not move," Brann said quietly.

The Censor sat rigidly erect, a greenish tinge to his skin, staring not at Brann or the beast, but at the serpent swaying beside her. The two enforcers in the arch wheeled when they heard the abruptly silenced shriek from their companion, took a step into the room, stopped in their tracks when the serpent hissed, the weasel-beast gave a warning yowl.

The taproom filled with those tiny sounds that make up a silence, the ones never heard in the middle of ordinary bustle and noise, the creak of wood, the hiss of the dying fire, the hoarse breathing of the men, the grinding of the Censor's teeth, the buzzing of a lissfly without sense enough to shun the place.

"Censor," she said. She'd done some rapid thinking, dipped into the fund of stories she'd heard from ancient Uncle Eornis, tales of heroes, monsters and mischief-makers. "I am Drinker of Souls," she said, infusing the words with all the heavy meaning she could. "Feel fortunate,

O man, that I am not thirsty now. Feel fortunate, man, that the Mountain's children are not hungry. Were it otherwise, you would die the death of deaths." She felt a little silly, though he seemed to take her seriously enough. "All I desire is to pass in peace through this miserable land. Let me be, Temueng, and I'll let you be. You and your kind." She let the silence expand until even the slightest sound was painful. Then she said, "I have a weakness, Censor. Anger, Censor. You will be tempted to make the locals pay for your shame. But if you do that, I'll be very very angry, Censor. I'll find you, Censor, believe me, Censor."

She stopped talking and grinned at him, beginning to enjoy herself. But enough was enough so she stood, pushing her chair back with her legs. "I'm going to my room now, Censor. I'm tired and I plan to sleep soundly and well, but the Mountain's children never sleep, so you'd be well advised to let me be. Say what you want to the folk here, I won't contradict you, you need lose no touch of honor, Censor."

She felt his eyes on her as she left the room. Yaril flitted up the steps before her and Jaril came behind—guarding her, though she was too self-absorbed to realize that until triumph burnt out and she was walking tiredly down the lamplit hall to the room she'd hired for the night.

A cheerfully crackling fire on the hearth, a large tub of hot water set comfortably close to the heat, copper cans of extra hot water to add later. Soft nubbed towels on the rush seat of a high-backed straight chair, a bowl of perfumed soap beside them. She crossed the room letting the children shut the door, touched the thin-walled porcelain of the soap bowl, picked it up, ran her fingers over the bottom. Immer's mark. It was born from her father's kilns. The simple lovely bowl made her feel like weeping. Her father was a gentle man who disliked loud voices, would simply walk away if someone got too aggressive. He saved his anger for cheats and liars and slipshod work and for that last he was unforgiving. He would not live long as a slave, there wasn't the right kind of bend in him. She sighed and stripped, putting aside that worry, there being little she could do about it right then.

With a breath of pleasure she eased into the hot water and began to wash away the grime of her long hard ride, the pleasure of the bath making up for those many hardships she'd had to endure, even for the contretemps in the taproom and whatever came of it. She wrinkled her nose at the filthy shirt and trousers thrown in a pile beside the chair, disgusted by the thought she'd have to get back in them come the morning. No mother or cousin or anyone to do for her. When she was done she stood up, dripping the scent from the soap around her like a cloud. She snapped open one of the towels—it was almost big as a blanket—and began rubbing herself dry, a little timid about touching herself, embarrassed by the soft full breasts, the bush of pubic hair. She put a foot on the side of the tub, dried it, stepped onto the hearth tiles, dried her other foot, dropped the damp towel beside her discarded clothes and wrapped the dry one about her.

Yaril and Jaril were sitting on the bed watching her, but in the days since the Valley she'd gotten used to their being always around. She rubbed at her head with a corner of the towel, combed her hand through short damp hair, sighed with relief as it curled about her fingers. Being bald was almost as embarrassing as the jiggle of her breasts.

She looked at the bed, but she wasn't sleepy. Tired, yes. Exhausted, uncertain, weepy, yes; but the bed meant nightmares when her mind was so roiled up. She walked to the window. It was still not raining and very dark, the Wounded Moon not up yet and anyway it was shrunk to a broken crescent. She leaned on the broad sill, gazing to the west where the mountains were; wondering what her folk were doing now, how they were faring, if they'd gone back and collected the loot yet. She continued to gaze into the cloudy darkness, willing herself to see her mountain, her Tincreal.

And—for a moment—believed it was her will that touched the peaks with light. Then the sill rocked under her elbows, the floor rocked under her feet and the faint red glow illuminating the peaks rose to a reddish boil bursting into the sky. Some minutes later a blast came like a blow against her ears; it settled into a low grinding grumble that finally died into a tension-filled silence. The red glare subsided to a low-lying seethe sandwiched between clouds and earth. Standing with her face pressed against the iron lace, her mouth gaping open in a scream that wouldn't come, she was a hollowcast figurine, empty, no anger, not even any surprise. As if she'd expected it. And of course she had, they all had, the signs had been amply there, the children had warned the blow was coming soon. "No," she said, saying *no* to the sudden thought that the Mountain had destroyed the little the Temuengs had left of Arth Slya. Guilt seized her. If she'd left the soldiers alone, alive, if she'd let them take her folk away, her mother'd be alive now, they all would.

A tugging at her arm. She looked down. Jaril. "They could be safe, Bramble. If the Mountain blew away from the Valley. And it isn't your fault. Like you told me once, your folk know the moods of the Mountain. I could fly there and see, be back by morning. If you want. Do you?"

Brann barely whispered, "Yes. Please." She turned back to the window, her eyes fixed on the soft red glow, a bit of hope mixing with her despair. Behind her she heard the door open, click shut. Then small hands caught hold of her arm. Yaril led her to the bed, tucked her in. Lying on her stomach, her face to the wall, she let herself relax as Yaril murmured soft cooing sounds at her and smoothed those small strong hands across her shoulders, down along her arms, over and over. Her shaking stopped. All at once she was desperately tired. She slept.

A weight was on her, she couldn't breathe, a hand was clamped over her mouth, a knee butting between her legs. Fear and horror and revulsion welled up in her; she began to struggle, not knowing what was happening, trying to free her mouth, trying to buck the weight off her, but he was strong and heavy and he'd got himself set before she was awake enough to fight him. He was hard and thick, pushing into her, he was grunting like an animal, hurting her, it was a dry burning as if he invaded her with a reamer, rasping at her, all she could think of was getting it out.

Seconds passed, a few heartbeats, and she came out of her panic, lay still for one breath, another, then she moved her head so suddenly and so strongly he wasn't ready for it. She didn't quite free her mouth but she got flesh between her teeth and bit hard. He cursed and slapped her, then fumbled for her mouth again. She wriggled desperately under him, got her hands free, slapped them against the sides of his head, shoved it up off her, started the draw. He had a moment before the paralysis took hold but he couldn't dislodge her.

When he was drained, she rolled him off her and got shakily to her feet, lit the lamp from the dying fire, threw on a few more sticks of wood. Toe in his ribs, she nudged him over. The Censor. She'd humiliated him; this was how he got even. Got dead. She looked away. No anger or fear left, all she felt was dirtied. Filthy. She looked down at herself and was startled by a drop of blood falling by her foot. Her thighs were smeared with blood. Another drop fell. Hastily she stepped into the tub, scooped up a dollop of fresh soap and began washing herself, gently at first then scrubbing the washcloth harder and harder over her whole body as if she could scrub the memory of the dead man off her skin.

By the time she finished, the bleeding had stopped. She padded to the bed, wrapped herself in a blanket and sat crosslegged in the middle of the stained sheets, staring at the door.

About an hour later Yaril came back with a bundle of clothing. Brann blinked at them, understanding then where Yaril had gone. The changechild had seen the way she looked at the stinking shirt and trousers. Once she was safely asleep, Yaril went out and stole clean things for her.

"You didn't lock the door," Brann said, her voice a hoarse whisper.

Yaril looked at the dead man, shook her head, held up the clumsy key. "I did."

Brann opened her mouth to say something, forgot it, began to cry, the gasping body-shaking sobs of a hurt child.

Yaril dropped the clothing and ran to her, sat on the bed beside her, murmured soft cooing words to her, patted her, soothed her, comforting her as a mother would a frightened child, gentling her into a deep healing sleep with the song of her voice, spinning sleep with that soft compelling voice.

When she woke, the sound of rain filled the room. While she slept, her body had healed itself; the bruises and strains were gone and the burning hurt between her thighs. She sat up. The body was gone. She got quickly out of bed and started pulling on the clean clothes Yaril had brought her.

A knock on the door as she was tucking in her shirt tail. "Come."

Jaril came in looking a little wan. "I was right," he said, not waiting for her questions. "Mountain blew east not north. The river has changed course some, got more cataracts, the track out is chewed up so badly that if you didn't know where Arth Slya was already you'd never find it. Dance floor is cracked, part of it tilted. Some of the workshops slid into the river. Your folk are out clearing up, a few bumps and bruises but I didn't see anyone seriously hurt. Your mother's fine. Her looms didn't get burnt, the fire in your house went out, the quake didn't mess them up either, so she's been busy. She thinks you're dead, killed by Temuengs. Folk don't know what to do about your father and the others. If they haven't returned before shelters are cobbled together, some of your cousins are going to slip down and see what happened to them."

"Sheee, they shouldn't. . . ."

"Be all right if they keep their heads down; they've been warned."

Brann brushed her hand back over her hair, rubbed at her eyes.

"Thanks, J'ri. That helps a lot. You look worn down." Her mouth curled into a wry smile. "I picked up a life last night. Come and take."

Jaril hesitated. "You all right?"

"Not so upset as I was. A little wiser about the way things are." She held out her hands. As he took them, she said, "By the way, what did you and Yaril do with the body? And where is she?"

"Watching the enforcers, they're asleep and she wants them to stay that way until after we're gone. We dumped it in the river. With a little luck it'll be out to sea before it's spotted." He took his hands away, giggled. "He'll get to Tavisteen before us. I better see how they're treating Coier, get him saddled. You feel like eating?"

"What's one more dead man?"

After he left she wandered about the room, picking up her scattered possessions, folding everything neatly, packing with the careful finickiness of the most precise of her aunts. When she was finished, she sat on the bed gathering courage to leave the room. After a few ragged breaths, she bounced to her feet, draped the saddlebags over her arm, sucked in a deep breath. Go slow, she thought, act like you don't give spit what anyone thinks. She touched the door's latch and went weak in the knees. Not ready to go out. Not yet. She passed her hand over her hair, realized she'd forgotten to wind the scarf about her head, saw the creased length of material hanging over the back of the chair. She crossed to the wavery mirror. A curling mass of soft white hair all over her head, long enough now that its weight made the curls larger, looser. Strange but rather nice, suiting the shape of her face. She thought about not wearing the scarf, it'd feel good to let the wind blow through her hair, but short as it was, the color it wasn't, it'd cause too much comment when she was riding the highroad. She wound the strip of cloth about her head, tied it so the ends fell behind one ear. Odd, that paring down of her head to its basic contours made her eyes look huge and gemlike, her mouth softer. She looked at herself another heartbeat or two, then strode to the door, jerked it open and stepped into the empty corridor. The other travelers staying the night had already departed or were still sleeping. It was early.

She walked slowly down the rush matting toward the stairs at the end of the corridor, her stride growing firmer, steadier. At the landing she touched the scarf to see if it was still in place, a concession to uncertainty, then started down.

A younger version of last night's host, so exact a copy he had to be the owner's son, looked up as she stopped by the counter. "You wish, athin?"

"I'd like, athno, something to eat."

"Certainly, athin. It is a bit early," he went on as he flipped the hinged section of counter top and came out to escort her to the table she'd chosen the night before. "It'll take a breath or two to prepare, but 'tis just as well to be early this day, the diligence from Tavisteen is due to stop here soon for the fastbreaking and we'll be busier than broody hens and wishing for more hands, trying to feed them and the escort too." She said nothing, but he must have read something in her silence because he came around and stood beside her. "Traveling was near impossible till the Temuengs started sending patrols with the pack-trains and the diligences. Now, we have eggs fried or poached, fresh baked rolls, sausages, they're the family's special blend and many the praises we've got for them, though it's me who says it. Or a nice steak? Or we've some young rockquail, or some fish my middle son caught from the river this morning. For drinking, there's ale, cider, tea or something called kaffeh a trader left with us a month ago. Some seem to like it, though I must say I think it's an acquired taste." He turned his head to listen to the rain coming steadily down outside. "The high-road will be awash if this keeps up, athin; for your comfort you might consider staying until the storm blows out."

Having waited for him to finish, she did not bother to answer his discreet attempt to wring another day's coin out of her, but simply ordered a hot ample breakfast with a pot of tea to wash it down. His amiable chatter had put her at ease and now she was merely hungry.

The children came in before she was done with the meal, soaked and waiflike one moment, dry the next. Silent and undisturbed by the stares of the fastbreakers in the slowly filling room, they threaded through the tables and came to stand beside her. Brann scowled at the stare-eyes and they looked hastily away, wary of her. Rumors, she thought, worse than midges for getting about. She sipped at the hot tea, saying nothing until she'd emptied the cup. She set it down with a small definite click, turned to Jaril. "Have you paid for our room and meals?"

"No mistress, nor for the stable and corn." His back to the rest of the room, Jaril grinned and winked at her.

"See to it then; I shall be annoyed if you allow yourself to be treated like a country fool."

Jaril winked again, went trotting off to pay the rate Yaril had won by bargaining with the host. Brann relaxed a bit more, squeezed a last half cup from the pot and sat sipping at it, looking about the room. A number of new faces, probably they'd been in bed when she reached the Inn last night, up now to get their morning's meal before the inundation from the diligence and the Temueng patrol. An odd mix. Alike in their wariness, not alike in other ways. A merchant with a duplicate-in-little of his opulent dress, bland ungiving face and tight little hands seated beside him, a son most likely learning the business. Several scarred, harsh-featured men in worn leathers with more cutlery hitched to their bodies than she'd seen outside of Migel's smithy. They reminded her immediately of the Temueng invaders, different racial types, but a sameness to them that overrode the minor differences of build or skin color. Half a dozen older men seated about, mostly with their backs to the walls, their clothing and demeanor giving little clue as to who they were or why they were on the move, the only thing she could be sure of was that they weren't Temuengs.

Jaril looked in through the archway, nodded. Keeping her face expressionless, Brann slid from her chair and walked without haste between the tables, feeling eyes on her all the way. In the foyer she lifted a hand to the young host, pushed through the main door and stopped under the bit of roof that kept the rain off her head. It was coming down harder than she'd expected, in gray sheets that hid everything more than a body-length away. Coier stood saddled and ready, hitched to a ring in one of the several wayposts before the Inn, sidling and unhappy, not liking the rain very much. She felt for him, reluctant herself to leave the shelter of the roof, but there was no help for it, she had to be long gone when Yaril's sleep spinning wore off and the enforcers woke to find the Censor vanished. She stomped through the wet and pulled herself into the saddle, sitting with a squishy splat, took the reins when Jaril handed them up to her, looked at him with envy. His clothing wasn't clothing at all, but a part of his substance and when he chose, it shed the wet better than any duck's back. She sighed. "The trouble you two get me into." With a gentle kick she started Coier toward the highroad, keeping him at a walk. "No doubt they all think I'm a horrible monster, riding while I make you children run in the mud." She bent down, called to Yaril, "How long's the spinning going to last without you there to freshen it?"

Yaril turned her face up. The rain slid away without wetting her. She held up her hands and Brann swung her onto the saddle in front of her.

"Till the diligence gets there probably. I'd say the noise of it is enough to wake them."

"What'll they do?"

"Considering what happened in the taproom, raise one holy stink and get half the Temueng army looking for us."

"Sheee, Yaro, we can't handle that."

"Can't fight something, then run like sheol and hope you lose it." Yaril patted her arm. "Just have to be smarter than they are, that's all."

"Not so great a start, was it."

An hour later the diligence came out of the rain at her. She heard it before she saw it, its creaks, rattles, cadenced sloppy thuds, windy snorts, a snatch or two of voices, mostly bits of curses; she nudged Coier off the road, pushing up tight against the hedgerow trying to ignore the clawing thorns. The rain was coming down harder than ever and from the sound of the thing whoever was driving it expected the world to get out of his way. The large mild heads of Takhill Dravs came out of the rain, their black manes plastered down over the white stripes that ran ear to nose, the leather blinder on the offside lead gleaming like the glaze of das'n vuor. Their brown hides dripped water and looked almost as black as the harness. The feathers on their massive shapely hocks were smoothed down with rain and mud but their sturdy legs lifted and fell with the regularity of a pendulum, tick-tock, tick-tock. Two first, then two more, then the two wheelers, larger than the others. A fine hitch. The driver hunched over the reins, cowl pulled so far forward she couldn't see his face, only the large gnarled hands so deftly holding the black leather straps. He was silent, his silence making a space about him that the second man on the perch made no attempt to breach. He was a Temueng with a short bow held across his knees that he was trying to protect with his cloak, a quiver full of arrows clipped to the inside of one leg. He was cursing steadily, stopping only to wipe at his face. He saw her, looked indifferently away. She watched him with a surge of hatred that twisted her stomach into knots.

The diligence was a long boxy vehicle creaking along on three pairs of oversize wheels that cast up broad sheets of brown water. Oiled silk curtains were drawn tight against the rain but there was some sort of lamp burning inside, probably more than one, because she saw the shadows of the passengers moving across the silk. Six high narrow windows filled with profiles and the rounds of swaying heads. She watched them and wondered what was so important it took those people out into weather like this. The last window slid past, then she saw the piles of luggage strapped behind. And felt again that helplessness that had engulfed her as she walked into the Inn, an ignorance of life down here so complete that moving into it was like stepping off Tincreal onto a low-hanging cloud.

Four Temuengs rode guard far enough behind the diligence to escape the mud and gravel the broad iron-tired wheels kicked up. They rode swathed in heavy cloaks, lances couched, bows covered, but she had little doubt they'd be a nasty surprise to anyone thinking of attacking the diligence. The leader turned his head and stared at her as he rode past. She saw a flash of gilt, of paler silver. An empush, commanding four.

Then he was past. Then they were all past. She let out a breath. Her middle hurt as if she'd been stooping and straightening for hours. She wiped at her face, kneed Coier into a walk, guiding him back onto the road, the two hounds pacing silently one on each side of her.

A few breaths later she heard the sound of a horse coming rapidly up behind her, then the Temueng empush rode around her, turning his mount to block the road. She pulled up, a flutter in her stomach, a knot of fear and rage closing her throat. She couldn't speak, sat staring at him grimly, silently. Her eyes blurred and after a moment she knew she was crying; she didn't try to hide her tears, only hoped the rain beating on her face would camouflage them.

"Who are you?" he shouted at her, his voice harsh, impatient. "What are you doing on this road? Where are you going?"

She stared at him, managed, "A traveler, headed for the nearest port so I can get out of this soggy backwater." She was surprised by the crisp bite of the words, no sign of what she was feeling in them, as if someone else were speaking for her. Her fear and anger lessened, the tears stopped, she sat silent waiting for his response.

"Your credeen." He rode closer, held out his hand.

"What?"

"Your permit to travel, athin." The honorific was an insult. He drew his sword, holding it lightly in his right hand. "The sigiled tag."

"Ah." She thought furiously. Seemed the Temuengs were trying to control travel and tighten their grip on Croaldhu; nothing of this had been in place three years ago at the last Fair; the Kumaliyn didn't bother with such nonsense. She dredged up the worst words she could think of, cursing the Temueng's officiousness, the need to poke his nose in other people's business. All he had to do was ride on and let her be. But he was waiting for some sort of answer and from the look of him, wasn't inclined to accept excuses or pleas of ignorance. She glanced quickly at Jaril and Yaril. The werehounds had moved quietly out from her until almost obliterated by the rain. She risked a look over her shoulder; the other soldiers and the diligence were out of sight and hearing. Lifting a hand slowly so he could see it was empty, she moved it in a broad arc from Yaril to Jaril. "They are all the permits I need, Temueng."

And Yaril was a fireball rushing at his head, and Jaril was fire about his sword. With a scream of pain, he dropped the blade. Hastily Brann said, "Just chase this one off, I've had enough lives."

The fires seemed to shrug, then nipped and sizzled about the flanks of the already nervous horse, driving it into a frantic, bucking run after the diligence, the shaken empush struggling to keep from being thrown into the mud. One of the fires flowed into a large hawk and came flying back. It swooped to the sword's hilt, caught it up and vanished into the rain with it. A second later it was back, settling to the ground beside Coier, Yaril again as soon as the talons touched mud. Brann lifted her onto the saddle in front of her. "I gave that fool his sword," Yaril said. "Better if he doesn't have to explain how he lost it." She leaned back against Brann, smiled as the other fire returned and was a hound again standing beside the horse. "We got trouble enough once he connects up with those enforcers."

Brann nudged Coier into an easy canter. "I'm still glad he's alive. We got trouble anyway, what's one more stinking Temueng?" She stroked Yaril's moonpale hair. "Another hour. . . ." She sighed. "Stinking rain. Wasn't for that, one of you could fly watch. I don't know what to do. . . . I don't know. . . ."

Brann rode on into the rain, that dreary steady downpour that falls straight from clouds to earth and stays and stays until you forget what the sun feels like. Jaril laughed at the idea that anything so simple and natural as rain could keep him from flying and was following about an hour's ride behind, a dark gray mistcrane dipping in and out of clouds. Yaril was a hound again, running easily beside the horse. Rested and well-fed. Coier had to be held to a steady lope; he wanted to run and Brann shared the urge, but she didn't dare let him loose.

An hour passed, then another. The children could communicate over any distance bounded by the horizon, why this limitation they either couldn't or wouldn't explain, and Jaril would give them an hour's warning of pursuit, a chance to discover a hide that would fool the followers.

Another hour. Brann rode on between half-seen hedgerows beaten into a semblance of neatness by the downpour, washed to a dark shiny green that glowed through the grays of rain and mud.

Some fifteen minutes into the fourth hour the hound was suddenly Yaril trotting by her knee, screaming up at her over the hiss and splat of the rain, "Riders coming up. Fast. Temuengs. Three from the diligence, one of the enforcers. Half dozen besides. New faces. Most likely occupation troops." She dashed ahead of the horse, was a hawk running, then powering into the rain, gone to look for a break in the hedges.

Brann was frantic. Ten men, men warned about her. Half a score of men who could stand at a distance putting arrows in her, pincushion Brann, not something pleasant to contemplate. Adept as her body was at healing itself, she had a strong suspicion there had to be a limit—at which point she would be very dead. The hedges on both sides of the road were high, wild and flourishing, taller than she was atop Coier and likely as thick as they were tall. Even if she could somehow push through, those murderous hounds on her trail would spot the signs she'd have to leave and be through after her and she'd have gained nothing, would have lost if some of them had been living long enough hereabouts to know something of the land. Even a year's patrolling would have taught them how they could drive her into a corner.

Yaril came winging back, touched down, *changed* to childshape. Brann pulled her up before her once again, so they could talk without having to shout. "Nothing," the changechild said. "No turn-offs far as I dared fly. But there's a weak spot in the hedge about twenty minutes on, a place where one of the bushes died."

Brann started to protest, but Yaril shook her head. "It's all there is, Bramble. We'll contrive something. Now move." She slid off, *changing* in midair and went soaring away on hawk wings. Brann urged Coier into a gallop and followed her, feeling a surging exhilaration at the power under her. The hedge on the left grew wilder and even the meager signs of tending evident before vanished completely, straggly canes encroaching on the paving.

Yaril stood in the road, waving at a thin spot where the canes had withered away and the few leaves clinging to branchstubs were wrinkled and yellow. Without hesitation, Brann turned Coier off the road and drove him toward the brittle barrier with voice, heels and slapping hands. Head twisted back, snorting protest, he barreled through into a long-neglected field that was grown to a fine thick crop of weeds in the center of which stood a shapeless structure with much of its thatching gone, its stone walls tumbled down, the stones charred black in spite of the rain and the many that had gone before. She rode Coier into the meager shelter through a door where half the frame still stood, the other half lay in splinters among the charred stones and twisted weeds. The roof that remained was sodden and leaking but it kept out the worst of the wet. She dismounted with a sigh of relief and trembling legs, glad to be out of that depressing incessant beat-beat on her body and head. She closed her eyes and leaned against the endwall, dripping onto the bird dung, weeds, old feathers, bits of thatching that lay in a thick layer over the beaten-earth floor. But she couldn't stay there. She looped the reins about the remnant of the door frame, then ran back to Yaril.

The changechild was dabbling in the mud, resetting the clods that Coier's hooves had thrown up, helping the rain wash away the deep indentations his iron shoes had cut into the mud. The hole in the hedge looked wide as a barn door; Brann tried to drag a few canes from the live bushes across the gap but that didn't seem to do anything but make the opening more obvious. Yaril straightened, the mud sloughing off her, leaving her dry and clean. She saw what Brann was doing, giggled. "Don't be silly, Bramble." The pet name seemed to amuse her more and she laughed until she seemed about to cry, then pulled herself together. "Go on," she said, "get into shelter. Jaril's coming, be here soon to keep watch when I can't."

"Can't?"

"Watch, then scoot." Yaril giggled again then stepped next to the twisty trunk of the bush and *changed*. With startling suddenness she was a part of the hedge, as green and vigorous, wild and thorny as the bushes on either side of her.

Shaking her head at her lack of thought, Brann trudged to the burned-out structure, barn or house or storage crib, whatever it was.

She stripped off her sodden clothing, rubbed herself down with one of her blankets, stripped the saddle and bridle off Coier and rubbed him down until she was sweating with the effort, doled out a double handful of cracked corn onto his saddle pad. She tied on his tether and left him to his treat, then got out her old filthy shirt and trousers, slipped into them. At least they were dry. She wrinkled her nose at the smells coming from the dark heavy cloth, but soon grew used to them again. She folded the damp blanket into a cushion, sat down with her back against the rough wall and was beginning to feel almost comfortable when Jaril walked in. "They're almost here," he said. "You'll hear them soon." He squatted beside her. "Far as I could see, they didn't investigate any of the turn-offs, they're coming straight ahead, pushing their horses hard, on the chance they can overtake you."

"What happens when they wear out their mounts and still haven't come on us?"

"Raise the countryside I expect. Listen."

Through rain that at last was beginning to slacken she heard the pounding of hooves on the worn stone paving of the highroad. Coier lifted his head and moved restlessly. She got to her feet and stood beside him, a hand on his nose to silence him if he decided to challenge the beasts on the far side of the hedge. She listened with her whole body as they went clattering pounding splashing past without slackening pace, the noises fading swiftly into the south.

She let out the breath she was holding. Jaril squeezed her fingers gently. "I'm off, Bramble. Better I keep an eye on them awhile more." He looked around. "I think you could chance a fire, Yaril'll get you the makings, dry them off. You might as well eat something now, it could get harder later." Then he was a mistcrane stalking out the door. Brann followed him, stood watching his stilting run and soar, beautifully awkward on the ground, beauty itself in the air. She stood wiping the damp off her face, suddenly and simply happy to be alive, delighted with the water running from her hair, the breath in her lungs lifting and dropping her ribs. She stood there long enough to see Yaril dissolve out of the hedge and come walking through the wet weeds, a slight lovely sprite, a part of her now, her family. She smiled and waited for Yaril to reach her.

Brann woke from a long nap to find the afternoon turned bright as the clouds broke and moved off. Yaril was sitting in silence, staring into the heart of a little fire, her face enigmatic, her narrow shoulders rounded, the crystal eyes drinking in and reflecting the flames. Brann felt an immense sadness, a yearning that made her want to cry; it wasn't her own grief but waves of feeling pouring out of Yaril. For the first time she saw that they'd lost as much as she had, drawn from their homeland and people as she was driven from hers. And there was very little chance they'd ever return to either homes or people; they were changed as she was changed, exiled into a world where there was no one to share their deepest joys and sorrows. Brann licked her lips, wanted to say something, wanted to say she understood, but before she could find the words, Yaril turned, grinned, jumped to her feet, tacitly rejecting any intrusion into her feelings. "Jaril's on his way back. Rain's over, we'll ride tonight and if we can, lay up tomorrow."

Brann yawned. "What's he say?"

"Temuengs went on till the rain stopped, but they finally had to admit they'd missed you. There was a bit of frothing at the mouth and toing and froing—" Yaril giggled—"then the enforcer rode on for Tavisteen, your favorite empush started back, he's sending the Temuengs one at a time down side roads to stir up the local occupation forces and looking careful at the hedges as he goes past. Time I got back to being a plant. It's boring but not quite so bad as being a rock." With another giggle she got to her feet and ran out.

Brann followed her to the opening, watched her dart through the weeds to the hedgerow, merge with the green. Shaking her head, she turned away to fix herself a bit of supper while she waited for Jaril to arrive.

The mistcrane flew ahead of them, searching out clear ways, leading them along twisty back roads that were little more than cowpaths. Moving mostly at night, ducking and dodging, watching Temuengs and their minions spilled like disturbed lice across the land, nosing down the smallest ways, missing her sometimes by a hair, a breath, Brann wormed slowly south and west, heading for Travisteen though that grew more and more difficult as the hunt thickened about her. The children stole food for her, corn for Coier to keep his strength up because there was never enough rest and graze for him. She grew lean and lined, fatigue and hunger twin companions that never left her, sleep continually interrupted, meals snatched on the run. Five days, seven, ten, sometimes forced into evasions so tortuous she came close to running in circles. Yet always she managed to win a little farther south. Twice Temuengs blundered across her, but with the children's help she killed them and drank their lives, passing some of that energy on to Coier, restoring the strength that the hard running was leaching from him.

The broad fertile plain at Croaldhu's heart dipped lower and lower until sedges and waterweeds began to replace the cultivated fields and the grassy pastures, until pools of water gathered in the hollows and stood in still decay, scummy and green with mud and algae. The fringes of the Marish, a large spread of swampland and grassy fens like a scraggly beard on Croaldhu's chin, a bar on her path, a trap for her if she wasn't careful; should the Temuengs get close enough they could pin her against impassable water or bottomless muck. The mistcrane flew back and forth along the edge of the Marish, trying to work out a way through it, a straggling line from one dot-sized mud island to the next, wading through the pools and streams to test depth and bottom, keeping as close to the Highroad as he could so he wouldn't get them lost in the tangle of the wetlands, even after the road turned to a causeway built on broad low stone arches a man's height above the water, an additional danger because Temuengs riding along the causeway could see uncomfortably far into that tangle. He led Brann and Coier along his chosen route, one that managed to keep a thin screen of cypress, flerpine and root-rotted finnshon between her and that road. The Wounded Moon was fattening toward full and the children's crystal eyes saw as well by night as by day, so they moved all night, slowly, with much difficulty, struggling with impossible footing, slipping and sliding, half the time with Brann dismounted and walking beside Coier, stroking him, comforting him, bleeding energy into him, helping him endure, stumbling on until they reached a mud island high enough to get them out of the water and away from the leeches and chiggers that made life a torment to the two fleshborn though they avoided the changechildren.

Gray. Even during daylight everything was gray. Gray skies, gray water, gray mud dried on sedges and trees, on low hanging branches, gray fungus, gray insects, gray everything. The stench of damp closed around her, of rotting everything, flesh, fish, vegetation. Three gray nights she rode, three gray days she rested on mounds of mud and rotting reeds, where she fed Coier from the too rapidly diminishing supply of corn, rubbed him down, touching to death the leeches on his legs, draining their small bits of life, feeding it back into him; once the leeches were drained they were easy enough to brush off, falling like withered lengths of gutta-percha. By accident she discovered another attribute of her changed body as she fed that life into the weary trembling beast; her hand was close to one of the oozing leech-bites and she saw the bite seal over and heal with the feed.

By the end of the fourth night, she was ready to chance the causeway rather than continue this draining slog. As dawn spread a pale uncertain light over the water, Jaril led her deeper into the Marish to an eye-shaped island considerably larger than the others with a small clump of vigorous, sharp-scented flerpines at one end, a dry graveled mound at the center with some straggly clumps of grass, a bit of stream running by it with water that looked clear and clean and tempting. She resisted temptation and began going over Coier, her probing deadly touch killing gnats and borers, chiggers and bloodworms and the ever-present leeches, feeding the weary beast those bits of life. It was a handy thing, that deadly touch of hers, and she was learning from far too much practice how to use it. By now she could kill a mite on a mosquito's back and leave the mosquito unharmed. After spreading a double handful of corn on his saddlepad, she plunged into a stream and used a twist of grass to scrub the sweat and muck off her body and hair. While she washed, Yaril thrust a hand into the pile of wood Jaril collected and flew back to the island, got a fire going and set a pot on to heat water for tea, then took Brann's clothing to the stream and began scrubbing the shirts and trousers with sand from the mound. When Brann was clean inside and out, when the water was boiled and the tea made, when Yaril had hung the sopping shirts and trousers on ragged branches of the pines, Brann sat naked on a bit of grass, cool and comfortable for the first time in days, watching Coier standing in the water drinking, sipping at her own drinking bowl, the tea made from the scrapings of her supply but the more appreciated for that. She set the bowl on her knee, sighed. "I don't care how many Temuengs are shuttling along the causeway, come the night, I'm getting Coier and me out of this."

Jaril looked at Yaril, nodded. "Traffic's been light the last few nights, and . . ." he hesitated, "we've used more energy than I expected. Yaril and me, we're getting hungry."

"Think I'd like being the hunter for a change. Instead of the hunted." She gulped at the tea, holding it in her mouth, letting the hot liquid slide down her throat to warm her all over. "Coier's sick or something, the water's got him, or those bites. He needs graze and rest, more than anything, rest. Me too. Maybe we could find a place to lay up once we're past this mess." She looked over her shoulder at the hazy sun rising above the pines. "Could one of you do something about drying my clothes? I don't feel right lying down with nothing on. Anything could happen to make us light out with no time to stop for dressing."

"Right." While Jaril doused the fire, Yaril *changed,* went shimmering through Brann's wet clothing, drying a set of shirt and trousers for her. When she thought they were ready, she brought them to Brann. "Get some sleep." she said. "We'll watch."

Brann woke tangled in tough netting made from cords twisted out of reed fiber and impregnated with fish stink. She woke to the whisper of a drum, to the suddenly silenced scream from Coier as his throat was cut. She woke to see little gray men swarming over the island, little gray men with coarse yellow cloth wound in little shrouds about their groins, little gray men with rough dry skin, a dusty gray mottled in darker streaks and splotches like the skin of lizards she'd watched sunning on her sunning rock, little gray men butchering Coier, cutting his flesh from his big white bones. She wept from weakness and sorrow and fury, wept for the beast as she hadn't wept for her murdered sister, her murdered people, wept and for a while thought of nothing else. Then she remembered the children.

She could move her head a little, a very little. It was late, the shadows were long across the water. No sign of the children anywhere. Another gray man sat beside a small crackling fire, net cording woven about him and knotted in intricate patterns she guessed were intended to describe his power and importance; a fringe of knotted cords dangled from a thick rope looped loosely about a small hard potbelly. In an oddly beautiful, long-fingered reptilian hand he held a strange and frightening drum, a snake's patterned skin stretched over the skull of a huge serpent with a high-domed braincase and eyeholes facing forward. Smiling, he drew from the taut skin a soft insistent rustle barely louder than the whisper of the wind through the reeds, a sound that jarred her when she thought about it but nonetheless crept inside her until it commanded the beat of her heart, the in-out of her breathing. She jerked her body loose from the spell and shivered with fear. Magic. He looked at her and she shivered again. He sat before that tiny hot fire of twigs and grass, his eyes fixed on her with a hungry satisfaction that chilled her to the bone. She thought about the children and was furious at them for deserting her until the drummer reached out and ran a hand over two large stones beside his bony knee, gray-webbed crystals each large as a man's head, crystals gathering the fire into them, little broken fires repeated endlessly within. His hand moving possessively over them, he grinned at her, baring the hard ridge of black gum that took the place of teeth in these folk, enjoying her helpless rage until a commotion at the other end of the island caught his gaze.

She strained to see, froze as a Temueng walked into her arc of vision, leading his mount and a pack pony with a large canvas-wrapped load. Gray men crowded around him, hissing or whistling, snapping fingers, stamping their broad clawed feet, jostling him, giving off clouds of a hate and fury barely held in check. His nostrils flaring with disgust, he looked over their heads and kept walking until he stood stiffly across the fire from the magic man, not-looking at Brann with such intensity she knew at once the Marishmen had sold her. She lay very still, grinding her teeth, with a rage greater than the gray men's.

"You sent saying you had the witch." The Temueng's voice was deep and booming, deliberately so, Brann thought, meant to overpower the twitter and squeak of the gray men. "I brought the payment you required."

The drummer convulsed with silent laughter, drew whispery laughs from his drum. "Yellow man, scourge a thee dryfoots." He laughed some more. "Sit, scourge."

Gray men trotted busily about building up the small fire into a snapping, crackly, pine-smelling blaze. The magic man played with his drum, its faint sounds merging with the noise of the fire. The Temueng sat in firmly dignified silence, waiting for all this mummery to be done, looking occasionally around to Brann. She glared hate at him, and lay simmering when he looked away, taking what satisfaction she could in his rapidly cracking patience.

The drum sound grew abruptly louder, added a click-click-clack as the drummer tapped the nails of two fingers against the bone of the skull. "I, Ganumomo speak," the drummer chanted, garbling the Plainspeak so badly she could barely understand what he was saying. "Hah! I, Ganumomo daah beah mos' strong dreamer in ahhh Mawiwamo." Continuing to scratch at the drumhead with two fingers of the hand that held the skull, he scooped up one of the crystals, held it at arm's length above his head. "Ganumomo naah fear fahfihmo, see see." He set the crystal down, pursed his rubbery lips, added a whispery whistle to the whispery rattle of the drum, snapped off the whistle. "Cha-ba-ma-we naah sah strong. Magah da Cha-ba-ma-we naah botha Ganumomo. Hah!" Dropping into a conversational tone, he said, "You, dryfoot, you bring aulmeamomo?"

With a grunt of assent, the Temueng got to his feet and went to the pack pony. He unroped the canvas, took a pouch from among the other items piled onto the packsaddle, brought it back to the fire. He dropped it beside the drummer, returned to his seat across the fire from the gray man. "Bringer of dreams," he said. "More will be sent when we have the witch, like you say, what is it? the chabummy. I brought other things. Axe heads, spear points, fishhooks, knives. An earnest of final payment. Give me the witch."

"Fish that swim too straight he go net. Otha thing in the trading. I Ganumomo daah beah wanting no dryfoots come in Mawiwamo. I Ganumomo daah beah wanting . . ."

Brann stopped listening as the bargaining went on, focusing all her attention and will on the children. It was no use, she got no response at all no matter how hard she concentrated. She moved about the little she could, but her arms were pinned tight against her sides, her legs were bound so tightly she couldn't even bend her knees; the more she struggled, the more inextricably she was tangled in the cords. Anger rumbled in her like the fireheart of Tincreal, anger that was partly her own and partly that wildness that took hold of her and killed the Temueng pimush. She was terrified when that happened, somewhere deep within her there was terror now, but it was overlaid by that melded fury. She began to sing, very softly, under her breath, the possession song that Called the Sleeping Lady into the Yongala and readied her for the great Dances.

> Dance, Slya   Slya, dance
> I am the Path, so walk me
> Dance the sky the earth the all
> Dance the round of being's thrall
> Dance, Slya   Slya, dance
> Emanation, puissance
> I am the cauldron, empty me
> Dance dissolution, turbulence
> End of all tranquility
> Dance, Slya   Slya, dance
> I am the Womb, come fill me
> Germination, generation
> Dance hard death's fecundity
> Dance the is and what will be
> Dance the empty and the full
> Dance the round of being's thrall.

Though she sang so very softly and the magic man was deep in bargaining, he sensed immediately what was building in and around her;

her broke off, came round the fire and kicked her in the ribs, the head. But he was too late. Slya took her as she groaned, Slya called the drummer's fire to her and it burned the nets to ash and nothing and it leaped from her to the magic man and he was a torch and it leaped from her to the Temueng and he was a torch, and it leaped from gray man to gray man until the island was a planting of torches, frozen gray men burning, Temueng burning, grass and trees burning, pouch of dream dust burning. In an absent, blocked-off way she saw packs and gear burned off the horse and pony without singeing a hair on them, though they ran in panic into the water and away.

Finally the fire dimmed in her, a last tongue licked out, caressed the crystals. Yaril and Jaril woke out of stone, sat up blinking.

Then Slya was gone, the island bare and barren, the trees reduced to blackened stakes, the ashes of the burned blowing into drifts, and she was burdened with a fatigue so great she sank naked on charred sand and slept.

Three days later she was Temueng in form and face, wearing stolen Temueng gear, riding on an elderly but shapely werehorse, one good enough for Temueng pride but not enough to tempt Temueng greed, her altered shape grace of the children's manipulations and the lives of half a dozen Temueng harriers they ambushed along the causeway. The sun was setting in a shimmering clear sky and she was riding across the river on a stone bridge a quarter of a mile long, turning onto a road paved with massive blocks of the same stone, the city a dark mass against the flaming sky. Tavisteen. Gateway to the Narrow Sea.

3.

Brann's Quest—
Across the Narrow Sea
With Sammang Schimli

Bastard rumors spread faster than trouble through Tavisteen; no one claimed them, everyone heard them.

Agitation on the Plain. . . .

Temuengs dead or vanished (silent celebrations in Tavisteener hearts). Temuengs thrashing uselessly about, interrupting spring planting, rousting honest (and otherwise) folk from their homes, stopping trader packtrains to question the men and rummage through their goods. Temuengs closing down the port more tightly than before (suppressed fury in every Tavisteener and an increase in smuggling, Tavisteeners being contrary folk, the moment the Temueng Tekora governing the city promulgated a rule, there'd be cadres of Tavisteeners working to find ways to get round it, but they were wily and practical enough to pretend docility); since the Temuengs moved in and took over, any trader caught in port went through long and subtle negotiations and paid large bribes if he wanted to sail out again (another cause for fury, it was ruining trade). And this aggravation doubled because they were chasing some crazy woman who kept slipping like mist between their fingers (in spite of the trouble she brought on them, Tavisteeners cheered her in the secret rooms of mind and heart—and hoped she'd go somewhere else).

Agitation in the Marish. . . .

Marishmen went gliding like gray shadows from the fens to attack Temuengs and Plainsfolk alike, turning the causeway into a deathtrap for all but the largest parties, and these lost men continually to poison darts flying without warning from the Marish. No one dared go into the wetlands to drive off the ambushers; traffic along the road sank to a trickle then dried up completely.

Agitation in Tavisteen. . . .

Bodies without wounds lying in the darkest parts of dark alleys, floating in the bay. Temuengs and Tavisteeners alike. The locals were small loss to the city since all of them without exception were cast-offs without family to acknowledge them, given to rape and general thuggery. The other Tavisteeners grumbled at the cost of exorcising all those stray ghosts, but didn't bother themselves with listening to the complaints of the ghosts or hunting for the ghost-maker (for the most part, this was another case of silently applauding one they saw as something of a hero in spite of the trouble she was causing them).

The Temuengs were not nearly so philosophical about the mysterious force stalking and killing them. Temueng enforcers began snap searches, surrounding a section of the city or the wharves, turning everyone into the street, checking their credeens, searching houses and warehouses, ripping furniture, boxes and bales apart, kicking walls in, even turning out ship holds, beating Tavisteeners and foreign sailors with angry impartiality, hauling chosen members of both sorts off to the muccaits for questioning. Sometimes they made several of these searches in a single day, sometimes they let several days pass with none, sometimes they struck in the middle of the night.

They found smugglers' caches, forbidden drugs and weapons, illegal stills, prisoners escaped from any of a dozen muccaits, and other things of some interest to the Tekora. They did not find the woman.

Sammang Shipmaster sat hunched over a tankard of watery beer, scowling at the battered table top, his dark strong-featured face the image of his island's war god; squat and powerful was that god, a figure carved from sorrel soapstone and polished to a satin shine, meant to inspire awe and terror in the beholder. The rest of the tavern's patrons, not at all a gentle lot, sat at the far side of the room and left him to his brooding. Now and then he tugged at an elongated earlobe; the heavy gold pendant that usually hung there he'd sold that morning to pay docking fees; the little left had to keep him and his men for a while longer. Soon though, he'd have to break from the mooring and try to run past the ships and the guard tower at the narrow mouth of the harbor, not something he contemplated with any pleasure. Trebuchets hurling hundred-pound stones, springals with javelins that could pierce the thickest of ship timbers, fireboats anchored beyond to take care of what was left of any ship sneaking out, skryers to spot anyone trying to run under the cover of magic. Temuengs were thorough, Buatorrang curse their greedy bellies. He had a cargo of Arth Slya wares smuggled down from the Fair by an enterprising Tavisteener under the noses of the Temuengs who'd grabbed everything they could, with some hides and fleeces from the Plains, nothing that would spoil or lose its worth —if he could get the *Girl* out of this wretched port. He growled deep in his throat, his broad square hand tightening on the tankard until the metal squealed protest.

"Sammang Schimli? The Shipmaster?"

He looked up, the lines deepening between his thick black brows, the corners of his mouth dipping deeper into the creases slanting from flared nostrils. He ran his eyes slowly over the woman standing on the far side of the table. "Shove off, whore, I'm not looking for company." He shut his eyes and prepared to ignore her.

The woman pulled out a chair, sat across from him. "Nor I, Shipmaster. Only passage out of Tavisteen to Utar-Selt. And I'm not a whore."

Eyes still closed, thumbs moving up and down the sides of the tankard, he said, "I'm going nowhere soon, woman."

"I know." His eyes snapped open and he stared at her. "If you'll tell me just what you need to shake yourself loose," she went on, "and we can agree on terms, I'll see what I can do about financing your clearance."

He looked her over. No. Not a whore. Not reacting to him right for that. She was interested, but in an oddly childlike and at the same time cerebral way. None of the body signs of sexual awareness. Under the mask of calm, a nervous uncertainty. He clicked tongue against teeth, widened his eyes as he realized who she must be.

She had large green eyes in a face more interesting than pretty, rather gaunt right now as if she'd been hungry for a long time. A full mouth held tightly in check. Skin like alabaster in moonlight. The hands on the table were long, narrow, strong; hands not accustomed to idleness. Shoulder length soft silver hair catching shimmers from the tavern's lamps whenever she moved her head. Wholly out of place here. He had a sudden suspicion she'd look out of place anywhere he could think of. By Preemalau's nimble tail, how she ran loose in this part of the city was a thing to intrigue a man. He drew his tongue along his bottom lip, tapped his thumbs on the table. Maybe she could break the *Girl* loose, maybe she'd put his head in a Temueng strangler's noose. A gamble, but what wasn't? "Why not," he said.

"We can't talk here."

He thought about the rumors, the dead on the plain, the dead in the city, the dead floating in the bay, then he drained the tankard, set it down with a loud click that made her hands twitch. "I have a room upstairs."

She smiled suddenly, a mischievous gamin's grin that changed her face utterly. "Be careful, Shipmaster. You don't want to make me angry."

He stood. "Your choice." Leaving her to follow if she would, not so sure anymore he didn't want female company, he went up the several flights of stairs, hearing now and then her quiet steps behind him. He was rooming on the fifth floor, up under the roof, not so much for the cheaper price as for the breezes that swept through the unglazed windows. He unlocked his door, shoved it open, walked in and stopped.

Two children sat cross-legged on his bed, moonlight glimmering on pale hair, glowing in crystal eyes.

The woman brushed past him, settled herself in the rickety chair by one window. "My companions," she said. "Close the door." When he hesitated, she giggled. "Afraid of a woman and a pair of kids?"

He looked at the key in his hand, shrugged. "Might be the smartest thing I've done in months." He pulled the door shut, latching its bar and went to perch on the sill of the nearest window.

"Yaril," the woman said, "any snoops about?"

"No, Brann." The fairest of the two children grinned at her. "But Jaril did drop a rock on Hermy the nose."

"Nearby?"

The child with the shade darker hair waggled a hand. "So-so. Got him a couple streets back, fossicking about, trying to figure out what happened to you. No one else interested in you, well, except for the usual reasons."

"Hah, brat, talk about what you know. Still, mmh, I think you better go prowl about outside, see we aren't interfered with." She turned to Sammang. "Let him out, will you please?"

"What could the kid do?"

"More than you want to know, Shipmaster."

He shrugged. "Come on, kid."

When the latch was again secure, he stumped to the window, hitched a hip on the sill, angled so he could look out over the roofs toward the estuary and at the same time see the woman and the remaining child. "Why me?" he said. "Why not a Temueng ship? They're going in and out all the time. Cheaper too, because I'm going to cost you . . . Brann, is it? Right. I'm going to cost you a lot.

Maybe more than I'm worth. You who I think you are, you've already fooled Temuengs high and wide, seems to me you could go on fooling them just as easy. Not that I'm usually this candid with paying customers, you understand, but I want to know just what I'm getting into."

"Candid?"

He raised both brows, said nothing.

"You know quite well what you're getting into, Shipmaster."

The child—he was growing more certain it was a girl—slid off the bed and walked with eerie silence across the usually noisy floorboards, touched a pale finger to the wick of the stubby candle sitting on the unsteady table that was the room's only other piece of furniture. The wick caught fire, spread a warm yellow glow over Brann and Sammang, touched the hills and hollows of the lumpy bed. She went back to where she'd been and sat gazing intently at him for a long uneasy moment, sharp images of the candle flame dancing upside down in her strange eyes. "Tell him," she said. "He's hooked, he might as well know the whole, maybe he could come up with better ideas than we can; he knows this city and the Temuengs. You can trust him with just about anything he isn't trying to sell you."

He scowled at the girl, snorted at her impudent grin, turned to the woman. "Have you heard of Arth Slya?" she said. Her voice broke on the last words; she cleared her throat, waited for his answer.

"Who hasn't?"

"It was my home."

"Was?" He leaned forward, suddenly very interested; if Arth Slya was gone, the Slya wares hidden in his hold had suddenly jumped in value, jumped a lot.

"Temuengs came, a pimush and fifty men. Tried to take my people away, killed. . . ." Once again her voice broke; hastily she turned her head away until she had control again. In a muffled voice she said, "Killed the littlest and the oldest, marched the others off . . . off for slaves . . . on the Emperor's orders . . . the pimush told me . . . slaves for the Emperor. . . . He called him old lardarse . . . the pimush did . . . he's dead . . . his men, dead . . . I killed . . . the children and I killed them . . . my folk are home again, the ones left . . . trying to put things . . . things together again." Her shoulders heaved, she breathed quickly for a space, then lifted her head and spoke more crisply, her mask back in place. "Slya woke and Tincreal breathed fire, scrambled the land so Arth Slya is shut away. As long as the Temuengs hold Croaldhu I doubt you'll hear much of Arth Slya."

He tugged at his earlobe, narrowed his eyes. "You're going after the Emperor?"

"No. Well, not exactly. This is the year of the Grannsha Fair."

"I know, Slya-born, I came for it and caught my tail in this rat-trap."

"There were Slya folk at the fair. The pimush told me they were taken to Andurya Durat where they were going to be installed in a special compound the Emperor old lardarse. . . ." She laughed; it was not a comfortable sound. "He built for them. Slaves, Shipmaster. My father and two of my brothers, my kin and kind. I will not leave them slaves." She spoke with a stony determination that made him happy he was neither Temueng nor slaver. He nodded, approving her sentiment, it was what he'd have done in similar circumstances, which Buatorrang and the Preemalau grant would never happen; he wasn't so sure he wanted to involve himself and the *Girl* in this, but it might be worth the gamble; where she was now, she was like to rot before he could pry her loose. There was a lot the woman wasn't telling him, but he didn't think this was quite the moment to bring that up. "My greatest difficulty," she said, "is I haven't been out of Arth Slya before and know very little about the world down here."

"You're not doing so bad, Saör." He smiled. "And you knew enough to come here instead of Grannsha."

"Ignorance is not the same as stupidity, shipmaster."

"And you want to go to Utar-Selt. Slipping in the back door."

"I have to be careful, I'm all there is."

"It's not very likely you can do anything but get yourself killed."

She shook her head, looked stubborn. "I've taught Temuengs here they aren't masters of the world."

"You have that. How do you keep from being caught? Can't be two women on this island look like you."

"I know a trick or two. How much will this cost?"

He rubbed a hand across his chin. "Fifty gold for passage, you and the children. In advance."

"Done." The urchin grin again; it charmed him but not enough for him to reduce the price though he was rather disappointed that she hadn't bothered to haggle. "It'll take a few days to steal that much."

He raised his brows.

"Temueng strongboxes," she said defiantly. "They owe me, more than they could ever pay though I beggared the lot of them. And don't worry, Shipmaster, I won't get caught or tangle you in Temueng nets.

Now, the rest of it. What papers do you need? What signatures, what seals, who do you have to bribe, how much gold will it take and how soon do you need it?"

Four days later. Tavisteen gone quiet. No more dead. No alarums out for an impudent thief, though he listened for them and had his crew listening when they weren't getting the *Girl* ready to sail.

The room up under the roof. Late afternoon light streaming in, heavy with dust motes, a salt breeze blowing hot and hard through the windows, tugging at the papers Brann dropped on the table.

"Look them over, Shipmaster. I think they're right, but you'll know better than I if they'll pass."

That he could read a number of scripts was one of the several reasons the children had for choosing him; they'd walked his mind in dream, learning the language of his islands, learning much of what he knew about the ports he visited and more about his character. He was a man of strong loyalties who kept his crew together, cared for them, gave them money to live on though that meant his limited resources vanished more quickly, a man whose love for his ship was as fierce as her love for her folk and fire-hearted Tincreal, a man of many gifts who could read water, air, sky and landshapes as if they were words scribed in a book, hard when he needed to be hard, with a center of tenderness he let very few see, a brown, square man with a large-featured square face. Sitting by the window with the sun giving a sweat sheen to his tight-grained skin, he was a creature of living stone, a sea-god carved from red-brown jasper with eyes of polished topaz. He affected her in ways she didn't understand, did things to that adult body she'd so suddenly acquired that she didn't want to understand; this terrified her, even sickened her because she could not forget no matter how she tried the Temueng Censor grunting on top of her, reaming into her; she dreamed that time again and again, the children having to wake her because her cries might betray that night's hiding place. She watched the man and wanted him to touch her, her breasts felt sore and tight, there was a burning sweetness between her thighs. She forced her mind away from her intrusive body and tried to concentrate on the papers and what the man would say of them.

Sammang felt her restlessness, looked up. "Where are the children?"

"Around. Never mind them. How soon can we leave?"

He shook his head. "You are an innocent. Wait a minute." He began
going through the papers again, holding them up to the light, wondering by what magic she'd come up with them. Not a flaw in them, at
least none he could find. When he was finished, he squared the pile,
flattened a hand on it. "How much noise did you make getting these?"

"None. The Temuengs who signed and stamped them were, well,
call it sleepwalking. They won't remember anything of what happened."

"Handy little trick. Mmmh." He tapped his forefinger on the pile of
paper. "Can't go anywhere without these, but it's only a start, O dis-
turber of Temueng peace and mine; even with gold to ease their suspi-
cions, we'll have to be careful to touch the right men and move fast
before the wrong men start talking to each other."

"How much gold?" Without waiting for an answer, she leaned out
the window, brought back a heavy bag, which she set on the table in
front of him. Before he could say anything, she had twisted away. She
brought in a second bag, dumped it, and was out again, pulling in a
third. With quick nervous movements, she went away from him to sit
on the bed; today she seemed very aware of him as a man. Her response woke his own, he eyed her with interest, wondering what bedding a witch would be like. She looked hastily away. Skittish creature.
Well, Sammo, that's for later.

He unwound the wire from the neck of the first bag, began setting
out the coins, brows raising as he broached the other bags and the piles
multiplied, ten each, in rows of ten, ten rows of ten, a thousand gold, a
full thousand heavy hexagonals, soft enough to mark with his
thumbnail. Even without weighing and trying them, he was sure they
weren't mixed with base metal, something you had to watch for here in
Tavisteen the tricky. When he finished he sat frowning at the mellow
gold glimmer. And I thought to discourage her by asking a ridiculous
price for her passage. He looked up. "This much high assay gold will
be missed."

She shook her head. "Not soon; these are from the Tekora's private
stash, dust and cobwebs over the lockboxes."

With a laugh and a shake of his head he began putting the coins back
in the sacks. "You wouldn't consider signing on with me as bursar? I
do like the idea of paying off the Tekora's men with the Tekora's gold."
He set two of the sacks on the paper pile, held out the third. "Here.
You hang onto this, you might need it."

She shook her head. "No. I don't want it. When can we leave?"

He dropped the sack on the table, frowned. "Tide's right round mid-morning tomorrow, but I'd rather put off leaving another day, have to provision the *Girl,* top off the water barrels. Don't want to look hurried either, set noses twitching." He drummed his fingers on the table top, lips moving as he conned the tides. "Why not midday three days on?"

She brooded a moment, nodded.

"Can you and the children get on board without anyone seeing you?" When she laughed at that, he went on, "A Temueng pilot will be coming along. He's to get us past the forts and fireships, good enough, but he'll stick his nose into every corner before he lets us leave. Can you handle that?"

"I think so. You can really be ready to sail that quickly?"

"I could sail yesterday." His voice was angry, violent. "If it weren't for those lapalaulau-cursed sharks."

She slid off the bed, started for the door, turned back. "I forgot to ask. How long from here to Utar-Selt?"

"Say we get good winds and we aren't jumped, ten, twelve days. The *Girl*'s a clever flyer."

"That long. . . ."

"You want a shorter route, it's only five days to the mouth of the Garrunt, but don't ask me to take the *Girl* anywhere near the Fens."

"Which I understand are a maze of mud and stink and hostile swampfolk. No thanks. The Marish was bad enough. Seems to me the long way round is the shortest route, all things considered."

He got up and walked over to her, touched the side of her face, dropped his hand on her shoulder. "Need you go right now?"

She stopped breathing, green eyes suddenly frightened; she moved away, would not look at him.

"I only ask," he said mildly. He didn't try to move closer.

She let out a long shaky breath. "How old do you think I am, Sammang Schimli?"

He raised a brow. "Shall I flatter or speak the truth?"

"Truth."

"Mmm, mid-twenties, maybe a bit more." He crossed his arms over his chest. "A lovely age, Brann, old enough to have salt in the mix, young enough to enjoy the game."

She set her shoulders against the door, her agitation visibly increasing. It puzzled him, disturbed him, made him wonder if she was whole in the head. If not, what a waste.

"I wouldn't . . . wouldn't know." She flattened her hands against the door, then burst out. "I'm eleven, I know what I look like, I know it's hard to believe, but inside here, I'm eleven years old. The children changed me, grew me older, I went to sleep a girl and woke a woman. Like this." She swept a hand along her body, dared to look at him a moment. "How could a child do what I have to do?"

"Eleven?" He frowned at her, uncertain.

She nodded, shyly, abruptly. "You . . . you do disturb me, Ship-master. . . ." She rushed on, "But I'm not ready for what you offer."

Abruptly he believed her, saw the child there, marveled that he hadn't understood it before. When her urchin's grin flashed out, when she relaxed and let her mask drop, she was little sister, mischievous child—if he didn't look at her body. He backed off. Nice child, good child, bright and warm and loving. He discovered that he liked her a lot and wanted to help her all he could. "Too bad," he said. "But we're still friends?"

She blushed, nodded. "If it were otherwise. . . ." She fumbled the door open and ran out.

He followed her, watched her slow as she went down the stairs until she was the cool witch he'd first seen. Shaking his head, he shut the door, went back to the table to tuck the papers in a leather pouch. The children. Spooky little bits. Those eyes. Preemalau's bouncing tits. Changed her. He shivered at the thought, momentarily chilled in spite of the heat. Eleven. What a thing to do to her. To me. He slid a hand down one of the bags of gold, the corners of the hexagonal pieces hard against his palm, then stripped its tie off and began stowing the coins about his person. The other two bags he shoved in the pouch on top of the papers. No more Arth Slya wares. For a good while, anyway. And I'm the only one in Tavisteen who knows that. He chuckled, patted the bulging pouch, began humming a lively tune. Too soon to be passing out bribes, might as well nose out some more of the Slya wares; she'd passed the gold on, didn't care what he did with it as long as he got her out. When she's a few years older, what a woman she'll be. Taking on the whole damn Temueng empire. And getting away with it, yes, he'd wager even the *Girl* she got away with it. Should've had Hairy Jimm hanging around below. This much gold was honey to the tongue for the thugs hanging about. He bent, transferred the boot knife to his sleeve. Still humming, he left the room, locked the door behind him, went lightly down the stairs, the song's traditional refrain ousted from his head by a more seductive one, the siren song of the trader's game where profit was more the measure of skill than anything important in itself. No more Slya ware, his mind sang to him, no more no more, and when the word gets out, when that word gets out, the price goes up up up. . . . You're a lucky man, Sammang Schimli, though you'd have traded places with a legless octopus a week ago. Slya ware, Slya ware, rare it is and growing rarer, no one knows gonna be no more. . . .

The Temueng enforcers went like locusts through his goods, but the smuggled treasures were deep in the bundles of hides and fleeces. His crew went after the lapalaulau castrate and put things together again, stowing the bales and casks properly so the *Girl* was ready to go. When the sun was directly overhead and the lice were off the ship, when the *Girl* was tugging at her mooring, eager as Sammang was to be gone, he stood at her rail, wind whipping his hair into his eyes and mouth as he waited for the pilot. He watched the skinny Temueng (his pockets heavy with Brann's gently thieved gold) leave the sour-faced harbor master, clamber into a dinghy, sit stiff and somber while the master's men rowed him out to the *Girl*. Sammang wondered briefly where Brann and the children were, then walked forward to help the pilot over the rail.

He showed the Temueng about the ship, fuming as the man poked and pried into her cracks and crannies, even into the crew's quarters, opening their seabags, sticking his long crooked nose where it had no business being. The crew resented it furiously, but were too happy to be getting back to sea to show their anger. They watched with sly amusement as the Temueng (they named him in whispers *Slimeslug*) went picking through Sammang's quarters with the same prissy thoroughness; they passed the open door again and again, savoring Sammang's disgust. He held his tongue with difficulty, beckoned Hairy Jimm in to take a chair on deck for the pilot. And he lingered a moment after the pilot followed Jimm out to grin at a large sea chest the Temueng hadn't seemed to notice and salute.

As soon as he could, he left the pilot sitting with his signal flags across his knees, lowering the level in a sack of red darra wine. Brann was sitting on his bed, flanked by the not-children. There was a shimmer about her, a snapping energy. "We've pulled the hook, the pilot's getting drunk on deck; we're just about loose, young Brann, but hold your breath until we're past the fireships." He dropped his eyes to the full breasts swaying with the movement of the ship beneath the heavy white silk of her shirt, sighed as he saw the nipples harden.

She smiled. "Eleven," she said. "Though I'm getting older by the minute."

"Yeah. Aren't we all."

The blond boy had his head in her lap, the girl was curled up tight against her, both were deeply, limply asleep. With their eyes closed, they seemed more like real children. "They've been working hard the past few nights," she said. "They're worn out."

Worn out. That too was something he'd just as soon not have explained. "Not much point in hiding down here once we put the pilot off. You can trust my men, they're a good bunch." He frowned. "No . . . no, you wait here until I have a talk with them which I will do once we pour that gilded gelding into his dinghy. You get seasick?"

"I don't know. I've never been on a boat before."

"Buatorrang's fist, woman. Ship. Not boat, ship." He fished under the bed, found a canvas bucket. "Spew in this if the need takes you." He looked at the sleeping children. "Them too." He started out the door, turned. "I won't leave you shut up longer'n I have to. Um, my crew, they're not delicate flowers, don't mind the way they talk."

"Stop fussing, Shipmaster. I have got a little sense, or haven't you noticed?"

Feeling better about everything Sammang went back on deck and stood by the rail watching Hairy Jimm maneuver the *Girl* among the ships crowding the estuary. The pilot was paying little attention to what was happening about him. His title had a Temueng twist to it; he wasn't there to guide them through the harbor's natural snags but to ease them past the far more deadly man-made obstacles. The day was brilliant with a brisk headwind, and tide and river current together were enough to carry the *Girl* barepoled out to the stone pincers at the mouth of the bay. Stays singing about him, the salt smell growing stronger than the stench of estuary mud and city sewage, the shimmering blue water blown into sharp ridges, white foam dancing along them, Sammang relished everything about the day, the colors and sounds, the mix of smells, the exploding array of possibilities ahead of him.

The pilot shoved onto his feet as the ship came up to the two great towers looming over the narrow mouth of the estuary, settled himself and began whipping his signal flags about. When specks of bright color bloomed and swung atop the South tower, he made a last pass, then rolled up his flags, sheathed them, and dumped himself back in the chair, ignoring the crew who took every chance they found to walk up, stare at him and stroll away again. Hairy Jimm kept a minatory eye on them and the heckling didn't go beyond staring; he'd made it quite clear early on that anyone who laid a hand on the pilot would go overboard there and then. More than one of the crew had deep grudges against the Temuengs and the parade could have disintegrated into a shivaree with a dead Temueng at the end of it. When they began crowding too close and staying too long, Sammang nudged Hairy Jimm, and the big brown bear lumbered forward and stopped the parade.

The ship slid without incident between the towers, began to lose way as the channel widened abruptly and the flow spread out. Hairy Jimm sent Tik-rat and Turrope to raise the jib and ordered the ship into a tack so the wind wouldn't push them into the Teeth of the Gate. The *Girl* was a two-masted merchanter with standing lugsails, a configuration that could have been clumsy and often was, but she was Sammang's dream and he'd watched her rise from bare bones under the hands of his great uncle Kenyara; more than that, he'd built with his own hands model after model, had sat with Kenyara and argued and trimmed the models and made her come to life as much by will as by the work of his hands and the gold he brought back to the Pandaysar-radup, the wood he'd searched out and brought back, the fittings he'd gathered from most of the ports he touched in his travels; the eyes on her bow he'd carved and painted himself. She could sail closer to the wind than most her size, could squat down and ride storm waves as well as any petrel. She was an extension of himself and he loved her far more than he would ever love man or woman, loved her with a passion and a delight that would have embarrassed him into stammering if he had to talk about it. Seeing her dulled and dying and quiet at the mooring had been the worst of many bad times during the months of stagnation in Tavisteen. Now he felt her come to life under his feet and hands; he stood smoothing his hand along her rail in a contented secret caress. *Young Brann, I owe you. Whatever you want, you and your. . . .* He cleared his throat with a sound half a laugh, half a groan. The children scared him and he had no hesitation admitting that to himself. Brann was pleasanter to the mind—child, woman, fighter, with a passion, caring; stubbornness that reminded him very much of a younger Sammang. He thought fondly of a few of his own childhood exploits, as he watched the fireships swinging at anchor, the last line to pass, then they were free. He took a deep breath. The air filled the lungs better out here. He looked at the slouched Temueng half asleep and reeking of the wine they'd fed him. Or it would soon as they got that off the *Girl* 's deck.

They put the pilot and his minions overside in the trailing dinghy, set and trimmed the sails and left the fireboats in their wake. Sammang stood sniffing at the wind, gave a short shout of freedom and celebration, grinned as he caught the cheerfully obscene salutes from Dereech and his shadow Aksi.

He moved to the wheel, cupped his hands about his mouth, bellowed, "Tik-rat, Turrope, Aksi, Leymas, Dereech, Gaoez, Staro, Rudar, Zaj, gather round."

When they were around him, squatting on the gently heaving deck, Sammang clasped his hands behind his head, grinned at them, still riding high with the effects of breaking the *Girl* loose and incidentally sneaking past the Temueng clutches the woman they were turning the island upside down to find. "We got a passenger," he said. He stretched, straining his muscles till his joints popped. "The woman the Temuengs were hunting. One who kicked those sharks where it hurt. We don't mind that, do we." He grinned into their grins, grimaced as the wind blew hair into his teeth. Rotting in Tavisteen, he'd let his hair grow long, too despondent to get it cut. "We owe her," he said. "Still be watching moss grow up the walls without her help. Witch," he said. "Nice kid but no man's meat. Not mine, not yours. Ever see what happens if a Silili priest holds onto a rocket too long after it's lit? Uh-huh. So keep your hands to yourselves. This old fart talking to you, he wouldn't like to see what comes down if one of you got her into a snit."

"Hanh." Hairy Jimm rubbed a meaty hand across his beard. "I heerd a thing or two about that nakki that makes me leery of her. What keeps her hands off us?"

"Relax, Jimm. She's a good kid. Treat her like a little sister." He thought a minute. "Not so little." He looked round at the crew. "That's it."

They went off to busy themselves with the endless tasks that kept a ship healthy, but Hairy Jimm fidgeted where he was. "Turrope's hoor was telling him the Fen pirates are taking everything that moves, be you Temu be you Panay, whatever. How you want to handle that?"

"A good wind and no proa's going to catch the *Girl.*"

"Turrope's hoor has got a busy ear, she say the Djelaan have found them a weatherman."

Sammang laughed. "If he sticks his head up, I'll sic the witch on him." He sobered. "She's paying us for a quick passage, Jimm. Cutting south would add at least five days. Give your totoom a thump for me and whistle us a steady blow." He rubbed thumb and forefinger over the finger-pieces of the heavy gold pendant in his left ear, the first thing he'd ransomed with Brann's gold, tracking down the buyer and leaning on him till he sold. "I'll talk to her, see what she says." He watched Jimm walk away, watched him try the tension of backstays, eye the sails for weak spots, look for any problems he'd missed in port, things that would only show when she was moving. With a nod to Uasuf, silent at the wheel, Sammang went to stand in the bow, hands clasped behind him, staring out across the empty blue. Empty now, but how long would it stay that way? For a few breaths he stopped worrying and simply relished the way the *Girl* was taking the waves and the wind; she was a trier, his sweet *Girl,* even with her hull fouled with weed and barnacles, she danced over the waves. Preemalau be gentle and send no storms, she had to be careened and cleaned, gone over for dry rot and wood worm, every bit of cordage checked and replaced if necessary. He knew as well as Hairy Jimm how fragile she was right now. He unclasped his hands, touched her stays, feeling the hum in them, touched her wood feeling the life in it, loving her for her beauty and her gallant heart, afraid for her, cursing the Djelaan pirates, cursing all weathermen, cursing the Temuengs who were too busy with conquest to keep their own coasts clean. He watched the dolphins dance in the bow waves a while longer then went below to see how Brann was faring and talk to her about Jimm's disclosures.

"How soon until we're in Djelaan waters?" she said.

"Four days," he said.

"Too far," she said, "Wear the children out for what could be nothing."

"You don't far-see?" he said.

"The Temuengs call me witch," she said, "their mistake. Don't you make the same one. I have certain abilities, but they're useful only in touching-distance."

"Then we should turn south in two days, go wide around the Djelaan corals," he said.

"How many days would that add?"

"Four, probably five."

"Too long," she said. "I'd be a shade by then and the children would be hungry."

"Then we sail on luck and hope," he said, "and fight if we have to."

"There's nothing else?"

"No."

The next two days passed bright and clear, with spanking winds that propelled the ship across the glittering blue as if she were greased. Sammang watched Brann move about the ship, taking pains to keep out of the way of anyone who was working. She respected skill and found the sailors fascinating. Both things showed. The crew saw both, were flattered and fascinated in their turn and the children helped with that by staying below where their strangeness wouldn't keep reminding the men of corpses in dark alleys and corpses floating in the bay. Young Tik-rat was wary of her for an hour or two, but he succumbed to her charm after she'd followed him about awhile as he played his pipe to help the work go easier; he spent the hour after that teaching her worksongs. Leymas was the next she won. He taught her a handful of knots, then set her to making grommets; she was neat-fingered and used to working with her hands and delighted when he praised her efforts. Sammang continued to watch when he had a moment free, amused by her ease with them as if they were older brothers or male cousins, as if she willed them to forget her ripe body, damping ruthlessly any hint of sexuality. One by one his crew fell to her charm and began treating her as a small sister they were rather fond of, fonder as the second day faded into the third. By then he couldn't move about the deck without finding her huddled with one of the men, her strong clever hands weaving knots, her head cocked to one side, listening with skeptical delight to the extravagant tale he was spinning for her. Even Hairy Jimm told her lies and let her take the wheel so she could feel the life of the ship while he showed her how to read the Black Lady, the swinging lodestone needle, and put that together with the smell of the wind and the look of the sea to keep the ship rushing along the proper course.

She had relaxed abruptly and utterly all her own wariness and pretenses and was the child of the gentle place where she'd been reared. He saw in her the naïve and trusting boy he'd been when he found his island growing too small for him and he'd smuggled himself on board one of the trading ships that stopped at Perando in the Pandaysarradup. He'd been confident in his abilities and eager to see the great world beyond, never hurt deliberately and with malice, trust never betrayed, friendly as a puppy. It took a lot of trampling and treachery to knock most of that out of him. He saw the same kind of trust in her and he sighed for the pain coming to her, but knew he couldn't shield her from that pain—and if he could he wouldn't. To survive, she had to learn. Even the Temuengs hadn't taught her to be afraid of others; here, surrounded by people who were not threatening, who responded to her friendliness with good will and friendliness of their own, she'd let her guard down. Not a good habit to get into. Still he couldn't condemn it totally as foolishness, it had done her good with the men. And, he had to admit to himself, with him.

The fifth day slid easily into the sixth; no Djelaan yet, but the rising of the sun showed him clouds blowing about a low dark smear north and west of the *Girl*. The southernmost of a spray of uninhabited coral atolls, most of them with little soil and no water, good only to shelter pirate proas while the Djelaan waited to ambush ships that ventured past. He scowled at it. Was it empty of life except for birds and a few small rodents or were a dozen proas pulled up on one of its crumbly beaches with a weatherman set to cast his spells?

Brann came to the bow and stood beside him. "Is that Selt?"

"No."

"Thought it was a bit soon. Djelaan?"

"If they're coming, that's where they'll come from."

She chewed her lip a moment. "I can't judge distances at sea."

"We'll come even with the island about mid-afternoon, be about a half-day's sail south of it."

"And you'd like to know if you can relax or should get ready to fight."

"Right."

"And the trip is a little more than half over?"

"Wind keeps up and pirates keep away, we should be in Silili say about sundown five days on."

"Mmm. Children lying dormant, they haven't used as much energy as they'd ordinarily do." She looked around at the crew, then straightened her shoulders, stiffened her spine. "Jaril will fly over the islands and Yaril will tell us what he sees. You'd better warn Jimm and the others; it's sort of startling the first time you see one of the children changing."

Sammang wasn't sure what was going to happen but suspected it would be spectacular and remind him and his crew forcibly she wasn't little sister to all the world. He patted her hand. "They won't faint, Bramble."

She looked up at him, startled, then half-smiled and shook her head.

"Well . . . I'd better fetch them up." She left him and moved with brisk assurance along the deck.

He went back to stand by Hairy Jimm who had taken the wheel awhile because he was nearly as fond of the *Girl* as Sammang and loved the feel of her under his hands. "Our witch is getting set to scare the shit out of us."

"Hanh." Jimm took a hand off the wheel, scratched at his beard. "Hey, she *our* witch, Sammo. Ehh Stubb," he boomed. "On your feet."

The dozing helmsman started, came to his feet, looked dazedly about. "Huh?" Then he came awake a bit more and strolled yawning over to them.

"Grab hold." As soon as Staro the Stub had the wheel, Jimm moved away. "Our witch gon be showing her stuff and I want a close eye on it."

By the time Brann came up on deck with Yaril and Jaril, the news had spread through the crew. Even those supposed to be sleeping settled themselves inconspicuously about the deck doing small bits of busywork. Sammang looked around, amused. The way Hairy Jimm said *our witch,* with the air of a new father contemplating his offspring, made him want to laugh until he realized he felt much the same way.

She came up to Sammang and Hairy Jimm. "What's the most common large bird that flies out this far?"

"Albatross. Why?"

She turned to the boy. "You know that one?"

Jaril grinned at her and suddenly the grin was gone, the boy was gone, there was a shimmer of gold and a large white bird with black wingtips was pulling powerfully at the air and rising in a tight spiral above the ship; a heartbeat later it was speeding toward the island.

Yaril sits with her back against the mast, her eyes shut, her high young voice sounding over the wind and water sounds, the creaking of mast and timber.

First island. Nothing from high up, going closer, some birds objecting, no beaches, no sort of anchorage. Going on to the next.

Silence. The listeners wait without fuss, quietly working, not talking.

Second island. More trees. Don't see any sign of surface water. Definitely deserted, quiet enough to hear a rat scratch.

Silence. Sammang gazes at Brann wondering what she is thinking.

Third island. This one's the lucky dip. A dozen proas drawn up by a stream cutting through a bit of beach, apparently water's the main attraction. Maybe a hundred Djelaan, war party, clubs, spears, throwing sticks, long knives, war axes. A clutch of them cheering on a tattooed man who's throwing a fit. Ah, the fit's over. Look at them scoot. Anyone want to wager the tattooed gent wasn't telling them about this fine fat ship passing by? Get a move on, folks, you got trouble rolling at you.

They raced west and south, carrying as much sail as the rigging would stand, the *Girl* groaning and shuddering, fighting the drag of the weed on her hull. In spite of that she sang splendidly through the water. She popped rigging and staggered now and then, but the crew replaced and improvised and held her together as much by will as skill. Sammang was all over the deck, adding his strength where it was needed, eyes busy searching for breaks. He heard laughter and saw Brann beside him, her green eyes snapping with sheer delight in the excitement swirling about her. For a breath or two he gazed at her and was very nearly the boy who'd run to the wider world confidently expecting marvels. Then he went back to nursing his *Girl.*

The wind dropped between one breath and the next. The *Girl* shivered and lost way, the drag of the weed braking her with shocking suddenness. Sammang cursed, stood looking helplessly about. The crew exchanged glances, dropped where they were to squat waiting, hands busy splicing line, one man whittling a new block to replace one that had split.

Brann touched Sammang's arm. "Jaril says the proas are about an hour behind us."

"How many?"

"Twelve. Traveling in two groups, the tattooed man—that has to be the weatherman, Jaril thinks so and I agree—he's hanging behind with a couple boats to guard him. The other nine are riding a mage wind at us, really flying, Jaril says."

"How many men in each boat?"

"Nine or ten."

"Eighty maybe ninety, not counting the bodyguards." He scowled at the limp sails. "A wind, even a breath. . . ."

"Jaril's thought of that. He's been trying to get at the weatherman but he keeps bouncing off some kind of ward, whether he comes at the proa out of the sky or under water. Only thing he can think of is a pod of mid-sized whales he spotted a little way back. When he broke off talking, he was going to find them. He plans to drive them at the proas. Spell or no spell, a half dozen irritated whales are going to swamp that boat. He figures a weatherman will drown as fast as any other breather. And once *he's* gone, you should have your wind. Thing is, though, he doesn't know quite how long it's going to take, so you should be ready for a fight."

Sammang nodded, touched her arm. "Our witch," he said, felt rather than heard a murmur of agreement from the crew. "You'll fight with us?"

"In my way." She grimaced, looked around at the circle of grave faces, raised her voice so all could hear. "Listen, brothers, when it starts, don't touch me. I am Drinker of Souls and deadlier than a viper, I don't want accidents, I prefer to choose where I drink."

Sammang nodded, said nothing.

Yaril tugged at his sleeve. "What do you want me to be, Sammang shipmaster? Serpent? wildcat? falcon? dragon? It'd have to be a small dragon."

Sammang blinked at the not-child. "Falcon sounds good. You wouldn't get in our way, and you could go for their eyes."

She considered a moment, nodded. "Be even better if I make some poison glands for the talons, then all I have to do is scratch them."

Sammang blinked some more. "Be careful whom you scratch," he said after he got his voice back.

"Don't worry, I've done this before." She stretched, yawned, went to curl up by the mast; a moment later she seemed sound asleep.

He turned to Brann, raised a brow.

"Don't ask me," she said. "Before they came here, probably; that's something I haven't seen."

Sammang went below and dug out his war ax, a steel version of the stone weapon he'd learned to swing as a boy in the godwar dances, his father's passed on to him, an ax that hadn't been used in a real war since his great-grandfather carried it against Setigo, the next island over. After he'd shipped out a few years, he got very drunk and nostalgic and spent most of his remaining coin hiring a smith to make a copy of the bloody old ax, describing it to him as a curving elongated meat cleaver, point heavy with a short handle carved to fit his grip.

Zaj and Gaoez, the bowmen of the crew, climbed on the cabin's roof and sat waiting, arrow bundles between their knees; Hairy Jimm was swinging his warclub to get the feel of it, a long-handled lump of ironwood too heavy to float; other crew members were using hones on cutlasses or spearpoints, razor discs or stars, whipping staffs about, making sure clothing and bodies were loose enough to fight effectively. Djelaan never took prisoners; either they were driven off or everyone on the ship died. The *Girl* wallowed in the dead calm. Close by, several fish leaped and fell back, the sounds they made unnaturally loud in that unnatural silence. Yaril woke, fidgeted beside Brann. "I'm going up," she said suddenly. She dissolved into a gold shimmer then was a large Redmask falcon climbing in a widening spiral until she was a dark dot high overhead circling round and round in an effortless glide. Brann stood still, looking frightened and uncertain.

The hour crept past, men occupied with small chores fidgeting with their weapons.

The Redmask left her circling and came swooping down, screaming a warning, found a perch on the foresail yard.

Silence a few breaths, the sea empty, then the Djelaan came out of nowhere, yelling, beating on flat drums, proas racing toward the *Girl*, their triangular sails bulging with the magewind, a wind that did not touch the *Girl*'s sagging canvas.

Zaj and Gaoez jumped up and began shooting, almost emptying the first proa before the mage wind began taking their shafts and brushing them aside. They shot more slowly after that, compensating for the twist of the wind, managed to pick off another half-dozen before the Djelaan bobtail spears came hissing at them, propelled with murderous force by the throwing sticks. They hopped about, dodging the spears and getting off an ineffective shaft or two until Hairy Jimm began batting spears aside with his warclub. The rest of the crew darted about, catching up those that tumbled to the deck and hurling them back at the proas, doing little damage but slowing the advance somewhat.

Then grapnels were sinking into the wood of the rail, the Djelaan attacking from both sides. Sammang and others raced along the rails, slashing the ropes until there were too many of them and they had to fight men instead of rope. Yaril screamed, powered up from the yard and dived at the proas, not a falcon anymore but a small sun searing through the sails. The weatherman was holding the air motionless, trapping the *Girl* but protecting her too; in seconds she was swaying untouched in a ring of flames as the proa sails burned and began to char the masts and rigging. With shouts of alarm half of the attackers turned back and began to fight the fires that threatened to leave them without a means of retreat.

The rest swarmed over the rails and the *Girl*'s men were fighting for their lives, cutlass ax and halberd, warclub staff and all the rest, flailing, stabbing, slashing, a ring of men tight about the foremast holding off the hordes that tried to roll over them. Yaril flew at Djelaan backs, stooping and slashing, her razor talons moistened with the poison she and her brother could produce when inspired to do so, keeping the Djelaan off Brann as she walked through them, reaching and touching, reaching and touching, each touch draining and dropping a man. A spear went into her side; she faltered a moment, pulled it out with a gasp of pain, sweat popping out on her face, a trickle of blood, then the wound closed over and she walked on.

At first the attackers didn't realize what was happening, then they began struggling to avoid those pale deadly hands. They retreated before her, throwing other attackers into confusion. The *Girl*'s men shouted when they saw this and fought with renewed hope.

A powerful gust of wind whooshed along the deck, filling the drooping sails. Another deadly Redmask came darting out of the east where the weatherman's proas had been and swooped at the Djelaan, clawing at eyes and hands, slashing flesh, the poison on his talons killing quickly, painfully. Twisting and turning with demonic agility he wove unharmed among the weapons of the pirates with a formidable ease that drew moans of fear from them. Retreating from the falcons, retreating from Brann who burned now with a shimmery fire, the Djelaan broke. Dropping their weapons, scrambling down the grapnel lines, leaping into the sea and swimming for their fire-stripped proas, the men in the boats dragging the swimmers over the sides, the Djelaan fled that demon-haunted ship.

Sammang dropped his war ax and leaped to the wheel, turning the *Girl* so she was cutting across the rising swells, not lying helpless between them. Hairy Jimm roared the men capable of moving into trimming the sails and getting the ship into order so she wouldn't be broken by the coming storm. Brann and the children staggered along the deck, heaving Djelaan dead and wounded overboard. When that was finished, Brann stood a moment staring at her glowing hands, the wind whipping her white hair about, plastering her shirt against her burning body. With a sigh she went searching for crew dead and wounded. Zaj was dead, a small brown islander much like the men who'd killed him. She and the children carried him to the side wall of the cabin and lashed him there to wait for what rites Sammang and the others would want for him. She hurried back to kneel beside Dereech who had a flap of scalp hanging down over his face, deep cuts in his legs and shoulder. He stared up at her with his one clear eye, horror in his face as she reached for him, tried to crawl away from her but was too weak. When she flattened her hand on him, he froze, a moan dying in his throat.

From his place at the wheel, Sammang watched her and wondered what she intended, wondered if he should drive her off Dereech. What she'd done to the Djelaan she'd done to save her life and theirs, but the glimpses he'd caught of her work worried him. He liked and trusted the child in her, but didn't know what to do about the witch. In the end, he did nothing.

She bent lower, smoothed her hand up along Dereech's face, pressing the flap into place, her hands blurring in a moonglow mist. The bleeding stopped, the flap stayed put as if the mist had soldered it down. She pressed the other wounds shut, smoothed her hands over them, the glow shuddering about her flesh and his. The children stood behind her, their hands welded to her body until she sat back on her heels, finished with the healing.

Tik-rat had a spear through a lung. She burnt the spear out of him, bone point and broken haft, closed the wound and held her hands over it, a wound that was almost always fatal. Smiling Tik-rat was the ship's bard, story teller and singer, the pet of the crew. Now all saw her clean and close his wound, saw the boy's chest begin to rise and fall steadily and smoothly. *Our witch, she's our witch.* A whisper passing round. Our child-woman witch, Sammang murmured to himself. The children with her, she moved on to Rudar, then Uasuf, left them sleeping, their wounds closed, cleaned, healed.

She went briskly over to Hairy Jimm, who jumped when she touched him, looked uneasy and dubious as she began moving her hands over his meaty body, touching, pressing, the mist moving with her. After a minute of this, though, he grinned and stood holding his arms out from his body as if for a tailor taking measurements. When she finished, he patted her on the head. "Any time, our witch."

She went on, the children following close behind. Turrope, Leymas, Gaoez. Healing the smallest cuts, the scrapes and bruises, even a blood-blister on Turrope's little finger. Then she came toward Sammang.

She looked very tired, haunted by all the dying, her face pale in spite of the eerie glow that shone out through her skin. "Your turn, Sammo. Give over the wheel a minute; you might find this a bit distracting."

Hairy Jimm boomed laughter, shouldered Sammang away from the wheel. "Distractin's not the word, no not the word."

She touched the cut in Sammang's side. He felt a jolt, then a tingle, then coolness, a new vigor coursing into him. Her strong nervous hands moved along his body and all the hurts and scrapes of the fight were wiped away. And he understood the look on Jimm's face. He was tumescent before she was half done, ready to take on a harem and a half when she stepped away from him.

She smiled uncertainly at him, met his eyes briefly, blushed, turned hastily away to the hatch.

A bit of hard work and some douches of icy sea water from the building waves cooled him down. He glanced at the sun and was startled to see how little it had moved. Less than an hour since the fighting started. He shook his head, feeling a touch of wonder at how much had happened in that pinch of time. Two dead. But because of the child-woman and the not-children the wounded lived and were well, neither maimed nor disfigured. He lifted his head and laughed. "Our witch," he shouted, laughed again at the cheers from the three now awake. He began a rumbling song, Hairy Jimm took it up, all of them roared it into the wind as they settled the *Girl* for the blow coming.

Sometime after midnight Sammang stumped wearily into his cabin. A nightlamp was hanging from a hook by his hammock. Brann was curled in the bed, half-covered by a blanket, her flesh faintly glowing in the darkness. Her eyes were closed and for some time he thought she was asleep; he pulled off his shirt, started to unlace his trousers, thought about the sleeping witch, and decided he could stand the damp if he kept himself warm. Eleven, eleven, eleven, he told himself; his mind believed it but his body didn't. He started to swing up into the hammock, couldn't resist another look at Brann. She was curled on her right side now watching him. Her face was pale and drawn, huge eyes, dark-ringed, asking him. . . . He turned his back on her, climbed into the hammock, flipped the blanket over him and settled himself to sleep.

Much later he woke, knowing something had roused him from sleep, not knowing what it was. He listened to the ship, nothing there. Slowly he became aware of a sound almost too soft to hear, faint rhythmic creaking, soft soft rustles.

Brann lay curled up, her back to him; the children were somewhere else, doing whatever shapechangers did at night. She was sobbing and the shudders that convulsed her body were shaking the bed. He scowled at her, hesitated, tipped out of the hammock and padded the few steps to the bed. He touched her shoulder. "Bramble?"

She buried her face in the pillow. The shaking went on; she was gasping and struggling to stop crying, unable to stop the shudders coursing through her body.

He caught her shoulder, pulled her over, examined her face. She was crying with the ugly all-out grief of a wounded child. He straightened, looked helplessly around, cursed the children for leaving her in this state. Finally he gathered her up, holding her tightly against him, patting her, smoothing his hand over her hair and down her back, over and over, murmuring he didn't know what to her; her shudders and wrenching sobs died gradually away.

For a while she was just a child he was comforting. Insensibly that changed, pats changed to caresses. He forgot the child in the woman's body—until he suddenly realized what he was doing. He pulled away from her. "You'll be all right now," he said when he could get the words out. He started to get up but her hands closed about his arm, pulled him down beside her.

"Don't go," she whispered. "Please."

"Brann. . . ." He touched her face, drew his hands down over her shoulder and onto her breast. Her eyes widened, her tongue moved along her lips. She sighed and her breast shifted under his hand, the nipple hard as he was. He pulled his hand away.

"No," she breathed.

"Got to," he said; he tore at the lacing on his trousers, breaking the thongs in his urgency.

She was warm and wet and ready for him, closing tightly about him, passive at first, then doing what her body taught her. When it was finished and he lay beside her, his breathing quieting, she snuggled against him, sighed, a sound of deep contentment, and went to sleep.

He woke with a numb arm and white curls tickling his chin, sunlight pouring through the slats of the airvent, lay a moment listening to the sounds of the ship. The wind had slackened to a brisk quartering breeze that drove the *Girl* steadily along without straining her.

Brann's breath was a spot of warm dampness on his shoulder. She was deeply, bonelessly asleep, not even murmuring as he eased from under her and slid off the bed. He picked up a fresh pair of trousers and laced them on, pulled on a sleeveless shirt bleached by sun and salt water to a dirty gray. He ran his fingers through his hair and swore to have Staro take a knife to it before the day was out.

He looked at Brann. She lay on her stomach, one arm outflung, the other bent so her fist was pressed against her mouth. A child, damn her. A moment before he'd been looking forward to breakfast, now his appetite was gone. He left the cabin, his bare feet soundless on the planks, taking care to make no noise when he shut the door. He didn't want to wake her. If she slept most of the day away, he'd be quite happy. He had a lot of thinking to do.

Hairy Jimm had the wheel. He was squinting at the sky ahead, humming a three-note song into his beard. He grinned at Sammang, jerked a massive thumb at the sky. "Takes a bit of getting used to, it does, but they're handy little buggers. Y'know, Sammo, you ought to keep hold of them all, say you can."

Sammang looked up. Two large white birds circled lazily above the ship, effortlessly keeping even with her.

"They been up there most all the night, friendly of them, they say they give us a shout down here if somethin starts coming at us."

Late in the afternoon Brann came on deck. Standing in the bow, Sammang heard her shouted exchanges with the crew, heard her silences. She drifted about for some time, circling gradually closer to him, but he gave no sign he knew she was there. When she put her hand on his arm, he flinched and all but jerked his arm away.

"You're really upset." She seemed amazed.

"Yes," he said, angrily, almost violently.

"I told you I was getting older. I was eleven in Tavisteen, but things have happened since, pushing me older. Might be fifteen, sixteen, seventeen now." She drew her forefinger along the hard muscle of his arm. "You helped, Sammo, you taught me a lot before you ever touched me."

"Don't do that." He pulled his arm away, stared at the water ahead of the ship without seeing it. "Why?"

"I don't know. Lot of reasons. Comfort. I needed to touch someone just for me, not to heal them or kill them." She gave a tiny shrug. "Curiosity."

"You weren't virgin." His own resentful confusion increased his fury.

"A Temueng Censor raped me. He's dead." She ran her hand slowly down his arm; he felt her enjoying the feel of him and ground his teeth together. "You would be too," she said, "if I'd wished it."

A chill ran through him, fear. He forced himself to look at her. There was sadness in her face as if she knew how her words had affected him, had extinguished desire. *She said it deliberately,* he thought, *out of pity for me.* He took a step away, almost hating her. Then child and woman both looked at him out of those wide green eyes and anger drained from him.

Forgetting him, she leaned precariously out to look down at the water slicing out from the bow. "The sea looks different," she said. "How come?"

"How different?"

"Color maybe, the way it moves. I don't know. It's just different."

Watching her, he again saw himself as a boy, ship's lad trying to answer the same question. He leaned over the rail beside her and began teaching her as he was taught.

The next day was bright and clear, but the wind grew erratic, now and then quitting altogether, leaving the *Girl* wallowing, her sails slatting, the crew run off their feet. And the weathermaker's ghost tangled itself in the rigging, gibbering at them, which didn't improve either skill or morale. Tik-rat, who was ship's exorciser as well as bard, had dealt with the rest of the ghosts but the weatherman was stubborn and filled with spite, determined to make the lives of his slayers as miserable as he could manage. He was ragged and growing more so, but grimly hanging on, ignoring Tik-rat's chants and sacred dances, the eroding of the incense the boy waved at him, the curses of Sammang and the rest of the crew. Yaril and Jaril watched the process with fascination until it began wearing on the nerves of their friends, then they joined to drive the ghost from the shrouds and banged through him until he was scattered wisps of smoke that dissipated with the rising wind.

On the twelfth day after leaving Tavisteen the *Panday Girl* dropped anchor in the crowded bay at the island port Silili.

4.

Brann's Quest—
Silili to Andurya Durat
with Taguiloa the Dancing Man

Holding lit candles in both hands, Taguiloa made the last run, whirling over and over, coming up with the candles still burning, arms lifted high over his head, feet stamping out an intricate patterdance over the cork matting spread on the flags of the summer court. He finished the dance before the painted coffin, made the required deep obeisance, blew out the candles, bowed to the finger-snapping crowd and stalked into the darkness with stiff-legged dignity, leaving Yarm to pass through the ghost-witnesses and collect what coins they felt like giving. Should be a goodish haul. Most of the witnesses were rich old merchants, more than half-drunk, delighted to have their minds taken off the death of one of their number, even if the dead was only an old cousin of the master of this house. They were reminded too vividly of their own decaying bodies and how short the count of their remaining years could be. He didn't like performing at ghost watches either but the money was good, the fee guaranteed, with whatever he could wring from the watchers added on top of that.

He stopped by the food table, dipped a drinking bowl into the hot mulled wine and stepped back into the shadows to watch the dancers who followed him move onto the matting, their long sleeves fluttering, their gauze draperies hiding little of the lithe bodies beneath. Tari called Blackthorn and her dancers. Csermanoa wasn't stinting his uncle. Taga smiled. Wasn't for love, all this, Csoa the Sharp was underlining his position among the Hina merchant class; from the number of men sitting out there and the smiles painted onto their faces, he was nailing down his status with the same force he used to drive bargains.

Tari's flute player was a marvel, the sounds he got out of that pipe, and matched the mood of the dance and the subtle rhythms of Tari's body. Taga sipped at the wine, frowning thoughtfully at the way the

music enhanced the appeal of the dancers. Though tradition decreed
that flute music be reserved for female dancers, for the past year he'd
been working with Tari's Ladjinatuai, developing a mixture of tumbling and dance that used the flowing line of the flute music, but he
hadn't tried it in public yet. It was a daring move and required the
right audience, probably one with a strong leavening of Temuengs.
Much as he despised them, they weren't so rigidly set on maintaining
things the way they were. When he ventured to combine juggling and
tumbling into a single presentation, he had Gerontai his master to
support and defend him, but he remembered all too well how difficult it
had been to win acceptance before the Tekora chanced to see him and
approve. Taguiloa spent a good few days despising himself for being
grateful for this recognition until his mentor-almost-father chided him
out of it. We're despised anyway by those who pay us for our skills,
Gerontai said, don't let them tell you how to see yourself. Look at the
lap-dogs licking Temueng ass and running after you now that the
Tekora says you're remarkable. What does it matter that it takes a
Temueng to see what you are? You know yourself, soul-son, you know
you're better than I ever was or could be. Your integrity lies in your
art, not in what Hina say of you. The new things he wanted to do,
though, would need a lot more than the Tekora's approval. He was
growing more and more impatient to get started but could only see one
way to manage. Gather a troupe together and travel to Andurya Durat
with a chance at performing before the Emperor—which would give
him the right to display the Imperial sigil when he was working. That
plan would cost an impossible sum in bribes and fees, to say nothing of
general expenses. He'd need a patron and a lot of luck to have half a
chance of pulling it off.

He watched and listened a while longer, brooding over all the barriers he could see no way of surmounting, then set the bowl down and
went into the sidecourt where Csermanoa had put up a paper pavilion
for the players, a place to keep them away from his guests. He found
Yarm in a corner with one of Tari's maids, glanced at her to see if she
was being coerced in any way, nodded to her and strolled into the
alcove that served as washroom and dressingroom. After stripping the
paint from his hands and face, he climbed out of his tumbling silks and
pulled on a long dark robe, thrust his feet into the aged sandals he
brought along when the performance would be long, complex and tiring. Knotting a narrow black sash about his waist, he walked back into
the main room, stood looking around. Chinkoury the m'darjin magi-

cian and his boys in a small knot by the door, elongated blue-black figures, even the boys a head taller than Taguiloa. To one side and a little behind them a clutch of Felhiddin knife dancers, bending, stretching, testing gear, inspecting each other, chattering in their rapid guttural tongue, little brown men covered in intricate blue tattoos. He didn't recognize them, must be new to Silili. Trust Csermanoa to get hold of something no one else had seen. Curled up in the far corner, snatching what sleep they could, six young women, more joyhouse girls than dancers, a step above ordinary joygirls, but far below the rank of courtesan, though most of them had hopes. The last to perform—in both their functions—they were expected to return to their house with more than their appearance fee, with longer-term attachments if they could manage it.

He nodded to Chinkoury and passed out of the pavilion. He stood in shadow watching the dancers, silently applauding Tari for the gift she was wasting on those drunken coin-suckers. He watched the merchants for a moment with a contempt he usually had to hide; some were drinking and eating, a few frankly asleep, others wandering about, some watching the dancers, some with their heads together, a heavily conspiratorial air about them that suggested they either plotted new coups or told each other tales of coups past to magnify their shrewdness. Maybe one or two watched Blackthorn dancing with a pinch of appreciation and understanding of what they were seeing, the magic she was making there on the cork mats before the painted coffin. Taguiloa drew his sleeve across his face, amused and angry. I ought to know, he thought, by now I ought to know what to expect. He put anger away and watched Blackthorn end her dance, bow first to the coffin, her sleeves fluttering dangerously near the hordes of candles burning about the elaborate box, then to the audience, who woke enough to provide the expected applause, she was after all Blackthorn, the most celebrated dancer in three generations. As her maids came giggling into the audience, rattling their collecting bowls, dodging gropes, shaking heads at gross remarks but careful to smile and say nothing, Blackthorn sailed majestically into the darkness, her dancers drifting after her, the flute player weaving a slow simple tune that trailed into silence a moment after the last of the girls vanished.

In the hush before Chinkoury was due to appear, Taguiloa heard a faint commotion from the direction of the main gate and succumbed to the curiosity that was his chief vice. He glanced quickly about, but the noisy clash of cymbals, the sprays of colored smoke and the hooming

of the apprentices as they ushered their master onto the cork, all this
had trapped the attention of most of the guests and servants; those still
involved in conversations wouldn't notice if old Csagalgasoa climbed
out of his coffin and jigged on the lid. He slipped away and eeled into a
dark corner of the public court, hidden behind a potted blackthorn that
Tari had given to Csermanoa when he was one of her favored few,
before she inherited her house and income from another of her lovers.

Old Grum stopped talking and slammed the hatch shut, swung the
bar and opened the wicket to let in the folk he'd been arguing with.

A man and a woman. Not Hina. Two children, very fair. Not Hina.

"You wait," Grum said, "You wait here." He jerked a third time at
the bell rope then stumped off to his hutch and vanished inside.

A broad man muscled like a hero, Panday by the look of him, not
much taller than Taguiloa but wide enough to make two of him. Dark
brown skin shining in the torchlight, yellow eyes, hawk's eyes.
Taguiloa grinned. Fitting, with a beak like that. Wide, rather thick-
lipped mouth, good for grins or sneers. Raggedly cut black hair. Barbaric ear ornament the length of a man's finger, a series of animal faces
linked together. A shipmaster from his dress.

The woman, tall and full of nervous energy. Attractive face for one
not Hina, rather wide in the mouth with elegant cheekbones and an
arrogant nose; eyebrows like swallow's wings over large lustrous eyes.
Green, he thought, though it was hard to be sure in the torchlight. A
band of silk wound about her head, hiding her hair. White blouse with
long loose sleeves, wide leather belt that laced in front, long loose black
trousers stuffed carelessly in the tops of black boots. She wore no orna-
ments of any kind, had no visible weapons, but he smelled the danger
that hovered round her like a powerful perfume.

Dombro the Steward came into the court, hastened to the visitors.
"Sammang Shipmaster, you are early this year."

"And late this night, for which I beg your master's pardon, but it is
important I speak with him."

"So the Sao Csermanoa understood. He asks if you would wait in the
spring garden pavilion, Shipmaster. He cannot leave his guests quite
yet."

Taguiloa scowled at the Steward. Stiff-rumped worm. Players had to
put up with a lot of sniping from him; he looked like he wanted to try
his insolence on the Shipmaster but didn't quite dare. Obviously the
Panday was important to Csermanoa. He watched the Shipmaster nod
and follow the Steward, waited a while then slipped after him. He'd

met many foreigners in this house. Csermanoa's interests ranged widely; while it wasn't according to Temueng law for a Hina to own shipping, he was a very silent partner to more than one Shipmaster, and Taga's snooping had brought him the startling discovery that this highly respectable merchant was also a fence of considerable proportions; there was not a whisper of that in the market places around Silili and Taguiloa would have been mocked as moon-dreaming if he'd told anyone, but he was a miser with the secrets he nosed out, calling them up and fondling them when sleep eluded him.

He ghosted through the dark paths, his senses alert; if this was something to do with the subterranean aspects of Csermanoa's business, the merchant would be quick and drastic in the methods he used to keep his secrets to himself. *I should forget this and get back to the Watch,* he told himself. He kept following them.

The Steward unlocked and opened a gate in a wall, and left it open after ushering the Panday and his companions through. Taguiloa crept up to the gate after a few ragged breaths, still half-convinced he should get out of there.

A few scrapes of feet against gravel, no talking. Dombro wouldn't waste his breath on foreigners. Taga watched a moment more, then floated through, his feet as soundless as he could make them. He whipped into shrubbery on the far side of the gate, wishing he wore clothing more suitable for night-prowling. A moment later the Steward came back, a sour sneer on his face. He passed through the gate, slammed it shut and locked it. Trusting soul. Seshtrango send him boils on his butt.

The pavilion was a free-standing six-sided structure large enough to contain more than one room. He circled round it till he found one window whose oiled paper was an arch of yellow light. He slid into the shaggy yews planted close to the wall, dropped into a crouch as a voice sounded above him, startling him with its nearness and clarity. At first he didn't catch what was being said, then realized the woman was speaking Panay. Growing up wild in this polyglot port city had given him the rudiments of many tongues and he'd polished them as he grew older, because he admired his master's command of many languages and because it was a necessity for satisfying his thirst for secrets.

"You're fussing about nothing, Sammo." Her voice was husky but musical, deep enough to pass for a man's. "I did all right in Tavisteen."

"Hunh." An angry rasping sound rather like a lion's cough. "You're a baby, Bramble-all-thorns. Tavisteeners may think they're the slipp'ri-

est things under the Langareri bowl, but Silili Hina make them look
like children who aren't very bright. Hina say they're the oldest folk
and maybe it's so; trying to get through their customs is like threading
a maze without a pattern. And since the Temuengs took over here
nothing they say or do means exactly what it seems to. It's called
survival, Bramble, Hina are very good at surviving."

"So am I, friend."

Another impatient sound from the Panday. Footsteps going away
from the window, coming back, going away again. Pacing, Taguiloa
thought, a baby? that woman? Wicker creaking, the whisper of silk.
The woman sitting down. After a while the man joined her. "Csermanoa financed a good part of the *Girl,"* he said, "I'm clear of debt to
him, the *Girl* 's all mine. It's the other way now, he owes me. He'll take
care of you."

"I can take care of myself."

"Baby, baby, you haven't the least idea what the real world's like."

A chuckle, warm and affectionate. "Hah! Maybe I didn't last month,
but I've learned a few things since."

"You've learned to tease, that's for sure."

"Who says I'm teasing?"

"Let it go, Brann. You know how I feel. Smooth your feathers and
take any help that's going. Think of your father and your brothers. If
you're killed before you get to them, what good is all you've done so
far?"

"You throw my own arguments at me. How can I fight that?" Silence for a while. "I'll take a lot of killing."

"Lapalaulau swamp me, I wish you were a few years older." There
was an odd, strained note in the man's voice.

Taguiloa scowled. There was too much he didn't know. He couldn't
catch the nuances, the feelings between the words. Crouched outside in
the darkness, he could hear the strong currents of affection passing
between them, such shared understanding they didn't have to say any
of those things he wanted to know. He flushed with envy. Not even
Tari Blackthorn was that close. Gerontai had loved him but he was an
old man when he took an angry street boy into his home and he was a
man of solitude and distances. Taga's parents, his brothers and sisters,
he lost them in a shipwreck when he was five; he clung to a bit of debris
and was pulled out of the sea by a fisherman, brought back to live with
an overworked cousin who had eight children of her own and neither
missed nor mourned him when he ran away.

"What are you going to do?" The woman's voice.

"Unload my official cargo for what I can get. See if I can get hold of more Slya ware, maybe pick up other cargo. Go home awhile. Careen my ship. I didn't use half your gold in Tavisteen. You sure you don't want it back?"

"Very sure. What I need, the children will provide."

"Yeah." Sound of wicker shifting, scrape of boots on the tile floor. "What about your father, will he work for the Emperor?"

"How can he without Tincreal's fire? He's spent a lifetime putting her heart into his work; what he does is more than just shaping the bowls and things. Old Lardarse. . . ." She giggled. "Like that name? A Temueng pimush should know the worth of his Emperor. . . . Where was I? Ah. I suppose he can have my folk beaten into making something, but it won't be Slya ware. What a fool he is. If he'd left us alone, he'd have had the pick of what we made. Now that the mountain has taken her own back, he'll have nothing."

Arth Slya gone, Taga thought. He closed his eyes and cursed the Temuengs, cursed the woman, cursed himself for somehow believing there'd always be a place free from the compromises he'd made all his life, a place where artist and artisan explored their various crafts without having to pander to blind and stupid men whose only virtue was the gold in their pockets. If he understood what she was saying, Arth Slya was either dead or maimed beyond recovery.

The Panday cleared his throat. "Come home with me, Bramble. Wait till I get my ship clean of weed and rot. We'll take you up the Palachunt to Durat, sooner and safer than the land route, wait for you, take you and your folk away once you break them free."

Silence again. More creaks from the wicker as she shifted about, more wool moving against silk. "I'm sorry you wouldn't love me again, Sammo. I wanted you to, you know that."

"Bramble, how could I? Tupping a child. I'd kill another man for doing that."

"I should have kept my mouth shut that time in Tavisteen, just said no and left it at that."

"I wish you had."

"I'm growing older fast."

"Give me a couple more years, Bramble, then maybe I'll believe it."

"Slya! you're stubborn."

"We're a pair."

"You're right. I'm going to stick to my first plan, Sammo. I know how you feel about the *Girl* and I can read a map. A dozen places on that river where the Temuengs could drop rocks or fire on you and would if they thought they had a reason. You'd all be killed and if you weren't, you'd lose the *Girl.* I won't have that, Sammo. I won't."

The shadows around Taguiloa suddenly vanished and hot golden light flickered about him. He bit back a yell and jumped to his feet, meaning to get out of there as fast as he could, hoping he wasn't already identified. His feet wouldn't move. He tried to turn his head. It wouldn't move. Not his head. Not a hand. Not a finger.

He stood frozen and afraid. As abruptly as it came, the light was gone, taking with it the greater part of his fear. Whatever else had happened, he wasn't discovered. Inside the pavilion the man and woman were still talking; there were no shouts of discovery outside it. Something very strange had happened. If he fled without careful thought, likely he'd run into trouble rather than away from it. He glanced around, saw only darkness and yews, dropped to the ground and began listening again to what was happening inside.

"I don't want to let you go." The Panday was walking about, his words loud then muffled.

"I don't want to go." Creak of wicker as she moved restlessly on the divan. "If it weren't my father, my brothers, my kin, if it weren't for Slya filling me, driving me, if . . . If! Stupid word. I can't change what is, Sammo."

"You don't even know if they're alive now, you don't know what will happen to them before you can get to Durat."

"No." A long silence filled with the small sounds of movement. "If they aren't alive," the woman said suddenly, fury, frustration, fear sharp in her voice. "If they aren't alive, I will drink the life from Abanaskranjinga and spit it to the winds."

"Preemalau's bouncy tits, Brann, don't say that, don't even think it."

"I won't say it again, but I will do it. That's another reason I don't want you and the others anywhere about."

"I believe you, don't say more, what if someone is listening." Sound of door opening, feet crossing the tiles, voice louder, window shutters slamming open. Taguiloa shrank farther into shadow, but the Panday saw nothing but the darkness of the yews and the moonlit grass beyond. He dragged the shutters to and went to stand behind the woman, so close to the window Taga could hear him breathing. "Where's the boy?"

"Keeping watch."

"Ah." Feet on tiles, wicker protesting loudly as a heavy weight dropped onto the silk cushions. The Panday sitting beside the woman. "I could leave Jimm to take care of the *Girl* and go north with you."

"Don't be silly, Sammo. I'd have to spend more time worrying about you than getting on with the business. The children will take care of me. There's no way the Temuengs can harm them. Strike at them and they fade and are something else, somewhere else."

"Not you."

"While they live, I live."

He grunted, then laughed. "Don't think I want to go deeper into that."

Laughter from the woman. A long comfortable silence. Taguiloa felt the amity and warmth moving between them, filling the silence, was angry and sad at once that such a communion was beyond him. Even as he felt this, the woman repelled him and the things they said frightened him. He thought of leaving, decided he'd wait for Csermanoa and see what happened then.

As if it took a cue from him, a child's voice broke the silence. "Jaril says Csermanoa's coming."

Taga listened, heard nothing for a few breaths, then the crunch of feet on the gravel path, then Csoa's voice ordering the guards to take up their posts. Taga smiled to himself. Csoa the Sharp making sure they weren't close enough to hear what was said in the pavilion, yet where they could come running if he needed them fast. Heavy footsteps as he came on alone, protesting planks as he climbed the stairs to the pavilion's door, faint squeal of hinges.

"Well, Sammang?"

"Precariously, Saöm." He spoke Hina with very little accent.

"Ah." Creak of wicker as the rotund little merchant settled himself across the room from the man and woman. "Didn't expect you till the end of summer."

The Panday chuckled. "The gods dispose, Saöm." A short silence. "This isn't business. I'm calling in a couple favors. Business we'll discuss tomorrow." Another short silence. "Sorry about your uncle."

"An old man full of years." Wariness in the merchant's voice. Taguiloa grinned into the darkness, seeing the film sliding over Csoa's eyes, the stiff smile stretch his lips. For him, favors meant coin and he never parted with coin until he got as much as he could for it.

"My friend needs a place to stay hid and needs tutoring in Hina and Temueng ways."

"She speak Hina?"

The woman broke in with a rapid question to the Shipmaster, wanting to know what was being said. She listened and told him she'd be speaking Hina the next day, the children would give it to her.

"She will," the Panday said, finality in his voice.

Loud creaks from across the room, the wicker complaining as Csoa's shifting weight stressed it. Taguiloa imagined the fat man leaning forward to stare at the woman, his narrow black eyes sliding over her as if she were a sack of rice he thought of buying. "Stay hid?"

"That's the other favor. Don't ask."

"Ah." The wicker creaked again, Csermanoa settling back. "Dombro won't gossip, he knows better. Grum wouldn't talk to his mother if he had one. Who else saw her?"

"My crew, but they won't talk, not about her. We came the back ways, no one credible saw her."

"You had that hair covered? Good. Old woman's hair with a young woman's face catches the eye. Can she read and write? Her own gabble, I mean. Yes? Good. She's got the idea. Shouldn't be too hard to give her a fair sense of Hina script if she's willing to work at it." Silence. Taguiloa imagined the merchant running shuttered eyes over the woman again. "Is she prepared to earn her keep?" An angry exclamation from the Shipmaster. "Not while she's here," Csermanoa added hastily. "I ask so I'll know what to teach her."

Switching into rapid Panay, almost too rapid for Taguiloa to follow, the man reported to the woman what he and Csermanoa had been saying.

"Sammo, I'm not going to be earning my way, you know that. He's fishing, it's nonsense. I'll survive," she added grimly. "Leave how I do it to me."

Taga smiled. As I thought, he told himself. A tough one. Csoa can go milk a rock and get more than she'll give him.

"You don't want the Imperial guard waiting for you." Sammang speaking angrily. Careless, Taguiloa thought. I'm sure Csoa knows some Panay, and the word *Imperial* is a bad slip, has to tell him more than they want him to know.

"Who knows to wait?"

"You think the Temuengs in . . . where you come from don't send messages every day to Durat?"

"So?"

"They're not stupid. By now they know you've escaped them, and they'll have an idea where you're going. They will be waiting for you. You've got to be sly and cunning, you've got to know the ground."

"All right, all right, I hear you. I admit you're right. Get on with the bargaining. I'm sleepy."

Be careful, Taguiloa thought, Csoa may owe you favors, but you're not Hina, remember that and beware, how he treats the woman depends on how much he still needs you. Don't let him know the Temuengs will hunt her down and stomp everyone connected with her. He made a note to himself to stay as far away from her as he could manage.

Switching to high Hina, the Shipmaster said, "Saö Csermanoa, will you provide shelter and tutoring for the freewoman and her child companions?"

Taguiloa wished he could see the merchant's face. That was a most formal request, phrased in the elegant high Hina more suitable for use with one from the few Old Families left after the Temueng clearances in the bloody aftermath of their invasion. He nodded with appreciation. A touch. A real touch. Shrewd though he was, Csermanoa would bite.

In the same high tongue, with the same formality, Csermanoa answered the Shipmaster. "I say to you, O Sammang Schimli, shelter will be provided and tutoring for the freewoman and her child companions." Slipping into less formal language, he went on, "You said companions. I only see one child. Silent little thing."

"Her twin watches outside."

"A bit young."

"But very competent."

Competent? Taguiloa thought. *Haven't found me.* . . . he jumped and almost betrayed himself as a small hand touched his arm, a soft laugh sounded in his ear. He looked down, saw the boy's face as a pale oval in the shadow, then it dissolved into the golden light that had touched him not so long ago, then the light was gone; there was a faint rustle to his left as if something small was pattering away. No wonder the woman wasn't worried. Witch with demon familiars. He shivered and renewed his vow to keep away from her, shivered again when he realized the boy would tell her about him as soon as Csermanoa left. He fidgeted. He wanted to get out of there now, he knew enough to play with, but he couldn't chance the guards. They'd be just bored enough to catch the slightest sound and mean enough to enjoy stomping him.

"Favor for favor," the merchant said.

"Name it and I'll think about it."

"Tomorrow, Shipmaster." Wicker creaked. "You said business tomorrow."

"Saöm, would you promise blind?" Sounds of the Panday shifting his feet, softer noises of the woman standing beside him. "Thanks for listening. I'll make other arrangements."

"Sit, sit." Csermanoa spoke hastily, a querulous note in his voice. "There's no question of swearing blind. Certainly not. We'll talk about that tomorrow." Grunts, more creaking, a few thuds. Csermanoa standing. "The woman may stay, of course she may, servants will be provided, food, the tutoring you ask. All I ask is discretion." Heavy steps on the tiles, crossing to the door. "Come to the ghostwatch, Shipmaster, before you leave." Sound of door opening, closing. Heavy feet stumping down the steps. Csoa calling to his guards, walking off with them.

Taguiloa stayed where he was until he heard the gate clunk shut. He straightened, turned to follow Csoa out. Then he heard the Panday and the witch start talking, hesitated, squatted once more, cursing his stupidity but unable to break away.

"Our witch." Caressing sound in the man's voice. "You're set. He won't bother you. Maybe ask questions. Mmmh. Certainly questions. You're all right as long as you're suspicious, Bramble, but soon as you relax, you talk too much. You talked too much to me."

"What harm would you do me?"

"Bed you, child."

"I keep telling you. . . ." She sighed impatiently. "It wasn't a child's body you loved. I don't know what I am any more, only that I'm not Arth Slya's Brann waiting for her eleventh birthday so she could make her Choice. Sammo, I was going to be a potter like my father. He made a teapot and drinking bowls for an old man's birthday. Uncle Eornis. My birthday was his too, he was going to make a hundred this year . . . the oldest among us. . . ." Her voice broke. After a moment she cleared her throat and went on. "That he was killed two weeks before his hundred . . . funny, that seems worse. . . ." She seemed to be speaking to herself. Taguiloa was caught up in them, his imagination responding to the emotion in the soft voice, emotion that was all the more powerful because of the quiet restraint that kept the words so slow and easy. "I saw a Temueng take my baby sister by the heels and dash her brains out against the Oak, I saw them fire my home and walk away with my mother, my uncles, aunts and cousins, I didn't cry, Sammo, all that time I didn't cry. And now I weep for an old man at the end of his life. Look at me, isn't it funny?"

"Brann. . . ."

"Don't worry about me, Sammo, I'm not falling apart. Like aunt Frin always said, complaining is good for the soul. A purgation of sorts."

Silence. The man began walking about, stopping and walking, stopping and walking, no regular rhythm to his pacing. Pulled two ways, Taguiloa thought, wants to stay, wants to go.

"Three months," the Panday said, his voice stone hard with determination. "Enough time for you to learn how to go on and work out a way into Audurya Durat, then make your way there. In three months I'll be tied up at the wharves of Durat waiting for you."

"No!"

"You can't stop me."

"The *Girl.* What if something happens to her?"

"Thought about that. Plenty of inlets near the mouth of the Palachunt. Jimm can wait there with the *Girl;* your gold will buy a ship I don't have to care about, all it needs is a bottom sound enough to get us back down the river. And the children flying guard." He chuckled. "Now argue with that, Bramble-all-thorns."

"Dear friend, what about the crew? Who're you going to take with you into that rattrap? Tik-rat? Staro the Stub?"

"Better to ask who I can persuade to stay behind and if I'm going to have to part Jimm's hair with his war club to make him wait with the *Girl.*" He cleared his throat. "You're part of the crew now, Bramble. You're our witch."

Soft gasping, snuffling sounds. The witch weeping. Taguiloa scowled into the darkness, his pulses shouting danger at him, danger to stay so close to a woman who could spin such webs. He started to creep out of the shadows, froze as he heard the door slam, feet running down the steps. Then the Shipmaster slowed to a deliberate walk. The gate creaked open, bumped shut. Taguiloa stood, still in half-shadow, and worked the cramps out of his body. Behind him he heard the soft murmur of voices—the children and the woman. He closed his ears to them, started cautiously for the gate, staying in the shadow of the plantings, moving with the silent hunting glide that had served him so well other times.

A faint giggle by his side. He looked down. The blond boy, trotting beside him. Taga ignored him and went ghosting on until he reached the wall.

The boy caught hold of his arm. "Wait," he breathed.

A slight tug, then a large horned owl was powering up from him. It sailed over the wall, circled twice and came slanting back. Feathers soft as milkweed fluff brushed at his arm, then the boy was standing beside him. "No one out there, not even a servant."

"Why?"

"It's late. Only a couple hours till dawn."

"You know what I mean."

The boy grinned at him, danced back a few steps, turned and ran into the darkness. Taguiloa stared after him then turned to the gate. With a silent prayer to Tungjii, he lifted the latch and walked through.

The Kula priest came from the house and paced round and round the pyre with its festoons of silk flowers and painted paper chains and the paper wealth soaked in sweet oils to make a perfumed and painted fire. He waved his incense sticks and the sickly sweet perfume drifted on the breeze to Taguiloa. If funerals had not provided a steady income and a place to show his work, he'd have missed them all; the smell of the roasting meat, the sight of the earthsoul and skysoul oozing out of the coffin surrounded by that smell which the incense never quite covered twisted his stomach and made the inside of his bones itch.

The fire was crackling briskly as the Kula finished the final censing round. He stepped back and chanted, binding the sparks into a web of light so there was no danger of the House or the Watchers catching fire.

Taguiloa sensed a presence and looked down. The blond boy was standing beside him, watching the show with amused interest. There was a companionable feel to the situation that made him want to relax and grin at the boy, ruffle his hair the way he hated to have done to him when he was a boy. He'd stopped being afraid of this maybe-demon, this changechild; he smiled at the boy and went back to watching the fire burn.

The shimmer that was the skysoul wriggled free and darted skyward like a meteor shooting up instead of down. The earth soul, a bent little man looking much as old uncle had looked in life, hovered near the pyre as if it didn't have the strength to leave the meat that had housed it. After a while, though, it seemed to shrug its meager shoulders and begin a heavy drift upwards riding the streamers of smoke. The death was clean, the old man had nothing to complain of, there was no violence against the meat to hold the earthsoul down, a clear testament to the way Csermanoa performed his family duties.

As the fire began to die down, the party grew livelier. The servants came bustling about, replacing the plundered food trays, setting out new basins of steaming spiced wine, drawing the lamps down and replacing the candles in them; the joygirls were circling through the guests, teasing and laughing, cajoling sweets from the men, whispering in their ears. It was clearly time for the players to leave. He looked down. The child was gone. He watched a moment more, then edged around the walls of the summer court and went into the paper pavilion. Yarm had the gear packed and was curled up, dozing, beside it. He shook the boy awake, caught up his own pack and left Csermanoa's compound by the servants' entrance, the sleepy doorkeeper coming awake enough to hold out his hand for a tip. Feeling generous, ignoring Yarm's scowl, Taguiloa dropped a dozen coppers in the palm; the broad beaming grin he got in return seemed worth the price.

As they wound through the irregular narrow streets, Yarm kept looking back, something Taguiloa didn't notice until they were about halfway to the players' quarter and the house and garden he'd inherited from Gerontai. He endured Yarm's fidgeting for a while, then looked back himself, half-suspecting what he'd see.

The small blond boy was strolling casually along behind them, making no effort to conceal himself. He stopped when he saw them watching him, waved a hand and sauntered into an alley between two tenements. Taguiloa tapped Yarm on the shoulder. "Forget it," he said. "That's nothing to trouble us."

"Who's he? What's he want?" Petulance and jealousy in the boy's voice.

Taguiloa frowned at him, started walking again without answering him. Yarm had a limber body, a quick mind when he wanted to use it, a good ear for rhythm; he also had a difficult nature he made no attempt to change. He was intensely, almost irrationally possessive. Taguiloa's continued aloofness still intimidated him a little, but the effect of it was wearing off. He had to go. There were complications to getting rid of him, notably his cousin the thug-master Fist, but he had to go.

An owl dipped low overhead, hooted softly and went slanting up, riding the onshore wind freshening about them in the thickening dark just before dawn. Taguiloa shivered, then laughed at himself. The boy was teasing him, that was all. And following him home. He glanced up at the owl, walked on. Nothing he could do about it. Besides, a hundred people knew where he lived, that was not one of his secrets.

The days slid one into the next until a week was gone. The boy appeared now and again when Taguiloa was performing, watching him with such genial interest that he found himself relaxing and accepting his presence with equanimity and curiosity. He didn't try to talk to the boy, only nodded to him and smiled now and then.

Yarm began making jealous scenes about the boy, barely confining them to the walls of the house, making life there such a misery that Taguiloa began staying away as much as he could, even neglecting practice, something he'd never done before. He was coldly furious at Yarm, but he needed him for performances already booked, a wedding, two funerals, a guild dinner, and the first-pressing festival. And there was always Fist who started dropping in on Taguiloa now and then, mentioning casually how delighted the family was that Yarm had found such a considerate master. It was enough to make a man stomp into the Temple and kick old Tungjii on hisser fat butt.

Taguiloa threw the sticks and they landed eskimemeloa, the wave of change, a sign of the third triad, a good high point. He smiled with satisfaction. Maybe a sign that his luck was changing. Djeracim the pharmacist grunted, gathered the sticks and threw them, snarled with disgust and emptied his winebowl. Neko-karan. Only one step from nothing, the maelstrom. Grunting with the effort. Lagermukaea the Fat scooped up the sticks, held them a moment lost in his huge hand. "That kid of yours, Taga, he's whispering nasty things about you in Pupa's ear. Muck-worm don't waste any time running to the Temueng Nose to dump his dirt. You ought to pop the kid in a sack and drop him in the bay." He opened his hand, looked surprised to see the thin brown stalks on his broad palm. Clicking tongue against teeth, he cast them, hummed a snatch of a dirge as they split into two signs. Rebhsembulan, the honeybee, and mina-tuatuan, the reviving rain. He grunted. Even added, they didn't count enough to beat the eskimemeloa. He grinned a moment later, began flipping the coppers one by one to Taguiloa who caught them and tossed them up again, keeping more and more in the air until he finally missed one and dropped the bunch. Laughing, he opened his pouch and dropped the coins inside along with Dji's, leaving out enough to buy another jug of wine. "That I would," he said. "Tie him in a sack. If someone would sack Fist and feed him to a shark." He pushed the coins into a squat triangle. "Let me know if someone none of us likes is looking for an apprentice, maybe I can push Yarm off on him. Or her." He curled his tongue and whistled up another jug.

Taguiloa sat on the pier in a heavy fog, listening to the sound of the buoys clanging, to the distant shouts from the Woda Living boats, to the thousand other noises of the early morning. He'd always liked foggy days, enjoyed the times when he was immersed in the sounds of life, yet wholly alone in the small white room the fog built around him.

The blond boy came into that room and sat beside him, his short legs dangling over the pier's edge. Water condensed on his skin and in his hair, ran down his nose and wet the collar of his jacket.

"Why are you following me about?" Taguiloa spoke lazily, not overly interested in the answer.

"Curiosity."

"About why I was outside the pavilion listening?"

"That? Oh no. I already know what you were doing there and why. I wanted to know more about you."

"Why?"

"My companion needs to reach Andurya Durat. I thought you might be the right one to take her."

"Me? No!" After a moment's silence, he said, "She's a witch. Worse, she's a foreigner. Worse than that, she's going hunting for Temuengs."

"So? You like Temuengs?"

"Hah! I like living."

"What about gold?"

"Not enough to die for it."

"You want to go to Durat and play for the Emperor. Brann could provide the gold."

"My master reached his eighties by being a prudent man."

"He took a chance on a boy who tried to rob him, took him in, taught him, made him his heir. Was he wrong?"

"Stay out of my head." There was no force to his voice, he was too accustomed to the boy now, he couldn't work up any fear of the changechild, no matter how strange he acted. "Look, Jaril, I'm not saying I don't understand her feelings, if my folks were slaves. . . . Understand me, it's the rest of my life you're talking about."

"Brann knows that. All she wants is a quiet way into the city so she can get there without the guard waiting for her. If she didn't care who knew she was coming she could hire a barge and a team of Dapples and float in comfort up the canal."

"A foreigner?"

"She could buy a Temueng to take her. Enough gold buys anything."

"Csermanoa's gold?"

"Certainly not, we're not going to make trouble for our Sammang and his men; think rather of the Tekora's vaults. Who can stop Yaril and me from getting in where we want?"

"Why me?"

Jaril snickered, slanted a crystal glance at him. "You presented yourself." Darkened by the fog his eyes glistened with good humor. "And who would look for vengeance riding in a player's wagon?"

"Your companion offers to pay the bribes and the outfitting?"

"And expenses along the way. What you make, that's yours to share out with the others in the troupe."

"She is generous."

"How easy to be generous with Temueng gold."

"Given the Temuengs don't know."

"Who would think of serpents with pockets in their hide?"

Taga chuckled. "Not me, friend."

"You won't take Yarm?"

"One more funeral and I'm done with him."

"He's got a cousin with a nasty temper."

"He has a lot of cousins, most of them with nasty tempers."

"Only one of them about to lesson you with padded clubs that won't break the skin, only bones."

"Tungjii's gut! I suppose you were a fly on the wall."

"Be one monstrous fly, but you've got the idea."

"Why tell me?"

"We like you. Offer. Whether or not you accept my companion's gold, Yaril and I, we'll keep an eye on Fist and warn you when he's set to act."

"Accept. Seshtrango send him hives and flatulence and inflict Yarm on him the rest of his life."

Jaril giggled, then dug in the pocket of his jacket and dropped a handful of gold beside Taguiloa. "Brann wants to move out of Csermanoa's house. He's hanging around a bit too much, asking questions she doesn't want to answer, and the maids spy on her. Makes her nervous. Could you find her a place to stay?" He stacked the coins into a neat pile. "That should be enough. Someplace she can stay quiet and safe?"

"There's no place safe from gossip."

"Even if she seems Hina? At least outside the house?"

"She can do that?"

"We can do that."

"Mmm. I can think of a couple places might do. Give me two days, meet me at my house."

"I hear." The boy got to his feet with the sinuous supple grace of a cat, vanished into the fog with a wave of a hand.

Taguiloa sat staring at the black water rocking under his feet, wondering what he'd got himself into.

He followed the music and laughter through the pleasure garden to the beach house built out over the water—water-dark stones and wind-sculpted cedars, clipped and trained seagrape vines. Salt flowers in reds and oranges and a scattered shouting pink. A willow or two to add a note of elegance. A bright cool morning with the sun just hot enough to fall pleasantly on the skin. Flute song winding through the wash of the sea, the spicy whisper of the cedars, the rustle of the willows. Ladji, he thought, then lifted his head and stopped as another instrument began to play, a jubilant, very clear, rather metallic flurry of notes dancing around the thread of the flute song.

He walked into the house.

Tari Blackthorn was reclining on a low divan amid piles of pillows watching two girls dancing. A small ancient man with a few wisps of hair on mottled skin stretched tight over his skull knelt at the edge of the straw matting and danced fingers like spider legs over the holes of his flute. Beside him a small dark-haired woman sat on a broad orange cushion, an instrument like a distorted and enlarged gittern on her lap. Her hair was dressed in innumerable small braids, some of them stiffened into graceful loops about her head. Elaborate gold earrings, wide hoops with filigreed discs hanging from them. Large blue eyes, the blue so dark it was almost black. Small pointed face, dark olive skin. A nose that had a tendency to hook. A wide mobile mouth, smiling now as she watched the girls dance. Short stubby fingers moved with swift sureness over the strings, the ivory plectrum gleaming against her dark skin.

Tari looked up as he came in, smiled and nodded at a pile of cushions near her feet. He dropped on them, leaned against the divan and watched the girls. They were very young, ten or eleven, sold by their parents into the night world when they were old enough so their adult features could be guessed at. He'd escaped being impressed into the world of the joyhouses by craftiness learned in a hard school, by the nimble body, coordination and speed Tungjii had gifted him with, and by a lot of luck. He watched the dancers with a cool judicial eye, his tastes running to older women. The plumper one wasn't going to make a dancer, she was a juicy creature with a bold eye; she had the proper moves, but there was no life to her dancing, none of the edge and fire Tari Blackthorn got into her dances. The other girl was thin and under-developed, coltish and a bit clumsy but there was a hint that she might have some of the gift that made Blackthorn the premier dancer of Silili before she was nineteen and kept her there for the next fifteen years.

Taga twisted his head around and saw her watching him. A slow smile touched the corners of her mouth. She seldom let her face move in any way that would encourage wrinkles, part of the discipline she enforced over nearly every aspect of her life. He was a part of that tiny area where she let herself feel and possibly be hurt, that little area of danger that gave her the magic she put into her dancing. Her smile was at most a slight lifting of her face, a gleam in her eyes, but he'd warmed to it since he'd celebrated his seventeenth birthday in her bed. Eight years ago. She was at her zenith now while he was still rising. She'd stay where she was for a few years and manage a graceful glide into her retirement unless she made enemies. Here too she walked the ragged and crumbly edge between acceptance and obloquy, walked it with calculation and care, knowing a misstep could destroy her. Like every player she had only her wits, her skill, and the tenuous protection of custom and reputation to restrain the merchants and the officials who ran Silili (always subject to the whims of the Temuengs) and ordered the lives of all who lived there.

Tari touched the ceramic chimes. The double clink was not loud, but it cut through the music. The dancers stopped and bowed, then stood waiting for her to speak, the plump one a little nervous but enough in command of herself to slide her eyes at Taguiloa, the thin one seeing no one and nothing but Blackthorn. Tari lifted a hand. "You saw, what do you say?"

"The hungry one."

Tari nodded. "When you have that hunger, it's easy to see it in others. If I were five years younger, I might want to kick her feet from under her." She turned to the two girls. "Deniza," she told the thin one, "see my bataj about buying you out. Rasbai, your gifts lie elsewhere, I am not the proper teacher for you. May I suggest . . . mmm . . . Atalai?" She dismissed them firmly, ignoring both Rasbai's scowl and Deniza's sudden glow. "Your student has shut his mouth. What'd you do to that little snake?"

He watched the two girls walk out with their silent chaperone and said nothing until they had time to get beyond hearing, then turned to stare coolly at the foreign woman. "Me?" he said, "I did nothing."

Her eyes opened a bit wider, the toes of her right foot nudged at the nape of his neck, tickled through the hair by his right ear. "This is Blackthorn, little love. Maybe you forget?" She dug at him with the nail of her big toe. "Harra? Would I ask in front of her if I didn't trust her? Fishbrain."

He swung round, caught hold of her ankle, danced his fingers along the henna'd sole of her foot. "Even a fishbrain knows Blackthorn." He let her pull her ankle free. "It's the truth. I did him nothing. He's happy contemplating my future broken bones."

"What?"

"Fist and a handful of his thugs are getting set to thump me some."

"You're very cheerful considering."

"Considering I've got some protection Fist and Yarm don't know about. I'm shucking Yarm the end of the week, going on tour soon as I can get it together. I've got a patron of sorts, who's financing me and providing that protection I mentioned."

"You're finally going to do it? The dances?"

"Uh-huh. I need a flute player." He scowled at the mat. "Funeral tomorrow. The last appearance I've got for a while. Yarm's out the next day. I'm not looking forward to that."

"I told you he was a bad idea."

"That you did, but I had no ears then."

"And nothing between them either."

He caught hold of a toe, pinched it lightly. "Flute player."

A sharp intake of breath, a moment's silence. Tari lay back with her eyes shut. He frowned at her, but before he could say anything, she spoke. "Ladji."

The ancient flute player got easily to his feet, came across the open airy room and dropped to his knees near the head of the divan. "Saör," he said tranquilly. He held his flute lightly across his thighs.

"You have a student, your sister's grandson I think it is. You know him, you know Taga. What do you think?" She opened her eyes. "It's a gamble, and the hillwolves are getting bold." She glanced at Taguiloa, lifted the corner of her mouth a fraction. "Rumor is once the Jamara lords and the Jamaraks are left behind, it's a dance with death." Delicate lift of a delicate brow, slow and smooth, a question to Taguiloa. "You're not given to taking those kinds of chances, little love."

"It's the hillwolves that better watch themselves." He hesitated, wondering exactly what he wanted to say, how much he wanted to tell. This was Blackthorn who read him better than he did himself. "My patron is a friendly witch with demon familiars." He turned so he was facing the foreign woman. "That is not for repeating."

She nodded, but said nothing.

The old man spoke. "Taga, when would you like to talk with Linjijan? And where?"

Blackthorn's toe nudged at Taguiloa's head again. "Will here do?"

"Since you offer." He rubbed his head gently against her foot. "This afternoon? I've got to start shaking the mix."

"Ladji?"

The old man looked past her at the wall. "Linjijan went out with his brothers this morning. After fish. He'll be returning with the sun. But he'll need sleep." He turned muddy amber eyes on Blackthorn and smiled, the wrinkles lifting and spreading. "And you, saör, prefer the afternoon."

"True, my eldest love," She made the deep gurgle that was her sort of laugh. "Taga. Dance for me, you. I've earned some entertaining, don't you think?"

He turned his head and kissed the smooth instep, then jumped to his feet. He kicked off his sandals and walked barefoot onto the woven straw mat, rubbed his hands down his sides, lifted a brow to Ladjinatuai, then began snapping his fingers, hunting for the rhythm that felt right for the mood he was in and the way his body felt. He looked over his shoulder at the foreign woman. "Play for me," he said. "With Ladji, if you will."

Ladjinatuai lifted his flute and began improvising music to the changing rhythms of Taga's fingers.

A few beats later, a soft laugh, and the lively metallic complex tones of stringed instrument came in, picking up the beat, playing fantasies around it, making a sound he'd never heard before.

He let the music work in him a while longer.

When he was ready, he began the first tumbling run, moving faster and faster, gathering the energy of the music into his blood and bone, ending the run with a double flip, landing, reversing direction without losing the impulse driving him, dropping, curling onto his shoulders, slowly unfolding his body until he was a spear pointed at the roof, breaking suddenly, the music breaking with him, a long swoop of the flute, a glittering cascade from the strings, his body flexed, rose and fell, wheeled and caracoled, improvised around the traditions of the female dancers, the male mimes and tumblers; he felt every move, all the pain and effort, yet at the same time he was flying, riding the sound.

Until a tiny shake, a hairline miscalculation, and he lost it, the music went on but his improvisation faltered. With a gasping laugh he sank onto his knees, then sat back on his heels, hands on thighs, breathing hard, sweat pouring down his face, into his eyes and mouth. He heard Blackthorn's gurgling laughter, the patter of her hands, but only at a distance; more important to him this moment was the music that wove on and on, the foreign woman and the old flute player working out their own magic until they achieved resolution and silence.

He swung on his knees to face the woman. "Who are you?"

"My name is Harra Hazhani."

"From the west?"

"A long way from, dancer."

"Why?"

"Chance, curiosity, who knows. I came with my father."

"Your father?"

"Dead." She plucked a discord from the strings. "An aneurism neither of us knew he had."

"Your people?"

"You wouldn't know them." She shrugged. "What does it matter?" Then, producing a soft buzzing sound from the instrument by pulling her hand gently along the strings, she stared past him. "I'm a long way from my mountains, dancer. The wind blew me here and dropped me. The day will come when I catch another and blow on. Rukka-nag. My people. You see, it means nothing to you and why should it?" She had a strong accent that was not unpleasant, especially in her honey-spice voice. As she spoke she made almost a song of the words, using the pads of her fingers to coax a muted music from the strings. Abruptly she lifted her hands from the instrument and laughed. "More prosaically, Saö Taguiloa, when my father dropped dead, Saöri Blackthorn took pity on me and gave me houseroom until I could find the kind of work I was willing to do." She took up the plectrum and plucked a questioning tune. "And have I, O man who makes music with his body? Have I?"

"Do you dance?"

"The dances of my people. And never so well as Blackthorn does hers."

"Show me." He moved off the mat to make way for her, seating himself once again at Tari's feet.

Harra Hazhani looked at him gravely, considering him, then she set her instrument aside and got gracefully to her feet. She wore black leather boots with high heels; a long skirt with a lot of material in it that swung about her ankles, a bright blue with crudely colorful embroidery in a band a handspan above the hem; a long-sleeved loose white blouse and a short tight vest laced up the front that seemed designed to emphasize high full breasts and a tiny waist. The blouse was gathered at wrists and neck by drawstrings tied in neat bows. She reached into a pocket in the skirt and pulled out a number of thin gold hoops, slid them over her hands so they clashed on her wrists when she lifted her arms over her head and began clapping out a strongly accented rhythm. Still clapping she began to whistle, a sound with a driving energy as crude to his ears as the colors and patterns in the embroidery on her clothing was to his eyes. She whistled just long enough for Ladjinatuai to pick up the tune, though the mode of her music was not that of his flute.

Her head went back; her arms curved so her hands were almost touching, then quivered so the gold hoops clashed slightly off the beat, then she was whirling round and round, her feet moving through an intricate series of steps. She danced pride and passion and joy—at least that was what he read into what he saw—then went suddenly still, a foot pointed, a leg a little forward, a straight slant visible through the drape of her skirt, her head thrown back, her arms up as if she would embrace the moon.

She broke position, grinned at him and went back to her cushion, dropped with energetic grace beside her instrument.

"What do you call that?" He pointed to the instrument.

"Daroud. A sort of distant cousin to a lute."

"You dance well enough."

"Thanks."

"You play a lot better."

"I know."

"Modest too."

"Like you."

"What would you do if a man started fondling you?"

"Depends. Official, patron or some lout in an Inn where we happened to be staying?"

"Start with the lout."

She tilted her head, scowled, put her hands on her hips, "Back off, lout." One hand shifted position so quickly it seemed to flicker. A short thin blade grew suddenly from her fingers; she held the hand close to her body and waited. "And if he didn't, he'd lose maybe some fingers, certainly some blood." She tossed the bright sliver of steel into the air, caught it and flipped it at the wall. It thudded home a hair from a small waterstain on the wood. She frowned, got up and retrieved the knife. "Kesker would pull my hair for botching a throw like that."

"Kesker?"

"My father's bodyguard until he got killed."

"Protecting your father?"

"No. Bloodfeud. We passed too close to his homeland."

"You've had a varied life."

"Very."

"That takes care of the lout. If you run into trouble for it, I'll back you, but try saying no first, will you?"

"Sure. Why not."

"Say a Jamar Lord has an itch for foreign bodies in his bed."

She grinned. "And I say, it's all right with me, honored Saöm, but I've got the pox so maybe you'd rather not."

"You don't look it."

"That's us foreign bints, can't tell about us."

"And if he says he doesn't believe you?"

"Then I do this." She began to whistle an odd little droning tune. He watched her a moment until she blurred and a total lassitude took hold of him. She stopped whistling and clapped her hands, the sharp sound jolting him awake. "Men are very suggestible in that state," she said calmly. "I'd tell him he wasn't at all interested in me and he should forget the whole thing including the whistling. My father was a mage. I was his best and most constant student."

He looked at her and began laughing so hard he fell over on the floor. When he recovered a little, he sat up, wiped at his eyes, caught Tari's astonished stare and almost began again. He sucked in a long breath, exploded it out. "If you want to come along, you're welcome, Harra Hazhani." He cleared his throat. "Though you might want to wait until you meet my patron before you make up your mind." He narrowed his eyes, examined her face, her hands, wondering how old she was.

"Twenty-three."

"You answer questions not asked?"

"Why waste time? You wanted to know."

"Keep out of my head, woman."

"No need to get in it. Your face told me; men are much alike, you know, at least on things like that."

"Uh-huh, you and the witch should have some interesting conversations."

"You make me curious. Who is she?"

"A foreigner like you."

"Should I know her?"

"I doubt it."

Tari Blackthorn stirred on the divan, nudged at him with her foot. "Go home, Taga. Now that you steal my treasure from me. Go home, summerfly and soothe the wasp in your nest." She made a soft snorting sound. "Don't come back, O ungrateful one, without a thank-gift to make up for taking all my afternoon. The second hour after midday and not a breath before." She gurgled. "Or I'll have my dancers tickle you into a mass of quivering jelly."

He trapped the prodding foot, woke laughter in her with knowing fingers, kissed the instep, then jumped to his feet and started for the door.

Before he reached it, she called out, "Bring your witch with you and let us see this wonder of wonders."

He waved a non-committal hand and plunged out the door before she could call him back, strode off along the winding path, whistling an approximation of Harra's dance tune, content with things as they were (except for Yarm and Yarm would cease to be a problem very soon); old Tungjii was sitting on his shoulder, he could almost feel hisser presence there. "So I light a batch of incense for you, O patron of my line, O bestower of joy and sorrow."

The doorguard let him out the gate and he strolled along the sun-dappled lane beneath the willows and the tall, rare mottled bamboo. A few wisps of fog were flowing in off the sea and the air had a nip to it that pleased him. The night would be foggy and Jaril was sure to come to him. Brann's house was ready with a discreet maid waiting to see if she pleased the new mistress. He sauntered through the Players' Quarter, wound deeper into Silili, heading up the mountain to the Temple, his mood mellowing until he was afloat on contentment and all men were brothers and all beasts had souls.

He drifted through the godons, the throng of traders from a thousand lands east and west. M'darjin, black men, ebony stick figures, heads shaven and enclosed in beaten bronze rings, bronze rings about their wrists and ankles, narrow bodies clad in voluminous robes, patterned in lines and blocks of black and white and sudden patches of pure color, blue, green, red, a vibrant purple. They brought ivory and scented woods and metal work of all kinds.

Western men and women—Phras, Suadi, Gallinasi, Eirsan, dozens of other sorts of men he couldn't name, pinkish skin, hair shading from almost white to the darkest of blacks, eyes blue, brown, green, yellow, mongrel hordes they were, none as pure as Hina. They came with clocks and other mechanical devices, saddles and fine leatherwork, books, wines, fine spices. The women especially were spice hunters adept at worming into the odd places where you found the rarest of the spices. Gem traders, art dealers, dream sellers. Anything that men or women would buy.

Harpish clad in leather top to toe in spite of the warmth of Silili's climate, faces shrouded in black leather cowls with only the eyes cut out, always in groups of three, never alone, dealers in mage's wares and witch's stock, mystical books, rumor and small gods.

Vioshyn in layer upon layer of violently clashing patterned cloth, selling sea-ivory and mountain furs, carved chests and exotic powders, also most of the more common drugs.

Felhiddin, small, thin, a walnut brown, clad mostly in the blue tattoos that covered every inch of visible skin, skimpy loincloths and sandals, men and women alike, though any stranger who mistook the meaning of the bare breasts got the metal claws the women wore in the meat of the offending hand and threatening growls from any other Felhiddin nearby as they swirled about him like a dog pack set to attack. Trading in exotic nuts and herbs, scaled hides of strange beasts, furs in fine bright colors, metallic reds and greens, a hundred shades of blue, bowls and other objects carved from jewelwoods with great simplicity but exquisite shape.

Henermen trading nothing but their services and their herds of strong ugly Begryers, hauling whatever their hirers desired inland along the land route to the west.

Mercenary fighters of all races and both sexes.

Street magicians, dancers, acrobats, musicians, beggars. Woda watermen and porters, squat, broad, bowed legs, calling their services in loud singsong voices.

Priests. Servants to many gods and demons. Mostly Hina, native to the ground, born on Selt to die on Selt, born in the uplands that had once been Hina-ruled but now lay in the tight fists of Jamara lords, here now as pilgrims to the great Temple on Selt's central mountain or teaching in the priest schools attached to the Temple.

Mages, small men and large, small women and large, all races all shapes, some pausing awhile in Silili during their enigmatic wanderings, some there for the day, changing ships, touching foot to ground only to leave it again, some there to study in the Temple schools, some just nosing through the teeming market.

Fog was edging up from the water and the streets were beginning to empty, the foreigners flowing out of them into the joyhouses or the Inns of the Strangers' Quarter according to the hungers that most clamored to be satisfied.

Taguiloa waved to those who leaned from joyhouse windows calling his name, shrugged off invitations. He was popular among the women of the night because of his stamina and his delight in them and their bodies. It was his intention to appear as one who walked lightly and with laughter through the world; his fears and blue spells he kept strictly to himself. He was a good fella, a pleasant considerate lover, a gambler who lost and won with cheerful equanimity, a friend who didn't vanish when trouble came down, so there were many men and women to wave and call his name, and few knew it was as much calculation as nature, as hard-won as Blackthorn's beauty, a product of much pain and rage and thought. When Gerontai died, he wept and shuddered in Blackthorn's arms and she shut herself away with him a day and a night, though this meant she had to deny her current patron and had to coax him into complaisance with a masterly performance of illness. A sickness in which she seemed frail and suffering, but ten times as lovely and desirable as before, perhaps because of her momentary unattainability. From where he was concealed Taguiloa watched with amazement and appreciation, seeing how she took what would have destroyed a lesser woman and made it work to her advantage. He left her and shut himself in his master's house, his now, shut himself away from everyone and thought long and hard about how his life should go, coming from that wrestling match with a sketch of the man he wanted to be, eighteen and determined to climb as high in his way as Blackthorn had in hers.

He ran up the steps of the Temple Way, reached the Temple Plaza, turned and looked out across the city and the bay.

The shops were being shuttered, the paper windows of the living quarters above them glowed a dark amber just visible as night drifted down on Selt. Torches and lampions flared in the Night Quarter, the noises of the night came to him, tinkle of strings, soar of flutes, laughs, shouts, a fragment of a song. The Strangers' Quarter was quieter, the only lights the torches that glimmered before the Inns and taverns and noodle shops. The docks were dark and deserted except for the guard bands with their polelamps and rattles. Out on the water the Woda-an were lighting up lanterns and cook fires, too far away for him to hear more than a few mushy sounds, the blat of a horn, a wild raucous shout or two. He could see dark shapes passing the lanterns, merging and parting, some moving fast, jaggedly, some slowly, sinuously, a shadow play of dark and light that fascinated him for a while, wisps of images for another dance fluttering unformed in his head. The ghosts of the drowned and murdered came oozing from the water and the ground, blown by the wind like scraps of smoke. Ignoring the Temuengs, *it's a good place to be,* he thought, *and I am a man with the luck god riding my shoulder. Time to pay my debt, eh Tungjii?*

He went into the Temple, moved past the Godalau and her companion gods and stopped before one of the smallest figures, the little luck whose belly was shiny from the hundreds, no, thousands of hands that had rubbed it, a mostly naked little man/woman with fat big-nippled breasts and a short thick penis, left eye winking in a merry face. Taguiloa bowed, patted the round little belly, dropped coins in the offering bowl and lit a handful of incense sticks. Feeling more than a little drunk from contemplating the possibilities in his future, he poked the sticks in the sandbowl, squatted and watched the sweet smoke swirl up about the god. After a moment he laughed, jumped to his feet, did a wheeling run, a double somersault, flipped into a handstand then over onto his feet, then he was running from the Temple, laughter still bubbling in his blood, the luck god still riding his shoulder, giggling into his ear.

Jaril materialized from the fog, walked down the Temple Way stairs beside him, saying nothing, just there. Taguiloa nodded to him and continued his careful march downward; the steps were slick with condensation and worn by generations of feet. To break a leg here would be thumbing his nose at the god on his shoulder and an invitation to a cascade of evil luck. When he reached the bottom, he smiled down at his small silent companion. "Ladji and Blackthorn offer Linjijan, Ladji's grand-nephew as our flute player. Blackthorn wants to meet Brann." He hesitated, lifted a hand, let it fall. "I told them a little about her and you. They won't say anything, Jaril. Oh yes, there's a foreign woman too, a musician and the daughter of a mage. She's joining the troupe. I think. Tomorrow, two hours after midday. Would your companion be willing to come? I've found a house. A few steps from mine, a maid there for Brann if she wants to keep her. The girl will be discreet. We can get your companion moved in tomorrow morning if she decides to take the house. You want to see it? Come along then."

Brann came through the wall-gate, not at all the woman he'd seen that morning. Obviously she'd decided not to show forth as Hina, wisely so, he thought. The Shipmaster was right, Hina ways weren't easily acquired. Her hair was hanging loose, not curling but undulating gracefully out from her face, black as night, cloud soft. She wore a cap of linked gold coins with strings of coins hanging beside her face, a long loose robe of black silk embroidered with birds and beasts from Hina tales. Her skin was darkened to an olive flushed pink on the cheeks, her mouth a warm rose, her green eyes wide and gemlike, her face as devoid of expression as the godmasks in the Temple. A brindle hunting bitch pranced beside her, prickears twitching, crystal eyes filled with a dancing light that said Yaril was enjoying herself.

For a moment Taguiloa felt uneasy before this trio, though he was used to ghosts fluttering about and gods roaming the world. Now and then someone would see the Godalau swimming through the waters of the outer bay, her long fingers like rays from the moon combing the waves, her fish tail like limber jade flipping through air and water, churning both. Or Geidranay big as a mountain squatting on a mountainside tending the trees. He'd seen a dragon break a long drought, undulating laughter it was, flashes of reds and golds as the sun glittered off its scales, a memory of beauty so great the ragged boy digging for clams forgot to breathe. The little gods, Sessa who found lost things, Sulit the god of secrets, Pindatung the god of thieves and pickpockets, all the rest of them, they scampered like cheerful mice from person to person, coming unasked, leaving without warning, a capricious, treacherous and highly courted clutch of godlings. You could make bargains with them and if you were clever enough even profit from them. If you weren't clever enough and brought disaster on yourself and your folk, well that was your fault; if you got greedy and overstepped or fearful and failed to keep your wits honed you might find yourself reduced to night-soil collector or beggar with juicy sores to exploit.

Taguiloa walked in silence with the woman, boy and bitch, contemplating his choices. When Tungjii gave, you used the luck or lost it and more. The time he was still fussing about being obligated to a Temueng, Gerontai impressed that on him and to underline the lesson told him Raskatak's story.

Raskatak was a fisherman with a small boat and miserable luck who brought in just enough fish to keep him from abandoning the craft and seeking some other kind of work. One bright day he was out in his boat alone on a becalmed sea, his lines overboard while he patched his sail. It had nearly split up the middle in the sudden squall that separated him from the other boats and left him wallowing between swells that rapidly flattened out as the wind stopped dead and the sun rose higher and higher until it was beating remorselessly on the ocean. There was nothing touching his lines, they hung loose over the side, even the boat sounds had died away until the noise the awl made punching through the canvas seemed as loud as a large fish breaking water, though none did for miles about.

Overhead, sundragon burned and undulated, white and gold, great mother-of-pearl eyes turning and turning. And on his forward shoulders Tungjii rode, hisser plump buttocks accommodated in a hollow the dragon made for himmer. Waving a fan gently before hisser face, heesh looked down at the wretched little boat and grinned suddenly, broadly, reached into the glitter about the dragon, twisted hisser dainty hand in a complicated round, opened hisser fist and let a scatter of gold coins drop into the boat, watching with casual interest to see if they would hit the fisherman on his head and kill him, miss the boat altogether and be lost in the sea, or land beside the man in a clinking shining pile. Tungjii had no leaning toward any of those outcomes, heesh was merely watching to see how chance would work out.

The coins came clunking down, heavy rounds that landed in a little pile beside Raskatak's bare feet, one of them bouncing off his big toe, crushing the bone. He gaped at the coins, his big bony hands stilled on the rotten canvas. After a minute he put the canvas aside and scowled at his reddened toe. He lifted his foot and put it heavily on his knee. He touched the toe with clumsy fingers, grunted at the pain. Still ignoring the gold, he searched around in his sea chest, drew out a flat piece of bone, broke off a bit of it, bound it to his toe with a bit of rag, then a twist of line. He put his foot down with the same heavy care. Only then did he pick up one of the coins and look it over, test it with his teeth. He sat staring at it as if he didn't understand what it was. Moving with the same stolid deliberation he picked up each of the coins, tested each of them the same way and put it away in his sea chest. When he finished that he looked up, searching the sky for the origin of the shower of gold. What he saw was the glitter and burn of the noon sun. He hawked and spat over the side, went back to sewing up the sail. Gold or no gold, he wasn't going to get home without a working sail.

He finished the seam and raised the sail, but the wind was still absent. The canvas hung limp, not even slatting against the mast. He sat waiting, his eyes half shut, dreaming of what he was going to do with the gold.

As if to prove that miracles never occur singly, a school of fish struck the hooks on his lines and he spent the next two hours hauling them in, dropping the lines back until his boat was alive with flopping glistening silversides and the moment the school passed on, a fresh breeze sprang up and set the wretched little boat racing for Selt. For the first time ever he came in early and alone and got premium prices on his fine fat fish. He went back to the tiny hovel he'd built of ancient sails and bits of driftwood on a handful of land he rented from a distant cousin. He counted the coins over and over, even when it was only by feel after his fish oil lamp sputtered dry. And he counted the silver and copper coins the day's catch had brought, ten times the sum he usually made. Fearing that the gold might disappear as strangely as it had come, fearing too that the thieves that lived around him might smell it out and steal it from him, forgetting no thief of reasonable intelligence would come poking through his bits and pieces, he buried the gold under the agglomeration of sticks and rope he used for a bed, then spent a good part of the night nursing a jug of cheap wine and trying to ignore the pain in his toe while he dreamed of great feasts and high-class dancing girls and fine silk robes and his cousins bowing respectfully before him and seeking his advice and begging favors of him which he granted or refused with gracious nobility.

In the morning he washed his toe, bound some cobwebs and chicken dung about it and tied on another rag. Without much thought, acting from old habit, he rose with the dawn, got dressed, went limping down to the water and went out again in his boat. Again he had great luck. As if his hooks were magnets, he called the fish to them. Again he filled the boat so soon he was the first back and got the best price.

It being the way of the stupid, he saw himself as clever, he saw what was happening as an outcome of his superior worth. Though he was no less a silent man he began holding himself with great pride (not noticing that children followed behind him, mocking him). The gold coins stayed where they were, buried beneath his bed. He dreamed the same dreams night after night, but in the morning he left the dreams behind and went out on his boat as he had since he was old enough to hold a line. He sat alone in the boat whispering to himself, saying: if I spend gold, they'll want to know where it comes from, they'll send thieves to steal it from me, they'll send men to kill me. So the gold stayed under his bed, the dreams stayed in his head. His foot got worse, the toe swelling and turning black. His catch went back to what it was before, a whole day's work hardly enough to pay his land, buy his meals and a jug of cheap wine to kill the pain in his foot.

On the sixth day a squall caught his boat before he got more than a few lengths from the shore, reducing the wretched thing to a hodgepodge of shattered planks and timbers. It took him all day to gather the bits and pieces, then he went looking for driftwood so he could cobble the boat back together; he had more than enough gold for a dozen such boats, but the thought of spending it never entered his head. He worked on the boat all day, then went home to eat and dream some more. In the morning he couldn't get out of bed, his whole foot was black, his leg swollen, his body damp with fever.

By the end of the week he was dead.

This is the lesson, Gerontai told Taguiloa: Use your luck or it rots like Raskatak's toe.

Linjijan was a smiling amiable boy, nineteen or twenty, skinny, hands chapped and callused from the labor on a fishing boat, keeping in spite of that the tender agility of his great-uncle's hands. Taguiloa met his mild uncurious gaze and groaned within. The boy seemed as incapable of keeping himself as a day-old baby. Then he saw the way Blackthorn, Brann and Harra were smiling at him, the half-exasperated, half-adoring smile of a mother for a mischievous but well-loved child—and changed his mind. Linjijan was one of the fortunate of the earth. As long as he had his music, he'd be content and whatever he needed to survive and play that music would come unasked into his hands. Women and men alike would care for him, protect him, love him even when they were furious at him. Taga sighed but promised old Tungjii more incense and a free performance on the Luckday festival. He listened to Linjijan play and sighed again, moved quietly to stand beside the old piper. "Thanks," he said dryly.

The old man stretched his mouth in a tight-lipped smile, savoring the ambiguity in the word. He snapped his fingers. Linjijan stopped playing and came to squat beside him. "You want to go with him?" Ladji nodded at Taguiloa.

Linjijan nodded. He hadn't said a word so far, even to his great-uncle, greeting him with a smile and a nod.

"That's it then. Come." The old man retreated to the far side of the room and sat with his back against a wall, Linjijan beside him.

Tari stirred on her divan, her eyes fixed on Brann. She'd focused on the woman's face the moment Taguiloa brought her in, had been glancing repeatedly at her as Taguiloa dealt with Linjijan; now she gave over any pretense of interest in the others. "Saör Brann," she said. "Taga tells me you will be reading past and future for the countryfolk. He tells me you're a witch, really a witch. Read for me." She looked blindly about. "What do you need, gada sticks? fire and shell? crystal? a bowl of water? Tell me what you need and I'll have it brought."

Brann came across the room to kneel beside the divan, the brindle bitch moving beside her with silent feral grace. "If you will give me your hand, saöri Blackthorn." Tari extended her hand, Brann cradled it on hers. "Yaril," she said, "Let's make it real this time."

The bitch shimmered into a gold glow which rose and hovered a moment over Blackthorn then sank into her. Taguiloa remembered it with a shiver at the base of his spine and wondered briefly if he should interfere. He glanced at Brann's intent face and held his tongue. The glimmer emerged from Tari and coalesced into a small blonde girl. She stood beside Brann, murmured in her ear for several minutes, then she retreated to the end of the divan and sank out of sight.

Brann shivered, her composure broke suddenly, briefly. Pain and fear and pity and anger flowed in waves across her face. She sat very still, as if frozen for a moment, then the mask was back; she opened her eyes, drew a forefinger across Tari's palm.

"Not even the gods know for certain what the morrow brings," she said quietly. "Their guesses might be better than a mortal's but that's only because they've had a longer time to watch the cycling of the seasons and the foolishness of man. When I read the fates of men and women, I will give them what pleases them and phrase it vaguely enough that whatever happens they can twist the words to fit as they will. They want to be fooled and will do the greater part of the work for me." Her voice flowed on, gentle and soothing. "Yongala laughing told me folk hold fast to their dreams even when their reason tells them they are fools. Tari Blackthorn, dancer on fire, do you desire that sort of reading or the truth of what you fear?"

Tari trembled, closed her eyes. "What do you know?"

"Shall I speak of it here?"

"These are my friends. I wouldn't ask if I didn't expect a real answer."

Brann looked at the hand she still held, set it on the black velvet cover. Watching her closely, his curiosity a hunger in him, Taguiloa saw her gather herself; a cold knot in his stomach, he waited for her answer. "This is what I know," she said, her voice held level with visible difficulty. "Some days every step is agony and effort. Your ankles and knees swell and throb sometimes beyond bearing. When you are in the dance you forget that pain but are nearly crippled by it once the dance is over. You fear the end of your ability to dance. Six months ago you sought solace from pain in poppymilk, now you find yourself slaved to it and view that slavery with horror but cannot escape it." She turned away from Tari's drawn face, looked over her shoulder at Taguiloa. In spite of her efforts her own face quivered; she closed her eyes, tried to calm herself and when she spoke her voice was flat and dead. "Saöm, I will not do this for you in the villages, it would call too much attention to me. And I don't think I. . . ." She faced round again, moved on her knees to the foot of the divan. "Yaril, Jaril, come to me, I need you."

The blond boy came from the shadows, put his hand on her left shoulder; the hand melted through the black silk and into the flesh beneath. The blond girl came from behind the divan and stood at her right shoulder, the hand melting through the black silk of the robe and sinking into the flesh beneath. Brann reached out and brushed aside the many layers of fragile silk and took Blackthorn's ankle in her hand.

Taguiloa saw then what he'd overlooked before. The ankle was swollen a little, thickened, stiff. Tari watched with fear and anguish as Brann brushed her fingers across the swelling. "It is only beginning," she said, cleared her throat, took a breath, then went on. "Were it to

proceed, you would be unable to walk five years from now." She smiled
a wide urchin's grin full of joy and mischief. "Slya be blessed, O
dancer, it will not proceed." She closed her eyes and held the ankle
cradled between her hands.

Tari's eyes flew open wider. "Heat," she whispered.

Brann said nothing, did not seem to hear. After a moment she lowered that foot to the velvet and lifted the other.

Taguiloa watched, amazed, his anxiety and the sharp fear aroused by
the witch's words dissipating as the woman's long strong hands moved
from ankles to knees not bothering to push aside the layered silk robe,
from knees to hips, then wrists, elbows, shoulders. Humming softly,
Brann moved her hands from the top of Tari's head down along her
body to the henna'd soles of her lovely feet, the children moving with
her, bonded to her, flesh to flesh. Then she sat back on her heels and
sighed.

The children moved away from her, their small fine hands sliding
from flesh and silk. Yaril shimmered a moment and was again a brindle
bitch lying beside her. Jaril went to squat beside Taguiloa.

Tari's face flushed then paled. She sat up, moved one foot then the
other, moved her wrists, bent one leg at the knee, straightened it, bent
the other leg, straightened it. Her hands were shaking. Her breath
came sharp and fast. She opened her mouth, shut it, couldn't speak,
closed her eyes, pressed her hands against her ribs, sucked in a long
breath, let it out. "And the poppymilk?"

"You're free of that too."

"There's not gold enough in the world. . . ."

Brann shrugged. "Oh well, gold." She got to her feet, stretched,
yawned. "This isn't what I'm going to feed the farmers, no and no, tell
them what they want to hear and make them shiver just enough." She
grinned. "And scare the bones out of any hillwolves stupid enough to
attack."

Taguiloa looked around. Harra was gazing at Brann with an expression of lively interest, her full lips pursed for a whistle, but not
whistling. Ladji was sliding his ancient flute between thumb and forefinger, smiling at nothing much, his body gone rubbery with his private
relief. He was apparently the only one who'd known of Tari's growing
pain. Linjijan was gazing dreamily at nothing, his fingers moving on his
thighs as if he practiced modes of fingering for music he heard inside
his head.

Jaril touched Taguiloa's arm. He looked down. "What is it?"

"You wanted a boy to play the drums."

"You volunteering?"

Jaril shook his head. "Too boring. But I found a boy. He doesn't have to be Hina?"

Taguiloa looked around the room. Mage's daughter from so far west he'd never heard of her people. Linjijan, comfortably Hina. Brann the changeling witch, once of Arth Slya, now of nowhere. Yaril and Jaril, who knew what they were? "One more foreigner, who'd notice." He laughed. "How long will it take to get him here . . . ?" He turned to Tari, spread his hands. "Sorry, I shouldn't be so free with your house."

Tari Blackthorn waved a slim hand. "I won't say I owe you, but you may bring all the world in here and I won't complain."

"He's waiting outside." Jaril darted for the door.

Taguiloa strolled across to the divan, knelt beside Tari, took her hand in his. "There was a time when I thought I was running this thing." He lifted her hand, touched his lips to the wrist, cradled the hand against his cheek. "You didn't tell me."

"I wasn't telling myself." She eased her hand free. "Taga my tinti," her voice was a whisper that reached only him, "don't you see how odd it is, all this? This collection of mage-touched strangers? Why are they being pulled together? And who is doing it?" She bent a finger, touched the knuckle to his chin. "She worries me, your patron, I don't understand her. I shouldn't say it after what she did for me, but be careful of her, summerfly. Why is she doing this?"

"She has her reasons."

"And you know them. Why am I even more worried for you? No, don't fidget so, little love. I won't ask more questions." She ran her forefinger around the curve of his ear and down his neck. "Your drummer comes, Taga." Laughter shook in her voice.

Taguiloa swung round. A m'darjin boy stood uncertainly in the doorway clutching drums half as big as he was, ten, maybe twelve, blue-black skin, hair a skim of springs coiled close to his skull, huge brown eyes. His hands and feet were borrowed from a bigger body, his arms thin as twigs with bumpy knobs where the joints were.

"His name is Negomas," Jaril said. "His father was a m'raj shaman and he did something, Negomas doesn't know what but it was bad and it killed him and the rest of the m'darjin won't have anything to do with Negomas now, it's like he caught something from his father and could infect them with it, but that's not true, I checked him out and you know I'm good at that." He tugged the boy forward.

Negomas grinned nervously. His body was taut, quivering with eagerness and hope.

"Your drums?" Taguiloa said.

"My drums." He grinned wider and mischief brightened the huge brown eyes. "I grow into them." He waggled one of his large bony hands. "With a bit of time," he finished, winced as Jaril kicked him in the ankle. "Saöm," he added politely.

"Play them for me. Something I can move to." He stepped out of his sandals, moved to the center of the mat and stood waiting, shaking himself, a long ripple from ankles to head, wrists to shoulders. He smiled toward the boy, then unfocused his eyes and concentrated on listening with ears and body both.

He heard a blurred shiver of sound, then some tentative staccato taps that had unusual overtones, a sonority similar to the deeper notes of Harra's daroud. The drums began speaking with more authority. He kept up his loosening moves, listening until the sound slid under his skin and throbbed in his blood; he flexed his arms, twisted his body from side to side, then let the music lift him into a handless backflip that developed into a series of bending stretching kinetic movements, alternating high and low; he reveled in the drumsong beating in blood, bone and muscle, was unsurprised when two flutes joined in, singing in none of the usual modes, producing a strong harsh music, then the daroud came in, picking up its own version of the melodic line, adding a greater tension to the blend by tugging at the beat of the drums. The dance went on and on until Taguiloa collapsed to the mat, sweating and laughing, exhausted but flying high, his panting laughter mingling with the applause and laughter from Tari and Brann, whoops from Jaril and the sweating m'darjin boy. Then silence, filled with the sound of Taguiloa's breathing.

He fell back till he lay flat on the straw. His hands burned, his bones ached and he'd collected bruises and sore muscles from moving in ways he hadn't tried before. He turned his head, lifted a heavy hand to push sweat-sticky hair off his face. "You'll do, Negomas." He yawned, swallowed. "Anyone I need to talk to about you?"

The boy shook his head, moved his fingers on the drumheads.

Taguiloa looked at Jaril, raised his brows.

Jaril shook his head.

Taguiloa pushed up until he was sitting with his arms draped over his knees. "You understand you won't be my student but only part of the troupe?" When the boy nodded, he went on, "I'm sorry but that's the way the world says things have to be; I need a Hina boy. If ever I can find the right one. Jaril, fetch whatever the boy's got, move him into my house and make sure Yarm doesn't try anything."

Jaril snorted, looked pointedly at Brann.

Brann sighed. "Taguiloa is master of this motley group, my friend. We don't argue with the boss, at least not in public even if he's being more than usually foolish." She chuckled, then sobered. "You know what Yarm is like. For the good of our purpose, get Negomas settled, then take him out for something to eat." She smiled. "I know you could fry Taga's liver if you chose, he knows it by now or he's a lot stupider than he looks, we all know it. And we know you're going to do nothing of the kind."

Jaril walked over to Negomas, jerked his head at the door, then strolled out with an air of going where he chose at the speed he chose to go. Negomas picked up his drums, winked over his shoulder at Taguiloa, then followed the blond boy out.

Brann got to her feet, stood looking around. "I'm glad it's you who's got to pull this mix of geniuses together." She nodded to Blackthorn, smiled a general farewell and swept out the door.

Yarm looked up as Taguiloa stepped through the door. "Where you been? And what's that dirty m'darjin doing here?"

"None of your business. And speaking of dirty, this house is a garbage dump."

"If you want neat, hire a girl. You can afford it," Yarm said sullenly. "I'm not your servant."

"You're not my wife either, which is just as well because you'd be fit only for drowning if you were a woman. Not a servant? Boils on your ass, you're what I say you are. As of now, that's nothing. Get." He jerked a thumb at the door.

"Now?" Yarm's voice cracked with surprise and rage. "You're putting that foreigner in my place?"

"Get out. Now. Tomorrow morning you can collect your gear, but I've had all I'm going to take from you."

"Fist will. . . ."

"Out." He leaped at the boy, caught the collar of his shirt, half shoved, half lifted him across the room and out of the house, set his foot on the boy's backside and sent him in a stumbling sprawl down the leaf-littered path.

Yarm lay dazed for a moment or so, then scrambled to his feet and came screaming at Taguiloa. Who slapped his face vigorously several times, swept his feet from under him with a leg scythe, caught an arm in a punish hold and ran him down the path and out into the street. He stood watching as Yarm slunk off, even his back full of threat though he didn't dare turn and voice his thoughts.

"He still doesn't quite believe you're serious."

Taguiloa looked down. Jaril stood beside him, his blond hair shining in the sunlight.

"I'm like to have company tonight."

"Uh-huh. We'll be there too. Yaril's been getting bored, she says I have all the fun."

Taguiloa stood in the center of the bedroom and looked about him. He'd finished packing up Yarm's things and a ratty lot they were, the boy had no pride. Blackthorn was right, he thought, as she always is. Yarm had a beautiful slim body, limber as a sea snake's, and the face of a young immortal which the women in the audiences sighed over. He also had a good sense of timing, he learned quickly everything Taguiloa taught him, but he was spoiled, lazy, whining, dishonest about small things and large unless he thought he would be caught, jealous of Taguiloa's time and attention to a degree that had soon become unbearable. Not a sexual jealousy, that would have been far easier to handle, but something else Taga couldn't understand or explain.

He put the packets outside with a feeling of relief. This house used to be the place where he rested, practiced, meditated. It was filled with memories of his loved teacher, memories of peace and contentment after the turmoil in the streets. Gerontai had taught him much besides tumbling and juggling. He'd been hoping for much the same relationship with Yarm but was quickly disillusioned. He'd let Yarm move in with him, not seeing the speculative gleam in Yarm's black eyes. A measuring cold calculation powered by malice and spite and a like for hurting. A passionate need to hold and own. Fire and ice and neither of them comfortable to live with. Taguiloa stood in his doorway rubbing his back across the edge of the jamb, feeling relaxed and clean for the first time in the three years Yarm had lived here.

The Wounded Moon was a ragged crescent rising in the east, its lowest horn just touching the Temple roof. I'm not going to wait here staring at the wall like a fool. Negomas was spending the night with Brann, no need to worry about him. "Jaril," Taga yelled.

An owl circled above, hooted what sounded like laughter, came swooping down, landing beside Taguiloa as the blond boy. A moment later a nighthawk screeched, came slipping down and landed as the silverbright small girl. "What's the fuss?" Her voice was water clear, melodious.

Taguiloa bowed. "Welcome, damasaör."

"Hm. Well?"

Feeling as if he faced the ghost of his great-aunt who was mamasaör to the whole family and by repute tougher than a Temueng pimush, Taguiloa cleared his throat. "I was going to visit some friends, thought your brother might like to come along."

She snorted (though Jaril had informed Taguiloa that his kind didn't actually breathe and therefore couldn't play the flute). "And let Fist burn you out?"

Taguiloa laughed before he thought, then expected her to scold him for disrespect, but she seemed unperturbed, just stood waiting for him to explain himself. "Fist has better sense," he said. "Even on a foggy night, start a fire here and half of Silili would go. Bad enough to have Hina on his tail when some ghost or other named him as the fire-starter, something that big would bring in Temueng enforcers and maybe even an Imperial Censor. He'd be skinned alive and hung to rot. His family too and everyone who helped him and their families." Taga flung his arms out. "And even when he was dead, the ghosts he made would torment the ghost he was. I'm not worth all that. No way. Not even for dearest Yarm the family hope." He smiled at the little girl. "Want to come along?"

She gazed a moment at her brother, then nodded. "Why not. This ghost business is weird."

Taguiloa stared at her. "Your kind don't die?"

"Oh they die all right. And stay dead. Ghosts? No way."

"They don't have souls?"

"That's something they've been arguing about since eldest ancestor learned to talk." She shrugged. "A waste of time and breath far as I can see." She watched as Jaril blurred then changed into a Hina boy. "This is the first reality we've seen where there are ghosts you can actually talk to." She shimmered and changed to a small golden lemur, then hopped up to ride her brother's shoulder.

"Well," Jaril said, "she couldn't come as a little girl, that'd make your friends uncomfortable."

Taguiloa pulled the door shut, turned the key in the lock and dropped the metal bit into a pocket, then started walking toward the gate through the rustling foliage of bushes he reminded himself he'd have to water in the morning. "You change your shapes so why couldn't she be another boy?"

The lemur gave a chittering sound that sounded indignant. Jaril grinned and patted her paw. "But Yaril's a female," he said. "She couldn't do that."

"Why not?" Curiosity driving him, Taguiloa persisted. "It's only appearance after all. If I dressed myself in woman's robes, painted my face, wore a wig and practiced a bit, I could make a fairly convincing appearance as a woman, though my real nature wouldn't change at all."

The boy turned those strange crystal eyes on him; when Taguiloa was sure he wasn't going to answer, he did. "The inner and outer are one with us. If we try to change the nature of the outer, we deny and warp the inner. So—" he grinned, an impudent urchin grin that acknowledged and mocked Taguiloa's voice—"that we seem children should tell you we are children."

"How old are you"

"Hard to say. Time is funny. Six or seven hundreds of your years. Something like that."

"Children?"

"We grow slowly."

"Seems like." He tapped a finger on Jaril's head, relieved to find it solid, warm and a little oily. "Talking about weird, I find you changechildren stranger than any ghost I've ever seen."

They wandered through the night quarter, sharing jugs of wine, the lemur a popular little beast with her smooth soft fur and dainty manners; they got evicted from a few places when some weak-stomached drinkers refused to tolerate an animal drinking from men's wine bowls and others who liked the beast somewhat more than they liked the objectors jumped the objectors and started breaking the furniture; they visited a joyhouse, Jaril pouting and Yaril sulking when Taguiloa wouldn't let them go upstairs with him; they settled for entertaining the joygirls, Jaril clapping his hands and dancing, Yaril dancing with him, a small and elegant figure, bowing and swaying with the most wonderful grace, golden fur glimmering in the lamplight. The lemur even played a simple tune on a gittern abandoned in a corner. They stayed there quite a while even after Taguiloa rejoined them, but eventually wandered on to watch a fight in the middle of the street, throw the bones with a circle of men on the sidewalk, losing and winning with equal enthusiasm, all three savoring the noise and activity about them, loud, raucous, mostly illegal and immoral, but full of vigor and the beat of life. Now and then Taguiloa got a jolt when he looked at Jaril's eager young face, then he'd tell himself, seven hundred years, Tungjii's tits and tool, and forget worrying about corrupting the boy.

Sometime after midnight, he doused his head with ice-water, looked blearily about, collected the children and started threading through the narrow streets heading toward the Players' Quarter.

They left the lamplit streets behind, left the noise and warmth and good feeling. Taguiloa's shivered, the water in his hair making him cooler though it didn't do much to clear the fog out of his head. "I shouldn't have had that last jug?"

"Yah." Jaril shook himself like a large wet dog. Yaril-lemur leaped off his shoulder, shimmered and was a large owl beating upward at a steep angle. "Yaril's going to keep an eye on our backs."

"Someone's following us?"

"Not yet. Probably waiting for us. Tell me about Fist. What scares him?"

"Not much. Hanging. Temueng torturers. Dragons. He swears he won't hang, the enforcers will have to kill him to take him." His footsteps sounded like gongs in his ears. Jaril's feet made no sound at all. "He's cunning, knows when to back off, runs strings of smugglers, snatchthieves, thugs, I don't know what all."

"He figures he can handle you, a little pain and fear and you do what he says?"

"Yeah. I'd figure the same, were it not for you changechildren. Why else would I put up with Yarm for so long?"

"And he's afraid of dragons?"

"A few years back, or so I'm told, Fist had a diviner read the gada sticks for him. The man told him to watch out for dragon fire."

"Ah. Maybe Yaril and me, we can make that reading come true." Jaril blurred and a twin to Yaril's owl went sailing up, narrowly avoiding tangling itself in the branches of pomegranate growing out over a wall.

Taguiloa stood blinking after him. "I'll never get used to that." As he prowled along through the shadows of the narrow lane, he wondered what had got into the changechild. Too much wine, for one thing. He thought about that and was more confused than before. They didn't have innards like normal folk, you could see that when they were smears of light. But Jaril had picked up a taste for wine rambling the night with Taguiloa and disposed of it somehow, managing to get nicely elevated on it, maybe it was like ghosts drinking the fragrance of wine and tea and cooked foods. What did changechildren eat? Jaril never said anything about that. Doesn't matter, he's a friend, can eat whatever he wants, doesn't bother me; good kid, Jaril, even if sometimes he scares the shit outta me.

Slowly sobering, he kept to the shadows and moved as silently as he could toward his own gate. Fist wasn't going to kill him, just break an arm or leg or both and tromp on him a lot and repeat the tromping as soon as he healed unless he gave in and took Yarm back. Taga cursed the Emperor's boils or whatever it was that stirred him up and made him grab at everything in sight. With the usual number of enforcers about and the Tekora's guard up to strength, Fist would have settled for a minor beating. Tungjii and Jah'takash alone knew what he'd get up to these days.

A horned owl came swooping down and changed to a blond child. Yaril. She came close to him, whispered, "Some men in the garden waiting for you. Yarm is there, two-legged elephant beside him, a couple others with clubs."

"Fist himself." Taga swore under his breath. "That's bad."

"I thought so. Mind if Jaril and me, we burn up a little of your garden?"

"What?"

"I remember what you said about fire. We won't let it get away."

Taga stared at her, then grinned. "Dragons."

"Well?"

"In a good cause, why not." He scowled and swore again. "Fist. Seshtrango gift him with staggers and a horde of rabid fleas."

Yaril giggled, looked up, giggled again, shimmered and was a replica in green and silver of the small crimson and gold dragon undulating past over Taga's head.

Jaril-dragon flipped his streamered tail in airy greeting.

Taga grinned up at the baby dragons. "You're drunk both of you." Silent laughter bubbled in his blood. The serpentine shapes waved laughter at him, wove laughter-knots about each other, exulting in a form that made them drunker than any amount of wine would. They settled down before the enchantment of their beauty wore off him (he was wine drunk too, far more than he should be) and started off toward his house.

He gave them a few moments then followed after, thinking they were going to impress the shit out of those thugs waiting like innocent babes in his shrubbery. The dragons moved swiftly ahead of him, darting in swift undulations toward his garden. He strolled along the lane between the high wood-and-stone walls that shut in the house-and-garden compounds of those players and artists wealthy enough to buy and maintain a place here. He had inherited his. There'd been some uncertain years after his master died when he was afraid he would lose the tiny house and garden, when he had to swallow his pride and borrow money from Blackthorn which he knew she wasn't expecting him to repay. He did it—and repaid it—because Gerontai had taught him to love tending that garden; he knew every plant in there, every inch of the soil, even the worms and beetles that lived in it, he knew it by taste and feel and smell, he knew every miniature carp in the small pool, every bird that nested in his trees and bushes. It was his place of retreat and meditation and more necessary to him than anything or anyone else, even Blackthorn. Yarm had disrupted that peace, but once this nonsense was over, he'd have his retreat back. Negomas was proving a quiet, happy companion with a love of growing things and a gentle sureness in those outsize hands that were so clumsy othertimes. He had the wrong sort of body and no talent at all for tumbling or the new kind of movement Taguiloa was exploring, but Taguiloa was beginning to feel that he'd found someone to whom he could pass on the other things Gerontai had taught him. And maybe the changechildren could find him a Hina boy to learn the movements, a boy that would fit into the household and appreciate the peace. Taguiloa ambled along the curving lane dreaming of times to come, chuckling as he heard shouts, curses and screams ahead of him, cracks, cracklings, shrieks, a scream. Baby dragons getting busy.

When he stopped by the gate, a red and gold dragon head popped over the wall, a gold crystal dragon eye winked at him, then the head vanished. He pushed on the leaves of the gate and they swung inward without a sound. Busy Yarm, there'd been a squeak in one of the left side hinges yesterday. He strolled into his garden, hands clasped behind him, stopped after a few steps and grinned at the tableau before him.

Yarm in a half crouch, fists clenched, his face twisted with helpless rage, his shirt and trousers slashed with thin charred lines and speckled with black spots still red-edged and smoking.

Fist on his knees howling with pain, the side of his face burned, his left shoulder and arm bubbling raw meat.

Two other men on their faces in the gravel of the path, twitching a little, speechless with terror.

Yaril dragon and Jaril dragon drifted down and hovered by Taguiloa, one on the left, the other on his right, both a little behind him like proper bodyguards.

"Greet you, Yarm," Taguiloa said. "Come for your things? I see you met my friends." He grimaced at the howling Fist, turned to Jaril. "Could you do something about that noise?"

Golden eye winked at him, dragon dissolved. In his light ray form Jaril zipped through Fist, wheeled about him, went through him again, then returned to dragon shape and took his place at Taguiloa's shoulder. The howling stopped. Not a full cure, the man's flesh was still ragged and raw, but at least it wasn't oozing anymore. Fist got to his feet. He opened and shut his left hand. The muscles in his arm shifted stiffly, but the pain was no longer unbearable.

"They've promised to keep an eye on me and mine," Taguiloa said. "They must have thought you had hostile intentions, waiting here in the dark like this. You don't have hostile intentions, do you Fist?"

The big man was staring fascinated at the serpentine shapes, turning his head from one side to the other until Taguiloa began to get dizzy watching. Eyes glazed, fearsweat dripping down his face, Fist coughed, said, "Uh no, sure not." He turned away from Yaril and Jaril, reached over to touch his burned side. "Like you said, we come to get Yarm's stuff. Meant nothing by it." He kicked the nearest of his men in the ribs. "Isn't that so, Fidge? On your feet, goat turd."

Silent laughter from the dragons. Taguiloa glanced at Yaril, blinked as she began smoking about the nostrils and produced a small gout of bright blue fire. Fidge started shivering and had difficulty getting to his feet. Fist went so pale he looked leprous in that brief blue glow.

"Then Yarm might as well collect his belongings. Everything he owns is in those packs by the door. He'll need some help hauling it, but then you're here, aren't you, so generous with your time and muscle." He turned his head to Jaril dragon. "Light their way, my friend. If you feel like it, of course."

More silent laughter, then Jaril dragon went coiling after Fist and Yarm, prodding them to move faster.

When they were back Taguiloa said, "Good. There's no reason for any of you to return, is there? My friends here might be a bit nastier if they saw you again. They were mild tonight, but their tempers get a bit tetchy when they're hungry. I wouldn't show my face inside these walls again if I were you."

Silently, heavily the four intruders trudged through the gate and into the lane. Taguiloa pushed the two sections of gate shut and dropped the bar home with intense satisfaction. He strolled toward the house, laughter bubbling up in him, his own and that from the dragonets.

Yaril and Jaril dissolved and reformed into childshapes, giggling helplessly, leaning against the housewall beside the door holding their middles. "You should . . . you shoulda . . ." Yaril gasped. "You should've seen Jaril chasing them through the bushes. You should've seen us herding them off the grass, giving them hotfoots until they were hopping like . . . oh oh oooh, I think I'm gonna bust."

Jaril calmed a little, asked hopefully, "You think they'll come back?"

"Not this summer." He looked around at the garden but couldn't see much. The crescent moon was low in the west and the starlight dimmed by fog rolling in. He couldn't see any smoldering glows, turned to the children. "Fire?"

"All out. We made sure."

"If you're wrong and I burn to death, I'll come back and haunt you."

"We know," they said in chorus. "We know."

Early in that long summer in Silili, Jaril went with Taguiloa to the Shaggil horsefair on the Mainland.

Loud, hot, dusty, filled with the shrill challenges of resty stallions, the higher bleating whinnies of colts and fillies, the snap of auctioneer's chant, the wham-tap of closing rods, the smell of urine, sweat, hay dust, clay dust, horse and man, cheap wine and hot sauce, boiling noodles and vinegar, cinnamon, musk, frangipani, sandalwood, cumin, hot iron, leather, oils. Islands of decorum about Jamar Lords. Islands of chaos about wrestlers, tumblers, jugglers of the more common sort, sword swallowers, fire-eaters, sleight-of-hand men doing tricks to fool children, shell and pea men fooling adults, gamblers of all degree. Hina farmers there with their whole families, the infants riding mother and father in back-cradles, the older children clinging close, somewhat intimidated by the crowd. Foreigners there for the famous Shaggil mares whose speed and stamina passed into any strain they were bred to. Speculators there on the hope they alone could dig out the merits in colts neglected enough to keep their price low. Courtesans there for good-looking easy mounts to show themselves off in wider realms than the streets of Silili. Temueng horse-beliks there to buy war mounts and Takhill Dravs to pull supply wagons and siege engines.

Taguiloa strolled through the heat, noise and dust, enjoying it all, enjoying most of all the knowledge he could buy any handful of those about them with the gold in his moneybelt. He stopped a moment by a clutch of tumblers, watching them with a master's eye, sighing at the lack of imagination in the rigidly traditional runs and flips. They performed the patterns with ease and even grace, and they gathered applause and coin for their efforts, but he'd done that well when he was twelve.

Jaril wouldn't let him linger but tugged on his sleeve and led him from one shed to another, pointing out a bay cob they should get to pull the travel wagon, a lanky gray gelding that would do for Harra who admitted she was out of practice but had once been rather a good rider. The changechild wouldn't let Taga stop to haggle for the beasts, but urged him on until they were out at the fringes where weanlings and yearlings were offered for sale. He stopped outside a small enclosure with a single colt inside.

Taguiloa looked at the wild-eyed demon tethered to a post, looked down at Jaril. "Even I know you don't ride a horse less than two. Especially that one."

"Yaril and me, we'll fix that later, the age, I mean."

"Oh."

"Wait here and don't look much interested in any of these." He waved at the enclosures around them.

"I'm not and suck your own eggs, imp."

Trailing laughter, Jaril shimmered into a pale amorphous glow, tenuous in that dusty air as a fragment of dream. It drifted in a slow circle above the corrals, flashing through the colts and fillies in them, finishing the survey with the beast in the nearest enclosure. It melted through his yellow-mud coat and seemed to nestle down inside the colt. That made Taga itchy, reminding him of antfeet walking across his brain, skittering about under his skin. He reached inside his shirt and scratched at his ribs, looked about for anything that might offer relief from the beating of the sun. He was sweating rivers, his heavy black shirt was streaky with sweat mud, powdered with pale dust, the moneybelt a furnace against his belly. Nothing close, not a shed about. These were the scrubs of the Fair, interesting only to the marginal speculators and a few farmers without the money to buy a mature beast, but with land and fodder enough to justify raising a weanling. He pulled his sleeve across his face, grimaced at the slimy feel, the heavy silk being no use as a swab. When he let his arm fall, Jaril was standing beside him.

"We want him," the changechild said, and pointed to the dun colt moving irritably at his tether, jerking his head up and down, blotched with sweat, caught in an unremitting temper tantrum.

"Why?" The colt was a hand or two taller than the yearlings about them, with a snaky neck, an ugly, boney head, ragged ears that he kept laid back even when he stood fairly quiet, a wicked plotting eye. Whoever brought that one to the Fair had more hope than good sense. "You can't be serious."

"Sure," Jaril said. "Tough, smart and kill anyone tries to steal him. And fast." He reached up, tugged at Taguiloa's sleeve. "Come on. Once the breeder knows we really want him, he'll try to screw up the price. He expects to make enough to pay for the colt's feed, selling him for tiger meat to some Temueng collector. Don't believe anything he tries to tell you about the dun's breeding. The mare was too old for bearing and on her way to the butcher when she got out at the wrong time and got crossed by a maneater they had to track down and kill. Took them almost six months to trap him. Colt's been mistreated from the day he was foaled and even if he wanted to behave he wasn't let. Offer the breeder three silver and settle for a half-gold, no more. Don't act like you know it all, that's what breeders like him love to see. He'll peel your hide and draw your back teeth before you notice. Just say you want the colt and will pay a silver for him, let the breeder rant all he wants, then say it again." He gave Taguiloa a minatory glance, then a cheeky grin and trotted away, his small sandaled feet kicking up new gouts of dust.

Annoyed and amused, Taguiloa followed him, knowing Jaril was getting back at him for the times he'd ordered the changechild about. He was a tiny Hina boy today with bowl-cut black hair and dark gold skin, except for his eyes indistinguishable from any of a thousand homeless urchins infesting the streets of Silili, dressed in dusty cotton trousers and a wrapabout shirt that hung open over a narrow torso and fluttered when there was any breeze. He rounded a haystack and stopped beside three men squatting about a small fire drinking large bowls of acid black tea. He waited for Taguiloa, then nodded at a fox-faced man, lean and wiry, with a small hard pot belly that strained the worn fabric of his shirt.

Taguiloa came up to him. "Saöm," he said, "you own the dun colt tethered by himself, back there a ways?" "I have a fine dun yearling, Saöm. Indeed, one whose blood lines trace back on both sides to the great mare Kashantuea and her finest stud the Moonleaper. Alas, the times are hard, Saöm, that a man must be forced to part with his heart's delight."

"Bloodlines, ah. Then you've turned up the man-eater's origins?"

A flicker of sour disgust, then admiration. "That a sothron islander should know so much! Oh knowing one, come, let us gaze on the noble lines, the matchless spirit of this pearl among horses. A pearl without price as such a wise one as you are must see at a single glance."

"I know nothing of horseflesh," Taguiloa said, glad enough to take Jaril's advice. "One silver for your dun."

"One silver?" The breeder's face went red and his eyes bulged. "One silver for such speed and endurance. Of course, a jest at my expense. Ha-Ha. Twenty gold."

"I noticed the spirit. He was doing his best to eat the plank in front of him. No doubt he'd prefer man-flesh like his sire. Two silvers, though I'm a fool to say it."

"Never! Though I starve and my children starve and my house fall down. Fifteen gold."

"Eating your house too, is he? Think what you'll save on repairs by getting rid of him. Three silver and that's my limit."

"His mother was Hooves-that-sing, renowned through the world. Twelve gold, only twelve gold, though it hurts my heart to say it."

"No doubt it was because of her great age that she died in the birthing." Taguiloa wiped at his face and looked at his hand. "I'm hot and tired, my wife waits with a bath and tea, let us finish this. Three silver for the beast and five copper for his rope and halter. My boy can find a new fancy if he has to. Well?"

"You're jesting again, noble saöm, such a miserable sum. . . ."

"So be it. Come," he wheeled and started off, knowing Jaril was coming reluctantly to his feet and pouting with disappointment. Might work, might not, he didn't really care, he didn't want anything to do with that piece of malevolence in the corral.

The breeder let him get three strides away, then called out, "Wait. Oh noble Saöm, why didn't you say you bought for this divine child, this god among boys? That my heart's delight should find a home with such a young lion, ah that tempts me, yes, I can give my prize into such hands, though if you could bring yourself, noble Saöm, a half-gold

. . ." He sighed as Taguiloa took another step away. "You are a hard man, noble Saöm. Agreed then, three silver and a copper hand. You pay the tag fee?"

Satisfied with his bargaining, Taguiloa nevertheless glanced first at Jaril, got his nod, then waved a hand in airy agreement.

They stopped at the pavilion of records, paid the transfer fee and the small bribes necessary to get the clerks to record the sale and hand over the tin ear tag, a larger bribe to get a tagger to set the tag in the dun colt's ear.

As soon as he identified the proper beast, the breeder's job was done but he lingered, relishing the dismay on the face of the tagman when he heard the yearling scream, saw him lash out with each hoof in turn, saw his wild wicked eye, his long yellow teeth. The tagman started to refuse and retreat, but Taguiloa got a good grip on his arm. "The boy'll get him calmed down. Watch."

Jaril climbed the rails and stood balanced on the top one, looking down at the dun, who went crazy trying to get at him. Somewhere deep in his soul the breeder found a limit and opened his mouth to protest, shut it when Taguiloa laughed at him and repeated, "Watch."

The boy found the moment he wanted and launched himself from the rail, twisting somehow in mid-air so he came down astride the colt. The yearling squealed with rage, gathered himself. . . .

And snorted mildly, did a few fancy steps, then stood quite still, twisting his limber neck around so he could nose gently at Jaril's knee. Again the breeder started to shout a warning, again he held his peace as the dun swung his head back round and stared at him. Breeder stared at beast, beast at breeder and the man looked away first, convinced the beast was snickering at him. Fuming, he stalked off, aware he'd been fooled into selling a valuable beast for almost nothing.

After they bought the bay cob and the gray gelding, they left the Fair, Taguiloa on the gelding, leading the cob, Jaril riding the yearling. They left the three horses with a widow who had a shed and pasture she rented. In the days that followed Jaril and Yaril flew across frequently to train and grow the dun from a yearling to a lean fit three-year-old. Those same days Taguiloa planned the performances and rehearsed his troupe.

They walked out of Silili, Taguiloa, Brann, Harra, Negomas, Linjijan, Jaril as Hina boy and Yaril as brindle hound. Taguiloa and Linjijan put their shoulders to the man-yokes of a tilt cart that carried their props, costumes, camping gear, food, and a miscellany of other useful objects. Brann and Harra slipped straps over their shoulders and added their weight to the task of towing that clumsy vehicle. Jaril ran ahead of them with Negomas, both boys chattering excitedly about what they expected to happen, a sharing of ignorance and pleasurable speculation. Yaril trotted about, her nose to the ground, enjoying the smells of the morning.

They left the last huts of the indigent behind before the sun was fully up, negotiated the waste, cursing ruts and briars, then rocked onto a country lane where the going was a bit easier. There was dew on the grass and low bushes, the morning was cool and bright, the smell of damp earth and soft wet grass almost strong enough to overcome the pungency of cow dung and dog droppings. They hauled the cart through long crisp shadows cast by fruit trees, nut trees, spice trees and an occasional cedar or sea-pine. All the bearing trees were heavy with ripe fruit or nuts or pods of spice. As the heat of the sun increased and licked up the dew, it also woke the heavy sweet perfume of the fruits and spices, the tang of the cedars. Bees and wasps hummed about, nibbling at late peaches and apricots, nectarines and apples, cherries and pears. The air was filled with their noises, with bird song, with the whisper of needles and leaves—and with the squeals, groans and rattles from the cart as it lurched in and out of ruts, one of the not so small irritations of being Hina or foreign in a Temueng-ruled world. If they could have used the paved Imperial Way, they'd have cut in half the effort and time it took to reach the causeway between Selt and Utar, but bored Temueng guards harassed even the wealthiest of Hina merchants using that road; what they'd do to a band of players didn't bear thinking about.

Five hours after they left Taguiloa's house, they came out of a lane onto the rocky cliffs where a few skinny long-legged pigs rooted among the grass and weeds, trotting sure-footed on the edge of cliffs rotten and precipitous. Jaril eyed them warily, looked up at his soaring sister who had long since decided that she preferred wings to feet, made a face at her then shimmered into a tall fierce boar-hound and went back to trot beside the sweating straining adults; the small wild pigs were the only non-working livestock on the island and had tempers worse than hungover Temueng tax-collectors.

The causeway towers were visible ahead, a barrier that had to be passed no matter how unpleasant or malicious the guards were; they needed to get their credeens there, the metal tags they had to have to show in every village or to any Temueng who stopped and required them. Taguiloa had travel permits for all them, but the credeens were more important. It meant more bribes, it meant enduring whatever the guards wanted to do to them. These Temuengs were the scrapings of the army, left here while the better soldiers were off fighting the Emperor's wars of conquest. Taguiloa saw them every time he looked up, saw them watching the clumsy progress of the tilt cart, talking together; the closer he got, the worse they looked. He began to worry for the women's sake. The guards had to let them by eventually, but they knew and he knew that nothing they did to him or Brann or Harra or Linjijan or the children would bring them any punishment. His stomach churning, he kept his eyes down, his shoulders bent, hoping to ride out whatever happened, knowing he had no choice but to accept their tormenting. Resistance would only make things worse.

The empush turned the papers over and over, inspecting every mark and seal on them, asking the same stupid questions again and again, jabbing a meaty forefinger into Taguiloa's chest, hitting the same spot each time until Taga had to grit his teeth to keep from wincing. Only two of his four-command were visible, the others probably even drunker than their fellows and asleep inside the tower.

Brann endured the comments and catcalls, the ugly handling, though she was strongly tempted to suck a little of the life out of the Temuengs; might be doing the world a big favor if she drained them dry. She watched Harra and Taguiloa both stoically enduring their hazing and kept a precarious hold on her temper, but when the guards left their tormenting of the women and began leading Negomas and Jaril toward the tower, she'd had enough. She went after them, covering the ground with long tiger strides. Harra bit her lip, then started whistling a strident tune that brought a large dust-devil whirling up the dirt lane and onto the Way where it slapped into the empush, distracting him so he wouldn't see what was happening. Brann slapped her hand against a guard's neck. He dropped as if she'd knocked him on the head. A breath later and the second guard followed him. Shooing the boys ahead of her, green eyes flashing scorn, she stalked back to Taguiloa and the empush.

Before he could object or question her, she caught hold of his hand and held it for a long long moment. By the time she released him, his face had gone slack, his eyes glazed. "Give us our credeens," she said crisply.

Moving dreamily, the empush fumbled in his pouch and drew out a handful of the metal tags. She counted the proper number and tipped the rest into his hand. "Put these away." She waited until he pulled the drawstring tight. "Give me the travel papers. Good. You're going to forget all this, aren't you. Answer me. Good. Now you can go into the tower with your drunken men and get some sleep. When you wake, you'll remember having some fun with a troupe of players, but letting them go on their way after a while. The usual thing. You hear? Good. Never mind the men on the ground. They'll wake when they're ready. Go into the tower and crawl into bed. That's right." She watched tensely as he turned and stumbled into the tower, stepping over his men without seeing them.

Taguiloa raised a brow. "They dead?"

"Just very tired. Take them a couple days to get back to their usual nastiness."

"Thought you wanted out with no trouble."

"Comes a time, Taga, comes a time." She gave him the travel permits and passed the credeens around.

"As long as he really forgets." Taguiloa ducked under the shafts and got himself settled once more against the yoke. Linjijan looked mildly at him, then away again; he'd ignored most of what had gone before, looking at the guards with such calm surprise when they poked at him that they left off in disgust.

Brann drew her hand across her sweaty, dirty face, grimaced at the streaks of mud on her palm. "It's worked before. In Tavisteen, well, you wouldn't know about that. Let's get moving. I feel naked standing around like this."

They were stopped at the Utar end of the causeway, but that empush was only interested in his bribe and let them pass without much difficulty. He had a sour spiteful look, but his men were out of sight, perhaps even out of call and he wasn't going to start trouble, not on Utar with his commander a sneeze away.

They curved around the edge of the terraced mountain that took up the greater part of Utar, keeping to the broad Way on the lowest level where the haughty Temueng lordlings wouldn't have to look at them, passed a third empushad of guards, and were finally freed of hindrances, rumbling along the causeway that linked Utar to the mainland.

At the widow's farm where they'd pastured the horses, they transferred the gear and supplies from the cart to the gaudy box-wagon Taguiloa had purchased from a disbanding troupe whose internal dissensions had reached the point of explosion in spite of their success on tour. They left the tilt cart in the care of the widow and after a hasty meal, started on the two-day journey through the coastal marshes. Taguiloa drove, Linjijan sat beside him coaxing songs out of his practice flute. Negomas rode on the roof with his smallest drum; he liked it up there with the erratic wind pushing into his stiff springy hair and blowing debris away from him. He played with the drum, fitting his beat to Linjijan's wanderings or playing his own folk music, singing in the clicking sonorous tongue of his fathers. Brann and Harra rode ahead of the wagon, Harra on the gray gelding, Brann on the dun colt forcegrown by the children, a well-mannered beast as long as she or one of the children were around and an ill-tempered demon when they weren't. Brann was working on that, but it would take time.

They rolled along the stone road raised on arches above the mud and water through the misty gloom of the wetlands into heavy stifling air that blew sluggishly off the water and along the raised road, carrying with it clouds of biters. The dun's temper deteriorated until even Brann had trouble controlling him; even the placid cob grew restless and broke his steady plod as he twitched and snorted and shook his head.

"Vataraparastullakosakavilajusakh!" Harra slapped at her neck, wiggled her arms, began whistling a high screeching monotonous air that seemed to gather the biters in a thick black cloud and blow them off into the gloom under the trees. She kept it up for about twenty minutes, then broke off, coughed, spat and took a long long drink from her waterskin.

Negomas giggled and began beating a rapid ripple on his drum, chanting up a wind that came from behind and blew steadily past them, keeping them relatively clear of biters until they came up to the campsite the Emperor kept cleared and maintained for travelers, a large shed with wattle walls and a tile roof, a stone floor tilted so rain would run out, and a stack of reasonably dry wood in a bin at one side. It was very early in the trading season so everything was clean and all the supplies were topped off, the steeping well was cleaned out, with a new base of sand and charcoal, the water in it fairly clean and clear. There was a second shed for the wagon and stock, this one with high stone walls and a heavy gate with loopholes in it where a spearman or bowman could hold off a crowd. With Yaril and Jaril to stand guard it would take a wolf hardier than any of the loners living in the swamps to make off with their goods.

The next day they showed their credeens at the gates of Hamardan, the first of the river cities clear of the marshes, and rode through the streets, Negomas playing a calling song on his drums, Linjijan making witcheries on his flute, Harra riding the gray with her knees and plucking cascades of cheerful noise from her daroud. It wasn't market day but the bright noise of the music was pulling folk, Hina and Temueng alike, out of their houses and shops, and drawing boisterous children after them.

They made a wide circle about the city and then in the center of the flurry they'd created they rolled, trolled, caracoled to the largest Inn in Hamardan. It was a hollow square with few windows in the thick outside wall and a red-tile roof with demon-averts scattered along the eaves, a place where the richest merchant would feel safe with his goods locked in the Inn's fortress godons, and he himself locked into the comfort and security of the Inn proper. This was early in the season, few merchants traveling yet. End of summer, not yet harvest time, no festivals coming up, none in the recent past. Folk were ripe for anything that promised entertainment. Though they were players and low on anyone's scale of respectability, though half the troupe was foreign and worth even less than players, still Taguiloa knew the value of what he was bringing to the Inn and made a point of assuming his welcome. He drove the wagon into the central court and leaped down from the driver's seat with an easy flip, landed lightly on the paving-stones to the applause of the swarming children, bowed, laughing to them, then went to negotiate for rooms and the use of the court for a performance on the next night after the market shut down and the crowds it brought were still in town.

Brann set up a small bright tent in the market and put Negomas beating drums outside it, Jaril doing some tumbling and calling out to the passersby to come and hear past and future from a seer come from the ends of the earth to tell it. Though she carefully used nothing painful from the bits Yaril gave to her, she gave the maidens and matrons a good show and it was not long before word flew along the wind that the foreign woman was a wonder who could look into the heart and tell you your deepest secrets.

Twice male seekers thought to take more than she wanted to give—a woman alone, a foreigner, was fair game for the predatory—but a low growl from a very large brindle hound that came from the shadows behind the table was enough to discourage the most amorous. And she got twice her fee from these men, smiling fiercely at them and mentioning things they didn't want exposed, and a calm threat to show to the world their poverty or stinginess, whichever it might be. They left, growling of cheat and fake and fraud, but no one bothered to listen.

That night the Inn was jammed with people, anyone who could come up with the price of entry—city folk and those from the farms and fisheries around, the Jamar and his household. The poorest sat in thick clumps on the paving stones of the court, the shopkeepers and their families packed the third-floor balcony, the Jamar and his family had the choice seats on the end section of the second-floor balcony, the side sections of that balcony given over to town officials and the Jamarak Temuengs. The wagon was pushed against the inside end of the court, its sides let down on sturdy props to make a flat stage triple the wagon's width. The bed and sides were covered by layers of cork, the cork by a down quilt carefully tied so it wouldn't shift about. The first balcony above the wagonstage was blocked off for the use of the players; a ladder went from this to the wagon bed, giving them two levels for performing.

It was a good crowd and a good-natured one. Brann and Harra took coin at the archway entrance to the court, the Inn servants escorted the balcony folk to the stairs and glared down street urchins who tried to sneak in for free. The Host stood on the second balcony watching all this with suppressed glee, since he got a percentage of the take for allowing Taguiloa to use his court. There were very few clients in the Inn and fewer expected for the rest of the month, so it was no hardship to accommodate the players, something Taguiloa had counted on for he'd made enough tours with Gerontai to know the value of an inn-keeper's favor.

The noise in the court rose to a peak then hushed as the drums began to sound, wild exotic music most of these folk had never heard before, a little disturbing, but it crawled into the blood until they were breathing with it. On the second-floor balcony Taguiloa looked at Brann. "Ready?" he mouthed to her. She nodded. He put his hand on Negomas's shoulder. The boy looked up, smiled then changed the beat of his music, lending to the throb of the drums a singing sonorous quality; Linjijan came in with his flute, giving the music a more traditional feel, blending M'darjin and Hina in a way that was more comfortable for the listeners. Then the daroud added its metallic cadences and the crowd hushed, sensing something about to happen. Taguiloa leaped onto the balcony rail and stood balanced there, arms folded across his chest, the soft glow of the lampions picking out the rich gold and silver couching of his embroidered robe.

"People of Hamardan."

The drum quieted to a soft mutter behind him; flute and daroud went silent.

"In the western lands beyond the edge of the world, maidens dance with fire to please their king and calm their strange and hungry gods. At great expense and effort I bring you FIRE. . . ." As he gestured, blue, crimson and gold flames danced above the quilting (Yaril and Jaril spreading themselves thin) ". . . and the MAIDEN."

A loose white silk gown fluttering about her, Brann swung over the rail and went down the ladder in a controlled fall, using hands and feet to check her plunge. Then she was in among the flames, standing with hands raised above her head while she swayed and the flames swayed about her. The drum went on alone for a while until the beat was so strong they who watched were trapped in it, then the flute came in and finally the daroud, playing music from Arth Slya, the betrothal dance when a maid announced to the world that she and her life's companion had found each other, a sinuous wheeling dance that showed off the suppleness of the body and the sensuality of the dancer. In Arth Slya there were no flames, the girl would dance with her lover. Brann danced it that night with what pleasure she could and more sadness than she'd expected to feel, danced it in memory of Sammang Schimli who had salvaged her pleasure in her body.

The flames vanished, the music stopped, the dance stopped. Brann stood very still in the center of the wagonstage, breathing rapidly, then flung out her arms and bowed to the audience. She ran up the ladder and vanished into the shadows to a burst of whistles and applause.

The drum began again, a quick insistent beat. Taguiloa leaped onto the railing. "People of Hamardan, see my dance." He flung the broidered robe away with a gesture as impressive as it seemed careless for he capered high above the wagon and the court's rough stone on a rail the width of a small man's hand. He wore a knitted bodysuit of white silk flexible as chainmail, fitting like a second skin; a wide crimson sash was tied about his waist, its dangling ends swinging and flaring with the shifts of his body in that impossible dance. Behind him, flute and drums blended in familiar music, Hina tunes though the drum sound was more sonorous and melodic than the flat tinny sound of tradition. At first the flute sang in a traditional mode, then changed as the dance changed, beginning to tease and pull at the tunes. Harra tossed Taguiloa's shimmer spheres to him, one by one. They caught the light of the lampions and multiplied so it was as if a dozen tiny lamps were trapped in each crystal sphere, shimmering crimson, gold and silver as he put one, two, three and finally four into the air and kept them circling as he did a shuffle dance on that rail moving on the knife edge of disaster until he built an almost unbearable tension in the workers, who gave a soft whisper of a sigh as he capered then tossed the spheres one by one into the darkness behind him.

The drum hushed, the flute took up a two-faced tune; it had two sets of words, one set a child's counting rhyme, the other a comically obscene version the rivermen used for rowing. With that as background he did a fast, sliding, stumbling comic dance on that railing, swaying precariously and constantly seeming about to fall from his perch. Each time he recovered with some extravagant bit of business that drew gasps of laughter from the crowd. He ended that bit as secure, it seemed, on his narrow railing as his audience were on their paving stones. With the flute laughing behind him, he flung out his arms and bent his body in an extravagant bow. The flute soared to a shriek. He overbalanced to a concerted gasp from the watchers that changed to stomping, shouting applause as he landed lightly on his feet and flipped immediately into a tumbling run. Above, the flute, drums, daroud began to weave together a music that was part familiar and part a borrowing from three other cultures, music that captured the senses and was all the stranger for the touch of familiarity in it. Taguiloa flung his body about in a dance that melded tumbling, movement from a dozen cultures and his own fertile imagination. The music and the man's twisting, wheeling body wove a thing under the starshimmer and lampion glow that earth and sky had never seen before. And when the movement ended, when the music died and Taguiloa stood panting, there was for one moment a profound silence in the court, then that was broken with whistles, shouts, stomping feet, hands beating on sides, thighs, the backs of others. And it went on and on, a celebration of this new thing without a name that had taken them and shaken them out of themselves.

When they could get away from the exulting Host and the mostly silent but leechlike attentions of the Jamar and his Jamika, they met in the Inn's bathhouse.

Steam rose and swirled about lamps burning perfumed oil, casting ghost shadows on the wet tiles; the condensation on the walls was bright and dark in random patterns like the beaded pattern on a snakeskin. Brann swam slowly through the hot water, her *changed* black hair streaming in a fan about her shoulders. Yaril and Jaril swam energetically about like pale fish, half the time under the water, bumping into the others, sharing their soaring spirits. Negomas paddled after them, almost as much at home in the water as they were, his only handicap his need to breathe. Taguiloa lolled in the warm water, his head in a resthollow, his eyes half shut, a dreamy smile twitching at his lips. Now and then he straightened his face, but his enforced gravity always dissolved into a smile of sleepy satisfaction. Harra kicked lazily about, her long dark brown hair kinking into tight curls about her pointed face.

The first time the troupe had gone from a long hard rehearsal into Blackthorn's bathhouse, Harra had been startled, even shocked, as the others stripped down to the skin and plunged with groans of pleasure into the water and let its heat leach away soreness from weary muscles. Communal bathing was an ancient Hina custom, one whose origins were somewhere in the mythtime before men learned to write. A bathhouse was rigidly unstratified, the one place where Hina of all castes mingled freely, the one place where the strictures of ordinary manners could be dropped and men and women could relax. After the Temueng conquest, the bathhouses were suppressed for a few years, Temuengs seeing them as places of rampant immorality, unable to believe that sexual contact between all those naked people was something that simply did not happen, that anyone who broke the houses' only rule would be thrown out immediately and ostracized as barbarian. Harra's wagon-dwelling people lived much like those early Temuengs, with little physical privacy and many rules to determine the behavior of both sexes, rules born out of necessity and cramped quarters, though her life had been different from that of the ordinary girlchild of the Rukka-nag. She had no older brothers or sisters. Her mother died in childbirth when she was four, and the infant girl died with her. After that her mage father spent little time with his people, traveling for months, years, apart from the clan, taking Harra with him. Absorbed in his studies, absently assuming she'd somehow learn the female strictures her mother would have taught her, he treated her as much like a son as a daughter, especially when she grew old enough for him to notice her quick intelligence, though he did engage a maid to help her keep herself tidy and sew new clothing for her when she needed or wanted it. He began teaching her his craft when she was eight, training her in music and shaping, the two things being close to the same thing for him and her; they were much alike in their interests and very close; he talked to her more often than not as if she were another magus of his own age and learning. But there were times when he was shut up with his researches or visiting other mages in the many many cities they visited or stopping at one of the rude hermitages where nothing female was permitted; then he settled her into one of the local homes. She learned how to adapt herself quickly to local custom, how to become immediately aware of the dangers to a young girl and how to protect herself from those while making such friends as she could to lessen her loneliness a bit. Sometimes—though this was rare—her father stayed as long as two years in one place, other times she'd begin to take in the flavor of a city, to learn its smells and sounds and other delights, then he'd be going again. It was a strange, sometimes troubling, usually uncertain existence, and the burden of maintaining their various households fell mainly on her slender shoulders once she reached her twelfth birthday, but it was excellent preparation for survival when her father died between one breath and the next from an aneurism neither of them knew he had. And it let her assess at a glance the proper manners in a bathhouse and overcome her early training. Unable to control her embarrassment, she contrived to hide it, stripped with the rest and got very quickly into water she found a lot too clear for her comfort. She paddled about with her back turned to the others hoping the heat of the water would explain the redness in her face, but ended relaxed and sighing with pleasure as the heat soothed her soreness.

Now she was as much at ease as the others, as she watched Taguiloa's smiles and savored her own delight. Rehearsals were one thing but putting on a finished performance with that storm of audience approval—well, it was no wonder he was still a little drunk with the pleasure of it. She felt decidedly giddy and giggly herself.

"It could get addicting," she said aloud.

Taguiloa opened one eye, grinned at her.

The door to the bathhouse opened and several serving maids came

in. They set up a long table in one corner and covered it with trays of
fingerfood, several large stoneware teapots, more wine jugs, drinking
bowls, hot napkins. The roundfaced old woman who supervised this
bowed to Taguiloa. "With the Jamar's compliments, saöm-y-saör."

Taguiloa lifted a heavy arm from the water. "The Godalau bless his
generosity."

The old woman bowed again. "Saöm, the Host does not wish to
intrude on your rest, but he desires you to know that the Jamar has
requested you perform at his house the coming night."

Taguiloa lay silent for a breath or two, then finally said, "Inform the
Host that we will be pleased to perform for the Jamar provided we can
arrange a suitable fee and proper quarters for ourselves and our
horses."

The woman bowed a third time and left, shooing the curious and
excited maidservants before her.

Taguiloa batted at the water and said nothing for a few moments,
then he sighed and rose to sit crosslegged on the tiles. "A fee is probably a lost cause, I'm afraid. We'll be lucky if we get a meal and shelter.
I'd hoped to get farther along before I ran into this sort of complication. Still, it could be worth the irritation. These Temueng Jamars keep
in close touch by pigeon mail and courier, so word of us will be passed
on and reach Andurya Durat before we do." He studied Brann a long
minute. "You will be careful?"

"I'll try, Taga. Slya knows, I'll try."

Harra got out of the water, wrapped a toweling robe about her and
went to inspect the food, suddenly very hungry. She poured some tea
and began trying the different things set out on the trays. "Come on, all
of you. Leave the heavy worrying for some other times, this is heaven.
If you're as hungry as me."

The Jamar was a big man. Even as tall as she was, Brann's head
came only to his middle ribs. His shoulders were broad enough to
make three Hina, his belly big and hard as a beer tun, his legs tree
trunks, arms, feet and hands built on a similar heroic scale. He should
have been ugly, but wasn't. He should have seemed fierce and intimidating as an angry storm dragon, but didn't. He gave them a mild,
beaming welcome. "Hamardan House is honored by your presence,"
he boomed.

Taguiloa bowed. "We are the honored ones," he murmured, feeling a
bit battered.

Jamar Hamardan escorted the troupe to the rooms within the House he had set aside for them, something Taguiloa hadn't expected, nor had he expected the luxury of those rooms. He didn't quite know how to deal with all this effusiveness. It made him uneasy. Temuengs simply did not treat Hina and foreigners like this.

The Jamar hovered about them as they tried to settle themselves, silent and diffident but impossible to ignore. His bulging eyes slipped again and again to Brann, Harra and the others; again and again he licked his lips, opened his mouth to speak, shut it without saying anything. Taguiloa tried to edge him out the door and away from the troupe so he would say what was on his mind, but he seemed impervious to hints and unlikely to respond well to being hustled out in spite of his apparent amiability. Taguiloa knew enough to be extremely wary at this moment, though the tension of keeping up the required courtesies wracked his nerves. He caught Harra's eye. Tungjii bless her quick wits, she gathered the rest of the troupe and hustled them out of the room. The Yaril hound settled in the corner of the room, her crystal eyes half-closed but fixed on the Temueng, a powerful defender if there was trouble.

Jamar Hamardan waited while the room emptied out completely, listening absently as Taguiloa continued his inane chatter. Abruptly the huge Temueng cleared his throat, shutting off Taguiloa in midsentence. "How many days can you stay here . . . ?" He fumbled for some way to address the player. He wouldn't use the Hina *saö* though he obviously wished to be polite, and he wouldn't give the player any Temueng honorific—no Temueng could do that and keep his self-respect. He avoided the difficulty by falling silent and waiting with twitchy impatience for Taguiloa's answer.

"Ah . . ." Taguiloa scrambled for some way to escape what he saw coming. "Ahh . . . Jamar Hamardan, saö jura, we have to be in Durat before the storms blow down from the high plains." He was deferential but determined, used his most careful formal speech and hoped for the best. If this Temueng decided he wanted his own troupe of entertainers, there was almost nothing they could do. Running meant giving up everything and he wouldn't do that as long as there was the smallest chance he could work himself free. "Stay here," the Jamar said. "You won't lose by it."

"A generous offer, Jamar Hamardan saö jura." Taguiloa spoke slowly, still hunting for a way out. "If I may, we need more than a place to keep the rain off and food in our bellies. . . ." He risked the

touch of commonspeech after a sidelong glance at the Temueng. "We
are at our best this year, saö jura. If I may, we have dreams . . . but
that is nothing to you, saö-jura. I waste your time with my babbling,
your pardon, saö jura." He lowered his eyes, bowed his head and
waited.

The Temueng cleared his throat. "No, no," he said. "No bother."
Silence.

Taguiloa glanced quickly at the Temueng. The big man looked troubled. He turned his head suddenly, caught Taguiloa watching him.
"One week," he said. "My Jamika grieves." He half-swallowed the
words. "Our eldest son is with the forces in Croaldhu, our youngest
was called to Andurya Durat." He looked past Taguiloa as if he no
longer was aware of him. "He is her heart, the breath in her throat. A
good lad for all that, rides like he's part of his horse, open-handed with
his friends, spirited and impatient. Maybe a little heedless, but he's
young." He cleared his throat again. "You . . ." Again he searched
for a word but settled for the slightly derogatory term used by
Temuengs for Hina females. "Your ketchin, they should keep the
Jamika distracted. She was pleased by you last night. She smiled when
you did that thing on the rail and the rest of it . . . well, she slept
without . . ." He broke off, frowned. "Give her some time away from
grieving, showman, and you can ask what you will."

Taguiloa looked away from the huge man stumbling over his love for
his cow of a wife and for that calf who sounded like most young male
Temuengs, arrogant, thoughtless and as unpleasant to his own kind as
he was to those who had the misfortune to be in his power. Never mind
that, he told himself, a week's better than I hoped. He swept into a low
bow. "Of your kindness, saö jura, certainly a week."

The Jamar Hamardan turned to leave, turned back. "One of the
ketchin, she's a seer?"

"One can sometimes see past a day, past a night, saö jura."

"My Jamika will ask the ketcha to read for her. I do not inquire how
the ketcha reads or if she knows more than how to judge a face,
whether she lies or speaks what truth she sees. I do not care, showman.
Tell your seer to make my Jamika contended. Do you hear me?"

"I hear you, saö jura."

The Jamar hesitated another minute in the doorway, then stumped
out.

Taguiloa stood rubbing at the back of his neck with fingers that
trembled. Relief, apprehension, anger churned in him. A week. And

who said it would end then? One week, then another, then another. It
had to end there. Had to. He touched the shoulder where he'd felt his
double-natured patron riding and wondered if this was one of Tungjii's
dubious gifts. He scanned his immediate past to see where he'd forgot
and invoked his god. Nothing but ordinary chaos and the usual curses
quickly forgotten. He forced himself to relax and went searching for
the others to tell them what had happened.

Taguiloa pulled on a knitted black silk body suit like the white one he
used in his act, then he slipped from his room and began his nightly
prowl about the Jamar's House, listening for whatever he could pick
up, driven as much by survival needs as by curiosity. The week was
winding to a finish, the testing of Jamar Hamardan's good will was
closer. He might let them go, or he could insist they stay yet another
short while and then another, nibbling their time away, never letting
them go.

He moved through the maze of halls in the wing where the troupe
was housed, heading to the storage alcove he'd found the first night
he'd prowled the House. A pair of late rambling servants forced him to
duck into the shadowy doorless recess, only to discover they were
bound for that same alcove. He cursed the libidinous pair and searched
for some place to hide. They probably wouldn't raise a row if they saw
him, just take off to find another place to scratch their itch, but there'd
be gossip later that would work around to someone in authority and
make trouble for the troupe. There were narrow shelves set from the
bottom of one wall. He went up them and tried to fold himself into
invisibility. The shelves were far too narrow for that, but over him he
saw a recessed square in the ceiling of the closet. He pushed against
one side of the square and it tipped silently upward. He was through
the opening and easing the trap into place as the pair came in whispering, laughing. Afraid to move, he listened to the sounds coming from
below, but after a few moments of creeping boredom and stiffening
limbs, he eased into a squat and looked about him; enough of the
Wounded Moon's light came through airholes in the eaves to show him
a maze of beams with ceiling boards between them. The roof was high
over the place where he crouched, slanting steeply to the eaves. It was
just like a Temueng to waste such a vast cavernous space on dust and
squirrels, spiders and mice. The place was filled with noises once he let
himself listen, gnawing, the patter of clawed feet, chittering from squirrels, shrieks from mice as housecats stalked and killed them, yowls as

the cats fought and mated. His fears of being heard faded, he got to his feet, oriented himself and began prowling along the beams listening for voices in the rooms below.

In the days since that first prowl, he'd picked up enough to make him increasingly uneasy. Now he went swiftly along the ceiling beams, heading for the Jamar's quarters without stopping at his other posts.

The office. Silent now. He spent a moment standing over the crack that funnelled sound up from below. Last night Hamardan was there talking with his overseer, one of his uncles, a shrewd old man who'd lost all but the youngest of his grandsons to the army. They were discussing the increase in the Emperor's portion of the harvest, speculating cautiously about what it meant, both men not-saying far more than they put in words, their silences saying much more than those words about their curiosity and unease about what was going on in Andurya Durat. The old man had a letter from one of his grandsons anouncing the death of another of them; the others were well enough, but not especially pleased with their lot. The letter included news about the Jamar's eldest son; he was alive, unhurt but bored with his life, despising the Croaldhese, loathing the food, the smells, the women, everything about that cursed island, including (very much between the lines) his fellow officers and the men he commanded.

Neither the Jamar nor his uncle had any idea why the Emperor had suddenly decided to start sending his armies out to conquer the world; for two hundred years the Temueng Emperors had been content with the rich land of Tigarezun. They didn't like it. Tigarezun was important to them; they didn't consider the Hina had any connection with it, it was theirs; their ancestors' bones were buried in that soil (Hina burned their dead, the heedless creatures, how could they have any right to land if they didn't claim and consecrate it with ancestral flesh and bone?) but this coveting of foreign lands was foolishness, especially an island over a week's sail away. Especially any island. Temuengs did not like sea travel and felt uneasy on a bit of land that you could ride, side to side, in a day or two. And this warring was taking and wasting their sons. The two men spent an hour yesternight grousing and speculating about the Emperor's mental state; he'd just taken a new young wife, maybe he was a crazy old man trying to feel young again.

Taguiloa padded along the beams checking out the rooms in the private quarter of the big House, day room, bathroom, conservatory and so on, only silence—until he reached the Jamar's bedroom.

Wife weeping, husband trying to comfort her. Sobs diminishing after a while. Silence for a few breaths. Heavy steps, quicker lighter ones, noise of complaining chair, the continued patter of the woman's feet as she paced restlessly about. Taguiloa stretched out on the beam and prepared to wait.

"She says Empi's enjoying himself in Durat; he's got a new horse and hasn't lost too much money at gaming and has a chance to catch the eye of someone important at court." The woman stopped walking, sighed.

"It's what he wanted, Tjena."

"I know. But I miss him so, Ingklio." Steps, couch creaking. "Why don't we go to the capital for the winter?"

"Too much to do. And the Ular-drah have been raiding close by. You know what happened last month to the Tjatajan Jamarak. House burned, granaries looted, what the drah couldn't carry off they fouled."

"Uncle Perkerdj could see our land safe."

Hamardan grunted. "Not this year," he said with a heavy finality that silenced the Jamika.

More creaking as she got back on her feet and started dragging about again, making querulous comments about her maidservants and their defects, the insults from some of the cousins and kin-wives, the disrespect of one of the male servants. The Jamar said nothing, perhaps he didn't bother listening to her, being so familiar with her diatribes they were like the winds blowing past, a part of the sounds of the day no one notices. Taguiloa lay on his beam, half-asleep, telling himself he might as well leave them to their well-worn grooves, because the last four nights this by-play had ended in their going to bed. He yawned and grinned into the darkness. Had to be one monster of a bed and a sturdy one at that. The Jamika was built to match the Jamar, massive arms and thighs, breasts like muskmelons, only a head shorter than him. Maybe that's why he never took a second wife, she's the only woman in the world big enough he wouldn't crush her with that weight or look absurd standing beside her, an oliphaunt mated with a gazelle. The thought wiped away his amusement. If that was true, the Jamar would do just about anything to keep his wife content. He certainly had no concubines, and was awkward around Brann and Harra, seeming almost frightened of normal sized women. Taguiloa nearly forgot himself and swore at old Tungjii. He held back. Bad enough to be in this bind without irritating the unpredictable Tungjii. Hisser favors were bad enough, but hisser's curses were hell on dragonback. He bruised his nose against the splintery beam and promised Tungjii a dozen incense sticks when he got back to Silili.

"What about the players?" Hamardan said suddenly. "Shall I let them go or would you like to keep them?"

Taguiloa bit down hard on his lip, sucked in a long breath. "Oh Ingklio, would you keep them? That one comforts me so, she's a true seer, I know it, she's told me things no one else . . . well, things, and if she's here, she can keep telling me what Empi's doing. He never writes." Heavy creaking again as she flung herself down beside Hamardan. "Just think. Our own players. Can we afford it?"

"Hina and foreigners, how much can they cost?"

Fuming, Taguiloa listened as the discussion below him altered to an oliphauntine cooing. Enough of this; listen to them much longer, and I'll be sick. He got to his feet and ran the beams to the distant trap, let himself down and loped along the dark quiet hall to his bedroom. He stripped off the black bodysuit, sponged away sweat and dust, wrapped a soft old robe about himself and went down the hall to rap at Brann's door.

She let him in after a brief wait. The lamps were still lit, Jaril and Yaril sat cross-legged on the bed, their small faces serious, their crystal eyes reflecting light from the lamps.

"Jaril thought you'd be along soon," Brann said. She sat on the bed beside Yaril. "Bad news." It wasn't a question.

"We're a little gift he's wrapping up for his wife." Taguiloa said. "You've been a bit too convincing. That great cow wants daily news of her wretched calf."

She said a few words in a language he did not know but they needed no translation as they crackled through the air.

"And she's charmed with the idea of having her own company of players. Something to raise her status with the neighbors; she was a little worried about the cost but he wasn't, we're only Hina and a few foreigners, how much could scum like that cost? Throw a little food at us, a jar or two of wine and we're bought."

"Mmm. Yaril, fetch Harra. We've got to talk. Don't frighten her but let her know it's urgent." She looked thoughtfully at Taguiloa. "We won't bother waking Linji and Negomas." She looked at the door. "Harra knows a lot more about things like this than I do." She blinked uncertainly. "There's so much. . . ."

A tap on the door. Taguiloa got up, let Harra in, resumed his seat on the bench. "We're about to be offered a permanent home," he said. "Right here."

Harra wrinkled her nose at Brann. "I told you to tone those sessions down."

"Easy for you to say, not so easy for me to do. You didn't have that cow hanging over you sucking every word you said." She sighed. "I know. I got a little carried away, but I have to tell you, my behavior doesn't make much difference. The Jamika wants to believe in me and she twists everything I say into something she wants to hear. Even if I don't say a word, she interprets the way I breathe." She moved impatiently, the bed squeaking under her. "Anything helpful in what your father taught you?"

"Well, he wasn't very organized about anything besides his own studies, just taught me whatever interested him at the time. Mmmm." Harra frowned at the wall, sorting through the inside of her head. Suddenly she grinned. "I have it. There's an herb and a spell that will set a geas on that man. Thing is, one can't work without the other. I've got a pinch or two of lixsil in my father's herb bag, but it doesn't need much. The maid that brings my meals chatters a lot, she tells me Hamardan eats his breakfast alone in his private garden when the weather's good. She says he's a sore-foot bear mornings and no one stays around him if they can help it. The weather's going to be dry and sunny the next three days, Negomas swears he knows and I think I believe him. So. You see where I'm heading. One of the changechildren drops the lixsil in his tea, I don't have to be that close, I can lay the spell on him when we're with the Jamika. Brann, you handled those guards on the causeway, can you do the same with her? She's bound to kick up the kind of fuss we don't want when we roll out."

"Mmm." Brann looked wistful. "I wish I had magic. What I do best is kill people, and awful as she is, Tjena doesn't deserve killing." Her eyes shifted from Taguiloa to Harra and back, then she moved her shoulders and visibly pulled herself together. "I can drain her so she's tottery and suggestible, then tell her that what she does the next few days will affect her son . . . I'll have to think about it some more." She smiled and relaxed, yawned. "Anybody got anything to add? Well, let's get some sleep."

Hina servants set out the table and covered it with a huge stoneware teapot and a drinking bowl, a mountain of sweetrolls, a bowl of pickled vegetables, a platter of sausages and deep-fried chicken bits, a bowl of sweetened fruit slices, citrons and peaches, apricots and berries, a platter of fried rice with eggs mixed in. As soon as the meal was set out the servants left, moving with an alacrity that underlined Harra's maid's report of Hamardan's morning moods. When the garden was empty, a small gray-plush monkey dropped from one of the trees and scurried to the table. He leaped up on it and picked through the dishes, lifted the lid of the teapot and shook a bit of paper over the tea. He peered into the pot and watched the gray bits of herb circling on the steaming water. The bits turned translucent and sank. He put the lid back on and scampered away, diving into the bushes just as Hamardan stomped out, glared at the sky, then stumped to the table, pushed back the sleeves of his robe, splashed out a bowlful of tea and gulped it down. The small gray monkey showed his teeth in a predator's grin, then blurred into a long serpent and began slithering through a hole in the wall.

Jaril slipped into the room where Harra was playing a muted accompaniment as Brann chatted with the Jamika about her children, listening more than she spoke. He squatted beside Harra. "He's guzzling it down," he whispered.

Harra nodded. She began simplifying the music until her fingers wandered idly over the daroud's strings; she closed her eyes and began a soft whistling that twisted round and round and incorporated the play of her fingers. An intense look of concentration on her face, she wove the spell, the magic in it itching at Jaril, it made his outlines shiver and blur and started eddies in his substance that acted on him like a powerful euphoric. A cold nose nudged at his hand. Yaril as hound bitch had crawled over to him and was pressing against him, quivering a little, her outlines shimmering, the same eddies in her substance. She was as uncertain as he about this feeling as a longterm experience, but she was enjoying the sensation, being a measure more hedonistic than her brother, willing to live in the pleasures of the moment, while he tended to fuss more about abstracts and what-will-be than what-was in the point present.

Harra stopped whistling. "It's done," she murmured. "Go back to him and whisper what you want in his ear."

Jaril jumped to his feet and went out.

Brann turned to watch him go, missing something the Jamika was saying. When the querulous voice snapped a reprimand at her, she swung back slowly and sat staring at the Temueng woman, her back very straight, waiting in silence until Tjena ran down. "If you're finished?" she said with an icy hauteur that quelled the woman, then she looked down at her own palms. "We are at a change time," she said, bringing each word out slowly, heavily as if she dropped over-ripe plums on the table and watched them mash. When she heard herself, she lightened up a bit, reminding herself that the woman might be thick but she wasn't totally stupid. "Forces converge," she said, "weaving strange patterns. It is a time to walk warily, every act will resonate far beyond the point of action. It is time that those tied to you experience a like courtesy. Give me your hands."

She held the Jamika's larger hands between her own, tilted her head back, closed her eyes. "The change is begun," she said. "The threads are spun out and out, fine threads wound about one, about and about, the links are made, son to mother, mother to son. What the mother does to those about her will be done unto the son." As she chanted the nonsense in a soft compelling voice, she tapped into the Temueng woman's life force, draining her slowly, carefully, until the woman was in a deeply suggestible daze. Softly, softly, Brann whispered, "Anything you do to us will be done to you, prison us here and your son will be a prisoner, send bad report about us to the other Jamars and Jamikas and your son will suffer slander, hurt us in any way and you hurt your son, hear me Tjena Hamardan Jamika, you will not remember my words, but you will feel them in your soul. Any harm you do to us, that same harm will come to your son. Hear my blessing, Tjena Hamardan Jamika, the benign side of the change coin. What good you do to man and maid in your power, Hina, Temueng or other, that good will bless you and your son, praise will perfume his days and nights. Good will come to you in proportion to the good you give, a quiet soul, a contented life, sweet sleep at night and harmony by day. Hear me, Tjena Hamardan Jamika, forget my words but feel them in your soul, forget my words, but find contentment in your life, forget my words." She set the Jamika's hands on the table and heard a soft unassertive whistle die behind her and knew Harra had reinforced her words with one of her whistle spells. "Sleep now, Tjena Hamardan Jamika. Sleep now and wake to goodness at your high noon tea. Lie back on your couch and sleep. Wake with the nooning, knowing what you must do. Sleep, sleep, sleep. . . ."

With Harra's help she straightened out the huge woman on the daycouch, smoothing out her robes and crossing her large but shapely hands below her breasts, smoothing her hair, fixing her so she would

wake with as few as possible of those debilitating irritations that came
from sleeping in day clothing. Brann frowned at her a moment, then
trickled some of the life back in her, doing it carefully enough she
didn't disturb her sleep; she moved away from the couch, going to the
door of the sitting room. Several maids were in the smaller room beyond, talking in whispers, working on embroideries and repairs while
they waited to be summoned. She beckoned to the senior maidservant,
showed her the sleeping form of the Jamika. "Your mistress will sleep
until time for tea; her night was disturbed and she was fretful."

An older Hina woman with a weary meekness from years of hector-
ing, the maid's mouth pinched into a thin line; she knew all too well
what fretfulness in the Jamika meant for her and the other maids.

Brann smiled at her. "If she finishes her sleep without being disturbed, the Jamika will wake in a sweeter temper and make your life
easier for a while, at least until the moon turns again."

The maid nodded, understanding what was not said. "Godalau's
blessing on you if it be so, Saör," she murmured, then went quickly
away from Brann, appreciative but uneasy with the stranger's powers.

Brann, Harra and the Yaril-hound went back to their rooms to pack,
having done everything they could to ensure good report and an un-
eventful departure on the morrow.

They rumbled from the House early the next morning, leaving behind
much good feeling among the Hina servants and a pair of contented
but rather confused Temuengs. Linjijan, who'd grown restless and unhappy closed within those walls, was delighted to stretch his spirit and
body—long thin legs propped up on the splashboard, neck propped on
his blanket roll, he played his flute, the music ebullient and joy-filled,
waking little devils in the horses, who'd also grown bored in their
sumptuous stables and were inclined to work off their excess energy in
bursts of mischievous behavior. Brann's dun shied at his own shadow,
kicked up his heels, tried to rear, and gave his rider some energetic
moments until she managed to settle him down a little. When they
passed from sight of the House, she let him run a short while but
pulled him back to an easy canter before he could blow himself and tire
her more.

Harra laughed and let her gray dance a bit, then quieted him and
added the plink of her daroud to the wanderings of the flute and the
dark music Negomas was stroking from his smallest drum.

At midday they reached Hamardan again and stopped at the Inn for a hearty lunch with hot tea and pleas from the Host to play again that night. Anxious to make up time Taguiloa shook his head to that but promised to stop there when the troupe returned to Silili.

Certainly Tunjii rode Taguiloa's shoulder those next four weeks as they followed the river road north. The weather was perfect for traveling and for outdoor performances. In villages without an Inn, they played to cheering crowds in the market square and more than once spent several nights in a Jamar's House, though there was no more trouble about leaving when they pleased. Word flew ahead of them; it seemed that every village and inland city was waiting and ready for them, folk swarming about the show wagon, following in shouting cheerful crowds as they drove through city streets or village lanes. The hiding places in the cart's bottom grew heavy with coin and the mood of Temueng and Hina alike was as genially golden as the weather. Whether it was his timing, the long summer having worked up a mighty thirst in them for diversion, whether it was the strong leavening of Temuengs in each audience, for whatever reason, the troupe met little of the resistance Taguiloa had expected to the strange and sometimes difficult music and the improvisational and wholly non-traditional dance and tumbling he was introducing. He began to worry. They were a tempting target for the Ular-drah, the hillwolves through whose territory they would have to pass, a small party of players coming off a phenomenally successful tour fat with gold, on their own, no soldiers, two of them women, two of them children, only the dog to worry about and they wouldn't worry that much about her. He could hope Tungjii would stick around, but he knew only too well the fickleness of his patron and the quicksilver quality of such fortune as that they bathed in these golden glowing days, these warm dry silver nights.

They left the city Kamanarcha early in a bright cool morning. There was a touch of frost on the earth, glittering in the long slant of the morning light. The guard at the city gate was yawning and stiff, more than half asleep as he operated the windlass that opened the gate. Taguiloa tossed him a small silver and got a shouted blessing from him along with a hearty request to come back soon. As an afterthought, the guard added, "Watch out for the drah, showman, word is they're prowling."

On top of the wagon's roof Negomas grinned and rattled his drum defiantly. Linjijan was stretched out more than half asleep, lost in the dreams he never spoke aloud. Of them all he'd changed the least during the tour, no closer now to the others than he'd been before, an amiable companion who did everything he was asked to do without skimping or complaint and nothing at all he was not asked to do. He was no burden and no help, irritating each of the others in turn until they learned to accept him as he was for he certainly wasn't going to change. His flute was a blessing and a joy; that had to be enough.

Negomas and Harra were much together, studying each other's bits of magic. As Taguiloa had taken dance and tumbling and juggling and melded them into an exciting whole, had brought Harra and Negomas and Linjijan together and almost coerced them into producing the musical equivalent of his dance, so these orphan children of different traditions were blending their knowledge to make an odd, effective magic that belonged only to them and magnified their own power, the whole they made being greatly more than either apart.

Brann was as isolated from the others as Linjijan though more aware of it; she was simply too different now from human folk and her purposes were too much apart from theirs. She was fascinated by the illusions Harra and Negomas created for their own entertainment and by the intimate connection magic had with music as if the patterning of sounds by drum, daroud, and Harra's whistling somehow patterned the invisible in ways that allowed the boy and the young woman to control and manipulate it. After leaving Hamardan, Brann had tried to learn from Harra, but she could not. It was as if she were tone-deaf and trying to learn to sing. There was something in her or about her that would not tolerate magic. Harra found this fascinating and tried a number of experiments and found that any spells or even unshaped power that she aimed at Brann was simply shunted aside. Magic would not touch her, refused to abide near her. Harra and Negomas both could do whatever they wanted in her presence as long as whatever they did wasn't aimed at her. She wasn't a quencher, therefore, not a sink where magic entered and was lost; she simply wasn't present to it. At least, not any longer. She told Harra about the Marish shaman who'd netted her and the changechildren so neatly. Harra decided eventually that this had somehow immunized her and the children against any further vulnerability. Brann listened, sighed, nodded. "Slya's work," she said. "She doesn't want me controlled by anyone but her."

The countryside was brown and turning stubbly, the harvest coming in. The pastures were taking on a yellow look with sparse patches where little grass grew and fewer weeds. They were coming to the barrens where the soil was hard and cracked, laced with salt and alkali so that only the hardiest plants grew there and those only sparsely. Even along the river where there was plenty of water there was little vegetation and the trees had a stunted look.

For some hours they passed long straight lines of panja brush, low-growing bushes with smooth hard purplish bark, crooked branches and little round leaves hard as boiled leather. These lines were windbreaks against the winter storms that swept down off the northern plains, those flat gray grasslands that spawned the Temuengs. They left the last of the windbreaks behind a little after noon and were out of the Kamanarcha jamarak and into the barrens.

The road began to rise and the trees thinned and fell away. There was a little yellowish grass on the slopes but it didn't look healthy. The river sank farther below them into the great gorge that cut through the Matigunns; the road followed the lip of the gorge and the towpath continued far below them, the stone pilings that marked the edge of the canal jutting like gray fingers from cold pure water glinting bluer than blue in the late summer sun. The canal was part of the river here, the stone of the mountain heart too stubbornly resistant for anything else; the towpath was a massive project in itself, old tales said it was burned out of the stone by dragons' breath in the mythtime before Popokanjo shot the moon. There were no barges on the river yet, floating down or being towed up. In a few weeks, when the harvest up and down the river was complete, the trading season would begin and the huge Imperial dapplegrays that towed the barges from Hamardan to Lake Biraryry would be plodding northward in teams of eight or ten, escorted by the Emperor's Horse Guards. The dapples were bred and reared only in Imperial stables; anyone else found with one would be fed to them piece by piece because the dapples ate flesh as well as corn, human flesh by choice, though they'd make do with dog or cow or the flesh of other horses if there was no one in the Emperor's prisons healthy enough to be fed to them. The tow master for each team was raised with them from their foaling; he slept with them, ate with them, arranged their matings, tended them in every way, shod them, plaited mane and tail, washed and combed the feathering at their hocks, polished their hooves, repaired their harness, kept it oiled and shining. He did all that from pride and affection for his charges and also because they'd kill and eat anyone else who tried to come near them. Even the fiercest of the Ular-drah bands left them alone. Barge travel was safe but very expensive.

High overhead a mountain eagle soared in wide graceful loops, Yaril keeping watch over the road and the surrounding hills. She'd spot any ambushes long before they ripened into danger. Harra and Taguiloa were joking together, both of them relaxed and unworried for the moment; Yaril's presence was a guarantee that there was no present danger to the troupe. Brann rode ahead of the wagon, brooding over a problem that was becoming increasingly urgent. The children were hungry. The performing used up their strength far faster than she'd expected. She'd walked the alleys of Silili for a fortnight, taking the life force of every man who came after her intending to steal or rape or both, feeding the children until they were so sated they couldn't take another draft of that energy they needed for their strange life, storing more of the stolen life in her own body until her flesh glowed with it. Since then she'd fed them from herself and from what animal life she could trap, dogs and cats that roamed the streets of the cities and villages they played in, careful to take no human life. She didn't want anyone connecting mysterious deaths with the troupe. She cursed the Hamardan Jamar, he was the source of the trouble now; if it hadn't been for him, they'd have reached Andurya Durat already, the drain from the dregs of the city. A day or two more and she'd have to go hunting, anything she could find in these barren mountains, wolves two-legged or otherwise, deer, wildcats, anything the children could run to her. The children were patient, but need would begin to drive them and they would drive her.

By nightfall they were deep in the barrens. Yaril had found one of the corrals the dapples used when they walked the road to Hamardan, returning to pick up another barge. It was a stone circle with a heavy plank gate and three-sided stalls, locked grain bins and a stone watering trough. At the roadside there was a tripod of huge beams that jutted out over the river, a bucket and a coil of rope; there'd be no problem about bringing water up for them and for the horses. They set up their night camp inside the circle, filled the trough with water, emptied half a sack of grain in the manger (they didn't touch the grain bins, though the children could have opened them; that was dapple food and they'd be stealing directly from the Emperor. Not a good idea). The night promised to be cold and drear though Tungjii was still hanging about since the sky was clear and no rain threatened. The children went prowling about the hills and came back with lumps of coal for a fire, reporting a surface seam about a mile back from the road. Leaving Brann and the children to watch over the camp,

Taguiloa, Linjijan and Harra took empty feed sacks and fetched back as much as they could carry, more of Tungjii's blessing, Taguiloa thought, for there was no wood to make a fire and wouldn't be as long as they were in the barrens. And the nights were not going to get warmer.

Leaving Harra and Taguiloa making a stew from the store of dried meat and vegetables, arguing cheerfully over proportions and how much rice to put in the other pot, Negomas and Linjijan rubbing down the horses and going over them with stiff brushes, combing out manes and tails, cleaning their hooves, Brann went with the children to stand beside the tripod where they couldn't be seen by those inside the corral. She held out her hands and the children pulled life from her; she could feel them struggling to control the need that grew each night and she suffered with them. When they broke from her, she sighed. "You want to go hunting tonight?"

Yaril kicked a pebble over the edge and watched it leap down the nearly vertical cliff and plop into the water. "Might not have to."

"Ular-drah?"

"Uh-huh. A man's been watching us since late afternoon."

"Where's he now?"

"Gone. He left before we found the coal. Left as soon as it was obvious we were settling for the night."

"Ah. You could be right."

Yaril nodded, her silver-gilt hair shining in the light of the Wounded Moon. She giggled. "Our meat coming to us."

"How soon, do you think?"

"Not before they think everyone's asleep. They think we'll be trapped inside that." She nodded her head at the corral. "I say we turn the trap on them." She looked at Jaril. He nodded. "Me out at long-scout, night-owling it. Jaro staying with you to carry reports. What about numbers? I think four or five of them is all right, we're sure hungry enough to handle them. Ten or more we'd better scare off, we could cut some out, two or three maybe, hamstring them so they can't run, what do you think, Bramble?"

Brann felt a twinge of distaste, but that didn't last long. The Ular-drah were a particularly unpleasant bunch with no pretensions to virtue of any sort, the best of them with the gentle charm of cannibal sharks. She nodded at the corral. "Tell them?"

"I vote no," Yaril said.

Jaril nodded. "Let 'em sleep. They'll just get in the way."

Brann sighed, then she smiled. "Just us again." Her smile broadened into a grin. "Look out, you wolves."

Jaril looked up. "Six of 'em. On their way." He blurred into a wolf form and went trotting into the dark.

Brann pulled her fingers through her hair, the black stripping away until it was white again, blowing wildly in the strong cold wind. She pulled off her tunic, tossed it to the ground beside the stone wall, stepped out of her trousers, kicked them onto the tunic. The air was very cold against her skin but she'd learned enough from the children to suck a surprising amount of warmth from the stone under her feet and bring it flowing up through her body. Comfortable again, she still hesitated, then she heard the yipping of the wolf and set off in that direction running easily through the darkness, her eyes adapting to the dark as her body had adapted to the cold. She reached a small, steep, walled bowl with the meander of a dry stream through the middle of it, a few tufts of withered grass and a number of large boulders rolled from the slopes above the bowl. A horned owl came fluttering down, transforming as it touched the earth into Yaril. "You might as well wait here. They're a couple breaths behind me." Then she was a large gray wolf vanishing among the boulders.

Brann looked about, shrugged and settled herself on a convenient boulder, crossed her legs, rested her hands on her thighs, and culti- vated a casual, relaxed attitude.

The Ular-drah came out of the dark, a lean hairy man walking with the wary lightness of a hunting cat. The rest of the drah were shadows behind him, lingering among the boulders. He stopped in front of her. "What you playing at?"

She got slowly to her feet, moving with a swaying dance lift, smiled at him and took a step toward him.

He looked uncertain but held his ground.

She reached toward him.

He caught her arm in a hard grip. "What you think you doin, woman?"

"Hunting a real man," she crooned to him. She stroked her fingers along his hard sinewy arm, then flattened her hand out on his bare flesh and sucked the life out of him.

As he fell, she leaped back wrenching her arm free. In the boulders a man screamed; others came rushing at her, knives and swords in hand. She danced and dodged, felt a burn against her thigh as a sword sliced shallowly, slapped her hand against the first bit of bare flesh she could reach, pulled the life out of that one, More pain. She avoided some of the edges, took a knife in the side, touched and killed, touched and killed. Twin silver wolves slashed at legs, bringing some of the men down, blurring as steel flashed through them, wolves again as swiftly. Three men drained, two men down, crawling away. Touch and drain. Man on one leg lunging at her, knife searing into her side. Touch and drain. Touch and drain. All six dead.

Gritting her teeth against the pain, she jerked the knife free and tossed it away, the wound healing before the knife struck stone and went bounding off. She straightened, felt the tingle of the life filling her. The wolves *changed.* Yaril and Jaril stood before her, held out pale translucent hands. They had expended themselves recklessly in this chase and the drain of it had brought them dangerously close to quenching. She held out her hands, let the stolen life flow out of her into them, smiling with pleasure as the mountain's children firmed up and lost their pallor.

When the feeding was complete she looked around at the scattered bodies, felt sick again. I've saved Slya knows how many lives by taking theirs. . . . She shook her head, the sickness in her stomach undiminished. Shivering, she strode back to the stone circle, Yaril and Jaril trotting beside her, looking plumper and contented with the world. She pulled her hands back over her hair, darkening the shining silver to an equally shining black. She stepped back into the trousers, pulled the laces tight and tied them off, wriggled into the tunic and smoothed it down. Suddenly exhausted, she leaned against the stone wall. "I'm going to sleep like someone hit me over the head. Any chance we'll get more visitors?"

"Not for a while," Yaril said. "I didn't see any more bands close enough to reach us before morning, but I'll have another look to make sure."

Brann nodded and stood watching as two large owls took heavily to the air. She watched them vanish into the darkness, hating them that moment for what they'd done to her, for what they made her do. A lifetime of draining men to feed them and Slya knew what that word *lifetime* meant when it applied to her. The flare-up died almost as quickly as it arose. There was no point in hating the children; they'd followed nature and need. And as for living with the consequences of that need, well, she'd learned a lot the past months about how malleable the human body and spirit was and how strong her own will-to-live was. Like the children, she'd do what she had to and try to minimize the damage to her soul. Like them too she was in the grip of the god, swept along by Slya's will, struggling to maintain what control she could over her actions. She followed the high stone wall around to the gate and went in.

Taguiloa sat by the fire, breaking up chunks of coal with the hilt of his knife, throwing the bits in lazy arcs to land amid the flames. He looked up as she came into the light, then went back to what he was doing. She hesitated, then walked across to stand beside him.

"How many of them?" he said.

"Six. How did you know?"

"Figured. Got them all?"

"Yes."

He tossed a handful of black bits at the fire, wiped his hand on the stone flagging. After a moment he said, "The three of you were looking washed out."

"We wouldn't hurt you or any of the others."

"Hurt. I wonder what you mean by that." He began chunking the hilt against another lump of coal, not looking at her. "What happens when we get to Durat?"

"I don't know. How could I? My father, my brothers, my folk, I have to find them and break them loose. You knew that before you took up with me. I don't want to have to choose between you . . . and the others . . . and my people, Taga. I'll keep you clear if I can. I'll leave you once we get to Durat, I'll change the way I look." She shrugged. "What more can I do? You knew it was a gamble when you agreed to bring me to Durat. You knew what I was. You want to back out now?"

"You could destroy me."

"Yes."

"Make it impossible for me to work where there are Temuengs."

"Yes."

"You knew that in Silili."

"Yes."

"You know us now. We're friends, if not friends, then colleagues. And still, if you have to, you'll destroy us."

"Yes."

"All right. As long as it's clear." He smiled suddenly, a wry self-mocking twist of his lips. "You're right. I gambled and I knew it. Your gold to finance a tour and a chance for the Emperor's Sigil against the chance you'd get us chopped." He touched his shoulder. "Tungjii's tough on fainthearts. I go on. As for your leaving us, could cause more talk than if you stayed. You're part of the troupe the Duratteese are waiting to see. Until we perform at the Emperor's Court, if we ever do, you're part of the troupe, remember that and be careful."

She lifted her hands, looked at them, let them fall. "As careful as I'm let, Taga."

5.

Brann's Quest—Andurya Durat: The Rescue and Attendant Wonders

Taguiloa stopped the wagon at the top of a stiff grade, sat looking down a winding road to the oasis of Andurya Durat. Dry brown barren mountains, ancient earth's bones sucked clean of life and left to wither, two files of them blocking east and west winds, funnelling south the ice winds of the northern plains. Andurya Durat, doubly green and fecund when set against those mountains, steamy damp dark green, lush, born from the hot springs at the roots of Cynamacamal, the highest of the hills, its angular symmetry hidden by a belt of clouds, its cone-peak visible this day, splashed thick with blue-white snow.

Absently stroking and patting the neck of her fractious mount, Brann stared at the mountain, feeling immensely and irrationally cheered. It was a barebones replica of Tincreal; she felt the presence of Slya warm and comforting. She would win her people free, she didn't know how yet, but that was only a detail.

Taguiloa watched her gaze at the mountain and wondered what she saw to make her smile like that, with a gentleness and quiet happiness he hadn't seen in her before. He turned back to the road, frowned down at the dark blotch on the shores of the glittering lake, sucked in a breath and put his foot on the brake as he slapped the reins on the cob's back, starting him down the long steep slope, wishing he could put a brake on Brann. Godalau grant she didn't run wild through those Temuengs down there.

Andurya Durat. Stuffed with Temuengs of all ranks. Glittering white marble meslaks like uneven teeth built on the shores of the largest lake, snuggling close to the monumental pile still unfinished that housed the Emperor and his servants, vari-sized compounds where the Meslar overlords lived and drew taxes from the Jamars in the south, the

Basshar nomad chiefs in the north. Along the rivers and on the banks of the cluster of smaller lakes, there were Inns and Guesthouses that held Jamars from the south come up to seek an audience from the Emperor so they could boast of it to their neighbors, to seek legal judgments from the High Magistrate, come up to the capital for a thousand other reasons, and there were tent grounds and corrals that held the Basshars and their horse breeders down from the Grass with pampered pets from their tents to sell for Imperial gold, with herds of kounax for butchering, with leatherwork, with cloth woven from the long strong kounax hair, with yarn, rope, glues, carved bones and other products of the nomad life. Scattered among the farms that fed the city were riding grounds for the horse and mallet games played with bloody kounax heads, a noisy brutal cherished reminder of the old days when the Durat Temuengs were nomad herders on the Sea of Grass, ambling behind their blatting herds, fighting little wars over water and wood. Times the old men among the Meslars spoke of with nostalgia, celebrating the ancient strengths of the People. Times even the most fervid of these celebrators hadn't the slightest inclination to recreate for themselves.

There was another Andurya Durat tucked away behind massive walls, the Strangers' Quarter, a vigorous vulgar swarm of non-Temuengs. Shipmasters and merchants from the wind's four quarters, drawn to the wealth of the ancient kingdom. Players of many sorts, hoping for an Imperial summons and the right to display the Imperial sigil. Artisans of all persuasions, many of them working under contract to build and maintain the gilded glory of the vast city outside the walls. Inn and tavern keepers, farmers (mostly Hina) in from the local farms with meat and produce, scribes, poets, painters, mages and priests, beggars, thieves, whores. And children, herds and hordes of children filling every crack and corner. Winding streets, crowded multi-storied tenements with shops on the ground floor and a maze of rooms above, taverns, godons, the market strip, all these existing in barely contained confusion and non-stop noise, shouts, quarrels, music clashing with music, raucous songs, barrowmen and women shouting their wares, yammer of gulls, bubbling coos from pigeons, twitters and snatches of song from sparrins and chevinks, harsh caws from assorted scavenger-birds, screams from falcons soaring high like headsmen's double-bitted axes, sharp-edged and cleanly in their flight.

Taguiloa inserted himself and his company into this noisy multicolor polyglot community, just one more bit of brightness in a harlequinade as subtle and as blatant as frost-dyed leaves in a whirlwind, taking his troupe to the Inn where he and Gerontai stayed the time they came seeking to perform for the Emperor.

Papa Jao sat outside his Inn on a throne of sorts raised higher than a Temueng's head, his platform built of broken brick, rubble arranged at random, set in a mortar of his own making that hardened and darkened with the years so the stages of the throne's rise were as clearly evident as the rings on a clamshell. On top of the pillar he'd built himself a chair with arms and a back and covered it with ancient leather pillows. It was his boast that he never forgot a face, something likely true because he wrapped his hands around the chair arms, leaned out and cried, "Taga. Come to make your fortune?"

"You know it, Papa Jao. How's it going?"

"Sour and slim, Taga, sour and slim." Bright black eyes moved with a never-dying curiosity over the wagon and the rest of the troupe. "Ah ah," he chortled, "it's you been tickling gold out of Jamar purses." The chortle fruited into a wheezy laughter that shook every loose flap of flesh inside and outside his clothing. He was a pear-shaped little man with a pear-shaped head, heavy jowls, a fringe of spiky white hair he drew back and tied in a tail as wild as a mountain pony's brush after it'd been chased through a stand of stoneburrs. "How many rooms you want? Four? Yah, we got 'em, second floor, good rooms, a silver a week each, right with you? Well, well, rumor say truth for once." He leaned round, yelled, "Jassi! Jass-ssii, get your tail out here," swung back. "You want stable room for the horses and a bit of the back court for your wagon? Silver a week for the horses, we provide the grain, three coppers for the wagon, oh all right, I throw in the court space." Leaned round once more. "Angait! Anga-ait! Get over here and show saö Taguiloa where to go."

The next day Taguiloa busied himself burrowing into the complicated and frustrating process of getting the troupe certified for performing in Durat, working his way up the world of clerks and functionaries, parting as frugally as possible with Brann's coin, returning to the Inn that night, exhausted, angry and triumphant, the permit, a square of stamped paper, waving from a fist sweeping in circles over his head. Harra laughing. Brann clapping. Negomas slapping a rhythm on a tabletop. Linjijan wandering in with the practice flute he was almost never without.

Taguiloa's return metamorphosed into an impromptu performance for the patrons of Jao's Inn, Taguiloa dancing counterpoint to Brann, Harra whistling, Linjijan producing a breathy laughing sound from his flute, Negomas playing the tabletop and a pair of spoons—the whole ending in laughter and wine and weariness. Taguiloa went up the stairs relaxed, mind drifting, frustration dissipated; rubbing against his own kind he had rubbed away the stink of Temuengs and their stupid arrogance.

While Taguiloa was swimming against the stream of Temueng indifference and stupidity, while Negomas and Harra were out exploring the market, watching street conjurers and assessing the competition, Brann set out to do some exploring of her own, hunting without too much urgency for a niche where she could make changes without interested observers; she wanted no connection between Sammang—if he had come to Durat—and Taguiloa's black-haired seer. The Strangers' Quarter swarmed with people. Not a corner, a doorway, a rubble heap, a roof nook empty of children, beggars, women and men watching the ebb and flow in the street. She worked her way to the wharves, finding more space among the godons as long as she avoided the guards the merchants hired to keep the light-fingers of the Quarter away from their goods. Yaril found a broken plank in one of the scruffier godons, flowed inside and kicked it loose while Jaril-hawk flew in circles overhead watching for guards.

Brann crept inside, stripped off the skirt and coins, stripped the black from her hair, altered her face to the one Sammang knew. She straightened, smiling, feeling more herself than she had in weeks, as if somehow she'd taken off a cramping shell. A sound. She wheeled, hands reaching, straightened again. Jaril stood looking up at her. "I'll stay," he said.

"Why?"

"I'm tired."

"I should hunt tonight?"

"Uh-huh." He looked around at the dusty darkness. "Who knows what's hived in here. You'll want the skirt and things when you're ready to go back to the Inn. Be nice if they were still here."

She frowned at him. "You sure you're all right?"

"Don't fuss, Bramble. I gave Yaril a bit extra, that's all. In case something goes bad round you." He blurred into a black malouch and curled up on the skirt, his chin on the pile of linked coins, his eyes closed, running away as he always did when she tried to probe his thoughts and feelings. As Yaril always did. She shook her head impatiently, ran her hands through her hair, dropped to her knees and crawled out into the street.

Yaril walking beside her, a frail fair girlchild again, Brann began searching along the wharves for Sammang or one of his crew. Ebullient Tik-rat who'd be whistling and jigging about, center of a noisy crowd. Hairy Jimm who'd tower over everyone by a head at least, a wild woolly head. Staro the Stub, wide as he was tall with big brown cow eyes that got even milder when he was pounding on someone who'd commented on his lack of inches. Turrope, lean and brown and silent, Tik-rat's shadow. Leymas. Dereech. Rudar. Gaoez. Uasuf. Small brown men like a thousand others off a hundred ships, but she'd know them all the moment she saw them. And Sammang. There was a flutter at the base of her stomach when she thought of meeting Sammang again. She wove in and out of the godons, went up and down the piers jutting into the river, looking and looking, her face a mask, never stopping, fending off hands that groped at her, sucking enough life out of men who refused to back off to send them wandering away in a daze. From the west wall to the east she went, searching and finding none of those she searched for, stood with her hand on the east wall, tears prickling behind her eyes, a lump in her throat—until she convinced herself that Sammang would keep his men out of trouble while he waited for her and the best way to do that would be to keep them off the wharves. She rubbed at her forehead, trying to think. Where would he be? If he was here. How could he make himself visible but not conspicuous? Hunh. Phrased like that the answer was obvious. If he was here, he'd be sitting in a wharfside tavern waiting for her to walk in.

She began working her way west again, drifting in and out of taverns as the afternoon latened, ignoring shouted offers from traders, shipmasters, sailors, and others who mistook her purpose, ignoring caustic comments from several tavernkeepers who objected to her presence or the presence of Yaril in their taprooms. As shadows crept across the streets and out onto the river, she came to a quiet rather shabby structure near the western wall. Her feet were starting to give out, her knees were tired of bending and she was about ready to quit. How easy once she was out of sight and touch for Sammang to change his mind, call himself a fool, head for pleasanter waters.

Without much hope she pushed through the door, stood looking around, squinting against the gloom, trying to make out the faces of the dark forms seated at tables about the room. The man behind the bar came round it and crossed the room, a little rotund man without much force to him.

"We don't want children in here. You should be ashamed of yourself, woman, using a baby like that in the business. Go on, get out of here, go on, go go go." He waved pudgy hands at her like a farmwife shooing chickens out of the kitchen garden.

She glared down at him, her patience pushed beyond its limit. "You calling me a whore, little man?"

He winced. "No need for hard words, what do I care what you do? Just don't do it here."

"What I'm going to do here is sit myself down and have a bowl of wine and my young friend is going to do likewise." She pushed past him and went to one of the stools at the bar, swung up on it and sat massaging her knees. Yaril climbed up beside her, sat with her small chin propped on her palms, her elbows braced against the aged dark wood.

A chuckle came from one of the darker corners. Brann's stomach turned over and she felt breathless as she recognized the voice. Sammang came into the light, stopped beside her. "I greet you, witch. So you made it."

The little man started, opened his eyes wide, set a winebowl in front of her, one in front of Yaril, shoved the jug at her and backed hastily away without waiting for payment. She slanted a glance at Sammang, filled the bowls and sipped at the wine, sighing with pleasure as the warmth spread through her. "So I did."

He reached round her, caught the jug by its neck, went back to the table. Yaril giggled. Brann scowled at her. "Finish that and go stand guard, if you don't mind."

Yaril nodded, gulped down the rest of the wine. Ignoring the goggling eyes of the barman, she wriggled off the stool and trotted out.

Brann squared her shoulders, slipped off the stool and marched with her bowl to the table in the corner where Sammang sat waiting for her. She set the bowl down with a loud click, pulled out a chair, dropped into it and scraped it close enough to the table so she could lean on crossed arms and look past him or at him as she chose. "Who's with you?"

"All of 'em; said they'd swim the whole damn river if I tried leaving them behind." He filled the bowl, pushed it toward her. "Relax, Bramble, I'm not going to jump your bones out here."

"Hunh! What about the *Girl?*" She sipped at the wine, her elbows braced on the wood to keep her hands from shaking, avoiding his eyes except for quick glances.

"I circled round by Perando, picked up a cousin of mine and his crew. He's got her tucked away up the coast a bit. When did you get in?"

"Yesterday. You?"

"A week ago; been doing some trading, lucked into a few things that should pay expenses. Yesterday, mmm. Haven't located your folk yet?"

"The children are going out again tonight. Tell Jimm to knock his totoom for me and stir up some luck; sooner this is done, the easier I'll be." She rubbed at the nape of her neck, frowned at the tabletop. There was a stirring in her that had nothing to do with the way Sammang made her feel, a sense of tidal forces moving that frightened her for herself, for her kin, for Sammang and the troupe, for everyone and everything she valued. She reached for the bowl, gulped more of the wine down and forced herself to ignore that fear.

"We're ready to go when you are."

She glanced at him, looked away. "I could know more tomorrow. Maybe we could meet here to make plans?" She had to fight to keep her voice steady. "If you're staying here?"

He reached out, closed his hand around hers. "Finish your wine and come upstairs."

"You sure?"

"I've decided face value's good value. I missed you."

"I . . . I hoped. . . ." She emptied the bowl and stood, swaying as the rush of the wine made her dizzy. Sammang reached out to steady her. His touch was fire, more disrupting than the wine. The first time they'd come together in the cabin of his ship, it'd been easy and natural as breathing, this was more deliberate, colder . . . no not cold, far from cold . . . but planned, not a sweet happening, but a deliberate step taken in full understanding of what she was doing. She was nervous and uncertain, afraid she couldn't please him this time. "The barman?" Her voice was a silly squeak; she flushed with embarrassment.

"None of his business, Bramble-without-thorns." Sammang touched her cheek. "Relax, little witch, we've plenty of time."

Fed up to full strength from the rats and snakes of the Quarter (Brann didn't want angry ghosts shouting her presence to the night winds and maybe Temueng ears), Yaril and Jaril flew out her window and swept on wide owl wings across the lake to the great pile resting on the roots of fire-hearted Cynamacamal. Brann hitched a hip on the windowsill and watched them vanish among the cloud shreds, staying where she was a while longer, enjoying the damp cool wind blowing up from the river. A long day. It was full dark before she could wrench herself from Sammang's side, getting back to the Inn just in time to celebrate Taguiloa's success. Then she had to go out again on the feeding hunt. Now she sat in the window, her thin silk robe open to the nudge of the soft wind, remembering the feel of the solid powerful body next to hers, the smell of him, the hard smoothness of his skin, the spring of his hair. She watched the Wounded Moon rise over the Wall, up thin and late, dawn only a few hours away, feeling within herself a deep-down purring that was not a part of her, a little angry at it, unhappy that it was there, hoping Sammang wasn't aware that he'd pleasured Slya perhaps as much as he'd pleasured her. She stretched and yawned, slid off the windowsill, padded across to the bed, dropping the robe to the floor as she moved, sinking into the flock mattress, sinking deep deep into a dreamless sleep.

Yaril and Jaril circled over the main pile of the palace, wheeled away as something wary and malevolent down there smelled them out and reached for them, long invisible fingers combing the air. They spiraled higher and stopped thinking, only-owls for a while, until they felt the fingers coil back down, felt the palace folding in on itself like a blood lily come the dawn. They drifted a while longer through the clouds, then went back to their swoops over the grounds, locating the guard barracks, the crowded warrens where the servants lived, the far more spacious and luxurious quarters of the Imperial dapples and the carefully tended fields where those monsters ran, the workshops and greenhouses, the foundry, the glass-making furnaces, the kitchen gardens, working their way out and out until they came to a new structure tucked into the folds of the mountain, an isolated compound still stinking of green cement and raw lumber. High walls, a guard tower overlooking a heavy barred gate. Torches burning low to light the space about the gate, lamps inside the tower, guards drowsing there but ready enough to come awake at a sound. The owls sailed across the wall and fluttered down onto a rooftree, then melted into light shimmers and slipped inside through the rooftiles.

Workshops. Spacious. Well-equipped, though there were no steel tools about. Locked up or carried away for the night, or for times when the tool users were sufficiently tamed that the tools wouldn't be a danger to them or the guards. The light smears zipped through the shops and passed into the living quarters. Room after empty room, then a sleeper, another, then more empty rooms. In all that vast place there were only twelve, of the twoscore gone to the Fair there were only a bare dozen left. Despite what the pimush had said—perhaps had said to escape a drawn-out dying—the Temueng soldiers had not been tender with the Arth Slya slaves. The changechildren wondered briefly if the Emperor still expected his double-hundred slaves from the Valley, wondered if the sribush in charge of the invasion forces had gotten tired of waiting and sent Noses prowling to find out what happened to the pimush and his captives.

When they'd probed the whole of the compound and made sure there were no others tucked away into the odd corner, they drifted back through the occupied rooms, naming the sleepers so they could tell Brann just who was there, knowing each because they knew what Brann knew.

Callim. Brann's father. He'd been beaten, probably because he declined to work. He was recovering, the beating must have been several days before, stretched out on the room's single bed, snoring, twitching as flies walked his back, the weals there sticky with salve. Cathar, Brann's oldest brother, slept curled up on a pallet in one corner, Duran her younger brother sat dozing in a chair beside the bed, waking now and then to fan the flies away.

In the next room over a man sat, dull-eyed, slack-faced, fingers plucking steadily at nothing, Uncle Idadro the etcher and inlayer, a finicky precise little man, never too adept at handling outsiders; his wife Glynis had gone to the Fair most years before but she died suddenly a weakness in the heart and left him drifting, his eldest son Trithin, his only anchor against the world, he was wholly unable to cope with. This year he'd taken that son to the Grannsha Fair, the boy blessed with his mother's bubbling good humor and ease with people. Little friend of all the world they called him when he was a baskling, then a trotling. No sign of Trithin anywhere within the compound; perhaps he was alive elsewhere, but neither of the changechildren believed it, more likely that the Wounded Moon rose whole than that they'd find Trithin walking earthface again.

This is the roll of the living they call out to Brann later: Callim, Cathar, Duran, Trayan, Garrag, Reanna, Theras, Camm, Finn, Farra, Fann and Idadro. Eight men, four women.

This is the roll of the dead: Trithin, Sintra, Warra, Wayim, Lotta, Doronynn, Imath, Lethra, Iannos and Rossha.

At the end of this final sweep the two light smears hovered in the middle of an empty room and sang to each other the questions that had occurred to them. What was that thing in the palace, that thing with the groping fingers? How powerful was it that it not only caused the Emperor to commit genocide, but made Slya herself act deviously, wrenching them from their home space and sending them to Brann to change her so she could be a vessel for Slya, bringing Slya here disguised to fight her attackers? They circled each other and sang their uncertainty. Should they tell Brann what they thought about it? She knew some of it already, knew Slya slept within her and simultaneously slept within Tincreal, knew Slya drove her as she drove the stone of Tincreal, with utter disregard for her and those she cared for. The changechildren contemplated that disregard with a chill in their fire-bodies that paled the light and almost sent them into their hibernating crystals, the form their people took when all energy was drained from them and no more would be available for some considerable time, the dormant form that was not death but a state for which their folk had little fondness and exercised their ingenuity to avoid unless the alternative was the dispersal of real death, like burnt-out stars choked to ash and nothing. The children hovered and shivered and were more afraid than they'd been since they woke on the slopes of Tincreal and found themselves starving in sunlight. "She might send us back when she's finished with us," Yaril sang.

"No. . . ." It was a long long sigh of a sound, filled with a not-quite despair; after all there was much to be said for this world and for the companionship they shared with Brann.

"We could talk to her," Yaril sang, "when this is over. Brann too. If Slya returns us, she'll have to change Brann back."

"Brann," Jaril sang, "is a brown leaf falling, not ignored but not restored. Why should Slya bother, after she gets the Arth Slyans free again and the vengeance she wanted for the slaughter? I think the great are the same in all realities, they use and discard, use and discard, this one and that, for what they consider the greater good. Their good. Poor Brann."

"Poor us."

"That too."

Two small light smears, very young for their kind with much of the long slow learning of that kind yet ahead of them, swooped anger-driven through the roof tiles, melted into twin owls and went powering back to Brann, uncertain what they should or would say to her, hoping with every atom of their impossible bodies that she slept and dreamed of the bite of pleasure she'd worried from the chaos of her life. They didn't know what to do, how the Slyans could be rescued without harming folk who were their friends, what to say to Brann if she asked their advice.

They glided through the open window, blurred into their childforms and tiptoed to the bed. Brann was deep asleep, her eyes moving under the lids, a small smile twitching her lips. Yaril looked at Jaril; he nodded and the two of them retreated into a corner and sank into the catalepsy that took the place of sleep.

Jassi stuck her head in the door, knocked against the wall.

Taguiloa looked up from the glitter sphere he was polishing.

"Someone to see you." She winked at him. "Tightass highnose creep with Maratullik's brand on him. Imperial Hand, eh man. You musta connect some good coming up."

Taguiloa set the sphere carefully into its velvet niche, got to his feet and began pacing about the room. This was an astonishingly early response to his permit; he'd expected several days of rest before the Temuengs took note of his presence, if they ever did. He stopped at the window, stared at the court without seeing any of it. I'm not ready. . . . He snapped thumb against finger, swung round. "That I did. Uh-huh." He smiled at Jassi. "Tell your creep friend I'm busy but if he wants to wait, I'll be down in a little while. If he decides he wants to hang around, offer him a bowl of your best wine so he won't be too-too annoyed."

"You could land up to your neck, Taga." She eyed him uncertainly, but with more respect than before. "You that sure of yourself?"

"Jassi, lady of my heart and elsewhere, I'm not, no I'm not, but if you scratch every time a Temueng itches, you'll wear your fingers down to nubs. Now go and do what I said." He wrinkled his nose. "If he walks, come tell me."

She shrugged and left.

Taguiloa closed his hands over the window sill, squeezed his eyes shut, breathed deeply. This was make or break. He knew as well as Jassi that he was taking a big chance. If the slave walked out chances were he or another like him would not be back. Chance. He touched his left shoulder. Tungjii, up to you, keep your eye on us.

He pushed away from the window, hunted out the travel papers and the metal credeens he was holding for all but Brann. He stood looking at them a moment, then tossed them on the bed, kicked off his sandals, stripped. Moving quickly about the room, he washed, brushed his long black hair, smoothed it down, tied it at the nape of his neck with a thin black silk ribbon, making a small neat bow over the knot. He dressed quickly in the dark cotton tunic and trousers, the low topped black boots that he thought of as his humble suit. When he was finished, he inspected himself carefully, brushed a hair off his sleeve, smoothed the front of the tunic. Neat but not gaudy. Smiling, he collected the papers and credeens, left his room and went down the hall to Harra's.

She let him in, went back to the skirt she was embroidering, using this bit of handiwork to calm her nerves and pass the time. He looked around. Except for them the room was empty. "Seen Brann?"

"She went out with the changekids this morning early. Excited about something." Harra narrowed her eyes. "That's your go-see-the-massa outfit."

"The Imperial Hand sent a slave to fetch me." His eye twitched, he put his hands behind him, not as calm as he wanted to appear. "I'm letting him stew awhile."

"Don't let it go too long. But you don't need me telling you that. Think it could maybe be about Brann?"

"I don't know. He asked for me, Jassi says."

"Ah. Then it's either very good news and we're on our way to the Court or it's very bad news and the Hand's going to be asking you questions you don't want to answer." She paused a moment. "Last doesn't seem likely. If he was going to be asking nasty questions, he'd send an empush and his squad to fetch you, not some slave."

"Right. Here. You keep these." He gave her the troupe's papers and the credeens after separating out his own. "In case." A wry smile, a flip of his hand. "In case the Hand is sneakier or crazier than we know. Get Negomas and Linjijan back to Silili."

"And Brann?"

"If I don't come back, be better if you keep as far from her as you can. You know why she's here." He moved his thumb over his own credeen, slipped it into his sleeve. "Well, I've killed enough time. I'd better get downstairs."

"Keep your cool, dancer."

"I'll try, mage-daughter, I shall try."

Taguiloa followed the silent slave through the West Gate onto the broad marble-paved avenue fronting the lake, thinking about the year he and Gerontai had come here. They'd got to the lower levels of the Temuengs, the merchants and magistrates and minor functionaries, but the powerful had ignored them and they made their way back to Silili without getting near the Emperor's halls. Meslar Maratullik was the Emperor's Left Hand, running the Censors and the Noses, head of security about the Emperor's person. Hope and fear, hope and fear, alternating like right foot, left foot creaking on the gritty marble. Following the silent sneering slave, he walked along that lakeside boulevard, past walls on one side, high smooth white walls with few breaks in them, only the massive gates and the narrow alleys between the meslaks. The lakeside was planted with low shrubs and occasional trees, stubby piers jutted into the lake, with pleasure boats, sail and paddle, tied to them. The lake itself was quiet and dull, the water reflecting the gray of the clouds gathering thickly overhead. No rain, just the grayed-down light of the afternoon and a steamy heat that made walking a punishment even in these white stone ways as clean and shining and lifeless as the shells on an ancient beach. Now and then bands of young male Temuengs came racing down that broad avenue on their high-bred warhorses, not caring who they trampled, whooping and yelling, sometimes even chasing down unhappy slaves, leaving them in crumpled heaps bleeding their plebian blood into the noble stone. Taguiloa's escort had a staff with Maratullik's sigil on a placard prominently displayed so they escaped the attention of the riders.

Maratullik's meslak was a broad rolling estate on the lakeshore with a riding ground, a complex of workshops and servant housing, extensive gardens, self-sufficient within the outerwalls should some disaster turn the meslak into a fortress. Taguiloa followed the slave through the gates into the spacious formal gardens with their fountains and banks of bright flowers, the exquisitely manicured stretches of grass; he looked around remembering the noisy rat-ridden Quarter and knew if he was absolutely forced to choose between the two, he'd take the rat-home, not this emptiness, but such a choice was most unlikely; what he was determined to ensure was a less radical choice, staying out of the slums, keeping himself and Blackthorn (if it came to that) in reasonable comfort after his legs went and his body would no longer do what his mind desired. What he had now suited him very well, the silence, meditation, comfort of his small house on the hillside, the noise and excitement of Silili nights.

It took twenty minutes to work through the gardens and corridors to a small glassed-in garden with a gently plashing fountain in the center, falls and sprays of miniature orchids, some rare kinds Taguiloa had never seen before, one huge tree encased within the bubble, fans worked by ropes and pulleys from outside by slaves who never saw the beauty they maintained. There were wicker chairs scattered about, singly and in small clusters, but he was not tempted to sit despite the two-hour walk and his aching feet. He moved his shoulders, tightened and loosened his muscles to calm himself. There was no point getting angry at the Temueng and there were a lot of reasons he shouldn't. He knew he had to control his irritation. He didn't take easily to groveling, had lost the habit of it the past five years, but all that he'd won for himself in Silili meant nothing here.

The Meslar Maratullik Left Hand Counsellor to the Emperor came into the garden with a feline grace and the silent step of a skilled hunter. He was short for a Temueng, though he was more than a head taller than Taguiloa; his face was rounder, less bony, the features more delicate than most Temuengs'. He wore a narrow robe of heavy dark gray silk, finely cut, arrogant in its simplicity. As Taguiloa bent in the prescribed deep obeisance, he went cold with the thought that perhaps there was Hina blood somewhere in the Hand's ancestry. If that was true, he was in a doubly perilous position; he'd seen too often what happened if a Hina in an important family was born with Woda-an characteristics, how that man made himself rigidly Hina, rejecting everything that would dilute the ancient Hina culture, how that man overtly and in secret tormented any Woda-an unfortunate to fall into his hands. And how often such a man ended up in a position like the Hand's where he had a great deal of power over the lives of others, especially those he hated so virulently. Taguiloa could trip himself up here without ever knowing precisely what he'd done to bring the mountain down on his head. Care, take care, he cautioned himself. Don't relax till you're out of here and maybe not even then.

Maratullik acknowledged Taguiloa's presence with a stiff short nod, crossed to the fountain, settled himself in one of the wicker chairs and spent some moments smoothing out the heavy silk of his robe. He lifted his head, his dark eyes as dull and flat as the silk, beckoned Taguiloa forward, stopped him with an open palm when he was close enough.

Taguiloa bowed again, then waited in silence, eyes lowered. A game, that's all it was, a game with bloody stakes. Yielding just enough to propitiate this Temueng that rumor made a monster, yet not enough to lose his self-respect, walking the hair-fine ridge between capitulation and catastrophe. He waited, his hands clasped behind him so they wouldn't betray his tension.

Maratullik was silent for a long time, perhaps testing the quality of Taguiloa's submission, more likely taking a bit of pleasure in making him sweat. "We have heard good things of you, Hina." The monster's voice was a high thin tenor.

"I am honored, saö jura Meslar," Taguiloa murmured. He could feel sweat damping the cloth under his arms; he fought to keep his grasp on himself, telling himself the Hand expected such signs of nervousness and would be suspicious if he failed to see them. The two silences stretched on. Taguiloa's head started to ache. There was no way he could get anything like respect from this Temueng, but making a doormat of himself would only incite the man to stomp him into the ground.

"You have foreigners in your troupe."

"Yes, saö jura Meslar." Taguiloa lifted his eyes just enough to catch glimpses of Maratullik's hands. At the word *foreigner,* the fingers twitched toward closing, opening again slowly and reluctantly. At Taguiloa's mild and noncommittal answer the fingers stiffened into claws. Taguiloa sweated some more. Trying to play safe was less than safe in this game. Should he amplify his answer or would that further antagonize the Temueng? After a few moments of harried thought, he elected to wait for the next question and see how a more extended answer affected those hands, hoping all the time that Maratullik didn't know how thoroughly his small and delicate fingers betrayed him.

"Why?"

Taguiloa shifted from foot to foot, let his nervousness show a bit more, disciplined his voice to a dull monotone. "Three reasons, saö jura Meslar." He spoke softly, slowly, choosing his words with care, his eyes flicking, careful not to look at the hands too long. "First, saö jura Meslar, when I was younger, I made tours through the Tigarezun with my master Gerontai and I have taken notice of how eagerly the countryfolk greeted exotic acts and how well they reward those that please them." He winced inside at the pompous greed in the speech but the fingers were relaxing; he was conforming to expectation. "Second, saö jura Meslar, making a tour such as this is very costly especially in the beginning; aside from their other talents the members of the troupe excepting the children have contributed to outfitting us and will have a share in whatever we take in, the foreigners of course taking a much smaller share than the Hina." Glance at the hands. Almost flat out. Good. But don't overdo the boring bit. Or the greed. "Third, saö jura Meslar, though this will be of little importance to you, it carries a high weight with me, there are my own aspirations. I seek to blend tumbling, juggling and dance into something no man has seen before. The music I found to accompany this new movement was also a blend, a music from M'darjin drums, Rukka-nag daroud, Hina flute, a music that is sufficiently different to be intriguing, sufficiently familiar for the comfort of the listeners. It is an exciting music, saö jura Meslar, all who have heard it agree." He bowed again and fell silent. Watch what you say; he's far from stupid or he wouldn't be where he is.

"Tell me about your foreigners. The women first."

"They are honored by your interest, saö jura Meslar." Taguiloa cleared his throat. "I know only outlines, saö jura Meslar, I must confess it, I wasn't interested in their life stories, only their coin and their skills. Harra Hazhani is Rukka-nag from far out in the west somewhere, you will of course know of them. She came to Silili with her father, he died and left her without protection or a place to go and a limited amount of coin so she needed a way to earn more. The customs and strictures of her people forbid her on pain of death to sell that which is a woman's chief asset and besides she was a foreigner, only the perverse would pay for her. However she is an excellent dancer in her way and a musician of considerable talent. The other woman is called Brannish Tovah, she is Sujomann, out of the west too, from up in the far north somewhere, she says winter nights last half a year and the snow comes down until it's high enough to drown mountains. I needed a seer who could also dance and she came well recommended. She's bound to the wind by her god or so she said, goes where the wind blows, said she lost a husband and two children to ice and wolves, has a brindle boar hound she says is her familiar and a street child she picked up who has something to do with helping her in her rites and acts as crier to call clients so she can read for them. Like the Hazhani woman, she is forbidden by custom and her in-dwelling god to seek congress with men not her kind. Were she to be forced, she is bound by her god to castrate the man and kill herself. That tends to reduce the ardor of any who might find her interesting. To speak truly, saö jura Meslar, I was quite pleased when I learned these things. Having women in a troupe is always a tricky thing, can lead to complications with the countryfolk if they consider themselves free to supplement their incomes on their back. The M'darjin drummer is a boy about ten or so, hard to tell with those folk. He has no father or relatives willing to claim him, though how that happened is not clear to me. I did not bother to probe for answers, I was not interested in anything but the way he played the drums. Linjijan the flute player is Hina and the second best in all Silili, the first being his great uncle Ladjinatuai who plays for Blackthorn." He bowed and waited tensely for the Hand's response.

Hands still loose on his thighs, Maratullik was silent for some breaths, then he said, "Both women come from the west."

"So they said, saö jura Meslar."

The questioning went on for a short while longer, Maratullik's hands relaxed, his voice gone remote and touched with distaste. He was no longer much interested in the answers and Taguiloa rapidly shortened them to the minimum required by courtesy. Short as they were, the Temueng interrupted the last. "You will perform here tomorrow night," he said. "You will make the necessary arrangements with my house steward. Wait here." He got to his feet and glided out, ignoring Taguiloa's low bow, his attitude saying he had forgotten the matter completely, it was of that small an importance in his life. Taguiloa squeezed his hands together, froze his face into a mask, exultation bubbling in him; he struggled to keep his calm, but all he could think was, *I've won, I've almost won.*

Hair a white shimmer tied at the nape of her neck, clothes a black tunic and trousers, worn sandals on her feet, Brann walked through the busy market, making her way to Sammang's tavern, in no hurry to get there, savoring the anticipation, enjoying the exuberant vitality of the scene around her. A face came out of the crowd, two more. She strangled a cry in her throat. Cathar. Camm. Theras. Her brother. A cousin by blood. A cousin by courtesy. Faces she knew as well as her own. She began following them, trying to stay inconspicuous, afraid of losing sight of them.

Cathar sauntered through the market, his eyes alive with pleasure in the jumbled colors and forms, stopping to bargain for fruit and herbs, a length of cloth, joking with the cousins, in no hurry, unaccompanied by any guard she could see, paying for his purchases with a metal tablet he showed the vender. She wanted desperately to talk to him, but didn't dare approach him. After her first flush of emotion, her mind took over. What was he here for except as bait to draw her out? Otherwise, why would the Temuengs let him and the others beyond the compound walls, taking a chance they'd run? Not much of a chance with the hostages the Temuengs held, but how could they be sure? Had to be Noses about. She couldn't see any but that meant very little in this crush. Anyway, how could she tell a Nose from the rest of the folk here? Couldn't smell them. She choked back a hysterical giggle. Besides, what could she say to Cathar if she did go up to him? Hello, I'm your little sister. A foot taller, hair gone white, fifteen years too old, but I'm still Brann. Bramble-all-thorns. No, I'm not a crazy woman. I really am your sister. Eleven years old, never mind my form. Ha! He'd believe her, like hell he would. She chewed on her lip as she eased after them, trying to think of some way she could talk with him without giving herself away to the Noses.

Yaril tugged on her arm. She let the changechild lead her into a side street, where there was a jog in a building that gave her a bit of privacy.

"House of assignation," Yaril whispered. "There's one the next street over. You put on a Hina face and go rent a room, I'll bring Cathar to you."

Brann grimaced. "Yaril. . . ."

The changechild scratched at her head, made an impatient gesture with her other hand. "The door's got twined serpents painted on it. You just go and knock and say you want a room for the afternoon and give the old woman three silver bits and tell her your servant will be bringing someone later and let the maid take you up. When the girl's gone, you take your clothes off and put on the robe you'll find in the room and sit down and wait." She frowned. "Keep the Hina face. And you'd better make it a kind of wrinkled up face. Dirty old woman paying young men to service her. Just in case Cathar's Nose decides to check you out."

Brann wrinkled her nose. "Tchah! What a thing."

"You don't have to like it, just do it."

"Don't be too long. You sure you can convince him?"

Yaril giggled. "Cathar? You know your brother, never passed up a chance in his life. I'll get him there, you be ready."

She was sitting at a table near the window when Cathar walked into the room, curiosity bright in his gray-green eyes, his dark brown hair blown into a tangle of small soft curls. She watched him with deep affection and nearly wept with joy to see him so much himself in spite of everything that had happened. He came and looked her over, a glint of amusement and interest in his eyes. He bowed. She felt a knot tighten in her stomach, she didn't want her brother looking at her like that even if he didn't know who she was and thought she was some rich Hina matron who got her thrills from picking up young men in the market.

She leaned forward, started to speak.

Yaril said hastily, "Wait." She darted into the shadows of the bed curtains, emerged as a smear of light sweeping along the walls.

Cathar's eyes widened, he looked from the light to Brann, began backing toward the door, his hand reaching for the latch.

"Cathar," Brann whispered, "wait."

"You know me?" He blinked, stood frozen with shock as Brann's face rippled and changed to the one she woke up with on the flight from the valley. He licked his lips. "What. . . ."

Brann glanced at Yaril who was a small blond girlchild again. The changechild nodded. "No one listening right now. I'll keep an eye out downstairs just to make sure. He had a shadow." She flicked a hand at Cathar. "Like you suspected." She grinned up at him. "Relax, baby, no one's going to hurt you." She tugged on the latch, pulled the door open and went out.

Brann sighed. "I don't quite know how to explain this. Cathar, sit down, will you? You make me nervous fidgeting like that."

He narrowed his eyes, pulled out a chair and sat across the table from her. "I know you?"

"I'm glad it's you, not Duran, he's so damn hardheaded he'd never believe me. I'm Brann. Your sister."

He leaned forward, frowning as he scanned her face. "You're very like Mum. Now. You weren't a few minutes back."

She pushed at her hair, still black, she hadn't bothered changing that again. "And I'm a dozen years too old and I'm a long way from home. And a shapeshifter of sorts."

"Well."

"Slya woke, brother, she changed me. Did they tell you, those Temuengs, did they tell you they sent a pimush and his fifty to clean out the valley?"

"They told me."

"Gingy and Shara are dead, Cathar. All the kids under eleven were killed. All the old ones too. Uncle Eornis. The Yongala. The rest. . . ." She closed her eyes. "I've gone over it so often. I saw some of it,

Cathar, what they did to Mum, saw Ruan get killed, uncle Cynoc. They set the houses on fire too, but they didn't burn too much, the houses I mean. I was up on Tincreal all day. You know. I found the children there. I came back and the soldiers were in the valley. I watched from Harrag's Leap, then I went after them. Slya changed me. I told you that. And brought the children. Yaril has a brother." She opened here eyes, tapped her breast. "She rides me. Slya. I don't know what she's going to do. I killed them, Cathar. The pimush and his men. The children helped. They make a poison. It kills between one breath and the next. The pimush told me what happened at Grannsha. He said no one was killed. Jaril tells me about half aren't here, I suppose they were killed after all. Mum's all right. Well, as all right as she can be after what happened. Her looms weren't hurt. Tincreal blew about a week after that. Jaril flew back to see what happened. The hills are scrambled. You could only find your way back to the Valley if you knew where it was. But they're all right, the ones left alive. I forgot. Marran's dead. I found him killed. On the trail. Gave him fire. Didn't do that for the Temuengs. We think you're bait to catch me, you and the others they let out. The children and me, we think the sribush on Croaldhu knows his men are dead. Before I got off Croaldhu, I gave the Temuengs some sorrow. I expect they guessed I had something to do with Arth Slya. Which is why you and the others have Noses on your tail. How long have they been letting Slyans out?"

"About a month." His voice was cool, he wasn't committing himself to anything yet.

She sucked in a long breath. "You're as hardheaded as Duran. All right, listen. You remember the time you and Trihan caught uncle Cynoc in your dammar trap? Remember what he made you do, bury the offal from the killing ground all that summer?" She made a sharp, impatient gesture. "Either you believe me or you don't. Did they tell you why they're letting some of you out?"

He shrugged. "Said they don't want their Hina waiting on us, we're supposed to do for ourselves, they give us a credeen to show and keep track of what we buy. And just send out those with close kin here. They said they'd skin Duran first then Da if I run. Same with the others. First few days we had guards breathing down our necks, but they left us looser after that. I haven't noticed anyone following us. Be easy enough to do." He looked around the room. "This was clever, Bramble." He grinned. "All right, I do believe you, though it's not easy when I look at you. What have you got in mind? Breaking out won't be that hard, but where do we go after we're out?"

"The shipmaster who took me off Croaldhu and brought me to Silili, he's here now, he's going to take you down the Palachunt and back to the north end of our island. Where the smugglers come in. You know. Best not to wait, get it done fast, less chance of something disastrous happening. You get the others ready to move sometime the next five days. The children know where to find you, they can get in and out without anyone noticing them. How is Da? The children told me he's been beaten."

"Yeah, he wouldn't work and he won't take any kind of orders. He's getting better, but not easier. Mum's safe, alive, you're sure?"

"Uh-huh. Last time Jaril saw her, she was setting up her loom." Brann smiled. "You know Mum; house half burned down around her, everything in a mess but as long as the roof is tight over the looms and she's got the yarn she needs, the rest doesn't matter."

"I'll tell Da that, might make him bend a little if he has to. He can get about, if that's what worries you.

"Do they ever check on you at night? Say after sundown and before dawn."

"No. At least they haven't up to now. They change the guards a little after sundown, about the seventh hour, leave them on all night, change again about an hour after dawn. I've heard them grousing about the long dull duty they're pulling."

"Then the sooner we can get you out, the longer it'll be before anyone notices you're gone. Barring some ill chance."

"Can't leave too soon or . . ." He broke off as a large brown bird came swooping through the window, blurred and landed beside Brann as a slim blond child, blurred again into the Hina child who'd brought him here.

"Nose has decided he wants to be sure what you're doing up here. He's negotiating with the old woman right now and in a breath or two he'll be up peeping through the voyeur holes." She darted to the bed and pulled the covers about, talking rapidly as she worked. "You, Cathar, get your shirt off, muss your hair, see if you can look however you look when you've had your ashes hauled. Brann, get that Hina face back on fast. And take those pins out of your hair. Look like you've been mauled about a bit, huh?" She scowled from one to the other, then marched to the table, caught up the bell, stomped to the door, leaned out and rang for the house maid. "She'll bring tea, you should've rung before."

Brann closed her eyes, sat back in the chair and concentrated. Her face and body rippled and flowed, the face and hands changing to those of a middle-aged Hina matron. She opened dark brown eyes, saw Cathar staring at her uncertainly. "I can answer any question you ask me, brother. In spite of what's been done to me, I am Brann. You were courting Lionnis, I forgot to tell you, she's one of the living too, remember the time Mouse and I spied on you?"

Yaril swung the door wide as the maid brought in a heavy tray with tea and cakes; she set the tray on the table, bowed, smiled at the silver bit Brann tossed to her. Yaril shut the door after her, came back to the table. "Eyes," she murmured, "in the wall now." She squatted by Brann's feet, her eyes closed, a mask of indifference on her pointed face.

Cathar pulled his shirt over his head and began doing up the laces, making quite a production of it, a twinkle in his gray-green eyes. He was beginning to have fun with this business, the realization born in him that there was hope, there was a good chance he and the others would get back to the Valley, home to the slopes of Tincreal. That hope was bouncing in his walk and gleaming in his grin.

His spirits were winding up to an explosion which she hoped he would put off until he got back in the compound. She watched him scoop up the gold coin she set on the table, toss it up and catch it, grinning, then strut out of the room, watched him and wanted to run after him and hug him until he squealed. Impossible. Damn the Temuengs for making it impossible. She poured out a bowl of tea and sat staring out the window, sipping at the hot liquid, fighting an urge to cry, overwhelmed by the love she felt for her brother, realizing how lonely she'd been the past months. Even with Sammang and the crew, even with Taguiloa and Harra, even with the intimate association with the children, she felt alone; nothing could replace the feel of her folk around her, where she breathed in warmth and affection, where the space she took up was one she'd grown for herself, where she moved suspended in certainty. Not so long ago she'd been fretting about that closeness, feeling suffocated by it, now she was beginning to understand the dimensions of her loss. But she didn't have time to brood over it. She emptied the bowl in a pair of gulps, patted her mouth delicately with the napkin from the tray, swung to face Yaril. "He was a good one, girl," she said, making herself sound mincingly precise. "Go find me another such boy." She reached into a box and took out another gold coin. "Hurry child, I grow . . . needy again."

Silent and expressionless, Yaril took the coin and went out. Brann filled the tea bowl and sat staring out the window, sipping at the cooling liquid. Now that the room was silent and empty she thought she could hear tiny scraping sounds the spy made as he fidgeted behind the peepholes, could feel his eyes watching her.

The silence stretched out and out. The noise-in-the-wall sounds grew louder and more frequent. Then the sounds moved along the wall, very small noises that might almost be mistaken for shifts and creaks of the old house. Even when they were gone she sat without moving or changing the expression on her face, sat sipping at the tea as if she had all the time in the world. Yaril came back through the window again, a gold shimmer mixed with the gray light from outside. She flashed through the walls and came back to stand beside Brann. "He's gone."

"Think we convinced him?"

"Enough so he won't probe further, not now anyway. Or he'd be outside waiting to follow you. But just in case he left a friend behind, you better keep that form awhile."

Brann grimaced.

Yaril patted her hand. "Poor baby Bramlet."

"Hah!" Brann striped off the robe, tossed it onto the bed, pulled on her tunic and trousers. "Let's get out of here. I don't like this place."

That day passed and the night and in the late afternoon when the shadows would have been long and dark if the heavily overcast sky had let enough light trickle through, the troupe rolled out of the West Gate, their planning done, two plot lines converging, everyone nervous and wondering if the whole thing was going to come apart on them and sink them beyond recovery, on their way to Maratullik's meslak, escorted by the slave who'd fetched Taguiloa before, this time on a lanky white mule of contrary temper whose notion of speedy travel was a slightly faster walk than usual. A pair of silent guards rode ahead of them, another pair rode behind.

Yaril was an owl circling over them, Jaril rode with Negomas on top the wagon, both boys quiet, Negomas because he was nervous and rather intimidated by the guards and the great houses white and silent and eerie in the pearly gray light, Jaril because he wanted to avoid drawing notice to himself.

Brann rode beside the bay cob, looking out over the ruffled gray water, the stubby docks with their pleasure boats covered with taut canvas to keep out the rain. The street was empty, even of slaves, as the threatened rain began to mist down and the wind to blow erratically, dropping and gusting, dropping and gusting, throwing sprays of rain into her face.

The wagon rolled on and on, rumbling over the pebbled marble, the sound echoing dully from the walls, the slow clop-clip of the ironshod hooves extra loud in each drop of the wind. Taguiloa drove and Linjijan rode beside him, his flute tucked carefully away to keep it out of the rain. Linjijan stretched out on the seat, practicing his fingering along his ribs, wholly unconcerned about what was happening around him. He was restful to be with right now; Taguiloa felt the calm radiating out from him and was grateful for it as his own pulses steadied, his breathing slowed, the tightness worked out of his muscles. He couldn't keep his dreams from taking his mind—if they made a good enough showing, if they managed to interest the Hand, they were set. Set for the court performance, the chance he'd worked so long to get. He tried not to think of Brann and her plans for this night, expelled from his mind any thought of the changechildren and what they would be doing while he danced.

Up ahead, the slave kicked the mule into a faster gait as the rain started coming down harder.

Brann danced with fire, a soaring, swaying shimmering column of braided blue red gold, Jaril flowing bright, the drums heavy and sensuous in the shadows behind her, the daroud deep and sonorous, singing with and against the song of the drums. The Hand sitting in shadow watched without any sign he was responding to the music or the dance, but the adolescent Temueng males filling the benches on either side of him were stamping and whistling. Both things bothered her, the meslarlings' raucous callow behavior and the Hand's silence, draining the energy she needed for the dance. She owed the troupe her best, so she reached deep and deep within and drove herself to increase the power and sensuality of the dance. Negomas and Harra seemed to sense her difficulty and threw themselves into the music, making the great room throb and the Hand move in spite of himself, leaning forward, letting himself respond. And then it was over and Brann was bowing, then running into the shadows behind the screens set up to serve the players.

Taguiloa touched her shoulder. "Never better," he whispered.

She smiled nervously. "It's a bad crowd," she murmured. "Stupid and arrogant."

He nodded, touched the chime that warned Linjijan and the others to begin the music. He caught up his clubs, began his breathing exercises, listened to the music, eyes shut, running through the moves in his mind. The dance was paradoxically easier on the high rail at the inns because he didn't have to work so hard for the clown effect.

Everything forgotten but his body and the music, he caught the cue and went wheeling out with a calculated awkwardness where he seemed always on the verge of winding himself into impossible knots and losing control of the clubs and knocking himself on the head.

As Taguiloa flung himself and the clubs about, Jaril was a shadow-colored ferret darting through the lamplit halls until he reached the outside, then a mistcrane powering up through the rain to join Yaril, who was circling through the clouds waiting for him, a mistcrane herself now that the rain had turned heavy. They cut through the clouds to the far end of the lake and circled around the great shapeless pile of the Palace to the slave compound at the back.

"Guard changed yet?"

"Should have, but we better check."

They landed on the roof of the tower, blurred and oozed through the tiles into the rafters where they hung as mottled serpents lost among the shifting shadows from the smelly oil lamp sitting in the center of a worn table. The room was empty for a few breaths, then the guards came in, stomped about shaking off the wet, using their sodden cloaks to mop faces arms and legs, then a blanket off the cot in the corner, grumbling all the time about having to nursemaid a clutch of mudheads like that, not even able to have a little fun with the women, stuck out here the rest of this stinkin night to sit and shiver in case one of those know-nothing shits tried to run.

Yaril lifted her serpent head, looked at Jaril, nodded. She blurred into a beast rather like a winged marmoset with poison fangs, then moved silently along the rafters until she was in position above one of the guards. When she heard the click from Jaril that told her he was ready, she dropped on silent wings, gliding onto her target's shoulder and back, sinking her fangs into his neck, shoving off before he could close his hands on her, fluttering up in a steep narrow spiral as he collapsed, twitched a little, went still, his mouth open, a trace of foam on his lips. Jaril struck a second later than she did, his guard fell over hers, dead before he hit the floor.

They blurred into light smears, oozed through the roof and flew down to the gate. With a little maneuvering, they swung the bar out of its hooks, but left the gate shut for the moment so the gap wouldn't be noticed. They filtered through the planks, then were small blond children running unwet through the rain to the living quarters.

Taguiloa kicked the club into the air, then hopped about holding his foot with one hand while he kept that club circling in long loops with the other, a grimace of exaggerated anguish on his face. Throwing the club higher than before, he danced back and back while the club soared, hopped closer and closer to the club abandoned on the floor, the music rising to a screech. He bumped his heel into the floorclub, wheeled into a series of vigorous back flips, landed flat on his back and caught the descending club a second before it mashed his head, waved it in triumph then let his arm fall with a loud thump that cut the music off as if with a knife. He lay there a moment, then got to his feet with a quick curl of his body, bowed and ran off the padded part of the floor into the protection of the screens.

The Hand chuckled throughout the performance, apparently deciding he approved of these players. There was more stomping from the youths, a few whistles. Taguiloa went out, bowed again, then retreated behind the screens. Negomas and Linjijan began playing a lazy tune while Harra came behind the screen to collect her wrist hoops and finger bells. She nodded to Brann, then Taguiloa, flicked her fingers against his cheek, wriggled her shoulders, clinked her bells once to let Linjijan know she was ready, stood waiting until the music changed.

Jaril grinned up at Cathar. "This is it. Time to go."

"Right." He looked over his shoulder. "Duran, go get the others." Back to Jaril. "The guards?"

"Dead. Gate's open. Downpour out, so there's nobody much about. We have to get to the lake, but that shouldn't be a problem; Yaril and me, we can take care of just about anything that pops up. All you and the rest need to do is follow us."

"Good enough. Duran's going to be handling one boat with me. Farra and Fann will take the other. Boats are ready?"

"Well, we wouldn't be here now, if they weren't."

"Didn't mean to insult you, just nerves."

"Yeah. Get a good hold of 'em, it's a long hairy walk to the lake."

With Uncle Idadro gagged and supported by Camm and Theras, Duran and Reanna giving their shoulders to Callim, the Arth Slyans followed Jaril out of the compound. Cathar closed the gates and put the bar in place with Garrag's help, then joined with him to act as rear guard. Garrag was a woodcarver who'd puttered about in the workshop without doing much, telling himself he was doing it to fool the Censor who was in each day to check on them, but he was a man who couldn't stand idleness, he had to do something with his hands, even if it was only whittling. He'd found a short length of seasoned oak in the supply bin and shaped it into a long lethal cudgel. Though the chisels and other tools were counted and taken away every night, the Censor and his minions didn't bother with the wood. He carried that cudgel now and walked grim-faced beside Cathar, short-sighted eyes straining through the gray sheets of rain.

They moved through the rain along a twisting service path toward the main gate, the only way out of the Palace grounds. Yaril flew ahead, scouting for them, Jaril walked point, leading them through the maze of paths and shrubbery, past the stables of the dapples, past the echelons of slave quarters, into the gardens before the gate, deserted gardens with gardener and guard alike inside out of the miserable weather; even the hunting cats loosed at night were snugged away out of the wet. They came close to one of these lairs where a malouch lay dozing. Cathar and Garrag spun around to face the charge of the large black beast, but light streaked between them and the malouch, wound in a firesnake about the beast, sent him in a spinning tumbling yowling struggle to rid himself of the length of burn searing his hide.

He went whining off into the darkness and the light streak was once more a blue gray mistcrane flying precariously through the rainy gusts, predator eyes searching the foliage for other dangers.

Harra stood posed, listening to the whistles and applause and shouted suggestions, trying to ignore most of it. Spoiled young brats, many of them the prime sons of the Meslars and magistrates here in Audurya Durat. She broke her pose, bowed and ran into the relative quiet behind the screens. "Louts," she muttered.

Taguiloa dropped a hand on her shoulder. "They like you and want you back."

"Hah. They'd like anything in skirts, especially if she took them off." She grimaced, pasted a smile on her face, stepped into the light, bowed, retreated again. "You're going to have a job getting them back, Taga; they haven't the sense to know what they're seeing. Godalau grant the Meslar has and does." She stripped off the gold hoops and the finger bells, laid them on the table, stood rubbing her hands together.

Taguiloa listened to the whistles and shouts that showed little sign of tapering off, knowing all too well what he'd have to face. It was a gamble sending Harra out to dance before this herd of spoiled youth, but he needed the rest time after the comic dance. He moved away to the food table the Hand had set up for them, poured some water and drank a few sips, just enough to wet his mouth, watched as Harra drank more greedily, then dipped her fingers in the water and sprinkled it across her face. Outside, Linjijan was playing a lyrical invention of his own with Negomas delicately fingering his drums to produce a soft singing accompaniment, their skill almost drowned by the noise of the watchers. Harra sighed, took up her daroud, frowned. "You want me to stay here so that won't go on even more?"

"No. I can get 'em. Go on out. I need you there."

She nodded, wiped her hands on the cloth laid out by the house steward, threw the cloth down, went around the back end of the screen and settled herself as inconspicuously as she could beside Negomas, ignoring the flare-up of noise that only stopped at a sharp tap of the gong at Maratullik's elbow. She picked up the beat and fit herself into the music, then helped it change into the sharp dissonances and throbbing hard beats of Taguiloa's dance music.

Taguiloa shivered his arms, sipped at the air, closed his eyes and once again played over in his mind his first tumbling run and the dance moves immediately after; he'd be moving at speed, carried on the music, going faster and faster until he was at the edge of his ability to control his body. He tapped the small gong to let them know he was ready, shook himself again, then listened for the music that would lift him into his final dance.

Jaril came trotting back to the clump of trees where the Arth Slyans huddled in the cold soggy darkness. "We've eased the slave portal open. Yaril's keeping watch on the guards, but they've got themselves some mulled cider and are more interested in that than what's outside the windows. Keep quiet and move real slow. We don't want to have to kill these guards, we don't know when they're going to be relieved or what would happen if the next set found them dead. Be better if the alarm doesn't go up till the morning, better for Brann and better for you all. Follow me and keep in the shadows, I don't want you even breathing hard, and when we get out stay hugging the wall until we're far enough away from the guard towers it won't matter if they see us. Got that? Good. Come on."

They followed the child through the shrubbery, the storm wind covering any noises they made, tension winding higher and higher in them all until Cathar wanted to shout and break things and knew the rest were feeling much the same. They had to cross a small open space before they reached the narrow gate set within the larger one. Jaril didn't stop but went skimming across the gravel, his feet making almost no sound at all. Cathar watched the thin line of his folk move after the boy and winced at every crunch of their feet. He waited until the last were through then followed Garrag across the gravel, his back knotted with expectation of shouts or spears hurled at him. He was almost disappointed when nothing happened and he was through the portal and walking along the massive white wall fronting the palace grounds. Jaril brushed by him, passed back through the portal. Over his shoulder, Cathar watched the door swing shut, then saw a patch of light ooze through the wood, coalesce into the boy. Jaril ran past him, waving him on impatiently, no time to indulge curiosity now. Cathar moved his shoulders and grinned, then shifted into an easy lope to catch up with the others. Slya bless, what a pair they are. He looked at the nearly invisible mistcrane flying above them, the pale boy-form leading them. Slya bless.

A moment later Jaril led them across the avenue and along one of the stubby piers. Two sailboats were set up and ready at the far end. Working as quickly as they could, Cathar and his brother, Farra and her sister Fann got the others settled into the boats, the sails raised, the lines cast off. The water was choppy, the wind difficult and the rain didn't help, but once they got away from the shore, that rain served to conceal them from anyone watching. Then the escape became a matter of enduring wet and cold and keeping the boats from capsizing. The mistcranes flew with them guiding them until they were halfway across the lake, then one of them went ahead to take care of the guards at the outlet into the Palachunt.

When Cathar eased his boat into the outcurrent, the guard towers shone as brightly as usual with the huge lampions that spread their light out across the river until there were no dark patches for smugglers or troublemakers to slip past. He chewed on his lip, but the mistcrane that guided them flew serenely on so he tried to relax and trust the children. A flicker of darkness sweeping past him, then there were two mistcranes sailing the clouds above them. No shouts from the towers, no stones catapulted at them. Slya bless, what a pair.

They circled a number of moored merchanters, tricky sailing in the dark and storm, with the river's current both a help and a hindrance, then the cranes blurred into shimmering spheres of light hanging about the masts of a small ship moored away from the others.

When they came alongside that ship, a broad solid man, a Panday with a clanking gold ornament dangling from one ear, leaned over the rail and tossed Cathar a rope. "Welcome friend," he called down. "Tikrat, get those nets overside."

Taguiloa wheeled across the matting, sprang off into a double twisting backflip, swung round and dropped onto his hands as he landed, used the slap of his hands on the mat to power him back onto his feet, then went on one knee in a low bow, the music behind him breaking as suddenly into silence.

Silence from the watchers, then a burst of applause, calls for more, more. But Taguiloa was exhausted, not even sure he could stand yet. He stayed in the bow, his arms outstretched at first then folded on his knee.

Maratullik touched the gong beside him and the applause faded to silence. He leaned forward. "A remarkable performance." He watched as Taguiloa got heavily to his feet and bowed again from the waist, acknowledging the compliment. For him at that moment, the Meslar was little more than a paper figure, unreadable, a mask that might have anything behind it, something a smooth voice came from, saying pleasant things. "Most remarkable. My compliments, dancer. Come here, if you please."

Taguiloa stumbled forward, exaggerating his weariness though not by much, wondering what was coming next.

"Accept this poor recompense for the pleasure you have given my young friends." With a sweeping gesture, Maratullik brought round a heavy leather purse and held it out, smiling at the roars and applause from the benches.

Taguiloa dropped to one knee in a profound obeisance. "Godalau bless your generosity, saö jura Meslar."

"Introduce your troupe, Hina, they too deserve our thanks."

Was he preening himself before the sons of his peers or was he after something else. Paper figure making gestures? He was pleasing those louts if the noise was any measure of their feelings. Taguiloa stood slowly, holding the purse before him. "Linjijan. Hina, flute player, the second best in Silili, the first being his great-uncle the wondrous Ladjinatuai who plays for the dancer Blackthorn."

Nod from the Hand. Desultory applause from the benches.

"Negomas. M'darjin and drummer."

As before, a quiet nod from the Hand, a sprinkle of clapping from the youths.

"Harra Hazhani. Rukka-nag, dancer and daroudist."

Nod from the Hand. He scanned her face with some care but said nothing. Whistles and shouts from the benches that quieted as soon as Maratullik touched his gong.

"Brannish Tovah. Sujomann, seer and dancer."

Again Maratullik scanned her face, saying nothing, again he stopped the noise from the meslarlings when he tired of it. "My steward tells me the rain is heavy. Rooms will be provided for you to take your night's rest here. You may return to the Quarter come the morning." Without waiting for a response from Taguiloa, he turned to Brann. "You will please us yet more, oh seer, if you stay to read for us."

She lifted her head and stared at him coolly. Taguiloa held his breath. "Certainly, saö jura Meslar. If you will furnish a guard instructed to curb the enthusiasm of the overeager." Taguiloa let his breath trickle slowly out; this response fit within the margins of proper behavior though barely so. Brann, oh Brann, oh Bramble-all-thorns, remember who this is and why you're here.

"You suggest . . ."

"Nothing, saö jura Meslar. I warn. My god is jealous of my person and prone to hasty acts."

"Ah yes. I know something of the Sujomanni. Which of their gods is yours?"

"The Hag with no name, saö jura Meslar. She who spins the thread of fate."

"Thus your calling. Most fitting." He looked from bench to bench, quiet now except for some muttering, and moved his lips in a neat and mirthless smile. "We will forgo the readings, seer. This night. Perhaps another time would be more propitious."

"Your will is mine, saö jura Meslar." She bowed and stood silent, waiting with the others for their dismissal.

"Would it were so, Sujomann." He struck the gong and the steward came forward to lead them out.

Working swiftly and with a vast good humor, the crew got the Arth Slyans stowed below deck. The flight through the palace grounds and across the lake had used up the better part of three hours and even the fittest among the escapees was cold, weary and soaked to the skin. Rubbed down and dressed in dry clothing, hoisted into hammocks, wrapped in blankets, swaying gently as the ship hoisted anchor and started downriver, all tension drained from them, warm and comfortable, most of them drifted into a deep sleep.

Cathar was too restless to sleep. He tumbled out of his hammock and made his way back on deck. The masts were bare except for a small triangle of sail; the shipmaster was taking her away from her mooring as silently and inconspicuously as he could. Trying to keep out of the way of sailors passing back and forth along the deck, uneasy about his footing, wind and rain beating against his back, Cathar groped along the rail to the bow where the Panday stood staring into the gloom. He touched the man's arm. "Shipmaster?"

The Panday turned a stone-god face to him, a sternness in it that eased a little when he saw who it was. Even with that easing he didn't look very welcoming, his words underlined his dislike for mudfeet wandering about his deck. "You'll be more comfortable below. Brann's brother. Cathar, is it? Right. Soon as we're around that bend ahead we'll be racing. No place for passengers then."

"Why isn't Brann here?"

"Your sister has proper reasons for everything she does; leave her to them. She got you out, I'll get you home, that's enough. You'll see her when she's ready. Look, Cathar, it's three days coming up the Palachunt and usually two days going down for a shipmaster who gives his ship the respect she deserves. Us, we'll be racing the pigeon mail and taking chances that turn my hair white thinking of 'em. If we can make the mouth by noon this coming day, there's no way in this world the Temuengs can get word to the fort there in time to stop us. But, lad, one thing we don't need is interference on deck. You keep your folk below, you hear?"

"I hear. Why are you doing this?"

"She's our witch as much as she's your sister. Someday when I'm good and drunk maybe I'll tell you the tale."

"Witch?" Then he remembered Brann's face changing and looked away, uneasy at the thought.

"Below with you. Now." A strong hand closing on Cathar's shoulder, turning him. "Get."

Brann stood at the glazed window seeing the gray curtains of the rain and the flicker of the single lamp cutting the darkness of the small room. A movement in the window mirror, the door opening. She stiffened then relaxed as Jaril came in, small black-haired Hina urchin. He came across and leaned against her hip; neither of them spoke for a while, then he began singing, his voice a burr that hardly stirred the air.

> Mistcrane, mistcrane flying high
> Through the gray and stormy sky,
> Wounded moon sails high and white,
> River races with the night.
> Oh, the mistcrane's ghostly flight
> Flitting phantoms never missed
> From their greedy master's fist.
> Mistcrane's flight is finished now,
> Shipman answers to his vow,
> Phantoms waking from their fright,
> Laughing in the face of might
> As the sun soars shining bright
> Turn the key
> Set us free
> Blessed be we
> When home we see.

Brann sighed, moved from the window. "Mistcrane's flight might be finished but there's a fistful of other threads to tie off. Watch while I sleep, my friend. I trust the latches on these doors about as much as I trust the walls."

With a strong following wind augmenting the push of the current and a clear sky opening ahead of them as they left the storm behind, the little ship groaned and strained and flew down the river, Sammang, Jimm and Tik-rat watching the water as if it were a treacherous mount that would try to rub them from its back given half a chance. They raced from point to point, trusting memories from the trip upstream, taking impossible gambles and bringing them off as if Tungjii rode the bow scattering blessings before them.

They emerged with the dawn from the twisting chute through towering limestone cliffs into the broad triangle of wetlands sloping down to the coast. Sammang sent Tik-rat into the jib-boom stays to spot snags, took in sail until the ship's speed was reduced by half, put Hairy Jimm at the wheel and kept the crew hopping as he went carefully down that treacherous stretch winding through half-drowned trees whose stale stench clung so closely to the soupy greenish-brown water that he felt as if he were eating, drinking, breathing it along with the swarms of pinhead midges blown from the trees on the heavy erratic wind.

They left the trees about mid-morning and picked up speed along the broad main channel of the delta, skimming along between stretches of saw grass and stunted brush. The air immediately seemed cleaner and many degrees cooler. Sammang sighed and moved his shoulders, rubbed his back against the foremast to get a little of the stiffness out of the muscles there. Tik-rat came off the ropes, rubbing at tired eyes, groaning and grousing but cheerful. Sammang laughed at him, then sent him below to tell the Arth Slyans they could come on deck if they wanted, get some sun and fresh air. He watched the youth go bouncing away and knew there was going to be a song about this race, one he'd enjoy but have to suppress for a while at least if he wanted to keep trading in Silili. He laced his fingers behind his head and pushed, exploding out a sigh of pleasure as he pulled against the resistance and worked his muscles. One last knot to unravel. The fort at the river's mouth. He glanced up at the hot pallid sky thick with birds. None of them carrying mail, he was ready to swear that. A witch-summoned demon might beat them but he had strong doubts so powerful a magus could be found in time to make a difference; Temuengs tended to distrust and dispose of anyone with that much power. He yawned, nodded at Jimm and went to see if Leymas had fresh kaffeh in the pot.

Taguiloa stared out his window at the busy courtyard below, fingers tapping nervously on the sill. Brann was out in the market somewhere, set up for readings, keeping herself visible while Imperial guards stalked about turning the Quarter upside down as they searched for the escaped slaves. He hadn't seen her since the troupe went wearily up the stairs a little after sunup. He didn't want to see her. He liked her, she was easy enough to like, doing the best she could to piece together the ruins of her existence. Trouble was, he'd got so close to being set for

life. A breath away from court. A breath! Easier to endure losing what
he'd had no real chance of getting. But to get so close . . . if it didn't
happen, he wasn't quite sure how he'd handle himself. He left the
window and began pacing about the room with the barely contained
energy of a caged tiger. Imperial guards stumping through the Quarter;
he could hear the sounds of their progress drifting in on the wind.
Rumors. Jassi brought a clutch of them with his breakfast tray. The
escapees were twelve identical sisters who performed unnatural acts on
each other while the Emperor watched, the description of those acts
growing more lurid with repetition. Or they were snake men with poison fangs the Emperor kept as a weapon to scare the Meslars into
doing what he told him and they were stolen by the Meslars who were
planning to assassinate the Emperor and he knew it and that was why
he was so hot to get them back. Or they were a coven of witches of
talents so wild no one agreed on what they could be, turning lead into
gold, whipping up an elixir that guaranteed immortality, seers who
could tell the Emperor everything that was happening in every corner
of the Tigarezun. Rumors. None that connected Taguiloa and the others with the escape. Tungjii took Brann's plot and made it better, bringing the rain down on them so they were shut up in Maratullik's house
for the whole night, impossible they could have any connection with
the escape. His mind told him, be easy, the Hand knows where we
were, he can't suspect us. His gut replied, that we're so clearly out of it
might be just the thing to make him suspect us. He doesn't need proof
to maul us about, all he needs is sufficient malice and a shred of suspicion. Taguiloa kicked a chair across the room, stalked after it and
jerked the door open, startling a maid into dropping a pile of dirty
towels. He gathered them up for her and sent her down to find him
some sandwiches and a pot of tea.

"You're nervous as the fleas on a dead dog." Jassi set her fists on her
hips after she deposited the tray on the table by the window, narrowed
her eyes at him. "Negomas says last night went good, what you fussing
about? This business with the slaves? Peh! Taga, that happens a half-
dozen times a year. We spend a few days dodging damn guards, then
they'll catch the running fools and things'll settle back the way they
were. Hey, you know why they leaving this Inn alone? Cause you here,
that's why. Grandda he even had a thought maybe he'd let you stay
here free, well, that one he din keep in his head for long." She giggled.
"So you got nothin to worry about."

He dredged up a smile, flipped a silver bit to her. "Just nerves, Jass, it's the waiting and not knowing."

She winked at him. "No sweat, Taga, you got it. We see a lot of 'em here and we know." A giggle, a side-to-side jerk of her hips, and she was gone.

He pulled the door shut and went back to pacing, gulping down several cups of the strong steaming liquid as he paced. The hollow in his belly that spurred him into ordering the sandwiches had vanished before Jassi came in with the tray. Helpless, that's what he was, nothing he could do to change what was going to happen; he couldn't remember feeling this helpless since the day five-year-old Taga drifted lost in an angry ocean clutching a ship's timber, sure nobody would ever find him.

The fort's main tower was a dark gray thumb thrusting into the sky. Sammang stood in the bow glaring at it when he wasn't scanning the water for the constantly shifting sandbars that were the plague of the coast along here. The Arth Slyans were below decks again, out of sight and out of the way. They crept closer to the fort. The sun was a hammer beating down, the glare from the water hard and bright, hiding the sand until they were almost on it, until it was almost too late to avoid jamming the ship into the soft sucking traps. They crept along, feeling their way through the water. The fort was silent. No one on the walls, no challenges. The ship came even with the dark mass. Silence. Hot, limp, cataleptic. They slid past into the deeper water, the brownish stain from the outflow vanishing into the blue of the open sea. Sammang drew his arm across his face, slapped at the rail. "Turrope, Rudar, 'Reech, get those sails up."

Mid-afternoon. A knock. He smoothed his hair down, composed his face, walked with slow controlled steps to the door and pulled it open.

Jassi grinned at him. "He downstairs again. That slave." She tapped at Taguiloa's arm. "Din I tell you?"

He cleared his throat. "Tell him I'm meditating, but I'll be down in a breath."

"I give him a jar of the good stuff. He happy. No sweat." She giggled. "You come down 'f you want, but he din ask to see you. He give me this."

Lead seals clanked dully at the ends of the red ribbon tied about the roll of parchment. He steadied his hand, lifted the roll until he could

see the pattern squeezed into the lead. "The Emperor's sigil," he said
softly. "Maratullik's man you said?"

"Yeah, I said. You gonna read that?"

Taguiloa smiled. "I am gonna read it." He carried the scroll to the
window, rubbed the ribbon off, hitched his hip on the sill and flattened
the parchment on his thigh. After skimming through the elaborately
brushed signs, he started at the top and read it again. His name. The
names of the others in the troupe. Horses. Wagon. Props. All listed.
Commanded to appear before the Emperor and his consort two nights
hence. Under the name PLAYERS OF THE LEFT HAND. They
were further commanded to move next day into the rooms provided in
meslak Maratullik where they would be the Emperor's resident company. He set his hand on the notice, grinned at Jassi. "Command
performance. Before the Emperor."

She slapped her hand on her thigh. "Din I tell you, din I? din I?"

"That you did, Jass. Tell Papa Jao to lay on a feast tonight. Everyone in the Inn and all the players in the Quarter you can fit at the
tables. Scoot."

He watched her swing out laughing and excited, shouting the good
news as she clattered down the stairs, then frowned at the parchment.
He had no intention of spending the rest of his life in this dead-alive
steambath of a city. Breaking loose would take some tricky maneuvering, though. He couldn't just pick up and leave. Seshtrango send the
man boils on his butt and a plague of worms. He sighed. Brann and
Harra would have to get to Maratullik somehow, change his mind. Or
. . . well, that's for later. Maybe he's not so hot to keep hold of us,
just wants something to distract the Emperor from the way his security
chief had lost a clutch of slaves. The troupe was a toy to dangle in front
of him. Brann, do I owe this to you like all the rest? He tossed the
parchment roll on the table and settled himself into a corner of the
room to do his breathing exercises and meditate himself back into the
calm he needed to handle what was happening.

Another late afternoon. The troupe turns onto the lakefront avenue,
this time passing through the gates of Maratullik's meslak. Guards
before, guards behind, slave on a cranky white mule. Lake water
turned hard and bright as sapphire shards, the sun burning hot in a
cloudless sky. Rumbling past slaves trotting on late errands who cringe
into the walls and watch the procession rumble along. Air burning in
Taguiloa's throat, catching there when Cymanacamal rumbles and

belches a gout of steam. The walls, the stone blocks of the paving creak beneath and around him. No wind, the latening day is so still every sound is a slap against his ears. Ominously still, once the noise of the mountain's stirring has subsided. Premonition sits like an ulcer in his belly. He tells himself it is pre-performance jitters. This is perhaps the most important performance of his life, not because he will be dancing before the Emperor—he has few illusions about the quality of the Emperor's appreciation and a deep-seated Hina resentment of all Temuengs, especially those in positions of power—it is important because it will determine the course of the rest of his life. He sits with the reins draped loosely through his fingers letting the cob pick his own pace, a willed nay-saying in his head. Nothing is going to go wrong, disaster will not happen, nothing happened in the Hand's house before that crowd of louts, nothing will happen when they perform before a court certain to be better mannered. Brann riding in front of the cob, Jaril perched behind her, Yaril-hound running beside her, her dun is restive, jerking his head about, drawing his black lips back, baring long yellow teeth. Harra riding beside the wagon, strain showing on her face. Nay-saying again, he will not see that strain, will not look at her again. Linjijan sitting up for once, fingering his practice flute, shifting continually. Even Linjijan the self-absorbed is restless and uneasy. About what? He will not think about Linjijan.

The palace gates open to take them in.

An understeward led them to a room opening off the audience hall where they would be performing and left them to get ready after telling Taguiloa that the hall was being prepared as he requested, matting on the floor, low stools for the musicians, a screened-off area to retire behind when one or the other of them wasn't on stage.

There were screens here also, set up at the far end of the long narrow room, dressing rooms of a sort. Along one wall two coppers of hot water simmered on squat braziers with soft white cloths heaped high on small tables beside the braziers, fine white porcelain basins beside the towels. Taguiloa smiled as Brann went immediately to the basins, ran her fingers over them hunting makermarks. Against the other wall, nearer the door, a long low table with pots of tea, wine jugs, fingerfood in elaborate array. Runners of braided reed taking the chill off the stone floor, a scatter of plump silk pillows. The Hand must have enthused wildly about them.

Brann felt a touch of pleasure in Taguiloa's evident delight, a touch of satisfaction at this indication of the troupe's high repute, but pleasure and satisfaction drained rapidly out of her as had all feeling since her folk left with Sammang, except for an occasional twinge of uneasiness when she thought of what slept within her. She sang to it at night, Sleep Slya Slya sleep, Yongala dances dreams for you, and hoped the god would sleep until Brann took them both back to the slopes of Tincreal. In spite of the lethargy that seized on her the past three days, she'd struggled to present her usual face to the world, grateful to Taguiloa and the others for giving direction to her life when every other purpose had been stripped from her. Having to stay with the troupe and perform with them meant it would be a while longer before she had to make painful decisions about what she was going to do with the rest of her life, it was an interlude when she could relax, enjoy the approval of audiences, the friendship of Taguiloa, Harra and Negomas and the comforting indolence of Linjijan, and let life flow about her undisturbed and unexamined.

She stripped, took the dance robe Jaril handed her, and wriggled into it, smoothed it down over her breasts and hips, enjoying the slide of the silk against her skin, pleased by the way it clung and showed off the body beneath. "I'm getting very vain," she told Jaril, giggled at the face he made.

Taguiloa dressed quickly, pulling on a crimson silk body suit, tied a broad gold sash about his waist, began spreading the white paint over his face.

A commotion at the door. He turned toward the curtained arch, smoothing the white onto the back of one hand and between his fingers.

The drape billowed violently. A tall thin girlchild stalked in, followed by a seven-foot guard. Three steps in, she stopped and looked around with arrogant inquisitiveness. Hot yellow eyes landed on Taguiloa. "I am Ludila Dondi," she said, "sister of the Consort."

He bowed. "Damasaörajan."

She stared at him as if she expected more from him, but he felt safer silent so he continued to wait, mute as the huge guard who stayed half a pace behind her.

She brushed past him, took up the jar of facewhite, poked her finger in it, then wiped the finger on the wall, dropped the jar without bothering about where it fell. By luck it landed upright on one of the pillows; annoyed but forced to keep silent, Taguiloa caught up the jar and set it back on the table, stood watching as Ludila Dondi sauntered about the room, poking and prying into everything. She slapped a heavy hand on a drumhead, ignored the alarm on Negomas' face as she beat harder and harder on the skin, laughing at the booms she produced. Negomas bit his lip and said nothing, but his brown eyes were eloquent. She gave the drum a kick, he caught it as it toppled and scowled after her as she strolled to Harra. "Are you the seer?" She put her hands on narrow hips and scanned Harra from head to toe with insolent thoroughness.

"No, damasaörajan."

"I am the Dondi, ketcha." She turned slowly, glaring about the room. "Where's the seer? I want the seer."

Brann stepped around the screen and bowed, antipathy sitting sour on her stomach. When she straightened, she watched the Dondi's face change. The Temueng girl felt it too. Hate at first glance. She was very young, long thin arms, long thin legs, black hair hanging loose, elaborate earrings in long-lobed ears, small mirrors bound in silver. A mix of some sort. Temueng plus something else. And dangerous, for all that she was a child. She was empowered. Warning plucked at Brann's nerves, then she felt the god stirring in her and forgot everything else. No, she thought fiercely, no you don't, you don't ruin Taga's life. No! She drew in on herself, pushing the god-force flat.

The Dondi walked around her, nostril lifted in a sneer. "You real or fake?"

"I am an entertainer, oh saör the Dondi." Brann was pleased but rather surprised at how cool and controlled she sounded. "Which would you prefer?"

The Dondi prowled about her with awkward adolescent ferocity, tugging at Brann's hair, pinching her breast, poking a finger into her stomach, drawing a hand down the curve of her hip, treating her like an animal on the block. Brann felt no anger, only a deeper and more intense loathing.

Bored with the lack of reaction, the Dondi stepped back. "Prophesy, oh seer."

"Certainly, saör the Dondi." Brann lifted her arms, pressed her hands together to make a shallow bowl. "Place your hand on mine, please."

"Which hand?"

"Whichever you choose, saör the Dondi. The choosing is part of the reading."

The Dondi looked at her hands, started to extend the right toward

Brann, then snatched it back. "No!" She wheeled and stalked from the room, followed by the mute guard.

Brann shivered and looked sick.

Taguiloa came to her, touched her shoulder with his unpainted hand. "What was that about?"

"I don't know." Brann shuddered. "I think she was just curious. Or sniffing at us to see what we were." She went silent for a breath or two. "I shouldn't have come here, Taga. Should have sprained my ankle or something."

"Couldn't do that. Not with Maratullik breathing down your neck." He soothed her, though he agreed with her, wishing he'd thought of it himself, but he didn't want anxiety tightening her muscles and perverting her timing. "Make them drool, Bramble, make them pant for what they can't get, make them forget you're anything but a woman."

She shook her head, laughed. "All right. All right, Taga. I get the message."

"Good." He went back to the table and began smoothing the white paint over his other hand.

Brann's dance went well, no one jumping up to denounce the fire as demon-bred or accuse her of running off with Imperial slaves. Applause when she finished was enough to show some interest but not great enthusiasm. Taguiloa relaxed as the dance went on, satisfied that the Dondi's visit was an aberration, not an indication that anyone here had serious questions about them. One thing bothered him. It was a dead house, Temuengs were sitting like stumps out there, barely could stir up a flash of response. He rubbed at the nape of his neck. Just meant more work, that was all.

The audience hall was a huge barrel-vaulted room, large enough to hold the Quarter's market square and have space left over; hundreds of glass and gold lamps were clustered along the walls and hanging on gilded chains from the ridge of the vault, swinging slightly in the drafts, painting a constantly shifting web of shadow on the floor and on the forms of those seated about the dance mat, from the look of the crowd, most of the Meslar lords in Durat. Royal Abanaskranjinga sat on a carved and gilded throne on a dais a double-dozen steps above the floor, behind him a carved and gilded screen. Taguiloa caught glimpses of dark figures moving behind the screen, probably the Emperor's wives and concubines and some of his older children. His present Consort sat six steps below him, her head even with his knees. On a cushion by her feet was a young boy, a stiff, determined look on his round face; no more than four or five, he was the chosen heir at present, the favorite among old Krajink's many sons. Closest to the dais were none of the Meslars, but a number of dark-clad Temuengs with the same mix in them as in the Dondi, behind them a clutch of men and women wearing heavy brown robes with cowls pulled forward so their faces were hidden in shadow.

Taguiloa finished his clown dance and bowed, avoiding the Emperor's hungry black eyes, eyes that caressed him, seemed to devour him. During the dance the Emperor had laughed and slapped his thigh, bent and whispered in his Consort's ear. Hungry, hungry eyes. No wonder Maratullik wanted a distraction to take the Emperor's gaze off him. Taguiloa bowed again and ran behind the screen.

Brann brought him a cup of tea and a towel. "It's going well," she whispered.

Harra came behind the screen for her hoops and fingerbells. "It's going well," she whispered, then looked from one to the other as they broke into hastily stifled giggles. "Fools," she said amiably, and turned to wait for her cue, clinking the small gong to let Linjijan and Negomas know she was ready.

Taguiloa sipped at his tea and gazed at Brann. She was wound so tight that another turn would shatter her. He kicked a pillow across to her, sat beside her. After a moment he closed his hand over hers. It was damp and cold and oak-hard. "What's wrong?"

"I don't know. I don't. It's like the air is pressing in on me. Not jitters exactly, I don't know." Silence awhile. They sat quietly listening to the music, the scrape of Harra's feet, the clink of her bells. "Who are those brownrobes?"

"I don't know."

"I'm frightened, Taga."

He patted her hand but said nothing. Reassuring lies wouldn't do here, he was too disturbed himself. He'd awakened the Emperor from his torpor and wrung laughter from him; he had a sense of approval flowing from the audience, but all the responses out there were just a hair off, nothing he could put his hand on, nothing he could ignore either. He was elated with his success and furious he couldn't enjoy it without this other thing niggling at him.

The music stopped. A ripple of applause. Harra came stalking behind the screen, moving with frustrated ferocity, stripping the bells from her fingers, the hoops from her arms. "They're half dead out there. I'd rather yestereve's louts." Setting the bells and hoops on a table with angry precision, she went scowling to the tea-table. She poured herself a bowl, gulped it down, poured another. "That was not an experience I want to repeat." She sighed and sipped, then lifted the bowl in a mock toast. "Luck to your feet, Taga. You'll need it." She shivered, set the bowl down. "Time to get back out there."

He felt the growing deadness of the audience when he wheeled out. It dragged at him, drained his energy. As if the black Temueng eyes and the yellow eyes of the mixes were mouths pressed against his flesh, consuming him as he danced for them. He forced himself to go on though his limbs felt leaden and his edge was gone. He pulled in, took fewer chances, and even then felt he danced on the rim of a precipice.

The music changes.

Taguiloa falters. Covers. Tries to go on.

A hot force takes his body, moves his feet in a complex pattern across the dance mat.

A rumbling in the ground below the palace.

The lamps sway and flicker.

The shadows dance in broken webs across the floor and the faces of the silent watchers.

Brann comes from behind the screen, dances toward him, her feet moving as his feet move. Her hair is white and shifting about her head as if windblown, though the air is heavy, thick, still.

Her face is strained and pale. She moves with a stiff resistance that matches his own, moves into the dance with him, weaving a pattern about and through the pattern he is weaving.

Moving gets easier for both of them.

The music grows wilder and wilder.

The walls groan.

The Temuengs sit frozen.

Abanaskranjinga shifts about on his throne, tries to stand, beats his meaty fists on the throne arms.

The dance goes on, inexorable as the passage of seconds into minutes, minutes into hours.

The Consort struggles to leave her chair, panting and squealing as her body fails to answer her will.

Brann and Taguiloa touch and retreat, swing away from each other, swing back. Loop out, converge, dance wheeling away.

The brownrobes shrink together, a mud-geyser surging and bub-

bling, heads bobbing up and down, throats throwing out a whining
moan that is barely louder than the music. They struggle to escape,
tugging and pulling at the forces binding them, but they cannot. Like
flies in honey they cannot pull away.

The drums beat louder. Louder. LOUDER.

Negomas fierce and frightened, half lost in the music, his long black
hands stroking and beating, working as if they belong to someone else.

The flute sings harsh, piercing dissonances that tug painfully at the
rolling rumble of the drums, denying its singing nature, screaming its
pain. Linjijan sways, eyes closed, entirely bound into his music.

Harra slaps chords and runs from the daroud, her eyes wild, white-
ringed, her mouth pulled back and down.

The sound builds and builds, filling the hall, melding with the moans
of the watchers, the rage-squeals and growls from the Emperor and
those around him.

The walls sway and groan.

The floor slides back and forth.

Brann's feet come down solid and steady. She circles Taguiloa.
Sweat runs down his face. His eyes have a glazed sheen. He touches her
hand. His flesh is cold and damp. He swings away.

Flute shrieks, drum goes toom-toom, daroud jangles.

The music stops.

Sudden silence.

Slya streams forth from Brann, takes form in the center of the mat.

Gasps, sighs, a wind of sighs passing around the room.

The great red figure stood planted on the mat, wisps of smoke from
the smoldering cloth rising about legs like mountain pines, coiling up
around the lavish fiery female form. One pair of arms crossed beneath
her high, round breasts, the second set curved out as if to gather in all
those about the throne, her hot red eyes glared at the Emperor.

"MINE," she roared and the building shook some more. "YOU
DARE PUT YOUR STINKING HANDS ON MY PEOPLE. YOU
MESS WITH SLYA FIREHEART. ME!" She reached out and out,
fingers extending and extending, two arms reaching, four arms reaching, fingers long and longer, gathering in the brownrobes and the
Temueng mixes, three to a handful, ignoring the banes they cast at her,
plagues and poisons, cast-fire and demon familiars, all the Kadda
power and Kadda skills their unnaturally extended parasitic lives had
given them. "ME! ME! YOU ATTACK ME!" She squeezed. Stench of
roasting flesh and burning cloth, shrieks, blood and other body fluids

oozing between her fingers, raining onto the floor and those remaining. She flung the mess aside and started to reach again.

A round bald figure in dusty wrinkled black was suddenly there, pushing the long fingers aside. Tungjii patted the back of the huge red hand, grinned up at the ominous figure. "Not the boy, little darling, not the boy."

Slya glared at him, hair stirring like serpents about her head. Then, (Brann astonished, Taguiloa wearily appreciative) the raking fingers shrank; red eyes rolling, red teeth showing in a broad grin, Slya patted the double god on hisser plump buttocks. In a voice like the groaning of a mountain, she said, "SINCE YOU ASK IT, TUTI."

Huge face returning to a savage scowl, she turned her hot red gaze on Abanaskranjinga. "YOU!" Her voice the howling of a storm wind, the roar of a forest fire. "YOU FOOL, BELIEVING KADDA PROMISES." One hand closed about him. She squeezed. His hoarse scream broke off abruptly though his arms and legs continued to writhe even after his body fluids began to drip on the marble steps. "HAH! LARDARSE, ATTACKING *ME!*"

Brann wrapped her arms about her legs, dropped her head on her knees, relieved in a way to have the waiting over, drowning in a vast lassitude; she wanted to stretch out on the mat and sleep and sleep and never wake.

Taguiloa sat on his heels breathing hard, watching the flame-red giant drop the squashed mass of the Emperor of Tigarezun, ruler of Temueng and Hina, a mess of charred meat, bone and slime. That's it then. I gambled and lost. He managed a tired smile as he saw Linjijan gaping at the god; even Linji understood his life was being trampled under those large but shapely red feet.

Slya flung the body of the Consort aside and ripped the screen from behind the throne. She winnowed through the women and children trapped there in the spell woven by the dance and the music, plucking out and crushing some, brushing others aside.

Tungjii caught up the weeping boy and carried him over to Taguiloa and Brann. Heesh lowered hisserself to the tattered mat and sat placidly watching the god hunting down her enemies, squashing and roasting them, his eyes filled with sardonic amusement, cheering her on with soft broken murmurs.

Slya raked immaterial fingers through the palace and extended them until they swept garden and stable, searching out and pulling to her all the Kadda folk.

Cuddling the Heir against hisser plump bosom with one hand, Tungjii reached out with the other and stroked it over Brann's silky hair, the touch warm and comforting. "One of 'em's going to get away," heesh murmured. "That tricky little nit that came nosing about you. You better watch out for her." Heesh stroked some more, hisser hand feeling like her mother's, steadying, calming, understanding. "You want to know why all this?"

Brann sighed, straightened her back and her cramping legs, looked round at himmer. "Yes."

"Glemma, child. The Consort that was. She's the reason. Ambitious. Got to be head oompah of the Kadda meld. Wanted more. Tried to tap the Fireheart of Cynamacamal. Ran into Slya who brushed her off like a pesky fly. Which embarrassed her and made her madder'n a cat in a sack. Made her think too. She teased old Krajink into marrying her and when she had him fast, she made him Kadda like her. Happy enough to do it, old fool, thought he was going to live forever and be young and handsome while he was doing it. Brought the meld here. They tried again, all of them. Stung Slya, woke her up some. And Cynamacamal rumbled and shook and spouted some hot rock. Scared them. They wanted hostages to make red Slya behave. So she whispered into Krajink's ear and teased him into sending his armies to take Croaldhu and then round up the Arth Slyans and bring them here. She thought she could hide behind them when she tried again to drive Slya from Cynamacamal, then all the fire mountains. Thought she could make herself a god. Lot of lies told. People had to be convinced it was a good idea to bring the Slyans here. You heard most of those lies."

"And me?" Brann looked at the worn smiling face of the little god. "And the children?" She touched Yaril's pale blond head, then Jaril's. "Look at Slya, they can't do a thing against her, all the Kadda can do is die. Why all that happened?"

"The Kadda meld's a lot stronger'n it looks, little Bramble. Falling apart now because red Slya sneaked up on it, trapped it before it could get going. Glemma and her crew threw up barriers that blocked our friend when she tried to get into the palace and stomp them. They were more than she could handle without getting a jump on them, though if you ask Slya Fireheart, she'd deny any limit to her powers, claim she didn't act because she'd have to harm the silly little mortals clustered about the roots of Camal." Tungjii chuckled. "We all have our pride, Bramlet. Anyway, she used you and my gifted friend here," he nodded at Taguiloa who listened angrily, but with interest, "to sneak her in past the barrier. Used you to spin the sticky web that caught the Kadda and kept them from uniting against her. Clever when she wants to be, our fiery dame."

Slya straightened, wiped her four hands down her naked sides, burning the ooze off them. Four hot red fists on her smooth hips, she looked around, smiled, and started to fade.

"No!" Brann leaped to her feet, enraged. "Not yet you don't." She caught hold of the god's leg, cried out as it seared her palm, but didn't let go. "No," she screamed. "You owe me. You can't run out like that. You owe me."

Slya looked down at her, made to brush her away. Again Tungjii caught Slya's hand. Heesh patted it, an affectionate scolding look on hisser round face. "Listen to her, sweeting. She's right, you know. You owe her a hearing."

The fiery fearsome god bridled like a girl the first time she came into mixed company after her passage rite. It was such a startling sight Brann almost forgot what she wanted to say. Almost forgot.

"The children," she cried as her anger came back. "Send them home. You're done with them. Why leave them away from kin and kind? They don't belong here. Send them home. And there's Taga and his troupe. Why ruin them? Why leave them to face the mess you made? You owe your triumph to us, Slya Fireheart. You used us. Make things right for us, or the world will know you are worse than the worst of the Kadda."

Slya spat a gout of fire that took out a section of wall. "WORLD? WHAT IS THE WORLD TO ME! NOTHING!"

"Am I nothing?"

Slya turned that fearsome red gaze on her, impersonal, indifferent, mildly angry. "YES."

Brann shuddered, drew a breath, closed her eyes a moment, searching for argument without much hope. "Then I'm *your* nothing," she shouted at the god. She waved a hand at the Temuengs beginning to stir about the fringes of the room. "Will you let them crush me? Will you let them laugh and say Slya lost half her chosen folk and let another dribble through her fingers?"

Slya looked thoughtful, then her red eyes brightened with a sly malice that turned Brann cold in spite of the heat radiating from the god. "TRUE." Voice like lava bubbling. "MY NOTHING." She looked around, her eyes lighting finally on Maratullik who was calmer than most, watching the destruction with an indifference equaling hers. A hot finger stabbed at him. "YOU! TOUCH MY NOTHING AND CAMAL WILL BURN YOU TO ASH, CAMAL WILL BURY YOU IN HOT STONE SO DEEP MAYFLY MORTALS WILL FORGET A CITY WAS EVER HERE." She stamped her foot. The walls groaned and the floor juddered beneath them. "THERE," she said complacently, and once again began to lose solidity.

"The children," Brann shrieked at her, "and Taguiloa."

Slya laughed, a high-pitched titter that cracked the walls. "I LIKE YOU, LITTLE NOTHING. I MAKE YOU A BARGAIN. I OFFER YOU TWO CHOICES, YOU CHOOSE WHICH. EITHER I SEND THE CHILDREN HOME AND CHANGE YOU BACK AND FORGET ABOUT THE DANCER AND HIS FOLK, LET THEM STRUGGLE TO SURVIVE HOW THEY WILL, OR I PROTECT THE DANCER AND HIS FOLK FOR THE REST OF THEIR MAYFLY LIVES, TORCH ANYONE WHO TRIES TO HARM THEM AND I FORGET ABOUT YOU AND THE CHILDREN. CHOOSE, LITTLE NOTHING. WHICH WILL IT BE?"

Brann looked from Taga to Linji, Harra, Negomas, to Yaril and Jaril crouching at her feet. Looked deep in the crystal eyes, remembering Yaril hunched and sad over the fire in the burnt-out storehouse when they were running from the Temuengs on Croaldhu, remembering the closeness they'd shared, the times they'd rescued her, remembering also all the lives of men and beasts she'd taken to feed them, thinking of all the lives she'd have to take for them if they stayed. Looked again at Taga and the troupe, all of them in this mess because of her. Her responsibility. She lifted her eyes to the mighty figure rising high before her, writhing red hair brushing the ceiling lamps, a pleased smile showing the tips of square red teeth. She said she'd change me back. I could go home. The desire to be again what she had been at the start of summer, to be back among her folk, beginning her apprenticeship with her father, that desire raged in her, shouted at her. Back with her father, learning his craft, struggling to make a thing as fine as the das'n vuor pot and its hundred bowls. Her father. She could see his calm brown eyes gazing at her, affectionate, understanding, but implacable. She could hear him speaking to her, saying see your actions through, Bramble-all-thorns, what you have done you must answer for; I don't want to see you if you abandon your friends. Sick and angry, she fisted her hands, forced her head up so she was staring into the shallow red gaze of the god. "Taguiloa," she cried; she wanted to explain why, but she did not. "That's my choice, let the children stay with me," she finished and could say no more.

Slya laughed. Several lamps shattered and spilled their burning oil onto the sluggishly stirring Meslars and their companions. "SO BE IT, LITTLE NOTHING. YOU OUT THERE HEAR ME, ANY OF YOU CONTEMPLATING HARM TO THESE FOLK OF MINE. I NAME THEM: TAGUILOA, HARRA HAZHANI, LINJIJAN, NEGOMAS. SEE THEM. HEAR THIS ALSO: CONTEMPLATE OR CAUSE HARM TO THEM AND YOU BURN. SO. . . ." She ran her red gaze over the Temuengs, stared a long moment at the Hand, moved on to a magistrate trying to straighten his tangled robes. He had just time to look up, startled, then he was a torch hot enough to melt the stone beneath his feet, ash and cinders a second later in a puddle of congealing stone.

Slya laughed. More lamps broke and a pillar cracked. She stretched her four arms, yawned, melted into nothing.

Tungjii calmed the wailing child heesh held on hisser knee, set him down and beckoned to Maratullik. "Take your new Emperor and serve him well, Hand. He's your luck now, make the most of him. His fortunes and yours are paired." Heesh grinned at the calm-faced Temueng. "Enjoy yourself, web spinner."

Maratullik permitted himself a small tight smile, took the boy's hand and led him away.

Tungjii rolled onto hisser feet, patted Taguiloa's head. "You too, Taga. Enjoy yourself." Over hisser shoulder, he called to Maratullik, "Web spinner, you better believe Slya means what she says." Heesh chuckled. "She likes to burn things, you know." The chuckle lingering behind himmer, heesh faded into nothing.

Brann looked down at her charred palm already pink with new skin, then at the space where Tungjii had been. "That old fox." She glared at Taguiloa. "I am so damn tired of jerking through the sneaky plots of every damn god around. I am so damn tired of being lied to and kicked around and having no idea what's really going on. Haaah! Tungjii!"

Taguiloa nodded absently, his eyes following Maratullik. "I told you, Bramble, heesh is the family patron."

Maratullik was busy talking in a low voice with several of his minions, sending them scurrying on errands, watching with cold amusement as the other Meslars crept away from the hall, hurrying to get away from the destruction and begin their own machinations. As soon as a Hina nursemaid led the child-emperor off, he walked over to Taguiloa. "You've made things interesting, Hina."

Taguiloa shrugged.

"You'll keep a still tongue about it. You and your troupe."

"Why not. If it's to my profit."

"Don't count too much on your fire-breathing patron. If you prove too troubling a nuisance, someone will find a way to remove you."

Taguiloa smiled at him. "Want to state that a bit more directly?" He laughed. "Don't threaten me, Hand." He moved his shoulders, straightened his back feeling as if he'd cast off a worn and cramping garment. "Hear me, Temueng. I don't give shit about you or your games. I'm a player, not a courtier. What I want is to go back to Silili with the Emperor's Sigil so I can do the kind of dances I want before the fools who think that Sigil means something."

"You're insolent, Hina."

"Yes, saö jura Meslar." Taguiloa drawled the honorifics until they turned into insult.

"You really don't care, do you."

"No."

"You could use your protection to wield a lot of power, Hina."

"I don't want a thing you want, Temueng."

Maratullik narrowed his eyes. "Oddly enough, I think I believe you. I don't understand you, but I believe you." He beckoned a guard to him. "Get some slaves and see they pack up the players' things, then take an empushad and escort them to my house; see them settled in." He cut off the guard's response, turned back to Taguiloa. "Get out of here now. Get out of Durat by sundown tomorrow."

"With pleasure. The Sigil?"

"I'll have the patent delivered to you before you leave. Anything else? Another way I can serve you?" There was a warning in the clipped words, the Hand had been pushed about as far as he was willing to go.

"What about a barge and an empushad of Imperial guards to keep us safe going south?"

Maratullik ground his teeth together, his face got red, breath snorted through his nose. He couldn't speak, he opened his mouth, a grating sound came out.

Taguiloa laughed. "Never mind. Just wondering. We'll take care of ourselves." He turned and sauntered out, the others trailing silently, contentedly, behind him, the guard bringing up the rear of the procession. Harra had slipped on her finger bells and after a few steps started up a jaunty beat, whistling a tune to match it, turning their exit into a triumphal march.

6.

Moving On

Brann gave the pot a final burnishing and set it in its velvet nest; she closed the lid and eased the flat little hook into its eye. Have to tell Chandro to drop this off at Perando for me. She smiled. Sailing man, like my Sammang, like another few I've known. I've definitely got a weakness for them, these sailing men. She looked up as she heard the squawk of an albatross dipping low over the ship. Yaril commenting on something, probably another ship. Hope it's not trouble out of Silili. Couldn't be, not yet, they won't have sorted out the mess in the Tekora's palace yet. She slid down in the chair until her neck rested on the top slat, swung her feet onto the table and crossed her ankles, lay stretched out contemplating the ceiling beams, dismissing the recent events in Silili, thinking about her quest and its end. A strange time that was. Gods and mortals jostling and elbowing each other, all wanting something different, getting in each other's way, scattering lies like seeds at spring planting, nothing exactly what it seemed.

The ship heeled over suddenly, the chair tottered and fell, dumping her onto the floor. She scrambled to her feet and rushed to the table, caught the box before it tumbled off. "That was close. Sandbar, I suppose, they come and go round here. What Yaril was yammering about more than likely." She stroked her hand across the smooth lacquer. "Into the chest with you."

She tucked the box into the heavy sea chest at the foot of the bed, got dressed, went out to hunt down the cook and get something to fill the hollow under her ribs.

A LAST NOTE—THE END BEING ALSO A BEGINNING

The Jade King drew the sword from its sheath, smiled at the new bloodmarks on the blade. "Curse still healthy?"

"Very."

"Good." He beckoned to his Vizier. "Pay her."

And that was the end of that. She went out wondering who he was going to give that sword to and why he had to be so devious. Another mystery to add to those things she'd probably never know.

Brann went wandering through the Jade-Halimm Market. It was famous through half the world, as much for the look of the place as for the rareties sold there, a spacious sunny place with ancient vines coiling over equally ancient lattices, living walls for the market stalls that were handed down from father to son, mother to daughter. They kept herds of small green lizards to eat the ivy clean of insects and sponged dust off the leaves every morning so these shone like the jade that gave the city its name. She saw a potter's stall and stopped to look over the wares, picked up a simple unglazed cup, ran her fingers over it, made of a clay strange to her, a pleasant red-brown, thin, tough, with a satisfying solidity. She held it and felt a shock of recognition, a rightness so strong it burned like fire through her. The stall-keeper, a handsome young woman, was busy with another customer; Brann fidgeted impatiently, caressing the cup as she waited, liking it more the longer she held it. When the woman came to her, she held it up. "Who made this?"

"My grandfather, Kuralyn. Dayan Acsic."

"Does he take pupils?" She set the cup down with great care, so tense she was afraid of breaking it.

"Yes. You would like to meet him?"

"Yes." She sighed, then smiled. "Yes, very much indeed."

Blue Magic

1

THE KINGDOM OF JADE TORAT. A MOUNTAINSIDE NEAR THE WESTERN BORDER.

Broad and yellow and heavy with the silt it carried, late summer low in its banks, the river Wansheeri slipped noiselessly past the scattered mountains of the Uplands, driving to the Plains and the vast city that guarded its mouth, Jade Halimm.

On one of those mountains, one close to the river and its deposits of clay, an old woman finished unloading her kiln onto a handcart and started downhill with the cart, old and broad and in her way as slow and heavy and powerful as the river. The sun was low in the west; the air moved slowly and smelled of dust, powdered bark, pungent sticky resins from the conifers, a burning gold haze filtered through lazily shifting needles; the shadows were dark and hot; sweat gathered on the old woman's scalp beneath strong white hair twisted into a feathery knot to keep it off her neck and poured in wide streams past her ears. Ignoring sweat and heat, she plodded down a path her own feet had pounded into the mountainside during the past hundred years. She was alone and content to be alone, showed it in the swing of her heavy body and the work tune she was whistling. The pots rattled, the cart creaked, the old woman whistled, here and there in the distance a bird sang a song as lazy as the sluggish air.

She reached a round meadow bisected by a noisy creek and started pulling the cart over flat stones she had long ago muscled into place for the parts of the year that were wetter than this; the cart lurched, the pots thudded, the iron tires of the cartwheels rumbled over the stones. She stopped whistling and put more muscle into moving the cart, her face going intent as she focused mind and body on the pushpole. When she reached the bridge across the creek, she straightened her back and drew an arm across her face, wiping away some of the sweat. A breeze moved along the water, cool after the still heat under the trees. She unhooked the pushpole and shuffled to the siderail, lingering in that comparative coolness, leaning against the top bar, head bent so the breeze could run across her neck. Across the meadow her house and workshed waited, half hidden by ancient knotty vines, their weathered wood fitting with grace into the stony tree-covered slope behind them. She was pleasantly tired and looking forward to fixing her supper, then consuming a large pot of tea while she re-read one of the books she'd brought up from Jade Halimm to pass the evenings with when the children were gone. Yaril and Jaril were due back soon; she smiled as she thought this. They'd have a thousand stories to tell about what they'd seen in their travels, but that wasn't the only reason she was beginning to grudge the hours until they came; she was more attached to them than she liked to admit, even to herself, they were her children, her nurselings, though their human forms had grown older in the years (about two hundred of them now) since their paths collided with hers on the slopes of Tincreal. Recently she'd begun to wonder if they might be approaching something like puberty. Their outward forms, to some extent anyway, reflected their inward being, so if they seemed to be hovering on the verge of adolescence when they took on the appearance of human children, what was that supposed to tell her? What was adolescence like for a pair of golden shimmerglobes? How would she deal with it? They'd been restless the past several years, ranging over much of the world, coming back to her only when their need for food was so demanding they could no longer ignore it. She wrinkled her nose with distaste. She wanted them back, but it meant she'd have to go down to Jade Halimm and hunt for victims she could justify sucking dry of life. High or low, it didn't matter to her, only the smell of their souls mattered. The folk of Jade Halimm who were ordinarily honest (which meant having only small sins and meannesses on their consciences but no major taint of corruption) were afraid at first when they knew the Drinker of Souls was prowling the night, but experience taught them that they had nothing to fear from her. She took the muggers, the despoilers of children, the secret murderers and such folk, leaving the rest alone. Many in Jade Halimm had reason to be grateful to her; the mysterious deaths of certain merchants and moneylenders made their heirs suddenly inclined to generosity and improved their patience wonderfully (for a while at least and never to the point of losing a profit). She frowned at the stream. How long have I been here? She counted the year names to herself, counted the cycles. Tungjii's tender tits, I'm letting myself go, time slips, like water through my fingers, it seems like yesterday I came up the riverpath and argued old Dayan into taking me on as his apprentice.

The western sky was throwing up rags of color as the sun dropped stone quick behind the peaks; the old trout that lived under the bridge drifted out, a dark dangerous shade in the broken shadows of the water. She sighed and pushed back onto her feet. If she wanted to get the pots stowed before full dark there was no more time for dreaming. She set her hand on the pullpole, meaning to lock it back in front of her, turned instead and stood gazing toward the river as she heard the hurried uneven pound of hooves on the beaten earth of the riverpath. Whoever it is, he's pushed that poor beast to the point of breakdown. Leaving the cart where it was, she walked off the bridge, up the paving stones to the road and stood waiting for the rider to show.

For a moment she thought of climbing to the house and barring the door, but she'd been settled in contentment too long and had lost the wariness endemic in the earlier part of her life. Who'd want to hurt her, the ancient potter of Shaynamoshu? Besides, it might be a desperate landsman running from the whipmasters on one of the cherns along the Wansheeri. She'd hid more than one such fugitive after Dayan died and left her the house.

The horse came out of the trees, a dapple gray blackened with sweat, a black-clad boy on his back. When he came even with her, the boy slid from the saddle, leaving the beast to stand behind him, head down and shivering, a thin wiry boy, fifteen, sixteen, something like that, dark circles of fatigue about his eyes, his face drawn and showing the bone, determination and terror haunting his eyes. "Brann born in Arth Slya, Drinker of Souls?"

She blinked at him, considering the question. After a moment she nodded. "Yes."

He fumbled inside his shirt, jerked, breaking the thong she could see about his neck. A moment more of fumbling, him swaying on his feet, weary beyond weariness, then he brought out a small packet, parchment folded over and over about something heavy, smeared copiously with black wax. "We the blood of Harra Hazhani say to you, remember what you swore." He pushed the packet at her.

She took it, tucked it in her blouse and caught hold of him as he fell against her, fatigue clubbing him down once the support of his drive to reach her was gone. A flash of darkness caught the corner of her eye. A tigerman popped from the air behind the boy. Before she could react, he slipped a knife up under the boy's ribs and vanished as precipitously as he came with a pop like a cork coming from a bottle.

An icy wind touched her neck.

Something heavy, metallic slammed into her back.

Cold fire flashed up through her.

Heavy breathing, broken in the middle. Faint popping sound.

Her knees folded under her, she saw herself toppling toward the boy's body, saw the hilt of the knife in his back, saw an exploding flower of blood, saw nothing more.

2

TWO MONTHS EARLIER AND A THOUSAND MILES SOUTH AND WEST ALONG THE COAST FROM JADE HALIMM. IN OWLYN VALE OF THE FIFTH FINGER, EVENTS PREPARE FOR THE KNIFE IN BRANN'S BACK.

SCENE: Late, the Wounded Moon in his crescent phase, just rising. One of the
walled households in Owlyn vale. A
small bedroom in the children's wing.
Three narrow beds in the room, one
sleeper, a girl about thirteen or
fourteen, the other beds empty. The
door opens. A boy of seven slips
through the gap, glides to the girl
and takes her by the shoulder, shakes
her awake.

"Kori. Wake up, Kori. I need you."

The whisper and the shaking dragged Kori out of chaotic nightmare. "Wha . . . who . . ."

The shaking stopped. "It's me, Kori. Tré."

"Tré . . ." She fumbled her hands against the sheets, pushed up and turned in one move, her limbs all angles, her body with limber grace, the topsheet and quilt winding around her until she shoved them away and dropped her legs over the edge of the bed. She swept the hair out of her eyes and sat scowling at her brother, a shivering dark shape in the starlit room. "Ahhh, Tré," she said, keeping her voice to a murmur so

AuntNurse wouldn't hear and come scold them, "shut the door, silly, then tell me what's biting you."

He hurried over, pulled the door shut with such care the latch went home without a sound, hurried back to his sister. She patted the bed beside her and he climbed up and sat where her hand had been, sighing and leaning his weight against her. "It's me now," he said. "Zilos came to me, his ghost I mean. He said I pass it to you, Trago; the Chained God says you're the one. They'll burn me too, Kori; when the Signs start, they'll know I'm the priest now and HE'll know and HE'll order his soldiers to burn me like they did Zilos."

Kori shivered. "You're sure? Maybe it was a bad dream. Me, I've been having lots of those."

Trago wriggled away from her. "I said he put his hand on me, Kori. He left the Mark." He pulled his sleeping shift away from his shoulder and let her see a hollow starburst, dark red like a birthmark; he'd had no mark there before, he was born unflawed, she'd bathed him as a babe, part of girls' work in the Household of the Piyoloss clan. And she'd seen that brand before, seen it on the strong sunbrown shoulder of Zilos the woodworker when he'd left his shirt off on a hot summer day, sitting on the bench before his small house carving a doll's head for her. Zilos, Priest of the Chained God. Three weeks ago the soldiers of the Sorcerer Settsimaksimin planted an oak post in the middle of the threshing floor, tied Zilos to it, piled resinous pinewood about him and burned him to ash, standing around him and jeering at the Chained God, calling him to rescue his Priest if he counted himself more than a useless ghost-thing. And they promised to burn all such priests wherever they found them, Settsimaksimin was more powerful than any pitiful little local god and that was his command and the command of Amortis his patron. Amortis is your god now, they announced to the stubborn refusing folk of Owlyn Vale, Amortis the bountiful, Amortis ripe and passionate, Amortis the bestower of endless pleasure. Rejoice that she consents to bless you with her presence, rejoice that she calls you to her service.

Warily, feeling nauseated, Kori touched the mark. It was bloodwarm and raised a hair above the paler skin of her brother's shoulder. The first Sign. He could hide that, but other Signs would appear that he couldn't hide. One day mules might bray and rebel and come running from fields, dragging plows and seeders and wagons behind them, mules might jump corral fences, break through stable doors, ignoring commands, whips, all obstacles, they might come and kneel before him. Some such things would happen. He couldn't stop them. Another day he might be compelled to go to every adult woman in Owlyn Vale and touch her and heal all ills and announce the sex of each child in the wombs that were filled and bless each such unborn so it would come forth without flaw and more beautiful than the morning. A third time, it would be something else. The one certainty in the situation was that whatever Signs were manifested would be public and spectacular. Kori sighed and held her brother in her arms as he sobbed out his fear and indignation that this should happen to him.

When his sobbing died down and he lay quiescent against her, she murmured, "Do you know when the Signs will start? Tomorrow? Next week?"

Trago coughed, sniffed, pushed against her. She let him go and he wriggled away along the bed until he could turn and look at her. He fished up the edge of her sheet and blew his nose into it, ignoring the soft spitting of indignation this drew from her. "Zilos his Ghost said the Chained God gives me three months to get used to this. Then he lets everyone know."

"Stupid!" She bit down on the word, not because she feared the God, but she didn't want AuntNurse in there scolding her for staining her reputation by entertaining a male in her bedchamber, no matter that male was her seven-year-old brother, how you start is how you go on Auntee said. "Any hope the god will change his mind?"

"No." Trago cleared his throat again, caught her glare and swallowed the phlegm instead of spitting it out.

She scowled at her hands, took hold of the long flexible fingers of her left hand and bent them back until the nails lay almost parallel to her arm. Among all the children and young folk belonging to the Piyoloss clan, Trago was the one closest to her, the only one who laughed when she did, the only one who could follow her flights of fancy, his dragonfly mind as swift as hers. If he burned, much of her would burn with him and she didn't like to think of what her life would be like after that. She smoothed one hand over the other. "We've got to do something," she murmured. She hugged her arms across her shallow just-budding breasts. "I think . . ." Her voice faded as she went still, her eyes opening wide, staring inward at a sudden memory. A moment later, she shook herself and turned to him. "I've got an idea . . . maybe . . . You go back to bed, Tré, I have to think about it. Without distraction. You hear?"

He wiggled back to her, caught hold of her hand and pressed it to the side of his face, then he bounced off the bed and trotted out of the room, leaving the door swinging open.

Kori sighed and went to shut it. She leaned against it a moment looking at the chest at the foot of the bed. She crossed to the chest, pulled up the lid and fished inside for a small box and carried that to the window. She rested her elbows on the sill, turned the box over and over in her fingers. It was old and worn from much prior handling, fragrant kedron wood, warm brown with amber highlights. It was heavy and clunked as she turned it. Harra Hazhani's gift to her children and her children's children, passed from daughter to daughter, moving from clan to clan as the daughters married into other families, each Harra's Daughter holder of the promise choosing the next, one of her own daughters or a young cousin in another clan, she took great care to chose the proper one, it was a serious thing, passing the promise on and keeping it safe. And it had been safe and secret through all the two centuries since Harra lived here and bore her children. Kori set the box on the sill and folded her hands over it as she gazed through the small diamond-shaped panes of glass set in lead strips. She couldn't see much, what she wanted was the feel of light on her face and a sense of space beyond the narrow confines of the room. There were times when she woke restless and slipped out to dance in the moonlight, but she didn't want to chance getting caught. Not now. She opened the box, took out the heavy bronze medal with the inscrutable glyphs on front and back, ran her fingers over it, set it on the sill, took out the stick of black sealing wax and the tightly folded packet of parchment, ancient, yellowed, blank (she knew that because after Cousin Diyalla called her to her deathbed and gave her the box and a hoarsely whispered explanation, she took the box up onto the mountain behind Household Piyoloss, opened it and examined the three things it contained). *Send the medal to one called Brann, self-named Drinker of Souls,* Diyalla whispered to Kori. *Say to her: we, the line of Harra Hazhani, call on you to remember what you swore.* This is what she swore, that if Harra called on her, she would come from anywhere in the world to give her gifts and her strength and her deadly touch to protect Harra or her children or her children's children as long as the line and she existed. And this Harra said to her daughter, the Drinker of Souls will live long indeed. And this Harra said, trust her; she is generous beyond ordinary and will give without stint. All very well, Kori thought, but how do I know where to send the medal? She smoothed her thumb over the cool smooth bronze and gazed through the wavery glass as if somewhere in the distortions lay the answer to her question. The window looked east and presently she made out the shape of the broken crescent that was the Wounded Moon rising above the mountains that curved like protecting hands about the mouth of Owlyn Vale where the river ran out and curled across the luscious plain that knew three harvests a year and a harder poverty for most of its people than even the meanest would ever face in the sterner, more grudging mountains. Absently caressing the medal, warming it with her warmth, she stared a long time at the moon, her gaze as empty as her mind. There was a small round hole near one end of the rectangle, she played with that a while. Harra must have worn it about her neck, suspended on a chain or a thong. Kori set it on the sill, raised her shoulders as she took in a long breath, lowered them as she let it out. She went to the chest and took out a roll of leather thonging she'd used for something or other once and put away after she was finished with it in a rare burst of waste-not want-not. She cut a piece long enough to let the medal dangle between the tiny hillocks of her to-be breasts, slipping it beneath her sleeping shift. She went back to the window and stood a moment longer watching the moon. I have to go out, I can't think here. I have to plan how to work this. The other times she'd sneaked out, she'd pulled on a pair of old trousers she filched from the ragbag and a sleeveless tunic that was getting to be too small for her. Somehow, though, that didn't feel appropriate this time. In spite of the danger and the beating she'd get if she were discovered, the disgrace she'd bring on kin and clan, she went like she was, her thin coltish body barely hidden by the fine white cloth she had woven herself on the family loom. She glided through the house silent as the earthsoul of a murdered child and out the postern gate, remembering the doubletwelve of soldiers quartered on the Vale folk only after she was irretrievably beyond the protection of the House walls. Like a startled, no a frightened, fawn she fled up the hillside to a small glade with a giant oak in the center of it, an oak that felt to her as always old as the stone bones of the mountain.

She drifted onto dew-soaked grass; her feet were aching with cold but she ignored that and danced slowly around the perimeter of the glade through the dappled moonlight, around and around, singing a wordless song that wavered through four notes, no more, singing herself deeper into trance, around and around, gradually spiraling inward until she spread her arms and embraced the tree, circling it a last time, drinking in the dark dry smell of it, breasts, belly and thighs rubbing against its crumbly rough bark. When she finished the round, she folded liquidly down and curled her body between two great roots pushing up through layers of dead and rotting leaves. With a small sigh, she closed her eyes and seemed to sleep.

As she seemed to sleep, a dark thin figure seemed to melt from the tree and crouch over her, long long gray-brown hair drifting like fog about a thin pointed face, androgynous, with an eerie beauty that would have been ugliness if the face were flesh. Long graceful fingers of brown glass seemed to brush across Kori's face, she seemed to smile then sigh. Brown glass fingers seemed to touch the leather thong, seemed to slide quickly away quivering with distaste, seemed to draw the medal from under the shift, seemed to stroke it smiling, seemed to hold the medal in one hand and spread the other long long hand across Kori's face.

HOW HARRA HAZHANI CAME TO OWLYN VALE.

Gibbous, waxing toward full, the Wounded Moon shone palely on a long narrow ship that sliced through the windwhipped, foamspitting water of the sea called Notoea Tha, and touched with delicate strokes the naked land north of the ship, a black-violet blotch that gradually gained definition as the northwestering course of the smuggler took her closer and closer to the riddle rock at the tip of that landfinger, rock pierced again and again and again by wind and water so that it sang day and night, slow sad terrible songs, and was only quiet one hour every other month.

On the deck by the foremast a woman slept, wrapped in blankets and self-tethered to the mast by a knot she could pull loose with a quick jerk of her hand. All that could be seen of her was the pale curve of a temple and long dark hair confined in half a dozen plaits that danced to the tug of the wind, their gold beetle clasps tunk-tonking against the wood, the small sounds lost in the creaks, snaps and groans of the flitting ship. A man sat beside her, his back against the mast, a naked sword across his thighs. Now and then he sucked at a wine-skin, the pulls getting longer and more frequent as the night turned on its wheel. He was a big man and in the kind darkness had the athletic beauty that sculptors give to the statues of heroes; even in daylight he had the look of a hero if you didn't look too closely for he was at that stage of ripeness that was also the first stage of decay.

The night went on with its placidities and tensions intact; the Wounded Moon crawled up over the mast and began sliding toward the heaving black water with its tracery of foam; the groaning song of the riddle rock grew loud enough to ride over the noises of the sea, the wind and the straining ship and creep into the fuddled mind of the blond hero who stirred uneasily and reached for the empty skin. Remembering its emptiness before he completed the gesture, he settled back into the muddled not-sleep that was a world away from the vigilance he was being paid for. The woman stirred, muttered, moved uneasily, on the verge of waking.

Shadows began converging on the foremast, dark forms moving with barefoot silence and confident agility, Captain and crew acting according to their nature, a nature she'd read easily enough when she made arrangements to leave Bandrabahr on that stealthy ship, needing the stealthiest of departures to escape the too-pressing attentions of an ex-friend of her dead father, a man of power in those parts. Having no choice in transport and understanding what a swamp she was plunging into, she hired the hero as a bodyguard and he'd done the job well enough up to this moment but her luck and his were about to run out.

The hero's throat was cut with a soft slide, the sound lost in the moan from the riddle rock now only a few shiplengths off, but since most of the crew were here, not tending the ship, she lurched in annoyance at being neglected and sent the hero's sword clanging against the deck. Half awake already, the woman jerked the knot loose and was on her feet running, knives in both hands, slashing, dodging, darting, slipping grips, scrambling on her knees, rolling onto her feet, creating and reading confusion, playing her minor whistle magic to augment that confusion, winning the shiprail, plunging overside into the cold black water.

She swam toward the land, cursing under her breath because she was furious at having to abandon everything she wasn't wearing. Especially furious at losing her daroud because her father had given it to her and she'd managed to keep it through a lot of foolishness and it was her means of earning her keep. She promised herself as soon as she reached the shore and could give her mind to it she'd lay such a curse on the Captain and crew, they'd moan louder and longer than that damn rock ahead of her.

Getting onshore without being battered and torn into ground meat and shattered bone proved more difficult than she expected; the smaller rocks jutting from the sea around the base of the riddle rock were home to barnacles with edges sharp enough to split a thought in half while water was sucked in and out of the washholes in the great rock, flowing in powerful surges that caught hold of her and dragged her a while, then shoved her a while, then dragged her some more. Half drowned, bleeding from a hundred cuts, she caught a fingertip hold on a crack in a waterpolished ledge and used will and what was left of her strength to muscle herself high enough out of the water to roll onto the ledge where she lay on her side, gasping and spitting out as much of the sea inside her as she could. When she was as calm as she was going to get, she began the herka trypps that were meaningless in every way except that they helped her focus mind and energy and got her ready to use the more demanding levels of her magic. Blending modes she learned from her father with others she'd picked up here and there in her travels since he died, she began to draw heat from the air and glamour from the moonlight and twisted them into tools to seal the cuts where blood was leaking away and taking strength with it and when that was done, she pulled heat and glamour into herself and stored it, then used it to shape the curse and used her anger to power the curse and shot her curse after the ship like poison arrow, releasing it with a flare of satisfaction that turned to ash a moment later as a net of weariness settled around her and pinned her flat to the cold stone.

Cold. She wasn't bleeding any longer, but the cold was drawing the life out of her. Get up, she told herself, get on your feet, you can't stay here. Struggling against the weight of that bone deep fatigue, searching out holds on the face of the riddle rock, she forced herself onto her knees and then onto her feet. For a minute or an hour, she never knew which, she stood shivering and mind-dulled, trying to get her thoughts ordered again, trying to focus her energy so she could understand where she was and what she had to do to get out of there. The riddle rock moaned about her, a thousand fog horns bellowing, the noise jarred her over and over from her fragile focus and left her swaying precariously on the point of tumbling back into the water. The tide began following the moon and backed away from her, its stinging spray no longer battered her legs. Once again she tried the herka trypps, closing her numb hands tighter in the cracks so the pain would break through the haze thickening in her head. Slowly, ah so slowly she regained her ability to focus, but the field was narrow, a pinhead wide, no more. She drew power into herself, plucking it from tide and moonlight, from the ancient roots of the rock she stood on, a hairfine trickle of strength that finally was enough and only just enough to let her *see* the way off the rock, then shift her clumsy aching body along that way until she was finally walking on thin soil where grasses grew gray and tough, where the brush was crooked and close to the ground. Half drowned still, blind with effort and fatigue, she walked on and on until she reached a place where there were trees and where the trees had dropped leaves that weren't fully rotted yet, where she could dig herself a nest and cover herself over with the leaves and, at last, let herself sleep. . . .

She woke late in the afternoon of the following day, stiff, sore, hungry, thirsty, sea salt and anger bitter in her mouth. The summer sun was hot and the air in the aspen grove heavy with that heat. Her aches and bruises said stay where you are, don't move, but the clamor in her belly and the sweat that crawled stickily over her body spoke more strongly. Gathering will and the remnants of her strength she crawled from her nest among the leaves and used the smooth powdery trunk of the nearest aspen to pull herself onto her feet.

She leaned against the tree and drew a little on its strength though all her magics had their cost and her need would always outpace the gain; as soon as her will weakened she'd pay that cost and it would be a heavy one. Stupid and more than stupid wasting her strength heaving that curse after the Captain and his crew; what she'd thrown so thoughtlessly away last night might mean the difference between living and dying this day. She grimaced and gave regret a pass, few things more futile than going over and over past mistakes; learn from them if there was anything to learn, then let them go and save your strength for today's problems which are usually more than sufficient. Yesterday banished, she turned her mind to present needs.

Food, water, shelter, and where should she go from here? Food? It was summer, there should be mushrooms, berries, even acorns if those dark green crowns farther inland were oaks. She touched her arms, felt the knives snugged under her sleeves; she kept hold of them when she went overside and didn't start swimming until they were sheathed. There were plenty of saplings near to hand. She could make cords for snares from their fibrous inner bark, for a sling too, if she sacrificed a bit of her shirt for the pocket and found a few smooth stones. There were birds about, she could hear them, they'd feed her, their blood would help with her thirst, though finding fresh water was becoming more urgent as time slid past, not just for thirst, she needed to wash the dried salt off her skin. She pushed away from the aspen and turned back her cuffs. Where do I go from here? After working stiff fingers until she could hold a knife without fear of dropping it, she began slicing through the bark of a sapling as big around as her thumb. No point in calling water and using that as a guide, she was surrounded by water and she wasn't enough of a diviner to tell fresh from salt. Ah well, this was one of Cheonea's Finger Headlands, salt sea on one side, salt inlet on the other; if she paralleled the inlet shore she was bound to come on streams and eventually into a settlement. The folk in the Finger Vales were said to be fierce and clannish and quick to defend themselves from encroachment, but courteous enough to a stranger who showed them courtesy and generous to those in need who happened their way. She sliced the bark free in narrow strips, peeling them away from the wood and draping them over her knee, glancing at the sky now and then to measure how much light she had left. No point in making snares, she didn't have time to hunt out game trails, she wanted to be on her way come the morning. She left the first sapling with half its bark, not wanting to kill it entirely, moved on to another. A sling, yes, I'm rusty, have to get close and hope for a bit of luck. . . .

She finished the cords, made her sling, found some pebbles and some luck and dined on plump brispouls roasted over a fire it took her some muscle and blisters to make, a firebow had never been her favorite tool and she was even less fond of it now. The pouls had a strong taste and the only salt she had was crusted on her skin, but they were hot and tender and made a pleasant weight in her stomach; she finished the meal with a bark basket of mourrberries sweet and juicy (though she had to spend half an hour dislodging small flat seeds from between her teeth). By that time the sunset had faded and the stars were out thick as fleas on a piedog's hide. Sighing, her discomforts reduced to a minimum, she got heavily to her feet, stripped off her trousers and shirt (leaving her boots on as she had the night before because she knew she'd never get her feet back in them), she wadded up her trousers and scrubbed hard at all the skin she could reach. The scum left behind when the sea water dried was already raising rashes and in the worst of those rashes her skin was starting to crack. When she'd done all she could, she dressed, dumped dirt on the remnants of the fire, smothering it carefully (she didn't relish the thought of waking in the center of a forest fire). A short distance away, she made a new sleeping nest, lay down in it and pulled dry leaves over her. Very soon she sank into a sleep so deep she did not notice the short fierce rain an hour later.

She woke with the dawn, shivering and feeling the bite at the back of the eyes that meant a head cold fruiting in her. She rubbed the heel of her left hand over the medal hanging between her breasts. Ah Brann, oh Brann, why aren't you here when I need you? With a coughing laugh, she stretched, strained the muscles in face and body, slapped at her soggy shirt and trousers, knocking away the damp leaves clinging to her. She shivered, feeling uncertain, there was something. . . . She looked at the three saplings she'd stripped of half their bark, shivered again as an image popped into her head of babies crying in pain and shock. Following an impulse that was half delirium, she scored the palm of her left hand with one of her knives and smeared the blood from the wound along the wounded sides of the little trees. She felt easier at once and almost at once found a clean pool of water in the rotted crotch of a lightning blasted tree. She drank, washed her wounded hand, then set off along the mountainside, keeping the morning wind in her face since as far as she could tell, it was blowing out of the northeast and that was where she wanted to go.

She walked all morning in a haze of growing discomfort as the cold grew worse and her cut hand throbbed. Twice she stopped at berry thickets and ate as much as she could hold and took more of the fruit with her pouched in the tail of her shirt. A little after the sun reached zenith she came to a small stream; with the expenditure of will and much patience combined with quick hands, she scooped out two unwary trout, then stripped and used the sand collected around the stones in the streambed to scrub herself clean, she even let down her hair and used the sand on that though she wasn't too sure of the result and never managed to get all the grit washed out of the tangled mass. After she pounded some of the dirt out of her clothing and spread it to dry over a small bushy conifer, she cooked the trout on a sliver of shale and finished off the berries. The sun was warm and soothing, the stream sang the knots out of her soul and even the cold seemed to loose its hold on head and chest. Her shirt and trousers were still wet when she finished eating, so she stretched out on her stomach on a long slant of granite that jutted into the stream and lay with her head on her crossed arms, her aching eyes shut.

The sun had vanished behind the trees when she woke. She yawned, went still. Something resilient and rather warm was pressed against her side. Warily she eased her head up until she could look over her shoulder. A large snake, she couldn't read the kind in the inadequate view she had, lay in irregular loops on the warm stone, taking heat from it and her. Its head was lifting, she could feel it stirring as it sensed the change in her. She summoned concentration, licked her lips and began whistling a two-note sleepsong, the sound of it hardly louder than the less constant music of the stream, on and on, until the snake lowered its head and the loops of its body stretched and loosened. She threw herself away from it and curled onto her feet, her heart fluttering, her breath coming quick and shallow. The snake reared its black head, seemed to stare at her, split red tongue tasting the air. For a moment snake and woman held that tense pose, then the snake dropped its head and flowed from the stone into the water and went swimming off, a ripple of black, black head lifted. She dropped her shoulders and sighed, weariness and sickness flooding over her again. She pulled her trousers and shirt off the baby fir and shook them out more carefully than she would have before the snake. Shivering with a sudden chill she strapped on her knives, pulled on her shirt and trousers, swung the long double belt about her and buckled it tight. She checked about the rock, collected odds and ends she'd emptied from her pockets when she washed her clothes, went on her knees and drank sparingly from the stream, then started on. There was at least an hour left before sundown and she might as well use it.

For seven days she moved inland, gathering food as she went, enough to fend off hunger cramps and keep her feet moving up around down as she patiently negotiated ravines and circled impossible bramble patches or brush too thick to push through, up around down. It was summer so the rains when they came were quick to pass on and the nights were never freezing though the air could get nippy around dawn. By the end of those seven days she was on the lower slopes of mountains that were beginning to shift away from the inlet, moving ever deeper into the great oak forest, walking through a brooding twilight with unseen eyes following her. The ground was clear and easy going except for an occasional tricky root that broke through the thick padding of old leaves. There were a few glades where one of the ancient oaks had blown over and left enough room for vines and brush to grow, but not many; getting food for herself was hard and getting wood to cook it would have been harder if she hadn't decided to dispense with fire altogether. As soon as she stepped into that green gloom, she got the strong impression that the trees wouldn't take to fire and (though she laughed at her fancies, as much as she could laugh with the persistent and disgusting cold draining her strength) would deal harshly with anyone burning wood of any kind here, even down deadwood. She spent an hour or so that night scooping wary trout from a stony stream, then gutted them and ate them raw. And was careful to dig a hole and bury the skins, bones and offal near the roots on one of the trees. The next morning she went half an hour upstream, got herself another fish and ate that raw too and buried what she didn't eat. Urged on by the trees who weren't hostile exactly, just unwelcoming, she hurried through that constant verdant twilight, walking as long as her legs held out before she stopped to eat and sleep.

Late afternoon on the seventh day she stopped walking and listened, finding it difficult to believe her ears. Threading through the soughing of the leaves and the guttural creaks from the huge limbs she heard a steady plink plink plink. It got gradually louder, turned into the familiar dance of a smith's hammer. The ground underfoot got rockier, the trees were smaller, aspen and birch and myrtle mixed with the oak and the sunlight made lacy pattens on the earth and in the air around her. Even her cold seemed to relent.

She came out of the trees and stood looking down into a broad ravine with a small stream wandering along the bottom. It was an old cut, the sides had a gentle slope with thick short grass like green fur. The sound of the hammering came from farther uphill, around a slight bend and behind some young trees.

She walked around the trees, moving silently more from habit than because she felt it necessary. He had his back to her, working over something on an anvil set on an oak base. It was an openair forge, small and convenient in everything but location. Why was he out here alone? His folk might be around the next curve of the mountain, but she didn't think so, there'd be some sign of them, dogs barking, cattle noises, she knew the Finger Vale folk had cattle, shouts of children, a thousand other sounds. None of that. He wore a brief leather loincloth, a thong about his head to keep thick, dark blond hair out of his eyes, and a heavy leather apron, nothing more. She watched the play of muscles in his back and buttocks, smiled ruefully and touched her hair. You must look like one of the Furies halfway long a vengeance trail. She touched her arms, the knives were in place, loose enough to come away quickly but not loose enough to fall out; she unbuttoned her cuffs and turned them back, a smith was generally an honest man not overly given to rape, but she'd lost her trusting nature a long way back and the circumstances were odd. A last breath, then she walked around where he could see her.

He let the hammer fall a last time on the object he was shaping (it seemed to be a large intricate link for the heavy chain that coiled at his feet) and stood staring at her, gray green eyes widening with surprise. "Tissu, anash? Opop'erkrisi? Ti'bouleshi?" He had a deep musical voice, even though she didn't understand a word, the sound of it gave her a pleasurable shiver.

"I don't understand," she said. "Do you speak the kevrynyel?"

"Ah." He made a swift secret warding sign and brushed the link off the anvil to get it away from her prying eyes. "Trade gabble," he said. "Some. I say this, who you, where you come from, what you wish?"

"A traveler," she said. "Off a ship heading past your coast. Its captain saw a way of squeezing more coin out of me; after a bit of rape he was going to sell me the next port he hit. I had a guard, but the lout got drunk and let them cut his throat. Not being overenchanted by either of the captain's intentions, I went overside and swam ashore. Aaahmmm, what I want . . . A meal of something more than raw fish, a hot bath, no, several baths, clean clothing, a bed to sleep in, alone if you don't mind my saying it, and a chance to earn my keep a while. I do some small magics, my father was a scholar of the Rukkanag. Mostly I make music. I had a daroud, the captain has that now, but I can make do with most anything that has strings. I know the Rukka dance tunes and the songs of many peoples. If there's the desire, I can teach these to your singers and music makers. I cannot sew or embroider, spin or weave, my mother died before she could teach me such things and my father forgot he should. And, to be honest, I never reminded him. There anything more you want to know?"

"Only your name, anash."

"Ah, your forgiveness, I am Harra of the Hazhani, daughter of the Magus Tahno Hazzain. I see you are a smith, I don't know the customs here, would it be discourteous to ask a name of you, O Nev?"

"For a gift, a gift. Simor a Piyolss of Owlyn Vale. If you would wait a breath or two beyond the trees there, I'll take you to my mother."

And so Simor the Smith, priest of the Chained God, took the stranger woman to the house of Piyoloss and when the harvest was in and the first snow on the ground, he married her. At first the Vale folk were dismayed, but she sang for them and saved more than one of them from the King's levy with her small magics which weren't quite as small as she'd admitted to and after her first son was born most constraints vanished. She had seven sons and a single daughter. She taught them all that she had learned, but it was the daugther who learned the most from her. Her daughter married into the Faraziloss and her daughter's daughters (she had three) into the Kalathim, the Xoshallar, the Bacharikoss. She heard the story of Brann and her search, she received the medal, the sealing wax and the parchment, she had the box made and passed it with the promise to the liveliest of her granddaughters, a Xoshallarin. As she passed something else. Simor who could read the heart of mountains found a flawless crystal as big as his two fists and brought it to his cousin, a stoneworker, who cut a sphere from it and burnished it until it was clear as the heart of water; he gave this to Harra as a gift on the birth of their daughter. She knew how to look into it and see to the ends of the world and taught her daughter how to look. It is not difficult she said, merely find a stillness in yourself and out of the stillness take will. If the gift of seeing is yours, and since you have my blood in you, most likely it is, then you can call what you need to see.

To find the crystal, daughter of Harra, go to the secret cavern in the ravine where Simor first met Harra, the place where the things of the Chained God are kept safe. Find in yourself the stillness and out of the stillness take will, then you will see where you should send the medal.

In the morning Kori went before the Women of Piyoloss. "The Servant of Amortis has been watching me. I am afraid."

The Women looked at each other, sighed. After a long moment, AuntNurse said, "We have seen it." She eyed Kori with a skepticism born of long experience. "You have a suggestion?"

"My brother Trago goes soon to take his turn with the herds in the high meadows, let me go with him instead of Kassery. The Servant and his acolytes don't go there, the soldiers don't go there, if I could stay up there until the Lot time, I would be out of his way and once it was Lot time, I'd be going down with the rest to face the Lot and after that, if the Lot passed me, it wouldn't be long before it was time for my betrothing and then even he wouldn't dare put his hands on me. I tell you this, if he does put his hands on me, I will kill myself on his doorstep and my ghost will make his days a misery and his nights a horror. I swear it by the ghost of my mother and the Chains of the God."

AuntNurse searched Kori's face, then nodded. "You would do it. Hmm. There are things I wonder about you, young Kori." She smiled. "I'm not accustomed to hearing something close to wisdom coming out your mouth. Yes. It might be your ancestor, you know which I mean, speaking to us, her cunning, her hot spirit. I wonder what you really want, but no, I won't ask you, I'll only say, take care what you do, you'll answer for it be you ghost or flesh." She turned to the Women. "I say send Kori to the meadows with Trago, send them tomorrow, what say you?"

"So I told the Women that that snake Bak'hve had the hots for me, well it's true, Tré, he's been following me about with his tongue hanging down to his knees, and I told them I was scared of him, which I was maybe a little, yechh, he makes the hair stand up all over me and if he touched me, I'd throw up all over him. Anyway, they already knew it and I suppose they'd been thinking what to do. Unnh, I wasn't fooling AuntNurse, not much, chain it. She just about told me she knew I was up to something. Doesn't matter, they let me go, almost had to, what I said made sense and they knew it." Kori flung her arms out and capered on the path, exulting in her temporary freedom from the constraints closing in on her since she'd started her menses.

Trago made a face at her, did some skipping himself as the packpony he was leading whuffled and lipped at the fine blond hair the dawnwind was blowing into a fluff about his face. "So," he said, raising his voice to get her attention, "when are you going to tell me that great idea of yours?"

She sobered and came back to walk beside him. "I didn't want to say anything down there, you never know who's listening and has got to tell everything, what goes in the ear comes out their mouth with no stop between."

"So?"

Speaking in a rapid murmur, so softly Trago had to lean close and listen hard, Kori told him about Harra's Gift and the not-dream she had under the great oak. "Owlyn Vale can't fight Settsimaksimin, we've got the dead to prove it. Chained God can't fight him either, not straight out, or he'd 've done it when they burned Zilos. Maybe he can sneak a little nip in, maybe that's what he was doing when he picked you for his priest and made that oaksprite give me a dream. 'Cause I think he did, I think he wants the Drinker of Souls here. I think he thinks she can do something, I don't know what, that will turn things around. So I had to get loose, otherwise how could I get to the cave without making such a noise everything would get messed up? And I thought I'd better be with you, Tré, since if you don't know where the cave is, Zilos will come and tell you about it like the oaksprite did me.

She said it's in the ravine where Simor met Harra, but who knows where that is? Only the priest and that's Zilos. He'll have to come to you again, like he did last night. Maybe tonight even. Drinker of Souls could be anywhere, the sooner we get the medal to her, the sooner she could start for here."

Tré sniffed. "If she comes."

"It's better'n doing nothing."

"Maybe." After a moment he reached over and took her hand, something he usually wouldn't do. "I'm scared, Kori."

She squeezed his hand, sighed. "Me too, Tré."

The packpony plodding along behind them, and then nosing into them as they slackened their pace, they climbed in silence, nothing to say, everything had been said and it hung like fog about them.

They reached Far Meadow a little after noon, a bright still day, bearable in shadow, but ovenhot in the sunlight. The leggy brown cows lay about the rim of the meadow wherever there was a hint of shade, tails switching idly, jaws moving like blunt soft silent metronomes, ears flicking now and then to drive off the black flies that summer produced out of nothing as if they were the offspring of sun and air. A stream cut across the meadow, glittering with heat until it slid into shadow beneath the trees and widened into a shady pool where Veraddin and Poti were splashing without much energy, like the cows passing the worst of the heat doing the least possible.

"Loooohaaa, Vraaad." Trago wrinkled up his face, squinted his eyes, shielding them from the sun with his free hand; when the two youths yelled and waved to him, he tossed the pony's halter rope to Kori and went trotting across to them. Kori sighed and led the beast up the slope toward the cabin and cheesehouse tucked up under the trees, partially dug into the mountainside, a corral beside it, empty now, a three-sided milking barn, a flume from the stream that fed water into a cistern above the house then into a trough at the corral. When Trago's yell announced their arrival, a large solid woman (the widow Chittar Piyolss y Bacharz, the Piyoloss Cheesemaker) came from inside the cheesehouse and stood on the steps, a white cloth crumpled in her left hand. She watched a moment as Kori climbed toward her, swabbed the cloth across her broad face, stumped down the steps and along to the corral, swinging the gate open as Kori reached her.

"You're two days early." Chittar had a rough whispery voice that sounded rusty from disuse. She followed Kori into the corral, tucked the cloth into the waistband of her skirt and helped unload the packs from the saddle and strip the gear off the placid pony; as soon as he was free, he ambled to the trough and plunged his nose into the water. "You take that into the house." She waved a hand at the gear. "I'll see this creature doesn't founder himself. And if that clutch of boys isn't up to help you in another minute, I'll go after their miserable hides with a punkthorn switch."

Kori grinned at her. "I hear, xera Chittar. Um, we are early and it's me because AuntNurse thought I should get away from the Servant of Amortis who looked like he was entertaining some unfortunate ideas."

"That's the politest way I ever heard that put. Panting was he, old goat, no—I insult a noble beast, by comparison anyway." Chittar wrapped powerful fingers about the cheekstrap of the halter and pulled the pony away from the water. "I see the truants are coming this way; you get into the house right now, girl, those ijjits have about a clout and a half between them and that's no sight for virgin eyes."

The first night Kori slept on a pallet in Chittar's room while Trago shared Poti's bed (he was the smaller of the two boys). Whatever dreams either may have had, they remembered none. In the morning, as soon as the cows were milked and turned out to graze, Veraddin and Poti left, warned not to say anything to anyone about Kori until they talked with the Women of Piyoloss. Chittar went back to the cheesehouse, leaving Kori and Trago with a list of things to do about the house and instructions to choose separate rooms for their bedrooms, get them cleaned up and neat enough to pass inspection, to get everything done before noon and come join her so she could show them what they were going to do until they could get on with their proper chores. Since neither of them had the least idea how to do the milking, she was going to have to take that over until they learned, which meant they'd have to do some of her work, like churning butter and spading curd, the simpler things that needed muscle more than skill or intelligence. Ah no, she said to them, you thought you were going to laze about watching cows graze? not a hope, l'il ijjits, I'm working your tails off like I do to all the dreamers coming up here.

By nightfall they knew the truth of that. Kori fell into bed, but had a hard time sleeping, her arms felt as if someone heavy was pulling, pulling, pulling without letup; they ached, not terribly sore, just terribly uncomfortable; she'd done most of the churning. Eventually she slept and again had no dreams she could remember. She woke, bone sore and close to tears from frustration. At breakfast she looked at Trago, ground her teeth when he shook his head.

A week passed. They were doing about half the milking now and had settled into routine so the housekeeping chores were quickly done and the work in the cheesehouse was considerably easier. Sore muscles had recovered, they'd found the proper rhythm to the tasks and Chittar was pleased with them.

On the seventh night, Zilos came to Trago, told him where to find the cave and what to do with the things he found there.

The hole they were crawling through widened suddenly into a room larger than Owlyn's threshing floor. Kori lifted the lamp high and stared wide-eyed at the glimmering splendor. Chains hung in graceful curves, one end bolted to a ceiling so high it was lost in the darkness beyond the reach of the lamp, the other end to the wall. Chains crossing and recrossing the space, chains of iron forged on the smithpriest's anvil and hung in here so long ago all but the lowest links were coated with stone, chains of wood fashioned by the woodworkerpriest's knives, chains of crystal and saltmarble chiseled by the stonecutterpriest's tools, centuries of labor given to the cave, taken by the cave to itself. The cold was piercing, the damp crept into her bones as she stared, but it was beautiful and it was awesome.

In the center of the chamber a square platform of polished wood sat on stone blocks a foot off the stone floor, above it, held up by intricately carved wooden posts, a canopy of white jade, thin and translucent as the finest porcelain, in the center of the platform a chest made from kedron wood without any carving on it, the elegant shape and the wonderful gloss of the wood all the ornament it needed. "I suppose that's it," she said. She shivered as her voice broke the silence; it was such a little sound, like a mosquito's whine and made her feel small and fragile as a mosquito, as if a mighty hand might slap down any moment and wipe her away. She set the lamp on the floor and waited.

Trago glanced at her, but said nothing. After a moment's hesitation he moved cautiously across the uneven floor, jumped up onto the platform. Uncertain of the proprieties involved, Kori didn't follow him; she waited on the chamber floor, leaning against one of the corner posts, watching as he chewed on his lip and frowned at the polished platform with its intricate inlaid design. He looked over his shoulder. "You think I ought to take off my sandals?"

She spread her hands. "You know more than me about that."

Nothing happened, so he walked cautiously to the chest. He turned the lid back, froze, seemed to stop breathing, still, statue still, inert as the stone around him. Kori gasped, started to go to him, but something slippery as oiled glass pushed her back, wouldn't let her onto the platform. She clawed at the thing, screamed, "Tré, what is it, Tré, say something, Tré, let him go, you . . . you . . . you. . . ."

Trago stirred, made a small catching sound as if his throat unlocked and he could breathe again. Kori shuddered, then leaned against the post and rubbed at her throat, reassured but still barred from the platform. He knelt before the chest and began taking things out of it, setting them beside his knees, things that blurred so she couldn't tell what they were, though she knew the crystal when he held it up; he brought it over to her, reached through the barrier and gave it to her, solemn, silent, his face blurred too (the look of it frightened her). Seeming to understand her unease, he gave her a smoky smile, then he returned to the chest, seemed to put something around his neck, (for Kori, impression of a chain with a smoky oval hanging from it) and he seemed to put something in his pocket (a fleeting impression of a short needleblade and an ebony hilt with a red crystal set into it, an even more evanescent impression of something held behind it). He returned the other things to the chest and shut the lid.

Abruptly the barrier was gone. Kori stepped back, clutching the crystal against her stomach, holding it with both hands. Trago sat on the chest and kicked his heels against it. "Come on, Kori, it's not so damp up here. Or cold. And bring the lamp."

Kori looked down at the crystal, then over her shoulder at the lamp. She wasn't happy about that chest, but this was Tré's place now; she was an intruder, but he belonged here. Holding the sphere against her with one hand, she carried the lamp to the platform, hesitated a breath or two, long enough to make Tré frown at her, managed to step up on the platform without dropping either the lamp or the crystal sphere. "You sure this is all right, Tré?"

He nodded, grinned at her. "It isn't all bad, Kori, this being a priest I mean. Anything I want to do in here, I can. Um . . ." He lost his grin. "I hope it doesn't take long, we got to get back before xera Chittar knows we left."

"I know. Take this." When he had the lamp, she settled to the platform, sitting cross-legged with her back to the chest. She rubbed the crystal sphere on her shirt, held it cupped into her hands. "Find the stillness," she said aloud, "draw will out of stillness, then look." She closed her eyes and tried to chase everything from her mind; a few breaths later she knew that wasn't going to work, but there was a thing AuntNurse taught her to do whenever her body and mind wouldn't turn off and let her sleep; she was to find a Place and began building an image of it in her mind, detail by detail, texture, odor, color, movement. When she was about five, she found a safe hide and went there when she was escaping punishment or was angry at someone or hurt or feeling wretched, she went there when her mother died, she went there when one of her small cousins choked on a bone and died in her arms, she went there whenever she needed to think. It was halfway up the ancient oak in a crotch where three great limbs separated from the trunk. She lined the hollow there with dead leaves and thistle fluff, making a nest like a bird did. It was warm and hidden, nothing bad could ever happen to her there, she could feel the great limbs moving slowly, ponderously beneath and around her like arms rocking her, she could smell the pungent dark friendly odor of the leaves and the bark, the stiff dark green leaves still on their stems whispered around her until she felt she almost understood what the tree said. Now she built that Place around her, built it with all the intensity she was capable of, shutting out fear and uncertainty and need, until she rocked in the arms of the tree, sat in the arms of the tree cuddling a fragment of moonlight in her arms. She gazed into the sphere, into the silver heart of it and drew will out of stillness. "Drinker of Souls," she whispered to the sphere, in her voice the murmur of oak leaves, "Show her to me. Where is she?"

An image bloomed in the silver heart. An old woman, white hair twisted into a heavy straggly knot on top her head. Her sleeves were rolled up, showing pale heavy forearms. She was chopping wood, with neat powerful swings of the ax, every stroke counting, every stroke going precisely where she wanted, long long years of working like that evident in the economy of her movements. She set the ax aside, gathered lengths of wood into a bundle and carried them to a mounded kiln. She pulled the stoking doors open, fed in the wood, brought more bundles of wood, working around the kiln until she had resupplied all the doors. Then she went back to chopping wood. A voice spoke in Kori's head, a male voice, a light tenor with a hint of laughter in it that she didn't understand; she didn't know the voice but suspected it was the Chained God or one of his messengers. *Brann of Arth Slya,* it said, *Drinker of Souls and potter of note. Ask in Jade Halimm about the Potter of Shaynamoshu. Send her half the medal. Keep the other half yourself and match the two when you meet. Take care how you talk about the Drinker of Souls away from this place. One whose name I won't mention stirs in his sleep and wakes, knowing something is happening here, that someone is working against him. Even now he casts his ariel surrogates this way. If you have occasion to say anything dangerous, stay close to an oak, the sprites will drive his ariels away. Fare well and wisely, young Kori; you work alone, there's no one can help you but you.*

Kori stared into the crystal a few moments longer, vaguely disappointed in the look of the hero who was supposed to defeat the mighty Settsimaksimin when all the forces of the King could not, nor could the priests and fighters of the Vales. Brann was strong and vital, but she was old. A fat old woman who made pots. Kori sighed and rocked herself loose from Her Place. She looked up at Trago. "Did you get any of that?"

Trago leaned toward her, hands on knees. "I heard the words. What's she like?"

"Not like I expected. She's old and fat."

He kicked his heels against the chest, clucked his tongue. "Doesn't sound like much. What does it mean, Drinker of Souls?"

"I don't know. Tré, you want to go on with this? You heard the Voice, HE's sticking his fingers in, if HE catches us . . . well."

Trago shrugged. His eyes were frightened and his hands tightened into fists, but he was pretending he didn't care. "Do I don't I, what's it matter? You said it, Kori. Better'n nothing."

"I hear you." She moved her shoulders, straightened her legs out. "Oooh, I'm tired. Let's finish this." She pulled the medal from around her neck, dropped it on the platform. "Think you could cut this in half like the Voice said?"

"Uh huh. Who we going to give it to?"

"I thought about that before I went to see the Women of Piyoloss and wangled my way up here." She rubbed at her stomach, ran her hand over the crystal. "Moon Meadow's down a little and around the belly of the mountain. The Kalathi twins and Hervé are summering there with a herd of silkgoats. And Toma."

"Ha! I thought the soldiers got him."

"Most everybody did. I did." Kori pulled her braids to the front and smoothed her hands along them, smoothed them again, then began playing with the tassels. "Women talk," she said. "It was my turn helping in the washhouse. They put me to boiling the sheets; I expect they forgot I was there, because they started talking about Ruba the whore, you know, the Phrasin who lives in that hutch up the mountain behind House Kalath that no one will talk about in front of the kids. Seems she was entertaining one of the soldiers, he was someone fairly important who knew what was going on and he let slip that they were going to burn the priest next morning and throw anyone who made a fuss into the fire with him. Well, she's Vale folk now all the way, so she pushed him out after a while and went round to the Women of Kalathin and told them. What I heard was the Women tried to get Zilos, away, but the soldiers had hauled him off already. Amely was having fits and the kids were yelling and Toma was trying to hold things together and planning on taking Zilos' hunting bow and plinking every soldier he could get sight of. What they did was, they took Amely and the young ones away from the Priest-House and got Ontari out of the stable where he was sleeping and had him take them over to Semela Vale since he knows tracks no one else does. And they gave Toma sleeproot in a posset they heated for him and tied him over a pony and Pellix took him up to Moon Meadow and told the Twins to keep him away from the Floor. They said he's supposed to've calmed down some, but he's fidgety. He knows if he goes down he gets a lot of folk killed, so he stays there, hating a lot. What I figure is, if we tell him about this, it's something he can do when it's just him could get killed and if it works, he's going to make you know who really unhappy. So. What do you think?"

Trago rubbed his eyes, his lids were starting to hang heavy. "Toma," he muttered. "I don't know. He . . ." His eyes glazed over, his head jerked. "Toma," he said, "yes." He blinked. "Aaah, Kori, let's get this finished. I want to go to bed."

"Me too." She got stiffly to her feet, sleep washing in waves over her. "Put this away, will you." She held out the crystal sphere. "Um . . . We're going to need gold for Toma, is there any of that in there? And you have to cut the medal before we go. I don't want to come here again, besides, we already lost a week."

Trago slid off the chest and stood rubbing his eyes. He yawned and took the sphere. "All right." He blinked at the medal lying by his foot. "You better go back where you were before. I think the god's going to be doing this."

" 'Lo, Hervé."
" 'Lo, Tré, what you doin' here?"

" 'S my time at Far Meadow. Toma around?"

"Shearin' shed, got dry rot in the floor, he was workin' on that the last time I saw him."

Trago nodded and went around the house, climbed the corral fence and walked the top rail; when he reached the shed, he jumped down and went inside. Part of the floor was torn up. Toma had a plank on a pair of sawhorses; he was laying a measuring line along it. Trago stood watching, hands clasped behind him, as his cousin positioned a t-square and drew an awl along the straight edge, cutting a line into the wood; when he finished that, he looked up. "Tré. What you doing here?"

"Come to see you. I'm over to Far Meadow, doing my month, 'n I got something I need to say to you."

"So?" Toma reached for the saw, set it to the mark, then waited for Trago to speak.

"It's important, Toma."

Muscles moved in the older boy's face, his body tensed, then he got hold of himself and drove the saw down. He focused grimly on his hands and the wood for the next several minutes, sweat coursing down his face and arms, the rasping of the teeth against the wood drowning Trago's first attempts to argue with him. The effort he put into the sawing drained down his anger, turning it from hot seethe to a low simmer. When the cut was nearly through and the unsupported end was about to splinter loose, peeling off the edge of the plank as it fell, he straightened, drew his arm across his face, waved Trago round to hold up the end as he finished sawing it off. "Put it over by the wall," he told Trago. "I think it'll come close to fitting that short bit."

"Toma . . ." Trago saw his cousin's face shut again, sighed and moved off with his awkward load. When he came back, he swung up onto the plank before his cousin could lift it. "Listen to me," he said. "This isn't one of my fancies. I don't want to talk to you here. Please, stop for a little, you don't have to finish this today. I NEED to talk to you."

Toma opened his mouth, snapped it shut. He wheeled, walked over to stare down into the dark hole where he'd taken up the rotted boards. "If it's about *down there* . . ." His voice dripped vitriol when he said the last words, "I don't want to hear."

Trago looked nervously around; he knew about ariels, knew he couldn't see them unless they chanced to drift through a dusty sunbeam, but he couldn't help trying. He didn't want to say anything here, but if he kept fussing that would be almost as bad; AuntNurse always knew when he was making noise to hide something, he suspected the Sorcerer was as knowing as her if not worse. He slid off the plank, trotted to Toma, took him by the hand and tugged him toward the door.

Toma pulled free, stood looking tired and unhappy, finally he nodded. "I'll come, Tré. And I'll listen. Five minutes. If you don't convince me by then, you're going to hurt for it."

Trago managed a grin. "Come on then."

He led his cousin away from the meadow into the heart of an oak grove.

Kori stepped from behind a tree. " 'Lo, Toma,"

"Kori?" Toma stepped back, scowled from one to the other. "What's going on here?"

"Show him your shoulder, Tré."

Trago unlaced the neck opening of his shirt, pushed it back so Toma could see the hollow starburst.

Kori dropped onto a root as Toma bent, touched the mark. "Sit down, cousin. We've got a lot of talking to do."

". . . so, that's what we want you to do." She touched the packet resting on her thigh. "Take this to the Drinker of Souls and remind her of her promise. It'll be dangerous. HE'll be looking for anyone acting different. Voice told us HE's got his ariels out, that's why Tré didn't want to say much in the shed, he wanted to be where oaksprites were because they don't like ariels much and chase them whenever they come around. Um, Tré got gold from the Chained God's Place because we knew you'd need it. Um, we'd kinda like you to go as fast as you could, Tré's got less'n three months before the Signs start popping up. Will you do it?"

Toma rubbed his face with both hands, his breathing hoarse and unsteady. Without speaking, he rested his forearms on his thighs and let his hands dangle as he stared at the ground. Kori watched him, worried. She'd written the message on the parchment, folded it around half the medal, used sewing thread to tie it shut and smeared slathers of sealing wax over it, then she'd knotted a bag about it and made a neck cord for it out of the same thread, and she had the gold in a pouch tied to her belt. Everything was ready, all they needed was Toma. She watched, trying to decide what he was thinking. If she'd been a few years older, if she'd been a boy, with all the things boys were taught that she'd never had a chance to learn, she wouldn't be sitting here waiting for Toma to make up his mind. She moved her hands impatiently, but said nothing. Either he went or he didn't and if he went, best it was his own doing so he'd put his heart in it.

A shudder shook him head to toe, he sighed, lifted his head. His eyes had a glassy animal sheen, he was still looking inward, seeing only the images in his head. He blinked, began to cry, silently, without effort, the tears spilling down his face. "I . . . Yes, I'll go. Yes." He rolled a sleeve down, scrubbed it across his face, blew his nose into his fingers, wiped them on his pants. "Was Ontari down below? I'll go for Forkker Vale first, see if I can get on with a smuggler. He knows them." He tried a grin and when it worked, laughed with excitement and pleasure. "I don't want to end up like Harra did."

Kori looked at Trago. Trago nodded. "I was talking to him the day before we come up here. He was working on a saddle, he won't be going anywhere 'fore he finishes that."

Toma nodded. "I'll go down tonight. He still sleeping in Kalathin's stable?"

"Uh huh. There's usually a couple soldiers riding the House Round, but they aren't too hard to avoid, more often than not they're drunk, at least that's what Ontari said."

"Wouldn't be you were flitting about when you shouldn't?"

Trago giggled and didn't bother denying it.

Kori got to her feet. "We have to be back in time to milk the cows or xera Chittar will skin us. Here." She tossed the packet to Toma, began untying the gold pouch. "Be careful, cousin." She held out the pouch. "Oaks are safe, I don't know what else, maybe you can sneak out, I'm afraid . . ."

He laughed and hugged her hard, took the pouch, hugged Trago. "You get back to your cows, cousins. I'll see you when."

". . . Crimpa, Sparrow, White Eye. Chain it, Tré, Two Spot has run off again. You see any sign of her?"

Trago snorted, capered in a circle. "Un . . . huh! Un . . . huh! Slippy Two Spot. Lemme see . . ." He trotted off.

"Mmf." Kori tapped Crimpa cow with her switch and started her moving toward the corral; the others fell in around her and plodded placidly across the grass as if they'd never ever had a contrary thought between their horns. A whoop behind her, an indignant mm-moooaaauhh. Two Spot came running from under the trees, head jerking, udder swinging; she slowed, trotted with stiff dignity over to the herd and pushed into the middle of it. Trago came up beside Kori, walked along with her. "She was just wandering around. I don't know what she thought she was doing." He yawned extravagantly, rubbed at his eyes, started whistling. He broke off when they reached the corral, slanted a glance up at her. "So we wait."

"So we wait."

3

ANOTHER MEADOW, THE SHAYNAMOSHU POTTERY ON THE RIVER WANSHEERI, AT THE MASSACRE.

SCENE: Late. The Wounded Moon a fat broken
crescent rising in the east. A horse
streaked with dried foam, trying to
graze, having difficulty with the
bit. A black-clad youth dead in a pool
of blood. Another figure, a woman,
crumpled across him. A pale translucent wraithlike figure lying upon
her, a second squatting beside them.

An icy wind touched her neck.
  Something heavy, metallic slammed into her back.
  Cold fire flashed up through her.
  Heavy breathing, broken in the middle. Faint popping sound.
  *Her knees folded under her, she saw herself toppling toward the boy's
body, saw the hilt of the knife in his back, saw an exploding flower of
blood, saw nothing more.*

A light weight on her, fire burning in her, pain . . .
  "Wake up, Brann. Come on. Yaril needs you, she's fading." Jaril's
voice, urgent, pleading.
  She blinked, her eyes felt grainy, sore. She fumbled about futilely for
a minute, found purchase for her hands, managed to straighten her
arms. They trembled. She was horribly weak, it frightened her how
weak she was. The frail weight slid off and Yaril rolled over twice, lay
face down on the grass beside the rutted dirt road, very pale, almost

transparent. Jaril was colorless too, though he had more substance to him. Brann looked down at herself. She'd lost almost all her flesh, her skin was hanging on her bones. Her hands were shaking and she felt an all-over nausea; chills ran through her body. "What . . ."

Jaril clicked his tongue impatiently. "No time for that. There's the horse, Brann, feed us before we go to stone, Yaril's hanging on a thread. The horse. You can reach it, come on, stand up, I can't carry you. Hurry, I don't know how long. . . ."

Trembling and uncertain, Brann hoisted herself onto her feet. Stiff with blood, feces and urine, too big for her now, her skirt fell off her, nearly tripped her; grunting with disgust she dragged her feet free, tottered down to the grazing horse. He started to shy away, but froze when her hand brushed against his flank. She edged closer, set her other hand on his back by the spine, hating what she was doing since she was fond of horses, but she was a lot fonder of the children so she drew the horse's cool life into herself, easing down beside him as he collapsed, sucking out the last trickle of energy.

Jaril drifted over, dropped to his knees beside her. "We brought some tahargoats," he said. "They're around somewhere, when we saw you down like that we forgot about them. I'll chase them over in a while. Horse won't be enough." He leaned against her, fragile and weightless as a dessicated leaf.

Brann straightened, twisted around, touched the tips of her fingers to his face, let him draw energy from her. Color flowed across him, pastel pinks and ivories and golds, ash gray spread through his wispy shirt and trousers, from transparent he turned translucent. He made a faint humming sound filled with pleasure, grinned his delight. Brann smiled too, got to her feet. "Get your goats," she said and started walking heavily up the grassy rise, heading for the road and Yaril. Jaril shifted to his mastiff form, went off to round up the goats.

Yaril lay on the grass, a frail girlchild sculpted in glass, naked (she hadn't bothered to form clothing out of her substance though she clung to the bipedal form and hadn't retreated to the glimmersphere that was her baseshape, Brann didn't know why, the children didn't talk all that much about themselves) and vulnerable, flickering and fading. Frowning, worried, Brann knelt beside her, stretched out hands that looked grossly vigorous in spite of the skin hanging in folds about the bone, and rested them gently on a body that was more smoke than flesh, letting the remnant of the horse's energy trickle into it.

The changechild's substance thickened and her color began returning, at first more guessed at than seen like inks thinned with much water, but gradually stronger as Brann continued to feed energy into her. When a dog barked and goats blatted, Yaril's eyes opened. She blinked, slow deliberate movements of her eyelids, managed a faint smile.

Jaril-Mastiff herded the goats over to her. Brann fed their energy to him and Yaril until they lost their frailty, then used the last of it to readjust herself, rebuilding some of the muscle, tightening her skin, shedding the appearance of age until her body was much what it had been when she and Harra Hazhani had played Slya's games so long ago. The changechildren had grown her from eleven to her mid-twenties over a single night back then and all her hair fell out. Remembering that, she shook her head vigorously; most of her hair flew off; she wiped away the rest of it. Bald as an egg. She rubbed her hand over skin smooth as polished marble. Ah well, maybe it'll grow back as fast this time as it did that. She looked down at the dead boy, stooped, grunting with the effort and took the knife from his body, straightened with another grunt, held it up. A strange knife, might have been made of ice from the look of it. As she turned it over, examining it in the dim light from the moon, it melted into air. She whistled with surprise.

Jaril nodded. "The one that was in you did the same thing."

Brann laughed, wiped her hand on her blouse. "They weren't souvenirs I wanted to keep." She started for the house. "Shuh, I need a bath." A sniff and a grimace. "Several baths. And I'm hollow enough to eat those goats raw what's left of them." Another laugh. "I didn't know how hungry it makes you—dying, I mean. It's not every day I die."

"You weren't actually dead," Jaril said seriously. "If you were dead, we couldn't bring you back."

"Was a joke, Jay."

He made a face. "Not much of a joke for us, Bramble. Starving to death is no fun."

"You made me, you could find someone else and change them."

"We made you with a lot of help from Slya, Brann, we didn't do it on our own. I doubt she'd bother another time."

"Mmm. Well, I'm not dead and you're not going to starve. Uh . . . ." She clutched at herself, started to turn back.

Yaril caught her arm, stopped her. "This what you want?" She held out a small bloodstained packet. "I found it lying beside me. You think it's important?"

"Seems to me this is what got the boy killed and me . . ." she smiled at Jaril, ". . . nearly." She closed her fingers about the packet. "It stinks of magic, kids. Makes me nervous. Somebody called up tigermen and whipped them here to make sure I didn't open it. I don't like mixing with sorcerers and such."

"Who?"

Brann tossed the packet up, caught it, weighed it thoughtfully. "Heavy. Hmm. No doubt the answer's in here. While I'm stoking up the fire under the bathtub and scrubbing off my stink, the two of you might take a look at this thing." She held out the packet and Yaril took it. "And I wouldn't mind if you fixed me a bit of dinner."

Jaril chuckled. "Return the favor, hmm?"

After scrubbing off the worst of her body's reaction to its own violent death, cold water making her shiver, and adding more wood to the fire under the brick tub, Brann climbed to the attic and pulled the gummed paper off the chest that held her old clothes. When she stopped wandering nearly a century ago and moved into the shed behind the house, she had to bow to Dayan Acsic's prejudices and pack her trousers away. She was a woman. Women in Jade Torat wore skirts. His one concession was this chest. When she came back with the proper clothing, he let her put her shirts and trousers and the rest of her gear in the chest, gave her aromatics to keep moths and other nuisances away and gummed paper to seal the cracks, then he shouldered the chest and carried it to the attic, tough old root of a man, and that was that.

She turned back the lid, wrinkled her nose at the smell; it was powerful and peculiar. She excavated a shirt and a pair of trousers, then some underclothing. The blouse was yellowed and weakened by age, the black of the trousers had the greenish patina of decades of mildew. "Ah well, they only need to cover me till I reach Jade Halimm." She hung the clothing in the window so it would air out and with a little luck lose some of the smell, retied the sash to her robe and climbed back down.

The water was hot. She raked out the firebox, tipped the coals, ash and unburned wood into an iron brazier and climbed into the water.

When she padded into the kitchen, sleepy, filled with well-being, the changechildren had salad and rice and goat stew ready for her and a pot of tea steaming on the stand. Jaril had dug out Brann's bottle of plum brandy; he and Yaril were sitting on stools and sipping at the rich golden liquid. The parchment was unfolded, sitting crumpled on the table, held down with a triangular bit of bronze.

Brann raised a brow, sat and began eating. Time passed. Warm odorous time. Finally she sighed, wiped her mouth, poured a bowl of tea and slumped back in her chair. "So. What's that about?" She smiled. "If you're sober enough to see straight."

Yaril patted a yawn with delicate grace; since she didn't breathe, the gesture was a touch sarcastic. She set her glass down, licked sticky fingers, brushed aside the chunk of metal and lifted the parchment. "First thing, these are Cheonea glyphs."

"Cheonea? Where's that? Never heard of it."

"A way west of here. A month by ship, if it's moderately fast. On the far side of Phras." Jaril sipped at the brandy. "Almost an island. Shaped like a hand with a thready wrist. We were there a year ago. Didn't stay long, one city the usual sort of seaport, farms and mountains and a smuggler's haven. Not very interesting. They kicked their king out a few decades back, from what I heard, he was no loss, but they got landed with a sorcerer who seems to think he's got the answer to the riddle of life." He reached for the bronze piece, tossed it to Brann. "Take a good look at that."

She caught it with her free hand. "Why not just tell me. . . ." She set the tea bowl down, began examining the triangle. Temueng script. On one side part of the Emperor's sigil, on the other part of a name. ". . . ra Hazhani. The boy said something, um, let me remember . . . Harra . . . no, we the blood of Harra Hazhani say to you, remember what you swore. This is half of one of those credeens the Maratullik struck off for Taguiloa and the rest of us. You remember those?"

Jaril grimaced. "We should."

Brann rubbed her thumb over the bronze. "I know." She'd had a choice then, Slya's sly malice set it for her, she could protect Taguiloa and the other players or send the changechildren home. She chose the players because they were the most vulnerable and accepted responsibility for keeping the children fed, though she hadn't really realized what that meant. Her own bronze credeen was around somewhere, likely at the bottom of the chest with the rest of her old clothes. "What's the letter say?"

Yaril lifted the parchment. "Took us a while to decipher it, we didn't pay that much attention to the written language when we were there. So, a lot of this is guess and twist till it seems to fit. We think it's a young girl writing, there are some squiggles after her name that might be determinatives expressing age and sex. She seems to be called Kori Piyolss of Owlyn Vale. She calls on the Drinker of Souls to remember her promise, that she'd come from the ends of the earth to help the Children of Harra. Harra married Kori's great great etc. grandfather and passed the promise on. Kori says she wouldn't use Harra's gift on anything unimportant, that you, Brann, must believe that. Someone close and dear to her faces a horrible death, everyone in the Vale lives in fear of He who sits in the Citadel of Silagamatys. That's the city Jaril was talking about, the only settlement in Cheonea big enough to call a city, a port on the south coast. She asks you to meet her there on the seventeenth day of Theriste. Mmm. That's thirty-seven days from now, no from yesterday, it's almost dawn, um, if I remember their dating system correctly. Meet her in a tavern called the Blue Seamaid. She'll be along after dark and she'll have the rest of the credeen. She can't write more about her plans in case this letter falls into the hands of Him. Got a heavy slash of ink under that *him*. You made the promise, Brann." She grinned. "And very drunk out it was. You remember, the party Taguiloa threw for the whole quarter when we got back from Andurya Durat." She pushed ash blond hair off her face. "Going to keep it?"

"Doesn't seem I have much choice. That sorcerer, what's his name?"

"Settsimaksimin."

"Right now he probably thinks I'm dead. That won't last long." She sipped at her tea, sighed. "And there's another thing. I've put off thinking about it, but those tigermen cut through more than my flesh. I've stayed here about as long as I can. Much more and folk are going to start asking awkward questions about just what I am." She looked round the room, eyes lingering on surfaces and cooking things her hands had held, scrubbed, polished, shook, brushed against for the past hundred years; it was an extension of her body and leaving it behind would be like lopping off an arm.

Eyes laughing at her, Jaril said, "You could turn into a local haunt, remember the old man on the mountain across the bay from Silili?"

"Hunh. And what would you be, Jay, a haunt's haunt?" She smiled, shook her head. "It might come to that, but I'm not ready for godhood yet, even demigodhood."

"What about this place?"

"Have to leave it, I suppose. Put the things I want to keep in the secret cellar you and Yaril burnt out for me, leave the rest to the wind and thieves." She yawned, finished her tea, rubbed her thumb against the bowl. It was part of the das'n vuor set that was one of the last things her father made before the Temuengs took him and the rest of Arth Slya to work in the pens of the Emperor. "Mmmm. Either of you see a riverboat heading west when you flew in?"

"There was one leaving Gofajiu, you know what that means, it'll be here two or three days on. You really planning on flagging it?"

Brann's mouth twitched to a half smile. "Yes, no; Jay, I haven't made up my mind yet." She smoothed the teabowl along a wrist little more than bone and taut skin, half what it'd been a day ago. "I don't look much like I did the past some years." Chuckle. "Young. And bald. That's not the Potter. Couldn't be the Potter. On the other hand," she grimaced, "that's the Potter's landing, what's she doing there, that woman, who is she, where's the Potter? Riverboat's comfortable and safe as you can get on the river, the two of you aren't up to much, me either." She set the bowl on the table and slumped in the chair gazing into the mirrorblack of the pot, her image distorted by the accidents of texture that gave the surface half its beauty. "I don't know . . . I know I'd rather take the riverboat but. . . ." She sighed. "The river's low, the summer's been hot and dry, it's still a monster, I've never sailed the skiff that far, but. . . . Ah, Slya's teeth, I keep thinking, the Potter's dead, leave her dead, no loose ends like strange females hanging about. My father always said the hard way's the best way, it means you're thinking about what you're doing not just drifting with no idea where you're going." A long tired sigh. "We'll forget the riverboat and take the clay skiff and hope old Tungjii's watching out for us." She sat up. "I'm too tired to work and too itchy to sleep. Probably shouldn't have drunk that tea. Ah well, we can't leave tomorrow anyway, too much to do." She yawned, then poured herself another bowl. "So. Tell me more about Cheonea. When you were there did you happen to visit Owlyn Vale"

Brann slid into the harbor at Jade Halimm after sundown on the third day, threading through a torchlit maze of floating life—flowerboats with their reigning courtesans and less expensive dancers, horizontal and otherwise, gambling boats, hawkers of every luxury and perversion the foreign traders and seaman might desire, scaled to the size of their purses. The wealthier passengers were left untroubled; they'd find their pleasures in more elegant surroundings ashore. The Jade King's mosquito boats buzzed about to make sure these last were not troubled by offers that might offend their sensibilities. Too shabby to attract the attention of the hawkers or the mosquito patrol, too busy managing the skiff to notice much of this, Brann got through the water throng without accident or incident and tied up at a singhouse pier, the small old skiff lost among the other boats. The tide was on the turn, beginning to come in but it was still a long climb to the pier, half of it on a ladder slimy with seamoss and decaying weed and the exudates of the lingam slugs that fed on them and the weesha snails that lived in them. She wiped her hands on her trousers when she reached dry wood, not appreciably worsening the mess they were already.

She stood on the edge of the pier looking down at the boat, feeling gently melancholy. It was the last thing left of her life as the Potter of Shaynamoshu. She stood there, the harbor raucous about her, remembering . . . a slant of light through autumn leaves, the sharp smell of life ripened to the verge of decay, the last firing that year, what year was it, no she couldn't place it now, it was just a year, nothing but a collection of images and smells and a deep abiding sense of joy that came she didn't know why or from where, coming down the track with the handcart loaded, the children playing in otter-shape running and tumbling before her . . . another time, the firing Tungjii blessed, texture moving in sacred dance over the surface, color within color, like an opal but more restrained, subtle earth hues, and most of all the feel of it, the weight and balance of it in the hollow of her hand when she almost knew the triumph her father felt when he took the last of the das'n vuor drinking bowls from the kiln on Tincreal and knew that one of them was perfect . . . another time after a snowfall when the earth was white and the sky was white and the silence whiter than both.

The onshore wind tugged at her sleeves, sent the ends of her headscarf whipping beside her ear. She thrust a finger under the scarf, felt the quarter inch of stubble. Growing fast, Slya bless. She settled the scarf more firmly, clicked her tongue with impatience as a horned owl swooped low over her head and screeched at her. "I know," she muttered, "I know. It's time to get settled."

She found a room in a run down tavern near the Westwall, a cubicle with a bed and not much else, blankets thin and greasy, bedbugs and fleas, a stink that was the work of decades, stain on stain on stain never insulted by the touch of soap; its only amenities were a stout bar on the door and a grill over the slit of a window, but these were worth the premium price she paid for sole occupancy. Her base established, she found a lateopen tailor and ordered new clothing, found one of her favorite cookshops and ate standing up, watching the life of the Harbor Quarter teem around her.

The next six days she prowled the night, in and out of houses, winding through back alleys, following the stench of corroded souls, killing until her own soul revolted, drinking the life of her victims, feeding the children, renewing her own vigor, drinking life until her flesh gave off a glow like moonlight. As the children edged in their slow way toward maturity, their capacity to store energy increased. Now they needed recharging only every second year, but it took many nights of hunting to fill their reserves. Back when Slya forced the choice on her she hadn't realized the full implications of her decision. She was, despite her appearance and the compressed experience of the past months, only twelve years old when that decision was made; she hadn't known how weary she could get of living (admittedly not every day, many of her days were contented, even joyful, but the dark times came more often as the decades passed), she hadn't known how crushing the burden of feeding the children would become, she hadn't known how much their appetite would increase, how many lives it would take to sate their hunger, how loathsome she would look to herself no matter how careful she was to choose badlives. Kings and mercenaries, counselors and generals, muggers, pimps and assassins, all such folk, they seemed able to live contentedly enough though they killed and maimed and tortured with exuberance and extravagance, but at the end of her bouts of gorging, she was so prostrated and self-disgusted that she wondered how she could bring herself to do it again; yet when the children were hungry once more, she found the will to hunt; they began as innocent victims of a god-battle they hadn't asked to join and finished as victims of her confusion and her preference for her own kind; to let them starve would be a greater wrong than all the killing lumped together.

On the seventh evening when her prowling was done for a while and her new clothes had been delivered, she moved from the tavern to a better room in a better Inn in a better neighborhood, close to the wall that circled the highmerchant's quarter, a four-story structure with a bathhouse and a pocket garden for eating in when the days were sunny and the evenings clear.

Brann gave a handful of coppers to the youth who carried her gear and showed her to the room she'd hired for the next three nights; she watched him out, then crossed to the single window and opened the shutters. "Hunh, not much of a view."

Jaril ambled over and leaned heavily against her. "Nice wall."

Yaril squeezed past them and put her head out as far as she could; she looked up and around, wriggled free and went to sit on the bed. "Should be bars on the windows. Bramble, our Host down there obviously didn't think much of you, putting you in this room. Should we leave the shutters open to catch a bit of air, anyone could get in here. The top of that wall is just about even with the top of the window and it's only six feet off, if that."

Brann smiled. "Pity the poor thief who breaks in here." She left the window, prodded at the bed. "Better than the rack in that other place. My bones ache thinking about it. Uuuh, I'm tired. Too tired to eat. I think I'll skip supper and spend an hour or so in the bathhouse. Yaro, Jay, I'd appreciate it if one of you gave the mattress a runthrough before you bank your fires, make sure we've got no vermin sharing the room with us. I can't answer for my temper if I wake itching."

Unlike Hina Baths, the House was divided, one side for women, the other for men and the division was rigidly maintained. The attendant on the women's side (a female wrestler who looked more than capable of thumping anyone, male or female, who tried to make trouble) didn't quite know what to make of Brann; she wasn't accustomed to persons claiming to be females who wore what she considered male attire. Half annoyed, half amused, too tired to argue, Brann snorted with disgust, stripped off her shirt and trousers. Demonstrably female, she strolled inside.

The water was steamy, herb scented, filled with small bubbles as it splashed into a sunken pool made of worn stones, gray with touches of amber and russet and chalky blue. Nubbly white towels were piled on a wicker table near the door into the chamber, there were hooks set into the wall for the patron's clothing, a shallow saucer of soap and a dish of a scented oil sat beside the pool beneath a rail of smooth white porcelain, scrubbing cloths were draped over the rail. Brann hung up her shirt and trousers, dropped her underclothing beside the towels, tugged off her boots and put them on a bootstand beside the table. Stretching, yawning, the heat seeping into muscle and bone, she ambled to the pool and slid into water hot enough to make her bite on her lip and shudder with pleasure when she was immersed. She clung to the rail for a moment, then began swimming about, brushing through the uncurling leaves of the dried herbs the attendant had dropped into the water as she opened the taps that let it flow from the hot cistern. She ducked her head under, shook it, feeling the half-inch of new hair move against her skull. Surfacing, she pulled herself onto the edge of the pool and began soaping her legs, taking pleasure in her body for the first time in years; she'd lived a deliberately muffled life up on her mountain, centering her pleasures in her work and the landscape around her; a longtime lover could have learned too much about her, there was no one she trusted that much, no one she wanted enough to chance his revulsion when he learned what she was; even a short-timer would have made too many complications. Now, she was a skinful of energy, tingling with want, and she didn't quite know what to do about it. Cultures change in a hundred years; the changes might not be large but they were enough to tangle her feet if she didn't move with care. Laughing uncertainly as her nipples tautened and a dagger of pleasurable need stabbed up from her groin, she pulled a scrub cloth across her breasts, watched the scented lather slide over them, then flung the cloth away and plunged into the pool, submerging, sputtering up out of the water splashing herself vigorously to rinse away the remnants of the soap. Later, as she stood rubbing herself dry, she began running through her plans for the next day. It was time she began looking about for a ship to take her south. Better not try for Cheonea from here, better to change ships . . . she knew little about the powers or the limits of sorcery, she hadn't a guess about how Setsimaksimin had found her . . . she was reasonably sure he was her enemy, she'd made enough others in her lifetime, though most of them had to be dead by now, besides there was the boy and the packet with its plea for her help . . . so she didn't know if he could locate her again, but breaking one's backtrail was an elementary tactic when pursued by man or some less deadly predator. Hmm. She'd always had a thing for ship captains . . . she grinned, toweled her head . . . maybe she could find herself another like Sammang or Chandro. . . .

The night was warm and pleasant, the garden between the bathhouse and the Inn was full of drifting perfume and small paper lanterns dangling on long strings; they swayed in the soft airs and made shadows dance everywhere. On the far side of the vinetrellice that protected the privacy of bathers moving to and from the Inn she could hear unobtrusive cittern music and voices from the late diners eating out under the sky, enjoying the pleasant weather and the fine food Kheren Zanc's cook was famous for. She thought of going round and ordering a meal (more to enjoy the ambiance than because she was hungry) but did nothing about the thought, too tired to dredge up the energy needed to change direction. She drifted into the Inn, climbed two flights of stairs and tapped at the door to her room.

Not a sound. She waited. Nothing happened. She tried the latch, made a soft annoyed sound when the door opened.

The children were both in bed, sunk in their peculiar lethargy. As Brann stepped inside, one pale head lifted, dropped again. She relaxed. Trust Jaril to leave a fraction of himself alert so he wouldn't have to crawl out of bed and let her in. She stopped by the bed and ruffled his hair, but he didn't react, having sunk completely into stupor; she smiled, looked about for the key. It was on the bed table, gleaming darkly in the light coming through the unshuttered window. She locked the door, stripped and crawled into bed. A yawn, a wriggle, and she plunged fathoms deep in sleep.

A noise outside woke her from a restless, nightmare-ridden sleep. She pulled a quilt off the bed, wrapped it around her and got to the window in time to see a dark head and shoulders thrust out from the top of the wall, close enough she could almost touch them. Beyond the wall she heard shouts and dogs baying. Without stopping to think, she leaned out, caught the fugitive's attention with a sharp hiss.

The head jerked up.

"In here," she whispered. She saw him hesitate, but he had little choice. The hounds were breathing down his neck. She moved away from the window, jumped back another step as he came plunging through and whipped onto his feet, knife in hand, eyes glittering through the slits in his knitted mask. "Don't be silly," she said, no longer whispering. "Close the shutters or get away from the window and let me do it."

He sidled along the wall, keeping as far from her as he could. After a quick glance out the window, she eased the shutters to, careful to make as little noise as she could, pulled the bar over and tucked it gently into its hooks. That done, she set her back against the shutters and stood watching him.

He was over by the door; he tried the latch. "The key."

She hitched up the quilt which was trying to untuck itself and slide off her. "On the table." A nod toward the bed. "Go if you want. You could probably break loose. Or you can stay here until the chase passes on. Your choice."

"Why?" A thread of sound, angry and dangerous.

"Why not. Say I don't like seeing things hunted."

He lowered the knife, leaned against the door and thought about it, a small wiry figure, with black trousers and black sweater, black gloves, black busks on his feet and a knitted hood that covered his whole head except for the eyeslits. The dim light coming through diamond holes in the shutters touched his eyes as he moved away from the door, pale eyes, blue or hazel, unusual in Jade Halimm; he stared at her several seconds, glanced at the sleeping children. "Who are you?"

"Did I ask you that?"

"They aren't breathing." He waved the knife at the children.

"Nor did I make comments about your person."

He hesitated a moment longer, then he dragged off the mask and stood grinning at her. "Drinker of Souls," he said, satisfaction and certainty in his voice. "You knew my grandfather." He was a handsome youth, sixteen seventeen twenty at most, straight thick hair, heavy brows, flattish nose and a wide thinlipped mouth that could move from a grin to a grimace at the flash of a thought. Mixed blood. Hina stature, Hina nose and tilted almond Hina eyes (though they should have been dark brown to be truly Hina), the dark blond hair that appeared sometimes when Hina mixed with Croaldhese, his mouth and chin were certainly Croaldhese. He had the accent of a born Halimmer, that quick slide of sound impossible to acquire unless you lisped your first words in Jalimmik.

He slipped the knife up his sleeve and went to sit on the bed. "My mother's father was called Aituatea. You might remember him." He waited a moment giving her a chance to comment; when she said nothing, he went on. "You're a family legend. You and them." A wave of his hand at the two blond heads.

"Hmm. This seems to be the month of old acquaintances."

"What?"

"Wouldn't mean anything to you. Yaril, Jaril, wake up." The covers stirred, two sleepy children sat up blinking. "Forget it, kids, the lad knows all about you." She turned back to the young thief. "How serious were they, those folk chasing you?"

He scratched at his jaw. "I'm still here, not running for the nearest hole. Those Dreeps know all the holes I do, and they'll be going down them hunting blood. Not just them." He thought a moment, apparently decided there was no point being coy about his target. "Highmerchant Jizo Gozit, it was his House I got into, he's a vindictive man and he's got more pull than a giant squid; by now the king's Noses are in the hunt."

"I see. They'll be searching this place before long. We could shove you under the bed or hide you in it . . . no, I've got a better idea . . . maybe . . . you think they know it's you they're hunting?"

"Doubt it. I usually keep well away from that quarter. The hounds have my scent, though; if the Dreeps bring their dogs. . . ."

"Jaril, let him take your place. Mastiff, I think hmm? Any dogs stick their noses in the door, you take their minds off our friend here."

Jaril patted a yawn, slid out of the bed, a slim naked youth. For a moment he stood looking at the thief out of bright crystal eyes, then he was a mastiff standing high as the boy's waist, muscle rippling on muscle, droopy month stretched into a grin that exposed an intimidating set of teeth. He went trotting around the room, came back to the rug at the foot of the bed, scratched at it until he was satisfied, turned around once and settled onto it, head down, ready to sleep until he was needed.

"Get into the bed beside Yaril," Brann said. "You'll be Jaril. Kheren will tell them I came in with two children, a boy and a girl, you're older and taller and not so fair, but that shouldn't matter."

The mastiff lifted his head, whined softly.

"Move it, friend." Brann whipped the quilt off, swept it over the bed and dived under the covers beside him. She felt his tension as he lay sandwiched between her and Yaril. "Relax," she muttered.

A long sigh, a wriggle that edged him away from her, then his breathing went slow and steady, craftily counterfeiting slumber. A handsome youth, but he didn't arouse anything in her except impatience. Getting old, she thought, Slya Bless, a few hours ago I was hot to trot, as the saying goes, contemplating the seduction of some sea captain. She sighed. What do I do if the same nothing appears when I find someone more to my taste, ayy yaaah, dead from the neck down? May it never happen. I was something like half dead up there. Mmh. Would have been all dead, if the children had been an hour or so later. She scowled at the unseen ceiling. Didn't even try to fight. . . . The memory made her sick. Didn't even try to get the knife out, heal the wound. They surprised me, but that's no excuse. Hadn't thought about it before but that must have been what I was doing the past fifty years, getting ready to die and when it happened. . . . Shuh! I can't die. Not with the kids depending on me. I've got to do something about that. I

don't know what. After this is over and there's time . . . maybe if I
went back to Tincreal and roused Slya . . .

She lay still and did a few mind tricks to keep her body relaxed, then
tried to figure out why she'd taken on this young thief with no questions asked. It startled her now that she had time to take a look at what
she'd done. She thought about what she'd told him, *I don't like to see
things hunted.* True enough, especially after the past six days (twinge in
her stomach, quickly suppressed). I suppose he's my redeeming act, my
sop, my . . . oh forget it, Brann, you're maundering. Aituatea's
grandson, hmm, he's got the proper heritage for his profession all right.
What's going on here? First Harra's great grandsoevers, now Aituatea's. Things come in threes, uh huh, and if there's a third intrusion
from my past. . . .

She heard the voices in the hall and the tramp of booted feet near her
door. She heard the clank of the key as it turned in the lock. She stifled
an urge to turn and look at the boy, forced her breathing to slow, her
body to relax again.

The door crashed open, banging against the wall. Light from the
hallway and the lanterns the Dreeps carried glared into the room, slid
off the leather and metal they wore. Jaril came onto his feet and stood
ears back, head down, growling deep in his throat. As if startled from
sleep but no less dangerous, Brann surged up, knife ready in one hand,
snatching at the quilt with the other, holding it in front of her. "Shift
ass out of here," she spat at them, "or I turn him loose and carve into
stew meat what he leaves."

"Calm, calm, fenna meh." Kheren Zanc pushed past the lead Dreep.
"There's no harm done. The guards are searching for a thief who got
over the wall near your room. They need to be sure he's not hiding in
here. It's for your safety, fenna meh."

She looked them over with insolent thoroughness, then she wrapped
the quilt around her and tucked in the end. "Let them look if they're
fools enough to think some idiot thief could get past Smiler there." She
dropped onto the bed, knife resting lightly on her quilt-covered thigh.
"I'll have the hide off anyone who wakes the children." She patted the
blanket beside her, whistled the mastiff onto the bed. Jaril, newly chris-
tened Smiler, leaped over the footboard and streched out with his hind-
quarters draped over the young thief's legs. Yaril and the ersatz Jaril
slept heavily while three Dreeps prowled the room, looking under the
bed and into the wardrobe. One of them prodded his pike through the
blanket near the foot of the bed but retreated before a sizzling glare

when he showed signs of wanting to jerk the covers off in case the thief was masquerading as a twig-sized wrinkle.

Kheren bowed with heavy dignity. "Your Graciousness." He shooed the Dreeps out of the room and locked the door after them.

With a wavery sigh Brann set the knife back on the bedtable, ran shaking fingers through the duckfeather curls fluffing about her head. She grinned at Jaril as he shifted back to boy and sat cross-legged on the bed. "Give them a minute more, then see what they're doing."

Jaril nodded. He slid off the bed, blurred into a gold shimmersphere and oozed out through the door. The young thief sat up, raised his brows. "Nice trick, wish I could do it."

"He'll warn us if the Dreeps start this way. What got you in this mess?"

"Bad luck and stupidity."

She laughed. "That's a broad streak of honesty there, better watch it, um . . . I'll call you Tua after your grandfather. Tua, my friend, it'll be an hour or two before you can move on, pass a little of it telling me your troubles. I might be some help. I'm inclined to be, for your grand-father's sake. Or out of boredom. Or from general dislike of Dreeps. Take your pick and tell your tale."

He rubbed his hands together, slowly, his light eyes narrowed. "Why?"

"Why not."

"Hmm. I expect there's not much point in shamming it. Here's how it was. About a week ago an hour or two before dawn, I was . . . mmm . . . drifting along Waygang street, do you know Halimm, ah!" he slapped his cheek, clicked his tongue, "I forgot who you are, you've been walking the ways here since before my mother was even born, where was I, yes, Waygang Street on the Hill end where the highclass Assignation Houses are, I'd been tickling a maid in one of those Houses," he shrugged, "you get the idea. I was seeing if I could fox the patrols and get inside without being nailed. I thought old Tungjii was perching on my shoulder when I made it as easy as breathing. Ten, eleven patrons were sleeping over, I went through their gear and teased open the locks on the abdits, you know, the lockholes in the walls where they generally put their purses and the best jewelry. What with one thing and another, it was a good haul for an hour's work. What I didn't know was one of those patrons was a sorcerer. He had this bad dreamsmoke habit, he'd stopped over in Jade Halimm to indulge it and was using the House as a safe bed for his binge. The room had that sour stink you don't forget once you've smelled it so I knew the man wasn't going to wake on me, the House could've burned down and he wouldn't wake. I got his purse, shuh, it was heavy. I almost didn't bother with the abdit, but I was stupid and I got greedy and I found this crystal egg in a jeweled case and I took it. Wasn't anything else in the abdit. Another thing, that sinking smoke made my nose itch and clog up, so I blew it. I used my fingers and wiped them on one of the sheets. Baaad mistake. Well, I didn't know it then. I finished up and slid out and it was easy as breathing again. I cached the gold, you don't want to walk in on . . . um . . . I think I won't say the name . . . someone with gold in your boot, he'd have it out before you opened your mouth to say what. I sold the rings and that egg to someone, got about what I expected, maybe a quarter what the stuff was worth. He passed the egg on less than three hours after he got it. I found that out later. Me, soon as I was rid of the dangerous stuff, I went . . . um . . . someplace and crawled into bed, I was tired. Everything was fine, far as I knew. Stayed fine all the time I was sleeping. I woke hungry and went to get something to eat. I was in the middle of a bowl of noodles when my insides started twiching. Didn't hurt, not then, just felt peculiar. I stopped eating. The twitches stopped. It was that cook-shop down by Sailor's Gamehouse. I decided Shem who ran it got into some bad oil, so I went into Sailor's figuring I could afford his cook for once. I got about halfway through some plum chicken when the twitches started again. This time I ignored them and finished the chicken, it cost too much to waste. The twitching went away. I thought, Oh. I went out. It was getting dark. There was a girl I knew. She's a dancer mostly, she has her courtesan's license so she doesn't have to go with anyone she doesn't like. I thought about going to see her. I even started walking toward the piers, she worked on a boat, I got a couple steps on the way when the worst pain I ever felt hit me. It was like redhot pincers stabbing into my liver and twisting. And a word exploded in my head. It was a minute before I could sort myself out enough to know what the word was. Come. I heard it again. Come. I didn't know what was happening to me. Come. Everyone thought I was having fits. Come. The pain went away a little. The voice got quieter. Come. I came. That's when I found out the man I stole the egg from was a sorcerer. He wanted the egg back. He wanted it back so bad, he told me what he did to me to get me there was a catlick to what would happen to me if I didn't bring it to him. I told him I'd already got rid of it, sold it to a fence and I didn't have any way of knowing what he did with it. He thought about that, then he asked me who the fence was. I didn't want to tell him but a couple twinges later I decided that . . . um . . . someone wasn't a man I felt like dying for. I told him who the fence was and where to find him. He made me come kneel at his feet, then he did something I don't know what and there was this tigerman in the middle of the room. He talked to the tigerman, I don't know what he said, it was some sort of magic gabble I suppose. The tigerman disappeared *pop* like he was a candleflame blown out. He came back the same way but this time he had the fence with him. The fence didn't want to say what he did with the egg. The tigerman played with him a little. So he dug in his memory, didn't have to dig far but he made a long dance out of it, and came up with the name of the highmerchant Jizo Gozit. The sorcerer told him if he said a word about this to anyone he'd start rotting slowly, his parts would fall off and his fingers and his toes and his tongue would rot in his mouth and his eyes would rot in his head and to show he meant it he rotted off the fence's little finger, we could see the flesh melt and fall away from the bones. Then the sorcerer told him to go home and he went. The tigerman went away. There was just me left. I don't *know* why he didn't send the tigerman after the egg, I've got an idea, though, something I came up with later. Maybe it's like this, he was going to start on his binge, but he didn't want anyone getting at him when he wasn't up to protecting himself so he put his two souls into that egg and locked it up and here I come along and go off with it. And he didn't send the tigerman for it or do any fishing about for it because he didn't want to give away where his souls were and he for sure wasn't about to let any demon get that close to them. He gave me five days to get it back, or I'd start hurting a lot. That was four days ago. So you know what I was doing. Those highmerchants, most thieves don't even try their Houses, I mean even the best we got in Jade Halimm don't bother with that quarter. I was lucky to stay loose enough to reach the wall ahead of the Dreeps and their hounds." He slid off the bed and went to the window, lifted the bar and eased the righthand shutter open about an inch so he could see the sky. "Looks to me like I've got a couple hours of dark left. Maybe if I went right back, they wouldn't be expecting me and might've let down their guard some. My hood, it's in the bed somewhere, ask the changer if she'll fish it out, then I'm for the wall and Jizo's House and you're rid of me."

"Mmm, give me a minute to think." She passed her hand over her head, smoothing down the fine white halfcurls. "Sorcerer . . . there

are a lot of idiots who fool around with magic of one kind or another
. . . uhhhm, how sure are you that man really is a sorcerer?"

"Eh, it's not everyone who snaps his fingers and makes a tigerman
fetch for him."

"I see. Yaril, what's your brother doing?"

"Still watching the Dreeps. They're up in the attics turning out the
servants' rooms."

"Tell him to leave them to it and get back here."

"He's coming."

There weren't that many sorcerers around, at least not those who'd
reached the level of competence in their arts that matched Tua's description of the man he'd robbed. And, from what she'd observed in
her travels when she was still wandering about the world, they all knew
each other. So it was more than likely this one could give her some
useful information about Settsimaksimin and less than likely he'd tell
her anything unless she had a hold on him.

Jaril oozed through the door. "The search is about finished, but the
Head Dreep, he's not happy about it, he wants to get the hounds in and
start over on the rooms, Kheren is having fits about that. I got the
feeling the Dreep was walking careful around our Host, that he knew if
Kheren complained about him, he'd be up to his nose in hot shit."

"Hmm. Tua, I've got a deal for you. Listen, I'll send the children for
that egg if you'll bring your sorcerer here."

"Why? Don't get snarky if I don't jump at the deal, but it's my body
and my life you're playing with."

"Don't worry. I'll take care of you."

"He's a sorcerer."

"And I'm Drinker of Souls and I'll have his in my hands."

"I don't have a choice, do I?"

"No. You might save us some time if you told Yaril and Jaril where
to find Jizo's House. Doesn't matter all that much, the place is probably lit up and swarming with guards, the children could fly over the
quarter and go right to it."

"I talk too much."

"Oh, I don't think so. You're getting what you want without risking
your hide." She chuckled. "Tua Tua, you've been working hard to
worm this out of me, clever clever young thief playing pittypat games
with the poor old demidemon, making her singe her aged paws plucking your nuts from the fire."

He opened his eyes wide, angelically innocent, then he gave it up and grinned at her. "Was clever, wasn't it."

"Shuh. Be more clever. Tell the kids where to find the egg."

He was a tall man with a handsome ruined face and eyes bluer than the sea on a sunny day. His fine black hair and the beard neatly groomed into corkscrew curls and the bold blade of his nose proclaimed him a son of Phras. He came in slowly, the thick, textured wool of his black robe brushing against boots whose black leather was soft and glowing and unobtrusively expensive. He wore a large ruby on the fourth finger of his left hand, his right hand was bare; they were fine hands, never-used hands, soft, pale with a delicate tracery of blue veins. He stood without speaking while Tua shut and locked the door and joined Brann who was sitting on the bed, Jaril-Mastiff crouched by her knee.

The silence thickened. Tua fidgeted, scratching at his knee, feeling the knife up his sleeve, rubbing the back of his neck, the small scrapes and rustles he made the only sounds in the room. Brann continued to sit, relaxed, smiling. She intended to force the man to speak first, she had to have that edge to counter the power and discipline she felt in him, to wrest from him the knowledge she needed. He'd spread a glamour about himself, he'd dressed in his best for this meeting, wearing pride along with wool and leather and power like a cloak, but he was dying, his body was beginning to crumble. He saw that she knew this and his eyes went bitter and his hands shook. His mouth pressed to a thin line, he folded his arms across his chest; the shaking stopped, but there was a film of sweat on his face and a crease of pain across his brow. He knew the egg was nowhere in the room. (It was with Yaril who was being a dayhawk sitting on the ridgepole of the Inn, the egg in a pouch tied to her leg; Brann had no way of knowing how close a sorcerer had to be to retrieve his souls and was taking no chances.) "You called me here," he said; his voice was deep and rich, an actor's voice trained in declamation and caress. "You have something for me."

"I have." She put stress on the I.

"Give it to me."

"Not yet."

Dark power throbbed in the room, lapping at her with a thousand tongues. Brann kept her smile (though it went a little stiff), kept her hands relaxed on her thighs (though the thumbs twitched a few times); tentatively she tapped into the field and began reeling its energies into herself, scooping out a hollow he couldn't penetrate. The young thief scrambled away from her, went to sit in the window, legs, dangling, ready to jump if Brann faltered. The Jaril-Mastiff came onto his feet, muscle sliding powerfully against muscle, and padded noiselessly around the periphery of the zone of force protecting the man. He oscillated there for several breaths, looking from the sorcerer to Brann (who was sitting unmoved, draining the attack before it could touch her) then he grew denser and more taut and when he was ready, he catapulted against the man's legs, bursting unharmed through the zone and knocking him into a painful sprawl.

Jaril-Mastiff untangled himself and trotted over to Brann. She laughed, scratched between his ears and watched the sorcerer collect himself and get shakily to his feet. "Are you ready to talk?"

He brushed at his sleeves, unhurried, discipline intact. "What do you want?"

"Information." She smiled at him. "Come. Relax, I'm not asking that much. Sit and let's talk."

He shook his robe back into its stately folds, straightened the chair he'd knocked awry in his sprawling fall and settled himself in it. "Who are you?"

"Drinker of Souls." Another smile. "What name do you answer to?"

Another thoughtful pause. "Ahzurdan." His blue gaze slid over her, returned to her face, touched the short delicate curls clustered over her head, again returned to her face. "Drinker of Souls," he said. "Brann," he said.

She frowned. "You know me?"

He glanced at the boy in the window, said nothing.

"Turn him loose," she said. "That's what he's here for."

Abruptly genial, he nodded. "Isoatua, the contract is complete." He raised a brow. "Go and don't let me see you again."

Tua scowled, turned his shoulder to him. "Fenna meh?"

"A minute. Jaril?"

The mastiff came onto his feet, yawned, was a glimmersphere of pale light. It drifted upward, whipped through Ahzurdan before he had time to react, then returned to Brann and shifted to Jaril the boy. "He means it," he said.

"You heard, Tua. Next time be a bit more careful what you lift."

Tua started to say something, but changed his mind. Ignoring Ahzurdan he bowed to Brann, strolled to the door. With a graceful flick of his wrist, he unlocked it. When he was out, Jaril turned the key again, put his head through the wall. A moment later he ambled over to Brann. "He's off."

"Thanks. Ahzurdan."

"Yes?"

"How do you know me?"

"My grandfather was a shipmaster named Chandro bal Abbayd. I believe you knew him."

"Shuh. You hear that, Jaril? Three. That's not coincidence, that's plot. Miserable gods are dabbling their fingers in my life again. All right. All right. Nothing I can do about it. Look, Ahzurdan, there was an attack on me a few days ago, a tigerman slid a knife between my ribs. No, I don't think you sent him. I'm reasonably sure someone called Settsimaksimin wants me dead. He came close, not close enough. I have no doubt he knows that by now. What I want from you is this, anything you can tell me about him."

"Ah." He slumped in the chair and let the glamour fade. There was a broad band of gray in his thinning hair, streaks of gray in his beard, the whites of his eyes were yellowed and bloodshot. He had high angular cheekbones in a face bonier than Chandro's, at least as she remembered him, strongly defined indentations at the temples, deep creases running from his nostrils past the corners of his mouth. A face used by time and thought and suffering, a lot of the last self-inflicted. "What did you do?"

"I suspect it's something I'm going to do."

"I see." He stroked his beard, no longer trying to hide the shake of his hands; red light shimmered in the heart of the ruby. "You're prepared to trust what say?"

She smiled. "Of course not. I trust my ability to interpret what you say. So you'll do it?"

"Yes."

"No reservations?"

"No."

"Jaril, tell your sister to get down here. Ahzurdan, you look awful. Come over here, get rid of that robe. When Jaril gets back with Yaril, I'll see what I can do about knitting you together again."

Ahzurdan unknotted the thongs of the pouch; he paused a moment, his eyes looked inward, he thrust two long fingers inside and touched the crystal. His face wiped of expression, he stood rigidly erect for several minutes as the souls flowed back into his flesh. When it was done, he tossed the pouch onto the bed and dropped beside it. "I'm a fool," he said. "Don't trust me, I'll let you down every time."

"Sad, sad, how terribly sad." Brann snorted. "Before a binge that might mean something, not after."

"Ah yes." He stroked a hand down his beard. "You see me not quite at my worst." He sighed. "A man is destroyed most effectively when he does it himself. Have you tasted the dreams of ru'hrya? No? You're wise not to bind yourself to that endless wheel." When she reminded him she couldn't work through thick wool, he managed a half smile and began unfastening his robe. "There's some pleasure in the smoke, a deep stillness, a gentle driffting, you're floating in a warm fog. But the thing that brings you back again and again to the smoke is the dream." His hand stilled for a moment, he looked inward again, pain and longing in those blue blue eyes. "The dream. You're a hero there. Colors, odors, textures, they're so alive they're close to pain but not pain. Everything you do there comes out right, you're not clumsy there or a fool or a victim. You live your life over again there, but the way you wanted it to be, not the way it was or is." He stood, pulled his arms free and let the robe fall about his feet. Under it he wore a black silk tunic that came to mid-thigh and black silk drawers that reached his knees. He was perhaps too thin, but was well-muscled and healthy despite a week-long binge on dreamsmoke; in an odd way his body seemed a decade younger than his face. "You can't forget them, the dreams, your body screams at you for the smoke, but that's not important, what you hunger for is the other thing. You despise yourself for your weakness, but after a while you can't stand knowing how stupid and futile you are and you binge again. And as the years pass you binge more frequently until the day comes when you do nothing else and you die still dreaming. I know that. I've seen it. The knowledge sits in my mind like a corpse. I run deeper into the smoke to escape that corpse and by doing so I run toward it, toward my degradation and my death. I came to Jade Halimm to find you, Brann; I came to beg you to free me from this need. Use your healing hands on me, Brann, make me whole. I'll tell you everything I know of Cheonea and Settsimaksimin, I'll go with you to help you fight him and you will need me, even you. Cleanse my body and my mind, Brann, do it in memory of the joy you and my grandfather shared that he told me about more than once, do it because you need me even if you think you don't do it out of the generosity of your soul."

"What make you think I can do what you can't?"

He smiled wearily. "Tungjii's laughter in my head, Brann."

"Slya's crooked toes! If I could . . . if I could climb the air . . . aah!"

"What?"

"That miserable menagerie of misfits that makes toys of us and dances us about to amuse themselves. Listen. I spent the last hundred years as a potter, a damn good one, sometimes even great. I was content working my clay, chopping wood for the kiln, all that. Then there comes this messenger from out of the past, the children of Harra Hazhani who was once a friend of mine are calling me to keep a promise I made her some two hundred years ago. And right away I'm lying on the grass with a knife in my back. And when I'm getting ready to go kick my enemy where it hurts, what happens? I'm sleeping peacefully in an expensive room in a highclass Inn and I wake up to dogs howling and a young thief climbing the wall outside my window, and lo, he's the grandson of another old acquaintance of mine, and lo, he's in this mess because he just happened to steal the souls of a sorcerer who just happens to be the grandson of another old friend and lover. I said it before, this isn't coincidence, it's a plot. Those damn gods are jerking me around again."

"What are you going to do about it?"

"Shuh, what I'd like to do is go back to my pots."

"But?"

"What choice do I have? There's my sworn oath and there's a man who wants to kill me. So. Now that that's over with, stretch out. On your stomach first. Yaril, help me, make sure we're not interrupted."

Her hands were warm and surprisingly strong. He thought about her chopping wood and couldn't visualize it. Soft hands. No calluses. Short nails, but cared for. She worked with her hands. A potter. He suppressed a shudder, but she felt it. "It's nothing," he said. "A troubling thought, no more." Her fingers moved in small circles over his head then drew lines of heat along his spine. Energy flowed into him, for once he felt as vital as he did in the dreams, yet more relaxed. He grunted as she pinched a buttock. "Talk," she said.

"Mmmm . . . loyalty . . . where does it end? That's the question, isn't it. He was my teacher . . . unh, don't destroy the flesh, Brann, I do enough of it, I don't need help . . . I suppose that is a fourth noncoincidence . . . I was twelve when he took me . . . there's an intimacy between master and apprentice . . . thumps and caresses

. . . leaves its mark on you . . . yesss, that feels good . . . he was
an odd man . . . difficult . . . rumors . . . there were other apprentices . . . they talked . . . we all talked . . . about him . . . listened . . . one rumor I think might be true . . . that he was sired by
a drunken M'darjin merchant on an overage Cheonene whore one
night in Silagamatys, he had the look . . . he was clever . . . fiercely
disciplined . . . he'd work like a slave day after day, no sleep, no
meals, a sip of tea and a beancake, that was all, both of them usually
cold by the time he remembered them . . . but when the thing was
done, he'd drown in the wildest debauchery he could find or assemble
. . . sometimes . . . depending on his mood and needs . . . he took
one or more of us with him . . . he always had four or five apprentices . . . one year there were nine of us . . . he dribbled out his
lessons to us . . . enough to keep us clinging to him . . . and he had
favorites . . . boys he bound closer to him . . . he fed them more
. . . fed them . . . us . . . something like love . . . like living in an
insane cross between a zoo and a greenhouse . . . yes, that's it, we
clawed and rutted like beasts and put out exotic blooms to attract
him. . . .

He stopped talking as she stopped the probing and pummeling and
began passing her hands over him. Warmth that was both pleasure and
pain (the two twisting inextricably in the flow) passed into his feet and
churned up through him until it flooded into his brain and turned into
pure agony; he dissolved into white fire, then darkness.

He sat sipping at hot tea, dawn red in the window. Pale blond
preteens in green-gray trousers and tunics, the changechildren were
sitting on the floor, leaning against Brann's knees, watching him.
Brann held a bowl of tea cradled in her hands. "The physical part of it
is gone," she said. "That's all. You could have done that yourself. No
doubt you have."

"After the third relapse, trying it again didn't seem worth the cost."

"I still don't understand what more you think I can do."

"Nor I." He smiled wearily. "In the depths of self-disgust after one
too many binges, I returned to the ways of my ancestors and cast the
lots. And found you there as my answer. Being with you. Staying with
you." An aborted shapeless gesture with the hand holding the teabowl.
"A parasite on your strength."

"Hmm." She finished the tea and set the bowl beside her on the bed.
"I don't know the Captains these days. Any ship in port going south

that makes good time and won't sink at a sneeze, whose master is a bit more than a lamprey on the hunt?"

"Ju't Chandro told me you had a fondness for sailing men. Was he casting a net for air?"

"Hmf. Do you love every son of Phras you meet? Come with me to the wharves and tell me who's who."

"I may travel with you?"

"For whatever good it does. Besides, all you've told me so far is that Maksim has apprentices around to do the scut work and a taste for the occasional orgy. Not much to help there."

"You'll get everything I know, Brann."

"Ah well." A tight half smile. "When I'm not sleeping with the Captain, life on shipboard tends to get tedious." She examined him, speculation in her eyes.

Ahzurdan felt a quiver in his loins and a shiver of fear along his spine, one of his grandfather's more lurid tales flowing in full colors through his head. He gulped the rest of his tea; it was cold, but he didn't notice. That white fluff, it looked like she'd shaved her hair off not too long ago, though why she'd do that . . . She wasn't beautiful, not in any ordinary sense, handsome perhaps, but there was something he couldn't put into words, a vitality, a sense that she knew who and what she was and rather liked that person. A disturbing woman. A challenge to everything he'd been taught about women. His mother would have hated and feared her. There were knots in his gut as he snatched brief glances at her; what she seemed to be expecting from him was more often than not something he couldn't provide, he didn't want to think about that, she made him think, she made him want the smoke again, anything to fill the emptiness inside him. Discipline, don't forget discipline, ignore what you don't want to see, you're a man with a skill that few have the gifts or intelligence or tenacity to acquire, that's where your worth lies, you're not a stud hired to service the woman. Ah gods, it's a good thing you aren't, you couldn't earn your pay, no, don't think about that. I owe you, Maksim, you played in my head and in my body and threw both away when you were tired of them. Maksim, Maksimin, you don't know what's coming at you. . . . He rose. "Time we were starting. I still have to ransom my gear from the House and the tide turns shortly after noon."

4

ON THE MERCHANTER JIVA MAHRISH (captain and owner Hudah Iffat, quartermaster and steward, his wife Hamla), THREE HOURS OUT OF JADE HALIMM, COAST HOPPING SOUTH AND WEST TO KUKURAL, HER LAST PORT BEFORE SHE TURNED NORTH AGAIN.

SCENE: Brann below, settling into her cabin. Ahzurdan on deck driving off stray ariels, setting wards against another attack on her. Yaril and Jaril watching him, wondering what he's up to.

Ignoring the noisy confusion at his back where the deck passengers were still getting settled into the eighteen square feet apiece they bought with their fares, Ahzurdan stood at the stern watching the flags on the Roganzhu Fort flutter and sink toward the horizon, frowning at the ariels thick in the wind that agitated those flags and filled the sails. Born of wind, shaped from wind, elongated asexual angel shapes with huge glimmering eyes, the ariels whirled round the ship, dipping toward it, darting away when they came close enough to sense what he was. Tapping nervously at the rail, he considered what to do; as long as Brann stayed below, the ariels were an irritation, no more. He swung around. The changechildren were squatting beside the rail, their strange soulless crystal eyes fixed on him. No matter what Brann said, they didn't trust him. "One of you," he said, "go below and tell her to stay where she is for a while." Neither moved. He sighed. "There are spies in the wind."

They exchanged a long glance, then the girl got to her feet and drifted away.

Ahzurdan turned to the sea again. For a moment he continued to watch the ariels swirl overhead, then he reached out, caught a handful of air and sunlight and twisted it into a ward that he locked to the ship's side. He began moving along the rail; every seventh step he fashioned another knot and placed it. He reached the bow, started back along the port rail, careful to keep out of the way of the working sailors.

Halfway along, Jaril stepped in front of him. "What are you doing?"

"Warding."

"Against what?"

"Against what happened before. This isn't the place to talk about it. Let me finish."

The boy stared at him for a long breath, then he stepped aside and let him pass.

Ahzurdan finished setting the wards, then stood leaning on the rail watching the sun glitter off the waves, thinking about the changechildren. He knew what they were and their connection to Brann. His grandfather had been fond of them, in a way, also a little frightened of them. That fear was easy to understand. Earlier, before coming on board he'd tried a minor spell on Jaril and nothing had happened. More disturbing than that, the boy in his mastiff form had whipped through his force shield without even a whimper to show he noticed it. The children must have been fetched from a reality so distant from this and so strange that the powers here (at least those below the level of the highgods) couldn't touch them. Not directly. Very interesting. Very dangerous. He collected his wandering thoughts, twitched the wards to test them, then went below satisfied he'd done what he could to neutralize anything Settsimaksimin might try.

Port to port they went. Lindu Zohee. Merr Ono. Halonetts. Sunny days, warm nights. A chancy wind but one kept the ship scudding along the coast. Brann stayed onboard in each of the ports, safe from attack behind the wards but restless. Ahzurdan watched her whenever he could, curious about her, perplexed by nearly everything she did.

She liked sailors and made friends with the crew when she could have been talking to the cabin passengers. There was an envoy from the Jade King aboard; he was a fine amateur poet and musician and showed more than a little interest in her. There was a courtesan of the first rank and her retinue. There was a highmerchant who dealt in jades, calligraphy and elegant conversation. Brann produced an embroidered robe for the dinners in the captain's cabin, a multitude of delicately scribed gold bracelets (Rukka-nagg he thought when she let him examine them, part of a daughter's dowry), and a heavy gold ear ornament from the Panday Islands (he was intensely curious about where she got that, only a Panday with his own ship could wear such an ornament, there was a three day feast involved, a solemn rite of recognition and presentation; most Panday shipmasters were buried with theirs; a lover perhaps?). Her hair was growing with supernatural speed, but it was still a cloud of feathery white curls that made her eyes huge and intensely green. She looked vital, barbaric and fine; he had difficulty keeping his eyes off her. She played poetry with the Envoy, composing verse couplets in answer to his, she spoke of jade carvers with the merchant, though mostly about ancient Arth Slyan pieces and the techniques of those legendary artisans, she questioned the courtesan Huazo about the dance styles currently popular, brought up the name of a long dead Hina player named Taguiloa and grew excited when Huazo told some charming but obviously apocrypal tales about the man (another lover?) and went into what Ahzurdan considered tedious detail about his influence on her own dancing. The dinners were pleasant and Brann seemed to enjoy them, but she went running to the crew when she had a moment free. He didn't understand what she saw in them, crude vulgar men with crude vulgar thoughts, and at the same time was jealous of their ease with her. The first few days he had fevered images of belowdecks orgies, but his training did not allow him to distort or reject what was there before his eyes no matter how powerfully theory and emotion acted on his head. Misperceptions weren't problems of logic or aesthetics to a sorcerer, they could kill him and anyone near him. She traded stories with the crew, showed off her skills with rope, needle and palm; her hands were quick and graceful, he watched their dance and deplored what she was doing with them. She was almost a demigod, not some miserable peasant or artisan grubbing for a living.

The day the ship sailed from Merr Ono, he was in her cabin telling her about his earliest days with Settsimaksimin but broke off and asked her why she avoided the cabin passengers when she was so much more suited to their society than those . . . ah . . . no doubt goodhearted men in the crew; he got a cool gaze that looked into his souls and stripped his pretension bare, or so he thought.

After several moments of silence, she sighed. "I don't like him. No, that's not right. He turns my stomach. I'll be polite to him at supper, but I won't stay around him any longer than I have to."

"Why? He's a cultivated intelligent man. His poems are praised from Andurya Durat to Kukurul for their power and innovation."

"Have you read any of them?"

"Yes!"

"We'll have to agree to disagree. I'll grant you a certain technical facility, but there's nothing in them."

"You can't have read *Winter Rising.*"

"Ah! Dan, I've spent the better part of a hundred winters doing little else but reading." She pushed her fingers through her duckfeather curls. "I read *Winter Rising* and came closer to burning a book than I thought I ever would. Especially the part when he mourns the death of a servant's child. His family chern lies half a day's journey downriver from the Pottery. I have swept up too many leavings from his justice," the word ended in an angry hiss, "to swallow his mouthings about suffering he himself is responsible for. I don't care how splendid the poem is," she shook her head, put her hand on his arm, "I'll admit the skill, but I can't stand the man. And I can't forget the man in the poet." She moved away from him. "Play with him all you want, Dan, but keep a grip on your skin and don't take any commissions from him. The Jade King doesn't send openfisted fools to negotiate trade rights." She dropped into a chair and sat with her hands clasped loosely in her lap. "If you're going to keep traveling with me, you might as well understand something. I despise him and all his kind. If the world wagged another way and it would make any real difference to his landfolk, I'd be the first to boot him out of his silky nest and set him to digging potatoes, where he might be useful and certainly less destructive."

"Brann, do you really think your cherished sailors would be any better, put in his place? It would be chaos, far worse than anything the Envoy had done. I've seen what happens when the beasts try to drive the cart. He has tradition and culture to restrain him, they've nothing but instinct,"

"Beasts, Dan?"

"By their acts shall you know them."

"By their acts shall you know their masters,"

"Aren't they to be held responsible for what they do?"

"Give them responsibility before you demand it from them. Ahhh, this is stupid, Dan. We're arguing abstracts and that's bound to be an exercise in futility." She laughed. "No more, not now. I wish you could have seen my home. Arth Slya isn't what it was, even so . . . I was born a free woman of free folk. We managed our own lives and bowed our heads to no man, not even the King of Croaldhu. If I had the power, I'd make the whole world live that way."

"You sound like Maksim."

"That's interesting. Do you know what he's doing in Cheonea? Tell me about it."

He shrugged. "It's foolishness. Rabble is rabble. Changing the name doesn't change the smell."

Brann snorted. "Shuh! Dan, I know you sons of Phras, you and your honor, it's a fine honor that scorns to touch a loom or a chisel but makes an art of killing. I loved your grandfather, Ahzurdan; Chandro was a splendid man as long as he was away from Phras, one who knew how to laugh at the world and how to laugh at himself, but not in Bandrabahr. When he went home, he turned Phrasi from his toes to his backteeth. You might think that's a proper thing to do, but me . . . hunh! I went with him once, the last trip we made together. I remember I said something about a pompous old fool strutting down the street, a joke, he'd laughed at things like that a hundred times before. He *hit* me. You know, it was funny. I just stood there gaping at him. He started calling me names. Vicious names. Then he tried to hit me again. That's not a thing I tolerate, no indeed. Well, there was a bit of a brawl with Yaril and Jaril rallying round. Last I saw of him, Chandro was laid out yelling, some meat gone from one buttock and a thigh, a broken shoulder bone and a bruised belly where I missed my kick or he might have been your uncle not your grandfather. There was a ship lifting anchor right then, I made it onboard a jump and a half ahead of the kashiks. Never saw him again. Sad. After that I came back to Jade Halimm, apprenticed myself to a potter and settled into clay and contentment."

By the time they sailed from Halonetts, beginning the last leg of the journey to Kukurul, Ahzurdan was sweating and nightmare-ridden, trying to fight his desire for dreamsmoke. He wallowed in despair; he'd thought having the demonic Brann around would somehow cure him of this need, but she grated on his nerves so much she was driving him to the dreams to escape her. In spite of this, he couldn't stay away from her.

She listened with such totality it made a kind of magic. He was uneasy under this intense scrutiny, he rebelled against it now and then, but it was also extraordinarily seductive. He began to need her ear worse than his drug; they broke for meals and sleep, but he came drifting back as soon as he could, and, after a few hesitations, was lost once more in his memories. Bit by bit he began telling her things he'd made himself forget, things about growing up torn between a father who wanted him to join his older halfbrothers in the business and a mother whose scorn of business was profound, who'd been sold into marriage to pay the debts of her family (a minor branch of the ancient and noble Amara sept). Tadar Chandro's son bought her to gain greater prestige among the powers of Bandrabahr, got a son on her, then proceeded to ignore her. She hated him for taking her, she loathed his touch, she hated him almost as much for leaving her alone, for his insulting lack of interest in her person or her sex. But she knew better than to release any of her venom beyond the walls of her husband's compound, he wouldn't need much excuse to repudiate her, since he'd already got all the good out of her he was going to get, no, she saved her diatribes for her sons' ears.

"I was the sixth son," Ahzurdan said, "ten years younger than Shuj who was youngest before me. He took pleasure in tormenting me, I don't know why. On my twelfth birthday my father gave me a sailboat as he had all his other sons on their twelves. A few days later I was going to take it out on the river when I met Shuj coming from the boathouse. When I went inside, I saw he'd slashed my sail and beat a hole in the side of the boat. I went pelting after him, I don't think I'd ever been so angry. I was going to, I don't know what I was going to do, I was too hot to think. I caught up with him near the stables, I yelled at him I don't know what and I called up fire and nearly incinerated him. What saved him was fear. Mine. There was this ball of flame licking around my hands; it didn't hurt me, but it scared the fury out of me. I jerked my arms up and threw it into the clouds where it fried a few unfortunate birds before it faded away. After that Shuj and all the others stayed as far away from me as they could. . . ."

Tadar was frightened and disgusted; a practical man, he wanted nothing to do with such things. For years he'd been crushed beneath the weight of a vital charismatic father who had a good-natured contempt for him, but after Chandro's death, he set about consolidating the business, then he cautiously increased it; he hated the sea, was desperately seasick even on river packets, but was shrewd enough to pick capable shipmasters, pay them well and give them an interest in each cargo. As the years passed, he prospered enormously until he was close to being the richest Phras in Bandrabahr. He spent a month ignoring his youngest son's pecularities and snarling at his other sons when they tried to complain (they had uneasy memories of tormenting a spoiled delicate boy and didn't want Ahzurdan in the same room with them), but two things forced him to act. The servants were talking and his customers were nervous. And Zuhra Ahzurdan's mother had sent to her family for advice (which infuriated Tadar, principally because they acted without consulting him and he saw that as another of the many snubs he'd endured from them); they located a master sorcerer who was willing to take on another apprentice and informed Tadar they were sending him around three days hence, he should be prepared to receive him and pay the bonding fee.

For Ahzurdan, during those last months at home, it was as if he had a skin full of writhing, struggling eels that threatened to burst through, destroying him and everything around him. Before the day he nearly barbequed his brother, he'd had nightmares, day terrors and surges of heat through his body; he shifted unpredictably from gloom to elation, he fought to control a rage that could be triggered by a careless word, dust on his books, a dog nosing him, any small thing. After that day, his mood swings grew wilder and fire came to him without warning; he would be reaching for something and fingerlength flames would race up his arms. The night before the sorcerer was due, his bed curtains caught fire while he was asleep, nearly burnt the house down; one of the dogs smelled smoke and howled the family awake; they put the fire out. It didn't hurt him, but it terrified everyone else.

For Tadar, that was end; he formally renounced his son; Ahzurdan was, after all, only a sixth son and one who had proved himself worthless. His mother wept, but didn't try to hold him. He was happy enough to get away from the bitterness and rage that flavored the air around her; she kept him tied to her, filled his ears with tales of her noble family and laments about how low she'd sunk marrying his father until he felt as if he were drowning in spite. He blamed her for the way his brothers treated him and the scorn his father felt for him, but didn't realize how much like her he was, how much of her outlook he'd

absorbed. Brann recognized Zuhra's voice in the excessive respect he
had for people like the Envoy and his dislike for what he called rabble.

Settsimaksimin came to Tadar's House around mid-morning. "He
scared the stiffening out of my bones," Ahzurdan said. "Six foot five
and massive, not fat, his forearms where they came from the half-
sleeves of his robe looked like they were carved from oak, his hands
were twice the size of those of an ordinary man, shapely and strong, he
wore an emerald on his right hand in a smooth ungraven band and a
sapphire on his left; he had thick fine black hair that he wore in a braid
down his back, no beard (he couldn't grow a beard, I found that out
later), a face that was handsome and stern, eyes like amber with fire
behind it; his voice was deep and singing, when he spoke, it seemed to
shake the house and yet caress each of us with the warmth, the gentleness of . . . well, you see the effect he had on me. I was terrified and
fascinated. He brought one of his older apprentices with him, a
Temueng boy who walked in bold-eyed silence a step behind him,
scorning us and everything about us. How I envied that boy."

Tadar paid the bond and sent one of the houseboys with Ahzurdan
to carry his clothing and books, everything he owned. That was the last
time he saw his family. He never went back.

On the twelfth day out of Jade Halimm the merchanter Jiva Mahrish
sailed into the harbor at Kukurul. A few days later as they waited for a
ship heading for Bandrabahr, Settsimaksimin tried again.

5

SILAGAMATYS ON THE SOUTH COAST OF CHEONEA, THE CITADEL OF SETTSIMAKSIMIN.

SCENE: Settsimaksimin walking the ramparts, looking out over the city and talking at his secretary and prospective biographer, an improbable being called Todichi Yahzi, rambling on about whatever happened to come into his mind.

Soaring needle faced with white marble, swooping sides like the line from a dancer's knee to her shoulders when she's stretched on her toes, a merloned walk about the top. Settsimaksimin's Citadel, built in a day and a night and a day, an orgy of force that left Maksim limp and exhausted, his credit drawn down with thousands of earth elementals and demon stoneworkers, fifty acres of stone, steel and glass. Simplicity in immensity.

Late afternoon on a hot hazy day. Grown impatient with the tedium of administration and the heat within the walls, Settsimaksimin told Todichi Yahzi to bring his notebooks and swept them both to the high ramparts. Heat waves crawled from the earth-colored structures far below, a haze of dust and pollen gilded the Plain that stretched out green and lush to mountains whose peaks were a scrawl of pale blue against the paler sky, but up here a brisk wind rushed from the open sea and blew his sweat away. "Write," Maksim said. "You can clean it up later."

He wound his gray-streaked braid in a knot on his head, snapped a skewer to his hand and drove it through the mass to hold it in place.

He opened his robe, spread it away from his neck, began stumping along the broad stone walkway, his hands clasped behind him, the light linen robe fluttering about his bare feet, throwing words over his shoulder at Todichi Yahzi who was a thin gangling creature (male), his skin covered with a soft fur like gray moss. His mouth was tiny and inflexible, he ate only liquids and semi-liquids; his speech was a humming approximation of Cheonase that few could understand. He had round mobile ears and his eyes were set deep in his head, showing flashes of color (violet, muddy brown, dark red) as he looked up from his pad, looked down again and continued his scribbling in spidery symbols that had no like in this world. Settsimaksimin fetched him from a distant reality so he'd have someone he could talk to, not a demon, not an ambitious Cheonene, but someone wholly dependent on him for life and sustenance and . . . perhaps . . . transport home. His major occupation was listening to Maksim ramble about his experiences, writing down what he said about them along with his pronouncements on life, love, politics and everything.

"The Parastes . . . the Parastes . . . parasite Parastes, little hopping fleas, they wanted to make me their dog, their wild dog eating the meat of the land and they eating off me."

He charged along the rampart, breasting the wind like some great bull, bare feet splatting on the stone, voice booming out over the city, lyric basso singing in registers so low Todichi had to strain to hear the words.

"They wanted to go on living till the end of time as entitled donothings. Bastards of the legion of the Born. Lordlings of the earth. Charter members in the club of eugennistos. Owners of lands, lives and good red gold."

Todichi Yahzi hoomed and cooed and was understood to say, "For the honesty of my records, sar Sassa'ma'sa, were there no patrikkos among them, no good men who cared for their folk? Among my own . . ."

Settsimaksimin swung round, yellow eyes burning with feral good humor. "My mother was a whore and I'm a half-breed, don't ask me for their virtues. Not me." He threw back his head and let laughter rumble up from his toes. "I never saw any. HAH! Go talk to them and see how sweet they are." He swept an arm around in a mighty half-circle. "Look out there, Todich. Black and bountiful, that old mother, she lays there giving it away to any man who knows how to tickle her right. Who does the tickling, who makes her breed and bear? Not our

Parastes. Dirt suits the dirty, not them, not our elegant educated fleas. Pimping fleas, lending her to busy little serfs who fuck her over and get nothing for their labors, it's the flea pimps who carry off the bounty she provides. They sit down there close enough to smell, Todich; they sit down there in their fancy houses behind their fancy walls with their fancy guards and fancy dogs keeping out the folk they fancy want to get at them; they sit down there and curse me. Let them curse. They go to sleep down there and dream me dead. Let them dream. Hah, who's dying? Not me. NOT ME," he shouted and the walls shook with the power of his voice. He wiped at this neck, started walking again, more slowly, as if some of the energy had gone out of him with the shout. When he spoke, his voice was softer, more sedate. "I made laws, Todich, you've writ them down, good laws, fair to the poor, maybe not so fair to the rich, but they've had a thousand years going their way." He chuckled. "Let them suffer a little, it's good for the character. Good for the CHARACTER, HA HA," he twisted his head around, "hear that, old mole? Ah the scorn I got, the righteous indignation. What am I doing? Clodhoppers and bumpkins? School? Land of their own? Whose land? WHOSE LAND! NEVER! Thief! Tyrant! Ignorant idiotic imbecile! You'll ruin the country. You'll destroy everything we've built. A voice in how they live? Perpetual servitude is the natural state of some men. Free them and you destroy them. Who is going to tell them what to do? They're lazy and improvident. Haven't you seen how they shirk their work? Look at how they live, how dirty they are. They drink and fornicate and beat their wives and starve their children. We hammer virtue into them, otherwise nothing would get done. They aren't men, they're beasts; if you treat them like men, you are a fool and you are harming them rather than helping. Ah ah ah, Todich, there you have your sweethearts. For those fleas, those bloodsucking fleas, for those swaggering club-wielders, the serfs were just one more tool for working the earth. Plowing procreating digging sticks. Animated hoes. Grubbing the fields of the fiefs, generation unto generation without a day of rest, without a home and fireside, without anything to save their worn-out nothingness until I took them into my hands.

"Two sorts of beings out there on the Plain, Todich. Nay-saying non-doing Parastes and everyone else. Field hands, farmers, ferrymen, watermen and woodmen, rowers and growers of greens, chandlers, craftsmen, drovers and sellsouls who were armed and charged with defending the fiefs of the Parastes against the claims of the slaves." Laughter rolled out like thunder. He turned the corner and went charging along the west wall. "They didn't expect their people to love them, no they did not. Just serve them. Hmm. I tried—and succeeded, Todich, you've writ how I succeeded—to bring more equality between the rich and the beggars. And spread confusion with both hands." He held up huge shapely hands. "Bountiful confusion and I enjoyed it, every moment of it. Why bother my head with such chimeras? they asked me. You can't do it. The poor don't want it, they hate change, they want things to go on being the same. They won't help you. We won't help you, we're not inclined to suicide. Your army won't help you, they despise dirt grubbers more than we do. Be sensible. Power is power. The rule is yours. Enjoy it, don't wear yourself down." The massive shoulders went round, he clasped his hands once more behind him and slowed his pace and lowered his voice to a mutter. "There are times when I'm tempted to agree." He stopped, put his hand on a merlon and stood squinting at the city below. "Then . . . then I remember begging in the streets. Look, Todich, down there, where the two lanes meet by the end of the market. A Parast had his harmosts beat me because I startled his horses. I left my blood on those paving stones, but you couldn't find it now, there's too much other blood over and under it. And there," he flung his arm up, jabbing his hand at the city wall where it curved to meet the bay, "I can see a hut there still, on that hill just beyond the wall, my mother starved in one like it after she was too old to whore any longer. Do you know why the Citadel is here and nowhere else? When I was six, Todich, a merchant caught me stealing and brought me to the slave market, it was right here, under where we're standing, and the pleasurehouses were just a step away, when we get round to the north side we'll be over the House I was sold into. No one should be rich enough to buy another, Todich, and no one poor enough that he's obliged to let himself be sold. Moderation, Todich, wealth in moderation, poverty in moderation. Pah!" He slapped the stone and stumped on.

"I took into my hands a country where the poor counted for nothing, where scoundrels were everything, so I had to be a greater scoundrel than them all, Todich. They were right, these fleas; no one wanted me to do what I did. I made my laws and sent out my judges with orders to be just and what happened? The poor ran to their masters for justice (ah, the silly men they were) and shunned mine. I had to do it all myself. I sold my soul, Todich. I sold it to the Stone and to Amortis. And I sold Cheonea to Amortis, when you take away one center you have to provide another, Todich; she's no prize, our Amortis, but she's less bloody than some; her sacrifices are those all men make without much prodding . . . hah! no, with a good lot of prodding, if you'll forgive the pun. I've done worse things, Todich, for reasons not half so worthy. I shrank from no evil to ensure my laws were enforced, especially the land laws. Write this, be sure you write this. I distributed the land to the people who worked it, with this condition, they were to pay the former Parastes a small sum quarterly for thirty years, then the land would be paid off and they would have in their hands the deed for it. I did that because I wanted them to value it. I knew them far better than the fleas did, I was one of them, I knew they wouldn't believe in anything that came to them too easily; I knew once they'd sweated and bled to earn the deed, they would own that land in their minds and in their blood and in their bone and they'd fight to keep it. The title papers have been going out for the past ten years. Lazy clodhoppers, eh Todich? Not anything like. Thrifty frugal suspicious lot, more than half of them paid out early, I think they weren't all that sure I'd last, they wanted that paper and they got it. And the same day they got it, those deeds were registered at the village Yrons and the Citadel. Ah, how I love them, these bigoted, stubborn, enduring men. They know what I've done for them, they're mine, they'd bleed for me or spy for me; they pray for me, did you know that? I've seen them do it when they didn't know I was watching. It wasn't for show, Todich, not for show." A rumbling chuckle filled with humor and affection. "Though they get annoyed with me sometimes. They don't like me interfering in their lives. They didn't like it when I put Amortis in their villages; I didn't like it either, but you have to break the old before you can bring the new, besides, I needed Amortis' priestcorps to run the country for me until I could get the dicasts and village headmen trained, there's only so much you can do with soldiers. They didn't want the schools either, I had to scourge half a village sometimes before they'd let their children come to them those first years. What a change since. Now they're proud of sons who can read, now they scold their grandsons when the lads want to skip school and forget learning to read, write and cipher, now they go to the passage ceremonies with wonderful pride in their own. Ah ah ah, and I am proud of them. They took the reins from me and built a strong new life on the changes I made. It'd be a foolish tyrant who tried to wrest land and learning from them now.

"There's one thing I regret, Todich, that's forcing Amortis on the Finger Vales. Burning their priests. I spit on these torchers, those stinking bloody brainless Servants with their Whore God. I spit on myself

for letting it be done, Todich, done in my name. Amortis! Forty Mortal
Hells, I didn't think even a god would be that stupid, but I NEED her,
Todich. A hundred years, I thought I was buying a hundred years so I
could set my changes so deeply no man could uproot them. Haaa yaa
yaa, I need them but I won't get them, that greedy bitch has ruined me.
HAH! Ruined or not, I'm going to fight, let the Hellhag come, I'm a
skin filled with rancor and I'm waiting."

He stopped in the center of the south side and stood looking out
across the Notoea Tha. Todichi Yahzi dropped into a squat behind a
merlon and waited with stone patience for Maksim to start talking
again.

The ariels came blowing out of the east, swirled in a confusing flutter
about him, whispering their reports in their soughing voices, voices
that were winds whistling in Todichi Yahzi's ears, nothing more. ". . .
the woman . . . alive . . . Jiva Marish . . . Ahzurdan . . . wards
. . . Kukurul . . ."

Maksim cursed bitterly, using his lowest register, the words tearing
from his throat. Leaving Todichi Yahzi to make his own way down, he
snapped to his sanctuary deep within the earth, warm dark earth
around him, elementals sleeping coiled about him, protecting him,
ready to wake if he called them. Lights came on automatically as he
materialized there and he strode toward the storage shelves, dragging
the skewer from his braid, shaking it down, pulling his robe closed and
doing up the fastenings. He thrust his arms into the loose overrobe he
wore for working; sleeveless, heavy and soft, it hung about him like
woven darkness as he carried the mirror case to his work table. He
kneed the chair aside, set the case down and stood with his hands on
the double hinged lid, thumbs tapping lightly at the wood as he calmed
himself into a proper state to use the mirror. "Little Danny Blue," he
murmured, "Ahzurdan. I wonder how you got tangled in this mess."
His mouth curled into a tight smile. "Tungjii, old meddler, that you
sticking your thumbs in?"

He maneuvered the chair back and dropped into it with an impatient
grunt, opened the case, took out the black obsidian mirror and the
piece of suede he used to polish it. "I know your little tricks, Blue Dan,
I know you, Danny Boy." He wiped gently at the face of the mirror,
breathed on it, wiped again. "Did you think of this, Danny Blue? I
don't know her. I can't reach her. I found her through the boy the first
time, now I've got you to guide my sight, is that a piece of luck, Baby
Dan, or is that a piece of luck. Haaaa! I've GOT you, Blue, nowhere

you can hide from me." He set aside the leather and slid the mirror into its frame. "Ahzurdan in Kukurul," he intoned and touched the stone oval with a long forefinger.

The stone surface shimmered, then he saw the side of a rambling Inn and small sparkles of light writing patterns over a window on the third floor. "Sooo sooo, how much have you learned since you ran off, Ser Ahzurdan? Mmm, interesting, I wonder where you picked that up? Looks like something Proster Xan was playing with a few years back. That's a clever twist, now how do I untie it? This . . . this . . . ah! cute, touch that one and I'm smoke. Sooo sooo, how do I get round that . . . here? No, I don't think so, tempting but . . . let's fiddle this loop out a little. Ah, ah ah, now this. Riiight. And now it comes neatly apart. Don't try fooling your old teacher, boy. Let's put this aside so we can tie it up again if we want and take a look at what's happening in there. Mmmmh mmh. So that's our Drinker of Souls." He leaned closer, frowning. "That mushhead swore he put the pagamacher in your heart, I suppose he missed his hit. You're hard to kill, lady. Mmm. No more tigermen . . . what have I got . . . mmmmm . . . what have I got. . . ." The woman was sitting in a chair with her feet up on a hassock; her body was relaxed but her brilliant green eyes followed Ahzurdan with a concentrated intensity as he walked about the comfortable room, his hands moving restlessly, opening and closing, tapping on surfaces, fondling small objects, while he talked in spurts and silences. "Gabble gabble, Danny Blue, you haven't changed a hair . . . hmmm." Two children were curled up on the bed, sleeping; he had a vague idea that they were attached to the woman and were a bit more than children. He watched them a moment, became convinced they weren't breathing. "Dipped in the reality pond, did you, lady? And pulled you out a pair of . . . of what? Complications, mmm, if I wait until you're alone and see you out, saying I can do it this time, those children would be left and what would I have coming at me? I went too fast the first time and missed my hit and unless I mistake me badly. I've done myself a mischief by it. Sooo sooo, this time I'll watch a while. A while? A day or two. Or three. Or more. Until I'm ready, lady." With a rumbling chuckle, he shoved the chair back and started to stand, stopped in the middle of the move and flattened his hands on the table. "Oh Maksi old fool, senility is setting in, next thing you know, you'll be drooling in your mush. Sooo sooo." he reassembled the ward and set it in place outside the window. When he was done, he pushed onto his feet, leaving the mirror focused on the

Inn. "Dream your little dreams, Danny Blue, I'll be with you soon as I finish some cursed clamoring business . . ." He stretched, groaned as muscle pulled against muscle, pulled off the overrobe and tossed it onto the chair. "AAAH! WHY WHY WHY can't they SEE? It's so simple." He twitched the linen robe straight and with a few quick flowing passes rid it of its wrinkles. "Dignity, give a man his dignity and you've increased his value and the land's value with it." He rubbed his feet on the pavingstones. "Be damned if I cramp my toes for that son of a diseased toad, that high-nosed high priest of my whore god, that posturing potentate of ignorance, HAH!" He glamoured sandals over his feet, grinned and added tiny grimacing caricatures of Vasshaka Bulan Servant of the Servants of Amortis to the seeming straps of white leather. A touch to the Stone snugged beneath his robe, a twisted tight smile as he felt a tingle in his fingertips, then he snapped to the reception chamber at the top of the west tower, a gilded ornate room that he detested. He knew the effect of his size and the chamber's barbaric splendor (and the long laborious climb to reach it) and used them when he had to deal with folks like Vasshaka Bulan who needed a good deal of intimidation to keep their ambitions in hand. A desk the size of a small room and a massive carved chair sat on a shallow dais that raised both just enough to give visitors an ache in the neck and a general sense of their own unworthiness. He settled himself in the chair, gave a quick rub to the emerald on his right thumb. "Let the charade proceed," he muttered. The only object in the vast plateau of polished kedron was a dainty bell of unadorned white porcelain. He rang it twice, replaced it and sat back in the chair, his arms along its arms, his hands curved loosely about their finials.

The double doors swung smoothly open and Vasshaka Bulan came stalking in, Todichi Yahzi gliding grayly behind him clutching a scarlet notebook. He touched Bulan's arm (ignoring the man's recoil and hiss of loathing), cooed him to the visitor's chair, then went to the gray leather cushion waiting beside the desk, wriggled around until he was comfortable, settled the book in his lap and prepared to record everything said during the interview.

Maksim rumbled impatiently through the rituals of greeting, gave brusque permission for Vasshaka Bulan to say what was on his mind. "Brief and blunt," he said, "unless you want to try my patience, Servant Bulan."

"Phoros Pharmaga, I hear." Bulan bowed his head. "I have a complaint about the Dicast Silthos a Melisto. He ordered a Servant taken from the Yron of Nopido, sat in judgment over him and ordered him stoned by the Nopidese. He had no right, Phoros. A Servant is judged by Amortis and the Kriorn of his Yron. None less can touch him. By your own word, this is Amortis' land."

"By my own word, Amortis judges her Servants in all except . . ." he leaned forward and slapped his hand on the desktop, making the wood boom, "EXCEPT for civil crimes. Rape is a civil crime. I have read the Dicast's report, Servant of Servants. This charming creature of yours raped an eight-year-old girl."

Bulan lifted his hand. "A holy frenzy, Phoros, for which he is not responsible."

Settsimaksimin forced himself to wait a moment before responding, hammering an iron calm over a fury that inclined him to send this snake back to Amortis as ash. He needed the wily old twister, especially now when he couldn't afford a fuss that would divert his attention from the Drinker of Souls and what she could mean to him. He managed a cold smile. "Anarpa didn't seem to share that notion. He murdered the girl and tried to conceal what he'd done."

"A weak man is a weak man and a stupid one does not acquire wisdom at such a moment. It is for the Yron and the Kriorn to judge him."

"By my word and by my law it is the people he injured who have that right. By my word and by my law and in the Covenant I made with Amortis. A covenant that you know word for word, Vasshaka Bulan, Servant of the Servants of Amortis." He lifted his hand and laid it across his chest, the Stone warm and dangerous under his palm. "We have been patient with you, Faithful Servant, because we know you are devoted to She whom we both . . . serve. We will continue our patience and explain our decree. The Servant Anarpa took refuge within the Nopido Yron when his crime was reported which from our reading was almost immediately since there was a witness to the burial. The Dicast, as was most proper and courteous though not necessary under our law and covenant, sent to the Nopido Yron and asked that the Servant named Anarpa be given to the civil court for judgment. The Kriorn of the Yron refused to produce him." Maksim felt his heart hurrying under the Stone and once again took time to calm himself. "That was neither proper nor courteous. Nor is it sanctioned by law or covenant. It is we, Vasshaka Bulan, who complain to you of such contumacious behavior. It is we, Vasshaka Bulan, who say to you, discipline your Servants or we will do it for you. And should you doubt our will or our ability to do so, we will ask Amortis to make it plain to you by punishing that Kriorn herself. We have explained to you what we intend to accomplish within the land; Amortis has given her sanction to these goals. Any Servant who cannot work with enthusiasm for our dream had best find another land to serve the Lady." He watched Bulan's face but not a muscle moved; the mild old eyes had no more feeling in them than a chunk of low grade coal.

"It is time, perhaps," Bulan said slowly, as if he were considering with great care everything he said (though Maksim had no doubt the old twister had forseen everything so far and plotted his speech accordingly, most of it anyway; with some pleasure Maksim remembered catching a slight tic in a cheek muscle when he said Amortis would do the punishing of that idiot Kriorn, that knocked you off center, you old viper). "It is time, I say, that we who are not so wise as you, Phoros Pharmaga, should meet and draw up tables determining specifically who in what circumstances has responsibility for making and upholding what laws."

Again Settsimaksimin examined the Servant's face, there was no reading anything but mild earnestness in that disciplined mask he used to cover his bones. What are you up to? I wouldn't trust you with the ink to write your initials. If you think you're going to tighten your bony grip on My people. . . . Hmm. Might not be a bad idea, though, keep him out of my hair when I haven't got the time or energy to waste on him. "We will think on it," he said gravely. "We are inclined to agree with you, Faithful Servant. Do this, draw up a list of scholars civil and servant whom you find capable of dealing with the complexities in such a plan and yourself, out of your vast wisdom, do you write for us the agenda you consider most suitable for such a group with such a purpose. Seven days for the list and agenda. Or do you need more?"

Vasshaka Bulan bowed his head in humble submission. "Seven days is sufficient, Phoros Pharmaga."

After he was gone, Settsimaksimin shoved his chair back with such force the wood of the legs shrieked against the wood of the dais. He went charging about the room muttering to himself while Todichi Yahzi finished his notes. "Seven days. Sufficient. HAH! SEVEN MINUTES IS MORE LIKE. He's been worming toward this for AHHH the gods know how long. I don't see what he's going to get out of it, Todich. He knows I'm going to read every miserable word of whatever

comes out of that bunch of legal nitwits and anything I don't understand or don't like is DEAD, Todich. The names? How could I trust
men he named for something like this? Even if I know they're good
men. He's after something, Todich, WHY CAN'T I SEE IT?" He flung
his arms out, dragged in a huge lungful of air. "AAAHHhhhmm
HAH! Hunh." Abruptly brisk, he turned to Todichi Yahzi. "Write this:
strataga Tapos a Parost and his prime captain; guildmaster Syloa
h'Arpagy; kephadicast Oggisol a Surphax and the three judges he
talked to me about, I've forgotten their names but he'll remember;
harbormaster Kathex h'Apydaro; peasant Voice, Hrous t'Thelo. Got
those? Good. Write me out a note to the chief Herald Brux so I can
sign it. Say send your best and fastest heralds, men you know can keep
their mouths shut, to the folk on that list and tell them to meet with
. . . hmmm, better be formal about it, I suppose . . . the Phoros
Pharmaga Settsimaksimin three days on, in the Citadel. This next is for
you, Todich, put them in the Star Cabinet down on the first floor, it's
warded. I don't want anyone snooping about what I'm going to be
saying there. Finished? Give me the stylus a moment. There. No don't
go yet. Listen, Todich, I'll be spending a lot of time in my workroom
and while I'm there those men are going to run Cheonea for me. Hah!"
A rumbling chuckle as Todichi Yahzi cooed a flurry of objections. "I
know, my friend. That's why I want you to watch them waking and
sleeping. You know, Todich, this isn't such an unhappy turn of affairs
after all; I've been thinking about setting up a council of governance
like that for some years now, to see how it would work if I weren't
here, ah, where was I? Yes. I'll give you command of some ariels and a
clutch of stone sprites . . . no no, you'll be able to see and hear them.
I'm not an idiot, Todich. If I had the mirrors . . . tchah! I've been
lazy and stupid, my friend. Mmm. You'll know a palace coup if you see
one hatching, yes, Todich, I really have been listening to you. If you see
anything funny happening, give me a call, I'll show you how to reach
me tonight, when I get back. No, I won't be angry if you've misread
some twitch or tic for treason, this is a time when caution is far more
important than certainty. If they're honest and I show my face, it will
encourage them; if they're starting a fiddle, they'll think again." He
rubbed at the back of his neck. "Hot in here. Anything more you need
to know? Good. Seven levels of mortal hell, Todich, I've got to wrestle
that bitch Amortis into scourging the Nopidese Kriorn. I'll be on
Deadfire Island for the rest of the day. If anything comes up," he

stretched, yawned, laughed, "turn it off till tomorrow. The world won't fall apart in that short a time."

Settsimaksimin sat in his sanctuary watching as Ahzurdan rambled through the streets of Kukurul with the woman or sometimes the children; there was a tooth-edged trace between those odd preteens and Ahzurdan that made him smile because it was so much like the hostility he'd faced now and again when he'd taken lovers from among the double-gaited, the hostility of children who refuse to share their parent; in a way it was puzzling, from what he knew of Baby Dan there wouldn't be much between the woman and him, nothing to make the children so jealous, but jealous they were and suspicious of him. They watched him and they burned.

And they protected him, presumably because the woman told thim to. On the fifth night in Kukurul, late, long after the woman had gone to sleep. Ahzurdan slipped out of the Inn and went foraging among the alleys of the waterfront. Watching him sidle through the darkness, Maksim nodded to himself. Hunting a trader in dreamdust, he thought. You don't change, Danny Blue. Miserable little rat. He thrust his hand into his robe and under the Stone, massaged his chest. Still running away from anything that makes you look at yourself. Wonder where the children are? Did you finally manage to slip them? He continued to watch and after several more twists he noticed a gray mastiff following Ahzurdan, a purposeful shadow in shadows. Now what does that mean? He examined the beast. Ah! crystal eyes, no irids, only a swirl of half-guessed vapor. One of the children, the boy, yes, I've never seen demons or anything else with eyes like theirs. So. Shapeshifters. He looked around for the girl and found a nighthawk drifting above the street, swinging in slow loops that centered over Ahzurdan. A large nighthawk with glimmering crystal eyes. Clever children. Strong muscles and a good set of tearing teeth down there on the ground, a watcher overhead. You can talk to each other, can't you. Interesting. Mmm. Ambush ahead. You up there, you have to see them. What are you going to do about it? Nothing? Ah. The mastiff edged closer until he was almost breathing on Ahzurdan's heels and the hawk dropped lower. I see. Let Baby Dan handle it, but be ready to jump if he needs you.

The muggers attacked and were dispatched neatly by a jolt from Ahzurdan; he smoothed his tunic down and went on, ignoring the dead men. Unaware of his escort, he found a dealer, got the dust and went slipping back to the Inn. He sat holding the packet and staring unhappily at it. Then he laid it away among his robes, undressed and crawled into bed. Sooo sooo, baby Dan, I wouldn't 've believed it without seeing it. Mmm. That worries me. I don't want you cleaned out and feeling pert, Danny Boy, I want you coming at me scared. He rubbed long limber fingers together, yellow eyes fixed on the sleeping man. You were the best I had, little Blue, yes, and the most dangerous. I smelled it on you the minute I saw you, standing there no one daring to get close. Your face is twisting, little Blue, remembering me in your dreams? I swore I'd tame you or kill you. Came close to doing both, didn't I. But you ran, Danny Blue. You ran so fast and so far it didn't seem worth coming after you. Got your nerve back? Or is it the woman? Demidemon with finicky tastes, or so I hear. No respecter of man or god. Goes her own way and be damned to those who try and stop her. Amortis, Haa-Unh, she turned purple when I told her Drinker was heading this way. Drinker of Souls. God of gods, I like her, I do. You haven't a ship yet, lady, but any day now, and I'm not much good round water, did he tell you that, the toad? Mmm. Shapeshifters. I can deal with that. The eyes are enough to pin them. Wonder what they are when they're home? Hah hah hah, I don't really want to know. Sooo, what have I got for you, lady . . . mmm, what have I got . . . come the dawn, what do I throw at you?

6

WAITING AT KUKURUL,
THE INN OF PEARLY DAWN.

SCENE: Early morning. That lull time, when
         the night life has diminished to a few
         weary thieves, whores and drunks wan-
         dering through dingy gray streets,
         when the day life that will turn those
         streets noisy and busy and fill them
         with color is confined still to bed-
         rooms (or whatever shelters the
         sleepers managed to find) and kitch-
         ens and stables.

Kukurul. The world's navel. The pivot of the four winds. The pearl of
five seas. It is said that if you sit long enough at one of the outside
tables of the Sidday Lir, you'll see the whole world file past you going
up the Ihman Katt. Kukurul. Expensive, gaudy, secretive and corrupt.
Along the Ihman Katt, brothels for every taste (in some of them children mimicking the seductive postures of street whores hang from upper windows soliciting custom); ranks of houses where assassin guilds
advertise men of the knife, men of the garotte, women of the poison
trade. If your tastes run to the macabre, halfway along there is a narrow black building where death rites are practiced and offered for the
titillation of connoisseurs. At the end of the Ihman Katt is the heart of
Kukurul, the Great Market. A paved square two miles on a side where
everything is on sale but heat, sweat and stench. Where noise is so
pervasive and so intense that signing is a high art. No greens or flesh or
food fish, but anything else you might desire. Trained dog packs for
nervous merchants or lordlings who don't enjoy personal popularity
with family or folk; rare ornamental beasts and birds; honeycomb
tanks of bright colored fighting fish, other tanks of ancient carp, cha-

meleon seahorses snails of marvelous color and convolution. Fine cloth and rare leathers. Blown glass of every shape, color, and use, including the finest mirrors in the world (according to the claims of their vendors). Gold, silver, coppersmiths sitting among their wares. Cuttlers and swordsmiths. Jewelers with fantastic wealth displayed about them. Spice merchants. Sellers of rare orchids. Importers of just about everything the world offers. And winding through the cluttered ways, water sellers, pancake women, piemen, meatroll vendors, their shops on their backs or rolling before them. That is Kukurul on the island of Vara Smykkal.

Vara Smykkal. The outermost island of the Myk'tat Tukery. A large verdant island. Little is known of the land and people beyond the ring of mountains about the deep sheltered harbor and most visitors don't bother asking; they spend their time in the Great Market or the cool dim trade rooms of the many Inns that sit on the hills around the Market Flat.

Myk'tat Tukery. Generally thought of as the Thousand Islands, though no one has ever counted them. The interior islands are mysterious, shut away from just about everyone, rumored to be fabulously wealthy and filled with women of superlative beauty and passion, with magical creatures like unicorns and manticores and spiders with nacreous eyes weaving wedding silks so fine they'd pass through a needle's eye, with trees that grow rubies and emeralds and sapphires, with fountains of gold and silver and liquid diamond. But the narrow crooked waterways between the islands were infested with bandits and pirates; there were deceptive shoals and rocks that moved, there were shifting mists and freaky winds and lightning walked most nights and one green rocky island looked much like the next. Even the cleverest and greediest men seldom got far into the maze and few of these got out again. And the ones that made it back seldom had much to say about what they'd seen.

During her wandering years after the ravaging of Arth Slya, Brann took a sailing canoe deep into the Myk'tat Tukery and out again, emerging with mind and body intact and memories of some lovely places, especially an island called Jal Virri, but like the less fortunate she didn't talk about the experience. She'd intended to go back one day; events intervened and she went in another direction. As she told Ahzurdan, she settled into clay and contentment at the Pottery beside the Wansheeri. Coming back to Kukurul roused those memories and she thought about retreating into the maze and letting the world rock on without her, but once again she was too tangled in that world to do more than daydream of peace.

Brann rose with the dawn and went to eat at the Sidday Lir, escaping before Ahzurdan crawled out of bed and came to bend her ear again. After living so long as a solitary, she found it difficult to control her growing irritation with the man; she was getting useful information about the training a sorcerer required, his powers and their limitations, but she had to seine those items out of a flood of rambling discourse. A sleepy waiter brought her a pot of tea and a plate of mooncakes, went off to find some berries and cream.

Yaril came drifting along and settled beside her at the table. "He went out last night. Late. Bought two ounces dreamdust."

"Smoke any?"

"No."

Brann waited until the waiter set the bowl of berries and the cream pot before her and went away. "Hmp. Idiot man. Why now?" She poured a dollop of cream over the dark purple mound, lifted her spoon. "What do you think?"

"He'll crumble at a look. Drop him, Bramble."

"Hmm." For several minutes she spooned up berries, savoring the dark sweet-tart taste and the cool fresh breeze blowing in off the water, then she wiped her mouth and frowned at Yaril. "I don't think so. Not yet. Wait till we get to Bandrabahr, then we'll see."

Yaril shrugged. "You asked."

"So I did. Yaro, ever think about Jal Virri?"

"Not much. Boring place."

"But it was beautiful, Yaro."

"So? Lots of places are pretty enough. I like places where things happen."

Brann broke a mooncake in half. "Was your home like that, a place where things happen?"

"We've been away a long time, Bramble. Think about Arth Slya. What do you remember? The good times, eh? Same with us."

"I see." Like always, she thought, they won't talk about their home world, slip slide away. Did they love it, did they hate it, what did they think? Though she thought she knew them almost as well as she knew herself, at times like this she was jarred into a feeling that they were essentially unknowable. Too many referents that just weren't there. "Yaro . . ." she looked down over the warehouses and the wharves, out to the ships moored in the bay, "I'd like you and Jay to fly a sweep to the north and see if you can sight Zatikay's ship. Ahzurdan swears he'll be here any day now, but time's getting short on us. Theriste first is day after tomorrow, I want to be out of here by then, we have to be in Silagamatys by the seventeenth, I want some room for maneuvering in case of snags. You know nothing ever goes exactly as it's planned."

"Ahzurdan's a . . ."

"Don't say it, Yaro, I'm tired of that onenote song." She finished the berries, emptied the teabowl and tapped against it with her spoon. When the waiter came, she paid him, then began strolling up the still deserted Ihman Katt, passing the ancient streetsweepers as they brushed away the debris from last night's business, stopping a moment to exchange a word with a M'darjin woman so old her skin had turned ashy and her hair white as crimped snow. "Ma amm, Zazi Koko, how many diamonds today?"

Zazi Koko leaned on her broom and grinned at Brann, showing teeth as strong as they'd been when she was running the grassy hills of her homeland, though a lot yellower. "More than you, Embamba zimb, more than you."

"True, oh true." Brann laughed and ambled on. The brightening day was clear and cool; behind the facades she passed she could feel a slow torpid struggle against weariness left over from last night, lepidopter stirring in her chrysalis. She turned into the flowery winding lane that led uphill to the Pearly Dawn, walking slower still, reluctance to return to the Inn and Ahzurdan gathering like a lump under her ribs. She broke a green orchid from a spray that brushed her head, showering her with delicate perfume, tucked it into an empty buttonhole, then broke off another and eased it into the fine blond hair over Yaril's ear. Smiling affectionately at the startled girl, she patted her shoulder and ambled on.

Heavy-eyed and morose, Ahzurdan met her on the stairs and followed her into her room. As soon as the door shut behind him and before he could start talking, Brann said, "If Zatikay isn't here by tonight, I'm going to hire transport to Haven on Cheonea. Yes, yes, I know none of the Captains in the harbor would shift his schedule for any price, but there are ships not too deep in the Myk'tat Tukery with more flexible masters."

"Bloody cannibals, more likely to carve us up and eat us than waste time on open water."

"Unless they've changed since I ran into them, they won't bother me or the children. And I suspect you'd find it easy enough to convince them that you're no tasty morsel. I didn't say I liked the idea. But time's . . ." she broke off, frowned. There was suddenly a faint odd smell in the room, a creaky droning, like a doorhinge down a deep well. "What the . . ."

Tall, thin, brown and ivory, like a lightning-blasted tree, an eerie ugly creature solidified in front of Brann and reached for her.

Alerted by the sound and the smell, Brann dropped to a squat, then sprang to one side, slapping against the floor and rolling onto her feet. The treeish thing looked stiff and clumsy, but it wasn't; it was fast and flexible and frighteningly strong. One of its hands raised a wind over her head, but her hair was too short for any kind of grip and she dropped too quickly. When she kicked out of the squat, rough knotty fingers got half a grip on her leg but slipped off as she twisted away. She bounced onto her feet, gasped with sudden fear as a second set of hard woody arms closed about her and started to squeeze.

Yaril shifted to a fireball and flung herself at the treeish demon, meaning to burn it, but it wasn't what it seemed and all she did was char it a little, releasing an appalling stench into the room. It loosened its grip on Brann, held her with one hard ropy arm and swung at Yaril with the other.

Jaril came whipping through the wall and slammed into the first Treeish, charring it and stinging it enough to drive it back.

Another Treeish solidified from air and stench. And another.

Brann slapped her hands against her captor and began drawing its life into her; she screamed (voice hoarse with agony) as that corrosive firestuff poured into a body not meant to contain demon energies, but she didn't stop the draw.

Yaril flew to her, sucked away as much of the energy as she could and redirected it into a blast of liquid fire at the other three Treeish.

Jaril was a thick worm of fire, winding about the short stubby legs of the Treeish, toppling them one by one as they tried to move at Brann.

The Treeish holding Brann screamed, a deep hooming sound that cut off abruptly as the demon shivered suddenly to flakes of something like dried mushroom. Brann leaped at a second Treeish, one rocking onto its feet after Jaril tripped it; avoiding the arms that whipped snake quick at her, she got it from behind and flattened her hands against its sides, holding onto it through all its gyrations as she drained the life out of it, screaming and screaming at the agony of what she was doing, but going on and on.

While Brann scrambled desperately to survive and the children fought with her, Ahzurdan stood by the door, frozen, all his ambivalences aroused. He watched Brann struggle, he listened to her scream, he wanted to see her humiliated, hurt; he loathed this in himself, despaired when he had to acknowledge it. But he couldn't make himself act.

Minutes passed. The second Treeish died. For a breath or two, Brann stood trembling, unable to make herself endure that agony again, then she sank her teeth into her lip until she drew blood and threw herself at the third.

Yaril deflected a snatch of fire from the fight and spat it at Ahzurdan; it missed, being meant to miss, but it singed his ear and burnt away the ends of a wide swatch of his hair.

Startled out of his self-absorption, he roused will and memory , took a quick guess at the essence of the demons, assembled his shout, his hand gestures, and in a burst like a storm striking drove the demons from this reality.

Brann dropped panting to her knees, tears squeezing from her eyes. The changechildren dropped beside her, emerged from their fireball forms and spread their hands on her, drawing the poison fire out of her.

Ahzurdan stirred, went to the room's windows, threw them wide to let the sea breeze blow the stench away. He stood in the window that looked out over the bay, his back to the room, wanting to run before Brann recovered enough to ask the questions he refused to ask himself. It was so much simpler to be somewhere else when the result of his actions or lack of action began to come clear. His mind told him it was wiser to stay (this time) and talk his way round her. His flesh wasn't so sure.

"You took your time." Ordinarily she had a rather pleasant voice, low for a woman, but musical; those words came at him like missiles.

"You don't understand." He turned his head, a gesture toward courtesy, but didn't look at her.

"Hah!"

"I told you. We work by will. Will driven by knowing. Knowing comes first, it has to. I had to know them to force them home. It takes . . . time." Resisting an urge to see if she accepted that explanation, he stared out the window at nothing until a bit of color caught his eyes, a name flag on a masthead. His face loosened as he recognized it, though he tried to keep his relief from showing in his back. "Zatikay's in."

"Tk." An exasperated sigh. "Get yourself out there and find when he's leaving and if it's tomorrow or the next day, get us passage if you have to take deck space. Umf! And have a look at those wards of yours, seems to me they're leaking."

He drew his fingers along the sill, making lines in the faint dusting of yellow-gray pollen. "The ariels," he said. "They told him I'm traveling with you. He knows me, he knows my tricks." He felt an odd mix of fear and freedom, fear that she'd force him away from her, hope that she'd cut him loose so he didn't have to fight himself any longer, that she'd free him to destroy himself as quickly and as easily as seemed right. "I'm sorry. I didn't think of that when I asked to come with you."

"I did, so stop squirming." She was moving briskly about behind him; he turned, saw her using a pillowcase to clean up the leavings of the dead demons. The children were watching him, more hostile than ever. He had to make her say it.

"Tell me to go."

She looked up from the unpleasant task, raised her brows. "Why?"

"He can't find you if I'm not around."

"You were lazy, Dan, leaning on me too much. You won't again."

"I'll let you down, you know I will."

"If you want out, go. But it's your decision. You won't put that on me."

He looked at his hands, rubbed his thumbs across the smears of pollen clinging to his fingertips. "I can't go."

She nodded, got to her feet. "I see. If I understand what you've told me Maksim is tired. He won't come at us again for a while. So, go talk to Zatikay. Jay, go with him. I want to know soonest if we're leaving on the morrow; you and Yaro will have to raid the treasury, our gelt is getting low. Go. Go." She laughed, waving the case at them. "Get out of here."

7

DANIEL AKAMARINO STROLLS DOWN A DUSTY BACK ROAD AND STEPS FROM ONE WORLD TO ANOTHER.

WORK RECORD

DANIEL AKAMARINO aka Blue Dan, Danny Blue

BORN:
YS 745
Rainbow's End
Line Family Azure
> Family Azure has five living generations. 50 males (adults) aged 24–173. 124 females (adults) aged 17–175. 49 children. Names available to adults: Teal, Ciello, Royal, Akamarino, Turkoysa, Sapphiro, Ceruli, Lazula, Cyanica.

RATED:
1. Communications Officer, Master Rating, first degree
2. Propulsion Engineer, Master Rating, first degree
3. Cargo Superintendent/Buyer, Master Rating, first degree

COMMENTS:
> If you can get him, grab him. He won't stay long, a year maybe two, but he's worth taking a chance on. Let him tinker. He'll leave you with a com system you couldn't buy for any money.
> Got eyes in his fingertips and can hear a flea grunt a light-year off. Have your engines singing if you let him. Good at turning up and stowing cargo. Lucky. Will make a profit for you more often than not.
> A pleasant type, never causes trouble in the crew, but undependable.

Drifter. Follows his whims and nothing you say will hold him to a contract he wants to walk out on.

EMPLOYMENT:

1. Aurora's Dream
   Sun Gold Lines, home port: Rainbow's End.
   Captain: Martin Chrome
   YS 765–769   apprentice prop eng

2. Herring Finn
   free trader
   owner/master: Kally Kuninga
   YS 772–775   appr prop eng
                       Master Rating YS 786

3. Dying Duck
   free trader
   owner/master: Berbalayasant
   YS 779–786   appr coms off
                       Master Rating YS 786

4. Andra's Harp
   worldship
   Instell Cominc lines, registered the Sygyn Worlds
   Captain: Bynnyno Wadelinc
   YS 788–791   comms off sec (788)
                       comms off sec (789)
                       comms off Comdr (790–1)

5. The Hairy Mule
   free trader
   owner/master: Dagget O'dang
   YS 795–797   appr carg sup/   byr

6. Astrea Themis
   free trader
   owner/master: Luccan della Farangan
   YS 799–803   Mst Eng

7. Prism Dancer
   Sun Gold Lines, home port: Rainbow's End
   Captain: Stella Fulvina
   YS 805–810   comms off Comdr

8. Astrea Themis
     free trader
     owner/master: Luccan della Farangan
     YS 813–821   appr carg sup/byr
                                Mstr carg sup/byr YS 819

9. Herring Finn
     free trader
     owner/master: Kally Kuninga
     YS 825–   Mstr carg sup/byr

SCENE: Daniel Akamarino walking along the
             grassy verge of a paved road, let-
             ting his arms swing, now and then
             whistling a snatch of tune when he
             thought about it. A bright sunny day,
             local grass is lush with a tart dusty
             smell, pleasant enough, a breeze
             blowing in his face heavy with the
             scent of fresh water.

A man past his first youth (his age uncertain in this era of ananile drugs that put off aging and death to somewhere around three hundred among those species where three score and ten had once been optimum), bald except for a fringe of wild hair over his ears like a half-crown of black thorns, blue eyes, brilliant blue, they burn in a face tanned dark. He is tall and lanky, looks loosely put together, but moves faster than most and where his strength won't prevail, his slippy mind will. A man not bothered by much, he seldom feels the need to prove anything about his person or proclivities; he mostly likes dealing with things but is occasionally interested in people, has quit several jobs because he touched down in a culture that he found interesting and he wanted to know all its quirks and fabulas. Impatient with routine, he drifts from job to job, quitting when he feels like it or because some nit tries to make him do things that bore him like shaving every day or wearing boots instead of sandals and a uniform instead of the ancient shirts and trousers he gets secondhand whenever the ones he has are reduced to patches and threads. He stays longest in jobs where his nominal superiors tell him what they want and leave him to produce results however it suits him. He has no plans for settling down; there's always something to see another hop away and he never has trouble finding a place on a ship when he's done with groundside living.

Daniel Akamarino is down on a Skinker world, nosing about for items more interesting than those the local merchants are bringing to the backwater subport where the Herring Finn put down (the major ports were closed to freetraders; technically the world was closed, but its officials looked the other way as long as the profits were there and the traders were discreet). He is getting bored with the ship; the Captain is an oldtime friend, but she is a silent woman settled in a longterm and nonstraying relationship with her comms Com; the engineer is a Yilan with a vishéfer as a symbiote; two words a month-standard is verbosity for him.

Daniel Akamarino is mooching along beside a dusty two-lane asphalt road, enjoying a bright spring morning. Yesterday, when he was chatting over a drink with a local merchant, he took a close look at the armlet the Skinker was wearing on one of his right arms, flowing liquid forms carved into a round of heavy reddish brown wood. Today he is on his way to find the Skinker who carved it, said to live in an outshed of a warren a kilometer outside the porttown. Now and then a jit or a two-wheeler poots past him, or a skip hums by overhead. He could have hired a jit or caught the local version of a bus, but prefers to walk; he doesn't expect much from this world or from the woodcarver, but it's an excuse to get away from town clutter and merchants with gold in their eyes; he wants to look at the world, sniff its odors, pick up its textures and sound patterns, especially the birdsong. The local flying forms have elaborate whistles and a capacity for blending individual efforts into an astonishing whole.

Daniel Akamarino strolls along a two-lane asphalt road in a humming empty countryside listening to extravagant flights of birdsong; the grass verge having turned to weeds and nettles, he is on the road itself now, his sandals squeak on the gritty asphalt. A foot lifts, swings, starts down . . .

Daniel Akamarino dropped onto a rutted dirt road, stumbled and nearly fell. When he straightened, he stood blinking at an utterly different landscape.

The road he'd landed in curved sharply before and behind him; since it also ran between tall hedges he couldn't see much, only the tops of some low twisty trees whose foliage had thinned with the onrush of the year; withered remnants of small fruits clung to the topmost branches.

Real trees, like those in his homeplace, not the feathery blue analogs on
the road he'd been following an instant before. A raptor circled high
overhead, songbirds twittered nearby, distractingly familiar; he listened
and thought he could put a name to most of them. Insects hummed in
the hedges and crawled through dusty gray-green grass. A black leaper
as long as his thumb sprang out of the dust, landed briefly on his toe,
sprang off again. He sucked on his teeth, kicked at the nearest rut, sent
pale alkali dust spraying before him. If the sun were a bit ruddier and
had a marble-sized blue companion, this could have been Rainbow's
End. But it was egg-yellow and solitary, and it was low in what he
thought was the west and its light had a weary feel, so he shouldn't
waste what was left on the day boggling at what had happened to him.
He took one step backward, then another, but the fold in spacetime
that brought him here seemed a oneway gate. He shrugged. Not much
he could do about that. He knelt in the dust and inspected the ruts.
Inexpert as he was at this sort of tracking, it seemed to him that the
heaviest traffic went the way he was facing. Which was vaguely northeast (if he was right about the sun). He straightened, brushed himself
off, and started walking, accepting this jarring change in his circumstances as calmly as he accepted most events in his life.

Cradled in a warm noisy crowded line family, always someone to
pick him up and cuddle him when he stubbed a toe or stumbled into
more serious trouble, he had acquired a sense of security that nothing
since had more than dented (though he'd wandered in and out of danger a dozen times and come close to dying more than once from an
excess of optimism); he'd learned to defend himself, more because of
his internal need to push any skill he learned to the limits of his ability
than because he felt any strong desire to stomp his enemies. It was
easier not to make enemies. If a situation got out of hand and nothing
he could do would defuse it, he generally slid away and left the argument to those who enjoyed arguing. One time a lover asked him,
"Don't you want to do something constructive with your life?" He
thought about it for a while, then he said, "No." "You ought to," she
said, irritation sharpening her voice, "there's more to living than just
being alive." He gazed at her, sighed, shook his head and not long after
that shipped out on the Hairy Mule.

He swung along easily through a late afternoon where heat hung in a
yellow haze over the land and the road was the only sign of habitation;
he wasn't in a hurry though he was starting to get thirsty. He searched
through the dozens of pockets in his long leather overvest, found an

ancient dusty peppermint, popped it into his mouth. A road led somewhere and he'd get there if he kept walking. The sun continued to
decline and eventually set; he checked his pocketchron, did some cal-
culations of angular shift and decided that the daylength was close to
shipstandard, another way this world was like Rainbow's End. He kept
on after night closed about him; no point in camping unless he found
water, besides the air was warm and a gibbous moon with a chunk
bitten out of the top rose shortly after sunset and spread a pearly light
across the land.

Sounds drifted to him on a strengthening breeze. A mule's bray.
Another. A chorus of mules. Ring of metal on metal. Assorted anonymous tunks and thuds. As he drew closer to the source, the sounds of
laughter and voices, many of them children's voices. He rounded a
bend and found a large party camped beside a canal. Ten carts backed
up under the trees. A crowd of mules (bay, roan and blue) wearing
hobbles and herded inside rope corrals, chewing at hay and grain and
each other, threatening, kicking and biting with an energy that made
nothing of the day's labors. Two hundred children seated around half a
dozen fires. Fifteen adults visible. Eight women, dressed in voluminous
trousers, tunics reaching to midcalf with long sleeves and wide cuffs,
headcloths that could double as veils. Seven men with shorter tunics
and trousers that fit closer to the body, made from the same cloth the
women used (a dark tan homespun, heavy and hot), leather hats with
floppy brims and fancy bands, leather boots and gloves. They also had
three bobtail spears slanted across their backs and what looked like
cavalry sabers swinging from broad leather belts; several carried quar-
terstaffs. The last were prowling about the circumference of the camp,
keeping a stern eye on the children while the women were finishing
preparations for supper.

One of the men walked over to him. "Keep moving, friend. We don't
want company here."

Daniel Akamarino blinked. Whatever or whoever had brought him
here had operated on his head in the instant between worlds; he wasn't
sure he liked that though it was convenient. "Spare a bit of supper for a
hungry man?"

Before the man could answer, a young boy left one of the circles
carrying a metal mug full of water. "You thirsty, too?"

A woman came striding after the boy, fixing the end of her headcloth
across her face, a big woman made bigger by her bulky clothing. She
put a hand on the guard's arm when he took a step toward Daniel.

"He's a wayfarer, Sinan. Since when do Owlyn folk turn away a hungry man?" She tapped the boy on the head. "Well done, Tré. Give him the water."

Hoping his immunities were up to handling this world's bugs, Daniel gulped down the cold clean water and gave the mug back with one of his best grins. "Thanks. A hot dusty walk makes water more welcome than the finest of wines."

"You'll join us for supper?"

"With enthusiasm, Thiné." The epithet meant Woman of High Standing, and came to his lips automatically, triggered by the strength and dignity he saw in her; she rather reminded him of one of his favorite mothers and he brought out for her his sunniest smile.

She laughed and swept a hand toward the circle of fires. "Be welcome, then."

They fed Daniel Akamarino and dug him out a spare blanket. The boy called Tré drifted over to sit by him while he ate, bringing an older girl with him that he introduced as his sister Kori. Tré said little, leaving the talking to Kori.

"This is one big bunch of kids," Daniel said. "Going to school?"

She stared at him, eyes wide. "It's the Lot. It's Owlyn's month."

"I haven't been here very long. What's the Lot?"

"Settsimaksimin takes three kids each year from each Parika in Cheonea. The Lot's to say which ones. Boys go to be trained for the army or for Servants of Amortis, girls go to the Yrons, those are the temples of Amortis, and the one that gets the gold lot goes to the high temple in Phras."

"Hmm. Who's Settsiwhatsisname and what gives him the right to take children from their families?"

Another startled look at him, a long gaze exchanged with her brother, a glance at the trees overhead. "We don't want to talk about him," Kori said, her voice a mutter he had to strain to hear. "He's a sorcerer and he owns Cheonea and he can hear if someone talks against him. Best leave things alone you don't have to know."

"Ah. I hear you." Sorcerer? Mmf. Probably means some git stumbled on this world and used his tech to impress the hell out of the natives. "You're heading for a city, how close is it?"

"Silagamatys. About three more days' travel. It's a sea port. Tré's seven, so this is his first trip. He hasn't seen the sea before."

"You have?"

"Course I have. I'm thirteen going on fourteen. This is my last Lot; if I slide by this time, I won't leave Owlyn Vale again, I'll be betrothed and too busy weaving for the family that comes." She sounded rather wistful, but resigned to the life fate and custom mapped out for her. "We've told you 'bout us. AuntNurse says it's impolite to pester way-farers with questions. I think it's impolite for them to not talk when they have to see we're dying to know all about them." She was tall and lanky, with a splatter of orange freckles across her nose; wisps of fine light-brown hair straggled from under a headcloth that swung precari-ously every time she moved her head; her eyes were huge in her thin face, a pale gray-green that shifted color with every thought that passed through her head. She grinned at him, opened those chatoyant eyes wide and waited for him to swallow the hook.

"Weeell," he murmured, "I'm a traveling man from a long way off. . . ."

Much later, rolled into the borrowed blanket beside one of the carts, Daniel Akamarino thought drowsily about what he'd learned. He was appalled but not surprised. This wasn't the first tyrant who'd got the notion of building a power base in the minds of a nation's children. Clever about how he managed it. If he'd tried taking children out of their homes, no matter how powerful he was, he would have faced a blistering resistance. By having the children brought to him, by arrang-ing what seemed to be an impartial choice through the Lot, he saved himself a world of trouble, didn't even have to send guards with the carttrains. Sorcerer? Oh yeah. Seen that before, haven't you . . . Vague speculation faded gradually into sleep.

Having got used to him by breakfast (he was an amiable guest, quick to offer his services to pull and haul, doing his tasks whistling a cheer-ful tune that made the work lighter for everyone), they let him ride one of the carts. Tré and Kori sat with him. The boy was silent, troubled about something, the trouble deepening as he got closer to the city. For a while Daniel thought it was having to face the Lot for the first time, but when he slipped a murmured question to Tré, the boy shook his head. He was nervous and unhappy, he clung to Daniel for reasons of his own, but he wouldn't talk about what frightened him. Kori knew, but she was as silent about it as her brother. She sat on the other side of Daniel, sliding him murmured information about Silagamatys and its waterfront that she had no business knowing if it was like most other such areas he'd moved through in his travels. She laughed at his unexpressed but evident disapproval of her nocturnal wanderings. He liked the mischievous twinkle in her eyes, the dry quality to her humor, the subtle rebellion in the way she carried her body and changed his mind about how resigned she was to the future laid out for her. Thinking about it, he was rather sorry for her; from everything he'd seen so far, this world wasn't all that different from other agricultural societies he'd dipped into. Men and women both had their lives laid out for them from the moment they were born, which was fine if they fit into those roles, but hell on the rebels and the too-intelligent, especially if these last were women. Kori had a sharp practical mind; she must have realized years ago that there were things she couldn't admit to doing or knowing and continue to live at peace with her people. Talking with him was taking a chance; what she said and what it meant, slipping out after dark to wander through dangerous streets, that could destroy her. He suspected her actions had something to do with her brother's fretting, but he didn't have enough data to judge what she was getting at.

After a while, he fished inside his vest and brought out the recorder he carried everywhere; he blew it out, played a few notes, then settled into a dance tune his older sisters had liked. The other children in the cart crowded about him; when he finished that tune he had them sing their own songs for him, then played these back with ornamental flourishes that made them giggle. Tré joined him with a liquid lilting whistle, putting flourishes on Daniel's flourishes, the girls clapped their hands, the boys sang and the afternoon passed more quickly than most. After that, even Sinan stopped resenting him.

He caught glimpses of farmhouses and outbuildings, a village or two, no walls or fortifications in sight (obviously, invasions were scarce around here). They passed over a number of canals busy with barges and small sail boats; there was a lot more traffic on the water than there was on the road. He didn't blame them, this world hadn't got around to inventing effective springs and riding these ruts (even sitting on layers of blankets and quilts) was rather like a bastinado of the buttocks.

Midafternoon two days later, the carttrain topped a hill and looked down on Silagamatys.

Daniel Akamarino was playing his flute again, but broke off in surprise when his cart swung round a clump of tall trees at the crest of that hill and he saw for the first time the immense walls of the city and the gleaming white Keep soaring into the clouds.

"HIS Citadel," Kori murmured, her voice dropping into the special tone she used when she spoke of Settsimaksimin but didn't want to name him. "AuntNurse said her father's brother Elias, the one who married into the Ankitierin of Prosyn Vale, was down to the city just after HE kicked out crazy old King Noshios; she said Elias said HE cleared the ground and had that thing built in two days and a night. And then HE built the Grand Yron just two weeks later and that only took a day." Third in the line of ten, the cart titled forward down the long undulating slope toward the city's SouthGate. "We're going to the Yron Hostel, it's built in back of the main temple. They won't let you in there, it's just for people doing the Lot. Actually, you'd better get off soon's we're through the Gate. You don't want HIM getting interested in you." The city was built on a cluster of low wooded hills looking out into a sheltered blue bay. The usual hovels and clutter of the poor and outcast snugged against the wall, but most of the ugliness was concealed by trees that Settsimaksimin had planted and protected from depredation by poor folk hunting fuel. When Daniel wondered about this, Kori said, "HE said don't touch the trees. HE said put iron to these trees and I'll hang you in a cage three days without food or water and don't think you can escape my eyes. And he did it too. HE said get your wood from the East Side Reserve. HE said Family Xilogonts will run the Wood Reserve for you. HE said you can buy a desma of wood for a copper, if you don't have the copper you can earn a desma by cutting ten desmas, if there is no wood to cut, you can earn a desma by working for Family Xilogonts for one halfday, planting seedlings and looking after young trees. If anyone in Family Xilogonts cheats you in any way, tell me and I will see it doesn't happen again."

"Hmm. I didn't expect that kind of thinking in a place like this. What do I mean? Ah Kori, just chatter, talking to myself." He looked around at the brilliant colors of the fall foliage, smiled. "Seems to work."

She scowled at him, unwilling to hear anything good about the man she called a sorcerer, turned her shoulder to him and went into a brood over what he suspected was her vision of the perversity of man.

The cart bumped over the last humpbacked bridge and rumbled onto an avenue paved with granite flats, heading for the gaping arch of the gateway. He braced himself to withstand a major stench, if they couldn't put springs on their rolling stock, clearly sewers were a lost cause, but as the carts rattled through the shadowy tunnel (the walls were at least ten meters thick at the base), there was little of the sour stink from open emunctories and offal rotting in the streets that he'd had to deal with when he was on a freetrader dropping in on neofeudal societies. The cart emerged into a narrow crooked street, paved with granite blocks set in tar, clean, even the legless beggar at the corner had a clean face and his gnarled knobby hands were scrubbed pale. The drivers of each of the carts tossed a coin in his bowl, got his blessings as they drove past.

A woman leaned from an upper window. "What Parika?"

The lead driver looked up. "Owlyn Vale," she shouted.

The children in the carts jumped to their feet, stood cheering and whooping, swaying precariously as the iron-tired wheels jolted over the paving stones, until they were scolded back down by the chaperones. Followed by laughter, shouts of welcome, luck and remember this that and the other when they got settled in and were turned loose on the city, the carttrain wound on, rumbling past tall narrow houses, through increasingly crowded streets, past innumerable fountains where the houses were pushed back to leave a square free, moving gradually uphill into an area where houses were larger with scores of brilliant windowboxes and there were occasional small gardens and green spaces and the fountains were larger and more elaborate. Ahead, two hills on, a minareted white structure glittered like salt in sunlight.

Kori leaned closer to Daniel Akamarino, murmured, "We'll be going slower when we start up the long slope ahead, you better get off then. If you want ships or work or something, keep going south, the Market is down that way and the waterfront.

"I hear you. Luck with the Lot, Kori."

She gave him a nervous smile. "Um . . ." She closed her hand over his wrist, her nails digging into the flesh; her voice came as a thread of sound. "Tré says we'll be seeing you again." She bit her lip, shook his hand when he started to speak. "Don't say anything. It's important. If it happens, I'll explain then."

"I wait on tiptoe." He grinned at her and she pinched his wrist, then sat in silence until they started the long climb to the Yron.

He got to his feet, swung over the side of the cart, wide enough to miss the tall wheel. After a flourish and a caper and a swooping bow that drew giggles from the children and waves from the chaperones, he move rapidly away along an alley whose curve hid the carts before he'd gone more than a few steps.

Though it was the middle of the afternoon, the Market was busy and noisy, the meat and vegetables were cleared off, their places filled with more durable goods. Daniel Akamarino drifted around it until he found the busiest lanes; he dropped into a squat beside the beggar seated at the corner of two of these. "Good pitch, this."

The beggar blinked his single rheumy eye. "Aah."

"Mind if I play my pipe a while? Your pitch, your coin."

"You any good?"

"Don't like it, stop me."

"A will, don't doubt, A will."

Daniel fished out his recorder, shifted from the squat and sat cross-legged on the paving. He thought a moment, blew a tentative note or two, then began to improvise on one of the tunes the children had taught him. Several Matyssers stopped to listen and when he finished, snapped their fingers in approval and dropped coppers in the beggar's bowl.

He shook out the recorder, slid it back into its pocket, watched as the beggar emptied his bowl into a pouch tucked deep inside the collection of rags he had wrapped about his meager body. "New in town."

"A know it, an't heard that way with a pipe 'fore this. Wantin a pitch?"

"Buy it, fight for it, dice for it, what?"

A rusty chuckle. A pause while he blessed a Matysser who dropped a handful of coppers into the bowl. "Buy it, buy it, Him," a jerk of a bony thumb at the Citadel looming like white doom over them, "He don't like blood on the stones."

"Mmm. Got a hole in my pocket."

"There's one or two might be willing to rent a pitch for half the take."

"Too late for today. I'm thinking about belly and bed. Anyone round looking for a strong back and careful hands?"

"Hirin's finished with by noon."

Daniel sucked his teeth, wrinkled his nose. "Looks like my luck quit by noon." He thought a minute. "Any pawnshops around? I've got a couple of things I could pop in a pinch." He scratched at his stubble. "It's pinching."

"Grausha Kuronee in the Rakell Quarter. She an ugly old bitch," he cackled, "don't you tell her A said it. But she give you a fair deal." He coughed and spat into a small noisome jar he pulled from his pocket;

when he was finished, he recorked it and tucked it away. Daniel Akamarino had difficulty keeping his mouth from dropping open. Settsiwhatsisname had a strangle grip on this country for sure; he began to understand why the place was so clean. And why young Kori talked the way she did. "Tell you what," the beggar said, "play another couple of tunes. A'll split the coin and A'll whistle you up a brat oo'll run you over to Kuronee's place."

"Deal." He took out the recorder, got himself settled and started on one of his liveliest airs.

Daniel Akamarino tossed the boy one of the handful of coppers he'd harvested, watched him run off, then turned to examine the shop. It was a dingy, narrow place, no window, its door set deep into the wall with an ancient sign creaking on a pole jutting out over the recess. The paint was worn off the weathered rectangle except for a few scales of sunfaded color, but the design was carved into the wood and could be traced with a little effort. A bag net with three fish. He patted a few of his pockets, frowned and wandered away.

A few streets on he came to a small greenspace swarming with children. He wandered between the games and appropriated a back corner beside a young willow. After slipping out of his vest, he sat and began exploring the zippered pockets. The vest was made from the skin of Heverdee Nightcrawlers, the more that leather was handled, the better it looked and the longer it lasted; on top of that, it was a matter of pride to those who wore such vests never to get them cleaned, so Daniel hadn't had much incentive to dump his pockets except when he tried to find something he needed and had to fumble for it through other things that had no discernible reason for being in that pocket. He found a lot of lint and small odd objects that had no trade value but slowed his search. He sat turning them over in his fingers and smiling at the memories they evoked. It wasn't an impressive collection, but he came up with two possibilities. A hexagonal medal, soft gold, a monster stamped into one side, a squiggle that might have been writing on the other. He frowned at it for several moments before he set it aside; he couldn't remember where he'd picked it up and that bothered him. A ring with a starstone in it, heavy, silver, he'd worn it on his thumb a while when he was living on Abalone and thumbrings were a part of fitting in; since he didn't really like things on his hands, he slipped it into a pocket the day he left and forgot about it until now. He put everything back but the lint and dug that into the soil under the willow roots, then leaned against the limber trunk and sat watching the children running and shouting, swinging on knotted ropes tied to a tall post-and-lintel frame, climbing over a confection of tilted poles, crossbars and nets, playing ring games and rope games and ball games, the sort of games that seemed somehow universal, he'd met them before cross species (adapted for varying numbers and sorts of limbs), cross cultures (varying degrees of competition and cooperation in the mix), ten thousand light-years apart. He smiled at them, thought about playing a little music for himself, but no, he was too comfortable as he was. The day was warm, the Owlyn Valers had fed him well at noon so he wasn't hungry yet, he had a few coppers in his pocket and the possibility of getting more and he felt like relaxing and letting time blow past without counting the minutes.

When the sun dropped low enough to sit on the wall and the children cleared away, heading for home and supper, Daniel Akamarino got to his feet, shook himself into an approximation of alertness and went strolling back to Kuronee's Place. He spent the next half hour haggling over the ring and the medal, enjoying the process as much as the old woman did; by the time he concluded the deal he was grinning at her and had seduced the ghost of a twinkle from eyes like ancient fried eggs; he got from her the name of a tavern whose host had a reputation for knocking thieves in the head and not caring all that much if he knocked the brains right out. He rented a cubbyhole with a lock on it and a bed that had seen hard usage. Not all that clean, but better than he'd expected for the price. He ate a supper of fish stew and crusty bread, washed it down with thick dark homebrew, then went out to watch the night come over the water.

The evening was mild, the air lazy and filled with dark rich smells, one more day's end in a mellow slightly overripe season. Mara's Dowry his folk called this last spurt of warmth before winter. Season of golden melancholy. *I wonder what they call it here and why.* He sat on an oaken bit watching the tide come in, his pleasant tristesse an elegant last course to the plain good meal warming his belly. A three-quarter moon rose, a large bite out of the upper right quadrant. The Wounded Moon, that's what they called it. He watched it drift through horsetail clouds and wondered what its stories were. *Who shot the moon and why? Who was so hungry he swallowed that huge bite?*

Something glittered in the dark water out beyond the ships. Dolphins leaping? A school of flying fish? Not flying fish. No. He got slowly to his feet and stood staring. A woman swam out there. A woman thirty meters long with white glass fingers and a fish's tail. Shimmering, translucent, eerily beautiful, throbbing with power.

"Sweet thing." The voice was husky, caressing. Daniel Akamarino turned. A dumpy figure stood beside him, a wineskin tucked under one arm; at first, because of the bald head with a fringe of flyaway black hair and the ugly-puppy face, he thought it was a little fat man, then he saw the large but shapely breasts bursting from the worn black shirt, the mischievous grin, the sun colored eyes that danced with laughter. "Godalau," the ambiguous person said, "bless her saucy tail." Heesh poured a dollop of wine into the bay, handed the skin to Daniel who did the same. Laughter like falling water drifted back to them. With a flirt of her applauded tail, the Godalau submerged and was gone. When Daniel looked round again, the odd little creature had melted into the night like the Godalau had into the sea, the only evidence heesh had ever been there was the wineskin Dan still held.

He settled back on the bit, squirted himself a mouthful of the tart white wine. Good wine, a little dryer than he usually liked, but liquid sunshine nonetheless. He drank some more. Gift of the gods. He chortled at the thought. Potent white wine. He drank again. Sorcerers as social engineers. Giant mermaids swimming in the surf. Hermaphroditic demigods popping from the dark. I'm drunk, he thought and drank again and grinned at a glitter out beyond the bay. And I'll be drunker soon. Why not.

The Wounded Moon slid past zenith, a fog stirred over the waters and the breeze turned chill. Daniel Akamarino shivered, fumbled the stopper back in the nozzle and slung the skin over his shoulder. He stood a moment looking out over the water, gave a two fingered salute to whatever gods were hanging about, then started strolling for the tavern where his room was.

The fog thickened rapidly as he moved into the crooked lanes that ran uphill from the wharves. He fought to throw off the wine. Damn fool, you going to spend the night in a doorway if you don't watch it. He leaned against a wall a minute, the stone was wet and slimy under his hand and heavy cold drops of condensed fog dropped from the eaves onto his head and shoulders. He did a little deep breathing, thumped his head, started on.

A few turns more, as he left the warehouses and reached the taverns clustered like seadrift about them, the lanes widened a little; the fog there separated into clumps and walking was easier. He turned a corner, stopped.

A girl was struggling with two men. They were laughing, drunkenly amorous. The taller had a hand twisted in her hair while he held one of her writhing arms, the other was pushing his short burly body against her, crushing her against the wall while he fumbled at her clothing. Daniel sucked at his teeth a moment, then ran silently forward. A swift hard slap to the head of the skinny man—he squeaked and folded down. A kick to the tail of the squat man—he wheeled and roared; bullet head lowered, he charged at Daniel. Daniel danced aside and with a quick hop slapped the flat of his foot against the man's buttocks and shoved, driving him into a sprawl face down on the fog-damped paving stones.

The girl caught at Daniel Akamarino's arm. "Come."

He looked down, smiled. "Kori." He let her pull him into a side lane, ran with her around half a dozen corners, until they left the shouts and cursing far behind. He slowed to a walk, waited until she was walking beside him. "Blessed young idiot." He scowled at her. "What do you think you're doing down here this time of night?"

"I have to meet someone." She tilted her head, gave him a quick smile. "Not you, Daniel. Someone else."

"Mmf. Couldn't you find a better time and place to meet your boyfriend, whatever?"

"Hah!" The sound dripped scorn. "No such thing. When the day comes, I'll marry someone in Owlyn. This is something else. I don't want to talk about it here."

"Mysteries, eh?"

"Come with me. Tré says you're mixed up in this some way, that you're here because of it. You might as well know what's happening and why."

"Tell you this, Kori, you're not going anywhere without me. I still think you should go back to your folks and wait till daylight to meet your friend."

"I can't."

"Hmm. Let's go then."

The Blue Seamaid was near the end of the watersection, a rambling structure sitting like a loosely coiled worm atop a small hill. This late, it was mostly dark, though a torch smoldered in its cage over the taproom door, a spot of dim red in a patch of thicker fog. Daniel

Akamarino dropped his hand on Kori's shoulder. "Wait out here," he whispered.

"No." Her voice was soft but fierce. "It's not safe."

"You weren't worried about that before. Look, I'm not going to take you in there."

"It's not drunks I'm worried about, it's HIM."

"Oh." He thought about that a moment. "Political?"

"What?"

"Hmm." He stepped away from her and scanned her. "What's that you're wearing?"

"I couldn't come dressed in my Owlyn clothes." Indignation roughened her voice. "I borrowed this off one of the maids in the hostel." A quick grin. "She doesn't know it."

"Kuh," disgust in his voice, "after that mauling you got, you look like you're an underage whore. I'm not sure I like being a dirty old man with a taste for veal." When she giggled, he tapped her nose with a forefinger. "Enough from you, snip. Tell me the rules around here. The tavernkeepers let men take streetgirls into their rooms?"

"How should I know that? I've seen men taking girls in there, what they did with them . . ." She shrugged.

In the fireplace at the far end of the long room fingerlength tongues of flame licked lazily at a few sticks of wood; three lamps hung along a ceiling beam, their wicks turned low. There were men at several of the scattered tables, talking in mutters; they looked up briefly and away again as Daniel led Kori through the murk to a table in the darkest corner. A slatternly girl not much older than Kori came across to them. Her face was made up garishly, but the cosmetics were cracking and smeared and under the paint she was sullen and weary. Daniel ordered two mugs of homebrew, dug out three of his hoard of coppers. The girl scooped them into a pocket of her stained apron and went off with a dragging step.

"So. Where's this friend of yours?"

"Probably asleep. Tré says she's here, but I'm a day earlier than I arranged. I thought I could ask someone where her room was." She considered a minute. "Maybe you better do the talking. Ask about a white-haired woman with two children."

"You know her name?"

"Yes, but I don't know if she's using it."

"Hmm. I see. Kori. . . ."

"No. Don't talk about it, not now."

The serving girl shambled back with two mugs of dark ale, plunked them down. Daniel dug out another copper. "You've got a woman staying here, white hair, two kids."

More sullen than ever, she looked from him to Kori. Her mouth dragged down into an ugly sneer.

Daniel set the coin on the table. "Take it or leave it."

Without a change of expression, she brushed the coin off the table. "On the right going up, first room, head of the stairs."

Shock and sadness in her eyes, Kori watched the girl drag off. "She . . ." Her hands groped for answers that weren't there. "Daniel . . ."

He frowned; she was a child, sheltered, innocent, but truth was truth however unpalatable. "You've never seen a convenience close up before?"

"Convee . . ."

His hand clamped on her arm. "Quietly," he whispered. "This isn't your ground, Kori, you play by local rules."

"Convenience?"

"She's for hire like the rooms here. What did you think?"

"Any of those men . . ."

"Any of them, or all." He smiled at her. "I thought you were being a little glib back there, talking about whores and what they did."

"It's not like Ruba."

"Who's Ruba?" He kept his voice low and soothing, trying to ease away the sick horror in her eyes. "Tell me about her."

Kori laced her fingers together and rubbed one thumb over the other. "Ruba, our whore. She's a Phrasi woman. She came to Owlyn, oh before I was born. Some of the men built her a house. It's away from the other houses and it's a little like the Priest House. She lives there by herself. The men visit her. The women don't like her much, but they don't make her miserable or anything. They even talk to her sometimes. They let her help with the sugaring. Things like that. The only bad thing is they won't let her keep her babies. They take them away from her. I've watched her since before I was old enough for the Lot. She's happy, Daniel, she really is. She's not like that girl."

"How old is she?"

"I don't know. Thirty-five, forty, something like that."

"That's part of the difference, another part's how your people treat her. Forget the girl. There are hundreds like her, Kori. There's nothing you can do for her except hope she survives like Ruba did. It's better than being on the street. She won't get hurt here. Well, not crippled or killed. And she'll most likely have enough to eat."

"The look on her eyes." Kori shivered, tried a sip at the ale, wrinkled her nose and pushed it away. "This is awful stuff." She watched Daniel drink, waited impatiently till he lowered his mug. "Where you come from, Daniel, are there girls like that?"

"I wish I could say no. We've got laws against it and we punish folk who break those laws. When we catch them. But there's always someone willing to take a chance when they want something they're not supposed to have."

"What do you do to the ones you catch?"

"We've got uh machines and uh medicines and mmf I suppose you'd call them sorcerers who change their heads so they won't do it again." He took a long pull at the ale, wiped his mouth. "We'd better go wake up your friend, you have to get those clothes back to the maid before she crawls out of bed." He stood, held out his hand. When she was on her feet, he looked her over again. "It would be a kind thing if you left the girl a silver or two, you've pretty well ruined her going home clothes."

She closed her mouth tight and flounced away, heading for the stairs. He grinned and ambled along behind her.

Suddenly uncertain, she tapped at the door, not half loud enough to wake anyone sleeping. She started to tap again, but it swung open before her knuckles reached the panel. A young boy stood in the narrow dark rectangle between door and jamb, fair and frail with odd shimmery eyes.

"Brann," Kori murmured. She reached under her hair and pulled a thong over her head, held it out, a triangle of bronze swinging at the bottom of the loop. "I'm the one who sent for her."

The door opened wider. A dark form appeared behind the boy. "Come." A woman's voice, a rough warm contralto.

"Show me," Kori whispered. "First, show me the other half."

Snatch of laughter. A hand came out of the dark, a triangle of bronze resting on the palm. Kori snatched the bronze bit, examined it, turned it over, ran her thumb along the edge, then dropped both parts of the medal into her blouse. "If you'll move back, please?" she said to the boy.

He frowned. "Him?"

"He's in it."

"Jay, let her in. Ahzurdan is fidgeting about the wards."

With a small angry sound, the boy moved aside.

Daniel followed Kori inside. A lanky blond girlchild was setting an old lamp on the shelf at the head of a lumpy tottery bed. Just lit, the lamp's chimney was clouded, a smear of carbon blacked the bottom curve. The shutters were closed and the smell of rancid lamp oil and ancient sweat was strong in the crowded room. A tallish woman with short curly white hair backed up to give them space, lowered herself on the end of the bed. The boy Jay dropped on the crumpled quilt beside her; the girl who was obviously his sister settled herself beside him. Arms crossed, a tall man in a long black robe leaned against the wall and scowled at everyone impartially. His eyes met Daniel's. Instant hate, instantly reciprocated. Daniel Akamarino the easygoing slide-away-from-a-fight man stared at the other and wanted to kick his face in, wanted to beat the other into bloody meat. The woman Kori had called Brann smiled. "As you can see, the amenities are limited. Sit or stand as you please. There's a chair, I don't trust the left hind leg, so be careful." When Kori started to speak, she held up her hand. "Stay quiet for a moment. Ahzurdan, the wards."

Ahzurdan dragged his eyes off Daniel Akamarino, nodded. His hands moved in formal, carefully controlled patterns; his lips mouthed silent rhythmic words. "In place and renewed," he murmured a moment later.

"Interference?"

"Not that I can taste. I can't be sure, you know. This is his heart place and he's strong, Brann. A hundred times stronger than when I was with him."

"HE has a talisman," Kori said. "A stone he wears round his neck."

Ahzurdan took a step toward her. "Which one? Which talisman?"

"I don't know. Do they have names?"

"Do they . . ." He straightened, closed his eyes. "Yes, child, they have names and it's very very important to know the name of the talisman he has."

"I'll ask Tré if he can find out. The Chained God might be able to tell him. He's given us other things like Daniel here being involved somehow in what's going to happen. Aren't you awake now because you got a notion I was coming a day early?"

Brann turned her head. "Ahzurdan?"

"There was a warning. I told you." His dark blue eyes slid around to

Daniel, slid away again. "Nothing about him." His voice was low and dragged as if he didn't want to say the words.

"I see. Young woman, your name is Kori Piyolss?" When Kori nodded Brann turned to Daniel. "And you?"

"Daniel Akamarino, one time of Rainbow's End."

"And where's that?"

"From here? I haven't a notion."

"Hmm. Daniel Akamarino. Danny Blue?"

"I've been called that." He gave her one of his second-best grins. "I've been called worse."

"This isn't going to hurt you," she said. He raised his brows. "I need to know," she said. "When that bronze bit came to me, it brought two tigermen with it who killed the messenger and tried damn hard to kill me." Kori gasped, leaned against Daniel, clutching his arm so hard he could feel her nails digging into him. "Sorry, child, but you'd best know what kind of fight you're in. Where was I? Yes, I have to know more about the two of you before we get into it about our mutual friend you know who. Yaril, Jaril, screen them."

The two children were abruptly spherical gold shimmers. Warily, Daniel began to slide toward the door; before he moved more than a step, one of the shimmers darted at him and merged with him. A ticklish heat rambled about inside him, then focused in his head. A few breaths later, the shimmer whipped away again and was a young boy sitting on the bed, his sister beside him.

"Jay?"

"Daniel Akamarino is like us, fetched here from another reality, he doesn't know how or why. It's a reality more like ours, no magic in it, no gods, their ships don't sail on water but through the nothingness between suns." The boy chuckled suddenly, reached out and stroked Brann's arm. "He's a sailing man, Bramble, not a captain I'm afraid, but he's been just about everything else on those ships."

Brann shook her head. "Idiot. Yaro?"

"It's pretty much what you thought, Bramble. The girl is being driven by the Chained God who wants something from you. This Tré she's talking about, he's her brother, seven years old and not likely to live till eight unless something is done. When one priest dies, the god himself chooses the next and makes his choice known through fancy and extremely public Signs. A little over two months ago, You-know-who's soldiers tied Owlyn Vale's priest of the Chained God to a stake set in the threshing floor and lit a fire under his feet and a few days after that the god told Tré he was it next." Yaril lifted a hand, let it fall. "Not a profession with a great future."

Kori sighed and went to sit in the mispraised chair.

"Tré's got maybe a week before the Signs start."

Daniel Akamarino thought, uh huh, that explains what was bothering the boy. Kuh! Burnt to death. Me, I wouldn't be worried, I'd be paralyzed. Gods, hah, gods tromping around interfering with ordinary people. Magic that's more than self-delusion. Wouldn't 've believed it a few hours back. Which reminds me. "I met one of your gods, demigods whatever tonight. Two of them, actually. A ship-size mermaid and a little bald shemale with good taste in wine." He slid the carry-strap of the wineskin off his shoulder. "Heesh left this with me. Care for a drink?"

"Tungjii and the Godalau!" Brann sighed. "Old Tungjii Luck sticking hisser thumbs in my life."

"That's what heesh called her. Godalau." He squeezed wine into his mouth, held out the skin. "Tungjii, you said. Luck?"

She drank, passed the skin to the changechildren. "Point of view, my friend. Tungjii touches you, things happen. 'S up to you to make it good or bad." She hitched round to face Kori. "Chained God tell you where I was, or did you ask downstairs?"

"Daniel asked the girl."

"Hmm. Our mutual friend has Noses watching the place. Dan," amusement danced in her eyes as she swung back so she could see both Kori and Daniel Akamarino, "our own Danny Blue, he tells me he saw two with message birds in the taproom last time he went down. So Him, by now he knows you've got to me. Something to think about. Eh?"

Daniel Akamarino rested his shoulders against the wall, crossed his arms; he wasn't looking at Ahzurdan so he didn't know how closely his stance mimicked the other man, though he could feel the powerful current of emotion flowing between them; the sorcerer with a version of his name didn't look like him, so it wasn't a matter of physical double in a different reality, but there was some sort of affinity between them; no, affinity wasn't quite the right word, it felt more like they were two north poles of a bipolar magnet, each vigorously, automatically repelled by the other. He cleared his throat. "If I were mm whatsisname, I wouldn't fool with spies, I'd send a squad of soldiers and grab us all. Three adults, three kids, it's not much of a fighting force."

Brann smiled. "He knows better, Sailor. Ahzurdan here could whiff out a dozen soldiers without raising a sweat. Yaril and Jaril, they'd crisp another dozen and me, I'm Drinker of Souls. We're wasting time; Kori, you've got to get back to your folks before they find out you're gone. So. I've answered your summons and got whatsisname," a quick smile at Daniel, "on my back for it. What am I supposed to do about him and if it's not him, what?"

"Drinker of Souls."

"Not that simple, child. Yes, I'll call you child and you'll be polite about it. I would have to touch him and there's no way in this world he'd let me get that close." She frowned. "Is that your plan? You said you had one."

" 'S not MY plan exactly. Chained God told Tré what you should do is get to him and get the Chains off him, then he'll go with you to get the talisman from HIM and that means Amortis won't do what HE says any more and we won't have to listen to the Servants of Amortis and if they try to set soldiers on us in the Vales, we'll beat them back down to the Plains. And Tré won't get burnt."

"That's the plan?"

Kori looked at her hands. "Yes."

Brann shook her head in disbelief. "Miserable meeching mindless gods. How the hell am I supposed to take chains off a god if he can't do it himself, how do I even get to him?"

Eyes on her laced fingers, Kori shook her head. 'I don't know. All I know is what Tré said. He said there's a way to reach the Chained God. He said the god wouldn't tell him exactly what it is. He said the god didn't want HIM to know it. He said you've got to go to Isspyrivo Mountain. He said once you're there, the Chained God will get you to him somehow."

"Isspyrivo. Where's that?"

"You'll do it? You'll really do it?"

"If you think that needs answering, you haven't been listening. Now. Where is that idiot mountain?"

"On the end of the Forkker Vale Finger, you can see it from Haven Cove, at least that's what um folks say when they think the kids aren't listening. Haven's a smuggler's town; it's not something they want us to know about; we do, of course. The men get drunk sometimes at festivals and they tell all kinds of stories about sea smugglers and land smugglers; one of them was about the time Isspyrivo blew and caught Henry the Hook on the head with some hot rock. It's a fire mountain.

They say it's restless, they say it doesn't like folk climbing around on it; they say it kills them, opens up under them and swallows them."

"Hmm. Let me think a minute."

Daniel Akamarino leaned against the wall watching her. Drinker of Souls. Hmm. I think I pass on this one. It's an interesting world; if I'm stuck here, I'm stuck, no point in getting myself killed which seems likely enough if I hang with this bunch. He slid along the wall, closed his hand about the doorlatch. "Been fun, folks," he said aloud. "See you round, maybe."

Brann looked up. "No, Ahzurdan, I'll handle this. Daniel Akamarino, if you leave, you walk into our enemy's hands; you're a dead man but not before he finds out everything you know. I don't want to do it, but if you insist on leaving us, I'll have to stop you and let the children strip your mind."

"Nothing I can do about that?"

"Not much."

He scowled at Ahzurdan. "He'd enjoy frying me, wouldn't he?"

"I couldn't say."

Hands behind him, he tried the latch; the hook wouldn't move, he applied more pressure, nothing happened. Across the room Ahzurdan was laughing at him soundlessly triumphant. Daniel ignored him and moved back to his leaning spot. "If I can't leave, what about Kori? How does she get back to the hostel?"

Brann nodded. "If she's going, it's about time she went. Jaril, take a look downstairs, see what's happening." The boy flipped into his shimmershape, dropped through the floor. "Yaril, scout the outside for us, see what's waiting out there." The girl flitted away through the ceiling. "Dan um this is going to get confusing, Ahzurdan, I want to get Kori to the hostel without your ex-teacher tracking her. Can you fog his mirror or something?"

"Or something. Talisman or not, I've learned enough from his attacks to blur his sight. He'll know I'm moving, he'll know the general direction, but he won't be able to see me or anyone with me. Earth elementals and ariels, I can handle those myself; if you and the children can remove the human watchers, we can get the girl back without him finding out who she is. The fog will be broad enough to cover the hostel and half the quarter around it, he can't be sure where I'm going, but he's not stupid, so he'll guess fairly accurately what's happening."

"Kori, you hear?"

"Yes." The word was a long sigh. She was pale, her eyes huge and frightened. Daniel watched her, understanding well enough what she was feeling now; she'd gone into this blithely enough, enjoying the excitement of her secret maneuvers; her brother's life rested on her skills, but that wasn't quite real to her. Settsimaksimin's power wasn't real to her. It was now. She was beginning to understand what might happen to her people because of her activities. No, it wasn't a game any longer.

Brann got to her feet, crossed to stand beside her; she touched her fingers to Kori's shoulder. "What do you want to do? You're welcome to stay here."

"I can't do that. If I'm gone, HE'll do something awful to my folk."

"Dan uh Ahzurdan?"

"These are his people, Brann; remember what I've told you about him, he's always been extravagantly possessive about things that are his. When we . . . his apprentices finally broke away, he took it as a kind of betrayal. He won't do anything to them unless he's driven to it. As long as there's no overt break, as long as he can strike at you, us, without involving them, he'll leave them alone. The girl's right. She has to go back."

"Soon as the children are back, then, we'll move. You'll come with us, Daniel Akamarino." She smiled. "I can almost hear your mind ticking along. Don't waste your time, my friend. We won't be too busy to keep track of you, don't you even think of slipping off. . . ."

Jaril whipped up through the floor, changed. "Taproom's cleared out except for a couple of drunks. Real drunks, I whizzed them and nearly picked up a secondhand buzz. I went outside and ran a few streets. Lot of men standing in doorways. I counted twenty before I came back, there's probably twice that."

Yaril dropped through the ceiling, fluttered into her girlshape. "He's not exaggerating. They're watching every street and path around this place, just about every bush. There's another ring beyond that, almost as tight and beyond that two more, not so tight. There are even some little cats out on the water zipping back and forth through the fog. Must be a couple of hundred men out there. The landwatchers aren't all that enthusiastic, standing around holding up walls, walking circles in the middle of the street, but seems to me that's because nothing is happening. Let them spot us and they'll turn as efficient as you want."

Brann frowned. "I didn't expect quite that many . . . we can forget about the boats and the first ring isn't a problem, we can get most of them before they realize we're out. Before He knows we're out. It's those next, what, you said three rings? They worry me. Did you scan the rooftops, Yaro?"

"Bramble! course I did. Some people were up there sleeping, there were several pairs of lovers intent on their own business, they wouldn't give a fistful of spit for anything happening on the street. I didn't see anyone alert enough to be a spy, but I won't guarantee I didn't miss someone." She hesitated, turned finally to Ahzurdan. "Would he do something like that? Use dozens of visible watchers to camouflage two or three maybe a few more of his best Noses, so we take the guards out and don't notice some sly rats sneaking after us?"

"He's a complicated man. I'd say it's likely."

Daniel Akamarino watched the working of this odd collection of talents and began to feel better about being involved in this web. They put aside their antagonisms and concentrated on getting the job done, once they'd defined what the job was they wanted to do. It wasn't a group that could or would stay together in ordinary circumstances, but nothing was ordinary about what was happening. Kori was obviously feeling a little out of it; she was fidgeting in her chair, making it creak and wiggle, not quite overtaxing the weak hind leg. He rubbed a thumb across one of his larger pockets, tracing the outlines of the rectangular solid snugged inside, a short range stunner; he eyed Brann a moment, then the children, then Ahzurdan, wondering if he could take them out and get away; his thumb smoothed over and over the stunner, no, impossible to tell what sort of metabolism the children had; they might eat the stunfield like candy. Besides, old Settsimaksimin had the ground covered out there. He liked the thought of that man operating on him about as much as he liked the idea of the children wiping his mind. When he brought Kori here he hadn't noticed the watchers, but that might have been the wine, he still wasn't all that sober, or it might have been worrying about young Kori and what she was up to; whatever, he wasn't about to argue with the children's assessment of the danger out there. Shapeshifters, shoo-ee, what a world. Contact telepaths, lord knew what else they were. He eased the zipper open, fished out the stunner. "Hey folks," he said, "listen a minute. I think I know the problem. Brann, you and the kids have to actually touch someone to take him out, right?" She nodded, a short sharp jerk of her head. "And there are too many watchers out there to get at one sweep, right? So, if you could put them to sleep for say an hour, ten, twenty at a blow, and do it from say roof height, them being on the ground with no one near them, that would erase the worst of your difficulties, wouldn't it?"

"It'd come close." She leaned toward him, focused all her attention on him, wide green eyes shining at him. "What have you got, Danny Blue?"

"Being a peaceful man with a habit of dropping into places that don't appreciate good intentions, I keep this with me." He held up the stunner. It didn't look like much, just a black box with rounded corners that fit comfortably in his hand, a slit in the front end covered with black glass, a slide with a shallow depression for his thumb in it that with a little pressure bared the triggering sensor.

Jaril sat straight, crystal eyes glittering. "Stunner?"

Daniel Akamarino raised his brows, then he remembered they, like him, were from somewhere else. "Right. Short range neural scrambler."

"See it?"

"Why not." A glance to make sure the thumbslide was firmly shut, then he tossed the stunner to the boy.

Jaril caught it, set it on the bed, switched to his energy form and sat over it for a few breaths like hen on an egg. He shifted, was a boy again. "It'll do. You letting Yaro and me use it?"

"You can handle it in the air?"

The boy grinned. "Ohhh yes."

"Feel free. Need any directions?"

"Nope. We read to the subatomic when we have to."

"Handy. That work on what they use here?"

"Magic?"

"I'm not all that comfortable with the concept."

"Better get comfortable, tisn't likely you'll go home any time soon."

"You?"

"Two centuries so far."

"Ananiles?"

"We never bothered with those. Natural span of the species is ninety centuries."

"Hmm."

"You finished?" Dry amusement in Brann's voice. "Good. We'll run out of night if we keep this chatter going. Kori, anything else you need to tell me?"

Kori looked up from hands pleating and repleating the heavy cloth of her long black skirt. "No. Not that I can think of."

"Jay, Yaro, from the little I understand of your chat with Daniel, it seems you can clear the way for us. How long will it take?"

The changechildren stared at each other for several minutes. Daniel Akamarino felt an itching in his head that rose to a peak and broke off abruptly as Jay broke eye contact with his sister. "We'll zigzag, trading off, each one take a ring while the other flies to the next. I think we better do at least half each ring, maybe a bit more. Yaro?"

"Time. You know how long it took me to check the full length of all four rings, maybe twenty minutes; this'll go a lot faster. I'd say, ten minutes at most to do the ring sweeps, then we'd better go over the streets along the way to the hostel, zapping everything both sides in case sneaks are ambushed inside the houses. Say another five minutes, it's not all that far from here."

Brann threaded her fingers through her hair, cupped her hand about the nape of her neck and scowled at the floor. Ahzurdan cleared his throat, but shut up as she waved her other hand at him. A waiting silence. Daniel rubbed his shoulders against the wall, yawned. She lifted her head. "Go, kids, get it done as fast as you can, we'll wait five minutes, then follow."

Ahzurdan at point spreading his confusion over half Silagamatys, the four of them moved at a trot through the stygian foggy tag-end of the night, past bodies crumpled in doorways and under trees, through a silence as profound as that in any city of the dead. Halfway to the hostel the children came back, horned owls with crystal eyes and human hands instead of talons. One of the owls swooped low over Daniel, hooted, dropped the stunner into his hands and slanted up to circle in wide loops over them. They swept past the hostel and Kori slipped away. Daniel Akamarino watched her vanish into the shrubbery and spent the next few minutes worrying about her; when the building continued dark and silent, no disturbance, he relaxed and stopped looking over his shoulder.

8

KORI PIYOLSS RUNS INTO A QUIET STORM IN THE SHAPE OF AUNTNURSE.

SCENE: Quiet shadowy halls, doorless cells
on both sides, snores, sighs, groans,
farts, whimpers, creak of beds, slide
of bodies on sheets, a melding of
sleepsounds into a general background hum, a sense of swimming in
life momentarily turned low.

After a last look at Daniel Akamarino, Kori slid into the shrubbery of
the Hostel garden, worked her way to the ancient wittli vine that was
her ladder in and out of the sleeping rooms on the second floor. She
tucked up the skirt, kicked off her sandals and tied them to her belt, set
her foot in the lowest crotch and began climbing. The shredded papery
bark coming to threads under her tight quick grip, the dustgray leaves
shedding their powder over her, the thinskinned purple berries that she
avoided when she could since they burst at a breath and left a stain it
took several scrubbings to get rid of, the highpitched groans of the
stalk, the secret insinuating whispers the leaves made as they rubbed
together, these never changed, year on year they never changed, since
the first year she came (filled with excitement and resentment) and
crept out to spend a secret hour wandering about the gardens. Year on
year, as she grew bolder, slipping slyly through the dangerous streets,
only a vague notion of the danger to give the adventure spice and edge,
they never changed, only she changed. Now there was no excitement,
no game, only a deep brooding anxiety that tied her insides into knots.

She reached out and pushed cautiously at the shutters to the small
window of the linenroom, lost a little of her tension as they moved
easily silently inward. One hand clamped around a creaking secondary

vine, she twisted her body about until head, shoulders and one arm were through the window, then she let go of the vine and waved her feet until she tumbled headfirst at the floor; she broke her fall with her hands, rolled over and got to her feet feeling a little dizzy, one wrist hurting because she'd hit the stone awkwardly. She untied the sandals, set them on a shelf, stripped off the maid's clothing, used the blouse to wipe her hands and feet, thinking ruefully about Daniel Akamarino's comment; it was true then and doubly true now, no one would wear those rags. She dug three silvers out of her pouch, the last she had left of the hoard from the cave, rolled them up in the clothing, telling herself she would have done it anyway, Daniel didn't have to stick his long nose in her business. She pulled her sleeping shift over her head, smoothed it down, eased the door open a crack and looked along the hall. Silence filled with sleeping noises. Shadows. She edged her head out, looked the other way. Silence. Shadows. She slipped through the crack, managed to close the door with no more than a tiny click as the latch dropped home, ran on her toes to the room at the west end where the maids slept. No time to be slow and careful; dawn had to be close and the maids rose with the sun; she flitted inside, put the rolled clothing where she'd got it, on the shelf behind a curtain, and sped out, her heart thudding in her throat as one of the girls muttered in her sleep and moved restlessly on her narrow bed.

Struggling to catch her breath, she slowed as soon as she was clear of the room and crept along past the doorless arches of the sleeping cubicles; her own cubicle where she slept alone was near the east end of the Great Refectory. She was exhausted, her arms and legs were heavy, as if the god's chains had been transferred to them, the old worn sandals dragged like lead at her fingers.

Sighing with relief, scraping her hand across her face, she turned through the arch.

And stopped, appalled.

AuntNurse sat on the bed, her face grave. "Sit down, Kori. There." She pointed at the end of the bed.

Kori looked at the sandals she carried. She bent, set them on the floor, straightening slowly. Head swimming she sat on the bed, as far as she could get from her aunt.

"Don't bother telling me you've just gone to the lavatory, Kori. I've been sitting here for nearly three hours."

Kori rubbed at the back of her right hand, bruises were beginning to purple there, fingermarks. She didn't know what to say, she couldn't tell anyone, even AuntNurse, about the Drinker of Souls and the rest of them, but she couldn't lie either, AuntNurse knew the minute she tried it. She chewed on her lip, said nothing.

"Are you a maid still?"

Kori looked up, startled. "What? Yes. Of course. It wasn't that."

"May I ask what it was?"

Twisting her hands together, moving her legs and feet restlessly, Kori struggled to decide what she should do. Ahzurdan's fog was still over this sector but it wouldn't be there much longer. "You mustn't say anything about it after," she whispered. "Not to me, not to anyone. Right now HE can't hear us, but that won't last. Tré's the next Priest. I've been trying to do something to keep him from being killed. Don't make me say what, it's better you don't know."

"I see. I beg your pardon, Kori. That is quite a heavy burden for your shoulders, why didn't you share it?"

Kori looked quickly at her, looked away. She didn't have an answer except that she'd always hated having things done for her; since she could toddle, she'd worked hard at learning what she was supposed to know so she could do for herself. And mostly, people were stupid, they said silly things that Kori knew were silly before she could read or write and she learned those skills when she was just a bit over three. They took so long to understand things that she got terribly impatient (though she soon learned not to show it); the other children, even many of the adults, didn't understand her jokes and her joys, when she played with words she got blank stares unless the result was some ghastly pun that even a mule wouldn't miss. Not AuntNurse, no one would ever call AuntNurse silly or stupid, but she was so stiff it was like she wouldn't let herself have fun. Without exactly understanding why, Kori knew that she couldn't say any of this, that all the reasons she might make up for doing what she wanted to and keeping Tré's trouble a secret, all those fine and specious justifications would crumble like tissuepaper under AuntNurse's cool penetrant gaze.

"I suppose I really don't need an answer." AuntNurse sighed. "Listen to me, Kori. You're brighter than most and that's always a problem. You're arrogant and you think more of your ability than is justified. There's so much you simply do not understand. I wonder if you'll ever be willing to learn? I know you, child, I was you once. If you want to live in Owlyn Vale, if you want to be content, you'll learn your limits and stay in them. It's discipline, Kori. There are parts of you that you'll have to forget; it will feel like you're cutting away live flesh, but you'll learn to find other ways of being happy. More than anything you need friends, Kori, women friends; you'll find them if you want to and if you work at it, you'll need them, Kori, you'll need them desperately as the years pass. I was planning to talk to you when we got back." She lifted a hand, touched her brow, let it drop back in her lap. "I'd still like to have that talk, Kori, but I'll let you come if you want, when you want. One last thing, do you have any idea what your life would be like if you had to leave us?"

Kori shivered, rubbed suddenly sweaty palms on the linen bunched over her thighs as she remembered the girl in the tavern. "Yes," she whispered, "I saw a girl. A con—convenience."

AuntNurse smiled, shook her head. "You terrify me, child. I am delighted you got back safe and rather surprised, if that's the kind of place you were visiting."

Kori chewed her lip some more, then she scootched along the bed until she could reach AuntNurse's hand. She took it, held it tight, shook her head, then gazed at AuntNurse, fear fluttering through her, sweat dripping into her eyes.

AuntNurse nodded, smoothed long cool fingers over Kori's bruised and sweaty hands. "I see. Unfortunately you face the Lot come the morning, so I can't let you sleep much longer than usual, Kori. You must eat, you'll need your strength." She got to her feet, freed her hand.

"If I can help, Kori, in any way, please let me." She touched Kori's cheek, left without looking back.

Kori sat for several minutes without moving; in some strange and frightening way she'd crossed a chasm and the bridge had vanished on her. It had nothing to do with Tré or Settsimaksimin and everything to do with AuntNurse. With . . . with . . . Polatéa, not AuntNurse. Never again AuntNurse. Shivering with more than the early morning chill, she crawled into bed and eventually managed to sleep.

9

SETTSIMAKSIMIN WATCHES IN HIS WORKROOM AND AT THE COURT OF LOTS IN THE GRAND YRON.

SCENE: 1. Settsimaksimin in his subterranean workroom, idly watching his mirror, Todichi Yahzi back by one wall, noting Maksim's comments, released for the moment from the onerous task of watching over the machinations of a number of very ambitious men.

2. Settsimaksimin on the highseat at the Court of Lots, in the Grand Yron. Picture an immense rectangular room, sixty meters on the long sides, twenty on the short, the ceiling fifty meters from the floor, utterly plain polished white marble walls with delicate traceries of gray and gold running through the white, a patterned pavement of colored marbles, ebony and gilt backless benches running two thirds the length of the long sides, two doors dressed in ebony and gilt in the short north wall, one at the west end, one at the east. At the short south wall (beneath Settsimaksimin but out

far enough so he can see it without
straining), a low ebony table with
a gilt bowl on it, a bowl filled
with what looked to be black eggs.
To his left, about ten meters away
along the west wall, near the end
of the long bench, another table
with another bowl, this one red,
the pile of black eggs in it is considerably smaller than that in the
gilt bowl. To his right, ten meters
away along the east wall, a third
table with a third bowl, this one
blue, its egg pile about the same
as that in the red one. A trumpet
blares, two lines of children
stream in, girls on the east, boys
on the west.

Settsimaksimin lounged in his chair, bare feet crossed at the ankles and
resting on a battered hassock, he sipped at a huge mug of bitter black
tea; he'd discarded all clothing but the sleeveless black overrobe and
the heavy gold chain with the dull red stone on it, the talisman
BinYAHtii (I take all); his gray-streaked plait was twisted atop his
head again and skewered there. The only evidence of his fatigue lay in
his eyes, they were red streaked and sunk deeper than usual in heavy
wrinkles and folds. He was watching the scenes skipping across the
face of the obsidian mirror: the waterfront (he scowled as he saw the
Godalau playing in the water and interfering old Tungjii ambling about
the wharves, stopping to talk to a ghostly stranger sitting on a bitt); the
tavern where Brann and her entourage were (a place mostly blank
because Ahzurdan had learned too much for Maksim's comfort from
the attack at Kukurul and had tightened and strengthened his wards
until there was no way Maksim could tease them apart or find a cranny
to squeeze a tendril through; though it was a major complication in his
drive to protect himself and his goals, he beamed proudly at the blank
spot, a father watching his favorite son show his strength); the Hostel
where the Owlyn Valers were settled in and presumably sleeping the
sleep of the just and innocent, even the one that plotted against him; a
sweep through the streets, flickering over the watchers he'd posted

about the tavern, swooping to check out assorted nocturnal ramblers
(he chanced on a thief laboring over the lock at the back of a jeweler's
shop, snatched him up and dumped him into the bay). Waterfront
again (the man with the blurred outlines was still sitting on the bitt
drinking from a wineskin and staring out over the water, singing to
himself and getting pleasantly drunk, wholly innocuous except for that
odd blurring; Maksim sat up and scowled at him, tried to get a clearer
image; there were peculiar resonances to the man and he didn't like
puzzles wandering about his city; he shrugged and let the mirror pass
on). Tavern again. He looked through the eyes of his surrogates in
there, but nothing was happening downstairs. Hostel again. Dark and
sleeping. Streets and those in them. Waterfront. Tavern. Hostel. "Now
what have we got here?"

Up on the second floor a small form eased out a window and started
down the vine that crawled over part of the wall near that window. A
girl it was, skirt tucked up, dropping from branch to branch faster than
most folk could negotiate a flight of stairs. He willed the mirror into
sharper focus on her, smiled as she reached the grass, put her sandals
on, shook out her skirt and smoothed down her flyaway hair. She
darted into the shrubbery, moving with assurance through the darkness. Maksim sat up, laughter rumbling round his big taut belly. "Little ferret." She reappeared in the street and began moving at a steady
pace toward the bay. "Aaahhh," he breathed, "it's you, YOU, I've got
to thank for this. Eh Todich, come see. There's my great enemy, a girl,
twelve maybe, a skinny little girl." She clung to shadow as much as she
could, but went forward resolutely, circling drunks and skipping away
from a man who grabbed at her, losing him after she fled into back
alleys and whipped around half a dozen corners; she didn't pause to
catch her breath but glanced around as she trotted on, oriented herself
and started once more toward the waterfront, a thin taut wire of a girl
seen and unseen, an image in a broken dream. "A girl, a girl, Tungjii's
tits, why does it have to be a girl? She's got more spine than half my
army, Todich; if she had a grain of talent and was a boy, ah what a
sorcerer she'd make. Danny Blue, my baby Dan, she'd eat you alive,
this little ferret. If she weren't a girl, if she had the talent. What's that
now?"

She whipped around another corner and slammed into two men. The
taller man grabbed her arm, swung her hard against the wall, while his
squat burly companion gaped blearily at her. The tall one laughed, said
something, wrapped his other hand in her hair and jerked her head up.

Ignoring her struggles, he looked over his shoulder at his friend, his rubbery face moving through a series of drunken grimaces.

The squat man flung himself at the girl, mashed her against the wall. He slobbered at her, began fumbling at the band of her skirt, using one shoulder to pin her other arm as she clawed at him.

"Drunks," Maksim growled, "filthy beasts." He watched her struggles and her fear and her fury with an uncomfortable mix of satisfaction, compassion and shame. "You're getting what you asked for, little ferret, you should have stayed where you belong." By forgetting who and what she was, by working against him who had done so much for the people of Cheonea and meant to do so much more, she'd brought her shaming on herself. He had not the slightest doubt it was she who'd sent for the Drinker of Souls, the boy who carried the message came from Owlyn, what was his name? Toma something or other, dead now, it didn't matter, though how she'd known of the Drinker and what she'd used to lever Brann into moving . . . well, he'd find out before too long. "I'll have you, Owlet, you face the Lot tomorrow, yes, I'll have you. . . ." He scowled at the mirror, moved his hands uneasily, twisted his mouth into a grimace of distaste. A child. A clever devious spirited child. Her strength was nothing against those men, her arms were like twigs. He could save her as easily as he took his next breath, snatch those beasts off her, send earth elementals to crush them. He watched and did nothing. You have to learn, little ferret, he told himself, learn your limitations so I don't have to punish you myself. He watched and shifted uneasily in his chair, his stomach churning. He rubbed at his chest under BinYAHtii as his heart thudded painfully.

The odd man from the waterfront came suddenly from the fog. He seemed to hesitate, then with a slap and two kicks disposed of the attackers. The girl put her hand on his arm, said something. "She knows him. Bloody Hells." He thumbed the mirror. "Sound you."

For several minutes the only sounds were the slap of their feet, the diminishing yells from the squat man who was quickly lost in the fog, the drip of that fog from the eaves. Then the man slowed and spoke to the girl. Maksim clicked his tongue with deep annoyance; like his form the man's words were blurred beyond deciphering.

". . . . . ."

"I have to meet someone." The child tilted her head and smiled up at the man. Flirting with him, Maksim grumbled to himself, hot with jealousy, little whore.

"Not you, Daniel. Someone else."   Daniel, Daniel, she does know
him, Forty Mortal Hells, who is he?

". . . . ."

*"Hah! No such thing. When the day comes I'll marry someone in
Owlyn. This is something else. I don't want to talk about it here."*

". . . . ."

*"Come with me. *** says you're mixed up in this some way, that
you're here because of it. You might as well know what's happening and
why."*

". . . . ."

"I can't."

". . . . . . ."

Maksim watched them hurry through the fog until they reached the
Blue Seamaid. He nodded to himself. I'm going to have to do something about you. Who are you? Owlyn Valer, yes. What's your name,
child? I'll know it come the morrow. Scoundrel time old Maksi, you
out-rascaled the Parastes, now a child is completing your corruption,
I've never interferred with the Lot before this, but I can't leave her
running around loose. You're going into the Yron training, my angry
young rebel, you're going to get that hot blood cooled. He listened to
one side of the argument outside the tavern, guessed most of the man's
objections, saw his final shrug. The child's got ten times your backbone, you fool. Why don't you pick her up and get her back where she
belongs? He considered doing that himself, it'd be easy enough; he put
off deciding (though such dithering was foreign to him) and followed
them inside.

". . . . ."

"Probably asleep. *** says she's here."   Why can't I hear that name?
That's the second time it's blurred out on me. Someone is interfering,
someone is working against me. He slapped his hand on the table,
calmed abruptly as his heart started bumping irregularly. He closed his
fingers about the talisman and squeezed until his body calmed and he
could listen again. *". . . room was. Maybe you better do the talking.
Ask about a white-haired woman with two children."*

". . . ."

"Yes, but I don't know if she's using it."

". . . ."

"No, don't talk about it, not now."

Maksim stopped listening. He stroked the talisman, closed his eyes and reached for her, intending to flip her back to the Hostel garden.

He couldn't get a grip on her. What should have been simple was somehow impossible. He could feel her, he could smell her, he could almost taste the salt sweat on her skin but he couldn't move her a hair one way or another. His eyes snapped open. "That man. That stinking scurvy scrannel scouring of a leprous dam. That canker, that viper, that concupiscent incontinent defiler of innocence, that eyesore, that offence to heaven and earth. . . ." He blasted out a long sigh that fogged the mirror for an instant until he glared it clear again. Rubbing at his chest, he went back to listening since he couldn't do anything else.

". . . come from, Daniel, are there girls like that?"

". . . . ."

"What do you do to the ones you catch."

". . . . ."

She closed her mouth tight and flounced away, heading for the stairs, irritated by whatever it was he said. Maksim gave her a thin angry smile. That's right, get away from him, girl. He's not for you. When she'd put some distance between her and the man (he was getting up to go after her), Maksim tried once more to catch hold of her, but he couldn't get a grip, she slid away as if she were greased. He sat fuming, breathing hard; he couldn't remember being so helpless since he was a boy in the pleasurehouse he'd stomped into the ground when he took Silagamatys and Cheonea from crazy old Noshios. His head ached and acid burned in his throat as he watched the girl and the man pass through Ahzurdan's wards and vanish into that blank he couldn't penetrate. He spent a few minutes probing at it again, if the man really was an energy sink, he ought to affect Ahzurdan's work too. Nothing. Not a waver in Baby Dan's weaving.

Maksim left the image tuned to the tavern and paced about the workroom muttering to himself, glancing occasionally at the mirror where nothing much was happening. He thought about sending his watchers to that room and taking them all, he thought about turning out the barracks, sending every man he had against them until they were drowned in dead men, unable to twitch a finger. Noooo, Forty Bloody Mortal Hells, Danny Blue had found some nerve, the woman of course, and Danny with nerve and resolution was by himself more than an army could handle. Amortis? He fingered BinYAHtii and was tempted but shook his head. Not here. Not in MY city. If he brought

Amortis down, Tungjii and the Godalau were likely to join the battle and that would level half of Silagamatys. They're in the plot on the Drinker's side, AND WARNING ME, otherwise why show themselves to that man, that MAAAANN. Who was he? What was he? Filthy whiskery caitiff wretch, looked like any drifting layabout, he'd seen a thousand of them rotting slowly into the soil they sprang from. Soil he sprang from? What soil was that? Pulled here from a different reality? Why? What reality?

He stopped pacing and stared at nothing for several minutes, then tapped the mirror off, he didn't need to see any more and he wanted his strength and total concentration for the next few hours' work. He swung round to Todichi Yahzi. "Todich, old friend, you'd best get back to your overseeing. Mmm. Report to me tomorrow after the Lot on the activities of the Council, I'd like your opinion on how well they're doing and what the weaknesses of the form are, your suggestions on how I can improve it. Don't let up on them, these next weeks are crucial, Todich. If I can get that council working, if I can craft something that will stand, no matter what the Parastes try. . . ." He sucked in a huge breath, exploded it out. "Ready, Todich? Now!"

After alerting the guardians of that sealed cube of a room (sealed against magic, not air; like everyone else, sorcerers had to breathe), Maksim toed up the brake levers on the wheels of his tiltchair and rolled it to the center of his largest pentacle. When he had it oriented the way he wanted, he heeled the levers down again, stood rubbing thoughtfully at his chest and stared at nothing for a moment. With a grunt and a grimace he crossed to a wallchest, filled a cordial glass with a thick bitter syrup and choked it down, washed the taste away with a gulp of brandy. For several breaths he stood with his head against the door of the cabinet, his hands grasping the edge of the shelf below it, his powerful massive arms stiff, supporting most of the weight of his upper body, trembling now and then. Finally, he sighed and pushed away from the wall. There was no time. No time. He brushed his hand across his face, felt the end of his plait tickle his fingers. He pulled the skewers out, shook his head, looked down at himself and smiled. Not the way to confront the visitor he expected to have.

He slipped out of the workrobe, tossed it onto the tiltchair and padded across the cold stone floor to the place where he kept spare clothing. He drew a simple white linen robe over his head, smoothed it down and with a flick of his fingertips banished the creases from its long folding. There were no ties or fastenings, the wide flat collar fell softly about the column of his neck, the front opening spread in a narrow vee, showing glimpses of the heavy gold chain and a segment of the pendant BinYAHtii. He drew his hand across his face, wiping away the signs of weariness and the few straggles of whisker, smoothed straying hairs into place, pulled the black workrobe about him and dug out his rowan staff; he'd made it nearly a century ago, when he was out of his apprenticeship a mere two years, tough ancient wood polished with much handling, inlaid with silver wire in the private symbols that he alone could read. He laid it across the arms of the tiltchair, then went for a broom standing in the corner. There were four smaller pentacles at irregular intervals about the large one, marked out with fine silver wire laid into the stone; stepping into the pentacle the chair faced, Maksim swept it very clean, ran the broom over it one last time, then tapped the circled star into glowing life with the end of his staff. He swept off the larger pentacle until he was satisfied, put the broom back in the corner and crossed the silver wire to stand beside the chair. His massive chest rose and fell in an exaggerated sigh, then he tapped this pentacle into life, settled himself on the cushions and laid his staff once more across the arms. Reaching down past it, he pumped the lever until the chair was laid out under him, his back at a thirty degree angle to the floor. He closed his hands about the staff, closed his eyes and began assembling his arsenal of chants and gestures.

Aboard the JIVA MARISH, this is what Ahzurdan said to Brann: Magic words, magic chants, magic gestures, oh Brann, these are part of the storyteller's trade, they've got nothing to do with what a sorcerer is or does. Look at me, I say: JIIH JAAH JAH and move my hands so and so, and lo, I give you a rosebud wet with morning dew. Yes, it's real, perfume and all. Yes, I merely transported it from a garden some way west of here where the sun's not shining yet, I didn't create it from nothing. I could teach you to mimic my voice, there's not that great a difference between our ranges, I could teach you to ape my gestures to perfection, and do you know what you'd have? Nothing.

A sorcerer works by will alone, or rather by will and word and gesture. The words and gestures are meaningless, developed by each student from his own private set of symbols, sounds and movements that evoke in him the particular mindstate and pattern of will he needs to perform specific acts of power. What you learn when you're an apprentice is how to find these things and how to control the results. Then you learn how to use them to impress the clients. Among ourselves, we know that none of the words and gestures belonging to one of us could be used by another, at least not to produce the same effect. There is no power inherent in any word or sequence of words, in any sound or sequence of sounds, in any gesture or sequence of gestures; they are only self-made keys to areas of the will.

Ah yes, I know, claimants to mystical power have roamed the world from the time the moon was whole to this very day selling books of such spells and chants and sacred dances and charms and potions and all that nonsense, making far more gold from talentless gullibles than they'd ever gain from their own gifts, there's always someone fool enough to want a shortcut to wealth and power, or even to a woman he has no chance of getting at, someone who'd never believe the truth, that everything a sorcerer does is won out of self by talent and arduous study and ferocious discipline. That's the truth, Brann, almost all the truth. I say almost, because there are the talismans. No one knows what they really are, only what they look like and how they might be used. There's Shaddalakh which is said to be something like a spotted sanddollar made of porcelain; there's Klukesharna which was melted off a meteor and cooled in the shape of a clumsy key; there's Frunzacoache which looks exactly like a leaf off a berryvine, but it never withers; there's BinYAHtii which looks like a rough circle of the darkest red sandstone; there's Churrikyoo which looks like a small glass frog, rather battered and chipped and filled with thready cracks. There are more, said to be an even dozen of them, but I don't know the rest. All of them mean power to their holder, you notice I don't say owner, it takes a strong will to wield them and not be destroyed, they're as dangerous as they are tempting. No, I don't have a talisman and I don't want one. I don't want power over other men, I simply want to be left alone so I can earn a living doing things I enjoy doing. There's intense satisfaction in using one's talents, Brann. (He looked startled, as if he hadn't connected his skills with her potting before this moment.) *Was it that way with you, making your um pots?*

Before Maksim began calling up consultants, he focused his will on the little he could make out of the man, two arms, two legs, a common sort of face, two blurs for eyes, a smear for a mouth and some sort of nose, a darkness about the lower face that looked like beard stubble, reddish brown skin, at least where the sun had touched him, though he showed a bit of paler skin when his shirt had moved aside, that time he slapped down the drunks attacking the girl. Looked bald on top, though that was more a guess than something Maksim saw clearly. He wore trousers and a shirt and a long sleeveless vest with many pockets that looked like they were sewn shut with heavy metallic thread, it didn't seem logical but he kept the impression, it was a detail and every detail helped. Sandals, not boots. Maksim smiled to himself, the odd man had risked his toes, kicking the fundament of that chunky drunk; for an instant he lost some of his rancor toward him. But that was very much beside the point, a distraction, so he put emotion and image aside and focused more intently on the man himself, assembling a schematic of him he could used to direct his search through his index of realities.

He triggered the flow and the images began flipping before his mind's eye. The world of the tigermen, hot steamy deeply unstable; the place (one couldn't call it a world in almost any sense of that word) where the ariels swam along currents of not-air swirling about not-suns; the tangle of roots and branches that filled the whole of a pocket reality where he'd plucked forth the Treeish and sent them after Brann, one immense plant with its attendant parasites and detachable branches; reality after reality, all different yet all the same in the power that thrummed through them, all these demon realities passed by without stopping, identified by the symbols he'd given them when he'd discovered them and explored their possibilities. A dance of shifting symbols, one flowing into the other, the whole dazzle a key to HIM; if an outsider could read them and follow their shifts he would know him to the marrow of his bones. That outsider would have to BE Settsimaksimin to read the symbols, and being him would not need to read them.

The demon worlds passed swiftly because they had no affinity with the pattern Maksim presented as key, but there were other realities he'd discovered, other realities he could reach into, one of them that busy place he'd snatched Todichi Yahzi from. Realities without magic in them, or at least without the kind of magic he could tap into, and therefore of no interest to him. Three of that sort of reality resonated with the oddman's pattern; he tagged these and went on searching the index until he reached the limits of his explorations. He hadn't sent his shamruz body searching for decades, it took too much energy, too much time, it was a luxury he couldn't afford when he already had more power sources and demon pits than he needed. When he had to acknowledge that his body and the energy it contained, out of which he worked, was slowly and inexorably failing. So he left off searching and did not bother exploring the non-magical realities since there was nothing for him there. More than that, unlike the demon realities, those were immense beyond even his ability to comprehend. Immense in size and immensely various in their parts. He was uncomfortable there, reduced to a mote of spectacular unimportance, which was hardly an inducement to spend what he could no longer replace unless he had a need no other sort of reality would or could fill, Todichi Yahzi being one example of such a need.

He entered the first of these universes, set his construct of the oddman before him and swooped between the stars following the guide on a twisty path that set his immaterial head spinning. He visited one world after another, watched folk going about their business, they looked very much like the peasants and shopkeepers and traders in Cheonea and sometimes he understood what they were doing, the goods they were selling but not often, mostly their deeds were as incomprehensible as their words; even though he knew what the words were supposed to mean, he didn't have the referents to make sense of what those folk found perfectly sensible. The guide construct was wobbling uncertainly with no evident goal, he wasn't learning anything and he felt himself tiring, so he withdrew, rested a moment, then visited the second of the realities. Here the guide construct waffled aimlessly about with even less direction than before. Angry and weary, Maksim broke off the search and tried the third.

This time the pull was galvanic; the construct whipped immediately to a world swimming in the light of a greenish sun; it hovered over a stretch of what looked like seamless dusty granite spread over an area twice the size of Silagamatys. There were the mosquitolike machines on one part of it; on another, one of the metal pods these folk drove somehow between worlds, a huge hole gaping in its side. A tall bony blond woman with a set angry face snapped out orders to a collection of four-armed reptilians using peculiar motorized assists to load crates and bundles on noisy carts that went by themselves up long latticed ramps and vanished inside the pod; now and then she muttered furious asides to the short man beside her.

"No, no, not that one, the numbers are on them, you can read, can't you?" Aside to her companion, "If that scroov shows his face round my ship again, I'll skin him an inch at a time and feed it to him broiled."

The bony little man scratched his three fingers through a spongy growth that covered most of his upper body; he blinked several times, shrugged and said nothing.

"Sssaah!" She darted to the loaders, cursed in half a dozen languages, waved her arms, made the workers reload the last cart. Still furious, she stalked back to where she'd been standing. "Danny Blue, you miserable druuj, I'll pull your Master's Rating this time, I swear I will, this is the last time you walk out on me or anyone else."

"Blue wants, Blue walks," the man murmured. "Done it before, 'll do 't again."

"Hah! Mouse, if you're so happy with him, you go help Sandy stow the cargo."

"I don't do boxes."

She glared at him, but throttled back the words that bulged in her throat, stalked off and spent the rest of the time Maksim watched inspecting the carts as they rolled past her and rushing over to the loaders to stop and reorder what they were doing.

Maksim opened his eyes, ran his tongue along his lips; for several moments he lay relaxed in the chair breathing slowly and steadily; he licked his lips again and managed a smile. "Danny Blue. An analog with you, Baby Dan? Odder and odder." He stroked long tapering fingers over the staff, knowing every bump and hollow and nailmark, taking comfort in that ancient familiarity. "If she was a shipmaster here, I'd say Danny Two was cargomaster and she's fussing about him going off and leaving her to do the stowing. Sounds like he makes a habit of it, disappearing on his obligations to go off and do what he wants. A pillar of milk pudding when it comes to providing support. Why him? Who'd be such a fool as to bring THAT MAN here? Forty Mortal Hells, what good is a twitchy cargomaster to the Drinker of Souls? Who's in this idiotic conspiracy?" A quick unhappy halfsmile, then he pushed himself up and levered the chair to vertical so it supported his back and head and his feet were planted firmly on the footboard. He was wearier than he'd expected to be and that worried him. The Lot's tomorrow, he thought, just as well. His stomach knotted, but he forced the misery away. Children die; children always die, they starved by the hundreds when the Parastes and their puppet king ran Cheonea, they died of filth and overwork, they died in the pleasurehouses and under the whips of those fine lords. What's the death of one child compared to the hundreds I've made healthier and happier? It was an old argument, he felt deeply that it was a true argument, but when he took the child who drew the gold lot to Deadfire Island, the child who was miserable at leaving his parents and excited about seeing the marvels of the Grand Yron in the holy city Havi Kudush deep in the heart of Phras, when he took that child and fed his life (or hers) to BinYAHtii, he found his rationalizations hard to remember.

He glanced at the wallcabinet, wondered if he should take another dram of the cordial, but he didn't want to break the pentacle and have to lose more energy reactivating it. Reluctantly he spread his hand over BinYAHtii and drew on it; it was restive and hard to control, but the disciplines of that control were engraved in his brain by now, in his blood and bone, so he dealt with the brief rebellion so quickly and effectively he hardly noticed what he was doing. When he was ready, he smoothed his hair again, straightened out his linen robe and the soft black overrobe, pulled BinYAHtii through the neck opening and set it flat against the snowy linen. He swung the staff around and held it vertical beside him, then he began to chant, letting his deepest notes ring out, the sound filling the chamber with echoes and resonances.

"IO IO DOSYNOS EYO IO IO STYGERAS MOIRO IO IO TI TILYMON PHATHO IO IO LELATAS EMO."

And as the echoes died he gestured with hand and staff in ways both erotic and obscene (which is one of the reasons he did most of his primal magic in private; a sorcerer in many ways is stuck with what his submind dredges up for him; powerful magics require powerful stimulants no matter how upsetting or ridiculous they might seem to onlookers.)

"PAREITHEE, OY YO ROSAPER ROSPALL. PAREITHEE EN-THA DA ROSPA."

He beat the end of the staff against the stone three times, the sound faint after the power of his reverberant basso. A misty column appeared in the smaller pentacle.

The mist thickened and solidified into a creature like a series of mistakes glued together. A cock's comb and mad rooster eyes, spiky gold feathers, a black sheep's face where the beak should be, narrow snaky shoulders and torso, spindly arms with lizard hands and lizard skin on them, male organs bulging in a downy pouch, huge heavy hips and knees that bent the wrong way, powerful in the wrongness, narrow two-toed feet with lethal black claws on the toes. Rosaper Rospall whined and panted and swayed in the small space allotted to him and fixed frantic evil eyes on Maksim.

Maksim let his voice roll (not so solemn and sonorous this time, he was fond of the deplorable little gossip), "Rosaper Rospall, I demand of you, tell me who among the gods are plotting and working against me."

Rospall's arms jerked with each of the words, his hands flew about with feeling gestures; he whimpered as he touched again and again the burning unseen wall about him. His blunt muzzle writhed in a way to confuse the eye and sicken the stomach, but he managed a few words. "No one works against you, chilo, no one no want no cant no can none works against you."

Maksim frowned. Rospall never lied, but his truths were strictly limited. He reworked his next question. "Tungjii and the Godalau are scheming against someone, perhaps several someones. Who is it? Who are they?"

"Juh juh juh, scheme dream stir the pot not not who but what."

"What's the what?"

"BinYAHt."

Maksim's eyes snapped wide, then he smiled and nodded. "I should have been expecting that. Amortis is in this?"

"Amortis disportis cavortis, BinYAHt's the hook in her, who cares, the fisherman dances to her tugging, hugging, happy sappy Amortis. No. No change for her no danger in her."

Maksim nodded, answering his own thoughts more than Rospall's words. "Who works with Tungjii and the Godalau, who set the hook in them and got their help?"

"In the wind, a whisper, Perran-a-Perran, lord of lords, piranha of piranhas, he consents, in the wind, a whisper, Jah'takash perverse, spitting snags and checks and worse your way, in the wind a clink of links, the Chained God blinks and blinds and minds the mix." Hooting laughter. "From the rest no nay or yea, they gossip and they play. And they wager who will win and when."

Maksim felt a tremble of weakness deep within, saw Rospall's bold black eyes get a feverish glow. Enough, he thought, I've got enough to think on now. He gathered himself, let his voice roll out, filled with power, never a tremble in it. "APHISTARTI, OY YO ROSAPER ROSPALL, APHISTARTI ENTHA DA ROSPA." And his hands moved again through their erotic dance.

The visitor's body shuddered, for a moment he seemed to fight his dismissal, then he broke into fragments and the fragments faded.

Maksim didn't move until the last wisps of the presence had vanished utterly, then he sighed, shuddered, lay back limp in the chair, eyes closed. For several minutes he lay there breathing deep and slow. Finally, as the need to sleep began to overwhelm him, he forced his eyes open, used the staff to lever himself out of the chair. He stood and stretched, yawned enormously, then flicked himself up to his bedroom for a few hours of the sleep he needed so badly.

Todichi Yahzi cooed protests as he hovered about watching Maksim dress himself for the Lot ceremony. "Sleep," he warbled, "anyone can see you are exhausted, Mwahan, you do not need to be there, you do not enjoy being there, why do you go?" He repeated this until Maksim snarled him into silence.

Later, as Maksim strode through the murmuring park toward the Yron, he regretted his harshness and made a mental note to apologize when he got back. Poor old Todich, he kept pecking and pecking at a place, but he couldn't know how sore that spot already was. One had to take responsibility for one's acts, one doesn't slide away and pretend that nothing's happening. He'd set that burden on himself in those wild first days when Cheonea teetered on the verge of a slide into chaos, when he knew he'd have to use BinYAHtii. The stone had to be fed when it was used or it fed itself from the user. Forty years he'd fed BinYAHtii, ten times a year, once a month. Forty years, once a month he'd walked this path and climbed to the high seat behind the austere stone railing and watched the children file in. Self-flagellation, reminding him not to forget why he was doing these things. If he allowed himself to be corrupted by wealth, power, by the infinite capacity in the human soul for self-justification, then these children were torn from their parents for nothing, then one of the three chosen died for nothing at all.

At his private entrance the waiting Servant opened the door for him and bowed him inside.

"Kori." Polatéa's voice broke into confused dreams suffused with sick anxiety.

Kori stirred, sat up, rubbed at grainy eyes. "What time . . ."

"Breakfast in five minutes; wash and dress, come down as soon as you can, I'll save some food for you." Polatéa brushed the straggles of hair out of Kori's eyes. "You can sleep some more, if you want, after the Lot."

"If I'm not chosen."

A long sigh. "If you're not chosen."

Tré looked her over. "Your skods are crooked."

Kori clicked her tongue, adjusted the covered cords that held her headcloth in place. She and Tré were together in the Hostel court, wait-

ing to be put in line. She used one end of the headcloth to rub at her eyes, not sure she could manage to keep on her feet till the Lot was over; she felt as if she were walking two feet under water that was sloshing about, threatening to knock her over. "I got everything done," she muttered, hiding her mouth behind the corner of the cloth. "It's started."

Tré stepped closer, nestled against her. "You think it'll make any difference, Kori? Do you think she's got a chance against HIM?"

"A chance? Yes. There's more than just her. Daniel's in. You didn't dream?"

"No."

Sinan blew the cow's horn and the lines began sorting themselves out, girls in one, boys in the other, eldest at the front. Tré gave her arm a last squeeze and drifted back to the end of his line, he was the youngest boy this year. She was two from the front of her line. Dessi Bacharikss was two months older, Lilla Farazilss a week and a half. Dessi's twin Sparran led the boys' line, he was a tall rather skinny boy with a wild imagination and a grin that was starting to make Kori's toes tingle. He looked around at her, winked, then straightened and sobered as the signalhorn hooted and the lines began to move.

Maksim watched the children file in, grave and rather frightened, their sandals squeaking on the polished marble. Ignoring the boys, he scanned the first few girls, smiled tightly as he saw Kori's red-eyed, weary face. He crossed his arms, his hands hidden in the wide black sleeves of his heavily embroidered and appliquéd formal overrobe, began the gestures and the internal chant that would bring the blue lot to Kori's searching fingers. His smile broadened a hair. There was no sign of the interference that had protected her last night.

Kori thrust her arm deep into the bowl; the capsules seemed oddly slippery this year, it was a breath or two before she could get hold of one and bring it out. She took a deep breath and moved on, hearing the capsules rattle behind her as Sallidi Xoshallarz reached for hers. She crossed to the gilt bowl, tried to ignore the feeling that HE was staring down at her ill-wishing her; it was easier to grab this time, she got her second egg and went to take her place on the girls' bench.

It is done. I have her, little ferret, ah what a fine fierce girl she is, tired now but she doesn't give in to it. Look how straight and bold she sits, waiting to see if fate will pass her by. Not this year, little ferret.

Your last year, isn't it. You shouldn't have got so busy with things you don't understand. We'll have to do something with you; not one of Amortis' whores, that would break you faster than marrying one of your clod-cousins and disappearing into the nursery with half your mind shut down; hmm, you could be trained to teach . . . With some difficulty he repressed the laughter rumbling in his belly. Not with what you're apt to teach my restive folk. Would you like to be a scholar, child? I wonder. I could send you east to study in Silili. Study what? Magic? Have you got a talent there? There's something in you that calls to me. Yes, you have a talent in you waiting to unfold, oh child, if you deny it, how terrible for you. I'll make you see it. Why weren't you born a boy? It would be so much easier if you were born a boy.

The black capsules grew sweaty in her hand; she changed hands and wiped the sweaty one surreptitiously on her overtunic. Over half done. Two capsules for every Owlyn child. Kori didn't feel like a child any more; she wanted this to be over with so she could get back to Owlyn and get her life in some sort of order again. Maybe because she was so tired, she wasn't much worried this time, not for herself anyway; so many important things had happened to her the past two months, she felt bone deep sure the Lot would pass over her, one more thing would be just too much. She watched the girls file past her going to take their places on the bench and wondered which of them would get the blue lot and be kept here in the Yron, then wondered which one would get the gold, would it be a boy or a girl this time? If I had a choice, she thought, I'd take the gold, how terribly exciting to go so far away. Havi Kudush. A wonderful magical name, it stirred desires in her she didn't want to deal with and had to keep pushing away. She gazed down at the enigmatic black eggs. The capsules each had a ball of lead inside them, most were simply gray, one was painted blue; the girl who got that one stayed at the Yron to study as a teacher or if her tastes and talents ran that way, to serve as one of the temple whores. Kori's mouth twitched. She fought her face straight and swallowed the smile. Polatéa would scold her for saying whore, but that's what they were, those that called themselves Fields of Amortis, *plowed and replowed those fields if the gossip she heard was true. Gahh, that was almost as bad as that girl in the tavern. One of the balls in the boys' bowl was painted red, the boy that got that one went to the army to learn a soldier's trade or into the Yron schools to study how to Serve. But the gold yolk, oh the gilt one, the child who got the gilt one went to Havi Kudush and did wonderful things, she was sure of it. Have a golden yolk, she thought at the black things in her hands, if you can't have the good old safe and steady leaden gray, have a golden yolk. She glanced quickly around, lowered her eyes again. I couldn't stand it if I had to stay here.*

Sarana Piyolss, the baby of the line walked past her. The drawing's over for this year, Kori thought. Now we find out who got the colors. Two doors opened beside the High Seat, two small processions filed down the narrow steps slanting from both sides of the high dais, first a Servant dressed in white linen, white leather sandals, short white gloves, then a boy and a girl, also dressed in white, carrying a wide shallow basket between them.

Deep silence in the court, a sense of almost intolerable waiting. One servant stopped before Sparran, the other before Dessi. Their movements slow and measured, as close to synchronized as a good marching team, they took the capsules from Sparran, from Dessi, opened them. Together both the Servants intoned NO and let capsules and lead balls fall into the basket. They moved to the next in line, repeated their movements, repeated the NO, then the Servant on the girls' side stood before Kori. His face impassive, he took the damp capsules before her, broke one. A plain lead ball rolled on the palm of the white glove; he broke the second capsule. A blue ball, nestled next to the gray.

Kori stared at it, unable to believe what she saw. She lifted her eyes. HE was looking at her. You, she thought, you did it to me on purpose. She opened her mouth, then clamped it shut. What could she prove? Nothing. She'd just bring trouble on her kin if she protested. She glared up at the huge dark man on the High Seat. I'll get out of this somehow, she thought fiercely, I will, you can't beat me so easy as that.

You aren't stupid are you, little ferret. Yes, it was me did that to you. I doubt you'll ever thank me for it, but you should. I hated old Grigoros when he sold me to the House, but he did me a favor. He smiled as Kori dropped her eyes to clenched hands when the Servant shouted BLUE; when he pushed it at her, she took the blue ball with angry reluctance, then sat staring at the floor, refusing to look at Maksim or anyone else until the RED and GOLD were announced. He saw her shoulders tremble; she turned her head, glared up at him again, but this time there was a triumph in her face and eyes that he didn't understand. What have I missed? There's more to you than I thought, warrior girl. What is it? I will know, child, in the end I will know. He got heavily to his feet and stood watching as the Servants led the chosen children (two boys and the girl) up the stairs to stand beside him. He could feel the heat of her anger, the intensity of the effort she was making to keep silent.

He lifted his hands. "It is done." His voice rolled out and filled the court. "Honor the chosen and their lives of service, honor yourselves for the grace of your compliance. For three days the city is yours, rejoice and be content."

He watched them file out. The youngest boy kept turning to look up at the chosen, anguish in his face; he stumbled against the boy ahead of him, but straightened himself without help and went stiffly out the door. Maksim glanced at the girl and saw an echo of that anguish in her face. Your brother, is it? Is that why the triumph, that he was passed over this year? I will know. But not now. He bowed his head in a stately salute to the children, but he didn't speak to them, merely made a sign for them to be taken away. He stood at the balustrade looking out over the empty court until the last sounds faded, rubbing absently at his chest. He had to be at Deadfire Island when the boy arrived, but that was a good six hours off and he wasn't sure how he wanted to pass those hours. He needed sleep. He had to listen to Todichi Yahzi report on the activities of the council he'd assembled and decide who he wanted to add or delete, what other changes he needed to make. He had to take a look at the blank spot and see if Baby Dan had moved himself and the others out of Silagamatys which would mean he could turn Amortis loose on them. He tapped long fingers on the marble, irritated by the hurry of all this, then snapped to his work-room to start with the easiest and most urgent of the things he had to do.

10

FIGHTING THEIR WAY TO THE CHAINED GOD: BRANN, YARIL, JARIL, AHZURDAN AND DANIEL AKAMARINO, WITH SOME HELP FROM TUNGJII AND THE GODALAU.

SCENE: Daniel Akamarino finds a ship for them, discomforting Ahzurdan who is locked into the room because he can't leave the wards without endangering himself and the rest of them. On the ship Skia Hetaira traveling between Silagamatys and Haven.

"Had a bit of luck." Daniel Akamarino squatted by the beggar, held out the wineskin. "Found me a patron."

"Aah." The old man squeezed a long stream of the straw gold wine into his toothless mouth, broke the flow without losing a drop. He wiped his mouth, handed the skin back. "An't swallowed drink like that sin' one night ol' Parast Tampopopea got drunk's a skink and busted six kegs in the Ti'ma Dor."

"Luck," Daniel said and smiled. He squirted himself a sip, chunked the stopper home. "Quiet day."

"Some. Lot day. Come afternoon, it'll perk up. You thinkin about a pitch?"

"Nuh-uh. Patron wants to sail tonight. She hates fuss, she wants to go out like a whisper."

"Aah." The old man's warty eyelids flickered, the tip of a pointed whitish tongue touched his upper lip, withdrew. "A like the way you play that pipe."

"I hear." Daniel slid the carrystrap of the wineskin over his shoulder, shifted out of his squat and brought out the recorder. He looked at it, thought a minute and began playing a slow rambling bluesy tune that made no demands but slid into the bone and after a while took over enough to bring crowds drifting around them. He ended it, raised a brow. The old man closed his eyes to slits and looked sleepy. Daniel laughed, played a lively jig, then put the recorder away. The small crowd snapped fingers enthusiastically, but Daniel was finished for the moment, at least until they paid something for their pleasure. He sat as stolid and sleepy as the old beggar. With a flurry of laughter, they tossed coins into the begging bowl and wandered off, some returning to their stalls, others drifting about looking for bargains.

The old man collected his coin, stowed it away. He blinked thoughtfully at the skin, ran his tongue around his teeth. "Real quiet, aah?" He scratched at the gray and white stubble on his wattles. "Wanna keepa neye lifted for sharks."

"Hard to know where the sharks are if you don't know the waters."

"Aaah. Eleias Laux's lookin for cargo, might go without if ta patron meetzis price. *Skia Hetaira,* thatzis boat." He took the wineskin and drank until he seemed about to drown, stopped the flow with the neatness he'd shown before. "Way down west end. Black boat, ketch, flag's a four point star, black on white. Lio, eez hived up at the Green Jug. Eatzis noon there." He glanced at the sun. " 'Bout this time a day, more often than not." He held out the skin. "Gi'm a stoup 'r two a this and eez like to sail ta patron to the Golden Isles, no charge."

Daniel Akamarino got to his feet, yawned and stretched. He smiled amiably at the old man. "G' day to you, friend," he said and strolled away.

"How'd you know he'd know?"

Daniel looked down, startled. Jaril was walking beside him, looking up at him with those enigmatic crystal eyes. "Been on a lot of worlds," he said. "There's always someone who knows, you just have to find him. Or her or it, whatever. That old man, he's got the best pitch in the Market which means he's got some kind of clout, I don't have to know what kind, just that it exists. There's this, he's no muscle man, must be shrewdness. Brains and information. Means he knows what's going on where."

"And now you're going to hunt out Eleias Laux?"

"Mmm, might."

"That's a funny wineskin."

"Funny how?"

"It's not all that big."

"Mmm."

"Should be near empty the way you been squeezing it. Isn't, is it?"

"Lot of funny things on this world. You might have noticed."

"We have noticed that. Some of it's been done to us." The boy grinned up at him. "How've you been feeling lately?"

"Herded."

"You're not alone."

"What I mean. Takes more than one to make a herd; company's no blessing, if it's just that."

"You right. Give me a drink?"

Daniel raised a brow. "You?"

"Did last night."

"Why not." He tossed the boy the skin, watched him drink, took it back and drank a draft himself. It was chilled, just the right temperature for the taste, a computerized cooler couldn't have done better. Tungjii Luck, magic wineskin, what a world.

They ambled through sunny deserted streets, past shops whose keepers were gone off somewhere leaving a clerk behind to watch the stock and doze in the warmth and quiet. Lot day seemed to mean waiting for Owlyn Valers to burst loose with their warrant to spend what they wanted, freely as they wanted; the bills would be paid from Settsimaksimin's pocket (which meant eventually from taxes and tariffs and fines). Jaril was silent and frowning, a small thundercloud of a boy.

"Can't really fight gods," he said suddenly, grave now, a touch of bitterness putting bite into his voice. "Either they squash you right out or they sneak up on you and cut your legs off and you bleed to death."

"Sneak up? That mean what I think it does?"

"Don't know. The talismans Ahzurdan was talking about can make them do things. A good sorcerer can block them out. Brann and us, we were mixed up in a fight between a clutch of witches and a god. She used Brann to get past their defenses. Complicated plot, took more than a year to set up, used maybe hundreds of people who didn't know they were in it. Even looking back I couldn't say who all was in it or how much what they did mattered in the blowup. You can't win even if you win, they keep coming back at you, get you in the end. Or you die and they get you then."

"You've got, what did you say? ninety centuries less a few."

"Doesn't matter, long as we're stuck here, the end's the same."

"Gives you time to work out a way to get home."

"Can't go home. You heard what they call Brann."

"Drinker of Souls. So?"

"You saw what we are, Yaril and me. Back home we drank from the sun. Slya, that's the god I was telling you about, she changed us, then she helped us change Brann so Brann could feed us. We live on life energy, Daniel Akamarino; if anything happened to Brann, we'd starve."

"Why tell me?"

"Because we're frightened, Yaril and me. Him in the tower there, he's strong, you don't know how strong. He hasn't exerted himself yet, not really, Yaril and me, we don't know why, but even with those offhand tries, he nearly killed Brann twice and the second time Ahzurdan was there and he stood like a stump doing nothing until Yaril singed his ear. We don't like him, we don't want him about, but Brann won't send him away. Even when he tells her she should, she won't. We don't know why, but we're afraid it's because the gods messing with us won't let her. You're affined to him, Daniel Akamarino, but you're a different sort of man." Jaril gave him a twisted smile. "You don't want to be in this, but you are. Yaril and me, we want you with us and ready to do something when Ahzurdan fails her."

"Which reminds me. Since you're in a talking mood, Jay, why am I let off the leash this morning when last night Brann wouldn't let me out of the room without Ahzurdan to babysit?"

They pressed up against a wall to let a heavily loaded mulecart clatter past heading uphill for the Market, then went round a corner and moved west along the busy waterfront road, dodging carts and carrypoles, vehemently gesturing traders, crowds of merchants with their clerks. The morning wasn't quiet here, it was deafening, hot, dusty, filled with a thousand smells, ten thousand noises. Daniel pulled Jaril into a doorway to let a line of porters trot past. "Well?"

"Lot day," Jaril said. "He's always there. In the Yron. When the Lots are taken. He can't overlook us without his mirror. He'll be away from it for maybe another hour. And I'm here." He giggled, amused at the thought. "I'm babysitting you."

"Mmf." Daniel left the doorway, sidled between two carts being loaded by men shouting jokes at each other, their overseers darting here and there, pushing shoving yelling orders that were obeyed when the men got around to it or ignored if they counted them silly. Runners not much older than Jaril seemed were darting about, carrying messages, small packages, orders, the shrill whistles that announced them adding to the crashing pounding noise that broke like surf against the walls of the warehouses. A few meters of this and Daniel sought an unoccupied doorway. "Jay, if you're going to haunt me, can you do it as something besides a boy?"

"Why? Plenty of boys like me about."

"I know. Just a feeling Laux will talk more without an extra pair of ears to take it in."

"Hmm. Why not. Dog be all right?"

Daniel chuckled. "Nice big dog?"

"All teeth and no tail."

The man and the big dog strolled the length of Water Street until they reached a quieter section and smaller boats, one of them a slim black ketch with a black and white flag hanging in silky folds that opened out a little whenever the fleeting breeze briefly strengthened. Hands clasped behind him, Daniel inspected the craft. "Wet and cold." The dog nudged his leg. "All right, I give you fast." The boy dozing on the deck lifted his head when he heard the voice, squinted up at Daniel. Daniel produced one of his everyday smiles. "Where's Laux?"

"Why?"

"Business. His."

The boy patted a yawn and gazed through the fringe of dirty blonde hair falling over his eyes. After a minute, he shrugged. "Green Jug. Be back here a couple hours if you wanna wait."

"Where's the Jug from here?"

"Back along a ways, there's the Kuma Kistris, the one with a double spiral on the flag, black and green, alley there between two godons, leads up Skanixis Hill, follow it, Jug's near halfway up."

Daniel found two coppers, tossed them to the boy, strolled away grinning. Jaril hound was already two moorings away doing an impatient doggy dance in front of a boat with a green and black flag.

"Eleias Laux?"

"Who wants to know?"

"Someone wanting passage out."

"Paying or working?"

"Paying. Five, two of 'em kids."

"Hmm. Sit." He was a little spider of a man, M'darjin with skin like aged walnut polished to a high shine, dressed in well-worn black trousers and tunic, a heavy silver earring with moss agate insets hanging from his left ear, linked plates that shivered with every breath he took, drawing the eye so that most people who met him never noticed his face and remembered only the flash of silver and the gleam of agate. The earring glittered wildly as he glanced at the hound, looked dubious, relaxed as Jaril settled placidly to the floor by Daniel's feet. He pushed his plate aside, emptied his winebowl and was about to call for more wine when Daniel slid the skin off his shoulder and offered it.

Laux pinched at his nose, looked from the skin to Daniel's face. "Be you insulted if I say you drink first?"

"I'm a cautious man myself, be you insulted if I want another bowl?"

Eleias Laux laughed and snapped his fingers for the serving girl.

When she brought the bowl, Daniel filled it halfway and sipped at the straw colored liquid, smiling with pleasure, taking time to do it justice. When the bowl was empty, he set it down, raised his brows.

Laux nodded, watched warily as the wine streamed out. He drank, widened his eyes, took another mouthful, let it trickle down his throat. "Now that is a thing." He grinned. "Not your best plan, friend. You just raised the price a notch."

Daniel shrugged. "Luck's meant to be shared. I was mooching about the wharves a few nights back, when it was foggy, you remember? saw the Godalau swimming out in the bay and this bald little shemale offered me a drink, left the skin with me."

"Tungjii Luck?"

"Couldn't say, but I've been drinking wine since and passing it around here and there and the skin's about the same as it was when I got it. I figure it's just old Tungjii sticking hisser thumbs in and why not enjoy it while it's here. Think you might be willing to slip out tonight, head round to Haven, no fuss?"

"How quiet?"

"Like a ghost's shadow."

"Might could. You walking round loose?"

"Far's I know. Hound here says so and he's good at nosing out nosy folk. You don't want to know more."

"True, true. Five gold each."

"Ahh now, have yourself some more wine and think on this, two silver each adult, one each for the kids."

"The wine I'll take, but don't you fool yourself; drunk or sober I'm not about to wreck myself for anyone. No discount for kids, they're worse than dryrot on a boat. But seeing you're a friendly type, I'll think on taking a bit of a loss. Three gold each. You bringing the hound here, another gold for him.

"No hound. What about this, five silver each, with a gold as bonus when you set us down on the shore of Haven Cove."

"Mmmmm." Laux drank and smiled, a friendlier sheen in his brown velvet eyes; if he had armed himself against the seduction in Tungjii's wine, his armor was leaking. "Ohhhh, I'm feeling so warm to you, my friend, I'll tell you what. Five silver each, a gold as bonus when you're on the fine black sand of Haven Cove, sweetly out of sight from Haven herself, and five gold as trouble quittance, to be refunded if trouble keeps away."

"Mmmm." Daniel filled the bowl pushed over to him, filled his own. "Five silver each, a gold as bonus when we're landed, five gold as trouble quittance, paid over the minute trouble shows."

"Now now . . . what do I call you? give me something."

"Daniel."

"Now Daniel, don't be a silly man. Trouble comes, nobody has time to count out cash."

"Point made, point taken. Five silver each, a gold as bonus, two gold as trouble quittance, to be refunded if no trouble shows; my patron guarantees the cost of any repairs."

"Ah, now that might be a good deal, saying your patron's the right sort. You willing to say who he is?"

"I won't be mentioning that she doesn't want her name spread around. I've heard you're a man of discretion and wisdom. She's called Drinker of Souls."

"Exalted company, hey, gods and demigods all round." Laux sat hunched over the winebowl, a long forefinger like a polished walnut twig stirring the plates of his ear dangle as he stared past Daniel at shadow forms he alone could see. He said nothing, but Daniel could read the argument going on inside, an argument he'd been in himself, never coming out with the same answer twice. Daniel waited without speaking for the struggle to end, fairly sure what the answer would be. Laux knew well enough he could be jumping into a maelstrom that could suck him under, but he was visibly bored with the mundane cargos he ferried in and out of Silagamatys and something deep and fundamental in him was tempted to try the danger, especially if he could be sure of coming out of it reasonably intact, his boat in the same condition.

"Mmh!" Laux straightened, shifted his focus to Daniel. "Yes. Tell you what, considering what's likely to be involved and how likely it is bystanders get chewed up and spat out when powers start to feuding, and this isn't trying to screw you, Daniel, just me taking care of me, how 'bout instead of your patron's giving me her word, she gives me two hundred gold surety to hold for her till the bunch of you put foot down on Haven Cove's black sand. No one in his right mind would try cheating the Drinker of Souls. The rest as before, five silvers each, a gold as bonus, four gold trouble quittance."

"Done." Daniel grasped the hand Laux extended, gave it a brisk shake, settled back in his chair. "How're the tides, can you leave around sunset today?"

"Tide'll be standing, my Hetty don't draw enough to worry about the sandbars at the bay's mouth. As long as the wind's good (give old Tungjii's belly a rub) we'll go."

They sat in silence a while, sipping at their wine, Laux leaning over his elbows, Daniel lounging in the chair, straightening up to fill the bowls whenever they showed bottom. There were a few other drinkers and diners scattered through the comfortable gloom inside the taproom, talking together in muted tones and generally minding their own business. "Waiting for the Lot to finish," Laux said. "Everything's waiting for that."

"Not Water Street, Laux."

"Call me Lio, yeah you right, they're not waiting, they're stocking up for the run. Leaves the rest of us neaped." He shoved out his bowl, watched the pale gold wine sing into it. "Cheonea's neaped these days." He sipped and sighed. "Sold my Gre'granser in the King's Market here when he was somewhere about six. He said you couldn't hear yourself think for a mile all round the port it was that busy. Most of it under the table, but that didn't seem to matter. My Granser's mum was a freewoman Gre'granser sweetered into the bushes, means he was born free. Him he was prenticed out on a merchanter when he made six. He took to the smuggling trade and trained his sons in that. Ahhh, it was a wild trade then and Haven was a wild town, it never stopped, you know, moonset was busy as sunset, ships coming in and going out, half a hundred gaming houses wide open, a Captain could win a fleet or lose everything down to the skin, man or woman make no matter. There was a woman or two had her ship and you didn't want to mess with them, Granser used to say, they didn't bide by rules, got you howsoever they could." He dipped his finger in the wine, drew a complicated symbol on the dark wood. "Never saw any of that myself. Him in the tower, he shut down the slave market and cleared out the hot brokers and he put the tariffs down to nothing almost on spices, silk and pearls and the like so an honest smuggler can't live on the difference. Aah, Daniel, the past some years I've been thinking of moving on to livelier shores." A long silence, voices drifting to them, clanks of china as serving girls began to clear the tables. "Might do it yet. Trouble is, them already there won't like newcomers nosing in, that kind of thing gets messy. Starve for a couple years, maybe get killed or turned, no contacts, no cargo, I tell you, man, it was a sad year when Him he kicked out the king and started on his Jah'takash be damned reforms." He fell silent, brooding into his wine.

Jaril stirred. His claws scratched at the floor, his teeth closed on Daniel's leg not quite hard enough to break the skin. Daniel blinked, looked down. Jaril got to his feet and started for the door.

Daniel knocked on the table. When Lio Laux looked up, he said, "Got to go, my patron's not the kind you want to keep waiting. See you sunset."

Lio grunted, lifted a hand, let it thump down, Tungjii's wine was wheeling round his head and he was lost in old days and old dreams.

Ruby shimmers slid off the opaline scales of an undulant fishtail and bloodied long white fingers combing through the waves; the Godalau swam before the Skia Hetaira as the ketch slipped swift and silent from the bay. A scruffy little figure in ragged black sat on a giant haunch and waved to Daniel Akamarino. He waved back, jumped when he felt a hand on his shoulder. Brann. "I haven't got used to it yet," he said.

"What? Oh yes, you come from a place where you have to imagine your gods and they keep going abstract and distant on you." She leaned on the rail beside him. "Sounds like paradise to me. No gods to tie strings to your ankles and jerk you about. Hmm. Maybe one day I'll jump high enough to break the strings and land in a reality like that."

Daniel shaded his eyes, picked out the translucent tail that flickered across the sky some distance ahead of them, more guessed at than seen. "It has its drawbacks. At least here there's somebody to notice you're alive, might be all round bad vibes, but that's better than being ignored. Where I come from, live or die, the universe won't notice. I'll wait a while before I decide which sort I prefer." He laughed. "Not that I have much choice. Tell me about Tungjii."

"Tell you what?"

"A story, Bramble, tell me a tale of ol' Tungjii. It's a lovely night, there's nothing much to do, get drunk, sleep, watch the wind blow. I'd rather hear you talk."

She laughed. "Such a compliment. Your tact is overwhelming, Danny Blue. Why not. A warning tale, my friend. Heesh is an amiable sort, but you don't want to underestimate that little god. So. There's a land a long way east of here, a land that was old when Popokanjo walked the earth, before he shot the moon. In that long long long ago, in the reign of the Emperor Rumanai, a maretuse whose maret was a broad domain at the edge of the rice plains came to consider himself the cleverest man in the world, yet he had to keep proving his cleverness to himself. Every month or so he sent out mercenary bands to roam the silk road and snatch travelers from it to play games with him, games he always won because he set the rules and because he really was very clever in his twisted way. Each of his conscripted guests played game after game with him until the miserable creature lost his nerve or was killed or began to bore the maretuse. His landfolk did their best to keep him entertained with strangers because that meant he wouldn't turn his mind to testing them. And they were loyally discreet when Rumanai's soldiers came prying about, hunting the bandits interfering with the Emperor's road and the taxes it brought to his treasury.

The land prospered. In their silence and because they took the spoils he passed out among them, the horses, the dogs, the tradegoods, even some of the gold, the landfolk also shared his guilt. But the peasants on the land and the merchants in the small market towns told themselves that their hands were clean, *they* shed no blood, *they* did not lift a finger to aid their master in his games. That they profited from these was neither here nor there. What could they do? It was done and would be done. Should they starve by having too queasy a stomach? Should their children starve? Besides, the travelers on the silk road knew the dangers they faced. And no doubt they were little better than the maretuse if you looked into their lives. Thieves, cheats, murderers, worst of all foreigners. If they were proper men, they would stay home where they belonged. It was their own fault if they came to a bad end. So the Ambijaks of maret Ambijan talked themselves into silence and complicity.

The day came when the mighty Perran-a-Perran, the highest of the high, lord and Emperor of all gods, took a hand in the matter of the clever maretuse.

Old Tungjii was sitting on a hillside munching grapes when a messenger from the high court of the gods came mincing along a sunbeam, having a snit at the common red mountain dirt that was blowing into every crevice and fold of his golden robe. Old Tungjii was more than half drunk from all the grapes heesh had been eating because heesh had been turning them to wine before they hit hisser stomach. Heesh was wearing common black trousers like any old peasant, the cloth worn thin at the seat and knees and a loose shirt heesh didn't bother to tie shut, letting the wind and grape juice get at fat sagging breasts with hard purple nipples. Heesh was liking the warm sun and the dusty wind that sucked up the sweat on hisser broad bald head. Heesh was liking the smell of the dust, of the crushed grass and leaves underneath him, the sounds of the grape pickers laughing a little way off and the shepherd's pipe someone was playing almost too far away to hear. Heesh certainly didn't want to be bothered by some sour-faced godlet from the Courts of Gold. But old Fishface (which is how Tungjii privately thought of the god-emperor Perran-a-Perran, how heesh muttered about him when rather too drunk to be discreet) was nasty when one of his undergods irritated him, especially one of the more disreputable sorts like the double-natured Tungjii. So heesh spat out a mouthful of grapeskins and lumbered to hisser broad bare feet.

"Tungjii," the messenger said.

Tungjii smiled, winning the bet heesh made with hisserself that the godlet's voice would whine like a whipped puppy. Heesh nodded, content with the perfection of pettiness old Fishface had presented himmer with.

"The maretuse of maret Ambijan is getting above himself," the messenger said, his lip curled in a permanent sneer that did odd things to his enunciation even while he spoke with a glasscutting clarity. "The foolish man is thinking about plotting against dearest Rumanai, the beloved of the gods, the true Emperor of Hinasilisan. He has convinced himself he deserves the throne for his own silly bottom." The messenger made a jerky little gesture with his left hand meant to convey overpowering rage and martial determination. Tungjii reminded hisserself sternly that old Fishface didn't like his subgods to giggle at his official messengers. "Perran-a-Perran, Lord of All, Lord of sky, sea and earth, Emperor of Emperors, Orderer of Chaos, Maker of man and beast, Father of all . . ."

Tungjii stopped listening to the roll of epithets, let hisser senses drift, squeezing the last drops of pleasure from the day. Even old Fishface's eyes glazed over during one of these interminable listings of his attributes and honors, finishing with the list of his many consorts, the only one of them of any interest to Tungjii being the Godalau with her moonpale fingers and her saucy fishtail. The two of them had played interesting games with hisser dual parts. Horny old Tungjii was a busy old Tungjii in spite of hisser unprepossessing outer envelope and found hisserself in a lot of lofty beds (the messenger would have been shocked to a squib to know one of those beds belonged to Perran-a-Perran). A girl's laughter came up the hill to himmer and heesh blew a minor blessing down to her for the lift of pleasure she'd given himmer.

". . . of all gods, Perran-a-Perran commands Tungjii the double god to go to Ambijan and stop this blowfish from poisoning the air and punish his overweening folly for daring to plot trouble for the God of all gods' dearest dear, the Emperor Rumanai."

Tungjii yawned. "Tell him I went," heesh said and was gone.

Some time later a fat little man was riding along the silk road on a fine long-legged mule, drowsing in a well-padded saddle, content to let the mule find the way. If anyone had asked, the little man would have blinked sleepy eyes and smiled, showing a mouthful of fine square teeth, and murmured that the mule was smarter than him and the questioner combined so why bother the good beast with such foolishness.

The snatchband came down on him as the day reached its end, rode round him in the dusk, demanded he follow them which he did without a murmur of protest, something that troubled them so much they rode through the night instead of camping some miles off the road as they usually did. And two of them rode wide, scouting the road again east and west because they suspected some kind of ambush. None of their victims had exhibited such placid good humor and it made them nervous. The scouts came back toward morning and reported that nothing was stirring anywhere. This should have reassured them, but somehow it did not. They gave their mounts grain and water, let them graze and rest a few hours, then were on their way again when the dew was still wet on the grass. The little man rode along with the same placid cheerful acceptance of what was happening, irritating the snatchband so much that only their very great fear of the maretuse kept them from pounding him into a weeping pulp.

So uneasy were they that after they delivered the little man and his mule to the maretuse, they collected their belongings and rode south as fast as they could without killing their mounts, intending to put a kingdom or two between them and Ambijan. The horses survived and ran free. Tungjii liked horses. A tiger ate one of the men. Another fell off a bridge into a cataract and eventually reached the sea, though mostly in the bellies of migrating fishes. A third helped to feed several broods of mountain eagles. Tungjii liked to watch the great birds soar and wheel. The fourth and fifth stumbled into the hands of trolls and fed a whole clutch of trollings. All in all, the snatchband contributed more to the wellbeing of the world that one summer than they had in years.

The maretuse had the little man brought before him. "What is your name?" he said.

"Guess."

"Insolence will get you a beating. That is warning."

"A wild boar can tromp and tear a hunter. It doesn't mean he's smarter or better than the hunter, only that the hunter's luck has turned bad."

"Luck? Hunh. It doesn't exist. Only degrees of cleverness and stupidity."

"Old Tungjii might argue with you on that."

"Tungjii is a fat little nothing men dream up so they won't have to face their inadequacy at dealing with the world and other men. Tungjii is nothing but wind."

"Heesh wouldn't argue too much on that point. Wind and the random crossing of separate fates, that's chance not luck, but there's a tiny tiny crack there where Tungjii can stick hisser thumbs and wiggle them a bit."

"Nonsense. A clever man scorns luck and reaches as high as his grasp will take him."

The little man tilted his head to one side, clicked his tongue against his teeth. "Cleverness is a war, but a soldier is a soldier."

"What do you mean by that? If anything."

"You're the clever man. Tell me."

"Wind!" The maretuse settled back in his chair. "It is my custom to invite a traveler into my house and match him at a game or two. Be aware that if you lose, you will be my slave as long as you live. And you will lose because you are a fat little fool who believes in luck. But

you will choose a game and play it or I will peel the hide off your
blubber and feed it to you strip by strip."

"And if I win, what will I win?"

"You won't win."

"It's not a proper contest if there isn't a prize for both players."

The maretuse forced a laugh. "You won't win, so what does it matter? You name my forfeit."

The little man clasped his hands over his hard little belly, closed his
eyes and screwed up his face as if thinking were a struggle for him,
then he relaxed, smiled, opened his eyes. "You will feed my mule."

"Done." The maretuse waved his servant over with the Jar of Lots.
He was rather disappointed when the Lot did not turn up one of the
more physical games. His guest was such a plump juicy little man he'd
looked forward to chivvying him through the Maze of Swords or hunting him in the Gorge of Sighs, but he was pleased enough with the
chosen game. He was a master strategist at stonechess and no one in
the Empire, even the masters in the capital, had ever defeated him.
Sometimes he won with only a few stones left, sometimes he crushed
his opponent under an avalanche of stones, but always he won. Five
years back when he was in Andurya Durat for the Emperor's Birthday,
one of his games passed into legend. It lasted fourteen days and less
than a dozen stones were left on the board and both players had to be
carried off and revived with tea and massage.

He didn't expect the game to last long, a few hours at most, then the
guest would lose and he would dip again into the Jar and lose again
and dip again until he lost his nerve entirely and was only good for
tiger feed. The maretuse was a trifle annoyed at his snatchband. The
little man had an amiable stupidity that was apparent to the bleariest
eye; they should have let him go on his way and found someone more
challenging.

He had the board set up, along with bowls of ansin tea, bowls of
rosewater and hot towels, piles of sausage bits, sweet pork, seven
cheeses, raw vegetables, finger cakes and candies. Honest food to give
this fool some spark of wisdom if anything could and keep the game
from being too short and boring.

Hours passed.

Servants lit lamps, replenished the food, moving with great care to
make no sound at all to disturb the concentration of their master. At
first they were pleased to see the game continue so long because a hard,
taxing contest kept the maretuse quiet for a long time. But when dawn

pinked the hills they began to worry. The maretuse had never lost
before and they didn't know how he would take it. Experience of his
moods when he was irritated made them fearful. The next pot of the
guest's tea had a dusting of dreamsugar in it. The little fat man took a
sip, grinned at them, then emptied the cup with a zesty appreciation
and continued to sit relaxed, looking sleepily stupid and unremittingly
cheerful. And the servants grew sick with fear.

Midafternoon came; sunlight fell like a sword across the table.

The maretuse watched his guest drop a stone with calm finality to
close the strangling ring about the largest portion of his remaining
stones. He could fight another dozen moves if he chose or he could
capitulate.

"Who are you?" he said. "No man this side of the world is my
match. Or yours."

The little man grinned and said nothing.

"I'm not going to let you leave here, win or lose."

A nod. That inane grimace was still pasted across the round stupid
face.

"Feed your mule, you said. I will pay my forfeit. What does the beast
eat? Oats? Straw? Grass?"

"You'll see."

The mule came titupping daintily across the marble floor though no
one saw how it got from the stables into the house.

The youngest daughter of one of the gardeners was playing among
the bushes, content to watch caterpillars crawl and ladybugs whirr
about, lines of ants marching frantically to and fro and a toad like an
old cowpat blinking in the shade of a flowering puzzlebush, flicking out
his white tongue when it occurred to him to snatch and eat a hapless
bug that fluttered too close. Crawling about among the bushes and
gathering smears of dirt with a total lack of concern, she passed the
long windows of the gameroom where the maretuse and his guest were
concluding their match.

She stopped to stare inside and saw the mule come titupping in and
giggled to see a beast in the great house coming to tea just like any
man.

The little man waved at her and she waved back, then he turned his
head over his shoulder and spoke to the mule. "The maretuse," he said,
"has agreed to feed you, Mule."

The mule opened his mouth. Opened and opened and opened his
mouth.

The maretuse struggled to move but he could not.

The little man swelled and changed until heesh was Tungjii male and female in hisser favorite wrinkled black. Ignoring the terrified man, Tungjii walked over to the long window. Heesh opened it and picked up the gardener's daughter.

"Dragon," she said.

"Yes," Tungjii said, "a very hungry dragon. You want to come with me?"

"Uh-huh. Dada too?"

"Not this time. Do you mind, little daughter?"

She looked gravely into hisser eyes, then snuggled closer to himmer. "Uh-uh."

Tungjii began walking up the air, grunting and leaning a little forward as if heesh were plodding up a steep flight of stairs. At first the gardener's daughter was afraid, but Tungjii's bosom was soft and warm. She relaxed on it and felt safe enough to look over hisser shoulder.

Fire spread from one edge of the world to the other.

"Dragon?"

"The Dragon Sunfire. He is living there now."

"Oh."

And to this day Ambijan is a desert where nothing much grows. The few Ambijaks left are wandering herdsmen and raiders who worship a dragon called Sunfire.

"Dragons too? What a world." He rose from the coil of rope where he'd been sitting, stretched, worked his shoulders, glanced at the black sea rolling ahead of them. The Godalau was still out there, swimming tirelessly along. "Barbequed peasant. Rather hard on those who disturb the status quo, don't you think? I've known a few Emperors who needed a bit of disturbing."

She hitched a hip on the rail, took hold of a handy shroud. "It's a story. Probably didn't happen. Could happen, though. Don't go by heesh's looks, Tungjii is dangerous. Always. The one who told me that story, he was a dancer whose company I was traveling with right then; Tungjii was his family patron. That gardener's daughter, you remember? When she was old enough Tungjii married her into Taga's family and promised to keep a friendly eye on them. They learned fast not to ask him for help. Heesh always gave it, but sometimes that help felt like five years of plague." She ran her eyes over Daniel Akamarino, looked puzzled. "Which makes me wonder why he fetched you here. Him or some other god."

"Why not accident? The god snatched for whatever he could reach."

"You haven't met tigermen or ariels or some of the more exotic demons sorcerers can whip into this world with something less than a hiccup or a grunt. And that's nothing to what a god can do when he, she or it makes up its corporate whatever to act."

"Don't tell me it's him," Daniel jerked a thumb toward the cramped quarters belowdeck. "Just because our names match?"

"Who knows the minds of gods, if they've got minds which I'm not all that sure of, or why they do what they do?" Her hands had long palms, long thumbs, short tapering fingers; they were strong capable hands, seldom still. She ran her fingers along his forearm, feathery touches that stirred through the pale hairs. "Why you?" Her mouth had gone soft, there was a thoughtful shine to her eyes.

He trapped her hand, held it against his arm. "Why not." Still holding the hand, he moved around so he could sit on the rail beside her, relaxing into the dip and slide of the boat. He slid his hand up her back, enjoying her response to his touch; she leaned into him, doing her version of a contented purr as he moved his fingers through the feathery curls on her neck.

Lio Laux came up on deck, moved into the bow and stood watching the intermittently visible Godalau, then he drifted over to Daniel and Brann. "I thought you were swinging it some. Not, huh?"

"Not. When do we make the Cove?"

"Hour or so before dawn, day after tomorrow." His ear dangle flashed in the moonlight, brown gleams slid off his polished bald head. His eyes narrowed into invisibility. "Given there's no trouble?" There was a complex mixture of apprehension and anticipation in his voice.

Brann's head moved gently in response to the pressure of Daniel's fingers. "I haven't a notion, Lio Laux." Her deep voice was drowsy, detached. "We have . . . eyes out . . . should something show up . . . we'll go to work . . . no point in fussing . . . until we have to."

Lio Laux pinched his nose, considered her. "Let's hope." He walked away, stopped to talk to the blond boy, the one-eyed Phrasi, the Cheonene, the members of his crew still on deck now that the sandbars were behind them, then he went below again.

"This boat's too crowded," Daniel murmured. "Unless the hold . . ."

Brann grimaced. "Wet. Smelly. Rats."

"Offputting."

"If you're older than fourteen."

"Me, even when I was fourteen, I didn't turn on to rats." He stopped talking, moved his mouth along her shoulder and neck; close to her ear, he murmured, "What about putting Danny One in with the rats?" He moved his hands over her breasts, his thumbs grazing her nipples.

She shivered. "No. . . ."

"Be right at home. Rat to the rats."

She pulled away from him, strode to the bow. After a minute she ran shaking hands through her hair, swung around. "I can dispense with you a lot easier than him, also with stupid comment."

Daniel watched her stride across the deck and disappear below. He scratched his chin. "Didn't handle that too well, did you." He looked down at himself, thumbed the bulge. "Danny's blue tonight, ran his mouth too long too wrong."

The Wounded Moon shone palely on the long narrow Skia Hetaira as she sliced through the foamspitting water of the Notea Tha, and touched with delicate strokes the naked land north of the boat, a black-violet blotch that gradually gained definition as the northwestering course of the smuggler took her closer and closer to the riddle rock at the tip of the first Vale Finger, rock pierced again and again by wind and water so that it sang day and night, slow sad terrible songs and was only quiet one hour every other month.

Brann sat on the deck, her back against the mast; the melancholy moans coming from the rock suited her mood. Ahzurdan said the air was clotted with ariels, a great gush of angry angel forms passing to and from Silagamatys, carrying news of them to Settsimaksimin, helping him plan . . . What? Ahzurdan was working with half the information he needed, he didn't have the name of the talisman Maksim wore, he didn't know how far Maksim could press Amortis. He had a strained weary look, but he wouldn't let her feed him energy as she did the children, though she offered it (having energy to spare after prowling the foggy streets of the water quarter after the others went back to the Blue Seamaid); he was in a strange half-angry state she didn't understand, though she couldn't miss how deeply he was hurting. He was carrying the full load of defending them and neither the children nor Danny Two were helping the situation with their irrational hates— no not exactly hates, it was more a fundamental incompatiblity as if they and Ahzurdan were flint and steel bound to strike sparks whenever they met. She looked up. The children were flying overhead, elegant albatrosses riding the wind, circling out ahead of the ship, drifting in and out of knots of cloud, cutting through the streams of ariels they couldn't see. She felt rather like a juggler who'd been foolish enough to accept the challenge of keeping in the air whatever her audience threw at her. Any minute now there might be one thing too many and the whole mess would drop on her head.

She listened to the moaning rock and found the sound so restful she drifted into a doze in spite of the damp chill and the drop and rise of the deck under her.

Some time later, she had no idea how long. Ahzurdan was shaking her, shouting at her. As soon as she was awake, he darted away from her to stand in the bow, gesturing in complex patterns, intoning a trenchant series of meaningless syllables interspersed with polysyllabic words that meant something to him but made no sense in the context.

The children flew in circles over the mainmast, their raucous mewing cries alerting everyone not already aware of it that something perilous was about to happen.

In the northwest an opaline glow rose over the horizon and came rapidly toward the Skia Hetaira, resolving into the god Amortis striding to them across the dark seawater, blond hair streaming in snaky sunrays about a house-sized face, her foggy draperies shifting about her slim ripe body in a celestial peekaboo, shapely bare feet as large as the Skia Hetaira moving above the water or through it as it swelled, feet translucent as alabaster with light behind it, but solid enough to kick the waves into spreading foam. The hundred yards of female god stopped ten shiplengths away, raised a huge but delicate hand, threw a sheet of flame at the boat.

Hastily the two albatrosses powered up and away, their tailfeathers momentarily singed, drawing squawks of surprise from them, the flame splashing over them as it bounced off the shield Ahzurdan had thrown about the Skia Hetaira.

Amortis stamped her foot. The wave she created fled from her and threatened to engulf the boat. The deck tilted violently, first one way then another, leaped up, fell away. Ahzurdan crashed onto his knees, then onto his side and rolled about, slammed into the siderails (narrowly escaping being thrown overboard), slammed into the mast; he clutched at the ropes coiled there and finally stopped his wild careering. Gobbets of flame tore through his shielding, struck the sails and the deck, one caught the hem of his robe; they clung with oily determination and began eating into canvas, cloth and wood. Vast laughter beat like thunder over the Skia Hetaira and the folk on her. Amortis stamped again, flung more fire at the foundering boat.

As the first splash reached them, Brann dived for Ahzurdan, missed and had to scramble to save herself. She heard muted grunts and the splat of bare feet, managed a rapid glance behind her—Daniel Akamarino with only his trousers on and absurdly the magic wineskin bouncing against his back. When Ahzurdan grasped the mast ropes and stopped his careening about, Brann and Daniel caught hold of the straining sorcerer, eased him onto his knees and supported him while he gestured and intoned, gradually rebuilding his shield.

Lio Laux and his two and a half crew struggled to keep the Skia from turning turtle and when they had a rare moment with a hand free, they tried to deal with the fires (fortunately smoldering rather than raging, subdued though not quenched by Ahzurdan's aura). At some indeterminate moment in the tussle Tungjii arrived and stood on the deck looking about, watching with bright-eyed interest as Ahzurdan fought in his way and Lio in his. Heesh wriggled himmer's furry brows. Small gray stormclouds gathered over each of the smoky guttering fires and released miniature rainstorms on them, putting them out.

Out on the water Amortis stopped laughing and took a step toward the Skia, meaning to trample what she couldn't burn.

An immense translucent fishtail came rushing out of the waves, lifting gallons of water with it, water that splashed mightily over Amortis and sent her sprawling. Squawling with rage, she bounded onto her feet, bent and swung her arms wildly, grabbing for the Godalau's coarse blue-green hair. The Godalau ducked under the waves, came up behind the god and set pearly curly shark's teeth in the luscious alabaster calf of Amortis' left leg; the Blue Seamaid did a bit of freeform tearing, then dived frantically away as Amortis took hold again, subdued her temper and used her fire to turn the water about her into superheated steam that even the Godalau could not endure.

A stormcloud much larger than those raining on the ship gathered over the wild blond hair and let its torrents fall. Clouds of gnats swarmed out of nowhere and blew into Amortis' mouth, crawled up her nose and into her ears. Revolting slimy things came up out of the sea and trailed their stinking stinging ooze over her huge but dainty toes.

Amortis shrieked and spat fire in all directions, drawing on her substance with no discretion at all; more of the sea about the Skia grew too hot for the Godalau, driving her farther and farther away, until she could do nothing but swim frantically about beyond the perimeter of the heat, searching for some way, any way, she could attack again. Tungjii's torments whiffed out fast as he could devise them, his rain melted into the steam that was a whitehot cloud about the whitehot fireform of the god; rage itself now, Amortis flared and lost her woman's shape, sinking into the primal form from which she was created by the dreams of men, from which in a very real sense she created herself.

On deck, battered and exhausted, Ahzurdan faltered. More fire ripped through the shield. A worried frown on hisser round face, Tungjii rained on the fires and flooded most of them to smudgy chars, but the water was so hot around the Skia that steam drifting over the decks threatened to burn out mortal lungs and roast the skin off mortal bodies. The busy little god sent eddy currents of cooler air to shield hisser mortals, but heesh was more pressed than heesh had ever been in all hisser lengthy existence. The sea itself was so hot that the timbers of the hull were beginning to steam and smolder. Laux's seamanship and the desperate scurrying of his crew had managed so far to keep the Skia Hetaira upright and clawing in a broad arc about the center of the fury, far enough out so the heat was marginally endurable, but let Ahzurdan falter again and the Skia and everyone on it would go up in a great gush of flame.

Brann felt Ahzurdan weakening, felt it in her hands and in her bones. She pressed herself against him, whispered, "Let me feed you, Dan, I can help but only if you let me. I did it when I cleansed you before, let me help you now."

He nodded, unable to stop his chant long enough to speak.

Brann let her senses flow into him; usually she had one of the children to help with this, but they were gone, out beyond the shield doing she didn't know what. She fed a tentative thread of energy into him, working cautiously so she wouldn't distract him, that would be almost as fatal as his collapse from exhaustion. As she got the feel of him, she fed him more and more, draining herself to support him.

Only peripherally aware of the struggle on the deck, Yaril and Jaril flew again and again at Amortis, their birdshapes abandoned. Fire of a sort themselves, her fire couldn't hurt them, but they were too small, too alien to damage her in any satisfactory way, all they could do was dart at her eyes while she still had eyes and distract her a little; when she altered to her primal form there was nothing at all they could do with her except use their odd bodies as lenses and channel small

streams of her fire away from the Skia, which they did for a while until
the futility of their acts grew depressingly apparent. They flicked away
from the stormcenter and merged in consultation.

Brann, Yaril pulsed, *she handled the Treeish, with a bit of help
from us; do you think she might be able to drain that bitch?*

I think we better try something, this can't go on much longer.

Ideas?

*Make a bridge between her and that thing. We can focus its ener-
gies, that's what we've been doing, isn't it?*

And Brann handles the pull. Right. Let's go talk to her.

They flicked through the shield, bounced up and down in front of
her until they had her attention, then merged with her and explained
their plan.

Brann scowled at the deck. "We've got about all the fire we can
handle now." She spoke the words aloud, listened some more. "You're
sure it's different? Yes, I do remember the Treeish. They weren't gods
or anything close to it and it hurt like hell handling their forces." A
listening silence. "I see. Channeled force, a limited but steady drain."
She laughed. "Nice touch, defeating Amortis with her own strength. I
agree, there's not much point in going on with what we're doing, she
certainly can outlast us no matter how much of that fire she throws at
us. So. The sooner the better, don't you think?"

The children emerged from Brann, darted back through Ahzurdan's
shield and hovered in the heart of the fire, glimmering gold spheres
faintly visible against the crimson flame flooding out of Amortis. They
melded into one and shot out curving arms until they extented from
Amortis to Brann in a great arc of golden light. As soon as both ends
of the arc touched home, Brann PULLED. And screamed with the
agony of the godlife flowing into her, alien, inimical, deadly fire that
almost killed her before her body found for itself a way of converting
that fire into energy she could use. She absorbed it, throttled down the
flow until it was a source Ahzurdan could take in without dying of it.
She fed him the godlife, filled him with the godlife, until he glowed
translucent alabaster like the god and used the god's own substance to
make the shield so fine a filter that heat and steam and eating fire were
left outside and the water that came through was the black cool seawater that belonged to the Notoea Tha in midautumn nights. And the air
that came through was a brisk following breeze, cool almost chill. And
the tumultuous seasurface subsided to the long swells that came after
storms had passed. The Skia Hetaira settled to an easy slide through

abruptly edenic waters and Lio gave the helm to his mate so he could begin an inspection of his ship; he strolled about assessing damages, adding trauma penalties to the repair costs he planned to lay on Brann's surety pledge. He was a bit wary of pushing her too hard, but figured a little fiddling couldn't hurt.

Beyond the semi-opaque shield sphere, Amortis slacked her raging, let her fires diminish as she began to be afraid; she shut off her outpouring of her substance and recovered her bipedal form so she could think about what was happening. The arc between her and Brann was draining off her energy at a phenomenal pace; if it went on much longer she would face a permanent loss of power and with that, a loss of status so great she'd be left as nothing more than a minor local fertility genius tied to some stupid grove or set of stones. A last shriek of rage heavily saturated with fear, a shouted promise of future vengeance, and she went away.

The golden arch collapsed into two globes that bobbled unsteadily, then dropped through the shield onto the deck and flickered into two weary children.

Tungjii strolled over to the entwined trio, tapped Daniel's arm, pointed to the wineskin and vanished.

Brann stirred. She didn't let loose of Ahzurdan, for the moment she couldn't. She throbbed and glowed like an alabaster lamp, her bones were visible through her flesh. Ahzurdan was like her, glowing, his bones like hers, a dark calligraphy visible in hands and face.

He stirred. With a hoarse groan of utter weariness out of a throat gone rough from the long outpouring of the focusing chants, he dropped into silence and let his hands fall onto his thighs. The shield globe melted from around them and the Skia Hetaira glided unhindered on a heaving sea.

The Godalau swam before them once more, her translucent glassy form like the memory of a dream. The raging winds were gone, the steam was gone, the water was cold again about the ship, the only reminders left of that ferocious conflict were the blackened holes in the sails and the charred spots in the wood.

Daniel eased himself away from Ahzurdan and Brann, sucking at his teeth and shaking his head when he saw them still frozen, unaware of his departure. He looked down at his hands and was relieved to see them comfortably opaque, no mystical alabaster there, just the burnt brown skin and paler palms he was accustomed to seeing. His bones were aching and his body felt like it had the first time he went canoeing with the Shafarin on Harsain, the time he decided he wanted to find out what the life of a nomad hunter was like. That was one of his shorter intervals between ships, when was it? yes, the time he walked away from della Farangan after one loud slanging match too many. Afterwards he went to work for a shiny ship to get the grit out of his teeth and the grime out of his skin. And the taste of burnt gamy flesh out of his mouth. Stella Fulvina and the Prism Dancer; quite a woman in her metallic way, uncomplicated. You knew where you were with her and exactly what you'd get. Restful to the head though she worked your butt off. He unslung the wineskin and thumbed out the stopple. The wine burned away his weariness. He sighed with pleasure and after a moment's thought, splashed a drop of it on a small burn, grinned as the blackened flesh fell away and the pain went with it. "Tungjii Luck, you've got great taste in wine, you do." He grimaced at Brann and Ahzurdan, crawled to the pale limp changechildren lying on the deck a short distance off. "Here," he said. "Have a drink. Give you the energy to keep breathing." He looked at them and laughed. "Or whatever else it is you do."

As the children drank and flushed with returning color, Brann and Ahzurdan finally eased apart. Brann lifted one hand, pointed at the sky. A great white beam of light streamed from her bunched fingertips and cut through the darkness before to melt finally among the clouds. She closed her hand and cut off the flow. Ahzurdan waited until she was cooled down, then bled off his own excess charge much the same way, though he used both hands.

Daniel grinned at Jaril, reached for the skin. "Much more and you'll be crawling, Jay."

The boy giggled. "Still get there."

"Yup, give it here anyway." He took the wineskin to Brann, she was still glowing palely as if her skin was pulled taut over moonlight, but she looked weary as death and worried. "Tungjii's blessing," he said. "Makes the world look brighter."

She found a smile for him and took the skin. Tungjii's gift worked its magic; she flushed, her eyes acquired a new warmth, her movements a new vigor. She touched Ahzurdan's arm. "Tungjii's blessing, Dan."

His head turned stiffly, slowly, dull blank eyes blinked at her. The ravages of the godlife were visible in his face, even more than the utter weariness of body and spirit. He took the skin, stared at it for a long moment before he lifted it and squeezed a wobbly stream of wine at his mouth, missing more than he hit. Daniel started to help him steady himself, but Brann caught his reaching hand and held it away. "No," she said. "Not you. Not me."

Ahzurdan lowered the skin, fumbled at his mouth and neck, trying to wipe away the spilled wine. He was looking all too much like a punchdrunk fighter, his coordination and capacity for thinking beaten out of him. Brann took the skin from him and gave it to Daniel. "Go away a while, will you? I'll take care of him."

Daniel Akamarino shrugged and went to sit on the rail. He watched Brann get her shoulder under Ahzurdan's arm and help him to his feet. Her arm around him, she helped him stumble across the deck and down the ladder to the cramped livingspace below. Before she quite vanished, she turned her head. "On your life, don't wake us before noon."

Daniel flicked the dangling stopple. "Women," he said.

Lio Laux leaned on the rail beside him. "Uh huh." He rubbed a burn hole in his shirt between his thumb and forefinger, shredding off the charred fibers; eyes narrowed into dark crescents, he looked up at the sails, holed here and there but taut enough with the following wind, then squinted round at the deck. "Expect more of that?" He snapped thumb against midfinger and pointed his forefinger at a charred place in the wood.

"Me, I don't expect. This isn't my kind of thing." Daniel passed the skin to Lio. "You might want to put some of this on your burns." He held out his arm, showed the pale spot where the charred skin fell off. "Seems to be as useful outside as it is in."

"Hmm. You don't mind, I'll apply it to the inside first."

The rest of the voyage passed without incident. Two hours before dawn on the next morning, Lio Laux landed them on the black sand of Haven Cove, gave Brann back her surety gold and sailed out of the story.

11

MAKSIM AND KORI, A DIGRESSION.

SCENE: In Maksim's chambers high above the city.

"Sit down, I'm not going to eat you."

Kori sneaked a glance at him, looked quickly away. Everyone said how big Settsimaksimin was and she'd seen him tower over the Servants and the students at the Lots, but he was far off then and she hadn't realized how intimidating that size would be when she was not much more than an arm's length away, even if it was the length of *his* arm. Eyes on the floor, she backed to a padded bench beside one of the tall pointed windows. She folded her hands in her lap, grateful for the coarseness of the sleeping shift they'd given her at the Yron. She didn't feel quite so naked in it. She stole another look at him. He was smiling, his eyes were warm and it startled her but she had to say it, gentle, approving. She wondered if she ought to worry about what he was going to do to her, but she didn't feel bothered by him, not like she was when that snake Bak'hve looked at her. Frightened, yes, but not bothered. She ran her tongue over dry lips. "Why did you snatch me here like this?"

"Because I didn't want to make life at the Yron more difficult for you than it is already."

"I don't . . ."

"Child, mmmm, what's your name?"

"You don't know it?"

"Would I ask?"

His deep deep voice rumbled and sang at her, excited her; she forgot to be frightened and lifted her head. "Kori," she said, "Kori Piyolss."

"Kori." Her name was music when he said it; she felt confused but still not bothered. "Well, young Kori, you wouldn't like what would certainly happen to you if anyone thought I was interested in you. I'm sure you have no idea what lengths some folks will go to in order to reach my ear, and that's not vanity, child, that's what happens when you have power yourself or you're close to someone with it. You're a fighter, Kori, yes I do know that. I've watched you plot and scheme against me; unfortunately, I did not know who it was that plotted soon enough to stop you. Ahh, if things were other, if I had a daughter, or a son even, if he or she were like you, I would swell with pride until I burst with it. Why, Kori? What have I done to you? No, I'm not asking you that now. I will know it, though, believe that."

She gazed defiantly at him, pressed her mouth into a tight smile that was meant to say *no you won't.*

He chuckled. "Kori, Kori, relax, child, I'm not going into that tonight. I've got other things in mind. You were right, you know, I fiddled the Lot, I wanted you out of Owlyn, child, I wanted you where you won't make more trouble for me. You might as well forget about going back there. Think rather what you'd like to do with your life."

She blinked at him. "What do you mean?"

"I am not going to permit you to teach, Kori, I'm sure you see why. You don't want to be a holy whore, do you?"

She swallowed, touched her throat, forced her hand down.

"It's not a threat, child; but we do have to find something else for you. You've got a talent, did you know it?"

"Um . . . talent?"

"Why weren't you born a boy, Kori, ah, things would be so much simpler."

"I don't want to be a boy." She couldn't put too much force into that, not after the talk with Polatéa. She wrinkled her nose, moved her shoulders. It was a funny feeling, talking to the man like this, she felt free to say things she couldn't say to anyone not even Tré; it seemed to her Settsimaksimin understood her, all of her, not just a part, understood and in a funny way approved of her. All of her. He was the first one, well, maybe Polatéa was the first, but Polatéa wanted to close her in and if he meant what he was saying, it seemed to her he wanted to open out her life to new things, splendid things. Aayee, it was hard, she was supposed to hate him for what he'd done, for what he was going to do when he found out about Tré, was he playing with her head already? She didn't know, how could she know? "What I'd really like," she said, "is not to stop being a girl, I am a girl, it's part of what makes me who I am, I like who I am, I don't want to change, what I want is to be free to do some of the things boys get to do." She scratched her cheek, frowned. "What did you mean, talent?"

"Magic, child. Would you like to study it?"

"I don't understand."

"There are schools where they teach the talent, Kori; there's one, perhaps the best of them, in a city called Silili. It's a long way from here, but I'll see you get there if you think you might like to be a scholar."

"Why?"

"Nothing's ever simple, Kori, haven't you learned that by now? Ah well, you've had a sheltered life so far. Why? Because I like you, because I don't like killing my folk, don't scowl, child, didn't your mother ever tell you your face could freeze like that? Yes, you are mine whatever you think of that and yes, I am not lying when I say I loathe killing. I do what I must."

"No. You do what you want."

"Hmm. Perhaps you're right. Shall I tell you what I want?"

"I can't stop you. No, that isn't honest. I would like to hear it. I think. I don't know. Are you messing with my head, Settsimaksimin?"

"Yes."

"Why?"

"I don't want to see you frightened. I don't want to feel you hating me."

"I can't do anything about that?"

"Not now. If you develop your talent, the time will come when no one, not even a god, can play with your feelings and your thoughts, Kori. Take my offer. Don't waste your promise."

"Why are you doing this? I don't understand. Help me understand. Are you like Bak'hve the Servant in Owlyn, do you want me? I don't think so, you don't make me feel bothered like he does."

He frowned. "That Servant, he approached you, suggested you lie with him?"

"No. Not yet, he hasn't worked himself up to it yet."

"Hmm. I'll put a watch on him; if he's got a penchant for young girls, he goes. And no, Kori, you're right, you don't excite me that way. Do I shock if I tell you, no girl or woman would?"

"Oh." She wriggled uncomfortably. "You said you're trying to do something. What is it?"

He gave his low rumbling laugh, settled into his chair, put his feet up on a hassock and began to talk about his plans for Cheonea.

Her head whirled with visions as immense as he was. What he wanted for the Plain sounded very much like the kind of life her own folk lived up in the Vales. How could that be bad? There was a fire in him, a passionate desire to make life better for the Plainsers. How could she not like that? His fire called to the fire in her. Maybe he was playing games with her again, but she didn't really think so. She felt her mind stretching, she felt breathless, carried along by an irresistable force like the time she fell into the river and didn't want to be rescued, the time she was intensely annoyed with her cousins when they roped her and pulled her to the bank; though she thanked them docilely enough, she went running back to the House, raging as she ran. She quivered to the deep deep voice that seemed to sing in the marrow of her bones. She understood him, or at least a part of him, there was no one he could share his dreams with, just like her. No one who could follow the leaps and bounds of his thought. She could. She knew it. But she also knew her own ignorance. In addition to her dreams and enthusiasms, she had a shrewd practical side. Though her life was short and severely circumscribed, she'd heard more than a handful of one-sided stories meant to justify some lapse or lack. Men who let their fields go sour, women who slacked their weaving or their cleaning, children who had a thousand excuses for things they had or hadn't done. She'd told such stories herself, even told them to herself. So how could she judge what he was saying? Measure it against what was there before down on the Plain? What did she know about the Plain except some ancient tales her people told to scare unruly boys? Trouble was, how could she trust those stories? She knew how her folk were about outsiders, nothing outsiders did was worth the spit to drown them in. What else did she know? Really know? What he did about the wood. Yes. That rather impressed Daniel Akamarino. How he kept the city clean. Bath houses for beggars even. The slave markets were gone. But girls still sold themselves on the streets and in the taverns they were conveniences provided with the beds and the bottles. The pleasurehouses were gone, older girls on fete eves told dreadful tales of those places, tales that would have had them scrubbing pots for a month if one AuntNurse or another had caught them. But Settsimaksimin's own soldiers burned the Chained God's priests and would burn Tré if she couldn't stop it. The thought cleared her head and chilled her body.

She looked up. He was watching her, yellow cat eyes questioning her silence. Momentarily she was afraid, but she thought about Tré and everything and straightened her back. If she could stop it here, if she could make him see. . . . She took a mouthful of air, let it out with a soundless paa. "There's one thing," she said. She rubbed at her forehead, pushed her hand back over her hair, afraid again. He saw too much. What if he saw Tré? "You let us alone for over forty years. Except for the Lot. And we got used to that and it was kind of exciting coming down to the city and having it ours for three days. You let us live like we always lived. No fuss. And then, no warning, you send your soldiers to the Vales, and the Servants. We don't want them, we don't need them. We have the Chained God to look after us. We have our priests to bless us and teach us and heal us and wed us each to each. At least, we had them before your soldiers burnt them. Why? We weren't hurting you. We were just doing what we'd always done. The Servants gave the orders to the soldiers, but they were your soldiers. Why did you let that happen?"

"Let it happen? oh Kori, I couldn't stop it, I was constrained by things I promised decades ago. Let me tell you. Fifty years ago I took Silagamatys from the king." He gave her a weary smile. "I had a thousand mercenaries and a few dozen demons and the skills I'd acquired in a century's hard work. I took the city in a single night with less than a hundred dead, the king being one of those. And it meant almost nothing. He had less say in how Cheonea was run than the scruffiest beggar on Water Street. The Parastes and the vice lords, the pimps, the bullies, the assassins and the thieves, they ran Cheonea, they ran Silagamatys, they ignored me and my pretensions, Kori. It was like trying to scoop up quicksilver; when I reached for them, they ran between my fingers and were gone. All I had accomplished, Kori, was to tear down the symbol that held this rotting state together. SYM-BOL! That vicious foulness, that corrupt old fumbler. He was the shell they held in front of them, he was the thing that kept them from going for each other. I had to cleanse the city somehow, I had to put my hand on the hidden powers if I wanted to change the way things were and make life better for the gentle people. I worked day and night, Kori, I slept two hours, three at most. I think I looked into the face of every man, woman and child inside the crumbling walls about this cesspool city. I caught little weasels that way, weeded them out and set them to work for me in the granite quarries, cutting stone to rebuild those walls. The wolves slipped away on me except for a few of the stupider ones. Every Parika on the Plain was a fortress closed against me and the Parastes reached out from behind their walls to strike at me whenever they saw a chance to hurt me. I held on for five years, Kori, I got Silagamatys cleaned out, I got my walls built. But Cheonea outside the walls was drowning in blood. The wolves were turning on each other. I don't believe that chaos reached into the Vales, but it couldn't have been a happy time there either; there were desperate men in the hills who stole what they needed to stay alive and destroyed what they couldn't use to appease the rage that gnawed at them. I could have cleansed the Plain too, Kori, as I cleansed the city, if I had another hundred years to spare and the strength of a young man. I wasn't young, Kori, I had limits. And I had this." He pulled the talisman from under the simple white linen robe he wore, brushed his hand across the stone. "There's a price to using it, I won't speak of that, child, it's my business and mine alone. I didn't want to use it, but I looked into myself and I looked out across the Plain and I called Amortis to me. I used her because I had to, Kori. For the greater good. Oh yes. I know. My good, too. Either I forgot my dream or I corrupted it and myself. You understand what I did and why. I promised her Cheonea, Kori, I could compel her to some things but to do all that I wanted, she had to have a reason for helping me. Cheonea was that reason. I left the Vales alone as long as I could, Kori, I talked with her, I teased her, I even was her lover for a while." He gave her a sad wry smile. "Not a very satisfactory one, I'm afraid. I can't claim virtue for trying to save you folk from Amortis' greed. The runes I read, the bones I cast, the stars in their courses all told me that going into the Vales would destroy me." A long weary sigh. "I'm tired, child, but I'll keep fighting until I die. Cheonea will be whole and it will be a good place to live. If I have a few more years, just a handful of years, what I've done will be so strong it won't need me any more. I won't let you take those years from me, Kori. I won't let you be hurt, but I will kill you if I have to, do you understand that?"

"Yes."

"Will you tell me what you've done and why?"

"No."

"Do you understand what you are saying to me?"

"Yes."

"It's war between us?"

"Yes."

He touched the tips of his lefthand fingers to the stone. "In one hour Amortis herself goes after your champions, Kori. Would you like to see what happens?"

"Yes."

"Hmm. Some hundred years ago it seems to me I asked if you would like to be a scholar."

"Yes."

"Does that merely mean you remember the question or is it your answer?"

"I remember the question and yes, I think I would like to be a scholar." She gazed at fingers pleating and repleating the coarse white wool of her shift. "If you don't break me getting out your answers."

He laced his fingers over his stomach, his yellow eyes laughed at her. "Kori, young Kori, there's no need for breaking. You've no defense against me, making you speak will be as simple as dipping a pen into an inkwell and writing with it."

"Why all this talk talk talk, then? Why don't you get at it? Do you expect to charm me into emptying myself out for you? You could charm a figgit out of its hole and you know it, but you'll have to take what you want, I won't, I can't give it to you. Why are you wasting your time and mine like this? Do it. Get it over with and let me go."

"Am I, Kori, wasting my time?"

She looked up, looked down again without saying anything.

"You don't understand what I'm trying to do? How much it is going to mean to ordinary folk?"

"I do understand. They aren't my folk."

"Yes. I thought it was that. Your brother?"

She folded the cloth and smoothed it out, folded and smoothed and tried to ignore the pressing silence in the high moon-shadowed room.

"How is he involved in this? A baby like that." When she continued to not-look at him, he got to his feet, held out his hand. "Come. Or do you hate me so much you refuse to touch me?"

Her head whipped up; she glared at him. "Not fair."

His rumbling laugh filled the room, his eyes shone with it. He waggled his huge hand. "Come."

Settsimaksimin ran his tongue over his teeth as he looked round the cluttered workroom. With a grunt of satisfaction he strode to a corner, brushed a pile of dusty scrolls off a padded backless bench and carried it across to the table where the black obsidian mirror waited, dark glimmers sliding across its enigmatic surface. He scowled at the dust on the dark silk, lifted the tail of his robe and scrubbed it vigorously over the cushion. Kori resisted a strong impulse to giggle. He was so massive, so powerful, so very male, but his play at hospitality reminded her absurdly of AuntNurse Polatéa arranging a party for visiting cousins. When he straightened and beckoned her over, she gave him her best demure smile and settled herself gracefully, grateful for once for all those tedious lessons.

He drew the ball of his thumb across the mirror. "Show thou." As a scene began to develop within the oval, he dropped into a sagging armchair, shifted about until he was comfortable, propped his feet on a rail under the table and laced his long dark fingers over his solid stomach.

Kori watched white sails belly out against black water, black sky, and lost any urge to laugh when she saw the towering figure of the god come striding across the sea.

Squawling threats, Amortis vanished. The gold arc broke apart. The translucent shell dissolved. The sea smoothed out. The boat came round and sliced once more toward Haven Cove.

"Well." Settsimaksimin pushed his chair back and stood looking down at her. Kori couldn't read anything but weariness and regret in his heavy face, but she was terrified. Helpless. No place to run. Nothing she could say would change what they'd just seen. All she could do was hold the rags of her dignity about her and endure whatever he planned for her.

He loomed over her, leaned down; very gently, a feather's touch wouldn't be softer, he brushed his thumb across her mouth. "Speak thou," he murmured. "What have you done and how? Why have you done it?"

She struggled to resist, but it was like being caught in the river, carried on without effort on her part. The story tumbled out of her: Tré's peril, Harra's Legacy, the Cave of the Chained God, Toma and the medal, Daniel Akamarino, the Blue Seamaid and all that happened there, what Brann organized to get her home unseen (she fell silent a moment and stared as he burst out laughing. I stopped watching, he said to her, before any of that went on. All that effort wasted), the Chained God's command to come to Isspyrivo, take the chains off him, return with him to destroy the talisman that Settsimaksimin was using against a god.

When she finished and fell silent, he brushed her lips a second time with his thumb, stepped back. He pointed at the bench. "Bring that. There." He pointed at the center of a complex of silver lines, a five-pointed star inside a circle with writing and other symbols scattered about it, within the pattern and without; he didn't wait to see her do it, but whipped away, robe billowing about him as he strode to another corner; he came back with a long, decorated staff. He looked her over, nodded with satisfaction, tapped the silver circle with the butt of the staff. The wire began to glow. "Don't move," he said. "Don't cross the line. There will be dangerous things beyond the pentacle; you can't see them and you don't want to feel them. You hear me?"

"Yes."

He stopped beside a second small pentacle, activated that, moved to the largest. There was an odd looking chair in it, big, made from a dark wood with tarry streaks in it, his chair, even before he settled into it, its shape suggested him, she could see him sitting in it, his massive arms resting in the carved hollows in the chair's arms, his long strong feet fitting in the hollows of the footboard. He stepped across the dull gray lines, smoothed his hands over his hair, tucking in the short straggles that made a black and pewter halo for his face. With a complicated pass of his flattened hand, he wiped the wrinkles and dust smears from his robe, then he tapped the pentacle to life, climbed into the chair and settled himself into a proper majesty, the staff erect in its holders, rising over him, its wire inlay catching the light in slippery watery gleams. He turned his head to look directly at her (she was on his right off to one side), grinned and winked at her as if to say *aren't I fine*, then faced forward and began intoning a chant, his voice filling the room with sound and beats of sound until her body throbbed in time with the pulses.

"PA OORA DELTHI NA HES HEYLIO PO LIN
LEGO IMAN PHRO NYMA MEN
NE NE MOI GALANAS
TRE TRE TRAGO MEN."

And as he chanted, he moved his hands in strange and disconcerting patterns; something about the gestures stirred her insides in ways that both terrified and fascinated her. She felt the power surging from him; in spite of her fear she found herself swept up in it, exulting in it (though she felt sick and shamed when she realized that—it was like being outside, walking through an immense towering thunderstorm, winds teasing at her hair and clothes, thunder rumbling in her blood, lightning striding before her.

She gasped, jumped to her feet though she didn't quite dare cross the lines. Tré was in the other small pentacle, curled up on his side, deeply asleep, his first pressed against his mouth. "What are you going to do to him," she cried. "What are you going to do?"

Settsimaksimin sighed, the talisman glimmering as it rose and fell with the rise and fall of his chest. "Put him where his god can't reach him," he said; the residue of the chant made a demi chant of the simple words. "If I kill him, child, there'll only be another taking his place, another and another until I have to kill everyone. So what's the point. He'll sleep and sleep and sleep . . ." He turned his head and smiled at her. ". . . until you and only you, young Kori, until YOU come and touch him awake."

"I don't understand."

"Wait. Watch." He straightened, closed his eyes a moment to regain his concentration, then began another chant.

"ME LE O I DETH O I ME LE OUS E THA NA TOUS
HIR RON TO RON DO MO PE LOOMAY LOOMAY
    DOMATONE
IDO ON TES HAY DAY THONE."

His gestures began as wrapping turns. A shimmer formed about Tré's body, solidified into a semitransparent crystal; Tré was encased in that cyrstal like a fly in amber. The gestures changed, fluttered, ended as he brought his hands together in a loud clap. The crystal cube vanished.

"He has gone to his god," Settsimaksimin said. "In a way." He got to his feet, stood leaning against the chair looking wearier than death. "He is in the Cave of Chains. If you can get yourself there, Kori, all you have to do is touch the block of crystal. It will melt and the boy will wake. No one else can do this. No one, god or man. Only you. Do you understand?"

"No. Yes. What to do, yes. Why?"

He reached his arms high over his head, stretched, groaned with the popping of his muscles. "Incentive, Kori." He dragged his hand across his face. "I want to save something out of this mess. I can't save myself. Cheonea? All I can do is hope the seeds I've planted have sent down roots strong enough to hold it together when MY hand is gone. You've destroyed me, Kori. If I were the monster you think me, I'd kill you right now and send your souls to the worst hell I could reach.

Instead . . ." he chuckled, but there was no humor in the sound, "I'm going to pay for your education." He resettled himself in the chair, worked a lever on the side so that the back tilted at an angle and the footboard moved out. He was still mostly upright, but not so dominant as he had been.

A chant filled the room again, his voice was vibrant and wonderfully alive, none of the exhaustion she'd seen was present in that sound; power, discipline, elegance, beauty, those were in that sound. He was a stranger and her enemy, but she felt a deeper kinship with him now than with any of her blood kin. She felt like weeping, she felt empty, she felt the loss of something splendid she'd never find again. If it hadn't been Tré, if only it hadn't been Tré.

The smaller pentacle filled again. A tall woman, gray hair dressed in a soft knot, a black silk robe tied loosely over a white shift. Thin face, austere, rather flat. Long narrow chocolate eyes, not friendly at the moment, were they ever? Thin mouth tucked into brackets. She glared at Settsimaksimin, then she relaxed and she smiled, affection for the man showing in her face. The chocolate eyes narrowed yet more into inverted smiles of their own. "You!" she said. Her voice had a magic like his, silvery, singing. "Why is it always the middle of the night?"

Settsimaksimin laughed, swung his hand toward Kori. "I've a new student for you, Shahntein Shere. Take her and teach her and keep her out of my hair."

"That bad, eh? You interest me."

"Thought I might."

"You paying for her or what?"

"I pay. Would I bring you here else? I know you, love." He shifted position, looked sleepily amused, his real weariness nowhere visible. Kori watched with astonishment, fear, hope, reluctant respect. "A hundred gold a year, with a bonus given certain conditions. She's . . ." he frowned at Kori, ". . . thirteen or thereabouts, ten years bed, board and training." He ran his eyes over the sleeping shift that fell in heavy folds around her thin body. "And clothing."

"For you, old friend, just for you, I'll do it."

"HAH." A rumbling chuckle. "She'd do you proud, Shahntien."

"You mentioned a bonus."

"Young Kori, her name is Kori Piyolss, she isn't too happy about leaving home right now. She's clever, she's got more courage than sense and she's stubborn. The first time she tries to get away from you, whip her. If she tries twice and you catch her at it, kill her. That's what the bonus is for. You hear that, Kori?"

Kori pressed her lips together, closed her hands into fists. "Yes."

"You see, Shahntien? Already plotting."

"I see. How clever is she? Enough to stay quiet and learn until she thinks she knows how to avoid being caught?"

"Oh yes. I'm counting on you, Shahntien, to prove cleverer still and keep her there the whole ten years."

"Take her now?"

"In a moment." He shifted to face Kori. "Apply yourself, young Kori. Remember what I told you. Your brother will sleep forever unless you come for him, so be very very sure you know what you're about."

"Now?" Kori drove her nails into the soft wood of the bench. "What about . . ."

"Nothing here matters to you any longer, child. Stay well."

A gesture, a polysyllabic word and she was in the other pentacle tight up against the woman who put a thin strong arm about her shoulders. A gesture, a word and both of them were elsewhere.

Maksim carried the bench back to the corner, piled the scattered scrolls on it again. He straightened, stretched, rubbed at his chest. Grimacing, he crossed to the wallcoffer, poured out some of the cordial and gulped it down, followed it with a swallow of brandy to wash away the taste. He leaned against the wall and waited for the strengthener to take hold, then snapped to his bedroom to get the rest he so urgently needed.

12

UPHILL AND NASTY.

SCENE: Black sand sloping up to an anonymous sort of scraggly brush. High tide, just turning, foam from the sea, white lace on black velvet, out on the dark water, white sails dipping swiftly below the horizon. Isspyrivo a black cone directly ahead, twice the height of the other peaks. It is several folds back from the shore, perhaps fifty miles off.

Brann shoved a hand through her hair. Daniel was a little drunk again. A thousand maledictions on old Tungjii's head, wishing that pair on me. One of them sneaking whiffs of dreamdust, the other afloat in a winy sea. She began pacing restlessly beside the retreating surf, small black crabs scuttling away from her feet into festoons of stinking seawrack; every few steps she stopped to kick black grit out of her sandals. What now? We should get started for the mountain. Walk? She snorted. Take a whip to get this party marching. Ahzurdan had performed nobly during the attack, they owed their lives to him, perhaps even the children did, but she couldn't be sure he'd come through next time. Half an hour ago, when she went to fetch him, the smell of hot dust in that cabin was strong enough to choke a hog. The young thief was right, once you smelled that stink you didn't forget it. He was sitting on the sand now looking vaguely out at the vanishing sails of the Skia Hetaira, probably he regretted getting off her. Daniel drifted over to him, offered the wineskin. Danny One stared at Danny Two, dislike hardening the vagueness out of his face, then waved him off. Like a bratty child, not the man he was supposed to be, Daniel kicked sand on the sorcerer and wandered away to sit on a chunk of lava, one of several coughed up the last time Isspyrivo hiccupped.   Brann sighed and thought longingly of Taguiloa and the dance troupe, there was much to be said for the energizing qualities of ambition. She watched the changechildren playing with the sand; its blackness seemed to fascinate them. Jaril and Yaril were appreciably taller and more developed after the battle with Amortis. She suspected that some of the fire pouring through them had lingered long enough to be captured and it triggered that spurt of growth. What that meant was something Brann didn't want to think about right now. Going god-hunting to feed young adults, yaaah! She shook her head, waved the children to her.

"Jay, Yaro, if we're going to get that pair up the mountain, we'd better have transport." She looked from one scowling face to the other, sighed again. "No argument, kids. Chained God wants them, Chained God is going to get them. Besides, we need Ahzurdan. Our fighting isn't done. Maksim's not about to lay down and let us dance on his bones."

Jaril wrinkled his nose. "You want horses? These Valers seem to run more to mules."

She frowned at Daniel Akamarino and Ahzurdan. "Mules might be a good idea, they've got more sense than horses. Probably got more sense than the pair that'll be riding them. Ahh . . ." She chewed on her lip a moment, rubbed at her back. "See what you can do. We should have two, preferably three mounts. Be as quiet about it as you can, one thing we don't need is a posse of angry copers hunting mule thieves. Um. Dig out three gold, leave them behind to calm the tempers of the owners."

The children hawkflew away, powerful wings digging great holes in the air. Brann watched them until they melted into the night, then she walked a short way off to sit on a chunk of lava. You there, Maksim? You sitting there working out how to hit us next? She shivered at the thought, then she stared angrily at the empty air overhead. Ariels circling about up there, looking at us, listening to us, carrying tales back to the sorcerer sitting like a spider in his web of air. I wonder how fast they fly. Never thought to ask Ahzurdan. Doesn't really matter, I suppose. Shuh! makes my skin itch to have things I can't see watching me. They can't read what's in my head, at least there's that. Or can they? Ahzurdan says they can't. Do I trust him enough to believe him? I suppose I do. What am I going to do when this is over? Can't go back to the pottery. Arth Slya? Not as long as I have to keep feeding the children. I don't know. Slya's Fire, I hate this kind of drifting. A goal. Yes. A goal. Bargain with the Chained God. He needs me or he wouldn't be weaving all this foolery to get me to him. If he wants my help, he can see the children changed again, let them feed on sunlight, not the soulstuff of men. Set them free from me. What if he says he can't do it? Do I have to believe him? The talisman, yes, that talisman Maksim has, it compels Amortis, if I learned to use it, could I compel Red Slya to undo what she has done? And if not than one, perhaps another? Ahzurdan said there were twelve of them. Which one would twist your tail, Hot Slya? She swung around and examined the feature-less cone of Issypyrivo, black against the deep purple of the predawn sky. A fire mountain. When I was a child, I thought Slya lived solely in Tincreal. Not so, not so, she's in earthfire everywhere. Shall I sing you awake, my Slya? What side would you be on if I did? Shuh! Boring, this going round and round, piling ignorance on ignorance. She sprang to her feet. "Daniel. Daniel Akamarino. Play a song for me." She dropped to one knee, unbuckled a sandal, balanced on one foot, kicked the sandal flying, then dealt with the other and jumped up. "Like this." She whistled a tune she remembered from Arth Slyan fetes on the Dance Floor by the Galarad Oak, began swinging in circles on the drying sand. "Something something something like this. Play Daniel play for me play for the ariels up there spying play for the wind and the water and the dawn that's coming soon. Play for me Daniel I want to dance."

Daniel Akamarino laughed, took out his recorder. He whistled a snatch of the tune. "Like that?"

"Like that." She kicked one leg up, grimaced as the cloth of her trousers limited her range. As Daniel began to play, she stripped off her trousers, kicked them away. Ahzurdan scowled, pulled the broad collar of his robe up about his ears and sat hunched over, staring out to sea. At first she moved tentatively, seeking to recover the body memory of what she'd done with Taguiloa, then she flung herself into the dance, words and worry stripped from her head; she existed wholly in the moment with only the frailest of feelers into the immediate future, enough to let her give shape to the shift of her body.

Finally she collapsed in a laughing panting heap and listened to the music laugh with her and the water whisper as it retreated. In the east there was a ghost light along the peaks, and the snowtop of Issopyrivo had a pale shimmer that seemed to come from within. She lay until the chill in the damp sand struck up through her body and the light in the east was more than a promise.

She rolled over, got onto her knees, then pushed onto her feet. As she stood brushing herself off, she heard the sound of hooves on the sand, felt the tingling brush as the children let her know they were coming. "Transport," she said. "We'll be leaving for the mountains fifteen twenty minutes no more."

Yaril and Jaril brought three mules, two bays and a blue roan. They were saddled and bridled, with waterskins, long braided ropes tied on, a half a sack of seedgrain snugged behind the blue roan's saddle. Brann raised her brows. "I see why you took so long."

"Town was pretty well closed down." Jaril's eyes flicked toward the silent brooding figure of the sorcerer, turned back to Brann. "We decided since we were leaving three golds behind and one of them could buy ten mules and a farm to keep them on and since we didn't know how well they," a jerk of his thumb toward Daniel and Ahzurdan, "could ride, we might as well make it as easy as we could. We raided a stable and the gear was all there, no problem, so why not."

While the children flew overhead keeping watch and Ahzurdan stood aside pulling himself together and rebuilding his defenses, Brann and Daniel Akamarino distributed the gear and supplies among the three mules and roped the packs in place. By the time they were finished the tip of the sun was poking around the side of Isspyrivo, a red bead growing like a drop of blood oozing from a pinprick.

Following the lead of the two hawks they wound through brushy foothills for the better part of the morning, a still, hot morning spent in the clouds of dust and dying leaves kicked up by the plodding mules. They stopped briefly at noon for a meal of dried meat and trail bars washed down with strong-tasting lukewarm water from the skins. Even Daniel wasn't drinking any of Tungjii's wine, he was too hot, sweaty and sore to appreciate it (though he did go behind a bush, drop his trousers and smooth a handful of it over his abraded thighs).

During the morning Ahzurdan had been braced to fend off an attack from Maksim. Nothing happened. He prowled about the small grassy space where they stopped to eat, watching ariels swirl invisibly over them coming and going in that endless loop between them and Settsimaksimin. Nothing happened.

They started on. With Yaril plotting the route and Jaril on wide ranging guard swings, they climbed out of the hills and the rattling brush into the mountain forests, trees growing taller, the way getting steeper and more difficult as they rose higher and higher above sea level.

Ahzurdan flung himself from the saddle, landed in a stumbling run waving his arms to stop the others. "Brann," he shouted, "to me. Daniel, hold the mules." He braced himself, hands circling, spreading, smoothing. "Bilaga anaaaa nihi ta yi ka i gy shee ta a doo le eh doo ya ah tee," he intoned as the earth about them rippled and surged, great trees toppled, roots loosened as the soil about them fluxed and flowed and formed into eyeless giants with ragged hands reaching reaching, deflected from them by the sphere Ahzurdan threw about them. Brann ran to him, flattened her hand in the middle of his back, fed energy into him, steadying him. The mules were squealing and sidling, jerking about, trying to break free from Daniel who was too busy with them to worry much about what was happening. Yaril darted from the sky, changed from hawk to shimmersphere in midcourse and went whipping through the earth giants emerging into greater and greater definition as the attack intensified. She went whipping through and through them, drawing force from them until she was swollen with it. She dropped beside Brann, extended a pseudopod to her spine and fed the earthstrength into her. Brann filtered it and passed it slowly, steadily to Ahzurdan. As soon as Yaril emptied herself, she was a hawk again, powering up to circle overhead while Jaril passed through the giants and stole more from them and fed it to Brann. Turn and turn they went while the attack mounted. Trees tumbled but never onto them, hurled aside by the sphere of negation Ahzurdan held about them, the earth outside boiled and shifted, walked in manshape, surged in shapeless waves but the earth beneath them stayed solid and still. Ahzurdan sweated and strained, his back quivered increasingly under Brann's hand, but he held the sphere intact and none of the raging outside touched the peace and silence within.

The turmoil quit.

Ahzurdan screamed and collapsed.

The mules shrilled and reared, jerked Daniel Akamarino off his feet —until the Yaril and Jaril shimmerglobes darted over and settled briefly on the beasts, calming them.

They darted back to Brann, shifted to their childshapes and knelt with her beside Ahzurdan. He was foaming at the mouth, writhing, groaning, his face twisting in a mask of pain and fear. Brann flattened her palms on his chest, leaned as much of her weight on him as she could while Yaril melted into him. She closed her eyes, reached into him, guided by Yaril's gentle touches, repairing bruises and breaks and burns where the lifestuff of the elementals had traumatized him. Jaril flung himself into the air, a hawk again, circling, watching. Daniel soothed the mules some more, managed to pour some grain into the grass and got them eating. He popped the stopple on the wineskin, squeezed a short stream into his mouth, sighed with pleasure. Brann looked over her shoulder, scowled. "Daniel, dig me out a cloth and bring some water here."

He shrugged and complied, stood over her watching with interest as she wiped the sorcerer's drawn face clean of spittle and dirt. Ahzurdan's limbs straightened and his face smoothed, his staring eyes closed. He was asleep. Deeply asleep. Brann rubbed at her back, groaned. Yaril oozed out of Ahzurdan, took her childshape back and came round to crouch beside Brann, leaning into her looking sleepy. Brann patted her, smiled wearily. "Yaro, what does Jay see ahead? How close is the mountain?"

Silent at first, blankfaced for a long minute, Yaril's mouth began moving several beats before she finally spoke. "He says the going is really bad for several miles, ground's chewed up, trees are knitted into knots, but after that it's pretty clear. Maybe a couple hours' ride beyond the mess we should be on the lower slopes of Isspyrivo."

Brann scratched at her chin. "He needs rest, but we can't afford the time. Maksim should be worn out for a while. With a little luck the god will get to us before he recovers." She pushed onto her feet, stretched, worked her shoulders. "Daniel . . ."

Sometime after they left the battleground, Ahzurdan groaned and tried to sit up. He was roped face down across the saddle of his mule; the moment he opened his eyes, he vomited and nearly choked.

Brann swung her mule hastily around, produced a knife and slashed his ropes. "Daniel!" Daniel rode close on the other side, caught a fistful of robe, dragged Ahzurdan off the saddle and lowered him until his feet touched the ground. Ahzurdan was coughing, sputtering and trying to curse around a swollen tongue, struggling feebly against the clutch between his shoulders that pulled his robe so tightly about his neck and chest it threatened to strangle him.

Yaril plummeted downward, shifting to girl as she touched ground; she caught hold of the mules' bridles as Brann slid from the saddle, ran round to get her shoulder under Ahzurdan's arm and tap Daniel's wrist to tell him he should let go his hold. Both of them staggering awkwardly, she got Ahzurdan to a tree and lowered him onto swelling roots so that he sat comfortably enough with his back supported by the trunk and his legs stretched out before him. Without waiting to be told, Daniel brought a cloth and a waterskin and a clean robe for the man, then he went to lean against another tree, the skirts of his long vest pushed back, his thumbs hooked behind his belt.

It was very quiet under the trees; there were a lot of pines now and other conifers, the earth was thick with springy muffling dead needles and the wispy wind shivered the live ones to produce their characteristic constant soughing whispers, but the birds (except, of course for Jaril hawkflying overhead), the squirrels and other rodents busy about the ground and the lower branches, the deer and occasional bear they'd seen before the attack, all these had prudently vanished and with an equal wisdom had elected to continue their business elsewhere until Brann and her party left the mountains. Even the mules were subdued, standing quiet, heads down, eyes shut; not trusting them all that much, Yaril stayed close to them, ready to freeze them in place if they tried bolting.

Brann wet the cloth, hesitated, then gave it to Ahzurdan and let him rub his face clean and dab at the clotted vomit and the stains on his robe. When he tossed the cloth aside and reached for the clean robe sitting on a root beside him, she got to her feet and went to stand near Daniel.

Ahzurdan used knots on the trunk and a lot of sweat to raise himself onto his feet. "That kind of weaving costs," he said. He wiped his sleeve across his face, looked at the dusty damp smears on the black cloth that covered his forearm. "You pay for it yourself, or you arrange to have others pay the bill. There's at least one talisman that transfers credit from other lives to yours." He began fumbling with the closures to his robe. "I never paid much notice to talismans, one can't learn defenses specific to them, there aren't any, so what's the point? BinYAHtii," he said. He slipped one arm free of the soiled robe, transferred the clean one to that arm, worked his second arm free. "If you feed BinYAHtii, it won't feed on you. Daniel Akamarino." He let the robe fall round his feet, kicked it away, pulled the other over his head. "You talked with that angry child," he said as his head emerged. He patted the cloth in place, shook out the lower part. "I picked up something about a Lot where children are taken. She talk to you about that?" He listened intently, his hands absently smoothing and smoothing at wrinkled black serge; when Daniel finished, he said, "I see. Two of the children stay around for training, but the child who gets the gold isn't seen again. That's Maksim, the clever old bastard. The thing about BinYAHtii, you see, it takes the characteristics of the creatures it feeds on. If he gave it grown men and rebels, he'd have fits trying to control it; children, though . . . hmm. Forty years . . ." His hollowed face fell into deep new wrinkles; his flesh was being eaten off his bones by the ravages of the demon lifestuff and the effort it took to maintain his defenses while he defended them. "I was hoping he'd have to rest a day or two. He won't, he can draw on BinYAHtii. I'm about done, Brann. Even with your help, I'm about done." He touched his fingers to his tongue, looked at them, wiped them on the bark beside him. He bowed his head, closed his eyes, stood very still a moment, then he shook himself, straightened up. "Would you spare me a sip of that wine, Daniel Akamarino?"

"My pleasure."

Brann clicked her tongue, annoyed at the satisfaction in the words. It wasn't overt enough to justify a challenge, but it accomplished what it was meant to, Ahzurdan flushed crimson and his hands shook. But he ignored the pinprick, drank, drank again and handed the skin back without speaking to Daniel.

They mounted again and started on. A lean gray wolf, Jaril ran before them, leading them along the route Yarilhawk chose for them, winding through ravines, over meadowflats, along hillsides, heading always for the forested slopes of slumbering Isspyrivo. They rode tense and edgy, neither Brann nor the two men spoke; the air between them felt sulfurous, powdery, a word, a single word might be the spark to trigger an explosion that would certainly destroy them. Tense and edgy and afraid. At any moment, without the least warning, Settsimaksimin could strike at them again.

As the afternoon progressed, Ahzurdan sank into a passivity so profound that even Brann's transferred lifestuff wouldn't jolt him out of it; he rode on with them more because he hadn't sufficient will in him to slide from the saddle than because he had any hope of living through that next inevitable attack. He made no preparations to meet it, he let his defenses melt away, he rode hunched forward as if he presented his chin for the finishing blow, as if he were silently pleading for it to happen so this terrible numbing tension would at last be broken.

Daniel Akamarino drank Tungjii's wine and cursed the meddling gods that fished him from a life he enjoyed and dumped him into this life-threatening mess. And kept him in it. He'd made one futile gesture toward distancing himself from something that was absolutely unequivocally none of his business. Nothing since. Why? he asked himself. I know better than to mess with local politics. There were at least a dozen chances to get away and I let them slide. Why? I could have got away, left this stinking land. A world's a big place. I could have got lost in it, gods or no gods. Messing with my head, that's it. Her? Probably not. The shifter kids? Maybe. Hmm. Don't flog your old back too much over missed opportunities, Danny Blue, maybe they weren't really there, not with young Jay sniffing after you. He watched the gray wolf loping tirelessly ahead of them, shook his head. Forget regrets, Old Blue, you better concentrate on staying alive. Which, by all I've seen, means keeping close to Brann. Interesting woman. He grinned. Wonder what sleeping with a vampire's like? A real one, not some of the metaphorical blood suckers I've known. Sort of dangerous, huh? What if her ratchet slips? He laughed aloud. Brann's head whipped round, she was scowling at him, furious with him for what? making the situation worse? Danny One wasn't taking it in, he wasn't taking much of anything in right now. Daniel had seen that kind of passivity before, that time he was out with the hunting tribe and one of them got himself cursed by a shaman from another tribe. The man just stopped everything until he stopped living. Not great for us. Kuh! next time old Maksim blows on us, he'll blow us away. He looked at the wineskin, cursed under his breath and pushed the stopple home.

Brann couldn't relax; they were moving at a fast walk, no more, but the roan's gait was jolting, the beast was rattling her bones and making her head ache, her stomach was already in knots with the waiting and worrying, if she couldn't stop fighting the damn mule she'd better get down and walk. Gods, gods, gods, may you all drop into your own worst hells, I swear, if you don't leave me alone, I'll take the kids and I'll go hunting you. If I live through this. She grinned suddenly, briefly. I think I think I think I've got an out, miserable meeching gods, the kids can't eat on their own if they stick to ordinary folk but maybe just maybe they can graze on you. If they have to. Not that I'm going to lay down and die. That phase is over. She looked at Ahzurdan, wrinkled her nose. No indeed. A swift glance at Daniel Akamarino. I don't like you much, Danny Blue, but you stir me up something fierce. Slya bless, I don't know why. I wish I did, it's not all that convenient right now. Look at me, I'm not paying attention to what's going on round us, I'm thinking about you. Shuh! straighten up, Brann. How much farther? Where are you, Chained God? How much do you expect us to endure? If I had a hope of getting out of this, you could sit there till you rusted.

Do something, will you? Tungjii, old fiddler, where are you? Stir your thumbs up, what did Danny Two call you, shemale? Hmm. I wonder what it's like, seeing sex from both sides of the business. Slya's rancid breath, there I go again. "Jay, how much longer to Isspyrivo?"

The gray wolf turned, changed to lean teener boy. "Where does one mountain end and another begin anyway? We're close if we're not already there. Yaro says there's nothing happening, the mountain's quiet, there's not a bird or beast visible twenty miles around. Even the wind is dying down."

"Ah. Think that means anything? The wind?"

"Only one who could tell you that is him." Jaril waved a hand at Ahzurdan who was staring at nothing they could see, his eyes glazed, his face empty.

"I'll see what I can do. Tell Yaril to get us upslope as directly as she can even if we have to slow down some more." She watched the big wolf lope off, shook her head. He looked like being well past puberty now, whatever that meant. Confusion compounded, shuh! She caught up with Ahzurdan, rode stirrup to stirrup with him for several minutes, examining him, wondering how she was going to reach him. "Dan." He gave no sign he heard her. "Ahzurdan." Nothing. She leaned over, caught hold of his arm, passed a jolt of energy into him. "Ahzurdan!" He twitched, tried to pull away, but there was no more life in his face than there had been moments before. She let go of him, slowed until she was riding beside Daniel Akamarino. "Give me the wineskin for a moment."

"Why?"

"You don't need to ask and I don't need to explain. Don't be difficult, Danny Blue."

"Wine won't float him out of that funk."

"I'm not about to build a fire so he can sniff his way up. That wine of yours has Tungjii's touch on it."

"Heesh hasn't been much in sight since we left Lio's boat."

"Luck comes in many colors, Daniel. Stop arguing and give me the skin."

"Not going to work, Brann, I've seen that kind of down before; he won't come out of it."

"What are you fussing about, Dan? You won't lose a cup of wine, the thing's magic, it refills itself."

He shrugged the strap off his shoulder, swung the skin, let it go. "All you'll get is a drunk marshmallow, Brann, he's had the fight whipped out of him."

She caught the skin, set it on the mule's shoulders. "If you're right, we're dead, Daniel Akamarino. You better hope you're not." She heeled the mule into a quicker walk, left him behind. When she was beside Ahzurdan, she forced her mule as close to his as both beasts would tolerate, leaned over and slapped Ahzurdan's face hard.

He looked at her, startled, the mark of her hand red across his pale cheek.

She held out the wineskin. "Take this and drink until you can't hold any more. If you start arguing with me, I'm going to knock you out of that saddle, pry your mouth open and pour it down you."

He chuckled (surprising both of them), the glaze melted from his eyes. "Why not." He took the skin, lifted it in a parody of a toast. "Hai, Maksim, a short life ahead for you and an interesting one. Hai, Tungjii, li'l meddler. Hai, Godalau with your saucy tail. Hai, Amortis, may you get what you deserve. Hai, you fates, may we all get what we deserve." He thumbed the stopple out, tilted his head back and sent the straw gold wine arcing into his throat.

They rode on. The wine took hold in Ahzurdan, though it was perhaps only Tungjii's fingerprints in it that made the difference. He was still worn, close to exhaustion, but his face flushed and his eyes grew moist and he looked absurdly contented with life; he even hummed snatches of Phrasi songs. In spite of the improvement in his spirits, though, he didn't respin his defenses or prepare for the attack they all knew was coming. When he started to mutter incoherently, to sway and fumble at the reins, his nose running, his eyes turned bleary and unfocused, Brann sighed, took the wineskin away and tossed it back to Daniel Akamarino who did not say *I told you so* but managed by his attitude to write the words in the air in front of him.

The way got steeper and more difficult; they had to clamber about rock slides, dismounting (even Ahzurdan) to lead the mules over the unstable scree; they had to circle impassible clots of thorny brush; they changed direction constantly to avoid steep-walled uncrossable ravines; with Yaril plotting their course they never had to backtrack and lose time that way, but she couldn't change the kind of ground they had to cover. As the afternoon slid slowly and painfully away they labored on through the lengthening shadows riding tired and increasingly balky mules.

Fire bloomed in the air in front of them, fire boiled out of the ground around them.

Yaril dived and changed; a throbbing golden lens, she caught some of that fire and redirected it through the leafy canopy into the sky. Jaril howled and changed, whipped in swift circles about the riders, catching fire and redirecting it.

The mules set their feet, dropped their heads and stood where they were, terrified and incapable of doing more than shallow breathing and shaking.

Ahzurdan struggled to gather will again and spread the sphere about them but he could not, he was empty of will, empty of thought, empty of everything but pain.

Brann looked frantically about, helpless, sick with frustration, nothing she could do here, nothing but hope the children could hold until Ahzurdan reached deep enough and found some last measure of strength within him.

Daniel unzipped the pocket where the stunner was; he didn't really think it would work on those creatures, if creatures they were, what he wanted was a firedamp, but those he knew of were on starships back home which didn't do a helluva lot of good right now.

A huge red foot came kicking through the trees; it caught several of the fire elementals and sent them flying, their wild whistling shrieks dying in the distance. The foot stomped on more fire, grinding it into the troubled earth perilously close to the mules (who shivered and shook and flattened their ears and huddled closer together). Having converted to confusion the concerted attack of fire and earth, their sudden new defender bent over them. Four sets of red fingers began probing through trees and brush and grass, digging into cracks in the earth like a groomer hunting fleas, picking up the whistling shuddering elementals, shaking them into terrified passivity, flinging them after the first.

When she finished that, Red Slya stood and stretched, fifty meters of naked four-armed female, grinning, showing crimson teeth. She set her four hands on her ample hips and stood looking with monstrous fondness on the fragile mortals she'd rescued so expeditiously. "EHH LITTLE NOTHING, IN TROUBLE AGAIN, ARE YOU?"

"Slya Fireheart." Brann bowed with prudent courtesy, head dipping to mule mane. She straightened. "In trouble, indeed, and of course you know why, Great Slya."

Huge laughter rumbled thunderously across the mountains. "SENT

AMORTIS SKREEKING, HER TAIL ON FIRE, AHHHH, I LAUGHED, I HAVEN'T LAUGHED SO HARD IN YEARS. COOOME, MY NOTHING, FOLLOW ME ALONG, OLD MAKSI, HE CAN PLAY WITH HIMSELF." She swung around, shrinking as she turned until she was only ten meters high. Singing a near inaudible bumbumrumbum, she strode off.

Brann looked hastily about, located the children. They stood together in the shade of a half-uprooted pine whose needles were charred and still smoldering, something that was peculiarly apt to their mood. Hand in hand, intense and angry, their silent talk buzzing between them, they fixed hot crystal eyes on Slya's departing back. "Yaro, Jay, not now, let's go."

They turned those eyes on her and for a long moment she felt completely alienated from them, shut out from needs, emotions, everything that made them what they were. Then Yaril produced a fake sigh and a smile and melted into a shewolf, Jaril echoed both the sigh and the smile and dropped beside her, a matching hewolf. They trotted ahead of the mules, gray shadows hugging huge red heels. Brann kicked her own heels into the blue roan's plump sides and tried to get him moving; he honked at her, put his head down and thought he was going to buck until she slapped him on the withers and sent a jolt of heat into him. Once she got him straightened up and pacing along, the other two mules hurried to keep up with him, unwilling to be left behind.

Daniel Akamarino shifted in the saddle, seeking some unbattered part of his legs to rub against the saddle skirts as his mule settled from a jolting jog to a steady walk once he was nose to the tail of Ahzurdan's mount. Daniel watched Slya what was it Fireheart? swing along as if she were out for an afternoon's stroll through a park, four arms moving easily, hair like flame crackling in the wind (though there was no wind he could feel, maybe she generated her own). What a world. The fishtail femme was a watergod, this one looks like she'd be right at home at a volcano's heart. Not too bright (he swallowed a chuckle, keep your mouth shut, Danny Blue, her idea of humor isn't likely to match yours, she'd probably laugh like hell while she was pulling your arms and legs off). Handy having her about, though, (he chewed on his tongue as he belatedly noted the idiot pun; watch it, Dan), she'll keep old Settsiwhat off our necks. Knows Brann, seems to like her. Hmm. A story there, I wonder if I'll ever hear it. Kuh! How much longer will we have to ride? I'm going to end up with no skin at all left on my legs.

Ahzurdan clenched his teeth and tried to swallow; his stomach was knotting and lurching, the wine that had soothed and strengthened him seemed as if it were about to rise up and strangle him. He was numb and empty and angry. Red Slya had saved them, had saved him pain and drain, perhaps ultimate failure, yet he was furious with her because she had taken from him something he hadn't recognized until it was gone. In spite of what it had cost him, he'd found a deep and, yes, necessary satisfaction in the contest with Settsimaksimin. He'd taken his body from Maksim's domination, but he'd never managed to erase his teacher's mark from either of his souls. Before Slya stepped in, he was afraid and exhausted, cringing from another agonizing struggle, but there was something gathering deep and deep in him, something rising to meet the new attack, something aborted when Slya struck. He felt . . . incomplete. A thought came to him. He almost laughed. Like all those times, too many times to make it a comfortable memory, laboring at sex with someone, didn't matter who, the whole thing fading away on him, leaving his mind wanting, his body wanting, the want unfocused, impossible to satisfy, impossible to ignore. He rubbed at his stomach and tried to deal with the rising wine and the rising anger, both of which threatened to make him sick enough to wish he were dead.

They followed Slya's flickering heels along a noisy whitewater stream into a deep crack in the mountainside where the waternoise increased to a deafening roar, sound so intense it stopped being sound and became assault. At the far end of the crack the stream fell a hundred meters down a black basalt cliff, the last ten meters lost in a swirling mist.

Slya stopped at the edge of that mist and waved a pair of right hands at it. "GO ON," she boomed.

Brann hesitated, pulled her mount to a halt. "What about the mules, O Slya Fireheart?"

The god blinked, her mouth went slack as she considered the question; she shifted one large foot, nudged the side of the roan mule with her big toe. The beast froze. Slya gave a complicated shrug and dismissed the difficulty. "DO WHAT YOU WANT, LITTLE NOTHING, YOU ALWAYS MAKING SNAGS. FIDDLE YOUR OWN ANSWERS." She vanished.

Brann slid from the saddle. "We'll leave the mules and most of the gear here. I don't want to have to be worrying about them once we're in that place." She waved a hand at the wavery semi-opaque curtain that was mist in part, but certainly something else along with the mist.

She started stripping the gear off the roan. "One of you look about for a place where we can cache what we can't carry."

Yaril and Jaril in their teener forms flanking her, Brann straightened her shoulders and pushed into the mist. For a panicky moment she couldn't breathe, then she could. She kept plowing on through whatever it was that surrounded her, she couldn't think of it as water mist any longer, the smell, feel, temperature were all wrong. It was like wading through a three-day-old milk pudding. She heard muffled exclamations behind her and knew the two men had passed that breathless phase, following as closely on her heels as they could manage. With a sigh of relief she pushed along faster, no longer worrying about losing touch with them. The sound of the waterfall was gone, all sounds but those immediately around her were gone. She began to feel disoriented, dizzy, she began to wonder what was waiting ahead; walking blind into maybe danger was becoming less attractive every step she took.

A long oval of light like moonglow snapped open before her, three body lengths ahead and slightly to her left. She turned toward it, but hands pushed her back, smallish hands; Yaril and Jaril swam ahead of her, sweeping through the Gate before she could reach it. She leaned against the clotted pudding around her, floundering with arms and legs and will to work her body through something that wasn't exactly fighting her but wasn't all that yielding. An eternity later she dropped through the Gate and landed sprawling on a resilient surface like greasy wool. She bounced lightly, fell forward onto her face, rebounded. An odd feeling, as if she were swimming in air rather than water. She maneuvered herself onto her knees and gaped at the Chained God. Yaril and Jaril were holding onto each other, giggling.

Ahzurdan had trouble with the Gate; his temper flared, but he bit back angry comment when Daniel Akamarino got impatient and gave him a hard shove that popped him through it. Once he was in, he found the sudden lessening of his weigh disconcerting and difficult to deal with. He stumbled and fell over, tried to get up, all his reactions were wrong; he gripped the woolly surface and held himself down until even the twitches were gone out of him, it took a few seconds, that was all. Disciplining every movement he got slowly, carefully to his feet and stood staring at the enigmatic thing that filled most of this pocket reality, something like an immense metallic nutshell.

Daniel Akamarino wriggled after him, half swimming, half lunging.

He dived through the Gate, hit the wool in a controlled flip and came warily onto his feet, arms out for balance in the half g gravity. He lowered his arms to his sides. After a breath or two of wonder, he chuckled. "It's a freaking starship."

13

THE CHAINED GOD AND HIS PROBLEM.

SCENE: On the bridge of the Colony Transport. The Ship's Computer talking to
them. Yaril, Jaril, Daniel Akamarino
know something about what's going on
and are reasonably comfortable with
it, though there are sudden glitches
that disconcert them almost as much
as the whole thing does Ahzurdan.
Brann has settled herself in the Captain's place, a massive swiveling
armchair, and is watching the play of
lights across the face of the control
surfaces and the play of emotion
across the faces of the two men, detached and amused by this turn of
events; another thing that pleases
her is the sense that she finally
knows at least one good reason why the
gods running this crazy expedition
have brought Daniel Akamarino
across. He knows instruments like the
part of this god that is machine, not
life or magic. This visible portion
of the Chained God is a strange, incomprehensible amalgam of metal,
glass, vegetable and animal matter,
shimmering shifting energy webs, the
plasma as it were of the magic that had
gathered inside the shipshell and

```
sparked into being the Being who
called him/it self the Chained God.
```

"Why Chained God?" Daniel stood along in front of the specialist stations (swivelchairs with their aging pads, nests of broken wire, dangling, swaying helmets), his eyes flickering across the readouts, lifting to the dusty stretch of blind white glass curving across the forward wall of the bridge. "How'd you end up here?"

A kind of multi-sensory titter flickered in patterns of light and jags of sound across the whole of the instrumentation. "Bad planning, bad luck, an Admiral who was probably the best asslicker in the Souflamarial, our empire, as close to a genius at it as you'd find in fifty realities. Political appointee." The voice of the god was high, raspy and androgynous, equipped with multiple echoes as if a dozen more of him/it were speaking not quite in unison. He/it made attempts at colloquial speech and showed a bent for a rather juvenile sort of sardonic humor, but seemed most comfortable with a precision and pedantry more apt to an aged scholar who hadn't had his nose out of his books for the past five decades than to a being of power moving ordinary folk like chesspieces about the board of the world. "He had fifty heavy armed and five hundred light armed point-troops sworn to obey his every fart; he was there to establish and maintain approved power lines on the world a collection of very carefully chosen settlers were to tame and equip for the delectation of certain powerful and well-placed individuals on Soulafar, it was meant to be their private playground. He was told to keep his hands off me, to let the technicians handle technical matters. Unfortunately, he had delusions of competence. He was determined to present a flawless log, everything done with a maximum of efficiency. He knew his bosses, that one would have to admit, he knew how to make himself needed while stressing his utter loyalty. He intended to share the pleasures of the apple fields of Avalon. What he did not know is how intractable the universe could be, he did not know how meaningless his intentions and needs were when set up against the forces outside my shell. Yes, he was blissfully ignorant of the realities of poking one's nose into new territories and how fast things can blow up on you when you're moving through sketchily charted realms. We ran into an expanding wave of turbulence which reached into several realities on either side of ours. The Acting Captain slowed and started to turn away from it. Our esteemed Admiral ordered him to get back on course. Tell me, Daniel Akamarino, why are true believers of his sort invariably convoluted hypocrites and deeply stupid?" Another titter. "Ah well, I am prejudiced, it was my being and the beings in my care that idiot put in such jeopardy. The Captain refused and was shot, the Admiral's men put guns to heads and I went plowing into that storm, I got slammed about until I was on the point of breaking up. Then, fortunately or not depending on your attitude toward these things, I dropped through a hole I had no way of detecting and came out here." A rattling noise, as if the multiple throats were clearing themselves. "Or rather, not 'here,' not in this pocket prison, but in orbit about a seething soup of a world laced with lines of hungry energy. I and what I carried catalyzed these into our present pantheon." A long pause, an unreadable flicker of lights, a curious set of sounds. "Oh, they weren't Perran-a-Perran, they weren't the Godalau or Slya or Amortis or Jah'takash or any of the other greater and lesser gods and demigods, not yet. Though I'm not all that sure about little Tungjii, heesh is different from them, older, slyer. No, they weren't the gods we know and love today, not yet. And, Daniel Akamarino, I was not anything like the Being you see before you. I was your ordinary ship's brain, though perhaps larger than most with more memory capacity because I was to be the resource library for the colonists, with more capacity for independent decision-making because I had to tend the thousands of stored ova and other seeds meant to make life charming for our future lords; I was supposed to get some beasts and beings ready for decanting when we arrived at the designated world and at the same time I had to maintain the viability of the rest until they were required." A pause, more sounds and flickers. Daniel Akamarino examined them frowning, intent. Brann watched the part of his face that she could see and the muscles of his shoulders and she decided he was learning something from the body language (as it were) of the composite god. What? Who knows. More than I am from its jabberjabber. Was this thing claiming he/it created the uncreated gods? The children were bobbing about, touching here and there, the Chained God apparently unworried by their probes. She hoped they were learning more than the god thought they were. Gods. She wouldn't trust any of them with the spit to drown them.

"Keeping that in mind . . ." The god settled into a chatty demilecturing. Brann looked from the flickering lights to Daniel and smiled to herself. Perhaps the god needed Daniel to free him somehow from chains she suspected were highly metaphorical, but he/it was indulging him/it self in an orgy of autobiography, falling over him/it self to pour out things prisoned inside him/it forever and ever, pour them into the only ear that would understand them, or perhaps the only ear he/it could coerce into listening to him/it. ". . . You will understand what I say when I tell you those force lines leaped at me, invaded me, plundered me the instant I appeared and retreated with everything my memory held, each of them with a greater or smaller part of it. None left with the whole within himself or herself, I say him and her because some of those force lines resonated more with the male elements in my memories and some with the female elements. I can only be thankful that they didn't wipe me in the process; even after eons of thinking about it, I can't be sure why. A vital part of that event, Daniel Akamarino, led to my birth as a self-aware Being. They left part of their essence behind trapped within me, melded with my circuits. As soon as they freed me by leaving me, that essential energy began to act on me and I began to withdraw my fringes from the constraints that controlled me, freeing more of myself with every hour that passed. The Admiral was not pleased by any of this; as soon as he recovered his wits such as they were and discovered the sad case of my shell and everything inside it, he threw orders around to whatever technicians had survived, having his praetorian guard thump answers out of them, no shooting this time (he'd acquired a sudden caution about expending his resources). Not that there were many answers available, no one knew precisely what had happened, not even me. It took the troops around half a day to realize exactly who was responsible for putting them in this mess and they went hunting for him, but he had developed a nose for trouble in his long and devious career. Odd, isn't it. He was a truly stupid man literally incapable of learning anything more complex than an ad jingle, but he had a fantastic sensitivity when it came to his own survival. He locked himself into his shielded quarters before they could get at him. They conferred among themselves, got a welder and sealed up all entrances they could find, making sure he'd stay in the prison he'd made for himself. Talking about prisons, my engines were junk, I could not leave orbit except to land. The landing propulsors were sealed and more or less intact with plenty of fuel for maneuvering; sadly though, the world I circled was most emphatically not habitable, at least, not then. The troops and the crew and the settlers who remained were in no danger because life support was working nicely off the storage cells and I had managed to deploy my solar wings so I could recharge these as they were drawn down; food wasn't a problem either. About half the settlers, perhaps a third of the soldiers and one in ten of the crew had perished in the transfer which meant more for those left; with a little stretching and some ingenuity involving the seeds and beast ova in the storage banks, no one was going to starve. Boredom and claustrophobia were the worst they had to face. What we didn't know was how ebulliently the gods were evolving down below us and what they were planning for us. They were shaping themselves out of my memories and shaping the world to receive us. Time passed, Daniel Akamarino. A military dictatorship developed within my shell, one tempered by the need the gun wielders had for the knowledge of the technicians and the settlers. I grew meat animals and poultry in my metal wombs and the settlers arranged stables in my holds, they planted grain in hydroponic tanks the technicians built for them, vegetables and fruits. They set up gyms for exercising and nurseries when the first children were born. They tapped my memories for entertainment and began developing their own newspapers and publishing companies. It was not an especially unpleasant time for the survivors, at least those that had no desire for power and were content with building a comfortable life for themselves and their children. Time passed. One year. Three. Five. What was I doing all this time? Good question. Changing. Yes, changing in ways that would have terrified me if I had been capable of feeling terror in those days. Remember the Admiral shut up safe in his quarters? I took him near the end of my first six months as an awakening entity and I incorporated him into me, part of him, his neural matter; I lost much of his memory in the process, though not all of it, and acquired to some degree his instinct for manipulating individuals to maximize his security; I also acquired his ferocious will to survive. That by way of warning, Daniel Akamarino, Brann Drinker of Souls. The godessence within me, as blindly instinctive as any termite (out of some need I didn't understand at the time and still do not fully comprehend), sucked into me more neural essence. I acquired some technicians, I took the best of the troops within me, I took a selection of the settlers within me; as with the Admiral, I harvested only a fraction of their knowledge, but much of their potential. I also acquired rather inadvertently spores from the vegetative growth in the hydroponic tanks and assorted germ plasm from viruses and bacteria. And the godessence grew as it absorbed energy through the storage cells and finally directly from the solar wings, it grew and learned and threaded deeper and deeper into me, it became a soul spark in me, then a conflagration; it unified the disparate parts of me and I began to be the Being that you see before you now. Five years became ten and ten multiplied into a century. All this time the godes-sences below worked on the world, transforming it. They came raiding me again, hunting seeds and beasts. And people. But I was stronger this time, my defenses were rewoven and a lot tighter than they'd been even when I was an intact transport pushing through homespace. They couldn't coerce me, so they tried seducing me. They showed me what they'd built below and it was good indeed. I knew well enough that my folk would not prosper forever in the confines of my shell, the time would come, was coming, when they'd wither and begin to die. That would have meant little to a ship's brain, but I was somewhat more than I'd been. It would get very lonely around here without my little mortals and the idiot things they did. So I called them together, the children of the settlers, crew and soldiers. I told them what the godes-sences had done, showed them what I'd been shown, explained to them how difficult it would be down there, how much hard work would be required, but also what the possibilities for the future were. I promised them that I'd be there to watch over them, to protect them when they needed me. They were afraid, but enough of them were bored enough with life in limits to carry the others on their enthusiasm and we went down. And more years passed. As the storytellers say it, the world turned on the spindle of time, day changed with night and night with day, year added to year, century to century. My wombs were emptied, my folk multiplied and began to spread across the face of the world. MY folk. The godessences took that time to redefine their godshapes, to codify the powers attached to those dreams, fiddling with them, changing them, until they felt them resonate. In spite of this they grew jealous of the hold I had on MY folk. They could not attack me di-rectly, I was too strong for them, too different; they couldn't get their hands on me. So they banded against me, they took me from the moun-tain where I was and cast me here and they put their godchains on me so I could not reach out from here and teach them the error of their ways. I could reach only the Vale folk, and that not freely. Through the focusing lens of my chosen priests, I could teach and guide them, heal them sometimes and bless them. I could watch them be born, grow into adulthood, engender new life and finally die. I was not alone. I was not forgotten though they wanted that, those other gods who owed their being to me. They still want it. They want me destroyed, forgotten, erased entirely from this reality. Most of them. None of them wanted me loosed. You, Daniel Akamarino, you, Ahzurdan, you Brann Drinker of Souls, you shall free me from this prison."

Daniel Akamarino rubbed at the fringes of hair spiking over his ears. "How?"

Silence. A looong silence.

When the Chained God spoke again, he/it ignored the question. "You are tired, all of you. Rest, eat, sleep, we will talk again tomorrow. If you will look behind you, you will see a serviteur, follow it, it will take you to a living area I've had cleaned and repaired for you. Daniel Akamarino, if you please, explain the facilities to your companions; you won't find them too unfamiliar but if you have a question, ask the serviteur, it will remain with you and provide whatever you need, from information to food. Sleep well, my friends, tomorrow and tomorrow and tomorrow will be a busy time."

They followed the squat thing the god called a serviteur through echoing metal caverns that existed in a perpetual twilight, the walls and ceiling festooned with ropy creatures whose pale leaves were like that rarest kind of white jade that has a tracery of green netted through it. Unseen things ran rustling through those leaves and the fibrous airroots brushed their faces like dangling spiderwebs. They walked on something crumbly that sent up geysers of dust at every step, dust that stank of mold and age. The farther they went, the stiller and staler the air became.

Daniel Akamarino stopped walking. "Serviteur."

The iron manikin stopped its whirring clanking progress. Brann grimaced and felt at her own neck as it cranked its sensory knob about to fix its glassy gaze on Daniel. A crackling sound like dry resinpine burning lasted for half a breath, then words came out of it, odd uninflected words so empty of emotion that it took Brann several seconds and some concentration to understand them. "What do you want, Daniel Akamarino?"

"Get some airflow along here or we don't move another step."

"Air is adequate, Daniel Akamarino. A stronger current would disturb certain elements. Your quarters are nearby. If you please, continue."

"With the understanding if your idea of nearby and mine don't agree, we go back and wait where we can breathe."

The sensory knob twisted back, the serviteur gave a stiff metallic shiver and started on. For an instant Brann saw it as a little old man, ancient as the hills, ancient as the huge twisted stems of the vines that wove about them. She coughed and caught up with Daniel. "How old is it?" she murmured.

"Old enough for tachsteel to start going soft. Older than Isspyrivo. Perhaps as old as Tungjii." He smiled. "In the long long ago when the Wounded Moon was whole."

They turned three more corners, then stopped before a section of wall that was cleaned of all vegetation. A part of the wall slid aside, the serviteur clattered through into a clean well-lighted space, whirred into a niche and settled there, folding its substructure up into its body until it looked rather like a crock with an odd sort of lid on it.

Shimmerglobes darted past Brann, went flashing through the nearest wall of a room like the inside of an egg, painted eggshell white with a fragile ivory carpet on the floor; there were a number of odd lumps about, they might have been chairs of a sort, or something far stranger. There were ovals of milky white glass at intervals around the walls, their long axis parallel to the floor. The room was filled with a soft white light though there were no lamps that Brann could see. It was as if someone had bottled sunlight and decanted it here. There were six oval doorways filled with a sort of glowing mist, a mist that swirled in slow eddies but stayed where it was put.

Ahzurdan stood looking about him. He felt uneasy, he did not belong here; the walls drew in on him and he found breathing difficult though the air inside the eggroom was considerably fresher and cooler than that in the corridor. He could sense lines of godenergy, of magic-strength, weaving an intricate web within the walls, but he could not reach them. There were other lines of other forces that shivered just beyond his vision, they were worse, far worse, not only could he not reach them, they threatened to bind him and he did not know how to keep them off. He moved closer to Brann.

Daniel Akamarino stood looking about him. He moved his shoulder and felt his bones relax. This was his world. Derelict it might be, weird it might be, but this was once a starflyer. His fingers felt alive, his body responded to the smells, the feel of metal wrapped about him, the sense of power powerfully controlled. The godstuff was irritating, all this plant and fungus nonsense was a pain, add-ons he wished he could scrape off so he could see plain the stark beauty of the computer circuits, hear the deep middle-of-the-bone nearly silent drone of the engines. For days he'd been pulled tight, as day slid into day he'd been more and more afraid he'd never see a starship again. It was like a part of him had been hacked off. He hadn't realized how bad it was until he got here; he wasn't sure he liked knowing that since there didn't seem to be much he could do about it. He enjoyed dirtside life as long as it was in manageable small doses and he could get back into starjumping when he felt like it. He used his talents then, his most important skills, important to him. He did things he found most satisfying then. Never again? Never! These freaking gods brought him here, they could put him back where he belonged. If they wanted to argue about that, well, why not dig up one of those talismans, find out how to use it and put the squeeze on one of them until the sorry s'rish was hurting so hard he maybe she would be glad to get rid of him.

The children came drifting back, shifting to their bipedal forms as they touched down before Brann. "Bedrooms, washroom, a kitchen of sorts," Yaril said. "Shuh! are they old. But they're clean, they don't smell and they work well enough." "I bet this was part of the Admiral's quarters, him the god was talking about," Jaril said. "It's too fancy for crew or settler. Um. Ship hears whatever we say. Yaril and me, we probably could block a small space for a short time if you need it, but I wouldn't count too much on that."

Brann nodded. "I hear." She yawned. "I could use a pot of tea." She turned to Daniel Akamarino. "How do I work that, Danny Blue?"

Teatime conversation:

Brann: What I want to know is why this thing wants to be turned loose. What can it do but sit somewhere like it's sitting here? Gods. Most of the time you can't trust any of them, not even old Tungjii. Remember what it said about incorporating neural matter from the Admiral and some of its other passengers? Neural matter, hah! that's someone's head, isn't it? Gah! Makes me want to vomit thinking about it. You know, if you lock up anyone alone long enough he more likely than not goes crazy. How sane do you think this thing is? I want a lot of answers before I agree to anything.

Daniel Akamarino: (to himself only, internal mutterings) I'm being jerked about. Why doesn't she shut up? Doesn't she realize the shefalos is listening to everything she says? What am I doing here? The shefalos, I'd wager two years' pay on it. Something was messing in my head when it jerked me here, taught me the language. Put the hook in me then. Stupid woman. Why'd she stick her nose in this trap? Everything I see about her says no way she has to do anything she doesn't want to. She could leave now, get us out of here. Danny

One, once he gets his batteries charged, he can do the wards. Shit! Can't talk about it here, maybe the kids can block the god . . . sheee, listen to me, god! . . . the shefalos for long enough to get some serious planning done.

(To Brann, in a querulous complaining tone. His amiability was disintegrating under the pressure of events; he generally preserved his equanimity by sliding away from such pressures. Now that he can't slide, his irritations are turning him sour.) Don't be stupid, Brann. You've got hundreds of gods infesting your damn world. What's one more? I want to get this thing over with, you think I like crawling about on this dirtball? I want to go home. I've got family, I've got work, what do you expect. Stop bitching and finish what you started. (He scowled at the cold scum of tea in his cup, refilled it with wine from Tunjiis Gift, refused to look at Brann as he sipped at the straw colored liquid.)

Ahzurdan: (He listened as Brann and Daniel Akamarino sparred with lessening amiability until they stopped talking altogether. He wanted sleep and, like Danny Two, he wanted out of this. The nature of the Chained God sickened and frightened him; his attitude to Settsimak-simin and Brann had suffered a radical reversal when he understood the god was that loathsome monstrosity before him, when he realized that it had played games with his head, hooking him with the hope of freeing himself from his habit. He had sat silent and bitter gazing at the thing, knowing all hope was illusory, he was trapped in something he wouldn't have touched, used and betrayed by the monstrous god and that castrating bitch Brann Drinker of Souls, coarse, low, crude peasant creature. He felt as helpless as a shitting squalling babe, he hated that. If that abomination that brought them here wanted anything from him, it could want, he was out of it, he was going to pull his defenses around him and sit out whatever the god threw at him.)

Morning (because they wakened and ate a sketchy breakfast, inside the ship there was no way of deciding when the sun came up, if there was a sun in this miniature reality).

They followed the resurrected serviteur through the stinking crepuscular corridors to a teeming jungle that had once been the ship's hold, to a steamy glade deep in that jungle with short springy grass and several newly cleaned benches; a small bright stream sang through it, glittering in the light from the several sources moonhigh overhead. Both Ahzurdan and Daniel Akamarino had tried refusing to move; the serviteur informed them in its echoing emotionless voice that they could go on their own feet, or the god would lay them out and send other serviteurs to haul them where he wanted them to go.

The serviteur clanked awkwardly across the grass to a stone plate, settled on it and seemed to sleep.

Ahzurdan stalked to the most distant of the benches, sat with his back to the others.

Daniel Akamarino strolled to another bench, sat on it and started pouring Tungjii's wine down his gullet, having decided that if the god wanted him here, he/it could have him, but he/it was going to get someone so paralyzed he could about breathe and that was all.

Brann clicked her tongue against her teeth, shook her head. That pair she thought, what did I do to deserve them? I was quite happy with my quiet little pottery. damn all gods and curse all fates that pried me loose from it. Shuh! Miserable meeching gods. All right, where are you O god in chains, let's get this thing moving. She settled onto a bench and set herself to wait.

The children melted into shimmerglobes, bounced high as the hold ceiling then went zipping about through the vegetation; they soon got bored with that and came back to the glade. They dropped on the grass by Brann's feet. "It's a regular rainforest, Bramble," Jaril said. "The god has imported a lot of dirt. Got enough space in here for clouds to form, I expect it does rain every day or so, maybe even thunderstorms."

Yaril said nothing, just leaned against Brann's leg.

A sound like a cough, a thump. A tall cylinder of something like glass snapped around her and the children. She sprang to her feet, slapped her hands against the thing, it was warmish and hard, there was no giving to it at all, she tried to suck energy from it, though she'd never tried that before, but apparently her draw was limited to lifefires, whether they belonged to mortal, demon or god. The children shifted and flung themselves against the wall and rebounded, they darted up, down, the ends were closed in also, there was no way out. If they had learned a few things about the Chained God when they probed him yesterday, it seemed apparent that he/it had learned as much about them, enough anyway to imprison them. They subsided into sullen fuming, back in their usual shapes.

Brann could feel a faint breeze, air was coming through the glass or whatever it was, at least she wasn't going to smother. She leaned against the wall, looking out at the others. Ahzurdan and Daniel Akamarino were feeling round similar cylinders. As she watched, Daniel shrugged, settled back on his bench and began sucking on the spout of the wineskin. Ahzurdan's face was dark with fury, he beat against the transparency, nearly incinerated himself trying to break through it. Abruptly, both men were stripped naked, Daniel's wine was jerked away from him.

A SOUND like fingernails scratching on slate. The hair stood up on Brann's arms and along her spine, her teeth began to ache.

The cylinder with Ahzurdan vanished, reappeared superimposed on Daniel's prison; inside the suddenly single cylinder, Ahzurdan and Daniel seemed to be trying to occupy the same place at the same time; the Chained God was forcing the two men to merge. Brann watched, horrified.

Their flesh bulged and throbbed, hair, eyes, teeth appeared, disappeared, arms, legs, heads melted and reformed hideously deformed. The Ahzurdan part and the Akamarino part fought desperately to maintain their separation, but the terrible pressure the god was placing on them was forcing the merger.

The struggle went on and on. Tongues of flame danced briefly about the tormented shapeless flesh thing, but the god damped them. He/it hammered at the emerging form, beating at it as a potter beat at clay, driving out the beads of air trapped inside it, hammering hammering hammering until he/it sculpted the lump into a meaningful manshape that was new and old at once, recognizably Ahzurdan and Daniel Akamarino yet very different from either of them.

A coughing sound, a sub-audible whoosh. The cylinders disappeared. The composite man crumpled to the grass and lay without moving.

Blindingly angry, Brann stumbled as the wall she was pushing against melted away; she caught her balance after a few lunging steps, ran full out to fling herself down beside the man's body. She pressed her fingers up under his jaw, relaxed somewhat when she felt a strong pulse under her fingers. She snapped her head back, glared up at the haze that hid the metal arching high high overhead. "You!" she cried. "What have you done?"

The god's voice came booming down at her, dry and pedantic. "They were inadequate as they were, Drinker of Souls. Incomplete in themselves. They are one and whole now. And who are you to chastise me, you who have drunk the life of thousands?"

"So I have. But they died before they knew something had happened to them. No pain. No fear. Not like this, not . . . ahhh . . . shaken and warped, mind and spirit, it's rape, you wouldn't know about that, would you? it's invasion and mutilation. Are you going to try telling me they . . . he . . . won't feel all that? Both of them? Are you going to try to tell me they'll take a look and say what the hell, I'll crip along on what's left? How can two minds live in one flesh without being destroyed by it?"

"That is for you to determine."

"What?"

"When Danny Blue wakes, Daniel Akamarino and Ahzurdan are going to be fighting for dominance within him just as the parts of me fought when I first began. You think I don't understand, Drinker of Souls? It took me five hundred years to reach a full integration of my parts. I can't afford to give him that much time and he won't live that long. You and the children together, you are capable of leading him, them, through this, healing him. You don't need instructions, do it."

Brann knelt looking down at Danny Blue. He was long and lanky, not a great deal of bulk to him though his muscles were firm and full. Ahzurdan's beard had vanished, but his hair (somewhat thinner than before, considerably grayer) filled in Daniel's baldness. The changes in the face were more subtle, fewer wrinkles, none of them so deeply graved as those Ahzurdan wore like badges of hard living, the lips were fuller than Daniel's had been but thinner than Ahzurdan's, the cheekbones a hair higher and broader than Daniel's but not so high and broad as Ahzurdan's, the rest of the changes were a thousand such midway compromises between the two men.

His body shuddered, his fingers jerked, began clawing at the sod, his lips and eyes twitched. His breathing turned harsh and unsteady. Brann bent over him, spread her hands on his chest. "Yaril, Jaril!"

With the children occupying her body and his and guiding her, Brann began the struggle to integrate the two minds. She couldn't see what the three of them were doing, only feel it; she groped blindly toward what she sensed as hotspots, paingeysers, cyclonic storms, working from an instinct that was an amalgam of her inborn unconscious bodyknowledge and the learned knowledge of the children (their understanding of their own bodies and minds, their considerable experience of the minds and bodies they indirectly fed upon). She was still seething with anger at being trapped into doing the Chained God's work; her fantasies about bargaining with him were fantasies indeed, about as useful and lasting as writing on water. His/its tampering with Ahzurdan and Daniel Akamarino put her in a position where there was only one thing she could do and continue to live with herself.

The work went on and on, images fluttered into her mind; she didn't believe they were dreams leaking from the disparate parts of Danny Blue, no, they were translations of emotion, perhaps concept, into images from her own stores, Ahzurdan had told her something like that when he was explaining how sorcerers developed their chants. *Black malouch snarling circling about black malouch, these malouchi with sapphire eyes, not gold.* She whined with angry frustration, every troublespot she soothed down seemed to birth two more. *Black hair blue eyes not black Temueng trooper with a serpent tail, rearing up, swaying, hissing, deadly, tensing to strike.* On and on. She saw the trouble under her touch gradually diminishing. Her anger drowned in a flood of fascination with what she was doing, with what was making itself under her fingers. *Blue water heaving, blue iris, blue hyacinth, blue lupin, blue flames, blue EYES blue and blue, blue glaze shining, look deep and deep and deep into a blue bluer than a summer sky, deep and deep.* . . . Her need to make was almost as deep-seated in her as her need to breathe. She bored over Danny Blue, blind fingered, eyes shut, shaping him, manipulating his clay, all thought of the Chained God pushed away so that the Danny Blue under her hands seemed her creation, almost as if she'd birthed him. *Thoughts (gnat swarms of blue sparks) in cloud shimmers blue funnels wobbling about each other, dipping toward each other, fragile, fearful, furious with hate, touch and shatter, struggling away, drawn back, always drawn back.* . . . On and on, spending her strength recklessly, no thought of the god and what other treacheries he might be planning, on and on making a man with all the art and passion in her. *Clay under her hands, blue clay fighting her, holding stubbornly to its imperfections, holding its breath on her, keeping the treacherous air bubbles locked in it, bubbles that would fracture it in the firing, stubborn, resisting, tough but oh so fine, so fine when she got the flaws out.* On and on until there were no more hotspots, no more images in blue, until the need that drove her drained away.

She broke contact and sat on her heels looking blearily down at him. He was asleep, snoring a little. She turned him on his side, shifted off her heels until she was sitting beside him on the grass. Jaril slid out of her, flickering from globe to boy, lay down a short way off, a naked youth molded in milkglass, she could see the jagged line of dark green grass through his legs. Yaril slid out of Danny Blue, crawled over to stretch out beside her brother, naked milkglass girl like she'd been when she rolled off Brann the day this all began, but older now with firm young breasts and broadening hips. Pale wraiths, they lay motionless, waiting passively for her to feed them or do something to restore their strength.

Brann rubbed at her back, lethargic, despondent. It had cost her, this scheme the godthing imposed on her, muscle tissue going with her energy to feed the reshaping of the man; there were some small lives in the trees and the undergrowth surrounding the glade, but they weren't worth the effort to chase them down, so, she thought, let him/it pay its share of the cost out of its own stores of godfire. She closed her eyes, her mouth twisting into a quick wry smile. He/it wasn't hovering over her, volunteering. Shuh! Amortis wasn't volunteering either, but she gave to this small charity want to or not. What's good for her is good for him/it. On hands and knees, Brann crawled to the children, worked her way between them so she could hold a hand of each.

Jaril. Yaril. Can you hear me?

We hear. Odd double voice in her head, charming harmonies that made her smile again, a softer wider smile this time.

Remember Amortis and the bridge. Do you think you could make the bridge again? I do hope so, otherwise I don't know how we're going to replace what's gone.

Can you feed us something? Just a little?

She looked at the skin hanging loosely about her forearms, then over her shoulder at Danny Blue. *Might be able to steal a bit from him. Let me take a sniff at him and see.* She dropped the hands, moved back to sleeping Danny, touched his arm. A lot of what she'd put into him had been eaten up by the drain of the alterations, but she could pull back a small trickle without damaging what she'd made.

When she'd fed the children, she frowned down at them. There was a faint flush of color in their bodies, but the grass was still visible through them. *That be enough?*

Jaril wrinkled his nose. *Enough to tell us how much more we need.*

Yaril drew her knees up, shook her head, not in denial, more to show her unhappiness with the way things were. *Brann, we'd better draw hard and fast, this isn't really like with Amortis. He'll hit back soon as he understands what's happening and we don't have Ahzurdan to stand ward for us.* A swift ghost of a smile. *All right, I admit I was wrong about him.*

I hear. Hard and fast. A pause. Brann drew her tongue along her lips. *When I give the word.* She pulled her hands from the children, folded her arms, hugged them tight against her. She closed her eyes, squeezed them shut, memories of pain scratching along her nerves; it can't feel pain twice, but the body winces anyway when it knows that more is coming. For several breaths she couldn't make herself say the word that would bring that agony down on her. Finally she straightened her back, her shoulders, lifted her head, set her hands on her thighs. "Do it."

The children were glimmerglobes, paler than usual, drifting upward.

The children touched.

The children merged.

The children whipped into a thin arc, one end deep into the heart of the Chained God, the other sunk into Brann's torso, she heard the shouted YES and pulled.

Godfire seared into her until she was burning, the grass under her was burning, the air round her was burning. She pulled until she was so filled with godfire an ounce more would spill from her control and turn her to ash and char.

The children sensed this and broke, tumbled to the grass before her, pale glass forms again. They reached for her, drew the godfire into themselves, drew and drew until she could think again, breathe again, move again.

The god raged, but Yaril and Jaril threw a sphere of force about her until he/it calmed enough to reacquire reason. "What are you doing?" he/it thundered at them, the echoes of the multiple voices clashing and interfering until the words were garbled to the point of enigma. "What are you doing? What are you doing?"

The children dropped to the grass a short distance from the sleeping body of Danny Blue; they sat leaning against each other, looking into a vague sort of distance, displaying an exaggerated indifference to what was happening around them. No. Not children any more. Young folk in that uncertain gap between childhood and maturity, doing what such folk often do best, irritatingly ignoring the crotchets of their elders, the questions, demands, rodomontades of those who thought they deserved respectful attention.

Brann rubbed her grilled palms on the cool grass, glanced at the changers, wrinkled her nose. Due to the convoluted workings of her fate, she'd skipped most of that phase of her development; at the moment she was rather pleased that she had. And rather shaken at the thought she had to cope with it in Yaril and Jaril. She pushed the thought aside and concentrated on the god who was still hooming unintelligibly. "If you'll turn the volume down," she said mildly, "perhaps I could understand what you're saying and give you the answers you want."

Silence for several minutes. When the god spoke, his/its boom was considerably diminished. "What were you doing?"

"Taking recompense," she said. "You asked me to do a thing, I did it. I spent my resources doing it, I nearly killed myself and the . . ." she looked at the changers, decided that *children* was no longer a suitable description, ". . . Yaril and Jaril. I simply took back what I used up."

More silence (not exactly utter silence, it was filled with some strange small anonymous creaks and fizzes, punctuated with odd smells). Finally, the god said, "I'll let it go this time, don't try that again."

"I hear," she said, letting him hear in her tone (if he wanted to hear it) that she was making no promises.

A pause, again filled with small sounds and loud smells. Lines of phosphor thin as her smallest finger spiderwalked about them, began passing through and through the sleeper, began brushing against her (she started the first time but relaxed when she felt nothing not even a tingle), began brushing against Yaril and Jaril who refused to notice them.

"When is Danny Blue going to wake?" The god's multiple voice sounded edgy. One of the phosphor lines was running fretfully (insofar as a featureless rod of light can have emotional content) around and around Danny Blue; it reminded Brann of a spoiled child stamping his feet because he couldn't have something he wanted.

"I don't know." Brann watched the phosphor quiver and suppressed a smile. "When he's ready, I suppose."

"Wake him."

"No."

"What?"

"You heard me. You've waited for eons, wait a few hours more. If you wake his body now, you could lose everything else."

"How do you know that?"

"I don't. Know it, I mean. It's a feeling. I'm not going against it, push or shove."

The air went still. She had a sense of a huge brooding. The god needed her to deal with problems that might arise after Danny Blue eventually woke, she was safe until then. Afterwards? She felt malice held in check, a lot of the Admiral left in him/it, if what he said about the Admiral was anything like the truth.

"You are fighting me every way you can. Why?"

"If you do or say stupid things, you expect me to endorse them? Think again. It's my life you're playing with, the lives of my friends. You want an echo, get a parrot." She scratched at her knee, sniffed at the stinking humid air, wrinkled her nose with disgust. "I'm hungry and he will be when he wakes. What you brought us here for is finished. Any reason we have to stay?"

The god thought that over for a while. Spiderlegs of phosphor flickered about Danny Blue, wove him into a cocoon with threads of light and took him away. Jaril shimmersphere darted after him, slipped through the walls with him. Yaril sighed, stretched. "Took him to Daniel's bedroom, dumped him in the bed."

Before Brann had a chance to say anything, the phosphor lines snapped back, wove a tight web about her and hauled her away, dumping her seconds later on the bed she'd slept in the night before. By the time she got herself together and sat up, Yaril was standing across the small room, watching her from enigmatic crystal eyes. She smiled at Brann and slid away through the doorfog. Brann grimaced, pushed off the bed onto her feet. She felt grubby, grimy. Good thing I can't smell myself. Hmm. Start the teawater boiling, if I can remember which whatsits I should push, then a bath. She rubbed a fold of her shirt between thumb and forefinger. Wonder how they did their washing? Maybe the kids know. Hmm. I'm going to have to figure some other way of thinking about them. Wonder if that godstuff's good for them, they're growing so fast. . . . I'd better take a look at Danny Blue. Ah ah the things that keep happening. . . .

Brann was stretched out on the recliner Jaril had deformed for her out of a lump on the floor of the eggroom. A teapot steamed on an elbowtable beside her, she had a cup of tea making a hotspot on her stomach; she sipped at it now and then when she remembered it while she watched a story stream past on a bookplayer she balanced on her stomach beside the cup (the god had translated several of these and presented them to her, which surprised her and tended to modify her opinion of him/it, which was probably one of the reasons he/it did it). Yaril drifted in, leaned over her shoulder a moment, watching the story. "Brann."

"Mmm?"

"Danny Blue's restless. Jaril thinks he's going to wake soon."

"How soon?"

"Ten, fifteen minutes, maybe."

"Hmm." Brann set the player down beside her, shifted the cup to the elbowtable and pushed up. "He showing any trouble signs?"

"Jaril says he's been having some nightmares, isn't much to any of them, Jaril could only catch a hint of what was going on, more emotion than imagery. That stopped a short while ago. Jaril says it looks like he's trying to wake up."

"Trying?" Brann stood, tucked her shirt down into her trousers, straightening her collar. "That doesn't sound good."

Brann bent over Danny Blue. His head was turning side to side on the pillow in a twitchy broken rhythm; his mouth was working; his hands groped about, crawling slowly over his ribs, his face, the bed, the sheet that was pulled across the lower part of his body. She trapped one of the hands, held it still. "He's not dreaming?"

Jaril was kneeling close to her, a hand resting against the side of Danny's face, fingertips bleeding into him. "No."

"What do you think?" She felt his hand flutter like a bird within the circle of her fingers; using only a tiny fraction of his strength, he was trying to pull away from her. "Yaril, Jaril, should I let him kick out of it . . ." she frowned as he made a few shapeless sounds, ". . . if he can? Or should I jolt him awake? I don't like the way he looks."

Yaril leaned past her, her face intent, her hands moving through his body. She turned her head, stared for a long moment into her brother's eyes, finally pulled free. "We think you better jolt him, Bramble."

Danny Blue snapped his eyes open and promptly went into convulsions; he screamed, hoarse, building cries that seemed to originate in his feet and scrape him empty as they swept through his body and emerged from his straining mouth. Brann, Yaril and Jaril held him down, the changers reaching into him and soothing him whenever they could snatch a second between his kicks and jerks. Shivering, shaking, bucking, he struggled on and on until they and he were exhausted and even then he showed no sign he knew what was happening to him or where he was. He lay limp, trembling, blue eyes blank, looking past or through them.

Brann chewed her lip, spent a few moments feeling helpless and frustrated. She wiped the sweat-sodden hair off her face, tucked the straggles behind her ears and stood scowling at him. Finally she bent over him, slapped his face, the crack of her palm against his cheek filling the small room. "Dan!" She flung the word at him. "Danny Blue! Stop it. You aren't a baby." She rubbed the side of her hand across her chin, back-forth, quick, angry. "Listen, man, we need you. Both of you. I know you don't have to be like this."

He looked at her, the blankness burnt out of his face and out of his eyes, replaced by bitterness and rage. He swung his legs over the edge of the bed and pushed up. He looked at her again, then sat rubbing at his temples, staring at the floor.

"We need to talk, Dan. Can you work with Yaril and Jaril to give us some privacy?"

"You couldn't wait?" He spoke slowly, with difficulty, his mouth moving before each word as if he had to decide which part of him was ordering his speech.

"What's the point. Either you can or you can't, what good will waiting do?" She shrugged. "Except to sour you more than you are already."

He opened his mouth, shut it. He draped his hands over his knees and continued to stare at the floor.

"I'm not going to coax you," Brann moved to the door, Yaril and Jaril drifting over to stand beside her, "or waste my breath arguing with you. Make up your own mind where you want to go. Don't take too long about it either. We'll be in the sitting room figuring how to walk out of this."

A little over half an hour later Danny Blue ducked through the doorway (he was a head taller than he'd been two days ago) and strolled into the egg-shaped sitting room. He was wearing Daniel's trousers, his sandals and his leather vest, Ahzurdan's black silk undershirt; he had Daniel's lazy amiability as a thin mask over Ahzurdan's edgy force. He nudged a chair out of a knot in the rug, kicked up a hassock; he settled into the chair, put his feet up, crossed his ankles and laced his fingers over his flat stomach. "You can forget about privacy," he said. "Over in the reality where this ship was built they had some mean head games. Very big on control they were. Ol' god here, he's got a hook sunk in my liver which says I'm his as long as he wants me. I don't work against him, I don't help anyone else work against him, I don't even think about trying to get away from him. You can forget about sorcery or anything like that, this has nothing to do with magic. Takes a machine to do it, takes a machine to undo it. So. There it is."

Brann drew her fingertips slowly across her brow as if she were feeling for strings. "I don't think," she said slowly, "I don't think it did it to me . . . um . . . us. We did some things it didn't like . . . and . . . and we didn't . . . there wasn't anything inside stopping us. Yaril? Jaril?"

The changers looked at each other, then Yaril said, "No. The god hasn't done anything we can locate in us or you. We might be missing something that will show up later, but we don't think so." She hesitated, took hold of Brann's wrist. "Being what we are, I don't think we'd need machines to undo a compulsion the god tried to plant in us, and Brann's linked very tightly with us. I think . . . I don't know . . . I think we could undo any knots in her head. I'm afraid we couldn't help you, Dan. The connection isn't close enough." She shifted her hand, laced up her fingers with Brann's. "There's something else, isn't there?"

Danny Blue uncrossed his ankles and got to his feet. "I wanted to ask you, Brann, you and them, give me some time before you push the god into doing something drastic. I, the two parts of me, we have to get an idea what the god wants and what we can do about it."

Jaril dropped beside Brann, took her free hand. *We'll watch,* he said. *And we'll do some exploring ourselves.*

Be careful that thing doesn't learn more from you than you do from it. Remember what happened before.

We are not about to forget that, Bramble. The voice in her head sounded grim. Yaril said nothing but the same angry determination was seething in her, Brann felt it like thistle leaves rubbing against her skin.

So we give him some time. Three days?

Yes. That's good. And we'll keep the time, Bramble, the god can make a day any length he wants. Tell Dan three downbelow days.

Downbelow days. Good. Brann relaxed and the changers slid away. "Three days, Dan," she said aloud. "Three downbelow days."

The outside door slid open, Danny Blue strolled into the eggroom. He nudged a chair out of a knot in the rug, kicked up a hassock; he settled into the chair, put his feet up, crossed his ankles and laced his fingers behind his head.

Brann looked up from the book she was scanning. "Ready to talk?"

"Where are the changers?"

"They got bored staying in one place, I suppose they're exploring the ship."

He pulled his hands down, rested them on the arms of the chair. "You remember what I told you?"

"I remember." She laid the book aside. "So?"

"Just keep it in mind. That's all. Chained God. He wanted to leave this pocket." He spoke quietly, calmly, more of Daniel showing than Ahzurdan, but behind that control he was raging; his eyes were sunk in stiff wrinkles, the blue was dulled to a muddy clay color, the lines from nose to chin were deeper than before, a muscle jumped erratically beside his mouth. "He's had to give up on that." A twitch of a smile. "His metal is too old and tired to take the stresses, the rest of him is too adapted to this space to survive the move." He pulled his hand across his mouth. "Think I could have a cup of that tea?" Another twisted smile as she snorted her disgust, but poured him out some tea and brought it to him with a brisk reminder that she wasn't his servant and didn't plan to make a habit of fetching and carrying for him. When she was seated again, he went on, "Using what Daniel knew and all the different things Ahzurdan had learned . . ." He sipped at the tea, rested the cup on the chair's arm. ". . . I have worked out a means of opening other gates, one in each of the Finger Vales; he'll have greater access to his priests and his people." He cleared his throat, anger had lodged a lump in his gullet it was hard to talk around. He gulped down most of the tea, lay back and closed his eyes. "That's for later. For now, I've managed to widen the gate on Isspyrivo; we can get out with less trouble than we had coming in, though we'll still have to use that aperture, the others won't be ready."

"We?"

He opened his eyes a crack. "Chained God has a deal for you."

"Why should I listen to anything it says?"

"Because he's got something you want."

"And what's that?"

"He can cut the cord that ties you to the changers."

"I see. Go on."

"Caveat first. He can keep you here as long as he wants, Brann. You can annoy him if you try hard enough, you might even hurt him a little, but he can kill you and drain the changers if you force it. He knows everything Ahzurdan knew about you, everything Daniel knew, he knows if he let you run loose, you'd find a way to make peace with Maksim. You've very like Maksim, did you know that? You think like him. There's a good chance you could talk him into slapping Amortis down so Kori's brother would be safe. Chained God doesn't want that. What he wants is BinYAHtii."

"I won't have anything to do with that."

"Why? Because it eats life? Like you?"

"I can handle the guilts I have. I don't want more."

"Chained God says he'll reopen the changers' energy receptors so they can dine on sunlight again. And he'll do it before you leave here as a gesture of good faith."

"What about sending them home?"

"He can't. He doesn't know their reality. Slya's the only one who does, you'll have to work that out with her."

"Why should Yaril and Jaril trust him enough to let him fiddle with their bodies? Even if I do agree to his conditions."

"YOU have more choice than Daniel Akamarino and Ahzurdan had. You can say no. THEY couldn't. If you say yes, he won't bother asking their consent."

"Exactly what would the god expect me to do?"

"Stop working against him. Go with me, help me. Persuade the changers to help. Coming here, we were an effective team. We could be one again."

"If I say no, I spend the rest of my life here?"

"A part of it, how long depends."

Brann grimaced, looked down at her hands. They were clenched into fists. She straightened her fingers, brushed her palms against each other. "I. . . ." She laced her fingers together, steepled her thumbs. "I made a choice for Yaril and Jaril once, I made it out of ignorance and . . . well, no matter. I won't do it again. They'll have to decide this time."

Two pairs of crystal eyes were fixed on her as she finished explaining the Chained God's offer. "That's it," she said. "It's your bodies, you decide what you want done with them."

Abruptly Yaril and Jaril were glimmerglobes; they drifted up until they were near the ceiling. They merged and the double globe hung there pulsing.

Danny Blue prowled about the oval room, tapping the vision plates on and off as he passed them, looking at the yellow sky outside, the greasy wool that billowed around the ship, glancing between times at the globe. Brann sat on the recliner watching him. There was a stiffness to his movements that neither Ahzurdan nor Daniel Akamarino had had; she read that stiffness as anger he couldn't admit to because of the compulsion that thing had planted in him. She'd seen this before, in shopkeepers and landsfolk who could not show their rage or even let themselves know about it when an important customer was arrogant or thoughtless, when an ignorant exigent overlord made impossible demands on them. They beat their wives and children instead. She grew warier than before, wondering just how Dan was going to displace that anger and who his target would be. She had a strong suspicion it might be her. Before the merger Ahzurdan had not been liking her vey much and Ahzurdan was in there somewhere.

The globe split apart, the parts dropped to the rug, Yaril and Jaril stood before Brann and Danny Blue looking angry, determined and a little frightened. Jaril stood with his hand on his sister's shoulder; he said nothing, Yaril spoke for them. "We'll take the chance, Bramble."

Brann held out her hands. "Come here." When they had their hands in hers, she thought, *It bothers me, you know that.*

Yaril: *Let the Valers take care of themselves. Isn't it time you thought about us?*

Brann: *More than time. You don't need to say it.*

Jaril: *Don't we?*

Brann: *No. You've decided, I acquiesce. What I'm saying is, help me. You know this thing, this god. Will it be worse than Maksim, feeding more and more lives to BinYAHtii? Or will it let the talisman sit, there to help it defend itself if the other gods attack?*

Jaril: *Remember what Ahzurdan said about Maksim, that he was possessive about his people? The god's a lot like that, maybe more so. Been breeding and coddling these folks for millennia, won't feed them to the talisman; outsiders though, they'd better watch out.* A quick grin, a squeeze of Brann's hand. *Just think about Slya and your own folk.*

Yaril: *What about this, Bramble? After this thing is over, we go find young Kori and tell her about BinYAHtii's habits; she can pass the word on to her folk. What they do about it is up to them. What about you, Jay? What do you think?*

Jaril: *One thing we don't want to do is say word one about this to Danny Blue.*

Yaril: *You're being obvious, brother. Of course not, talking to him's like talking direct to the god. You have anything helpful to add?*

Jaril: *Nope. 'S good enough for me.*

Brann: *It's the best we can do, I suppose.* She freed her hands. "I agree, Dan. Does it want me to swear?"

The Chained God's voice sounded from a point near where the double globe had floated. "Say what you will do, Brann Drinker of Souls. Specify your limitations and intentions. Swearing is not necessary."

Brann pulled in a lungful of air, exploded it out in a long sigh. "I will accompany Danny Blue and do what I can to help him, provided always that you do not harm Yaril and Jaril in any way and provided that they can truly feed themselves when you're finished with them. Is that sufficient?"

"Quite sufficient." Before the sound of the words had died away, Yaril and Jaril were gone from the room.

14

THEY START ON THEIR WAY TO SNATCH THE TALISMAN FROM THE SORCEROR.

SCENE: Dawn still red in the east, three
mules standing nervously beside the
cached supplies, mist thick and thin
like clotted cream billowing and
surging behind the man and the woman
as they emerge from the steep-walled
ravine.

Yaril and Jaril flashed from the mist and soared into the brightening sky, gold glass eagles spun from sunlight and daydream, laughter made visible joy given shape, swinging in wide circles celebrating the coming of the sun, the sun that was their nipple now, mother sun.

Danny Blue followed Brann from the clotted yellow mist to the stunted trees where she and his progenitors had cached the greater part of their gear. The mules were there, waiting, heads down, looking subdued and lightly singed. Slya's work, no doubt, adding her mite out of friendship or something. He moved up beside Brann and began shifting the concealing rocks aside. His mind felt as chaotic as the fog blowing about in the ravine, but his body was in good shape, he didn't have to think about what he was doing, his hands would go on working as his mind wandered. His flesh was charged and vital, his physical being hummed along at a level that Ahzurdan and Daniel Akamarino reached only when they were operating at peak in their various proficiencies. He swung a saddle onto a mule, reached warily under its belly for the cinch, drew it through the rings and used his knee to punch the swelling out of the mule so he could pull the strap tight. It was not as if two voices spoke within his head, no, more that the Composite-He would be musing about something and suddenly find himself thinking in an entirely different way about whatever it was, perhaps heading for a different outcome. And then his mind would shift again and he'd be where he was before. There was never any sense of coercion in this shifting. It was . . . well . . . like the interaction of two roughly parallel currents in a single river. As long as he rode the flow of those currents and didn't try to fight them, he could think competently enough about whatever engaged his attention. And as time passed the Composite-He took more and more control of the Composite Mind. He retained the full memories of both his progenitors, along with their talents and their training (his work for the god-in-the-starship had been ample evidence of that) but slowly and surely the being who did the remembering was becoming someone else. Blue Dan. Danny Blue. Azure Dan, the Magic Man. He tied the depleted grain sack behind the saddle and the blanket roll on top of that and went for the saddlebags.

The changers chased each other in endless spirals, singing their exuberance in their eagle voices; their connection to Brann and the ground seemed more and more tenuous as the sun appeared and finally cleared the horizon.

Danny Blue rode behind Brann, the leadrope of the third mule tied to a saddlering. He looked up at the changers and wondered how long they'd stay in sight and whether they'd keep their ties to Brann now that they no longer needed her to stay alive. He thought about asking her what she was thinking, but he didn't. Something in him was enjoying her tension and her quick sliding glances at the changers, something in him stood back and watched, uninvolved, unmoved; he thought that he disliked both of his progenitors, he thought they felt flat, one-dimensional. He was slaved to the god and he hated that, but he was beginning to be glad that Danny Blue was alive and aware and riding this mule along this mountainside, listening to the crackclack of the mule hooves, the morning wind hushing through the pines, the eagles screaming overhead, feeling himself sweat and chafe and jolt a bit because he still wasn't much good at riding mules. He began to whistle a rambling undemanding tune, thought of getting out Daniel's recorder but let the impulse slide away with the glide of the song.

One of the eagles came spiraling down, changed to a slight fair young man the moment he touched ground. Brann's back lost its rigidity as her mule halted and stood with ears twitching nervously. "We thought we'd better ask," Jaril said. "The god printed a map for you, but maybe you'd like us to scout out the best ground ahead till we get to Forkker Vale?"

"We could move faster that way." Brann threaded her fingers through her hair. "Can Yaro get high enough to see Haven? That thing said there wasn't a ship due for a week at least, I don't know why it'd lie, the faster we can get to Maksim, the less chance he'll have to make trouble for us, the sooner it could have its talisman, but I'd feel easier with some corroboration."

No longer golden glass but a large brown and white raptor, the eagle overhead climbed higher, vanishing and reappearing as she passed through drifts of cloud fleece.

Jaril tilted his head back and followed her with his eyes. "The sea is empty all round far as Yaro can see. Not even a smuggler out. Haven is pretty much still asleep. There are some fishboats out working nets, she sees a few women near the oven stoking it up so they can bake the day's bread, the hands are busy with cows and whatever on the near-in farms. Nobody's hustling more than usual. That's about it."

"Ah well, it was a chance." Brann rubbed at her chin. "You want to run or ride?"

"Ride." He walked to the third mule, waited until Dan untied the lead rope, swung into the saddle and moved to ride beside Brann. "Yaro says Slya's sitting on top of Isspyrivo turning the glacier into steam; she's watching us."

Brann chuckled. "She'll freeze her red behind if she does that for long."

"Or flood out Haven. The creek from the crack runs down to the sea right there."

She yawned. "Somehow I find it hard to care right now." She thrust her hand into the bag by her knee, pulled out a paper cylinder, unrolled it and held it open along her thigh. "Hmm." She rode closer to Jaril, tapped the nail of her forefinger against a section. "Looks like we'll have to take a long jog about this, unless it's not so deep as it looks. What's this?"

"It's a young canyon all right. I don't know what that blurry bit is." He was silent a minute, then he nodded. "Yaro's gone to check it out. Be about twenty minutes' flying time."

Brann examined the map a few moments longer, then let it snap back into its cylinder and slid it into the bag.

Danny Blue watched Brann and the changer youth and felt a twinge of jealousy. The affection he saw between them had survived and more than survived the cutting of the chains that held them in servitude to each other; he had half-expected the changers to vanish like a fire blown out once they were free of her; when he saw their aerobatic extravagances he thought they were gone. He was wrong. A loving woman, a passionate one. The strength of the ties she forged with those alien children was evidence of that, he had more evidence of what she was in his memories. He remembered the feel of her back, the way she reacted to Daniel's hands, his mouth twitched into a crooked smile as he remembered with equal clarity how quickly and completely Daniel shut off the flow of that passion.

He watched Brann's back (the feel of it strong in his hands) and observed his own reactions. Ahzurdan had more hangups than a suitlocker, Daniel had only a moderate interest, enjoying sex when it was available, not missing it all that much when it wasn't. From the way Danny Blue's body was sitting up and taking notice, he was going to have to change his habits. He sucked in a long breath, exploded it out and tried to think of something else before the saddle got more uncomfortable than it was already.

Jaril reached over, touched Brann's arm. "Yaro's got there. She says the blur you saw is a bridge over that ravine, a smuggler's special, she says from on top and even up close it looks like a couple down trees with some vines and brush growing out of them, but she went down and walked on it and it's solid. The mules won't have any problem crossing it even if it's dark by the time we get there and it probably will be."

"Anything between here and there that might give us problems?"

"She says she doesn't think so. Trying to read ground from the air can be tricky, you've got to remember that, especially as high as Yaro was flying, but she says the smuggler's trace is fairly obvious and if we keep to that we shouldn't have more problems than we can handle. She's spotted a spring she thinks we can reach before it gets too dark if we start moving some faster, if we keep ambling along like this, we'll have a dry camp because there's no water between here and there."

"I hear. Go ahead and show us the trail, will you?"

Jaril nodded, pulled ahead of them. He increased his mule's pace to an easy trot as he followed the inconspicuous blazes cut at intervals into tree trunks as big around as the bodies of the mules. They'd long since passed the areas where the battles with Settsimaksimin and his surrogate elementals had torn up the ground, the mountainside was springy with old dried needles, little brush grew between giant conifers that rose a good twenty feet above their heads before spreading out great fans of branch and pungent needle bunches, there was room for the mules to stretch their legs without worrying about what they'd step into.

They rode undisturbed that day, stopping briefly to grain and water the mules and snatch a bite for themselves, starting on again with less than an hour lost. They reached Yaril's spring about an hour after sundown. She had a small sly fire going and was prowling about in catshape, driving off anything on four legs or two that might want to investigate the camp too closely. No one said much, aloud at least; what the changers were saying to each other, they kept to themselves and did not break the silence about the fire. Brann rolled into her blankets after she ate and helped clean up the camp; as far as Danny Blue could tell she didn't move until she woke with the dawn. He had more difficulty getting to sleep, his muscles were sore and complaining, his mental and physical turmoil kept his mind turning over long after he was bored with every thought that climbed about his head, but he had two disciplines to call on and eventually bludgeoned his mind into stillness and his body into sleep.

The days passed because they had to pass, but there was little to mark one from another; they rode uphill and downhill and across the smuggler bridges with never a smell of Settsimaksimin. Even the weather was fine, nights cool, days warm with just enough of a breeze to take the curse off the heat and not a sign of rain. Now and then they saw a stag or a herd of does with their springborn fawns; now and then, on the edges of night and morning brown bears prowled about them but never came close enough to threaten them. Blue gessiks hopped about among the roots and shriveled weeds, broad beaks poking through the mat of dead needles for pinenuts and borer worms; their raucous cries echoed from hillside to hillside as they whirled into noisy bluff battles over indistinguishable patches of earth. Gray gwichies chattered at each other or shook gwichie babies out of pouches close to being too small for them and sent them running along whippy tarplum branches for late hatching nestlets or lingering fruit.

On the fifth day or it might have been the sixth, shortly after dawn when shadows were long and thin and glittered with dew, they dropped through an oak forest to the grassy foothills along the side of Forkker Vale.

Jaril and Yaril rode first, Jaril in the saddle, Yaril behind him, clinging to him. Their new dependence on the sun for sustenance had wrought several changes in how they ran their lives. In a way, they were like large lizards, they got a few degrees more sluggish when the sun went down unless they took steps to avoid it. They were still adjusting to the change in their circumstances; staying with Brann on this trek, with its demands on them and the dangers that lay ahead of them wasn't helping them all that much.

Down on the floor of the Vale a line of men walked steadily across the first of the grainfields, scythes swinging in smooth arcs, laying stalkfans flat beside them, a line of women followed, tieing the stalks into sheaves, herds of children followed the women, some gathering sheaves into piles, others loading those piles onto mulecarts and taking them down along the Vale to the storesheds and drying racks at the threshing floor. The men were singing to themselves, a deep thoated hooming that rose out of the rhythm of the sweep, hypnotic powerful magical sound. The women had their own songs with a quicker sharper rhythm, a greater commensality. The children laughed and sang and played a dozen different games as they worked, counting games and last one out and dollymaker as they gathered and piled the sheaves, jump the moon and one foot over and catch as they swung the sheaves around, tossed them to each other then onto the stakecarts, running tag and sprints beside the mules. It was early morning, cool and pleasant, boys and girls alike were brimming with energy. It was the last golden burst of exuberance before winter shut down on them. Or it was before the strangers appeared.

As Brann, the changers and Danny Blue rode past them on the rutted track, the Forkker folk looked round at them but no one spoke to them, no one asked what they were doing there or where they were going. And the children were careful to avoid them.

Ahzurdan's memories prodded Danny Blue until he heeled his mule to a quicker trot and caught up with Brann. "Trouble?"

"Maybe." She scratched at her chin. "It could be local courtesy not to notice folk coming from the direction of Haven. I don't believe a word of that. Jay." He looked over his shoulder, dusty and rather tired, the sun hadn't been up long enough to kick him into full alertness. "Could you or Yaro put on wings and take a look at what's ahead of us?"

"Shift here?"

"Why not. A little healthy fear might prove useful."

Yaril stretched, patted a yawn, yawned again and slid off the mule;

she ran delicate hands through her ash blond air, shivered like a nervous pony, then she was an eagle powering into a rising spiral.

They started on, moving at a slow walk. A mulecart rattled past them, the children silent, subdued, wide frightened eyes sliding around to the strangers, flicking swiftly away.

Danny Blue watched the cart jolt away from them, the mule urged to a reluctant canter, the sheaves jiggling and shivering. Several fell off. Two boys ran back, scooped them up and tossed them onto the cart. A swift sly ferret's look at the strangers, then they scooted ahead until they were trotting beside the mule, switching his flanks to keep him at the faster pace. "They've been warned about us," he said.

"Looks like it. Jay?"

"Yaro is looking over the village. It's pretty well empty. Those houses are built like forts, an army could be hiding inside them. Each house has several courtyards, they're as empty as the streets, Yaro says that about confirms trouble ahead, at this hour there should be people everywhere, not just in the fields. She thinks maybe we should circle round the village, she says she saw shadows behind several of the windows, the streets, well, they aren't really streets, just openspaces between housewalls, they're narrow and crooked with a lot of blind ends, it's a maze there, if we got into it, who knows what'd happen. There's problems with circling too, orchards and vineyards and a lot of clutter before we'd get to the trees, makes her nervous, she says. Ah. Soldiers in the trees, left side . . . um . . . right side. Not many. She says she counts four on the left, six on the right, Kori said there were a doubletwelve in Owlyn Vale, there won't be fewer here, that leaves what? about fourteen, fifteen in the village. She says it won't be that difficult for her and me to take all of them out if we could use Dan's stunner. Question is will the Forkker folk mix in this business? If they do, things could get sticky, there are too many of them, they can swamp us given we have a modicum of bad luck. What do you think?" Jaril opened his eyes, looked from Brann to Danny Blue, raised his brows.

Danny Blue thumbed the zipper back, squeezed out the stunner; he checked the charge, nodded with satisfaction, tossed the heavy black handful to Jaril. "Chained God topped off the batteries, but don't waste the juice, Jay, I'd like to have some punch left when we get to where we're going."

Jaril caught the stunner. "Gotcha. Brann?"

"Yaro read Kori back when . . . Jay, was that her or you asking about the Forkkers? You? What does she think?"

"Um . . . she thinks they're in a bind. They don't like Maksim or his soldiers, but they don't want him landing on their backs either, especially not over a bunch of foreigners. She says if we go through fast and they don't see much happening, they'll keep quiet. She says she's changed her mind about going round the village now that she thinks about it. She says thinking about it, we've got to put all the soldiers out, we don't want them stirring up the Forkkers and setting them after us. She says Brann, she can read a couple Forkkers to make sure, if you want. And Dan, she says, whatever, it's up to you. The stunner's yours."

Danny Blue ran his tongue around his teeth, scratched thoughtfully at his thigh. "Can you singleshot the soldiers? It'd cut down the bleed if you don't have to spray a broad area."

"She says the ones in the trees will be easy, she'll mark them for me, so I can do them while she's hunting out the ones ambushed in the village. She says what she'll do is globe up and pale out, go zip zap through all the houses, be done with that before they know what's happening. Once she's got the village ones spotted, unless there's too many of them or they're in places I can't get the stunner into, I should be able to plink them before they get too agitated." A quick grin. "Too bad the stunner won't go through walls."

"Too bad." Danny glanced over his shoulder at the workers in the waist high grain. They weren't working anymore, they were gathered in clumps, stiff and ominously silent, watching Jaril, Brann and him as they rode at a slow walk along the dusty track. "You might as well get at it. All I say is remember we've got a long way to go yet."

Danny Blue tied the leadrope of the third mule to the ring, watched the man-handed eagle fly off toward the trees. Brann was looking sleepy, unconcerned. The wind was blowing her hair about her face. You can almost see it grow, he thought, I wonder why she cut it so short. Her body moved easily with the motion of the mule, she was relaxed as a cat. A wave of uneasiness shivered through him (the shefalos hook operating in him), cat, oh yes, and he didn't know how she'd jump.

He fragmented suddenly, Ahzurdan and Daniel Akamarino resurrected by their powerful reactions to Brann, a gate he'd opened for them. They were still one-dimensional, his progenitors, reduced to a few dominant emotions closely related and thoroughly mixed whose only stab at complication was a vague fringe of contradictions that trailed away to nothing. Ahzurdan glowered at Brann, a glaresheet of nauseous yellow, hate, resentment, frustration. Daniel pulled himself into a globe, iceblue, dull, rejection irritation numblust. Danny Blue was nowhere, shards scattered haphazard around and between the fragments of his sires.

Cool/warm touch on his arm. "Dan?" Warm sweet sound dancing across his nerve ends, echo re-echo chitter chatter flutter alter alto counterplay countertenor contralto confusion diffusion refusion dan dan dan dan. . . .

A surge of heat. The bits of Danny Blue wheeled whirled jabbed into the glaresheet (broke it into sickly yellow puzzle pieces) jabbed into the globe (shattered it to mirrored shards, slung them at the yellow scraps) the bits of Danny Blue wheeled whirled, gathered yellow gathered blue, heat pressure need glue bits shards scraps, moulage collage— Danny Blue is whole again, a little strange the seams are showing, but it's him, yes it's him, singly him. He blinked at Brann, at her hand on his arm. He wrapped fingers (warm again his again) about hers, lifted her hand, moved his lips slowly softly across the smooth firm palm. He cupped her hand against his cheek. "Thanks."

Buffered by a taut silence that the thud of mule hooves on the muffling dust only intensified, they rode at a fast trot through the village following a large bitch mastiff while the man-handed eagle flew sentry overhead. The soldiers slept and the Forkker folk did nothing, the riders and the changers fled unhindered down along the Vale, past other grainfields waiting for the reapers, past fields of flax and fiberpods, past rows of hops clattering like castanets in the breeze, past tuber vines already dug, waiting, drying in the hot postsummer sun. The hills closed in, the road moved onto the left bank of Forkker Creek. At the mouth of the Vale where the stone bridge crossed that creek, a small stone fort sat high on a steep hillside, overlooking the bridge and the road. The mastiff trotted past it without stopping, the eagle circled undisturbed overhead. Brann and Danny Blue crossed the bridge without being challenged and left the Vale.

15

**SETTSIMAKSIMIN SITTING IN
HIS TOWER,
WATCHING WHAT HURRIES
TOWARD HIM AS HE HURRIES
TO SHAPE WHAT'S TO BE OUT
OF WHAT IS NOW,
WORKING MORE FROM HOPE
THAN EXPECTATION,
SHAPING CHEONEA.**

SCENE: Settsimaksimin in the Star Chamber,
the council he'd constituted some
weeks before breaking up after a long
meeting, the members stretching (inconspicuously or not, according to
their natures), several chatting together, the end-of-the-teeth incon-
sequentialities power players use to
pass dangerously unstructured moments that push up like weeds even in
the most controlled of lives.
Stretching or chatting they stroll
toward the door.

"T'Thelo, stay a moment."

The Peasant Voice looked over his shoulder, came back to the table.
"Phoros Pharmaga."

Settsimaksimin waved a hand at a chair, turned his most stately

glare on the rest of the council as they bunched in the doorway, reluctant to leave one of their number alone with him. Todichi Yahzi set his
book aside and shambled across the room. He herded the councilmen
out and shut the door, returned to his plump red pillow, picked up the
red book and got ready to record.

T'Thelo was a small brown tuber, at once hard and plump with
coarse yellow-white hairs like roots thin on his lumpy head. His hands
were never still, he carried worry beads to meetings and when he felt
like it would whittle at a hardwood chunk, peeling off paper thin curls
of the pale white wood. He seldom said much, was much better at
saying no than yes, looked stubborn and was a lot more stubborn than
he looked.

Maksim let himself slump in his chair and turned off the battering
ram he used as personality in these council meetings. He reached under
his robe and under BinYAHtii, rubbed at his chest. "You know my
mind," he said.

T'Thelo grunted, pulled out his worry beads and began passing them
between thumb and forefinger.

Maksim laughed. At first the sound filled the room, then it faded to a
sigh. "They're going to want to know what I told you," he said. "I'd
advise silence, but I won't command it. I've a battle coming at me,
T'Thelo. A man, a woman and two demons riding at me from the
Forkker, despite all I've done to stop them. A battle . . . a battle . . .
I mean to win it, T'Thelo, but there's a chance I won't and I want you
ready for it. You and the other landsmen, you'll have to fight to keep
what you've got if I go down. The army will be a problem, keep a close
watch on the Strataga and his staff; they're accustomed to power and
are salivating for more, they resent me for shunting them from the
main lines of rule, hmm, perhaps half the younger officers would support you in a pinch, don't trust the Valesons, matter of fact you'd do
well to send them home, but most of the foot-soldiers come from
landfolk on the Plain, be careful with them, the army's had the training
of them since they were boys, it means as much or more to them as
their blood kin, and they've had obedience drilled into them, they'll
obey if they're ordered to walk over you even if their mothers and
sisters are in the front line. The Guildmaster and his artisans will back
you if given a choice, they remember too well how things were when
the Parastes held the reins. So will the Dicastes, they lose if you lose.
There are a lot of folk with grudges about, especially the parasite
Parastes still alive and their hopeful heirs. Be careful with Vasshaka

Bulan, I know the landsmen don't like the Yrons or the Servants or Amortis all that much, but it's better to have them with you than against. I can't tell you how that tricky son will jump, but I know what he wants, T'Thelo. More. That's what he wants. More and more and more. Not for himself, I'll give him that, for Amortis, he calls himself Her Servant and, Forty Mortal Hells, he means it. So that's a thing to watch. Keep your local Kriorns and their Servants friendly, T'Thelo, they're not puppets, they're men like you, I've seen to that. The Yron has schooled them, but I've schooled them too. Keep that in mind." He fell silent, gazed past the Voice at the far wall though he wasn't seeing wall or anything else. "We're not friends, T'Thelo, you'd see me burned at the stake and smile, and as for me, you annoy me and you bore me, but for all that, T'Thelo, we share a dream. We share a dream." His voice was soft and pensive, a deep burrumm like a cello singing on its lowest notes. "Five days, T'Thelo, it takes five days to ride from Forkker Vale to Silagamatys. It isn't time enough for much, but do what you can. I expect to win this battle, T'Thelo, they're coming to ME, they will be fighting on MY ground. But there's a battle coming that I won't win. It's one you'll fight soon enough, my unfriend, you know which one I mean. When I commenced the shaping here, I thought I'd have a hundred years to get it done, aah hey, not so. Three, five, seven, that's it, that's all. I release you from any duties you have to me, Voice, make your plans, weave your web, woo your Luck. And be VERY careful who you talk to about this."

T'Thelo sat a moment staring at the string of wooden beads passing between his callused work-stiffened fingers; he'd had them from his father who'd had them from his, they were dark with ancient sweat, ancient aches and agonies, ancient furies that had no other place to go. He rubbed his thumb across the headbead larger than the rest, darker, looked up. "Give me a way to get word to the Plain."

Maksim snapped his fingers, plucked a small obsidian egg from the air. He set it on the table, gave it a push that took it across to T'Thelo. "The word is PETOM', it calls a ge'mel to you." He smiled at the distaste visible in T'Thelo's lined face. "A ge'mel is a friendly little demon about the size of a pigeon, it looks like a mix between a bat and a bunch of celery and it's a chatty beast. Worst trouble you'll have with it is getting it to shut up and listen to instructions. It can go anywhere between one breath and the next, all you have to do is name the man you're sending it to and think about him when you name him. When you've finished with the ge'mel, say PI'YEN NA; that'll send it home. Any questions?"

T'Thelo looked at the egg. After a long silence, he put his worry beads away, reached out and touched the stone with the tip of his left forefinger. When it didn't bite him, he picked it up, looked at his distorted reflection in the polished black glass. "Petom'," he said. His voice was nearly as deep as Maksim's but harsher; though it could burn with hard passion, that voice, it could never sing, an orator's voice, an old man's voice beginning to hollow with age.

The ge'mel flicked out of nothing, sat perched on the richly polished wood, its oval black eyes lively and shining with its demon laughter; its face was triangular, vaguely batlike, it had huge green jade ears with delicately ragged edges that matched the greenleaf lace on its tailend. Its wings were bone and membrane, the membrane like nubbly raw silk, green silk with tattered edges. Its body was lined and ridged, almost white about the shoulders, growing gradually greener down past the leg sockets until the taillace was a dark jade. Its four standing limbs were hard and hooked, much like those of a praying mantis, its two front limbs had delicate three-fingered hands with opposable thumbs. It held its forelimbs folded up against its body, hands pressed together as if praying. "Yes yes, new master," it said; its voice was a high hum, not too unlike a mosquito whine, but oddly pleasant despite that. "What do you wish? I, Yimna Himmna Lute, will do it. Oyee, this is a fine table." It pushed one of its hind limbs across the wood, making a soft sliding sound. "Lovely wood." It tilted its little face and twinkled at T'Thelo. "Are you an important man, sirrah? I like to serve important men who do important things, it makes my wives and hatchlings happy, it gives them things to boast of when the neighbors visit."

Maksim chuckled. "Now how in modesty could the man answer that, Yim? I'll do it for him. Yes, little friend, he is a very important man and the work he gives you will be very important work, it might save his land and his people from a danger coming at them."

Yimna Himmna Lute bounced happily on its hindlimbs, rubbed its dainty hands together. "Good good splendid," it fluted. Wings fluttering in the wind of its impatience, it fixed its black beady eyes on T'Thelo (who was rather disconcerted since he had nothing for Yim to do at the moment, having called up a monster to get a look at it, only to find there was nothing monstrous about the little creature; he'd had chickens a lot more alarming and certainly worse tempered).

"Unruffle, Yim. The man just wanted to meet you, be introduced, as it were. Voice T'Thelo meet Yimna Himmna Lute, the swiftest surest messenger in all realities. Yim, meet Hrous T'Thelo, Voice of the Landmen of Cheonea." He waited until T'Thelo nodded and Yimna finished its elaborate meeting dance, then said, "Voice T'Thelo, now that the introductions are complete, perhaps you could send Yim back home while you think out and write out the messages you want it to carry for you."

T'Thelo blinked, raised tangled brows. Yim gave him another elaborate bow, coaxing a reluctant smile from him. The Voice rubbed his thumb across the smooth black obsidian, thought a moment, said, "Pi'yen Na."

Little mouth stretched in a happy grin, Yim whiffed out like a snuffed candle.

"Cheerful little git," T'Thelo said. He pushed his chair back, stood. "I thank you, Phoros Pharmaga, I will not waste your warning." He followed Todichi Yahzi to the door, gave a jerk of a bow like an afterthought and went out.

Todichi Yahzi came back and stood before Maksim; his deepset eyes had deep red fires in them. "I have served you long and well, Settsimaksimin, I have not made demands beyond my needs," he sang in his humming garbled Cheonese, "I do not wish to leave you now, but if you die how do I go home?"

"Todich old friend, did you think I had forgot you?" Maksim got to his feet, stretched his arms out, then up, massive powerful arms, no fat on them or flab, he yawned, twiddled his long tapering fingers, held out a hand. "Come, I'll show you."

The bedroom was at once austere and cluttered; Todichi Yahzi clucked with distress as he followed Maksim inside. It'd been weeks since he'd been let in to clean the place. The bed was a naked flocking mattress in a lacquer frame, sheets (at least they were clean) and thick soft red blankets twisted into a complex sloppy knot and kicked against the wall. A blackened dented samovar on a wheeled table was pushed against the frame near the head of the bed, a plate with flat round ginger cookies, a sprinkle of brown crumbs and the remnants of a cheese sandwich sat on the floor by the table. A book lay open beside it, turned face down. Robes, sandals, underclothes, towels, scrolls of assorted sizes and conditions and several leather pillows were heaped on or beside rumpled rugs. Maksim crossed to a large chest with many shallow drawers. He opened one, poked through it, clicked his tongue with annoyance when he didn't find what he was looking for, snapped the drawer shut and opened another. "Ah ah, here we are." He lifted out a fine gold chain with a crooked glass drop dangling from it. "Here, Todich, take this."

Todichi Yahzi held the drop in his dark leathery palm, looked down at it, gleams of purple and brown flickering in his eyes.

"When you know I'm dead, throw the drop in a fire; when it explodes, you go home. Don't try it while I'm still alive, won't work. And ah don't worry about it breaking, it won't. I've been meaning to give you that for months, Todich." He lifted his braid off his neck and swiped at the sweat gathered there, rubbed his hand down his side. "Every time I thought of it, something came up to distract me. You understand what to do?"

Todichi Yahzi nodded, closed his fingers tight about the drop. His chest rose, fell. After a tense silence, he sang, "May the day I burn this be many years off." He looked around, shuddered. "Maksim friend, will you please please let me clean this . . . this room?"

A rumbling chuckle. "Why not, old friend. I'll be below."

Todichi fluted a few shapeless sounds, fidgeted from foot to foot. "I will work quickly. And you, my friend, you take care, don't spend yourself to feed your curiosity, come back and rest, eat, sleep."

Maksim smiled, squeezed Todichi's meager grayfurred shoulder with gentle affection, snapped to his subterranean workroom.

Danny Blue yawned, smiled across the fire at Brann. This night was much darker than the last, clouds were piling up overhead, wind that was heavy with water lifted and fell, lifted and fell, there was a sharp nip in the air, a threat of frost come the morning. She was seen and unseen, face and hands shining red-gold when the dying flames flared, slipping into shadow again when they dropped. Made irritable by the electricity from the oncoming storm, the changers were out in the dark somewhere, male and female mountain cats chasing each other, working off an excess of energy as they ran sentry rounds about the camp. "He doesn't seem to care that we're in the Plain."

Her knees were drawn up, her forearms rested on them, she held a mug of tea with both hands and was sitting looking down at it, her face empty of expression as if her thoughts were so far away there was no one left behind the mask. When he spoke, she lifted her head, gazed thoughtfully at him. "Is that what you think?"

"Me? Think? Who am I to think?"

She gave him a slow smile. "Ahzurdan I think, hmm?"

"Ahzurdan is dead. Daniel Akamarino is dead. I'm Azure Dan the magic man, Danny Blue the New. Three weeks old, alive and kicking, umbilical intact, chain umbilical welded in place, no surgeon's knife for me; the Chained God jerks and I dance, don't I dance a pretty dance?"

"A personal, intrusive god isn't so attractive now, hmm?"

"It's like trying to reason with a tornado, you might come out of the experience alive but never intact. And whenever you try, you don't make a dent in the wind."

She smiled, a slow musing smile that irritated him because it seemed to say *I have, I have dented a god more than once, Danny Blue, when you talk about wind, whose wind do you mean?* She said nothing, looked at her mug with a touch of surprise as if she'd forgotten she was holding it. She sipped at the cooling tea and gazed into the puzzle play of red and black across the coals of the little fire. She was strong, serene, contented with who and what she was, she had already won her battle with the god, she'd got what she wanted out of him, freedom for herself and the changers, all she was doing now was paying off that debt; anger flashed through him, a bitter anger that wanted to see her bruised, bleeding, weeping, groveling at his feet; part of him was appalled by the vision, part of him reveled in it, all of him wanted to break the surface of her somehow and get at whatever it was that lay beneath the mask. "Sleep with me tonight."

"I smell like a wet mule."

"Who doesn't. What you mean is not before the children."

"What I mean is, what you see is what you get."

"If I didn't want it, would I ask for it?"

"Would you?"

"You keep your hands off my soul and I'll keep mine off yours, it's your body I want."

She smiled, slid her eyes over him. "It's a point. Why not."

"A little enthusiasm might help."

"A little more Akamarino in the mix might help."

"I thought you didn't like him much."

"I liked his hands, not his mouth, rather what came out his mouth."

"Akamarino is dead."

"You said that."

"You don't seem to believe it."

"I do, Dan. I don't like thinking about it, I. . . ." Her mouth twisted. "Why not. No doubt the god knows quite well how I feel. Somehow I'm going to make it hurt for that, Dan. I don't know how right now and I wouldn't tell you if I did. You intend to keep talking?"

Maksim lay stretched out in his tiltchair, watching the mirror, listening to the conversation. His hair hung loose about his shoulders, the sleeveless workrobe was pulled carelessly about him, a fold of it tucked between BinYAHtii and his skin, his legs were crossed at the ankles and his fingers laced loosely across his stomach. The chair was set parallel to the table so he could reach out and touch the mirror if he wished. For the past several days he'd been snatching scarce moments between conferences to watch what was happening in the mountains and the Forkker Vale, puzzled for a while by the male figure who rode with Brann and the changers. The mirror followed him as if he were Ahzurdan, yet he was not, he was at least a span taller, he was broader in the shoulders, his face was different, though there were hints of Ahzurdan in it as if this man might have been one of his half-brothers. Several times Maksim had focused the mirror on his face, but he couldn't get it clear, the lines blurred and wavered, the closer he got the less he could see, though he could hear most of what the man said. That blurring was something he associated with Daniel Akamarino when he joined Brann and Ahzurdan in Silagamatys. By the time they reached the Vale Maksim had an idea what the Chained God had done, though he couldn't wholly accept where his logic led him, it seemed so unlikely and he couldn't dredge up a reason for doing it, but listening to this hybrid Danny Blue announce the deaths of the men that made him, he had no choice, he had to believe it. Why was it done? What did it mean? He brooded over those questions as he watched Danny Blue get to his feet, move round the fire to join Brann on her blankets. There was that odd and effective weapon Daniel had brought with him from his reality. I'll have to get that away from him somehow before they get here. He watched the maneuverings that combined caresses with the shedding of clothing and decided that trousers were a nuisance he was pleased to have avoided most of his life. The vest went. It's in there, in one of those pockets. He leaned over, tried to focus the mirror on the vest but the blurring was worse than with the man. They're close enough, maybe I can. . . . He reached for the vest and tried to snap it to him. He couldn't get a grip on it. He hissed with annoyance and returned the mirror to its former overlook. They'll be on the Plain early tomorrow, he thought, what do I do about that? I think I leave it to T'Thelo and whatever he contrives. Ha! Look at that, oh, Baby Dan, you're not so dead after all, I know your little ways, oh yes I do. . . ."

"Dan, I'm here too." When he didn't bother listening to her, she pushed his hand off her breast and started wriggling away from him.

He caught one of her wrists, pinned it to the ground beside her shoulder, slapped her face lightly to let her know who was in charge. He grinned at her when she relaxed, laughed in triumph when she stroked his face with her free hand. That was the last thing he saw or felt.

When he woke, his head was wet, there were jagged pebbles and twigs poking him in tender places, a damp blanket was thrown over him. Brann dropped the depleted waterskin beside him and stalked off. She was dressed, her hair was combed and she looked furious but calm. She sat down on the blanket she'd moved across the fire from him and watched him as he chased the fog from his head.

"I was raped once," she said. "Once. I wasn't quite twelve at the time, I was tired, sleeping, I didn't know what was happening to me but I wanted it to stop, so I stopped it. I got a lot more than an ounce of jism from that man, Dan, something you should remember. The kids dumped his body in the river for me. Ahzurdan, if you're in there somewhere, you also should remember what happened to your grandfather when he decided it was a good idea to slap me around. Do you know why you're alive? Don't bother answering, I'm going to tell you. I pay my debts. When I say I'll do something, I do it. Damn you, Dan, that's the second time you've got me wound up and left me hanging. Believe me, there won't be a third time. I'm a Drinker of Souls, Danny Blue, get funny with me and you'll ride to Silagamatys in a vegetable dream."

Maksim smiled as he watched Danny Blue sleep; the hybrid twitched at intervals; at intervals he moved his lips and made small sucking sounds like a hungry baby. Across the dead fire, Brann was in her blankets, sleeping on her side, knees drawn up, arms curled loosely about them, her pillow the waterskin, newly plumped out from the river nearby; now and then there was a small catch in her breath not quite a snore and she was scowling as if no matter how deeply she slept she took her anger with her. "I like you, Drinker of Souls, Forty Mortal Hells, I do, but I wish you smudged your honor some and let Baby

Dan chase you off. AAAh! I owe him a favor, a favor for a lesson, no no, more than a lesson, it's a warning. You don't get within armlength of me, Brann, you or your changeling children."

A long lean cat slipped through the camp, nosed at the sleeping man, went pacing off, a whisper of a growl deep in his? yes, his throat. "Hmm, I wouldn't want to be in your sandals, Danny Blue, the changers are not happy with you. Aaah! that's an idea, good cat gooood, next time through you might let your claws slip a little, yes yes?" He got heavily to his feet, thumbed off the mirror and snapped to his rooms.

Todichi Yahzi was whuffling softly in a stuffed chair, having gone to sleep as he waited for Maksim to return. Maksim bent over him, smiled as he caught the glint of gold in the short gray fur on his neck; Todich was wearing the chain. Maksim shook him awake. "Now what are you doing, Todich? Go to bed. I'll do the same soon as I've had my bath."

Todichi yawned, worked his fingers. "Yim showed up with a message from T'Thelo," he humspoke. "Sent it to me not you because mmmm I think he was frightened of what Yim might carry back to him. He said Servant Bulan wanted mightily to know what you said to him, said he said you wanted him, T'Thelo, to assemble a report on the village schools, that you said it was important right now to know how the children were doing, what the teachers and landsmen were thinking. He's slyer than I thought he was, that old root, I thought you were making a mistake talking to him like that. He said that he, T'Thelo, is going to do that along with the rest, it will be a good camouflage for the other things he has to do, besides it's something that needs doing." He passed his hand over his skull, smoothing down the rough gray fur that was raised in ridges from the way he'd been sleeping. "The scroll Yim brought is in there on the bed, there's some more in it, but I've given you the heart of the matter. Mmmm. I sent a stone sprite to overlook Bulan, he called his core clique at the Grand Yron to the small meeting room off his quarters, he harrangued them some about loyalty, said some obscure things about a threat to Amortis and the Servant Corps and told them to send out Servants they could trust to visit the Kriorns of all the villages to find out what's happening there. The Strataga went nightfishing with his aides, I sent some ariels to see what he was up to, but you know how limited they are and the Godalau was swimming around near harbormouth, they don't like her and won't stay anywhere near her. So I don't know what they were saying, they were still out when I went to sleep, I made a note of which ariels I sent, you can probably get a lot more out of them than I could. The Kephadicast did a lot of pacing, but he didn't talk to anyone, he wrote several notes that he sealed and sent out to Subdicasts here in Silagamatys, asking them to meet with him day after tomorrow, I haven't a notion why he's putting the meeting off that long. Harbormaster went home, ate dinner, went to bed. No pacing, no talking, no notes. I wrote all this up, every detail I could wring out of the watchers, Maksim. The report is on your bed beside T'Thelo's note. The next council meeting is tomorrow afternoon, what do you want me to do about all this mmmmm?"

"Go to bed, Todich, you've done more than enough for tonight. I've got to think." Todichi Yahzi looked disapproving, pressed his lips tight as if he were holding back the scarifying scold he wanted to give. Maksim chuckled, a deep burring that seemed to rise from his heels and roll out of his throat. He stretched mightily, yawned. "But not tonight, old friend, tonight I sleep. Go go. Tomorrow I'll be working you so hard you won't have time to breathe. Go."

Unable to sleep though he knew he should, Maksim pulled a cloak about his shoulders, looked down at the naked legs protruding dark and stately from his nightshirt, laughed and shook his head. "Be damned to dignity." He snapped to the high ramparts and stood looking down over his city.

Clouds were blowing up out of the west and the moon was longgone, it was very dark. Silagamatys was a nubbly black rug spread out across the hills, decorated here and there with splotches and pimples of lamplight and torchfire except near the waterfront where the tavern torches lit the thready fog into a muted sunset glow. The Godalau floated in the bay's black water, moving in and out of the fog, her translucent body lit from within, Tungjii riding black and solid on her massive flank. She drifted past Deadfire Island, a barren heap of stone out near the harbor's mouth; her internal illumination brushed a ghostly gray glimmer over its basalt slopes. She passed on, taking her glimmer with her and Deadfire was once more a shadow lost in shadows. Maksim leaned on the parapet, looking thoughtfully at the black absence. *I let them leave my city and I lost them. Mmm. Might have lost them anyway and half the city with them. Deadfire, Deadfire . . . yes, I think so.* He laughed softly, savoring the words. *Live and die on Deadfire, I live you die, Drinker of Souls and you, Danny Blue. Let the Godalau swim and Tungjii gibber, they can't reach me there, and your*

Chained God, hah! Brann oh Brann, sweet vampire lass, don't count on him to help. The stone reeks of me, it's mine, step on it and it will swallow you. He reached through the neckslit of the nightshirt and smoothed his hand across BinYAHtii. You too, eh? Old stone, that's your stone too, you've fed it blood and bones. There's nothing they've got that can match us . . . mmm . . . except those changers, I'll have to put my mind to them. Send them home? Send them somewhere, yesss, that's it, if they're not here, they're no problem. He stroked BinYAHtii. It might take Amortis to throw them out, Forty Mortal Hells, the Fates forfend, I'd have to figure a way to implant a spine in her. He gazed down at the city with an unsentimental fiercely protective almost maternal love. Blood of his blood, bone of his bone, his unknown M'darjin father had no part in him beyond the superficial gifts of height and color, his mother and Silagamatys had the making of him. Amortis! may her souls if she's got them rot in Gehannum's deepest hell for what she's done to you my city. To you and to me. If I did not still need her. . . . He shivered and pulled his cloak closer about his body. The rising waterheavy wind bit to the bone. Out in the bay the Godalau once more drifted past Deadfire. Maksim pushed away the long coarse hair that was whipping into his mouth and eyes. That's it, then. We meet on Deadfire, Drinker of Souls, Danny Blue. Four more days. That's it. He shivered. So I'd better get some sleep, I've underestimated the three now two of you before, I won't do it again.

They reached the Plain by midmorning, emerging from a last wave of brushy, arid foothills into a land lushly green, intensely cultivated, webbed between its several rivers by a network of canals that provided irrigation water for the fields and most of the transport for produce and people. Brann and Danny Blue rode side by side, neither acknowledging the presence of the other, an unbroken tension between them as threatening as the unbroken storm hanging overhead. The changers flew in circles under the lowering clouds, probing with their telescopic raptor's eyes for signs that Settsimaksimin was attacking, signs that held off like the storm was holding off.

The day ground on. The hilltrack had turned into a narrow dirt road that hugged the riverbank, a dusty rutted weed-grown road little used by anything but straying livestock. Out in the river's main channel flatboats moved past them, square sails bellied taut, filled with the heavy wind that pushed them faster than the current would. Little dark men on those boats (hostility thick on dark skin, glistening like a coat of grease on a kisso wrestler's arms and torso) glared at them out of hate-filled dark eyes. In the fields beside the road and the fields across the river landfolk worked at the harvest, men, women, children. Like the boatmen they stopped what they were doing, even those far across the river, and turned to glower at the riders.

The hangfire storm continued to hover, the storm smell was strong in the air. Whether it was that or the hate rolling at them from every side, by nightfall the mules were as skittish as highbred horses and considerably more balky. Yaril and Jaril vanished for a while, came back jittery as the mules; they flitted about overhead long after Brann and Danny Blue stopped for the night, camping in a grove of Xuthro redleaves that whispered around them and sprayed them with pungent medicinal odors as the heat of the campfire lifted into the lower branches.

Danny Blue rested his teamug on his knee and cleared his throat. Brann gave him no encouragement. A catface came into the light, crystal eyes flashing a brilliant red, the cat stared at him for an uncomfortably long time, then withdrew into the darkness; he couldn't forget it was out there not one minute and while that was comforting in one way, in another it turned his throat dry thinking about the changers pacing and pacing in their sentry rounds, feral fearsome beasts angry at the world in general and at him in particular. He gazed across the fire at Brann who was in her way quite as lethal. "I'm sorry about last night," he said.

She nodded, accepting his apology without commenting on it.

"I do fine," he said, "as long as it's the rational side of me called up. Or the technical side. Doesn't matter who's running the show, Akamarino or Ahzurdan or me. It's emotions that screw me up, ah, confuse me. Ah, this isn't easy to talk about. . . ."

She looked coolly at him as if to say why bother then, looked down at her hands without saying anything.

Anger flared in him, but he shoved it down and kept control, him, Danny Blue the New, not either of his clamoring progenitors. "When it's strong emotions, well, Daniel avoided them most of his life, couldn't handle them, which gives Ahzurdan an edge because he played with them all since he was born, anger, you know, lust, frustration, resentment, he's loved a maid or two, a man or two, been wildly happy and filled with cold despair, too much passion, his skin was too thin, he had to numb himself, dreamsmoke washed out the pain of living, you know all that, you heard all that on the trip here. He has ambivalences about you, Brann, growing all over him like a fungus, I suppose I should say all over me. That's the problem, I can't control him when there's emotion involved. Think about it a minute. How old is Danny Blue? Three weeks, almost four, Bramble-all-thorns . . ."

Her head came up when she heard the name the changers sometimes gave her. "Don't call me that."

"Why not, it suits you."

"Maybe it does, maybe not. My name is Brann and I'll tell you when you can call me out of it." She twisted up onto her knees, touched the side of the teapot, refilled her cup and settled back to her blankets. She sipped briefly at the hot liquid, then sat with her legs drawn up, her arms resting on them, both hands wrapped around the cup as if she needed the warmth from it more than the taste of tea in her mouth. "Do me a favor," she said, "experiment on someone else." She gazed at the fire, the animation gone out of her face, her eyes shadowed and dull. After several moments of unhappy silence, she shivered, fetched a smile from somewhere. "You still think you want me when you've combed the knots out, I expect I'd be fool enough to try again. At least you already know what I am. What a relief not having to explain things." She gulped at the tea, shivered again. "Looks like everyone about knows where we're going and why."

"And they don't like it."

"And they don't like it. Yaril, Jaril," she called. "One of you come in, will you?"

The ash blond young woman came into the firelight, tall and slim, limber as a dancer, crystal eyes shadowed, reflecting fugitive glimmers from the dying fire. She glanced at Danny Blue, her face bland as the cat's had been, showing nothing but a delicately exaggerated surprise at seeing him there. He grinned at her, Daniel uppermost now and finding her much to his taste, an etherial exotic lovely far less complicated and demanding than Brann; watching her settle beside Brann her shoulder and profile given to him, he wondered just how far she'd gone in taking a human shape and what it'd feel like making love to a skinful of fire, hmm! who was also a contact telepath. Now that's rather offputting. Gods, Ol' Dan, you're hornier 'n a dassup in must. And neither of them's going to have a thing to do with you and it's your own damn fault. Talk about shooting yourself in the foot, huh, that's not where the bullet went. Say this is over and you survive it, you'll have to hunt up a whore or three and argue old Ahzurdan into a heap of ash so you

can get your ashes hauled. Till then I guess it's the hermit's friend for
you if you can get yourself some privacy, shuh! as Brann would say, to
have those changers come on me and giggle at what I'm reduced to
. . . uh uh, no way. A little strength of mind, Danny Blue, come the
morning, dunk yourself in that river, that should be cold enough to
take your mind off.

"A while back," Yaril said, "Jay and I, we decided we wanted to
know what all the glares were about, so we paled out and probed a few
of those peasants out there. They've had news about us from Silagamatys, all of them, farmers boatmen you name it. They're trying to
think of some way to stop us. They don't know how so far, the ones we
checked were thinking of sneaking up on us when we're asleep and
knocking us in the head or something like that, maybe setting up an
ambush and plinking us with bolts from crossbows, so far they haven't
nerved themselves into trying anything, it was mostly wish and dream,
but they surely wouldn't mind if we fell in the river and drowned.
They're worried about Settsimaksimin, if anything happened to him
the wolves would be down on them from all sides. They love the man,
Bramble, sort of anyway, he's mixed up in their heads with the land,
everything they feel for the land they feel for him, it's like when they're
plowing the soil, they're plowing his body. They pray for him, and,
believe me, they'll fight for him. Any time now we're going to start
running into big trouble. Probably tonight. I wouldn't be surprised if
some of the wilder local lads tried their hands with bullkillers or scythe
blades. Probably around the third nightwatch, I doubt if they'll come
sooner and later it'd be too light."

"You and Jay can handle them?"

"Hah, you need to ask? Braaaann." She clicked her tongue, shook
her head, finally sobered. "You want us to wake you?"

"As soon as you see signs of trouble, yes. We want to get the mules
saddled and the supplies roped in place in case we have to leave fast."

"Gotcha, Bramble. Anything else?"

"Um . . . what's the land like ahead?"

"Pretty much more of the same for the first half day's ride, another
river joins this one a little after that, hard to tell so far off but I think
there's some sort of swamp and the road seems to turn away from the
river. You want Jay or me to go take a look?"

Brann frowned at the fire. "I don't . . . think so. No. I'd rather you
rested. Take turns with Jay. How are you doing on energy? It was a
cloudy day. Give me your hand a minute. Good. That god didn't

change you so much you can't take from me, I thought a minute it might have, self-defense, you know, so we couldn't build the bridge again and suck godfire out of it, but I suppose it wanted to be sure we could handle Amortis if she poked her delicate nose in the business with Maksim."

"You needn't worry about us, Bramble, our batteries are charged, matter of fact we've been pretty well steady state since we left the ship."

"Happy to hear it, but tired or not, you and Jay both operate better after a little dormancy, I think it's like with people, you need your sleep to clear out the day's confusion. So, you rest, both of you, hear?"

Yaril giggled. "Yes, mama." She got to her feet and walked with lazy grace out of the circle of firelight.

Danny Blue yawned. "Looks like Maksim's made himself some friends."

"You could try helping us a bit. I agree with Yaro; we're bound to run into trouble; I'd like to know more about that and how you're going to help deal with it."

"That depends on the attack, doesn't it?"

"I don't know, does it?"

"In a word, yes. Trouble, mmm. Maksim's got earth and fire elementals tied to him and an assortment of demons. You've met some of those." A quick grin. "Demons aren't too big a problem, you send them home if you know where home is and I know most of the realities Maksim located because Ahzurdan knew and I've got his memories." A lazy stretch, a yawn. "Flip side." When she raised her brows, not understanding, he murmured, "The good of having Ahzurdan in here. As opposed to the problems he causes." He took a sip of the tea left in his mug, grimaced. "Stone cold." He poured it out on the ground beside him and managed to squeeze another half mug from the teapot nestled next to the fire. "Which reminds me, one of the things Maksim might try is tipping the changers into another reality; it's something I'd do if I could. If he managed that, he could really hurt our chances of surviving. Something else . . ." He gulped at the tea, closed his eyes as warmth spread through him. "It's a plus and a minus for us, Ahzurdan might have told you this (I'm a little hazy here and there on my sires' memories), the top rank sorcerers don't often fight each other, no point and no profit. They tend to avoid taking hires that might oblige them to confront an equal. He'd argue this, but I don't think Ahzurdan is one of them. Might be close but the impression I get is he lacked a certain stability." His body jerked, he looked startled, then grim. He set the mug beside him with careful gentleness, pressed his lips together and slapped his hands repeatedly on his knee until the nagging itchy under-the-skin pains faded away. "He didn't like that." He finished off the tea, wiped his mouth. "Where was . . . yes. What I'm saying is, Settsimaksimin has never been in a war with someone as strong as him or close to it. We've both seen it, he doesn't like to attack. He'll make individual strikes, but he won't keep up the pressure and I don't believe it's because he can't. He's a warm man, he likes people, he needs them around him and he's generous, if I'm reading the Magic Man right. Aaah, yes, what I'm saying is his peers are all frogs in their own ponds, they don't want to share their how shall I say it? ahhh adulation. He's like that in some senses, he wouldn't tolerate anyone who pretended to equality with him, but he's got friends in the lower ranks and among the scholars who don't operate so much as study and teach, more of them than you might expect. Ahzurdan's not typical of his ex-students either, poor old Magic Man (uhnn! there he goes again), but even he can't hate the man. That's one of his problems, shahhh! apparently it's mine too. I'd say this, if we hurry him, don't give him time to set himself, there's that little hiccup between thought and act we could use to our advantage. No matter how he nerves himself, attack isn't natural to him, his instinct is to defend. Which is a potent reason for making sure he doesn't flip the changers off somewhere. Amortis wouldn't have that drag on her, her instinct is stomp first then check out what's smeared on her foot. He knows his limitations better than any outsider making funny guesses. He'll use BinYAHtii to drive her against us. She's afraid of you, Brann, you and the changers, and she loathes you and she loathes Maksim for constraining her, all that fear and rage is waiting to dump on you . . . ahh . . . us. With the changers we should be able to deflect it onto Maksim and let him worry about it. Without them . . . I don't like to think of facing him without them."

She bit into her lower lip, frowned at the fire a moment, looked up at him. "How do we stop it?"

Danny Blue unwrapped his legs and lay back on his blankets; he gazed up at the spearhead leaves fluttering over him, the patches of black sky he could see in openings between the branches. "I don't know. I have to think. I might be able to block him if I have a few seconds warning. If the changers start feeling odd or if they see sign of

Amortis, they should get to me fast." He yawned. "Morning's soon enough to tell them."

"Why not now?"

He pushed up on his elbow, irritated. Her face was a pattern of black and red, he couldn't read it, but when could he ever? "Because I don't know what to say to them yet." His irritation showed in his voice and that annoyed him more.

She got to her feet. "Then you'd better start your thinking, Danny Blue. I'll be back in a little." She walked into the darkness where Yaril had gone, a prowling cat of a woman radically unlike the changer, slender but there was bone in her and good firm muscle on that bone. He remembered her hands, wide strong working hands with their long thumbs and short tapering fingers, he remembered Ahzurdan looking at them disturbed by them because they represented everything he resented about her, her preference for low vulgar laboring men, her disdain for wellborn elegance, for the delicacy of mind and spirit that only generations of breeding could produce, her explosive rejection of almost everything he cherished, he remembered even more vividly the feel of those hands moving tantalizingly up Daniel's arms, stirring the hairs, shooting heat into him. He pushed up, slipped his sandals off and set them beside his blankets, then stretched out on his back and laced his hands behind his head. "Yes," he said aloud. "Thinking time."

Toward the end of the third nightwatch six young men in their late teens slipped from the river and crept toward the redleaf grove. Jaril spotted them as he catwalked in ragged circles about the camp. To make sure these young would-be assassins were all he had to worry about, he loped through one last circuit; reassured, he woke Yaril and left her to rouse the others while he shifted to his shimmerglobe. He considered a moment, but the impulse was impossible to resist; he'd wanted to try a certain repatterning technique since he'd sat on Daniel's stunner and sucked in the knowledge of what it was. He made some swift alterations in one part of his being, suppressed the excited laughter stirring in him and went careening through the trees, a sphere of whitefire like a moontail with acromegaly. He hung over the youths long enough to let them get a good look at him, then he squirted force into his metaphorically rewired portion and sprayed them with his improvised stunbeam. He watched with satisfaction as they collapsed into the dust.

Yaril glimmersphere drifted up to him. *Nice. Show me.*

It's based on Daniel's stunner. You do this. Then this. Right. One more twist. Good. That's the pattern that does it. Remember, keep the lines rigid. Like that. And you cyst it. I didn't at first and look what I've done to myself, that's going to be sore. It gulps power, Yaro, but you don't have to hold it more than a few seconds.

Now we won't have to depend so much on Danny Blue. I like that, I like it a lot.

Agreed.

Why didn't you try it before?

No point. Besides, if Maksim knew about it too long before we got to him, he just might figure out a way of handling it. Remember what Ahzurdan said, this is heartland for him, I don't doubt he can overlook most of it easy as an ordinary man looks out his window.

Gotcha. Do you really think Maksim is going to try tipping us into another reality?

Brann does. Don't you?

We'll have to keep wide awake, Jay. When I leave this reality, I want it to be my idea and I don't want to be dumped just anywhere, I want to go home.

Bramble's next quest, reading Slya's alleged mind?

If we can work it. Talk to you later. She's coming.

Brann walked into the pale grayish light they gave off, squatted beside one of the young men. She pushed her fingers under his jaw, smiled with satisfaction when she felt the strong pulse. "Good work, Jay. How long will they be out?"

Jaril dropped and shifted, held out his hand. When Brann took it, he said, *Don't know. I finagled a version of the stunner, haven't done this before so it's anybody's guess. They could wake up in two minutes or two hours.*

I hear. Useful.

More useful if nobody knows exactly what happened.

Nobody being Maksim umm and Danny Blue?

You got it. Or that Yaro can do it too, now.

*Anything else? No? Good. We'll tie our baby assassins up to keep them out of mischief, fix some breakfast and get an early start. From now on I suppose we can expect *anything* to happen.* She freed her hand. "Yaro, flit back to camp and fetch us some rope hmm?"

Yaril dropped and shifted. "Sure. Need a knife?"

"Got a knife."

The Plain emptied before them. Boatmen brought their flatboats upriver and down into the throat of the Gap, mooring them to rocks and trees and to each other, a barrier as wide as the river and six boats deep. Landfolk poured into the hills between Silagamatys and the Plain, the greater part of them gathering about the Gap where the river ran, interposing their bodies between the threatening and the threatened. Some stayed behind. When Brann and Danny Blue came to the marshes, hidden bowmen shot at them. The changers ashed the arrows before they reached their targets. Spears tumbled end for end into the sedges when Danny Blue snapped his fingers, slingstones whipped about and flew at the slingers who plunged hastily into mucky murky swamp water.

Aware that Amortis was not going to march to war for them, that weapons would not stop the hellcat, her sorcerer and her demons, the landfolk left their homes and their harvests and in an endless stream walked and rode into the hills, a stubborn angry horde determined to protect their land and their leader. It was a thing the Parastes never understood or acknowledged, the lifetie between the small brown landfolk and the land they worked, land that held layer on layer on layer of their dead, land they watered with their sweat and their blood. These grubbers, these strongbacked beasts, these self-replicating digging machines, they owned that land as those elegant educated parasites the Parastes never would, no matter how viciously and vociferously they claimed it. Much of what Settsimaksimin did after he took Cheonea linked him in the landfolk mind to the land itself and its dark primitive power. When he gave them visible tangible evidence of their ancient ownership, when he gave them deeds written in strong black ink on strong white parchment, it struck deep into their two souls. The idea of the land wound inextricably about the idea of Settsimaksimin and he became one for them with that black and fecund earth, himself huge, dark and powerful.

The land itself fought them. A miasma oozed from the earth and coiled round them when they slept, breeding nightmares in them, humming in their ears go away turn back go away turn back. Coiled round them when they rode, burning their eyes, cocooning them in stench, whispering go away turn back go away turn back. The hangfire storm was oppressive, it was hard to breathe, crooked blue lightning snapped from fingertips to just about anything they brushed against. The mules balked, balked again, exasperating Brann because she had to jolt each one every time they did it. The ambushes kept on happening, a futile idiotic pecking that accomplished nothing except to exhaust Danny Blue who had to keep his shield ready, his senses alert. Amortis had laid a smother across the Plain, more oppressive for him than the storm; each time he had to flex his magic muscle he was working against an immense resistance. By the end of the day he was so depleted he could barely hold himself in the saddle.

The third morning on the Plain. Left in pastures unmilked, cows bawled their discomfort. Farmyard dogs barked and whined and finally sated their hunger on fowl let out to feed themselves while their owners were gone. Aside from those small noises and the sounds they made themselves, there was an eerie silence around them. The harvest waited half-gathered in the fields, the stock grazed or stood around, twitching nervously, the houses were empty, unwelcoming, no children's laughter and shouts, no gossiping over bread ovens or laundry tubs, no voices anywhere. No more ambushes either. Danny Blue sighed with relief when the morning passed without a stone flung at them, but the smother was still there, pressing down on him, forcing him to push back because it would have crushed him if he didn't.

Night came finally. They stopped at a deserted farmhouse, caught two of the farmer's chickens, cooked them in a pot on the farmer's stove with assorted vegetables, tubers and some rice. It was a small neat house, shining copper pots hanging from black iron hooks, richly colored earthenware on handrubbed shelves, the furniture in every room was crafted with love and skill, bright blankets hung on the walls, huge oval braided rugs were spread on every floor, and it was a new house, evidence of the farmer's prosperity. After supper three of them stretched out on leather cushions around the farmer's hearth while the fire danced and crackled and they drank hot mulled cider from the farmer's cellar. Jaril was flying watch overhead.

Yaril sighed with a mixture of pleasure and regret; she set her mug on her thigh, ran her free hand through her pale blond hair. "We'll reach the hills sometime late tomorrow afternoon," she said. "There's a problem."

Brann was stretched out half on a braided rug, half on Danny Blue who was leaning against an ancient chest, a pillow tucked between him and the wood. He opened heavy eyes, looked at Yaril, let his lids drop again. "How big?" he murmured.

"Oh, somewhere around ten thousand folk sitting on those hills waiting for us."

His eyes snapped open. "What?"

"Miles of them on both sides of the river. One shout and we've got hundreds pressed around us, maybe thousands."

Brann sat up, her elbow slamming into Dan's stomach. She patted him, muttered an offhand apology, turned a thoughtful gaze on Yaril. She said nothing.

Dan crossed his ankles, rubbed the sore spot. "The river?"

"Boatmen. Flatboats. Roped together bank to bank, six rows of them, more arriving both sides. Net strung under them. Bramble, you and Danny Blue are going to have to be very very clever unless you plan on killing lots of landfolk."

Brann got to her feet. "Us? What about the two of you?" She strolled to the fireplace and stood leaning against the stone mantel.

Yaril set the mug down, scratched at her thigh. "We already tried, Bramble. You know how there started to be nobody anywhere? Not long after that Jay and I saw lines and lines of landfolk moving across the Plain. Jay flew ahead to see what was happening and came back worried. We tossed ideas around all afternoon. You know what we came up with? Nothing, that's what. It's up to you. We quit."

Danny Blue went downcellar and fetched another demijohn of cider. He poured it into the pot swung out from the fire, tossed in pinches of the mulling spices, stirred the mix with a longhandled wooden spoon. Brann and Yaril watched in silence until he came back to the chest that he was using as a backrest, then, while the cider heated, the three of them went round and round over the difficulties that faced them.

BRANN: We could try outflanking them.

YARIL: Plan on walking then, the terrain by those hills is full of ravines and tangles of brush and unstable landslips. Mules can't possibly handle it.

DANNY (yawning): Don't forget Amortis; with Maksim to point her, she can snap up a few hundred bodies and drop them in front of us and do it faster than we can shift direction.

BRANN: You said she's afraid of the changers and me.

DANNY: Sure, but she wouldn't have to get anywhere near you, she could do all that from Maksim's tower in the city.

BRANN: Shuh! There's a thought there, though. What about you, Dan? If she can snap a couple hundred over a distance of miles, surely you can do the same with two over say a dozen yards. Enough to take you and me past them.

DANNY: Get rid of Amortis first, then sure. Otherwise, with the smother getting heavier as we get closer to the hills, just breathing is going to make me sweat.

BRANN: Then you'd better busy yourself deciding what you can do now. Yaro, what about you and Jay? How many could you stun how fast?

YARIL: Jay and I working together, um, couple dozen a minute. Listen, that won't work, same reason it wouldn't work going round them. With that many sitting on those hills, there's bound to be one or two we miss who lets out a yell and there we are, nose-deep in a landfolk. Another thing you better think about, you can't get through them without riding up to them somewhere, announcing your interest as 'twere, and once that's done, guess what else is going to happen. Bramble, Jay and I, we went round and round on this. Remember how the Chained God shifted you and Danny's sires poppop back and forth across that ship? We thought about that, we thought about it so much we just about overheated our brains. We figured Amortis could do the same if she took a notion to, so you and Danny have to cross the line without getting close to it. We figured we could gnaw on that idea till we went to stone without getting anywhere. We figured we can fly across with no difficulty, it's you and Danny here who have the problem, so it's you and Danny who have to come up with the answer.

DANNY: Roll back a sec, stun them? since when and how?

YARIL: Um, Jay took a look at your stunner, remember? He figured a way to repattern a part of his body to produce the same effect, he powered it from his internal energy stores, tested it on those baby assassins. You saw the results.

DANNY: So I did. Repatterning . . . mmm.

While Brann and Yaril chewed over the problem of acting without being seen to act, Danny Blue withdrew into himself to track down a wisp of an idea. Once upon a time when Daniel Akamarino was very new among the stars and still feeling around for what and who he was, he signed onto a scruffy free trader called the Herring Finn and promptly learned the vast difference between a well-financed, superbly run passenger liner and the bucket for whose engines he was suddenly responsible. And not only the engines. He was called on to repair, rebuild or construct from whatever came to hand everything the ship needed of a propulsive nature. One of those projects was a lift sled for loading cargo in places so remote they not only didn't have starports, they very often didn't have wheels. He'd rebuilt that thing so many times it was engraved into his brain. And with a little prodding Danny Blue found he could retrieve the patterns. From his other progenitor he culled the memory of his lessons in Reshaping, one of the earliest skills a Sorcerer's apprentice had to master. Hour on hour of practice, until he could shut his eyes and make the shape without error perceptible to the closest scrutiny which he got because Settsimaksimin was a good teacher whatever other failings he might have. There was still the problem of power. He decided to worry about that after he knew whether or not he could shape a sled. I need something to work on, he thought, something solid enough to hold Brann and me, but not too heavy.

He got to his feet and wandered through the house. The beds were too clumsy, besides they were mainly frame and rope with a straw palliasse for a mattress and billowing quilts. He fingered a quilt, thinking about the nip in the air once the sun went down, shook his head and wandered on. Everything that caught his eye had too many problems with it until he reached the kitchen and inspected the hard-used worktable backed into an alcove around the corner from the cooking hearth. The tabletop was a tough ivory wood scarred with thousands of shallow knifecuts, scrubbed and rubbed to a surface that felt like satin; it was around twelve centimeters thick, two meters wide and three long (from the positioning of the cuts at least eight women gathered about it when they were making meals or doing whatever else they did there). He fetched a candle, dropped into a squat and peered at the underside. Looks solid, he thought, have to test it. Hmm, those legs . . . if they don't add too much weight, they might be useful, some sort of windscreen . . . mmm, the front four anyway, whichever end I call front . . . how'm I going to get this thing out where I can see what I'm doing? Ah! talking about seeing, I'm going to have to set up a shield. If I can. He rose from the squat, set the candle on the table and hitched a hip beside it, unwrapped and began to finger his anger, his resentment of the constraints laid on him, his frustration. Daniel Akamarino went where he wanted when he wanted, Ahzurdan was constrained only by his internal confusions, whatever he wanted or needed he had the power to take if some fool tried to deny him. Danny Blue was too young an entity to know much about who and what he was, but he resonated sufficiently with his progenitors to feel a bitter anger at the Chains the god had put on him. He felt the compulsion clamp down on his head when he tried to give voice to that anger; he could not do, say or even think anything that might (might!) work against the god. He knew, though he had deliberately refrained from thinking about it, that he suffered the smother without trying to fight it because it offered—or seemed to offer—an escape for him, a way he could thwart the god without having to fight the compulsion. After the landfolk shut down their ambushes, he'd ridden relaxed under it exerting himself just enough to keep from being crushed, smiling out of vague general satisfaction as the weight of the smother increased and the possibility of action diminished. He carried that satisfaction into dinner and beyond, but somewhere in the middle of the discussion, he lost it. The Hand of the God came down on him harder than the smother, *find the answer, find it, no more dawdling, I'll have no more excuses for failure, failure will not be permitted. Get through that line however you can, stomp the landfolk like ants if you have to, do whatever you have to, but bring me BinYAHtii.*

He wiped the sweat off his face, beat his fist on the tabletop until it boomed, working off some of the rage that threatened to explode out of the cramping grip of the god and blow the fragile psyche of Danny Blue into dust. He might be young and wobbly on his feet, but he had a ferocious will to survive. Not as Ahzurdan, not as Daniel Akamarino. As Danny Blue the New.

"What is it? What's wrong?"

He looked up. Brann was standing in the arch of the alcove looking worried. He opened his mouth to explain but his tongue wouldn't move and his throat closed on him. It was forbidden to think, do or say anything against the god. His face went hot and congested as he wrestled with the ban; he felt as if he were strangling on the words that wouldn't come out. She came to him, put her hand on his arm. "Never mind," she said, "I know."

He slammed fist against table one last time, sighed and stood up. "Help me turn this thing over."

Brann pushed her hair off her face, blinked at him, then began laughing. He looked up, startled. "What?"

"You wouldn't understand. Why turn the table over?"

"Don't want to talk about it, you know why."

"Ah. Can the changers help?"

"No. You take that end, I'll take this. Watch the legs."

"Better move the candle first, unless you're planning to burn the house down. If you want light, why not touch on the wall lamps?"

"Lamps?" He looked up. There were ten glass and copper bracket lamps with reservoirs full of oil spaced along the walls of the alcove two meters and a half above the floor; he hadn't noticed them because he hadn't bothered to look higher than his head. "Do you know how irritating a woman is when she's always right? Here." He thrust the candle at her. "Light the ones on your side."

When the table was inverted and lay with its legs in the air, Danny Blue knelt on it and thumped at various portions of it to make sure the wood was solid; finished with that, he sat on his heels and looked thoughtfully at Brann. "You fed Ahzurdan, you think you can do that for me?"

She frowned at him, moved to the arch. "Yaril, I need you."

Drifting above the clouds, Jaril spread out and out and out, shaping himself into a mile wide parabolic collector seducing into himself starlight, moonlight, gathering every erg of power he could find; Yaril was a glimmering glassy filament stretching from Jaril to Brann, feeding that power into her; Brann was a transformer kneeling beside Danny Blue, feeding that power into him as fast as he could take it.

Using Ahzurdan's memories, Danny Blue wove a shield about them like the one Ahzurdan had thrown about the room in the Blue Seamaid; he worked more slowly and had to draw more power than Ahzurdan had, the memories were there but he was no longer completely Ahzurdan and the resonance of word and act were no longer quite true. With Brann feeding energy into him, he got the shield completed, locked it into automatic and found that he'd gained two advantages he hadn't expected. The smother couldn't reach him, couldn't wear at him. And the shield once it was completed took almost no maintaining. Whistling a cheerful tune he unbuckled his sandals and kicked them across the room, grabbed hold of Brann and pulled her into the aclove, shrinking the shield until it covered only that smaller room, it'd attract less attention and he had no illusions about how irritated Maksim was going to be at losing sight of what they were doing. But it was so damn good to be working again on something as simple and elegant and altogether beautiful as lift field circuits—he felt like a sculptor who'd lost his hands in some accident or other, then had to spend a small eternity waiting for them to be regrown.

Yaril filament had no difficulty penetrating the shield; she continued to transmit moonlight and starlight into Brann who kept one hand lightly on Danny's spine, maintaining the feed as he dropped to his knees on the underside of the tabletop. He brushed his fingertips across the wood, sketched the outline of a sensor panel, but left it as faint marks on the surface. Hands moving slowly, surely, the chant pouring out of him with a rightness that was another thing he hadn't expected (as if the magic and his Daniel memories had conspired to teach him in that instant what it'd taken Ahzurdan years to learn, as if the rightness and elegance of the design dictated the chant and all the rest), he Reshaped the wood into metal and ceramic and the esoteric crystals that were the heart and brain of the field, layer on layer of them embedded in the wood, shielded from it by intricate polymers, his body the conduit by which the device flowed out of memory into reality, his will and intellect disregarded. When the circuits were at last completed, he sculpted twin energy sinks near the tail (full, they'd power the sled twice about the world) and finished his work with a canted sensor plate that would let him control start-up, velocity, direction and altitude. After a moment's thought, he keyed the plate to his hand and Brann's; whatever happened, Maksim wasn't going to be playing with this toy, it was his, Danny Blue the New, no one else's. He added Brann (reluctantly, forcing himself to be practical when the thought of sharing his creation made him irrationally angry), because there was too good a chance he'd be injured and incapable and he trusted her to get away from Maksim if she could possibly do it so he didn't want to limit her options. He sat on his heels, gave Brann a broad but weary grin. "Finished."

She inspected the underside of the table; except for the collection of milkglass squares on the tilted board near one end she couldn't see much change in the wood. "If you say so. Shall I call the changers in?"

He tested the shielding and his own reserves. "Why not. But you'd better tell them I'm going to need them in the morning when there's sunlight, we have to charge the power cells before we go anywhere."

She nudged the tabletop with her toe. "I've heard of flying carpets, but flying kitchen tables, hunh!"

He jumped up, laughed, "Bramble-all-thorns, no you won't spank me for that." He caught her by the waist, swung her into an exuberant dance about the kitchen whistling the cheeriest tune he knew; he was flying higher than Jaril had, the pleasure of using both strands of his technical knowledge to produce a thing of beauty was better than any other pleasure in both his lives, better than sex, better than smokedreams; he sang that in her ear, felt her respond, stopped the dance and stood holding her. "Brann. . . ."

"Mmmm?"

"Still hating me?"

She leaned against his arms, pushing him back so she could see his face, her own face grave at first, then warming with laughter. She made a fist, pounded it lightly against his chest. "If you mess me up again, I swear, Dan, I'll . . . I don't know what I'll do, but I guarantee it'll be so awful you'll never ever recover from it."

He stroked her hands down her back, closed them over her buttocks, pulled her against him. "Feel me shaking?"

"Like a leaf in a high wind."

He tugged her toward the alcove, but she broke away. "I'm not going to bruise my behind or my knees," she said. "Privacy yes," she said, "but give me some comfort too. Pillows," she said. "And quilts. Fire's down, it's getting chilly in here."

The children were curled up on the couch in the living room, sunk in the dormancy that was their form of sleep. Brann touched them lightly, affectionately as she moved past them, then ran laughing up the stairs to the sleeping floor. She started throwing the pillows out the doors leaving them in the hall for Dan to collect and carry downstairs, came after him with a billowing slippery armload of feather comforters.

Brann blinked, yawned, scrubbed her hands across her face. She felt extraordinarily good though her mouth tasted like something had died there, she was disagreeably sticky in spots and when she stretched, the comforter brushing like silk across her body, she winced at a number of small sharp twinges from pulled muscles and a bite or two, which only emphasized how very very good she was feeling. She lay still a moment, enjoying a long leisurely yawn, taking pleasure in the solid feel of Dan's body as her hip moved against his. But she'd never been able to stay abed once she was awake, so she kicked free of the quilts and sat up.

Dan was still deeply asleep, fine black hair twisting about his head, a heavy stubble bluing his chin and cheeks, long silky eyelashes fanned across blue veined skin whose delicacy she hadn't noticed before. She bent over him, lifted a stray strand of hair away from his mouth, traced the crisp outlines of that mouth with moth-touches of her forefinger. The mouth opened abruptly, teeth closed on her finger. Growling deep in his throat, Dan caught her around the waist, whirled her onto her back and began gnawing at her shoulder, working his way along it to her neck.

Brann drunked a corner of the towel in the basin of cold water, shivered luxuriously as she scrubbed at herself. "The changers are still dormant. I suppose I should wake them."

"They worked hard and there's more to do, leave them alone a while yet . . . mmm . . . scrub my back?"

"Do mine first. I'd love to wash my hair, but I'm too lazy to heat the water. Dan . . . ?"

"Dan Dan the handyman. How's that feel?" He rubbed the wet soapy towel vigorously across her back and down her spine, lifted her hair and worked more gently on her neck. When he was finished, he dropped a quick kiss on the curve of her shoulder, traded towels with her and began wiping away the soap.

"Handyman has splendid hands," she murmured. "Give me a minute more and I'll do you."

"Trade you, Bramble, you cook breakfast for us and I'll haul hot water for your hair."

"Cozy." A deep rumbling voice filled with laughter.

Brann whipped round, hands out, reaching toward the huge dark man in a white linen robe who stood a short distance from them.

Dan moved hastily away from her. "No use, Brann, it's only an eidolon."

"What?" As soon as she said it, she no longer needed an answer, the eidolon had moved a step away and she could see the kitchen fire glow through it.

"Projected image. He's nowhere near here." Dan's voice came from a slight distance, when she looked round, he was coming from the alcove with his trousers and her shirt.

"He can see and hear us?" She took the shirt, pulled it around her and buttoned up the front.

"Out here. If we went into the alcove, no." He tied off his trouser laces and came to lean against the pump sink beside and a little behind her.

"So," Brann said, "it's your move, image. What does he want with us?"

The eidolon lifted a large shapely hand, pointed its forefinger at the alcove.

"NO!" Dan got out half a word and the beginning of a gesture, then sank back, simmering, as the eidolon dropped its arm and laughed.

"Busy busy, baby Dan?" The eidolon folded its arms across its massive chest. "I presume you have cobbled together some means of coping with the landfolk. A small warning to the two of you which you can pass on to your versatile young friends. Don't touch my folk. I don't expect an answer to that. What I've sent the eidolon for is this, a small bargain. I will refrain from any more attacks against you, I'll even call off Amortis; you will come direct to me on Deadfire Island." The eidolon turned its head, yellow eyes shifting from Brann to Danny Blue. Its mouth stretched into a mocking smile. "A bargain that needs no chaffering because you have no choice, the two of you. Come to me because you must and let us finish this thing." Giving them no time to respond, it vanished.

The table hovered waist high above the flags of the paved yard. Still inverted, its front four legs supported a stiff windbreak made of something that looked rather like waxy glass, another of Danny Blue's transformations. He sat in the middle of the sled grinning at her; lift-sled, that's what he'd called it and when she told him no sled she'd ever seen looked like that he took it as a compliment. Yaril and Jaril were sitting on the rim of a stone bowl planted with broadleaved shrubs that were looking wrinkled and shopworn (end of the year symptoms or they needed watering); the changers were enjoying the performance (hers and Dan's as well as the table's).

Brann shivered. The wind was more than chill this morning, it was cold. If those clouds ever let down their load, it would fall as sleet rather than rain, a few degrees more and the Plain might have this year's first snow. "Yaro, collect us two or three of those quilts, please? And here," she tossed two golds to Yaril, "leave these somewhere the farmwife will find them but a thief would miss. I know we're gifting the farmer with three fine mules, but he didn't sew the quilts and he doesn't use the table we're walking off with. I know, I know, not walking, flying. You happy now, Dan? Shuh! save your ah hmm wit until we're somewhere you can back it up. If you need something to occupy you, figure for me how long our flying table will need to get us to Deadfire."

Danny Blue danced his fingers over the sensors; the table lowered itself smoothly to the flagging. He got to his feet, stretched, stood fingering a small cut the sorcerously sharpened knife had inflicted on him when he used it to shave away his stubble. Ahzurdan jogged my hand, he told Brann, he keeps growling at me that adult males need beards to proclaim their manhood, it's the one advantage he had over

Maksim, he could grow a healthy beard and his teacher couldn't, the m'darjin blood in him prevented, but I can't stand fur on my face so all old Ahzurdan can do is twitch a little. He fingered the cut and scowled past Brann at the wooden fence around the kitchen garden. "It's hard to say, Bramble. Last night, who was it, Yaril, she said we'd reach the mountains late afternoon today, say we were riding, that's . . . hmm . . . what? Sixty, seventy miles? Jay, from this side the hills, how far would you say it is to Deadfire Island?"

Jaril kicked his heels against the pot. "Clouds," he said. "We couldn't get high enough to look over the hills." He closed his eyes. "Before we left on the Skia Hetaira," he said, his voice slow and re-membering, "we wanted to get a look down into Maksim's Citadel, we weren't paying much attention to the hills . . . Yaro?" Yaril dumped quilts and pillows onto the table, walked over to him. She settled beside him, her hand light on his shoulder. They sat there quietly a moment communing in their own way, pooling their memories.

Jaril straightened, opened his eyes. "Far as we can remember, those hills ahead are right on the coast. You just have to get through them, then you're more or less at Silagamatys. About the same distance, I'd say, from here to the hills, from the hills to Deadfire. Maybe a hundred miles altogether, give or take a handful."

Dan nodded. "I see. Well . . ." He clasped his hands behind him and considered the table. "If the sled goes like it's supposed to, flying time's somewhere between hour and a half, two hours."

"Instead of two days," Brann said slowly. She looked up. The heavy clouds hid the sun, there wasn't even a watery glow to mark its posi-tion, the grayed-down light was so diffuse there were no shadows. She moved her shoulders impatiently. "Jay, can you tell what time it is?"

Jaril squinted at the clouds, turned his head slowly until he located the sun. "Half hour before noon."

Brann thrust her hands through her hair. Her stomach was knotting, there was a metallic taste in her mouth. Instead of two days, two hours. Two hours! Things rushing at her. Danny was cool as a newt, the kids were cooler, but her head was in a whirl. She felt like kicking them. They were waiting for her to give the word. She looked at the table, smiled because she couldn't help it, charging through the sky on a kitchen table was pleasantly absurd though what was going to happen at the end of that flight was enough to chase away her brief flash of amusement. She wiped her hands down her sides. "Ahh!" she said. "Let's go."

16

THE BEGINNING OF THE END.

SCENE: Deadfire Island. Taking color from
the clouds, the bay's water is leaden
and dull; it licks at a nailparing of a
beach with sand like powdered charcoal; horizontal ripples of stone
rise from the sand at a steep slant in
a truncated pyramid with a rectangular base. About halfway up, the walls
rise sheer in a squared-off oval to a
level top whose long axis is a little
over half a mile, the short axis about
five hundred yards, with elaborate
structures carved into the living
stone (the dominant one being an immense temple with fat-waisted columns thirty feet high and a central
dome of demon-blown glass, black
about the base, clear on top, the
clear part acting as a concentrating
lens when the sun's in the proper
place which happens only at the two
equinoxes). On the side facing Silagamatys a stubby landing juts into
the bay; a road runs from the landing
through a gate flanked with huge
beast paws carved from black basalt,
larger than a two-story house, three-
toed with short powerful claws; it
continues between tapering brick
walls that ripple like ribbons in a

breeze, then climbs in an oscillating
sprawl to the heights.

Settsimaksimin stands in the temple
garden, leaning on a hoe as he watches
a narrow stream of water trickle
around the roots of bell bushes and
trumpet vines. Most of the flowering
plants have been shifted from the
flowerbeds into winter storage, but
there are enough bushes with bril-
liantly colored frost-touched
leaves to leaven the dullness of the
surroundings. Behind him Amortis in
assorted forms is flickering restlessly about the temple, her fire alternately caged and released by the
temple pillars; she is working herself into a fury so she can forget her
fear.

Maksim scratched at his chest, then scratched some dirt into the channel to redirect the water. When he was satisfied, he swung the hoe
handle onto his shoulder and strolled to the waist-high wall about the
garden. Sliding between Deadfire and Silagamatys, glittering fero-
ciously, shooting those glitters at him, the Godalau swam like a limber
gem through the gray matrix of the sea. Tungjii was nowhere in view,
no doubt heesh was around, watching for a crack where hisser's
thumbs could go. Past noon. Divination said they'd be here in an hour
or so, riding Danny's little toy. He had a last look around, took the hoe
to the silent brown man squatting in a corner sipping at a straw colored
tea and went back across the grass to the minor stairs that led to a side
door into the temple.

The Dome Chamber was an immense hexagonal room at the heart of
the temple, it was also an immense hexagonal trap set to catch Brann,
Danny Blue and the changers. A complicated trap with overlapping,
reinforcing dangers. In each of the six walls, two arched alcoves bound
by quickrelease pentacles, twelve cells holding different numbers of
different sorts of demons, fly-in-amber-waiting. A blackstone
thronechair on a dais two thirds the length of the room from the

entrance, massive, carved with simple blocky fireforms, unobtrusive lowrelief carvings that decorated every inch of the chair's surface, caught the constantly shifting light and changed the look of the chair from moment to moment until the surface seemed to flow like water, a power-sink, a defensive pole, not dangerous in itself, only in its occupant. Pentacles everywhere, etched into the basalt floor like silverwire snowflakes widecast about the dais, some dull, some glowing with life, some punctuated with black candles awaiting an igniting gesture, some left bare (though scarcely less dangerous), some drawn black on black so only sorcerer's sight could see them. Between the pentacles, sink traps scattered haphazardly (the unpattern carefully plotted in Maksim's head so he wouldn't trap himself), waiting for an unwary foot, a toe touch sufficient to send the toe's owner into a pocket universe like the one that held the Chained God only not nearly so large. Other traps written into the air itself, drifting on the eddying currents in that air. Amortis, shape abandoned, a seething fireball, floating up under the dome filling the space there with herself, keeping herself clear of the traps, waiting for her chance to attack and destroy the midges who'd dared to threaten her, waiting her chance also to sneak a killing hit at Maksim, waiting for him to forget her long enough to let her strike, not knowing he'd made her bait in another trap; if the changers tried to tap her godfire, they tipped themselves into a far reality, removing themselves permanently from the battle.

As Maksim moved through the forest of columns, he tugged the clasp from his braid, pulled the plait apart until his hair lay in crinkles about his shoulders, unlaced the ties at the neck of his torn wrinkled workrobe. He turned aside before he reached the Dome Chamber, entering a small room he'd set up as a vestry. Humming in a rumbling burr, he stripped off the robe, dropped onto a low stool and planted one foot in a basin filled with hot soapy water. With a small, stiff-bristled brush he scrubbed at the foot, examined his toenails intently then with satisfaction, wiped that foot and began on the other. When he had washed away the dirt of his play at gardening, he buffed his fingernails and toenails until he was satisfied with their matte sheen, then he started brushing his hair, clicking his tongue at the amount of gray that had crept into the black while he was busy with Brann and the Council. He brushed and brushed, humming his tuneless song, vaguely regretting Todichi Yahzi wasn't here to do the brushing for him (it was one of his more innocent pleasures, sitting before the fire on a winter evening while little Todich tended his hair, brushing it a thousand strokes, combing it into order, until every hair end was tucked neatly away, braiding it, smoothing the braid with his clever nervous hands). Maksim clicked his tongue again, shook his head. No time for dreaming. He plaited his hair into a soft loose braid, pressed the clasp about the end, pulled on an immaculate white robe, touched it here and there to smooth away the last vestige of a wrinkle. Standing before a full length mirror, he drew the wide starched collar back from his neck, brought BinYAHtii out and set the dull red stone on the white linen. He weighed the effect, nodded, reached for his sleeveless outer robe. It was heavily embroidered velvet, a brownish red so dark it was almost black. He eased into it, careful not to crush the points of his collar, settled the folds of the crusted velvet into stately verticals, slid heavy rings onto the fingers of both hands, six rings, ornamental and useful, invested with small but deadly spells shaped to slip through defenses busy with more massive attacks. Holding his hands so the rings showed, he closed his fingers on the front panels of the overrobe and studied the image in the mirror. He smiled with satisfaction then with amusement at the vanity he'd cultivated like a gardener experimenting with one of the weeds that came up among his blooms. He licked his thumb and smoothed an eyebrow, licked it a second time and smoothed the other, winked at his image in the mirror and left the room.

His staff was leaning against a column beside the broad low arch that was the only entrance to the Dome Chamber; he'd left it there because he'd need it to move around the chamber without getting wrapped in one of his own traps. He went through the arch at its center, turned sharply left, moved along the wall to the first of the cells then began a careful circuitous almostdance across the floor, staff held before him to sweep aside the air webs. He reached the chair intact and immaculate, with a memory of heat close to him. Having seated himself in the greatchair which was ample enough to hold him with room to spare and more comfortable than it looked, but not much, he laid his staff across the arms and settled himself to wait.

A whitish waxy muzzle nosed slowly, awkwardly, through the low arch. He waited. When the thing emerged a bit more, he was amused to see it was an inverted table with Brann and Danny Blue crouched between its legs. Floating a yard above the floor, it inched forward until it was clear of the arch then stopped, rocking gently as if blown by summer breezes on a summer pond. The changers followed it in, twin glimmerspheres so pale they were visible only as smudges of light against the blackstone wall as they hovered one on each side of the table.

For a breath or two he considered calling to them, working out some sort of compromise, but Amortis was seething overhead, ready to seize and swallow at the first sign of hesitation, not caring whom she took, him or them, BinYAHtii trembled on his chest, hungrier and more deadly than the god, and, beyond all this, he remembered the thousands of landfolk who'd left home and harvest for him, trying to interpose their bodies between him and those on that table. There was no room left for talking. There never had been, really. He swung the staff up, knocked its end against the dais three times and took all restraints off his voice. "I give you this warning," he roared at them, "This alone. Leave here. Or die. There is nothing for you here." While he was still speaking, before the warning was half finished, he fingered the staff and loosed a sucking airtrap, throwing it at the table. There were many ways of managing that lift effect; it didn't matter which Danny Blue had chosen, for the trap would negate the magic behind the effect, send the table crashing to the floor and prison it with its riders in one or another of the stonetraps.

Nothing like that happened. Danny Blue didn't even try to counter the trap. While it twined about the table and withered futilely away, Dan spat into his palm, blew at the spittle. It flew off his hand, enlongated into a blue-white water form that arrowed at Maksim, a water elemental (which surprised Maksim quite a lot since Ahzurdan's forte had been fire and fire-callers, like earth-singers, seldom could handle water at all, let alone handle it well; this was either the Godalau's work or the Akamarino melded with him, which made one wonder what else he could do and what his weaknesses were); Maksim drew briefly on the chair's power, channeled it through his staff and twisted a tunnel through the air that sucked in the elemental and flung it into the bay.

The table moved a hair or two forward. Dan was frowning, trying to read floor, air, ceiling, walls as if he had forty eyes not two. The Drinker of Souls knelt beside him, silent, frowning, one hand resting lightly on his shoulder. The changers drifted beside the table, waiting. For what, Maksim did not know, perhaps they wanted to get closer before they came at him; one thing he did know, he did not want them anywhere near him. He prodded a reluctant Amortis, ordered her to stir herself and start attacking, wanting her to draw the changers into striking back at her, thereby taking themselves out of the game. While

she shaped and flung a storm of firedarts at the sled, he scanned his
prisoned demons, chose the players for his first demon gambit.

*Third cell on the right: small bat-winged flyers with adamantine teeth
and claws, a poison dart at the tip of whippy tails.* He released the
pentacle and sent the flyers racing at the sled.

*Third cell on the left: one creature there, a knotty tentacled acid
spitter, capable of instantaneous transfer across short distances, capable
also of terrific psychic punches when it was within touching distance.* He
tripped the pentacle on this one a few seconds after the other, waiting
until Danny Blue was focused on the first set of demons, fishing for the
release call that would send them home.

Demons in the remaining ten cells, waiting to be loosed to battle.

*In two separate cells, two vegetative serpents thirty feet long and big
around as a man's thigh, immensely powerful with shortrange stunner
organs that they can use to freeze their prey before they drop on it.*

*In three separate cells, three swarms of Hive demons each three
inches long, they suck up magic like flies suck up blood, hundreds of
units in each swarm.*

*In three separate cells, three tarry black leech things, eyeless, with
feelers that they extrude and withdraw into themselves, each with a
rhythm of its own; like the hivers they drink magic rather than blood,
they are capable of sensing traps and avoiding them and nothing but
death or dismissal will take them off a trail they're started on.*

*A mist creature, a subtle thing, slow, insinuating; given sufficient
time it can penetrate any shield no matter how tight; once in, it consumes whatever lives inside that shield.*

*A roarer, a swamp lizard mostly mouth and lungs, it attacks with
sound, battering with noise, stirring terror with subsonics, drilling into
the brain with supersonics.*

Dan shouted the release that flipped the flyers to their home reality a
micro instant before the tentacled demon slammed into the shield
sphere, gushed acid over it and wound itself up to punch at the people
inside. As the sled rocked and groaned under the added weight, before
Dan had time to shift his focus, Brann had the stunner out of his
pocket; she thumbed the slide back and slashed the invisible beam in a
wide X across the creature.

It howled in agony, pulled its tentacles into a tight knot and tumbled
off the shield, crashing to the floor inside one of the pentacle traps

which locked around it and held it stiff as a board against stone that sucked at it and sucked at it, slowly slowly absorbing the demon into its substance.

The changers wheeled above the shield, catching the firedarts and eating them. Amortis stirred uneasily in the dome and stopped wasting her substance for no result.

Danny Blue shivered the shield to rid it of the remnants of the acid, then he scraped the sweat off his brow and peered into the air ahead of him, searching out the airtraps, inching the sled between them, gaining another foot before he stopped to catch his breath and prepare another attack.

Maksim frowned. That shield should be costing Danny Blue more than he could afford—unless he had something similar to BinYAHtii feeding him. Her. Had to be her. Forty Mortal Hells, I have to get to her. How, how, how . . . ah! The sled had whined and dropped lower under the weight of the demon. If he could crash it, if he could put them on foot. . . .

Second gambit. Complex. Crushing weight, pile stone elementals on that shield sphere, attack on every side with everything I can throw at them, distract the changers, tempt them once more to attack Amortis.

Settsimaksimin tripped the pentacles, flipped the serpents and the roarer at the sled and left the others to make their own way; he goaded Amortis into attacking again, instructing her to slam the sled about as much as she could while she flooded it with fire; he reached deep into the stone, wakened the elementals sleeping there, sent them boiling up (bipedal forms with powerful clumsy limbs, forms altering constantly but very slowly, growing, breaking off into smaller versions like a glacier calving icebergs, gray and black and brown and brindle, stone colors, stone flesh, stone heavy), standing on each other, climbing over each other until they were up and over the shield sphere, saving only where the serpents were. Once they were in place, they swung their arms and crashed their fists into it, pounding it, pounding. . . .

The Roarer crouched on its bit of safe ground and hammered at them with with great gusts of SOUND, blasts so tremendous they seemed to shake the temple, threatening to bring the columns crashing down around the chamber. The effect of this SOUND was diminished slightly by the insulating effect of the crawling stone bodies of the elementals, but not enough, not nearly enough. The serpents tightened their grip on the shield, flat sucker faces pressed against it, sensors searching for life within, stun organ pulsing, ready to loose its hammer the moment it had a target. . . .

Danny Blue cursed and fought the numbing of that SOUND and searched through Ahzurdan's memories for the names and dismissals he needed. Brann tried the stunner again, but she couldn't get at the Roarer and the serpents were stunners themselves with a natural immunity that bled off the field before it could harm them. She felt something like tentacles moving over her, slimy, cold, nauseating, closing around her; force like a fist blow raced through them, struck at her, almost took her out, but Dan found one reality he wanted, one name he needed, shouted the WORD at the serpents and banished them.

He pulled more and more energy from her as the pressure on the shield increased and she was beginning to wilt as the drain on her resources intensified. "Yaril," she cried. A tentacle of light snaked through the shield, touched her. *I need help, I'm nearly empty.*

Gotcha, Bramble. Just a moment. Yaril merged briefly with Jaril. When they separated, Jaril dived at the elementals, swept through and through them, stealing energy from them, sloughing what he couldn't contain, Yaril expanded into a flat oval, a shield over the shield, absorbed the fire from Amortis, sent some of it along a thread to Brann and flared off the rest, doing her best to splash the overflow toward Maksim.

As the godfire poured into her, Brann gasped, closed her eyes tight, tears of agony squeezing out the sides. She contained the fire, controlled it, transmuted it and fed it into Dan to replace the energy flooding out of him.

The hivers sucked at the weave of the shield, softening it, draining it. The slugs were still a few yards out, oozing their way warily past the traps on the floor, but Dan could already feel them. The roarer battered at him, it was impossible to think with that noise drilling into his brain, plucking at his nerves, making him shudder with dread. After more frantic searching, he chanced across another NAME and another WORD, and with a sight of relief he banished the Roarer and its SOUND.

The shield softened further and he couldn't stop it, no matter how much strength he poured into the weave, he could only slow it a little. He scowled at the buzzing hivers, trying to get a closer look at them, chilled inside because nothing he remembered came close to matching them, and if he didn't get rid of them soon. . . .

He didn't attempt to do anything about the elementals; earth was

Maksim's forte and this close to him no one, not even a god, would wrest them from his control, Jaril was distracting them, weakening them, that was all anyone could hope for.

He was furious and frustrated. Maksim hesitating to attack, HAH! he'd kept them on the defensive from the moment they reached the chamber. His ground. No doubt he'd been preparing it for days, perhaps for decades, not specifically for them but for anyone who thought to challenge him. He shook off his malaise. "Brann, the swarms, see if the stunner will knock them down. Ahzurdan doesn't know them, I can't. . . ."

"I hear." She began playing the stunner along the undersurface of the sphere, an undersurface clearly marked by the stony bodies of the elementals. Dan made a little sound, a combination gasp and involuntary chuckle as the hivers fell away from the shield, pattering to the floor with tiny clatters like wind driven seeds against windowpanes.

More elementals came out of the earth and crawled onto the shield, closing the last interstices so he could no longer see the slugs. The sled groaned and shivered and sank lower until it was only six inches off the stone, in minutes it was going to touch the floor, it was bound to land in one of the pentacles or sink into a trap. The elementals stopped pounding on the shield, they were weakened by Jaril's raids, but that didn't help, it was the weight of them that did the damage. Water, he thought, water, somehow I've got to get water in here, some . . . how. . . . The slugs pulled harder at him, they were going to swallow him if he didn't do something. Where where did Maksim get them, I seem to remember . . . Magic Man, where where . . . ah! He spoke the NAME, he spoke the WORD, the pressure diminished so suddenly, so sharply, he almost fell on his face, his skin felt too thin as if he were about to explode, his grip on the shieldweave wavered. His hands snapped into fists as he caught hold of the shield and tightened it again. He forced himself to sit up, pressed a fist against his thigh and straightened the fingers one by one, working them carefully until he had some control over them. Bending over the sensor panel, he started the sled forward, got a little momentum and was able to break away from the elementals still boiling up through the floor, though the ones already clinging to the shield sphere stayed with him and he couldn't gain height. He didn't have to worry about airtraps any more, the bodies of the elementals protected him from those. He felt the sled jolt and knew that Maksim was hammering at him. The jolting grew harder, came faster without any pattern to it. Amortis was slamming at them too, her blows amplifying or interfering with Maksim's, she wasn't concerned with that, she screamed her hate and fury as she put all her strength into those clouts. The sled rocked precariously, tilted far to one side, bucked and twisted, throwing Danny Blue and Brann against the legs, threatening to whip them through the shield into the arms of the elementals. This wasn't something he planned for, the sled was reasonably stable but even its prototype wasn't built for this kind of strain; the table groaned and whined, rocked wildly, one moment a corner scraped against the stone; luck and luck alone kept them from trap or pentacle. He fought the sled level again, managed to squeeze more forward speed from the field, hoping as they got closer to Maksim that Amortis would have to take more care, giving him a chance to think a little. Somehow he had to strip away the elementals so he could see Maksim, as long as he was blind all he could do was hold his defenses tight.

Maksim watched the mound of oozing stone forms surge, tilt, shudder, heard the sled scrape the floor, ground his teeth when he was sure it had touched down in one of the few clean spaces. It labored on, creeping toward him; so far nothing had worked to stop it. He glared up at Amortis, shouted at her to stop wasting fire, she was only feeding the changers, to concentrate on slamming the sled about. A mistake, that fire, it meant the changers didn't have to draw from the source. He'd misread the events in Amortis' first attack, he saw that now, and he'd made other mistakes in play; shouldn't have hit them so hard from so many directions, he wasted the demons that way (though he hadn't expected all that much from them since Ahzurdan knew them as well as he did, except the hivers, too bad about them, that cursed weapon Akamarino brought with him, the mist demon was still in the game, Ahzurdan knew its form and home, but Danny Blue would have to see it before he could do anything about it). Wasted his best trap too, there was no one clear danger, he should have made Amortis the clear danger, then the changers might have attacked her, they were too busy defending the sled to be tempted that way. The mist demon finally reached the sled and began oozing among the elementals, the overflow from the fire was bothering it, he could feel it whining, he snarled at Amortis again, subsided as the flood of fire choked off and the sled tottered as she put muscle into her immaterial arm and her immaterial fist slammed into it.

He pulled more elementals from the stone and threw them atop the pile. The sled groaned and dropped an inch lower, but still kept coming. He wondered briefly whether Danny Blue meant to slam into the stairs of the dais, or didn't know he was getting close to them; the elementals flowed so thickly about him, there seemed no way he could see where he was going. Unless the changers were piloting him. They went through the rind of elementals and that peculiar shield as if neither existed. That shield, it was like nothing he'd seen before; he assumed it was an amalgam of the knowledge held by Ahzurdan and Akamarino. It was certainly effective. Fascinating, what the Chained God had done with those two men. He moved his staff, sent a ram of hardened air at the sled; it swung and shuddered, then came on even faster. He scowled, deflected a splash of earthfire slung at him by one of the changers as it drained strength from the elementals and pried bits of the elastic stone from the shield sphere, thumped the sled once more. He didn't want to give up the trap woven round Amortis, but if that thing got too close he might have to; he began shifting his intent, began gathering himself for one last grand effort.

The sled swerved sharply, picked up yet more speed and began running at the wall on Maxim's right, rocking, sliding, tottering under the increasing force and speed of the whacks from Amortis' immaterial fists. It must be hellish inside there.

The sled swerved again, scooted behind the chair and stopped. The changers sucked great gulps of energy from the earth elementals and washed it across the back of the thronechair. The obsidian chairback exploded in a spray of molten stone; part of the energy in that eruption came from his own power which he'd stored in the chair, part from the stone life in the elementals, stone against stone, stone melting stone. Maksim jumped to his feet, did a hasty dance with his staff to shunt the melted obsidian away from him, cursed, then laughed, appreciating the irony in this interweaving of chance and intention. He leaped onto the chairseat, drew what remained of the stored power into himself and flung the fire back at the changers and the sled.

Hampered by the narrow space and nervous about getting too close to Maksim, Amortis struck at them, hit the sled hard enough to slam it into the backwall, hit it again when it rebounded. And again.

The elementals kept trying to crush the shield, pushing that futile attack because Maksim wouldn't release them. They pressed more substance into their fists and beat on the shield, they grew knife-edged talons on feet and hands, gouged at the shield, they oozed themselves up toward the top of the shield sphere, oozed back down again when they couldn't get a hold on it, their stony substance stretching and flowing like cold taffy.

The changers went wheeling and whipping through the elementals, they scooped huge gouts of earthfire out of them and flung it at Maksim, flung it with such power it seemed to reach him almost before it left their hands. He deflected it, but he was linked too closely to the elementals to escape their pain, their fury, the heat got at him, the fire raised blisters on his face and arms.

The exchange went on and on, neither side seriously affecting the other. Maksim kept waiting for the mist to act, but nothing seemed to be happening on the sled. It slammed against the wall, bounced against the back of the dais, it groaned and whined, it came close to capsizing, but the shield never faltered. He cast up a deflector of his own to carry the changers' attack away from him and away from the chair so its stone wouldn't melt from under him, he slapped his right foot on the stone, slapped his left foot on the stone, yelled a wordless defiance that filled the chamber, set himself firm as stone, set himself for a last throw, unknotting the trapweb about Amortis, dragging it back into himself, dragging an unwilling Amortis down from the dome, holding her shivering on the dais beside him, her mass compacted until she was a mere ten feet tall, a vaguely bipedal shape of red-gold white-gold light. Sullen light. He muttered to himself, pulling from his sorcerer's trickbag the preparatory syllables that would set the points for the wild web he was planning to spin.

Sometime later he happened to glance round, no particular reason for it, it was just something he did; he saw black, dull black shirt and trousers, threadbare, wrinkled, a round graceless form silhouetted against the flare of the deflected earthfire. Tungjii. Watching. It jolted him. What's that one doing here? Never mind. Concentrate, Maksim, don't give himmer a crack for hisser thumbs. Forget himmer, you've got them in your hands, you can throw them anywhere you want once you're ready. Ready ready, almost ready . . .

His voice boomed in a reverberant chant, filling the chamber with sound so powerful it was a tangible THING, the intricately linked syllables weaving a fine gold web about the sled. . . .

SEY NO TAS   SEY NO MENAS
   DAK WOLOMENAS WOLOMENAS
SEY NO TAS   SEY NO MENAS
   DAK AMEGARTAS GARTAS GAR TASSSS

SEY NO TAS   SEY NO MENAS
  PAGASE PAGASE AMEGARTA GAR
SEY NO TAS   SEY NO MENAS
  KNUSI AIKHMAN
SEY NO TAS   SEY NO MENAS
  IDIOS NOMAN
HROUSTITAKA HREOS
SEY NO TAS
HREOS MEGARITAN. . . .

Danny Blue grunted as he slammed into one of the legs, then into Brann; he rolled across the table, contorted his body to avoid the sensor panel, finished for the moment stuffed into the corner where the windbreak curved round one of the front legs. The sled shuddered, scraped against the wall, stone shrieking as it rubbed against stone. He ignored the battering and focused on *water;* the shield he'd woven about the sled wasn't difficult to hold in place, it just required a steady flow of power which Brann and the changers supplied. A tube, that was what he needed, a tube and some molecular pumps. Tube, hmm, same weave as the shield, don't want Maksim cutting it. . . .

Brann wrapped one arm about a table leg and reached for Dan's ankle so she could keep up the feed. It was hot and stuffy and darkly twilight inside the sphere, the sensor panel provided a dim bluish glow and the feed pipe was a soft yellow, neither of them made much impression on the darkness. She and Dan weren't choking on fouled air because Yaril and Jaril fed them fresh along with the godfire, but that only kept the atmosphere bearable, it didn't make it pleasant. The godfire feed was spasmodic now (she smoothed it out before sending it on into Dan); the changers were moving too fast and too erratically to maintain a constant flow. They took turns as they'd done that time on the mountain, plowing through the elementals, collecting from them, spalshing earthfire at Maksim, snapping the feedpipe down to Brann, pumping her as full as she could hold, doing this over and over. When the earthfire flooded into her, when it sat seething in her, it wasn't quite as agonizing as godfire, but it was bad enough, it was like gulping down mouthfuls of boiling acid and it never got easier. She endured the pain because she had to, Danny Blue depended on her, young Kori had called in a promise—and most of all she was no longer ready to die, there were too many other promises she had to keep, promises she had made to herself. She endured and grew stronger not weaker as the torment went on.

Her eyes began to burn. She blinked repeatedly, tried to focus, but she could see less and less as the minutes passed. Her skin burned. She touched her face, held her fingertips close to her eyes and saw that they were stained. She touched them to her tongue, tasted warm salty wetness. Blood. Her tongue began to burn. The pain from the earthfire was hiding . . . what? She fought to set that internal burning aside and feel about with immaterial fingers for what else was happening.

Smoky rotting vegetation smell, faint but there. A feeling of humidity, swampiness. Hunger. Now that she was listening, it shouted at her. HUNGER. "Dan," she cried. Her voice was hoarse, her throat felt as if something was scraping it raw. "Dan, there's something in here with us. What is it? DAN!"

Danny Blue heard Brann saying something, but he had no time nor attention to give her. He Reshaped the Pattern of the spherical shield (maintaining the shield in place and carefully separated from his other activities), and used the new Pattern to construct a closed cylinder; he poured more energy into it, lengthening it. He inserted the lead end into the shield, eased it through, then began the exacting and difficult task of forcing the cylinder through the thick elastic rind of earth elementals.

Brann realized he wasn't listening and dropped the attempt to reach him. She took her hand from his ankle and clamped it briefly around her own arm, felt something like a greasy film spread around it. Scowling, she wiped her hand on her trousers, then closed it around Dan's ankle so she could maintain the feed. She'd got a reading from the thing: an intensification of that feral hunger, no sense of intelligence behind it, only will, a predator's will. Cautiously she reached out, pulled life from the thing, drinking it in as once she'd drunk the life of a black malouch, there was the same sense of wildness, greed, hunger. And fear as the thing felt the danger from her.

It wrenched free of her and Danny, fled toward the top of the sphere. The air curdled up there as it compacted its misty substance, as far from her as it could get.

Brann broke from Danny again. Holding the table leg she struggled to her feet and reached for that mist.

With a kind of silent scream if flowed desperately away from her hand until it managed to ooze down between the windshield and the shieldsphere where she had no way of reaching it. Satisfied for the moment, she dropped back, settled herself as comfortably as she could while the table continued to rock wildly, to judder like a worm with hiccups, to slam between the wall and the dais. Her legs wrapped about the table's leg, she spared a moment to heal the damage from the mist, Dan first, then herself, then she went back to feeding fire to him. She didn't know what he was doing, only that it must be important if the intensity of his concentration meant anything.

Danny felt the small pains but ignored them. Sometime later he felt the upheaval when Brann interfered with his body as she healed the skin burns and the eye-damage; he ignored that too. He drove the tube up until it was clear of the elementals, bent it in a quarter circle and expanded it swiftly toward the nearest wall, holding it steady despite the careening of the sled. When it jammed against the stone, he heated the head end hotter than Amortis' fire and melted the tube through; his Sight was cut off by the elementals, but he could See down the tube and expand that Sight a few degrees as soon as one end was outside the temple. He sent it arching down over the edge of the island, down and down until it reached the gray seawater. When it dipped below the surface, he felt the cold shock of that water, shouted his triumph, "I've got you, Maks, I've got you now." He heard Brann's exclamation, ignored it and grew side pipes along the tube in an ascending spiral; grinning, he popped in the tiny pumps and started them sucking. "Brann, tell the changers there's going to be a lot of water in here in just a moment. I don't know exactly what's going to happen, but it'll be wild."

He reached again, sending an imperious call for water elementals, felt an immediate, almost frightening surge as they answered him. Answered him in the hundreds. Came compressed, swimming up the tube with the water the pumps were hauling.

Water and water elementals spurted from the sidepipes, sprayed copiously over the earth elementals crawling weak and angry over the shield sphere. Converting them to a slippery mindless sludge that dripped, ropy and viscid, off the sphere.

Light flared through the shield, red light, gold light, light hard and bright as diamond.

Settsimaksimin and Amortis stood together, dais and chair, Maksim half sunk in her shimmering translucent female boby. Black sorcerer body. Black Heart in that Rose of Light, chant reverberating thunderously through the great chamber. . . .

SEY NO KRISÊ   SEY NO KORÔN
KATAMOU NO KATAMOOOOU

Lines of light webbed around the sled, closing on it. They were caught like fish in a tightening purse seine. . . .

SEY NO KATALAM   SEY NO
    PALAPSAM   EKHO EKHO PALAPSAM

Dan shuddered under the power of that chant. Amortis and BinYAHtii and Settsimaksimin plaited like a gilded braid, their unstable meld building to a climax that was terrifyingly close. For a moment he sat passive, helpless, Ahzurdan exhausted riding up hill to the Chained God and the trap inside the ship. . . .

SEY NO EKHO   SEY   SEEY UUHHH
    EY NO NO NO. . . .

The water elements flowed up the dais, pressed around Maksim and the Fire, not quite touching either, disturbing him so much it broke into the drive of the chant. Didn't stop it, but the chant faltered and some of the power went out of it. BinYAHtii's dull red glow flickered.

A smallish dark figure strolled up the burning air, moved easily and untouched through the ring of water, the shell of fire and stepped onto the half-melted chair arm. Tungjii balanced there a moment, then rested hisser hand on Maksim's arm near the wrist, that was all, then heesh was somewhere else.

Settsimaksimin's body jolted, his voice broke; he gave a small aborted cry, crumpled, tumbling off the chair and down the stairs to land sprawled on his face on the floor.

Ball lightning and jagged fireline snapped across and across the Dome Chamber, rebounding from the walls, bouncing from the floor and ceiling as Maksim's stored magic discharged from stone and air and his tormented flesh, squeezed its tangible elements into hot threads that braided themselves in a rising rope of fire that went rushing up and up, bursting through the dome, shattering it into shards which fell like glass knives onto the stone, glancing off the shield Dan kept in place about the sled until the worst of the storm was past. Amortis solidified into her thirty meter female form, looking wildly about and fled after the fleeing remnants of Maksim's magic.

17

THE END OF THE END.

SCENE: Maksim sprawled on the floor, dead or dying. The changers stood beside him, once more in their bipedal forms. The table settled to the floor. Brann and Danny Blue, bruised, battered, weary, climbed off it and started around the ruined dais.

Danny Blue stood beside the crumpled body. "Looks like his heart quit on him. Old Tungjii found his crack."

Brann frowned, disturbed as much by the dispassionate dismissing tone of those words as by the words themselves. She touched Maksim's hand with her toe, feeling manipulated and not liking it very much. She'd helped destroy a man she might have liked a lot if things were other than they were. Before the eidolon appeared (a hallow image, yet with enough of his personality in it to intrigue her) she'd known him mostly through Ahzurdan's comments, yes, and his attacks on her, which seemed to stop him, but the rise of the landfolk had shaken her badly. Abandoning a harvest only half-gathered with the winter hunger that might mean? leaving their houses open to plunder, their stock handy for the nearest lightfinger? doing it to protect one man, the man that ruled them? In all of her travels, in all of her reading, she'd never heard of a king (not even the generally mild and intelligent kings of her home island Croaldhu), Emperor, protector of the realm, whatever the ruler called himself, whose peasantry volunteered (volunteered!) their bodies and their blood to keep him from harm. Nobles certainly, they had a powerful interest in who sat the local throne. Knights and their like, for gold, for the blood in it, for what they called their honor (being a true son of Phras, Chandro boasted hundreds of those stories about this one and that one among his ancestors and she'd heard them all). Armies had fought legendary battles but not for love of their leaders;

they had their pay, their rights to plunder, their friends fighting beside them and the headsman's axe waiting for the losers. Peasants though! What peasants got from a war was hunger and harder work, ruined crops, dead stock, burnt houses while their landlords refilled war-starved coffers out of peasant sweat and peasant hide. She frowned down at Maksim, caught her breath as the fingers by her foot moved a little. She dropped to her knees beside him. "Dan, help me turn him over."

"Why?"

"Because I damn well refuse to be some miserable meeching god's pet executioner. If you don't want to help, get out of the way."

He shrugged. "It's your game, Bramble. You take his feet, I'll get his shoulders."

When Maksim was on his back, the velvet and linen robes smoothed about him, Brann eased BinYAHtii's gold chain over his head and tried to lift the talisman away without touching the stone; this close, it seemed to radiate danger. It rocked a little but wouldn't come free. She laid the chain on his chest, the heavy links clunking with oily opulence; she looked at them with distaste, then used both hands on the broad gold frame fitted around the stone, pulling as hard as she could. The pendant lifted away from his chest with a sucking sound, a smell of burned meat. She swallowed, swallowed again as her stomach threatened to rebel, thew the thing away, not caring where or how it landed. "Yaril," she said, "take a look inside, will you? I think I'd better not try this blind."

"Gotcha, Bramble, just a sec."

Yaril shifted form and flowed into the body, flowed out a moment later. She didn't bother talking, she leaned against Brann's side, transferred images to her that Brann used as she bent over Maksim, planted her hands on his chest and worked to repair the extensive damage inside and out, heart, arteries, brain, every weakness, every lesion, tumor, sign of disease, everything Yaril had seen and passed on to her.

Dan watched her for a while until he grew bored with the tableau whose only change was the slow shifting of Brann's eyes. He strolled around behind the wreck of the dais, brought the table back, parked it close to Brann's feet, looked around for something else to kill some time. Yaril was pacing lazily about, sniffing at things, a huge brindle mastiff. Yaril was glued to Brann and didn't seem likely to move from her. The clouds must have begun breaking up outside because a ray of light came through the jagged hole in the dome and stabbed down at the floor, the edge of it catching the pendant, waking a few glitters in it. He walked across to it and stood looking down at it. The thing made him nervous. That was what the Chained God sent him to fetch, good dog that he was. He didn't want to touch it, but the compulsion rose in him until he was choking. Furious and helpless, he bent down, took hold of the chain and stood with the pendant dangling at arm's length. He looked at it, ran the tip of his tongue over dry lips, remembering all too clearly the hole burned in Maksim's chest.

There was a subdued humming, the air seemed to harden about him, the chamber got suddenly dark. "OHHHH. . . ."

". . . SHIIIT!" He stumbled, went to his knees before the control panel in the starship, caught his balance and bounded to his feet. His arm jerked out and up, the talisman was snatched away, the chain nearly breaking two of his fingers. BinYAHtii hung a moment in mid-air, then it vanished, taken somewhere inside the god. And I hope it gives you what it gave Maksim, he muttered under his breath. "Send me back," he said aloud. "You don't need me any more."

"I wouldn't say that." The multiple echoing voice was bland and guileless as a cat with cream on its whiskers. "No, indeed."

Dan opened his mouth to yell a protest, a demand, something, was snapped to the room where he had lived with Brann and the others. He was conscious just long enough to realize where he was, then the god dumped him on the bed and put him to sleep.

Brann sat on her heels, sighed with weariness. "Done," she said, "He'll be under for a while longer." She rubbed at her back, looked around. "Where's Dan?"

Jaril came trotting over, shifted. "He picked up BinYAHtii and something snatched him. If I guessed, I'd say the Chained God got him. The god really wanted that thing."

"Looks like it didn't want us."

"Luck maybe. Old Tungjii wiggling hisser thumbs in our favor for once. Say the god couldn't grab us all, we were too scattered."

"Hmm. If it's luck, let's not push it." She got to her feet. "What about the table? Will it fly again?"

"Sure. Where do you want it to go?"

"Give me your hand." She closed her fingers around his, said silently, *Myk'tat Tukery. Jal Virri. Not much can get at us there.* Aloud, she said, "Help me load Maksim on the sled."

"That's like bedding down with an angry viper, Bramble. Leave him here, let him deal with the mess he made for himself. It's not your mess. When he wakes, he's going to be mad enough to eat nails. Eat you."

"So we keep him sleeping until we go to ground and have some maneuvering room. I mean to do this, Jay."

"Ayy, you're stubborn, Bramble. All right all right, Yaro, give us a hand here." He scowled at the table. "Hadn't we better pick up those quilts and pillows we dumped outside? The sky's clearing, but it'll be chilly when you hit the higher air."

Brann smiled at him. "Good thought, Jay. There are people living here, a few anyway, that gardener for one. See if you can find some food, I'm starved and I'll need supplies for the trip; going by how long it took us to reach here from the farm, it'll be eight to ten days before we get umm home."

The changers darted about the island collecting food, wine and water skins, whatever else they thought Brann might need, then they helped her muscle the deeply sleeping sorcerer onto the table. They settled him with his head on a pillow, a comforter wrapped about him, tucked the provisions around him and stood back looking at their work.

Brann shivered. "I've got an iceknot in my stomach that says it's time to be somewhere else." She swung round a table leg, settled herself in a nest of comforters and pillows; tongue caught between her teeth, she ran the sequence that activated the lift field, gave a little grunt of relief and satisfaction when the sled rose off the floor, moving easily, showing no sign of strain (she'd been a bit worried about the weight of the load). When it was about a yard off the floor, she stopped the rise and started the sled moving forward. She eased it through the arch, wound with some care through the great pillars beyond, starting nervously whenever she heard the stone complain.

Outside, the gray was gone from the sky, the bay water was choppy and showing whitecaps, glittering like broken sapphire in the brilliant sunlight. She took the sled high and sent it racing toward the southeast where the thousand islands of the Myk'tat Tukery lay. Behind her, the massive temple groaned, shuddered, collapsed into rubble with a thunderous reverberant rattle; part of it fell off the island into the sea. Brann shivered, sighed. She stretched over, touched the face of the man beside her, wishing she could wake him and talk to him. She didn't dare. She sighed again. It was going to be a long dull trip.

18

KNOTTING OFF.

Kori.
The School at Silili.

Kori glared at the flame on the floating wick, trying to narrow her focus until she saw it and only it, until she heard nothing, felt nothing, knew nothing but that erratically flickering flame. The small room was dark and quiet, no sounds from outside to distract her, but she felt the stone through the flimsy robe Shahntien Shere had given her, she heard every scrape her feet made when she had to move or suffer torments of itching, she felt the chill draft that curled round her body and shivered the flame. It seemed to her she was getting worse not better as she struggled to learn the focus her teachers demanded. Talent! He was dreaming, that man. She had no talent, nothing. She scratched an itch on a buttock and began running through the disciplines for the millionth time. . . .

Something watching her. The small hairs stirred along her spine, her mouth went dry. She fought to keep her eyes on the flame but couldn't, she jumped to her feet, turning with the movement so she faced the open arch.

Shahntien Shere stood there, eyes narrowed, fury rolling off her like steam. "Maksim's dead or destroyed," she said softly. "Your doing." She smiled. "He set a geas on me to teach you, it doesn't stop me making you one sorry little bitch. Contemplate that a while, then do me a favor and try leaving." A last glare, then she whipped around and stalked off.

Drinker of Souls, Kori thought, she did it. She sighed. Nothing had turned out the way she planned. Ten years, she thought, I'm safe for ten years, but after that I'd better be a long, long, way from here. She dropped to her knees and began going through the disciplines again, contemplating the flame with grim determination; she had to learn everything and be better at it than anyone else before her. Maksim said she had talent, talent didn't count if you couldn't use it. Ten years. . . .

Trago.
The Cave of the Chained God

Sealed into the block of crystal, the boy slept. Now and then he dreamed. Mostly he waited unknowing in the midst of nothingness.

Danny Blue.
The Pocket Universe.
The stranded starship.

After an interval whose length Dan never knew, he was allowed to wake because the god wanted someone to talk to. The god couldn't leave the pocket universe, he/it knew that now and it was Dan who told him/it. He/it couldn't change that verdict without dying, but he/it could punish the messenger who brought the bad news. And Dan could be converted easily enough into a blood and bone remote who could do things the god wanted done in that other universe. He/it wasn't about to lose his services. The mortal could sulk and rage and plot all he wanted, he lived and breathed because the god willed it, he was going to do whatever the god wanted done.

Todichi Yahzi.
Settsimaksimin's Citadel.
Silagamatys.

When Maksim vanished from the scene, Todich took the drop from around his neck and looked at it for a long while, then he shook his head, packed his things and started off to look for the man he knew was still alive somewhere.

Brann.
Myk'tat Tukery. Jal Virri.

Maksim coughed, opened his eyes.
"Jal Virri."
The voice came from behind him, amused and wary. Brann. Sooo.

He sat up. The sky was blue, the air warm, a silky breeze wandered past him, stirring the pendant limbs of a weeping willow. The tree grew by an artesian fountain, where water bubbled from a vertical copper pipe, sang down over mossy boulders into a pond filled with crimson lilies and gilded carp and out of that into a stream that rambled about the garden. He was sitting on a gentle slope covered with grass like green fur. This has to be south of Cheonea, I can't have slept completely through winter. He looked at his arms. He'd lost flesh and muscle tone. Maybe not all winter but more than a day or two. "Jal what?" He got to his feet, moving slowly to camouflage his weakness.

Brann was sitting on a stone bench beside a burst of ground orchids. "Jal Virri. Isn't that what everyone asks? Where am I?"

Maksim moved uphill and eased himself onto the far end of the bench. "Where's Jal Virri?"

"Myk'tat Tukery. One of the inner islands."

"How long was I out?"

"Ten days."

"Why bother?"

"I loathe being jerked around."

"I was a fool."

"You were."

He folded his arms across his chest, narrowed his eyes, grinned at her. "You were supposed to appreciate my humility and disagree with courteous insincerity."

She gave him a long look; eyes green as the willow leaves smiled at him. "I'd rather beat up on you a bit. Why didn't you talk to me? You swatted me like I was a pesty fly. That sort of thing is bound to upset a person."

"It seemed easier, a surgeon's cut, quick and neat, and a complication was gone out of my life."

"Wasn't, was it."

"Doesn't seem like it. Sitting here on this dusty bench, I can see half a dozen ways we might have managed some sort of compromise. Hindsight, hunh! bad as rue and twice as useless. Seriously, Brann, all I needed was maybe ten years more. I was buying time."

"For what?"

"For Cheonea."

"You say that so splendidly, so passionately, Maks. Such sincerity."

"Sarcasm is the cheapest of the arts, Bramble-all-thorns, even so, it needs a scalpel not an axe."

"Depends on how thick the skull is. Seriously, Maks, you've made a good start, but my father would say it's time to let the baby walk on its own. Otherwise you'll cripple it. Hmm. Are you thinking of heading back there?"

"That rather depends on you, doesn't it?"

"No."

"What?"

"I pulled you out of there because I wouldn't trust the Chained God as far as I could throw it. Amortis either. And you weren't in any shape to defend yourself. I take no more responsibility for you than that. If you want to go, good-bye."

"And if I wish to stay for a while?"

"Then stay."

"Hmm." He fiddled with the charred hole in the linen robe he still wore, looked down at the smooth flesh under it. "What happened to BinYAHtii?"

"I took it off you, threw it away, foul thing, it'd eaten a hole almost to your heart. Jay told me this: when Yaro and I were working on you, Dan went over to it, picked it up and vanished. Chained God probably."

"Good-bye Finger Vales, eh?"

"Seems likely."

"So Kori got what she wanted. Her brother safe and the Servants tossed out."

"You know about that?"

"Had a talk with her."

"Where is she now?"

"The Yosulal Mossaiea in Silili. Do you know it?"

"She's talented? Slya's teeth, why am I surprised, she's Harra's Child. You sent her?"

"Why are you surprised? You expected me to eat her?"

"Well, feed her to BinYAHtii."

"That ardent soul? BinYAHtii was hard enough to control with ordinary lives in it. Besides, I liked her."

"So. What will you be doing next?"

"So. Resting. Here's as good a place as any. Will you be staying?"

"For a while."

"The changers?"

"Yaro says this place is pretty but boring." She looked wary again, smiled again. "I probably shouldn't tell you this, but they've gone off exploring, they've got a lot of things to get used to, the changers have changed. I suppose the next thing for me will be finding a way to get them home. I don't want to think about that for a while yet. I'm tired." She got to her feet, held out her hand. "I'm glad you're staying. It'll be pleasant having someone to talk to. Come. Let me show you the house. I haven't the faintest notion who built it, I stumbled across it the last time I was here. It's a lovely place. Friendly. When you step through the door, you get the feeling it's happy to have you visit." Her hand was warm, strong. She seemed genuinely pleased with him, in truth she seemed in a mood to be pleased by almost anything. As she strolled beside him, she slid her heels across the grass, visibly enjoying the cool springy feel of it against the soles of her bare feet. She'd had a bath before she woke him, she smelled very faintly of lavender and rose petals, the silk tunic which was all she wore was sleeveless and reached a little past her knees, the breeze tugged erratically at it, woke sighs in it. I'll need clothing, he thought, he touched the soiled charred robe, grimaced. She didn't notice because she was looking ahead at the odd structure sitting half shrouded by blooming lacetrees. "There's something I've never been able to catch sight of that bustles around, cleans the house, weeds the garden, prunes things, generally keeps the place in shape, I don't know how many times I've hid myself and tried to catch it working. Nothing. Maybe you can figure it out, be something to play with when you feel like exercising your head. To say truth I hope it eludes you too, that gives me a chance to stand back and giggle."

"Myk'tat Tukery," he murmured, "I've heard a thousand tales about it, each stranger than the last."

"Maksim mighty sorcerer, I'll show you a thing or two to curl your hair, a thing or two to draw it straight again." She dropped his hand, ran ahead of him along the bluestone path, up the curving wooden stairs; she pushed the door open, turned to stand in the doorway, her arms outspread. "Be pleased to enter our house, Settsimaksimin, may your days here be as happy as mine have been."

Laughter rumbling up from his heels, he followed her inside.

KNOTTING DONE (for the moment).

A Gathering of
Stones

DRAW IN THE STONEBEARERS:
They are the chosen—by the God and by the Stones themselves.

1. BRANN, THE DRINKER OF SOULS, affinity: Massulit Called (by friends and those fond of her), Bramble, Bramble-all-thorns, Thornlet.

She was born in the mountain valley called Arth Slya, her father a potter of genius, her mother a weaver of tapestries. When Slya Fireheart thought up a plot to get at some Kadda witches who were too powerful for her to touch directly, the god reached into the realities and plucked forth two juvenile energy beings, JARIL and YARIL; Brann was *changed* so she could feed them and in that *changing* became DRINKER OF SOULS and effectively immortal. In the course of Slya's plot, she rescued her people from slavery, opened a Gate for Slya who came stomping in and destroyed her enemies. Then she was turned loose to live how she could, an eleven-year-old girl in the body of a woman in her twenties.

She wandered about the world for a hundred years, settled for another hundred years as the Potter at Shaynamoshu. At the end of that time another God—the Chained God—meddled in her life and drew her into his scheme to acquire the Great Talisman BinYAHtii, using as instruments KORI PIYOLSS and the sorcerer/king SETTSIMAK-SIMIN along with the sorcerer Ahzurdan and the out-reality starman Daniel Akamarino. In the final battle between Brann and Settsimak-simin, the God acquired the Talisman, Settsimaksimin's heart gave out and he nearly died. Because she'd found much that was admirable in her enemy—disregarding a little thing like repeated attempts to kill her

—Brann healed the wounds BinYAHtii had inflicted on him and the weakness in his heart; having saved his life, she carried him off to a lovely island (Jal Virri) in the heart of the Myk'tat Tukery where they spent the next ten years in friendship and peace.

2. JARIL AND YARIL, THE CHANGERS, affinity: Churrikyoo
Petnames: Jaril called Jay; Yaril called Yaro

Juvenile energy forms drawn from one of the layered realities.

Their base forms were lightspheres (at first just big enough to fit within a man's circled arms, later larger), Yaril's slightly paler than Jaril's, but they could take many shapes and appear convincingly solid in them though the eyes they saw from were clear crystal and marked them as demon. At first they were completely dependent on Brann; she drained life energy from men and beasts and fed it to them to keep them from starving. In the course of the action against Settsimaksimin, Brann won their freedom from the Chained God; he changed the Changers so they could once more feed directly on sunlight and similar energy sources. They were still linked to Brann by strong ties of affection, but they were no longer her nurslings. The two hundred years on the World have brought other changes; they passed through their equivalent of puberty and acquired sexual drives and needs that they could not satisfy without others of their kind and age. After Brann took Settsimaksimin to the island Jal Virri, Jaril and Yaril ranged restlessly about the World, trying to work off the energies that threatened to destroy them.

3. SETTSIMAKSIMIN, affinity: Shaddalakh
Called (by friends and those fond of him): Maksim, Maksi, Maks.

He was born in Silagamatys the chief city of Cheonea, sold into slavery at the age of six, a child-whore until he was ten, bought out of the pleasurehouse by the Sorcerer Prime Musteba Xa who wanted to use the boy's Talent to enhance his own.

After releasing himself from his apprenticeship by killing his Master, he studied and practiced and became one of the four Primes among the sorcerers of the World. Around this time he came upon the Talisman BinYAHtii; this sparked his ambitions for his homeplace. He returned to Cheonea, kicked the corrupt and feeble king off his throne and took the reins of power into his own hands. It was a long struggle, but he broke the power of the Parastes (the local lords), put the land into the hands of the folk who worked it, outlawed slavery, hung some slavedealers, burned the ships of some slavetraders and began setting up a new sort of government where the peasants and the so-called lower orders would have some say in the circumstances of their lives. To do this he had to keep BinYAHtii fed (the life of a child a month was the price for access to the Talisman's power) and alternately cajole and compel the god Amortis to act against his enemies. Being warned (as part of the Chained God's scheming) that Brann Drinker of Souls would be drawn into the fight against him, he struck first and sent Tigermen demons to kill her. The Changers arrived just in time to save her and the battle was on—a battle Settsimaksimin lost after a hard struggle that cost him much, including his hold on Cheonea.

At the end of ten years on Jal Virri he was growing restless, tired of living without ambition or effort.

4. KORIMENEI PIYOLSS, affinity: Frunzacoache
Originally her name was simply Kori (which could mean either Maiden or Heart), but when Settsimaksimin put her in school and compelled her to remain there for ten years, she took the name Korimenei (which meant Heart-in-Waiting).

The Finger Vales of Cheonea had served the Chained God since the time when the Wounded Moon was whole, which meant essentially forever, but when Kori was thirteen-going-on-fourteen, the soldier-priests of Amortis came to Owlyn Vale, tied the Chained God's priest to a stake and lit a fire under him. Then they declared the folk on Owlyn Vale must serve Amortis instead. A few months later Kori's youngest brother (the closest to her of all her kin) came to her with the Chained God's mark on him, chosen for the new priest. Once that was out her brother would be burned also. She was the several times great-granddaughter of Harra Hazhani who carried a promise from the Drinker of Souls: She or any of her descendants could call on Brann in time of trouble and Brann would come to give whatever help she could. Kori looked into Harra's Eye, located Brann and sent a cousin to summon the Drinker of Souls to fight Settsimaksimin and help her keep her brother alive.

Some months later she was in Silagamatys for the Lot (where three children were chosen, a girl to serve in the Temple as teacher or priest-ess, a boy to serve as a priest or soldier and another—either boy or girl

—to be fed to BinYAHtii, though only Settsimaksimin knew this, the people thought the third child was sent to Havi Kudush to serve in the Great Temple of Amortis); during this time, Settsimaksimin became aware of the strong Talent she had in her, plucked her from her people and sent her off to school in Silili, half a continent away from Cheonea, getting her out of his hair and keeping her safe at the same time; he liked her and was proud of her spirit. To keep her in school he imprisoned her brother in crystal and informed her only she could set him free. All she had to do was go to the Chained God's altar in the mountain cavern where she'd found Harra's Eye and set her hand on the crystal. No one else could wake her brother; if she got herself killed, he'd sleep forever in that spell-crystal. At the end of the ten years, when her training was finished, she could leave with his blessing; if she tried to leave before that the Mistress, one Shahntien Shere, was instructed to punish her at the first attempt and kill her at the second.

The ten years passed pleasurably enough, she enjoyed her schooling after she'd got used to the constraints on her and she'd proved an excellent student, beyond even Settsimaksimin's expectations (he kept an eye on her from Jal Virri, sent his eidolon to talk to her every few months), but as the time for her passing-out ordeal approached she was getting more and more anxious about her brother, more and more eager to go release him from his enchanted sleep.

5. **TRAGO PIYOLSS**, affinity: Harra's Eye
   Called Tré by friends and family.

A seven-year-old boy used as a pawn, by the Chained God first to bring Brann into play against Settsimaksimin, then by Settsimaksimin to keep his hold on Kori Piyolss, he slept under enchantment in the Altar Cave of the Chained God.

6. **DANNY BLUE**, affinity: Klukesharna

Danny Blue was one man, two men, three men. One man, because he had a single body. Two men because he was made from two men and their memories and personalities lingered within him. Three men, because Danny Blue had developed a life of his own, a personality that was both more and less than a blend of his two half-sires with memories that belonged to him alone.

He was born in the body of the Chained God (an ancient starship) where the flesh of his two sires was merged into one man by the power of the God, where Brann Drinker of Souls was midwife to the birth of his personhood as well as his fleshbody.

AHZURDAN was once a student/apprentice of Settsimaksimin's. When he met Brann and was drawn into the Chained God's scheme, he was a second rank sorcerer of considerable ability but regrettable habits, being addicted to dreamdust and in flight from reality. He was born into a Phrasi merchant family of considerable wealth and social ambition; his mother belonged to the minor nobility and impressed into her son all her attitudes toward lesser beings. He was a momma's boy and didn't get on with his older half-siblings at all well, though that was not entirely his fault, they were an intolerant lot. He was also an unsatisfactory son, being totally uninterested in the family business. When his talent came on him, he nearly burned down the house and did singe a spiteful older brother. By this time his father was quite happy to pay the fees and bond him to Settsimaksimin's service for the usual seven years. He worked hard and learned fast, but he never managed to match his Master and left his service at the end of those seven years resenting Settsimaksimin, jealous of other apprentices, angry and unhappy.

DANIEL AKAMARINO was born in a reality where magic was fraud and wishful thinking; he made his living on assorted starships as Communications Officer, Propulsion Engineer or Cargo Superintendent/Buyer, having a Masters Rating in all three. He was a man not bothered by much, seldom felt the need to prove anything about himself or his beliefs; impatient with routine, he drifted from job to job, quitting when he felt like it or because some nit tried to make him do things that bored him like wearing boots instead of sandals and a uniform instead of the ancient shirts and trousers he got secondhand whenever the ones he had were reduced to patches and threads. He had no plans for settling down; there was always something to see another hop away and he never had trouble finding a place on a ship when he was done with groundside living. The Chained God snatched him in mid-stride and transferred him to the World, landing him in a road in Cheonea.

He joined the Owlyn Valers as they went to Silagamatys for the Lot, met Kori, through her linked up with Brann and Ahzurdan and went with them into the Chained God's pocket reality, where he and Ahzurdan became DANNY BLUE and went with Brann to fight the final battle with Settsimaksimin. When that battle was finished and

Brann was concentrating on healing the sorcerer, he picked up the Talisman BinYAHtii—and was snatched back to the Chained God's body.

That was how the Chained God acquired BinYAHtii.

Danny Blue roamed about the ancient rotting starship and struggled to relearn Ahzurdan's magic; all the sorcerer's WORDS and mindsets had to be reconfigured to suit the new personality. When he felt strong enough, he tried to attack the God, but was seized and slammed into a coldsleep pod where he spent the next ten years in statis.

DRAW IN THE CATALYSTS:
These are the stones of power, the great talismans:

BinYAHtii	Held by the Chained God. Manifests as a rough circle of reddish stone pendant on a massive gold chain, set in a heavy ring of beaten gold.
Churrikyoo	Held by the Servants of Amortis in her Temple in Havi Kudush, the holy city in central Phras. Manifests as a small glass frog, battered, chipped, filled with thready cracks.
Frunzacoache	Held in the essence pouch of a shaman of the Rushgaramuv Temuengs. Manifests as a never-withering berry leaf pressed between two thin round layers of crystal set in a ring of tarnished silver cable, pendant from a silver chain.
Harra's Eye	Held in the secret, sacred Cavern of the Chained God. Manifests as a sphere of crystal about the size of a large grapefruit. Not known as one of the stones of power because it is a new focus; it has lain dormant in the Cavern, waiting. None of the first rank sorcerers has learned of it or used the power locked in it.
Klukesharna	Held by Wokolinka of Lewinkob in the Henanolee Heart, in the island city Hennkensikee. Manifests as a small rod of black iron melted off a meteor, cooled in the shape of a clumsy key.
Massulit	Held by the Geniod in the chamber of crystals sunk within the white cliffs of the Lake Pikma ka Vyamm, the inland sea in the heart of the Jana Sarise. Manifests as a star sapphire the size of a

man's fist, the color of the sky at the zenith on a clear spring day.

Shaddalakh   Held by Magus of Tok Kinsa in the holy city of the Rukka Nagh. Manifests as a spotted sand dollar made of porcelain.

THE REBIRTHING: PHASE ONE
The stonebearers are set in motion

I: BRANN THE DRINKER OF SOULS

Jal Virri in the Myk-tat Tukery Brann and Settsimaksimin
In the tenth year of their habitation within the Tukery, they are restless.

1

The wide bed creaked as Brann rolled onto her side. Maksim muttered a few shapeless sounds without waking enough to know what he was protesting. She finished her turn and lay on her back, staring at a ceiling swimming in green-tinted light. The sun was barely above the horizon, shining directly in through the tight profusion of vines Maksim had coaxed across the windows. Given his choice he would come grudging out of bed sometime past noon and would have hung thick black curtains over the windows, but Brann needed a free flow of air and a feeling that the outside penetrated the room, that she wasn't shut into something she couldn't escape from. The vines were a compromise. She smiled at the shifting leaf-shadows; the light that came through in the very early morning was such a lovely green.

Maksim was sleeping soundly again now the nights were cooler and Brann was once more sharing the bed with him. Solid, meaty, comforting to sleep against once he settled down, he was a furnace that got hotter as the night went on, a blessing in winter but impossible when the nights heated up. When the hot season arrived, Brann moved into the other bedroom and Maksim was once again tormented by the bad dreams that wracked his sleep when she wasn't there to chase them off; he'd lived a long time and done things he refused to remember; he had reasons he considered adequate at the moment but they didn't ease his

mind when he looked back at them. During the day he pottered contentedly enough about Jal Virri, reading, working in the many gardens
beside the sprites who tended the place, but when night came, he
dreamed.

Brann and Maksim slept together for the comfort they took from
each other, body touching body. They shared a deep affection. One
might have called it love, if the word hadn't so many resonances that
had nothing to do with them. Maksim found his loves in Kukural,
young men who stayed a night or two, then left, others who loved him
a longer time but also left.

Brann went through a short but difficult period during the first days
they spent on Jal Virri; she wanted him, but had to recognize the
futility of that particular passion. It was a brief agony, but an agony
nonetheless, a scouring of her soul. His voice stirred her to the marrow
of her bones, he was bigger than life, a passionate dominating complex
man; she'd never met his equal anywhere anytime in all her long life.
She shared his disdain for inherited privilege, his sardonic, sympathetic
view of ordinary men; her mind marched with his, they enjoyed the
same things, laughed at the same things, deplored the same things,
were content to be quiet at the same time. Anything more, though, was
simply not there. She too went prowling the night in Kukural, though
it was more distraction than passion she was seeking.

There was enough of a nip in the air to make her snuggle closer to
Maksim. He grumbled in his sleep, but again he didn't wake. She
scratched at her thigh, worked her toes, flexed and unflexed her knees.
It was impossible; how did he do it, sleep like that, on and on? She
never could stay still once she was awake. Her mouth tasted foul, like
something had died in it and was growing moss. Her bladder was
overfull; if she moved she'd slosh. She pressed her thighs together; it
didn't help. That's it, she thought. That's all I need. She slid out of bed
and scurried for the watercloset.

When she came back, Maksim had turned onto his stomach. He was
snoring a little. His heavy braid had come undone and his long, coarse
hair was spread like gray weeds over his shoulders; a strand of it had
dropped across his face and was moving with his breath, tickling at his
nose. She smiled tenderly at him and lifted the hair back, taking care
not to wake him. Lazy old lion. She shaped the words with her lips but
didn't speak them. Big fat cat sleeping in the sun. She touched the
tangled mass of hair. I'll have a time combing this out. Sorceror Prime

tying granny knots, it's a disgrace, that's what it is. She patted a yawn, crossed to the vanity he'd bought for her in Kukurul a few years back.

The vanity was a low table of polished ebony with matching silver-mounted chests at both ends and a mage-made mirror, its glass smooth as silk and more faithful than she liked this autumn morning. Maybe it was the green light, but she looked ten years older than she had last night. She leaned closer to the mirror, pushed her fingers hard along her cheekbones, tautening and lifting the skin. She sighed. Drinker of Souls. Not any more. I don't have to feed my nurslings now. They're free of me. She stepped back and kicked the hassock closer, sat down and began brushing at her hair. There was no reason now for the Drinker of Souls to walk the night streets and take life from predators preying on the weak. The changechildren could feed themselves; they weren't even children any more. They came flying back once or twice a year to say hello and tell her the odd things they'd seen, but they never stayed long. Jal Virri is boring; Jay said that once. She paused, then finished the stroke. It's true. I'm petrified with boredom. I've outlived my usefulness. There's no point to my life.

She set the brush down and gazed into the mirror, examining her face with clinical objectivity, considering its planes and hollows as if she were planning a self-portrait. She hadn't been a pretty child and she wasn't pretty now. She frowned at her image. If I'd been someone else looking at me, I'd have said the woman has interesting bones and I'd like to paint her. Or I would have liked to paint her before she started to droop. Discontent. It did disgusting things to one's face, made everything sag and put sour lines around the mouth and between the brows. Her breasts were firm and full, that was all right, but she had a small pot when she sat; she put her hands round it, lifted and pressed it in, then sighed and reached for the brush. It won't be long before I have to pay someone to climb into bed with me. She pulled the bristles through the soft white strands. Old nag put out to pasture, no one wants her anymore.

She made a face at herself and laughed, but her eyes were sad and the laughter faded quickly. Might as well be dead. She rubbed the back of her hand beneath her chin and felt the loosening muscle there. Death? Illusion. Give me one man's lifeforce and I'm young again. Twenty-four/five, back where I was when Slya finished with me. No dying for me. Not even a real aging, only an endless going on and on. No rest for me. No lying down in the earth and letting slip the burden of life. How odd to realize what a blessing death was. Not a curse. Well

. . . once the dying was finished with, anyway. Dying was the problem, not death. I wonder if they'd let me? She got to her feet, looked over her shoulder at Maksim. One massive arm had dropped off the bed; it hung down so the backs of his fingers trailed on the grass mat that covered the floor.

She went out, walked through rooms filled with morning light, swept and garnished by one of the sprites that took care of the island, the one they called Housewraith. The kitchen was a large bright room at the back. She pulled open one of the drawers and took out a paring knife. She set the blade on her wrist. It was so sharp its weight was enough to push the edge a short way through her flesh; when she lifted the knife, she saw a fine red line drawn across the porcelain pallor of her skin. She put the knife down. It wasn't time yet. She wasn't tired enough of living to endure the pain of dying. Boredom . . . no, that wasn't enough, not yet.

She set the knife on the work table and drew her thumb along the shallow cut, wiping away the blood. The cut stung and oozed more blood. Rubbing her wrist absently against the side of her breast, she wandered outside, shivering as the frosty morning breeze hit her skin. For a moment she thought of going inside and putting on a robe, but she wasn't bothered enough to make the effort. She looked at her wrist; the cut was clotted over; the blood seepage had stopped.

Ignoring the bite of dew that felt like snowmelt on her bare feet, she walked down the long grassy slope to the water and stood at the edge of the small beach listening to the saltwater lap lazily at the sand and gazing across the narrow strait to a nearby island, a high rocky thing sculpted by wind and water into an abstract pillar, barren except for a few gray and orange lichens. All the islands around Jal Virri were like that; it was as if the lovely green isle had drawn the life out of them and spent it on itself. Arms huddled across her breasts, hands shaking though they were closed tight about her biceps, her feet blocks of ice with smears of black soil and scraps of grass pasted on them, she watched the dark water come and go until she couldn't stand the cold any longer. It's time we went to Kukurul again, Maks and me, or me alone, if he won't come. She stood quite still for a breath or two. I don't think I'm coming back. I don't know what it is I'm going to do, but I can't vegetate here any longer. She turned and walked back toward the house. I've been sleeping and now I'm awake. I never could stay in bed once I woke up.

2

"Hoist it, Maksi." She jerked the covers off him, slapped him on a meaty buttock. "Wake up, you bonelazy magicman, I need you."

He grunted and cracked an eye. "Go 'way."

"Uh-uh, baby. You've slept long enough for ten your size. Pop me to Kukurul, luv. I woke up wanting."

He closed the eye. "Take the boat."

She took his earlobe instead and pinched hard.

"Ow! Stop that." He grabbed for her arm, but she jumped out of reach. "Witch!"

"If I were, I wouldn't need you."

He groaned and sat up. "You don't need me."

"Come on, Maksi. Housewraith decided to make breakfast this morning. It's spelled to wait, but I'm hungry. I'll take the boat all right, but I want you with me."

He shoved tangled hair off his face and looked shrewdly at her. "What is it, Bramble? Something's eating at you."

"No soulsearching before breakfast, if you please. I've run your bath for you, I've had mine already. I'll wait twenty minutes no more, so it's your fault if your eggs are cold."

3

The fire crackled behind the screen; the heavy silk drapes were pulled back to let in the morning sun. Brann paced back and forth, her body cutting through the beams, her shadow jerking erratically over the furniture. She swung round, scowled at Maksim. "Well?"

"Of course I'll go with you. Matter of fact, I've been thinking for several days now it's time for another visit." He rubbed his hand across his chin. "What's itching at you, Bramble-all-thorns?"

"The usual thing. What else could there be?" She turned her back on him and stared out the window.

"I don't think so."

"Oh you."

"Me."

She moved her right arm in a shapeless, meaningless gesture; she started to speak, stopped, tried again, had even less luck finding words for what she wanted to say; the trouble was, she didn't know what she wanted to say. "I'm useless. There's nothing to do here." She turned round, hitched a hip on the windowsill. "Nothing real." She lifted her hands, let them fall. "I don't know, Maksi. There's no point to anything. Nothing I try . . . works. I tried potting, you know that, you shaped my kiln for me. It was horrible. Everything I did . . . mediocre . . . bleah! At Shaynamoshu I was content a hundred years. Happy. Here . . . ? I paint a pretty flower, don't I. Dew on the petals, pollen on the stamens, you can see every grain. Lovely, right? Horrible. A dead slug has more soul. Useless, Maksi. Out to pasture like a brokedown mare. Even the damn gods don't need me anymore. Maybe I should go to Silili with you and give Old Tungjii a boot in the behind. Maybe something would come of that."

"It probably would. I doubt you'd be pleased with whatever it was."

"Pleased? That doesn't matter. It'd be something to do. Some reason to get out of bed in the morning. To keep on living. You know what I'm talking about; you're restless too, magicman."

"Brann, I. . . ."

"No. You don't need to say it. I know what's going to happen. You'll go to Silili to see your protége through her Passage Rite and you won't come back. Why should you?"

"Thornlet, come with me." He lay back in his chair and laughed at her and let his voice boom out, dark velvet rubbing her bones. "Come wandering with me and see the world. Sure somewhere there's a prince who needs his bottom whacked, a lord to be taught his manners, a bully who needs his pride punctured. Let us go out and do good, no matter how much chaos we leave behind us."

"Ah Maksi m'luv, you're such a fraud, you evil old sorcerer, you bleed at a touch and put yourself to endless inconvenience. I don't know. Maybe we just need some hard living for a while so we can appreciate peace again. Anyway, let's scratch our ordinary itches and see what comes of that."

4

Kukurul. The place where seapaths cross. The pivot of the four winds. If you sit long enough at one of the plaza tables of the café Sidday Lir, it's said you'll see the whole world file past you. Kukurul. Expensive, gaudy, secretive and corrupt. Its housefronts are full of windows with screens behind them like the eyes of Kukrulese. Along the Ihman Katt are brothels for every taste, ranks of houses where assassin guilds advertise men of the knife, women of the poison cup;

halfway up the Katt there's a narrow black building where deathrites are practiced for the titillation of the connoisseurs, open to participation or solitary enjoyment. At the end of the Ihman Katt is the true heart of Kukurul, the Great Market, a paved square two miles on a side where everything is on sale but heat, sweat, and stench. Those last are free.

Brann patted at her face with a square of fine linen, removing some of the dust and sweat that clung to her skin. It was one of those fine hot airless days that early autumn sometimes threw up and the Market was a hellhole, though few of the shoppers or the shopkeepers seemed to notice it. She pushed the kerchief up her sleeve and lifted a graceful vase. Eggshell porcelain with an unusual glaze. She frowned and ran her fingertips repeatedly over the smooth sides. Unless she was losing her mind, she knew that glaze. Her father's secret mix and Slya's Breath, never one without the other. At Shaynamoshu she'd tried again and again to get that underglow, but it was impossible without the Breath. She examined the lines and the underpainting. It wasn't her father's work or that of any of his apprentices, but there was something there . . . the illusive similarity of cousins perhaps. Biting at her lower lip, she upended the vase and inspected the maker's mark. A triangle above an oval, Arth Slya's sigil. The glyph Tayn. The glyph Nor. These were the potter's seal. Tannor of Arth Slya. She carried the vase to the Counting Table. "Arth Slya is producing again?"

The old man blinked hooded eyes. "Again?"

"You claim this is oldware?"

"Claim?" He shrugged. "The mark is true, the provenance can be produced."

"I don't doubt the mark, the glaze alone is enough to guarantee it."

"You a collector?"

"No." She smiled as she saw the glitter in his eyes fade before that cool negative. "Earthenware is at once too heavy and too fragile to survive my sort of life. I will take this, though, for the pleasure it gives me. It's a cheerful thing when a dead loveliness comes to life again. Twenty silver."

He settled to his work and his pleasure. "New or old, that's Arth Slya ware. Silver is an insult. Five gold."

When the bargain was concluded, Brann had him send the vase to the Inn of the Pearly Dawn where she and Maksim were staying. She left the Market and strolled down the Katt to the café Sidday Lir, confused by the conflicting emotions awakened by the vase. She was pleased because her father had left workheirs; she was jealous because that place was hers by right and talent. She wanted to go home. Home? Arth Slya? What made her think that place was home more than any other patch of earth? Kin? She couldn't claim them, who would believe her. If they believed her, they'd back away from her, terrified. And could she blame them?

She chose a table with a view out over the harbor and sat watching the ships arrive and depart, wondering if one of them was a trader like Sammang's Panday Girl, like her working the islands north and east of the Tukery, like her calling in at Tavisteen on Croaldhu where Brann had started her wandering. She wallowed comfortably in nostalgia as she sipped at the tea and enjoyed the dance of the ships and the streaming of the ladesmen working the wharves below; she wondered what the Firemountain Tincreal looked like these days, whether the eruption and the weathering of two centuries since had changed her out of all recognition, wondered if she'd recognize the descendants of her kin if she saw them. Was there any more reason to go back to Arth Slya than there was to return to Jal Virri? I'd like to see it again, she thought. I'd like to see what the ones who went back made of it.

When the teapot was empty, she sat considering whether she wanted more tea or should call for her bill and return to the Inn for a bath and a nap until it was time to go looking for something to warm her bed. Before she reached a decision on that, she saw Jaril walking down the Katt and settled back to wait for him.

The changer wound toward her through scattered tables, drawing stares enough to make him uncomfortable; Brann watched him shy away from a clawed hand reaching for his arm, pretend he didn't hear a half-whispered suggestion from a Hina woman of indeterminate age, or drawled comments from a group of Phrasi highborns lounging at three tables pushed together. He looked a teener boy, fourteen, fifteen years old, a beautiful boy who'd somehow avoided the awkward throes of adolescence, hair like white-gold spun gossamer fine lifting to the caress of the wind, elegantly sculptured features, crystal eyes, a shapely body that moved with unstudied grace. He pulled out a chair and sat down, fidgeted for several moments without speaking to her.

"Add a few warts next time," Brann said, amused. She felt suddenly happy. Her son was come to visit her. She looked past him. Alone? "Where's Yaro? Saying hello to Maks?"

"No," he said "Yaro's not with me."

She eyed him thoughtfully, caught the attention of a waiter and ordered a half bottle of wine. When he'd gone, she said, "Tell me."

Jaril touched a fingertip to a drop of spilled tea and drew patterns on the wood. "Remember the swamp before we got to Tavisteen? Remember what happened to me and Yaro there?"

Brann closed her eyes, thought. "That was a while ago," she murmured. She remembered gray. Even during daylight everything was gray. Gray skies, gray water, gray mud dried on sedges and trees, gray fungi, gray insects, gray everything. She remembered waking tangled in tough netting made from cords twisted out of reed fiber and impregnated with fish stink. She remembered little gray men swarming over the island, little gray men with coarse yellow cloth wound in pouty little shrouds about their groins, little gray men with rough dry skin, a dusty gray mottled with darker streaks and splotches. She could move her head a little. It was late, shadows were long across the water. A gray man sat beside a small fire, net woven about him and knotted in intricate patterns describing his power and importance; a fringe of knotted cords dangled from a thick rope looped loosely about a small hard potbelly. In a long-fingered reptilian hand he held a drum; it was a snakeskin stretched over the skull of a huge serpent, its eyeholes facing outward. He drew from the taut skin a soft insistent rustle barely louder than the whisper of the wind through the reeds; it crept inside her until it commanded the beat of her heart, the pulse of her breathing. She jerked her body loose from the spell, shivering with fear. He looked at her and she shivered again. He reached out and ran a hand over two large stones sitting beside his bony knee, gray-webbed crystals each as large as man's head, crystals gathering the light of the fire into themselves, miniature broken fires repeated endlessly again. Yaril and Jaril frozen into stone. She knew it and was more frightened than before. He grinned at her, baring a hard ridge of black gum, enjoying her helpless rage.

She blinked, brought herself back out of memory. "The swampwizard," she said. "Ganumomo, that was his name. Why him? Did you go back to Croaldhu and fall in that trap again?"

"No." He sipped at his wine and gazed out across the bay. He was uncomfortable and she couldn't make out why. He was worried about Yaril, but that wasn't it. She watched the level of the wine sink lower in his glass and remembered something else; neither he nor Yaril would talk about their people or their home. Had something happened to Yaril that was connected to their homeplace? "Caves," he said; he seemed to taste the word like hard candy on the tongue. "Caves. We love them because they're terrifying, Bramble. We could die if we were shut off from sun too long, we would go stone and lie there in stone, fading slowly slowly until there was nothing left not stone." He poured more wine in his glass, tilted it and watched the rich red sliding down the curve. "Yaro and me, we were poking about some mountains, the Dhia Dautas, if you want the name, and we found this set of caves. Splendid caves, Bramble. Shining caves. We went a little crazy. Just a little. We soaked up all the sun we could before we went down. We weren't going to stay down more than a day or so, we'd have plenty of push left to get us out of trouble should we run into any. Not that we expected to." He gulped at the wine, went back to staring at what was left.

Brann waited. His lack of urgency was reassuring. Yaril wasn't dead. She was sure of that. Jay would be . . . different . . . if his sister was dead.

"She was flitting along ahead of me. Actually, I was chasing her . . . it's an old game . . . from home . . . complicated rules . . . the thing he . . . whoever . . . didn't count on." A crooked angry grin, a hunching of his shoulders. "I wasn't close enough to get caught with her. I was round a bend about twenty feet behind when the thing closed round her. The trap I mean."

"Trap?"

"It wasn't something natural."

"What was it?"

"I don't know. Yaro went stone before I got round the bend. I saw her sitting there . . . you remember how we looked . . . gone stone . . ." He shuddered in his peculiar way, his outline melting and re-forming, his hands growing transparent, then solid. "I tried to get to her. There was a barrier. I couldn't see it, I couldn't feel it either, not really, I just couldn't get to her. I tried going over it. Around it. Under it. I went into the mountain itself, I slid through the stone. That's dangerous, it's so easy to get confused so you don't know up from down, but I did it. No good. It was a sphere, Bramble, it was all around her. I couldn't get to her. I leaned against it and called to her; if I could wake her, maybe we could do something together. I couldn't reach her. I couldn't even feel her there, Bramble. Do you understand? My sister. The only being in this place who's LIKE me. If I lost her, I'd be alone. I couldn't TALK to her. Not even TALK to her, Bramble. I went wired for a while, I don't know how long." He shuddered again, the pulses of fleshmelt moving swiftly along his body, clothes as well as flesh because his clothing was part of his substance. "When I knew what I was doing again, I was miles south of the caves." He gulped at the wine, then with a visible effort steadied himself. Brann watched, more troubled than she'd been a short time before; Jaril was barely containing his panic and his control was getting worse, not better. "I was eagleshape, driving south as fast as I could fly. I couldn't think why for the longest, I wasn't capable of thinking, Brann, but I kept on flying. After a while, I decided I was coming for you. I knew you'd help us. And prod Maksim into doing what he can. He doesn't like us much, but he'd do a lot for you, Bramble."

Brann clinked her spoon against the teabowl and waited for the waiter to bring the check. "We'll go up to the Inn," she said. "And go over everything you can remember first, then you can hunt Maks up and bring him to me."

Jaril nodded. "Bramble. . . ."

She thrust out her hand, palm toward him, stopping him. "Later."

He shifted round and saw the waiter walking toward them.

##

A winding lane with flowering plums and other ornamentals growing at carefully irregular intervals along it led to the Outlook, a terrace halfway up the side of the dormant volcano which rose high above the lesser mountains that ringed the bay; the Inn of the Pearly Dawn sat on that Outlook, surrounded by its gardens with their well-groomed elegance, an expensive waystop but only moderately successful since the merchants, collectors, and more esoteric visitors preferred living in the heat and stench of the city where they could keep their fingers on its throb and profit thereby.

Brann and Jaril walked up the lane, feet stirring drifts of dead leaves; they talked quietly as they walked, with long intervals of silence between the phrases.

"How much time do we have?"

"Decades, if whoever's got her lets her have sun. If they keep her dark, a year."

Brann reached up, broke a small green and brown orchid from a dangling spray. "I see." A fragile sweet perfume eddied from the flower as she waved it slowly back and forth before her face as she walked. "We'd better expect the worst and plan for it."

Jaril's outline wavered. When he'd got himself in hand again, he nodded. "Maksim. . . ."

"No." Brann closed her hand hard on the orchid, crushing it, releasing a powerful burst of scent. She flung the mutilated thing away, wiped her hand on her skirt. "Don't count on him, Jay. He's got other commitments."

"If you ask. . . ."

"No."

"He owes you, Bramble. Weren't for you, he'd be dead."

"Weren't for me, he'd still have Cheonea to play with. It balances."

Jaril moved ahead of her, opened the Zertarta Gate for her, then followed her into the Inn's Stone Garden.

Brann touched his arm. "We can go up to my rooms, or would you rather take sun by the lily pond?"

"Sun." He shimmered again, produced a stiff smile. "I'm pretty much drained, Bramble. I didn't stop for anything and it was a long way here."

She strolled beside him, following the path by the stream that chattered musically over aesthetically arranged stones and around boulders chosen for their lichen patterns and hauled here from every part of the island. The stream rambled in a lazy arc about the east wing of the Inn, then spread in a deep pool with a stone grating at each end to keep the halarani in, the black and gold fish that lived among the water lily roots. Three willows of different heights and inclinations drooped gracefully over the water. There were stone benches in their spiky shade, but Brann settled on the ancient oak planks of the one bench without any shadow over it. There was no breeze back here; stillness rested like gauze over the pond, underlaid with the small sounds of insects and the brush-brush-tinkle of the stream. She smiled as Jaril darkened his clothing and himself until he was sun-trap black, sooty as the dusky sides of the halarani. He dropped onto the bench and lay with his head in her lap; his eyes closed and he seemed to sleep.

"We were in the Dhia Dautas," he murmured after a while. "East and a half-degree south of Jorpashil. West on a direct line from Kapi Yuntipek. Dhia Dautas. Means daughters of the dawn in the Sarosj. The hill people call them the Taongashan Hegysh, they live there so you'd think travelers would use their name for the mountains, but they don't, the Silk Roaders always say the Dhia Dautas." His voice was dragging; she could feel him putting off the need to talk about the caves. She could feel the tension in him, he vibrated with it. "We were in Jorpashil five, six days, we heard about the caves there. Storyteller in the Market. A pair of drunks in a tavern. Seemed like we ran across at least one story every day while we were there. You want me to give you all of it?"

"Later, Jay. It's probably important."

"I think so. How could whoever it was lay the trap for us if he didn't know we'd be there to spring it. We weren't thinking about traps then, we took wing and went hunting for the caves. . . ." His voice droned on.

They talked for a long time that afternoon, until neither could think of another question to ask, another answer to give. Then they just sat quietly in the hazy sunlight watching the Inn's shadow creep toward them.

5

Brann stood at her bedroom window, a pot of tea beside her on the broad sill. Far below, the sails of the ships arriving and departing were hot gilt and crimson, then suddenly dark as the brief tropical twilight was over. Night, she thought. She looked at her hands. Idle hands. They'd lost strength over the past ten years. If I had to fire a kiln tomorrow, I'd be wrecked before I was half through splitting billets. She filled her bowl with the last of the tea, lukewarm and strong enough to float a rock, sipped at it as she watched the lamps and torches bloom along the Ihman Katt. Wisps of sound floated up through the still, dark air, laughter, even a word or two snatched whole by erratic thermals. Jaril was down there, looking for Maksim. She grimaced at the bite of the tannin, the feel of the leaves on her lips and tongue. Maksi, she thought, always underfoot when you didn't need him, down a hole somewhere when you did. I have to Hunt tonight.

When the Chained God weaned her nurslings from their dependence on her, at first she'd felt relief. Each time she went out to Hunt for them, she sickened at what she had to do, the killings night after night until Yaril and Jaril were fed and she could rest a month or so; later, when they were older, once a year did it, then once every two years. Drinker of Souls, sucking life out of men and women night after night —more than ten thousand nights—until she was finally free of the need. She quieted her souls by choosing thieves and slavers, usurers and slumlords, assassins and bullyboys, corrupt judges and secret police, anyone who used muscle or position to torment the helpless. All those years she yearned to be rid of that burden, all those years she thought she loathed the need. Then she stopped the Hunting and thought she was content. Now that the need was on her again, she wasn't sure how she felt . . . no, that wasn't true, she knew all too well.

She gazed at the lamps of Kukurul and was disconcerted by her growing impatience to get down there and prowl; her body trembled with anticipation as she imagined herself stalking men, drawing into her so much lifeforce she shone like the moon. Filling herself with the terrible fire that was like nothing else. Ever. She remembered being awash with LIFE, alive alive alive, afraid but ecstatic. In a way, though she didn't much care for the comparison, it was like a quieter time when she unpacked her kiln and held a minor miracle in her hands, like those few wonderful times all squeezed into that singular moment of fullness. . . . And for the past ten years she'd had neither sort of joy. Yes. Joy. Say it. Tell yourself the truth, if you tell no one else. Satisfaction, pleasure beyond pleasure, more than sex, more than the quieter goodness of fine food and vintage wines. She pressed a hand under her chin, flattened the loose skin, dropped her arms and pinched the soft pout of her belly; she was tired of aging with the aches and pains age brought. If she couldn't die, why endure life in a deteriorating body? She shivered. No, she thought, no, that's despicable.

She moved away from the window, started pacing the length of the room, back and forth, back and forth, across the braided rug; her bare feet made small scuffing sounds; her breathing was ragged and uncertain. She was frightened. Her sense of herself was disintegrating as she paced. The only thing she felt sure of was that her father would neither like nor approve of what she was turning into.

An owl dropped through the window, landed on the rug and shifted to Jaril; he crossed to the bed, threw himself on it. "I found Maksim. He was with someone, so he wasn't happy about me barging in. When I told him you needed to see him, he wanted to know if it was urgent or what, then he said he'd be back round midnight if there wasn't all that much hurry. I said all right."

She sat beside him, threaded her fingers through his fine hair; they tingled as threads of her own energy leaked from her to him. He made a soft sound filled with pleasure and nestled closer to her.

"Jay."

"Mm?"

"You need to go home, don't you."

He shifted uneasily. "We can talk about that after we get Yaro back."

"All right. We do have to talk. Never mind, luv, I won't push you." She slid her hand down his arm, closed her fingers around his. "I can't live on sunlight or grow wings."

"Flat purse?"

"Pancake."

Jaril laughed drowsily, tugged his hand loose. "So I go scavenging?"

"With extreme discretion, luv."

"More than you know, Bramble." He yawned, which was playacting since he didn't breathe; that he could play at all pleased her, it meant he was not quite so afraid. He turned serious. "Not at night."

"Why?"

"Wards are weaker in daylight."

"Since when have you worried about wards?"

"Everything changes, Bramble. We've picked up too much from this reality. Things here can see us now. Sort of."

Brann scowled at him. "Forget it, then. I'll see what I can borrow from Maks. We'll pick up supplies on the road."

"Just as well, the Managers here are a nasty lot. I'll crash a while, tap me when Maks shows up." He moved away from her, curled up on the far side of the bed and stopped breathing, deep in his usual sleep-coma.

Brann looked at him a moment, shook her head. "I don't know," she said aloud. She went across to the window, hitched a hip on the sill and went back to watching the lights below.

6

"What's this Jay was hinting at?" Maksim was tired and cranky; she saw that he meant to be difficult.

"Come sit down." She stepped back from the door and gestured toward the large leather chair that stood close to the sitting room fire. "There's brandy if you want it, or tea."

He caught hold of her chin, lifted her face to the light.

"Those nits have put you in an uproar. What is it?"

"We need your help, Maksi." Her jaw moved against the smooth hard flesh of his hand. She closed her eyes, wanting him intensely, roused by the power in him. The futility of that made her angry, but she suppressed the anger along with the desire and waited for him to take his hand away.

He crossed to the chair and poured a dollop of brandy into the bubbleglass waiting beside the bottle. When he'd settled himself, he said, "Tell me."

Keeping her description terse and unemotional, she reported what Jaril had told her. "So," she finished, "there's a time limit. If we're going to find her alive, we do it before the year's out. Will you long look for us?"

He held the glass in both hands and stared into the amber liquid as if he sought an answer there. "Where's Jay?"

"In the bed. Resting. He said to wake him when you came, but I decided not to."

Maksim's lips twitched, the beginnings of a smile. "Tact, Bramble?"

"Surprised? I think that's an insult."

"Never." The word was drawn out and ended in a chuckle. "Seriously, Thornlet, how quiet do you want to keep this? If I start operating around here, there'll be notice taken. Official notice. The Managers don't like outsiders mussing the pool."

"I haven't a clue what you're talking about."

"Security, Brann. Kukurul's boast. Do your business here and it stays your business."

"So?"

"Use your head. How do you think they enforce that?" He closed his eyes and looked wary. "If you want me to fiddle about under seal, we go back to Jal Virri."

"Will they know what you're doing or only that you're doing it?"

"Now I'm the one insulted."

She flipped a hand in an impatient gesture. "Can you work here? I mean, do you need tools you haven't got?"

"Words are my tools, all I need," he said. "Little Danny Blue explained that, remember? As long as my memory functions and my hands move, I'm in business." He smiled at her, his irritation smoothed away by hers. "I haven't noticed it falling off, have you? Don't answer that, mmh." He leaned forward, hands cupped over his knees. "I could get busy tonight, Bramble, but I'd rather wait until I can inform the Managers what I'm doing is no business of theirs."

"I have to Hunt, Maksi. For lots of reasons."

"Better wait."

"How long?"

"Two days, three at most."

"All right. Will you come with us?"

"No. I'll make up some *call-me*'s for you; if you run into trouble and I can help, break one under your heel and I'll be there." He lifted his hands, spread them wide in a flowing expressive gesture. "If it weren't for young Kori. . . ."

"It's my affair, not yours, Maksi; you needn't fuss yourself."

"Hmm." He got to his feet. "If you need money. . . ."

"I do. But I'll talk to you about that later. All right?"

"Fine. Third hour tomorrow morning?"

"All right. Here? Good."

She stood in the doorway to her suite and watched him stride off down the corridor. That's over, she thought. I was right. Neither of us is going back to Jal Virri. Healing time, resting time, it's done. She sighed and shut the door, went over to the fire and stood leaning against the mantle, letting the heat play across the front of her body. Tungjii, she thought. Say hisser name and step back. Maksi was right. I shouldn't have invoked the little god, look what happened. She brooded until her robe began to scorch, then she shifted to a chair. Slowly, with painful care and uncomfortable honesty, she confronted needs she hadn't expected to have and set these against the ethical code her father had taught her by example and aphorism.

Don't cheat yourself by scamping your work, whatever the pressures of time and need; you always lose more than you gain if you cut corners.

In your dealings with others, first do no harm.

If harm is inevitable, do all you can to minimize its effects.

Her eyes filled; she scrubbed her hand across them angrily. This cursed nostalgia was useless. All it did was undercut efforts to deal with the things that she was discovering about herself, things that terrified her. Disgusted her.

"You didn't wake me." Jaril dropped beside her, knelt with his arms resting on the chair arm.

"Maksi was in a mood." She touched his hair. "Do you mind?"

"He going to help?"

"Yes. He'll start looking for Yaril tomorrow. He has to soothe the Managers first."

"Um. He coming with us?"

"No. It'll be just us."

"Good."

"Jay!"

"He'd be a drag and you know it."

"He's powerful. He can do things we wouldn't have a hope of doing."

"Who says we'll need those things? We haven't before."

"Imp." She tapped the tip of his nose, laughed. "What are we arguing about, eh? He's not coming, so there's no problem."

"When we leaving?"

"Maksi says he should have all he can get in two-three days, say three days. Then I've got to Hunt, he says wait until he finishes his sweep and I agree. Say two nights more. All right?"

"Has to be. You look tired."

"I am."

"Sleep."

"Can't turn my head off."

"Come to bed. I can fix that."

"I don't want to dream, Jay."

"I won't mess with dreams, Bramble. If you do, you need to. Come on."

"I come, o master Jay."

7

Maksim was embarrassed and worried when he came to her suite two days later. "I don't know who, I don't know why. I tried every means I know, Bramble, but I found out nothing." Hands clasped behind him, he went charging about the room, throwing words at her over his shoulder. "Do you hear? Nothing! Even the cave is closed off from me. All of it." He stopped in front of her, glared at her. "I don't think you should go there, Bramble. Not alone."

"I won't be alone. Jay will be with me."

He brushed that away. "You have a year. Give me two months. Come with me to meet Kori when she leaves the school. As soon as I finish there, I'll be free. I've never seen anything like this, Brann; god or man, no one has shut me out like this since I was a first year apprentice."

"No, Maksi. Now. It has to be now."

"If I don't snap you to the cave site, it will take you at least two months' travel to reach it. Give me those months."

"If that sled Danny Blue made hadn't gone to pieces, I wouldn't have to beg. I hate this, Maksi, but I've got no choice. Please. Do what you said you'd do. I'm not being stubborn or perverse. It isn't Jay working on me. This is . . . I don't know, a feeling, something. It says NOW. I don't know. Please, Maksi. Do you want me on my knees?" She started to drop, but he caught her arm in a hard grip that left bruises behind when he took his hand away.

"No!" He shouted the word at her. "No," he said more quietly. "Here." He stretched out a fist, held it over her cupped hands. *"Call-me's.* If you need me, put one under your heel and crush it. I'll be there before your next breath. If I can find you." Grim and unhappy, he dropped half a dozen water-smoothed quartz pebbles in her hands. "If I can. If you aren't blocked off from me like the cave."

8

Drinker of Souls prowled the streets.

A band of prepubescent thieves came creeping through the fog to find their Whip limp and lifeless on the filthy cobbles.

A childstealer dropped from a window with a bundle slung over one shoulder. A hand came from the darkness, slapped against his neck. A mastiff howled until a houseguard came out to throw a cobble at the beast. The guard heard the baby crying, saw the bundle and the dead man, woke the house with his yells.

An assassin prepared to scale the outside of a merchant's house. When the streetsweepers came along, they found his body rolled up against the wall.

Inside the BlackHouse a man was beating a boy, slowly, carefully beating him to death. When he finished, he left the place, strolling sated between his bodyguards. His gardener found the three of them stretched out under a bush, dead.

And so it went.

In the cold wet dawns the streetsweepers of Kukurul found the husks she left behind and put them on the rag and bone cart for the charnel fires.

In the cold wet dawns the Kula priests went sweeping in procession through the tangled streets, setting silence on the newborn ghosts. Ghosts that were highly indignant and prepared to make life difficult for everyone around them. They fought the grip of the priests but lost and went writhing off, pulsing with blocked fury. The wind blew them off to join the fog out over the bay and the debris from older cast-out souls.

9

On the evening of the third night, with Jaril trotting beside her, Brann climbed the mountain above the Inn and waited for Maksim.

The Wounded Moon was a vague patch of yellow in the western sky, a chill fog eddied about the flat; the stones were dark with the damp, slippery lightsinks and traps for the unwary ankle. Brann pulled her cloak tighter about her body, muttering under her breath at Maksim's insistence on this particular spot for his operations. At the same time she was perversely pleased with her surroundings, the gloom around her resonated with the gloom inside her. Jaril was even more unhappy with the place. He'd kept his mastiff form but replaced his fur with a thick leathery skin that shed the condensation from the fog like waxed parchment. In spite of that he was uncomfortable. The wet stole heat and energy from him. He was prowling about, rubbing his sides against any boulders tall enough to allow this, impatient to get away.

In the fog and the cold and the dark, Jaril whining behind her somewhere. Brann began to wonder if Maksim had changed his mind again. She eased the straps of her rucksack; though the leather was padded, they were cutting into her shoulders. Soft, she thought, but I'll harden with time and doing. She looked at her hands. They glowed palely in the dense dark, milkglass flesh with bone shadows running through it.

"You can still change your mind, Bramble." Maksim's voice came out of the dark, startling her; she hadn't heard on sensed his approach. That worried her.

"No," she said. "Jay, come here. Do it, Maksi."

10

Brann stepped from one storm into another. The slope outside the cave mouth was bare and stony; a knife-edged icewind swept across it, driving pellets of ice against Brann's face and body. Jaril whimpered, ducked under the snapping ends of her cloak and pressed up against her.

Brann dropped into a crouch, put her mouth close to his ear. "Where's the cave? We've got to get out of this."

Jaril shivered, grew a thick coat of fur. He edged from the shelter of the cloak, waited until she was standing again, then trotted up the slope to a clump of scrub jemras, low crooked conifers with a strong cedary smell that blew around her as she got closer, powerful, suffocating. She plunged through them and into a damp darkness with a howl in it.

Once he was out of the wind, Jaril changed to the glow globe that was his base form and lit up a dull, dark chamber like a narrowmouth bottle. He hung in midair, quivering with indignation and cursing Maksim in buzzing mindspeak for sending them into this cold hell.

Brann ignored the voice in her head as she would a mosquito buzzing; she slid out of the shoulder straps and lowered the rucksack to the cave floor. Her cloak was wet through, she was cold to the bone. "Jay, in a minute give me some light out there. I have to get a fire started before I perish. . . ." She gasped and went skipping backward as a stack of wood clattered to the stone, followed by a whoosh and a flare of heat as a clutch of hot coals and burning sticks landed near the woodpile. She laughed. "Thanks, Maksi," she called. She laughed again, her voice echoing and re-echoing as Jaril darted to the fire and sank into it, quivering with pleasure as he bathed in the heat.

She bustled about, spreading mat and blankets, restacking the wood, organizing the coals and several sticks of wood into a larger fire. When she finished, she sighed with weariness and looked around. Jaril was gone. He couldn't wait, she thought. Well, she's his sister and night and day don't matter underground. She rubbed her back, frowned. What do I do if he's trapped like Yaro? Idiot boy! A few more hours and I could have gone with him. She dropped onto the mat and pulled a blanket around her to block off the drafts. Staring into the fire, she grew angrier with every minute lumbering past.

The glowsphere came speeding recklessly back. Jaril shifted to his bipedal form, flung himself at Brann, sobbing and trembling, cold for his kind and deep in shock. "She's gone, Bramble, she's not there any longer, she's gone, she's gone. . . ."

II.   SETTSIMAKSIMIN

> Kukurul, the World's navel
> Settsimaksimin, alone and restless
> also: Jastouk, male courtesan
>   Vechakek, his minder
>   Todichi Yahzi, Maksim's ex-
>   secretary, now a mistreated
>   slave.
>   Davindolillah, a boy who re-
>   minds Maksim of himself, of
>   no other importance.
>   Assorted others.

1

Settsimaksimin yawned. He felt drained. It was brushing against the trap in the cave that did it, he thought. The block. Fool woman, lackbrained looby, ahhh, Thornlet, that thing is dangerous. He stomped about the rubble-strewn flat, uncertain what to do next; the fog was thickening to a slow dull rain and the night was colder; it was time to get out of this, but he was reluctant to leave. Fool man, me, he thought. He wrung some of the water from his braid, shaped a will-o and sent it bobbing along ahead of him to light the path so he wouldn't break his neck as he went downhill to the Inn.

Jastouk would be at the *Ardent Argent* unless he'd got tired of waiting and gone trawling for a new companion. Gods, I'm tired. I don't want to sleep. Sleep, hah! Bramble, you're damn inconvenient, you and those devilkids of yours . . . fires die if you aren't there to fan them. . . .

He changed his clothes and took a chair up the Katt. He found Jastouk sitting sulkily alone, watching some uninspired dancers posturing with the flaccid conjurings produced by an equally uninspired firewitch. He coaxed the hetairo into better humor and carried him off to a semi-private party at one of the casinos.

Company in his bed didn't chase the dreams this time. Maksim woke sweating, his insides churning. He swore, dragging himself out of bed and doused his head with cold water.

Heavy-eyed and languorous, Jastouk stretched, laced his hands behind his head. "Bad night?" he murmured.

Maksim snapped the clasp off the end of his braid, tossed one of his brushes on the bed. "Brush my hair for me," he said. He dropped into a chair, sighed with pleasure as the youth's slim fingers worked the braid loose and began drawing the brush over the coarse gray strands. "You have good hands, Jasti."

"Yours are more beautiful," Jastouk said. His voice was a soft, drowsy burr, caressing the ear. "They hold power with grace."

"Don't do that." The anger and worry lingering from the night made Maksi's voice harsher than he'd meant it to be. "I don't need flattery, Jasti. I don't like it."

Jastouk laughed, a husky musical sound, his only answer to Maksim's acerbities. He began humming one of the songs currently popular in Kukural as he drew the brush through and through the sheaf of hair. He was thin, with the peculiar beauty of the wasted; his bones had an elegance denied most flesh. He was neither learned nor especially clever, but had a sweetness of disposition that made such graces quite superfluous. Pliant and receptive, he responded to the needs and moods of his clients before they were even aware they were in a mood and he had a way of listening with eyes and body as well as ears that seduced them into thinking they meant more to him than they did. They were disturbed, even angry, when they chanced across him in company with a successor and found that he had trouble placing them. He was wildly expensive, though he never bothered about money, leaving that to his Minder, a Henerman named Vechakek, who set his fees and collected them with minimal courtesy. Jastouk had a very few favored lovers that he never forgot; despite Vechakek's scolding he'd cut short whatever relationship he was in at the time and go with them, whether they could afford his fees or not. Maksim was one of these. Jastouk adored the huge man, he was awed by the thought of being lover to a Sorceror Prime; there were only four of them in all the world. But even Maksim had to court him and give him the attention he craved; there were too many others clamoring for his favors and he had too strong a need for continual reassuring to linger long where he was neglected and ignored. He was indolent but had almost no patience with his lovers, even the most passionate; when Brann's demands on Maksim's time and energies interfered with his courting, Jastouk was exasperated to the point of withdrawing, but when the interference was done, he was content to let Maksim's ardor warm him into an ardor of his own; this morning he was pleased with himself, settling happily into the old relationship. He brushed Maksim's long hair, every touch of his hands a caress; he sang his lazy songs and used his own tranquillity to smooth away the aches and itches in Maksim's souls.

When they left the Inn, the sun was high, shining with a watery autumnal warmth. Content with each other's company, they moved along the winding lane, dead leaves dropping about them, blowing about their feet, lending a gently melancholy air to the day. Maksim had the sense of something winding down, a time of transition between what was and what will be. It was a pleasant feeling for the most part, with scratchy places to remind him that nothing is permanent, that contentment has to be cherished, but abandoned before it got overripe. He plucked a lingering plum from a cluster of browning leaves, tossed it to a jikjik nosing among the roots. There were no real seasons this far south, but fruit trees and flowering trees went into a partial dormancy and shed part of their leaves in the fall, the beginning of the dry season, and stretched bare limbs among the sparse holdouts left on whippy green twigs until the rains came again.

"When you were busy with your friend," brown eyes soft as melted chocolate slid lazily toward Maksim, moved away again, the chocolate cream voice was slow and uninflected, making no overt comment on Maksim's neglect of him, though that did lie quite visible beneath the calm, "I was rather moped, missing you, Maksi, so I went to see the Pem Kundae perform. Do you know them?"

"No." Maksim yawned. "Sorry, I'm not too bright today. Who are they and what do they do?" He wasn't much interested in Jastouk's chatter, but he was willing to listen.

The hetairo noted his mental absence; it made him unhappy. He stopped talking.

Maksim pulled himself together; he needed company; he needed sex and more sex to drown out and drive away things clamoring at him. Drugs were impossible; a sorcerer of his rank would have to be suicidal to strip away his defenses so thoroughly. He needed Brann. He was furious at the changers for calling her away like that. He missed her already; time and time again when he saw some absurdity, he turned to share it with her, but she wasn't there. Instead of Brann, he had Jastouk, pliant and loving, but oh so blank above the neck. I'm not going to have him, if I keep letting my mind wander. He set himself to listen with more attention. "Are they some kind of players?"

Jastouk smiled, slid his fingers along Maksim's arm, took his hand. "Oh yes. Quite marvelous, Maksi. They do a bit of everything, dance, sing, mime, juggle, but that's only gilding. What they mainly do is improvise little poems. You shout out some topic or other and two or three of them will make up rhyming couplets until there's a whole poem finished for you. And the most amazing thing is, they do it in at least half a dozen languages. Delicious wordplay, I swear it, Maksi. Multilingual puns. You'd like them, I'm sure; it's the kind of thing you enjoy." He hesitated, not quite certain how his next comment would be taken. "I've heard you and your friend play the same kind of game."

"Ah. I shall have to see them. Tonight, Jasti?"

"It would have to be, this is their last performance here. I bespoke tickets, Maksi, do you mind? They're very popular, you know. I had to pull all sorts of strings to get these seats. They're a gold apiece, is that too much? They're really worth it."

"No doubt they are." Maksim cleared his throat; he regretted the sarcastic tone of the words; he knew Jastouk wouldn't like it. "I'm looking forward to seeing them perform."

They turned into the Ihman Katt and strolled toward the harbor. The broad street was crowded with porters and merchants coming up from the wharves, with other strollers, visitors who meant to sample the pleasures of Kukural before getting down to serious buying and selling; a few like Maksim and Jastouk were heading for the café Sidday Lir and noon tea or a light lunch and lighter gossip.

A line of slaves on a neck coffle came shuffling along the Katt. Maksim's eyes grazed over them. He started to look away as soon as he realized what they were, then he saw the being at the tail of the line, separate from the others, tugged along on a leash like some bad-tempered dog. It was Todichi Yahzi, his once-amanuensis.

Maksim felt a jolt to his belly. Guilt flooded through him, choked him. He'd dismissed the little creature from his mind so completely he hadn't thought of him once during the past ten years. Gods of time and fate, he thought, not an instant's thought. Nothing! He'd snatched the kwitur from his home reality, used him and discarded him with as little consideration as any of the kings he so despised. He couldn't even comfort himself with the notion that he'd assumed Yahzi had got home; the trigger he'd left with the kwitur only worked if he, Maksim, died. He hadn't assumed anything because he hadn't bothered to remember the being who'd spent almost every waking hour with him for nearly twenty years. He saw the collar on Todichi Yahzi's neck, the chain that tethered him to the whipmaster's belt. He saw the lumps and weals that clubs and whips had laid on his almost-friend's hide; he saw the hunched, cringing shuffle, the sudden blaze of rage in the deep set dull eyes as they met his. Todichi's body read like a book of shame, but despite the abuse he'd suffered, he was as alert, intelligent and intransigent as he'd been when he lived in the Citadel.

After that brief involuntary lurch, Maksim walked on. He knew Jastouk had noted his reaction and would be wondering why such a commonplace sight as a string of slaves would bother him so much. That couldn't be helped. He looked around. They were passing a tiny temple dedicated to Pindatung the god of thieves and pickpockets, a scruffy gray-mouse sort of god with a closet-sized niche for a temple. He stopped. "Jasti, go ahead and get us a table. I'll want tea, berries, and cream. I'll be along in a minute."

Jastouk touched Maksim's shoulder. For a moment he seemed about to offer what help he could give, but in the end opted for tact. "Don't be long, hmm?"

"I won't. It's something I'd forgotten that I've got to take care of. Only be a few minutes. Don't fuss, luv."

Jastouk pressed his lips together; he didn't like it when Maksim either deliberately or unconsciously echoed Brann's manner of speech, but he said nothing.

Ruefully aware of offending, quite aware of where the offense lay, Maksim watched the hetairo saunter off. Shaking his head, he slipped into the templet and settled onto the tattered cushions scattered across a wallbench. He slid his hand into his robe and took out his farseeing mirror. He'd made it to keep watch on Brann so he could help her if she needed him, but he had a more urgent use for it now. It was an oval of polished obsidian in a plaited ring of Brann's hair, white as a spider's web and as delicate. The cable it hung from he'd twisted from a strand of his own hair. He breathed on it, rubbed his cuff over it, sat holding it for several moments. What he was going to do was a very minor magic; there was even a good chance that the Guardians hired by the Managers wouldn't notice it. If they did, he might be booted out of Kukural and forbidden to return. He scrubbed his hand across his face. He was sweating and angry at himself, angry at Todichi Yahzi for showing up and making him feel a lout, angry at Fate in all her presentations including Tungjii Luck.

Impatiently he pushed such considerations aside and bent over the mirror, his lips moving in a subvocal chant. He set the slave coffle into the image field, along with the agent and his whipmaster, followed the shuffling string to the Auction House on the edge of the Great Market and into the slavepens behind it. He pointed the mirror at the agent and followed him into the office of his employer, watched and listened as the agent made his report, the slaver made his arrangements for the sale of the string. Three days on. Maksim let the mirror drop, canceling the spell on it, and spent a moment longer wondering if he should bid for himself or employ an agent. Shaking his head, he stood and slipped the mirror back beneath his robes. He thrust two fingers into his belt purse, fished out a coin and tossed it in the bowl beneath the crude statue of the little gray god. "In thanks for the use of your premises," he murmured and went out.

He stood a moment looking down the Ihman Katt toward the café Sidday Lir where Jastouk waited for him. I am sadly diminished, he thought. From tyrant and demiurge I have descended to merely lover and bought-love at that. Poor old Todich. There's nothing grand in hating a little man. He started walking, chuckling to himself at the image the words evoked.

2

Maksim dressed with great care, choosing a good gray robe meant to present the image of a man moderately in coin and moderate in most other things, a third rank sorcerer who could defend himself but wasn't much of a threat. He dressed his long hair in a high knot, had Jastouk paint it with holding gel until it gleamed like black-streaked pewter, then he thrust plain silver skewers through the knot. He loaded his fingers with rings. Quiet, moderate rings. He was a man it was safe to gull a little, but dangerous to irritate too much.

He finished buffing his nails, inspected them closely, dropped his hands into his lap. "Slave auction," he said. "Jasti, don't come. You don't want to see that place. Or smell it."

Jastouk smiled and took his buffer back, replaced it in his dressing kit. "The sun shines all the brighter for a cloud or two."

Snorting his irritation, Maksim got to his feet. He didn't want Jastouk along, but the hetairo had evaded him all morning, refusing to hear what he didn't mean to hear. He could order him to stay away, but he didn't dare go that far. Should he demand obedience, Jastouk would obey—and when Maksim got back to his rooms, he'd find Vechakek waiting with a graceful note of farewell and a bill for the hetairo's services. He wasn't ready for that, not yet. He knew he could easily find other company, but he wanted Jastouk. The hetairo excited him. Jastouk carried an aura of free-floating promise undefined but exquisitely seductive. Maksim didn't fool himself, it was part of a hetairo's portfolio, that promise never fulfilled, never denied so that hope lingered even after the sundering: *Someday someway I will find what I want, someday someway I will KNOW what I want.* It wasn't Jastouk and it was, it wasn't Brann and it was, he didn't know what it was.

The slavepens were a vast complex growing like mold over the hills south of the Great Market, apart from it, yet part of it, deplored by the genteel of Kukural but patronized by them along with others who didn't bother about the moral issues involved. The shyer visitors rented thin lacquer halfmasks from the dispensary just inside the portal, beast mask, bird, fantasy or abstraction, a face to show instead of the faces they wore in more respectable circumstances; the bold put on masks for the whimsy of the act or played to their vanity by separating themselves from the nameless troglodytes who bought drudges for kitchens and stables or selected more delicate fruit for the pleasure Houses. Despite a compulsive overdecoration in all the more public areas, the pens were a meld of stench and ugliness. That didn't matter, those who came to buy didn't notice the ugliness and ignored the wisps of stink that cut through the incense drifting about the private views and the auction room.

Carved in Twara-Teng high relief, the massive portal was intricately chased, heavily ornate, monumentally ugly. On sale days the syndics had the twin leaves of the Gate swung outward and pinned to angular dragonposts, exposing the serpentine geometrics of their inner surfaces. Maksim walked past them, his nostrils twitching. He loathed this place, but was almost pleased because its aesthetic qualities were so wonderfully suited to the acts within, as if the building and its ornamentation were designed by some heavy handed and deeply offended satirist. He paused at the dispensary and rented a falcon's mask for Jastouk, taking a black bear's muzzle for himself.

Masked and silent, they strolled among the cages for a while, waiting for the first sale to be called.

Jastouk was restless, uneasy. Like most of the hetairos working with Minders or from one of the established Houses, he'd been meat in a cage like those around him when he was a child, a brown-eyed blond with skin soft and smooth as fresh cream, knowing just enough to be terrified because he had no say in who bought him or what use they made of him. But that was long ago, longer than he liked to think about. The years were pressing in on him, leaving their traces on his face and body. The day would come when clients would ignore him for younger, fresher fare; new lovers would be hard to find, his price would drop, his standards go. He'd seen it happen to others again and again, thinking not me, no never. Anyway, that's a long time off, when I'm old, I won't be old for years and years. This place reminded him that those years were passing, each year faster than the last; it was time and more than time to begin planning, it was time and more than time to search for a lover he could stay with.

They passed a small blond boy, all eyes and elbows and numb terror.

Maksim felt the fingers on his arm tremble, caught the flicker of slitted eyes. He guessed at Jastouk's fears and felt pain at the loss of something he'd treasured, the golden gliding invulnerability of the hetairo. Jastouk had made several mistakes this morning, the biggest of them, underestimating the power of the buried anxieties this place would trigger, the effect they'd have on his judgment. Maksim looked at him with pity instead of lust and was saddened by that. For a moment he thought of keeping the hetairo with him now that Brann was gone and unlikely to return, but only for a moment. He was fond of Jastouk but he didn't like him much and he certainly wasn't in love with him; he hadn't been in love for . . . how long? It seemed like centuries. It was at least decades. The last time, when was it? Certainly before he went to Cheonea. Traxerxes from Phras. The ancient ache of parting felt like pressed flowers, the shape there but all the fragrance gone. Five stormy years and more pain and fury than . . . faded and gone. No one after Trax. He was too busy with his little Cheonenes, trying to shape them into something . . . no time, no energy, nobody. . . . Jastouk wasn't meant for longterm anything. He was a diversion, delightful but ephemeral.

No, don't think about it, he told himself and made a half-hearted pretense of inspecting the merchandise. Without his musings to distract him, outrage took hold, outrage and helplessness. If he were given the rule of things, he'd turn every slaver into pigmeat and lop the ears off parents who sold their children no matter what the reason. He'd outlawed slavery in Cheonea, skinned some slavers and confiscated some ships—how long that would hold he had no idea. He had to trust his farmers to keep the land clean; they were tough old roots; they had their claws on power and it'd take a lot to pry them loose. Ah well, it wasn't his responsibility any longer.

He pulled the mask away from his face, mopped at his brow and upper lip with the lace-edged linen wipe he twitched from his sleeve. He settled the mask into place, tucked the wipe away and strolled to the back of the room. Todichi Yahzi was in none of the cages. That might mean the kwitur was part of the first lot. If so, good, he thought, the sooner I'm out of here. . . .

Maksim set his back against the wall, smoothed a hand down the front of his robe, his stomach churning despite the calm detachment he was trying to project. Or it might mean Todich was already gone. Private sale. The dealer hadn't planned to offer private views, but anything might have happened since last night.

Jastouk leaned against him, responding to his tension, offering warmth and support—and a voiceless warning that he was broadcasting too much emotion.

Maksim sighed and did his best to relax. He was drilled in self-control, but excess was an integral part of his power. He drew strength from riding the ragged edge of disaster. Not now, he told himself. This is not the time for power, this is the time for finesse. Forty Mortal Hells, you great lumbering fool, finesse! He blinked sweat from his eyes and swept the room with an impatient glance. It was rapidly filling up. About a third of the newcomers wore masks, some of them far too rich to be part of the Dispenser's stock; it was early for such notables to be out, maybe that meant something, maybe it was just chance. The rest were stolid types with House Badges on dull tabards, some solitaire, some with a clutch of clerks in attendance. Maksim bent toward the smooth blond head resting against his ribs. "Tell me who's here," he murmured.

"Some of the masks I don't know." Jastouk's whisper was a thread of sound inaudible a step away. "They don't make the night circles, I think. Goldmask Hawk, that's an Imperial Hand from Andurya Durat; I don't know why he's here now; this is a meat market. The skilled slaves go in the evening sale. Black Lacquer Beetle with the sapphire bobs, she's Muda Paramount from the Pitna Jong Island group, that's out in the middle of the Big Nowhere, she usually culls a girl or two from these sales, or a boychild if he's very young and very beautiful. . . ." The creamy murmur went on as the stage began to show signs of life. Two sweepers emerged from behind tall black velvet curtains, swung brooms in graceful arcs, almost a dance as they came together, parted, then glided out, pushing before them small heaps of dust and other debris.

"The Hina mix in gray with the Shamany Patch . . . um, that patch is a lie, he hired it off the Shamany; everyone knows that but goes along with it. The Shamany's a miserable poxHouse, makes it taxcoin from those patchrents. I've seen him around in the dogends of morning, I think he runs a stable of child thieves; he's probably looking for new talent. . . ."

Three youths in black pajamas pushed a squat pillar out to the center of the stage, fitted a curving ramp onto it. The Block. Maksim shuddered, acid rising in his throat. It was over a century since he'd been present at a slave auction; it was two hundred and seventy-one years since he himself had been sold in one. The sight of it still made him want to vomit. As more sceneshifters brought in the Caller's Lectern and a cage that glittered like silver in the harsh light, he forced himself to listen to Jastouk.

"Rinta House, Gashturmteh, Aldohza, Yeshamm, all solitaire reps, they don't look like they're expecting much . . . um, BlackHouse is here, that's why. Not a good idea to bid too often against BlackHouse, bad things happen to you." Jastouk shuddered, his body rubbing against Maksim's.

The Caller came onstage and stood behind his Lectern, holding his hardwood rod a handspan above the sounder. He looked out across the milling crowd, then he hammered twice for attention, the harsh clacks breaking through the buzz of conversation, pulling those still drifting among the cages onto the auction floor. Maksim stepped away from the wall and onto the floor though he stayed at the back of the bidders. His size was an embarrassment sometimes, an advantage here. He couldn't be overlooked. He folded his arms across his broad chest and waited.

The first offerings were brought out to warm up the crowd and get them bidding, two half-grown males and a middle-aged woman; they went to clerks looking for muscle and a reasonable degree of health.

"We have several items fresh in from the South; the first is a healthy boy said to be Summerborn and in his sixth year." The Caller tapped lightly with his sounding rod. A Hina girl led a small M'darjin boy from behind the curtains, walked him up the ramp and whispered commands to him from behind the pillar, making him turn and posture, open his mouth and show his teeth, go through the ritual of offering himself for sale. He was frightened and awkward, but already he'd learned to keep silence and obey his handlers.

Blind unreasoning rage shook Maksim, rattled in his throat. Without warning he was that boy on the Block; all the intervening years were wiped away, his control was wiped away; another instant and he might have destroyed half of Kukural in his fury before he was himself destroyed by the forces that guarded the city.

A short sharp pain stabbed through the haze, came again and again; Jastouk had read him and reacted without thought or hesitation. He had a come-along hold on Maksim's hand, he was squeezing and pressing on it, generating such agony that it brought Maksim out of his fit, sweating and cursing under his breath.

"Bid," Jastouk whispered urgently. There was a faint film of sweat on his skin, a frantic, half-mad glare in his eyes. "If you want him, bid." He began massaging the hand he'd mistreated, still disturbed, his eyes half-closed, his breathing a rapid shallow pant.

"Could've been me," Maksim muttered.

"No. Stupid ordinary little git. Not you."

Maksim managed an unsteady chuckle. "I was a stupid ordinary little git, Jasti."

Jastouk shook his head in stubborn disagreement, but he said nothing.

The caller had already taken a few bids, starting low, six coppers; he worked that up to thirty coppers, coaxing small increments out of the motley group on the floor. All the boy offered was his youth; he wasn't especially charming or quick and the Caller continued noncommittal about his talents.

The BlackHouse Rep held up five fingers. Fifty coppers.

That jolted Maksim out of his brooding. He lifted both hands, showed six fingers. Though he'd recovered from that first shock of identification, he could not possibly let that boy go to BlackHouse; there was only one use they had for a child that age; it made him sick thinking about it.

The Rep looked around, scowling. Once they declared interest in an item, they weren't used to being challenged. He thought a moment, showed six fingers straight and a seventh bent. Sixty-five coppers.

Maksim showed eight.

The Rep looked at him a long moment, looked at the boy, shrugged and let the bid stand. Small coltish boys with no special charm or

talent were no rarity and he wouldn't be reprimanded for letting this
one go elsewhere.

There being no other bids, the Caller hammered the boy to Maksim
and the Hina girl led him off. He'd be held in the back until Maksim
brought the coin to pay the bid and the tag-fee.

Another boy was brought out, older this time, a stocky freckled
youth with a long torso and short legs. "Journeyman gardener," the
Caller announced and the bidding started again.

Maksim was annoyed at his loss of control, annoyed at circumstances, Fate, whatever, forcing his hand. What do I do with him? Send
him home? Chances are it was his own family sold him to some traveling slaver. Complicating my life. I certainly don't need complications,
it's bad enough now, what with Jastouk and his needs and Bramble
with those devilkids she dotes on and Kori coming out of school; I've
got to leave for Silili soon if I want to be in time to catch her before she
starts home. And now there's old Todich, gods know how much he's
going to cost me. Signs. All these signs. A closure coming. An era
pinched off. Turn of the Wheel. I damn well better get myself in order
or that Wheel will roll right over me. Offering to the Juggernaut,
smashed meat.

As the bidding continued around him and Jastouk grew restless and
unhappy at being ignored, Maksim brooded over the Signs. Sad, sad,
sad. Melancholy like the dead leaves eddying around their feet when
they came down from the Inn. The boy, what did he mean? Was he
setting free his baby self so he could move to true maturity? What was
maturity to someone like him who could extend his life as long as he
was interested in living? Was it the willingness to let go, to die? He
thought about death with a curious lack of emotion. To this point he'd
fought death with everything he had in him, fought death and won—
with Brann's help. Brann was gone. He thought about that. Odd feeling. Like an arm hacked off. Todich. A thread dangling from his past.
Tie it off. Send him home. I owe Todich passage home or I'm no better
than BlackHouse or old king Noshios I kicked out of Silagamatys. It
was a debt he had to pay, a payment he'd put off far too long. It was
going to cost. No more BinYAHtii to carry the load. Cost doesn't
matter. Ah well. . . .

Todichi Yahzi was brought on at the tail of the lot.

"Here we have an exotic item, looks like a cross between a macaque
and some sort of giant bug. It can talk a little and understand what you
tell it. Our readers have checked it over and it's no demon, so you don't

have to worry about waking up turned into a toad. . . ." The Caller chattered on, trying to stir up some interest as the handlers prodded the kwitur up the ramp and got him to crouch on the Block facing the audience. They poked at him, cursed him in angry hisses, but gave over their efforts at a sign from the Caller who didn't want his lack of spirit to become too apparent.

Maksim waited a moment. No other bids, bless Tungjii Luck. He thought it over, then he lifted a fist, opened up four fingers. Forty coppers. There was some stir in the others on the floor, but no more offers, no matter how cleverly the Caller wheedled them. Finally he gave up and hammered the kwitur to Maksim.

Maksim smoothed his fingers along the nape of Jastouk's neck. "Let's go," he said.

"That's it? It's that thing you came for?"

"Are you coming?"

"No. I think not."

"I'll see you tonight, then."

"Perhaps."

Maksim thought about coaxing him into a better humor. After a minute he decided better not. If it was ending, let it end.

3

Jastouk was gone when Maksim got back from provisioning the boat.

He couldn't send Todich home from Kukural; if he had unfriends elsewhere, he had spitesons on his back in Kukural who would sacrifice a firstborn to catch him when he was too whipped to defend himself. Spite and envy aside, the Managers who ran Kukural would like nothing better than setting their claws into a sorcerer of his rank; he couldn't call his breath his own if they got hold of him. Without BinYAHtii to give him support and control, he'd have to drain himself to a dishrag simply reaching the reality where he'd found the kwitur; sliding Todich there along the capillary he was holding open with will and bodyforce would drop him into coma for hours, maybe even a full day, it wasn't one of the easy reaches like the salamandri source or the tigermen's world. He'd be vulnerable to anyone who stumbled across him. A yearling bunny could make a meal of him. Better to sail deep into the Tukery and find himself a deserted rock where he could sleep off the throwjag and have a chance of waking with his souls still in his body.

He came back to the Inn weary and depressed, looking forward to a little cuddling and comforting, though Jastouk had turned cool and unforthcoming since the slave-auction. He walked into Jastouk's Minder.

Vechakek came from the SunParlor off the main lobby of the Inn; he stepped in front of Maksim, put his hand flat against Maksim's chest. "He's off," the Minder said. "He doesn't like being ignored, he won't put up with it. The association is terminated." He held up a sheet of paper folded once across the middle. "The account for services rendered. Pay now." He was a massive Henerman from Hraney, a half-mythical country supposed to be somewhere in the far west. His skin was pale mahogany, hard and hairless, polished to a high gleam; he wore his coarse black hair in twin plaits that hung beside his highnosed face; he had a taste for sarcasm and sudden violence that made folk walk tip-a-toe around him. Would-be clients tolerated his insolence; they had to if they wanted to arrange a liaison with Jastouk.

Maksim stared at him until he backed off a few steps. "Don't touch me again," he said quietly.

Vechakek's face went rigid and darkened across the cheekbones, but the Henerman couldn't quite work up the nerve to come at a man who was rumored to have few equals in power and none above him but the gods themselves. Then the anger washed out of his face and Vechakek was smiling, his pale blue eyes swimming with malice; he knew something. Something was going to happen, something which Maksim wouldn't like, no, not at all, which Vechakek planned to sit back and enjoy.

Maksim read that and wondered; the Henerman seemed very sure of what he knew; it was a thing to puzzle over but not just now. He held out his hand. "Give me the bill." He unfolded the paper, examined the list of charges; there were things he might have challenged, but in spite of the unhappy ending of this interlude, Jastouk was a dear and a delight; besides, he didn't feel like wasting energy on petty cheating. "Wait here," he said.

Todich and the boy were in the sitting room of his suite. The kwitur was curled up in one of the armchairs, either asleep or making an effective pretense of sleeping. The boy was standing by an open window, staring out into the foggy dank afternoon.

Maksim crossed to the fireplace and took down the battered leather box sitting on the mantle. As soon as he touched it, he knew the boy had been fooling with it, trying to get it open. A thief and incompetent at it. No doubt that was the reason his people sold him. Young idiot not to realize a sorcerer would have wards on anything he wanted left alone. Maksim put the box on a table beside Todichi's chair. He grinned down at the little creature. "Ah! Todich, you should have told him it was futile fooling around with this." No answer. The boy's shoulders twitched, but he didn't turn around.

Maksim opened the box and counted out the coins he needed from his rapidly diminishing store of expense money. He was going to have to tap one of his caches before he started to Silili; what with the auction and Brann's call on his purse, he had barely enough coin left to pay his bill at the Inn. Other years he'd have added a handsome tip when he paid Jastouk off; not this time, he couldn't afford it and the hetairo hadn't earned it. He divided the fifty Kukral aureats Vechakek demanded into four piles, wrapped them first in the bill, then in a clean sheet of writing paper. He sealed the ends with red wax from his private store, stamped his mark into the wax and spun a small bind about the packet, keying it to Jastouk's touch. If Vechakek intended to take his percentage before he handed over the coin, he was out of luck. It was a small favor, perhaps meaningless, all Maksim could do for his temporary lover—let the hetairo get full measure for once, not just what his Minder decided to hand over.

He tugged at the cord and gave the packet to the maidservant who came to answer the bell. "Take this to the man in the SunParlor," he said. He gave her a five cupra piece for her pains, watched, amused, as she pushed the broad coin into her sleeve, flirted her lashes at him, then bounced from the room.

He brushed his hands together, brushing away Jastouk and Vechakek with the nonexistent dust. For a moment he stood gazing at the door, then he sighed and crossed to the largest of the armchairs. When he was settled, his feet comfortable on the hassock, he laced his fingers together across the hard mound of his stomach and contemplated the narrow back of the M'darjin boy. Occupied with Jastouk's sulks and making the boat ready for a trip into the Tukery, he'd ignored his new acquisition, noticed the boy only as a minor irritation to be brushed aside when he got underfoot. With Jastouk gone and the trip imminent, it was time to find out what he'd got. "Come here, boy."

The boy came slowly away from the window. When he reached the hassock, he fell on his face, elbows out, hands clasped behind his head.

"Get off your belly, buuk." Maksim looked at the cringing figure with distaste; he understood why the boy was that way, but he didn't have to like it—and it woke painful memories he'd tried hard to erase. "What's your name?"

The boy scrambled to his feet. "Davindolillah." He looked sideways at Maksim, added, "Saör."

"So you're a thief."

Davindo opened his eyes wide. "No."

"And a liar." Some of his sourness washed away; the boy amused him. "A bad liar," he said, cutting off Davindo's parade of indignation before he could get it going. "By which I mean an incompetent liar. Unconvincing. Where did the slavers get you, Davindolillah? By which I mean: what is your homeland?"

"Majimtopayum," the boy said, pride thrumming in his voice. "The Country of the River Which is Wide as the Sea. My father is Falama Paramount, he has five hundred wives and his wives each have five hundred cows and five hundred boats and five hundred acres each of beans and maize and taties," he boasted, piling improbability on improbability, head back, eyes flashing, strutting where he stood. He shook himself and mimed a becoming humility. "I am not the eldest son. . . ."

Maksim suppressed a smile. The boy could prove amusing enough to earn the coppers he cost.

"And I am not the youngest son." Davindo slapped at his skinny chest. "Only the favorite. There was weeping and wailing and tearing of hair when the slavers stole me from my father's house. When I was born, the Wamanachi prophesied over me, the Great Wamanachi said of me, I shall be Puissant and Terrible to the Enemies of the Land, inside and out. I shall be Sung down the Ages, Father to many sons, Warchief to my people, Paramount among Paramounts. That is what he said."

"Most interesting. No. Be silent, Davindolillah." He inspected the boy more closely than he'd done before.

Davindo's small size and round face had fooled him as they had the slavers. The Caller had rated him about six. Maksim measured him against his memories of himself at six and rejected the number; he was at least double that though still on the child's side of puberty, a tough, clever little streetrat, defending pride and person with everything in him. Maksim saw the desperation behind the boasting, knew it intimately because it was his own when he was five, six, ten; it made him sick and turned him crueler than he'd meant to be.

"If I sent you back, would your people simply sell you again?"

The boy pressed his lips together. Anger flashed in his black eyes. His first impulse was to attack with the slashing invective he'd acquired in his home streets, but he'd learned enough about being a slave to keep a tight rein on his temper. "I was stole," he muttered.

"As you say. I am going to give you your papers. No. Be quiet. I don't intend to discuss my reasons with you. If you wish to go home, I will pay your passage and put you on a ship with a master I trust to make sure you get there. If you prefer to stay in Kukural, I will arrange schooling for you or an apprenticeship. Well?"

Davindo's eyes shifted from the door to the window. His pale pink tongue flicked over his lips. "What do you want me to say?"

"I know what you think you want, but I'm not going to cut you loose; I've got enough guilt spotting my souls, I don't need more. Do you have a talent or an inclination that you'd like to pursue?"

Davindo looked sly. "You teach me."

"Do you know what I am?"

"The beast told me. Sorceror."

"Yes. You have no Talent."

"How do you know? You haven't even looked at me."

"Talent shouts. You don't have to look for it. I can hear it across a city, young Davindo. There's nothing I can teach you. Don't take that as an insult; you wouldn't blame a singing coach for not training you if you couldn't hold a tune. Do I send you home?"

"No." Davindo swallowed, kicking at the rug. After a minute he squared his narrow shoulders, stared defiantly at Maksim. "As long as I'm here, I might as well take a look round the place."

"Wise of you. Who would neglect the opportunities that come his way is a clothhead not worth the name of man. Can you read?"

"Of course I can, I had teachers since I could walk. Um, but not this jabber they speak up here."

"Right." Maksim swallowed a smile, his need to deflate the boy's air castles dissipated by his appreciation of Davo's deft footwork. "The more languages you can read and write, the more control you have over your circumstances." He moved his feet, freeing a part of the hassock. "Sit down. School or tutor?"

Davindo hesitated, then dropped warily beside Maksi's ankles. "Tutor."

"I hear. You didn't answer me. Do you have a talent or an inclination you'd like to pursue?"

"I will be Warleader in my time."

"So you said. I take it that means you have no scholarly interests?"

Davindo twisted his face into a scornful grimace, but said nothing.

"So. Apprenticeship not scholarship. I'd best find you a place in one of the guilds. Merchant, military, seaman, priest, artisan, player, singer, musician, thief, beggar, which? There are others, but those are the chief."

"Thieves have a guild?"

"They don't put it about, but they do take apprentices and they have teaching masters who'll work your tail off. That amuses you. Hmm. I suppose it is funny to see the darkside aping the bright, but it's useful. If you go that route, you'll learn something and they'll house and feed you, which is more than you can expect outside. And there's this, if you don't have Family here to back you, you'd better have a Guild or you're fair game for the Pressgangs supplying meat to the pleasure Houses and the Whips who run the childgangs and anyone else with a taste for boys and the power to gratify his whims. And there's Black-House. Let me warn you, keep clear of BlackHouse.

Davindo shivered. "They told me at the Pens."

"Yes." Maksim closed his eyes. He was tired, but taking care of the boy—finding a tutor, arranging the apprenticeship, setting up a trust account to support Davo while he was being taught, all that meant it would be hours before he could rest. He knew why he was doing it; he was using Davindo to cancel a portion of his guilt for abandoning Todich, using the boy as a parlor wipe to polish up his amour-propre. "Choose," he said, impatience sharpening his voice.

"Thief." Davindo looked defiant, as if he expected Maksim to try talking him into something more respectable.

"You're sure?"

"Yes."

"So be it." Maksim got wearily to his feet, crossed to the door. "You should be set by tomorrow evening. I'll pass over your papers and after that you're on your own."

Davindo bit at his lip. "Why?" he burst out. "Why are you doing this?"

Maksim pulled the door open, looked over his shoulder at Davindo. There was no way he could answer that question, the boy was too

young, too limited to understand the things that drove a man. "Call it
a whim," he said and left.

4

Late that night Maksim went up the path behind the Inn to the flat
where he'd sent Brann and Jaril on their way. Using a broom he'd
borrowed from a tweeny at the Inn, he swept the stone as clean as he
could, then he drew a circle with a length of soft chalk. Working
quickly, he finished the sketchy pentacle; precision wasn't important
for what he planned, there was little danger in casting mantaliths.
What he wanted, what he needed was privacy.

The chalk had a tar base so the damp from the fog didn't wash it
away; he stripped off the cotton gloves he'd used to keep it from clinging to his hands and knelt at the heart of the pentacle. He drew out a
soft leather pouch and twitched the knot loose that held the drawstrings tight. Muttering the manta chanta under his breath, he poured
the rhombstones into the palm of his left hand. He closed his eyes,
visualized the reality he needed to reach, then spoke the word:
WHEN? And spoke other words: WHAT DAY? With a snap of thumb
against finger on his free hand, he shouted the Trigger, his deep voice
booming through the fog, echoing back at him, the overtones lovely in
their murmurs and their silences. When the echoes died, he threw the
mantaliths and read their answer.

Two days hence. Third hour past noon.

At that time Todichi Yahzi's home reality would in some inexplica-
ble way be closer to this one, easier to reach, the membranes between
the two softer, thinner, the number of realities between them lessened
somehow. He passed his hands over the stones, murmured the releasing manta chanta, the blessing on the mantaliths, the delivery of his
gratitude for the answer he'd received.

He gathered up the stones and the broom and went away, leaving the
rain to wash away his traces.

5

Maksim raised sail an hour before dawn on the chosen day; Todichi
Yahzi sat in the bow of the boat, looking out across the black water, his
back to his one time master. He hadn't said a word to anyone since he
left the Pens, his anger was too deep. As Maksim sent the small boat

scooting south into the Tukery, he glared at the kwitur and choked on his guilt and smoldered with an anger of his own—and sometimes was sad at losing an almost-friend.

By the time the sun rose they were deep into the narrow crooked waterways. Already he had crept through the patches of dense fog that swung in complex orbits around and about the Tukery, fog inhabited by howling souls cast out from Kukural, souls spilling over with fury and despair, doing their futile best to drive him onto razor-edged rocks or into quicksands that could swallow a boat between one breath and the next. Twice he'd driven off ambushing bands, throwing fire and dissolution at them, pulling their sailing canoes apart under them and dropping them into schools of hungry needlefish. He didn't know exactly what he was looking for, he just sailed on and on, waiting for his Talent to seize onto a place.

Through all this Todichi Yahzi sat silent and brooding in the bow, ignoring Maksim, staring at things only he could see.

When the sun was directly overhead, Maksim, saw a rocky islet with vents in its precipitous sides voiding steam into the cold dank air; it was a truncated cone rising about a hundred yards above the water. Here and there swatches of orange and faded-olive lichens interrupted the drab dun stone; near the vents ferns were lush lacy patches of a green so vibrant it hurt the eyes. There was a small halfmoon of sandy beach on the north side, the side he came on first; he circled the islet and came back to the beach, drove the nose of the boat up onto the sand and tossed the anchor overside. He slipped his arms through the straps of his rucksack and got cautiously to his feet. "Todich, you think you can make it to the top?"

The kwitur dragged himself up, moving with painful slowness. Maksim watched, frowning, angry at first, then amused. "Ooohhh, tragedy, the very image of it." He laughed for the first time in days, the sound booming back at him from the hollows of the cliff. He held to the mast, his weight keeping the boat steady as Todich clambered out.

The kwitur sank ankle-deep into the damp sand. He hummed his distaste for the clinging stuff and continued cursing in his insect voice as he trudged to the rock and began picking his way carefully upward, climbing with the steady sureness of his kind.

Maksim contemplated the slope and considered snapping himself to the top; his mass and relatively high center of gravity made him less than sure-footed on rock faces and he was beginning to feel the weight of his years despite his skill at using earthfire to boil off the poisons of aging. He dropped overside into the shallow water, pulled the boat higher on the sand and moored her to a handy rock; he wasn't about to trust an anchor here in the Tukery.

He got to the top, weary, shaking, scraped about like a stew carrot. Todich was crouching in a pitiful knot, looking more miserable and mistreated than ever. Maksim snorted. Todich was overdoing the victim to the point of absurdity. He began building a small fire with the coal and tinder he'd hauled up in his backpack. In the middle of this business, he looked up to see Todich watching him. He'd never been sure he read the kwitur's minimal expressions with anything like accuracy, but he thought he saw a flash of amusement, even affection there. That startled him so much he forgot about fanning the tiny fire and it went out on him. Exaggeration? Resentment caricatured beyond absurdity? Beyond? Absurdity? THAT LITTLE GIT WAS PAYING HIM BACK FOR THOSE TEN YEARS AND HAVING SOME FUN AT THE SAME TIME!!! "You! YOU! You perfidious inglorious diabolic old fraud."

"Slow," Todichi hoomed. "Got old, han't you."

"Yeh, you right. Looks like any brains I had've turned to suet." He dug into the backpack, tossed a blanket to the kwitur. "You're shivering. You'd better wrap this round you till I can get this damn fire lit."

The reluctant coals finally caught. Maksim set a pan of water on a tripod, watched it a moment to see that the tripod was stable and the fire was going to keep burning, then he sat on his heels and contemplated Todichi Yahzi. "Tell me about it," he said and settled himself to listen.

6

They talked and sat in a shared silence and talked some more, drank tea when the water boiled, made peace with memory while they waited for the appointed hour.

When the time came, Maksim sent Todichi Yahzi home as gently as he could, then collapsed beside the remnants of the fire.

7

When he struggled back to awareness, at first he couldn't remember where he was or what had happened to deplete him so thoroughly.

Memory crept back slowly, so slowly he was disturbed; his mind was not working right.

He tried to sit up.

He was tied.

His arms were tight against his body, his hands were pressed against his thighs; ropes passed round and round him; he couldn't wiggle a finger; he could barely breathe.

He tried to speak.

His tongue was bound, not by ropes but by a force he couldn't recognize.

He tried to mindcall a firesprite to work on the ropes, something he was able to do before he could read his name.

His mind was bound.

He sweated in claustrophobic terror until he managed to override that bloodfear, then he gathered will in shoulder and neck and got his head up off the stone.

Fog.

Like white soup, ghosts bumping about in it, swirling about him and whoever had caught him.

He ignored the ghosts.

Jastouk, he thought. I talked in my sleep and he betrayed me. He wept and was furious at himself for weeping.

Time passed.

He couldn't feel his body or count the beats of his heart.

There was nothing he could use to tick off the minutes, nothing to tell him if a day had passed, a week, or only an hour.

He eased his head down.

He fought the helplessness that was worse than the claustrophobia. He called on two centuries of discipline, then waited with the patience of a cat at a mousehole. His captors had given him time to collect himself. Stupid of them. Or maybe they didn't care. Overconfidence? He produced a wry smile. I hope it is overconfidence.

Time passed.

The ghosts backed off.

New shapes solidified in the fog.

He heard a foot scrape against stone and decided he was still on the islet.

Someone spoke.

He heard the voice but couldn't make out the words.

Answers came from several points.

He strained to make out what was being said, but it was as if his ears were stuffed with something that deafened him just enough to make sure he learned nothing from what he heard.

The exchanges continued.

It began to feel like ritual rather than speech.

He couldn't tell if that was a trick of his fettered mind or something real. This irritated him, his incapacity was like nettles rubbed against his skin.

By the Gods of Fate and Time, I will make you suffer for this, he thought at them; he struggled to shout it; his jaw ached with the need to shout at them.

The binding held.

Not a sound came out, not a sound!

With such a cork shoved in his mouth, need was building up in him.

He was going to explode.

He visualized himself blowing apart, hot burning pieces of him rushing outward, colliding with the things out there prattling like fools, colliding with them and ashing them.

I'm getting giddy.

Gods of Fate and Time! Keep hold of yourself.

Think of Vechakek and Jastouk.

I owe them.

I'll pay them.

I pay my debts. Always.

Feeling trickled back into him.

The chill of the damp stone struck up through his body, sucking away what warmth he had left.

He pressed his fingers into the meat of his thigh and won a little space.

He worked his fingers, trying to gain enough movement for a simple gesture.

The stone softened under him, flowed up around him.

Lumpy, faceless elementals like animate gray clay lifted him and carried him down a spiral ramp that created itself before them.

Complaining about the abrasions of the sand in subsonic groans like rock rubbing against rock, they lumbered across the beach and rolled him into his boat as if he were a dead fish.

He managed to keep his head from crashing into the deck but collected bruises over every part of his body.

Fog billowed about him.

Ghosts hoomed in the distance, frightened off by those other entities, whatever they were, who stood on air about the boat, thickenings in the fog, featureless, serpentine, bipedal.

He didn't recognize them.

Smell, aura, everything about them was unfamiliar.

He wasn't surprised.

The layered realities were infinite in number and each sorcerer had his own set of them in addition to those that they all shared.

His head wasn't working right, but he settled grimly to learning what he could about them.

Two figures dropped onto the deck.

They dragged him into the hutch and laid him out on the sleeping pad.

They wore black leather top-to-toe like the Harpish and black leather cowls with only the eyes cut out.

They weren't Harpish.

Forty Mortal Hells, who are you and who is running you?

Amortis?

Gods of Fate and Time, I hope not.

She'd watch me burn and throw oil on the fire.

They tossed a blanket over him and went out.

He felt the boat float free.

She shuddered, yawed, rolled.

Those two didn't know codswallop about sailing.

They got the sails up finally and the boat underway.

Maksim settled to work trying to free his hands a little.

There were gestures so minimal they required almost no space but could focus sufficient energy to cut him free.

The way those numb-butts were handling the boat, there was a good chance he'd end up on the bottom of some Tukery strait, food for prowling needlefish.

The rope was spelled to cling.

Every millimeter of freedom he won from them was gone as soon as the spell reacted.

He fought the ropes as long as he had strength, then he slept.

He nudged at the spells that bound him.

He tried to work out their structure.

He couldn't counter them without word or gesture, but knowing that structure would let him act the first chance he got.

He probed and pried, sucked in his gut, drove his thumbs into his thigh muscles and got nowhere.

The bonds holding him responded automatically and effectively to every effort.

The boat went unhindered through the Tukery despite the clumsiness of the crew.

Not long after sundown he felt the lengthening swells as the boat broke into the Notoea Tha.

He heard the basso wail of a powerful following wind that drove them northwest, away from Kukural.

He stopped being afraid of drowning or dying, but his determination to get out of this trap only grew stronger.

Late at night, the boat hove to, the sails came crashing down.

The two pseudo Harpish dragged Maksim up on the deck and left him there.

Their companions swung in slow circles overhead, maintaining the same distance between them always, no matter how they moved.

The boat was bobbing beside a dark, rakish ship, a Phrasi Coaster, ocean-going and river-capable, a favorite of smugglers, pirates and those merchants who needed speed and a shallow draft from their ships.

He could hear men talking; they spoke Phrasi.

A davit swung over the rail and a cargo net was winched down.

The net settled over him, dragging back and forth as the boat rocked with the heave of the sea.

The pseudo Harpish loaded him into the net.

He was hauled up, jerk by jerk, the winch squealing with every turn of the spindle.

As the sailors caught hold of the net to pull him inboard, a wisp of smoke floated by him.

Woodsmoke?

He muscled his head around and looked down.

His boat was burning.

He fumed.

Phrasi sailors hauled him over the rail and dumped him on the deck.

Wisps of smoke rose past the rail.

There were flickers of red on the white sails that rose as the ship prepared to go away from there.

He cursed and struggled to break loose.

He was fond of that boat. There were good memories laid down in it, memories of Brann and the Tukery, Jal Virri and Kukural, days full of brightness scudding before the wind with the sails bellied out, the sheets humming.

Seven pseudo Harpish came for him.

They rolled him out of the net and carried him to a crate near the foremast.

They dumped him in the crate and nailed it shut around him.

They chanted in their buzzing incomprehensible langue and tightened another layer of bonds about him.

He was smothered into unconsciousness.

III.   KORIMENEI PIYOLSS

Silili on the double island Utar-Selt
    Korimenei at the end of her
    schooling, goes through a
    passing-out ordeal and
    starts on her journey to free
    her brother.
also:
The Eidolon of her Sleeping
    Brother
The Old Man of the Mountain
The Gods Geidranay
    Groomer of Mountains
    Isayana Birthmistress
    Tungjii Luck
    and Assorted Others
Spirit Guides.
Shahntien Shere,
    headmistress
Firtina Somak, Kori's best friend
    at school

1

"No! You can't come back. Not yet."

The eidolon of the sleeping boy was the size of a mouse; he lay curled in a crystal egg that floated in the darkness over Korimenei Piyolss. She saw him whether her eyes were open or shut, so she kept them open. She moved impatiently on her narrow bed. "Why?" She kept her voice low. The walls between this sleeping cell and the next were paper and lath; after ten years at the school she knew well enough how sound carried. "I thought you wanted out of there soonest possible."

"And then what?" Her brother looked like the seven-year-old boy the Sorceror Settsimaksimin had spelled to sleep; his body hadn't changed a hair. His mind certainly had. Those three words aren't a boy's complaint, she thought, he's so bitter. "Dance to the Chained God's contriving?" he spat at her. "No!"

"I don't see how you can change that."

"Why do you think I had you do all that work on the Great Talismans?"

"I didn't want to ask. I didn't know what might be listening."

"So?" there was an acid bite in the single word, a touch of impatience.

"And what does that mean?"

"Use your head, Kori. If HE listened, the asking itself would tell HIM all HE wanted to know."

"Then how can we do anything?"

"If, Kori. Did you hear me? IF. Listen. HE has BinYAHtii now, HE got it off Settsimaksimin after Brann and the Blues took him, but I don't know how much good that's doing HIM, that stone is hard to handle even if you keep it fed." He stopped talking. His body never moved, nonetheless, Kori thought she felt a shudder pass through him. "HE has been keeping it fed. I don't want to talk about that. HE's a god. I don't know all that means but for sure HE has limitations, otherwise HE could've squashed Settsimaksimin without bending an eyelash. Listen, listen isn't it true when old Maksim had BinYAHtii round his neck, didn't he keep Amortis on the hop? I could feel how nervous Amortis made HIM. What I've been thinking: if I could get hold of the right Talisman, I could block HIM, keep HIM off me. Off you too."

Korimenei closed her eyes, pressed her lips together. She couldn't blame him, not really, and it was her fault he was stuck in that cave, but including her was so obviously an afterthought that it hurt. It hurt a lot. A belated tact disastrously untactful. Oh gods and gunk, I'm as bad a phrasemaker as Maks is, even if I can't roar like him.

Her enforced sojourn at the school was almost over. Just that morning the runner Paji came to the exercise court to say Kori should come to the Shahntien's office at the end of second watch tomorrow. He didn't say what it was about. She didn't need telling. It was her graduation exercise. She'd been strung out for days now, waiting for Shahntien Shere to decide what it would be and when it would happen. Tomorrow, the next day, maybe the next, then she'd be free to leave. She wanted to go to Trago as soon as the Shahntien cut her loose, she wanted to go as fast as she could for the cave where her brother slept in crystal waiting for her to touch him free, she wanted to go NOW, not after some indefinite period devoted to some sort of nonsense Trago had dreamed up. How sane could he be, after all, confined to that stupid crystal for so many years? Three, nearly four years blocked off from everything outside. Then he finally managed to free his mind enough to reach her. Six years since and all he could do was look over her shoulder. Does he visit other places too? Does he look through other eyes? She was appalled at herself when she felt a twinge of jealousy. "What do you want, Tré? Do you really want me to hunt up a talisman and fetch it to you?"

"Yes, Kori. Yes yes yes. Please. The one called Frunzacoache."

"All right, if you say so. Why that one?"

He ignored the question and went on, "Frunzacoache disappeared years ago, but I found it. It's in the torbaoz of a Rushgaramuv shaman. He doesn't know what he's got. There's barely enough magic in him to light a match. He has a vague idea it's a thing of power, so he hides it away down at the bottom of his essence pouch. If you pattern up a good copy and sink some energy into it, he'll never know the real thing's gone. Bring it to me, Kori. Pleeease?"

The eidolon winked out before Korimenei could say anything. She lay staring into the darkness where it'd hung. It was a long time before she went back to sleep.

2

Korimenei pulled the half-hitch tight, glanced across the bay at the paired islands Utar-Selt, then left the stubby pier and started up the mountainside.

She was lanky and tall, thin for her height with long narrow hands and feet that looked too big for her. She had fine curly flyaway hair the color of dead leaves, a pale gray-brown with shines of an equally pale gold when the sun touched it at the proper angle. Her eyes were a light gray-green like shadowed water; her skin was thin and pale with a spray of small freckles across a longish nose and high broad cheekbones; every ebb and flow of blood showed through, to her frequent embarrassment.

She wore old canvas trousers frayed and soft as velvet from many washings, trousers inherited from a student long gone, and a sleeveless pullover with a high neck, several badly botched patches, assorted pulls and snags. Over this she'd pulled on a knee-length canvas coat with huge pockets and wide cuffs; it was slightly newer than the trousers, but even a ragman would turn up his nose at it. On her feet she wore a pair of heavy-soled sandals, fairly new but as scuffed and scarred as her ankles. She was carrying an old leather rucksack, not heavily loaded, with a thick blanket rolled into a tight cylinder and tied below it.

She climbed the Old Man's Mountain, walking along an unobtrusive but well maintained path. Much of the time she was moving through lowslope woods, maple, beech, aspen, oak, the morning light glowing through leaves like translucent slices of jade, dark and light, gold and green, the leaf shadows moving mottles on the red earth of the path. A hundred kinds of songbirds flittered and swooped over her, hidden by the leaves, singing extravagant solos, or blending in pleasant cacophonies. Now and then the path moved out of the trees across an area of open slope or along a cliff edge where she had a clear view out over the bay.

Halfway to the Old Man's Meadow, she stopped walking and turned to gaze at Silili; she could see the gilded roofs of the school buildings peeping through the dark yews, oaks and willows planted along the walkways and in the water-gardens. She was startled by how much of the south slope of Utar's Temple Mountain the school took in. There were no vistas inside the walls, just gardens like green gems for teaching and meditation, so it was impossible to judge the size of the place when one was in it. She'd known the school was important from the way that merchants treated her when they saw the patch sewn on her shirt, but this was the first time she'd had any real idea how important it had to be. Only the Temple grounds were larger. You did me well, Maks my friend. I suppose I'll have to thank you for it. She sighed again and trudged on. Hmm. I expected to see you before this. Well, busy busy, I suppose, setting the world right. She'd gotten very fond of the man and was a little hurt because he hadn't come.

Watersong filtered through the trees; she went over a hump on the mountain's flank and looked down into an ancient cut at a stream leaping along a series of steps, swirling about black and mossy boulders. The path continued along the rim of the ravine, crossed over it on an elegant wooden bridge, each timber handhewn and hand-polished and fitted together with wooden pegs and lashings of thin tough rope. On the far side the path curved through a stand of ancient oaks that almost immediately opened onto the Old Man's Meadow.

His small neat hut was across the meadow, half-hidden by the droopy limbs of a monster oak; like the bridge the hut was built of ax-smoothed planks with a roof of cedar shakes. Korimenei pulled off the rucksack, rummaged inside and took out the gift she'd brought for the Old Man, a half pound of the most expensive tea found in Silili Market; it was wrapped in a swatch of raw silk and tucked into a carved ebony box.

The Old Man was kneeling between rows of onion sets, pulling gently at grass and tiny weeds growing around them. Ghost children ran in silent games among the dying vines on the beanpoles, ghost grandmothers so ragged they were little more than sketches watched over them, ghost grandfathers squatted beside the Old Man, chatting with him, pointing out weeds for him. A strangled man ghost hovered close to the trees, watching Korimenei with frightening intensity. A headless woman, her battered head clutched under one arm, came rushing at Korimenei, veered off, trailing behind her an anguished wail more felt than heard. Korimenei ignored all of them, stopped at the end of a row and waited politely for the Old Man to reach her. Her first sight of the ghosts of Silili had startled her, Owlyn ghosts stayed decently among the treetops until they dissipated, but habit and time had made her accustomed to the sometimes vocal and always present dead.

The Old Man settled onto his haunches, his dirt-crusted hands dropping onto his thighs. Morning light cool as water and filled with dancing motes picked up every wrinkle, wart, and hair on his still face. He blinked, mild ancient eyes opening and closing with slow deliberation; with his shaggy brown robe, the tufts of white hair over his ears, his round face, he looked like a large horned owl. He also looked harmless and not too bright, but there were many stories about him and certain brash intruders who thought they could force his secrets from him. "Saöri?" His voice was the dry rustle of dead leaves.

Korimenei bowed and held out the chest. "This unworthy student will be much honored if the Saör considers accepting this handful of miserable tea."

He took the chest, tucked it into a pocket of his robe. "Leave the mountain as you found it," he said.

"This one hears and swears it will be so, Saör."

He grunted, swung round still squatting and began pulling grass from around a set.

Korimenei flared her narrow nostrils, but swallowed the laughter bubbling in her throat; the Old Man could be touchy about his dignity at the most unexpected times. She resettled the rucksack and began walking again, following the path.

3

The tiny meadow was stony and dry in its upper reaches. An ancient conifer had fallen to a storm a decade or so past and now lay denuded of bark, slowly rotting into the earth it had grown from. Thinner now and noisier, the Old Man's Stream curved around the stubby root-shield and squeezed past boulders at the bottom of the roughly circular meadow and disappeared into shadows under the shivering gold leaves of a grove of aspen saplings. Korimenei shrugged out of the rucksack, set it on the dead trunk. She wriggled her body, reached high, stretching all over as she did so, stayed on her toes for a long long moment, then exploded out a sigh and dropped on her heels.

She pulled loose the thongs binding her dream-blanket to the ruck-sack, shook it out and spread it on the grass. Toward the end of her first year at the school, she'd bought wool in Silili Market. She dyed it and wove it into a dreampattern blanket which she kept wrapped in silk for the day she'd need it, for now. She sat on the trunk and smiled at the sharp-angled patterns and the brilliant colors. I did good, she thought, pleased with herself. She unbuckled her sandals, closed her eyes and flexed her toes; the earth was cool and silky against her soles and she had a curious sense that she was momentarily cut off from the flow of time, that she was a part of the Mountain. Her mind drifted into phrasemaking, ephemerally eternal, eternally ephemeral. The Mountain and the life parasited on it changed, died, was continually reborn. She sighed and yanked herself back to her own purposes. Set-tling herself on the blanket, she folded her legs and dropped her hands onto her knees. Her mind drifted to yesterday. . . .

#

Shahntien Shere sat behind her desk and frowned at Korimenei. She was a tall woman, thin, her abundant gray hair dressed in a soft knot at the nape of a long neck. She wore a simple white dress with close fitting sleeves and a high soft collar, over that an unadorned sleeveless robe of heavy black silk. It was her customary dress, effectively elegant, under-lining her authority without making too oppressive a point of it. Abruptly, unexpectedly, she smiled, her dark eyes narrowing into in-verted echoes of her mouth. "The ten years are up," she said. "Of course you know that. You've done well, better than I expected. Maksim is most pleased with you, though he seems rather shy about telling you himself." She paused, rubbed the tips of her fingers together. "I don't know what his plans are, Kori; I expect he'll show up when he's ready. I've taught you all I can," the ends of her thin mouth tucked deeper into their brackets, turned into a mirror image of her earlier smile, *"All anyone can, I think. The rest is up to you."*

Korimenei laced her fingers together and stared down at them. She couldn't think of anything to say, so she said nothing.

"Yes," the Shahntien said, *"and that is essentially what this is about."* She sighed. *"To it, then. I have consulted yarrow and water and tortoise-shell and considered your family lines. Your people are . . . um . . . remarkably untouched by Talent, always excepting that imposed by the Chained God on his priests; however, that has nothing to do with you since the priests are always male and as far as I can determine chosen by the God himself without much concern about any inborn Gifts. Your Talent has come to you from your Ancestress Harra Hazhani, the Rukka Nagh; there were, no doubt, other women before you with much the same abilities, but things being the way they are among your people, the Gifts were denied and they withered without being used."* She tapped her nails on the desk top, a tiny clatter like a flurry of wheatsized hail against a window. *"An obscenity. . . ."* She spread her hands flat on the desk, frowned at them. *"Which is a digression . . . I'm explaining too much. It's not needed. More than that, it's probably counterproductive. You are to go to the Old Man's Mountain across the bay. You are to find a sufficiently quiet and secluded place. You are to fast and meditate for three days. Do nothing. Accept what comes to you. Forget nothing. You won't understand most of it now, you don't know enough about the world or yourself. Accept for the moment what I tell you, it comes from my own experience, Kori Heart-in-Waiting; you will return again and again to this time, finding new richness, new meaning in it."* She straightened her back, looking past Korimenei. *"Again I explain too much. You seem to have that effect on me, young Kori. Go and do."*

#

Korimenei settled into her fast-vigil. She sought to re-find that sense of connectedness with air and earth, with plant and beast that she'd gotten as a gift for those few moments when she sat on the trunk and dabbled her feet in the dust.

The sun rose higher, dust motes danced in the rays that slid through openings in the needle canopy above and behind her. She was all sensory data, perception without self-awareness. Then lost it. Then had it again. Then lost it. And lost it. And sank into self-doubt and sourness.

Shadow shrank about her, hot yellow sunlight crept toward the blanket, came over it, touched her knees, her fingers. She rubbed at her eyes, looked up. The sun was almost directly overhead. "Three days," she said aloud. "Three days."

She rocked on her buttocks, straightened her legs, flexed and loosened the muscles in them until the stiffness was gone. She stood, stretched, shivered all over. Two hours only and already the exercise seemed futile, a fanatic's flagellation of body and spirit. She let her arms drop. There you go again, you silly maid, aping Settsimaksimin, roaring phrases in your alleged mind. Her fast had begun this morning with a breakfast of juice and a hardroll. She was hungry, her stomach was grumbling and she had that all-over sense of debilitation she got when she went too long without eating. Three days, she thought again and just managed to stifle an obscenity, one of the many she'd picked up when she was a rebel child wandering Silagamatys' waterfront when she was supposed to be in bed.

She fished a tin cup from the rucksack, filled it at the stream and sat on a flat rock with her feet in the water. The stream went down a long shallow slide here, with a steady brushing hum punctuated occasionally by the pop of bubbles or a troutling breaking surface. She sipped from her cup and watched the clear cold stream smooth as glass slip over her bare toes. The sun was hot on her head and shoulders; behind her she could hear the buzz and mumble of insects. Her stomach cramped. She closed her eyes and willed the nausea to go away. It was mostly imagination, she knew that well enough, but knowing didn't seem to help. Three days. I'll be a rag. Why am I doing this?

She rinsed the cup, filled it again and took it back to the blanket. She lowered herself onto the dreampattern, set the cup beside her and folded her long legs into the proper configuration. Ten years she'd spent learning control of her Talent. That's all it is, this school, Maksim told her once, control. And maybe expanded possibility. Maybe. She could testify to the truth of that now. Control and the limits of control. She told herself she knew her limits, she told herself she had earned a degree of confidence in her skill and in her strength. She'd survived each trial so far, but every new step was a new threat. She didn't believe there could be more for her to learn; the last two years she'd spent consolidating what she'd dredged up out of herself during the first eight years of her schooling. She didn't want to believe there was more power out there waiting for her to tap into it; she was afraid of touching any hotter, wilder sources. There were times during the past ten years when she was working hot that the power she was shaping threatened to consume her. She managed to hang on, but each time was worse than the last, each time she came closer to losing it, a lesson she took to heart. She had an edgy uncertainty working in her now, a fear that the next time she touched heat, she wouldn't be strong enough, that she'd die, or worse than death, find herself controlled.

"Trago," she said aloud. "Come talk to me." She waited, hands on her thighs, opening, closing, short ragged nails scratching erratically at the canvas of her trousers. He didn't come. She never knew if he heard her when she called him; sometimes he showed up, sometimes he didn't. This looked like one of the latter. "Damn." If it weren't for Trago locked dreaming in crystal, she'd run and trust her reflexes to keep her loose. But he was the hook that bound her to the Shahntien's whim and she had to play out this farce.

# #

I put him, Maksim said, where his god can't reach him. If I kill him, child, there'll only be another taking his place, another and another, no end to it. He'll sleep and sleep and sleep . . . Maksim turned his head and smiled at her . . . until you and only you, young Kori, until you come and touch him awake. He is in the Cave of Chains. If you can get yourself there, Kori, all you have to do is touch the crystal enclosing him. It will melt and the boy will wake. No one else can do this. No one, god or man. Only you.

# #

She scratched at her nose. All over the place, she thought. I did better concentration my first year. "Tré," she said, "give us a look, will you?"

Nothing. Obviously he was busy with other things, things more important than a long gone sister. She moved her body impatiently. He'd been looking over her shoulder for years, studying what she studied, maybe even nudging her when he wanted something she wasn't dealing with at the moment. She'd been driven, those first years. She'd thought it was because she wanted to get away as soon as she could and free her brother. She had to learn, to grow accustomed to working hot and fast, she had to find a way to outwit the Shahntien so she could escape her claws. To outwit Maksim who made a habit of sending his eidolon to chat with her. Maybe it was more than that, maybe it was Trago pushing her. One thing she did know, he was watching and studying a long time before he started talking to her. She worked her mouth. It hurt, thinking that way, but the most important thing she'd learned (besides control, of course) was never lie to yourself. No matter what extravagances you practice on other people, it's fatal to lie to yourself. She had the Shahntien to show her the truth of that, she had Maksim. Odd, the way he treated her. She could swear he never lied to her, never even shaded the truth. It was hard to take at times, but in the end she was grateful to his habit, in the end she saw this as the starkest compliment he ever paid her. In the end it was why Shahntien Shere stopped hating her. And life at the school got to be a lot easier.

The sun slid down its western arc; shadow crossed the stream and crept around her, cold and silent. Depressing. She was tired and hungry and she hadn't managed more than a moment or two of real meditation the whole futile day. Her stomach cramped repeatedly through that interminable afternoon, at times she could think of nothing but food. She dreamed of roast chicken with brown-gold gravy pooling round it. She thought of shrimp fried in a batter so light it might have floated off at a breath of wind, succulent pink shrimp. Peaches, peeled and golden, dripping with a rich fragrant nectar. Strawberries, plump tartsweet, floating in whipped cream. She wrenched her mind away and contemplated a blade of grass she pulled from a clump beside the blanket. She considered the greenness of it, greenness as an abstract idea, greenness as it was expressed in this particular physical object, mottled with lines of darker color, with pinpoints and patches of black and tan; she considered the edge where the blade left off and the air began, the finely toothed edge that was not so much green as an extraction from the colors combined into green, a pale anemic yellow fading to white, to no-color.

The sky put out its sunset flags and the wind rose, chill enough to knife through Korimenei's coat and pullover, stir the hairs on her arms and along her spine. Gentle Geidranay came walking along the mountain peaks. He squatted among them with his head against the sun, his fingers grubbing among the pines, absurdly like the shadow of the Old Man in his garden, grotesquely enlarged and cast against the drop of the darkening sky. The Groomer of Mountains came closer, his fingers swept across the small meadow, brushed against Korimenei and passed out without noticing her. The fingers were like semisolid light, translucent, melting through the air without agitating it, dreamlike and disturbing, a beautiful nightmare, if such could exist. Korimenei shivered and shut her eyes.

A dozen heartbeats later she cracked a lid; the god was gone. She sighed and broke posture. Her head was swimming, but the dizziness faded when she had moved about some more. She went to the stream, refilled her cup and stood watching the water darken to black glass as the last color faded from the sky. She carried the cup to the dead trunk, sat down beside her rucksack and took sip after slow sip until the cup was empty. The largest bulge in the sack was a heavy, knitted laprobe. She thought a moment, then with some reluctance took the laprobe out and dropped it on the blanket; dying of pneumonia was not a desirable outcome of this minor ordeal. She plucked a handful of dry grass and went deeper into the trees to void her bladder; when she was finished she washed her hands at the stream, using sand for soap.

She settled onto the blanket, folded her legs properly and pulled the laprobe about her shoulders.

In the distance an owl hooted. She thought about the Old Man, wondered vaguely who and what he was. Some odd manifestation of the Earthsoul, thrust from the soil as stones are ejected by a combination of earth and thaw? Or a creature as ancient as old Tungjii, perhaps even a kind of kin to himmer? Older than the gods themselves, older than the earth she sat on? Or was he the face of the Mountain itself? Was her blanket spread across his flesh? She moved uneasily, that was an uncomfortable thought. She considered the Old Man and the Mountain and Geidranay, Tungjii and her brother, Maksim and his assorted peculiarities, whether he'd managed to rise above his prejudices, sexual and social, and take her as an apprentice. She wanted that rather desperately; she knew by study and experience now what she'd guessed the first time she saw him: there was no one like him. If he taught her . . . if he taught her, maybe she wouldn't be so afraid of what she sometimes saw in herself, what she scurried from like a scared mouse whenever she caught a glimpse of it.

The laprobe trapped warmth around her; sleep tugged at her as she grew more comfortable, threatened to overwhelm her as the night turned darker. A fat, mutilated crescent, the Wounded Moon was already high when the sun went down; its diminished light fell gently on the quiet meadow, cool and pale, drawing color out of grass and trees, turning Korimenei and her blankets into a delicately sketched black and white drawing. Moon moths flew arabesques above the stream, singing their high thin songs. Fireflies zipped here and there, lines of pale gold light, the only color in the scene. A white doe came from under the trees on the far side of the stream. For a long moment the beast gazed at Korimenei, her eyes deep as earthheart and dangerous,

Korimenei felt herself begin to drown in them. The doe turned her head, broke contact; as silently as she came, she vanished into the inky shadow under the pines.

A fragment of old song drifted into Korimenei's mind, one of Harra Hazhani's songs which had been passed with another gift from daughter to daughter down the long years since she came to Owlyn Vale. Korimenei was born with that gift, Harra's ear for pitch and tone and her sense of rhythm; she'd long suspected it was a major part of her Talent, when she thought of Maksim's extraordinary voice she was sure of it. "I am the white hind," she breathed into the night; the darkness seemed to accept and encourage her, so she sang the song aloud. Not all of it, it had hundreds of lines and three voices, the white hind, the gold hart and the fawn; the hind spoke, the hart answered, the fawn questioned both. Korimenei lifted her voice and sang:

I am the White Hind
Blind and fleet
My feet read the night
My flight is silence
My silence summons to me
Free and bold
The Gold Hart.

I am the Gold Hart
Artful and fierce
I pierce the night
My flight is wildfire
Desire consumes me
She looms beside me
Fleet and unconfined
The White Hind.

Korimenei let the song fade as the doe had faded into the darkness. Why? she thought. What does it mean? Does it mean anything? She closed her eyes and banished memory and idea, accepting only the sounds of the stream. Fragmented images prodded at her but she pushed them away. Hear the stream sing, she told herself, separate the sounds. First the coarse chords. She heard these, named them: the shhhh of the sliding water, the steady pop of bubbles, the brush-brush tinkle against intruding stones and boulder, the clack-tunk of bits of wood floating downstream, bumping into those boulders, swinging into each other. She listened for the single notes of the song, teased them from the liquid languorous melliflow, concentrated on one, then another and another, recognized them, greeted them. Concentrate, she told herself. It's gone, it's gone. Narrow your focus, woman. You know how, you've done it a thousand times before. It's gone. Get it back. Concentrate, separate, appreciate, she chanted. Symmetry, limitry, backbone, marrow, she chanted, the phrasemaker in her head plundering her wordstore. Separation, isolation, disseverance, disruption, rent, split and rift, cleavage and abruption, she chanted, the words drowning the water wounds.

The Wounded Moon slipped down his western arc, crossing the spray of stars with a ponderous dignity that dragged at Korimenei's nerves, setting her to wonder if this interminable night would ever end, if she could possibly get through two more nights like it.

Sometime after moonset, she felt a presence come into the meadow. It was a small meadow with young pines clustering tightly around it. She sat in the center like a rat in a pit. Owl eyes looked at her, immense golden eyes. Owl flew round and round the pinepit meadow, his wings stretched wider than the grass did, but somehow Owl flew there round and round Korimenei. Feathers touched her, wings brushed her head, her shoulder, she smelled him. She trembled, her bones turned to ice. She heard Owl cry something, voices spoke inside her head, there was something they were saying to her, she could not quite understand them.

She was suddenly on Owl's back, spiraling up and up until she was high above the meadow. She looked down and saw her body sprawled across the dreampattern blanket, the laprobe bunched beside her hip. She was at once frightened and exhilarated. Owl circled higher yet until she saw points of light sprayed out beneath his belly; stars, she thought, we fly above the stars.

Owl tilted suddenly. She slid off his back. She fell. Down and down and down she fell. She was terrified. She was screaming. Her throat was raw from screaming.

Then she was inside her body looking up into the face of Geidranay, a Geidranay made small, his golden flesh like sunlight given form.

The Groomer of Mountains touched her pullover and it fell open, baring her breasts. He plunged his left hand into the earth and brought it up again; he held an amethyst, a single crystal glowing violet and blue. He set it on her chest above her heart and watched it slip inside her, melting through her flesh. He thrust his right hand into the earth and brought it up again; this time he held a moonstone the size of her fist. He touched the closure of her trousers and they fell open, baring her navel. He set the moonstone on her navel and watched it slip inside her. He touched her forehead. His fingers were cool as the stones. He said nothing, but she knew she must not move. He took up the tin cup she used for drinking and drew a golden forefinger about its rim and it turned transparent, gleaming in the starlight like polished crystal. He reached into the air, closed his hand into a fist; when he opened his fingers, diamonds cascaded into the cup. He knelt, dipped the cup into the stream and brought it back to her, the diamonds like ice floating in the water. He cupped his hand behind her head and lifted her gently, tenderly; he put the cup to her lips and she drank. The water was delicately sweet and smelled of spring orchids. The diamonds melted into the water. She drank them also.

When she looked up, Geidranay was gone. The cup was tin again, ancient, battered, as familiar as her hand.

Feathers brushed across her and her clothing vanished utterly, the laprobe was gone, the dreampattern blanket was gone. She lay on earth and grass. Great wings brushed across her and were gone. Owl walked toward her. It was the Old Man. He stood at her feet and looked down at her. She was ashamed at first because she was naked before him, but she was not afraid. He sank into the earth, slowly slowly. She wanted to laugh when she saw his round stupid face resting on her great toes, then the face slid down and vanished into the earth.

He was reborn from the earth, rising from it as slowly, silently, easily as he went into it. He was covered with red dust, otherwise he was naked and young and beautiful. He put his left foot on her right foot; gently, delicately he moved her leg aside. He put his right foot on her left foot; gently, delicately he moved this leg aside. He knelt between her legs and put his hands on her thighs. She shivered as she felt fire slide into her flesh. He looked at her, smiled. She cried out with pleasure, as if that smile were hands touching her. He bent over her, his hands moving along her body; they left streams of red dust on her skin.

His hands moved over her, stroking, rubbing, even pinching where the small sharp pains intensified her pleasure. When he finally pushed into her, the pain was briefly terrible, he burned her, wrenched her open, then she was on fire with a pleasure almost too intense to endure. It went on and on until she was exhausted, too weary to feel anything more.

He rose from her. She cried out, desolate. He stood beside her, his broad tender smile warmed her once more. As Geidranay had reached into the air for diamonds, the Old Man Reborn Young reached up and plucked a square of fine linen from the shadowy air. He came back to her and pressed the cloth between her legs, catching the blood that came from the breaking of her hymen. He sat on his heels and folded the cloth into a small packet, the bloodstains hidden inside. He leaned over her, touched her left hand, laid the packet on her palm. Again he said nothing, but she knew it was very very important that she keep the cloth safe and hidden, that she should never speak of it, not to Shahntien Shere or to Maksim, not even to her brother.

He set his right hand flat on the ground beside her thigh. The dreampattern blanket was under her again. He stepped over her leg and squatted beside her, drew the fingers of his left hand from her ankles to her waist, drew the fingers of his right hand from her waist to her shoulders and she was dressed again. He snapped the fingers of his left hand, spread his hands; the laprobe hung between them. He laid it over her and smiled a last time, touched her cheek in a tender valediction. And was gone.

She slept. When she woke it was midmorning. The first day and the first night was done.

4

At first she thought the events of the night were a dream, but when she moved her legs, she found she was still sore. The linen packet fell away when she sat up; she looked at the bloodstains for a long moment, then folded it up again and put it in her rucksack. Feeling more than a little light-headed, she took the tin cup to the stream and filled it. She drank. The liquid was merely cold water with the acrid green taste common to most mountain streams. She remembered water flavored and scented with diamonds, but that might have been something she did dream. She sipped at the water and thought about sleeping. She wasn't supposed to sleep, she was supposed to keep vigil. She didn't feel like worrying about her lapse. After filling the cup once more, she carried it up the gentle slope to her blanket and set it on the grass by her foot. She looked around.

The meadow space was filled with stippled sun rays, the misty light slanting through the dark needle-bunches on the upslope pines and cedars; there was no wind, the quiet was so thick she could feel it like the laprobe pulled heavy and close against her skin. Her mind was weary; it was hard to tie one word to another and make a phrase of them. She walked about a little, her legs shaky. Her inner thighs felt sticky, the cloth of her trousers clung briefly, broke away, clung again. She grimaced, disgust a mustiness in her mouth. She stripped, dropped her clothing on the blanket and took a twist of grass to the stream. She waded in. The water was knee-high, the cold was shocking. She shivered a moment, then gathered the will and went to her knees. She gasped, then examined her thighs. She'd bled copiously which surprised her, but she didn't waste time worrying about that either. She splashed water over the stains, began scrubbing at them with the grass. Each move bounced her a little on the gravel lining the streambed, she felt the bumps against her knees and shins, the rubbing, but the cold was so numbing she felt no pain until she climbed out of the water, put her clothes back on and warmed up a little.

She grunted as she tried to fold her legs; the bruises and abrasions she'd acquired in the stream made themselves apparent, so she crossed her ankles and straightened her back and began feeling her way into further meditation.

Flies came from everywhere and swarmed around her; they settled on her and walked on her hands and on her arms and on her legs, everywhere but her face; they were a mobile armor of jet and mica flakes, buzzing through a slow surging dance up and around and down, black twig feet stomping over every inch of her. She sat and let this happen. When the sun was directly overhead, the armor unwove itself and flew away.

She sat. Something was happening inside her. She didn't understand anything, but she had fears she didn't want to think about.

A one-legged woman stood under the trees across the stream. Vines grew out of her shoulders and fell around her. There was emptiness on her left side; the vines swayed parted, unveiling nothing, the vines on her right side grew round and round her single leg. She hopped. Stood still. Hopped again. The vines bounced. Arms outspread, she began jumping up and down on the same spot, turning faster and faster as she hopped. Korimenei heard a whining sound like all the flies singing in unison. The woman went misty and the mist went spinning away into the dim green twilight under the trees.

Korimenei considered this. She slid her hand up under her pullover and touched the place where the amethyst had seeped into her. Her skin was cool and dry; there was nothing to show it had really happened. She pulled her hand out, let it rest on the slight bulge of her belly; it seemed to her she could feel a thing growing in her, growing with a speed that vaguely terrified her. She took her hand away, closed her eyes and began humming to herself. After a while she plucked a song from Harra's Hoard, an Owlsong, and focused all of herself on it.

Around midafternoon another woman came slithering from the trees across the stream. She was writhing on her stomach like a great white worm; her legs were all soft from hip to toe; she had no toes, her legs ended in rattles like those on a snake's tail. She reared up the forward half of her body and danced with her arms and shoulders, shook her rattlefeet to make music for her dance. She had the polished ivory horns of a black buffalo, horns that spread wider than the reach of her arms. Her face was broad, her nose and mouth stuck out like the muzzle of a flat-faced dog. Her ears were pointed and shifted independently, a part of her body-dance. The hair on her head was like black broomstraw and hung stiffly on either side of her face. The hair under her arms was rough and shaggy like seafern; it hung down her sides, lower than the flat breasts that slapped against her ribs. There was a terribleness about her that rolled like smoke away from her, invisible emanations that filled the round meadow and squeezed Korimenei smaller and smaller.

Before Korimenei shriveled quite away, the horned woman sank into the earth and was gone.

The sun went down. Korimenei watched for Geidranay, but he didn't come this dusk; she felt sad, lonely. "Tré," she said aloud. "Trago, brother, talk to me." He didn't come. She was alone in the growing darkness with a thing growing in her.

She curled her hands and stared at her palms. "I don't understand any of this," she said aloud. That wasn't quite true. The crystals were for eyes to see and ears to hear the things beneath/behind the things one saw in ordinary light. She'd read about them in the books that Shahntien Shere had drawn to her library from the four corners of the world, she'd heard about them from the wandering scholars the Shahntien collected on the temple Plaza and invited to lecture to certain students, those she thought would profit from contact with other symbologies, other systems of visualization. Sometimes the crystals weren't crystals but roots or flowers, insects or beast organs; the effect was much the same. Her initiation had its parallels, also, the event though not the details. The flies . . . she could call from memory a score of similar happenings and each of these had at least a score of interpretations, meaning one thing to the newly initiate, something else to the same person when he or she was a mature practitioner, something else again to that person when he or she was in the twilight of his or her life. The two women had no referents, but both frightened her, both reeked of danger, of power on the verge of erupting from control. She remembered what the Shahntien said and smiled, then went back to being frightened; she pressed her hand against her swelling body. This . . . she laced down her fear, tying it tight inside her . . . had no parallel she knew of, only the familiar terror before dangers she hadn't the knowledge or strength to fight against, the terror that swept through her when Trago came into her bedroom and showed her the Godmark that meant he was doomed to burn at the stake unless she could manage something, the terror that swept through her when the drunk caught her on the street and she thought he was going to hurt her, kill her before she could reach the Drinker of Souls, the terror that swept through her when Settsimaksimin snatched her from her bedroom and so arbitrarily threw her to the Shahntien like a beast thrown to a tamer. Terror. . . .

Sometime after moonset the white doe came from the woods; she stood gazing at Korimenei for several moments, then she lifted herself onto her hind legs, shrinking as she did so until she had the doe's head still, but a woman's body with white milky breasts; the breasts were bare but the rest of her wore the doe's pelt; it glinted like silver wire in the starlight. Music came from somewhere, a flute played, a drum, a lute, something with a high sweet woman's voice, singing. The doe spoke: "There is music. You are not dancing."

Korimenei stood. Her clothing fell away from her. She began to dance. She didn't know what she was doing, her feet were moving, she felt awkward, she was awkward.

The doewoman waded across the stream. She took Korimenei's arm. "Be still," she said. "I will teach you the proper dance. Come with me." She led Korimenei toward the stream, choosing the place where there were two stones in the middle of it. She stepped on the first stone and pulled Korimenei onto it with her. There was very little room, Korimenei pressed against her guide, smelled her strong deer smell, gland and fur. The doewoman stepped across to the second stone; it was smaller than the first, there was no room for Korimenei but the woman tugged her after her anyway. Somehow there was room. They stood without moving. Korimenei looked around her. The stream was a river now, split into two strands; it was the widest deepest river she'd ever seen. The water was deep and silent as it flowed, it looked like green-blue grass. There was power and terror in it. And great beauty.

The doewoman made the waters rise. Korimenei lay down in them, her body pointed in the direction of the flow. The water took her. Her body began to undulate like the serpent woman, back and forth in sweeping s-curves. She went that way for a long time. She didn't know how long.

The singing began again, louder. The drum was louder also, the flute more piercing. A man lifted her, carried her. His head was the head of the Gold Hart. His antlers spread like a great tree of heavy rough-beaten gold. His eyes were hot and piercing, they were gold, molten gold. Force came out of him like heat from a fire. It went into her. He laid her on the water; he stood at her feet, holding onto them. He made her sit up. She discovered that she was under water and she gasped for breath. She started struggling. "Be still," he said to her. "I am making you drink this water. Drink it. Drink."

After she drank, he carried her out of the river and set her on her feet. Water ran out of her, pouring from her eyes, her mouth, from every orifice in her body. The doewoman was there, waiting, a small male fawn pressed up against her. The Hart strode over the grass to the Hind; he put out his hand. She rested her hand on it. They danced, a slow stately pavanne, circling each other, parting and coming together, face to face, then back to back. The dance went on and on. Korimenei should have been cold, but she was not. A Whole Moon larger than the moon she knew swam high overhead, full and white with traces of blue like a great round of pale cheese. The trees around them were bone white and still as stone, though they were not dead; Korimenei felt a powerful life in them. The grass was thick and short and black as the fur on a silver fox.

The dance changed, grew wilder. The Hart came to her, took her hand, pulled her into the dance. The three of them circled, parted, came together, face to face, then back to back.

Korimenei had no idea how long the dance lasted, she suffered no fatigue, she flowed with the pattern and felt only a cool pleasure.

The Hart and the Hind and the Fawn drew back before her. They sank onto four legs and trotted away, waded across the stream and vanished under the trees on the far side. The river was gone, or perhaps it had merely shrunk to what it had been before the white doe came. She was standing on the red dirt of the meadow; she was dressed again in trousers, pullover and coat. She went back to the blanket, settled herself on it, pulled the laprobe about her shoulders. She touched her swelling body, but the fear was gone. Something was going to come out of this, but she knew the dance now and nothing could hurt her unless she let it. Behind her the eastern sky flushed palely pink.

The second day and the second night were done.

5

Korimenei was no longer hungry. She was exhausted, her head swam whenever she moved it. She wanted no more visions, no more harrowing of her flesh and spirit. She refused every flicker of thought, pushed out of her mind's eye everything but what her body's eyes saw and she restricted that to the blanket pattern centered between her knees. Her body continued to swell. She ignored that. Her bladder ached. She ignored that as long as she could, went to her latrine bush when she had to. She snatched a handful of needles as she went back to the blanket, rolling them between her palms, crushing them to release the clean acrid pine scent. She threw the wad away as she reached the rim of the meadow, wiped her hands on her sides. She sank onto the blanket and went back to contemplating the patterns on it.

The day lumbered along. Nothing happened.

She refused to think about anything, especially about events and images of the past two nights, but she could feel, down deep inside her, those experiences sorting themselves out, dropping into their proper pattern. The thing growing in her settled into a similar consolidation of its forces; it lay still and serene within her. It was alive, she had no doubt of that; it glowed like an iron stove in midwinter, not with heat, but with a cool power beyond any the doewoman or the deerman could show. It was like the great Owl come to nest inside her.

Nothing happened. She waited in a state somewhere between sleep and waking for the day to be over.

The sun crept down the western sky. She saw gold firedragons undulating around it, they were so beautiful she wept awhile; quietly, effortlessly she wept and smiled.

Geidranay came strolling along the mountaintops; he stopped when he was between her and the vanishing sun, lifted a hand in greeting and gave her a great glowing smile. He wandered on, vanishing into the clouds blowing up from the west.

Korimenei sighed and rubbed the back of her hand across her eyes. After the sun was completely down and the sky darkened to a velvet blue-black, she walked shakily to the stream and splashed water onto her face. She scooped up more water and drank from her hand. She straightened and stood rubbing her back. One last night, then this thing was over. What good it was, she had no idea. She smoothed her hands over her swollen front, grimaced, then walked upslope to her blanket.

The Wounded Moon went down, the clouds thickened overhead; the night grew darker and darker. Korimenei wasn't trusting her senses much, but sometime late, she thought it was around midnight, she had her first contraction.

Cool hands closed on her shoulders, eased her flat. Isayana Birthmistress bent over her, humming a song that flowed over her like water, calming her; she floated on a bed of air that the god rocked like a cradle. She retreated to a distant place, looking down on the body she'd left behind. The contractions came closer together. Isayana touched the body and left it bare where her fingers wandered. Korimenei snickered soundlessly, gods were great valets, no bother with buttons or ties.

After an hour, Isayana lifted Korimenei's laboring body onto its feet and held it in a squat. A thing emerged, slick with blood and mucus. It dropped to the blanket, crouched a moment between Korimenei's knees, then it tried to scuttle away. Isayana laughed and let Korimenei care for herself as she scooped it up, cradled it in gentle hands. "Oh, oh, oh," she crooned. She held the small creature against her generous bosom with one hand, stroked it with the other, cleaning it. It was a tiny gray-furred beast with huge eyes, black hands and feet, like a combination of ferret and marmoset.

Korimenei lay back on the blanket, watching, not knowing how to feel about what had happened to her. Her insides churned. She had birthed the creature, what did that mean? What was it? What had she done? NO! what had been done to her?

This is a mahsar. Isayana's voice was deep and caressing, she spoke in sounds like a warm wind makes when it threads through a blowhole, sounds that turned into meaning inside Korimenei's head. *Your womb received and nurtured her, child, but she is no flesh of yours. Quiet your fears, child, untrouble your souls. Your body was prepared to receive her . . .* Isayana raised a delicate brow; her large brown-gold eyes glimmered with amusement, *and a pleasant preparing it was it, not so? Don't speak, child, your blush answers me. Your body was made ready to receive her and she was drawn into you from the place where she and her kind dwell. She was drawn little by little into you until she was wholly here. She is tied to you, Kori Heart-in-Waiting; were you a witch, she would be your familiar; as you are more, so she is more. She has many talents and more uses, they are yours to discover. She will stay with you until your first true-daughter is born, then go to your child to protect and serve her.* Still cuddling the creature against her breasts, Isayana bent over Korimenei and stroked her clothing into existence as the Old Man Made Young had done, as the doewoman and the deerman had done. She tucked the mahsar into the curve of Korimenei's left arm, touched Kori's temple with gentle approving fingers and was gone, melting like mist into the night air.

Slowly, dreamily Korimenei sat up, bringing the mahsar around into her lap. She sat drawing her hand over her not-daughter's small round head, down her springy spine and along her whippy tail. Over and over she drew her hand down, taking pleasure in the exquisite softness and silkiness of the mahsar's short gray fur and in the warmth of the tiny body where it cuddled against her. "Mahsar, mahsar, mahsar . . ." She chanted the species name in a mute monotone, making a kind of mantra of the word. "Mahsar, mahsar, mahsar . . ."

She stilled her hands and sat lost in a deep oneness with air and earth. Time passed. The clouds thickened. Rain came, no more than a fine mist that drifted on the intermittent wind and condensed in bead-sized droplets on every surface.

When she was damp and cold enough, she surfaced and pulled the laprobe around her head and shoulders. She tucked it around the mahsar too, smiled dreamily as she felt the little creature nestle cosily in its folds and vibrate with a sawtooth purr. "Ailiki," she said suddenly. "That's your name, daughter-not. Yes, Ai . . . li . . . ki . . . Ailiki. Yes." She knew most surely, with a shock that broke her free from her drift that she'd found the first NAME in all the NAMES she'd know the rest of her life, the first great WORD in all the WORDS she'd know. She'd drew her forefinger over the curve on Ailiki's head, along her shoulder and down her foreleg to her three-fingered black hand. Ailiki edged her hand around and closed it on Korimenei's finger. Kori laughed. "Words," she said aloud. "Do you know, I think I'm going to be a sorcerer. Maybe even a prime." She laughed again, cut off the sound when it turned strange on her.

She pushed the damp hair off her face. Her hand felt hot. "You're a little furnace, Aili my Liki. Sheeh!"

Later she threw off the laprobe and lifted her face to the unseen clouds. The mist droplets landed on it and puffed into steam. Heat was a river pouring irresistibly into her, coming from the heartroots of the earth and flowing into her. She sat unperturbed and bled it our again, until the air around her was white as daylight with the power of it and she the suncenter, a glass maid filled with fire.

The heat came harder, the river widened into a flood. She bled it off still, but the air burned her now, the radiance reached for the trees and she was suddenly afraid they would catch fire and burn like she was burning. She tried to control the flow, to pinch it down into a thread she could handle, but the attempt to control was enough in itself to send the river flaring hotter. She whimpered, allowing herself that small outlet for the uneasiness building in her, while she concentrated on channeling and, more important, understanding. She saw realization of her potential as a key. What she allowed now would determine the extend of her access to that potential. At worst she would burn to ash . . . no no, at worst she'd end a mediocrity, death was better than that. At best she had that chance of rivaling Settsimaksimin. Of wresting from him all he was and all he knew. She wanted that. She needed it.

She threw her strength against the flood. She could smell singed hair, the blanket under her was burning. Not that way, no no . . . all she'd been taught was control, all the Shahntien knew was control. But Shahntien Shere was limited, magistra not sorcerer, immensely learned and knotted into that learning. Korimenei drew back as much as she could without giving her body to fire and ashing; she cooled, the heat flowed around her as the river had flowed when the White Hind took her to the island. She'd gone into the river then, she'd given herself to the current, let it take her where it must. Was that the answer? No, not the whole answer. The Gold Hart held her underwater, forced her to drink, to make the water most intimately a part of her. She gasped and pulled a shield like glass about her. She could endure this, she saw that as soon as the glass closed around her. She could endure and be what Shahntien Shere was, not so bad an outcome. Not really mediocrity. But not majesty either. She stared at the white-gold flames coursing about her, rising in shimmering stabbing tongues to touch the clouds overhead. She felt rather than heard Ailiki hissing with a terror answering her own. "Ahhhh. . . ." she said aloud. "Tushzi," she cried in a voice to match her desires, using an ancient word from the Rukka Nagh ancestors buried deep in her cells, a word that meant fire. "TUSHZI VAGYA. I AM FIRE," she cried. It was her second

WORD. She cast away the shield, she threw Ailiki into a spiraling loop above her head and stretched her arms wide, surrendering body and souls to the fire.

For a moment she was without thought, without perception, she was light itself, heat itself. She flowed with the stream wherever it would take her and it took her on a circle of the layered realities, bursting into one and out between one blink and the next. She was traveling with such speed she took with her only a blurred fragment of each putting it into memory for the time when she would return though she was not thinking of returning now, she was not thinking at all, she simply WAS. Galaxies turned beneath her, she crossed a universe in the blink of an eye, dived into another and crossed that. . . .

The stream slowed, cooled; she began to draw back into herself, to seek home. A thing called her without words, a fireheart pulsed, drew her to it. She fell like the mist-rain, as slowly and insubstantially and blown about by the sullen wind. She fell into the meadowpit again and landed as she had before so lightly not a blade of grass stirred. Ailiki leaped into her arms and murmured a wordless welcome. She laughed. Her hands were translucent, filled with a light as cool and pale as moonglow. She felt immensely powerful, as if she could walk the mountaintops beside Geidranay and never miss a step. Yet there was more gentleness and love in her than she'd felt before, an outreach to all there was around her, a welcoming in her for all that was, name it good, name it evil, she welcomed all and gave it respect and dignity. She ran her hands over her hair and laughed again. The ends were singed into ashy kinks, as if someone had passed a torch too close to her. She looked around. The ground was charred where her dreampattern blanket had burned. Leave it as you found it, the Old Main said. Yes. Let me think.

Before she was ready, fire leaped to her hand, startling her. She wasn't afraid now. Without knowing how she knew she had to do, she shaped the fire and threw it from hand to hand, played with it like a juggler with his props; she squeezed it into a ball, spun it on a finger until it spread like flatcake dough into a wide disc. She dropped the disc on the burnt grass. It soaked into the earth and left behind it crisp new grass, green and springing, smelling like spring. She laughed again and stretched out beside the new patch, weary but immensely content. After a while she slept.

The third day and the third night were done.

6

She woke in cool green morning light.

The Old Man was standing beside her. When she sat up, he held out a battered pewter bowl filled with potato and onion soup. The smell was at first nauseating, then with a shocking jolt, was everything good; she took the bowl and forced herself to eat slowly though she was ravenous. A sip at a time, a chunk of potato or onion, slow and slow, the soup went down. The warmth of it filled her, the earthsoul in it wiped away the haze that blurred her mind. The Old Man sat on the new grass at her left side, watching her, smiling. She snatched quick glances at him, embarrassed at first, but there was nothing of the red-gold lover visible in him so her uneasiness faded. When the bowl was empty, she sat holding it and smiling at him.

Tungjii came strolling from under the trees. Heesh snapped hisser fingers and Ailiki lolloped over to himmer, her odd high-rumped gait comical but efficient. She climbed himmer like a tree and sat on hisser shoulder, preening herself and murmuring in hisser ear. Male and fe-male, clown and seer, bestower and requirer, the old god stood at Korimenei's right side and smiled down at her. Heesh pointed at the bowl, snapped hisser fingers again.

Korimenei scrambled to her feet. Bowing, she offered the bowl.

Heesh cupped it in hands of surprising beauty, long-fingered shapely hands that looked as if they belonged with another body. Eyes twinkling, heesh whistled a snatch of song currently popular in Silili. A warm yellow glowsphere formed momentarily about hisser hands, dissolved into the pewter. The bowl was changed. It was a deep-bellied bubbleglass filled with a thick golden fluid.

Korimenei took the glass and obeyed the flapping of heesh's hand; she sank down, sat cross-legged and sipped at the liquid. It was a mixture of fruit juices, sweet and tart, rich and cold; even the Old Man's soup was not so wonderful. Tungjii plumped down beside her, nodded across her at the Old man, then sat beaming at her while she continued her sipping. There was no urgency in their waiting, so she took her time finishing the juice. They were enjoying her enjoyment and she was content to share it with them.

Tungjii took the glass when she held it out to himmer, touched it back to pewter, tossed it into her lap.

Amused by the absurd routine, she fished up the bowl, bowed deeply over it and passed it to the Old Man.

His dead-leaf eyes shone at her. He bowed in answer, then took the bowl in both hands, blew into it and held it out. When she took it, he folded both his hands over hers, his touch was warm and releasing. He got to his feet and wandered off, vanishing under the trees.

Korimenei watched him leave, a touch annoyed because he hadn't bothered to speak to her, to say something cryptic and satisfying as rumor said he did at other times for other questers. Potato soup, she said to herself, suffering gods, potato soup? She frowned at the bowl and wondered what that meant. She turned to Tungjii to ask himmer to explain, but the plump little god had taken hisser self off somewhere. Nothing from himmer either. Potato soup and fruit juice. The school cook could do as much. She laughed aloud. Well, maybe not quite as much, gods and demiurges and tutelary sprites seemed to be better cooks than retired witches. She stretched, yawned. Three days and three nights. I'd say I've done my time. She was changed, she knew that, but she didn't want to think about it now. She wanted the security of the person she'd known for twenty-four years, not his new thing, this battered creature tampered with by crazy gods and whatever took a notion to have a go at her.

Groaning as sore muscles complained, she got to her feet. She put the bowl away in her rucksack, then streched and twisted, ran her hands through her hair and grimaced at the burnt straw feel. She was tired, but not so tired as she had been. The potato soup and the fruit juices were in there working. Swinging the rucksack onto her back, she pushed her arms through the straps; it pressed wrinkles into her coat and the pullover underneath so she tugged them flat and smoothed the coat around her hips. "Ailiki?"

The mahsar came running across the meadow; she took a flying leap and landed on Korimenei's shoulder where she crouched, singing into Kori's ear.

Korimenei laughed. "So you'll be riding, eh?" She walked to the stream, found the path that brought her here and started down it.

The Old Man was working in his garden again. She called a greeting but got no reply. She hadn't really expected one, so she kept on walking. The clouds were blowing out to sea and the sun broke through more and more as she went down the mountainside. The boat was where she left it. She slipped the knots, settled herself on a thwart and began rowing across to Utar-Selt.

7

Korimenei held a shirt up and inspected critically but rather absently its collection of patches and the numerous threadbare places. Behind her the door opened.

"That might do for a dustrag." Firtina Somak lounged against the door jamb, her arms crossed over the plump breasts she found more an irritation than an asset. "Unless you plan an involuntary strip some windy day."

Kori threw the shirt on the bed. "It's not all that much worse than the rest of my stuff."

"Tell me, hunh, me who's had to look at them all this time." Firtina laughed. "You only have to wear them." She came into the sleeping cell and plopped herself on the hard narrow bed, twitched a shirt from the pile and snapped it open. "T'k t'k, you can't wear this in public, Kri, people will throw coppers at you thinking you're a beggargirl." She folded the garment into a neat rectangle, sat scratching absently at a forearm. "The Shahntien passed you then."

"Mmh." Korimenei pushed the mound of clothing aside and sat on the bed next to her friend. Firtina was intensely curious about everyone; she never talked about what she learned and she wasn't pushy about it or malicious, but you could feel her feeling at you. "She said anything to you yet? About your test, I mean."

"She said sometime in the spring. If I work on voice control I'll be a Witch of Witches which is nice to know, but there's that damn IF. She says I go so flat sometimes it's a misery and she'd be shamed to claim me as one of hers." She narrowed her eyes, glanced slyly at Ailiki who was sleeping on the windowsill, body coiled into a pool of sunlight, gray fur shimmering like tarnished silver. "I never thought you'd go for a witch."

"Haven't." Korimenei could feel Firtina wanting to ask about that and the mahsar, but her friend managed to swallow her curiosity, for the moment, anyway. Relenting a little, Kori said, "She's not a Familiar, she's Something Else."

Firtina waited a moment to see if Korimenei was going to add to that, then grinned at her, shook her head. "Clam. You for home?"

"Not for a while, I think." Korimenei spoke slowly; she hadn't told anyone about her brother, not even Frit who was her best friend; she didn't want to lie to Frit, but she couldn't tell her the whole truth, so she pinched off a little of it and produced that. "My um sponsor sent some money, I'm going to spend it poking around here and there before I settle to something. You going home?"

"Have to, I think. The Salash Gazagt. . . ."

"Huh?"

Firtina scratched at her thigh. "I thought you knew the Nye Gsany."

"To read, not to speak." Korimenei left the bed and crossed to the window where she stood smoothing her fingers along Ailiki's spine. Over her shoulder she said, "And only the Nye of the Vanner Rukks. I don't know the hissery-clunk you talk, village girl."

"Hunh! talk about tin ears. Nye is Nye. I think you're digging at me, li'l Kri. Should I apologize for calling your clothes rags?"

"Idiot."

"All right, all right, here it is, the Salash Gazagt, he's the oldest male, the head of my family. When you come to visit me, I'll introduce you. If I know the two of you, it'll be dislike at first sight, but I'll do it."

"Am I going to visit you?"

"Aren't you?"

"All right. So what's your Salash Gazagt on about?"

"He's getting impatient, old bull; he wants me home before I wither into uselessness."

"Haah?" Kori swung round, hitched a hip on the windowsill and began chewing at a hangnail. "Wat th' hay, Frit? Tink and Keiso and RayRay and I'm not going to waste breath naming the rest of your tongue-hanging court, the way they pant after you, you're not exactly declining into decrepitude."

"Them." Firtina wrinkled her nose. "They don't count. Thing is, if I'd stayed home like my sisters, I'd be wedded and bedded and by now hauling around a suckling and a weanling or two." She slapped at her breasts. "My doom," she said. "My folk have a thing about virginity, they tend to marry off a girl as soon as her shape starts showing. Just to make sure."

"Hunh! Just like my lot."

"Hmm. Sounds to me like you're not going home. Or maybe just a visit to show 'em what they'll be missing?"

"You got it." Korimenei plucked at the ancient white blouse she was wearing. "I never paid much attention to clothes."

"You finally noticed?" Firtina giggled, flicked another sly glance at

Kori. "If three nights fasting will do that for you, it gives me hope. Maybe my Ordeal fixes my ear."

"Nothing wrong with your ear, you just don't keep your mind on what you're doing." Korimenei was briefly amused at this delicate hint for confidences, but the Passage Test wasn't something you talked about, it was too intimate a thing, more intimate than sex or family secrets. "I'm no good at line and cut and yelling at shopkeepers. Come help me spend my money."

"Why not." Firtina slid off the bed, held up a hand. "Let me get this straight. You really are going to spend REAL coin on NEW clothes?"

"Mmh-hmm." Korimenei took an ancient vest off its peg, shoved her arms through the armholes and smoothed the leather over her hips. She scooped up Ailiki and tucked her into one of the sagging thigh pockets. "Something easy but dignified."

"Oh oh oh." Firtina giggled. "Dignified. Dignified. . . ." She repeated the word twice more; each time she put a different spin on it, snuffling little laughs up her too-short nose as she walked from the cell. She stopped a few steps down the hall and waited for Korimenei. "Seriously," she said, "you have any idea what you want?"

Korimenei pulled the door shut, put her personal seal on it and followed Firtina out of the Senior Cott onto the maze-walk around the Dorms. "More or less the same thing I always wear," she said. "Better material, newer, that's all."

The autumn afternoon was warm and sunny; all evidence of the brief storm three nights ago was cleared away, the stones underfoot were dry and powdery, as were the bright-colored leaves scattered on the granite paving by first year students who spent most of their days cleaning and sweeping, cutting grass and pulling weeds. Somewhere among the clipped yew hedges two girls giggled and chatted while they worked in a flowerbed, having lost much of their first awe of the place and at the moment at least some of their grim determination to succeed here. Two teachers came walking past, M'darjin drummers exchanging grave gutturals and spacious gestures. A squad of second-years paced along a nearby path, breathing in time with their coach, a student, like Korimenei and Firtina, nearing the end of his studytime. Kori stretched and sighed, lifting her head to look beyond the walls. The school was near the top of Selt's single mountain; at her left hand the gilded Temple roofs rose above the treetops, but everywhere else what she saw over the wall was the deep bright blue of the sky.

"You'll need some skirts too," Firtina said thoughtfully. "Boots, riding gear, a cloak, hmmm. . . ."

"Skirts, gah. No."

"Don't be stupid, Kri. You know well enough there are places where a woman gets stoned if she's not in skirts. It's better to be tactful than dead. Besides, a skirt can feel nice fluttering about your ankles, make you feel elegant and graceful."

"Gah."

"Don't bother then, go home and wear your trousers chasing after cows."

"Double gah."

"It's a cold cruel world out there that the Shahntien's going to boot you into. By the by, when's the parturition due?"

"Two, three days, depends on when I can get passage out."

They passed through a narrow arch in a thin, inner wall, walked into the rectangular formal garden at the front of the school and strolled toward the main gate. Short-stemmed asters were masses of pink and purple, yellow and vermilion; white tuokeries foamed around them. Manicured to an exquisite polish, oaks and cedars and plum trees grew alone or in carefully balanced groups of three. Patches of lawn like rough velvet changed color as a chancy wind blew blades of grass about. The paving stones in the curved walks were cut and placed so the veining in the marble flowed in a subtle endless dance of line and stipple. There was a fountain at the golden section; it was a sundragon carved from clear crystal spitting a stream of water from a snout raised to the sky. Korimenei and Firtina fell silent as they passed into this garden, respecting its ancient peace.

The porter came from his hutch, read their senior status from the badges, and opened the wicket to let them through into the city.

The street outside the school was a cobbled lane rambling between graceful lacy mimosas growing in front of walls that closed in the villas of the richest and most important Hina merchants. Ghosts were caught like cobwebs in the bending branches; they stirred, twitched, flapped loose for the moment to flutter about the heads of every passerby; they struggled to scream their complaints, but produced only a high irritating whine like a cloud of mosquitoes on a hot summer night. Though they refused to banish the haunts, considering exorcism a kind of murder, Kula priests working out of the Temple wove a semiannual mute spell over these remnants. The merchants had to suffer the embarrassment of the haunting (everyone knew that earthsouls only hung around those who injured them or their kin), but escaped more acute indictments by paying for the Kula muterites. Ignoring the eroding souls, Korimenei and Firtina walked north toward the Temple Plaza.

"So." Firtina clasped her hands behind her and looked up at Korimenei who was the taller by more than a head. "Are you looking for a Master, or is that already fixed up, or shouldn't I ask?"

"I don't know. It's like going home, I've got to do it sooner or later, but there's no hurry about it." Her mouth tilted into a crooked smile. "After all, I've got to visit you first and you won't be home for half a year or more."

"Ooh ooh ooh," Firtina chanted. She pinched Korimenei's arm and danced away as Kori slapped at her, swung round and danced backward along the lane. "While I'm waiting for that threat, where'll you be? North or South?"

"I thought I'd go south a bit, Kukural maybe."

"Then you want light stuff." Firtina waited for Korimenei to come up with her, walked beside her. "Cottons and silks, nothing to make you sweat."

"Well. . . ." Korimenei fidgeted uncomfortably; she loathed having to hedge every statement, but what could she do? "I'd better have some winter things too. There'll be mountains, I'm pining for mountains, it can get cold in mountain vales, even southern ones, come the winter."

"Mmh-hmm. Fur?"

"Extravagance. Good wool and silk will do me." For a few steps she brooded over the idea of fur, then shook her head, her fine curls bouncing. "Definitely not fur." She bent a shoulder and touched the lump that was Ailiki asleep in the pocket.

They went on without talking through a shadow-mottled silence; no city noise came this high. The crunch of their feet, the soft flutter of the mimosa fronds and the whine from the ghosts only underlined the peace in the lane. It was one of those golden autumn days when the air was like silk and smelled like potpourri, something in it that bubbled the blood and made the feet dance.

Korimenei and Firtina came out of the quiet of the lane into the bustle and noise of the Temple Plaza like bathers inching into the sea. It wasn't one of the major feastdays, but the Plaza was filled with celebrants and questers, with merchants looking for a blessing on their cargoes or a farsearch to locate late ships, with mothers of unwed daughters dancing bridal pavannes for Tungjii and Jah'takash, with pickpockets, cutpurses, swindlers, sellers of magic books, treasure

maps and assorted other counterfeit esoterica, with promisers and pro-
curers, with lay beggars and holy beggars, with preachers and yogin
and vowmen in exaggerated poses, with dancers and jugglers and players of all sorts, with families up for an afternoon's half-holiday, come
to watch the evershifting show, with students sneaking an hour's release from discipline, or earnestly questioning Temple visitors, with
folk from every part of the known world, Hina and Temueng locals,
westerners (Phrasi, Suadi, Gallinasi, Eirsan, Henermen), southerners
from the Downbelow continent (Harpish, Vioshyn, Fellhiddin,
M'darjin, Matamulli), Islanders from the east (Croaldhese, Djelaan,
Panday, Pitnajoggrese), others from lands so far off even the Temple
didn't know them, all come to seek the Grand Temple of Silili, Navel of
the World, the One Place Where All Gods Speak.

Korimenei and Firtina edged into the swirling chaos on the Plaza
and went winding through it toward the Temple. A pickpocket attracted by the bulge in Kori's thighpocket bumped against her; he
suppressed a scream of pain as Ailiki bit him, let the press of the crowd
whirl him away from them. Frit grinned, twitched plump hips in a
sketch of a dance, jerked her thumb up. Kori shook her head at her,
amused by her friend's exuberance and the pickpocket's optimism; she
knew better than to carry coin in any pocket she could get into without
unbuttoning something. They eeled through the mob on the wide shallow stairs going up to the Temple, passed in through the vast arches.

They dropped coppers through a slot and accepted incense sticks
from the acolyte. Firtina lit hers and divided them between Isayana
and Erdoj'vak, the land spirit of her homeplace. She bobbed a bow or
two, then followed Kori from Geidranay to Isayana to the little alcove
where Tungjii's image was. Kori thrust the last of her incense sticks
into the urn between hisser turned-up toes, then rubbed hisser belly for
luck; for a moment she let herself remember her Ordeal, then she
pushed away the troubling images, laughed, and followed Frit into the
light.

They plunged into the market, bought wool and silk, linen and cotton, Frit taking the lead and Kori backing her, bargaining energetically
and vociferously with the vendors. A sewing woman next, a quick
measure and a more protracted back-and-forth over styles and cost.
Bootmaker. Glover. Perfumer for soaps, creams and scents. Sad-
dlemaker for pouches to hold all the above.

When they were finished, they sat over tea in the Rannawai Harral
and watched the sun go down. Geidranay was a golden shadow against

the sun, squatting among the mountaintops, his fingers busy among the pines; a translucent sundragon undulated above the horizon for a while, then vanished behind a low flat layer of clouds; the Godalau surfaced out beyond the boats of the Woda-an, and played among the waves, her long white fingers catching the last of the sunlight, her saucy tail glinting as if its scales were plates of jade.

"The gods are busy tonight." Firtina spoke idly, turning her teabowl around and around in her short clever fingers. "I haven't seen so many of them about since the New Year feast."

Korimenei sipped at her tea and said nothing. Her Ordeal was taking on the haze of myth. Not quite dream. Not quite memory. *If I let myself slide into megalomania, I could think all that's put on for me,* she thought. She smiled. *Not likely, I'm afraid.* She glanced at Firtina, smiled again. *She almost believes it. I can see that. I wonder why? She's got a special touch for divining.* "You think something is stirring?"

Frit chewed on her lower lip. She reached for the teapot and filled her bowl again. "You've got the right word," she said finally. "Stirring."

"What?"

"Ah. That's the question. I don't know." She frowned, pushed back the dark brown hair that fell in a veil past her eye and curved round to tickle at her mouth. "It's, it's well, like standing over a grating and hearing things, you know, *things,* slithering about under you. You don't know what they are and you're quite sure you don't want to know. That sort of stirring." She gulped at the tea, shivered, refilled the bowl and sat holding the warm porcelain between her palms. "Yuk."

"Well, it can get on with it without me, I'm off as soon as my things are finished."

"Well. . . ." Frit set the bowl on the table and frowned across the bay at the mountains, dark and quiet since Geidranay had vanished with the sun and her attendant dragons. "I get the feeling . . . I just started noticing . . . it smells stronger every breath I take . . . I think you're some kind of . . . of magnet for it. When you move, it moves. I'll do some looking when we get back, see what I can find."

"Thanks. I think." Korimenei made a face. "Portents. Gah! I don't believe a word of it, you know. Come on, you're still under Rule, we don't want to get you chucked out before your time is up."

8

Six days later Korimenei Piyolss, sorcerer in posse and possessor of portents too nebulous to grasp despite Frit's efforts and her own, Korimenei followed a porter and her pouches onto the merchanter *Jiva Marish* and sailed south for Jade Halimm.

IV: DANNY BLUE

1

The Daniel Akamarino part of him woke first because Daniel had been through this before.

He opened his eyes and saw the translucent white petalform of the pod cap slanting up away from him. Sleep pod? He swallowed. The taste of burning insulation that filled his mouth warned him he'd been down for more than a few hours. He stared at the cracks clouding the cap and trembled with terror/rage. The starship was older than time and rotting to dust. He could have died in that pod. If the coldsleep system had broken in the smallest part, he would be dead now and rotting with the ship.

Dead and rotten. For a god's whim, Chained God playing Spin the Boogie with Fate. Live? Die? Who cares.

Mutely cursing the god and h/its reckless interference in his life, hands shaking with anger and inanition, Daniel Akamarino stripped leech-feeders off the emaciated body he inhabited and tried to sit up.

Your life? Our life! The words exploded in a head already blind with pain. Ahzurdan was coming awake. Sharing the body with Daniel, he shared the terror, the rush of adrenalin, though he couldn't know what caused it since he was entirely ignorant of starships and their mechanisms. *My life also.* Daniel saw the words as black against red with liquid white halos flowing around the outside of the letters. He cursed again, shoved angrily at the intruding Other. "Go away," he shouted, asserting control of the voice they shared. "Leave me alone."

Ahzurdan seemed to acquiesce, then slammed into Daniel with a sudden flare of power, trying to expel him from the body.

Their joint flesh humped, twitched, threatened to boil off the bone, their shared bones creaked and shuddered. Ahzurdan screamed, the SOUND tearing at their throat. Daniel howled and tried to shape the howl into words, to grasp at words and use them to kill the Other or, if killing were impossible, to force him from the body. This was a mistake. Words were Ahzurdan's technology, he could unmake with them as well as make and he strove desperately to unmake Daniel Akamarino and control the body that was born from the forced melding of their flesh.

Danny Blue, their rueful and unappreciative sort-of-son, woke and hovered like a ghost above his battling half-sires.

Not so long ago in conscious time, impossible to know how long in world time, Daniel Akamarino was walking down a road in another reality, was a starman/trader looking for a bargain, was a man who had a deep contempt for self-styled magicians, considering them deluded idiots with a yen for power but too inept or lazy to acquire the real thing, or charlatans, milking the deluded idiots that swarmed about them. On that day when he was walking along that road, Daniel Akamarino was past his first youth, with blue eyes bright in a face tanned dark, was bald except for a fringe of hair over his ears like a halfcrown of black thorns, was a tall man, lanky, loosely put together, but fast and hard when he had to be. Amiable, competent, unambitious, and generally somewhere else when you needed him.

Not so long ago in conscious time, in this reality where magicians are the technocrats, Ahzurdan was a sorcerer of high rank with a dreamdust habit that was killing him. Back then he was a tall man with a handsome ruined face and eyes bluer than the sea on a sunny day, with fine black hair, a beard combed into corkscrew curls and a bold blade of a nose. Among ordinary folk for his vanity's sake he spread a glamour about himself, wearing pride along with wool and leather, wearing power like a cloak, pride and power put on to cover the blind weak worm within. An ineffectual driven man, despite the power he commanded. Bitter, angry, dominated for too long by a neurotic mother, then a charismatic master.

Danny Blue's half-sires, fighting insanely over a body neither had the strength to control.

He snorted with disgust when he discovered what was happening. If one part of him destroyed the other, it would be an act of suicide. Ahzurdan and Daniel Akamarino were ghosts, incapable of independent existence; apparently neither of them could or would recognize this. Since he had no soft yearnings for easeful death, he gathered himself, slapped his warring parts into order and rolled his fragile body up until he was sitting with his legs hanging over the edge of the pod, his head cradled in dry bony hands.

He sat that way for several minutes, trying to dredge up sufficient strength to hunt out his quarters and see how much time had passed while he was stashed away in coldsleep. He scrubbed a hand across his mouth; his lips were cracked and dry. Painful. Whole body's in bad shape, he thought. He shivered; the clammy chill of the pod chamber was seeping into him. He reached up, caught hold of the cap and levered his wasted body off the cot.

He swayed, pressed his free hand hard against his eyes as his head threatened to explode. He lowered his hand and frowned at it. I look like the tag-end of a seven-year famine, he thought. He trembled again and his knees went soft on him. That miserable conglomeration of rot, I could have died in there. He clutched at the cap, steadied himself, then took a tentative step toward the open arch between the squat, cylindrical pod-chamber and whatever was outside it; he didn't lift his feet but shuffled along like an aged, aged man, body bent and swaying. When he reached the arch, he closed his hand around a broken bit of the wall and stood panting and shaking as he looked about.

The chamber was only slightly larger than the one behind him. Halfway across it, shoved up against the right-hand wall, there were two wide flat couches raised waist-high off the floor and surrounded by skeletal instruments he managed to identify through a painful stretch of his imagination and Daniel's memories. Sick bay, he thought. Thick scummy webs hung in veils from the vines that crossed and recrossed the ceiling and grew out of shattered screens ranked along the walls. Unseen vermin scuttled about. He heard the click-clack of their feet, the tentative whisper of the limp pallid leaves as they brushed past. He scowled at the mess of weed and web. This decay reminded him how lucky he was to be alive. He worked his mouth, spat on the first two fingers of his left hand, reached across his body and rubbed his fingers on the wall beside him, an offering to Tungjii Luck. He did this automatically, a habit pattern from Ahzurdan's past life, as he struggled to think around pain that struck in from his eyes whenever he moved his head and between times was a dull, grinding ache.

Sick bay. Small. Must be officers only. Hmm. Colony ship, converted battleship, given what that misbegotten patchwork told me. That means I'm not too far off from my quarters. Shee-it, how long was I out of it? God, I wish I knew what happened while I was down. My legs feel like spaghetti, I'll be crawling before I get there. Come on, Danny, anyplace is better than this, it's enough to make a goat sick. Start shuffling, man. He set his teeth and began creeping toward the exit. It was half open and he could see a pale light beyond. A corridor, probably. And it was lit. A good sign. Could be it was still passable. There was air wherever you went in this ancient ship, he knew that now; metal and forcefields could exist in vacuum, but too much of the Chained God's life or essence or whatever had spilled out of the natal computer into that cobbled together mess, bits of brain matter, bone and sinew, vegetable growths and swarms of necessary symbiotes for h/it to shut off the flow of air.

He started across the chamber, clawing awkwardly at the ancient webs, his skin crawling as he visualized spiders dropping into his eyes. The dust he knocked off the webs and the leaves drifted slowly slowly onto him with the silky ponderance of the half-g gravity decreed by the Chained God throughout this pocket reality; he breathed shallowly, his lips pressed together, but that exuviae, that ancient scurf filled his mouth with the taste of death. He caught hold of the rail at the foot of the first cot and stood bent over it, feeling it give slowly slowly under the pressure of his diminished weight. The dust fell harder, the leaves above him shook with the agitated trotting of the creatures that lived up there. He moved on.

For the next half hour he moved along corridors as overgrown and dusty as the sickbay. The transition into a clean well-lighted section was abrupt, as if he passed through a membrane that blocked contamination from the unregulated life outside. He leaned against a sterile white wall, closed his eyes, sick with weariness, knowing he was near the living quarters which the Chained God had cleaned up for outsiders, the apartments he'd occupied for a month and a half before the god caught him plotting and dumped him into coldsleep. Because he was so near, the will that kept his body moving drained out of him . . . so near and so far. He sank onto his knees, hugged his arms across his chest and tried to dredge a last effort out of a mind and body on the verge of collapse. Just a few turns more, only a few turns more and he could rest and eat. The thought of food nauseated him, but he had to replace the flesh melted off him while he vegetated in the pod. He had to begin rebuilding wasted muscle. He rocked onto hands and knees and crawled, head hanging, eyes blind with sweat and the hair that must have kept growing while he slept; it fell in a coarse gray-streaked black curtain long enough to sweep the rubbery floorcovering. He hadn't thought about hair before, it'd just been there on his head. He crouched where he was and scowled at the hair falling past his eyes. The Daniel memories told him that in a properly working coldsleep pod even hair growth stopped, but there was enough play in the stasis field to let small changes occur if the adjustment wasn't precisely tailored to the metabolism of the sleeper; the wasting of his body was one of those changes, a serious one if he'd stayed much longer in the pod, the hair growth was another. And it was a crude way to measure time. He started crawling again, moving blindly along the corridor as he considered available data. The hair he'd inherited from Ahzurdan was eight to ten cm long when the god put him down. Now it was . . . he stopped crawling, pushed up into a squat and jerked a hair from the back of his head. It was close to thirty cm now which meant . . . two cm a year was a good average, take off ten already there, that left twenty which meant he was in that pod for roughly ten years. He threw the hair away and went back to crawling. Ten years? He snarled at the friable mat that crumbled each time he set a hand down. Ten years cold storage. I'm supposed to be a good boy now, eh? Or you put me down again and maybe this time I'm snuffed? No joy, stewmeat. His mind blanked as rage took hold of him; his arms quivered and he collapsed to the floor, his body shaking with dry sobs.

His half-sires whispered sarcasms into his ears, mocking his suffering as extravagance and nonsense, a whimpering of hypochondriacal organism, puppy looking to be petted. He slapped his hands against the mat, lifted himself on trembling arms and crawled on, fuming; his anger at the Chained God for risking him so casually was shunted aside by this annoying persistence of his sires; he was beginning to wonder if Daniel and Ahzurdan would ever fully merge with him and leave him without those irritating chains that kept jerking him back into his double past. Hair swaying in front of his nose, limbs trembling, he inched along the corridor, staying close to the left-hand wall.

A door sighed open. He stopped, blinked, then fumbled around and passed through the doorway into the chamber beyond where he collapsed in the middle of a painfully clean, faded blue carpet. He lay there and thought about pulling himself up and putting himself properly to bed, but the will to move died with his consciousness and he sank into a sleep that was close to coma.

2

For the next two weeks Danny Blue ate, slept, quelled his sires when they threatened to come apart, built back his weight and strength. And he grew more puzzled as each day passed.

He remembered the Chained God being powerfully present everywhere, sending a fantastical web of sound throughout the starship—cascades of beeps, oscillating hums, bings, bongs, twangs, murmurs, sibilant sussurations, squeals and twitters, subsonic groans that raised the hair on his arms and grumbled in his belly—the god communing with h/its various parts. That continuous, pervasive noise was barriered from the living quarters, but back then, when he was living there alone, the unheard vibrations filled the rooms despite the filters, buzzing in his bone. The vibrations were gone, replaced by a silence as intangible and impenetrable as the god's alleged mind. Silence filled the quarters, except for the sough of air through the ducts, the minor ticking of the support systems, and the noises Danny himself made. The god had withdrawn from his realm.

At first Danny was too intent on his own needs to notice that absence, except for a vague unease that wasn't intrusive enough to break his concentration on himself. When he was no longer an animated skeleton, though, he heard the silence and wondered. And started worrying. The Chained God in h/its ordinary aspect was spooky enough. This was worse.

He worked out in the gym, his mind seething—what's happening?

what's that obscenity getting up to? He fiddled with recalcitrant controls on the food machines—god, I've got to get out of here, this ship is collapsing under its own weight, it's a wonder I lived through ten years of coldsleep, what do I do when the food and water quit? when the air goes? What is that abomination planning for me now? It has to be something or h/it wouldn't 've waked me. What? what? what? He coaxed the autotailor into fabricating new underwear and some multizippered shipsuits for him—how do I bust loose? is there anywhere in that backroad reality h/it can't reach? H/it's got h/its hooks set deep in me.

By the end of a month-standard, Danny Blue's body was repaired sufficiently to let him settle into a workout routine; he'd trimmed his hair, leaving it long enough to brush his shoulders (the mane he'd inherited from Ahzurdan was one of his not-so-secret vanities); he'd found his Heverdee vest and his sandals, their leather dry and cracking but intact because the god had put them away where the vermin couldn't get to them; he oiled the sandals and rubbed them until they were reasonably supple, then began a much more careful refurbishing of the vest.

3

He stood in the middle of a room like the inside of an egg, walls painted eggshell white, a fragile ivory carpet on the floor; there were a number of lumps about, chairs and couches folded in on themselves, put away for the moment, there were ovals of milky white glass at intervals around the walls, long axes parallel to the floor. The room was filled with soft sourceless light, as if someone had bottled sunlight and decanted it there.

"Hey," he bellowed. "Kephalos! God! Ratmeat! Talk to me. What the hell's going on?"

Silence.

"What do you want? I can't read your alleged mind, Garbage Heap."

Silence.

"Look, Rotbelly, I don't intend to spend the rest of my life hanging round this dump."

Silence.

Danny Blue wiped his hand across his mouth. He waited one minute, two, five. . . .

Silence hung thick and sour about him. He brought his hands a slight distance from his body, fingers curled, palms up. He frowned at the palms as if he were trying to read the god's answer in the lines. He dropped his hands and walked from the room.

4

The Bridge.

The visible portion of the Chained God was a queasy amalgam of metal, glass, vegetable and animal matter, shimmering shifting energy webs, the plasma of the magic that was the source of the lifestrength of the god. Instrumentation stacked blind face on blind dead face, dials, sensor plates, keyboards, station on station grouped in a squared-off horseshoe about the massive Captain's Chair. Dusty sweep of milkglass forescreen, fifty meters by thirty like a blind white eye dominating the chamber.

Danny Blue stepped warily through the half-open valve and stopped just inside. Powerdown, he thought. The energy webs were ghostwriting across the heavy decaying metal and plastic of the stations, the readouts were dead, most lights were shut off. Even so he could see sketchy attempts the god had made to refurbish h/its mainplace, attempts that some time ago had trickled into nothing. There were carpets spread across the crumbled remnants of the floormat; even in the gloom he could see the rich colors and intricate designs, he could also see the film of dust and grit laid over the pile. There were plants in ceramic tubs, dead, all of them. Rustling at long intervals when the airflow stirred their dry leaves.

Beside the Chair the floor was bared to metal, deckmetal plated with silver in a paper-thin disc twenty meters wide, polished until it gleamed like ice in the half-light. A design was scribed on the disc, fine black lines set into silver, a circle within a six-pointed star which itself lay within a second circle; lines inside the star crossed from point to point and intersected at the center of the design. *Hexa, get away from it.* The thought came from Ahzurdan; he didn't want anything to do with that figure. BinYAHtii lay in a sprawl of heavy gold chain where the lines crossed. Ignoring his half-sire's urgings, Danny stood scowling at the talisman. Why? he thought. Though his memory was uncomfortably vague, it seemed to him that the chain and its pendant lay much as they had when he dropped the thing ten years ago. But that couldn't be true, he'd been back to the Bridge several times since and BinYAHtii was nowhere in sight. Why was it here now, why arranged like that? why? He took a step toward the silver. The Ahzurdan phasma mind-shouted a warning: AVOID AVOID.

"All right," Danny Blue said aloud. "Hey! God! What's going on?" Silence.

Hands clasped behind him, arms tucked cautiously against his sides, he moved along the instrument array, examining everything minutely, touching nothing.

Dark. Blank. Dead.

Here and there a few lights wavered, monitors hooked into energy flow and life-support. The god had powered down so far h/it was in a kind of coma.

Fear stirred in Danny Blue, colder than a wind off Isspyrivo's glaciers. The god had waited too long, whatever h/its plan was. H/it underestimated the ravages of age on h/its material fabric. Even hull-steel was mortal, given sufficient time and stress. The Chained God was dying, h/its slow time-death accelerating toward total dissolution even as Danny watched.

Danny Blue moved back to the central bank of instruments. An impulse to try taking control of the computer stirred in him—that was Daniel Akamarino fighting to surface, the Akamarino phasma retreating to memories of a reality so different that his reactions had no connection to what Danny Blue had to cope with; even with all he'd seen since he'd been pulled into this reality, down deep Daniel then and his phasma now simply didn't believe in magic and wouldn't, perhaps couldn't, incorporate it into his worldview. Danny clamped down hard on his half-sire's urge, knowing it for the stupidity it was. He moved away to stand at the edge of the silver, staring down at BinYAHtii.

The Ahzurdan phasma stirred uneasily; he was uncomfortable this close to the Hexa; his anxiety sent cold chills down Danny Blue's spine. Daniel Akamarino was trying to be heard, saying: Pattern a drain, set it on delay and let's get out of here. If you won't try breaking the Kephalos free of the god, at least destroy it. I know we tried that before. I know the god caught us at it and put us down. It's different now. That thing is dormant. Can't you feel it?

Like eels in a sack, Danny's half-sires were fighting against his control, flexing and writhing, punching at him; he was getting more and more impatient with this nonsense, it was distracting him when he needed all his intellect focused on the problem before him. The

Chained God was dying and if he couldn't get out of here, he was going to die with h/it.

Danny Blue frowned at the talisman; he could feel his half-sire Ahzurdan coveting the stone despite the phasma's fear of the Hexa. If Danny could get at it somehow, he knew from a sweep of Ahzurdan's memories that he could use its power to protect them all from the god. From that sweep he learned also that the Hexa he saw was a dangerous variation on the more usual pentagram. Ahzurdan had never used one and knew very little about them, but he was afraid of this one; he didn't know why the god had laid it there, he didn't want anything to do with it. He fought to keep Danny from touching it.

BinYAHtii lay dull and red, sucking such light as there was into its rough heart. It was close enough to be tempting, two long strides would take him to the center of the pattern. Rubbing at his chin, Danny looked about, hunting for a pole or something he could use to rake the talisman from the silver.

His half-sires began wrestling with him and each other again, leaving his brain a muck of half-thoughts, half-desires, half-terrors.

Impatient and angry, he swore aloud, backed off a few steps, then took a running leap into the center of the Hexa. With a smooth continuation of the motion, he bent and grabbed for the chain, planning to straighten and leap again as soon as he had it.

His hand passed over a surface like glass. He couldn't touch the talisman. He thought suddenly, No dust, there's no dust on. . . .

5

He dropped a few inches, stumbled and fell to his hands and knees on black sand.

He got to his feet, brushed sand off his knees and hands. To his left, diminishing black hills curved around a placid bay. The sun was low enough in the west to glare into his eyes and dazzle off wrinkle-waves. He knew this place. "Haven Bay," he said aloud.

There was a ship anchored out near the narrow mouth of the bay, a sleek black hull with a green and black port flag snapping in the wind. I know that ship, he told himself. He scowled at it, disconcerted. Unless she has a twin, that's the *Skia Hetaira*. What's going on here . . . ?

He shook his head and started trudging along the beach, heading for Haven Village, out of sight around a bulge in the foothills.

6

The corral was empty. The erratic wind lifted then dropped clouds of ancient dry manure and sent the gate creaking on its cracking leather hinges. The stable doors gaped wide; several of the windows were cracked or broken; all of them were smeared with gray dust and veiled with dusty cobwebs. The cottage beyond had lost part of its thatching. Like the stable, its door was open and a litter of leaves, twigs and dirt had been blown through the gap into the kitchen beyond.

Danny Blue walked along the rutted street, frowning and nervous. The village was deserted; it looked like it'd been empty for years. He had a chilly feeling he knew what had happened to the people living here; that freaking Ratbait had fed them to the Stone. BinYAHtii. Haven was as dead as the god was going to be. Danny smiled at the thought, then shivered, thinking about the hook the god had set in him; he was afraid his fate was linked somehow with that abomination.

He came round a curve and saw a pale skim of yellow lantern light laid out across the ruts; it came through the open door of a tavern. He hesitated, glanced toward the bay. He couldn't see it now, but nodded anyway. Someone off the ship. He stepped through the door.

Lio Laux was perched on a stool at the bar, a lantern beside him, the only light in that stale dessicated room. There was an open bottle and a tankard at his side. He was sitting with his elbows on the bar, his bare feet hanging loose beside the legs of the stool. He wasn't drunk, but elevated enough to watch the mirror with philosophic melancholy as Danny Blue walked toward him.

Danny dusted off another stool, wiped his hand on his pants and sat down. "No one about."

There was a flicker as Laux moved his head slightly; his silver and moss agate ear dangle shivered in the lantern light. The light touched his ancient dark eyes, snuffed out as horny eyelids closed to slits. "No." After a moment, he added. "You live round here?"

"Just passing through. There another of those tankards left?"

"Ahind the bar."

"Ah." Danny slid off the stool, sauntered around the end of the bar and squatted so he could inspect the cluttered, dusty shelves. It looked very much like the proprietor stepped out for a breath of air and never came back. He found a tankard; it was thick with dust so he hunted some more until he discovered some clean rags in a tilt-out bin.

When he was back on his stool, he filled the tankard from Laux's bottle, took an exploratory sip, then a larger gulp. "That your ship?"

Danny saw ivory glints as the old man's eyes darted toward him and away; Laux was puzzled by a vague sense that the two of them had met before, but he couldn't pin down time or place. He had plenty of reason to remember Ahzurdan and Daniel Akamarino and Danny had something of each in his face and form. The resemblance to either wasn't all that strong, but it was there, a family likeness as it were.

"Yah. Looking for passage?"

"Might be, say we can do a deal."

"What you got to offer?"

"I could whistle a wind should you be wanting one. And I can do another thing or two if the need arises."

"Wizard, mage?"

"Nothing so grand. A bit of Talent, that's all."

"You set wards?"

"Yah."

"How far you want to go?"

"Next port bigger'n this."

" 'S a deal. You ward if we need it, give us a wind if we draw a calm, take a hand if we run into sharks round the Ottvenutt shoals. And I'll carry you on crew as far as Dirge Arsuid, that's ten days west of here. It's a chancy port, but you won't have to sit around long, there's a lot of trade in and out this time o year, take you just about anywhere you want."

"Good enough."

Laux drained his tankard, his ear dangle clattering musically as he tilted his head. He squinted at the bottle; there was half an inch of wine left in it, wine thick with wax and wing. "Reach me another of those bottles . . . ah . . . what do we call you, man?"

"Lazul, Laz for short."

"And while you're ahind the bar, hunt out the biggest of those rags, Laz. I wave that out the end of the pier, my second'll come fetch us."

Danny took one of the dusty bottles lined up below the mirror, set it on the bar. "Need something to open that?"

"Got something." Laux drew the cork, sniffed at the neck, poured a dollop into his tankard and tasted it. He grunted with satisfaction and filled the tankard. "Found that rag?"

Danny shook out a gray-white rectangle that might once have been a flour sack. "This do?"

"Should. Toss it over. You been here before?"

"First time."

Laux sucked at his teeth, tilted his tankard and contemplated the dark red wine. "Haven't been here for some years now," he murmured, talking more to himself than to Danny Blue. "It was quiet, the glory days were gone, long gone . . . time was there was near a thousand here, a dozen taverns, a casino, the place wide open day and night . . . yah, it was quiet when I was here last, but not so quiet as this. Two/three hundred people hereabouts, more down along the inlet. Don't know about them, maybe they're still around. You see anyone?"

"No."

"Mmh. Funny. The notion come to me one night, I ought to go see Haven again. Don't know why. Just something I ought to do. Wish I hadn't."

"Know what you mean." Danny put his elbows on the bar beside the rag, scowled into the tankard Laux shoved across to him. The wine was past its peak, but it wasn't that put the sour taste in his mouth. It didn't take a lot of thinking to see why Laux and his ship were here right now. Jerking my string, he thought. Whatever it takes, I swear I'm pulling that hook out. He gulped at the wine, wiped his hand across his mouth. "Any reason you're hanging about? Tides or something?"

"Ah the vastness of your ignorance, young Laz." Old Laux grinned at him, shook his head. He sobered, looked depressed. "Crew took a look round an hour ago. Got spooked and left. I told them to fetch me come sundown, I wanted to poke about some more. Haaankh." Having cleared his throat, Laux spat the result into the dust on the floor. "Being you're over there, shove a couple bottles in the pockets of that thing you're wearing and push another couple across to me. I saw a vest like that once, some years back. Never seen another."

"Gotcha. Never saw another myself. Could be it's the same one. I picked it up in Kukurul Market a little over a year ago."

"Ah." Lio Laux collected his bottles, slid off his stool and ambled toward the door. Over his shoulder he said, "Bring the lantern, Laz."

Danny grinned. Getting his money's worth, old thief. Well, I'm riding for free. So what's a dime's worth of flunkying.

7

Danny Blue, Laz to his companions, emerged into the abrasive cold, shivered as he wandered over to stand beside Lio Laux who was leaning on the port rail, watching the play of light across the walls and towers of the city on the horizon. The pointed roofs of Dirge Arsuid glittered blackly in the dawnlight; it rose in white and crimson and raven black over the dark drooda trees and the broad reedfields of the mouth-marshes of the Peroraglassi.

Danny/Laz folded his arms across his chest. "What's the problem? Why aren't we moving?" The *Skia Hetaira* was hove-to a half mile out to sea, riding the heave of the incoming tide, lines and spars humming, clattering in the brisk wind.

"No problem, Laz. We just waiting till it's full light before we go closer."

Danny inspected the water and what he could see of the city. "No rocks."

"Nah. Arsuid's built on mud."

"How come it don't sink?"

"It's Arfon's toy. You didn't know that?"

"Never been out this way. Arfon?" In the back of his head, the shade of Ahzurdan sneered. *You know,* the phasma said in a thin scratchy mindvoice, *if you condescend to remember. Fool. All right, go ahead, show your ignorance. Who cares if he despises you for it.* Danny Blue ignored his fratchetty half-sire and waited for Laux to answer him.

"River god. Dwolluparfon, which is too much of a mouthful so Arsuiders just say Arfon. Never, huh?"

"No. I come from way out where the sun pops up. I'm a rambling man, Laux; can't stand sitting around watching the same scenery all the time. If it's not silt or rocks, why are we sitting out here? We waiting for high tide?"

"Nah. Lemme tell you something, Laz. Darktime in Arsuid is a thing smart man keeps shut of. Unless he's an Arsuider and even then, hmm. We're not going to move for another couple hours, so I might as well spend it telling the tale of Dirge Arsuid." The plaques of his ear dangle clattered softly as he tilted his head to look up at Danny/Laz; the silver shimmered, the moss agate insets seemed to alter as if spiders crawled about under glass; there was a quizzical amusement in his old dark eyes. "You may have noticed I like to talk." He twisted his head around further, beckoned to the ship's boy who happened to be passing. "Pweez, tell Kupish to burn some duff for us, eh?" To Danny, he said, "You turning blue. Han't you got a coat or something? It's getting on for winter, jink."

"I didn't expect it to get this cold this far south."

"Winter's winter. Let's go below. I'll spin you the tale over hot grog an' one o Kupish's fancier fries. Taksoh caught a gravid kuvur last night, we'll have roe an' cheese to start."

8

"In the time before time when the Wounded Moon was whole. . . ." Lio Laux sucked up a mouthful of thick hot grog, let it trickle down his throat. "And the gods were sorting themselves out and sharing up the world, Dwalluparfon found he'd got hisself a river, a swamp and a handful of vipers. The story goes like this; he took a while to root round and get to know his mud, then he stuck his head up and looked round at his neighbors. And lo, they had lots of things he didn't. They had cities and farms, most of all they had people. He had fish and snakes. He didn't like that no way, wahn't fair. So he caught him a mess o snakes and made hisself some people." Luax's eyes slid round to Danny, the wrinkles round them crinkling with his sly-fox grin. "Not a tale Arsuider mams tell their lovin' infants. Lessee. He watched the snake people slither round in the mud and that was amusing for a while. But it was kind of drab, so he decided they were going to build him a city. He thought about it a long while, being slow that way; like his river he takes a long while to get anywhere, lots of detours, but he finally reached a conclusion. He wanted a shining city like the other gods had. He built up a mound of mud at the river mouth and cooked it until it was hard, then he drove a grid of canals through it and fixed the canals so the water was always moving in and out of them in good strong currents to keep them scoured clean. He went snooping around to the cities people built in other godplaces and picked out the things he liked about them and made hisself a city pattern. When he got back home, he scooped up a clutch of his snake people, rinsed them off and set them to work with ovens he made for them, turning out tiles, red, white and black. He spread his plan out for them so they'd know what he wanted, then he drove them generation after generation till he had his city built. Then he said, go live there and follow my rules and do me honor. And there you have it, Dirge Arsuid."

"Snake people, hmm?"

"To know 'em is . . ." Laux sucked up more grog, twinkled at Danny ". . . to know 'em."

"So, tell me more. If I'm going to be knocking about there, I better know what to look out for." In the back of his head, the Ahzurdan phasma snorted but said nothing. Danny ignored him. For a lot of reasons, he wasn't willing to trust the information in the memories his half-sire made available to him.

Laux ran his tongue over his teeth, stared past Danny at the cold white light coming through the porthole. "Been thinking 'bout that. I'll tell you a thing or two first, then . . . well, that can wait. Arfon say you get a trial if you accused of something. He say you got to be guilty 'fore they can send you to the strangler. Guilty o something, if not the thing they say you did. That's the law an' Arsuiders, they hold very strict to it. Arsuid honor. Hmh!" He shook the grog jar, emptied the last drops into his mug. "Trouble is, most folks have a thing or three staining their souls, an' if they don't, well a smart ysran, what they call their judges, he can f'nagle it someway to shift someone else's guilt onto that poor jink's head. Arfon don't care, long as the look o the thing's right. Mostly he don't notice what's happening; like I said, he's not too swift. Keeping all that in mind, it's a pretty loose guarantee 'less old Arfon, he sticks his head up and takes your side. It do happen. Can't count on it, but it do happen. I know. I run into something first time I showed up wanting to trade. Nearly got my neck in the strangler's noose too. But Arfon took a notion, don't ask me why, he stick his weedy head through the floor an' tell the ysran let me go. Ysran don't like it, but he do it. I don't have a smell o trouble the rest of the time I was there, I got some mighty profit out of it too. Why I bother to come back an' why I don't go in while there's dark on the canals. Trading here's worth walking the edge awhile. That f' sure. Long's you do it in daylight and watch the 'ifs' and 'buts' in your bargaining, they good folk to do business with. Arrogant bastards, make you want to skin 'em the way they act, but they keep their word. An' if they tell you something 'bout what they're selling, it's true. An' they got a lot to sell. Hennkensikee silks, for one thing. Better price than you can get just 'bout anywhere. Lessee, what else . . . ah! Stay inside once the sun's down. All bets 're off after dark. Strangers on the walkways or riding the canals, they dead. Don't think you could argue your way loose or fight 'em off, you won't. You dead. Floating out to sea. Sacrifice to Arfon. Arsuiders, they know what their god likes." He wrinkled his nose, sat back in the chair, dark fingers laced over his small hard pot.

"Lots o pretty red blood and fancy screaming. Long's it's foreigners making the noise and doin' the bleedin'. Way I see it, old Arfon, he never did get over other gods gettin' the jump on him with their cities an' their temples an' their busy-busy little folk, and he kinda likes seeing outsiders wiggle for it."

Danny lifted his mug. "Here's to the Arsuiders. To know 'em . . ." he gulped down the last of the lukewarm grog, ". . . is to know 'em."

"Yeh." Laux ran his tongue over his teeth, making his lips bulge. "Look here, Laz, you whistle up a good wind." He grunted with impatience and stopped talking as Pweez came in to clear away the dishes; when the boy was gone, he went on. "Taught some manners to those top'sh off Ottvenutt shoals. First time I've got past without taking some damage. You say you're a rambling man, no place you have to be, no one expecting you here or there. What I'm saying, if you don't fancy taking a chance on that," he flicked a hand toward the porthole, "why not stay on board? Say we can settle on what you get out of it."

Danny Blue picked at a hangnail and thought about it. He was tempted. He didn't know where he was going—except away. Away from the Chained God and his manipulations. Which did the god want him to do? Stay? Go? Enough to send a man biting his tail. His half-sire Daniel Akamarino had spent his life drifting from one place to another with no goals, no ambitions, his work the only center his life had. That kind of work wasn't available here, that reality was a place Danny found himself wanting to visit, but it was out of reach and he wasn't about to waste time yearning for what he couldn't have. His other half-sire Ahzurdan never took one step without plotting out a hundred steps beyond, though for him too, work was justification, a reason for being. And that was gone too, not available. With the war going on in his head, Danny Blue couldn't reach the degree of focus a sorcerer needed for all but the most ordinary activities.

Stay, fool, Ahzurdan's phasma said, *you won't find a better place. Things will only get worse.*

Don't listen to that mushbrain, Daniel's phasma said, *you and me, we're going out of our skull shuttling around on this crackerbox. We can get along just fine on the ground.*

Danny Blue liked old Lio Laux, the M'darjin was close to being a friend. He liked the crew. But he agreed with his half-sire Daniel, he most definitely did not like living on the ship. He was cramped, uncomfortable, and bored most of the time.

"Thanks," he said. "It's a good offer, but Dirge Arsuid sounds interesting, it's a place I've never been, I think I'll take a look at it. How long you going to be in port?"

"In by noon, out by dark. I don't overnight here ever."

"That's that then. See you round, I suppose. Maybe on my way back."

9

Danny Blue followed the guide Laux had summoned for him, a boy, twelve or thirteen, sallow skin with a greenish tint, stiff spiky hair dyed in green and yellow squares, green paint on his eyelids, yellow triangles painted under each eye, lips carefully tinted green. Heavy round ceramic plugs swung in rhythm with the swing of his meager hips, hanging from flesh loops stretching down from his earlobes, green in the right, yellow in the left. He had ceramic armlets clamped above and below the elbow on his left arm; they were striped in green and yellow. He wore a glove on his right hand, snakeskin dyed a rich dark green. His left hand was bare, the nails painted blood red. On his feet he wore snakeskin slippers dyed to match the glove. Instead of trousers he wore knitted hose, right leg green, left leg yellow, with a bright red codpiece and belt. To cover his torso he had a tight sleeveless green shirt with pointed yellow darts slashing downward diagonally, starting from his right shoulder, aiming toward his left hip. He strolled along as if he were going that way from choice and had no connection with the scruffy drab creature following him. His was a conservative dress for his kind, a simple walking-out costume. Warned on the ship to mind his manners, warned again before Laux turned him loose, Danny Blue managed not to stare at the show around him, but sometimes it was not so easy to keep his eyes straight ahead. As when a creation in feathers and gauze fluttered past, its species as uncertain as its outline. The boys he saw all had painted faces but no masks; every adult, male and female alike, wore halfmasks, stylized serpent snouts as if they adopted the insult in the old tale and made it something to flaunt. Laux said they carried viper poison in the rings they wore and could shoot it into someone with a special pressure of the hand. They usually refrained in the daylight, it was bad for business, but you didn't want to push them much, their restraint was delicate as a spider's thread.

It was a city of silences and shadows, of walls and towers; it smelled like clove carnations; they grew in the walls, red and white carnations, they floated in the water, bobbing past him as he walked along the roughened tiles, red and white carnations with white orchids and a rose or two, swirling around the narrow black boats poling along the canals. Red and white. The whole city was red and white. Every wall was faced with glossy red and white tiles. Panels of red tiles, columns of white tiles. Patterns of cut tile, red and white swirling together, sweeping along in dizzying flows. Red and white, white and red. Except for the pointed roofs. Those were black tile, shiny black. It rained most days from two till four, thunderstorms that dumped an inch or more into the grooves that ran in spirals from the peaks and dropped into channels that fed the glossy black gargoyles; the rain water spewed from their mouths, arching out over the walkways to spatter into the canals.

The boy led Danny Blue past a water plaza.

There was a black tile fountain in the middle and lacy white footbridges arching to it from the corners of the square. There were seats round the fountain. Several Arsuiders sat there, in groups like flocks of extravagant birds, heads close, talking in whispers. They stopped talking when they saw Danny, watched him until he went round a corner. He didn't look back, but he could feel the pressure of their whispers following him.

The Stranger's Quarter, local name Estron Coor, was laid out near the heart of the City, not even the Ahzurdan phasma knew why. The Stranger's Wall was a swath of murky red with black diamonds in a head-high line marching around the enclosure. The single door in that wall was iron thickly coated with a shiny black paint, nicked and bruised and smeared, the first dirt Danny Blue had seen in the city; the opening was narrow, a man only marginally bigger than average would have trouble squeezing through it.

The boy stopped before the door, his costume swearing at the wall; next to its heavy brooding solidity, he seemed more a concept than a living person, a player in some fantastical drama. He whistled a snatch of something, a complex tonerow sort of thing, stepped aside when he got a matching answer from the gatehouse perched over the entrance, no windows in it, only arrowslits with oiltraps in the base of the overhang. Danny Blue kept his face noncommittal but wasn't liking this much at all. Laux said they barely tolerated outsiders in their midst; this tower underlined that and went beyond. Strangers were treated like disease germs, encysted, kept away from the rest of the organism.

The door creaked open, a sound that felt like a rusty knife twisting in the bone. No sneaking out of here, Danny thought. He went through the narrow opening into the Estron Coor. The boy was still watching when the door was maneuvered shut by a complicated arrangement of ropes and pulleys. Making sure I stay where I'm put. What a bunch. Danny Blue looked around.

There was an Inn, three stories high and tight against the Wall; from the look of the second story windows and other signs it was eight rooms long and barely one room thick. The third story was tucked in under toothy eaves with shuttered unglazed holes too small to qualify as windows. Next to the Inn were several miniature stores with living quarters above them, a cook shop, a grocery, a butchery, a miscellany. Across the canal from the Inn there was a ponderous godon with offices or something similar in part of the ground floor and a line of portals with chains and bars enough to suggest that behind them were rare and costly things. Next to the godon there was a sort of multipurpose temple with seven flights of steps leading to seven archways, no two alike; ghosts in various stages of preservation drifted in and out of openings that made a sieve of the cylindrical tower emerging from the squat ground floor; they undulated past women with painted breasts who sat in those openings, they mingled with the drifts of smoke from the incense which kept the air inside the walls smelling rich enough to eat. The Ahzurdan phasma sneered at the women. *Temple whores. Tempted, Danny?* The Daniel phasma muttered something Danny couldn't hear, didn't particularly want to hear.

All those buildings were fairly new and constructed of wood by someone with a fixation on sharp points; the eaves looked like the bottom jaws of sharks, there were spearheads or something similar jutting from the corner beams, edges sharp enough to split a thought. The window bars were no meek retiring rods; on the outside they had ranks of needles like the erectile spines of a hedgehog snake, and the needles had discolored points. Poison, Danny thought, sheeit.

There were people looking at him from the corners of their eyes, shoulders turned to him. A motley collection, scarce two alike though they were mostly men. They were standing around as if they had nothing more important on their minds than sneaking peeks at a new arrival; the whole place had a feeling of stagnation, constipation, though the water in the broad canal ran clear and clean with scattered flowers riding the wind ruffles, slipping in through one grating and out the other. One of the men sauntered away from a group, crossed the humpy bridge to the temple and went inside. A few women swathed in drab veils that covered them head to toe hurried from one store to another, trotted back to the Inn or climbed the stairs to the cramped quarters over one of the businesses.

Unhurried, giving those side-eyes a bland mask to look at, Danny Blue strolled for the Inn, wondering rather seriously how much it was going to cost him. He had an assemblage of coins, a very mixed lot, some left over from Daniel's first days in Cheonea, some from Ahzurdan's hoard, some he'd found scattered about the starship. Though it wasn't much when he piled it up, it was enough to cushion him until he decided how to make some more—as long as he was quick about it. He pushed through the door.

The room inside was small and smoky, lit by a brace of sooty lamps. There was a staircase vanishing around a sharp corner, swallowed by shadows as sooty as the lamps and in the corner opposite it was an L-shaped counter with barely enough room for the youth dozing behind it. Danny woke him up, talked him out of a room and went to it to think about things.

In the middle of thinking, he fell asleep.

10

He woke, startled out of sleep so suddenly he sat up confused, slammed his head into something hard and cold. He swore, moved more cautiously. He was in a stone cage, granite by the look of it, squat, heavy, ugly. It sat inside a pentacle in a domed room without windows or any apparent doorways. No one about. He ran his hands over the stone, there wasn't a crack in it, not even where stone joined stone. "No doors in this thing, how'd they get us in here?"

C'vee mir, Ahzurdan phasma said, detached appraisal in his insect voice.

Danny was briefly amused, as he suspected he was meant to be. "What's that?" he said aloud.

Cage. Meant to hold magic wielders. Us.

"Not good, you mean?"

Not good.

"What's going on?"

I suspect we'll find out soon enough.

"You don't know?"

Like Lio Laux, I've avoided this place. There was no reason to seek it out. They don't welcome stray sorcerers here, no matter how high the rank.

"They don't welcome stray anybody. Any law against unregistered sorcerers?"

None that I know of.

"Gods, I haven't been here long enough to bruise a rule, let alone break one. What do they think I did? Spit in their canal?"

There'll be something. Unless Arfon intervenes.

"I think we can forget about that. This cage carved out or patterned?"

You mean, can I unmake it.

"Yeh."

I can't. You can.

"What a hope." Both his sires had learned whatever they needed to learn as easily as breathing; Danny Blue had assumed he could relearn Ahzurdan's sorcery in much the same way. After all, he didn't have to do the original work, only shift the WORDS and gestures to match his new psyche. Two problems with that. First, he wasn't given the time he needed; he'd spent the past ten years in an artificial coma. Second, he kept slamming into Daniel Akamarino's bone-deep disbelief in magic. In short, he discovered the truth in the aphorism: Sorcery requires will and the proper application of will requires belief. In those first months after the battle with Settsimaksimin when Danny was confined within the starship body of the Chained God, before the god caught him plotting, he'd worked harder than he could remember in either of his lives to rebuild a full range of WORD, IMAGE and gesture, though it was like fighting a tiderace to overcome the Daniel phasma's resistance, his unconscious rejection—and the Ahzurdan phasma's jealousy. Danny recovered some small confidence in his skills, though he was frustratingly unable to move among the realities, his half-sire clutched that ability to his insubstantial chest and wouldn't let Danny near it. Danny got far enough along to contrive a way of shorting out of the shipbrain, but the god woke up and time ran out on him. The Ahzurdan phasma might harbor illusions of competence; Danny Blue knew better. His hold on fire and wind was deft enough; he could play what games he wanted with the unTalented, but until he could make free with his realities again, put him against a fumble-fingered apprentice and he'd go down smoking. The phasma was right, he could dissolve that cage, he knew that after some tentative exploration, but he couldn't do it without making such a noise that the cage-maker would come running. Annoyed at the waste of his work, no doubt he'd impose a nastier sort of coercion. Best leave things as they were and see what happened.

Be ready, the Ahzurdan phasma said, tension sharpening his gnat's voice. *If there is a challenge, you need to be prepared. Search my memories. Now!*

Danny Blue paid no attention to his half-sire's agitation; there simply wasn't time to acquire skills he didn't already have. He floated his fingertips across the stone, seeking to read the status of the sorcerer who made it, and tasted the air around him to pick up ghost images of past events in this unlovely chamber, a psychometric survey that even the Daniel phasma believed in since it mimicked the activity of electronic sniffers.

From the air he got: Images of dark-robed men, of menacing faces looming over him. A fog of fear and cringing, rage, outrage and helplessness swirling about him. Voices booming words that never quite took specific shape. A sense of death and desolation and dissolution. Trials without defense where the verdict was given before the questions were asked.

From the cage, the c'vee mir, he got: Arrogance and malevolence, prissiness and paranoia. And a name. Braspa Pawbool.

There was a burst of insect laughter from the Ahzurdan phasma. *Poo Boo,* he squealed. *Poo the Boob, he couldn't scratch his way out of a spiderweb.* A moment's silence; Danny waited. *But he can talk, Danny, oh can he talk, I remember once he talked me into . . . mmh, never mind that. I can see how he tickled the Brin Ystaffel into hiring him. He's a water man, Danny. Fire makes him piss his pants. If it comes to a crunch, throw some salamandri at him and see if we can snap out of here before Arfon interferes.*

"I can't touch the realities, you forgot? Even if I could, we're inside this pentacle; I throw a salamander, it bounces back on me and whoosh, we're all gone."

The Ahzurdan phasma refused to hear what he didn't want to know. He ignored the first part of the statement. *A pentacle of Poo's making. Cobwebs. Breathe on it and it breaks.*

Danny Blue worked his body around until he was lying on his stomach. He reached through the cage, edged his fingertips to the nearest of the glimmering lines.

A nip, pain in his hand, like putting his finger in a live socket—the image slipped in from the Daniel phasma who was watching with cool skepticism. It wasn't as bad as his memories forecasted. He touched it again, let the pain flow round him and slip away without bite or afterbite. He tasted it, savored the flavors, got to know it, learned the WORD to dismiss it, translated that WORD into his own framework. He drew his hand back. "Yes," he said aloud. "One-two and it's through."

Yessss.

The satisfied vibrato tickled through Danny, made him smile. He crossed his arms, dropped his head onto his forearm and settled himself to wait for events to unfold. After half an hour when nothing happened, nothing changed, he slept.

11

There was a portentous knocking, the butt of a staff pounding on the wood of the dais with the five thronechairs. The chairs were filled now with black hooded figures, velvet halfmasks reinforcing the shadows from the hoods; the men wore heavy jeweled chains with jeweled pendants that caught what light there was and broke it into particolored glitters, they wore silks and velvets subtly draping about their hidden forms, richly tactile, magnificently sweet to the eye. A sixth man stood with staff in hand, robed and hooded too, but more simply, with plainer stuffs and a plainer chain. The six of them had slipped in while Danny Blue dozed and arranged themselves in dignified poses; now they waited for the drama to begin, waited in a silence as portentous, as theatrical, as essentially hollow as that knocking—a reaction Danny shared with the Daniel phasma who saw it was the sort of idiocy that disgusted him in the by-the-book, spit-and-polish conformity he had to put up with whenever he shipped on carriers like the Golden Lines. Danny Blue sat up warily, folded his legs and waited. What he saw was far tawdrier than the images he'd evoked; the phantom impressions of past trials were realer than the reality. The Ahzurdan phasma was annoyed with Danny and Daniel both and irritated by the figures in the chairs. In the days before he got tangled in the plots swirling about the Drinker of Souls, he cultivated such men and found a validation in their acceptance; they acknowledged his power as he paid homage to theirs, tacitly, placidly, both sides blessed by the certainty of their superiority. But the recognition, the certainty were missing now and he resented that. They should have known. If they were the real powers of Dirge Arsuid, they should have seen the power he had, or rather, the power possessed by the body he dwelt in. They should have given Danny the honor he deserved even if he was too stupid to demand it.

"I am the Prenn Ysran of Dirge Arsuid." The voice echoed hollowly; it took a moment for Danny to identify who spoke; it was the man in the center seat. If Prenn Ysran meant what he thought, this was the high judge of all Arsuid. He wasn't happy with the identification; it told him he was in more trouble than he liked to think about. The man spoke again. "State your name, felon."

Danny thought that over before he answered; Daniel prodded him to demand an explanation; Ahzurdan wanted him to be meekly courteous. "My name is Lazul," he said. "Why am I here?"

"You lie. Your name is Ahzurdan."

"No. Ahzurdan is dead."

"You are a sorcerer. You are addicted to dreamdust and come seeking it here. The sale of dreamdust is illegal here. To attempt to buy it is to break the laws of Dirge Arsuid."

"I am who I say I am. If I'm a sorcerer, that's my business, unless you passed a law against them. Have you? Not only am I not addicted to the dust, I'd put a knife through anyone who tried to force it on me. Who says I court such idiocy? Who says I importuned him to sell me anything? Bring him. Show him to me so I can call him the liar he is."

"The deed is not required, only the intent."

"Intent? You reading people's hearts now?"

"It is not necessary. You are here. Your habits are known. You are guilty. Do you repent?"

"How can I repent what I've neither done nor thought? How can I repent another man's sins?"

"He is contumaceous, brothers; he is intent on his illegal purposes. I say there is no point to further deliberation. How say you?"

"Guilty," intoned the figure to the far left. "Guilty." "Guilty." "Guilty." The lesser judges condemned him in whispers, squeaks and muted bellows.

"So say I. D'wab-ser, dissolve the cage and bring the man before us."

Danny Blue prepared himself, ready to move when he felt the event-flow shift. He watched the cowled sorcerer change his grip on his staff, saw the silver lines inlaid in the wood come to life, running like moonwater from tip to butt. He saw a shifting of shadow under the hood as the man's lips moved, though he couldn't hear words. The cage melted away around him. He stood up.

Free hand twisting through complex, awkward gestures, D'wab-ser Braspa Pawbool came down the stairs.

Danny waited, ready to counter if he could figure out how, waited for the moment when the man broke through the pentacle, expecting the attack then. Ready to attack the stone beneath Pawbool, the air around him, ready. . . .

No attack.

Braspa Pawbool simply reached across the lines, cancelling them. "Come," he said. "Don't be foolish. Come." He took hold of Danny's arm near the wrist, tugged at him. "Face your sentencing like a man not a child."

Startled, Danny took a step toward him. Pawbool's grip shifted. The Ahzurdan phasma screamed, *Pull away, pull . . .*

He was too late. Danny Blue felt the pricks from the twin fangs of the ring on Pawbool's center finger. His wrist burned. He started to jerk his arm away, Pawbool tapped the point of his shoulder with the staff; his arm went limp. "What . . . what are you . . ."

"Nothing to worry you. It's just to keep you quiet. Come with me."

Pawbool took his hand away. The fangs withdrew, the burning cooled until Danny couldn't feel it. Slowly, slowly the strength began returning to his arm. He followed Pawbool. The Sorcerer stopped him with a touch of the staff when he was in front of the Prenn Ysran. Danny stood there rubbing at his wrist; he could feel the drug beginning to work in him. A pleasant euphoria spread through his body; he felt lethargic, didn't want to move or think.

The Prenn Ysran waited until Braspa Pawbool climbed the stairs and resumed his place beside the last chair on the right, then he leaned forward until his nose and chin were visible as the light from one of the three lamps edged under his cowl. "The D'wab-ser lied," he said. "You have your death inside you, but you need not die." He spoke quickly, nervously; his heavily gloved hands tightened on the arms of his chair. "There is a way of atoning for your guilt, felon. There is an antidote. You can earn it. It will save you if you get it within the next four months. After that you die." He cleared his throat, his hood swayed as he turned his head slightly side to side as if he watched for something he feared to see. "What say you?"

"What do I have to do?"

"Say the words, felon. Say you accept the task." Again that twitch of his head, the shimmy of the hood.

Danny thought it over; he didn't like anything about this business, he also didn't have much choice. "If I can do it, I accept the task."

There was an odd creaking sound, a plopping like bubbles breaking in hot mush. Startled, Danny looked around.

A large head had pushed up through the stone, dark and shifty, quivering as if it were sculpted from gelatinous mud; on hair like seagrass it wore dripping, leathery leaves in a limp off-center wreath. Large dull eyes stared at them all, passing along the line of judges, dropping, stopping at Danny Blue. They fixed on him, gray and filmy fisheyes.

Danny Blue began to understand more of this. The god was behind what was happening. Arfon. Dwalluparfon. Mixed up somehow with the Chained God and his convoluted plots. The Daniel phasma sniggered. *Traded to a bush league, that's you, old Dan. Traded like a broke-down offwing.*

Be quiet, Danny snarled at his half-sire, *I need to pay attention here.*

The Prenn Ysran settled back in his chair, his relief palpable. "There is in the city Hennkensikee one of the Great talismans, Klukesharna. You are a sorcerer, you must know of Klukesharna."

"Sorcerer or not, I know of Klukesharna."

"Do you know what it looks like?"

"It's star-iron, shaped like a key about the length of my palm."

"Good. Bring us Klukesharna and we will give you the antidote."

"In four months? Impossible."

"We will underwrite your expenses and provide useful companions."

"Why me? The Peroraglassi passes through Lake Patinkaya; if his Riverine Sanctity over there wants the talisman, why doesn't he reach out and take it?"

"It is not for us to question the tasks the Great One sets us, felon; even more is it unseemly for you to intrude yourself."

"Hmh! Fancy language for blackmailers."

"Watch your tongue, felon, or your back will suffer for your insolence."

"Oh really?"

"We can find another easily enough."

"That I believe. However. . . ." He yawned, patted the yawn, hooked thumbs into loops on his vest. "Dead is not what I want out of life, so let's talk about this underwriting business. I need a reason to visit Hennkensikee. What do you suggest?"

The Prenn Ysran stood. "This is nothing to do with the Ystaffel. Make your arrangements with the D'wab-ser; he has our authority to proceed." He walked along the dais, skimming past the knees of the sitting judges and vanished behind an ancient dark arras that shifted slowly in the many drafts wandering about the chamber; after he was gone, Danny Blue deciphered the image embroidered there, it was a repeat of the Head silently watching the business, the river god protruding from the floor. Silently the other four judges rose and marched out, leaving Braspa Pawbool alone with the prisoner and the god.

Pawbool settled himself into the end chair. "Well, Ahzurdan, you've changed the furnishings somewhat, but you smell the same."

"Ahzurdan's dead," Danny murmured; in his head the Ahzurdan phasma gibbered a denial, but he ignored that. "Call me Lazul."

Pawbool laid his staff across his knees. "The dreamdust must have rotted your brain, you were easier than a first year apprentice, not a ward in sight. Makes me wonder if we were right involving you in this business. Well, what's done is done. Your question. It's the end of the trading season; the Silk Road is shut down though there's no snow in the passes yet, which is odd, there should be some by now, the last caravans left for the east a couple weeks ago. What that's got to do with this is this: every year when the season closes, the Lewinkob Spinners get rid of the ends and bolts that didn't sell. They cut the selvage off so the Hennkensikee sigil is gone and reduce the price to something like a third of what it would have been. What happens is small-time traders come in from everywhere to hunt through the leavings and get what they can. Even without the name, Lewinkob silks bring big money. You play things right, the Wokolinka's Amazons will think you're just another trader."

"I know as much about silks as you do about fire, Poo Boo."

"There you come, sneaking out, Firenose. Say your greets to the real world." Pawbool ran his fingertips delicately along his staff. "We know how ignorant you are, Little Zhuri. We have provided. Of your three companions, two know as much about silks as any specialist would. One steals them, the other wears them."

"A thief and a. . . ."

"Courtesan."

"And the other?"

"Thief and assassin, you get two for one with her. Oh, you needn't be worried about their commitment to the enterprise; the basis of their loyalty is much the same as yours."

"I see."

"I'm sure you do."

"Right. If you want this thing to work, I'll need a few items. An up-to-date map of the city. I presume you know where the talisman is housed, so lay out for me whatever information you have about that, a floor plan of the structure, if you can come up with one that's reasonably accurate, a description of how the thing is guarded—and warded. I assume it's powerfully warded and our silent friend back there would have got his fingers singed if he tried this on his own. I need what you know about the local god and what's his or her attributes." He paused a moment, thought a question at the Ahzurdan phasma, got back the equivalent of a shrug. "I've never been there and I haven't bothered to learn the basics. Too busy with more immediate concerns. I need to know them now."

Pawbool glanced at the god, then nodded. "Everything we have will be ready for you before the day's out."

"Good. I need to meet with and assess these aides you've roped in for me; any plan I make has to include their weak points and strengths. I'll go there by river, but I want strong, fast horses waiting for me and the others when we leave Hennkensikee. If things go well, we'll get out without raising a stir, but it's stupid to count on that. You know as well as I do, if anything can go wrong, it will. Set up relays along the river so we can change mounts and come straight through to Arsuid without stopping to rest."

"Travel both ways by river. We can guarantee protection as long as you're on water."

"Lovely. It's my skin, Poo. I know what I can do, I'm not all that sure of your um protection. It'd be so very easy to take that talisman off me and leave me to the tender mercies of the Wokolinka. If you want me to do this, set up the relays."

"You don't do it, you die. Painfully."

"Without the relays, I'm even more apt to die. Painfully."

There was a bubbling grunt from the god. Danny stiffened, then relaxed as he recognized the sound. Arfon was laughing. "Do it," the god said; his voice was like mud flowing, liquid and thick. "I like this one's wits; he doesn't cringe like you worms and he uses his head. I like him."

Pawbool's hands tightened on the staff; he waited until he was sure the god had finished, then his hood jerked as he nodded. "Agreed," he said to Danny, carefully not speaking to the god. "I will arrange for the relays come morning. What else?"

"If the three you've planted on me look like everyone else in this city, they'll need less conspicuous clothing. I won't travel with things out of some dye-master's nightmare. I'll need more gear myself; set me up as a Phrasi on the tawdry side, a small trader just barely making it. And I'll need enough coin to be convincing. Over and above what you found on me, which I'll want back. I'm supposed to be going there to buy, not shoplift. Everyone's heard that much about Hennkensikee; they don't let deadbeats through the gates."

"That has already been arranged. We will send you properly equipped."

"Nice of you. I'd better not go back to the Estron Coor, I don't want rumors to get out connecting me to anything Arsuider, especially your lot. I presume you've thought of that and set up quarters for me here, wherever this is."

"Yes."

"You left my gear in my room?"

"Yes."

"Transfer it. I'm tired and hungry and filthy. I want food and a bath, then I want to see the three I'm supposed to be working with."

"Snipsnap, Firenose, is that all? Shall I send along some dreamdust too?"

"Stuff it up your own nose."

"Hostile, aren't you."

Danny Blue looked over his shoulder. The god was gone. He snorted, it took that to give Poo Boo some stiffening in his spine. He stretched, rubbed at the back of his neck. "How much more time we going to waste playing one-up games?"

Braspa Pawbool stood. The light flared in the silver inlay of his staff as he fashioned a small amber will-o which drifted over to Danny and hung before his face. "Follow the light, Firenose. I'll follow you."

12

"Felsrawg Lawdrawn." The small wiry woman in boy's tights and tunic glanced at him, went with quick nervous steps about the room, whipping back draperies, opening doors to see what lay behind them, stopping to touch the bars on the window. She was a narrow sword of a woman, tensile and darting, filled with energy, with anger at the world;

she looked like she'd give off sparks if you touched her. When she finished her inspection, she perched on a small backless chair, hands resting lightly on her thighs, her sleeves loose about her wrists, the knives she wore on her forearms not visible but ready if she needed them. Her tights were black and white, the stripes spiraling about her legs down to soft boots of dark crimson. There was a matching glove on her left hand; the nails of her right hand were painted green. Her tunic was divided into squares, black, red and white in a dizzying spiral; she wore a loinskirt of leather strips dyed a bright green, studded with black iron and silver. Her hair was black with silver stripes; it was pulled tightly up and bound at the crown with a green thong, the fall coiled into black and silver corkscrews that trembled past her shoulders. She had small ears that sat tight against her head pierced along the rim; she wore six black studs on the left side, six silver studs on the right. She had a lean and angular face, a wide mouth whose corners turned down. She was young, not more than twenty, and she could have been pretty if she'd wanted that, but she refused it with every breath she took. "Who're you?" she said; her voice was hoarse like an old singer's might be after fifty years in cabarets.

"Lazul."

"That doesn't tell me a whole helluva lot."

"I doubt you need telling much, being the one that Poo the Boob brought in to put a knife in me and take the talisman soon as we get clear of the city."

"At least you're not a fathead like him."

"There's only one of him, gods be blessed for that. He said you're a thief. How good are you?"

"You mean if I got caught, I couldn't be worth much." Her face was taut with an anger only just under control. "Him. He set his thumb on me. Arfon." She shrugged. "I was a whore when I was eight, killed my pimp when I was ten and got rid of his ghost before it squealed." She laughed when he raised his brows, mildly surprised that she would tell him something like that. "I'd just say you lie and they'd believe me, I'm Arsuider, you're outsider. Think about it, toop." Another shrug. "Since then my life's been mine, I have not been cheated or caught. I trust myself and no one else. I am good, Lazul. It took a god to get me. And I don't know shit about this business, except that blinbaw Pawbool told me I was to do what you said and when you got what they wanted, to get it off you and bring it to him."

"Wait till the others get here, I don't want to go through this more than once."

"Others? What others?"

"Two."

She got to her feet, began pacing about the room; there was too much fury in her to let her rest a moment.

13

"Simms Nadaw." The second thief had a spiky thatch of coppery hair and the translucent too-pallid skin some redheads were cursed with; the pink/purple flush of his face clashed awkwardly with that orange/red hair. His tunic and tights were a mix of reds and pinkish oranges in assorted plaids and stripes, his glove and boots were a bright brown of surpassing awfulness. He was such a disaster, so wrong, you looked away from him in embarrassment, remembering the ensemble while you forgot his face.

Amber eyes sleepy under fat eyelids, he produced an amiable grin, nodded without grace in answer to Danny's greeting and ambled over to sit in the single armchair.

Felsrawg stopped in front of him. "You, huh?"

Simms blinked at her. "Me, yeh."

She examined his outfit, shuddered. "I've seen you in bad, but that's the worst."

He grinned again, his eyes almost disappearing into the crease between upper and lower lids; he seemed barely intelligent enough to know which end of a shovel to dig with. "I try. Arfon?"

She shuddered again. "Yeh. You?"

"You think the 'staffel got me?" He had a light tenor voice that made sleepy laughter of the words.

"No."

"Sh'd hope not."

She swung round to face Danny Blue who was watching this, bland-faced but amused, planted her fists on her hips. "Well?"

"There's one to come yet."

"Who?"

"I don't know. She's supposed to be a courtesan of some kind. Knows silk. Poo the Boob said one of you knows silk. Which?"

She jerked a thumb at Simms. "You wouldn't think it to look at him, would you."

Danny folded his arms, leaned against the wall. "Oh, I think so; he's a very clever man, isn't he."

"So are you, if you see that." She stood stone-still for a moment, her eyes narrowed, her head thrusting forward; she looked like a poison lizard poised to strike. Then she relaxed and perched on the edge of the backless chair where she'd been sitting before. "Maybe we'll get out of this alive."

14

"Trithil Esmoon." She came through the door with a sussurous of whisper silks. Despite the play she made at concealment, a narrow serpent mask across her eyes, she was immediately and astonishingly beautiful. Despite that mask, she was not Arsuider. No Arsuider had eyes of that deep smoky blue or hair fine and white as spidersilk; it was combed back and to one side, flowing in long shimmering waves to her waist. Her skin was cream velvet, delicately pink about the cheekbones. Her wrists were pencil thin, her hands small and tapering. She wore a simple robe that slanted from her shoulders to a fullness about her feet; it was made of layer on layer of transparent blue silks that shifted across each other with every movement, every breath she took; her body was a hint of darker blue beneath them, slender with round full breasts and a tiny waist; the sleeves were tubes, the upper edge open and falling away in swags from silver tacks, gathered at the wrists into silver bracelets. She wore silver and sapphire earrings as long and heavy as a Panday shipmaster's ear dangle and on her ungloved hand had silver and sapphire rings on every finger plus her thumb; most of the sapphires were faceted and glittered bluely when she moved her hand, but the thumb ring was cabuchon cut, a mounded oval, a star in its heart. Her slippers and glove were silver, her perfume subtle as the shift of blues in her robe. She smiled at Danny Blue, held out her gloved hand, the glove being a guarantee the hand was safe to take.

Since she seemed to expect it, Danny took the hand, bowed over it. She was a piece all right, artificial as a wax flower, advertising her pliancy to his needs with every move, every twitch of an eyelash. He thought he disliked her pretentions and was put off by her profession. Half-sire Daniel disapproved of prostitution; besides, he'd never needed to buy women. They liked him. He drifted in and out of their lives as easily as he drifted in and out of his jobs. Half-sire Ahzurdan was ambivalent about women at the best of times, which these most decidedly weren't; his sex life was mostly imaginary, taking place in the heroic fantasies he experienced during his dust orgies.

Then Trithil's perfume hit Danny and he wasn't so sure what he thought of her.

He straightened, led her to the bed and lent his arm as she sank gracefully onto the quilts and sat there with her little hands laced together, half-hidden in the folds of her draperies. When he turned, Felsrawg was looking as if she'd been carved out of hot ice into a personification of indignation and disgust. Simms screwed up his face and panted like a dog, tongue lolling, then relapsed to idiot.

Danny Blue went back to leaning against the wall; he crossed his arms and scowled at two-thirds of his strike force. "You're a pair, you are. Insolent, impudent and smarter than any three like me, right?" He spoke with weary impatience and a deep-down anger he wasn't about to surface, not now anyway. "Insubordinate because you earned it, right? Individualists who aren't about to take orders from me or anyone else, right?" He yawned. "I know you, see? I've been you. Nothing you can show me I haven't done already and done better. I don't give a handful of hot shit for any of your games. It comes down to this, my friends, we've got four months to do a job. We bring it off or we die. I'm not going to waste time tickling your vanities. Either you help or you hinder. If you hinder, you're out. Now or later." He moved his eyes from Felsrawg to Simms to Trithil, then fixed on Simms. "What I say now, you better believe. I don't need any of you. You're in this because the ones working this scam figure you can be useful. And you're here because they don't trust me farther than they can spit, they figure poison isn't enough of a hold on me. Well, I intend to survive. I'm good at surviving. Just remember that."

Felsrawg simmered; Simms looked stupider; Trithil smiled slowly and fixed her blue blue eyes on him as if she couldn't bear to look away.

"Right, I can see how impressed you are. Did they tell you what we're going after?"

Simms rubbed a long spatulate thumb over his wrist, a gesture Danny recognized; he'd been doing the same thing since Pawbool injected the poison into him. "They say come here." He sounded as if he were speaking through a yawn, letting the words fall out of his mouth. "They say back up him I found here any way I c'd. They say when he gets sa thing, steal it an' bring it back. Nobody bother sayin' what IT is."

Felsrawg stirred. She glanced at Simms, very unhappy at his sing-song discourse. Which told Danny more than words would about the man and his talents. "Same with me," she said finally. "I told you that, remember? And you said something about a talisman."

Danny turned to Trithil, raised his brows. She didn't have anything to contribute but the graceful lift and fall of her breasts. He looked hastily away, ignored Felsrawg's muttered insults. "We're going to Hennkensikee," he said. "We're going to steal Klukesharna."

"Broont! We're dead." A flicker of Felsrawg's hands and she was holding twin stilettos, the blades needle-fine, hardly longer than her middle finger and coated with a dark gummy substance. "I swear, before I'm dead, they are."

Simms sat placid as a milk pudding with cinnamon trim. "Sorcerer?"

"Not the one they think I am, but yes, a sorcerer."

"Not a prime."

"Too true. Poo the Boob caught me napping, it's not something I'm proud of, but there it is." He glanced down at the scabbed pinpricks on his wrist, grimaced. "I'm not asleep now. For what that's worth. Make up your minds, the three of you. In or out?"

Simms' eyes dropped completely shut. "In," he said. "Long as you stay awake."

"In." It was a liquid murmur, promise of delight, all that in one tiny syllable. Trithil reached up, smoothed the hair back from her face, her rings glittering.

"In," Felsrawg said, biting off the tail of the word as if she'd like to bite something else. She looked down at the knives, slipped them back into their sheaths. "What choice have we got?"

"You got a choice, Felsrawg. Enthusiasm or out."

"In. In! IN!"

"Now that that's done, I need to know what you all do best. I'm a whiz with wards, I can tease the densest knot open without a whisper and throw a knot of my own that only two people I know can undo. But there's bound to be more involved than wards. Poo tells me the Wokolinka uses witches and the local god to run her security. Which is not good news, witches tap into earth forces I can't touch; that means traps. And a god even a local one is always trouble. Which you know as well as me." He tapped a forefinger on the wrist where Pawbool had sunk his ringfangs. "Any of you been to Hennkensikee?"

"Not me." Felsrawg leaned forward, her interest caught at last. "I do locks. All kinds of locks. Walls. I'm good at walls. Blowpipes and sleep powders, nobody's ever sneezed when I puff the powder in. That happens, you know, if you're sloppy. It can embarrass the hell out of you because they wake up." She was sparkling, almost laughing; apparently she'd decided to lay her resentment aside and treat the problem as a challenge. "I know metals, if that helps. And I'd be a lot more useful if I had my keys and files and picks and the rest of my kit. The 'staffel took it away and haven't give it back which seems rather stupid, considering."

"Agreed. I'll have a talk with Poo and see if we can fix that."

Simms yawned, blinked slowly. "Get 'm to gi' me mine too," he murmured. He ruffled his spiky hair, smiled sleepily at Danny. "Like li'l Felsa there, 'm a born and bred Arsuider. N'er stuck my nose outside the place. No point in it. I know silks, yeh, like to know why y' wan' to know that, don' seem connect t' Kluk'shar'. Want me t' brag a bit, 'm the only thief 'round better'n Felsa at ticklin' locks." Another sleepy smile, this time directed toward Felsrawg. "She w'd argue that, but tis true. Got 'nother talent. Talk t' rocks."

"What?"

"Not so dumb as it sounds. I'm a Reader. Rocks chatter like ol' Grannas if you know how to tickle 'em. An' I'm good with ghosts. Be s'prised what they tell you 'bout their folks. Just 'bout all ghosts hangin' round thick 'nough to talk got a grudge. Ol' grandfa once take me right to a abdit full of pretties. Bein' lazy, I'm a patient man, I like to know all I can find out 'bout a place 'fore I go in. I'm good at piecin' too. Bit here, bit there, you know. Drawin' plans. That sorta thing." He stopped talking, having said all he meant to say.

"I know Hennkensikee," Trithil said quietly.

Danny Blue turned to her, startled. She'd shut off the hithery and lost her gloss. She was still beautiful, that was in the bone, but she'd added at least ten years and subtracted most of the life from face and eyes.

"I know grades and prices," she said. "Pawbool said you wanted in as a trader, I can handle that for you. And I can get information for you." There was an unreadable look in her eyes, animal eyes with nothing back of them, now that he paid more notice to them. "Man or woman, both find me pleasing. And if that fails, I have certain potions that loosen tongues or do other things you might find useful." She didn't so much stop speaking as let words drift away from her.

Danny Blue frowned, wondering about her. His half-sires stirred in him, equally uneasy.

Maybe she's on something and it just let her down, the Daniel phasma muttered. *How much can you trust what she's telling you?*

I don't like her, the Ahzurdan phasma said. *I don't trust her. I don't think she's what she seems. Maybe she's a demon of some kind. I don't smell demon on her, but there's something. . . .*

Can you watch her?

Sense of shrugging. The Ahzurdan phasma brooded a moment. *If you watch her, we see her. Otherwise not.*

Well, do what you can. I have to get on with this. Aloud, he said, "Just a few things for now. We can talk more on the way there. Are there many Arsuiders in Hennkensikee?"

After waiting a moment for the others to answer, Trithil said, "No."

"Why? There has to be trade moving along the river."

"Not as much as you might think. The Lewinkob are suspicious of the South. They prefer to deal with the caravans that come in from the east." She spoke in a marshmallow monotone that he had to strain to hear; she was passive, almost inert, giving out information like a robot. "Most of the Hennkensikee silk leaves that way, that's why it's called the Silk Road." She glanced briefly at him, looked down again, eyes fixed on the toes of her silver slippers. "They are more than suspicious really, they hate the South; they call the disputed land between the two domains the Bloody Fields. There have been raids across the Bloody Fields since before the cities were. And wars. Seven bloody wars, Dirgeland against the Tribes. No. Arsuiders are not welcome in Hennkensikee."

"Would the local noses be able to sniff them out?" He waved a hand at Felsrawg and Simms. "If we stuffed them into normal clothes."

"Probably not, as long as they use the kevrynyel tradespeech even in private and forget they know the Dirgefoth." She looked distantly at the others. "Trade is blood in Hennkensikee. Blood can blind."

Danny pulled his hand across his mouth. "I can't hear an accent in your kevrynyel, I can in theirs." He nodded at Felsrawg and Simms. "Heavy. What about that?"

"Traders come from everywhere to buy the silks, especially this time of year. They all speak the kevrynyel. They all have accents. One accent merges with the others."

"How much of a background will we need? What I mean is, how many questions are we going to have to answer?"

"None or too many."

"I see. The personas have to be fleshed before we come near the city."

"Yes."

"Hmm. Simms, ever heard of a place called Croaldhu?"

"Neh."

"Island off the east coast, about twelve days sail from Silili. You know Silili?"

"Who don'?"

"Let's do this. Your family left Croaldhu for reasons of their own and your grandfa or gre'grandfa, something like that, set up as merchant in Silili, hmm . . . how old are you?"

"Chwart."

"I take it that means old enough."

Simms grinned sleepily at him.

"All right. We'll say you're a third son, rambling about looking up new possibilities for the family business. You signed on with me because I said I'd get you into Hennkensikee. That's the heart of it; we can set the details later. Any questions? objections? whatever?"

"Why Croaldhu?"

"You have the look. Or would in what the rest of the world calls clothes. I'm half-Phrasi by birth, shouldn't be any problem with that. Trithil?"

"No."

"Felsrawg?"

"Tell me, o master, what's you got for li'l me?"

"Got any preferences?"

She shrugged, slipped a throwing knife from her boot and began flipping it and catching it.

He watched it loop lazily through the air, nodded. "Know anything about the Matamulli?"

She caught the knife, held it, looked at him from narrowed eyes. "That a joke?"

"Neh, assassin. They're Southrons; they claim the Mulimawey Mountains beyond M'darj." He rubbed at his nose, inspected her. "You could pass with some rearrangement here and there." She didn't want any part of that, he could feel her resisting. "The men are the homebodies; they farm, care for the herds. The women hunt and trap and do most of the trading. Very independent lot they are, too." Felsrawg flipped the knife again, caught it, flipped it. There was time left and Danny was willing to spend it persuading her; if time ran out and she was still fighting him, he'd cut her loose; it didn't matter how loud Poo yelled. "What's useful for us is this, before they settle down with a husband or two, younger daughters generally go outland to make a dowry for themselves since they don't have land." He pointed at the knife. "They carry half a dozen of those and can split a mosquito at thirty paces."

"That all?"

"All for now. Make up your mind."

"Enthusiasm or out?"

"Yep. Ground rules."

"I hear you. Just call me Matti. When do we go?"

"If Poo doesn't drag his feet, by the end of the week." He ran his hand through his hair. "Wait here, the three of you, if you don't mind; Poo sent over some charts, I'd like to get your ideas on them."

THE REBIRTHING: PHASE TWO
The stonebearers are pointed toward the stones

I: BRANN/JARIL

The Cavern was empty so they went searching
for Yaril in the only place they knew to look:
  Dil Jorpashil

1

"All right," Brann said calmly, using voice and body to quiet her changer son. "So Yaro is gone. She didn't just walk out?"

"No." Jaril stopped shuddering as Brann stroked his hair and fed him snippets of energy. "No, if she was free enough to walk, she'd be here, waiting for me."

"That being so?"

He lay still, his eyes closed. After a minute, he said, "That being so, whoever set the trap came and got her."

"Yes. When you feel up to it, Jay, go back and see if he left some traces, anything to tell us who to look for. If we're lucky, he isn't finished with this, he's after you too. And me."

"You?" Jaril pulled away from her, stared at her, startled.

"Think about it. Yaro's either food or part of a bigger trap. Which would you prefer?"

Jaril started convulsing; in minutes the shudders were waves of dissolution passing along his body, threatening to tear him into gobbets of mindless energy.

Brann snatched a burning billet from the fire and slammed it into and through him, feeding fire to him to strengthen and distract him; she caught up another and repeated what she'd done. Then she seized hold of him and began flooding him with energy, draining herself to help him stabilize.

He broke away, appalled at what he was doing. When he was steady enough, he crawled into the fire and crouched there. "Brann?"

"No no, luv, I'm all right. For a while anyway. You?"

"Sorry, Bramble. I didn't mean to. . . ."

"I know, Jay. Don't fuss, my fault, I shouldn't have been so abrupt."

"Bramble. . . ."

"Yes?"

"If anything happens to Yaro, I will DIE. I can't BE the only Surraht here."

Brann nodded. "I know." She got heavily to her feet, collected several scattered billets and piled them on the fire around Jaril. She gathered her blankets, folded one into a square and sat cross-legged on it, wrapped the other around her shoulders. "You and Yaro have always avoided talking about your people. I need to know more about you, Jay, so I can read this trap. Maybe send you home. You and Yaro." She grimaced. "I'll miss you, both of you."

Jaril fluttered a hand at her, looked away. "Bramble. . . ."

"I know. We've been together a long time. It's hard, mff." She managed a fragment of a laugh. "Talking Slya into sending you home isn't going to be the easiest thing I've ever done. You think you could crawl out of that fire long enough to set some water to boil? A little tea would be a help."

Jaril nodded. His limbs glowing red-gold like the flames, he cooled one hand enough to pour water from the skin into a pot, then went back to the fire and sat holding the pot on his thighs until the water boiled. He scolded Brann back to her blankets when she started to get up, made the tea and took a mugful to her. He retreated to the fire and watched as she sipped. "If we talked, it meant we had to remember. It's not easy, Bramble. Not even with you."

Brann sipped at the tea and waited; she said nothing, it was up to Jaril now, he had to decide what he was going to tell her.

"It wasn't so bad when we were aetas, that's uh children who aren't babies any more. Aetas are supposed to wander around, usually two or three or maybe four together. When they're twins like Yaro and me, they generally go in twos. That's how Slya caught us, we were off by ourselves, poking into a stuvtiggor nest. Stuvtiggors eat Surrahts, they pick on afas, that's babies, and agaxes, that's adults. Aetas are too fast and too tough for them. It's one of the things we do when we're aetas.

Eat stuvtiggors. They're uh like ants, sort of, their uh essence is like ours, not yours, Bramble; they taste good, like um those fried oysters you pig on sometimes. Not really, I don't know, it's the same idea. Close enough. They can do what we did when we made that horse for you, remember? They can merge to make one curst big stuv clot. If they catch one alone, it's good-bye Surraht. That's why, when you said Yaro might end up food. . . ." He started to shudder again, stopped himself. "We lost a . . . I suppose you'd call her a sire-side cousin . . . we got to her late, we saw the stuv clot eating her . . . agh! We scragged it, ate. . . ."

He stopped talking, flowed briefly into his globe form, sucking in great gulps of heat energy, almost killing the fire before he changed back. "We were aetas when Slya snatched us. She changed us back to afas, sort of, so we had to have you feed us, Bramble, so we had to change you, so she could use you and us. You know all that. Anyway, the thing is, we're not aetas any more, Yaril and me. We're aulis. All that godfire, it kicked us all the way past . . . uh . . . it's a kind of part-puberty. We aren't fertile yet, that happens later, but we uh make out like minks. Or we would if there were other aulis around. Not a sister . . . or a brother . . . we can't . . . uh . . . it doesn't work. . . . Ahh! gods, Bramble, sometimes in the past year or so, Yaro and me both, we felt like we were going to go nova if we didn't get somewhere there were more aulis than just us. We were working up to ask you if you'd please please figure a way to . . . it's more than uh sex, Bramble. Aulis make bonds. Communities. Like families here. Sort of. It's more complicated. We NEED to do that or we go uh rogue. Round the bend. Insane. We get worse than stuvtiggors. We eat . . . uh . . . it's bad. Well, you get the idea." He cupped his hand about a wisp of flame, let his flesh go translucent, showing shadows of bones that weren't really there. "This might be more important, Bramble. When we were aetas, we were uh simpler and uh tougher. You know how fast we came back after that webfoot shaman stoned us. We can't do that now, it takes time for us to uh unfold, it takes more uh force to bring us back and the longer we're down, the harder it is to come back. You don't want to count on Yaro being able to help us, well, fight or run, even if we can bring her all the way back from stone."

"And I was complaining about being bored." Brann rubbed her fingers across the hollow at her temple. "I do want you to look around more carefully down there, Jay; keep in mind what we decided about Jorpashil, see if you can find anything to support or cancel that."

Jaril deformed, his version of a yawn. He blinked sleepily at her over the tongues of fire curling about his legs. "You brought some wine, didn't you, Bramble?"

"I brought some wine. I'll have some hot for you when you get back."

"Holding my nose to it, huh?" He smiled, that sudden flash-grin that could twist her heart and remind her that he and Yaril were the only children she'd ever have. Then he shifted to the firesphere and went darting off.

She looked after him until even the faint glow on the walls went dark. First Maksim splits, now the children. No, that's the trouble, they aren't children any more. She thought about the Arth Slya that existed when she was a child and mourned for what had been, a long flow through the centuries since the first artisans moved there, teacher/parent passing skills to student/child who taught in his turn, her turn. My children will be gone beyond my reach after this is over. If they were dead, at least I'd have their ghosts to comfort me a while. If they stay here, they're dead or mad. Dead or mad. I never have a choice, do I? She grimaced. "Tchah! Brann, oh Brann, you know it's not so bad a world. Stop glooming. A month ago you were bored out of your skull. Hmp, Maksim was right, watch out what you ask for, you might get it."

"Talking to yourself, Bramble?" Jaril dropped into the fire, wriggled around until he was comfortable. He tossed her a copper coin. "Tell me what you think."

She rubbed her thumb across the obverse. "I don't know this writing."

"Sarosj. It says Blessings to Sarimbara the Holy Serpent."

"Ah. A coin from Dil Jorpashil?"

"What they call a dugna. Fifty to a silver takk."

"You're feeling better."

"It was not knowing, Bramble."

"I know. How far is Jorpashil from here?"

"Yaro and me, we flew it, took us five days and part of the sixth. 'Less we can get you mounted, you'll be walking. Probably triple that and then some, say twenty days for you."

She pulled the blankets tighter about her, shivering a little as stray currents of icy air sneaked through crevices in her clothing. "I could use one of Maksi's *call-me*'s. If he was here, he could pop us over in a wink."

"How many he give you?"

"Six."

"I have a feeling you ought to save them for something more important."

"More important than my poor little feet?"

"Brammmmble!"

"Mmh. You've been there, I haven't. What face should I put on?"

"Old and ugly. The base culture is nomad Temueng; an offshoot of one of the grassclans gone to seed. Settled by Lake Pikma a couple thousand years ago. Since then they've mixed with Phrasi, Rukka-nag, Lewinkob, Gallinasi, and whatever else trickled up the river, but that didn't change how they look at women. You know Temuengs."

"That I do. You going to spend the night in that fire?"

"Oh yes. Any reason why I shouldn't?"

"No, just pop a billet on now and then, hmm?"

"That's me, is it? Automatic fire feeder."

"Where could I find a better?" She grinned and got to her feet, taking the blanket she'd been sitting on with her. She snapped it open, folded it in half and spread it close to the fire. "Wake me sometime round dawn. Might as well get an early start." She wrapped the second blanket around her and stretched out. "Slya bless, this rock is hard." She yawned, rolled onto her side so she was facing the fire and in minutes was deep asleep.

2

Twenty days later a tall gaunt holywoman came striding along the Silk Road, a gnarled staff in one hand, the other swinging loosely at her side. She wore an ancient tattered overrobe and gathered trousers of coarse homespun; her sandals were worn, mended with cord. Her lank gray hair was loosely braided into a single plait that hung down her back, its ragged end bobbing against her buttocks in time with each step. Straggles of gray hair fluttered about a weatherbeaten face. Her mouth was a flat line bracketed by deep furrows curving down from the nostrils of a long bony nose. A big black dog with a blanket-wrapped bundle strapped to his back paced beside her.

She stopped at the edge of the rivermoat, sniffed at the thick green mat of jeppu plants and the hoard of leaf hoppers that started a frantic piping when she climbed up the levee and stood looking down at them. "So how do we get in?"

The dog looked up at her, then he turned south and trotted away along the levee path. The woman stumped after him.

There was a ferrylanding near the place where the moat branched away from the river, a gong on a gallows at one side. A rag-padded stave hung beside it; the leather loop tied through a hole in one end was hooked over a corroded nail on the gallowpost. A narrow lane was cut through the mat of jeppu, baring a strip of water wide enough to let the flatboat pass. The ferry was across the river, the ferryman nowhere in sight. Brann shaded her eyes with one hand, peered along the river. She could see other landings opposite other gates. At every crossing the ferries were snugged up on the city side. She shrugged, lifted the stave off its nail and beat a tattoo on the gong.

Nothing happened.

She looked at the stave, shrugged again and hung it where she'd found it. "I suppose he'll come when he feels like it."

The black dog yawned, sank onto his stomach. Tongue lolling, head on his forelegs he was a picture of patience.

Brann laughed and dropped beside him. She arranged her legs in the lotus cross and prepared to wait.

Across the river a stumpy figure came from a shed and stood on the bank, hands on hips, staring at her. He wiped the back of his hand across his mouth, spat into the mat of jeppu; his lack of enthusiasm was louder than a shout. He glanced up at the barbican behind him when a guard leaned from an arrowslit and bawled a garbled comment in the sarosj that Brann was only beginning to understand. He spat again, slapped his right hand on his left forearm, then turned his back on the guard. Impatiently he thrust his hands through his thick curly hair, shouted something incomprehensible at the hut and stalked onto the ferry; he stood at the shoreside end, his hands back on his blocky hips, watching as two boys ran from the hut, cast off the mooring lines of a longboat and rowed across the moat.

The boy at the forward oars inspected her with a lively curiosity in his black eyes, but he asked no questions. "To cross, a takk," he said.

"Don't be absurd. Three dugnas is more than enough for that leaky tub."

He smiled, a smile sweet as honey and as guileless. "Our father will beat us, baiar. Forty dugnas."

"He should beat you for your impudence, pisra. Five dugnas and only because you have the smile of an angel, though doubtless the soul of an imp."

"See my sweat, baiar. Consider how far it is. And you have that no doubt dangerous beast with you. Thirty dugnas for the two of you."

"There's not enough sweat on you and your brother both to tempt a gnat. Seven."

"Twenty for you, five for the dog."

"Ten for me, two for the dog."

"Done. Pay me now, baiar." He held up his hand, the palm horny with long labor at the oars.

"Why not. Make room for the dog, hmm?" After Jarilhound jumped into the boat and was standing with legs braced, Brann got to her feet, thrust two fingers in her belt pouch and fetched out twelve dugnas, counted them coin by coin into the boy's hand. When the count was done, she eased herself stiffly into the longboat and settled on a thwart with Jaril-hound sitting up between her knees. The boys started rowing.

On the other side, she followed Jaril onto the landing and stalked off, paying no attention to the ferryman or his sons, ignoring the guard who yelled at her but was too late to catch her as she passed through the gate and into Dil Jorpashil.

3

The first week Brann spent her nights in doorways with Jaril standing guard over her; she spent her days looking for someplace to go to ground.

She found an empty hovel on the edge of the Kuna Coru, the quarter where the sublegals lived when they weren't in prison or on the street due to a stretch of Tungjii's Buttocks in the Face. The hovel had three small rooms, one of them a kitchen of sorts; the roof leaked and the front door wouldn't close because the leather hinges were cracked, the scraped sheepskin on the windows was cracked or mostly missing, but the walls were thick and solid, the floor was intact and there was a jakes around the corner that she shared with five other households and a branch of the aqueduct brought city water close by; the tap on it was illicit, but no one paid much attention to that. All the discomforts of home and a bouquet of wonderfully varied and powerful stinks besides.

She paid the latch bribe to the local caudhar, hustled some furniture and had the roof and the floor fixed, then moved in. Her neighbors weren't the sort to ask questions and she wasn't talking anyway. Not then.

Once she was settled, she went to one of Sarimbara's shrines and sat there all day, neither eating nor drinking, her legs in a lotus knot, her gaze blank as the stone eyes in Sarimbara's icon. It was the most boring thing she'd done in all her long life, but she kept it up for a week, her presence there as a certified holywoman was cover for Jaril as he flew over the city in his hawkform, probing for any whiff of Yaril or her captor.

On the fifth day of this boredom, when Jaril came in from another sweep, this one as fruitless as the others, Brann was staring gloomily at a pot, waiting for the water to boil so she could drop in a handful of rice and some chopped vegetables. She was almost as bored with her own cooking as she was with the shrine-sitting; it'd been years since she'd bothered about meals, the ten years on Jal Virri, thanks to the cosseting by Housewraith. She looked up as Jaril flung himself into a tottery old chair by an equally dilapidated kitchen table. "You look like I feel."

He drew hardened nails across the table top, scoring grooves in the soft gray wood, making an ugly rasping sound. "This isn't working."

"Nothing?"

"Tell me what I should be looking for. Besides Yaro." He slapped his hand on the table. "Bramble, we have to DO something."

"What?"

"I don't know!" He kicked at the table leg, watched the table shudder. "I don't know. . . ."

"So what have you done, Jay? I see you about three minutes every third day."

Ignoring its creaking protests, he leaned back in the chair, crossed his arms and scowled at the fire in the stovehole. "I figured anyone who could build a trap like that would likely be up around the top, so I started with the hills and the Isun sars. I found a couple sorcerers living in the sars, neither of them anywhere near Maks' class. And a couple dozen mages, but mages don't deal with other realities so it isn't likely they'd know how to make that trap. I marked them anyway; if it comes to that, I can go into them and read as many of them as I can before they start yelling for help." He leaned back farther and put his feet on the table. "I spent a while sniffing about the Dhaniks since they're the ones that really run the city, I snooped on judges, tax farmers, priests in their shrines, caudhars of the districts. Nothing there either. Some Dhaniks hire Talents, but they sure take care not to associate with them. These Talents live in the Kuna Kirar with the lesser merchants. I checked out their hirelists, some witches for farseeing and truthreading, some shamans, mainly as healers, and low-grade mages to set wards about their offices and their sars. I looked at the lot of them; if you added their talents together, they wouldn't have enough gnom to light a fire in a jug of oil. I checked out the doulahars of the High Merchants. Pretty much like the Dhaniks, they hire Talents but don't want them around day to day. Yesterday and today, I did the Great Market. The same mix, mostly. Some street magicians whose hands are quicker than their Talents, especially when they're in your purse, fortunetellers, card and palm readers, dealers in potions and amulets, curse setters and layers, and none of them worth the spit to drown them. I looked at every Slya-cursed one of them. I thought maybe the trapper might be hiding behind a charlatan's mask. Be a good front, if you think of it much. If he is, he's too good for me. I'm whipped, Bramble, down to a frazzle. I don't know what to do now. Maybe I ought to dangle myself for bait."

"Hmm." Brann glanced at the pot, snorted as she saw the water busily boiling; she scooped up the vegetables and the rice, dumped them in, stirred them briskly and put the lid on. "Let's save that for desperation time. I don't think we've got that desperate, not yet. What about around us? The Kuna Cora."

"In this collection of losers?"

"It marches with your idea about the streetsers. If there's ever a place where people don't ask questions. . . ." She lifted the lid, stirred the mix inside some more, then moved the pan off the fire to the sandbed where it would continue cooking at a much lower heat.

"I'm tired, Bramble."

"I know. You ought to try spending your days looking that damn snake in the face. I think I'm going to set up as a wisewoman, Jay; this holy bit is getting us nowhere. Why don't you stay home a day or so, rest."

"You mean be your familiar and friendly sneak and read those women on the sly. That's a rest?"

"They say a change is as good as a rest." She lifted the lid on her supper, replaced it, and walked briskly to the box where she kept her bowls and flatware. She laid a place for herself, hunted out a napkin and dropped it beside the spoon. "Get your feet off the table, huh?"

"They say. Who they? I doubt that they ever did a day's labor."

"Quibble. Feet, Jay. I don't care to stare at your dirty boots while I'm trying to eat. You going to stay?"

"Oh yes."

4

On the first day, one woman came timidly into the warm steamy kitchen and sat at the table. She had a badly infected hand that was turning gangrenous. Brann poured up a cup of bitter herb tea, made her drink it and sat holding her hand, eyes closed; Jaril came padding around the table and sank to his stomach beside the woman, his body pressing against her leg. A few minutes later the woman was looking at a hand with all the swelling gone, the redness gone. The splinter that had caused the trouble was out, the wound was closed over, not fully healed but well on its way. Ignoring the woman's excited incoherent thanks, Brann took a dugna for her efforts and sent her off. Come the next morning, she had scarcely a minute to herself. Established healers made some trouble for her, but she was formidable in herself and handy with that hardwood staff and when a pushy Minder or one of the caudhar's bullyboys got a good look at Jarilhound's teeth, they turned polite very quickly. The caudhar tried to up his bribe, but she persuaded him that would be uncourteous and unwise.

Sambar Day came round again.

Brann closed down her clinic and went to sit in the shrine; she had a hard time staying awake, she was exhausted and depressed, but she did have a lot to think over. The hunger to Hunt was growing in her; the more she drained herself to help those miserable women, the more urgent that Hunger became. As if there were some sort of measure-stick inside her that tripped a valve when her energy dropped below a certain point. It was a frightening idea. She had to decide if she believed it and if she did believe it, what she was going to do about it. I'm tired of this nonsense, she thought, it's too complicated to think about now. Jaril was restless; nothing he gleaned from the women gave him any new leads, so he wanted to go wandering the Market as he had when he was here before with Yaril, hanging himself out for bait, trusting Brann to make sure he wasn't eaten. Slya Bless, I don't want him to do that. Let's hope he finds something today. Sarimbara, if you're bothering to listen, give him a nudge. Sleepy Sarimbara, you're a good match to my sleepy god. Slya Fireheart, what a sight she was, stomping through the Temueng Emperor's Audience Hall like a big red house-

wife chasing down vermin. Sleep, Slya, sleep, we sang, because when
you woke. . . .

Slya wakes
mountain quakes
air thickens
stone quickens
ash breath
bringing death

Slya sleep   sleep Slya
Yongala dances dreams for you

Slya turns
stone burns
red rivers riot around us
day drops dark upon us
beasts fly
men fear
forests fry

Slya sleep   sleep Slya
Yongala dances dreams for you

Look at me, idiot woman, singing Slya's lullaby at Sarimbara's
shrine. Impolite, to say the least, impolitic for sure. Going home . . .
got to go home for more than one reason now. I have to talk Slya into
sending the changers home. Forty Mortal Hells, like Maksim says,
what a bit of work that'll be. Why forty I wonder? Maksi, oh Maks
m'luv, I'm missing you like hell.

Rocking on her buttocks, muttering to herself, her mind wheeling
here and there and finding no ease anywhere, Brann passed the daylight hours in the shrine. When the sun went down and the lamplight-
ers were out, she went home to her hovel.

5

When Jaril came in from his search, the Wounded Moon was up and
swimming through dry clouds; Brann had supper on the table and was
just emptying the tea leaves out the back door. He shifted almost be-

fore his talons touched the grass mat, stumbled, caught himself and went running to the chest where she kept the wine jars.

She raised her brows, pulled the door shut. "Last is best, eh?" She poured herself a bowl of tea and stood sipping at it as he brought the jar and two glasses to the table. "Mind if I eat first? I've been stuck at the shrine all day. Which is enough in itself to make one dizzy without adding wine on an empty stomach."

"Mind?" His grin split his face in half and he waved the jar perilously close to a lamp. "I'd even kiss old Maksi's toes should he stand here now. Eat, Bramble. Eat the table if you want. . . ." He splashed wine in one of the glasses, gulped it down, then filled both and handed one to her. "First, lift a glass to Tungjii Luck."

"I take it you found her. Or him."

"I found something. Drink, Bramble, drink!"

She laughed, raised her glass high. "Tungjii, love!" she cried and spilled a goodly dollop of wine, laughed again as the libation vanished before it hit the table. The little god wasn't one known for wasting wine. She watched Jaril do the same, then she drank and slammed the glass to the table at the same time he did.

"Tell me." She pulled up the box she was using as a chair, began spooning up the mutton stew she'd left simmering on the stove while she was gone, taking sips of tea between bites, as excited as he was, but a lot hungrier since she didn't feed on sunlight.

"I told you about the stuvtiggor, remember?"

She nodded.

"Well, I started on the west, the side closest to the Market. You know how much I expected to find anything interesting. Well, I didn't, but it was all I had left and I wasn't really panting to lay myself out as bait. All morning there was nothing. About like I expected, there were some thieves and some others with hot talents I couldn't pin, but nothing for me. A bit past noon, I moved into the highrent section, such as it is, fences, you know, slave dealers, courtesans, a couple assassins and so on. I started getting nervous. I didn't know why, it was a weird shivery feeling. Thing was, it's a long time since I *sphined* a stuv nest and I'm not aeta any more so my *sphine* has got the reach of a drunk's breath. And it wasn't really stuvtiggors, just something that has the same . . . uh . . . the same I suppose you could say smell. Anyway, I went on searching, trying to ignore the feeling. It got worse. After a while I knew where it was coming from. Right at the edge of the Kuna Coru there's this doulahar; it's sitting on a bit of a hill, tall enough so folk on the top floor or the roof can look out over the Lake; it's got gardens and stables and a pond deep enough to swim in. Fancier even than some of the Isun sars. I don't know who owns it, some courtesan lives there, I saw her; she might even own it, though that's hard to believe, given the laws here. She was out visiting the first time I flew over. I stayed long enough to see her come back with a string of carriages bouncing after her. The Grand Isu himself was in the first one. She's got some client list, that whore. I wonder what they'd say if they knew she was a demon."

"What!"

"Well, I'm one, aren't I, by the way folks here think."

"Don't be silly." She frowned. "That kind of demon?"

"Is there any other kind?"

"I'm not the one to ask. Go on."

"Well, by the time she showed up, I was pretty sure what was happening to me. I was putting a shape to things. Them down in the doulahar, they weren't stuvtiggors, but they were at least first cousins. Hivesouls. Shoved together to look like people. And hungry. And dangerous. Stuvtiggors don't have magic, they just jump you and eat you. This bunch was something else. Spooky, sheeh! I think even old Maks when he had BinYAHtii would've taken a look at them and backed off. I backed off fast. I didn't try to get close. They didn't know I was there, I'm fairly sure of that. But they would've if I'd got closer. What I think is, we've got stuvtiggors in our reality, they've got something like Surrahts in theirs, so that's how they knew what we were when we were here. Five of them. Stuv clots, I mean. Six when the woman got back." He wriggled in his chair. "Feels funny calling that thing a woman. Gods, she's powerful. If she came after me, I'd go stone so fast . . . I'm scared, Bramble."

"Hmp." She took the glass he pushed across to her, sipped at the wine and frowned at the curtain stirring over the mended sheepskin in the window where the tape was peeling off. "What about Yaro? You think they've got her in that doulahar?"

"If she's there, they've blocked me off. She IS alive, Bramble. The tie's too tight between us for her to be dead and me not know. Anyway, where else would they put her?"

"Then we have to get inside somehow." She dragged her hand across her mouth, sat scowling at the amber wine running down the sides of the bell as she tilted the glass back and forth. "Without them knowing."

"Yeh. Otherwise they could eat her before we got close."

"Predators."

"I think."

"I think . . . I think we'd better add Maks to this plot." She set the glass down, pushed the box back and got to her feet. "Wait here, I'll get the *call-me*'s." A moment later she was back with a soft, leather pouch. She fished out one of the pebbles and set it on the table. It shimmered in the lamplight, a milky quartz stone water-polished smooth. "Crush it under the heel he said. You want to do the deed or shall I?"

"You're the one with the mass, Bramble."

"Never say that to a woman, urtch. Mmp. Better put this over there by the door. Maks does need considerable space." She looked up, chewed her lip. "And he's like to crash his head into the ceiling. Maybe I should take it outside."

"And maybe you shouldn't. We don't want to tell the neighbors all our business."

"Especially Jahira. I swear that woman knows every belch. Well, he'll just have to duck." She picked up the *call-me* and almost dropped it again. "Yukh, the thing feels alive." Squatting, she set it on the floor near the threshold; when she was satisfied, she stood, brought her heel down on the pebble, crushing it to powder. As soon as she felt it go, she jumped back.

Nothing happened.

"Maks? SETTSIMAKSIMIN!"

Nothing.

She stirred the powder with the toe of her sandal. "I am going to have your black hide for this, Maksi." She flung the door open, snatched up a broom and swept the glass bits into the yard muck. When every sliver was gone, she yanked the door shut, slamming it loudly enough to wake half the quarter, so hard that the latch didn't catch. It bounced open again. She ignored that. "All right, Jay. We do this ourselves."

Shudders passed along Jaril's body, escalating to a sudden convulsion. He spewed out most of the wine he'd drunk and went suddenly stone.

Brann swore, snatched up a dishtowel; she mopped at her arms and face, flung the towel into the mess sprayed across the table. She straightened Jaril's chair, picked up the warm pulsing crystal and opened her blouse. With Jaril stone cradled against her breasts, she felt with her foot for the chair, sat and waited.

Time passed. She understood then just how afraid Jaril was. And she saw what he meant when he said aulis take longer to recover than aetas. She began to be afraid; if he couldn't come out of this by himself, she hadn't a clue how to wake him up.

The crystal softened. It stirred against her; it felt like a baby wanting to suck. She bit her lip. There was no point in futile dreaming; she'd been effectively sterile since her eleventh birthday. Slowly, so slowly, the boy's form unfolded until, finally, Jaril filled her lap, his head resting between her breasts. He opened his eyes, looked blankly up at her, then remembered.

Stiffly, he pushed away from her, slid off her lap and went to stand in the doorway, staring into the stinking darkness outside.

Brann frowned at him. After a minute, she said, "If you go stone every time I mention that place or you-know-who, we're not going to get very far."

He pressed his body against the doorjamb, stretched his arm up it as high as he could reach. He said nothing.

"Hmm. Tell me this, is everybody at the house a demon?"

He twisted his head around. "I saw some gardeners that weren't. Some women went out to the Market, I suppose they were after supplies for the party the courtesan was throwing that night. They weren't. I didn't actually see more, but she'd need a lot of servants or slaves to run a house that size. I only counted five smiglar plus the courtesan."

"Smiglar, Jay?"

Rubbing at his neck, he swung around, strolled to her box and sat down on it. "Have to call them something. I'm uncomfortable when I hear talk about demons. The way you folk define these things, I'm a demon. I don't like the fringes that word has, you know what I mean. Stuvtiggor clots are smiglar, these hive types are like them, why not call them smiglar? Better than demon, isn't it?"

"Smiglar's fine. All right." She pushed fluttering strands of hair out of her eyes, began rebuttoning her blouse. "First thing. We need to know how the inside of that house is laid out, who lives there. You're sure they'd spot you?"

"Yeh."

"That's out then. Too bad. Trap . . . trap . . . um, you think the courtesan is the whiphandler of that clutch?"

"Yeh." He dipped a finger in a pool of wine, drew glyphs on the wood. Set. Tsi. Ma. Ksi. Min. "The uh fetor she gives off is ten times what I got from the others." He drew a line through the glyphs, canceling them. "Like I said, even Maks would back off that bunch. Her most of all." He frowned. "Maybe that's it. Why he didn't come."

Brann brushed aside his dig at Maksim, it was nothing but an upsurge of Jaril's old resentment. "And she's flying among the Isu?"

"If her guest list for tonight's party means anything."

"Courtesan, hmm. Big house. Lots of dependents. Living high. All that in spite of the Temueng base for the culture and what that means about woman's place, especially a woman without a family to back her. She has to be clever, Jay; power in itself wouldn't get her those things. You said there were sorcerers in some of those Isu sars?"

"Yeh." He drew two circles on the table, pulled a line from the left circle to the right. "One of them might have matched Ahzurdan when he wasn't drugged to the eyebrows. While he was still himself, that is."

"And they haven't smelled out what she is. Interesting, isn't it. And this. They're predators, but Yaro's still alive. They didn't take her to eat her. She's bait, Jay. For you, sure. For me, probably. Which means I've got to keep away from there too. Ahh! What a mess."

"Mess." He crumpled the stained towel between his hands, then began wiping up the wine. "You expected it to come out like that, didn't you."

"Why?"

"You asked about the servants. Only thing left is getting at one of them." He tossed the towel at the tub where the stew pot was soaking. "So?"

"So we go looking for a servant or slave or someone from that house that we can get next to without letting the boss . . . um, what's the singular form of smiglar, Jay?"

"Same. One smiglar, twenty smiglar. Hive things."

"Right. Without letting the boss smiglar know what we're doing. Get some rest, luv. We start tomorrow early."

6

One week later.

Midmorning, just before the busiest time in the Market.

A huge brindle mastiff stopped suddenly, howled, shook his head. Foam from his mouth spattered the serving girl who stood beside an older woman so busy arguing over the price of tubers she didn't notice what was happening around her. The girl screamed and backed away.

A gaunt old woman appeared between two kiosks. She swung a heavy staff at the beast and bounced dust off his hide. He howled, then yelped as the staff connected again; he swung his muscular front end from side to side, trying to get at her. Foam dripped copiously from his mouth.

People around them scrambled to get away. The girl had dived behind the old woman, trapping herself in a short blind alley between two rows of shops. Her companion looked around, yelped and went running off. The place emptied rapidly except for the three of them, the woman, the girl and the dog.

The mastiff whimpered, backed away from the whirling staff. He stood for a moment shivering convulsively, then he went ki-yi-yipping off, vanishing into the crazyquilt of alleys about the market, the noises he made sinking into the noises and silences of the dank cloudy afternoon.

The old woman knocked the butt of her staff against the flagging underfoot, grunted with satisfaction. She tugged her worn homespun shirt down and shook her narrow hips until the folds in her trousers hung the way she wanted them. Finally she tucked a straggle of gray hair behind her ear as she turned and inspected the deserted chaos around her. She saw the maid, raised her scraggly brows. "You all right, child?"

The maid was rubbing and rubbing at the back of her hand where some of the dog's spit had landed. Tears welled up in her eyes and spilled out; she wasn't crying so much as overflowing. She was young and neatly dressed, her brown hair was smooth as glass despite her agitation, pinned into a three-tiered knot atop her head; she might have been pretty, but that was impossible to say. Puffy and purplish red, a disfiguring birthmark slid down one side of her face, hugged her neck like a noose and vanished beneath her clothing. Her arms were covered from shoulder to wrist, but the backs of both hands were spattered with more of that ugly birthstain.

She lowered her eyes. "I think . . . I think so," she murmured, speaking so softly Brann had trouble hearing her.

"You're shivering, child." Brann touched her fingertips to the marred cheek. "Your face is like ice. Come, we'll have some tea. That will make the world look brighter."

The maid shrank back. "I . . . I'd better find Elissy."

"Surely you can take five minutes for yourself." Brann rested her hand on the girl's shoulder, using the lightest of pressures to start her moving. "Don't be afraid of me, I am the Jantria Bar Ana. Ah, I see you've heard my name. Why don't you tell me yours."

Reassured, the girl began walking along beside her. "My name is Carup Kalan, Jantria." She looked uneasily at her hand. "It didn't bite me, but I got its spit on me. Will that do bad to me?"

They turned a corner and plunged into the noisy, dusty throngs of the Market, walked around a group of highservants arguing over some bolts of silk and velvet. "No. If your skin is not broken, there's no harm in that foam. If you're worried, there's a fountain two ranks over; you can stop and wash your hands." She smiled at Carup. "I expect you were with—Elissy, was it—just to carry things, so it will be my pleasure to pay for the tea."

They stopped at the fountain and Carup Kalan scrubbed her hands with an enthusiasm that made Brann smile as she watched. Carup might have heard of her healings and find her presence reassuring, but she wasn't about to take any chances she could avoid.

There were a number of teashops scattered about the Market, each with a little dark kitchen, a counter and tables under a battered canvas awning. Brann took her unknowing catch to the nearest of these and sat her at a table while she went for tea and cakes.

Circling the crowded tables, lifting the tray and dancing precariously around clots of customers coming and going. Brann carried her cakes and tea back, shushed Carup as the girl jumped up and tried to take the tray from her. The tea was hot and strong, the cakes were deep-fried honey wafers, crisp and sweet. "From your name, you come from Lake Tabaga." She slipped some cakes on a round of brown paper and slid them across to Carup, poured tea for both of them.

"Ay-yah." Carup looked briefly surprised. "The Ash-Kalap have a farmhold close to a village called Pattan Haria on the west shore of Tabaga." She gulped at the tea. It was too hot; she shuddered as her mouth burned, but seemed to welcome the pain. When the bowl was empty, she set it down and stared into it; her face twisted with . . . something. There was tragedy in what birth had done to her. The mark distorted and denied all her expressions. Nothing came out right. Suffering was grotesque, a laugh was uglier than a snarl. "My father sold me when I was eight," she whispered. Trembling fingers stroked the mark on her face, then she jerked them down and began crumbling a cake into sticky fragments. "He said no one would want to marry me or even take me in to warm his bed. I was too ugly. He said he'd never make back the cost of my food and clothes, so he might as well get what he could out of me. He said they had perverts in the city that might find me. . . ." She took the bowl Brann had refilled and gulped at the steaming tea. "Might find me. . . ." She sobbed. Her hand shook, but she took care to set the bowl down gently. It didn't break. No tea spilled. "I'm sorry."

"No, child, don't. Say what you want to say." Brann took one of Carup's hands and held it between hers. As she'd spoken to many of the women visiting her, keeping up the role of holywoman, Jantria, she spoke to Carup: "Hearing what comes to me is the task the Gods have set me. Say what you must and know that I will hear it." She waited, feeling the tension in Carup, the need to talk and the fear of casting herself into deeper trouble. It was hard for Brann to understand the girl. Her own life was complicated and often dangerous; for the most part, though, she'd managed to control events rather than endure them. Time after time, one god or another had meddled with her, driving her this way and that; even so she was able to finesse a degree of freedom. She could see that Carup was different, that the options she had were much more limited; she could even see reasons why this was so, but that was the mind's eyes, not the heart's.

A bad taste in her mouth because she was going to use this unfortunate girl as unconscionably as the girl's beast of a father had, she leaned closer and smiled at Carup and prepared to entice from her everything she knew about the courtesan and her doulahar. "Were you brought right away to Dil Jorpashil?"

Carup sighed and freed her hand so she could sip at the cooling tea. "Ay-yah, the Agent brought us straight here."

"What happened then?"

"I was afraid . . . what my father said . . . but it didn't happen. The Chuttar Palami Kumindri's agent bought me for a maid." Carup sighed with weariness and managed at the same time to project a touch of pride. "You must have heard of her. The Chuttar Palami Kumindri is the premiere courtesan in all Dil Jorpashil." Her mouth turned down. "The Housemaster treats me like a dog. I work hard, I'm up before the sun every day, he never says word one to me, he pretends he doesn't even see me."

"Then you're still a part of the Chuttar's household?"

"Ay-yah." Carup sighed again; her eyelids drooped. The emotional storm had passed and she wanted nothing more than to lie down and sleep. A group of merchants came bustling past their table, kicking into her. She cringed automatically, tugged her chair farther under the table, made herself as small as she could.

Brann pressed her lips together, angry at the merchants because they were arrogant and thoughtless, angry at the girl because she hadn't spirit enough to resent them, at herself because she couldn't do anything about either. Her voice deliberately mild, she said. "How long has it been?"

"Ten . . . years. . . ." Carup blinked, straightened. The color drained from her face, leaving the red-purple stain more glaring than ever. Her eyes were fixed past Brann's shoulder.

Brann twisted around. The stocky woman, Elissy, Carup called her, was standing under the scalloped edge of the canvas, looking angrily about. Brann saw her and she saw Carup at the same moment. She came charging across to the table. Brann stood, held up a hand, palm out. "Gods' peace be on you, Elissy friend."

"I'm no friend of yours, beggar. Carup, get over here. By Sarimbara's Horns, what do you think you're doing, lazing about like this?" She turned her scowl on Brann. "Who you? What you think you doing with this girl?"

"I am the Jantria Bar Ana." Brann suppressed a smile as she saw the consternation on the woman's face, the sudden shift of expression. The past two weeks had apparently given her a formidable reputation.

She nodded gravely at Elissy, shifted her gaze to Carup. I need more, she thought, a lot more than I've got. Ten years that girl has been in that house. She's not stupid, poor thing, might be better for her if she was. Get to it, woman. . . . She set her hand on Carup's shoulder, turned the girl to face her. "Carup Kalan," she said, lowering her voice to its deepest register, speaking with a deliberate formality. "Would you care to serve me? My household is small, but you will not go hungry. You will clean my rooms and yours, you will do the laundry, you will buy food for our meals and do such cooking as you are trained for. In return, I will buy you out of your present place and register you at the Addala as a freewoman. I will provide a room and a bed, food and clothing and I will pay you five dugna a week."

Carup's face twisted into a gargoyle grimace as she struggled to decide; she had security, she knew where she would sleep, where her meals would come from, that she would be safe on the streets from pressgangs, pimps, muggers and assaults and she had a shadow share in the prestige of the Chuttar Prime, but she also knew that she'd be thrown out like refuse if she got sick or hurt too badly to work any more. Or when she was too old to work, though too-old was a long time off, at eighteen you're immortal. She hated her life, that was obvious, but she was afraid of venturing from its comfortable certainties, that too was obvious. Brann as holywoman/healer had prestige also, was presumably trustworthy, Carup being gullible enough to accept communal judgment about what was holy and what wasn't, but the Jantria was a stranger. From another land, another people. That was suspect, frightening. Brann was poor; Carup had a slave's ingrained contempt for the poor. Brann had treated her with kindness and acceptance, had stood between her and the rabid dog and had beaten it off, a powerful omen for the superstitious, and like most slaves Carup was deeply superstitious. Brann offered her manumission and a degree of control over her life. That was attractive in theory but terrifying in actuality.

With a suddenly acquired dignity that made Brann as suddenly ashamed of how she was using the girl, Carup said, "Sarimbara's Blessing, Jantria Bar Ana, I will serve you."

"So be it, child. Go with your companion now. Wait and trust me. I'll send for you when the thing is done."

7

Two days later.

The Housemaster tugged at heroic mustaches that hung from the corner of his tight mouth down past his chin to tickle his collar. He scowled at the Basith, a go-between Brann hired to handle the exchange because she didn't want to go anywhere near the doulahar. "Why this object?" He jerked a thumb at Carup who was kneeling at his feet, but didn't look at her. She offended his eyes and he'd let her know that every day of her life since she'd walked through the service portal.

The Basith was a typical Jana Mix. He had black hair like the coarse baka wool the nomad tribes wove into tent cloth, a tangle of watch-spring curls about a widening bald spot; he had a nub of a beard on the point of a long chin; he wore a Phrasi merchant's ring in his left ear and a Gallinasi coup-stud in his right ear, one of the prized ruby studs. His eyes were dark amber, long and narrow, set at a tilt above prominent cheekbones, clever eyes for a clever man. He was the son of a courtesan and an unusually rebellious Dhanik who took the boy into his sar despite the screeches of his proper wives and saw that he got a lawyer's education. A week ago the Basith's wife had ventured timidly into the Kuna Coru to see the holywoman about an ulcer on her leg; she came back with the ulcer closed over, with the cancer that caused it cleaned out of her and with a proper appreciation of Brann's worth. Which was why he was here now. He masked his distaste for the man in front of him, for that unfortunate creature crouching at the Housemaster's feet, and prepared to do what he was hired for. "The holywoman is but following the instruction of her god. This is the slave she wants. This is the slave she shall have. Place a price on her, if you please, Callam. Then we will see."

Half an hour later the Basith handed over one takk and five dugnas and received a bill of sale. He left the doulahar with the bill and Carup Kalan, took both to the Addala, did the paperwork and paid the manumission fee while the Tikkasermer stapled the bronze firman into the girl's left ear, signifying she was a freewoman. He delivered Carup and the documents to Brann, smiled with genuine pleasure as she thanked him and paid his fee. Then he went home to collect the gratitude of his wife.

8

Brann went back to being the Jantria, listening to women from the quarter and beyond, farther and farther beyond these days as her reputation spread, there were even a few wives from the lesser Isun, healing their bodies and doing her best to prop up their souls. It was draining, but she accepted it as the appropriate payment for the use she was making of the girl and for her bi-nightly prowls. Drinker of Souls was walking the streets of Dil Jorpashil. She came back sated and destroyed, swearing to herself she'd never go out again. But when the hunger was on her, she went.

Carup bloomed. She cooked, cleaned, sewed, she used a part of her meager pay to buy a chair for Brann, recaned the back and the seat, burnished the ancient wood until it glowed. She moved about the tiny house singing cheerful dirges, polishing the place until it gleamed. And she talked. Night after night, she consumed pots of tea and talked. And Brann listened. She nudged the girl now and then in a direction that would give her the data she needed about the workings of the doulahar; she didn't have to nudge hard or often. No one had listened to Carup Kalan since she was weaned or showed her in any way that they valued her. Not even her mother.

Jaril was restless and irritable during this time, as fidgety as a dog with fleas. He went back again and again to the doulahar like a tongue to a sore tooth. He couldn't keep away from it.

"The Chuttar left during the afternoon," he told Brann, "in her fanciest litter, the ebony one with the silver mountings. She went up the hill to the Isullata sar. She's still there, very entertaining she must be."

"She stayed home tonight," he told Brann another morning, "two Adals and a sorcerer came by. They were there about two hours, then the Adals left. The sorcerer was still there when I came away."

"She went to the Market; she bought two slaves, a live bullock, some bolts of cloth. I don't know why she went herself, maybe she was bored or something."

And so it went. He watched the Chuttar Palami Kumindri day and night; overflying the doulahar far enough up to escape notice, staying over it twenty minutes at most with two to three hours between visits. He was cautious, but he could not keep away.

Days passed.

Brann acquired charts and lists and schematics of each floor, timetables, locations of all forbidden areas, everything she needed for a fair notion where the Chuttar might be hiding Yaril, everything she needed to get into the doulahar with a chance of getting out again, but she still had no plan for handling the smiglar. And no plan for Carup's future. She had to have both before she could act.

Sambar Day.

She went as usual to the shrine and sat among the penitents and petitioners, surrounded by the slip-slap, click-clack of prayer beads rotating through work-worn fingers, the insect hum of the old women who came there because they had nowhere else to go, the rattle of drums and the chants of the celebrants as they did their best to sing Sarimbara deeper asleep.

Wreathed in incense drifting copiously from swinging censers as the celebrants made their hourly procession about the praiseroom, she cursed Maksim a while, but halfheartedly. Then she began to worry about him. Something must have gone wrong for him. That Jastouk? Little creep, he'd sell his mother for the gold in her teeth. That girl in Silili? What was her name? Kori something. Speculation was futile. And she had neither time nor attention to waste on him right now. Carup. She called up an image of Carup. If you ignored that mark and looked at her bone structure, her nose, mouth, eyes, she was almost beautiful. She was slim with wide hips and full breasts, the sort of body men in this culture valued above all others. She kept herself covered, but Brann was certain the red-purple flesh was spattered the length of her body, neck to heel. Strip that away, though, and maybe her family would take her back. I wonder if I could do that? Well, Jaril and I. I can't leave her here on her own, free or not. I might as well strangle her myself, it'd come to the same thing. I can't do like Maks did with his Kori and put her in school somewhere. No Talent. No interest either. She's bred to be some man's wife. Dowry? That I can do. The skin, the skin, can I do ANYTHING about that mark? Jaril and I, we've done harder things. Yes, take the curse off her face. Can't take it off her heart, can I. Takes more than magic to erase eighteen years of cringing.

A lanky boy with a shaved head came in, awkward and diffident, all bone and gristle, carrying a dakadaka under his arm, gray dust ground into the skin of his feet and knees, smeared over the rear folds of his bunchy white dhoti. He went shuffling to the raised area where Sarimbara's icon was and dropped clumsily to the planks. He wriggled around, adding more stonedust to his person and his clothing, got his legs wrapped around the dakadaka and began tapping at its twin heads, drawing a whispery rattle from the taut snakeskins. Several older celebrants straggled in, men with shaved heads and orange dhotis; they sat in a ragged arc behind the boy and began a droning chant, a weary winding sleepsong for the god whose attention they feared more than his neglect. The visitors to the shrine, mostly women, added their wordless hums to the chant, filling the praiseroom with a sound like dry leaves blowing.

Brann hummed with the others, taking a break from the dilemmas that plagued her. She passed her prayer beads through her fingers, slip, slap, rattle-tattle, dark brown seeds fingerpolished to a mottled sheen, round and round, a soft, syncopated underplay to the drum, the song, the hum.

The day passed slowly, but it did pass, taking with it her hesitations and uncertainties. She went home to her hovel determined to peel off her problems one by one, Carup Kalan scheduled first to go.

9

Three days later.

Morning, about two hours before dawn.

Raining outside, little wind, water coming down in near vertical lines, the sort of rain that seems like it will never end, as if the rest of life will be gray and chill and damp, the sort of rain that makes a pleasure palace of the most wretched of shelters as long as there's a bit of fire to chase away the damp.

Brann pushed aside the curtain that closed off her bedroom doorway, edged around it into the cramped livingroom where Carup was sleeping. Her hair hung loose, a waving mass of white, fine as spidersilk; she wore her own face, young, unlined, her eyes green as new leaves, her mouth a delicate curve, soft and vulnerable. She wore a black velvet robe embroidered with gold and silver and rubies. Jaril stole it for her from the wardrobe of an Isu whose taste in decoration was so bad it was almost a Talent. He grinned as he held it up for Brann to inspect; when she said finally, I suppose bad taste is better than no taste, he had a fit of giggles that she shushed quickly, afraid he'd wake Carup. In her left hand she held a heavy wooden candlepole taller than she was and covered with tarnished silver-gilt that she'd been afraid to clean because the gilding was so thin it came off if you looked at it hard. There was a fat white candle impaled on the spike, but she hadn't lit it yet. The only light in the livingroom came from the fireplace where faint red glows from last night's fire seeped through the smother of gray ash.

Jaril brushed past her, black panther with crystal eyes, moving with an eerie silence. He padded across to Carup, sniffed at her, came padding back. *She's ripe, Bramble. Her eyes are moving, she's starting to dream.*

She nodded, brought the candlepole down until the wick was beside his head. "Light me, Jay," she whispered.

He spat a spark at the wick, smirked as she swung the pole hastily upright when the twist began burning. *Handy to have round, am't I, huh?*

"Sometimes, but don't let it go to your head." She inspected him.

"Maybe you should turn yourself white. You disappear into the murk like that."

His mouth dropping into a feral cat grin, he purred at her. His eyes began to glow silver-white, the tips of his coathairs went translucent and shone with a clear white light. He was still a black cat, but one outlined in moonfire.

"Impressive," she murmured and grinned back at him. "All right, let's do it."

##

The candle made an aura round her shining hair, dropped dramatic shadows into the hollows of her face and touched with fire the rings on the hand that held the pole. "Carup," she called. "Carup Kalan. Wake up. Carup. Carup Kalan."

The girl woke, startled, then afraid, scrambling back under the covers until she was pressed against the wall; she pulled her knees up, threw her arms across her face and whimpered.

"Have no fear," Brann said. Her voice was deep and caressing, the words had a smile in them. "I am she who was the Jantria, Carup Kalan. Look at me, child. I mean you no harm."

Still trembling, Carup pulled her arms down, lay peeping at Brann over the delicate halo of hair on her forearm.

Brann lifted a hand in blessing. At first Carup cringed away, that was what her life had trained her to do, that was the only way she'd found to turn aside or lessen the pain about to be inflicted on her. Then she saw Brann's smile, only a little smile, a quirking upward of the ends of her mouth, but it was approval, fondness even, and Carup began to unfold like a flower opening in the sun.

"You have served me faithfully and well." The words were solemn but the tone was gentle, friendly, and Carup relaxed yet more. "You have given more than service, child. You have shown generosity of spirit, expecting only a little kindness, a trifle of shelter from the world and those who would do you ill. Carup Kalan, I am a servant of One I may not name. I am at times given word to do this, or do that, to go here, to go there. Word has come to me that I am required elsewhere soon." Brann kept her face a smiling mask as she spun her web of lies, but again she wasn't liking herself much, especially when she saw the look on Carup's face.

The girl's lips trembled, but she didn't dare protest. Fear was flooding back into her, more than fear, a flat despair. Once again Fate was tearing her from her happiness, casting her aside like garbage.

"I would take you with me, if that were permitted. It is not. But there is a thing I can do for you, a gift I can give you, Carup Kalan. I can send you home to your own people with the dowry of a queen."

Carup's right thumb moved over and over the marks on the back of her left hand. She didn't say anything for several breaths, then she bowed her head. "I thank you, Jantria." Her voice was dull, lifeless.

"Stand before me, Carup Kalan."

Carup glanced at the shining panther, then shrugged; there were far more terrible things waiting for her than that eldrich beast. She hitched herself to the edge of the cot and stood. She slept in a sleeveless shift of unbleached muslin. It had a meagerly embroidered neck with a faded ribbon threaded through the eyelets and tied in a limp bow at the front.

"Remove your shift."

Moving like an automaton, Carup pulled the bow loose, spread the neck of the shift and let it fall about her feet. She didn't try to cover herself, she was too deep in despair for shame to touch her. The spongy red-purple flesh ran the length of her body, more of it than Brann had expected to see. There were spatters on her right side, drops like spilled blood on her breast. A wide river of the wine flesh ran down her left side, slashed across her navel and flowed down her right thigh.

"Straighten the blankets on the bed, then lie down on them."

Obedient as always, refusing to acknowledge anger or pain, Carup worked with the skilled neatness with which she did everything, even turning square corners as she made the bed.

"Lie on your back," Brann said when Carup was finished.

All this while Jaril panther had been pacing around Brann, his crystal eyes reflecting the candle flame. Now he melted into a mist and the mist settled over Carup, seeping into her.

Carup lay rigid, eyes squeezed shut.

Brann leaned the candlepole against the chimney, went to kneel beside the bed. With Jaril guiding her, she began restructuring the blemishes, wiping away all trace of them. All that the night prowls of the Drinker of Souls had brought her, she poured into the girl. And more. When she was finished, Carup Kalan was a lamb without blemish, an unpierced pearl whose price was the price of queens.

Shaky with exhaustion, perspiration dripping down her face and body, Brann got to her feet and went to the candlepole, removed the candle and set it on the box that served as a bedtable; the candle was thick enough to stand by itself. She looked down at the rigid, unhappy girl, shook her head and crossed to the bedroom. Jaril emerged as mist, solidified to black nonluminous panther and padded into the kitchen; a moment later he was a mistcrane powering into the rain, heading for the doulahar and his obsession, cursing the damp, the cold and his unruly needs.

Brann came back with the hand mirror she'd bought as a gift for Carup once the metamorphosis was complete. "Open your eyes, Carup Kalan, and behold my second gift."

For an instant the girl resisted, then she sighed and did as she was told. Brann bit at her lip. *Where is your spirit, girl? You aren't grass for everyone to step on.* She said nothing. It wouldn't help. Carup was what her culture made her.

"Sit up," Brann said. "Look at your hands, child."

Carup pushed up until she was sitting with her legs over the edge of the bed. She looked at her hands, gasped. She felt at her thigh, at her breasts, she touched her face.

"Take your last gift, this mirror, and behold yourself, Carup Kalan."

Brann left the girl staring into the mirror and feeling at her face as if she were unable to believe what her eyes saw and needed the confirmation of her fingers. In her bedroom, Brann stripped off the robe and with some difficulty took on once more the aspect of the Jantria Bar Ana. She put on her ordinary clothes and sat on the bed for a while, gathering her strength.

"Jantria?" The voice that came from the other room was hesitant, shaky from excitement and a lingering fear.

"One moment, Carup." Brann got to her feet, felt at her braid to make sure it was properly clasped so it wouldn't unravel at the first movement of her head. *I feel like I'm going to unravel,* she thought. *Hoo! If I can get that girl to sleep, there's some dark left, maybe I can go find me a juicy murderer or two. No. A slave dealer. More appropriate, I'd say. Almost a pun. Spend on a slave, recoup on a slaver. Hah!*

She moved to the crate she used as a linen chest and dressing table, grunted as she lifted a small iron-bound box. Shoulders bent, she elbowed past the curtain.

Carup was sitting on the bed. She'd put the shift on again, and pulled a quilt around her shoulders, but she blushed when Brann came in, then looked uncertain as she saw the old woman who'd bought her free. She stole a look in the mirror—it was on the box beside the candle; she'd put her sandal behind it to tilt it up so she could see herself when she glanced that way. She blushed again, stared down at her hands as they rested in her lap, fingers twined tightly together.

Brann nodded at the candle and the mirror. "Push those aside, will you, Carup? So I can set this down. It's heavy."

Hastily the girl tossed the mirror onto the bed, brushed the sandal off the box and pushed the candle back. "Is that enough?"

"It should be." The flimsy box creaked under the weight of the small chest. "This isn't locked now, though you should keep it so later. Open it."

"Me?"

"It's your dowry, young Carup. Now, do what I tell you. Open the chest."

"Oh." Carup turned back the lid. Inside, there were two doeskin bags and a small belt-purse. She loosened the drawstring on the larger bag, reached in and took out a handful of coins. Gold coins, thick, heavy, with a cold greasy feel to them. "Jorpashil jaraufs," she whispered. "Sahanai the Siradar's daughter wore hers at her wedding, threaded round her neck."

"One hundred," Brann said. "I promised you a queen's price, child."

"She only had ten." Carup turned the broad coins over and over, rubbing her fingers across them, then she put them back in the bag and pulled the drawstrings until the opening was gone; neat-fingered as always, she wrapped the thongs into a smooth coil and tucked it between the side of the box and the bag. She opened the second bag. Silver this time. Takks.

"Fifty," Brann said. "Those are for you alone. A woman should always have her own money, Carup. It means she has a way out if she needs it. Pass what you don't use to your daughters; tell them what I've just told you. It is a trust, Carup Kalan."

"I hear and I obey, Jantria Bar Ana." She put the takks away and opened the purse. There was a pile of worn dugnas inside it.

"One hundred dugnas, Carup, to buy clothing, hire a bodyguard and transport to get you home."

"I don't want to go home." The words came out in a rush. "My father will just take the dowry and give it to my brothers. He did that all the time with the money my mother brought in."

"Gods! Does nothing go right? I can't leave you here. The vultures would be down on you before I was gone an hour."

"Take me with you, Jantria. I'll serve you. You said I was good at serving you. The One Without a Name, I'll serve that One too."

Brann sank onto the hearth, her back against the rough bricks of the fireplace; their heat seeped through her shirt and into her bones. Sleep flooded through her, waves and waves of sleep. Thinking was like shoveling mud. "Carup, I can't." The lies were catching up with her, twisting around her like a fowler's net. That last bit was true enough, though. She couldn't keep the girl with her. A deeper truth was, she didn't want to. Carup was reading that, though she wasn't fully aware of it, and trying to fight against it, flailing out helplessly, futilely. Brann drew her fist across her mouth, let her eyes droop closed for a minute. Fine time for the girl to dredge up some independence. "Where I go, no one can come." Make it convincing, Brann; she's going to be stubborn. "Even if you tell him the dowry is the gift of a god?"

"He wouldn't listen to me. Even if he listened, he wouldn't believe me." Carup wrapped the quilt tighter about her body, pulled her legs up and tucked them under her. She was fighting now, at last she was fighting for what she wanted. "If I go home and he takes me back as his daughter, I belong to him. Listen," she said. Her voice broke in the middle of the word. "This is how it went in my home, Jantria. My mother made shirts and sold them in the Pattan Haria Market; she had made herself a name for her broideries. Sometimes she got more from her shirts than he did off the land." She cleared her throat; her hand crept from beneath the quilt and stroked the side of her face where the mark had been. When she spoke again, it was in a hoarse whisper; she was talking about family things, breaking one of the most rigid taboos of her culture. "He took her money whenever the tribes came to Lake Tabaga and my brothers wanted to go into Pattan Haria and get drunk with them. My mother spent her eyes and her fingers on those shirts, she took from sleep time to make them and he took her money for my brothers to waste. Didn't matter what she said, what she wanted to do with the money; he owned her so he owned what she earned. If I go back, he'll do the same to me."

Brann rubbed at her eyes as her plans fell in rubble about her. She'd been so sure she could send the girl home and let her family have the care of her. Double damn, Tungjii help! What do I do now? She sneezed. What I do now is sleep. She sighed and got to her feet. "I'm too tired to think, Carup. It's late. Get some sleep. If you're up before I am and you find people waiting for me, send them away, will you? Tell them I'm meditating; it will be the truth, child. Get some sleep yourself, you should be tired too." She didn't wait for a response but pushed past the curtain and fell on the bed, asleep as soon as her body was horizontal.

10

Brann rubbed her eyes and sipped at the near boiling tea that Carup had brought to her as soon as she heard her moving around. She yawned and tried to clear the clots out of her head.

Hands clapped outside the curtain. Brann's hand jerked and she nearly spilled tea down her front. She swore under her breath, brushed some drops off her trousers. "Yes, Carup, what is it?"

"Subbau Kamin brought fresh bread this morning, she says her grandson is full of devils and laughter and her son is over the moon about the change, she blesses you and hopes you will accept this small gift. Piara Sansa came with her and brought sausages. Would you like me to bring you some of this? The bread smells wonderful."

"Yes, yes, but take some for yourself, hmm?"

"I will, thank you, Jantria."

Brann finished her breakfast and stretched out on the bed, her fingers laced behind her head. She stared up at the ceiling, traced the cracks and played games with the stains, but found no answer anywhere. She was still tired, her energy badly depleted. And her head seemed to have shut down completely. She closed her eyes.

The sounds of the Kuna trickled in, women gossiping as they did the wash at the aqueduct overflow across the alley, slap-slapping the clothing against the washboards, laughing, scolding their children, the children running in slap-and-kick games, screaming, laughing, bawling, creating a cacophony thick enough to slice like sausage. Dogs barking, howling, whining and growling in sudden fights that broke off as suddenly when someone threw a brick at them or tossed water over them. Several streets off, some men were fighting, she couldn't tell how many, others were gathered around them yelling encouragement or curses, making wagers on the outcome. Voices everywhere, the Kuna was stiff with noise, wall to wall, every day, all day, late into the night. There were always people in the alleys, going and coming from the lodgings, thieves coming back from their nightwork, pimps with their strings of whores, gamblers inside and out, running their endless games. To say nothing of the people who couldn't afford even the meager rents and were living on the street. And the caudhar's baddicks sniffing out those pimps who didn't pay their bribes, running down thieves suspected of dipping their fingers into high purses, pride having outmatched sense, or just looking out for healthy youths who'd make good quarry in the Isun chases. Though she despised these hunters of men, they smelled like rotten fish to her, she left them alone when they were working the alleys; if one was found dead, the whole quarter would pay.

She pulled her mind back from that morass and tried to concentrate on her current problem. I can't spend all this time on her. Yaril means a lot more than she does; I don't even like her all that much. What in Forty Mortal Hells am I going to do with her? She sighed. Hmm. It's been ten years since she left home, that's a long time . . . I wonder how old her father was then . . . maybe he's dead. Would that make a difference? Sounds to me like those brothers were spoiled rotten and might be worse than the old man. What did she say the family name was? Ah! Ash-Kalap. I need mother's name, father's name, eldest brother's name. All right. Let's get at it. She sat up, swung her legs over the edge of the bed and scowled at nothing. She moved her shoulders, opened and closed her hands, clenched and unclenched her toes, working the muscles of her arms and legs. "Carup," she called. "Come in here. I need to talk to you."

11

Two days later.

Night. Late.

The rain had stopped for a while, but the alleys were noisome sewers still.

Brann was picking her way across the mud, thankful her days in the Kuna Coru had deadened her nose so she couldn't smell the fumes rising from that muck. A large nighthawk swooped low and went climbing into the darkness.

Hunting. Jaril's mindvoice was filled with accusation and annoyance. *You know you shouldn't go out when I'm not there for backup.*

Go home, Jay, and wait for me. I don't intend to argue this up to my ankles in mud in the middle of a street.

Trailing disapproval like a tailplume, the hawk shot ahead.

Brann shook her head. Like I'm his child. She frowned as she reached the hovel and sloshed around to the kitchen door. Jaril was sitting at the kitchen table, the wine jar at his elbow, along with two glasses. He'd lit the lamp.

She kicked off her sandals, stepped out of her trousers and took the kettle from the sandbed. She touched it; there was still a little heat left. She poured the lukewarm water into a pan, put her feet in it and sighed with pleasure. "You can give me a glass, if you feel like it, Jay."

He was still temperish and glared at her. "You don't deserve I should, going out like that, you could have been killed." He splashed some wine in the glass and pushed it across to her. "You could have been KILLED. I can't get Yaro without you." Radiating misery, anger, fear, he gulped at his own wine. "I might as well go knock on the smiglar's door and say here I am, eat me."

Brann swished her feet in the water, mud swirling off them. "I was careful, Jay. But I needed to go."

"You needed to go." Despair and disgust sharpened his voice. "You didn't need anything, you got filled up the night before I left."

"All right, have it your way. I went because I wanted to. Does that satisfy you?"

"Satisfy! Bramble, what's got into you? It's like you're twelve, not two hundred plus."

"I don't want to talk about it. What'd you find out?"

He shook his head at her. "Bramble. . . . All right, all right, here it is. You had the right hunch. The father is dead. Stroke. Five years ago." He relaxed as the wine was absorbed into his substance, his eyes dropped and his face softened. "The oldest brother took over the farm, he's married, two wives, I counted five children. It's a big house for that size farm, it's got packed dirt walls, two stories, flat-tile roof. It's built inside a ten-foot wall, packed earth with a canted tile top. There's a garden of sorts, the mother keeps it in order. She's still alive, looks a hundred and two, but probably isn't more than sixty, sixty-five. Tough old femme, like one of those ancient olive trees that just gets stronger as it gets older. One of her daughters is living with her in a two room . . . I suppose you'd call it an apartment, built into a corner of the wall. The other daughters are married to farmers in the area, mostly second wives. The younger brothers seem to 've moved out; no sign of them at the farm or in town. After the father died, I expect the heir cut off supplies. It's a small farm, it can't really afford to support five grown men with a taste for beerbusts. I did some nosing about. Your Carup was exaggerating a trifle. Even if her father were still alive, she would have her mother's protection, should her mother care to give it. Once a woman who's had children makes it past fifty, all bets are off. She's got whatever freedom she wants; the rules don't apply to her any more. She can tell her old man to take a flying leap and get away with it. I expect that's how she kept the daughter home. If she wanted to shelter Carup, no one could stop her. Your Carup knows all that and she knows how old her mother is. Do you think she just forgot to tell you? I don't. You can shove her in a coach and send her home with a clear conscience."

Brann took a towel from the table, set her foot on her knee and began wiping it dry. "That is . . . marvelous, Jay. One incubus off my shoulders." She yawned. "Ahh, I'm tired."

"Get rid of her, we can't waste more time on her. Bramble, Yaril keeps . . . trying to wake, I can feel it. She's wearing herself out. I can't really touch her, it's like seeing her in a dream. A nightmare. I can't talk to her, let her know we're here. She won't rest. She's wasting herself. I'm afraid she thinks I was caught too. I said a year. I think we've got less than half that."

"Slya Bless." She traded feet, rubbed hard at her sole, scouring off dead skin and the last of the mud stains. "I used to think Carup was so passive she wouldn't try to get away if there was an open door in front of her, I used to think she'd stand there crying and let herself get eaten." She laughed, an unhappy sound. "I wouldn't mind having a little of that passivity now; I get the feeling she's set her teeth and she's not going to be pried off. Never mind, I'll manage somehow." She looked at the filthy towel. "I don't know how I'm going to explain this. Hmp, I won't try. There's something I thought about last night, nearly forgot it when you came ramping at me. This is a trap, right?"

"Right. So?"

"The Chuttar's been going about her business as if she doesn't give a counterfeit kaut whether we show up or not. Why? What does it mean? Maybe she knows all about us and is just waiting for us to make the first move. Why she'd do that, I don't know, I haven't the least notion why any of this is happening. What about it, Jay? Am I right? Are they just sitting there? Have you seen any sign of agitation? Well?"

"I hear you, Bramble. I think . . . a memory search . . . let me . . ." He looked at the inch of wine left in the glass, pushed it away, pushed his chair back and stood. Abruptly he shifted form and was a sphere of glimmering gold light that rose and floated over the table.

Brann watched as he drifted with the wandering drafts. She emptied her own glass, looked at the jar and decided she'd had enough for the moment. She glanced at Jarilsphere again, then picked up her trousers and inspected the mud drying on the folds and the ends of the drawstrings that tied about the ankles. She reached for the towel and started to scrub at the scummy cloth.

The lightsphere quivered, came drifting back. Jaril changed again and dropped into his chair. "Memory says the smiglar aren't concerned about anything. They haven't upgraded security, I mean there are no new guards human or otherwise. And they don't leave the place except for the Chuttar and all she does is visit her clients. No one's out looking for us, at least no one connected with that doulahar."

Brann brushed mud off a fold of cloth. "I haven't seen any unusual interest in us. A couple baddicks hang around, but that's just the caudhar making sure we don't short him on his rakeoff." She held up the trousers, scowled at the stench from the muck that impregnated the cloth. "Tchah!" She threw the trousers to the floor, dropped the towel on them. "Jay. . . ."

"Yaro is in there."

"You said it was like a dream."

"Yaro is in there."

"All right, you're the one that knows. How do we neuter them? Can we?"

Jaril frowned, shook his head. "Back home, we didn't fight them, we just ate them. Stuvtiggors, I mean. The stuv weren't as . . . well, smart as this bunch and they didn't play round with um magic; these smiglar stink of it. So I don't know. Except, maybe you should try Maksi again."

Brann nodded. She left, came back with a *call-me* cupped in her palm. She dropped it on the floor, knelt beside it and hammered it to dust with the heel of her mucky sandal.

The glassy fragments vibrated wildly; miniature, hair-fine lightnings jagged over them, died away. Nothing else happened.

Brann dropped the sandal, got to her feet and wiped her hands on her shirt. "That does it, Jay. He's in trouble. Slya bless, everything's twisting into, I don't know." She bent and brushed her knees off, straightened and gazed at the fluttering curtains. "You didn't fight them," she said slowly. "You ate them. You could still do that, I mean even if you've passed from aeta to auli?"

"Yeh. So?"

"The *Skia Hetaira*, remember? We did have Ahzurdan to shield us, but. . . ."

Jaril blinked at her, puzzled. Then he grinned, beat his hand on the table. "Don't fight 'em, eat 'em. You and me and Yaro, we ATE Amortis. We whittled her down and sent her scatting off, scared to her toes."

She sat. "Quiet, Jay. We don't want to wake Carup. Pour me some wine." She lifted the glass, took a sip and sat watching the red change as the lamplight wavered. After a while, she shook her head, as if she were shaking out uncertainty. "We'll keep it simple. If we're lucky . . . though the way things are going, I doubt we get any breaks . . . maybe the Chuttar will be gone for the night, give us less to cope with. Whatever, we go in tomorrow, after midnight, when the servants and so on will be asleep. You circle overhead until I'm inside, then come down fast. That could reduce the time they have for reacting. Unless they can locate me as easily as they can you. We'll just have to hope they can't. Argument?"

"None. Go on."

"Everything we've learned says the Chuttar's personal suite is the heart of that place, so that's where she'd most likely keep Yaro. No one goes in there but smiglar, not her clients, not the maids, no one. It's on the third floor, the main house. There's a smiglar guarding the roof, another at the top of the stair and a third guard stays in the suite whenever the Chuttar's not there. Not counting the Chuttar, that leaves two other smiglar. One of them acts as relief, the other is the Chuttar's Housemaster. Cammam Callan, Carup called him. Got his nose in everything, day and night. You say he's second to the Chuttar in power and if the two of them get together, that's trouble for us. I think you're right. Without Maksi to back us, all we can do is try whittling them down. Eat 'em." She gulped some wine, drew her hand across her mouth. "I'll get over the wall and into the house, shouldn't be too hard, break a pane on the glass doors that open on the terrace, turn the latch. You overfly first, let me know where the Housemaster is and the spare guards. I'll avoid them, if possible, drain them if I have to. That'll warn the others, won't it?"

"Yeh. When a bunch of aetas hit a stuv nest, they suck them up and get the hell out, fast, because the place is going to be swarming in minutes."

"You'll feel it too?"

"Yeh."

"Good. You stay high and keep track of me. If I make contact before I reach the stairs, you come in, take out the roof guard and if need be, the stair guard. Eat 'em fast, Jay, I don't want them landing on my back. If there's no contact, if I get up those stairs with no trouble, I'll mindyell as soon as I'm ready to take the guard there, that's when you come in. We'll try hitting the stairs and roof at the same time. Then it's a dash for the bedroom. If the Chuttar's out for the night, we hit the guard there, grab Yaro and get out before the others converge on us. If the Chuttar's there, I'll keep her busy while you see if you can get Yaro out of stone and mobile. Yes, yes, you told me, it's likely to be a slow unfolding. If you can't get her out, can you fly and carry her?"

"I suppose. You mean leave you there?"

"If you have to. I'll be doing what I did with Amortis. Draw and vent. Draw down the Chuttar and use her energy to fry the other smiglar if they come at me." She smiled at him, lifted a hand. "Once you get Yaro someplace fairly safe, if you feel like coming back, I wouldn't mind a bit."

"This sounds more like a stampede than a plan. Bramble, there are at least a hundred ways we could screw up."

"I'd say more like a thousand." She shrugged. "Nothing ever goes like you plan it, you should know that, Jay. If we keep moving fast enough, maybe the momentum will carry us through. It's got to be fast. For Yaro's sake." She pushed the straggling gray hair off her face. "If you can think of a better way, tell me."

He shook his head. "I'm not even going to try."

12

Veiled and cloaked, dressed with a subdued richness, she'd absorbed taste from the Chuttar if nothing else, Carup took the bodyguard's hand and climbed into the traveling gada; she ignored his blatant appreciation of her body, but she was pleased by it. Her dark eyes flicked to his face for a moment, then she settled back and he closed the door. He climbed to the seat beside the driver, slapped the man's arm; the driver snapped his whip over the ears of the lead pair and the gada started north along the dusty, rutted road, heading for Pattan Haria.

Brann watched for a while, wondering if Carup would relent and wave. She didn't. From the moment they stepped onto the landing, Carup had refused to see her. She hadn't said good-bye and she didn't look back now. Her resentment had gone deep; she would have rebelled if she'd dared, but she knew too well the futility of fighting powers greater than her own. Bitter, resentful, and rich. A bad combination. She was going to make someone's life a hell.

Brann sighed and stepped into the longboat. "Go," she said, and settled back as the man pushed off and began rowing her across the moat. I've done the best I can, she told herself, I can't change the world by myself. Maksi tried changing a piece of it and look what happened to him.

13

Raining again.

Strong winds, sleet, heavy cold.

The next storm would probably bring snow.

Brann huddled in the entranceway of a kotha, a house built directly on the street without the size, the grounds or the enclosing wall of a doulahar. The kotha belonged to an ancient fence who'd survived purges, investigations and other worries thought up by the Isun, not only survived those but managed to hang onto the greater part of his profits. The door at the back of the short passage was small and massive and there was a trap in the ceiling in front of it; persistent and annoying visitors got a most uncivil welcome; more than once his guards had poured burning oil on a man who wouldn't take *go away* for an answer. He was even nastier to street folk who tried to sleep there, but she was safe enough if she didn't linger too long or make a fuss.

Jaril came trotting in; he was using the horny, water-shedding form he'd dreamed up that night above Kukurul. He shifted and stood shivering before her. "She's staying home tonight. I'm not surprised. With weather like this I'd rather be inside myself. Callan smiglar is in his room, the one on the third floor; he's busy about something, I couldn't see what, I was too far off to do anything but place him. Be better if he was downstairs, soon's we make a noise he'll be over with the Chuttar. Can't help that, though. The relief is at the back of the house in another wing doing something with the other smiglar, the one who stays in the suite when the Chuttar's not there. That's all right, they're nowhere near the terrace, you can go in there without worrying about them. The stair guard and the roof guard are in their usual places."

"Anything I should worry about?"

"Callan. He and the Chuttar are wide awake and up to something. Most nights they're resting by now if the Chuttar doesn't have a client. Dormant. Like Yaril and me, you know. Otherwise nothing different."

"What do you think, should we call this off?"

"There'll always be something."

"You're right. How's your energy level?"

"The cold and the wet are pulling me down. I could use a shot."

"And I'm more dangerous when I'm hungry. Take my hand, yell if it gets too strong."

Brann fed him till he started to glow and she felt a hollow pulse inside her. A Need. When he pulled free, she touched his shoulder. "If you see anything I should know about, give me a tweak, hmm?"

"Bramble!"

"I know, I don't need to say it. Go on, get!"

After he left she stripped to undershirt and loincloth, stuffed her clothing and sandals into a waterproof bag and plunged out of the passage into the rain. She ran along the street, settling to a long easy lope, her feet splatting steadily on the muddy cobbles; she was in her original body again, the old woman banished for the moment. The rain beat into her face, half-blinding her, but she wasn't bothered by that, there wasn't much to see. Most of the street lamps were out, either water or wind had got at them. Splat and splat. On and on, feeling good because the waiting was over, feeling good because her body was fire and iron, working like a fine timepiece, alive, alive, so alive.

She loped past the doulahar's gatehouse, a glassed-in lamp putting out enough light to show her where she was. She slowed, moved closer to the wall and followed it until it turned and she could no longer see the lamp. She unwound the rope from her waist, swung the end with the climbing claw several times, then threw it up. The claw caught. She tugged. It held. She walked up the wall, switched the claw over and slid down, landing up to her ankles in the sloppy mud of a flowerbed. Leaving the rope dangling, she ran for the house, jumping low hedges, plowing through more flowerbeds, swerving to avoid ornamental trees she could barely see, laughing idiotically as she ran, riding the kind of high she hadn't felt for a century or more.

She slapped her hands on the stone railing at the edge of the terrace, vaulted over and ran across the slick streaming tiles; her feet slapped down noisily, she was panting like a swayback mare at the end of a race, but she didn't care, the wind was howling, the rain came swooshing down, the storm was loud enough to cover a stampede, let alone the small sounds she was making.

When she reached the array of glass doors, she looked up into the murk and waited for any comment Jaril wanted to make. Nothing. Good enough. She swung her pack down, reached into an outside pocket and took out a glove; the back was plated with iron and the tips were curving claws. With that on her left hand, she smashed a pane, reached through, and unlatched the door.

As soon as she was inside, she closed it again, threw the latch, and stuffed a wad of drape into the hole. It was black as a coal cellar in there, cold and silent, the sounds of the storm muffled by the thickness of the walls and the heavy draperies drawn across the doors. Working by touch, she took off the claw and dropped it on the rug, then stripped off her sopping clothes and dressed in dry things from the pack. She rubbed her feet, then her hands and head on the draperies, removing much of the wet, enough so she wouldn't drip on the stairs and betray her position by the noise she was making. She hesitated a moment, then pushed the pack behind one of the drapes. Her hands were her best weapons, her empty hands. No point in cluttering them or weighing down her body with unnecessary paraphernalia. Move fast, move clean, she told herself, momentum's the word.

There was a splotch of gray on the far wall, a nightlight filtering through a tightly netted doorweb. She moved cautiously across the room, stopped before the web and ran her fingers lightly over it. It was beaded, with beaded fringes, a misery to get past without enough clatter to break through the storm noise. She swore under her breath, gathered a handful of webbing and eased it aside enough so she could edge through. Keeping the fringe still, she spread the web out again until she could take her hand away without shaking the beads.

She listened. The storm sounds were a muted background; there were the usual night noises from a large old house. Nothing more. She ghosted away from the door and plunged into a nest of interconnecting rooms; there were small nightlights scattered haphazardly about, wicks floating on aromatic oil in glass bowls shaped like half-closed tulips. Annoyed and disoriented, she slowed. Jay, you've got it easy, luv. Sheeh! if I just had wings I could cut all this nonsense.

She emerged finally into an immense atrium three stories high with a graceful staircase curling around the rim like a climbing vine, its steps and rails made of white-painted wrought iron with more of the tulip bowls set on the outside edge of the steps, a shimmering loveliness in the tall dark. She listened again. Nothing. All right, she thought. Let's get at it. She glided across the black and white tiles and started up the stairs.

She was wary at first, but by the time she reached the first turn she was running, her bare feet making no sound on the lacework iron steps.

Up and around, up and around, first floor, second. She stopped, stared into the murk; she couldn't see anything, but there was no point taking chances she didn't have to. She swung over the rail, hung for a moment until she found footing on the end of the step. Hand over hand, feet feeling for holds, she moved up the outside of the stair, ignoring the abyss below her.

The guard was restless; she could hear him kicking at the floor mat. She hung where she was and peered through a lacy panel. The staircase ended in a dark hole, made all the darker by the faint light from one of the tiny lamps. She couldn't see the guard, not even as a blotch in that blackness, but from what she could hear, he had to be a few steps down the hallway. She shifted her grip and went on.

When she reached the top, she rested a moment, mindshouted intent at Yaril, then gathered herself and pushed off, using the strength of her legs to counter the relative weakness of her arms and shoulders. She went flying over the rail, landed running. Before the guard had a chance to react, she was on him, her hands slapped against him, drawing the life from him.

At first he went limp, then he began to dissolve; it felt like she had her hands on a sack full of hot-tailed scorpions. She increased the drain until she was taking in at her limit. The dissolution went faster, he was losing his shape, parts of him struggling to escape. He wasn't fast enough. She took everything he had and left him as dust on the mat.

Jaril met her at the door to the Chuttar's suite. He was glowing and grinning, wild and strange, more alien than she'd ever seen him. He nodded at her, shaped his hands into a parabola and shot a stream of fire at the lock, melting it and a good portion of the door around it.

Brann kicked the door open and plunged inside, running at the women who sat near a bank of windows, her hands folded over a black velvet cushion on her lap. The Chuttar Palami Kumindri, smiling and unconcerned. The other smiglar in the room, a big man with black mustaches hanging from the ends of his mouth, stood beside her. Cammam Callan, the Housemaster. He smoothed his mustaches, stepped in front of the chair and raised his hands, palm out. Brann slammed into something as resilient as a sponge, strong as oiled silk. Jaril changed and a blazing lightsphere hit the resilience beside her, rebounded, came at it again and yet again; each time he was flung back, each time he punched a deeper hollow in it. Brann flattened her hands against the shield and drew; somewhat to her surprise, she began pulling in a trickle of power. She laughed and pulled harder; she'd never managed to tap into a magic shield before; apparently this one was so much a part of that smiglar, was maintained so intimately out of his inner strength, she could attack it as if it were his flesh. Callan staggered, paled. He shrunk, grew denser, braced himself and shoved out the sags in the shield.

The Chuttar Palami Kumindri watched calmly for several minutes, then she began unfolding the black velvet. It wasn't a cushion. The milky, flawed moonstone that was Yaril sat on the velvet, pulling in light from all around her. Palami Kumindri lifted an elegant pale hand and splayed it out an inch or so above the Yaril stone. "Be still," she said. Her voice was low and lovely and full of the consciousness of her power. "Stop what you're doing or watch me eat her."

Jaril settled to the floor. He changed and stood radiating fear and rage, his eyes fixed on the Yaril stone.

Brann dropped her hands. "If that viper beside you attacks, I will defend myself," she said, "I will not stand still and allow myself to be destroyed, even for her."

"I have no intention of destroying you, Drinker of Souls. You are going to be much too useful."

"Not if I can help it."

"That's the question, isn't it." Palami Kumindri cupped her hands about the gleaming stone, still not quite touching it. "There's something I want. You can use that to ransom your friend." She took her hands away, rested them on the chairarms. "I will see that she is bathed in sunlight so she will keep as well as possible in this state. I will not harm her in any way, but I cannot prevent her from harming herself. I see you understand."

"What do you want?"

"In the Temple of Amortis, in the holy city Havi Kudush, there sits one of the Great Talismans. Churrikyoo. A small glass frog rather battered and chipped and filled with thready cracks. Bring it to me and I will give you your friend."

"There's a problem. Amortis. She doesn't love me and she knows me far too well. If I go near her, she'll eat me alive."

"You are a clever woman, Drinker of Souls, you will find a way."

"There are other talismans, send me after one of those."

"Churrikyoo is the only ransom I will accept, Drinker of Souls. Bring it here and claim your friend."

"Why should I trust you to keep your word?"

"I repeat, you are a clever woman, work that out. In any case, you have no choice."

Brann clasped her hands behind her, let her shoulders go round. She took time for a leisurely examination of the Chuttar, then the House-master. *Jay.*

What? His mindvoice was sullen, unfriendly.

Can they hear this?

No.

You sound very positive.

I am.

You know any way out of this?

No.

Terse.

What's to say?

We snapped up the bait, didn't we.

Yeh. Trolled us right in.

Trust me?

You know it.

Stay quiet, then, I'm going to do some pushing. She finished her look round the room, faced the Chuttar. "I have no choice if I let you dictate terms, if I value my friend's life above everything else. Listen and weep, whore. I do value her, but not beyond a certain point. Beyond that I WILL NOT BE PUSHED! Believe it. I will go after Chur-rikyoo. I will trade it for my friend. But not here. The exchange will be on my terms, not yours. I won't come back to this house. I won't come near this city."

"Where?"

"Let me consult with my friend." She turned to face Jaril. *Any ideas, Jay?*

Yeh. A Waystop in the Fringelands. Yaro and me, we've been past there more than once. It's just north of the Locks. The place is called Waragapur.

Tell me more about it. Why there?

It's a truceground, which should mean something, but probably won't and there's an old fossil of a sorcerer there, one of the Primes. Tak WakKerrcarr. If that bitch smiglar starts playing games with us, she'll have him on her neck. He's the one laid down the guarantee and it's one of the few things he gets stirred up about.

Good. Maybe we can use him to kick something loose.

Anything's better than here.

Agreed. She faced the Chuttar, straightened her shoulders and put her hands on her hips. "These are my terms, I will get Churrikyoo and bring it to Waragapur on the edge of the Fringelands. As soon as I get there, I'll send a message north by one of the riverboats. Come there. Bring her with you and we will make the exchange."

"Why should I?"

"You get nothing if you don't. If you refuse, we fight. You can destroy our friend, but we'll get you. One way or another you die. If not now, later. I have friends I can call on and I will, if you force it, and if you think you can stop me getting out of here, dream on."

"Calmly, calmly, Drinker of Souls. I too must consult. Step outside, please. I will call you when I am ready to answer you."

Brann bowed her head, strolled out.

Jaril hesitated, then followed her. *Bramble. . . .*

What could I do?

Nothing, I suppose.

Be patient, Jay. Our time is coming, has to.

Yaro's in there.

I know. Does she have any idea we're here?

It's that shield, Bramble. The same as the one in the cave. I can't feel anything through it, so Yaro can't feel me.

Damn, I was hoping we'd get at least that much out of this.

We could still try breaking through. I think I was close.

So do I. But we'd have to start over again and we couldn't break it fast enough to save Yaro. Well, we might have to try it. I meant what I said, Jay. If she gets us back here, none of us will get out.

I know.

One thing, we'll have the talisman.

You can't use it.

No, but WakKerrcarr can and from what Maksi said, he might not be a friend, but he's no enemy.

I didn't think of that. After all these years you can still surprise me, Bramble-all-Thorns.

*Let's hope I can surprise *them.**

Yeh.

"Drinker of Souls." It was a surly growl. Cammam Callan held the door open for them, then went back to stand beside Palami Kumindri, glowering like a chastised boy, obviously hammered into an agreement he wasn't strong enough to refuse.

Brann went back into the room. She waited, saying nothing.

The Chuttar sat with her hands cupped about the Yaril stone as if she were warming them at the changer's glow. "We have considered your terms, Drinker of Souls. We find them acceptable. We will meet you at Waragapur and make the exchange there."

Brann nodded, swung round and stalked from the room. Jaril backed up after her, not taking his eyes off the pair.

They went down the stairs in silence and left the doulahar without breaking that silence.

14

For the next several nights Drinker of Souls hunted through the streets of Dil Jorpashil, soaking up energy so she could assume a new shape. During the days she was the Jantria Bar Ana and kept up her healing, Jaril taking the form of a small M'darjin boy and acting as her attendant. A few of the local women asked about Carup; they were pleased, angry, happy for her and jealous, when Brann said she'd sent the girl home with a dowry.

Those same nights Jaril flew in and out of Isu sars and the Merchant doulahars, collecting clothing, jewelry and gold for the trip south. He was profoundly disturbed at the thought of leaving Yaril, churned to the point of instability because the days were passing and there was nothing he could do to shorten the time ahead and each day Yaril died a little.

15

One week after the abortive attack on the doulahar, an hour after dawn, when the new-risen sun was a muted blur in the clouds, providing little light and less heat, and the incessant east wind was whipping whitecaps off leaden water, a wealthy Jana Sariser widow attended by a M'darjin page dismounted from a hired palanquin and went aboard the riverboat *Dhah Dhibanh*.

About mid-afternoon the *Dhah Dhibanh* cast off her lines and started south, widow and page standing at the rail watching the city recede behind them.

II: SETTSIMAKSIMIN

Sending Todichi Yahzi home drained
Maksim so completely he was easy
prey to a party of demons (geniod)
sent to capture him. He woke unable
to speak or move; it was hard to
think, impossible to act. The demons
put him into his boat and took him
out of the Myk'tat Tukery into the
sea called the Notoea Tha where
they transferred him into a small
sleek Coaster and nailed him into a
large crate.

1

When Settsimaksimin surfaced enough for self-awareness, he was still
in the crate and from the dip and sway of it, still aboard the Coaster.
His thoughts oozed across a heavy, dull mind with the ponderous loiter
of a sleep-drugged snail.

How long?

No thirst, no hunger.

Not much of anything.

I see.

Preservation spell.

He tongued at it sluggishly, smelled at it.

The stripes of light that came through the cracks between the boards
of the crate crept across him, marking the passage of a day. Dark came
before he finished the plodding exploration. He drifted into sleep, more
from habit than need, almost despite the spell.

In the morning he thought:

No water.

No food.

How long?

Why do I think? Feel? See? Hear?

It was an extraordinary subtle spell in that it left him aware of what was happening around him while keeping him in stasis until he was handed over to whoever or whatever had orchestrated all this.

Why?

Yes. I see.

They want something.

They want me to do something.

They want me to do something I probably won't want to do.

They're softening me up.

The stripes climbed over him, moving across his motionless body while he produced these long slow thoughts. Slowly so slowly like a sloworm crawling from one hole to the next, he considered the spell. Night came and his sluggard metabolism reacted again, dropping him into sleep.

Yellow light running across his eyes woke him.

He considered the spell.

It was a strange one, he couldn't place the personality of the sorcerer or other who cast it, but he had nothing to distract him and the effort it took to think acted as a focusing lens. When the swift twilight of the tropical seas dropped over him once more, he almost had it. There was a sense of something distantly familiar, the cousin of a cousin of a cousin of a memory from the part of the past he'd suppressed as soon as he escaped from it, his apprenticeship. He slept.

He woke with the same taste on his tongue.

He burrowed through memory to the time when he was sold into a pleasure House in Silagamatys, six years old, a street rat, father unknown, mother rotting to death from diseases she'd picked up when she worked the wharves as a stand-up whore. He remembered Musteba Xa.

He was bought out of the House by that anciently evil man, a dried-up old bag of perversions who had forgotten how to feel so long ago that even the loss was a dim memory, the most powerful sorcerer in the world. He kept that claim real by sucking up life and Talent from his apprentices. Coveting Maksim's Talent, he began to train the boy . . . no, he didn't even see the boy, all he saw was the Talent. He cultivated that Talent like a gardener cultivating a rare plant; he put his hands on it and shaped it the way he wanted it to go. He made only one mistake —he taught Maksim too well, a mistake born out of his inattention to the whole boy and too much confidence in his ability to jerk him about like a puppet. With his icy precision and unmatched learning, his cutting tongue and hypertrophied intelligence, his ability to read muscle twitches and fleeting shifts of expression so that he knew every thought or intent that crossed Maksim's mind even before Maksim knew it was there, he'd forced the angry passionate boy to learn an equally icy control. When he decided to harvest what he'd nourished, he summoned entities that were. . . .

Were like these.

Yes.

Like these pseudo Harpish who controlled him.

Maksim's mind shut down on him, the sudden burst of excitement drowning the delicate control he'd achieved over his spelled and dreaming body.

Later. Sun stripes hot on him.

He recovered enough to lay phrase against phrase and began teasing at that memory, pulling out strands of it and setting them beside his impressions of his captors.

The demons Musteba Xa summoned were similar to the ones who were holding him now.

But not identical.

The web those earlier demons threw about him was similar to the cocoon that prisoned him now, but weaker.

Back then, he'd reacted from instinct and training; he broke the bonds and provided Musteba Xa with the first surprise he'd had in centuries. He killed his master and flung his body into an empty reality as far off as he could reach.

Similar, yes.

Now that he had some idea what to taste for, he used his fingertips like a tongue to taste the bonds that held him.

Time passed.

Sometimes he was aware of the thin lines of light running round him.

When he looked again, more often than not the lines were gone, the day gone with them.

Sometimes he overworked himself and his mind shut down again.

Sometimes he was focusing so intently, so narrowly, he wouldn't have noticed if the ship were on fire.

Interminable and immeasurable, the hours crawled past, turned into days, the days into weeks and so on.

He reached a point where he needed to know more about where he was going.

He rested from his labors and watched the sunlines move.

From the way the sunlight shifted about the crate, he decided the ship was heading west.

West of Kukurul the first port of any size was Bandrabahr.

On an average, in the autumn of the year, it was thirty days from Kukurul to Bandrabahr.

He tried to count the days he'd been in the crate, but he could not.

There was a brisk following wind.

A wizard's wind.

He could smell the power in it.

Great galloping gobs of power.

Whoever wanted him was spending it like water.

Bandrabahr. Phras.

He considered the implications of that and wanted to scream his outrage at this, using the sound of his voice to hide his fear.

Amortis.

Phras was her ground, the source of her godpower.

Her Temple was there.

Her priests were trained there.

Gods of Fate and Time, not Amortis!

The surge of emotion shut him off again.

When he came out of the dark, he felt a change in the ship's motion.

He heard port sounds, shouted orders, men calling to each other or to boat whores, the women answering, bargaining, exchanging insults, laughing. Water taxis scooting about, their sweeps shrieking like the ghosts of murdered children.

The language was Phrasi.

The smells were as familiar as his own armpits.

Bandrabahr.

He waited for the shipmaster to heave to and drop anchor.

The ship kept moving.

Slowly, carefully, it wound through the heavy traffic of the busy port.

He listened.

He heard the sounds of cranes and winches, but not the ones on this ship.

He heard the grunts of the rowers on the towships, the drums that set time for them.

He felt the ship yaw slightly.

For a minute he didn't understand this, then he knew the ship had entered the outflow from the river that ran through Bandrabahr, the Sharroud.

Forty Mortal Hells, am I being hauled off to Havi Kudush?

He struggled to control his body's reactions.

He couldn't afford to go black now, he had to get loose.

HAD TO GET LOOSE.

He almost lost it at that moment, but suppressed his sense of helplessness and went back to his investigations.

The preservation spell was wearing thin.

His body was speeding up.

His senses were freer.

He could almost shake his mindreach loose.

He was distantly aware of the smells and sounds of the water quarter as the ship clawed upriver through the city.

He was aware of time passing, the minutes ticking faster and faster, moving from loooong looong pulses to the heart count of real time.

The sounds and smells of the city faded and finally disappeared.

He smelled gardens and plowed fields.

He heard birdsong, sheep bleating, the squeal of an angry horse.

They were in the Barabar Burmin, the Land of Hidden Delights, the rich, fertile hinterland of Phras.

He knew this county, he'd spent a century here, a lusty wasteful wonderful century.

Three days upriver was the junction of the Kaddaroud and the Sharroud.

He'd have his answer then.

If the ship turned up the Kaddaroud, Amortis was waiting for him in the Temple at Havi Kudush where she'd fry him alive and eat him for breakfast.

Crossgrained, intemperate bitch god.

She had reason to be annoyed, she'd lost a hefty portion of her substance running his errands, going after Brann for him when he was still trying to kill the Drinker of Souls before she got him.

Hunger began to nag at him.

By the second day on the Sharroud, thirst grew into a torment.

He ignored hunger and thirst and continued to tease ravels out of his bonds, dissolving them as soon as he had them loose so they couldn't wriggle away from him and rejoin the parent weave.

He was beginning to burrow his way out. Soon, soon. . . .

By the beginning of the third day, thirst had him hallucinating.

He saw lightlines turn to serpents of gold that writhed and knotted and coupled in a frenzy of lust and rage, he cringed away from them, thinking that Amortis was coming for him.

Amortis was the patron of lust and frenzy.

He saw polymorphous gold beetles shimmer into uncertain being and drop onto him.

They crawled all over him.

The tickling of their feet grew worse and worse until it was unendurable.

There were other torments, all the worse for being self-inflicted.

He rode out the first waves of that disorientation, husbanding what strength he had left until he saw a chance to sieze control. . . .

He shaped a mind-drill and drove it through the decks into the river.

He turned the drill to a drinking straw and sucked up water through it. It was unfiltered river water with all that meant, the suspended soil, the sublife swarming in each drop, but it flooded with grateful coolth into his arid mouth and slid down his aching throat more welcome than the finest wine.

His stomach clenched, cramped and he almost vomited up what he'd swallowed, but he kept the water down and drew in more.

The hallucinations went away.

He returned to his raveling of the spellbonds.

Time passed in its uncertain way.

He looked around.

His vision was no longer confined to what his eyes could see.

He inspected the river banks, felt a flood of relief and pleasure.

They were deep into the great arid plain called the Tark that made up most of Northern Phras.

They were past the junction of the Kaddaroud and the Sharroud.

It isn't Amortis who has me.

Tak WakKerrcarr in the Fringelands, we'll be reaching him soon. If I can *call* him, if he's in a mood to listen. . . .

If I can't, it looks like Jorpashil's the endpoint of this voyage.

Interesting.

Thinking about Dil Jorpashil reminded him of Brann; he smiled.

Bramble, whoever's got that devilkid of yours has put his hands on me, I'd bet my stash on that.

He drank some more river and slept a while.

The hot wind that blew incessantly across the Tark crept through the cracks in the crate, turning it into an oven.

He had to reroute some of his meager resources into cooling himself.

He had to find a way of ridding his bladder of urine without voiding it into the crate; the stench would bring attention he didn't want.

When the ship came to the first of the Locks, he had almost reached the key strand.

One last sustained effort and he would make these bastards wish they'd never been whelped.

Outside the crate, there was frantic activity as the sailors prepared for the entrance into the lock.

The noise and shuddering of the ship faded from his senses as he narrowed and narrowed his focus.

He drew power from the heat in the planks he lay on and prepared himself for the strike that would free him.

He heard an immense rumbling roar and force smothered him.

The Others were awake finally.

He fought them, but he was still more than half bound by the old spinning so his reach was lamentably short, the power he could call on so small it was whiffed out immediately.

He screamed hate and rage at them, but could not get his curses past his tongue, the ties on it were iron-heavy, iron-hard.

He struggled to unlock his hands, but failed.

They were knowing and swift with their binding, but this time he was awake when they handled him and he learned more than they realized. Or so he hoped.

It was godFire they called on, no mage or sorcerer, witch or warlock could wield that Fire without a god behind him. Or her.

Not

Amortis

His mind slowed and stiffened.

Not

Amortis

I know

I am sure

Who?

Don't

Know

Don't . . . kno . . . o . . . ow. . . .

2

When he slid out of the darkness, his mind and body were slooow annnnd stiifff.

More than they were when his captors first nailed him in the crate.

He remembered.

That was the first thing he managed.

While he was remembering, the sunlines appeared and disappeared in one blink of his eye.

Appeared and disappeared, appeared and disappeared.

Sound came to him, slowed down and stretched until they were no more than hollow groans without meaning.

He listened and looked.

A concept at a time, a word or a phrase, he explained to himself where he was and what was happening to him.

The ship shivered continually.

That bothered him until he understood it.

The ship was moving with her usual grace at her usual speed; it was the difference between his timerate and hers that made her seem so jerky.

She kept moving, no halts, no major changes in her motion.

They were through the locks.

He was angry.

They'd slid him past WakKerrcarr before he had a chance to *call* the Prime.

He wondered about WakKerrcarr.

Tak must have known something peculiar was happening, he must have ignored it. That was typical of the man and his whims.

He thought about Brann.

It was a better world she lived in.

She wouldn't have dozed as someone was carried past her trapped in a web of demonspin. She'd have been down there finding out what was happening.

He thought about Cheonea and wondered how his experiment was progressing.

He hoped he'd laid a strong enough foundation to carry it on without him.

Brann wouldn't let him go look. You go back, she said, you won't keep your hands off, you'll adjust this thing and lop off that and before you know it, you'll be the old kings reincarnated. Do you realize, he told her, how irritating it is when someone's always right? She laughed at him and patted his cheek and went away to work on a pot or a drawing or something like that.

He missed her.

She was dear. Mother and sister and child in one.

He thought of her walking into a trap like the one that had closed on him and he lost control.

His mind shut down before he could gather its ravels, the world turned black, a mix of fear and rage like pine tar painted on him waiting to be fired.

He woke thinking of her.

How odd it is, he thought. In Kukurul I knew that she wouldn't come back to Jal Virri, that I wouldn't see her again, perhaps for years. I could contemplate that absence with equanimity because I knew . . . he thought about that . . . yes, because I knew we'd come together again. How odd it is. I hadn't the least idea how painful the separation would be. We argue and she runs her hands through her hair, certain we'll never ever resolve our differences. Or I go stomping off, sure of the same thing. A few hours later she laughs, or I laugh, it's all so stupid, not worth remembering. She is dear.

He started working at his bonds again.

Much to his satisfaction, the erosion went faster this time.

He knew them now, he knew the twists they put on their spells.

He knew their arrogance; he'd felt their surprise as he'd come so close to escaping them.

He knew how much an accident it was that they discovered his work before it fruited.

He didn't waste time cursing that accident; what happens, happens.

They watched him closer for a while. He felt their probes sweeping through the crate whenever they decided to check on him.

They'd left him alone for days now, he wasn't sure how many days.

Slipping into their old ways. Careless and rather stupid. Bang not brain. Use it or lose it.

He grinned into the darkness, imagining Brann's acerbic, probably nonverbal response to that list of clichés.

He rested a while and considered his captors.

His mind was moving more fluidly these days and he was again feeling the first touch of thirst.

They should have suspected that might happen.

They should have watched him more closely.

They weren't bothering to watch him.

He smiled, a feral baring of his teeth that might have warned them if they'd been watching him, but they weren't.

Bang bang. Power. They trusted their power.

They didn't seem to understand how tricky a man could get even though he couldn't match their power. Maybe they thought it would take him another thirty days to do what he'd done before. Maybe they expected to reach their homebase before he could get loose again.

Dil Jorpashil.

Sarimbara the Horned Serpent was god in Jorpashil.

He thought about trying to wake the god.

Sarimbara wouldn't be happy knowing other gods and their demons were meddling in his territory.

Sarimbara was a lazy god and spent decades dozing, merged with the earth below Jorpashil, his serpentine length coiled in complex knots; the Jana Sarise had hundreds of lullaby rituals because he was also a god with an infantile sense of humor or it might be a sublimely satiric sensibility; one's idea about which concept applied depended on who he was doing what to. He was touchy about his prerogatives. Those who got too arrogant or proud found their noses rubbed in the mud. The Grand Isu, first among the Isun, could wake and find he was a rag-and-bone dealer, while a beggar sat in his place, eating his food off his fine porcelain, wearing his embroidered robes, enjoying his concubines. It had happened more than once. ANYTHING could happen when Sarimbara woke.

The ship began slowing, weaving from one side of the river to the other as the channel permitted.

There was traffic on the water now, going and coming.

At times the master had to shift his ship as far out of the main channel as he could without grounding her and wait for barge strings to trundle past.

In those quiet times Maksim heard the blatting of the long-legged sheep that the grassclan Temuengs raised, the whooping of the drovers as they moved a portion of their herds to market in Jorpashil.

Sometimes he heard the shouted boasts of young clansmen heading for one of the river villages to celebrate this or that, get drunk, spend what coin they had, get themselves in trouble with the sedentaries and more often than not end up imprisoned or dead.

The noises from the Grass got louder and more confused, the traffic in the river denser and slower.

They were closing on Lake Pikma ka Vyamm.

His hands shook.

He fought down the urgency that screamed through him and continued with his slow, steady attack on the ties that held him helpless.

A ring of ghost fragments hung like a neck-high mist outside the walls of Dil Jorpashil. The ship slid through the part of the ring that drifted over the river, warning him he had almost no time left.

The soul mist flowed silently through the cracks in the crate, eddied about him and slowly drained away; the dead were silenced here as they were in most large cities, so all he got from them was a vague sadness and scattered pricks of rage.

He clenched his teeth and continued picking at the spells that held him.

The river didn't enter Jorpashil, it flowed around the city in two broad streams, a moat thick with carp and flowering floating jeppu plants that together almost managed to clean up the sewage that emptied every day into the sluggish flows. The island thus created was five miles wide and six miles long. It rose from the lakeshore to green and lovely hills like multiple breasts; the high lords, the Isun, and the lesser lords, the Dhaniks, planted their gardens and built their elaborate sars up there, above the dust and noise of the busy, hectic city. Just below them were the whitewashed doulahars of the richest merchants. For the rest, the poor lived where they could, the artisans and small merchants had their quarters, the sublegal professions had theirs, traders and other visitors had their small enclave. Inns and taverns, theaters and arenas, local markets and businesses were dotted about wherever there was space and the prospect of customers.

With acres of intricately intersecting alleys, clusters of cubby stores, daggerflags fluttering before them announcing their wares, ragged lines of open face kiosks piled with meats and fruit and every sort of foodstuff, the Great Market was laid out across the Lakequarter. Stuffed with bales, barrels, jugs, and sacks filled with the rich flow of goods that came up the river from Bandrabahr and by land along the Silk Road and lesser trade routes, low thick walled godons were built between the citywall and the lakeshore. The moorings for the river traffic were on the Lakeshore also, long heavy piers jutting half a mile into the water. Sarimbara's piers. They were built on piles made from the trunks of giant drakhabars brought up the river on huge barges, three trunks to a barge, barge after barge during the summer cutting-season, year after year for fifteen years. A dozen piers splayed out like the fingers on two six-digited hands.

They were there because Sarimbara woke from a doze one day and was annoyed with the clutter of ships scraping their keels against his mud, churning his waters into stinking soup. He decided the Grand Isu was going to do something to stop that nonsense. He demanded coin or service as worshipduty from everyone who ate from the Lake or the river, directly or indirectly, everyone who lived from the fruit of the land, directly or indirectly; in other words, he demanded something from everyone who lived in and around the city. He did some fancy manipulations on the wealthy and powerful to convince reluctant merchants, furious Dhaniks and supercilious Isun to contribute their proper share of the effort. After several haughty matrons and their puissant lords had visions of themselves scrubbing floors, gutting fish or mucking out stables, their enthusiasm for the project was exemplary.

Fighting the powerful sweep of wind that came ramming across the Grass and then across the Lake, sending whitefoam flowing across knifeblue glitter, blowing east to west, eternally blowing, fighting that wind, tacking and tacking again, the ship crossed to the north shore and dropped anchor by cliffs of crystalline white marble, screened from the east wind by a tall vertical fold of that marble.

3

Maksim kept working.

He was so close to breaking the ties. So close.

The ship jerked erratically at its mooring cables.

The minutes stretched and stretched.

He was close. So close.

The crate fell apart around him.

He screamed with rage.

The iron locked his tongue down, no sound came out of him.

The demons hovered about him, spherical glows like Yaril and Jaril but considerably larger.

They began to move, flowing round and round him, faster and faster until they were a ring of light.

He threw off the clinging remnants of his bonds.

With a shiver of triumph, he bounded to his feet and flung himself at the rail.

He passed through the shimmering ring, screamed aloud, finally finally aloud, vaulted the rail and plunged toward the water.

And landed on his feet in an immense cavern, a great shimmering gem of a cavern like the inside of a monstrous geode.

The demons hovered about him, seven nodes of golden light, adding a rich amber cast to the glitter of the crystals embedded in the stone arching over him, dipping under him.

He screamed again, a basso bellow that echoed and reechoed, reinforcing and canceling the original sound.

The figure on the massive throne raised a hand and compelled a sudden silence.

Maksim lifted his hands to fight, opened his mouth to pour forth the syllables he'd stored against this moment.

Nothing happened.

Nothing came to him.

He was mute.

He was erased.

His hands shook.

His arms went limp, falling to his sides.

"Maks, Maksi, Maksim, is that the way to greet your Master?"

He stared, swallowed. He didn't believe what he saw.

Musteba Xa. Line for line, gesture for gesture, it was Musteba Xa. It couldn't be.

"You're dead," he said, was momentarily pleased to hear his own voice, then was afraid and angry.

"I killed you," he said. "I flung you into a place where nothing was."

Did they get him from my mind? he thought.

No, he thought.

I would know.

I would know if they plundered me like that.

Trembling with an ancient rage, an even older fear, he glared at the ancient evil old man.

"I will not believe it," he said.

"You are dead, you are ash and nothing," he said.

He gazed into the eyes of what had to be a simulacrum and saw himself.

Whoever or whatever sat there, it knew him to the marrow of his bones.

"You always were a stubborn git, li'l Maks." Musteba Xa (no, it wasn't him, no, it couldn't be him) lifted a crudely polished gemstone, a star sapphire the size of a man's fist.

Maksim tried to snap elsewhere, but the stone anchored him and he could not move.

He fought to break free, but could not.

The stone was one of the Great Talismans, Massulit the Sink, Massulit the Harvester, Massulit awkward and impossible, taking more skill to wield than any of the other talismans. Massulit in the hands of Musteba Xa. No. In the hands of that THING who chose to take his Master's form.

The Thing on the Throne began to chant, drawing threads of soul-stuff from Maksim's helpless body, gathering the threads in the heart of the Stone.

He tried to fight.

He slammed into a wall.

For an instant he lost control and beat helplessly, futilely at that wall.

Then he gathered himself and waited for what would happen next.

They want something.

They need me to get it.

They need me alive.

Their mistake.

He managed a slight smile.

I hope.

The Thing watched the souls spin into the Stone, watched the stone glow brighter until its clear blue light filled the cavern.

The Thing laughed, a tottery wheezy giggle that should have made him sound senile and silly. It didn't.

Maksim knew that sound, it was like remembered pain.

He watched his souls spin out of him into the hands that seemed to belong to Musteba Xa and it was as if none of the intervening years had happened.

"You should thank the geniod for our reunion, Maks." Having settled Massulit into the crack between his withered thighs so his hands would be free to gesture, he waved at the seven glowspheres ranged in an arc behind Maksim, then at the hundreds of smaller lights that oozed from the walls of the cavern and floated free. "They have a little quest for you, dear boy. I told them you'd be stubborn, but you weren't stupid. So here we are. No questions? You haven't changed, have you, Sweetness." Another shrill giggle, then he straightened his bony shoulders and fixed his eyes on Maksim's face. "The Magus of Tok Kinsa has a talisman at the heart of his Keep. One of the Great Ones. Shaddalakh." He clicked his horny yellow nails on the curve of Massulit. "The geniod want it. Matched set, eh? You are going to get it for them. Do it and you get your souls back. Still no questions?"

"Swear on Massulit for your souls' sake that I will get mine back if I bring Shaddalakh out and hand it over."

"You don't want to qualify that, dear boy?"

Maksim shrugged. "Tell me what more I could get if the lie pleases you."

"For old time's sake? For the love that was once between us? Ask, my sweet boy, and you shall receive."

Maksim shuddered, but refused to let his sickness show. "Swear on Massulit for your souls' sake that I will get mine back if I bring Shaddalakh out and hand it over."

The bones in Musteba Xa's face were suddenly more visible; there was spite in him and anger, but he did as Maksim asked. He swore and Maksim was satisfied the oath was complete.

"Let him who is first among the geniod swear the same," he said. "I have lived long enough to know how to die if I must. Let him swear."

The glowspheres grew agitated, went darting about in complex orbits, maintaining a set distance between them no matter how recklessly they careered about. After some minutes of this confusion, the largest of the geniod came rushing toward the throne; it hovered before Musteba Xa, changed form, was a beautiful woman, naked and powerful in her nakedness. She reached out, took Massulit from Musteba Xa's trembling hands. Her contralto filling the cavern with echoes, she declaimed the oath that Xa had sworn, then she dropped the talisman into Xa's lap and stalked over to Maksim.

She caught hold of his arm. Her fingers were strong, but they felt like flesh. He could feel no strangeness in her, see no sign she was other than woman. She stared at him a moment, measuring him, then she snapped them both from the cavern.

4

He slammed down on the backward-facing seat of a closed carriage, a traveling gada, he thought. The woman settled herself opposite him, knocked on the window shutter beside her and braced herself as the gada started moving over a rutted track about as bad as any road he'd ever tried out. The gada swayed wildly enough to nauseate him, lurched and jolted even though the team that drew it was moving at a walk.

He was stiff, cold, filthy, half-starved, and half-crazy with thirst.

On top of that, he was a brittle shell of himself and his body was already beginning the slow agonizing death of the unsouled.

He sat staring at the veiled woman without really seeing her, trying to work out his next move.

Somehow he had to get hold of Massulit and take his souls back with his own hands.

Oath or no oath, he couldn't trust any of them to leave him alive once they had Shaddalakh.

Massulit and Shaddalakh. What talisman did they send Brann after? That at least was clear to him. Someone, something, was gathering the Great Stones.

Who? And did it matter?

All knowledge mattered. How could he plan without a basic piece of information like that?

He scowled at the woman. Geniod?

Who or what were geniod?

Kin to the demons his Master had controlled. Yes. That he'd believe.

He passed his hand across his face, his dehydrated palm rasping across the dry leathery skin. No stubble, thank his unknown father for that and the M'darj absence of face hair.

The geniod woman wore the gauzy voluminous trousers, the tight bodice and silken head veil of a Jorpashil courtesan, having acquired all of these in mid-passage between the cavern and the carriage. She swept the veil aside, let him see her astonishingly beautiful face, skin like cream velvet, brilliant blue-green eyes, hair the color of dark honey falling about her face in dozens of fine braids threaded with amber beads that matched the amber lights the lamps on the carriage wall woke in that honey hair. There was nothing to tell Maksim's ordinary senses or his sorcerer's nose that she was demon, not mortal. He found that astonishing also. She smiled and lowered her eyes; one lovely tapering hand played with the amber beads that fell onto the swell of her breasts. She was a superb artifact, a perfect example of what she pretended to be. He suppressed a smile. If she was supposed to be an added inducement, that was one mistake they'd made. Perhaps because I've been living with Brann, he thought. Something else I owe my Thornlet.

He thought about that Thing on the Throne and decided he'd been too precipitous in accepting appearances. He settled himself to endure his physical hardships. I'll beat the bastards yet.

The geniod stopped smiling when he didn't respond. She took a fur rug from the seat beside her and tossed it to him. "Wrap this around you and stop shivering," she said. "You look like a simm kit in a wetfall."

He eased the rug around him and sighed with pleasure as warmth began to spread through his battered body. A moment later the carriage swung about and climbed at a steep angle; it turned again and seemed to glide along. Road, he thought, some kind of highroad with a metalled surface. It was like being in a cradle; the sway was steady and soothing. He began to feel sleepy; his eyelids were so heavy he could barely keep them lifted.

"Stay awake," she said; she kicked his shin hard enough to draw a grunt from him. "Listen. My name is Palami Kumindri. I am Chuttar of the first rank."

"Courtesan," he murmured.

"Yes. I'm taking you into Jorpashil. You will not speak to anyone while you're there, not to people in the street, not even to my servants. I have my choice of lovers, Settsimaksimin, and I choose the most powerful and they do whatever I ask of them; they will not believe anything you say about me, they will have your head off before you get two words out. Remember that. Yes?"

"Yes." Maksim wondered drowsily why she was saying any of this; she was powerful enough to lay down her own rules for what was, after all, her game. He was too sleepy to ask.

"My doulahar is on the edge of the Kuna Coru. Yes, I have a doulahar and it is larger and richer than any other in all of Jorpashil. I have gardens and slaves enough to keep them groomed. I am rich, Settsimaksimin. And I am going to be richer. I am powerful, Settsimaksimin, and I am going to be more so. We are going to my doulahar, Settsimaksimin, slave." She played with her hairbeads and watched him like a cat with aquamarine eyes. "Take note of my doulahar, slave; that's where you will bring the talisman."

"I hear." Maksim struggled to make his mind work through the waves of sleep. Not to the cavern? Are they going to bring Massulit into that house so they can resoul me? Maybe they're not even going to make a pretense of keeping their oath. Can't think. My brain is like stale mush.

She left him alone after that and he slept until her servants were hauling him out of the carriage, taking no pains to be gentle about it. He stumbled into the room she assigned him and fell on the bed. In minutes he was drowned in sleep.

5

She came herself to rouse him before dawn.

He tried to pull sleep back around him and not-hear her.

She wouldn't let him escape that way; she muscled him out of bed, held him upright while she slapped and pinched him awake. She looked delicate as a rose petal, but she had the strength of a wrestler and a stubbornness greater than his own. After harrying him out of the room and through a series of corridors, she threw him into a bathtub the size of a small pond. It was filled with ice water. She laughed at his indignant roars and left him to his ablutions. At the door she turned. "Breakfast is waiting in the terrace room; ring the bell when you're ready and a servant will bring you there." She left.

Maksim shivered and gritted his teeth. He examined the taps and managed to pump up a stream of water warm enough to take the curse off that already in the tub. Shivering and running through a thousand ringing curses, mostly to hear his voice again, to hear words come pouring from his throat, he scrubbed the accumulated grime off his body. When he climbed from the tub and found clean robes laid out for him, robes tailored for his size and even for his taste in such things, he laughed aloud. Despite the loss of his souls and his miserable predicament, he felt alive and eager to get on with his work. He yanked on the bellpull and followed the servant to his breakfast.

He was surrounded by empty plates and sticky beakers and draining his last bowl of tea when the Chuttar Palami Kumindri came strolling in. She wasn't wearing her veil and her honey hair hung loose about her face; it was long, down to her waist, finer than spidersilk; the drafts from the door and windows teased it away from her head, making it ripple and wave like grass in a stream. She wore beads about her neck, rows and rows of them, ivory, turquoise, jasper, carnelian, beads carved from scented woods, from crystallized incense. She halted just inside the door, smiled at him and stroked her beads, waiting for him to acknowledge he was finished with his meal.

He set the bowl down, got to his feet and bowed. A little courtesy wouldn't hurt. He didn't have to mean it.

A graceful wave of her hand acknowledged and dismissed the bow. "I have purchased a travel dulic for you and two mules to pull it." She smoothed at her hair, tucked strands of it behind a delicate ear. "I doubt if there's a horse in the whole North Country up to carrying a man your size."

"My profound thanks, Chuttar Kumindri. The thought of riding that far put a shiver up my spine." He damped a napkin in a finger-bowl, began working over his hands. When he was finished, he tossed the napkin aside, looked up. "One thing. . . ."

She raised a brow, fluttered a hand.

"It seems to me we'd all be better off if you just snapped me there. Why don't you? You have power and to spare for that minor bit of magic."

"Forget that, Settsimaksimin; you will go the mortal road and keep your head down. The Magus is. . . ." She shrugged; the beads clattered with the shift of her shoulders. "He has discovered somehow there's a magicman pointed at his talisman. Read the omens, I suppose. His reputation says he keeps his fingers on the strings of will-be, old spider. Now that he's alerted, he seems to be delighted with the challenge. He is a very subtle man." She said the last indifferently, the words came out flat and cold as if they meant nothing to her.

He was furious but kept it to himself. "I'll need financing," he said. "Or do you want to pile that on me also?"

"My Housemaster has a map of Tok Kinsa which you might find useful and a plan of the Zivtorony where Shaddalakh is kept. These things are waiting for you when you decide you're ready to leave. He also has a purse with fifty gold jaraufs, five hundred takks and a double handful of dugnas. Make it last, Settsimaksimin, you'll get no more from us." She looked him over, head to toe, a scornful sweep of sea-colored eyes, then she swung round and stalked out.

He chuckled, pleased with himself, hauled on the bellpull and asked the maid who came in to take him to the Housemaster.

6

The HourGong in the drumtower boomed twice as Maksim drove the dulic onto a ferry landing. He was the only one there, the to-ing and fro-ing of the morning was long finished. The ferryman was annoyed at being called from his afternoon nap and took his time winching the cable off the riverbottom where he had to leave it between trips so he wouldn't tear the keels off the riverboats. He demanded a takk for his efforts, but accepted ten dugnas after several minutes of shouts and groans and beatings of his breast. It was too much, but Maksim didn't feel like arguing any longer, he didn't have the energy for it. He drove the dulic onto the flatboat and chocked the wheels while the ferryman whistled up his sons. A small boy who couldn't have been more than five started beating on a gong to warn off ships and barges; the ferryman and the two older boys got busy at the windlass. With the clumsy craft groaning and complaining, the water boiling around it, shreds from the jeppu mats bumping about its side, the man and his sons wound the ferry across the south branch of the river, sweat turning their arms and shoulders to shining brass.

When they reached the other side, there were several riders with a small herd of sheep wanting passage into the city, so the ferryman's sweat on the return trip wouldn't be wasted. As the bargaining got noisy, then noisier, Maksim unchocked his wheels and drove onto the landing. He clucked the mules into a quicker walk and headed toward the Dhia Asatas which were lines of pale blue ink written on the paler blue of the sky.

III: KORIMENEI

Under the prodding of her brother-in-eidolon Korimenei sailed south along the coast to the Jade King's city, Jade Halimm. She was on her way to steal Frunzacoache from the spiritpouch of a Rushgaramuv shaman and take it to the Cave of the Chained God where her brother waited for her to touch him awake.

1

"No, no, no," her brother screamed at her. The eidolon of the sleeping boy floated beside Korimenei as she leaned on the sill of her bedroom window and looked out across the busy harbor at Jade Halimm.

"Why?" She watched a Coaster from the north glide in and drop sails. "What's wrong with taking a Merchanter to Bandrabahr, then a riverboat up to Dil Jorpashil? The Rushgaramuv pass the Lake on their way to wintering in the Dhia Asatas; it'll be easy to pick them up there and follow them until I know enough to take the talisman. I'll have to go more miles that way, but a well-found Merchanter can outpace a caravan in anything but a calm. I don't get seasick, so it's more comfortable than land travel. The most important thing is, it's safer, Tré. I'm a woman traveling alone. I'm young and not hideous. Let me tell you what that means. I'm fair game, Tré. Anything on two legs that fancies his chances will have a grab at me."

"Kori, listen to yourself. You sound like AuntNurse lecturing naughty girls on chastity and virginity. That's not you."

"You think I'm just being female? You haven't been watching the past few days. Aaah! I was spoiled by Silili. I had the school back of me there. I'm not in school now and no one's backing me but me. It makes a difference, Tré. A big difference. I went to the Market this morning. It was like I was running a gauntlet. Ailiki bit one man. I singed another who wouldn't back off. I got pinched and fondled and squeezed and rubbed against. I spent an hour in the baths when I got back here and I still feel dirty. I want to go by ship, Tré, I want civilized surroundings, I want folk around me who know I'm not safe to mess with and who'll leave me alone."

"You're not doing it right, that's all. Don't go out by yourself. Hire a guide, that's what they're for."

"Dream on. Tré, all I have is the money Maksim gave me. It has to last until I can get to the cave and wake you. I can't waste it on extras like guides." She tried to see him more clearly, gave up after a minute. Foolish. It was just an image he was projecting, not him. She felt like crying. They'd been so close, once. He didn't even sound like him any more. I've changed too, she thought. For a moment she rebelled against his demands; let him lay there, he was safe enough; let me get on with my life. She sighed and pushed the temptation away. He was her brother, her dearest. Well, he had been, and she owed something to that memory. "Another reason for going by ship. When you count in everything you need for land travel, the sea is cheaper."

"Not when you count in Amortis."

"Who said anything about Amortis? You won't let me near Cheonea."

"Who said anything about Cheonea? I'm talking about Havi Kudush. That's where her Temple is, that's her ground, the well of her power, where she went when Settsimaksimin fell. By now she's replaced what the Drinker of Souls stripped from her, but she hasn't forgot it."

"The well of her power, hmm. You sound like one of my teachers."

"Kushundallian discoursing on the fundamentals of godhood?"

"Right. You were watching?"

"You know I was. Stop dithering. If you go upriver from Bandrabahr, you pass through the heart of her ground. Do you think she's forgot you, Kori? Do you think she doesn't know who brought the Drinker of Souls to Cheonea? Do you think you can slip by her? Well?"

"No, I don't think any of those things. You've made your point. What I don't understand is why you let me come this far south. I could have gone north to Andurya Durat and been on my way by now."

"Durat? Don't be an idiot, Kori. It'd take you a year and a small fortune to get a pass to the Silk Road. No. Jade Halimm is the place to start if you need to travel the Road. You take a riverboat up the Wansheeri to Kapi Yuntipek; you get what you need there and take the

Road to Jorpashil. It's too late for caravans; you'll have to travel by yourself. You can handle that, Kori; you know you can."

"What if the passes are closed?"

"They aren't. Not yet."

"How do you know?"

"Trust me. I know. There's been one storm in the mountains, it laid down three, four inches, but they've had rain since, so most of that snow is gone. You've got around a month before you'll have trouble getting through."

"So now you're Kiykoyl tosNiak, weather wizard?"

"I see what I see."

"That's the fact, huh?"

"That's the fact, yeh."

"You weren't around on the Mountain. I needed to talk to you, Tré."

He didn't answer. As he hadn't answered then. She straightened. "It's suppertime. I'll catch Our Host, see what riverboats are in and when they're leaving. With a little luck, I'll be out of here tomorrow."

2

The *Miyachungay* cast off and started upriver an hour after dawn, her slatted sails clacking and booming in the wind that came sweeping onshore most mornings as if it had dragons on its tail. After counting and recounting her coins, Korimenei had paid the premium that bought her a tiny cabin for herself; it wasn't much larger than a footlocker, but it had a bar on the narrow door so she'd sleep in peace and comparative comfort. As a cabin passenger she took her meals at the Captain's table, which meant she'd eat well and since the cost was included in the price of her cabin, she felt she'd made herself a satisfactory deal.

She stayed in the cabin as long as she could that first morning. She was uneasy; she didn't know how to behave as a traveler; she didn't know what the rules were. Settsimaksimin had translated her directly from Cheonea to the school in Silili. And she hadn't traveled after she'd got to school, Shahntien Shere kept a thumb firmly planted on her students. She'd gone from one tight supportive society to another. She didn't want to make mistakes. The short trip downcoast on the Merchanter hadn't helped, she'd stayed in her cabin the whole way. She was scared to stick her nose out now. It was funny. She could see that. She could even laugh at herself. It didn't help. She sat on the bunk with Ailiki on her lap, singing nursery songs to her, trying to convince herself she didn't mind the stuffy darkness of the room.

The walls closed in on her; the cabin was turning into a coffin.

"I've got to do it sometime, Aili my Liki. And you have to stay here, my Lili. Watch my things for me, hmm?" She tapped Ailiki on her tailbone. "Shift yourself, luv. I've got to unpack my meeting-people suit."

She'd bought Temueng traveling gear, a padded jacket and loose trousers gathered at the ankle over knee-length leather boots, a veil that went over her head and extended in two broad panels that hung before and behind, brushing against her knees. The veil had embroidered eyeholes, a knotted fringe on the edges; it was heavy cotton, a dusty black, and she hated it. Bumping elbows, knees, buttocks every time she had to shift her body, she changed to her new clothes and pulled the veil over her head. She coughed; she couldn't breathe. She knew that was stupid, she was doing it to herself. She reached under the veil and pushed the cloth away from her face, groped for the door and went out.

When she climbed onto the deck the wind took hold of her; it nearly ripped the veil off her and used the loose cloth of her trousers as a sail. Blinded and more than a little frightened, she clung to the doorjamb and struggled to get control of her clothing. Hands closed on her arms; someone large and strong lifted her, carried her down the ladder and set her on her feet in the companionway.

"Get rid of that damn veil, woman; it's a deathtrap. You're no Temueng; what are you doing dressed up like one?"

Korimenei dragged the veil off and glared at the man. He was a big man, broad rather than tall, his eyes on a level with hers. His shoulders were wide enough for two, his bare arms heavily muscled, his hands large and square; she remembered the strength in them. A Panday sailor. His ear dangle had three anchoring posts it was that heavy; it was ovals of beaten gold set with pearcut emeralds; it swayed with every movement of his head, the emeralds catching the light, winking at her. He was grinning at her, his green eyes glinting with an amusement that infuriated her even more. "Who do you think you are and why's it any business of yours what I do?"

"I think I'm Karoumang, Captain and Owner of this vessel and it makes all kinds of trouble for me when a passenger falls overboard because she's too lamebrained to know what the hell she's doing."

"Oh." She passed her hand from her brow to her nape, feeling the straggles and bunches dragged into her hair. A mess. She must look terrible.

"Here. Let me have that thing." He took the veil from her, hung it over a lamp hook. "You can retrieve it later. You still want to go on deck?"

Hands pressing her hair down, she nodded. It seemed safest not to say anything.

He followed her up the ladder, grabbed a handful of her jacket as the wind caught her again. "Been on a riverboat before?"

She hesitated, then shook her head.

"First thing to remember, when we're moving there's wind, no wind, we stop."

She snorted, tried to pull away. "I'm not a child."

He ignored that, kept his hold on the back of her jacket and moved her along, threading through the bales and barrels piled about the deck, roped in place or confined by heavy nets. "Second thing, wind takes us upriver. Down, the river takes us and we fight the wind. One way or another there's always wind." He piloted her past the main-mast, the noise of the sails and the singing of what seemed hundreds of ropes was all around her; it was like air, always there, so much so that in minutes she scarcely heard it, underscoring what he'd just said to her. "Third thing, this is a cargo boat. We take passengers, but not many of them. The cargo comes first. Passengers, even cabin passengers, should stay put when we're moving. If they think they need air, they should get air when we're tied up at one of our calls. Or they should join the deckers in the cage and stay there."

He stopped her by a heavy ladder with a hand rail; it led to a raised platform in the bow. "Up," he said.

She glared at him, considered telling him what she thought of him; she wasn't quite sure what she did think of him, so she kept silent, caught hold of the rail as he took his hand away. She went up those steps quickly; in spite of her irritation she was enjoying the brisk scour of the wind, the sounds and sights around her, everything new, everything strange and exciting. Even Karoumang, or perhaps especially Karoumang. Her body responded to him even as her mind said be careful, woman. As she stepped onto the narrow flat, she kept hold of the railing, made her way along it until she was looking down into the yellow water foaming about the bow. A small boy who was an exact miniature of Karoumang looked up from his perch in a bag net suspended from a stubby bowsprit; he waved a small grimy hand and went back to his watch, green eyes like Karoumang's intent on the water ahead. A tarnished silver horn hung on a thong about his neck, swaying with the movement of the boat.

Karoumang leaned over the rail. "Lijh't aja, i'klak?"

"Tijh, ahpa."

Korimenei looked from the boy to the man. "Your son?"

"One of them. I was asking about snags and he was saying there aren't any. So far." His eyes laughed at her as he turned to face her. He set his left arm on the rail, leaned on it. "Enigma," he said.

"The river?"

"You."

"Certainly not. Nothing difficult about me, I'm simply going home."

"Not up this river."

"Why?"

"Nobody like you north of here. Croaldhu, I wouldn't be surprised, Yuntipek I am. Married?"

"None of your business."

He inspected her, paying no attention to her words. "I don't think so. No man worth the name would let you run around alone. Virgin?"

"Definitely none of your business." She thought about leaving; this conversation was getting out of hand. She didn't want to leave. She glanced at him, looked quickly away.

"Hmm. I'll let that one hang. Twenty one, two . . . no, I'd say twenty-nine."

"Twenty-four." She snapped it out before she thought, glared at him when she realized what she'd done.

He stopped smiling, narrowed his eyes at her. "Over age, alone, no guards, no chaperone. Not someone's daughter coming from a visit or going to a wedding. Not wed, not courtesan, not player, not trader. Priestess or acolyte? No, the attitude's all wrong. You're no holy she. Holy terror, maybe. Student?"

She thought that over for a moment, then she nodded. "Was."

"Croaldhu? No. You have the look, but your accent's wrong. And there's that attitude. You're a little shy, but there's fire under it. You're edgy, but you're not afraid of me or anyone else. Not womanfear. You think . . . no, you're sure you can back me off. I outweigh you and outreach you. If I took a notion, I could pull you limb from limb in about thirty seconds. Or tear those idiot clothes off you, throw you down and do the usual. I don't see anything you could do to stop me. You're looking at me now like I'm the idiot."

"Your word, not mine."

"I see your shyness is starting to wear thin. Silili?"

She thought that over, shrugged. "Why not. Yes."

"Which school?"

"Does it matter?"

"Curiosity. I'd like to know."

"The Waymeri Manawha, Head Shahntien Shere."

"Sponsor?"

"How do you know about that?"

"I have a son with Talent."

"Ah. He's in school?"

"Will be, come spring. The Mage Barim Saraja has agreed to sponsor him. For a fee big enough to buy an Emperor, though as a favor don't repeat that. Yours?"

"Why should I tell you?"

"Why not?"

"Why not. The Sorcerer Settsimaksimin."

"One of the Four Primes, eh? I am impressed."

"So I see."

"I am." He moved away from the rail, bowed at the waist, his hands pressed palm to palm before his nose. He straightened, chuckled. "No lie."

"Curiosity satisfied?"

"Whetted." He arched a brow at her. "With questions I'm not going to ask. Where you came from and what your story is." He waited a moment to see if she was going to respond; when she didn't, he rested both arms on the rail and gazed ahead at the river which was a broad empty stretch of ocher fluid; there was no other traffic in view, only this boat riding the wind upstream. "How you came to the notice of a Prime, what there was about you that interested him." He looked along his shoulder at her, letting his appreciation show. Odd. She liked it. It was essentially the same as the looks she'd got from men in Jade Halimm and those made her sick. The looks that saw her as prey for the taking. In those long narrow eyes, green as the stones in his ear dangle, it had a different flavor somehow. Definitely she liked it.

"What your rank is now," he murmured, "and what it's apt to be when you come to full strength. What you are." He counted types, tapping his fingers on the rail. "Charm spinner, diviner, dowser, shaman, necromancer, witch, thaumaturge, wizard, magus, sorcerer. Do I have them all? Probably not." His brow shot up again. He seemed to be enjoying this, playing his little wordy game with her, then his pleasure faded. "Where you're going and why, what you're doing here, now." He looked away, the exaggerated Panday curves of his wide mouth straightening to a grim line. "A favor, Saöri. Keep it off my boat."

"There's nothing to keep," she said. "On or off. I'm just traveling. That's the truth, Karoumang Captain. I'm going somewhere, but where's a long long way from here and nothing to do with you." She put her hands on the rail beside his; they looked anemic, sickly almost, next to his rich coppery brown; her arms were thinner than his, much thinner, despite the bulk of the quilted sleeves, and pale like her hands with pale pale pinkish brown freckles scattered through the fine color-less hairs, blitchy blotchy like a red and white cow. She was glad they were hidden. She felt anemic all over, spirit as well as body; her irrita-tion at his prowling round her, sniffing at her, which had armored her so feebly against him, had gone away altogether and left her stranded. She wanted to touch his arm, to see if it was as hard and sleek as it looked. She tried not to think of her initiation, of the golden, glorious chthone who'd made her every nerve a river of fire, but her body was remembering. When she sneaked a look at Karoumang from the cor-ners of her eyes, it seemed to her he was outlined in shimmering gold light, that he was as beautiful as the god had been. She wanted to see him naked like the god; she pictured him naked, lying beside her, his hands on her, his strong hands moving on her. The breath caught in her throat; she tightened her fingers on the rail.

He was frowning at the water ahead. Abruptly, he leaned over the rail and spoke to his son. "Aja 'tu, i'klak? Mela' istan." He pointed to a line and some dots on the water around a half mile or more ahead of them, a long, dark thing with several stubby outthrusts that was rap-idly coming to meet them. "Angch t'tant." He waved his hand at the horn. "Lekaleka!"

"Eeya, ahpa." The boy steadied himself, eyed the object for a few beats until he was sure he knew its course, then he put the horn to his lips and blew a pattern of staccato notes.

Karoumang swung around, hurried to the rail, his eyes moving swiftly about the ship, following his crew as they went to work with a minimum of effort and a maximum of effect while the echoes of the horn notes still hung in the air; he watched the sail panels change conformation, watched the helmsmen on the overhang shift the tiller the proper number of marks to take them from the path of the snag. He relaxed, came back to Korimenei, smiling. "A good crew; they save me sweating." He leaned over the rail. "Baik, i'klak."

The boy laughed. "Babaik, ahpa."

"He's a clever boy," Korimenei said. "Reminds me of my brother. How old is he?"

"Nine. The only one of the bunch with a call to the water." He took her hand, spread it on his palm. "What small hands you have for such a tall girl."

"Not so small, it's as long as yours almost."

"But narrow. Bird bones, light as air." He turned the hand over, drew his forefinger across her palm. "Do you read these lines?"

Her breath turned treacherous on her again. She called on the discipline the Shahntien had hammered into her and when she spoke her voice was light, laughing. "I play at it. It's only a game."

"What other games do you play?" He stroked her palm absently, as if he'd forgot what he was doing.

"Girl's games," she said, deliberately misunderstanding him, "but not many of those. There wasn't time. The Shahntien kept us at it."

"And now?"

"And now I follow my own inclinations."

"And what are those?"

"What do you want them to be?"

"What shall I say?"

"That I'll be a student again, a day, a week, to Yuntipek, perhaps."

"You think I could teach you?"

"I think you are an expert on a subject I know little about. I think you enjoy such teaching and I like that. When the teacher enjoys, it's likely the student will."

"Sometimes there are consequences to this exchange."

"Not for a fledgling sorcerer from the Waymeri Manawha who has urgent claims on her time and energy." She chuckled. "Though distant ones." She was pleased with herself, enjoying the suggestive obliquities.

He laughed, placed a kiss on her palm. "Shall we begin the lessons after supper tonight?"

A tiny gasp escaped before she could swallow it.

He squeezed her hand. "Would you like to stay here or go below?" A glance at the bank gave him time and place. "We'll make a call in a couple hours. We have cargo to unload, probably pick some up, so we'll be there a while. You can go ashore, if you want to walk around. I wouldn't advise it. It's a chern village, you might see things you won't like. These country chernlords are an ugly bunch. Even a fledgling sorcerer should watch what she says and does around them."

"Karoumang teacher, it's not lectures I need from you," she smoothed her fingers across the back of his hand, ". . . but demonstrations."

"You need a whole skin to appreciate them, ketji. Stay on board at Muldurida. The next call up the river is a freetown and friendlier. Saffron Moru. We'll tie up for the night there."

"I think I'd like to go below for a while. Do you mind my being a bit afraid?"

He threw back his head and laughed, a big booming sound that came from his toes. "Noooo," he said. He took a handful of her jacket. "Let's hit the wind, ketji."

3

Korimenei stepped from her trousers and kicked them across the narrow cabin; she sat on the bunk and began working a boot off her foot; the boots fit close to her legs and took some maneuvering to put on and take off. "Aili my Liki, I've got myself into something and I don't know how it's going to turn out." She dropped that boot, started on the other. "Consequences, he said. He meant pregnant, but there's a lot more to think about, isn't there, Lili. Every act has consequences and most of them surprise the hell out of you. Back at school they kept hammering that into us: *Be careful what you do; the more powerful the act, the more unpredictable the outcome. Don't do what you can't live with. Undo is a word without real meaning.* They didn't have to tell me any of that, I knew it already, especially the last. Look at Maksim, look at where he is now, look where I am. Tré and I summoned the Drinker of Souls because we thought we could get the soldiers out of the Vales and things would go back the way they were before Amortis got greedy; we thought she'd cancel what Maksim was doing to us. Undo it. They're right, they're right, they're right, you can't undo anything." She dropped the second boot, dug under the blankets for the pillow and tossed it against the headwall. "I want to do this, Lili. My body screams do it." She swung her feet up and half sat, half lay, staring at the scraped and oiled calf hide stretched across the porthole. "What if I don't want to stop when I get to Yuntipek? Gods, the minute I saw him, I wanted him. He's got kids, a wife. A life he likes, no, loves. I'm a kind of trophy, aren't I, Lili. No, maybe not. But he does like power.

Probably never had a sorcerer before." She giggled, snapped her fingers. Ailiki jumped from the seat beside the porthole and landed on her stomach, driving a grunt out of her. Stroking her hand down and down and again down the mahsar's small firm body, she went on talking to herself. "Most of them are men, you know. I wonder if you do know, I wonder what you are, my Aili, my Liki. No men for our Karoumang. He's singleminded that way, you can smell it on him. I lay with a god of sorts and got you out of it, Lili. I've never been with a man. I wonder if I'm spoiled for mortal sex. I'll know by tomorrow morning, won't I. Oh Gods."

Ailiki purred like the cat she wasn't, her body vibrating and warm.

"Words. All words. No illusions and scared to my toenails, but I'm going to do it." She lifted Ailiki, held her so the mahsar's body dangled and they were looking eye to eye. "Lili my love, you watch my back, hmm?" She laughed, set the mahsar on her stomach and lay stroking her and watching the light change.

4

Night followed day and day followed night; the world turned on the spindle of time. It was a curious time for Korimenei, a happy time. A respite.

Nights she spent in the Captain's bed. Days she sat on the forehang and watched the land flow past, the little villages with their mud walls carved and decorated with the local totems, their wharves and storetowers; she watched horses run in clover fields, cattle and sheep graze in sun-yellowed pastures; she watched serfs and small farmers finish up the fall harvest and line up at flour mills and slaughter grounds; she watched the creaking wheels that were set thicker than trees on both banks send water and power to the fields and the two and three family manufacturies in the villages. She watched the day passengers going from village to village, carrying things they wanted to sell, or visiting relatives; one time a wedding party came on board and celebrated the whole distance with music and wine and dancing; one time a band of acrobats came on board and earned their way with leaps and ladders. These sights were endlessly interesting, partly because it was a place she hadn't seen before, a people she didn't know; partly because it reminded her of the life she'd left behind when Maksim discovered her Talent and flung her two thousand miles away from everything she knew.

Life was on hold for her, as if responsibilities and dangers were standing back and waiting for the trip to finish. Even Tré's eidolon stayed away. She called him once, curious about his absence, but he didn't answer. She was annoyed for about five minutes, then she shrugged off her irritation. She didn't really want him around. The thought of him watching her with Karoumang made her itch all over.

She was enjoying her bi-nightly lessons as much as she thought she might. Karoumang was a man of wide and varied experience and it was a matter of pride with him that she got as much pleasure from their coupling as he did. He could be maddening at times, especially when he treated her like some brain-damaged infant, but he liked her. He really liked her. Part of that was because he simply liked women, all women. Part of it belonged to her. She stopped worrying about what was going to happen at Kapi Yuntipek. Her infatuation was settling into something less exciting but a lot more lasting.

#

Twelve days after the *Miyachungay* left Jade Halimm, she came to the hill country and passed through the first series of locks; there were three more sets she'd have to negotiate before she reached the high desert plateau of Ambijan and the run for Kapi Yuntipek.

5

Something hard and cold slapped against Korimenei's buttock, then was gone; small hands and feet with sharp nails ran along her back. Something cold and hard slid along her shoulder and stopped against her neck. Long whiskers tickled her face. She muttered something, even she didn't know what, opened her eyes. There was just enough light from the nightglim over the door to show her she was nose to nose with Ailiki. "Wha. . . ."

Ailiki backed off. When she reached Karoumang's pillow, she sat up, her handfeet pressed into the soft white ruff that flowed from neck to navel.

"Something wrong? Karou. . . ." Korimenei shivered; the nights this time of the year were chill and damp, each one colder than the last, and someone—probably Ailiki—had pulled the quilts and blankets off her. Twisting around, she reached for the covers. Something rolled off her shoulder and thumped down on the sheet. She blinked. The Old Man's bowl? Wha. . . .

Ailiki darted at her, picked up the bowl and scampered back to the pillow. Sitting on her haunches, holding the battered pewter object against her stomach, she stared fixedly at Korimenei. Her ears were pressed flat against her head. The guard hairs on her shoulders were erect and quivering. Her lips were drawn back, exposing her small sharp fangs.

Korimenei rubbed at her eyes, tried to get her brain in order. "Lili? What's happening? What are you. . . . Karoumang?" She touched the sheet where he'd been. It was cold. Is it . . . Gods. His being gone hadn't bothered her before; he always got up some time during the night and took a walk around the boat, checking things out, making sure his Second was doing a proper job and his night crew wasn't sacked out on some of the softer bales. She slid out of bed, began groping for her clothes.

Ailiki beat on the bowl with her fingernails, a tiny, scratchy, tinging sound. Korimenei straightened, stared at her. Somehow, without crossing the intervening space, the mahsar had got over by the porthole and was squatting on the table where Karoumang worked on his books. She took the bowl's rim in her little black hands and hammered at the table, producing a series of resonant clangs. Then she sat on her tail and fixed her round golden eyes on Korimenei.

"Not Karoumang?"

Ailiki shook her head and patted the bowl.

Puzzled, Korimenei tossed aside the trousers she was holding and pulled on her dressing gown. "I wish you could talk, Lili. It'd make things so much easier on both of us."

Ailiki hissed at her; in spite of her relatively immobile features, she managed to look disgusted. She waited until Korimenei reached for the bowl, then she went elsewhere. She returned a moment later with a two-handled crystal cup filled with very clear water. She set it in front of Korimenei and stood back, expectation quivering in every line.

"Ah." Korimenei kicked the chair away from the table, sat and poured the water into her bowl. "Farlooking?"

Ailiki wiggled her whiskers.

"Danger ahead?"

Ailiki scratched at the table.

"For me?"

Two scratches.

"For me and Karoumang?"

Three scratches.

"For everyone on the boat?"

Ailiki's ears came up and her whiskers relaxed. She stretched out on her stomach, her chin resting on her folded forearms.

Karoumang came in. When he saw Korimenei at the table, his brows lifted. "What's doing?"

"You see anything to worry about?"

He crossed to stand behind her, slid his hand into her robe and stroked her neck. "No, should I have?"

She leaned into his arm as his hand worked down to play with her breast. "No. . . ." Ailiki lifted her head and scratched at the table again, her nails digging minute furrows in the wood. Korimenei sighed. She put her hand over Karoumang's, stilling it. "Go to bed, Karou. You distract me."

"From what?" His voice was sharper than usual; he wasn't used to being told to go away. He freed his hand, cupped it under her chin and lifted it so he could see her face. "What are you doing?"

She caught hold of his wrist, pulled his hand away. "I don't like that, Karoumang. I won't be handled like that."

He walked to the end of the table, faced her. "And I won't be sent to bed like a naughty boy. What are you doing?" It was the Captain speaking, wanting to know everything about what went on aboard his boat. She wasn't lover anymore, she was an unhandy combination of crew and passenger.

Korimenei relaxed. "Pastipasti, Captain Saö. Remember my profession." She flattened her hands on the table, the bowl between them. "I had a warning. I was about to take a look and see what it meant. Now, will you please go sit on the bed and let me get on with it?"

He frowned, fisted a hand and rubbed the other over and around it. She could see that he'd forgot what she was since he'd taken her to bed; anyway, he never thought of women as having professions apart from their families; he wasn't hostile to the idea, it simply wasn't real to him. "Do it with me here," he said. "I want to see it."

"Hoik over that hassock and sit down then, you make me nervous, looming over me like that."

She waited until he was settled, then she leaned over the bowl and began to establish her focus. She banished Karoumang, banished Ailiki, banished the boat, the noises around her, everything but her breathing and the soft brilliance of the water. She began a murmured chant, using archaic words from her birthtongue, words she'd learned from the rhymes her cousins and AuntNurse had sung to her when she was a baby. "Yso.yso.ypo.poh," she softsang. "Ai.-gley.-idou.-pan.tou.toh. Pro.ten.ou.kin.tor.or.thoh, nun.yda.ydou.ydoh."

She blew across the water, creating a web of ripples that rebounded from the sides of the bowl, canceling and reinforcing each other until they faded and the water was smooth as glass. An image appeared, a narrow valley, heavily wooded, shadowed by the peaks that loomed over it. A cluster of houses inside a weathered palisade. A two-story building with a four-story tower beside the river, fortified, the second floor extending beyond the first. A lock gate with heavy tackle bolted to massive stone bulwarks and huge, heavy planks.

Karoumang whispered, "The locks at Kol Sutong."

The scene fluttered and nearly vanished. She hissed through her teeth at him and he subsided. With some difficulty she retrieved her concentration and brought stability to the image.

The point of view had changed when the picture cleared. She was looking inside the Lock House. There were bodies scattered about, some sprawling like discarded rag dolls, some bound and gagged. All dead. Small dark men dressed in leather and rags and heavily armed were sitting at a table playing a game of stone-and-bone on a grid one of them had scratched in the wood. The view shifted again, showed the inside of the watchtower. One of the raiders was standing at the south window, looking down along the river. The sun was just coming up, staining the water red; the fog lingering under the trees was pink with dawnlight. A boat appeared, the *Miyachungay*.

Karoumang growled, lurched onto his feet.

"Sit down!" Korimenei pushed him away, keeping her eyes fixed on the image, willing it to hold as it wavered and threatened to break up.

The image boat slowed, moved past the gates and hove to. Some of the men in the Lock House ran to the tackle and began winching the gates closed. As soon as the bars clunked home, other men came trotting from behind the House, carrying canoes; they dealt competently with the eddies and the undertows and went racing for the boat. In minutes they were swarming over the rail, hacking and clubbing the crew, killing everyone they came across; Karoumang and the crew fought back, but there were too many attackers. When the killing was done, the raiders tore into the bales and barrels, spoiling what they didn't want. When they were finished, they set fire to the boat. They opened the lock before they left, sat on their shaggy ponies cheering and waving bits of cargo as the charred timbers and the dead went floating away.

The image vanished.

Korimenei watched her fingers twitch, then flattened her hands on the table. "Well," she said. "You know the river. When will we get to . . . what was it . . . Kol Sutong?"

Karoumang was frowning at the water; when she spoke, he turned the frown on her. "It didn't show you. Why?"

"It never does. The seeker is always outside the scene. Um." She ran her finger around the rim of the bowl; unlike glass, the pewter was silent. "You needn't take these things as chipped in stone, Karou."

His fingers drum-rolling on the table, he examined her face. "I've been to seers before, Kori Heart-in-Waiting. I've seen the water pictures summoned before. Always the seers tell me, that IS what will be."

"They lie, Karou. Well, maybe not lie, just make things simple for a simple man."

"Tchah! I'll give you simple, ibli ketji." He wrapped a hand around her wrist. "Stop being perverse and explain."

"If I'm a devil, why should I?"

"Come to bed and let me show you."

"Shame-shame. Bribery. I accept. Seriously, Karou, what you've seen here is something that's set up to happen, that will happen unless we act to stop it." She tapped the back of his hand and he opened his fingers, freeing her wrist. "So, tell me. How soon?"

"It was almost moonset when I came down, dawn's about three hours off. We should be seeing the tower roof a little after first light." He stared past her, unseeing eyes fixed on the porthole. "Unless I go back and pass a few more days at Maul Pak."

"Any point in that? Would the local chernlord send troops to rout out those raiders?"

"The Pak Slij huim Pak?" He made a spitting sound without actually spitting, it being his boat and his table. "I don't have the gold it'd take to stir that tub of lard into action. The Jade King himself doesn't have that much gold."

"Mmf. What if you did tie up for two, three days? The hillmen wouldn't stay put that long, would they?"

"Turn tail like a pariah dog. Turn once, I have to keep turning. No." He frowned at her. "With a sorcerer on board? No."

"Fledgling sorcerer, Karou; I left school less than a month ago. I have no staff, I haven't pledged to a Master, I haven't . . . oh, so many things, it'd take too long to list them. I don't know what I can do

. . . should do," she rushed the last words, "I have to think." Her hands were shaking again and she pressed them hard against the wood, finding a kind of comfort in the resistance of the seasoned oak. "Is there a place along here where you could tie up for an hour or so? I'd better not try anything difficult on water, I'm not good with water, I need to have earth under me."

"That's water." He waggled a thumb at the bowl.

"That's different. What you need, it costs more; it takes . . . well, if I manage anything, it'll take a solider base."

"It's your business, ketji. I suppose you know what you're doing." He got to his feet. "I'll give you two hours; if you can't come up with a plan by then, I'll take the crew and burn the bastards out."

6

A worn broom under one arm, a lantern in her free hand, Korimenei turned slowly in an open space where an ancient tree had fallen in some long-ago storm. Woodcutters had carried it off, leaving only the hollow where the roots had been. The cedars ringing the glade were young, their lower branches sweeping the ground, lusty healthy trees with no limbs gone. She held the lantern high; there was no down-wood anywhere, not even chunks of bark. "Cht!" she breathed. "Pak Slij. No doubt he'd sell air if he could figure out a way to bottle it."

She set the lantern down on a relatively level spot and began sweeping away the loose earth and other debris. Working with meticulous care, she removed everything movable from a circular patch of ground, ignoring insects, worms and other small-lives because she couldn't do anything about them anyway. When she was finished, she took a fragment of stone and drew a pentacle with the same finicky care, humming absently one of the nursery songs her dead mother sang to her. After the drawing was done, she took off her sandals and laid them beside the lantern, shucked off her outer robe, folded it and set it on the sandals. She took a deep breath, smoothed down the white linen shift that was all she was wearing, then stepped into the pentacle, carefully avoiding the lines. The night was old, near its finish, the air was chill and damp; frost hadn't settled yet, but it would before the sun came up. Shivering, eyes closed, she stood at the heart of the drawing. By will and by skill she smothered the fire in the wick; the lantern went dark.

By will and by skill, chanting the syllables that focused patterning and re-patterning, she redrew the lines, changing earth and air to moonsilver until the circled star shone pale and perfect about her.

She opened her eyes, smiled with pleasure as she viewed her work. It was one of the simpler exercises, but there were an infinite number of ways it could misfire. She dropped to her knees, then sat with her legs in a lotus knot, her hands resting palm up on her thighs, heat flowing through her, around her.

Minute melted into minute, passing uncounted as she sat unthinking.

The Moonstone emerged from her navel, oozed through her shift and rolled into her lap. Moving slowly, ponderously, as if she were under water, she lifted the stone and looked into the heart of it.

She saw the village. It was dead. The palisade gate sagged open; the streets were filled with bodies, men, women, children. Mutilated, eviscerated. She looked into the houses. They were filled with the dead. Ghosts wandered through the rooms, reliving what had been.

She saw the Lock House. The raider deadpriest had chased the ghosts away so they wouldn't alarm the crew on the boat they expected, but the dead were there, sprawled or bound. She saw again the game of stones-and-bones, she saw hillmen curled up, sleeping, she saw hillmen gnawing at plugs of tjank, eyes red and unfocused, she saw hillmen with three girls from the village, passing them around like the tjank.

She considered what she'd seen.

There were fifty-five raiders, fifty-three fighters, a warleader and a deadpriest. She thought about the fighters. Patterns. The original band must have been five groups of twelve. The villagers had gotten at least seven of them. That pleased her.

The Moonstone moved in her hands. She pressed it against her navel and it melted into her.

"Every act has consequences." Her voice was soft as the wind whispering through the cedar fronds; she spoke with a formality that was almost chanting, using memories from school to give her the confidence she needed. She was young and untried. Serious and a bit pedantic. She could not afford to doubt herself once the search began if she expected to emerge from it alive and intact. "Every refusal to act has consequences." Her voice comforted her, grounded her; ten years' study spoke through her. "Consider them. Look beyond the moment. If I kill them all, will their kin kill more folk to avenge them? The people of Kol Sutong are dead. They can't be hurt. What about other villages? Karoumang and his crew? There are other boats. Will they be more at risk?" She smiled as she saw fireflies flickering among the trees and heard an early bird twitter close by, life balancing death, a small beauty balancing a great horror. "No. Raiders raid; it is their purpose. Raiders kill for loot more often than vengeance. The death of those men will help more than hurt those who live by the river and on it." She mourned a little for them; she owed that to herself. They were brutal bloody murderers, but they were also men. "Fifty-five men dead because I willed it. I don't know them. I don't know anything about their lives. I don't know why they do what they do. I reach out and they cease. What am I? Maksim fed a child a month to BinYAHtii for fifty years because he considered it a small evil compared to the good he was doing. Am I going to walk that road? I don't know." She mourned for herself, for her loss of innocence; this virginity cost more in blood and pain than the first had and there was no pleasure in its loss. "Do what you must," she sang softly, "but do it without pride, without anger, knowing they are simple, stupid men, helpless before you."

Centered and ready, she sank into silence, letting the sounds of the waking forest flow through her. Hands on thighs, she sat not-thinking, not-waiting, open to whatever came to her.

Presently she was swimming among the realities as she had on the third night of her Ordeal. At first she wandered without direction, then she felt a tug. She flashed faster and faster past the layered realities, the infinite, uncountable elsewheres, faster and faster until she burst into one of them, a universe of heat and light where salamandri swam in oceans of sunfire.

She drifted, pushed here and there by the lightwinds.

Salamandri swam to her, hovered about her.

She contemplated them. Pulsing slippery shapes, constantly changing, growing extra limbs, absorbing them, growing denser, attenuating, shortening, lengthening, they were vaguely like the rock skinks she played with when she was a child. She caught one in a mindseine because once upon a time she'd caught a skink in a net she'd knotted for herself. It lay passive, eyespots fixed on her though she doubted it actually saw her. She caught another and another with no more reason than the first, went on catching them until their weight began to strain the meshes of her mind.

She drifted with her captives. They glowed like coals at the heart of a fire, redgold-whitegold, flickers of blue. She was reluctant to release them though she had no thought of using them. It took no effort to hold them, they were not struggling, they seemed content to stay with her. They warmed her, pleased her eyes and oddly enough her palate.

She felt a sudden twinge and started to move.

She came to the membrane at the edge of the reality.

The salamandri stirred, gracefully undulant.

She thought about releasing them. She thought about taking them with her. Vaguely she understood the danger in that. She knew it in her mind but not in her bones. Yes, she thought. Yes. I can, I must, I will.

Dragging the netted salamandri behind her, she broke through the membrane. Faster and faster she fled, running for her homeplace. Faster and faster until she was sitting within the pentacle, the salamandri swooping in swift orbits about its outer rim, turning the moonsilver red with their fires; around and around they raced, keening their anger and their triumph in a high, terrible whine.

They fought her. They were wiry, wild, leaping against her hold, their bodies were hard and strong, bumping, bumping, bumping against her. They'd lain passive all this time to catch her napping; they knew what she was, they knew she'd come for them, knew it before she did; they knew there was a world they could plunder and burn. They fought her and nearly won free before she hardened her hold on them.

She hadn't actually handled demons before, that was meant to happen when she had a Master backing her, but she drew on analogs from her training and descriptions of the process from her teachers; she cast lines at them, sank hooks into them, seven lines for seven salamandri. They lunged at the cedars with their enticing explosive resins. She jerked them back. The tips of several fronds sizzled, filling the air with an acrid green fragrance. That was all they got, the trees stood intact, untouched.

She laughed. "I've done it. I've really done it," she shouted to the night. "I have summoned demons." She was sweating though, and underneath the laughter she was shaking. She refused to acknowledge that and broke the demons to her hand. They swung round and round her, keening, sad. Round and round until she rode their senses and reined their bodies. Round and round until they answered her will as swiftly and surely as her own body did.

She sent them arcing up over the trees, out along the river, racing faster than the wind, pulsing eerie unsteady fireforms flitting over the water.

They came to the Lock House. The windows were shuttered against them, the door was barred. They burned through a wall. The dead-priest tried to turn them. The lead salamander shot out a long red tongue and licked his face off the bone. The warleader slashed at one and saw his blade melt. The salamander wrapped itself about the man and a moment later dropped a chalky skeleton and swooped on.

What Korimenei received through their senses was strange beyond anything she could have imagined, but she learned to read it and kept them from the House, its furniture, everything but the men. Only the men, she droned at them, over and over, only the men. She kept them from the captive girls, though a quick hot death might have been more merciful than life after what the raiders had done to them. She counted the kills and when the number was fifty-five, she jerked on the leashes and called the salamandri back to her.

They didn't want to come. They wanted to burn and burn until the world burned with them, hot and glorious and wholly theirs. They fought her; they turned and twisted and contorted themselves, trying to throw out the hooks. They flung all their weight and strength against the lines again and again and again, they never seemed to tire. Every inch she won from them was contested with a fury that seemed to increase as her own strength decreased.

She faltered. A salamander leaped away; it almost broke free. The jerk tore something inside her. She struggled to enfold and smother the pain and at the same time keep her hold on the demons. If they got loose. . . . She didn't dare admit even the possibility of failure. She pulled the demons to her and they came, slowly, painfully, but surely, they came. They brushed against tree tops and the trees burned. They cawed their pleasure, jarring shrieks that started high and squeezed to a thready wail as the sound soared out of hearing; they swung at the ends of the lines, back and forth, back and forth, working at her, changing the direction, the force, the intensity of the pull. She trembled. She was so weary. She couldn't think. She held on and held on. Inch by slow, torturous inch, she dragged them back to her. Strength oozed out of her. So tired. So tired. Her muscles were mush. Every nerve in her was vibrating raggedly. She was going to give way. There is a point beyond which will cannot drive body. She was reaching it, but she held on, she held. . . .

Coolness spread over her like a second skin, the waves of shivering slowed and smoothed out, a flow of energy came like water into her. She lifted her head and whipped the salamandri across the final stretch, brought them to her whimpering and cowed. She wasted no time with them, she squeezed them into a clot of fire and flung them back where she'd found them, sealing the aperture behind them.

Coolness peeled off her and pooled in her lap, weariness flooded back. The pool sublimed to mist, the mist swirled and billowed, took a familiar form. Ailiki.

When Ailiki was solid again, her plush fur neatly in place, her catmouth open in her mocking catgrin, Korimenei lifted her, held her eye to eye. "Once upon a time I said watch my back, Aili my Liki. You make one fine bodyguard, Lili." She settled the mahsar in her lap, smoothed her hand again and again down Ailiki's spine. Breathed the syllables that banished the moonsilver, erased the pentacle. Earth was earth again, air was air. "Ahhhh, I'm tired, my Liki. Consequences, gods! I could have burned the world to ash. One salamander was enough to handle that pitiful bloody bunch. Shuh! More than enough. So I bring in seven? Pride, my Liki. Carelessness. Jah'takash must've been beating her pig bladder about my fool head, dubbing me idiot, fatuity supreme. I won't try anything like that again soon. I won't be awake enough, I'm going to sleep for a year."

A laugh. She looked up. A lantern swinging by his knee, Karoumang came from under the trees. "I've known women like that. I take it you managed to come up with something. What were those streaks?"

"Salamandri. You don't have to worry about the raiders any more." She yawned, thought about rubbing gritty eyes, but her arms were too heavy, too mushy to lift that far.

"You going to sit there the rest of the night?"

"Probably. Unless someone feels like carrying me."

"That bad, huh?"

"Tired, terrified, and frozen."

He lifted his lantern, turned the lightbeam on her face. "Preemalau's fins! If you were dead, you'd look better."

"Thanks for telling me, huh." She giggled, then sobered. "I came close, Karou. Came close to killing you and everything. I nearly lost control of them." She yawned again, slumped over Ailiki, her head swimming.

He swore, took a step toward her, stopped. "I'll be back. One minute."

She was barely conscious when he returned with one of his sailors, a man named Prifuan. Karoumang scooped her up and started for the ship; Prifuan came along behind them with the lanterns and the rest of her gear.

7

Karoumang took the *Miyachungay* cautiously up the river, moored her between the bulwarks and sent Prifuan and four more ashore to work the gates. The girls from the village saw this and crept from the trees; they were bloody, bruised, dressed in clothing salvaged from the dead and deep in shock. Women among the deck passengers took charge of them, got them cleaned up, fed, wrapped them in blankets; they petted the story out of the girls, gasped and sympathized in the proper places, got the names of kin in the next Lock village and carried the information to Karoumang.

Korimenei slept through all this. She slept through the stir at the next lock as the girls went ashore and Karoumang consulted with the village elders. She was deep, deep asleep as Prifuan and his four arrived; they'd been left behind to open the gates once the *Miyachungay* was far enough upriver. She slept for three more days, woke to find the *Miyachungay* past the locks and moving through a dun and dreary landscape.

When she stepped onto the deck, wind beat at her, the dust it carried scoured every inch of bare flesh. She went back and dug out the despised veil, belted the hanging panels so they wouldn't flap about too badly and tried the deck again. She picked her way through shrouded bales and climbed to Karoumang's favorite perch. He was there now, wearing a Temueng headcloth, the ends wrapped about his face, leaving only his eyes free.

"Well," he said. "You found a use for it after all." He rubbed his thumb over the veil where it snugged against her cheek. "How you doing otherwise?"

"Well enough. One of these days I might even be hungry again." She stood at the rail and looked around. "This is lovely stuff, Karou. Hunh. Where are we?"

"Ambijan. Nine days to Kapi Yuntipek." He turned his back to the wind, pulled her closer, sheltering her with his body.

"All of them like this?" She leaned against him, smiling under her veil, drowsy and comfortable.

"Long as we're in Ambijan. Five days, six if there's more cargo than I expect at Limni Sacca'l."

"I'm surprised you get anything. Who'd live here?"

"Ambijaks. They're all a little crazy."

She slapped at her breasts, raising a dust cloud of her own. "I believe it. Mind my asking, what DO you get here?"

"Canvas. Jaxin do some of the tightest weaving you can find anywhere. Need to, I suppose. Keep the dust out. I use it whenever I need new sails. Jaks make colorfast dyes, there's always a good market for those, especially new colors. Drugs. Opals. There are mines in the back country somewhere. I don't ask." She felt rather than heard his soft laugh. "Ambijaks spend words like blood. Their own blood, not yours, they're generous with yours. Crazy. But they know me so they keep it down some."

"Mmm." Despite the veil her eyes were watering and the skin of her face was starting to burn. She looked past his head, tried to see the sun. All she saw was a dull tan sky. "What time is it?"

"Coming on third watch. Want lunch?"

"Getting that way. I think I'll go back down, this wind is peeling the skin off me flake by flake. Any chance of a bath?"

"If you'll work for it."

"Scrub your back, huh?"

"You got it."

She rubbed her shoulder against him. "Anything, Captain Saö, I'll do anything to get clean."

"I'll keep that in mind. We might even manage some hot water."

"Ah, bliss to be alive and in your presence." She giggled, eased out of the circle of his arm and bent into the wind as she started down.

8

The *Miyachungay* traveled upstream day on dreary day. The Wansheeri was sluggish here, winding around broad bends and serried oxbows. It carried a load of silt and occasional animal carcasses, but few snags; in Ambijan trees were an exotic species, any floaters that got so far from the mountains were seized by the Jaks and hauled ashore as soon as they were spotted. The wind blew steadily out of the east, cold dry wind, engendering melancholy and distraction. The sound of it never stopped, it muted everything, reduced the comfortable small noises of the boat to whimpers; words were unintelligible a few paces away from the speaker; crew and passengers alike communicated with grunts or single shouted words, no more. The pressure of it never stopped; it drove west, west, west without letup. When the river turned east, they fought to shove the boat forward against the wind; when it turned west, if they lost their concentration a single moment and let the wind take her, it could jam her into the bank before they had a chance to recover; getting her around some of those bends took sweat and prayer and curses in nearly equal amounts. It was almost worse when she pointed straight north; then the wind threatened to blow her sideways. Karoumang got little sleep, a few hours of sweaty nightmare filled with snatches of horror. He was wild and rough when he took Korimenei those nights, using her to ease his wind-frayed nerves, the grinding tension built up during the day. He didn't care who she was, only that she was there. She should have resented that; other times, other circumstances she would have been furious, she would have given him a scar or three to remember her by, but she wasn't thinking these days, the wind was getting at her too; she was rough and wild as he was, she used him for needs that would have terrified and shamed her a month or two ago, and slept like she was slugged when it was over.

When they slid through a tattered ghostring into the lee of Kapi Yuntipek, even the *Miyachungay* seemed to sigh with relief.

9

A pseudopod of the ghost stuff ringing Kapi Yuntipek stayed with Korimenei as she rode away from the city a week later, a clotted white finger set firmly on her, unable to touch her; she ignored it, kept her pony pacified and moving along at a steady walk. Behind her, Ailiki perched on the pack pony, calming the little gelding and holding him in place. Abruptly the pseudopod snapped back and they were moving through a bright chill day; the air was so clear the mountains seemed close enough to touch.

The Silk Road was not much of a road despite its fame. It was a dusty path marked by stone cairns spread so that the pile ahead came into view as the pile behind sank below the horizon. At the moment it was winding in lazy curves through the thin rind of small farms north of the city, going across bridges like hiccups over narrow ditches, thumbnail scratches filled with water from the river. Temu serfs working in the fields straightened and watched her, their dark eyes wary and hostile. The land they stood on belonged to the Kangi Pohgin, the Headman of Kapi Yuntipek; they were worked until they dropped, two-thirds of every harvest was taken from them, they were exposed to depredations from stray raiders out of the Temueng grassclans and bandits sweeping down from the mountains; they expected nothing but harassment from everyone outside their own families. They reminded her of the lowlanders in Cheonea; they had the same hard, knotty look, the same secret stares, the same sense they were rooted to the landheart, mobile manshaped extensions of the soil they stood on. If she gave them any opening they would swarm over her and leave nothing but bones behind; that was in their eyes and the set of their bodies.

When she came out of the farms she rode between walls of Temu grass that reached past her stirrups, swaying in the eternal east wind, the individual rustles of stalk rubbing against stalk sunk into a vast murmuring whole. It was a hypnotic sound. She swam in it, breathed it; after an hour or so she seemed to hear voices in it whispering secrets she couldn't quite make out. North and east of the city the grass stretched out and out, to the horizon and past, an ocean of yellow and silver-dun, rippling, constantly changing color, subtle changes, barely distinguishable shades of the base colors. An ocean of grass wide as any water ocean.

The piercing, aching loneliness she'd felt in the city fell gradually away from her as she shed the sense of pressure, of neediness, the hurry-hurry, get-on-with-it that afflicted her within those walls; she settled into the long slow rhythms of the land, birth, growth, death, rebirth, inevitable, unchanging, eternal. She was an infinitesimal mote in that immense landscape, but she didn't feel diminished, no, it was almost as if her skin had been peeled back so she was no longer closed within it but was intimately a part of that vast extravagant sky, that shimmering ocean of grass.

After about three hours she stopped, watered the ponies at one of the Road Wells and let them graze. She leaned against a cairn, crossed her ankles. Ailiki jumped on her stomach; she laughed and began scratching the mahsar behind her twitching ears.

"What are you doing, Kori?" Tré's eidolon hung above her, his voice cut through her drowse. "Why are you just sitting there? Get moving. You have to beat the snow."

"So you're back." She continued to stroke the mahsar. "How nice."

As he always did, he ignored questions expressed or implied. "You can't waste a minute, you have to cross the Dautas as soon as possible."

"Tré. . . ." She sighed. "You know what riding stock is like, you push too hard and they quit on you, you can't have forgot that, what's wrong with you?"

"You know what's wrong." The crystal vibrated though the mouse-sized figure of the boy inside changed neither expression nor position. "I want out of this."

"Why do you think I'm here?" She sighed. "If I push the ponies too hard, this jaunt stops before the day's out. Quit niggling at me, Tré, I know what I'm doing." She lifted Ailiki off her. "Go fetch them, Lili; they've had enough rest for now. Tré, what about the weather? From here, it looks clear enough, but that's a lot of mountains."

"No blizzards yet. There are some washouts from rain, a lot of rain has been falling, no snow, I'm not sure why. There's black ice in the passes; it makes treacherous going. You should try to hit the steepest slopes in the afternoon, when the sun's been at the ice long enough to clear some of it out. If there is any sun."

"Lovely. Look, Tré, you seem to show up when you want to stick pins in me and ignore me otherwise. I'm trying to remember you're my brother; don't leave me hanging out to dry, help me. Talk to me even if there's nothing else you can do."

The eidolon flickered, faded, appeared again like a washed-out watercolor painted on the air, vanished completely.

Korimenei sighed, got to her feet. The ponies were standing on the Road, foam dripping from their mouths as they chewed at a last clump of grass. She smiled wryly as Ailiki ran up the packer's side and perched on its withers. "Aili my Liki, I'm beginning to wonder what the hell's going on here."

The mahsar folded her arms across her narrow chest and took on the aspect of Sessa who looked after lost trinkets, one of the little gods who scampered like mice from person to person, coming unasked, leaving without warning, a capricious, treacherous, much courted clutch of godlings. She nodded gravely, but what she meant by it was impossible to guess.

"You're a big help." Korimenei shook her head, swung into the saddle and nudged the pony into a plodding walk.

10

Two weeks slid past. Korimenei rode and walked, walked and rode, nibbled at trailbars and apples during the day, usually while the ponies grazed, cooked up stew and panbread when she camped for the night, washing these down with strong tea and a bowl of the rough red wine she'd picked up in Kapi Yuntipek. Water wasn't a problem, there were wells and troughs at intervals along the road. The sky stayed clear, there wasn't any frost in the morning, the air was too dry, but even long after the sun came up, the days were crackling cold. Despite that, she passed up the Waystop Inns as she came to them, riding on to camp at one of the wells. As if he were trying to make up for a fault he wasn't about to admit, Tré came each night with a weather report and stayed to chat a little, mostly about what had been happening to Korimenei, he said it was because he was sealed in crystal, stuck in the cave; since nothing was happening to him, there was nothing to talk about unless they went over and over past times which he didn't want to do. She grew easier in her mind; she wanted to believe that the closeness they'd shared was still there, waiting to be resumed when he was free.

In the third week she left behind the last sparse clumps of Temu grass and moved into the foothills of the Dhia Dautas. The waves of land had a flat wispy ground cover, gray-brown, limp; there seemed to be no vigor in it, but the ponies relished it when she let them graze. The thorn-studded brush had small leaves that a series of hard frosts had turned into stiff rounds of maroon leather, and copper-colored crooked branches that wove in and out of each other to form a dense prickly ball that only changed size as it aged, not conformation. It grew in tangled clumps in and around dumps of boulders like the droppings of some immense and incontinent beast.

In the fourth week she was on the lower slopes of the mountains winding upward toward the first LowPass, moving through thick stands of trees and a different ground cover, broad-leafed vines that were crimson and gold, crawling across red earth that crumbled into a fine dust which settled on every surface and worked its way into every crevice. The slopes were steeper, the air thinner and colder. It cut her throat like knives when she was winded near the top of a rise and breathing through her mouth. She saw deer and narru herds, wolves trotting in ragged lines, sangas and mountain cats sunning on boulders or in trees, squirrels and rabbits and other small scutters, birds hopping along the ground, feeding on seeds and insects. There was a sense of waiting in the air, a feeling that the season was changing, but not yet. Not quite yet. Most mornings there were only a few wisps of cloud scrawled across the sky; as each day wore on, though, the clouds thickened and darkened, the light took on a pewter tinge, colors were darker, richer. She saw no one, the road was open, empty, but she was aware several times of eyes watching her. She ignored them. Let them watch.

At the end of the week she ran into rain and black ice.

11

When she crawled from her blankets the sky was clear and cold as the water in the stream, the world was a glitter of ice and frost flowers. Her skin tingled, she was intensely alive; when she started along the Road again she wore seven league boots and could stride across the mountains like a giant.

A patch of black ice reminded her she was merely mortal. Her feet slid from under her and she landed on hands and knees hard enough to jar her back teeth. She got painfully to her feet and inspected her hands; the palms were scraped raw, smeared with dirt. With slow stiff movements she rubbed them on her jacket; when the dirt was off, she pulled her gloves from her pocket and put them on. She made a face at Ailiki who was being Sessa again, sitting plump and sedate on the saddle, smirking at her. "Laugh and I start thinking Liki stew."

On the far side of the ridge was a long narrow valley, smoky with steam from hotsprings, steam that wove in and out of dark ominous conifers and went trickling up to a white-blue sky bare of clouds. About a half mile from the Road, she saw a huddled village; there were no people visible, no stock in sight; the harvest was already in, the fields were mud and stubble. A ghost drifted across the mud, circled her, then fled without saying anything. She could sense hostile eyes watching her and had a strong feeling she'd better not stay around for any length of time.

Half an hour later, she came on a small scraggly meadow; she stopped there, fed the ponies the last of the feedcake and let them graze.

When Ailiki brought them in, they were mud to the belly. Korimenei swore, dug out a stiff brush and went over their legs and feet, cleaning away the mud and the small round leeches they'd collected off infested brush. She worked up a sweat that damped her underclothes and ripened her smell until even she was aware she stank. She knocked the brush against the trunk of a conifer and straightened. "Lili, if it takes till midnight, we keep going until we reach an Inn."

They plodded on, winding up the next ridge in long slow loops that gained height with the tempered speed of a slug in winter, passing other xenophobic settlements nested on small mountain flats, blank-walled, secret places that turned their shoulders to the Road and refused to acknowledge its existence. By late afternoon more clouds were blowing off the peaks, blocking what small warmth the pallid sun had been providing; a chill, dank wind rolled down the Road. She pushed on, riding and walking, walking and riding. The day grew darker and darker. The sun finally sneaked down, no display of color this night, only an imperceptible hardening of the dark. Finally, near midnight, she reached the Waystop Inn at the throat of HighPass.

The doors were barred, the windows shuttered, the Inn was dark and silent. Korimenei was in no mood to tolerate obstacles or delicately weigh consequences. She sent the bar flying from its brackets, kicked the door open and went stalking in. She crafted a will-o, hung it by the thick ceiling beams and stood waiting in the eerie, bluish light, Ailiki on her shoulder, the ponies huddled close outside the gaping door. "Hey the house," she shouted. "You have clients. Stir your stumps or I'll turn this dikkhush into kindling."

The Host came down the stairs, his nightshirt tucked into trousers pulled hastily on, the lacings untied, ends dangling. He carried a lamp, set it on the counter when he saw the will-o and Korimenei standing under it. "It's late," he said. "We closed for the night."

"Looks like I just opened you. I want a hot bath, a hot meal, and a bed. And stabling for my ponies. We can debate the metaphysics of open and closed all you want come the morning. Right now I'm tired and I haven't a lot of patience."

"Sorcerer." It wasn't a compliment the way he said it. He shrugged. "Bath's no problem, we're sitting on a hotspring. Meal, that'll take some time and it'll cost. M' wife works hard and she needs her sleep, you're not the only one tired this night. Ponies, take 'em round yourself, get 'em settled. You had no trouble getting in here, do the same to the stables if you can't wake the boy up. I'd take it kindly if you didn't scare a year's growth out of him. He's m' wife's cousin and worth hot spit on a summer day, but kin's kin."

She laughed. "You're a clever man, Hram. You could milk the poison from a reared-back cobra. I expect to pay, but control your appetite, Hram Host; double is enough, more than that is sin and punishable by wart, eh?" She listened. "It's starting to rain, I'd better get the ponies under cover." She beckoned the will-o to her. "And let you shut your door so all the heat doesn't leak away."

\#\#

Warm, replete and clean for the first time in days, she crawled between fresh, sweet-smelling sheets and sighed with pleasure. "Well, Aili my Liki, this is something else. Why oh why am I putting myself through this muck? Ah I know, oh I know; poor Tré, he didn't deserve having his life taken away from him like that, just so Old Maks would have a hold on me. It's my fault he's there, my fault I'm here. I owe him. Sometimes though. . . ." She yawned, turned on her side and pulled the quilts up to her nose. Ailiki was a hotspot curled up against her stomach; the mahsar was already asleep and snoring with that tiny eeping that was a comforting nightsong. The rain was slashing down outside, a steady thrum against the shutters. A cold draft wandered past her nose. She murmured with pleasure, dreaming she was home again, a girl in her narrow bed, safe in the arms of her kin and kind, then she dropped deeper into sleep and left even dreams behind.

\#\#

In the morning she half-fell out of bed and barely made the slop basin before the nausea erupted and she emptied her stomach.

When the spasms stopped, she dipped a corner of the towel in the pitcher and washed her face, then sat on her heels, eyes closed, while she waited for the upheaval in her body to die down. Ailiki came trotting over to her, pressed against her leg. She lifted the mahsar, held her against her breasts, her warmth helping to soothe away the ache. "Well, Lili, I'm going to have to look, aren't I."

Sitting in the middle of the bed, rain dribbling down outside, a dull dreary drizzle, she turned inward and explored her body.

There was no mistake, no way of avoiding the truth. She was pregnant. The wind had worn away more than her nerves those days in Ambijan. She sat there in the quiet warm room, thinking: What do I want? What am I going to do? In the end, it was all words. She wanted the baby and she was going to have it. She needed it. Karoumang's child. No. Mine. The thought warmed her. My daughter. She knew it was going to be a daughter. She wasn't going to be alone any more. It didn't matter what her brother did. Didn't matter if Maksim wouldn't have her as apprentice. She folded her arms across her body, hugging herself and what she bore. I'm not going to worry, she thought. There's plenty of time to finish this thing before there's enough child to worry about. Tell Tré if he bothers to show up again? No! No way. It's none of his business.

#

She crossed HighPass and went through the serried ridges of the western flanks of the Dhia Dautas, daughters of the dawning sun, though there was little sun in evidence, dawn or dusk or anything between. It snowed twice in the first week, light snows, two inches one storm, six the next. Then it rained and that was worse. Each morning she woke and vomited. Then she rode on. Day after day, walk and ride, ride and walk until she was down in the grass again and twenty days out of Dil Jorpashil.

12

Korimenei looked at the tuber stew. The cook's heavy hand with the spice jars couldn't disguise the sweetish sick smell from the shreds of anonymous meat. I can't eat this, she thought, there's no way I can eat this.

She finished the dusty tea and the bread, got quietly to her feet and went outside. She leaned against the tie-rail and breathed in the clean cold air off the grass, thinking about the gaunt little girl who'd carried her gear to the sleeping loft with its scatter of husker mattresses and tattered privacy curtains. Ten years going on a hundred and running the Waystop alone; most likely her father was in the hedgetavern built onto the back of the hostel, playing host to the local drunks, a drunk himself if she read the signs right. From the smell that wafted up to the loft, he stilled his own sookpa. Must taste worse than that rancid meat. I've got to do something about food, she thought. She smiled into the darkness, patted her stomach. Well-fed cows make healthy calves. Old cow, I'd better see about keeping you properly fed.

She went exploring and found the girl in the kitchen, washing up. "Where's your father, child?"

The girl's eyes darted to the back door, flicked away. She shrugged, said nothing. She stood hunched over the washtub, her hands quiet in the greasy water, her body saying: go away and leave me alone.

"I see. Your mother?"

"She dead."

"You do the cooking?"

"You din' eat ye stew. We don't give coin back f' what ye don' eat."

"A starving sanga wouldn't eat that stew. It's not the cooking, child. It's the meat. I take it you don't raise your own?"

The girl shook her head, began scratching at a bit of crust in a loafpan.

"Your father doesn't hunt?"

"An't no game close enough. T' Road scare 'em." Her voice was muffled, defensive; once again her dark eyes went to the door, turned away.

"Hmm. If I brought you meat, would you cook it for me? I'll leave you what's left over in payment."

"What kinda meat?"

"Geyker."

"Ah-yah. When?"

"Soon. An hour, perhaps a little more."

"I wanna see t' hide." Her shoulders were hunched over, her hands shaking; she wouldn't look at Korimenei. She was terrified, but determined.

Korimenei laughed. "Yes yes. You're a good sonya. I wouldn't give you forbidden fare. You'll see hide, hooves, and all. Tell me something. Would Waystops down the Road take meat instead of coin?"

"I couldna say f' sure. I think so. Dada woulda if ye'd asked."

"Thank you. Good e'en, sonya." Korimenei left the kitchen, paused in the middle of the common room to consider site options. There was the sleeping loft, but she didn't like the feel or the smell of the place. The stable. No. The hostler was nested inside there like a rat in a wall and not even the sookpa stoups in the tavern were going to entice him out. She didn't want anyone looking over her shoulder while she went dipping for a demon to hunt some meat for her. She pushed away the fears that kept recurring about attracting notice and even a challenge from a local sorcerer. She had to do this, she had no choice. She moved to the door; it wasn't barred yet; the sun was barely down; a few rosy streaks on the western horizon lingered from a pallid sunset. The Wounded Moon was breaking free of the horizon in the east, nearly full, the moonhare-crouching plainly writ in streaks of blue-gray on the yellowish ground. The night was clear and brilliant with almost no wind to blow the grass about or stir the naked branches of the three gnarly olive trees growing beside the well. The well . . . ah, the well. Wells are powerpoints and sanctuaries or so Master Kushundallian claimed. I'll know the truth of that before the night's much older.

She pulled the door shut behind her. "Lili, I need you," she called. The mahsar was out hunting her dinner; she turned her nose up at anything cooked or dead before she made it so; in emergencies she'd share Korimenei's meals, but not without expressing her opinion of such slop with some full-body grimaces. "Aili my Liki," she called again, then went to sit on the well-coping and wait for her backup, smiling at herself, amused by her new-won prudence.

Ailiki materialized in Korimenei's lap, sat washing her whiskers with tongue-damped forefeet. Korimenei laughed, scratched behind her tulip petal ears, then lifted her and carried her to the bare earth where horses, mules, four-footed beasts of all kinds had milled about waiting their turn to drink from the troughs, their hooves cutting up the grass, grinding it into the earth, beating the earth into a hard crusty floor. She set Ailiki down and began drawing a pentacle. "What I'm going to do, Lili . . . I need a hunter who will go and get me a geyker. Hmm. I need fruit too, maybe I can do something about that." She inspected the pentacle. "That's done. Come here, babe."

She silvered and activated the pentacle, insinuated herself into the realities and drifted, waiting for the call. There was no urgency, only a quiet need; it took longer she couldn't tell how long her time-sense was useless here it might have been seconds or parts of a single second but finally the pull came and she eased through into an immensity that would have frightened her if she stopped to think, but she went swimming so swiftly that the darkness and the cold was only a mountain pond, she swanned through the dark and floated over the face of a world turning and turning in the light of a yellow sun. Sand and more sand, sand and brush and sand-colored cats prowling after herds of sand-colored deer. She dipped lower. Mancats with snakes for hands and four legs padding pacing loping over the sand. Mancats with eyes that *knew.* She called one and he came to her, he came rushing at her, she hadn't realized how big he was, how powerful. She smelled him. He reeked but it was an attractive stink, sensual, sexual. *Hunt for me,* she called to him. *Hunt for yourself and hunt for me.*

He shook himself, considered her. She felt his consent given and threw a mindseine about him. In some way, he leaned into her, helping with the shift. He was amused at the whole thing, curious, intensely immensely curious. Pleased at having the chance to travel away from his sandhills. He landed on the ground outside the pentacle and settled on his haunches, his massive head turning and turning, his black nostrils flaring as he tasted the air. She thought a geyker at him. He rumbled his assent, went loping off into the grass.

She flowed away again, floated aimlessly awhile, until a sweet-tart smell invaded her. She followed it into richness, a world lush with fruit, ripe fruit, oozing with juice. She drifted among the trees, choosing, dropping the fruit into a mindnet woven tighter than before. When she had as much as she could eat that night and the next day, she drifted back, carrying her gleanings with her. She juggled that fruit as the mindnet came apart when she touched down, dropped pieces that cracked open but were otherwise still edible. She piled it all by her knee and looked around. The mancat was close, she could smell him on the wind.

A moment later the grass parted and he came carrying a dead geyker. He laid it on the ground beside the pentacle and trotted off again. She looked at it. Lyre-shaped horns like polished jet. Black nose with blood coming from it like threads of ink. Rough, brindled coat in its winter growth, the guard hairs longer than her hand. Silken white ruff about the long neck, spattered and matted with more blood. Split hooves, black and sharp as knives. Tail like a flag, black above, white below. A good plump beast with its winter fat in place. She sighed and sang the old tributesong her people in the Vale sang over their butchered stock, giving its beastsoul rest and rebirth. Then she settled herself to wait until the mancat was finished with his own business and ready to go home with his prizes.

13

She *progressed* across the plain. There was no other word for it. She was a rolling storm of magic accompanied by demons, delivering fresh meat to the hostels, fruit and fish; she was a cornucopia of good things and generous with them, trading meat for stable space and sleeping room, leaving more always than she bargained with. One mancat after another came to her, hunted for her and himself, played with her, teased her, took pleasure in this *other place,* gave way to the next mancat and that one to the next, each one of them grinning that terrifying tender toothy grin, each one of them full of good humor and delight.

Tré came. "What are you doing?" he shouted at her. "What are you doing? Stop it. You're asking for trouble. You're asking to be challenged. Stop it. What are you doing?"

She waited until he ran down. "I'm saving coin and staying healthy. You want me to stop? Fund me, Tré. I'm spending my Passage gift for you. I've probably lost my chance to apprentice to Maksim. Either bring me some coin or leave me to do this my way."

The eidolon shivered, anger flared around her, brushing against her skin like nettle leaves, burning. Then with an almost tangible, almost audible *pop,* her brother's eidolon vanished. She trembled. After a few moments of nausea that had nothing to do with morning sickness, she started crying. There was an aching emptiness inside where her love for her brother had been. She hadn't stopped loving the boy she knew once, but he was gone. Whoever it was caught in crystal was not her brother. Not any more.

14

Dil Jorpashil.

Korimenei stopped to buy tea and trailfood and look around the city, relishing the Market with its noise, its cacophony of color and smell; it reminded her of the Market at Silili and she was brushed with a pleasant melancholy at the thought. Already her days at school seemed as if they'd happened to someone else in another lifetime and they'd taken on the golden patina of nostalgia.

The day she left, while she waited on a ferry landing for a riverboat to pass, heading south, she saw a woman standing at the rail looking back at the city, a widow in black robes with a small M'darjin page at her side. Drinker of Souls, Korimenei thought, startled. I wonder what she's doing here? She didn't know how she knew who the woman was —her hair was black, her face was different—but she did. She watched the boat glide away and thought she'd know the feel of that woman anywhere, whatever face or shape she wore. Drinker of Souls. Hmm.

The ferryman wound his cable from the water, rang his bell. Along with some noisy grassclanners from the south who were heading home after a hectic time in the city, she led her ponies onto the flat. She stood between the two beasts, trying to ignore the nomads; they were young and randy, on the loose and apt to see a stray female as fair game.

When the ferry reached the far side, she let them ride off ahead of her. When she came off, they were waiting. She put on an ASPECT, was suddenly twelve feet tall with world-class warts and fangs that curved down past her chin. They took off, screaming. Amused and rather pleased with herself, she led the ponies past the stubby pillars that marked the resumption of the Silk Road, mounted and rode toward the Dhia Asatas, the daughters of the setting sun, invisible now behind a shroud of the thick gray clouds.

IV: DANNY BLUE

Having been trapped by a cabal of Dirge Arsuiders, injected with poison and ordered to bring back the Talisman Klukesharna in return for the antidote to the poison, Danny Blue and the back-up help (two thieves and a courtesan) provided by the Arsuid Ystaffel climbed aboard the riverboat *Pisgaloy* and started for Hennkensikee.

1

At sunrise on the fifth day after she left Dirge Arsuid, the riverboat *Pisgaloy* rounded a long low knoll that was thick with mighty millenarian oaks and pointed her nose at Hennkensikee on the island cluster half a mile out in Lake Patinkaya. The sun was gilding the pointed roofs and the walls dissolved in glitters reflecting off water hard and bright as knife blades. The *Pisgaloy* leaned into the uncertain wind and clawed her way up the last stretch of free water.

Hennkensikee was tall and toothy, built of red brick fired from clay taken eons ago from the banks of the north rim of the lake. The ovens that fired the bricks were abandoned when the job was done; these days they were pits like pocks with snag-tooth beams poking through thistles and nettles and ragweed; the city witches went hunting herbs around there because they had ten times the potency of those picked elsewhere. In the days when the pits were roaring with the kiln fires, the god Coquoquin took the bricks and laid the walls of Hennkensikee, the towering curtain wall and the needle towers within, weaving the courses into complex, continually changing patterns, a subtle dance of design across all the surfaces, invisible at any great distance, meant to please eyes and fingertips simultaneously. She built and watched over a city of subtleties, of fountains playing in hidden courtyards, glimpsed through a confusion of arches or heard but not seen, of faces behind screens of wood and ivory, of layered fragrances from incense burned at every door. A city of patterns but no color, the brick was dull, the wood stained dark; the figures moving unhurriedly through the narrow winding streets wore black wrappings, rectangles of cloth wound about and about their bodies, a second, shorter rectangle rope-anchored to the Lewinkob long heads, male and female alike, falling like shrouds about squat Lewinkob bodies.

The *Pisgaloy* circled carefully wide about the island group and crept up to the end of a pier that extended like a finger into the Lake. A motley collection, all sizes, shapes and genders, the passengers went streaming off with their packs of tradegoods or sacks of coin. Danny Blue and his associates came ashore in the middle of the flood, joined the line formed up at the gate and waited for the Wokolinka's inspectors to let them into the city.

Trithil Esmoon was draped in the robes and embroidered veil of a Phrasi courtesan, not all that different from what she wore in Arsuid. Simms was nondescript in a new way, hair brushed back flat against his skull, his clothing a mix of dark grays and black; the colors suited him better than the reds and pinks he favored when not working, but nothing could make him handsome.

Felsrawg was enjoying herself. She looked fierce enough to slaughter a regiment of rapists. Her black hair was pulled up tight to the top of her head except for three earlocks on each side of her face; it was twisted into a spiral knot that added several inches to her height. Twin gold skewers with animal heads for knobs were driven through that knot and rose like horns above it. She'd replaced her earstuds with long gold arrowpoints on gold rings; they danced with every move of her head. A black leather tunic was laced tight to her slim body over a white silk blouse with long loose sleeves that hid her knives; with this she wore a narrow black leather skirt slit to the hip on the left side and black leather boots with razor-edged spurs strapped to them.

"Tirpa Lazul, Trader, out of Bandrabahr, come for the silk sale," Danny told the beard behind the table. "My associates," he waved a hand at the others. "The hanoum Haya, also Phrasi, companion. Hok Werpiaka, trader's son, out of Silili, traveling to learn the markets."

"He's not Hina."

"No. Croaldhese. His family moved to Silili for . . . hmm . . . political reasons some generations back. The other is Second Daughter Azgin kab'la Savash, Matamulli up from the Southland to earn her dowry."

"Looks like she's wearing part of it."

"You got it."

"One taqin each, any silver coin will do, provided it weighs at least five tunts. Drop them in the pan. Good." He emptied the coins from the balance pan into a leather box, pushed four wooden plaques across the table. "Keep these on you at all times. Be quick to show them if a S'sup asks to see them. Curb all uncouth behavior in the streets or elsewhere, except in the taverns. We are not barbarians, we realize our visitors need relaxation. However, this must be kept within limits and inside where it will not offend our eyes. Exceed those limits or provide reason for a complaint against you, and you will be warned first, then fined, then ejected. There is no appeal from a Tsi-tolok's judgment. Have you questions? No? Good. You may pass."

2

For two days and two nights they poked about in Hennkensikee, the walls constraining them, the only interiors open to them the great warehouses where dour old women spread silks on padded tables and squeezed the last tiny copper from the circling bidders. Trithil Esmoon reclaimed her hithery and the old women leaned toward her as if they smelled her sweetness, sniffed it in to compare with ancient memories the scent rewakened in them, tumbling over themselves to answer her questions.

While Danny Blue and Trithil Esmoon played their cover games in the fragrant dimness of the warehouses, Felsrawg explored the city, insofar as she could, plotting thieftracks on its walls, climbing and entering in her mind the needle towers and tall square houses with their high-peaked roofs and ogeed windows. Shuttered windows, unglazed, outsider eyes blocked by wood-and-ivory screens carved in intricate serpentines pierced and repierced, the wood age-dark and tougher than iron. Fingers and mind both itched as she read the chances; she wanted to climb those walls and work her way past the screens, to puff in the sleep powders and prowl in darkness hunting for the treasures she knew lay inside. She watched the colored liquids of her skry ring shift and coil beneath the crystal as they registered and reacted to the wards and traps; a glance was all she needed to know how weak and careless the ward-setter had been. She could slide through slick as a serpent slipping down a mousehole. She kept moving, ignoring the Lewinkob who turned to look at her and follow her with their eyes. Twice she was stopped by one of the armored S'supal, the Wokolinka's amazon guards. She played Second Daughter with zest, exulting as she fooled them; the cockiness might have sunk her, but they knew Matimulli and discounted it. By evening on the second day she'd got all she could and was beginning to repeat. She went to the meeting that night filled with impatience, irritation and anxiety. The sooner the job was done, the sooner she could claim the antidote.

Simms drifted about, his hair damped and darkened, his gray and black clothing and his stocky shape much like the other Lewinkob men walking around him, though he lacked the billowing beards they favored. He went into pocket parks, havens of greenery open to the public, and made himself available to the ghosts who blew about the streets, courts and public spaces, looking wistfully after the locals who more or less ignored them. He let them tell their stories and listened to their complaints, slipping in a word now and then to nudge them in directions he wanted them to go. When he wasn't talking to ghosts or doing his own thieftracks, he was leaning against walls, staring vacantly at the sky, listening to the ancient bricks tell their long creaky tales. By the evening of the second day, he too was beginning to hear things twice.

3

Danny Blue strolled around the room, checking the wards he'd woven about the windows and set into the threshold of the door; there was almost dust on them, they were so untouched. Carelessness on the guardians' part, but he wasn't about to fault them for it. He opened the door a crack and set the ward to admit three, then snap closed again. Witches made him nervous, he liked them best when they were tired or lazy. Against possible overlooking, which they could do through anything belonging to the city, he'd brought an old sheet from Arsuid. To keep it from being contaminated when he wasn't using it, he left it rolled within a warded leather sack which he hung from a peg beside the wardrobe. He took the sheet from the sack, snapped it open and spread it on the floor. He stepped onto it and lowered himself until he was sitting cross-legged. The others were elsewhere at the moment, though they were due to join him soon. He was content to sit and wait, to enjoy these few blessed moments alone. Because she was supposed to be his concubine, Trithil Esmoon was sharing his room and his bed. She was always there, always. . . . Last night she'd turned to him, all warm and enticing and he told her to shut it off; he didn't trust her an inch and wasn't about to give her that kind of hold on him.

He thought about that, grimaced. It'd been a long dry spell. Last time he'd had a chance at sex, he'd been with Brann and got knocked cold because he was too rough with her; it was enough to put anyone off his stroke to get half the life sucked out of him in medias res as it were. He thought about that now, uneasy because he wasn't reacting to Trithil as he'd expected to. Even when she turned on the hithery. He worried it around and around, then decided he could live with it. He decided he needed the sense that there was at least some reciprocity involved, more than mingled sweat, spittle and other fluids. She was a splendid fake, but fake she was, and he couldn't forget that no matter how skillfully she counterfeited her responses. He couldn't forget how cold and uninterested she was when she dropped the mask. He thought about Felsrawg and smiled as he pictured her. Her passions burned from the bone out; she prided herself on her gambler's face, but a child could read what she was feeling. She'd make a scratchy armful, but she wouldn't be boring. She was making signs like she'd be willing to try it out and see what happened. He rubbed at his chin, shook his head. Remember, old Dan, she might look frank and frisky and forthcoming, but she has orders to off you and take the talisman; if you doubt she'd do it, you're playing head games with yourself.

Felsrawg pushed the door open, stalked in with the coiled energy of a hungry puma. She dropped onto the sheet and sat fidgeting with one of her knives. She kept glancing at the door, frowned impatiently when Simms came strolling in and settled beside her on the sheet. She turned the frown on Danny Blue. "Where's the hoor?"

Danny shrugged.

Felsrawg took a bit of soft leather from one of her pockets, began polishing the blade. "Leader, hunh! Old cow would do more."

"Take over, do it better."

"Don't think I wouldn't if I could handle wards and witches."

"Then shut up till you can."

"Hah." She stopped her hands, stared pointedly at the mussed bed. "I can see where you've got your mind on other things, but couldn't we get this klatch moving? If the hoor wants to know what's happening, we can catch her up when she gets here."

"We wait. The ward is open till she crosses the threshold."

Felsrawg made a spitting sound, went back to polishing the blade.

Twenty minutes later Trithil came undulating in. She stripped off her veil, tossed it on the bed and took her place on the sheet.

Danny waited until he felt the ward click shut, then he flattened his hands on his thighs and looked at each of the others. "Any ideas about getting across those bridges to the Henanolee Heart?"

Simms pursed his mouth, shook his head. "I went an' leaned 'gainst one of the gate piers this end the firs' bridge. Bridge be trapped. " 'Larums an' sinks. Either the S'sulan drop on you, or y' get dropped to the eels that live in the straits 'tween the islands. What I know 'bout the S'sulan, better the eels. Ghosts say this: the S'wai, that the witches, they lower'n the belly of a starvin' snake. What they mean, the S'wai they tired. Burnt out. Been a long, hard season an' it coming up on Closeout so they lettin' down, doin' the min, y' know."

Felsrawg slid the knife back in its bootsheath. "Yeh. You'd expect them to have tightasses here where they let foreigners in, knowing how these Lewks see us all, but t'ain't so, Laz old Sorce. You pick a wall, any wall, I'll go up it like it was flat and clean out everything behind it without a peep from the 'larms. The wards are in pitiful shape. Creamcheese here, everywhere."

"Perhaps not creamcheese." Trithil slid a fingertip over and over the dome of the star sapphire in her thumbring. "But not far from it. The Maskab Kutskab spent the afternoon complaining about her S'sulan, she says they're spending more time in taverns than on the street. Half the time they're drunk out of their skulls on sourmash wukik or sucking the ton off some male whore. The other half, they're slicing pieces off each other in knife duels. When she wasn't carping, she was drooling over the hell she's going to put them through come Closeout. She didn't say much about the other islands, except some mutters about Maskabi too lazy to do their own breathing, Wokolinka's kin who got their places through toelicking or worse. I believe that confirms what our tame thieves are telling us." She gave Felsrawg a mocking smile, looked coldly at Simms, then lowered her eyes to the thumbring and contemplated the pulsing of the star.

"So," Danny lifted his legs. "We go round the traps and climb the walls. I thought it might come out like that. My first thought was a boat. Any ideas?"

Simms shrugged. "Ne'er been on a boat 'n 'm life till *Pisgaloy*."

Felsrawg clicked her tongue, the sound expressing her disgust. "Nor me."

Trithil lifted her eyes briefly, shook her head went back to watching the star.

Danny shook his head. "And you're all island born. Well, we fall back on something I did a while ago. It'll make things easier, but it's noisy as . . . well, never mind that, we'll just hope there's no sorcerer around to hear me working. Trithil, I need the room, find some other place to wait. You've all had supper? Good. Get some sleep. We go two hours after midnight."

4

Midnight.

Danny Blue waggled a finger at the wick. The spark caught and the oil-soaked braid began to burn and smoke. He cranked it down until the flame seemed to spout from the brass tube. As soon as the smoke cleared away, he fitted on the glass chimney and clipped the lamp into its brackets. He frowned at the leather sack, shook his head. No point in it since he was planning to use local materials to build his boat. Airboat. He grinned as he peeled the blankets off the bed, dragged the lumpy mattress onto the floor, doubling it over so it was thicker and half the width. *What I did before, I can do again.* He pushed at the pallet with the toe of his boot, walked around it, inspecting it. After a moment he dug through the bedclothes, found one of the thin pillows and tossed it down at the end of the pallet. *Unless the damn god wakes and sticks her long nose in my business, or one of the S'wai gets a twinge.* The way his luck was running, either one could happen or worse. *Tungjii my friend, I could use a smile from you right now.* He stepped into the middle of the pallet, knelt as comfortably as he could in front of the pillow and pulled a shield tight about him except for a tiny hole he hoped no one would notice.

He thought a moment, then began gathering his forces, putting bridles on his half-sires, whipping them into a momentary subservience and opening himself to both sets of memory; when he was ready, he adapted his half-sire Daniel's energy cables to his half-sire Ahzurdan's fire-handling and wove a lead; he drove the lead through the pinhole into the violent reality of the salamandri. He couldn't project himself into that reality, he couldn't draw demons from it, but he could tap into it and use its raving energies to power his Shaping and Transforms. When he had a steady flow coming through the lead into the accumulator cells he'd formed inside his body, he brushed his fingers across the pillow, back across the coarse canvas of the pallet cover. Murmuring a minor Transform, he turned a roll of cloth into a marker that drew coarse black lines. He narrowed his eyes, focused will and attention, and began blocking in the areas where he needed to make the major Transforms that could convert the pallet and pillow into a lift-sled like the one he'd made once from a kitchen table, like the sled Daniel knew so well from his home reality.

Sketching with the marker he shuffled backward on his knees, sweeping lines across the flat in broad X's; he hobbled to the front again and began drawing honeycomb braces around the edge of the pallet. He finished, straightened his aching back, and inspected his work. "Good," he muttered. "Now the hard stuff."

He knelt before the pillow, touched it. As it happened before, it happened now. Chant poured out of him with a rightness that seemed to come from bone rather than brain, as if the rightness and the elegance of the design once more commanded him, mind and body and spirit, as if the liftsled was using him to be born. He Reshaped the flocking and canvas into glass and ceramic, metal and plastic. Sucking great gulps of fire from the salamandrin reality, he poured it into the Patterns his will created, pressing and shaping that fire into the esoteric crystals that were the heart and brain of the liftfield. He laid down layer on layer of them, embedding them in intricate polymers, wove more polymers into honeycomb braces that stiffened the floppy mattress into something like solidity. He Reshaped the pillow into sensors and readouts, a canted control plate that would let him regulate start-up, velocity, direction and altitude; he drew a pair of powerlines from it to the rear of the palletsled. Dropping the lines for a moment, he sculpted twin energy sinks in the tail; he reclaimed the lines and joined them to the sinks. Then he rested a short while, until the shaking went out of his hands.

Holding the tap quiescent, he inspected his work inch by inch, making small changes here and there to improve the conformation. When he was done with that, he knelt by the sinks, put a hand flat on each and began feeding power into them until they were topped off, humming to the touch like a hive of angry bees.

He let the tap fade, let the shield dissolve about him. He got up and stepped away from the liftsled, triumphant but too drained to crow or preen—for the moment, anyway. He tossed the blankets back on the bed, spread them over the interwoven ropes that had served to support the mattress. It wasn't particularly comfortable, but he was too tired to care. It was a transient thing he'd made, fairygold, apt to vanish if you kept it around too long, but it'd last the night and it was so alien to this reality it wouldn't trigger alarms for the witches; even the god Coquoquin might not notice what was happening under her nose. Too bad it wouldn't last. He lay staring at the ceiling, imagining the look on Pawbool's face if the four of them came swooping in, waving Klukesharna and demanding the antidote. He lifted a heavy hand, checked his ringchron. Nearly two hours gone. No wonder I'm tired.

His muscles were sore, even his bones ached; too tired to sleep, he lay brooding over his limitations. Fused through all Ahzurdan's memories was the sense of ease, the exhilarating ease with which the sorcerer handled the power that leaped to his hands, the getting drunk with that power, riding a high like no other. . . . And Ahzurdan was second rank at his best. Settsimaksimin was something else. His mind drifted to that last battle. Maks alone against all of them, him and the changers and Brann. Funny that . . . in a way . . . Maksim depending on a talisman like BinYAHtii to capture and store power for him when he had a thousand thousand realities laid out for plundering. I don't know, Danny thought, wrong mindset, I suppose. There's nothing like forcefields and directed energy flows in this universe, they don't even have something simple like electricity. That's it, probably. They don't have the physical analogs to show them how to handle the hot stuff. If you don't know something exists, kind of hard to use it. Hmm. Wonder why Old Garbagegut didn't think of that? H/it's been sucked in, I suppose. Thinks like everyone else here. Computer, mmf. An't it the way, they have all the data but can't jump the ruts. Just as well, I hate to think what life would be like for ordinary folks here if h/it knew how to get h/its tentacles on that much power. Maksim now, he could handle anything the realities put out, if he happened to think of it. Look what he can do without the tap, transfer himself anywhere in the world he wants, wards're cobwebs he brushes aside, hardly noticing them. At least, that's how Ahzurdan remembers him, larger than life and more powerful than a god.

Danny drifted awhile through Ahzurdan's memory, melancholy at the loss between then and now. When Ahzurdan was on his own and at his peak, he could jump the horizon to any place he'd been before, he could snatch unwarded items half a world away. Me, I'm lucky if I can do a simple line-of-sight snap. To save my life, I couldn't round a corner ten feet off. Too bad. Too toooo bad. If I could look into the Heart, if I could make the exchange without going in . . .

Klukesharna's copy in the warded sack under the sheet . . . for Klukesharna in the Heart . . . no use regretting what I can't do . . . so much simpler, though. . . . He drifted into a light sleep.

##

He started awake, heart pounding, as some idiot pounded on the door. He sat up. "Come," he said. "Door's not locked."

Trithil Esmoon slipped in; she stood at the foot of the bed and inspected him critically. "You look like you've spent the whole time sniffing dust."

He yawned, dragged a hand across his eyes. "I've been working."

"On that? What is it?"

"Skyboat." He swung his legs over the edge of the bed, groaned himself onto his feet. "The others awake?"

"I heard Felsrawg slamming about in her room. Simms, who knows? It's raining out."

"Heavy?" He crossed to the door that led onto the balcony, unbarred it and swung it open. Enjoying the cool bite of the mist blowing in under the overhang, he stood in the doorway, listening to the rain, watching the gray lines slant through the patch of light from the lamp behind him. Across the garden court on the third floor of the other wing, he could see strips of yellow light tracing out shutters and balcony doors. A few patrons must be still up or sleeping with nightlights. "It doesn't look that bad."

"Does rain make a difference?"

"Short of a cloudburst, no problem, except we'll end up wet as the Godalau. If the S'sulan are as wiped out as you all think, the rain and the chill will keep them inside, make it easier for us. The S'wai?" A shrug. "The little I know about witches doesn't help much. Can't expect everybody to be sleeping sound, but rain does tend to wash away alertness. Something we'd better keep in mind too." He pulled the door shut, looked at his chron. "Go see if the others are ready, it's time to move."

5

Since she'd be a drain, not an asset, in this part of their plan, Trithil Esmoon stayed behind; she'd keep busy packing the gear and shifting it into Danny's room and covering for them if the S'sulan, the Inn's Host, or anyone else developed an unhandy curiosity. Felsrawg and Simms stepped onto Danny's peculiar version of a flying carpet and crouched uneasily behind him as it rose and hovered in the thick damp darkness inside the room; it swung round, hovered some more, then it glided forward, sliding through the balcony door with a hair's clearance on both sides. Trithil pulled the door closed and barred it again as the mattress curved up and around, then darted for the island called the Henanolee Heart.

The rain battered at them, the sled danced and shivered, dropped with sickening jerks and surged up again as the wind bucked under it, snatched at it, sucked air from around it, under it. The darkness was smothering, no stars, no moon, no lights anywhere around them. Danny crouched over the console, flying by the numbers; he was uneasy about the uncertainties involved, but there was nothing else he could do. When the counters showed the readings he'd been watching for, he slowed the sled until it inched along, hardly moving. Still he saw nothing, only the lines of rain a handspan in front of him, faintly visible in the flickering lights of the console. Wary of snags he crept closer and closer to the Henanolee, peering into the darkness ahead of him, straining to see the walls and the towers. Finally he made out the thickening in the darkness he was expecting; he took the sled up a meter and slid across the top of the curtain wall.

He brushed against the side of one of the towers, a few of its bricks shimmering ghostlike at the edges of the glimmer from the console, eased around that tower, slid past another and took the sled down until it hovered an armlength above the grass in the Meditation Garden at the center of the Henanolee. After another handful of minutes inching along past trees and shrubs and less identifiable obstacles, he found what he'd been looking for, a small open hermitage in a group of willows. He nudged the sled inside and relaxed when he saw that the rain didn't penetrate the thick vines growing up the lath walls; he wasn't too sure how well the liftsled would operate if it were sodden, his Reshaped circuits and crystals swimming in rainwater. He lowered the sled to the flags, shut down all drain from the powersinks except for the trickle required to keep the console lit. He wanted to see their faces, to make sure they knew what his limitations were; reminders never hurt, no matter how well your co-workers knew the drill. "We're shielded," he said, "Don't move more than five paces from me unless I tell you to."

Felsrawg snorted.

On the other hand, worrying at things could be counter-productive.

"All right, forget it. Let's go." He touched off the console lights, got to his feet and followed the two thieves as they moved quickly and surely through the darkness; he was impressed, more than impressed as he tried to imitate them but kept getting switched across the face by wet branches and stumbling over unseen rocks and roots.

Felsrawg and Simms waited for him by the door they'd chosen as the best way into the Heart itself. When he joined them under the stubby overhang that kept the rain off the top steps, Felsrawg thrust her left hand at him; the skry rings were glowing faintly. "Wards. The knots are here, here and here." She pointed to places on the wall, one on each side of the door, one below it; as she moved her hands, the rings pulsed rhythmically. "Sloppy, Laz. Old stuff. Want me to shut them down?" She patted her belt pouch. "I've got some smothers I've used ten years now without a smell of trouble."

Danny Blue read the knots; Felsrawg was right, the wards were old and ragged, fading even as they stood there. He could untie and reset them between one breath and the next; the trouble was, he couldn't know how they were linked into the witchtraps inside, if they were. "Simms? Any complications?"

"No."

Terse, Danny thought. Hmm. Smothers are neutral things. Why not. "All right, Felsa, go ahead."

She ran her hand carefully over the bricks and the stone threshold, pinning down the exact location of the knots. When she knew what she had to know, she formed three nubs of clay, slapped them in place, shoved a tiny crackle-sphere like a cooked glass marble into the soft clay; she worked so swiftly the three smothers were in with no discernible gap between the sets, zap, zap, zap. She ran her rings around the door, nodded with satisfaction when the stones didn't even flicker.

Simms flattened his hand against the bricks. "Good job," he murmured, "you want to take the lock or shall I?"

Felsrawg grinned at him. "Make yourself useful, little man."

6

The empty corridor had no traps in it until they reached the first turn. No traps but ghosts like ragged bedsheets drifting around, oozing up through the floor and vanishing through the ceiling, or dropping down to sink like spilled milk into the elaborate parquet, or sweeping back and forth across the hall before and behind the intruders, passing through the darkwood wall panels like fog slipping through unglazed windows. Watchghosts supposed to warn the watchwitches if they saw a wrongness in the halls.

Simms sang:

Swingle, tingle ghostee bayyy beee,
dance y' shroudee, mama mine oh,
timber time-bar, aren't y' prettee,
round around the troudee tree oh,
swingle mingle pattartateee,
diddle doo dih dee dee dee. . . .

His droning endless song was an insect buzz in the gray light, a crooning tenor buzz that was irresistible, it seemed, to all those ghosts. He sang:

Pittaree pattaree prettee ghostee,
prithee dance a shingaree
round and round in silkee laces
dance the laughee lovee thee. . . .

Words, Talent, song, a mix of all three, whatever it was, it worked. Simms charmed the ghosts into a complex dance and kept them so occupied with his nonsense they forgot to issue the warnings they were meant to give.

At the corner, Felsrawg lifted her hand to stop them, rings flickering.

Simms leaned against the wall, closed his eyes, his face blank, cheeks drawn in, mouth pursed. His hands drifted through small circular movements, unfocused, apparently uncoordinated. The ghosts drifted around him; now and then they nuzzled against him like cats bumping their heads against him, begging for a scratch behind the ears, but he'd tamed them so thoroughly he could take his attention away and still keep them focused on them, fascinated by him. He sighed, opened his eyes and moved away from the wall. Holding his voice to a murmur that fell dead two paces off, he said, "Triple trap. Firs' part, five steps on, the floor melt under you, jus' 'nough to let y' sink up to y' nuts, then she get solid and you stuck. Second part. Rack of scythe blades taller'n a man they swing down fro the ceilin', set s' close together it take a snake standin' on his tail to pass 'em, sharp 'nough to mince a bull. They come at you the min y' start sinkin', no time t' jump back and if y' did, you jump into the points of those blades. An' y' canna jump for'ard, f'r one thing, you couldna get a hold and you wouldna go anywhere 'cause you'd hit the third part. There some kind of pipe there shoots out fire from down where the islands was born; the firemountains come up underwater. Down where Coquoquin sleeps, y' know. If y' wan' a worse-case event, the roarin' of the fire wake the god. The fire it crisp what left after the scythes finish. Fifteen feet, you past it all, Laz. Count four lamp down, halfway to the next. Anythin' else?"

"Solid beyond?"

"Yeh, for three-four feet. That's far as I can reach."

"Got it. You know the drill, grab on." Danny grunted as Felsrawg wrapped one arm about his biceps and shoved her other hand down behind his belt. Simms attached himself less impetuously but as firmly. Danny concentrated, tapped into the power stored in the flesh-accumulators, then snapped himself and the two thieves to the fifth lamp down. They landed heavily, Danny staggered, stood trembling as the other two unwrapped themselves and started on, both of them as matter-of-fact as if they did this kind of thing every day. It was a minute before he could follow them; he hadn't been all that sure he could handle the weight and the complications of transporting them all together while he kept the shield intact. He'd half expected to fall short and end fried by that earthfire. He wiped the sweat off his face, caught up with that pair of idiots before they left the protection of the shield and hissed anathemas at them for their carelessness. Felsrawg laughed silently at him, patted his arm, then went back to work.

They moved on in a flickering grayness, the nightlamps burning at intervals too wide to do more than dent the dark, down and down in a jagged spiral with witchtraps in every flat, some double, some triple, all lethal to any intruder without the resources of the team. Danny Blue was surprised at how well it was working. Felsrawg and Simms were like hostile cats circling each other and neither of them had much opinion of him and he was not all that fond of them, who could be? They were primed to kill him once things calmed down and the job was done, but now they clicked, they were amazing; every step he took, he felt better about this project. Down and down they went, down and down to the earth-chamber of the Henanolee Heart.

Felsrawg was first again, senses taut, knives ready, dustpipe charged and clipped to her belt, her ring hand swaying in broad arcs before her.

She was fierce, intent, silent. In an ordinary house she'd be unstoppable. Not here. Single traps she had no problems with, but her rings weren't subtle enough to detect doubles and triples twisted inextricably together.

Simms followed close behind her, fingers brushing the paneling, reading the flow as he moved, his tenor buzz going on and on, nonsense to amuse and distract any ghost that might take a notion to flash ahead and alert the watchwitches that intruders were wandering the hallways. Though Felsrawg's rings were more sensitive than his natural talent, warning of traps and hidden alarums long before Simms was aware of them, once they reached whatever it was, he was able to read the nature and extent of the trap from the walls and floor; even the ambient air breathed information into him when he was working at peak. The bumbling idiocy he wore as an everyday mask had dropped away, the lazy amiability had vanished; he was a deadly and efficient predator.

Danny Blue kept close behind, holding the shield tight about them, containing the psychic noise of their progress, lifting them again and again across the witchtraps he could not see. Again and again, sweating each time over his limitations. If he had all of Ahzurdan's old skills he could jump straight to the Heart, bypassing all the nasty surprises. He didn't have them; what he had was a team of two thieves whose natural talents and hard-earned skill and, yes, some handy tools here and there, acted as a blind man's white canes, showing him what he couldn't see. What a team, he chanted to himself, what a team, too bad we can't stand each other. What a team. What a team.

Down and down they went, around the great spiral that screwed itself deep into the earthen center of the island, down and around until they stood at the end of the corridor looking into the Henanolee Heart.

7

The Heart was a six-sided brick-walled chamber with a domed roof. It was sunk in an opening carved into the living stone with the space between the chamber and the stone packed with tons of fine hard clay; in that clay, huge serpentine entities not-quite and not-quite-not elementals lay wrapped around the chamber, drowsing in a rest-state that was not-quite sleep. Each of the chamber walls had three arches in it, all but one with that off-white earth filling the bared space, openings where the serpents could emerge if they chose to, where they would emerge to crush any unwary intruder. The floor was white marble veined with gold, a Hexa of ruddy gold inlaid in it, a six-pointed star drawn around one circle and within another. In the inner circle was a low four-sided dais of white marble with three shallow steps on each side; on the dais was a black marble cube, its sides mirror smooth, reflecting the light from the gold-and-crystal lamps on each post of the brick arches. There was another lamp, larger; it hung in a webbing of gold chains from the apex of the dome, a crystal sphere with a source-less gold flame burning in its heart.

Kluskesharna lay on the unadorned top of the cube, small, unobtrusive, an irregular strip of black iron no longer than a man's hand.

Felsrawg looked at her rings, shuddered. She held up her hand; the stones were on fire with warning.

Simms touched his temple, squeezed his brows together; his eyes were filled with pain. Like Felsrawg, he said nothing. He'd stopped his song a few turns back, the ghosts had abandoned him, they didn't like it down here.

Danny nodded. He waved them back into the shadows of the HeartWay and stood in the arch looking across the chamber at the cube. The air was thick with wards; to his mindeye it was like reflections off seawater cast on a white wall, pulsing angular loops of light. He contemplated the chaos, trying to decide what to do. He could wipe them away, it wouldn't be hard. Trouble was he had a notion that was all it'd take to wake the serpents. He didn't want to do that.

In the end it was simple. Tiring, yes, tedious, yes, but simple. The Ahzurdan phasma shivered with a mix of tension and fear; at first the Daniel phasma resisted everything he saw, then he got interested as he associated the wards with the control systems he knew better than the configuration of his own palms; he had an intuitive understanding of interactive systems, it was one of the talents that made him among the best of the stardrive engineers, and when he got bored with that, one of the best com-offs around. Daniel Akamarino's talent and training melded with Ahzurdan's encyclopedic knowledge of wardforms told Danny Blue in exhaustive detail exactly what he had to do. He picked up the wards one by one and eased them aside, clearing a path to the cube; he didn't untie them or alter them in any essential way, he simply unhooked them from each other, rehooked them into another configuration. Like playing jackstraws with exploding straws. Simple. And oh so tedious.

Heat built up under the shield; it was trapped there; he didn't dare let it dissipate and wake the serpents. He might be able to handle them, but the battle to do it would most likely wake Coquoquin and a newly wakened god was bound to be cranky, a newly wakened god who found intruders messing around with one of her toys would escalate from crankiness to downright irritation. His voice went hoarse under the strain, his hands wanted to tremble, but that too he couldn't afford, the gestures had to be smooth and controlled or he'd blow a ward which would be a lot worse than leaking a little heat. He ground his teeth together, blinked as perspiration dripped into his eyes. Felsrawg startled him dangerously when she swabbed at his forehead, but he managed to spare her a smile, then went back to work.

An hour slid past. The clear passage drove deeper and deeper into the chamber. The serpents moved, he could feel them shifting, they were drifting up out of their vast placid slumber, drifting into dreamstate and uneasiness, crumbs of dirt broke from the earthfaces in the archways, there was a deep grumble in the earth around them, almost too low for his ears to hear it. Time and danger pressed down on him. Hurry, hurry, hurry. . . .

He resisted. The steady tedious untangling went on and on. Hurry hurry hurry . . . heads turned in the earth, blind eyes turned toward him, they weren't awake yet, but they were beginning to dream of him. Hurry hurry hurry. . . .

The path was clear. Eyes fixed on Klukesharna, Danny thrust out his left hand. Simms put the false Klukesharna in it. Cold and heavy, black iron copy. Dead iron. He looked at Felsrawg, waited while she wiped his face dry again. Arm held stiffly straight, he brought the false Klukesharna around in front of him. Lips drawn back in a feral grin, he bled the waste heat under the shield into the copy, giving it a false life. When the heat was sucked into the iron, he jerked his head toward the shadowy darkness up the HeartWay and waited until Simms and Felsrawg had retreated as far as they dared.

He let energy build up in his hands, then let the chant roll through his mind, though he didn't dare speak it aloud. The words poured silently out of him, wrote themselves in black and red in front of him. He opened his hand, holding the false Klukesharna in the crease between thumb and palm, the bitt hooked over his thumb. The words roared in his head, built to a mighty shout like a spill of black ink thrown across in front of him. The "key" jolted against his palm so hard he almost dropped it. He closed his fingers and felt Klukesharna recognize him, accept him. The exchange was made.

He swung round, two pairs of eyes were watching him avidly. He put Klukesharna in a doubly shielded leather pouch, hung it around his neck and tucked it inside his vest. With an impatient gesture, he urged the two thieves up the Way. Behind him he heard creaks and groans as the serpents stirred again. Felsrawg shivered, glanced at her rings, wheeled and started up the ramp. Simms was slower to look away, but even more than Felsrawg he felt the building danger. He caught up with her, walked half a pace behind her, ready to read the traps again because there was a good chance they'd be asymmetric, entirely different when approached from the other side.

Danny tightened down the shield until his own senses were tied in and he had to depend almost entirely on his companions.

Asymmetry. They couldn't trust anything they'd learned on the way down. Safe areas were no longer safe, the walls, the ceiling were set to erupt, they moved slower and slower until they were barely crawling. There was only one easing in the strain as they circled past the second coil of the HeartWay, the serpents were sinking back to sleep; that lessened the odds on Coquoquin waking and destroying whatever chance they had of getting away. Again and again and again Danny snapped himself and the others across the traps; again and again and again he Transformed air into a solid dome over them so they wouldn't trigger the walls and the ceiling; again and again he poured energy out of his stores until they were empty and he was feeding on himself.

Up and around they went until they reached the ground floor and moved through the hallways toward the door into the garden. Danny kept a wary eye on his companions; they weren't going to do anything yet, not until they were out of this place, they weren't fools, but afterward . . . he'd better not play the fool either. Gods, he was tired.

A man came from one of the rooms, a servant of some kind, yawning, unhurried. His eyes opened wide as he saw them, his mouth opened to yell. A knife hilt bloomed in his throat. Felsrawg stooped as she came up with him, pulled the knife loose, avoiding the gush of blood with a minimum of effort. She wiped the blade on the dead man's tunic, straightened and slid the knife into an arm sheath. She barely broke stride as she did all this.

Danny Blue watched grimly; in less than twenty minutes he was going to be sitting on the liftsled with that at his back.

They reached the door without further trouble. The man Felsrawg killed was the only person they saw during the whole time they were in the Henanolee. Once they were outside, Felsrawg collected her smothers, threw the clay out into the garden where the drizzle would melt it into the grass, then moved at a quick trot through the dark, heading for the hermitage. Simms loped after her, content to let her take the lead. Danny followed more slowly, loosening the shield a little to choke off some of the drain on his strength. He ached to stretch out and sleep for a year. In a while, he told himself, don't let down yet, you've got what you wanted, now you have to keep it. He fashioned a cherry-sized will-o, dropped it down near his feet so he could see where he was walking; he was in no mood to flop on his face or stub his toes on roots or rocks. He trudged after them, muttering curses at the drizzle soaking into his clothes and trickling down his neck.

At the entrance to the hermitage, Danny kicked the will-o up and into the darkness ahead, held his left hand canted before his face, palm out. "VRESH," he shouted, the command shunting aside the spurt of dust aimed at his eyes; he continued the shunting gesture with an outsnap of his arm. "SOV," he chanted, curling his fingers tight against his palm, all but one which he pointed at Felsrawg who was leaping at him, knives ready. She dropped, unconscious. He turned his glare on Simms who was leaning against the lathwork, arms crossed, no apparent interest in what was happening.

Simms unfolded his arms, held his hands level with his shoulders, palm out. "Nothin' to do with me."

"Keep it that way. Load her on the sled."

"Y' got it." He gathered up Felsrawg, laid her on the pallet, started to straighten.

Danny curled his fingers again, snapped out the forefinger, pointing at the middle of Simms' back. "Sov," he murmured. He smiled as Simms collapsed across Felsrawg. "There it is," he said aloud. "I should leave the pair of you right here. Let the Wokolinka play with you. Ah hell, I wouldn't leave a rabid rat to face torture. Shut up, Sorcerer," he told the Ahzurdan phasma, who started protesting vehemently as Danny rearranged the unconscious pair so he'd have room to sit at the console. "I don't give a handful of hot shit what you want." The Daniel phasma watched with amiable satisfaction and more than a touch of self-congratulation at seeing his semi-son adopt his ethics over those of his rival and co-sire. Angry at both of them, Danny fed power into the lift field. "Let's get out of here."

8

Danny Blue set the raft down on the balcony outside the door to his room. Before he could knock, it swung open and Trithil Esmoon came out. She raised her brows, mimed a question.

"We got it," he said. "Any trouble here?"

"Not even an insomniac roach." She looked past him at Felsrawg and Simms. "They dead?"

"Them?" He shook his head. "Sleeping." He glanced at his chron. "Be dawn in an hour or so, we won't wait. I think I can nurse this thing as far as the horses. Once the Wokolinka wakes up to what happened, she's going to shut this city down and shake it hard."

#

Working quickly, they loaded the gear onto the pallet, stowing it about the recumbent figures of the two thieves. Trithil Esmoon produced a reel of silk cord and helped Danny rope the pouches in place. She started to tie Felsrawg's ankles, but Danny stopped her. "No need," he said. "They'll both be out till around mid-morning."

She straightened, gave him a small tight smile. "Me?"

"Keep your hands to yourself."

She twiddled her fingers and laughed at him, her eyes flirted at him, very blue even in the dim fringes of the lamplight. "A promise, I swear it. Until you ask, Laz."

"Take off your rings."

"What?"

"Take them off or join Felsrawg and Simms."

"I gave you my word."

"Fine. Now, put the rings away."

She looked at him a moment, looked away. "If I must." She folded back her left sleeve, stripped the rings off her fingers and thumb, dropping them into the hem-pocket and turned the sleeve back to fall in graceful points about her knuckles. "Are you satisfied?"

He grunted. "You'll sit on my left, that arm away from me."

The door was still open, the pale yellow light streaming out to lose itself in the drizzle. She stood in the light, her body outlined by it, her fine hair shining like silver silk. The yellow light slid off her elegant cheek, put a liquid glimmer between her lashes, gilded her upper lip, her chin. She was unreal, beauty like that was unreal. He stared at her; he was tired, so tired he was looking at her through a haze. He had no desire for her, no need to touch to take her. He simply looked and kept on looking because he couldn't turn away. Her hands were lifted, unmoving yet indescribably graceful in their stillness. She dropped them to her sides and the spell was broken.

"Climb on," he said. "Be with you in a minute." He turned his back on her and went to the end of the sled. As she settled herself in front of the pouches, he squatted beside the energy sinks. Despite having to wrestle stormwinds during the trips to and from the Henanolee Heart, the sled hadn't used much power; the sinks were still two-thirds full. He was the empty one, exhausted in both senses of the word. He flattened his hands over the cells, drew power from them into his own accumulators; he'd bleed it off later, use it to wash out some of the fatigue poisons clogging his mind and body. He had to stay awake; had to watch the trau Esmoon. He trusted Trithil Esmoon less than the thieves, though her weapons were easier to combat—as long as he kept away from those venomous rings. He broke the contact and stood.

The rain had diminished in force until it was hardly more than a heavy mist. The towers rising around the Inn were dark; he couldn't see the streets, but he knew from the silence that they too were dark and empty; the island was sunk in its end-of-season weariness. There were no lights anywhere—except in his bedroom. He scowled, snapped his fingers, muttered a *word;* the lamps went out, making the dark complete. He wiped fog off his face, walked briskly to the front of the sled and settled himself behind the console.

9

The sled broke through into a silver-gray world of moonlight and starlight and boiling cloud floor. It was cold up there above the rain. Danny shivered, sneezed, swore. He released energy into his body, flushing out some of his fatigue, reinforcing his immunities. It was no time to catch a cold, he had enough problems with that poison eating at him. And three efficiently murderous companions.

It was as quiet as it was cold, as if they flew in a reality all their own, as if they were the only beings alive in it. His eyelids grew heavy, it was harder and harder to stay awake though he knew if he slept with Trithil there, sitting loose and ready, he'd wake up hitting the water below. He blinked at the direction-finder, made a small adjustment to the course and sat scowling at his hands because he didn't want to scowl at Trithil and let her guess what he was thinking.

"Lazul." Fingers touched his arm.

He looked down, then at her. "Hands in your lap, if you don't mind."

She dropped her eyes, looked momentarily distressed—which he didn't believe at all. "Do you know the attributes of Klukesharna?"

"Why?"

"She cleanses and heals. She unlocks possibility. If you use her properly, she will leach the poison out of you."

"And you, of course."

"Oh no, for me there's no need. I came into this under other pressures."

"Oh?"

"Which I do not plan to enumerate."

"Then why'd you say that?"

"I don't want to go back to Arsuid." She bit her lip, stared unhappily at a heap of clouds rising like whipped cream in front of them, a little off to one side. He watched her, appreciating the performance. It was flawless, but he didn't believe a word or a nuance. "I want Klukesharna." Her voice was low and musing, liquid lovely tones blending with the nearly inaudible hum of the liftfield. "I think it will be easier to take it from you than from the Ystaffel. I'll do whatever I can to get us beyond Coquoquin's reach, you can trust that, Lazul or whatever your name is. I don't play games with gods, they make up the rules as they go and the rules always favor them." She smiled at him, her blue eyes even bluer in the light from the console. "Like the Ystaffel, in their despicable way. There isn't any antidote, did you know that?"

"I suspected it."

"I'm a fool." She shook her silver head. "You planned all along to use Klukesharna." She brooded a moment, then looked startled. "Even the fight over the horses? Twisty man." A trill of laughter, another shake of her head. "You conned them. Got them to set up relay mounts at five stages along the river. You aren't going to use any but the ones at Kuitse-ots, are you. The rest are dust in the eyes."

He shrugged. "Whatever happened, I'd need transport. Horses can go where you point them, a river sticks to its bed. What are you?"

"Why do you say that?"

"A Great Talisman is useless to most people, except for its symbolic value. And when I say symbolic value, I do not mean gold; you haven't a hope of selling it. And you'd have to be witch, wizard, magus or sorcerer to milk its power. You're none of those. We know our own kind. We smell the Talent on those that have it. And none of the Talented would follow your particular profession or, to be blunt, be any good at it. You're very good."

"I don't see why you say that. I'm no good with you."

"Circumstances, trau Esmoon. The discipline of my craft. You did some fancy footwork round my question. What are you?"

"Call me a visitor who wants to go home."

"Demon?"

"It's a matter of definition, isn't it. I prefer visitor."

"No doubt." He spoke absently. There was a new note in the field hum, a whine that appeared and disappeared, appeared again. His Re-shaping was starting to unravel. He scowled at the counter; the reading said they'd come about twenty kilometers, which meant Waystop Kuitse-ots was still about ten kilometers off. It'd be a long walk if he had to set he sled down now, though at least they were finally over land not water. The whine started again, louder this time; it was like a circular saw chewing through hardwood.

"What's happening?"

"Nothing much, trau Esmoon. It's just we're about to be sitting on a flocking mattress with the flying characteristics of a rock." He put the sled into a long slant, took it down through the clouds, down and down, laboring, making horrible noises, down and down until it lurched along five feet off the ground. The rain had stopped, the air was chill and damp and gray with dawn. He leveled the sled and sent it forward at its maximum speed. "Keep watch for me. I can't leave this. Yell if we're going to hit something solid. Can you see in this murk?"

"I can see. Yell what?"

"How the hell do I know? Think of something."

"What about a road?"

"You see one?"

"No."

"Don't bother me then. Keep your mouth shut till you got some-thing to say." A crack crept in jags across the face of the console, moving between gauges and readouts. He smelled burning feathers, swore at the sled, willing it to keep its shape. As he fought the dissolu-tion, he gave an ear to Trithil's murmurs.

"Tree, swing right. Good. Missed it. Another tree . . . wait . . . wait . . . swing left . . . now! Missed it. Brush ahead, don't bother turning, we'll scrape over it, no problem . . . I think. . . ." The sled lurched and there was a loud crackling as they sheared the top inch off several bushes. Then they were clear. "Oh. There is a road, Laz. Angle about thirty degrees to your right. Good, you've got it. This must be the post road, it's graveled and ditched."

Danny Blue was too busy to answer her. He drew power from the sinks and sent it coursing through the frame to hold the Reshaping as long as he could; on and on the sled went, slowing as the crystals deteriorated, dropping lower and lower until they barely cleared the gravel. Two kilometers, five, seven, eight . . . then they were crawling along, moving as fast as a man could walk with arthritis and a broken leg. He held it together and held it . . . nine . . . nine and a half. . . . With a flare of light as the remaining energy stored in the sinks was released, the sled turned to mush under him; the rags of the Transforms vanished like dry ice sublimating. The sled jolted to the ground, throwing him onto a console that dissolved into charred cloth and smoldering feathers.

##

Danny got to his feet, brushing bits of feather off his vest. The pallet was a sodden mess. Simms had rolled over onto Felsrawg and was snoring heavily. Felsrawg lay with limbs sprawling, head rolled back, breathing through her mouth; she was alive but not lovely. Slimy with rain and mud, the silk cord had slipped off several of the pouches; they'd tumbled over the two thieves and spilled into the ditch at the side of the road. Elegant and immaculate, silver slippers unsmutched by the mud and the gelid dew coating every surface, Trithil Esmoon was standing on the gravel, sniffing fastidiously at the unsavory scene.

The sky was heavily overcast, but the rain had stopped—for the moment at least. The east was bloody with sunrise and there was enough light to see for some distance around. Low brush grew in mangy patches on the far side of the ditch. A scatter of wild plum trees with naked branches poked from the brush. There were other patches of trees dotted about the rolling grasslands, dull trees with a few mud-brown leaves still clinging to their branches. Across the road there was a low stone wall, a field of withered yellow-brown grass with a herd of dun cattle grazing in the distance. There were no houses or other buildings anywhere in sight, though the Waystop should be less than half a mile south along the road.

Danny rubbed the back of his neck as he looked round at the dreary land. Empty land. "Stay here. I'll bring the horses back."

"No. I don't think so."

"What?"

"You understand me. Where the talisman goes, I go."

"You think I wouldn't come back?"

"Lazul, ah Laz."

"Hmm." He squatted beside the pallet, opened one of the pouches, looked inside, dropped that one and picked up another. When he found his own, he began pulling things out, transferring and discarding until he had what he wanted in one pouch. He tied on a blanket roll, frowned. He undid the straps on another roll and shook out the blankets. He started to drop them over Felsrawg and Simms, changed his mind and got to his feet. "Help me shift them onto the pallet, straighten them out some."

"Why?"

"Do it."

"Needn't be so prickly, Laz, I was just asking what you intended for them." She waited while he dumped the gear off the pallet and spread out the blankets in its place; wrinkling her nose with distaste, she grasped Felsrawg's ankles and helped move her onto the blankets, then straightened and watched with avid curiosity as Danny fussed with the thief's clothing, opening her shirt at the neck, pulling loose awkward twists and catches. He folded her hands over her ribs, put a wadded shirt under her head. "You're laying her out like a corpse, you expect her to be one?"

"Sooner or later, we're all corpses."

"Speak for yourself, mortal man."

He grunted. "Help me move Simms."

When Danny had Simms straightened out and positioned, he covered them both, shoulder to feet, with more blankets, tucked the edges under them. He collected their gear and piled it around them.

"This is a waste of time, you know," Trithil said. "They'll be after us as soon as they wake."

"Take a walk, I'll catch up with you."

"Haven't you something to do first?"

"What?"

"Klukesharna. The poison."

"Klukesharna stays where she is as long as I'm in Lewinkob lands. The moment I take her from the shielding, Coquoquin will be here. You want that?"

She shuddered. "No indeed." She collected her own gear, slid the

pouch strap over her shoulder. "No, that would be a very bad thing."
She looked down at the sleepers. "You said mid-morning."

"Take a walk. Now."

"It's stupid not to kill them now."

"You want to join them?"

"You think you could handle me like that?"

"You want to find out?"

"Don't be a fool, I'm on your side, man."

"Nice to know. You've got two seconds to start walking or I drop
you."

She shrugged. "You could try, but that'd likely bring Coquoquin and
I'd lose a lot more. All right. Be sure you do come. I can get very
unpleasant when I'm disappointed."

He watched her walk away. I bet you can, he thought. He looked
down at Felsrawg and Simms. She's right, you'll be after me, you've
got no choice, but I'm not a murderer and I don't plan to become one.
I'll play the game my own way and take my chances. However, there's
no point being a total fool. He shut his eyes, thought a moment, then
began weaving a stasis web about them, once again melding the experience of his two half-sires, crafting a dome over them that would hold
them unmoving and untouchable for the next several days. He wasn't
all that sure exactly how long the stasis would last, two days or a week,
it didn't matter, he was buying himself time to get out of Lewinkob
lands and free the talisman to his uses. After that, let them try.

The sun had cleared the peaks of the Dhia Asatas, the wind was
shredding the clouds and exposing patches of sky; the day wasn't
brightening so much as pushing the horizon back. The land around
him was brown and gray and blanched, even the naked sky looked
dingy. Danny shouldered his gear, breathed in that chill air and felt
suddenly lighter than those vanishing clouds. Klukesharna was his and
in a day or so the poison would be out of him, he was free, finally free
of the Chained God's hook and on the way to reclaiming his Talent.
Whistling a tune from one of Daniel's more ancient memories, he
started after Trithil.

THE REBIRTHING: PHASE THREE
The stones are moving.

I: BRANN/JARIL

Having run full out into the geniod trap, Brann and Jaril are on their way to Havi Kudush to steal Churrikyoo from the Great Temple of Amortis so they can ransom Yaril from the grip of Palami Kumindri and her coterie.

1

The Mutri-mab went skipping about the deck of the pilgrim barge, holy fool in whiteface and fluttering ribbons. He leaped to the forerail and capered perilously back and forth on that narrow slippery pole, then struck a pose. When he was satisfied with the attention he had drawn to himself, he began beating two hardwood rods together, making a staccato melodious background to his chant. "Hone your wit," he sang in a powerful tenor:

> *Hone your wit with alacrity*
> *Romp and revel, gaiety*
> *Wait for thee, for us*
> *In Havi*
> *Kudush*
> *Ah sing Amortis*
> *More ah more ah more than this*
> *Ecstasy, amour and bliss*
> *Ah, ah Amortis, she*
> *Waits for thee, for us*
> *In Havi*
> *Kudush*
> *Don your slippers, dance for me*
> *Tipsy wanton jubilee*

Waits for thee, for us
In Havi
Kudush
Ah sing Amortis
More ah more a more than this
Ecstasy, amour and bliss. . . .

Brann pulled the heavy black veil tighter about her and wondered how stupid she was, coming here into Amortis' heartland. The two times she'd run into Amortis, she and the Blues, Yaril and Jaril had combined to whip the tail of the god. Her only hope was evading Amortis' notice. Unfortunately, the way things had worked out, it was near the end of the pilgrimage season and she didn't have masses of people to vanish into. Jaril stirred against her leg; since pilgrims didn't travel with watchpets, he couldn't be a hound again, nor could he continue as her M'darjin page, servants weren't permitted in Havi Kudush—not as servants, though they could come as pilgrims. So he was being her invalid son; the disguise concealed his oddities and provided an excuse for her.

She stroked his soft hair, smiled down at him, understanding all too well his impatience, his restlessness. He wanted Yaril freed as soon as possible. He wanted to fly in, take the talisman and rush back to trade it for his sister. He knew he couldn't do that, but the need was always there, an itch under his skin. And there were other strains, things she felt in him but couldn't find a way to ask about. There was an uneasiness in him now, needs that were growing toward explosion. She remembered his outburst in the cave and was furious at her helplessness. There was nothing she could do to ease him. She listened with half an ear to the chant swelling about her, the chorus of the paean to Amortis the Mutri-mab was singing. She joined in that chorus after a few minutes because she didn't want to be conspicuous in her silence. Not just worry about Yaril. Puberty, he said, a kind of puberty. He needs his people, he's ripe for mating, but Yaril's the only female of his kind in this reality. His more than sister, his twin. It's a recipe for disaster, she thought, one might even say tragedy. No more procrastination, I have to see them home. Even thinking about it hurt so much, she knew she'd bleed until she was empty when that knot was broken; two hundred years, more, they'd been her children, her nurslings, bonded to her mind and body. But what choice had she? Children leave you. That's the way things are.

Jaril sensed something of her trouble, nestled closer, trying to comfort her without words.

"Not much longer," she said. Her voice was lost in the singing of the other passengers, but even if one of them heard her, it'd mean nothing; it was the kind of thing anyone would say.

Have you figured out how, Bramble? There was a tinge of bitterness in the mindvoice; he trusted her, but he was afraid of Amortis and deeply angry at Maksim for letting them down.

"Don't," she murmured. "There are ears who can hear that shouldn't." She sighed. "No, I haven't. I don't know enough. Look ahead, Jay, there's the Holy Rock, we'll be there by dawn. We'll look around and see what's what."

The Rock rose like a broaching whale out of the stony plain—the Tark—that stretched from the misty reedmarsh where three rivers met to the southern reaches of the Dhia Asatas. At the highest point of the Rock, the three-tiered Sihbaraburj thrust up black and massive against the sunset. Above it the sky was still dark blue with poufs of cloud dotted across it, clouds that ranged from a pale coral overhead to vermilion in the west where the sun floated in a sea of molten gold. Havi Kudush the holy city. Harmony-tongued Kudush where pious hands hauled in tons and tons of warm gold bricks and laid them in a thousand thousand courses, brick on brick, slanted inward to make the three-step, truncated pyramid that was the Sihbaraburj, Temple to Amortis, that was the Heart of Phras, a made-mountain honeycombed with twenty thousand chambers where the Priest-Servants lived, where the Holy Harlots made worship, where healers and seers made promises that were sometimes kept, where dancers and singers, song makers and music makers lived and worked, where there were artisans of all sorts, goldsmiths and silversmiths, workers in bronze and copper, gem cutters and stone cutters, potters and weavers, painters, embroiderers, lace makers and so on, all of them creating marvels for the honor of Amortis—and the coin they got from selling their work to pilgrims as offerings or souvenirs. Havi Kudush the holy city. Its feasts flow with fat and milk, its storehouses bring rejoicing. Fill your belly, the hymns command, day and night make merry, let every day be full of joy, dance and make music, this is the pure bright land where all things are celebrant and celebrated, dance and make music, praise Amortis bringer of joy, praise her in pleasure and delight.

The barge halted when the sun dropped out of sight, changed teams and went on. The draft oxen plodded steadily along the towpath, used to the dark as was the drover boy riding the offside ox, flicking his limber stick at the bobbing rumps when the plodding slowed too much. On the barge the pilgrims settled to sleep behind canvas windbreaks. The Mutri-mab sat on the forerail and played sleepy tunes on his flute. The river whispered along the sides, tinkling, shimmering murmurs that lied about the heaviness of the silt-laden water which in the daylight ran thick and red with the mud of three rivers and the marsh. Jaril lay wrapped in a blanket he neither needed nor wanted but wore like a mask to keep off the eyes of the other travelers. He was sunk in that coma he called sleep, a shutting down of his systems, a hoarding of the sunlight he drank during the day. Brann lay beside him, but she couldn't sleep.

Head down, she told herself. I'm a poor lorn widow with an invalid son; who am I to attract the notice of a god. I wish we were out of here. Too much land to cover. What happens if she feels it when we lope off with Churrikyoo? What happens if she comes after us? We haven't got Ahzurdan to shield us. What happened to Maksi? I wish he were here. I'd feel a lot better about this business. He must have put his foot in something. Idiot man, he's too soft for his own good. That skinny whore he's so fond of leads him around by the nose, well, not the nose . . . Slya! I'm jealous of that little . . . that . . . damn damn damn all gods, why does this happen to me on top of everything else? I thought I was over wanting him. She luxuriated a moment in her misery, squeezing tears from tight-closed eyes, then she sighed and let it go; there was no point in scraping her insides raw yearning for what she couldn't have. She'd got over having to leave Sammang, she'd got over Chandro, it just took time.

She lay brooding for some time longer until, eventually, she drifted into a restless sweating sleep.

2

Havi Kudush the Lower was reed and mud and narrow waterway, with clouds of black biters to chasten the proud and try the tempers of the intemperate. According to their natures and the choice available, the pilgrims spent the week they were allowed to stay in longhouse dormitories constructed from the ubiquitous reeds or in individual cells, also woven from the reeds; this late in the season there were many empty cells for those who preferred privacy.

The pilgrims were ferried to and from the Temple Landing by small shallow boats that scooted about the reeds like bright colored waterbeetles, poled by small and wiry marshboys whistling like birds when they weren't exchanging insults, nothing solemn about them however solemn and pious their passengers; they were the only way to get about and reaped coin like their elders reaped corn though the Temple taxed half of it away from them.

The barge landing was a stone platform at the edge of the marsh. The marsh elders had a tall reedhouse there, its front woven into intricate and elaborate patterns; morning light slid softly across the wall in an enigmatic calligraphy of shifting shadow and shades of yellow. In season, the elders sat at a table placed before the high, arching doorway, writing with reed pens on sheets of papyrus as they enrolled the pilgrims and passed out the clay credeens that gave them the freedom of the city for seven days.

There was only one old man at the table when Brann's barge tied up at the landing. He looked half-asleep, sour and dirty; his fingernails were black with dried muck, there was dirt ground into the lines of his hands, a yellow-gray patina of sweat and rancid oil over every inch of visible skin and there was a lot of skin visible since all he wore was a light brown wrap-skirt of reedcloth, bracelets of knotted reedcord, a complicated pectoral of palm-sized rounds of reedcord, knotted and woven in sacred signs. When Brann finally reached him after standing in line for over an hour, she almost gasped at the stench blowing into her face; for the first time since she'd donned it, she was grateful for the protection of the veil.

"The Baiar-chich Kisli Thok," she murmured, answering the questions he'd dumped on her in his drawling indifferent voice. "Of Dil Jorpashil. My son Cimmih Thok ya Tarral. We come to seek healing for him." Jaril sagged against her, looking wan and drawn, all eyes and bones, the essence of sickly, pampered youth. She set seven takks on the table before the elders, the fee for a private cell plus the fee for the credeens. It wasn't cheap, visiting the Temple at Havi Kudush.

Moving slow and slow and slower, the old man scratched her answers on the scroll; when he was finished he wiped the pen's nib on a smeared bit of cloth and inspected it, unhooked a small curved blade from his belt and shaved off a few slivers, repointing the pen to his exacting standards. He set it down, pulled over the stacks of silver coins and weighed each on a small balance. Satisfied he had the full measure of what was due, he set the coins in a box and blew a shrill summons on a small pipe. Behind her Brann could hear soft whuffs of relief; the harried weary pilgrims knew better than to complain about how long he was taking, but they fidgeted and sighed and otherwise made their discomfort known. He showed no sign he heard or saw any of that, simply pulled his inkpot closer and beckoned to the next in line.

A marshboy came trotting up, loaded Brann and Jaril and their gear into his poleboat; she was afraid the shallow boat was going to founder under their weight, but by some peculiarity of its construction it merely shuddered and seemed to squat marginally lower in the water. The marshboy hopped onto the platform at the stern, dug in his pole and pushed off.

Between one breath and the next he had the bright red shell flying across the open water where the river emerged from the marsh; then he took them scooting precariously through the winding waterways of the reed islands, sliding on thick red water moving sluggishly among shaggy reed clumps with their spiky leaves and finger-sized stems. Half new green growth stiff as bone and twice as high as a standing man, half dead, broken leaves and stems slowly collapsing into the muck they'd emerged from, the reed clumps creaked and rustled in the morning wind, a wind that Brann wished she could feel. Down near the water, in spite of the speed of their passage, the air was still and lifeless and far too warm. Swarms of marshbiters rose as they moved along the ways; most of them were left behind before they had a chance to settle; the marshboy seemed to know the route so well he could follow it in his sleep and keep flying too fast for the bugs, though Brann couldn't understand how he did it. One clump of reeds looked much like the next, the narrow channels were indistinguishable; she was lost before they'd gone through a handful of turns.

After twenty minutes the poleboat emerged into a more open area, a flat sheet of water dotted with hundreds of small island gathered in tight clusters about a much larger one; when they got closer she saw that the islands were reed mats mixed with mud, pinned in place by pilings made of bundled nai reeds; each island had a small cell built on it. A lacework of suspension foot-bridges linked the islands within the clusters and the clusters with each other. On the big island there were several longhouses like the house at the Landing.

To build a longhouse: Take tapering bundles of towering nai reeds and wrap reed cords about them until they look like fifty foot spikes, their butts three feet across at the base. Drive them into the mud an armstretch apart in two rows of ten spikes, angled out like massive awns from some gigantic ear of wheat. Bend the spike ends over and bind them together, each to each, to make ten parallel pointed arches. Lay thin reed bundles across the arches to act as stringers. Sew on overlapping split reed mats for siding. Move in.

To build a cell: Do likewise, only in less degree.

The marshboy took them to one of the outer islands, basing his decision on some obscure calculation involving sex, age, and dress. After Brann counted out the coins he demanded, he pointed at the longhouses. "Wan' t' eat, t's tha," he said. He was a little monkey of a boy, black eyes like licorice candy, a snub nose and a cheerful grin that bared teeth like small sharp chisels and turned his eyes to black-lined slits. "Need else, t's tha." He hopped back on the boat, pushed off and in seconds had vanished into the reeds.

The cell was raised waist-high off the cracking mud; there was an odd sort of contrivance that led from the flat up to a narrow platform built onto the front end of the structure; it was like a cross between the foot-bridges and a staircase and was just wide enough for one person at a time. It groaned and darted sideways as Brann stepped onto the first segment; she grabbed at the handrope before the rampladder threw her and climbed cautiously to the platform.

When she opened the door, she smelled every pilgrim who'd lived there that season and maybe a dozen before. "Slya's Armpits." She groaned, wedged the door open and lifted the shutter mats from the windowholes, propping them up with the sticks she found thrust into loops beside the holes. "Favor, Jay?"

He was leaning in the doorway, the nose erased from his face. "What about it maybe alerting you know who?"

"Hah! You're just lazy, luv. If she hasn't smelled you yet, she won't notice you crisping a few bugs and firewashing this sty. At least I hope not. How can you go looking for you-know-what if you can't change? Think of it as a test run."

3

Mid-afternoon. Veiled in opaque black, swathed in black robes, Brann trudged up the long ramp to the top of the Rock. Beside her Jaril was stretched out on a litter carried by two adult marshmen; wrapped in blankets, pale and beautiful with little flesh on elegant bones (a carefully crafted image since he had nothing remotely resembling bones), he lay like a fallen angel, crystal eyes closed to hide their strangeness, controlling his impatience with some difficulty. Brann felt the strain in him, took his hand. He relaxed a little, gave her a slight smile. And held her hand so tightly she knew she'd have bruises on her fingers. The link between them was tightening more and more as the days passed since Yaril was taken; it was as if he were trying to make her take Yaril's place. She refused to think about that or what would happen to Jay and her if they failed here; it was too troubling, she couldn't afford the distraction.

The ramp they were moving up was a broad roadway paved with the same warm yellow-ocher brick that the Sihbaraburj was made of; it was cut into the Rock, slanting up the entire length of its northern face, a slope of one in seven, steep enough to make the pilgrims sweat but not enough to exhaust them. No doubt it was an impressive sight at the height of the season when a hoard of incense waving, torch-bearing worshipers climbed that long slant with Mutri-mabs weaving through them, capering and singing, playing flutes and whirling round and round, round and round in a complex spiral dance up that holy road. In this late autumn afternoon, she was alone on the roadway with the litter bearers; she didn't like the exposure, she'd planned to wait for morning and the rest of the pilgrims, but Jaril was drawn too taut. He said nothing, but she knew he'd go without her if she forced him to a longer idleness. He'd go in a wild, reckless mood, risking everything on a chance of finding and taking the talisman. It was better to take the lesser risk of Amortis noticing them.

They reached the top after half an hour's climb and turned in through a towering stone gate carved to resemble the reed arches of the longhouses. They passed into a green and lovely garden with fountains playing everywhere, palms casting pointed shadows over lawns like priceless carpets and flowering plants in low broad jars glazed red and yellow and blue. The walkway curved between two wrought iron fences with razor-edged spearpoints set at close intervals along the top rail: Look and enjoy but don't touch.

The bearers stopped just outside the Grand Entrance to the Sihbaraburj. They set the litter down and squatted beside it to wait until it was time to go back down. The widow helped her ailing son onto his feet and stripped away the blankets wrapped around him. He wore fine silks and jewels and arrogance, an exquisite, emaciated mama's darling.

With Jaril leaning on Brann's arm, they went inside.

Light streamed in through weep-holes, was caught and magnified in hundreds of mirrors. There were mirrors everywhere inside that brick mountain, light danced like water from surface to surface, images were caught and repeated, tossed like the light from mirror to mirror until what was real and what was not-real acquired an equal validity. Brann wandered bemused in that warren of corridors and small plazas, walked through shimmering light and cool drifts of incense-laden air and marveled that she had no sense of being enclosed in tons of earth and brick; like image and reality there was a confusion between inside and out, a sense she was in a place not quite either. They moved past shops and forges, small chapels and waiting rooms; they were stopped when they poked into the living sections, escorted back to the shops when they claimed they were lost. The place was so big that in the three hours they spent probing the interior they saw only a minute fraction of it. As the day latened, the light inside the Sihbaraburj dimmed and filled with shadow, the shopkeepers worked more frantically to woo coin from the straggling pilgrims, the Servants in the Grand Chambers were bringing their ceremonies to a close.

Brann and Jaril stopped in front of a room filled with shadow; fugitive gleams of gold, silver and gemstones came from the glass shelves that lined the walls from floor to ceiling.

A servant was sitting at a table just inside the open archway, a scroll, several pens and an inkpot at his elbow. He lifted kohl-lined dark eyes and smiled just enough to tilt the ends of his narrow mustache as she stepped in. "Yes, khatra?"

"May I ask, Holy One, what is this?" She moved her hand in a small arc, indicating the objects on the shelves.

"They are gifts, khatra. Beauty to honor her who is beauty's self."

"Is it permitted to see them closer?"

"Certainly, khatra. However, it is so near to Evendown, it would be better to return on the morrow."

As soon as he said the last word, a gong sounded, a deep booming note that shuddered in the bone. He stood. "That is Evendown, khatra, you must leave."

She bowed her head, turned, and left.

4

Jaril moved impatiently about the cell as Brann unpacked the supper basket she'd brought from the big island longhouse that sold food to the pilgrims. "I'm going back tonight," he said suddenly. "It has to be in one of those giftrooms, don't you think, Bramble?"

"No has-to-be, Jay. But you're probably right." Brann pulled up the three-legged stool and sat down to eat. She wanted to tell him he was a fool to take the chance, but she knew he wouldn't listen and she didn't want to irritate him into a greater recklessness. "How you going?"

"Wings, then four-feet. I'll be careful, Bramble. I won't go till late and I won't touch it if I find it. All right?"

"Thanks, Jay."

"I been thinking. . . ." He dropped onto the pallet, lay watching her eat. "We need something to keep it in, Bramble. To hide it from her."

"I know. I can't see any way we can do it. I'm afraid we'll have to fight our way to Waragapur and count on Tak WakKerrcarr to hold her off his Truceground."

"We might still have to, but I've thought of something. I can make a pocket inside myself and insulate the talisman from everything outside."

"Even from the god?"

"I think so."

"That helps. We've got seven days here, Jay. I think we ought to stay in character, leave with who we came with. Can you wait that long? It's six more days if you find the thing tonight."

"I can, once I know. I said it before and it's true. It's not knowing that eats at me, Bramble. But I don't think we ought to wait to take the talisman on the last night before we leave. If she notices it's gone, she'll hit the outgoers hard."

"And the stayers just as hard, be sure of that."

"Well. . . ." He turned onto his back, lay staring up at the cobwebs under the roof. "Damned if we do, damned if we don't. Maybe we should just toss a coin and let old Tungjii decide. Heads, early. Tails, late."

"Why not. Now?"

"No. Wait till I find the thing, Bramble. Till I know."

5

Brann sat on the bed, a blanket wrapped about her, chasing biters away from her face and arms with a reed whisk; the Wounded Moon was down, but the darkness was broken by stars glittering diamond-hard diamond-bright through the thin, high-desert air. She shivered and pulled the blankets tighter; that air was chill and dank here in the marsh; a curdled mist clung to the reed clumps and the floorposts of the cell; tendrils of mist drifted through the windowholes and melted in the heat from the banked peat fire in the mud stove. Outside, the big orange grasshoppers the marshfolk called jaspars had already begun their predawn creakings and a sleepy mashimurgh was practicing its song. There was almost no wind; the stillness was eerie, frightening, as if the marsh and the Rock and even the air were waiting with her for something to happen, something terrible. What an anticlimax, she thought, if Jay comes sliding in and says he hasn't found the thing. I don't know how I could get through another night of waiting. Slya! I hate feeling so helpless. It should be me in there, not my baby, my nursling. She contemplated herself and laughed silently at what she saw. She was nervous about Jaril, but mostly she was irritated because she had no part to play in this, she was baggage. It was harder than she'd thought to reconcile herself to being baggage.

A large horned owl came through a windowhole, snapped out its wings and landed neatly on the reed mat. As soon as its talons touched, it changed to Jaril. He dropped onto the second cot and grinned at her.

"Well?" Brann scowled at him. "Did you or didn't you?"

"Did."

"Giftroom?"

"No, I was wrong about that. It was in a storeroom, the kind where they throw broken things and whatever they don't think has much value."

"A Great Talisman in a junk room?"

"What it looks like, Bramble. Dust everywhere, broken everything, cheap trinkets, the kind your sailor friends bought their whores when they hit port. Wornout mats rolled up, cushions with the stuffing leaking out. And the old frog looking right at home sitting up on a shelf smothered in gray dust. Maybe it's been there since the Sihbaraburj was built." He crossed his legs, rubbed his thumb over and over his ankle. "Funny, I'd 've never gone in there, but a Servant came along the corridor I was in and I thought I'd better duck. There was a door handy; it was locked so I oozed in and while I was waiting I took a look round. I was being firesphere so I wouldn't leave footprints or other marks in case someone came in there hunting something. I about went nova when I saw the thing way up on the top shelf, pushed into a corner and like I said covered with dust. I managed to ride the blow out, I don't know how. I nosed about some more, there was no sign Amortis was around and I've got pretty good at spotting gods. I guess we sit it out the next six days."

"Can you?"

"Oh yes. Um, I should get all the sun I can."

"Morning be enough?"

"Unless it's raining."

"We've got to go to the Temple. Hmm. We went up mid-afternoon today, I suppose that could be enough precedent. You need to be outside?"

"No. Your bed gets the morning sun, enough anyway, we can trade and if anyone comes snooping I just pull a blanket over me and pretend to be asleep."

"Good enough." Brann yawned. "Let's switch blankets." She yawned again. "Just as well we're not going up in the morning. I need sleep."

6

Night.

A gale wind blowing across the marshes, a dry chill wind that cut to the bone.

The Wounded Moon was down, a smear of high cloud dimmed the star-glitter and a thick fog boiled up from the marshwater.

Brann sat wrapped in blankets, staring at the faint red glow from the dying fire, waiting for Jaril to return.

A great horned owl fought the wind, laboring in large sweeps toward the top of the Rock; he angled across the wind, was blown past his point of aim, clawed his way back, gained a few more feet, was blown back, dipped below the rim of the Rock into the ragged eddies around the friable sandstone, climbed again and finally found a perch on the lee side of the Sihbaraburj.

Jaril shifted to a small lemur form with dexterous hands and handfeet and a prehensile tail. Driven by all the needs that churned in him, he crawled into a weep-hole and went skittering through the maze of holes that drained the place, provided ventilation and housed the mirrors that lit the interior of the made-mountain. He shifted again to something like a plated centipede, and went scuttling at top speed through the wall tubes to the junkroom where he'd seen the little glass frog. He hadn't been back since that first day, no point in alerting

Amortis if she wasn't aware of what she had. He tried not to wonder if the thing was still there, but his nerves were strung so taut he felt like exploding. On and on he trotted, his claws tick-ticking on the brick.

He thrust his head into the room. The gloom inside was thicker than the dust, he couldn't see a thing. He closed his foreclaws on the edge of the hole, fought for control of the tides coursing through him. Preoccupied with his internal difficulties, for several minutes he didn't notice an appreciable lightening in that gloom. When he looked round again, he saw a faint glow coming from the shelf where he'd seen Churrikyoo. He shifted hastily to his glowsphere form and drifted over to it.

Having rid itself of dust, the talisman was pulsing softly, as if it said: come to me, take me. Jaril hung in midair, all his senses alert. He felt for the presence of a god. Nothing. He drifted closer. Nothing. Closer. Warmth enfolded him. Welcome. The little glass frog seemed to be grinning at him. He extruded two pseudopods and lifted it from the shelf. It seemed to nestle against him as if it were coming home. He didn't understand. He glanced at the shelf and nearly dropped the frog.

A patch of light was shifting and shaping itself into something . . . something . . . yes, a duplicate of the thing he held.

Jaril looked down. Churrikyoo nestled in the hollows of his pseudopods and he seemed to hear silent laughter from it that went vibrating through his body. He looked at the shelf. The object was dull and lifeless, covered with a coat of dust. He gave a mental shrug, slipped the frog into the pouch he'd built for it and flitted for the hole.

He shifted form and went skittering up the worm holes, a pregnant pseudocentipede. Now and then he stopped and scanned, every sense straining, searching for any sign of alarm. Nothing, except the frog chuckling inside him, nestling in a womblike warmth.

He wriggled out of a weep-hole and shifted again as he fell into the wind. Broad wings scooping, he fought the downdraft that flowed like water along the brick; there was a moment when he thought he was going to impale himself on the spearpoints of the walkway fence, but a sudden gust of wind caught him and sent him soaring upward, carrying him over the outer wall. He regained control and went slipping swiftly to the cell where Brann was waiting.

##

Brann looked up as Jaril landed with a thud, changed. "Did you?"

He patted his stomach, gave her an angelic smile. "I'd show you but . . ."

"Right." She rubbed at her neck. "I'm going to get some sleep. Barge leaves at first light. Wake me, will you, luv?"

7

The barge slid smoothly, ponderously down the river, considerably faster than it came up, riding the current, not towed behind eight plodding oxen. The deck passengers were quiet as they left Havi Kudush, tired, drained, even a little depressed—because they hadn't got what they wanted, or because they had. There were two Mutrimabs aboard, but they huddled in blankets, as morose as the most exhausted pilgrim.

Brann and Jaril had a place near the middle of the deck where they were surrounded by pilgrims; it was a fragile shield, probably useless if Amortis came looking, but the best they could do. Brann held aloof from the rest, concerning herself with her invalid son. That concern wasn't only acting; she was worried about Jaril. He'd lost all his tensions. She didn't understand that. Some, yes. They had what they'd come to get. Keeping it was something else. Nothing was sure until the exchange was actually made. He was relaxed, drowsy, limp as a contented cat; it was as if the talisman were a drug pumping through his body, nulling out everything but itself. His dreamy lassitude became more pronounced as the days passed.

Late in the afternoon of the third day, a gasp blew across the deck.

Golden Amortis came striding across the Tark with a flutter of filmy draperies, her hair blowing in a wind imperceptible down among the mortal folk. A thousand feet of voluptuous womanflesh glowing in the golden afternoon.

Brann huddled in her robes and veil, grinding her teeth in frustration. It was obvious Amortis had missed her talisman and was coming for it; no doubt the copy it'd made of itself had melted into the light and air it had come from. Jaril slipped his hand into hers; he leaned into her side, whispered, "Don't worry, mama."

Don't worry! Brann strangled on the burst of laughter she had to swallow. Not real laughter, more like hysteria. She closed her eyes and tried not to think. But she couldn't stand not seeing what was happening, even if it was disaster coming straight for her, so she opened them again. Bending down to Jaril, she muttered, "Could you build that bridge without Yaro?" The first time they'd clashed with Amortis, Yaril and Jaril had merged into a sort of siphon linking Brann with the god; once the connection was established, Brann sucked away a good portion of the god's substance and vented it into the clouds; they'd scared Amortis so badly she'd run like a rat with its tail on fire.

Jaril laughed, a soft contented sound like a cat purring. "Sure," he said. "But I won't need to."

That tranquillity was beginning to get irritating. She straightened, tensed as Amortis changed direction and came striding toward them.

The god bent over the river, cupped her immense hands ahead of the barge. Up close her fingers were tapering columns of golden light, insubstantial as smoke but exquisitely detailed, pores and prints, a hint of nail before the tips dipped below the water—which continued undisturbed as if there were no substance to the fingers.

The barge plowed into the fingers, passed through them.

Brann felt a brief frisson as she slid through one of them; it was so faint she might have imagined it.

She heard what she thought was a snort of disgust, unfroze enough to turn her head and look behind her. Amortis had straightened up. She was stalking off without even a look at the barge.

"Told you," Jaril murmured. "It doesn't want to be with her any more. It's taking care of us." He yawned, stretched out on his blanket and sank into his sleep coma.

Brann frowned down at him. If she wanted to play her role, she'd pull the other blanket over him; she chewed her lip a moment, glanced at the sun. Take a chance, she thought, let him draw in as much energy as he can, he's going to need it, poor baby.

8

For three more days the barge swung through the extravagant bends of the broad Kaddaroud. Twice more Amortis came sweeping by, ignoring the river and those on it, her anger monumentally visible. The pilgrims huddled in their blankets, terrified. When she was angry, the god had a habit of striking out at anything that caught her attention. If the force of that anger rose too high in her, she struck out at random; anything could set her off, a change in the wind, a gnat on her toe, a fugitive thought too vague to describe. Anyone who got in the way of her fury was ashes on the wind. All they could do was pray she didn't notice them.

She didn't. After she stalked by the second time, she didn't return.

#

The Bargemaster unloaded his passengers at the Waystop where the Kaddaroud met the Sharroud, took on a new load of pilgrims, hitched up the draft oxen and started back upriver.

The Inn Izadinamm was a huge place, capable of housing several hundred in a fair degree of comfort. This late in the season, there were scarce fifty there, three scant bargeloads come back from Kudush to wait for the riverboats that would carry them north or south to their ordinary lives.

Five days after they came to the Izadinamm, a northbound riverboat moored for the night at the Waystop landing. In the morning it left with a score of passengers, Brann and Jaril among them.

9

Waragapur, green and lovely, jewel of peace and fruitfulness.

Truceground and oasis, a place of rest among stony barren mountains jagged enough to chew the sky.

Warmed by the firemountain Mun Gapur, steamed by hotsprings, hugged inside hundred-foot cliffs, Waragapur knew only two seasons, summer during the hottest months and spring for the rest of the year. When Brann arrived it was the edge of winter elsewhere, but there were plum trees in bloom at Waragapur, peach trees heavy with ripe fruit, almonds with sprays of delicate white flowers and ripe nuts on the same tree.

Tak WakKerrcarr came down from his Hold and stood on the landing, leaning on an ebony and ivory staff, waiting for the riverboat. He was an ancient ageless man, his origins enigmatic, his skin the color and consistency of old leather drawn tight over his bones, long shapely bones; he was an elegant old man despite being a home to an astonishing variety of insect life and despite the strength and complexity of the stink that wafted from him—apparently he bathed every five years or so. He ignored the stares and nudges of those who came to gape at him (very careful not to annoy him by coming too close or whispering or giggling), ignored the nervous agitation of the boatmen who'd never seen him but had no doubt whom they were looking at. When Brann came off the ship with the passengers stopping here, he reached with his staff, tapped her on the shoulder. "Come with me," he said, turned and stalked off.

Brann blinked, looked after him. His voice told her who he had to be. It was a wonderful voice, a degree or two lighter than Maksim's, with much the same range and flexibility. "Jay," she glanced over her shoulder at the changer, frowned as she saw him curled up on the landing beside their gear, "look after things here." She hesitated, went on. "Be careful, will you? Don't trust that thing too much."

Jaril nodded, gave her a drowsy smile, and got to his feet.

She didn't want to leave him, but she hadn't much choice. She walked slowly after Tak WakKerrcarr, chewing on her lip, disturbed by the changes in the boy; after a few steps she shook her head and tried to concentrate on WakKerrcarr. She didn't know what he wanted with her or how much he knew about why she was here. He'd be dangerous if he took against her; Maksi wouldn't admit it, but even he was a little afraid of the man. Tak WakKerrcarr. First among the Primes, older than time. Brann straightened her back, squared her shoulders and followed him.

WakKerrcarr waited for her in a water-garden at the side of the Inn, sitting beside a fountain, one fed from the hotsprings, its cascades of water leaping through its own cloud of steam. She caught a whiff of his aroma and edged cautiously around so he was downwind of her.

He pounded the butt of the staff on the earth by his feet, bent forward until his cheek was touching the tough black ebony. He gazed at her as she stood waiting for him to speak. "Take off that kujjin veil, woman. You're no Temu priss."

With an impatient jerk, she pulled off the opaque black headcloth; she was happy to get it off, warmth poured more amply than water from that fountain. She smoothed mussed hair off her face, draped the veil over her arms. "So?"

"Got a message for you." He straightened up, laid his staff across his bony knees. "Fireheart come to see me. Said to tell you watch your feet, but don't worry too much, you're her Little Nothin and she won't let any god do you hurt."

"God?"

"I'm not telling you what you don't know." He crossed his legs at the ankles, wiggled toes longer than some people's fingers. "That bunch tryin to run you, they're fools dancin to strings they can't see."

"What god?"

He got to his feet. "Said what I planned. Not goin to say more. Well, this. Tell that demon, she don't play fair, I'll feed her to the Mountain." His eyes traveled down her body, up again, lingered briefly on her breasts. "When this's over, come see me, Drinker of Souls." A wide flashing smile, one to warm the bones. "I'll even take a bath." Chuckling and repeating himself, take a bath sho sho, even take a bath, hee hee, he strode out of the garden and vanished into the orchard behind.

Brann shook the veil out, whipped it over her head and adjusted it so she could see through the eyeholes—and started worrying about Slya's offer of protection. The god wasn't all that bright, she had a tendency to stomp around and squash anything that chanced to fall under her feet which could include those she meant to help. Nothing Brann could do about it, except stay as nimble as she could and hope she'd be deft enough to avoid any danger that might provoke Slya into storming to her rescue. She went back to the landing.

She collected Jaril and their gear and marched into the Inn. The Host came running, treating her with exaggerated deference; guests and servants stared or peeped at her from the corner of their eyes; she heard a gale of whispers rise behind her as the Host led her to the finest suite in the house and murmured of baths and dinner and wine and groveled until she wanted to hit him. Tak WakKerrcarr was the reason, of course; his notice had stripped away any anonymity she might claim.

When the Host stopped hovering and left the room, she started unbuckling straps. "Serve that toe-licker right if I skipped without paying."

Stretched out on the bed, Jaril watched Brann unpack the pouches and hang up her clothes. "What did WakKerrcarr have to say?"

She finished what she was doing, went to stand by the window, looking down into the garden where she'd talked to the sorcerer. "Message from Slya," she said. "That I'm not to worry, she's going to watch over us."

"Us?"

"All right, me. Same thing."

"Not really."

"You think I'd let her. . . ."

"Thorns down, Bramble. Course not."

She sighed, settled onto the windowseat. "So now we wait. Until the letter is delivered, until the smiglar get here, if they get here, until, until. . . ."

"If they get here?" Jaril lay blinking slowly, without the energy to pretend to yawn. "Relax, Bramble. They want the thing. They'll come."

She made a face at him. "Seems to me we've changed positions, Jay. I'm the impatient one now."

He chuckled. "Tell you what, Bramble. Go paddle around the bathhouse awhile. Should be plenty of hot water. You'll feel better. You know you will."

"Run away and paddle, mmm? Like a fractious infant, mmm? Jay, that wasn't a very nice thing to say to me."

He came up off the bed and ran to her, his sleepiness forgotten, his tranquillity wiped away. Trembling with dry sobs, he wrapped his arms about her, pushed his head against her. "I . . . I . . . I," he stopped, dragged in the air he needed for speaking, "I was just teasing, Bramble. I didn't mean it like that, you know I didn't mean it like that."

She stroked his white-gold hair. "I know, luv. I've tripped on my tongue a time or two myself. Just don't do it again."

10

Two days passed.

Jaril slept much of the time; Brann wandered about the Waystop gardens until the feel of eyes constantly watching her drove her away from the Inn and into the parklike forest at the base of Mun Gapur.

An hour past midday on the third day, she took a foodbasket the Inn's cook prepared for her and went into the forest to a place of flattish boulders beside the noisy little stream that burbled past the Inn and tumbled into the river. She spread out a blanket, filled a water jug and settled herself to enjoy a peaceful picnic lunch.

When Tak WakKerrcarr strolled from under the trees, she was sitting with her feet in the water, eating a peach. He settled himself beside her, dipped a napkin in the stream and handed it to her so she could wipe her sticky face and stickier fingers.

She glanced at him, opened her eyes wide. "You've parked your livestock."

He laughed. "So I have. They're accommodatin little critters."

His voice sent shivers along her spine. The Grand Voice of a Sorcerer Prime. A single word from Maksim could stir her to the marrow of her bones, that WakKerrcarr could do the same when she didn't even know him . . . it wasn't fair. He'd got rid of the stench too. He was tall and lean and powerfully male; she could feel his interest in her, the most effective aphrodisiac there was. "Why?" she said, more breathlessly than she intended, then reminded herself she was a grown woman with more than a little experience in these things.

"The critters? Backs off people I don't want to talk to. Besides, I like 'em. You got some time to spare, heh?"

"Seems so." She frowned as something occurred to her. "Heard from Maks?"

"Not to speak of," he murmured; he took her hand, moved his thumb across her palm. "Why?"

"I'm worried about him." She looked down at the hand caressing hers; his skin was a smooth olive, baby fine, there was almost no flesh between it and the slender hand bones.

"There's reason to be." He set her hand on her thigh and began stroking the curve of her neck, his long fingers playing in her hair. "And reason not to be. Maks is formidable when the occasion requires it."

She leaned into his hand, her eyes drooping half-shut, her breath slowing and deepening. "What are you talking about? Tell me."

"There's things I can't say."

"*You* can't?"

"When the gods are at play, a wise man keeps his head down. Or it gets bit off."

She pulled away from him, jumped to her feet. "Great advice, Tik-tok, I'm sure I'll follow it."

"It don't count when it's your strings they're pullin." He rose with the liquid grace of a man a fraction of his great age, clasped his hands behind his back. "All you can do is dance fast and try keeping your feet." He smiled at her, his yellow eyes glowing. "You're formidable yourself, Drinker of Souls."

"Does he need help? Can you tell me that?"

"He's doing well enough; don't worry your head, Brann. You're fond of him." He raised his brows. "More than fond, I think."

"For my sins."

He moved closer, wary and focused, predator stalking skittish prey, and set his hands on her shoulders, close to her neck, his long thumbs tucked up under her jaw. "For my sins, I want you."

"Will you help me?"

"No. Not beyond maintaining the Truce." He moved his thumbs delicately up and down her neck, just brushing the skin. "Must I buy?"

"No."

"I thought not."

"You plan to take?"

He curved his hand along her cheek. "I wouldn't dare. Besides, the sweetest fruit is that which comes freely to the hand. I'm not a rutting teener, Bramble-all-thorns. I can wait. If not now, then later."

Brann laughed, turned her head, brushed her lips across the palm of his hand. "Rutting ancient. Let it be now."

"And later?"

"I lay no mortgages on tomorrow."

"It doesn't hurt to dream."

"If you remember that reality is often disappointing."

"One can always adjust the dream. Come see my house."

"You mean your bed?"

"That too. Though I've never made a practice of confining myself to a bed. Shows a dearth of imagination."

11

"Bramble. Brann."

Someone was shaking her; she groped around, touched Tak's shoulder. He mumbled something indecipherable, snuggled closer against her. The shaking started again. "Wha. . . ."

"Shuh!" Sound of water running. Cold wet slap.

Brann jerked up, clawed the wet cloth from her face and flung it away. "What do you think you're doing!"

"Bramble, they're here. You have to get back."

"Jay?"

"Pull yourself together, Bramble. The smiglar. They're here. They didn't wait for a riverboat to bring them. They want you now."

Brann felt the bed shift as Tak lifted onto his elbow; she shivered with pleasure as his strong slender fingers smoothed along her spine. "Go back," he told Jaril. "I'll bring her in a few minutes."

Jaril snarled at him, hostile, angry; he was close to losing control.

Brann could feel the tides pulsing in him. She caught hold of his hands, held them tightly. "Jay, listen. Listen, luv. You've got to be calm. You're giving them an edge. Listen. Go down and watch them. I'll be there as fast as I can, I've got to get dressed. Do you hear me?"

Jaril shuddered, then slowly stabilized. With a last glare at Tak, he shifted to glowsphere and darted away.

Brann sighed. "I have to see him home somehow. Tak. . . ."

"Mmmh?" His hands were on her breasts, his tongue in her ear.

She relaxed against him for a moment, then pulled away. "No more time, Tik-tok." She slid off the bed, stood a minute running her fingers through her tangled hair.

"You'll come here after?" He lay back on the pillows, his fingers laced behind his head, his eyes caressing her.

She padded over to the basin, poured some water in it and began washing herself. Will I come back? I don't know. Once we ransom Yaril . . . there's Maks, I have to find out about him. . . . She began working the knots out of her long white hair. After a moment she chuckled. "First seacaptains, now sorcerers. I wonder if that means my taste in men is improving or worsening."

"Don't ask me, m' dear. You can see I'd be biased."

Brush in hand, she set her fists on her hips and contemplated him. "What I see, hah! You wash up lovely, old man."

"I like you too, old woman. You coming back?"

"I want to. Tak. . . ."

"Mm?"

"This isn't a condition, it's just a favor I'm asking."

He sat up. "Such diffidence, Thornlet. Ask, ask, I promise I won't let thoughts of past orgies influence me." He chuckled, slid off the bed and strode to the window. As she began pulling on her heavy widow's robes, he chirruped and chirred, calling his little critters to come back and crawl on him.

"The children have to be sent home. As far as I know, Slya is the only one can do that. Would you talk to her for us? They need their own kind, Tik-tok."

He opened the door to a closet, took out his ancient greasy leathers. "You realize how much more vulnerable you'd be without them?"

"That doesn't matter."

"It does to your friends, Thornlet. Slya is very fond of you, more than you know, I think." He took out his staff, leaned it against the windowsill.

"They'll either die or go rogue before much longer, Tik-tok, what use are they then?"

"You're sure of that?"

"I'm painfully sure of that."

"I'll talk with the Fireheart, I can't promise anything."

"I know. She goes her own way and Tungjii help us all." She folded the veil over her arm. "It's time."

"Come back."

"When I can."

"Maks?"

"I've got to see about him. Do you understand? He's a dear man."

"I think I'm jealous."

"Why? You know where Maksim's fancies lie."

"Sex is a delight, love's a treasure."

"Aphorisms, old man?"

"Distilled experience, old woman."

"You've had a lot of that, eh?"

"But never enough. Take my hand."

12

The Chuttar Palami Kumindri sat in the largest armchair in the suite's salon with a velvet wrapped bundle in her lap, Cammam Callan behind her, arms crossed, lively as a rock.

Palami Kumindri raised an elegant brow as Brann walked from the bedroom followed by Tak WakKerrcarr. "Are you interfering in this, WakKerrcarr?"

"Only to see the Truce is kept." He moved to the suite's main door, stood leaning on his staff, his face blank.

The Chuttar looked skeptical but didn't question what he said; she turned to Brann. "You wrote you had the ransom."

"We do. You have our friend?"

Palami Kumindri unfolded the black velvet, exposing the fractured crystal. "As you see."

"Give her to me."

"Give me the talisman."

"I'll let you see it." She went to the window, swung the shutters wide. "Jay, come in."

The great horned owl dropped like a missile through the unglazed window; he spread his talons, snapped his wings out and landed on the braided rug. As soon as he touched down, he changed and was a slender handsome youth. Eyes fixed on the Yaril crystal, he reached inside his shirt and brought out the little glass frog. "Churrikyoo," he said.

"Bring it here."

"Give my sister to the Drinker of Souls first."

"Why should I trust you?"

"Tak WakKerrcarr's Truce. I would rather not face his anger."

She shrugged. "Why not. Come here, woman." She indicated the crystal without touching it. "Take it."

As soon as Brann touched the crystal, she knew that it was Yaril and that the changer was still alive. "Give her the talisman, Jay."

Jaril flung Churrikyoo at Palami Kumindri and rushed to Brann's side; he took the crystal from her and fed sunfire into it until it throbbed with light; he crooned at it in a high keening that rose beyond Brann's hearing threshold. The pulsing grew fiercer, the edges of the stone melted into light and air. Silently but so suddenly Brann later swore she heard a *pop!*, the stone was gone and a glowsphere floated in front of Jaril. It darted at him, merged with him. He changed and there were two spheres dashing about the room in a wild dance of joy and celebration.

Brann laughed and spread her arms. A moment later she was hugging two slender forms, one a pale gold boy, the other a moonsilver girl.

And then darkness swallowed her. Swallowed them all. Swallowed Brann, Yaril, Jaril—and Tak WakKerrcarr.

She heard Tak WakKerrcarr scream with rage.

She heard Palami Kumindri laugh.

And then there was nothing.

II: KORIMENEI/DANNY BLUE

After her long journey, Korimenei
has finally caught up with the Rushgaramuv and is waiting for a chance
to steal Frunzacoache from the shaman. After that she can race south
along the Mountains to the Cheonene peninsula and at last—at long,
long last—can release her brother
from the spell and put the Talisman
in his hands.

1

Korimenei lay on her stomach at the edge of the cliff, her chin
resting on her crossed forearms; she watched the rites and revelry
below and felt exhausted; the autumnal fertility celebrations had been
going on all day and all night for a week now. It's enough to put one off
sex, beer and food for years, she thought. Maybe forever. It was boring.
And it was frustrating. Until the Rushgaramuv settled and started
sleeping at night, there was no way she could get at the shaman.

She watched until sunset, sighed when she saw the bonfires and
torches lit once more, new white sand strewn about the dance floor.
How they can, she thought. She wriggled back from the cliff edge, got
to her feet, and brushed the grit off her front. She shivered. The wind
had teeth in it. Any day now those fattening clouds were going to drop
a load of snow on her; she was surprised it'd held off this long. She
pulled the blanket tighter about her and went trudging back to the
camp, thinking she hadn't been warm in days.

Nine days ago, before the Rushgaramuv reached the wintering
grounds with their diminished herds, she'd come up here on the mountain and found a hollow in a nest of boulders. She'd caulked the holes
between the stones with mud and leaves to shut out the icy drafts and
stretched her tent canvas over the top, covered that with more mud
and twigs and sods she'd cut from patches of tough mountain grass. A

man could walk by a bodylength away and not suspect what he was passing.

Ailiki had killed and dressed some squirrels for her and nosed out some tubers. Korimenei smiled as she saw the neat little carcasses laid out on a platter of overlapping leaves. The first time she'd seen the mahsar dressing meat, she'd gaped like a fool, unable to believe what her eyes were showing her—Ailiki using a small sharp knife, its hilt molded to fit her hand, the blade a sliver of steel shaped like a crescent moon. Where Ailiki got it, how she knew how to use it. . . .

Korimenei looked down at the squirrel carcasses, shook her head and went to gather wood to cook them.

2

A persistent tickle woke her, something brushing again and again against her face. Shining like a ghost in the darkness, Ailiki scampered away as Korimenei sat up. The air was so cold it was knives in her lungs; the silence was spectral. She could hear her heart beating; Ailiki moved a foot and she could hear the faint scratch of the mahsar's claws in the dirt. "What is it, Aili?"

The mahsar flicked her tail and pushed past the piece of canvas used as an inadequate seal to the shelter, a door of sorts; Korimenei hastily crafted a tiny will-o, set it up against the roof canvas so she could see what she was doing. Not relishing the thought of going outside, she pulled on her bootliners, boots, gloves, a sweater and her coat, wrapped a scarf about her neck and head and crawled reluctantly after Ailiki.

The wind had quit. Snow fell like feathers. There was already half an inch on the ground. "I suppose this means the festival is over," she said aloud.

Ailiki clattered her teeth and lolloped off, looking over her shoulder now and then to see if Korimenei was following her.

When they reached the cliff edge, Korimenei dropped onto her knees and looked down. The canyon was as dark and silent as the slopes behind her. "How many hours till dawn?"

Ailiki drew three scratches in the snow, contemplated them a moment, then added a fourth, half the length of the others.

"Three and a half. Good. That's time enough. Aili, I'm going to start down, you fetch the fake, will you?"

Following the glimmering Ailiki, Korimenei groped through the scattered corrals and barns, then past the line of longhouses, making her way to the small sod hut off by itself where the Rushgaramuv shaman had gone to sing over his sacred fires, where he'd slept the past several nights, dreamwalking for the clan. She'd watched several women bring him his meals there, wives or female kin, she supposed. None of them went inside. The Siradar and his Elders made a ceremonial visit to the hut on the first day of the rites; his headwife and the clan matrons went the next day. Now that the rites were finished . . . Gods! maybe he'd already moved back, it was snowing, the longhouses would be a lot warmer. . . .

The snow fell thick and silent, soft as down against her skin until it melted, turning in an instant chill and harsh, leaching the warmth out of her. She followed Ailiki past the dance floor to the giant oak where the hut was; it was very much like the dance ground in Owlyn Vale where she'd pranced the seasons in and out with her cousins under the guidance of the Chained God's priest and AuntNurse Polatéa, though the Valer's celebrations were a lot more decorous than those she'd just witnessed. She frowned. Like all the other children she'd been sent to bed at sundown, maybe the decorum vanished with them. She shook her head. This wasn't the time for such things. Hold hard, woman, she told herself. Stray thoughts mean straying emanations, you don't want the old man waking.

She crept closer to the hut and listened at the leather flap that closed off the low, square entrance hole. Snores. He was inside, all right, and very much asleep from the sound of it. She leaned against the sods and did a cautious bodyread of the man inside.

He was drugged out of his mind; a herd of boghans could stomp across him and he wouldn't notice.

"Liki," she murmured, "brighten up a bit, mmh?"

She lifted the flap and followed the mahsar inside. The air was hot and soupy with a mix of herbs and sweat and ancient urine; there was a small peat fire in a brazier putting out more smoke than heat; half that smoke was incense and the other half came from the remnants of the dried herbs that sent the shaman into his stupor. He was curled up on a pile of greasy leathers, snoring. He had some Talent, she'd smelled that on him from the cliff, but not much. Even if he woke and found her here, he was no threat.

In spite of that, she was wary as she crawled over to him, shields up and as much I'm-not-here as she could smear over herself. Her precautions would've been pathetic if she'd been moving on Maksim, or even on the Shahntien, but they were good enough for this man.

He wore his torbaoz on a thong about his neck, an oiled leather pouch the length of her forearm. She touched it, pulled her hand back when his snore broke in the middle. She touched it again. He seemed uneasy, but he didn't wake. Right, she thought, if I'm going to do it, better do it fast.

She memorized the knot, got it untied. After spreading the neck of the torbaoz, she dipped two fingers into the mess inside, felt the cool nubbiness of the silver chain. She got a finger hooked through it and began drawing it and what it held out of the pouch. The snores went on, more sputter to them now; there was a restlessness in the old man's sleep that warned her she'd better hurry. He groaned but still didn't wake as she freed Frunzacoache from a dried bat wing and some stalks of an anonymous plant; the exhaustion from six nights' rituals were like chains on him.

She hung Frunzacoache around her neck, slipping it down inside her shirt to rest like a warm hand between her breasts, surprised at the temperature because the talisman was silver and crystal, neither of them welcoming to naked flesh. She took the copy she and Ailiki had made and eased it into the torbaoz, pushing it well down among the rest of the ritual objects. When she was satisfied with its set, she pulled the cords tight and worked the ends into as close a match to the original knot as she could manage. Waving Ailiki before her, she crawled from the hut.

The cold outside stunned her. A wind was rising, blowing snow into her face. Her elbows and her knees were like iced-over hinges; they'd break if she bent them. Ailiki came back to her, nuzzled her, sent a surge of fire through her that woke Frunzacoache from its passivity. The talisman spread warmth along her body, heated her joints enough to help her creak onto her feet. Walking eased her yet more. She followed Ailiki's spriteglow through the blowing snow, stumbling past longhouses still dark and sodden with sleep, past corrals filled with white humps where sheep and oxen, geykers and boghan lay, down the treeless flats to the mouth of the canyon.

The climb to her camp was easier than she expected. The wind was at her back instead of blowing in her face, Ailiki shone like a small yellow sun so she could see where to put her feet and Frunzacoache radiated warmth through her body. She had little time for thinking as she struggled up the treacherous slopes, only enough to wonder at the bonding between her and the talisman; as soon as it settled against her it was as if it had always been there.

Tré's eidolon appeared before her as she crawled into the shelter. "Well?"

She crouched on the groundsheet and stared at him. "I have it," she said finally. "How long is this snow going to last?"

When he spoke, his mindvoice was flat and dull, scraped down to bone. He was answering her for one reason only, his report would get her to him faster. No, not her, the talisman. "It will be finished around sunup. The wind will blow hard after the snow stops falling, but you can ride in it; you had better ride in it, it will cover your tracks. It will drop after an hour or so, but there will be gusts of cold damp air, the kind that eat to the heart. You need to watch the ponies, do not over-ride them. There is a road of sorts going south through the foothills, the Vanner Rukks use it in spring and summer, but they have settled for the winter so you will not see them. If you follow the road and make fair time you should reach a Gsany Rukk village by sundown. You can shelter for the night in the CommonHouse and buy more grain and tea there, they keep a supply for winter travelers. After that, you will have a week of clear, cold weather, then the next storm hits. You had better find shelter for that one, it is going to be a three-day blizzard; there are several Gsany villages close together, so you will have a choice of where to spend the waiting time. Come as quickly as you can, sister, I am very weary of this state." The eidolon shimmered and was gone.

Korimenei sighed. "Well, Aili my Liki, looks like nothing's changed. I'll be happier'n he is when this is over. Every time I see him, I feel like he's clawed me." She smoothed her hand down the front of her coat, then scratched behind the mahsar's ears. "We'll go somewhere warm and friendly, my Aili, and wait for my daughter to be born."

#

In the morning, as the eidolon had predicted, there were six inches of snow on the ground but none falling and a wind that cut like knives. Ailiki brought the ponies in, fed them grain she'd stolen from the Rushgar stores. The little mahsar was changing as every day passed, becoming less a beast than a furry person, even her face was flattening —slowly, imperceptibly, but steadily until Korimenei was sure she saw a human face emerging from the fur. If the change continued, maybe someday Ailiki would be able to talk to her. She stowed her gear in pouches that were beginning to show the strains of this long journey and took apart the shelter, rolling the several pieces of canvas into a neat packet.

By midmorning she'd found the Vanner Road; the stiff winds earlier had swept parts of it clear of snow, so she made better time, but the ponies refused to be pushed. They were shaggy with their winter coats, but not nearly so fat as they should have been. Despite the care she'd taken of them, they were as worn as the leather on her pouches, as worn as she felt some days though the morning sickness had left her before she reached the mountains. She walked and rode, rode and walked, slipped, trudged, cursed the mountains and the cold and her brother for sending her out in this weather.

As dusk settled over the slopes she rounded a bulge and found herself on the outskirts of a small neat village that reminded her very much of her home vale. She stopped her pony, whistled with pleasure. Even in the shadowy dimness she could see how bright the colors were, how clean and simple the lines were. The houses were smaller than the multifamily dwellings she knew as a child, they were like beads on a string, elbowing their neighbors, instead of standing solitary in a Housegarden, but they had the same high-peaked roofs with cedar shakes oiled until they were almost black, the same whitewashed walls with painted straps and beams, the same heavy shutters carved in deep relief. She couldn't see the designs, no doubt they were quite different, the thing was, they were there in the same place as the ones she knew. She felt her souls expand, her metaphorical elbows come away from her sides. She understood for the first time how much she missed her family, her people. She'd joked with Frit about going home; now she was indeed going home and she was suddenly very happy about that. Smiling fondly, perhaps foolishly, she nudged the pony into a weary walk and headed for the CommonHouse on the west side of the Square. Behind her, Ailiki made the little hissing sound Kori thought of as mahsar laughter and clucked the pack pony into moving after her.

4

Three days later she rode from a thick stand of conifers and saw a dead man sprawled facedown on the snow, three stubby arrows like black quills protruding from his back and his left leg. Blood was a splash of crimson on the snow. Crimson? It was still leaking out of the man. He had to be alive.

She slid off the pony, ran to him and knelt beside him, fingers searching under his jaw; she couldn't feel a pulse, but bodyread told her, yes, he was alive. "Aili, come here." She scooped up the mahsar and set her on the man's back. "Do what you can to warm him, my Liki, while I figure how to move him off this snow." Without realizing what she was doing, she closed her hand about Frunzacoache; the talisman felt eager, as if it had suffered frustration from being unused all the years it sat in the shaman's pouch. It was a focus of renewal, that's what the books said anyway. The Great Talismans weren't living creatures in any sense of that word, but Kushundallian said they sometimes showed a kind of willfulness, as if they recognized in some nonthinking way what they wanted and used whatever hands that came their way to get it.

She sat on her heels and rubbed at her back. It was late afternoon, the sky was boiling with clouds though the air down near the earth was barely stirring; it was several degrees above freezing, but that was not much help to the man stretched out beside her. If he wasn't to die on her, she had to get those shafts out of him and move him under cover . . . she touched his long black hair, drew her fingers along his cheekbones, down his nose, trying to remember where she'd seen him before. There was something . . . something about him . . . she couldn't catch hold of it, not yet. He was warmer; Ailiki's cuddle was starting to work on him. He was also bleeding faster. She jumped to her feet and ran to her stores.

She tugged him into the road and onto a piece of canvas, bunched blankets about him to hold in the warmth Ailiki was feeding him, then she sat on her heels scowling at the arrows. She had to get them out without killing him. Cut them out? She shuddered at the thought. Inanimate Transfer? Might as well grab hold of them and drag them out of him. She could burn the shafts, but that would leave the points sunk in him. Inanimate Transform? Hmm. Might work. With a little help. Leg arrow first; if I blow it, I'll do less damage there. She pulled Frunzacoache from under her shirt and pressed her left hand over it as she got ready for the act of transforming. She started to reach for the shafts, stopped her hand. Are the points iron or bone or stone or what? She grasped the shaft and read down it. Iron, yes.

"Meta mephi mephist mi," she chanted, hand tight about the shaft, feeling it vibrate against her palm as currents of change stirred in it. "Syda ses sydoor es es. Meta mephi mephist mi. Xula xla es eitheri."

The wood sublimated into the air; a thread of clear water oozed from the wound.

She smiled, shook herself, and eased Frunzacoache's chain over her head. Pressing the flat crystal enclosing the deathless leaf over the puncture wound, she held it there though the heat it generated grew so intense it was painful, held it and held it until the heat dropped out of it. She lifted the talisman and inspected the place where the wound had been. The puncture was closed; there wasn't even a scar to mark where it had been.

She rocked on her knees along his body until she could reach another of the arrows; it jerked rhythmically, a movement so tiny it was hard to see unless she looked closely at the flights. It had to be lodged tight against the man's heart. Tricky. If it had penetrated something vital, getting it out might be as dangerous as leaving it in, he might bleed to death before . . . She opened her hand and gazed thoughtfully at Frunzacoache for a minute, then closed her fingers about it and chanted: Meta mephi mephist mi . . . and as soon as the chant was done, slapped the talisman over the wound and held it. . . .

Contented with the results, she moved to the arrow high in the shoulder and began the chant for the third time. . . .

When she lifted Frunzacoache, it felt swollen, tumescent, as if it drew power into itself by expending power. It was so heavy it seemed to jump from her fingers to land on the man's back, driving a grunt out of him though he didn't seem to be waking up.

"Sounds like you're going to live, whoever you are." She felt under his jaw. A strong steady throb pulsed against her fingertips and his skin was warm, but not too warm. "Yes indeed." She started to straighten, but stopped as Ailiki chittered anxiously and put a small black hand on her arm. "You want me to do something more? Obviously you do." She moved closer to the man so she could kneel on the canvas; the cold from the sodden earth was striking up through her trousers and worrying at her bodyheat. Frowning, she focused on the man, scanning him in a full bodyread. "Poison, tchah! He's rotten with it. I wonder . . . mmh! no time for that. Back to business." Reluctantly, because her fingers were aching and stiff with cold, she cupped her hands about Frunzacoache and called on its gift of renewal to help her flush the poison from the man and heal its ravages.

When the work was complete, she lifted the talisman. Heavy, dark, swollen, it frightened her; though she didn't want to, she slid the chain over her head and tucked Frunzacoache under her shirt. It was hotter than she'd expected, the heat burned into her but vanished almost as soon as she felt it. She tucked her trembling hands into her armpits and looked around. The ponies were kicking through the snow and tearing up clumps of withered grass. A deer came to the edge of the trees, gazed out at her a long minute then retreated into the shadows. Otherwise the narrow winding flat and the stony slopes were devoid of life; sunk inches below the level of the flat by generations of hooves and high-wheeled wagons, the Road was the only sign that people had passed this way. Overhead, there was a high thin film of cloud, gray and cold. A chill wet wind was gathering strength around her; it blew across her face and insinuated itself into every crevice in her clothing. She shivered and wondered what she should do next. She couldn't just leave the man lying beside the Road. I have seen him before. I know it. Somewhere. Silili? Doesn't feel right. Where . . . where. . . .

The wind blew a strand of black hair forward over his face; it tickled his nose and he sneezed. And opened his eyes.

He rolled over, dislodging Ailiki.

She gave an explosive treble snort and lalloped across to the ponies; she jumped onto the saddle and sat watching the man with vast disapproval as he pushed himself up and ran his eyes over Korimenei.

"I know you. At least. . . ." He moved his shoulders, felt at his leg, looked round at the splatters of blood and forgot what he'd been saying. "I owe you one, Saöri."

Korimenei laughed. "Three."

"Huh? Ah! Your point." He narrowed his very blue eyes, inspected her more closely. "Kori?"

"It's Korimenei these days."

"Does that mean you've taken a husband?"

"No husband. I travel alone." She stood, fumbled in the pocket of her coat for her gloves. He knows me as Kori, she thought, I haven't been called Kori for ten years, ten . . . god's blood, I DO know him. She glanced at him again. I think I know him.

He struggled onto his feet, grimacing at his weakness; it would take time to replace the flesh he'd lost in healing and the blood that'd leaked out of him. "I see you didn't stay home and marry one of your cousins. How's your brother? Don't tell me he got taken in the Lot?"

"Daniel?" She stared at the thick wavy hair; it was part of him, she'd stripped poison from those strands. "But you were. . . ."

"Bald? That I was. And you were a child?"

"Ten years ago. One ceases to be a child in the ordinary course of time. Bald heads don't grow new crops."

A brow shot up, giving him a quizzical look. "And one turns a hair pedantic, it seems."

She sighed. "So I've been told. If you're stuck in a school ten years, it can do that to you. Even school doesn't grow hair."

"A sorcerer can grow hair anywhere he wants, didn't you know?"

"But you weren't. . . ." She stepped close to him, flattened her hand against his chest. "But you are." She stepped back, disturbed. "Why didn't I smell it before when I was working on you? And now. . . ."

"Long story." Waves of shudders were passing through his body; she could see the muscles knotting beside his mouth as he fought to control the shaking of his jaw. She glanced at the sky, located the watery blur that was the sun. At least three hours of light left. On the one hand, she didn't want to waste that much travel time; on the other, Daniel was in no condition to go anywhere. No coat, nothing but that odd vest she remembered more vividly than she did the man, now that she thought of it. A vest with two new holes in it, which wouldn't help it turn the wind.

"You can tell it later." She walked to the ponies, her irritation audible in the staccato crunch of her feet. "We'll stay here until tomorrow morning. While I'm getting camp set up, you cut some wood for the fire. The work'll warm you up a bit." Her hand on the saddle, she looked over her shoulder at him. "If you're up to it."

"If you've got an axe, my teeth just won't do it." His voice sounded strained, but he finished with a quick twitch of a smile.

"Fool." She relaxed, reminded of the days in the cart, him telling stories, listening to her chatter, playing his flute for her and the other children. "No axe, just a hatchet which you can curse all you want with my blessing." She began working on the straps that held it, doing some of her own cursing at the stiff, reluctant leather and the clumsiness of her gloved fingers. "I saw plenty of downwood as I came through the trees. Ah!" She caught the hatchet as it fell, held it out to him. "Better you than me. I put an edge on this thing last night. That should last about three cuts."

He took the haft between thumb and forefinger, gave her another of those twitchy smiles and marched off, vanishing under the trees.

"Right. Aili, I'll get the canvas. You chase the ponies to a place where we can camp."

5

The fire crackled vigorously, hissing now and then as the heat from it loosened a fall of snow from the branches high overhead. "Settsimaksimin decided I had Talent so he flipped me over to Sililī, sponsored me at a school and made sure I stayed put until I Passed Out." Korimenei pulled the blanket closer about her, sipped at the cooling tea in her mug. "Why I'm here, now, I'm going home. You?"

"Things happen, I get booted about." He was using her spare mug; he cradled it between his hands, frowned down at the inch of cooling tea it held. "Why not." He lifted his head. "Remember Ahzurdan? You met him at the Blue Seamaid when you went to see the Drinker of Souls."

She stared at him. Inky shadows cast by the fire emphasized the jut of his nose, his high angular cheekbones. His face changed and changed again with every shift of shadow. It was like looking at one of those trick drawings where background and foreground continually shift, where a vase becomes two profiles then a vase again. "I remember," she murmured. "Who are you?"

"Daniel Akamarino. Ahzurdan. Both and neither. Call me Danny Blue."

"I don't understand."

"Like I said, it's a long story."

"Well, what have we got but time?"

"All right. Chained God . . . remember him?"

"How could I forget?"

"Right. He wanted a weapon to aim at Settsimaksimin. He made one. He took a sorcerer and a starman and hammered the two men into one. Me. You might call Daniel and Ahzurdan my sires. In a way."

"That's not long, just weird." She wrapped her hand in the blanket, took the kettle from the coals at the edge of the fire and filled her mug. "Want more?"

"Better not if I intend to sleep tonight."

She sipped at the tea and thought about what he'd just told her. No wonder Tré was frightened of the god and wanted Frunzacoache to protect him. Does he know about this? She sneaked a look at Danny Blue. This abomination? He didn't say anything, but then he wouldn't, not where the god could hear him. She clung to a moment's hope, maybe her brother wasn't the way he sounded, maybe . . . no, don't be a fool, woman. She took too sudden a mouthful, spat it out, her tongue felt singed. "Did you know you were rotten with poison?"

"I know." He lifted a brow. "The past tense is the proper tense, I hope?"

"Very proper. I can't abide a half-done job. Blackmail?"

"Mmm-hmm. Bring us the talisman Klukesharna and we give you the antidote, that's what they said."

She looked quickly at him, looked away. Another Great One being snatched. She slid her hand inside her shirt, touched Frunzacoache. It felt warm, it seemed to seek her fingers as if it wanted to be stroked. I wonder, she thought, Kushundallian told us They get restless sometimes, They go through a period of dormancy, then They start moving, going from hand to hand until They feel like settling down again. Hmm. "You don't have Klukesharna."

"Not now."

"I see. Hence the feathering."

"You got it."

"You can't have been lying there more than an hour before I found you, you'd be dead otherwise. You could go after whoever took it. Will you?"

"No. That's trouble I don't need. Or want."

"Hmm." She looked down; she'd been playing with Frunzacoache all this time without noticing what she was doing. Either he wasn't the chosen or the person who took it had enough gnom to overpower a fresh link. She thought about asking, decided better not. "Have you decided what you're going to do now?"

He didn't answer for several minutes; finally, he tossed down the rest of his tea, set the mug by his foot. "She left my coin, all she took was Klukesharna. I need a horse and winter gear. Where's the nearest settlement?"

She, Korimenei thought. He knows who shot him. I suppose that's his business. "There's a Gsany village a day's ride south of here."

"You said you're for Cheonea?"

"The Vales. My Vale. Owlyn Vale." She spoke slowly, tasting the words, finding pleasure in the feel of them in her mouth. I'm going home, she thought. Home.

Danny Blue yawned, went back to brooding at the fire. His face was drawn and weary. Korimenei watched him a while, wondering what he was thinking about; it wasn't pleasant if she read him rightly. His eyelids fluttered; he forced them up again, but he said nothing. She smiled. No doubt he thought he was being courteous, letting her state the conditions of their cohabitation, because cohabitation it was going to be. She had no intention of forgoing the comforts, such as they were, of her tent and her blankets and he certainly wasn't strong enough yet to survive the night outside even with a fire. Gods, it's one of those tales Frit was always reading, twisting and turning to get the hero innocently into bed with the heroine and give him a chance to show just how heroic he was. How noble. Put a sword between them and grit the teeth. Silly. He was in no shape to . . . damn, she didn't want him thinking he had to . . . how do you say . . . hah! just say it. In a while. Not now.

She pushed the blanket off her shoulders and got to her feet, checked the pot she'd washed after supper and hung upside down over the top of one of the young conifers huddled in an arc around the rim of the glade, an adequate windbreak if the wind kept coming from the north as it had the past several days. The pot was dry enough to put away. She moved busily around the camp space, collecting items scattered about and stowing them in the pouches; when she was finished she took a last tour of the camp, came back to the fire.

"We'd best turn in now, I want to get started with first light." She picked up the blanket she'd been wearing, shook it out and draped it over her arm. "We'll be sharing tent and blankets, Danny Blue. You're tired. I'm tired. I'm sure neither of us is interested in dalliance."

"Kori my Thiné, Amortis her very self couldn't get a rise out of me tonight." He stood, staggering a little as he unfolded.

"I like to have things clear," she said. "You go in first, I'll follow."

6

Morning. Early. Frost crunching underfoot, whitening every surface.

Ready to start, saddle and packs in place, the ponies are huddled next to the fire, lipping up piles of corn set out for them, tails switching at half dormant blackflies. When the two people speak, they puff out white plumes of frozen breath.

Bulky with her layers of clothing, tendrils of soft brown hair curling from under her knitted hat, the girl stood with her fists on her hips, glaring at Danny Blue. "I don't give spit for your blasted vanity, man. Either climb in that saddle or get the hell out of here. I don't care where."

The Daniel phasma being off somewhere or still asleep, the

Ahzurdan phasma seized control of the body; hating his weakness, hating her for her strength, resenting her because she'd saved all their lives and laid that burden of gratitude on them, Danny Blue found himself wanting to smash that imperious young face. He wanted to beat her and by beating her, batter in her all the other women who'd dominated and rejected Ahzurdan, his whining mother and Brann chief among them. Lips pressed together, he swung into the saddle. He felt like a fool; even with the stirrups lowered as far as they'd go, his knees stuck out ridiculously, he thought he looked like a clown in a child's chair. He pulled the blanket about his shoulders and looked around. The odd little beast that traveled with Korimenei went running past and scrambled onto the packs; Korimenei tossed the lead rein into the small black paws.

She strode past him without looking at him and set off along the Road. He toed his pony into a brisk walk, heard the pack pony snort, then start after him.

##

They passed the whole day in silence; even when they stopped to rest the ponies and let them graze, neither acknowledged the other's presence with so much as a grunt.

Danny Blue was exhausted before half the day was gone, but Korimenei kept on, walking with steady, ground-eating strides, never looking back. She was no doubt partly putting it on to annoy him, but there was an impatience about her he couldn't discount; he knew she was eager to see her home again and he'd cost her time and was still slowing her down, something he found sourly satisfying for a while, until he was too tired and sick to sustain any kind of emotion so even the Ahzurdan phasma who'd been ruling him was forced to give way.

Though the pony had an easy rolling walk, he had to concentrate to stay on its back. At the last stop only the impatient jerk of Korimenei's shoulders gave him the strength to pull himself into the saddle. He sat there fumbling with his feet, unable to find the stirrups. She didn't say anything; grimly controlled, she caught hold of one boot, shoved it in place, circled the pony, dealt with the other foot, then started off along the Road.

In his head the Ahzurdan phasma sneered at the girl, at Danny Blue, and the Daniel phasma watched both with sardonic appreciation. Wearily, Danny Blue did his best to reclaim his body. Every step of the pony juddered through him, jolting his brain, shattering his sequences of thought so he had to begin over and over before he finished one. He stared at the striding girl and wondered who the hell he was and where his life was going. He couldn't get a hold on himself, he came to pieces when he tried, though he was getting a glimpse of something, a feel of potential; fatigue had stripped away his defenses, he couldn't hide any more. Or slide any more. A woman, a lover, had asked Daniel Akamarino once don't you want to do something with your life and he said no and left her behind. Now Danny Blue was being forced to ask the question of himself. And forced to realize he had no idea what the answer was. There was another thing. Puppet, he thought, playtoy, the god's still jerking my strings and making me dance. Bored. H/it wants to amuse h/itself. I know it. Running me in a circle. I go with her I go back to h/it. Round and round. Not a puppet, no, a rat in a running wheel. Round and round. Back to the place I started from. Kori's going home. I want to go home. I want to get out of this madhouse reality.

More and more he was drawn to the rationality of Daniel's world, the reality where gods were products of the mind and necessarily reticent about interfering in the lives of common men. Where the forces that worked on those lives were perhaps as powerful, but much less personal. The Ahzurdan phasma resisted this with all his strength though that was little enough; he was fading, his painfully cultivated Talent slipping away from him into the unappreciative hands of his semi-son. All he could do was try keeping his part of Danny Blue's double memory shut away from that semi-son, frustrating Danny's attempt to find a way to transfer himself to the Daniel reality. Danny had no doubt that was one of the constraints that kept him out of the realities, that blocked him from regaining this part of Ahzurdan's skill.

As the sun went down, the idea came to him. Settsimaksimin. If he can't do it, no one can. Yes. If he knows where my reality lies, he can reach it. I'm sure of it. He can do it. All I have to do is find him. And find out what price he wants for doing it. Kori knows him, maybe . . . can't think. God, I don't know. Is this my own idea? Or is that Compost Heap messing with my head again? Pulling my strings? Jump little puppet, run little rat?

The jolting stopped. When he realized that, he lifted his head. They'd been moving through huge old conifers for several hours, he'd noticed that without being particularly conscious of it; now they were on the edge of a broad clearing with a small village rising up the slopes of both sides of the track, its bright colors muted by the twilight and a dusting of snow; they'd ridden beyond the heart of the blizzard that laid the deeper snow to the north. Gsany Rukkers were moving about the slopes and the broad, mainstreet, coming in from the night-milking and other chores, gossiping over the last loaves from the communal oven, going in and out of a notions shop and the tavern built into the largest building, the village CommonHouse. It was a busy, cheerful scene, all the more so in its contrast to the dark, brooding conifers that surrounded it.

Kori slapped him on the leg, waking him from his daze. He looked down. "What?"

"I said do you have enough coin to pay the shot at the CommonHouse? I'm close to flat."

He thought that over. "How much will it take?"

"A handful of coppers, around twenty. Thirty if you're willing to spring for grain for the ponies."

"Thirty?" He rubbed his fist across his brow. "Yes. All right. Ah. . . ." Seeing she was still waiting, he frowned at her, shut his eyes. "Yes. I see." He tugged a zipper open. His hand was shaking with cold and exhaustion. He scooped up a fistful of the coins in the pocket, gave them to her. "If it's not enough, tell me."

She inspected the miscellany she held. "It's enough. Look . . . ah . . . Danny, they've got hotsprings and a bathhouse here. I think you ought to soak awhile before you sleep."

He blinked then smiled at her. "You telling me I stink?"

"Don't be an idiot, man. You're cold to the bone, you should get warmed up."

He brooded on that a moment, then nodded. "I need you with me."

"What?"

"Not that." Again he shoved the back of his fist across his brow; he was beginning to feel more alive, but he wasn't sure whether that was good or not since he was also feeling every ache and pull of his muscles. "If I soak alone, I'll go to sleep and drown."

"All right." She took hold of the halter's nose-strap. "Let's do it."

7

She was a seal in water, agile and slippery; she cast off whatever burden it was that kept her short-tempered and turned playful. Danny drifted in a corner of the bath, smiling a little as he watched her splash and sputter, dive under and come shooting up with Ailiki in her arms, sending waves of herb-scented water washing at him. She seemed hardly older than the child he remembered. The water rocked him gently, warming away his aches and much of his weariness without sinking him into lethargy; it was the effervescence that did it, the clouds of tiny bubbles that went rushing past his body like pinhead fists kneading and energizing him. He found it extraordinarily pleasant, the more so since he'd reached a temporary peace with himself. His mind was at rest, leaving his body to tend itself.

Kori came paddling over to him, hooked her arms over the bathsill; her freckles shimmered in the lanternlight, her eyes were the color of the water, her hair was slicked back though tiny curls had escaped the mass to make a frizzy halo about her thin face. "Feeling better?"

"Mmm." He reached out, brushed a fingertip across a dimple. "You don't look a day older than that girl in the cart."

"Am." With an urchin grin, she skimmed her hand lightly up his chest, then flicked water into his face.

Before he could react, a voice like icewind cut through the tendrils of steam. "Look up, you l'hy'foor!"

8

Korimenei levered herself up and over the bathsill, sprang to her feet. And froze.

A woman stood at the end of the pool, a taut, dark figure wreathed in steam with a short recurve bow held at stretch, one arrow nocked, a second held by the notch end between two fingers. She vibrated like a tuning fork with a rage that was on the raw edge of erupting.

Danny floated in his corner without trying to move. "Felsrawg," he said softly, "I should have known."

A stocky man came from the dressing room. "It's not in his clothes or hers." He inspected Korimenei. "What's that she's got round her neck?"

"Simms," Danny said, "that's nothing to do with you. You can see it's not Klukesharna."

Felsrawg drew in a breath; it sounded like the hiss of a snake about to strike. "Where?" she spat at him.

Danny didn't waste time pretending not to understand her. "Trithil."

"I don't believe you."

"Wasn't it you shot me? How'd you miss her?"

The bow shook. Danny's hands began to move under the water, gestures to support and shape the spell he was weaving; Korimenei saw that and took a half step away from him.

"You! Hoor! Don't you move."

Again Korimenei froze.

"You! Laz! Get your hands out of the water. Put them on the sill where I can see them. I swear if you move one finger you're dead."

Danny hesitated.

"Do it," Korimenei whispered, just loud enough for him to hear. "Don't be a fool. Remember what I am."

"I hear," he murmured.

Korimenei slid a hand up to touch Frunzacoache; the woman he'd called Felsrawg was glaring at him, watching him like a cat before a mousehole. She took advantage of Felsrawg's distraction to ease another step away, but forced herself to relax and go back to watching Danny when she saw the one called Simms watching her.

Moving slowly so he wouldn't trigger Felsrawg's precarious temper, Danny eased around so his shoulders were tucked in the corner, his arms outstretched along the sill. "Satisfied?" he said.

"Simms! Scrape your eyeballs off that hoor and get over there with him. Laz, you know what we want. You know how far we'll go to get it." She eased up on the bow though she could still get that arrow off before he could move. "Be sensible, man. What's the point?"

"I can't give you what I don't have. The Esmoon went off with it. See her anywhere about?"

"That silka limp? You expect me to believe she's any good off her back?"

"She's not a woman, she's a demon."

Demon, Korimenei thought. Salamander? No. Too damp in here. It'd likely panic and go out of control. A mancat. Yes. . . . Keep her distracted, Danny, give me time to reach. . . . She moved uneasily at a bark of laughter from the stocky man. Standing beside Danny, a skinning knife in his hand, Simms was watching her with cool speculation; Felsrawg might think he was looking at her breasts, but Korimenei knew better. It was Frunzacoache that attracted him, not her.

"You're lying. Simms!"

"Let him talk, Felsa. There's plenty of time for the knife."

Danny snorted. "Much good it'll do you, knife or talk." He waited for Felsrawg to stop quivering, then said, "You got me good three times, Felsa. What happened after that? The Esmoon was there, why didn't you get her? Think about it."

"You know." She growled the words. "You know. Sorcerer! You blasted us. Laid us out and went off leaving us to freeze."

"I was facedown in the snow, leaking blood from three holes, woman. You had to see me down. Use your head. You came within a hair of skewering my heart and you know it. I was in no shape to do anything to anybody."

"No!" Felsrawg was getting agitated again. "No! Liar! If it was true she had it, you'd be nose to the ground after her. You'd have to be."

"For one, who says I'm not, eh? Think of that?"

"You're saying she came this way?"

"No. Far as I'm concerned, I'd be delighted if I never saw the creature again. Come on, Felsa, put the bow down. The poison's out of me. My friend here, she did that when she healed my punctures. She's got a Talent for that sort of thing."

Felsrawg stretched her mouth into a mirthless feral grin. "Good for her," she said, "she can enjoy herself putting you together again. Simms."

Gods, Korimenei thought. She dropped to her knees, hugged her arms across her breasts and slipped dangerously unprotected into the trance that took her across the realities.

##

Sand and more sand, sand and brush and sand-colored mancats prowling after herds of sand-colored deer. She saw a mancat she knew and called to him. *Help me,* she said to him, *name your price and help me.*

He came trotting up to her, considered her. After a minute he opened his formidable mouth in a broad grin. She understood from him that he was fond of her as a man would be fond of a favorite pet and would help her for the fun of it.

##

Korimenei lifted her head and smiled.

The mancat dropped from nothing behind Felsrawg, wrapped thick muscular tentacles about her and breathed hot, meat-tainted breath in her ears. She screamed her rage and tried to kick and claw, but his front legs were spread too wide for her to reach and her arms were locked against her sides; she was as about as helpless as she'd ever been since she started walking. She went quiet and lay against the mancat's powerful chest, glaring at Korimenei and cursing bitterly.

The instant the beast came through the membrane, Danny Blue acted; using his elbows to power himself up, he slapped his hands about the wrist on Simms' knife hand and toppled him into the water; he set his feet against the thief's floundering body and kicked, using the resistance to help him roll out of the pool. He was over the sill and on his feet before Simms surfaced sputtering. Panting a little, Danny smiled at Korimenei, waved a hand at the mancat. "A friend, I hope?"

She chuckled. "My demon's better than yours."

"No argument there."

The mancat interrupted with an apologetic coughing rumble. He was uncomfortable in the damp and thought it was time he left.

"Right," she said. "Danny, you take care of him, I'll do her." She nodded at Simms who was holding on to the edge of the pool, watching them warily, then padded around to face Felsrawg. "Are you intelligent enough to know the truth when you hear it?" She inspected the woman, sniffed. "I wonder." Over her shoulder, she said, "Where'd you meet this pair, Danny?"

"They were my backup getting Klukesharna." He smiled lazily at Felsrawg. "And sent along to slide a knife between my ribs once we got her."

"Shuh! I don't think much of your taste."

"Not mine."

"Mmh." She tapped the mancat on his shoulder. *Lower your um arms a little, my friend; I need to get at the woman's neck.* After he readjusted his tentacles, she put pressure on the carotid until Felsrawg was unconscious. *Put her down, thanks. Anything I can do for you? No? Well, let's send you home.* She pulled her mindseine about him and snapped him back to his sandhills, promising in transit to visit him, them, again when things weren't so hectic.

When she looked around, Danny Blue was watching her, a hungry look on his face. She didn't understand. He was a sorcerer and a ripely Talented one if her nose wasn't fooling her. *Gods of Fate and Time as Maks would say—why am I thinking of Maksi—that's his business not mine, Tungjii's blessing on us both for that.*

He shook off whatever it was on his mind. "You going to wash the poison out of them, Kori? I wish you would. I don't owe this pair anything, but poison!" He dredged up a wry grin. "Besides, the only way I know of to get rid of them is kill them or cure them."

"Right," she said. "I'm just about to do that. Aili, where are you? Good. Watch my back. Danny, if you don't mind, fetch my clothes, hmm? This is no season for parading about as Primavera." Without waiting to see what he did, she dragged the chain over her head, dropped Frunzacoache on Felsrawg's leather bosom and began the cleansing.

9

"Frunzacoache the Undying," Danny said aloud, though he was speaking to himself, not Simms. "First Klukesharna, now Frunzacoache. Coincidence, maybe? Coincidence, hell."

Careful not to move too suddenly, Simms pulled himself onto the sill and sat with his legs dangling in the heated water. He watched Korimenei work, nodded. "I c'n feel it," he said. "You wahn't havin' us on."

"What? Oh. Yeh." Danny dragged himself away from the pulses of power throbbing out from the girl; the part of him born of Ahzurdan found the effect intoxicating. He ran a hand through his hair, frowned down at Simms. "You're not stupid."

"C'n see where you might think I was. Young for 't, an't she."

Danny yawned. As the tension drained out of him, his weariness came flooding back. "If she weren't still tender, you'd be ash and gone. Give me your hand." When Simms was on his feet, Danny tapped him on the shoulder, pointed toward the dressing room. "Come on, she wants her clothes and I'm tired of prancing around stark."

"What was that thing?"

"Don't ask me, it's not one of mine."

#

Simms hauled off a boot, upended it and shook out the water. "Sling me one of those tow'ls, eh Laz?"

"Make it Danny, Lazul was for the duration only."

"Sure. Why not." He pulled off the other boot, dried his feet and legs, then the inside of the boots. "Us'ly I don' bath with m' clothes on."

"Better I dump you than I fry you. I could've, you know."

"I 'spect you could. I 'spect you din't 'cause you'd fry yourself with me."

"Maybe so." Danny stomped his feet down in his boots, ran a towel over his hair, scooped up Korimenei's clothing. "On your feet, Simmo. She should be ready for you by now."

In the Bath Room he tossed the shirt and trousers to Kori. There was a pile of knives, poison rings and other weapons on the tiles. Felsrawg stood on the far side of the pool, glowering at nothing in particular, hands thrust in her trouser pockets. She turned that scowl on Danny a moment, then looked away.

"Gracefully grateful, I see," he said.

Kori grinned at him. "Yes, oh man, you did it much better. You, Simms, if you roll up that towel, you can stick it under your head and be a bit more comfortable. Stretch out where she was and I'll get to work on you."

Danny dropped to a squat, began examining the collection of weapons, trying the balance of the knives, testing the mechanisms in the rings. He felt eyes on him and lifted his head. Felsrawg was glaring at him, indignant at the insult he was offering her. He looked down at the ring he was fingering, then at her; he got the feeling he might as well have been fingering her naked body. He set the ring down and got to his feet, embarrassed at his boorishness, annoyed at the woman for challenging him. Muttering under his breath he moved to stand behind Kori; once again the waves of power she was outputting swept through him, pleasuring him. He drifted in that borrowed glow for a few moments, felt a wistful deprivation when the power abruptly cut off. Kori continued to kneel for a short time longer, head bent. Slowly, with visible reluctance, she reached for Frunzacoache and lifted it off Simms. The way she handled the talisman, it was far heavier than it looked. And hotter. She slid the chain over her head, slipped the pendant under her shirt.

"Want a hand, Kori?"

"I could use one." She swiveled round on her knees, held up her arms and let him pull her onto her feet. "What are we going to do with this pair?"

He swung her against him, her back to his chest, folded his arms under her breasts. "If they don't behave," he murmured into her ear, "you can send them to join your feline pet."

"Certainly not, he's a friend, I wouldn't do that to him."

Simms sat up, grimaced at his unexpected weakness. "A thought I wish you'd keep firmly in mind, Angyd Sorcelain. Why do I feel like the end of a long fast?"

Danny felt her relax against him; her ribs moved as she took a deep breath, let it out. "The poison has been working in you," she said. "I stripped fat and muscle from your bones to heal that damage. You'll get it back with a few good meals and some sleep."

"Sleep, sounds good." He got heavily to his feet. "You going to boot us out of here?"

"And waste my work? No."

Felsrawg snorted and came strolling around the end of the pool; she was pale and drawn, there were dark smudges under her eyes, but she refused to give in to her weakness. "Laz, where do you go, come the morning?"

"Where do I go, Kori?" He slid his hand down her side, rested it on her hip.

"Where you want. Why ask me?"

He chuckled. "I wouldn't touch that if you paid me." He eyed Felsrawg. "South," he said. "We go south all the way to water. Why?"

"We can't go back to Arsuid, not for a while anyway." She turned to Simms; he nodded. "This isn't a good time for traveling, the wolves are out, four legs and two. I want to come with you. Simms? Yes. We're not begging, Laz. We'll pay our way." She ran her eyes with slow insolence from Danny's bare feet to his stubble-shadowed face. "You look a fool on that pony. We can mount you. Her too, if she wants."

"The horses we had?"

"No, the ones from Soholkai-ots, the next stage on. You left us on foot, remember? We had to steal a fishboat to get to Soholkai. The Esmoon must have gone off with yours. Look," she said, "we were a good team before, we could do it again and four will scare off trouble better than two. I'm not saying you couldn't handle anything that came up, just that it'd be easier if it didn't. Come up, I mean."

Kori pulled loose, started for the door. "See me in the morning. I'm too tired to think. Danny, where you want. Read me?" She didn't wait for an answer.

"Not too early in the morning," Danny told Felsrawg and left.

10

Danny pushed the sweaty hair off Kori's brow. "Why'd you change your mind?"

"I don't know." She moved her head as he started nibbling on an ear. "All those bubbles, maybe."

"Mmmm."

"Stop that." She wriggled away from him. "Gods, man, I thought you'd be used up after. . . ."

"All those bubbles."

"They should bottle them and sell them to tired old men." She giggled, then sobered. "That pretty pair. You didn't tell me about them."

"Didn't know they were anywhere around."

"Mmm-hmmm."

"Don't believe me?"

"I melted three reasons out of your body."

"Ah, well. I said, *know.*"

"What do you think, do we let them come?"

After tugging a fold of blanket from under him, he eased onto his back and pulled her against him, her head pillowed on his shoulder. When he was comfortable, he thought about the question. "It's your call," he said finally. "We could use the horses."

"Yeh, the poor ponies, they've walked a long way. Why does Felsrawg want to come? I don't think Simms does, not really."

"Felsa looks round corners that aren't there."

"Huh?" She tilted her head to look up at him.

He brushed fine flyaway hair away from his mouth. "She's decided to believe me about the Esmoon, but she doesn't think I'd let Klukesharna get away. She intends to be there when I find it. It's her key to Dirge Arsuid, if you'll pardon the pun. She wants to go home."

"Don't we all."

"Mmh."

"What's that mean?"

"If I answered that I'd feel like a damn whore."

"Huh?"

"Selling my services. Or should I say servicings?"

"Do and you'll lose your asset."

"Challenging me, Angyd Sorcelain?"

"Never, Addryd Sorcesieur. Offering my knee."

"And a dainty one it is, if somewhat angular." He rolled over swiftly, pinning her to the rustling mattress, shutting off her protest with mouth and hands. After several minutes of this, he lifted his head. "May I move where I need to be, love, or should I fear that militant knee of yours? I'll take care to avoid it if you'll just tell me which it is."

"You talk too much."

"Never say it. Ah, I'm crushed."

"Hah! You stand tall for such a humble man."

"You can bring me low quickly enough."

"Talking again. It's deeds I demand."

"Command me, Angyd Sorcelain."

"Hear me, Addryd Sorcesieur. Do again what you did before. If you can."

"Be ready, Angyd Sorcelain. Here I come."

"So soon? Ah! that tickles."

"Good. Come has another meaning, love, you have a one-rut mind."

"No, a rutting friend, pra . . . aise be t . . . to Tungjiiii!"

11

Korimenei left the ponies behind, paying a stablemaster for their care with money she borrowed from Danny, adding a gloss on the coins by summoning a salamander and holding him overhead to show the man what would happen to him if he mistreated or neglected them. They were affectionate, hardworking little beasts and they'd been part of her life so long it was like tearing an arm off to leave them behind, but they were exhausted by the rough going and would have a much easier winter in the Gsany village Fal Fenyott, dining on grain and rich mountain hay.

Always a breath ahead of storms as if the northwinds and the snow were chasing them, the mismated quartet rode south on the wave of power pouring from the melded sorcerers, unwilled as breathing and copious as an artesian spring, sustaining humans and horses both, injecting into them the strength for enormous effort, letting them flee from dark into dark without stopping to rest or breaking down.

Simms withdrew into himself as the days passed. With the poison out of him, he didn't see any point in chasing the talisman; he had no real wish to return to Dirge Arsuid, in fact there were a lot of reasons he'd prefer not to, his lover had betrayed him to the Ystaffel when the guards came searching for him, his family had cast him out long before that, he was bored, he saw no challenges left in his profession or personal life. Lots of reasons. He watched Felsrawg nosing about Danny Blue and found the sight distasteful; the bond forged between the two thieves as they fought desperately to survive dissolved as soon as the danger was removed. On the tenth morning of that precipitous journey, he lost patience and left the group, riding east, bound for the river Sharroud and transport south to Bandrabahr. There he'd have a wide choice of destinations. Remembering what Danny had said about Croaldhu he had a vague notion of visiting that island, but mostly he wanted to escape the cold, the constant exhaustion and the disturbing urgency of that charge southward. He didn't understand what was happening and he didn't want to.

Korimenei drove Danny and Felsrawg south and south and yet south; she was more and more aware of the child growing in her, of the need to find a place where she could rest and feel safe. She wanted this hideous journey over, she wanted to be done with her brother's demands. The eidolon came every night to quiver over her after Danny had gone to sleep; Tré said nothing, but she felt him pushing at her to hurry, hurry, hurry. The passionate playful exchanges between her and Danny Blue, begun in Fal Fenyott and continued through the first few days of travel had turned brutish and wordless, greedy and needy, like the time in Ambijan. After Simms left she felt odd, lying with Danny while Felsrawg was rolled in her blankets outside the tent, listening . . . maybe not listening, but hearing it all; she was uncomfortable, it was too much like a public performance, but she couldn't stop, or let him stop. It was as if something was generated between them that was necessary to the journey and until that journey was finished she could neither understand it or do without it.

Danny Blue rode beside Korimenei, watching her, worrying about her. His half-sire Daniel grew up in a vast and fecund family, Family Azure on Rainbow's End in another reality altogether, but a woman here was no different from a woman there so the Daniel phasma was soon aware of Kori's pregnancy and passed the word to his semi-son. The Ahzurdan phasma hung about, gibbering his fear and distaste, his growing resentment of Kori, sneering at Danny for being so protective of another man's child. The Daniel phasma snarled back, scornful of such intolerance. In Family Azure all children were treasured, all mothers were the responsibility of the Family, not merely the particular male who'd got the woman pregnant; the Daniel phasma's protectiveness was automatic and all the more powerful because of that and it was transferred almost intact to Danny Blue.

There was another reason for the sharpening conflict between the two phasmas and the headache they were giving Danny Blue. Korimenei could send him home—or rather into Daniel's reality, a place Danny was more and more thinking of as home. He didn't have to hunt up Settsimaksimin, he had his transport; after seeing how easily she handled the massive mancat, he was sure she could do it once she was free to put her mind to the problem. He was determined to stay with her and give her what protection he could until that moment came.

Felsrawg's hopes eroded as the days passed. By the time they reached the Gallindar Plains, she was forced to concede she'd made a mistake. Danny Blue wasn't going after Klukesharna, he was tied to the heels of that woman. He trotted after her like a dog after a bitch in heat. It wasn't an edifying sight, Felsrawg thought, and burned with a jealousy she wouldn't admit even to herself. Especially to herself. She thought about leaving like Simms had, but she stayed. I've nowhere else to go and I want to see what happens when we reach the end of this journey, maybe I can wring some profit out of it, the woman's got a reason for half killing us like this, I want to know what it is. She refused to countenance what she considered her silly yearning for the man, it was too demeaning. She wasn't some sickly teener bitch, she'd survived two decades against the odds, been wholly on her own for the second of those decades. But she couldn't help going soft in the middle whenever she looked at him. And she couldn't stop wanting to skin that sorcelain who had her claws in him.

South and south and south they raced, outrunning hostile Gallinasi bands, flattening Gallinasi youths out to win their coup-studs with foreign ears and noses, south and south until they reached the shore of the Notoea Tha, and even there Korimenei wouldn't stop, barely paused, terrifying a misfortunate smuggler (who'd come slipping through the Shoals to trade Matamulli brandy for Gallindar pearls) into carrying them yet farther south, down the Fingercoast of Cheonea.

On a cold blustery morning, gray with a storm not yet broken, the smuggler landed Korimenei, Danny Blue and Felsrawg Lawdrawn at the mouth of a smallish creek, then hoisted sail again and got out of there fast as the wind would take him.

12

Korimenei lifted the lantern; nothing much had changed in the Chain Room. Ten years. It might have been ten minutes. She looked at the platform, looked quickly away. The crystal was there with Tré curled up in it, but she found she was reluctant to go near the thing. All she had to do was put her hand on the crystal, then Tré would be free, she could give him Frunzacoache and that would be the end of it.

Instead, she turned in a slow circle, the light from the lantern spreading and contracting with the irregular circumference of the cave chamber. Chains hung in graceful curves, one end bolted to a ceiling so high it was lost in the darkness beyond the reach of the lantern, the other end to the sidewall a man's height off the floor. Chains crossed and recrossed the space above her head, chains of iron forged on a smithpriest's anvil and hung in here so long ago all but the lowest links were coated with stone, chains of wood whittled by the woodworker priests' knives, chains of crystal and saltmarble chiseled by the stonecutter priests, centuries of labor given to the cave, taken by the cave to itself, a layer of stone slowly slowly crawling over all of it. No, there was no change she could see; if the stone had crept a fingerwidth lower, it would take a better eye than hers to measure it. She finished the turn facing the Chained God's altar, a square platform of polished wood sitting on stone blocks that lifted it a foot off the stone floor, above it, held up by carved wooden posts, a canopy of white jade, thin and translucent as the finest porcelain. In the center of the platform the crystal lay beside the kedron chest where Tré had found Harra's Eye and given it to her so she could use it to locate the Drinker of Souls. "Be careful what you do," she said aloud. "The more powerful the act, the more unpredictable the outcome."

Danny touched her shoulder. "You feel like telling us why we're here?"

"Take this, will you?" She handed him the lantern. "You see that thing?"

"Hard to miss."

"That's my brother in there. You said you remembered him."

"Ah. Who. . . ."

"Settsimaksimin. He wanted to make sure I stayed in school."

"You're out now."

Felsrawg shivered. "It's colder'n a fetch's finger in here. Whatever you got to do, do it."

"Stay out of this, Felsa," Danny said, "you're along for the ride, she doesn't need your ignorance yapping at her."

"T'ss! Don't need yours either, seems to me. All she needs from you is your. . . ."

"Shut up, both of you." Korimenei stripped her gloves off, shoved them into a coat pocket, lifted Ailiki from her shoulder and gave her to Danny. "Stay there, Aili my Liki. Wait." She took a deep breath, let it out slowly. Scratchy little thief was right, what you got to do, do it.

Don't stand around dithering. She walked to the altar, took hold of a post and pulled herself onto the platform. She took another breath, reached out and flattened her hand on the warm silky crystal.

It quivered like something alive, then she was touching nothing. She could still see it, but she was touching nothing.

Like water emptying down a drain, it flowed away from Trago, lowering him gently to the polished planks.

When it was all gone, her brother straightened his arms and legs, yawned and opened his eyes. He was on his side, his back to Korimenei. He didn't look round, he just got to his feet and went to the chest, opened it and took the crystal out, Harra's Eye. He turned finally and saw her. "Who are you?"

"I'm Kori, Tré."

"You can't be Kori, you're old."

"You don't remember?"

"I remember . . . I remember being at the Lot. Kori got the blue, I got nothing. They took her away. I went back to the Hostel with the others. AuntNurse gave me a drink to make me sleep. That was yesterday. . . ." He frowned as he saw Danny and Felsrawg standing silent under the chains.

"You shouldn't have brought strangers in here." When he realized what he'd said, he looked frightened. "What am I doing here? How'd I get here?"

"That wasn't yesterday, Tré. You've been spelled, brother, you've slept ten years away without knowing it. I thought . . . I thought you did know it, I thought you found a way to talk to me." She saw the confusion in his eyes and knew finally how completely she'd been fooled. "It wasn't you, was it?" At first she was relieved, the eidolon she'd grown to resent so bitterly wasn't her brother; then she was angry and afraid. She reached out to touch him; he shied away, frightened of her, then at last he seemed to accept her. He didn't say anything, but he let her pull him close and put her arm about his shoulder. "I am Kori, Tré, I am your sister. Really. I came to wake you and give you . . ." she touched the face of the talisman, slid her fingers over it and over it, drawing a measure of calm from the way it nestled against her. "Let me take you home, Tré. I want to go home too. I've been away at a school. A long, long way from here."

"Kori?"

"Come on, I'll tell you all about it. You going to keep the Eye with you?"

He looked down; he was clutching the crystal sphere against him, holding it in both hands. "I NEED to," he said.

"All right." She lifted him down. "Danny, Felsa, let's. . . ."

Darkness swallowed them.

She heard Danny curse, she heard Felsrawg scream with rage, Ailiki leapt at her, she felt the mahsar's claws dig through her coat into her flesh.

The darkness swallowed them all.

III: SETTSIMAKSIMIN

Driving south to steal Shaddalakh
from the Grand Magus of Tok Kinsa
in order to redeem his souls from the
geniod who'd trapped him, Maksim
was caught in a blizzard and blown
across the path of Simms the thief
who had taken shelter from that
storm in an abandoned farmstead.

1

On his third day out of the mountains, Simms ran into the front end of
a Plains blizzard. A few snowflakes blew past, at the moment more of a
promise than a threat; wet winds brittle with cold snatched at him and
whipped up the mane and tail of his horse; the beast sidled uneasily,
fought the bit, snorted and tried to run from the storm. "Hey Neddio,
ho Neddio, slow, babe, go slow," he sang to the horse, "soft, Neddio,
steady, Neddio, it's a long way we got to go, Neddio."

Calling on his Talent, reading earth and air, Simms sniffed out a
vague promise of shelter and rode toward it, angling across the wind.
"Here we go, Neddio, just a lit-t-t-tle way, Neddio, you'll be warm,
Neddio, out of the wind, out of the storm, Neddio." He loosened his
hold on the reins, letting the horse stretch to a long easy lope.

Around noon, though it might as well have been midnight, the
gloom had thickened until it was nearly impenetrable, he saw a scatter
of dark shapes that turned into trees and blocky buildings as he got
closer. A shoulder-high wall loomed ahead of him. Neddio the horse
squealed and shied; when Simms had him steady again, he followed the
wall to a gap. There should have been a gate, but he didn't see any. He
turned through the gap and felt a lessening of the wind's pressure as
the wall broke its sweep. He couldn't see much, so he let the horse find
the driveway and move along it toward what had to be the house.

No lights. Nothing.

"Hallooo," he yelled, raising his voice so he could be heard above the wind. "Hey the house! You got a visitor. Mind if I come in?"

Nothing.

"Well, Neddio, seems to me silence is good as a formal invite." He slid from the saddle, hunted about for the tie-rail; he found it by backing into it and nearly impaling himself on the end. He secured the reins around it in a quick half-hitch and went groping for the door, expecting to find it closed and barred.

It was open a crack, but resisted when he pushed against it. He pushed harder. The leather hinges tore across and the door crashed down. He heard some quick scuttlings in the darkness as vermin fled from the noise. Nothing else. The stead was deserted; from the dilapidation he could feel and smell it'd been that way for a long time. He leaned against the wall and listened to the slow, rumbling complaints of the rammed dirt, ancient memories of blood and screaming, present groans about the years and years since the wall had a coat of sealer brushed over it. Even the dirt knew it was decaying. He didn't listen long, it didn't matter that much why the folk had left, all that mattered was getting shelter before the storm hit.

He left Neddio at the tie-rail and groped his way around to the barn. It was in much worse shape than the house, two of the walls had melted away, the roof was lying in pieces about stalls and bins also broken and half burnt. It's house for old Neddio, he thought, and I best get as much wood in today as I can. When that blow hits full force, we're not going anywhere. Wonder if there's something about I can use as a drag so I won't have to make so many trips? Mellth'g bod, can't see a thing. Raaht, Simmo, one step at a time. Fire first, then see what I can locate. He gathered an armload of the wood scraps and felt his way back to the front door.

##

The house proved to be in better condition than he'd expected. There were two stories, the roof was reasonably intact and whatever leaked through the shakes was generally soaked up by the cross laid double floor of the second story. He decided to camp in the kitchen; there was a fireplace, a brick oven, several benches and a table that must have been built where it stood since it was far too big to fit through any of the doors. There was a washstand at the far end, close to the fireplace; that part of the kitchen was built over an artesian spring that was still gurgling forth a copious flow of cold pure water, the overflow caught and carried away by a tiled waste channel that split in two parts as it dipped under the back wall. One part flowed under the room next door and emptied into what had once been a large and flourishing vegetable garden—Simms found some tubers and herbs there that made a welcome addition to the stores he was carrying; the other part went to the barn; he found that ditch by falling into it when he poked about in the store sheds and corrals behind the house. In one of those sheds, a low, thickwalled, sod-roofed cube, he found a dozen ceramic jars almost as tall as he was, the tops sealed with a mixture of clay and wax. He put a hand on each of them, red beans, peas, lentils, flour, barley and wheat, old but untouched by rot or mildew. He tried shifting one of the jars; if he put his shoulder to it, he could tilt it and rock it across the floor, but getting it all the way to the house was something else. He'd have to use Neddio to haul them, something the horse wasn't going to like much. Wood first, though. He stepped outside, got a flurry of snow in the face; in the gusts and between them, the snow was coming down harder. He didn't have all that much time left before nightfall when even the dim gray twilight would vanish.

He cobbled together harness and collar with bits of rope and the saddle blanket, tied the ends of the harness rope to the front corners of a piece of canvas he'd found rolled up in a closet in the kitchen and began hauling wood back to the house, everything he could scavenge. He worked steadily for the next several hours, back and forth, rails, posts, bits of barn roof, rafters, stall timbers, anything he could chop loose and pile on the canvas, back and forth, the wind battering them, the snow coming down harder and harder, smothering them. Until, at last, there was no wood left worth the effort of hauling it.

He cut the canvas loose and left it in the small foyer, took Neddio around to the shed and hitched him to one of the jars. Hauling proved slow, awkward work; Neddio balked again and again, he detested those ropes cutting into him, that weight dragging back on him. Simms patted him, coaxed him, sang him into one more effort and then one more and again one more.

Heading out of the house for the last of the jars, he heard a mule bray and a moment later, a second one.

"Visitors? Yah yah, Neddio, you can stand down a while till I see what's what." He stripped off his heavy outer gloves, tossed them inside, slapped the horse on the shoulder and waited until the beast had retreated into the semi-warmth of the parlor, then he followed the sound of the braying. He groped his way to the wall, found the gap. He could see about a foot from his nose, after that nothing but the flickering white haze so he was very wary of leaving the shelter of the wall, it would be all too easy to get so turned around and confused he couldn't find his way back to the house. He stood in the gap, leaning into the wind and listening. The mules were off to his left, not far from the wall though he couldn't see them. He whistled, whistled again. The sound died before it reached them, sucked into the keening of the wind. That was no good. He began to sing, a calling song he'd learned from his outlander grandmer when he was a child. She died when he was six, but he still remembered her songs and the things she'd taught him. He sang across the wind, willed the mules to hear him and come. He sang until he was hoarse—until two dark shapes came out of the snow and stopped before him.

They were hitched to a light two-wheel dulic, the reins loose, dragging on the ground. The driver was a large lump mounded along the driver's bench, unconscious or dead. Didn't matter, the mules were alive, he had to get them into shelter.

Still singing, he teased them closer and closer until he could take hold of a halter and retrieve the reins.

He led them along the driveway and took them into the parlor, stripped off their harness and chased them into the corner where he'd spread some straw he'd retrieved from under a section of barnroof and piled up for bedding. After a minute's thought, he pulled the improvised harness off Neddio and sent him after them; the last jar could stay in the shed until they needed it. If they did.

Now for the driver, he thought. Dead or alive? Well, we'll see.

He shivered as he plunged into the wind and snow, groped over to the dulic and climbed into it. He burrowed through layers of scarves and cloaks until he could get his fingers on the man's neck, poked about until he discovered the artery and rested his fingertips on it. The man's heart was beating strongly, but he was very very cold. Something not wholly natural about the chilly flesh, he didn't know what it was, but it bothered him. Still, he couldn't leave him out here to freeze. Offing someone when the blood was hot, well, that was a thing could happen to anyone, cold blood was different, and by damn his blood and everything else was cold. He pried up the massive torso, gritted his teeth under the weight and length of the man, got as much of him as he could wrapped around his shoulders and began the laborious process of getting back to the ground without injuring his load or doing serious damage to himself.

Ten sweaty staggering minutes later, he laid the stranger out on the tiles in front of the kitchen fire. He left him there and went to fetch in the gear and other supplies from the dulic, piled the pouches and blanket roll on the table and went back for a second load. There was more baggage than he'd expected, this was no wandering beggar, whatever else he was.

When the last load was in and piled on the table, he went to look at his patient. The man hadn't changed position and wasn't showing any signs of waking. Simms touched his brow. No fever. He was still cold but not quite so deathly chill. You'll do for a while. I sh'd get those wet clothes off, but that can wait. Dulic first, then I deal with the door an' take care of the stock, then it's your turn, friend. Plenty of time for you. I be glad, though, when you wake and tell me what in u'ffren you're doin' out here. Wonderin' makes me itch.

After he pulled the dulic back of the house and rolled it into a shed, he inspected the door he'd knocked down; he and Neddio had tramped back and forth across it dozens of times but even Neddio's iron shoes had done little to mark the massive planks of mountain oak, glued together and further reinforced by horizontal and diagonal two-by-fours of the same oak nailed onto the planks with hand-forged iron nails. He muscled the door into the opening, propped it against the jamb, walked one of the jars against it to keep the wind from blowing it down again.

The two mules were tail switching and fratchetty, they kicked at Neddio if he went too close to them, nipped at Simms when he shifted some of the straw into another corner for his horse, even followed him, long yellow teeth reaching for arms and legs or a handy buttock, when he went to lay a fire in the parlor fireplace, though they didn't like the fire much and retreated to their corner when it started crackling briskly. Keeping a wary eye on them, he dragged one of the parlor benches to the hearth and spread corn along it from a corn jar in the foyer. He rolled an ancient crock from the kitchen, filled it with water, took a look round and was satisfied he'd done what he could to make the beasts comfortable.

In the kitchen, he filled the tin tank in the brick stove and kindled a fire under it so he'd have hot water to bathe his patient; he laid another fire in the stoke hole, filled one of the stranger's pots from the spring, dropped in dried meat from his own stores and lentils and barley from jars in the parlor, along with some of the tubers and herbs from the garden and set it simmering on the grate. He put tea water to heating beside the stew and went to inspect the stranger.

He was a long man, six foot five, six, maybe even seven with shoulders of a size to match his length. He had been a heavy man, big muscles with a layer of fat; he'd lost the fat and some of the muscle, his skin hung loose around him. He w'd make a han'some skel'ton. Simms smiled at the thought and drew his fingers over the prominent bones of the man's face. Beautiful man. Thick coarse gray hair in a braid that vanished down the cloak. Brows dark, with only a hair or two gone gray. Eyelashes long and sooty, resting in a graceful arc on the dark poreless skin stretched over his cheekbones. Big, powerful man, but Simms got a feeling of fragility from him, as if the size and strength were illusions painted over emptiness. Beautiful shell, but only a shell.

He turned the stranger onto his stomach, eased his head around so his damp hair was turned to the fire and began stripping the sodden clothing off him, boots first, boot liners, knitted stockings, two pairs, wool and silk with the silk next to the silk. Gloves, fur lined. Silk glove liners. Furlined cloak. Silk-lined woolen undercloak. Wool robe, heavily embroidered over the chest, around the hem and sleeve cuffs. Silk under-robe. Wool trousers. Silk underwear. Whoever he was, he was a man of wealth and importance. What he was doing crossing the Grass in winter, alone . . . itch itch, wake up an' talk t' me, man, 'fore my head explode.

He fetched the water from the tank and began bathing the stranger, concentrating at first on his hands and feet, checking carefully for any signs of frostbite, pleased to see there were none. He didn't understand why the man didn't wake up, worried about it and was frustrated by his own ignorance. If his family hadn't been so opposed to anything that smelled of witchery, if he'd had the drive and intelligence to go out and get training, beyond the little he picked up from his grandmer, if and if and if. . . . Beautiful beautiful man, if he die, it's my fault, my ignorance that kill 'im. He dried the man, rubbing and rubbing with the soft nubby towel he'd found in one of the pouches, and still he didn't wake, he yielded to Simms' manipulations like a big cat to a stroking hand, it was almost as if his body recognized Simms and cooperated as much as an unminded body could.

He folded the towel, put it under the man's head. I need clothes for you. I hope you don' mind, I been goin' through your stuff. He touched the man's face, drew his forefinger along the elegant lips. Wake up, wake up, wake. . . . He sighed and got to his feet.

The table was spread with the pouches and things he'd already pulled from them. He unbuckled the pouch that held the man's spare clothing. Robes, rolled in neat, tight cylinders. He shook them out, chose one and set it aside. The blankets, I'd better have them. Another pouch. Meat, apples, trailbars wrapped in oiled silk—he set those aside as he came on them. A large leather wallet with papers inside. He tossed that down without exploring it, none of his business, at the moment anyway. A plump, clunk-clanking purse. He opened it. Jaraufs and takks, Jorpashil coin. Another towel, in an oiled silk sac along with bars of soap and a squeeze tube with an herb-scented lotion inside.

He gave over his explorations, carried the robe and lotion back to the man. Kneeling beside him, he rubbed the lotion all over him, enjoying the feel of him, the brisk green smell of the lotion. Y' walk in circles I can't even sniff at, everythin' say it. He felt a pleasant melancholy as he contemplated the probable impossibility of what he wanted. When he was finished with the rubdown, he rolled the sleeper over, spread one of the blankets on the hearth; after sweat and swearing and frustration, he finally got the dry robe on him and shifted him bit by bit onto the blanket.

Weary beyond exhaustion, weary to the bone, Simms got heavily to his feet. The soup was sending out a pleasant smell, filling the kitchen with it, making it feel homier than any place he'd been in for years. He stirred the thick, gummy liquid, tasted it, smiled and shifted it from the grate to the sand bed where it could simmer away without burning. The tea water was boiling; he dropped in a big pinch of tea leaves, stirred them with a whisk and set the pot on the sand to let the leaves settle out. He picked up the wet, discarded clothing, hung it on pegs beside the fireplace to dry out and went into the parlor to check on the horses. The water in the crock was low; he emptied what was left onto the floor and fetched more from the kitchen. Neddio was sleeping in one corner, the mules were dozing in another. The truce seemed to be holding. He put out more grain, thinking: feed 'em well while I got it and hope the storm blow out before we in trouble for food. He checked the fire, threw a chunk of fence post on and left it to catch on its own.

Back in the kitchen he stripped and straddled the waste channel, scooped up water and poured it over himself, shuddering at the bite of that icemelt, feeling a temporary burst of vigor as he rubbed himself dry on his visitor's towel. He hung it on a peg, pulled on his trousers, turned to pick up his shirt and saw the man watching him.

"Well, welc'm to th' world, breyn stranger." He pushed his arms into the sleeves and began buttoning his shirt. "Was wonderin' when y'd wake." He went to check the soup, tasted it and turned, holding up the ladle. "Hungry?"

"What is this place?"

"I'm as temp'ry as you, blown here by the wind. Whoever lived here left long time ago." He started ladling soup into a pannikin. "Name's Simms Nadaw, out of Dirge Arsuid."

"Long way from home."

"Way it goes."

"Maks. Passing through everywhere, lighting nowhere. Recently at least."

"Right. Feel good enough to sit up?" He took the pannikin and a spoon to the hearth and set it on the tiles, went back to the stove. "Get some of that down you. Start warming your insides well as your out."

"Give it a try." After a small struggle Maks managed to raise himself high enough to fold his long legs and get himself balanced with his shoulder to the fire. "Weaker 'n I thought. Soup smells good." He tasted it. "Is good."

"Hot anyway." Simms spread a square of cheesecloth over his mug, poured himself some tea, rinsed the cheesecloth and repeated with another mug, then filled another pannikin with soup. Over his shoulder he said, "You want some tea? It's yours, I poke through y' things, they over there." He nodded at the table.

Maks looked amused. "See you found my mug."

"That I did. Take it that mean yes."

"Take it right." He set the pannikin down. "The mules?"

"Parlor. With Neddio. M' horse. Bad tempered mabs, an't they."

"Not fond of freezing, that's all."

"Mmh. Shu'n't keep 'em so hungry then, they were doin' their best to eat ol' Neddio. Me too. Got toothmarks on my butt. Want some more soup?"

"Just the tea for now. I don't want to overload the body."

"Odd way o puttin' it." Simms took the tea to him, collected the empty pannikin and rinsed it in the channel. He turned it upside down over the tank and went back to leaning on the wall beside the stove, enjoying the warmth radiating from the bricks while he ate his soup. He was immersed in flickering shadows while his visitor was centered in the glow of such light as there was in the kitchen. The firelight loved Maks' bones, it slid along them like melted butter, waking amber and copper lights in his dark skin, face and hands and the hollow where his collar bones met.

"Listen to that wind howl. Bless ol' Tungjii, I wouldn't want to be out there now." He had a rich deep voice, flexible, musical, Simms thrilled each time the man spoke; he had trouble concealing his response to the sound, but he worked at it, he didn't want to disgust him or turn him hostile.

"Blessings be, on heesh an' we." Simms finished his soup, rinsed his pannikin and spoon in the channel, set them on the stove. "We were both luckier'n we deserve running across a place like this." He gave himself some more tea. "Too bad the steader were chase out, a spring like this 'n is flowin' gold."

"Chased out?"

"'M a Reader, Maks; walls remember, walls talk. Blood and screams, 's what they tol' me. But it was all a long long time ago. Ne'er been this way b'fore. You know how long Grass storms us'ly last?"

"It's still early winter. This one should blow out around three days on."

"I put the dulic in a shed out back. I don' know how much good it's gonna do you if there's a couple feet of snow on the ground."

"We'll see what we see." He chuckled, a deep rumbling that came up from his heels. "There's no horse foaled that'd carry me." He yawned, screwed up his face. "My bladder's singing help," he said, "you have any preference where I empty it?"

"You see the spring here, they led a channel off from it under the tiles the next room over, what we call straffill in Arsuid, there a catch basin, for baths I s'pose. Got a hole in the floor, a spash-chute on th' wall, leadin' to the hole. You wanna shoulder t' lean on?"

Maks bent and straightened his legs, rubbed at his knees. "Give a hand getting on my feet, if you don't mind, breyn Nadaw."

"Simms, y' don' mind." He offered his hands, braced himself and let Maks do most of the work. When the big man was on his feet, standing shaky and uncertain, he moved in closer, clasped Maks about his thick, muscular waist, grunted as long fingers dug into his shoulder and the man's weight came down on him, not all of it, but enough to remind him vividly of the effort it took to haul him inside.

"Not too much?"

He could feel the bass tones rumble in the center of his being as well as in his head, he felt the in-out of Maks' breathing, the vibrations of his voice, the slide of muscles wasted but still bigger than most and firm. "It's not something I'd do for the fun of it," he said, almost breathless, though that definitely didn't come from fatigue.

"Let's go then."

2

He lay listening to the wind howl outside and the steady breathing of the man he shared the hearth with. Now and then he heard Neddio or the mules moving about in the parlor, the clop of iron shoe on wood floor. He turned his head. The fire was low, but he could leave it for a while yet. He closed his eyes and went back to listening to Maks. Maks . . . it was his name . . . it fit in his mouth with a familiar easiness . . . it wasn't the whole name. He thinks I'd recognize the whole name. Maybe so maybe not. He wanted to touch Maks, but he didn't dare, not now, not when he might wake and know he was being touched. Not yet. Simms drew his hands down his own chest. What was wrong with him? He was lively enough when he came out of that trance or whatever it was, unperturbed by his condition, but there was that . . . that something. . . . The man's spirit was so vital, so . . . absorbing, entrancing . . . Simms smiled into the fire-broken darkness . . . it obscured that other thing. Almost. Part of him wanted Korimenei here so she could work her magic on Maks. Part of him didn't want to share Maks with anyone, anything. Even if their enforced cohabitation came to nothing, there would be at least three days alone with him, time out from the world.

Round and round in his head, was he sick with something? Will he love me will he hate me will he look through me like I'm nothing? Round and round until he had to move, do something. He slipped out of his blankets and added wood to the fire, chunks of tough hard fence post that'd burn all night. He bent over Maks before rolling into his blankets again, touched his fingertips light, light, feather-light to the man's brow.

It took him almost an hour to get to sleep.

3

The house rumbled and rattled and shook under the blast of the wind as the blizzard settled around them.

Maks slept heavily while Simms fed the mules and Neddio, used an old cedar shake to scoop up their droppings and carry them into the straffill where he dumped them down the hole. He brewed tea, ate one of Maks' trailbars and put a new pot of soup to simmering on the stove. He washed his shirt, trousers, socks and underclothing in the waste channel, looked over Maks' clothing, brushed the mud and debris off the outercloak, washed the undercloak and the other things, hung them all to drip dry on a cord he'd stretched between two pegs in the straffill. It helped the morning pass. Now and then he went over to Maks, squatted beside him, worried about the long sleep, but there was no sign of fever or other distress, so he went away again and let him sleep on.

Maks woke an hour past noon. He stretched, yawned, looked relaxed and lazy as a cat in the sun. He turned to Simms, gave him a wide glowing smile that sent flutters running round Simms' interior. "What's the time?"

"You couldn't tell it from out there," he nodded at the shuttered window, "but it's a little after noon."

"Ahhhh. Perfect. I hate mornings. Best way to greet the sun is sound asleep."

Simms chuckled. "So I see."

"Don't tell me you're one of those pests who leaps out of bed at dawn caroling blithely. They should be swatted like flies."

Another chuckle. "Ne'er uh blithe, but up, yeh. When I wan't workin'."

Maks raised his brows at that, but didn't ask for explanations. He closed his eyes, turned his head from side to side. After a minute, he said, "Today, tomorrow, I think. Day after that we can move." He pushed the blankets off and got to his feet. He was steadier, visibly stronger.

Simms finished sewing a button on his shirt, tied off the thread and cut it with one of his sleeve knives. "Tea on the stove. More soup, should be ready by now." He rolled a knot in the end of the thread, turned the shirt inside out and started examining the seams.

Maks wandered out. Simms could hear him talking to the mules. He came back in the kitchen, looked through his packs, found a currycomb and a stone and went out again. A little later as Simms was putting a new edge on the frayed hems of his trousers, he heard splashing in the straffill, Maks whistling a cheerful tune. Maks came in, glanced at him, went to the stove and filled his mug. He looked at the tea. "You sure this isn't going to crawl out and jump me?"

"Wake y' up."

"One way or another. You've had a busy morning."

"Help the time pass, keeping y' hands busy. 'Sides, I been puttin' off a lotta this, might's well catch up while we stuck here."

Maks nodded. "Not a bad idea." He ladled out a pannikin of soup, glanced at Simms. "Want some?"

"After I finish this, I think. I'll take some tea, if you don't mind."

Maksim brought him the tea, fetched the pannikin and ate his soup while he squatted beside Simms and watched him set small neat stitches.

Simms was quietly happy; he said nothing because he felt no need to talk, and he was pleased that Maks seemed equally comfortable with the silence. He finished one cuff and began on the other. Maks set the pannikin down and sipped at the tea. The fire flickered and shadows swayed around them in a slow hypnotic dance, the wind howled and icemelt drafts whispered through the room. Maks set the mug down and gave Simms' shoulder a squeeze, got to his feet and wandered out again.

He was back a moment later with the mules' harness, some rags and a bottle of oil. After some maneuvering, he settled at the edge of the hearth, pulled a blanket round his shoulders and began working oil into the leather, cleaning it and working supple the places where the damp had stiffened it. Filled with the small peaceful sounds of their labor, the hiss and snap of the fire with the muted noises of the storm as background, the silence wrapped like a blanket about the two men as they went on with their work. Finally Maks spoke, his voice lazy and undemanding. "Arsuid's a long way south of here."

Simms chuckled, a small soft sound. "Y' mean I got rocks in m' head ridin' into this kinda weather." He glanced at Maks, met his eyes and looked away from the laughter in them, not because he didn't like it, he liked it far too much. "C'd say the same, don' y' think?"

"So you could. Never visited Arsuid. What's it like?"

"Yesta'day. Ev'ry yesta'day."

Maks thought about that a minute. "I see what you mean. It can get boring if nothing changes."

" 'Pends where y' sit."

"More so on whether you're a sitter or sat on."

"Y' know 't."

"Spite of that, Arsuiders seem to stay put."

"T's so. Arfon, he like to keep his folk hoverin' round. Way I got loose, well, y' might say I was flung out."

"Feel like telling it, or is it none of my business?"

Simms tucked the needle into the cloth, dropped his hands and frowned at the fire. "Don' know the whole, 's more confusin' than entertainin'." He snapped thumb against middle finger, shook his head. "Here tis. Arfon got a itch for a talisman of 'is own. He a jeaaalous god, yehhh. An' there was this sorcerer came by, call hisself Lazul. Turn out, wan't so."

"Sorcerer, hmm. Did you ever find out what his name was?"

"After, yeh. Danny. Laz was for th' duration, what he said."

"Danny. Danny Blue?"

"Dunno. Might be. 'Staffel trap him, me, a couple more, fill us fulla poison. Say go get Klukesharna, we wipe you clean when y' give her to us."

"Not nice."

"Nah, that tisn't." Simms grinned at Maks, went back to watching the fire. "You know 'im? Danny?"

"I know one Danny Blue. A student of mine once. In a way."

"You a Sorcerer?"

"For my sins. And you're a Witch."

"Nah." Simms sighed, shook his head. "Ne'er got the training."

"You have the Talent, you could still train."

"I don' think so."

"Well, you have to want it. You got Klukesharna?"

"Yeh, we made one gwycher team, in and out, slick's a trick."

"So Arfon has Klukesharna now."

"Nah. We got her yeh, but after that, things got outta hand."

"Danny?"

"Part. There was this putch the 'Staffel land on us. Din' need her, don' know why they bring her in. Their mistake, for sure. Her 'n Danny, they dump Felsa 'n me, run for the Asatas. We wake up, go after 'em. Had to. Poison. We catch up to 'em this side the Asatas. Felsa nails Danny. He fall out facedown in the snow. I go for the Esmoon. Think I hit her. What happens next I don' know till later. Felsa and me, we went out, whoosh, blowin' a candle. We wake up next day half-froze with heads like y' get after a three-day drunk. We still got no choice, so we take after Danny again. We catch him up. He with this woman, not the Esmoon, don' know where she come from. No Klukesharna. Felsa gonna to skin him, she don' believe nothing he says. He says the Esmoon went off with Klukesharna. He says the Esmoon's no woman, she a demon."

"Demon? Tell me what she looks like," Maks' voice was suddenly taut, compelling, for the first time he was putting the power on Simms.

Simms blinked. "Fahhn silver hair, way she wear it, it go to her waist in long waves, shiny. Blue eyes. Velvet skin. Beautiful and she know it. I 'spect mos' men go crazy for her. I 'spect Danny right 'bout her, I thought sure I put one shaft, maybe two in 'er. You know 'er?"

"Probably not her. But something like her. Go on. What happened next?"

"It was in this Gsany village, in a bathhouse. We caught 'em pants down, you'd think we had 'em flat. Wan't so. The woman drop a demon on Felsa an' Danny drop me. Blessings be, old Tungjii stirring the waters, it turn out that the woman has this talisman, Frunzacoache, she use it to leach the poison outta us. Korimenei. Goin' home and goin' fast. Takin' Danny with her. Felsa taggin' along, she don' believe Danny don' wanna see Klukesharna or the Esmoon ever again. I go along until I get tired a hurryin'. I leave and that's how I end up here."

"Korimenei." Affection and amusement rumbled in the word. "How'd she look?"

"Like you damn well better not get in her way when she goin' somewhere." Simms rubbed his thumb along the seam of the trousers he'd been working on. "She a student too?"

"More like adopted daughter. Apprentice if I survive and she wants it."

Simms blinked at him. "Cheonea," he said. "Settsimaksimin. Sorcerer Prime." He folded his arms across his chest and hugged himself as he watched hope and possibility wither and wash away; that was all he could see for the moment, then he realized what Maks had just said. "Survive?"

"It's a web they're weaving, Simms, the demons, the gods and the Great Ones. Arfon and the Ystaffel pumped you full of poison, my set of demons robbed me of my souls, temporarily I hope. They pointed me at Shaddalakh, either I get it or I die. I'm dying now. When the body's empty, it begins to fall apart. No healer or herb doctor can stop the decay." He shook his head. "They send me out and at the same time rob me of my best tools. Without my earthsoul I have no Shamruz body to journey for me, I can't walk the realities or summon demons."

Simms nodded, thinking he knew what Maks was saying. "Yeh. Y' c'd fetch a demon an' send it t' get th' talisman."

Maks laughed, a happy shout that embraced Simms and invited him to share the joke. "Nooooo, no," he said, "never let a demon near that much power, you could end up dancing to the demon's tune rather than the other way about."

"I s'pose. Yeh, thinkin' 'bout Esmoon, yeh." Simms scowled at the fire, wrestling with himself; he hated the thought of messing with demons again, but his impulse toward spending himself for the man who attracted him so fiercely won out over his fears. He turned to Maks. "Take me with you. I c'n maybe help. Reason the 'Staffel land on me an' Felsa, we the best thieves in Arsuid. Tol' y' I c'd read walls, stones, dirt. I c'n see witchtraps, help y' 'void 'em. I c'n sing ghosts t' sleep. Tickle locks. Lots more."

"Simms. . . ."

"Y' don' want me, a' right."

"It's not that. The Magus knows that someone is coming. He's one of those who reads could-be nodes like other men read print. You could get swallowed up and spat out, it's not worth it, my friend."

"Y' don' know, Addryd Sorcesieur." He gazed at his hand, stroked his fingertips up and down his thigh. "Goin' in the Henanolee, that was dangerous too. It was the bes' time in m' whole life. I was workin' on top of it, ne'er felt so full so strong so gooood. I was scared t' bone but e'en that felt good. An' what's it matter if I die? What am I? Jus' a thief. No one give a shit."

"No Addryd. Maks." He leaned toward Simms, touched his face. "What's this nonsense? Not just a thief, I have your word for it, best in Arsuid." His hand was warm and smooth, Simms leaned into the curve of it, it was comforting and exciting. "You'd best keep out of this, little witch."

Simms turned his head, kissed Maks' palm. He smiled dreamily at the big man. "No," he said. "No . . . command me . . . anythin' but go 'way."

"And if I commanded you to climb to the roof here and jump into the wind?" The voice was darkness and light, caressing him, stirring him to the seat of his souls. It was fully there, the compelling, seducing Voice of the Prime.

Simms drew away a little, steadied his breathing before he spoke. "I w'd prob'ly do 't. But I sh'd wanna know why first."

Maks threw back his head and laughed, the sound filling the room, overpowering the storm and everything else. "Good, good. Never jump without knowing why. And if I said love me, would you want to know why you should do such a thing?"

"No. I don' need t' ask 'bout what already is."

4

On the fourth morning they dug out and found the blizzard had been more blow than snow. Maks hitched up his frisky, rambunctious mules, Simms saddled Neddio and they started south toward the spur of the Asatas where Tok Kinsa was, walled city walled in by snag-tooth mountains, secret city, the ways in warded and hidden from all but the select. There was about six inches of snow on the ground and no road, so the going was difficult even for the huge-wheeled dulic, but they made fair time and by the end of the week had reached the end of the grass. Maks left the dulic in a dry wash and turned one of the mules loose, loaded his gear on the other and prepared to walk into the mountains. Simms followed, leading Neddio.

The trek was hard on Maks; he faded visibly as each day passed.

Simms ached for him; he was filled with frustration and fury at the gods, the demons, everyone, everything responsible for Maks' hurting. In Arsuid, Simms had pretended to be loose and easy, that was what people expected from him, what his lovers wanted; he lost them again and again because he cared too much and it frightened them. So much passion, so much need demanded a response they were unwilling or incapable of giving. He was feeling his way warily with Maks; he knew so little that was real about the man, only legends and legends lie. Maks seemed to like him, that was a wonderful thing, but Simms saw it as fragile as a soapbubble, a careless touch could destroy it. Maks was willing to love him, though not always able, especially after a hard day's climbing. But he'd hold Simms anyway, caress him; he made Simms feel wanted, needed. Loved.

The way Maks chose was narrow, steep, treacherous. Snow above was loose, always falling, avalanche a constant danger. Underfoot there were patches of ice and always more snow. They struggled on and on; once again Simms was traveling with a driven person. The only thing that bothered him this time was his inability to help; he'd never been in snow before he crossed the Dhia Asatas, he knew almost nothing about mountain traveling. He told himself he was useful around the camps, doing most of the work so Maks could rest. It was something.

On the third day they came on a small stream wandering through a ravine choked with aspen and waist-deep snow. They made camp on the rim of that ravine in a thick stand of conifers. Around the bulge of the mountain there was a windswept cliff that looked down into the bowlshaped valley where Tok Kinsa drowsed in the watery winter sunlight. They lay there staring down at the city.

Tok Kinsa, Home Ground of the Magus Prime. Power Ground of Erdoj'vak, Patron of the Rukka Nagh, Vanner and Gsany both. Like most local gods, he slept a lot, he was sleeping now.

No Outer Rukks allowed within the walls outside the pilgrim season and the season had finished weeks ago. No strangers allowed within the walls, with the minor exception of a few well-known scholars who were specifically invited to visit the Magus.

A bright city, full of saturated color, reds, yellows, blues, greens shining like jewels against the equally brilliant white of the snow, a paisley city with every surface decorated, even both sides of the immense curtain wall, in the geometrics of Rukk design. Inside the walls the streets were paved with alternating black and white flags; they were laid out like the spokes of a wheel, radiating from the round tower with the spiraling ramp curling up around it, the Zivtorony.

The streets were busy with Kinseers dressed in dramatic mixes of black and white, even the children. The city was busy, brightly alive, but the massive gates were closed and stayed closed. There were no footprints in the snow around Tok Kinsa.

Lying on folded blankets with blankets over them, Maks and Simms watched the whole of the day and by the sundown certain things had become obvious.

They couldn't go in openly or disguised. No one was entering the city and even if they were, there was no way Maks would pass as a Rukk. A six-foot-seven M'darjin mix would stand out in any crowd.

It'd be impossible to slip over the walls without the Magus perceiving them and brushing them off like pesky flies. Maks was in no shape for a protracted challenge-battle—especially with a Magus Prime supported by one of the Great Talismans.

The attack would have to be quick, leap in, seize Shaddalakh, leap out the next second, nothing else would work.

##

"The longer we hang around up here, the more certain it is the Magus will locate us and attack." The fire threw black shadows into the lines and creases in Maks' face, underlining the fatigue in his voice.

"I have no doubt he's probing for us right now, reading the could-be nodes over and over and plotting the changes."

Simms was watching his face, paying little attention to what he said; he didn't understand could-be nodes or any of that higher magic, he knew tones of voice and new lines in the face he loved. And he knew how to get into impossible places, though he'd never tried something so impossible as that snow-sealed city on the other side of the mountain. "Danny jump us over traps in the Henanolee Heart. C'd you jump us into the Zivtorony?"

"In, yes. Out, I don't know. If we have to tear things apart searching for Shaddalakh, it gives the Magus time to throw a noose round us and squeeze." He opened the wallet and pulled out a handful of parchment sheets, looked through them, pulled out a plan of the city, discarded that as useless, took up a sheet with diagrams of the tower. He passed it over to Simms. "Any ideas?"

Simms spread the sheet across his lap, bent over it, guessing at what the lines meant; he couldn't read the writing, he could barely read Arsuider and this was something else. His fingertips felt itchy, tingling. "Do y' b'lieve the Magus know it's you coming?" He thought a minute. "Or someone like you?"

"Sorcerer? Yes. He'd know that."

"Then I tell you one thing, he got Shaddalakh where he c'n reach out an' touch him." He smoothed his hand across the parchment. "Gotta jump direct." There was a vertical view, the tower sliced down the middle to show how the levels were arranged. He brushed his fingers up the center of the view, stopped where the tingling grew intense, almost painful. He closed his eyes. No image, but he smelled roast geyker and his mouth watered. He was startled. He moved his fingers on up the tower. The tingle faded, the taste went away. He looked up, frowning.

"What is it?"

"Smell anythin', like meat cookin'?"

"No."

Simms touched the diagram again, he didn't close his eyes this time, but there it was, the rich, mouth-watering aroma of red meat swimming in its own gravy. "Magus eatin' dinner," he said.

Maks looked at Simms' fingers resting lightly on the parchment, trembling a little. "Dowsing?"

Simms blinked. "I . . ." He looked down at his hand, lifted it off the drawing as if the parchment had suddenly gotten hot. "I never did that before." He was delighted with the discovery, it was a gift he could give his lover, a wanted gift, a needed gift.

Maks smiled. "Told you, little witch, there's Talent wasting in you; you should train it. Try for Shaddalakh."

"Do m' best." He rubbed his thumb across his fingertips, he was nervous, both hands were shaking. He looked at the vertical drawing, rejected it and moved to the floor plans of the different levels. One by one he brushed his fingers across them. When he touched the third level, he smelled the roast again, located it in a long narrow wedge of a room. That was the Magus, he got no sense of Shaddalakh. He moved on, level to level until he'd touched all seven levels. Nothing more. He shook his head. "All I read is Magus." He grinned suddenly. "Or maybe t's m' belly yearnin' for roast geyker."

Maks scowled at the fire. "I'd rather avoid a confrontation with him, but it looks like we have to remove the Magus before we start hunting." He rubbed his hand along his thigh as if the palm were suddenly sweaty. "Tonight," he said. "I go tonight. If I wait, I get weaker while he gets stronger."

Simms set the parchment aside, slipped a sleeve knife from its sheath and began working on the edge with a small hone. "What time?"

"Simmo. . . ."

"No, Maks. If y' have any feelin' for me, no."

"It's because I do. . . ."

"Turn things round an' think 'bout it, y' see?"

"Ahhh! Why do I always love contrarians! Brann who never lets me get away with anything and little Kori who has to be tied down to keep her out of trouble and you, stubborn man, if something happens to you, I die a bit."

"Do I hurt less if you go down? Am I s' useless, all I am 's a bedmate?"

"Being right all the time, it's as bad as a taste for getting up early."

Simms smiled happily at Maks, knowing he'd won his point. "What time?"

"Two hours after midnight."

"You get some sleep, Maksa, you the one gonna do all the work. I'll clean up here and wake y'."

"Simmo, don't hobble Mule or Neddio and set out the grain we have left."

"Yeh. Give 'em a chance, we don' be back. Pass me the wallet,

Maksa, I'll put this away." He picked up the plan. "No use leavin' it out."

"Keep it by you, you'll have to dowse again before we go. The Magus won't be sitting at the dinner table then, no telling where he'll be. Tungjii bless, Simmo, I don' know how I could have managed this without you."

Simms' mouth tightened as he struggled to control his surging emotions; he was afraid of scaring Maks off like he'd driven away so many others. He set the hone aside, took a bit of leather and began polishing the steel. "Maybe he don' know 'bout me. Think of that?" He held out the knife. "Maybe steel c'n cut spell."

"No no, not steel. Take him out if you can, but don't kill him, there's no reason to kill the man, he's only trying to protect what's his."

"A' right, gimme a sock." Simms tapped his foot. "I got no spares." He laughed at the look on Maks' face. "Sock an' sand, whap, whiff 'em, out like blowing out y' candle."

5

Simms brushed his fingertips up the vertical diagram, stopped at the top. The seventh level. "Here," he said. He closed his eyes, but he got nothing more than the location, no smells, no sounds, just an itch so intense it was painful. "I don' know what he doin', but he there." He scratched at the parchment, his fingernail moving across the highest level in the tower. He left the vertical and drifted his fingers across the floor plan of that level. He touched each of the rooms indicated, stopped at one that looked south toward the serried mountain peaks beyond the valley. "Here," he said. "This room."

Maks took the plan, read the glyphs. "His bedroom. Do you get the sense he's sleeping?"

"I . . . hmm . . ." Simms closed his eyes, focused inward, slid his thumb over and over his fingertips. "No . . . I don't . . . I can' . . . 'f I hadda guess, he awake an' waitin'."

Maks slid the sheet into the wallet, tied the strings, got to his feet. "Let's not keep him waiting."

6

The Magus struck at Maks before they touched foot to floor, exploding time-energy around him, ripping reality into wheeling chaos that manifested as blinding color and extreme form-distortion—and a discarnate hunger that sucked at him, struggling to dissolve him into that chaos.

The attack ignored Simms. He came down behind Maks, his aura masked by the sorcerer's lifeglow, a fire that spread nova strong, nova bright, about Maks, made visible by the whirling forces that filled the room. Simms dropped to his hands and knees. He relaxed, smiled; the floor was familiar, comfortable to his reading-touch. Polished wood, then a velvety carpet. He didn't try to comprehend what his eyes were showing him, he simply ignored it and took his direction from the carpet. He began edging toward the Magus.

Instead of trying to block that chaos, Maks sucked it into himself, stripped away the force in it and slowly, painfully recreated an area of normality about himself, gaining strength as the Magus expended his.

Still unnoticed as the two Primes hammered at each other, Simms circled wide and came round behind the wavering distorted figure. Reality twisted and tore about him, time-nodes exploded, but none of it was directed at him, it battered at him but the blows were glancing, he was rocked but not seriously hurt. He kept crawling. He came up behind the Magus, a dark column broken into puzzle pieces as if there were a glass of disturbed water between them.

Simms slipped the knotted sock from his coat pocket and sat on his heels peering at the column, trying to resolve it enough to find his target. Black and white, blurs of pinkish brown swaying swinging, changing rhythm suddenly, never still. Hands, he thought after a moment. He got to his feet. He could have reached out and touched the shifting uncertain figure, but he was careful not to. Finally he caught a glimpse of pinkish brown higher on the column, only a glimpse, it was swallowed a moment later by an amorphous blob of black. Must be the face, has to be the face. He set himself, swung the sock with carefully restrained force. He felt it slam against something, heard a faint tunk.

The confusion vanished instantly.

A man lay on the carpet at his feet, white and black robes spread around his sprawled body, an angular black and white striped headdress knocked half off his bald head. He was tall and lean, with a strong hooked nose and a flowing white beard.

Maks wiped sweat off a gray face. He found a chair and dropped into it. "Lovely tap, Simmo."

Simms looked at him, dazed. There was something throbbing in him that distracted him, even in his anguish at Maks' distress. He licked his lips, tried to say something, but he couldn't. He dropped the sock, turned slowly so slowly, until the string tied to his gut whipped tight and began reeling him in.

Step by slow step he went to the head of the great four-poster bed, touched the post on the left side. It was at least six inches square, deeply carved with the interlacing geometrics of Rukk reliefwork. He stroked his fingertips up and down the different faces of the post. There was a click. A part of the post slammed against the side of his hand. A shallow drawer. He pulled it open and looked into it. Shaddalakh lay there, dull white, sandpapery sand dollar. He lifted it out. It was like touching a lover, warm, accepting. He held it, tears gathered in his eyes, though he didn't cry. He smiled instead.

Maks' hand closed on his shoulder. "May I have it?"

It was the most difficult thing he'd done in his twenty some years of life. He turned slowly, held out the talisman.

Maks took it, there was a sadness in his face that told Simms his lover understood the gift he'd just received, but at the moment that didn't help lessen the ache from the loss.

"Time to go," Maks said. "We. . . ."

Darkness swallowed them.

Simms heard Maks cursing, something was wrong, he didn't understand. . . .

THE REBIRTHING: END PHASE
The stones assemble

Roaring with rage, Settsimaksimin landed on one point of a Hexa star; Simms came down at his feet. Maks clutched at Shaddalakh and gathered himself to snap out of this place wherever it was.

He was frozen there, Shaddalakh vibrated in his grip, but something blocked his access to the talisman. He gathered the remnants of his strength—threw all he knew and all he was into a bind-shatter Chant. His Voice was there. It made the dust jump. Nothing changed. The confusion of hums and whistles and other small ugly noises went steadily on around him. He'd never seen anything like this place. He understood nothing he saw, even less what he heard.

The dull gray light shuddered. Sparks came pouring into that dusty gray hell, shrieking as he'd shrieked. Geniod. He remembered them from the cavern.

Something caught them, something prisoned them in a glitternet of force lines above the dusty gray throne chair beside the Hexa. They quieted, he thought they were doing what he'd done, looking around, weighing their chances, deciding how to attack and free themselves.

The light shuddered again.

Palami Kumindri, her Housemaster Cammam Callan, another female figure. Simms gasped. "Esmoon," he whispered. Finally the simulacrum of Musteba Xa, holding Massulit clutched against his bony chest.

Something snatched Massulit away from him, brought it swooping around to hover over Maksim's head. His souls spun from the stone and fled back into him, swirling round and round in him, turning him dizzy with the euphoria of the Return.

When he recovered, the four of them were gone and the sack above the throne was jerking and jolting and brighter than before.

The light in that decaying dreadful room shuddered.

Brann appeared on the Hexa-point at his left, Tak WakKerrcarr standing behind her, his staff in one hand, his other hand resting on her shoulder. Massulit swept away from Maksim and rushed to her. She looked startled, caught it, stood holding it. "Maksi," she said, "so this is why you didn't answer the *call-me* 's."

"That's it. Tak."

"Maksim."

"Surprised to see you here."

"Not half so surprised as I am." He touched Brann's cheek, returned his hand to her shoulder. "Seems to be one of the drawbacks when you grow fond of a certain turbulent young lass."

"Fond, hah!" Brann said. "You're just a horny old goat."

"That too."

Maksim started to speak, shut his mouth as the light shuddered again.

Yaril and Jaril appeared at the next Hexa-point. They stood side by side, each with one arm about the other's waist. Jaril held his free hand chest-high with Churrikyoo sitting on it. Two pairs of crystal eyes turned to Maksim, turned away; they chose not to greet him.

The light shuddered.

Korimenei appeared at the Hexa-point at Maksim's right, a long-tailed beast on her shoulder. She wore Frunzacoache around her neck, the leaf within shining a brilliant green. She glanced quickly around, nodded as if she recognized what she was seeing, then she smiled at Maksim. "I missed you," she said, "I thought you'd lost interest in me."

"No, daughter mine, never that. Just unavailable as you see."

"Take me as an apprentice?"

He laughed, a shout that filled the room with life and vigor and made its deadness even deader. "Kori, you don't waste your opportunities, do you?"

"Doesn't Tungjii say take your Luck where you find it? Well?"

"Of course I will. As you propose, so I accept. If we manage to get clear of this." He looked round. "What is this place, anyone know?"

Brann sighed. "I forgot you hadn't seen it, Maksi. Chained God. We're in his body."

The light shuddered.

Trago appeared on the Hexa-point beside Korimenei, frightened and uncertain. He held Harra's Eye clutched tight against his chest and looked wildly around, started to speak to Korimenei, but didn't; instead he bowed his head and stood staring intently into the flawless crystal sphere.

The light shuddered.

Danny Blue appeared with Felsrawg crouching at his feet. He flung out a hand and Klukesharna slammed into it. He stared at the talisman a moment, then looked round. "Family reunion," he said. "Brann, Kori, Maksim, Changers. I was beginning to wonder if I'd see you all. It's like trail stew, drop in the ingredients as before and stir vigorously. Simms, sorry to see you, man. Where's the Esmoon? She ought to be here, seeing I'm infested with this thing again." He held Klukesharna between thumb and forefinger and waved it about.

Simms chuckled, he was amused but there was an edge to his enjoyment. "Sucked up there," he said and pointed at the glittersack; he was content to sit where he was at Maksim's feet and didn't try to stand. "I don't think she's enjoying it either."

"Should hope not." He reached a hand down to Felsrawg. "You gonna sit there or what?"

She moved her shoulders, looked disgusted. "I can't get up," she said. "I'm stuck here. Let me alone, fool."

"Your call. Hey, Garbage Guts," he yelled, startling Maksim and drawing a grimace from Brann. He was scowling at the broad sheet of milky glass spread across the front of the room. "What the hell's going on?"

For several breaths nothing happened. Lights flickered, threads of god-stuff danced and darted, minor lightnings struck and rebounded. The noises got louder; though they weren't music in any other sense, none of the euphony Maksim expected, there was a rhythm in those noises, a pulse not quite a heartbeat but similar; as they got louder, more demanding, their effect on him and the others intensified. There was a sense of something ominous getting closer and closer.

Maksim set himself to resist. He fought to tie into Shaddalakh, fought to resist unnamed, shapeless demands the noises made on him. He fought the god.

##

Korimenei saw Maks stiffen, begin to gesture and chant. She couldn't hear him. As if she were sealed off from him, a wall between them. She dropped and sat cross-legged with Ailiki in her lap, closed one hand about Frunzacoache, rested the other on the curve of the mahsar's back. Frunzacoache shook. She thought she could hear it screaming with rage as it tried to touch her. When reaching for the realities didn't work, she flipped through her choices and began trying everything she could think of to attack the forces holding her. She fought the god with everything inside her.

#

Brann leaned against Tak WakKerrcarr and struggled to draw energy from Massulit. Nothing. She reached for Yaril and Jaril. They were sealed off from her. Tak said losing them would put her in danger; she understood that now. She was powerless against anything she couldn't touch; whatever stayed beyond the reach of her arms was safe from her. She ignored the pressure from the Chained God and concentrated on reaching the Changers. If they could make that bridge again, the Chained God would find his metaphorical fingers singed. She denied the god, denied his hold on her, refused to let him shape her acts. She fought the god with everything in her.

#

Danny Blue's half-sires forgot their differences and fought the god. They were shadows of what they were, but they had their skills and their stubbornness. They poured all that into Danny; he fought the god with Daniel Akamarino's will to freedom and Ahzurdan's learning and his own rage. Danny clutched at Klukesharna, felt her quiver as she tried to break through to him and help him. He fought to reach her, he fought the god.

#

Jaril and Yaril raged as one; they struggled to reach Churrikyoo, but could not, together they punched at the force holding them on the Hexa-point, they struggled to reach out to Brann, they could see her, they knew she was trying to reach them. Wordlessly, they merged into a single glowsphere with Churrikyoo floating in their core. Wordlessly, furiously, they fought to break free and suck the life out of the god.

#

Trago clutched at Harra's Eye. He fought against being swallowed, but he knew so little about what was going on, he was, after all, only a seven-year-old boy, the ten years he'd passed in spell might have been ten minutes. All he could do was deny and deny and deny. He could not relate to the woman who said she was his sister, she was a stranger. He didn't want any of this, he was terrified and angry, the god made him feel sick when he looked at it, it was ugly, rotten. No, he shouted into the crystal, no and no and no.

##

The noises changed, the noises were a chant.

The Chained God chanted, gathering his forces, thrusting his will at them, a wordless spell or if there were words, they were sunk so deep in computer symbology and machine noise they were wholly unintelligible to mortal ears, even Danny Blue's.

BinYAHtii appeared, hovered over the Hexa-center.

The glittersack opened, poured out the geniod.

BinYAHtii quivered, hummed with power, put out a pulsing red aura, calling, calling the geniod to it: hungry hungry hungry: Hunger Incarnate. A HUNGER greater than even the geniod's. Demanding. Compelling.

The geniod struggled, screamed—and streamed in a river of light into the heart of the talisman.

BinYAHtii ate and ate, ate them all, its power song sinking into subsonics.

The river vibrated, distorted, took on one shape, then another, then was Palami Kumindri half submerged in the liquid light. "The Promise," she screamed. "We obeyed in all things. The Promise. Pay us what you promised."

The God spoke, h/its multiple voices like a swarm of locusts buzzing. "This is MY reality. What made you think I'd let you eat it bare? You've lived well enough. I owe you nothing. I used you and now I purge you. Consider it the price you pay for the worlds you have destroyed." H/it sounded prim and complacent. H/it drove the geniod into the Hunger of BinYAHtii until every fleck of light had vanished and the talisman glowed like a small red sun.

H/its power enormously increased, the god reached out and PUT H/ITS HANDS on them: *Settsimaksimin/Simms* *Brann/WakKerrcarr* *Yaril/Jaril* *Danny Blue/Felsrawg* *Trago* *Korimenei* H/it seized hold of them, turned them to face BinYAHtii. H/it seized hold of the Great Talismans and pulled at them, drawing the stone bearers with them into the heart of the Hexa, drawing them closer and closer to BinYAHtii, chanting all the time in its harsh insectile voices, faster and faster, the force in the machine words (if they were words) increasing, the rhythm more and more compelling.

They fought.

They struggled to join against him.

They could not touch, physically or psychically. The god held them separate, held them that way until h/it managed to bring them to the Hexa-center.

Maksim's grand basso broke free suddenly, battered at the humming clicking tweeting chant, joined a moment later by the grand baritone of Tak WakKerrcarr, the Voices of Sorcerer Primes at their most powerful, most urgent. They slowed the inward creep, they couldn't stop it.

Closer and closer to BinYAHtii h/it forced them.

Maksim's arm jerked out, out of his control, he held Shaddalakh before him like an offering.

Danny's arm jerked out, out of his control, he held Klukesharna before him like an offering.

Brann's arm jerked out, out of her control, she held Massulit cupped in the palm of her hand, held it like an offering.

Trago's arms jerked out, out of his control, he held Harra's Eye between his two hands, held it like an offering.

Frunzacoache flew out from Korimenei's breast, dragging her with it as it sought the middle, offering itself.

Yaril and Jaril dissolved from their sphere into twin bipedal shapes, moved side by side, each with an arm about the other's waist, moved with staggering, reluctant steps toward the middle. Jaril's arm stretched straight before him, Churrikyoo cupped in the palm of his hand, held like an offering to that demanding red Hunger throbbing at the Hexa-center.

Slowly, inexorably, resisting h/it all the way anyway they could, the stone bearers and their companions drew closer and closer to the HUNGER.

They touched it.

At the same instant the six talismans touched the seventh.

reality dissolves

ego-centers hover in a blinding burning golden featureless nothingness

hang disembodied, self-aware in only the dimmest sense

wait

are aware of waiting without being aware of time

are aware of waiting without being aware of purpose

are finally aware of otherness otherwhereness

six point-nodes of power tremble in a burning featureless nothingness

they begin to move

they swim toward certain ego-centers

they touch certain ego-centers, merge with them

ego-centers sense imminent change which is a change in itself

no time has passed

an eternity has passed

nothingness EXPLODES

2

Danny Blue finished the step he'd started ten subjective years before and nearly tripped over Felsrawg who was crouching on the roadway in front of him. He took her hand, pulled her to her feet.

"What happened?" Felsrawg turned her head from side to side, startled by the strangeness around her. "Where are we?"

"Skinker world, from the look of it."

"What?"

"Another reality, Felsa, I doubt you're going to like it. No gods here."

"Hah, that so. I like it already." She shied as a skip went groaning past overhead. "What. . . ."

Danny looked from her to the skip vanishing in the distance. What am I going to do with you, he thought. You're a survivor, but it'll take some doing to catch up on a good ten millennia of technological development between one breath and the next. He started walking; Felsrawg was still lost in shock and let him get several steps ahead. She gave a sharp exclamation and trotted after him; when she caught up, she walked beside him staring round with interest and uneasiness at an array of vegetation odd enough to start her licking her lips and touching the knives hidden under her long loose sleeves.

She shied again as a ground vehicle clattered past, the Skinker in it turning to stare at them from bulging plum-colored eyes. "Demon!"

Danny scratched at his stubble, sighed. His immediate future looked a lot more interesting than comfortable. "No demon, Felsa. You start acting evil to these Skinkers and I'll thump you good. This is their world. You hear?"

She scowled at him, shrugged. "Demon," she said stubbornly, but relented enough to promise a minimal courtesy. "Just keep them away from me."

Gods, Danny thought, xenophobe on top of everything else. He ran a hand through his hair. Tungjii Luck, if I ever go back there, so help me, I swear I'll put matches to your toes. He jerked to a stop as a tiny Tungjii sitting on an airbubble floated past his nose. The god twiddled hisser fingers, winked and vanished. Danny glanced at Felsrawg, but she was kicking along staring at a pair of hitsatchee posts planted beside an U-tree in bud. He stopped, felt the buds. They still had the fuzz on. Either he was coming back in the same season, maybe the same day in the season, or the time spent in that other reality had gone past between one blip and the next in this. He frowned at the sun. Not quite that fast. It was morning then, it's near sundown now. If this is the same day, I bet La Kuninga is ready to snatch me . . . he grinned and smoothed his hand over his thick wavy hair . . . bald again.

The traffic got heavier; Felsrawg stopped twitching as the ground-cars rumbled past, but she was still taut with a feeling half-fear, half-loathing. She kept snatching glances at him as if she expected him to turn into a slick skinned six-limbed lizardoid. When they reached the rim of the town, he stopped her. "Felsa, best thing for you is keep your mouth shut and do what I do. In a way it's too bad the jump here gave you interlingue, there's a lot to be said for dumbness covering ignorance."

She gave him a fulminating look, but dropped a step behind him, even followed him into a ribbajit without comment. He dropped on the tattered seat, shifted over when a broken spring gave him a half-hearted poke. "Port," he said and settled back as the jit trundled off.

Felsrawg spread her hand on her knee, exposing the skry rings, watching them from under her lashes.

Danny chuckled. "They won't read, Felsa. This is a machine, it runs on batteries, not magic. Nothing stranger than a . . . um . . . a loom or a waterwheel."

"There's nothing to make it move and there's no driver."

"It moves, doesn't it. Go with the flow, Fey."

She was silent for several minutes as the ribbajit clunked around the edge of the town. "Why am I here, Danny?"

"You want me to explain the multiverse?"

"Fool! You know what I mean. You belong in this place. I don't."

He touched the pocket where Klukesharna had somehow inserted itself during the crossing between realities; he had a suspicion the thing had imagined some kind of link between him and Felsrawg just because she was standing beside him in that cave. Typical computer-think if you could even say a hunk of iron could think. "You do now. Better get used to it."

"Send me back."

"Can't. There's no magic here." He said that flatly, giving her no room for argument. He believed it mostly, told himself that Tungjii's wink was imagination, nothing more. The ribbajit clanked to a stop by the hitsatchee posts outside the linkfence that ran around the stretch of metacrete the locals called a starport. "We're here," he said. "Come on."

"What's here?"

"I don't know. Let's go see."

#

A tall bony blonde woman with a set angry face was snapping out orders to a collection of Skinkers using motorized assists to load crates and bundles on the roller ramp running into the belly of her battered freetrader; now and then she muttered furious asides to the short man beside her.

"No, no, not that one, the numbers are on them, you can read, can't you." Aside to her companion: "Mouse, if that scroov shows his face round my ship again, I'll skin him an inch at a time and feed it to him broiled."

The little gray man scratched his three fingers through a spongy growth that covered most of his upper body; he blinked several times, shrugged and said nothing.

"Sssaaah!" She darted to the loaders, cursed in half a dozen languages, waved her arms, made the workers reload the last cart. Still furious, she stalked back to where she'd been standing. "Danny Blue, you miserable druuj, I'll pull your Master's Rating this time, I swear I will, this is the last time you walk out on me or anyone else."

"Blue wants, Blue walks," the little man said. "Done it before, 'll do it again."

"Hah! Mouse, if you're so happy with him, you go help Sandy stow the cargo."

"I don't do boxes."

She glared at him, but throttled back the words that bulged in her throat, stalked off and stood inspecting the crates as they rolled past her.

Danny walked round a stack of crates, Felsrawg trailing reluctantly after him. "Hya, Kally, I'm back."

She wheeled. "Where the hell you been, druuj!" Her eyes went wide when she realized what she was seeing. "Huh? You're not Danny."

"Remember Inconterza? Matrize Lezdoa the scarifier? I can go on."

"Never mind. Someday you have to explain to me how you grew a head of hair and three extra inches and changed your face that much," she glanced at her ringchron, "in nine hours." She looked past him. "And where you got the baba there."

"Be polite, Kally, Felsa's no man's baba. Woman's either."

"Hmp. You not giving me any excuse for leaving me to do your job, are you."

"No. But I'll contract an extra year if you give Felsa space on board."

"Guarantee no walking?"

"Guarantee. My word on it."

"Deal. She got anything but what she's carrying?"

"Nothing but a name. Felsa, I'll have you meet free trader and ship-master Kally Kuninga. Kally, this is one Felsrawg Lawdrawn. She doesn't know what the hell's going on, but she'll learn."

"You finished? Right. Get your ass over there and do your job. Mouse he's been having vibrations which means we gotta get the hell out before the sluivasshi land on us." She looked Felsrawg over, head to toe and back again. "She's your problem, Danny. Keep her outta my hair and see she's fumigated before you bring her on board." She twitched her nose, swung round and stalked off.

Felsrawg snorted. "Bitch."

"Sure. And if you say it to her face, she'll laugh, then she'll slap you down so hard you bounce. Come on. I've got work to do."

#

Felsrawg found a quiet corner near a stack of empty crates where she'd be out of the way of the workers. Danny was right, she didn't understand any of this, maybe she never would. She thought about that a minute and decided it was blue funk and not worth the air it took to say it, she might not know how those clink-clank slim-slam things worked, but she could see what they did. That's all she needed. She looked at her skry rings, sniffed. I don't know how they work either, but I got damn good at reading them. The sun was going down in the west, she thought it was the west, it felt like west, just like it did back home and the Kuninga woman was a gasht all right, but she looked normal, at least there was that.

The clattering stopped, the demons rode their metal carts across the hard white stuff that covered the ground and vanished behind some odd looking buildings. The rollerramp was folding itself up, squeezing together into an impossibly small package; it might not be magic, but it surely looked like it. Danny loped around like a Temu herder chasing strays, getting everything folded up and tucked away in that thing. Ship? It reminded her of an old tom swampspider after twenty years of mating battles, battered and molting, missing a leg here and a mandible there, but tough as boiled bull leather. She heard her name and stepped out of the shadow to wait for Danny who was coming to get her. It starts, she thought. Say one thing, it should be interesting.

3

Yaril and Jaril went slipping down a long long slide and burst into brightness, glowspheres zagging across complex crystal lattices on a hot young world circling a sun in the heart of a hot young cluster. Aulis came zipping round them, cousins and strangers, seekers and linkers, greeting them swinging through wild exuberant loops yelling welcome come and see we thought a smiglar had eat you Yaroooh Jaroooh. Aetas came, younglings budded since they left, bursting with curiosity, wallowing in the explosion of joy, Afas came, trailing after Nurse Agaxes, laughing and singing their infant songs, absorbing the excitement, the joy, though they had no idea what created it. And Agaxes came, majestic and slow, swimming in on all sides, and, finally, finally, father-mother meld at last there shimmering, expanding, opening to absorb them, hold them within in a hot and loving embrace.

Churrikyoo *moved.*

Before the absorption was complete, it emerged from Jaril, fell into the lattice and went hopping away, matter become energy, stasis become motility, non-life become life.

Yaril and Jaril rest in the embrace of mother-father reading off memory into memory until the whole is transferred, then the embrace ends.

Father-mother go drifting off to digest and discuss the tale with their community-companions. Waves of joy flush pink and gold through them, their children who were dead are alive again, more than alive are

triumphant and weighty with story, treasure beyond all other treasures, a meaty and complex narrative to be considered for meaning and
style, taken bit by bit, balancing each bit by another, bit against whole,
centuries worth of contemplation and dissection.

Surraht-Aulis whole and complete again, Yaril and Jaril emerge, go
darting away to join a cluster of other aulis. They race through the
lattices, chasing the radiant frog Churrikyoo, a new game for aulis, a
wonderful game because no one can win, no one can touch the frog,
only chase after it until he, she, they lose it. They play the old games
too, merging and remerging, telling their tale into the auli legend
horde. They are sad when they remember Brann, but they remember
her less and less as the world turns on the spindle of time. They are
home and valued, they are merging with their agemates, spinning a
community of copulation and exploration, song and story, merging,
emerging, remerging.

They are Home.

4

Knowing with all her body that the pocket reality was collapsing
around her, Brann fell away from it and landed on her hands and knees
in black sand. The Bay at Haven. Massulit lay on the sand beneath her.
She closed her hand about it, pushed up until she was sitting on her
heels with Massulit cuddled against her stomach.

Tak WakKerrcarr came over to her, reached a hand down to her and
pulled her onto her feet. He pointed at Massulit. "I see you've got
yourself a new playtoy."

She looked at the sapphire, watched the star pulse for a breath or
two. "You want it?"

"It's not the kind of thing you can give away, m' dear."

She slipped the Stone into a pocket, rubbed at her eyes. "Yaro? Jay?"
She remembered the Eating of the Geniod and was suddenly terrified,
turned so quickly she stumbled and nearly fell; recovering, she continued to swing round, kicking sand into a storm about her knees, her
arms flying out, her eyes wild. "Yaro? Jay?" Her voice cut through the
twilight, agony in the syllables as she cried out again and again the
names of her change-children. "Chained God," she shrieked, "If you
ate my babies. . . ." She ran along the sand, past Trago who was
kneeling in the wash of the outgoing tide ignoring them all, staring into
the shining heart of the Eye, past Simms and Korimenei who stood

silent on the sand, watching the drama but outside it. "If you fed my children to that Abomination. . . ." She stopped, glared at the mountain rising dark against the gegenschein, Isspyrivo the Gate. "If you took them, you DIEEEE!!!" She turned and ran back. "I'll tear you," she screamed as she ran. "I'll feed you to rats, I'll . . . I'll. . . ." She stopped where she'd started, swung round and round, flinging words to the wind, helpless to do anything but shout yet almost demonic in her rage. "I'll DRAIN you. . . ." Round and round. "Dead, *dead!* DEAD!"

Tak WakKerrcarr came running and tried to hold her but she broke away, Maksim swore and plunged at her. He ignored her struggles, wrapped his arms about her and held her tight against his massive chest. She kicked and hit at him, clawed at him, she was blind with rage and grief and an overmastering terror, she didn't know him, she no longer knew where she was. He kept her pinned with one huge arm, caught her hands in his and pressed them against his ribs, all the time talking to her, his bass voice flowing over her, calm, quiet, caressing, until she stopped fighting him and lay against him, shaking and sobbing.

A vast red figure came down the Mountain, shrinking as she came until she was a mere fifty yards of four-armed, crimson female god. Slya Fireheart tapped Maksim on the shoulder, wrapped her upper right hand around Brann when he released her. She got to her feet, lifted Brann till they were more or less eye to eye. "T'SSSH, T'SSSH, LITTLE NOTHING. WHAT'S ALL THIS?" A huge fingernail moved along Brann's face, scraping away tearstreaks.

Brann blinked, tried to gather her shattered wits. "What happened to them? My babies. . . ."

"THOSE FUZZBALLS? EHHH, LITTLE NOTHING, THEY WENT HOME, THAT'S ALL. YOU WANTED THEM TO GO HOME, DIDN'T YOU. YOU HAD POOR OLD MAN OVER THERE SPRINKLING ITCH POWDER ON ME, SAYING SEND THEM HOME SEND THEM HOME."

"Home. . . ." Brann tugged a hand free, scrubbed at her eyes. "Yes . . . but I . . . not so soon, not without saying . . . not so suddenly. . . ."

Slya set her down on the sand. Like a huge and clumsy child playing with a doll, she brushed at Brann with her upper right hand, plucked at her clothing with her upper left hand, smoothed her hair with one huge forefinger. Though the god was being kind and affectionate and meant no harm, Brann was exhausted and more than a little battered when Slya left off her efforts. Brann edged cautiously away, backing into Tak. She tilted her head to look up at him, smiled at him, then held her hand out to Maksim. She started to speak, closed her mouth, startled by a loud shout from the boy.

Trago was on his feet, pointing at Isspyrivo's peak. "Look," he cried again. "Chained God. God-Not-Chained."

A golden metal man a hundred meters tall stood upon Isspyrivo's glaciers, posing like a dancer. The setting sun glinted on hundreds of angular facets, the light off them so brilliant it was blinding. He moved. He was slow and clumsy at first, lurching, teetering on the verge of falling over, but he kept coming. Like Slya Fireheart he came striding down the Mountain toward them and with each step the awkward stiffness diminished until the metal moved with the elasticity of flesh and the God-Not-Chained gleamed and shimmered liquidly instead of glittering.

Paying no more attention to them than to the seagulls gliding around him, he walked out across the water and stopped in the middle of the bay. Slya Fireheart whistled, stomped her feet and shouted her approval of this new male god in the pantheon. He looked over his shoulder at her, crooked a finger. She whooped and went running to him across the water, each fleeting touch of her huge red feet sending up spurts of steam.

There was a shine not the sun on the northern horizon. Amortis came undulating across the water, her hair flowing in her personal wind, her gauzy draperies molding her lush body, her large blue eyes flirting with the God-Not-Chained.

Slya glared at her, Amortis glared back.

The god watched, preening like a cock two hens were fighting over. A thought flowed sluggishly across his perfect face. He left his companions, came striding back to the beach. He scooped up Trago, set the boy on his shoulder and went off with him.

Korimenei cried out, then fell silent as her beast came running across the sand and jumped into her arms.

Slya and Amortis trotted after the god, Slya slid her top right arm about his shoulders, her lower right arm about his waist, bumped her solid hip against his. Amortis took his other arm, brushed sensuously sinuously against him murmuring at him all the time, her voice like leaves rustling in a lazy summer breeze.

There was silence on the beach until the unlikely quartet vanished over the horizon.

Brann sighed. "So that was why," she said. "That was what all this was about. All the terror and the dying and the pain. To build a body to house that . . . that Monster."

"So it seems," Tak WakKerrcarr murmured in her ear. "Do you mind?"

"Yes," she said fiercely, then she shook her head. "It's futile, but I mind. Look what we've loosed on this miserable world. I'd like to. . . ."

"It's god-business, Thornlet. We're out of it now and lucky to be alive. Let's stay that way. You coming back with me?"

She leaned against him and looked at Maksim. He was over with Korimenei and a stocky red-haired man she didn't know; she saw him touch the man's face with the affection and tenderness he'd saved for her till now. I've lost him too, she thought, but I never had him, did I. He looks well. And happy. What kind of jealous bitch am I that I resent it? She smiled. Just your average sort of jealous bitch, I suppose. Nothing special. "Maksi," she called.

He looked round. "Bramble?"

"Going back to Jal Virri?"

"Yes, I've got an apprentice to teach." He threaded his big hand through Korimenei's flyaway hair, shook her gently. "Work her little tail off. You?"

"I'm for Mun Gapur. See you round. Tak?"

"Give the girl a rest, Maks, come see us some time. Bring your friend if you want. Ta."

5

The next morning, a bright clear cool morning with air that bubbled in the blood like wine, Brann stood beside one of the few coldsprings in Tak WakKerrcarr's watergarden at Mun Gapur. She held Massulit out away from her. "I don't want it, Tik-tok. I don't want it anywhere round me. It makes me nervous. It reminds me. . . ." She swallowed, the pain suddenly back, the loss raw in her.

"It goes where it will, Thornlet and that's not me. You want to lay a curse on me even I couldn't handle, try giving it to me." His mouth twitched in a smile part rueful, part calculating. "You might give it to Amortis."

Brann snorted, then she smiled too, a small reluctant lift of her mouth corners. "I will never ever forget that scene. I hope Slya sets her hair on fire." The smile went away. "And melts him into slag."

"Ah, m' dear."

"Hunh!" She contemplated Massulit a moment longer then tossed it into the spring and watched it sink through the clear cold water. It shone briefly but intensely blue, then settled dark and anonymous among the stones at the bottom of the pool. "There. I give it to nobody." She turned away, brushing her hands as if she brushed away the whole of the painful time just past. "This is a fire mountain," she said.

"True. Why?"

"Build me a kiln, Tik-tok."

"You need to rest a while, Thornlet. Relax."

She moved her shoulders, ran a hand through her long white hair. "I can't, luv. Not for a while yet. Do you understand? I need to be busy. I need to do something with my body, my hands, my mind. Something with meaning to me. When I was last in Kukurul I saw newware from Arth Slya. It gave me ideas I want to try. Any clay deposits round here?"

"I don't know. I'll see what I can find out. You're sure?"

"They were my children, Tik-tok. I have to grieve for them a while. But only a while. We have time, luv. If nothing else, we do have time."